Praise for Olivia Goldsmith

'A scorching Hollywood tale sprinkled with real names for authenticity . . . In classic ''sex-and-shopping'' style, Mary Jane Moran spends a fortune reshaping her looks and re-emerges drop-dead gorgeous to slay Tinseltown'
Peterborough Telegraph

'*Flavour of the Month* empties the Hollywood laundry basket and holds up each sordid item for our inspection: rapacious agents; crinkly-eyed Lotharios who, on reaching 50, suddenly trade the Joy of Sex for the Joy of Fatherhood: drink-sodden divas holed up alone in their echoing mansions – and girls, more and more girls, each more beautiful than the last'
Sunday Telegraph

'Far sharper, far wittier and far hipper than her older sisters Judith Krantz and Jackie Collins'
US Entertainment Weekly

'A sexy, wickedly funny novel'
Publishing News

Flavour of
the Month

'All right, doctor,' she said looking directly at him.
'Now you understand the situation. So. What would
it take to make me truly beautiful?'

The doctor looked out the window of the hospital
building. 'There would be a great deal of surgery
involved,' he began. He turned from the window
and looked at her. 'And there would be body scars.
Scars that would never fade and simply couldn't be
disguised.' He paused. 'And there would be discomfort. Undeniably. And it would take time. Time for
multiple procedures, and healing in between. There
are no guarantees. Work on this scale is painful. And
costly.'

'But you could do it?' she asked. 'It would be
possible?' Her voice caught for a moment. She
stopped there, took a breath and continued. 'They
all told me you were the one. That you work
miracles. You can make me beautiful?'

The doctor folded his hands over the file on the
otherwise barren desk. 'From the preliminary x-rays
and the results of the work-up, I think so.'

She let out her breath, slowly and shakily. She
licked her lips. 'Would it take more than two years
and sixty-seven thousand dollars?' she asked.

'I'm not sure. Perhaps. Why do you ask?'

'Because that's how much time and money I've
got,' she said, and pushed her opened purse, filled
with cash, across the desk to him.

Olivia Goldsmith is the author of *The First Wives Club*,
her wildly successful first novel which is now an
international bestseller. She has yet to become
Flavour of the Month.

**OLIVIA
GOLDSMITH**

---

*Flavour
of
the
Month*

Mandarin

To Paul Eugene Smith
On land, on sea, or in the air

A Mandarin Paperback

FLAVOUR OF THE MONTH

First published in Great Britain 1993
by William Heinemann Ltd
This edition published 1994
by Mandarin Paperbacks
an imprint of Reed Consumer Books Ltd
Michelin House, 81 Fulham Road, London SW3 6RB
and Auckland, Melbourne, Singapore and Toronto

Reprinted 1994 (twice)

Copyright © Olivia Goldsmith 1993
The author has asserted her moral rights

A CIP catalogue record for this title
is available from the British Library
ISBN 0 7493 1585 7

Printed and bound in Great Britain
by Cox & Wyman Ltd, Reading, Berkshire

Acknowledgements

I would like to express very special thanks to Nancy Robinson, my secretary, critic, and friend. Without her cheerful and brilliant support I would have surely drowned in the second revision. Not to mention the third, fourth, fifth and sixth. Sincere thanks also to:

Brendan Gunning for his peerless editorial assistance

Todd Harris of the William Morris Agency, who introduced me to Hollywood and taught me the maxim 'the agent always gets screwed'

Dr. Michael Sachs, whose understanding of women and beauty is only matched by his brilliance as a surgeon

Dr. Richard Gulian for the time he made for me, explanations he went over, and invaluable help he gave with the technical aspects of plastic surgery

Bill and Ann Johnson for their early readings and their generous comments on the draft

Dwight Currie and Michael Kohlman for their friendship, humour and the research help they offered

Ruth Bekker for her insights on the New York acting scene

Diana Hellinger for tireless enthusiasm and encouragement way beyond the bounds of friendship

Georgiana Francisco for her insider's view of L.A.

Jane Scovell, who knows everyone and everything, and is my pal

Ellen Hall who helped in so many ways, and mailed out the manuscript, time after time

Bill Hall, who finally got the job done, and beautifully!

Matilda Tucker, for her unconditional love and helpful suggestions for revamping chapter one

And, as always, Curtis Laupheimer and Justine Kryvin for everything

Lastly, thanks to all the women in Hollywood, both actresses and those behind the scenes, who so generously shared their experiences and their pain. Your truth is stranger than my fiction. I only hope I have not betrayed your trust.

Note from the Author

'Call me Ishmael – and call me often.'

I once knew a Hollywood agent, strictly small-time, who had that printed across the bottom of his business cards. Not that most people get the joke. And not that Ishmael Reiss did much business, but it wasn't because of the bad Melville allusion. Remember, this is the town where Bob LeVine, CEO at International Studios once asked, 'Hamlet? Isn't that the Mel Gibson vehicle?'

Writers – Melville, Faulkner, even Shakespeare – don't get much respect out here. You've heard the one about the dumb starlet? She was so stupid she slept with a writer to get a part. Of course, in the Hollywood food chain, writers are at the very bottom – the economic equivalent of career plankton.

That is, most writers – novelists, screenwriters, gag writers, or TV scriptwriters. But not all. I'm a writer, I chose to live out here, and I get respect. Well, it isn't mother love, but it beats the hell out of scorn and abuse. They may not like me, but they respect me, because they fear me. And I earn a lot of money.

Most people know who I am, and most people will say they don't like me. 'Laura Richie, what a cat!' they say, and that's when they're being polite. But as long as they buy my books, I don't care. Anyway, they don't actually know me – I'm just a famous name to them.

I'm famous for writing about the famous – a kind of celebrity hybrid, like Robin Leach. Funny about his name, isn't it? People call both of us leeches, but they also call me 'Richie the Bitchy.' An unfortunate coincidental assonance. Hey, it could be worse – 'Kitty Litter,' for example. Still, those who call names also lap the stuff up faster than I can research and write it.

It takes a lot of work. And I take pride in my work. It's biography. It's fact, not conjecture, not hearsay, not my opinions and my prejudices. I've got plenty of those, of course, but I keep them to myself, at least as much as any writer consciously can. I do a careful and complete job. I'm a plodder.

Well, I admit that as a life's work it's not Rheims Cathedral or even a biography of George Washington Carver, or Von Hilshimer, or Churchill. But comparatively few people are interested in the greats. Or even the near-greats. They prefer the ingrates.

So, if writers get no respect and no interest, what does?

Beauty. America is a country that worships only three things: money, youth, and beauty, and if you have the latter two, you can parlay them into the former. Beauty is youth. Beauty doesn't die, or at least it gives that impression.

What is new is that for the first time in history, money can buy beauty. And that somebody did.

Beauty begets money, money begets power. Sometimes. And everybody wants to read about beautiful women.

I know. My first book was Marion Anderson: A Black Artist's Struggle. *It was based on my doctoral thesis. It sold 2,216 copies. I'd worked on it for five years. But, hey, she wasn't beautiful. My last book,* Cher! *sold a half million copies. That's hardback. Multiply it times twenty-two dollars (of which I get fifteen per cent) and then call me names, if you want to. My banker calls me 'Miss Richie.' And for him I'd endorse my royalty cheques 'Richie the Bitchy' if it sold one extra copy. Plus, Bob LeVine and Mike Ovitz and April Irons return my calls. And invite me to their parties. It's nice to be noticed.*

And it took long enough, to get to be a known commodity. A Laura Richie book sells. Fame. It's weird, but useful. Fifty-nine per cent of Americans know who Donna Douglas is – she played Elly May Clampitt in The Beverly Hillbillies *– but they can't name even one Nobel Prize winner. Think about it. Hey, I didn't make this society, I'm only trying to live here. And I live well, and quietly. Of course, not too quietly. It wouldn't sell the column or the books. I've been on* Donahue, *and* Oprah *and* Geraldo *and* Sally Jessy *and a hundred radio call-in shows. But despite that and my picture on the back of my books, I still manage a private life. Know why? Because a writer – even a famous writer – could never be famous enough to lose all privacy. Actors, yes. Entrepreneurs, models, athletes, even notorious prostitutes, royalty (no matter how minor or spurious): they become celebrities.*

Women usually gain celebrity by being beautiful. Men because of their wealth or achievements. Funny how that works. Then the people who struggled up out of the morass of obscurity into the celebrity sunshine gain recognition but lose their lives to the public.

Because America is addicted to fame. Celebrity is more important to Americans than achievement, but the public's adulation is a two-edged sword. They build you up but they'll knock you down, too. That's part of my job. Knockin' 'em down. Once I started writing celebrity exposés – ones that told the whole truth – I found a market niche that can never be filled. Because America wants the dirt on those they worship: the stories of abuse, bankruptcy, incest, battering, addiction, and pain. The ugliness behind the beauty. A grim fairy-tale. My public. The seamier it is, the better they like it.

For women, the story usually begins with looks: a beauty in search of an audience. We are what we look like. But beauty isn't enough. For Jahne, Sharleen, and Lila, a trinity of names that have now become legendary, it all started with a lipstick. Well, more than a lipstick. A fight about lipstick. But I'm getting ahead of myself.

So, let me guide you through the tale. Permit me to point out all the places of interest. After all, who knows celebrity or Hollywood better than I? I promise you a great story and no one could tell it completely, from the beginning to the end, as I can. Because I was there. And there's never been a Hollywood saga like it.

Laura Richie
Halfway, Wyoming
199–

Obscurity

The first real problem I faced in life was that of beauty.

Mishimo Yukio

The way I look at it is, folks, if you wake up and you're ugly, you know what real pain is. That ain't fun. So I don't want to hear from 'I think it's real difficult to be good-looking and be an actress' . . . Give me a fucking break.

Don Simpson

If there is a defect on the soul, it cannot be corrected on the face. But if there is a defect on the face and one corrects it, it can correct the soul.

Jean Cocteau

1

New York winters are not kind to Broadway gypsies, Mary Jane Moran thought, not for the first time that day. She fought a sudden gust of biting wind to open the heavy glass door to the unemployment office. She walked into the cavernous grey room, ignoring the various direction signs hanging by wires from the ceiling, and, as she had done every week for the last six months, took her place in an already long line, this time behind a very short woman. I just hope she's not a talker, Mary Jane thought.

Mary Jane released a deep sigh as she surveyed the familiar scene. There was the usual smattering of laid-off seasonal workers and blue-collar types, but, for the most part, she guessed that a lot of the applicants were very much like herself – young and energetic, probably talented. But in New York most talented people didn't earn their livelihoods in the arts. They suffered instead. She thought again, as she always did at times like this, of the old showbiz joke: The guy at the circus who sweeps up the elephant shit starts feeling really sick and goes to the doctor. After dozens of tests, the doc tells him he has good news: 'Nothing serious, though very rare. Seems that you're severely allergic to elephant shit. Just avoid it and you'll be fine.' 'But I can't!' cries the guy, and explains his job. 'So, quit,' the doctor tells him. The guy is stunned. 'What! And give up show business?'

Like the guy in the joke, Mary Jane couldn't quit, despite her growing allergy to elephant shit. She usually felt compassion for the down-and-out writers, the dancers, the actors and singers, but not today. Too much elephant shit, and I've got my own troubles, she thought, and began rummaging in her large vinyl bag. She dug out a Mounds bar and a dog-eared paperback copy of *Queenie*, resigning herself to the long wait.

The woman in front of her half-turned towards Mary Jane and said, 'Hi. Rotten weather, isn't it?'

Mary Jane peered over the top of her book at the tiny woman in

3

what looked like a child's tan car coat, the kind with rope-and-wood closures. She looked only a step or two above a bag lady: none too clean, and a bit dazed or crazed. Mary Jane's boyfriend, Sam, always called her a 'dreck magnet,' because every kind of dullard and maniac approached her for a handout or a conversation. Still, she couldn't bring herself to be really rude to this tiny woman. Secretly, Mary Jane identified with every old, lonely woman she saw. Fear of my future? she wondered, and shrugged. 'Yeah, I hate it when it rains or snows on my reporting day. It makes the animals in their cages even more testy than usual,' she said, nodding towards the bored bureaucrats behind the counter. Well, that was enough talk. No need to encourage her. 'And I'm in no mood for anyone right now.' Mary Jane went back to her book as the woman shuffled around in her oversized galoshes and faced forward, pulling herself tighter into her coat.

It was several minutes before Mary Jane realized she had been reading the same sentence over and over. Shit, she thought, I was a little harsh. The woman was just trying to pass the time. Tapping her gently on the shoulder, Mary Jane said, 'Want a piece of gum?' The woman hesitated, looked at Mary Jane, then accepted and smiled. Her teeth made Mary Jane wince.

The woman unwrapped the Dentyne and popped it in her mouth. 'I'm a little anxious.' Motioning with one hand, she indicated the counter, yards before them. 'I'm afraid of what I'm going to hear when I get up there.'

Mary Jane laughed. 'Join the club,' she said. 'I think I've blown my wad, but I figured I'd come back today, just in case they make a mistake and give me one more cheque.'

The woman sighed, nodded.

'What do you do when you're working?' Mary Jane asked.

'I'm a writer, but I was working as a word processor at a law firm until I got laid off. And you?'

'I'm an actress,' Mary Jane told her. 'A currently unemployed but once-working actress. I had one big chance off-Broadway three years ago, got rave reviews, you should forgive the cliché, then nothing.'

'What was the show?' The woman seemed genuinely interested.

'*Jack and Jill and Compromise*. I was with the show for over a year.' Mary Jane felt herself grow depressed. 'I haven't gotten any attention since then.' Well, it was worse than that, but, she reminded herself, she didn't have to spill her guts to this complete stranger.

'Next!' they both heard at the same time. The old lady waved at Mary Jane as she shuffled off to the long counter before her. 'Good luck,' she said over her shoulder.

Mary Jane shifted once again on her cold and wet feet, watching as the interviewer began flipping through her files. She watched the old woman's face when the interviewer shook her head. Poor thing. What hole in the wall would she scuttle into? Had she really been a writer or was she just delusional?

After she watched the old lady slump and wander off, it was Mary Jane's turn at bat, time to receive the surly warning that her benefits ended in another two weeks. Mary Jane Moran walked out of the unemployment office at Twenty-sixth Street and Sixth Avenue and pulled her dun-coloured down coat tightly around her big-boned body. Two hours and forty minutes in line for a hundred and seventy-six bucks. After pausing a moment in the doorway to gather herself together, she began the long trudge up to St. Malachy's Church on West Forty-sixth Street for the repertory-group rehearsal. Her moon boots, cheap foam covered in vinyl, squished in the icy grey slush puddles, sending new currents of wet cold darting through her feet. Then it started to snow. Great! she thought. Why not just crucify me and get it over with? She pulled the scarf that was wound around her head farther forward to help shield her exposed face from the big wet flakes. She pushed her mittened hands deep into the pockets of the worn coat and kept trudging uptown.

She was used to the cold. She felt she'd always been out in it. Mary Jane had been raised in Scuderstown, New York, by her grandmother. Her parents had been victims of a car wreck. Mary Jane could only dimly recall the argument between her drunken father and mother, the lurch of the car, the screech of the tyres, the shattering glass. Then nothing. Except she clearly remembered the cold – it had been a December night – and then how she shivered in the hall of the hospital, a shaken four-year-old probably in shock, who was ignored while the medical staff clustered around her father and her mother.

Her mother had died. Her father had been severely brain-damaged and sent off, eventually, to a veterans' hospital. But she, at four, had been reluctantly taken in by her father's mother, her only living relative, and spent her childhood and teen years in a ramshackle farmhouse in upstate New York, the unloved, unwilling guest of the bitter old woman. It had been cold in the winters, almost as cold indoors as out, and she hated the cold then as she did now. She thought of the old lady at unemployment in her thin coat and shivered.

At Herald Square, she noticed that the Christmas decorations were still up at Macy's. By December 1, she was sick enough of Christmas cheer but now, in January, after the holiday season she had just survived, she wished Christmas had never been invented. The looks on the people coming out of the department store supported her view. Everyone hates it, she thought. It's just that no one will say it and stay off the bandwagon when it rolls around. I didn't. She sighed, remembering the call from her grandmother. Another poor, unloved old woman.

'I'm sick, Mary. I think I've got the flu. I can hardly get out of bed. I wouldn't ask you if I didn't have to, Mary.' Grandma only called her by her name when she wanted something. Otherwise it was simply 'you.' 'Could you come up for a few days and take care of me?' *After all, you are a nurse.* Grandma didn't say it, but it was implied. And, despite the rage, despite every feeling that made her want to fling the receiver back onto its cradle, to get an unlisted number, to run away, change her name, and never go back, the old guilt prevailed.

So, on December 24, Mary Jane had gone by bus to the one person she wanted most *not* to be with. Christmas in New York would have been glum enough, with Sam going to spend it in Sarasota with his parents, but being back in the shack outside Elmira, taking care of the sick old lady was a nightmare. It somehow made Sam's failure to invite her to join him even more hurtful. Was he ashamed to have her meet his parents? Mary Jane sighed.

Sam, wonderful as he was, was difficult. He'd been married once, when he was really young, and his wife had left him. That was his reason, he said, for hating marriage. Mary Jane didn't mind – not really. She had him, so why need a ring? But if they'd been married, wouldn't he have brought her to Florida? Wouldn't she know his parents by now? Any in-laws were preferable to her out-law grandma. It had been a miserable Christmas.

And it wasn't as if Grandma had been grateful. She never was. Instead, she alternately coughed up phlegm and carped. 'You've gained weight, I think. Look at me, skin and bone, but you, you've always been fleshy. On my food, on my pension, on my food stamps and Social Security, you got fleshy. Fleshy and conceited. Thought you were better than other people. Scuderstown not good enough for you. Nursing not good enough for you. Couldn't be a practical nurse. Had to get that useless R.N., then you don't even use it. Miss Actress. Got any jobs lately? Haven't seen *you* on TV or nothing. What happened to that show you was in?' It went on and on, unbearably, ceasing only when enough bourbon and Nyquil put her grandma out for the night. It had been almost more than Mary Jane could bear.

Bethanie was so pretty, Mary Jane had to work hard at not resenting her. She was the type her grandmother had admired, while the old woman ridiculed Mary Jane's own looks.

I should be grateful for being healthy, she told herself. I should be grateful that I'm smart. Not everyone is. For some reason she thought of a high school classmate Margery Heimann, who hadn't been able to name the capital of New York State, even though Scuderstown was only forty miles from Albany. *That* was dumb.

But, then, Margery was one of the prettiest girls in Scuderstown Regional High School, and Mary Jane could and did imagine what it might be like to have all the boys follow you with their eyes and fight to sit next to you on the school bus.

That had always been part of Mary Jane's problem, she figured: her imagination was too good. As a teenager she couldn't just sit there in the back of the gym at the pep rallies like the other lumpy farm girls, who seemed contented as cows. Mary Jane watched the cheerleaders, Margery Heimann among them, and could imagine what it would feel like to cavort in front of the crowd in those cute little skirts, and she was sure she would like the feeling. She also imagined, even then, how Lady Macbeth felt as she walked into the dark bedroom to commit murder, how Anna Karenina felt when she heard the train coming, and how Alice Adams felt when everyone ignored her at the dance. Oh, yes, even back then she could imagine *that* easily.

But *that*, she reminded herself wryly, didn't take very much imagination, since everyone at school *had* ignored Mary Jane. She had walked through the halls, a clumping ghost as far as all the boys and the popular girls were concerned. She was plain. Big nose. Beetle brow. Thick, lank hair. Thin lips. She decided then that there would be no easy way for her, no helping hand.

She'd have to do it herself. Boys wouldn't help her, her grandma wouldn't help her. She'd have to do it all herself.

And she had. Nursing school, on scholarship, to get out of Scuderstown. And then acting classes, and the almost hopeless

7

round of agents, auditions, day jobs, cattle calls, small parts, and rejections. It had taken so many, many years to prove herself, but at last she'd had a hit, been recognized, been accepted, been paid to do the work she loved. And she'd even been loved by a man who was both brilliant and handsome. Yet somehow it seemed she was losing it all, that it was turning to elephant shit.

An icy wind blew down Broadway, forcing Mary Jane into a doorway, where she tried to get her breath and a moment's rest. Standing there watching people catching cabs, she once again asked herself that question, the one she knew the answer to, the same answer every time she asked. What am I doing this for? Give it up, the voice inside her, her grandmother's voice, said. You don't even have bus fare, your boots are leaking, your coat is five years old and coming apart at the seams, and you're walking through a snowstorm to get to your acting group, which doesn't pay anything but demands fifty hours a week from you. You must be crazy.

But she knew she wasn't. She was doing what she had always wanted to do. As a kid back in Scuderstown, acting had saved her life. She was in all the school plays, always in the character parts – Regina in *Little Foxes*, Mrs. Webb in *Our Town* – and she'd been good. Hell, she'd been better than good. She'd been *real*. It had showed her the real way out – out of Scuderstown and Elmira, out of her unbearable life. She knew her grandmother wouldn't pay for college or acting school, and she had no money, and no way of earning a living. She had been forced into nursing school, but she had hated it. It was acting she loved, had always loved. It was in acting that she lost herself, found friends, gained herself. But now, once again, she would be forced to nurse just to earn some money.

There had been a time, not so long ago, when she thought that the day jobs were finally over, that at last she'd be able to earn a living acting. She'd been cast in a little two-character play, *Jack and Jill and Compromise*. She played a dumpy, middle-aged loser sales clerk who does a one-night stand with a down-and-out salesman, and the two fall in love. It all took place with them naked, in bed, on an almost bare stage, and it had been what she had always dreamed of – the vehicle that moved her up into the modest success of a working actress. Then, wonder of wonders, it had been praised by the critics, it had moved to a big off-Broadway house, and for almost two years she'd played the role of Jill, the role she'd created. Best of all, it was sold to the movies, and one of the producers, Seymore LeVine, met with her, nearly promising her the role.

She'd dreamed, back in Scuderstown, but she'd never been daring enough to dream of the movies. So, despite her very real success, her grandmother, Margery, and all the rest of Scuderstown was unaware of her triumph. They were not off-Broadway denizens, to say the least. But a *movie*. Everyone would see her. It would be a vindication, and, for the first time in her professional life, there would be some money in it. The play would bring her everything she'd ever wanted.

Because it had also been the play that had brought her Sam. He'd written and directed *Jack and Jill and Compromise*. He'd cast her and directed her and – miracle of miracles – he'd fallen in love with her. Then, almost six months ago, when Hollywood bought it, he'd negotiated to get to direct the movie. And he'd told her that she'd get to do Jill on the screen. It was a gritty, real, everyday tragic part. And it would be hers. Forever.

Sam had flown out to L.A. for the negotiations. He called her every night at first, then every other. Then, for almost a week, she didn't hear from him. She'd been nuts. At last, she got his note, 'Forgive me. I did the best I could. I'll be back in four days.'

Two days later, she read in *Variety* that Crystal Plenum was considering playing Jill. Mary Jane hadn't been able to get out of bed for twenty-four hours.

It was only her friend Neil Morelli who had gotten her through it. 'They're assholes,' he told her, while she lay, face down, silently weeping. 'Listen, you remember what the Taoists say about this?'

'No. What?' she sniffled.

'Shit happens.'

She sat up, wiped her nose. 'Yeah,' she agreed. 'And Hindus say, "This shit has happened before."'

Neil smiled, his weasel face almost looking good. 'Here, eat some of my rigatoni in pesto sauce. Crystal Plenum is a bimbo. She'll flop. Listen, *you* made Jill. *You* brought her to life. No one who ever saw you will forget that.'

'Yeah. And no one will ever see me again.' The sadness overwhelmed her, and she turned away to cry.

'Hey. You'll get another part. Remember what the critics said? "Evanescent. Pathos without a scintilla of sentimentality." Even fuckin' John Simon said you were transcendent, and he hates *everyone*. Fuck Hollywood. Fuck Sam. Fuck 'em all. Hey, while you're at it, how about fucking me?'

'Oh, Neil.'

'All right. Maybe later, after you've wiped your nose again.' He handed her a fresh Kleenex. 'So, how about a blow job?' he asked as she took the tissue. She grimaced at him and blew her nose.

'There's a good girl. Still, the next time you *do* a blow job, I've got a little hint: don't use your nose, use your mouth, and don't blow, suck. Got it? It's guaranteed to improve your popularity. Might even get you a part.'

Neil, her best friend, held her when she cried, made her laugh, fed her pasta. He was a great friend, but he'd been wrong. She hadn't gotten cast in anything since *Jack and Jill and Compromise*. Sam returned, shamefaced and guilty, and she tried to accept and understand. Of course he had no choice. Of course Hollywood wanted to cast the hottest woman in town, Crystal Plenum, in the part. And when Crystal Plenum accepted the role, Mary Jane tried not to resent Sam for rejoicing. For the last six months, she *had* tried to forgive him, while she watched his career surge forward. She *had* to forgive him, or she'd lose him. She loved him, and she knew he'd done the best he could. Hollywood simply didn't want fat, plain, almost middle-aged women on the screen. As far as she could figure, America didn't want them anywhere. Mary Jane shivered and pulled her old coat around her.

Sam had tried to make it up to her as best he could. He minimized the importance of the Hollywood trips for casting and preproduction prep, and he even began a new production – an off-broadway revue that she'd be featured in. But he resented her depression.

She shivered again. The wind *was* getting colder. At Times Square, she walked west through the theatre district. Ugly, tawdry, with old handbills peeling from older brick walls, dark, urine-reeking alleys – but the part of town she loved. It was Wednesday, matinee day, she realized as she noted all the late-afternoon activity under the theatre marquees, the comely crowd preparing to face the storm and wend their ways home to Westchester and Long Island. Mary Jane looked up at the enormous sign over the Plymouth Theater announcing *Dead Stop*. She had auditioned for it. No dice. Now she thought with envy of all the happily employed actors sitting in the warmth of an after-show glow in their cosy dressing rooms.

Since *Jack and Jill* had closed, she had felt lost. And now she was afraid she might be losing Sam as well. He was all taken up with the movie, while she sank deeper and deeper into her misery. She watched him prepare for his trips to the coast, and she hated herself as she clung to him before he left and when he returned, as he would tonight.

Sam hated clinging. It was probably why he was meeting her at the rehearsal. A cling-reduction strategy. It would be the first rehearsal with Sam in weeks. He'd run the group for nearly four years. And with him out on the coast, they all felt lost. But he'd be back now, for a while, and she'd pull herself together. She'd pull herself together and not resent that he would soon be leaving her for months, and try not to feel that he was leaving her for good. He'd asked her to come, she reminded herself. Maybe I shouldn't have refused. The snow was turning to sleet. At least there would be no sleet out in L.A. No sleet and no work, she told herself.

At last, drenched, she crossed Eighth Avenue, passed the two black whores who stood shivering in a Burger King doorway, and came to the entrance of the parish house of the St. Malachy's Church. She pushed her way through the heavy wooden doors. Father Damien, the actors' priest, stood inside talking with a parishioner and turned a startled face to her.

'Mary Jane, you're soaking wet.' The white-haired old man reached around her and helped her remove the snow-laden coat. He is always at hand to help an actor, she thought gratefully, and was moved by his concern. 'What happened?'

'Father, don't ask. I'm an unemployed New York actress, and you're my guardian angel. That's all I know.' Holding her wet, torn boots by the edges and throwing her old coat over her arm, she bumped open the door to the stairs with her wide behind and said, 'They better have some hot coffee ready down there, Father, or there'll be blood on the walls.'

2

Sam Shields unfolded his sweater and threw it down on the bed. His trip back from L.A. should have tired him out, but he felt full of energy. And flying MGM Grand was a nice way to travel: nothing but first-class seats, and no one but first-class people. The studio had picked up the tab, *and* sent him to the airport in a Rolls limo. That was the purest luxury – going top-drawer OPM – on other people's money. No more steerage for Sam Shields.

It was about time, too. Money – other people's or his own – was never a commodity Sam had much access to. Growing up on the North Shore of Long Island, in a tiny rented house that was always so damp that the wallpaper scrolled off the walls, where there was never enough money for proper clothes or a good cut of meat (but where there was always a bottle of Beefeater being poured by either his mother or his father), Sam had learned both what quality was and also how to do without it. Nice people wore Brooks Brothers, not suits from Robert Hall, so, if there wasn't money for a quality new blue blazer, he wore the old one until his arms had pushed so far below the sleeves that it looked as if he had rolled them up. His father, a failing advertising man, had once been a golden boy at Doyle Dane, back when that was *the* place for a clever Yalie to be. His mother had done her two years at Smith and then donned white gloves at Katie Gibbs. Both lanky and good-looking, he fair, she dark, they met at the office and married a month later.

What had it been like for them back in the fifties, when women wore hats and gloves, everyone drank Manhattans, and the city was a glistening pearl? Did they feel then the way he felt now, as if the world were opening up for him? He wondered if they had ever had a chance at the brass ring, and if they knew when, the exact moment, they missed it. Because for the two of them, after the first heady days of wine and roses, it was steerage all the way. Copywriting was beneath Philip, but what could he do that wasn't? He talked about writing, but he never did it, and his wife never stopped resenting that. After a lot of time and a lot of booze, Phil couldn't even write copy anymore. And Sam's mother, that deb with a heart of steel, must have realized that, despite her husband's pedigree and pretensions, she'd bet on the wrong horse. Sam's parents reminded him of characters from a failed Fitzgerald novel: those who lived at the edge of the beautiful social world but never got to the centre. Nowhere near it. And it was cold at the edge.

Sam hated Fitzgerald novels.

His parents had taught him to feel superior to everyone to whom he didn't feel inferior; to look down on Jews, on Italians, and especially on the Irish. Blacks weren't even in the picture. He was taught to revere the Whitneys (his father's distant relations), the Harrimans, the Vanderbilts, the Roosevelts, and all their cousins, aunts, in-laws, and dependents. And, as if he were the monied scion of a great family, he was sent to Deerfield and Yale (both on scholarship), his father's alma maters. Then he, too, had toiled in obscurity, with the fear that he would fail as his father had failed.

Now that had all changed. He smiled as he reached into the suitcase and lifted out his crumpled jacket. It was an old black linen one – he always wore black – and much too summery for New York in winter. But it had worked in L.A. *Everything* had worked in L.A. He and April had clicked, the rewrites were coming along nicely, and it looked as if they might go into production as early as May. If they were lucky with casting, it could happen.

Ah, casting. There was the rub. *Jack and Jill* was a gritty play, a slice of life. He'd seen it as *film noir*. Well, he still did. Not that it didn't have humour, pathos, the whole nine yards. But it was a dark story. A true story. And aren't all true stories dark?

Well, his was. Long Island boy moves to big city, starves, lives for the theatre, writes good plays, is ignored, almost gives up, writes one more, makes good. Sam shrugged, tired of unpacking, and dumped the rest of his dirty clothes onto a heap in the corner. Normally he'd leave the laundry at Mary Jane's. But not as things stood right now.

For the last two years, they'd lived together at her place most of the time, but Sam had been careful to keep his loft on East Nineteenth Street. It was important to him to have his own space to retreat to, and just as important for Mary Jane to know. It kept their boundaries clear. They were lovers, but he'd never made it a secret that he kept his options open.

He went to the other side of the loft and hit the flashing button of his answering machine. It whirred, then beeped, then clicked, and then Mary Jane's voice filled the room. 'Not back yet? I hope your flight was okay. I've got to go down to Unemployment. In this weather! Call when you get in. I leave at eleven thirty.' The machine beeped. Sam looked at his watch. Twelve forty-five. He'd missed her. Just as well. He shook his head. She sounded fine, but still made him uncomfortable. Guilty.

Because there *was* the dark side. And it was Mary Jane. Not that she was some *femme fatale*. Sam had to smile. Oh, he'd had more than his share of those: neurotic, haunted, narcissistic actresses who tortured him. He'd married Shayna when he was only twenty-three and let her torture him for four years. Then he'd been a wild man, but after a year or so of the bar scene he'd found Nora, to drive him equally crazy. Who was more beautiful, Shayna or Nora? Who was more selfish? Impossible to call. After Nora there'd been a string of lithe, perfect women, all with dancer's bodies, wonderful breasts, lovely lips, and tender, lying eyes. They'd either bored him or driven him crazy. Those were the two modes he'd known.

Until Mary Jane. At thirty-six, he'd just been beginning to think that he might be a failure, and his last play expressed that. He *was* Jack: desperate and afraid. Afraid of another soured affair, afraid of another big break that went nowhere, afraid that if this play went down the toilet he wouldn't have another in him. And in walked Mary Jane. Talented. Oh, more than talented. She took the part; hell, she fuckin' *owned* the part of Jill. She made it live. Onstage, he couldn't take his eyes off her. Working with her was so exciting. There wasn't a nuance that escaped her. And she knew her craft. She could hit the emotional peak, then nail a gag with perfect timing, night after night. She always made it look new, fresh.

Offstage, of course, she was nothing to look at. He had never taken her down to meet his judgemental parents. He imagined the mother's eyes giving Mary Jane the once-over. Half Irish, half Jewish, and the worst of each. Sam could imagine his mother's grimace, followed by the tight smile that would never reach her eyes. Mary Jane would not pass muster.

But he found that she was someone to talk to. Unlike the beauties, she listened, she responded, she was warm, loving, and always honest. Sam groaned aloud. Yes, she was honest, and he valued honesty and truth, although he couldn't seem to manage much of either one himself lately. Jesus Christ, why was life like this? It was some kind of cosmic practical joke: you can't get what you want without sticking it to someone else.

Well, once upon a time, three years ago, Mary Jane *was* what he wanted. He had to keep reminding himself of that. Oh, it might have started as a pity fuck, but she blew him away. She was hot, and right there. She'd bailed him out with her warmth and her performance, and it was so touching to see how much she obviously loved him. He had been moved by her passion, and her gratitude, and when he compared it to the coolness and self-interest of Shayna and Nora and all those pretty, difficult girls that came before, he felt happy for the first time.

Mary Jane asked for nothing, and she gave him everything. If there was an imbalance in that, he had felt too comfortable to question it. Not that he hadn't had a few relapses. He'd slept with a few cuties, but it was pleasant, even powerful, to go back to Mary Jane. It let him off the hook with them. And he had promised her nothing. Absolutely nothing. He'd always been clear about that. Still, she grew on him. It became natural to stay at her house: it was comfortable there, with a soup always cooking on the back burner, and his laundry sorted and folded and even ironed. He'd had a chance to regroup, to lick his wounds. It was like going back to the womb. Her big body was motherly. And she believed in him the way his own thin, beautiful, wasted bitch of a mother never had. Mary Jane's belief and talent sustained him. They worked together all day, intense in the *Jack and Jill* rehearsals, and then they comforted one another at night. She might be the first and only woman that he'd ever really loved. He'd even been tempted to ask her to marry him. Not that he was the marrying kind.

She'd brought him luck. When the play hit, it was her performance that got raves, that drew in the crowds. They moved it to a larger theatre, but were still Standing Room Only. He knew she was a cinch for the Obie. She believed *he'd* get one, or maybe two. They had: Best Actress, Best Play, Best Director.

So, instead of slitting his throat before he was forty, as he'd planned, he was flying out to the coast and making a movie. He'd held out for getting to direct it. His agent was sick about it: she didn't like to work for her money, but in this case she'd had to. No sale of *Jack and Jill* unless he, Sam Shields, got to direct. And, finally, Hollywood had gone for it.

But he wasn't going to get to enjoy the triumph. No. Because

Hollywood was definitely not going to risk sixteen million dollars on a plain, fat, unknown actress for the lead, even if the role called for one, even if it was, as they said, 'a small film.' It was a part of the deal from the get-go. Crystal Plenum was interested. If she signed, it was a guaranteed money-maker. So he got to be the bad guy, to break the news to Mary Jane. Try being happy looking at spaniel eyes that followed you everywhere, spaniel eyes that said, 'It's all right to kick me. I'm used to it.'

He knew that she must resent the shit out of him, but she'd never say so. It was the one dishonesty she'd ever tried. She had simply accepted. And her voice on the taped message seemed fine, normal. But it didn't play. Jesus, how it didn't play. Thank God he'd never proposed.

So, here he was, sorting his own laundry in his own dusty apartment. Because he couldn't face those spaniel eyes. She hadn't landed anything else since *Jack and Jill* closed. Christ! That, at least, wasn't *his* fault. He was coming to believe that she *wanted* to be a victim. And that she was punishing him by not allowing him to enjoy his success.

The message machine beeped again. 'Hi, Sam. It's Bethanie. I wondered if we could get together again.' The breathy voice paused; then she giggled. 'I mean I'd like to. I'll be home all day before rehearsal tonight. Bye.'

Shit. The troupe had rehearsal scheduled. He had almost forgotten. Jesus, after the sun and studios of Los Angeles, he wasn't sure he could handle St. Malachy's basement tonight. And, to be honest, the revue he was throwing together, though a crowd pleaser, was really just a bone. The machine beeped again.

'This is Sy Ortis of Early Artists calling Mr. Shields. Please call our Los Angeles office at 566–0111.' Sam raised his brows. Sy Ortis *himself* had called? Wait until my agent hears this: that I'm being called by the biggest power broker in L.A.! Sam thought of the old Industry joke: A writer comes home to find the police and the fire department at his house. A detective greets him with the news that his agent has gone berserk, come to his house, raped his wife, killed his kids, and burned the place down. The writer looks stunned. 'My agent came to my house?' he asks.

Well, Sy Ortis hadn't quite come to his house, but he *had* made the call himself, not delegated it to some effeminate assistant. Sam played the message again, just to be sure. God, he thought, I really am hot. Well, he was happy with his representation, but he would call Sy back. He scribbled down the number.

There was one more message. 'Hi, big boy. And I'm talking to your dick when I say that. Hope the flight was fine. Give me a call.' Sam smiled. April Irons was so secure she didn't bother to say who it was. He'd better erase this tape. Not that Mary Jane came to his place often, but just in case.

The thought of her once again wiped the smile from his face. Because, despite April, despite the others, he did love M.J. He hoped she would decide to come to L.A., though he was ashamed of her. But he also knew that he needed her, now more than ever. Despite the heat, despite the shot he had at the big time, despite the buzz, or maybe because of it all, he was afraid. Afraid he'd lose his shot at the brass ring. Bungle it, and wind up living his life out in obscurity. Ah, well, he'd see M.J. tonight. That would be soon enough. And in the meantime, perhaps he *would* pay a visit to Bethanie.

3

Mary Jane went down the stairs to the cavernous church basement that, for the last fourteen years, had been used as a rehearsal hall and showcase theatre. Thank God for the warmth, she thought, walked into the large room, and stood for a moment, taking in the delicious sounds of actors gathered for a production.

The vast room was low-ceilinged, with pillars breaking the big space into several areas. The walls were painted church-basement green, the floor a grey vinyl tile. Folding chairs of every design, colour, and condition lined the perimeters of the room. At the far end was a small raised stage. A shabby deep-red curtain hung open, displaying the narrow backstage space and the klieg lights. Several people were already huddled in a small circle, running lines. Two women were adjusting the height of the lights, although the show was far from ready for lighting. Mary Jane spotted a table off to the side which held a big pot of coffee and several open boxes of supermarket cakes and chocolate-chip cookies. Thank God! Empty carbohydrates and caffeine!

Sipping from a chipped mug, chewing one cookie and clutching another, she finally smiled. Mary Jane loved the animation, the excitement, whenever actors gathered in a room. Despite all her years in the New York theatre scene, she never took it for granted. An actor could *never* afford to take the opportunity to work for granted, even if it was, as here, unpaid. Because this ensemble group was *good*. Sam ran it, wrote for it, directed it. After he'd come back from L.A. the first time, almost seven months ago, he'd promised everyone that his next trip to California was only temporary, and that he'd come up with the idea for this revue. After directing *Jack and Jill*, he'd be back. Sam could never be happy in L.A., the town of false happy endings. His work was too real, too gritty, too involved with the realities of living life in good faith. The troupe had already had a few minor successes, along with the major one of *Jack and Jill*. If the rest of the actors felt any resentment or envy of Sam, they lived with it. Because you never knew what casting agent or director might turn up in the audience.

She sipped the coffee again and felt herself thawing out. Everyone here is just like me, Mary Jane thought. She had known some of these people for almost a dozen years, and to her they were family. We're all broke or just hanging on, all more or less talented, and we're all determined to make it. Some would look and see a roomful of actors, but it was also a roomful of waiters, cab drivers, speech coaches, word processors, and bartenders. Everyone with a day job. What we do for love of the theatre, she sighed.

'Mary Jane.' She turned to see Bethanie Lake, the newest member of the ensemble, walking across the floor with a fresh pot of coffee. The girl glowed. Mary Jane watched the young woman as she swayed, balancing the coffee. Though she wasn't very good, she *was* very pretty. Mary Jane never would have voted her into the group, but Sam had lobbied for her. And Mary Jane respected his judgement. Plus, Mary Jane thought ruefully, Grandma would vote for Bethanie.

Mary Jane had never forgotten her grandmother's child rearing: the poor food, the humiliation of the cheap, dirty clothes, the remarks and the scorn she got from grandma and the other girls at school. But worst of all had been her own awareness that her grandmother had been right – cruel, but right – when she called Mary Jane fat and ugly and a ridiculous dreamer.

She remembered sneaking into the dark, mildewed bathroom of the farmhouse to check on her reflection, hoping for some contradiction of her fears. She would turn on the light, a single sixty-watt bulb that extended from the wall over the bathroom mirror without benefit of a shade. She would open the shallow drawer in the chipped Formica vanity beside the sink and scrabble amidst the old hair clips, broken scissors, and half-used tubes of ointments, looking for the hand mirror. It had been a double-sided one, with a cracked magnifying glass on the back, two ancient rubber bands holding it together. Clasping it in her right hand, Mary Jane had to open the medicine cabinet so that it stood out from the wall, its age-speckled mirror facing the toilet. Then Mary Jane would climb up onto the commode seat and crouch there. It was the only way she could see her profile, and, awful as it was, it mesmerized her.

Each time, before she looked, she had paused for a moment, closed her eyes, and whispered one last prayer. Her heart always pounded, and her palms were always moist. Then, each time, she held the mirror in her left hand, angling it so that she could just manage to peer into it and see her profile reflected back at her in the larger, medicine-cabinet mirror. And each time her heart sank.

Her nose jutted out in a high arch from her forehead, her thick eyebrows almost meeting there. Then the nose flared out into a fleshy blob over her thin lips. Her chin, what there was of it, receded into her neck. Her cheeks were too full, formless chipmunk pouches. Except chipmunks were cute, she had thought. Chipmunks were attractive. Her face was unbalanced, horrible.

Each time that she crouched there and stared at her reflection, hot tears had filmed her eyes, as they did now. And each time she had, in the end, turned back to the mirror to face her enemy. Her eyes, still teary, big and brown, had stared at her from under the beetle brows. Windows to the soul, she'd thought. What good did it do her to have pretty brown eyes? So she could see how ugly she was? Nice joke, God.

At thirteen, Mary Jane Moran had known a few things. She had known that she was smarter than most of the kids in school. That wasn't hard in a place like Scuderstown, New York. Let's face it, she had been smarter than most of the teachers, too. But she hadn't let it show if she could help it. People didn't like you if you were smarter than they were. Her grandma had always called her 'Miss Smartypants,' and made it sound not like a baby word, but like a real insult. Mary Jane also had known that her grandma didn't love her. And that she was ugly, and probably would stay so. So, then, nobody would love her. Ever.

Now pretty Bethanie refilled Mary Jane's mug. What skin! That glow! She looked as if she'd just had sex! 'Oh, bless you, Bethanie. How could you tell I needed it?' Mary Jane sipped the hot liquid and moaned with relief while Beth helped her arrange her wet garments on a chair behind her.

'So. Tell me. How was Unemployment?'

Mary Jane paused for a moment. Had she mentioned to Bethanie that today was her reporting day? She didn't think so. How had she known? Well, it wasn't important. Mary Jane shrugged.

'Pretty much as I expected, Beth. It's the end of my twenty-six weeks. The well's going dry.'

'I'm sorry, Mary Jane. Is there anything I can do to help?'

She was very sweet, Mary Jane knew. Pretty, not too talented, but very sweet. Mary Jane had seen a thousand of them. They all had thin thighs and cute names. Bethanie was newly arrived in town, and filled with ambition and awe. Too bad that, despite Bethanie's face and body, she'd never make it. In New York you had to be able to read before you could act. But, hey, Mary Jane thought, you never can tell. There's always television.

'You can't help any more than you just did. Thanks for the coffee.' Looking around the noisy room, she asked, 'Is Sam here yet?'

'Yes, we've been here about an hour. Oh, we've come up with a wonderful scene for you and me to do together.'

We? Mary Jane thought, and sighed. Another starry-eyed actress in love with her director. Mary Jane had gotten used to it. She looked around for Sam, but he wasn't anywhere among the bustle that she could see. 'That's great, Bethanie, I'd love to work with you. What kind of thing is it?'

'Well, it's sort of a spoof on a magic act. It could be good.' Bethanie was all enthusiasm. 'You know, I've wanted to work with you since I first joined the company. You're so, I don't know, so *professional*. I know I've learned a lot from you already, just watching you. I feel the older, you know, the more *experienced* actresses have so much to offer, like role models.'

Great. Thirty-four years old, never been in a Broadway production, and I'm referred to as a 'role model.' Why doesn't she just roll out the wheelchair? That's it, Mary Jane thought. Today qualifies as the worst day of the year and it's only January. Stifling

20

a groan, she turned as she heard Sam's voice raised over the buzz in the room. Just hearing him warmed her better than the coffee had.

'Okay, everybody, let's settle down. We have a show to do.'

Mary Jane moved with the others to the circle of chairs in the centre of the space, glad that her conversation with the deadly Bethanie had been interrupted. She looked over to Sam and smiled, and he nodded. She wasn't surprised. He had never been demonstrative in public. Well, he'd say hello later, at home, in bed. Now the work of improvisation, rehearsal, scripting, and more rehearsal would start up again. Together, this group of ragtags would create a polished theatrical work, a showcase for all their talents. They were working on an idea of Sam's – to do a spoof of a variety show as in the days of television, but to show the backstage story as well. The working title was *Snow Business*.

Mary Jane loved the idea. But, of course, that was why she loved Sam. He was brilliant. Funny, brilliant, and hers. So what if every now and then he was tempted by the latest little item? Sam had insisted, from day one, that theirs would be an open relationship. Mary Jane simply closed her eyes to his dalliances. Not that there had been any that she was *certain* of. As she took a seat, Mary Jane looked across the room at Sam, caught his eye again, and winked, but he didn't wink back. Well, he was being the serious director again, she thought. Remember, he comes home with *me*, not with any of *them*, she reminded herself for the thousandth time.

She loved watching him in the theatre setting, loved drinking him in without his noticing. Tall and lanky, he moved with grace, like a dancer, Mary Jane thought. His usually pale skin was tanned from the California trip, and the two-day growth of beard and the black turtleneck sweater he favoured reminded her, as always, of some Italian film star of the fifties. His long, silky black pony tail offset his slightly receding hairline. He was very aware of his hairline, and she sometimes caught him measuring it in the mirror. It may bother him, but not me, she thought.

He'd be leaving for L.A. soon. What will I do then? she asked herself. Though she'd forgiven him for not being able to cast her in the film, Mary Jane wasn't sure that she could bear to watch stoically while *Jack and Jill and Compromise* was made without her, and she doubted she'd get any work on her own in L.A.

'Let's face it,' she'd said to Sam, 'I'm not the L.A. type.'

'That's *why* you'll get work,' he insisted. 'Character parts. I can almost guarantee it. You're so fucking talented, even the morons out there will see it.'

'Seymore LeVine didn't see it,' she reminded him.

'Oh, Seymore's just a producer. He's an asshole.'

'It's my impression that it's the assholes who do the casting,' Mary Jane had said drily.

Sam had been more than disappointed; he'd seemed angry that she wouldn't say she'd come – angry and *guilty*, a lethal mix – so maybe she shouldn't risk the long separation. After all, Crystal Plenum had a reputation. And, to be honest, with Sam gone, Mary Jane had nothing going for her here. Worst of all, she wasn't sure she could bear being without Sam for months. He had made her life worth living.

Sam was handed a note by one of the troupe. He looked up, and that was all he needed to silence the room. 'First an announcement,' he said. 'This Saturday's dinner will be at Chuck Darrow and Molly Closter's place, in the East Village, Sixth Street, past Avenue A. As usual, the hosts will provide the pasta, everyone else brings the wine, bread, and dessert.' The tight circle turned to the couple and clapped lightly. Mary Jane almost always found the Saturday Movable Feast to be warm and homey. And Molly was her closest girlfriend. I'd hate to leave this. This *is* my family, she told herself, as she looked around at the friendly, bantering crowd, caught Molly's eye, and smiled. Then Mary Jane's gaze fell on Bethanie, but *her* huge grey eyes were staring at Sam, waiting for his next word. Has he slept with her? The thought was a little flicker of poison, like a serpent's tongue.

But she didn't want to think about that. She and Sam did have a strict agreement that he would never sleep with any of the women she knew, so even if he did sleep around it wouldn't seem real to her. She'd only heard of his infidelities by innuendo. One 'friend' or another mentioned vague things from time to time. But she'd never discussed it with Sam.

And why should she? she thought. She wasn't a hundred per cent sure, and, anyhow, he loved *her*. That much she knew. He had nurtured her acting craft, encouraging her for almost three years. And still was. If it had hurt her when he insisted she'd get character work in L.A., it had also buoyed her. She'd never be an ingenue, but he still believed in her.

Still, what was that in Bethanie's gaze?

I've got to stop this, Mary Jane said to herself firmly, letting

Sam's voice bring her back to the business at hand. Anyway, if anything was up in that department, her pal Molly Closter would let her know.

'We have four scenes in front of the curtain put together so far for the revue, and six backstage scenes,' Sam began telling the now attentive group. 'We still need a few more variety-act skits to round out the show. I have an idea myself, but I would like to hear some of yours.'

Before anyone could answer, the door from the stairs crashed open and Neil Morelli came bounding in. 'I got it! I got it!' he screamed.

The group rose as one and ran to him, everyone hugging and talking at the same time. Neil Morelli, Mary Jane's best friend, obviously had gotten the TV pilot he had read for last month! Another one of us has made it, thought Mary Jane as she ran to him along with the others. Neil might be a little crazy, but he had a good heart. He was one of the cleverest comedians she had ever known. And she had known many – a few in the biblical sense.

The congratulations bubbled on. Taking her turn, Mary Jane threw her arms around Neil's skinny neck and said. 'Oh, Jughead, I couldn't be happier if it happened to me. You deserve it.'

Neil managed to scoop her up and gave her a little twirl. 'Thanks for all the rehearsal time you gave me,' he said. 'How 'bout a French kiss?' He planted a loud wet smack on each of her cheeks. The crowd laughed; he bowed, then turned back to her. 'You're next, you know.'

Mary Jane smiled wanly at this. In all her years of trying to get jobs as an actress in New York, every time someone else made it, he or she always said the same thing to her: 'You're next.' But she never was. She thought that *Jack and Jill* had been her shot, but the phone wasn't ringing off the hook.

Sam, the only one who hadn't crossed the floor to Neil, did so now. 'Good luck,' he said, extending his hand. Neil took it – reluctantly, it seemed to Mary Jane. They weren't great friends, but had always tolerated one another, if only for her sake. Sam smiled at Neil, his eyes cold. 'We're all very happy for you, Neil. Now, if no one objects, let's get back to work. I have an idea for a short skit for the show. A magic routine.'

Everyone groaned. Magic! Mary Jane thought. Well, I guess it could be worse. It could be a mime act.

'Hey, this is a democracy. I'll let you all judge. Then I'll decide.'

Everyone laughed. 'Mary Jane, Beth, Neil. Front and centre. I'm going to walk you through it.'

Sam outlined the blocking of the skit to each of them. Neil was the magician; Beth and Mary Jane were to play the obligatory assistants. Neil, always ready to take centre stage, gave up his moment of glory and, stripping out of his coat, did the walk-through, not knowing where it was going. As Sam directed, Neil placed Mary Jane in the imaginary box and said 'Ta-da.' Mary Jane did the classic one-arm-in-the-air, one-on-the-hip gesture of the magician's assistant. She got a laugh. Sam grinned at her. At the cue, Neil threw a sheet over the box. Then, ad-libbing, Neil went into an abracadabra spiel, playing to the crowd. Selling it. Meanwhile, Sam grabbed Mary Jane's hand, pulling her from behind the sheet. Without urging, Bethanie quickly took her place.

Then, with a big flourish, Neil pulled off the fabric. Bethanie perfectly aped Mary Jane's ta-da movements. The members of the troupe sat in silence for a moment, then erupted into laughter. At the sidelines, Mary Jane stood still. She wasn't certain what had happened. But fear flickered somewhere around her stomach. What was the joke? Then someone said it out loud. 'I get it. "Before" and "After."'

Mary Jane stood as if rooted to the spot, stunned by the realization. Her cheeks reddened with humiliation; tears stung her eyes. She was afraid to look at Sam, or anyone. How could he? she thought. Why? Why? Sure, she was a trouper about her looks. The part of Jill was that of an unattractive woman. Everyone knew it. She herself made self-deprecating jokes. But this was different. He knew how she really felt. Was that cheap joke worth her pain? Sam couldn't be so insensitive as to think that this wouldn't hurt.

She forced herself to scan the throng. They're my friends, she thought, my family. And they're laughing at me.

But not everyone was laughing. Molly Closter was looking at her with pity. And now so was Bethanie, who blushed and turned away. Mary Jane also felt a hot flush of shame. Pity felt worse than ridicule.

Then Neil Morelli held up his hands and called out Sam's name. The group's reaction calmed. Sam looked over at him as the group followed suit.

'I don't get it, Sam,' Neil said. 'I mean, what's so funny?'

Sam opened his mouth, but before he could explain, Neil interrupted. Mary Jane could see he wasn't having any of it. And he was starting a roll. Oh, no, Neil, she thought. Let it go. Don't be a hero for me. Just let me sit down, creep away.

'A transformation? Short, dark Mary Jane turns into tall, blonde Bethanie? Jeez, it's politically incorrect, but, even worse, I don't think it's very funny. I mean, it's been done. Wait a minute, Sam. I got a better idea. Let's change the scene just slightly, so it's not such a cliché. I think we can get a better laugh. A role switch. A *woman* magician, Sam. And *you* go in the box. She says "Ta-da," you disappear, and, in *your* place, Rick here pops out.'

Mary Jane, like all the others, looked over at one of the newer troupe members. Rick, the kid with a full head of golden curls and a body sculpted to perfection. Mary Jane saw Rick dip his head down a bit, then shrug. Some of the group laughed, and Molly Closter and another woman clapped.

Sam looked coldly at Neil, then smiled. Despite her shame, Mary Jane could see Sam was raging behind his pasted-on smile. Everyone watched Neil as he walked casually across the room and took his coat from the back of a chair. 'Come on, Mary Jane,' he said, as he began to put it on.

Mutely, she shook her head. That would make this all worse. She'd been waiting for Sam to come back from L.A. for two long weeks. She had so much to discuss with him tonight. And she wanted him to hold her, to be with her. Where would she go if she left Sam and her family? If she took this too hard, if she let them see her shame, she could never come back. Now Neil was pushing her into a corner. She backed away and shook her head again.

'Well, all right, then,' Neil sighed. 'But I'm out of here for good.' As he reached the door to the stairs, he turned and spoke only to her.

'I meant it, Mary Jane. You are by far the most talented actress I've ever met. You *are* next,' he said, and closed the door behind him.

4

In the search for an obscurity capital of the world, Lamson, Texas, would be a major contender. Grim and seemingly endless, Interstate 10 stretches from El Paso to San Antonio and has got to be one of the most depressing, dismal drives in the whole United States. Each dot on the map is an excuse for a town more dusty, faded, and dead than the one before. I, Laura Richie, know that, because I had to stop at so many of them, doing this research. But Lamson doesn't even rate a dot on the map. And in Lamson, the most obscure homes were in the trailer park beside the highway.

Sharleen Smith jumped off the dented yellow school bus and began to walk quickly along the dusty highway. She kicked small stones ahead of her with the toes of her Keds, puffing the dry dirt in low clouds around her feet. She turned off the main road and away from the other students, down the littered side street, towards the haphazard collection of decrepit trailers at the end, pulling at the red ribbon holding her pony tail as she went. She shook out her long, white-blonde hair, running her fingers through the loosened mass.

The groan she usually felt in the back of her throat, the groan she usually let out as she neared the tin box of a trailer she shared with her brother and father, was replaced today by a low hum of pleasure. Today nothing could bother her. Not even Sueanne Skaggs, who'd come to school on Monday in a new T-shirt. It had Sharleen's picture on it and a line below it that said, 'Just say no.' Sueanne had given one to all the boys on the football team. But Boyd, the captain and Sueanne's ex-steady, *he* didn't wear *his*. And none of the team would dare to if he didn't.

Sharleen couldn't quite figure out why Sueanne and all the girls hated her. Of course, she was poor, and she knew she was ignorant. Maybe even stupid. But she was really pretty. At least she *thought*

26

that she must be. Momma had always told her she was. But then Momma had left a long time ago.

If she was still pretty, the girls didn't seem to like her for it. Maybe it was her clothes. She tried to dress like the others, but she and Dean didn't have much, and that was a fact. Still, her red sweatshirt was clean, and her hair ribbon was pressed, and her jeans didn't have no more holes in 'em than the other girls'. But it seemed like they *bought* their jeans with holes, while hers came naturally. That made all the difference, she reckoned. Sharleen winced for a moment. Even with the thought of Boyd glowin' in the back of her mind, it didn't feel good, knowing the other girls hated her. But the boys sure didn't.

Sharleen skirted the trailer next door, ready for the snarling dog on a chain, remembering, too, when the pit bull used to run loose. Six years the dog had known her, but it still reacted with fury when she approached. Only her brother, Dean, could quiet the beast down. Well, Dean could make any animal love him. 'Shut up, Wally,' she told the snarling dog, feeling sorry for the creature. She knew what it felt like to be trapped and beaten. Poor Wally; its owner, a nasty biker, had never dignified the animal with a name. Only she and Dean called the dog Wally.

'Oh, shoot.' Her father's aged pickup truck stuck out from behind the end of the lot. The angle at which it was parked and the door left open told her that he was not only home but also drunk. She sighed. Nothing ever changed in Lamson, Texas. She paused for a moment, right there in the dusty road, and took out the Bible her momma had left her. She opened it blindly, then let her eye fall on the page. It was in Psalms, the prettiest part of the Old Testament. It was Psalm 21, and she read it through. All right, she told herself, then went to the door of the trailer and opened it quietly, not wanting to wake him if he was passed out. 'Please, oh, Lord, let him sleep,' she prayed. She didn't want tonight to be ruined.

His smell hit her as she stepped inside, a rank mixture of body odour and beer. She could make sure he had fresh-washed clothes, but she couldn't make him change them often or take a shower. Luckily, though, there wasn't a sound in the trailer. She realized he must be in a stupor, because she also smelled the overlay of cheap bourbon he drank only when he was into a real bad bender.

She turned on the light in the cramped living room where she slept. She sighed with relief to see that her father had made it to

27

his own room in the back and bypassed the convertible sofa bed.

Sharleen welcomed this time alone. Dean worked over at the feed-and-grain store after school let out. Tugging off her sneakers without untying them, she stepped out of the worn jeans and pulled the bright sweatshirt over her head in a single motion. Taking a towel from one of the hooks she used as a closet, she tiptoed towards the bathroom for her few luxurious moments of privacy. But before going in, she pressed her ear against the thin door of the room her father slept in, to confirm what she knew. Yep. His snores rattled like a snake in a bucket.

She closed the equally flimsy door to the tiny bathroom, and once again bemoaned the broken lock. Sharleen had no privacy. Though Dean was supposed to share the bedroom with their father, he most often wound up sleeping on the sofa with Sharleen. Not that she minded. She would feel safer now if Dean were home, knowing that *he* would keep an eye on her father while she showered. Still, Dean in his own quiet way demanded a lot of attention. Perhaps it was better like this. She reached into the cramped bathroom and turned on the water, hoping that there was some. Lamson Trailer Park's well occasionally went dry, or the pump broke. When she felt the first sting of the stream, she adjusted the temperature, pulled the cheap plastic curtain on the shower stall aside, and stepped in.

She let the water fall on her head and down her sleek hair to her shoulders. Her hair turned darker as the water ran down it to her breasts. Her nipples hardened as the water touched them. She turned slowly with her eyes closed. The water played at the small of her back, her buttocks, down her long, tapered legs to her feet. She felt good. Well, I might not be smart or rich or anyone important, but thank the Lord I'm pretty. Bein' pretty made Boyd like her. She was just like Momma, who had been pretty. Men liked Momma. All men except her daddy.

Sharleen could still picture Momma. She didn't have a photo of her or nothin', but she remembered her real well. Thinkin' of those times made her sad. She could still remember hiding with Dean in the red dust under the trailer, listening to her daddy and her momma above, hearing Momma being beaten. It had been a familiar sound, an awful sight, terrifying, but in a way even more terrible to think about. Sharleen still remembered the last time. Momma had come back from the laundry where she worked, still in her pink uniform, her hair batted up under the hairnet, tiny tendrils twisted at her temples, limp from the heat. Old tennis sneakers were on her feet, small holes at each pinky toe, worn by the three-mile walk each way between the laundry and the trailer. Down by her side she carried a plastic bag, holding the white shoes she polished each morning. She looked real tired, but when Dean showed her the tiny pup he'd found that day, she'd smiled.

Until Daddy had come home.

Sharleen and Dean had so often hidden from their dad, breathing into each other's ears, blocking out the sounds of the screams. The gentle hum of their breaths had always calmed her. She hummed now. She closed her eyes, letting the water run over her. It was almost as comforting as Dean's hand, the comforting rhythm he used as he stroked the back of her head, their bodies pushed tightly against each other. That day, the day of the puppy, had been real bad. She thought of how they rocked in rhythm with their breaths. The memory of the warmth of his body against hers, the fear that was a knot in her throat, now made her moan softly. His hand always went to her secret place and held it as she moved against him. The rocking caused them both to utter long slow moans. The sounds from the rest of the trailer, the fighting and the screams, would seem far away.

They spent that night in the dirt under the trailer, while the screaming continued, followed by silence. Somehow, the silence was worse, and they trembled until they finally slept.

Sharleen remembered their last morning together. Momma had come to find them. 'Sharleen, Dean. Are you there, kids?' Her voice was a whisper. Sharleen knew without being told that they were not to wake their father.

'We're here, Momma. Dean, come on, let's get up.'

Dean had rolled over and crawled out from under the trailer. Sharleen followed, brushing the dust off her as she started up the steps. Momma stopped just inside the door, and Sharleen saw her in the light. One side of her face was swollen and red. Her right eye was black and blue and puffy. The other was swollen shut. Dean froze, and Sharleen tapped his shoulder gently. Nothing else she could do.

'Go wash up, Dean, but be quiet,' she said. 'Don't wake him.'

When Dean went into the bathroom, Sharleen went to Momma and put a hand up to her face. Her mother winced and drew back. Sharleen had never seen her hurt so bad.

'Momma, it's bad,' she said gently, as if breaking news to her mother. 'You're hurt *real* bad this time, Momma.'

'I know, honey. It feels real bad this time.'

'We gotta go to the hospital, Momma.'

'No, honey. We'll just ask Jesus to take care of me and the puppy.' Momma took out a shoe box, the puppy lying twisted inside it. Sharleen didn't have to ask. Momma knelt, and so did Sharleen, who first got her mother the little Bible. Then Dean joined them. Sharleen even now remembered how he looked at the box and how his eyes got big, so very big.

'Is it sleepin'?' he asked.

'No, Dean. She's in heaven now, with Jesus. She's Jesus' puppy now.' Dean knelt beside them, and their mother whispered some words.

After breakfast, only Frosted Flakes and water 'cause there was no milk, Momma walked Sharleen and Dean to the school bus. Sharleen saw that her mother had put on her one good dress. It was bright blue with a white collar.

And she was carrying a cardboard suitcase. Sharleen knew then that her life was about to change, but couldn't imagine it getting worse. As Dean moped alone up ahead, their momma spoke real serious to Sharleen. It made Sharleen feel like a grown-up.

'Sharleen, honey, Momma's got to go away for a while. I can't take you two with me, but I'll come back for both of you as soon as I get a job and a place for us to live. You know you wasn't my natural-born daughter, but I love you like my own. Dean is my blood, but I got to leave him, too. He's only your half-brother, but I want you to love him like a true sister. I've only been your stepmomma, but I love you like flesh.' She handed Sharleen the little Bible. 'Keep this now, till I come back. No, honey, don't cry. You got to be strong. Jesus is going to watch over you. I promise you that. You talk to the Lord, and he'll take care of you while I'm gone.' She paused, wincing at the pain in her face. 'I want you to promise to take care of Dean. He ain't as smart as you.'

Sharleen listened in silence, knowing that there was nothing she could say. She'd known all along that her momma could not live through any more beatings. Her momma had no choice. Sharleen was glad she was getting away. And, being such a good girl, she didn't stop to think that there would be no one for her now. No one except Jesus, who she couldn't see, and Dean, who she had to take care of.

'Don't say nothin' to Dean until tonight. I don't want no fuss,' Momma said.

Sharleen nodded, and she and Dean got on the school bus. She turned around in the rear seat to look back at her mother. The frail woman raised her hand and waved twice, then turned very quickly and walked along the main road in the opposite direction, towards the Trailways bus stop near town. Sharleen had turned forward in her seat after she lost sight of her mother. She wouldn't cry. She just wouldn't. Because, once she started, she thought, maybe she'd never stop. She had bit her lip, then turned to her brother. 'Dean, I'm going to take care of you now,' she told him. He said nothing for a while, then just leaned his head against her shoulder and closed his eyes.

'It was a real good puppy,' was all he said.

Sharleen remembered it all, standing there under the thin trickle of the shower. She hadn't heard anything, lost in the memory of her momma and the sensation of the falling water. But suddenly Daddy was holding open the shower curtain with his shaking hand, his odour filling the steamy stall with his intrusion.

'What the hell are you doing?' her father growled. 'Wakin' me up. You crazy?'

She jumped at the voice and backed up to the rear wall of the tiny tin shower stall. Her practised eye measured her father's condition. Drunker than ever. It had been eight years since her momma had left, and her daddy had been mean and drunk for all of them. But he'd never done *this* before. Please, Lord, she thought. Please.

'Daddy,' she managed to breathe, trying not to show her fear. 'Wait a minute and I'll be right out.' She squeezed past him while he watched her nakedness. She took the towel off the peg on the wall and, feeling less vulnerable with it wrapped around her, walked towards the living room to the safety of her clothes and the outside door.

She heard the motion before she felt it. His hand fell like a stone on her wet head. Then he grabbed a handful of hair and he pulled her back, back towards the smelly den of his bedroom. The towel fell, leaving her bare. She screamed at the suddenness and the pain, and tried to stop him by holding on to the slippery handle of the old refrigerator. He reached around her and, with his free hand, wordlessly pried her fingers loose.

She went limp out of instinct, hoping he would have to loosen his grasp, reposition himself to carry her, but instead he just pulled her along the floor by her hair. The first words escaped her lips since the struggle had begun. 'Noooo!' she shrieked. 'No, Daddy, no!'

He stunned her silent with a slap of his broad, calloused hand, hitting flat across her face. 'Don't start with that, you little tease. I know what you are. Heard 'bout them T-shirts over to school. Struttin' yourself around in those tight pants. Tossin' your hair like some kinda Jezebel.'

As he dragged her down the hall, she went limp again. Then her father scraped her over the threshold of his door, and he let her fall at the foot of his bed. Holding a sheet around her, she started to scramble to her feet.

But he was too fast for her. He lashed out, quick as a striking snake, and threw her over his knee, viciously ripping away the sheet.

'I'll teach you some respect for me if I have to beat it into you,' he told her. Face down in the rank bedclothes, she tried to struggle off his lap.

'Please, Daddy, no. I'm sorry,' she cried, but his hand slapped her across her bare buttocks, hard. 'Please!' she cried again, but he hit her harder. When she tried to struggle up, he put his other hand on the back of her neck, pushing her head so hard into the mattress that she could barely breathe.

Her bare butt already stung, but once he had her pinioned helplessly he slapped it again and again and again. 'Little slut,' he cried. 'Tease. Just like your mother. How many of them boys you fucked? Boyd Jamison and who else? No-good little slut.' He grabbed one of her reddened buttocks and squeezed it viciously. Sharleen screamed at the pain and the shame of it.

'Don't you make one sound,' he warned her, swinging away at her again, and, despite the unbearable hurt, she didn't. After a time, he slowed down, then he stopped, but he still kept his one hand on her neck, pinning her. She felt smothered, and had to tell herself to keep breathing, small little breaths, despite the choking feeling in her throat and chest.

Then, with a chill of horror, she felt her father's hand move up between her legs, touching her *there*, in her private place. He grabbed a handful of her hair, there, down below, and tugged it. 'You let the boys up under your skirt?' he asked, his voice thick.

'No, Daddy,' she choked out.

His hand blessedly moved away, but then it was back to cup her right breast, hanging down over his left knee. 'You let them touch your titties?' he asked.

'No,' she cried again. His hand closed over her nipple, and he pinched it between his thumb and forefinger. The sharpness of the pain shot through her. 'You sure?' he asked.

'I'm sure,' she sobbed.

'Good,' he told her. 'Be sure you don't. Else you'll be a whore like all the rest of 'em.' He stood up, tumbling Sharleen, naked, onto the floor. He looked down on her with disgust.

'Get yerself decent. I'm going out,' he told her, and was gone.

Sharleen stumbled out of the close room and returned to the shower. The hot water had run out, but she hardly felt the difference. She stood in the cold flow, let it run over her back until the hurt cooled a little, then stepped out and carefully patted her raw skin with the thin towel. Thank God, Dean wasn't home, she thought. At sixteen, he weighed 185 pounds and was six-foot-two. She knew that Dean could hurt the old man, and once again knew she could never tell Dean of this. But Daddy was getting worse and worse. She flushed with the shame of it, feeling again her father's hand on her body. Worst of all was what she had felt against her belly while he hit her: her father had pressed his erection against her. She was afraid for herself, and also for what might happen to Dean if he knew. He'd fight their daddy, and then Daddy would kill Dean. He needed her to protect him, and she had promised her mother that she always would.

She put her hands up to her forehead, pulling back her hair as if she could pull the ugliness from her mind, and began, slowly, to dress in the skirt and blouse she had carefully made for what she was hoping would be an important occasion. With a trembling hand, she managed to put on lipstick in front of the flyspecked mirror nailed to the kitchen cabinet, then stopped for a moment to will herself to calmness. Lord, grant me this, she prayed. She had looked forward all week to her date with Boyd Jamison tonight, and wasn't going to let *anything* take away from it.

Sharleen took yesterday's meatloaf – mostly bread crumbs, not meat – from the refrigerator, cut off two big slices, and placed them in a pie tin. She scooped out the rest of the leftover instant mashed potatoes and added them, as well as a small can of creamed corn. She covered this all with aluminum foil and left it in the oven, then wrote a note to Dean telling him how to warm up his dinner and that she was going to the dance at the school. She didn't mention anything about Boyd or a date.

Turning back to the mirror, she examined her neck to make

sure there were no telltale signs of her father's attack. There were none, except her sore behind and her still-trembling hands. On the outside, Sharleen looked just perfect. So she left the trailer to wait for Boyd, in front so he wouldn't have to sound his horn.

5

Theresa O'Donnell has been world-famous for over thirty years. We know about her movie career, her mansion, her disastrous marriage, her failing career, her brilliant comeback, her slide, and even more than most of us would like to about her famous drunks. But it's hard to remember that only three years ago no one had heard of her daughter, Lila Kyle. Our fascination with the life-styles of even the rich and fading let us in on Theresa's latest album attempt, the perfume she was launching, and her troubles with the IRS. But not her daughter. And Theresa liked it like that.

A reader who didn't already know what was going to happen to Mary Jane and Sharleen might wonder how these two females are linked, and whether Laura Richie had not – as we say in the trade – lost control of her material. But you, gentle Reader, are savvy enough to have known from the beginning how these two are to be bound in a knot of fame, sexuality, and merchandising unmatched by any circus since the days of P. T. Barnum. And of course you would be wondering about the third part of the trinity, the most famous – or infamous – of them all.

The Rolls Corniche purred through the west gate of Bel Aire, moved up the hill effortlessly, swung slowly into the gently curving driveway, and came to a stop under the porte cochere. Lila Kyle opened her door, jumped out, and strode up the wide, cracked Carrara marble steps, through the enormous carved wooden door, slamming it behind her. She looked about at the once-grand foyer, the huge crystal chandelier, the curving staircase. 'It's not home, but it's much,' she murmured to herself, and headed upstairs. Her mother's housekeeper came into the gallery from the dining room, the expression on her face a combination of surprise and anger, just as Lila hit the first step to her bedroom suite on the floor above.

'Lila,' Estrella called out from below. 'Don't slam the door. I've told you a hundred times.'

Lila stopped, her hand holding tightly to the alabaster banister. She turned slowly towards Estrella, swinging her stuffed handbag over her shoulder. Lila wasn't only the daughter of a world-famous mother. Her father had been Kerry Kyle, the matinee idol of the forties and fifties. She was going to have to get into it with this bitch – *again*. When was Estrella going to get it? Glaring down at the Mexican woman, Lila said, 'Are *you* telling *me* what to do, Estrella? In *my* home?' Lila walked slowly back down one step, paused there, then said, 'You're way out of line. Anyway, you're only the *housekeeper*, you know? Hired help. And I'm *not* nine years old, for chrissakes.' Lila watched as Estrella's face flushed. It was a look that was becoming increasingly familiar to Lila. Like that teacher in school she'd had to straighten out that time. Or the saleswoman at the Rodeo Drive boutique. Panicky. Embarrassed to be reminded that they were only staff. Which was all they were. Because Lila had decided a long time ago that you couldn't buy these bitches' friendship, but you *could* demand their respect. Too bad her mother had never learned that lesson.

When she was satisfied that Estrella was in her place, Lila turned and began to retrace her steps. As she continued to walk up the stairs deliberately, she called over her shoulder, 'And send me up something to eat after my swim. You know, something I'll enjoy. Give it some *thought*, Estrella.'

Lila walked through the sitting room of her suite and through the double doors to her bedroom. She tossed her bag on the bed, wiggled out of her tight jeans and three-hundred-dollar silk jersey T-shirt, and walked into the bathroom. Without pausing, she turned on the sauna. While it was heating up, she moved to the huge walk-in closet and took down the chenille robe she favoured, threw it around herself, then went down the hall to the bedroom on the opposite side of the house to look out over the pool. It was the room her two 'sisters,' the wooden dummies that Theresa had made famous on her TV show, shared. The puppets lay in their twin beds staring at the ceiling. She wrinkled her nose at the smell of mildew that had gathered in the unused room. Why the fuck does she have to let it go like this? Lila thought. It's not that the Puppet Mistress's money was gone – Lila knew it wasn't. But Theresa was getting creepy, letting help go, not keeping things maintained. Jesus,

Estrella and Perez were the only household help they had, and most of the time Estrella just sat on her fat brown ass and watched TV with Theresa. The bitch is losing it, Lila thought. Well, that's not *my* problem. So long as the money is there.

Leaning out the window, she was able to see the entire pool area. From up here, it didn't look too bad. It was when you got close, and saw the cracks in the pool tile, or the overgrown weeds next to the pool house, that you knew that Theresa was ready for more than just her fucking close-up, Mr. DeMille. One of these days, Lila figured, Bill Holden's corpse would be floating out there.

The house had been built by a very big star in the thirties. In those days, before he'd gone out of style and bankrupt, the actor had set the standard for wretched excess in Hollywood, which most people in this town today had succeeded in topping. At the height of her career, Theresa O'Donnell had bought the place, and restored the house and grounds to their former splendour. But that was a long time ago.

Now Theresa O'Donnell, like the guy who'd preceded her, was over the hill. No more musical-comedy roles, no more movies, no more stupid TV shows or even recordings. Still, she held on to what she had – a hefty income from very carefully managed investments – but the glamour life was gone. Some people had said that Theresa was gone, too, but not Estrella, her resident fan, or the circle of ageing men – the Court of the Faggot Queens, Aunt Robbie called them – who loved to come over to Theresa's and dress up. Jewellery, makeup, wigs. Dresses and shoes. Trying on and changing. Imitations of Judy Garland being topped by Bette Davis. With the final coup de grâce: impressions of Theresa singing her theme song, 'The Loveliest Girl in the World.'

Lila scanned the lounge chairs around the perimeter. Good, she thought, no one's there. I'll have it all to myself. None of the usual bunch of her mother's hangers-on and moochers (although Lila knew that even they had been thinning out the last few years). Those few who remained were falling apart as badly as the house. But there was a new development: the faggots were being replaced by what Lila thought of as the Cinema Dweebs. All those young guys with glasses and hollow chests, who came from places like Akron, and wanted to write a book about the symbolism of breasts in Frank Tashlin's comedies of the 1950s. They ogled Lila and worshipped her mother. A lot of good it would do them. All

Theresa wanted was to sit in the screening room and watch her old movies endlessly. *The Lady's in Red, Cruising Down to Buenos Aires*. All the old crap that Lila herself used to watch. And, of course, *Birth of a Star*.

At least Kevin was different. He might have come to interview Theresa, but once he'd seen Lila he had stayed to talk to her. He was working on his film masters at UCLA, but he didn't look like a Cinema Dweeb. He looked great — tanned, fit, and very handsome. And he was smart. He came from back east somewhere, and he'd read like a million books. He gave her *East of Eden*, and she read it, even though she'd seen the movie. Kevin was interesting. And now that she'd dropped out of Westlake, Lila was bored.

Kevin paid attention to *her*. He played tennis with *her*. He jogged with *her*. He took *her* down to the Long Beach Marina and sailed out to Catalina. Stuff her mother was too old or too drunk to do. He was polite to Theresa, but he listened to all Lila's complaints about her, and he agreed. And sometimes he put his arm around Lila, though he never did anything more.

It felt good. He was taller than she was — the Dweebs came only up to her chest — and even more athletic, and it felt okay — just to be held. That was all she wanted, and that was all Kevin asked for.

Still, when Theresa had cooked up the idea of their marriage, Lila had been enraged. Kevin was her secret. Just for her. And, after all, she was only seventeen, too young to get married. Plus, it was none of the Puppet Mistress's goddamn business. It was embarrassing. Kevin might not be that interested in her. But, without even telling Lila, the Puppet Mistress spoke to him and got it all settled. At least *she* thought she had.

Just as she thought she had the reception all arranged. Theresa chose the date — to coincide with the start of the hiatus of the television shows — so they would have the biggest attendance possible. And the caterer was to be the one used by Jack Wagner's wife for all her parties. Theresa was knocking her brains out trying to make a decision between Ed McMahon and Pat Sajak for master of ceremonies. Lila could tell she had begun planning this as the beginning of another comeback caper. But Lila also knew there wouldn't be any reception, not to mention a comeback. Because Lila wasn't going to perform for the Puppet Mistress yet again, just so that Theresa could make a splash with Industry people. If Theresa wanted another job, let her get it herself.

But marrying Kevin was Lila's ticket out of this mausoleum. Lila didn't know where Kevin was now, but she assumed he was up at the tennis courts with his instructor. Even though Lila was starting to feel bored, she was glad to have him occupied for a while. Sometimes she just had to be alone. People, even Kevin, closed in on her. She wasn't in the mood. The Puppet Mistress had promised her that this would be accepted by Kevin, after the wedding. It had better be. Lila padded on her bare feet back to her room, and stripped down to her panties to sit in the welcome dry heat of the sauna. The thick door made her feel safe. Sweat began to bead the top of her chest and drip down her beautiful breasts. She'd been taking hormones that Theresa had gotten for her since she was ten, but on her sixteenth birthday, she'd also had implants – her mother's sweet-sixteen gift to her. Now they were perfect – round and upthrust, with tiny pink nipples that pointed high. They hadn't hardened with scar tissue or anything, the way some girls' had. Still, she didn't want anyone touching them but herself. She thought about Kevin again, and getting married. He hadn't squeezed her breasts. He'd never tried. Or done anything worse. Sometimes she felt he understood something about her that she didn't know about herself. Maybe that was enough.

More than anything, Lila wanted to get out of this crazy house, away from her mother and the madness and the fights. She needed Theresa to support her until her own money became available. But that might not be until she was twenty-one. One more disservice her father had done her, a trust fund that wouldn't kick in for another four years. She was dependent on her mother till it did. And the only way her mother would let her go was if she were married. 'A girl needs a man around, honey. Keeps the wolves from the door,' Theresa had said. 'And it looks bad, a girl your age moving out on her own. No one can say I didn't look after you, that I haven't been a perfect mother.'

Well, that was it. Theresa and her image – God knows, Lila wanted out of the house. But Lila was also afraid. Kevin was the best of the guys she'd met, and better than Mother's court, other than Aunt Robbie, of course. Kevin wasn't as mean as the others, maybe because he was young and good-looking. The rest of the Court of Dweebs or old and flabby fairies were ugly ones at that. Something happened to them when they reached a certain age, Lila thought. Something that made their mouths form into perpetual sneers. She wasn't going to wait around to see that happening to

Kevin, though. This was only a temporary solution, after all. Until her trust fund kicked in.

But, God, I don't *want* to get married. I want to get the fuck away from here, but I don't want to get married, Lila thought. Kevin's nice and all, and very understanding. She could *talk* with him — nothing too deep, but she had no one else to talk to at all. Except Aunt Robbie, but he was older, and he also loved her mom. And Kevin liked the movies — like she did — and enjoyed them without having to figure out symbolism and all that shit. That was something else they had in common. Mother had told her that Kevin would never force her to do anything. He would be very gentle, Theresa said. Or, if she wanted, he would leave her alone. He understood.

Sometimes Lila felt as much like a puppet as Candy or Skinny. Once she had hated them, had been jealous of them. Now she could almost feel sorry for them.

Slowly, she sat up and rubbed her skin roughly with a thick towel, then walked out of the sauna. She went to her bureau and opened a locked drawer with a key that she kept on a chain around her neck. She took out the three bottles of pills and arrayed them on the top of the dresser. She didn't have to look at the labels — she'd memorized them since before she was eleven, for chrissakes. She knew each one by shape and colour. And she had the dosage schedule down pat. What to take on what days. She took them out of the bottles, went to her bathroom sink, and swallowed the combination, washed down by a glass of water.

One of them — the one she had to take least frequently — always left a bitter aftertaste. Lila rinsed her mouth out with mouthwash, then returned to the bedroom, locked all the vials away, and pulled out the black Versace bathing suit she liked best. Inching on the tight spandex over her underpants wasn't easy, but at last she stared at herself in the full-length mirror and managed to smile. Then she left the room and headed for the pool.

Lila lay back on the chaise longue, the water droplets pooling around her on the white canvas cover. She felt the tension easing out of her, the effect of the hot sauna and quick swim. A shadow fell over her closed eyes, and her heartbeat quickened.

'Kevin?' she asked, opening her eyes, shielding them with her hand against the late-afternoon sun.

'No, mees, just Perez.'

Lila recognized her mother's latest (and oldest) yardman. 'Have you seen Kevin?' she snapped.

'No, mees. He was here 'bout an hour ago, but he leave. I don't know where.' He continued, 'Eet's okay I treem the hedges here, Mees Lila?'

'With this whole fucking place falling apart, you have to work *here? Now?* Go find yourself something else to do. This isn't show-time, for chrissakes.' Perez gave her the creeps, the way his eyes followed her whenever she was outside. He always seemed to be working right around her. She had told the Puppet Mistress to set him straight, but Lila guessed that she hadn't: *no one* worked cheaper than Perez. But Lila couldn't tolerate him.

Kevin was usually in the pool at this time of afternoon. He'd play tennis for an hour in the morning, then two more hours' practice in the afternoon with his instructor, one Theresa had hired, then he'd swim the pool for fifty laps. She liked that about him, the way he took care of his body. Exercise. Vitamins. They had *that* in common, too. And she liked to watch him in his tennis shorts, his Speedo swimsuit. He would come over to her in the afternoon on his way to the bathhouse to change out of his tennis clothes, and bend to kiss her as he went by, leaving the salty taste of his sweat on her lips. Sometimes, before she'd left Westlake, he'd pick her up after school. Every girl in school hated her for that. He *was* gorgeous.

But now Lila was lonely. Where the fuck was he? She stood up and pulled her robe closed. She decided to go back into the house, maybe go look for him. As Lila neared the door, she thought better of it. She didn't want to run into her mother, so she curved around the side of the building, past the solarium, intending to go in through the kitchen and up the back stairs to her room. The door to the unused solarium was closed, but the transom was open, and a mumble of voices came filtering through. Perez? she thought.

The low laugh was familiar and welcome. She twisted the knob and pushed in the door. 'Kevin?' she asked as it swung open. In the half-light of late afternoon, there were figures moving in the shade over by the rotten wooden potting table.

'Kevin?' she asked again. And then she saw clearly. He was leaning over the table, his strong arms bracing him, and he was naked. His tennis instructor was behind him, his back and bare ass to Lila, and he was moving, his white shorts in a puddle at his feet.

'Do you like it?' Bob asked, as he made another thrust with

his hips against Kevin's bare ass. 'Tell me you like it,' Bob teased.

'Yes,' Lila heard Kevin laugh. 'Yes, you bastard.' He grunted then, and so did Bob.

Lila felt the coldness stab at her heart and lungs. She stopped breathing for a long moment. The grunting continued, and then a groan. More than anything else, it was the disgusting sounds they were making that immobilized her. She made a sound herself. Kevin was the first to notice her.

They separated, slowly, breathing hard. Lila was breathing hard, too. She thought she might throw up. Kevin reached for his tennis shorts and said, 'It's not what you think, Lila. I love *you*, baby.'

But Lila was already screaming. 'I could kill you both,' she cried, her voice a shriek, sounding unnatural in her ears. The horror, the *meanness* of it was more than she could bear. 'I trusted you, Kevin. We were supposed to get married. *But then you do this*!' she screamed.

'Calm down, babe. Just calm down. Hey, I thought you knew, that you understood. I mean, this isn't a *surprise* to you, is it?' Kevin held out his hands, palms up, waiting for an answer.

Bob zipped up his white shorts, smoothed back his sweaty hair while looking at his reflection in the glass wall, then stepped past Lila. It appeared he had seen all this before. Turning to Kevin, he said, 'Same time tomorrow? Call me,' and left.

Lila stood there, shocked into silence until her breathing slowed. 'I despise you, you fucking faggot.' Lila turned to the door and opened it for him. 'You're no different than those disgusting old nellies that hang all over my mother. I should have known. I want you out of here. Now.'

Kevin stepped back, as if slapped. Then his face hardened. 'Yeah, you're right. You *should* have known. And Theresa told me you did, that it was all taken care of. Freedom and respectability for you, a nice income for me. I guess we're *both* fucked. *None* of us gets what we want now. Not even your mother.' He shook his head and walked through the open door. 'It could have all worked out. But – *someone* fucked up. And it wasn't *me*.' He was about to close the door behind him, then stopped, reconsidered, and smiled. 'No hard feelings?'

Lila pushed the door shut on him, then stood in the same spot for what seemed like a long time. She wasn't shaking, not a tremble. It was just that she couldn't seem to move, to think. At last, from behind her, from the door now open at the other end of

41

the solarium, she heard Theresa's voice. 'Better take him as he is, pet. He's the best *you're* ever going to do.'

Lila spun around. 'Oh, my God! Why didn't you tell me? You lied to me. I hate faggots, you *know* that. You said he didn't *want* that. You said . . .'

'What I *said* was, he doesn't want *you*.' Theresa paused. 'Just the good life. I said that he'd leave you alone. You'd be safe with him. We both would.'

'Why didn't you come right out and tell me, then?'

Theresa, as she so often did, ignored the question. 'It was a one-in-a-million deal and you blew it. I did it all for you, Lila.'

'But it's *my* life!'

'And *my* money! And *my* house, and *my* clothes on your back. You wanted to drop out of Westlake. Okay, I let you. You want to move out? I was letting you. But not without someone around to take care of you. Not to live some wild kind of life and start rumours. So I arranged it. I set it up. I found him, I paid him, and *this* is the thanks I get? After all I've sacrificed to keep you safe. To give you security.'

'Spare me, Mother. Next you'll be telling me Candy and Skinny are more grateful than I am.' Lila took a deep breath. She wouldn't cry. She was too angry, but the anger was cold. It had frozen all her tears. She looked at Theresa, the wreck of a star. 'The truth is, you're jealous of me. You're jealous, and you have been for a long time.'

'Jealous! That's a laugh! *I'm* Theresa O'Donnell. *I'm* a star. *I'm* famous. *You're* the one who's jealous of *me*!'

'I can get famous, Mother. You can't get young!'

Quick as a flash, Theresa struck out and slapped Lila, hard, across the face. Lila gasped, reached up to her cheek, took a step towards her mother, towering over her, then stopped. Her voice became low, deep, and frightening. 'You will *never* do that again. I'm certain of that. Because, if you do, I'll kill you. And you're not worth it. I'm *sick* of you. Sick of your constant manipulations. I'm not a puppet. For chrissakes, I'm not even your goddamn *daughter*.'

Theresa's face went ashen. 'Don't you *dare* say that to me. Or to *anyone*. *Ever*!' Specks of spittle had formed on the corners of Theresa's mouth.

Lila turned to go. 'I'm leaving.' She turned her back and began to walk back to the house.

'Don't you *dare* leave! Where are you going to go?' the Puppet

Mistress screamed behind her. 'You can't be on your own. You don't have a dime. And who's going to take *you* in?' Lila heard her mother's voice shrieking now. 'Don't you *dare* leave, Lila. You have no place to go.'

Sobbing now that her back was turned, Lila kept on walking away.

6

To understand this story, you've got to know Neil Morelli. Everyone knows him now, but no one knew him before that big Emmy award night. Now he's infamous, but back then he was just another stand-up comic trying to get a break and a sitcom of his own. Mary Jane's best friend, and a guy dying for recognition, he was one of the hungry hordes of New York entertainers trying for a ticket to the big time.

When Neil Morelli left the scene of Mary Jane's church-basement humiliation, he went on to work. Maybe someday she'd get wise – and notice the man in her life who really loved her. Now he couldn't be depressed about it. Bouncing off the elevator into the law firm's offices on the twenty-eighth floor of the Rockefeller Center skyscraper, he passed the receptionist behind an enormous cherry-wood desk. She sat amidst antique Sheraton tables and English hunt prints on the silk-papered walls, but he raced down the hall to the Word Processing Department. After working as a temp for three years in some of the most prestigious law firms in New York City, Neil had arrived at what he called his Ethnic Inversion Proportional Decorating Theory. He thought of it again as he rushed down the hall – the more Jewish or Italian partners in the firm, the more WASPy the furnishings – laughing to himself as he usually did. After all, a stand-up comic had to be his own best audience. With more than half of the partners here at Minster and Creed either Jews or guineas, the place looked like the queen herself supervised the decor. Yeah, he cracked to himself, but which queen?

Grinning, he opened the door at the end of the hall and walked into the fluorescent-lit interior, three rows of computer work-stations, six stations in each row, spread out before him in the windowless room. The noise level and the Spartan Formica work areas were in stark contrast to the sedate richness seen by clients. Ah, backstage at the law office.

Well, no more backstage: it would now be a soundstage for him. He had been waiting for this moment for three long years.

Dana was sitting at the supervisor's desk in the front, as usual. Neil breezed by her with an airy 'Hi,' dropped his backpack on the floor next to his desk, and waved a general hello to his co-workers. He saw Dana lower her glasses to the tip of her skinny nose and beckon him to her desk with an exaggerated curl of her index finger. At that moment, she reminded him of the nun in the fourth grade at St. Dominic's, Sister Helga. Neil had succeeded in getting his classmates to refer to her as Sister Hell Bent. Once the old crow had stood him up in front of the class and asked him where he thought his shenanigans would land him. 'Show business,' he cried, and the whole class laughed. The laugh was worth the beating he got later.

Now he waited for Dana. Like Neil, she considered herself in show business. Unlike Neil, she was kidding herself. A string of failed auditions did not constitute a career. She'd tried to be an actress, but she'd been both stupid and lazy, and now she was bitter. During his first days at the firm, she'd been warm and the soul of sympathy when he bombed over and over. It was only when he kept it up that her attitude changed. And Neil *had* kept it up, for over seven years now, doing a stand-up comedy routine at every club in town, starting with open-call nights only, midweek. He'd honed his material, worked all the way to weekends in the better clubs, and he had felt Dana's envy every time she asked him how he was doing.

If the envy had been mixed with respect, Neil supposed he could have tolerated it. But when Neil got his first paid gig, Dana's attitude took a turn for the worse. If once they had shared a camaraderie, from the night he got the twenty-five dollars for his bit at a retirement dinner on Long Island, Dana withdrew and seemed to take a perverse pleasure in making his job at the law firm hell. Because, while he'd moved up the club circuit, she'd only moved up the scut-work ladder. Now she was Queen of the Scut Work. Third-shift manager of a word-processing centre. Big deal. But it gave her enough power to guarantee that any really shit typing got assigned to him. Statistics. Tables. Footnote corrections. Neil swore she saved them up. Twenty-five bucks, for chrissakes, Neil thought. She's made my life miserable over twenty-five bucks.

But it wasn't just the twenty-five dollars. When he'd gotten the shot on *Letterman*, she'd begun the crucifixion. And since she'd gotten wind of the pilot, she'd been murder. But no more. Neil smiled to himself.

'You're late – again,' Dana warned as she neared his desk.

'I know. I'm sorry,' Neil said. All eyes were on him, though typists' fingers continued to fly. He made sure his face showed the proper contrition. No gags, no funny lines. He knew how to play an audience. He turned to the crew at their monitors. 'Hey, guys, what's the difference between a vulture and a lawyer?' They were ready for the gag. 'One's a lice-ridden scavenger that lives off the unfortunate.' He took a beat. 'The other's a bird.'

The crowd went wild, but Dana didn't even blink. 'That's the third time this week, Neil, and today's only Wednesday.'

Neil kept a straight face. The line's good and the bitch doesn't even know it, he thought.

Dana lowered her voice. 'I can't keep covering for you with the day manager,' she said. A total lie. The day manager only knew what Dana told him. 'I'm talking to you as a friend, Neil. Let's face it, this pays a lot more than retirement dinners, Letterman's scale, or free drinks at The Comic Strip.'

That's the good girl, open wide. For weeks now, it had taken all his willpower not to mention the sitcom pilot again. She must have figured it died, like her hopes. She wouldn't see this one coming. 'I know,' he said. 'But I won't be doing retirement parties for twenty-five dollars anymore, Dana.'

He could see her cheer up, the sick bitch. 'So, you're finally giving it up. Well, I can't say I blame you. I know you haven't had many bookings lately. You're better off here. *This* is your bread and butter.'

Now, this is getting too sweet, he thought. Time for the old one-two. 'Oh, I also won't be working *here* anymore.' The typists' fingers slowed down. Some actually stopped typing altogether.

'What? Why not?' Dana asked.

'Because,' he said, standing, then stepping back with his arms stretched up overhead, 'I GOT A TV SHOW IN L.A.!'

The other word processors, a motley crew of losers and misfits, applauded and stamped and shouted their congratulations. Only Dana looked nonplussed. So Neil waited for silence, returned his face to its sombre look, and spoke to her in a normal tone. He didn't need to shout. The whole room was still. Not a key was struck. 'I'd like to give you fifteen minutes' notice. I quit,' he said, as he grabbed his bag and began to walk to the door. Dana's jaw dropped. He turned around and decided to give his co-workers one more lawyer joke. He'd been doing one a day for six months, saying he believed it to be his equivalent of a marathon. 'Why does New York have all the lawyers and New Jersey have the toxic waste?' he called out to the room. Everyone but Dana had stopped working and was smiling at Neil in anticipation.

'WHY?' they yelled.

'Because New Jersey won the toss,' he told them, and opened the door to gales of laughter. Before he stepped out into the hall, he turned for a final time to Dana. She had managed a smile, but it was forced on tight lips, her face rosy with envy and humiliation.

Pay-back time. 'Keep punching them keys, Dana.' Neil smiled. 'Remember, its *your* bread and butter.' He closed the door and walked down the hall to the elevators, whistling.

Neil let himself back into his apartment, dropped his bag and the mail on the kitchen table, and took a beer from the refrigerator. He didn't normally drink, but today he was celebrating. Recalling Dana's face as he closed the door, he raised the bottle of beer in a toast, took a gulp, then made an imaginary checkmark in the air with a moistened index finger. He pushed one of the packing boxes off a kitchen chair and sat down, flipping through his mail. Bills, more bills, and a funny postcard from his sister, Brenda – the lesbian. The wall phone rang beside him, and he reached up and grabbed the receiver while continuing to sift through the envelopes.

'Hello.'

'Hey, Neil, I finally got you. Where've you been?' the cheery voice asked.

'Who's this?' Neil asked, his tone sweet.

'Nate.'

'Nate? Nate who?' Neil asked in the same syrupy voice.

'Nate. Nathan Fishman, for chrissakes. Your agent.' Nate's voice had lost a little of its friendly tone.

'Nate *Fishman*. Well, holy shit,' Neil said, now pretending excitement. 'I didn't recognize your voice. It's been so long. You must have gotten my – what, twenty, thirty messages, right?'

'Listen, Neil, I've been busy. But I heard the good news. I hear you got the pilot. See, kid? I said stick with me. We did it.'

Neil's voice dropped. '"We," you scumbag? "We"? Where was the "we" when I heard about the gig? Where was the "we" when I wanted to get in touch with the producers? Where was the "we" when I begged you to lend me the plane fare to fly out to L.A. to test? No "we," Nate, unless you're talking "we we." Because you pissed on me, Nate. And now you're fired.'

There was dead silence at the other end of the line for a minute, then a forced laugh. 'What do you mean, fired? This is a gag, right, kid? After all I did . . .'

'You didn't do shit for me, Nate. We had lunch a couple of times in the past year – *both* of which I paid for, by the way – I signed something three years ago, and you've been collecting ten per cent of everything I earned since, including my fucking word-processing job *and* the two-fifty out of the twenty-five dollars for my first gig. I booked the jobs, not you. You never got me a job, and most of the time you didn't return my phone calls. But you cashed my cheques, right on time, every month.'

'So you get a break and then walk away from me?' Nate's voice rose with indignation.

'You're a loser and a slime bucket, Nate. Think about it.'

'*I'm* a loser? *You're* the fucking loser. You're going to L.A. to make a pilot? Big fuckin' deal. They make five hundred pilots a season, asshole. What makes you think yours is going to go network, or even get syndicated? You'll be back here in a month, pounding on my door.'

'I just picked up my messages from my answering service,' Neil yelled, holding up two pink slips as if Nate could see them. 'And guess who they're from? Sy Ortis. "I'd like to talk to you about representation at your earliest possible convenience." *Sy Ortis*, Nate. Early Artists. That's why they call the firm that. They get the talent Early, when we're just about to take off. *Two* messages, Nate. And I think they deserve a call back! So fuck off, small time.' Neil banged the receiver back on the hook, took a deep breath, then made another invisible checkmark in the air.

He sat in silence for a moment, trying to regain his composure. Now the bastards were coming out of the woodwork to take credit for having discovered him. Well, fuck them. I did it myself. I'm the one that knocked on doors and took the abuse. I'm the one that got stiffed for pay by the worms that run the clubs.

He thought of Sal Condotti at Horizon's Star the other night.

After Neil had finished his act, Sal had come up to him and offered Neil his hand.

'I always knew you could do it, Neil. That's why I gave you weekends so soon after you started. I could tell quality.' Sal pumped his hand. 'So, whenever you want to break in your new routine, just let me know. I'll give you a Saturday night – and top billing.'

'Gee, thanks, Sal. I sure appreciate that. And could I get a raise, too? Could you let me have maybe fifty-*five* dollars instead of fifty?' Neil had kept a smile on his face.

'A raise? *You* should be paying *me*, for chrissakes,' Sal had said automatically. Talk money and he always went into his 'what-I-done-for-you' routine. '*I* gave you your break, and now you want to soak *me* for more money?' Sal smiled but shook his head sadly.

'Not *more* money, Sal,' Neil said. '*Some* money. You haven't paid me for the last three weeks. I mean, it's just as easy not to pay me fifty-five dollars as it is not to pay me fifty, right?'

Sal laughed and slapped Neil on his back. 'You're a riot, Neil. Okay, let's say fifty-five dollars. Would that make you happy, kid?'

Neil stared at the ceiling for a moment, as if considering Sal's offer. 'Nah,' he said, and stepped away from Sal. 'But I tell you what would make me happy. I'd be happy with a hundred dollars at Catch A Rising Star.' Neil began to walk to the door. 'And that's what I'm getting Saturday night *there*, Sal. Fuck yourself, Sal, you cheap wop. Drop in and see my new routine, if they forget to lock the cage.'

Sal's smile disappeared, and his voice went very low. 'Hey, *gumba* – don't burn all your bridges. You might need them when you cross the Styx into Hades.'

'I'll never be playing the sticks again, *paisano*. And that includes this toilet.' Neil had said, and walked out onto Second Avenue.

Remembering it now, Neil made another checkmark in the air of his kitchen, and smiled to himself. They were adding up, he thought, and then remembered to add Sam Shields to his list. Neil felt bad leaving Mary Jane and the troupe, but it was a pleasure to toss his success at Sam in front of the rest of them. The self-important bastard acted as if the group was his personal property. Humiliating Mary Jane in front of them all. *And* cheating on her left and right, not that Mary Jane would let herself see it. Neil sighed.

Why does someone like Sam wind up with someone like Mary Jane? he thought, for the seven or eight millionth time. She isn't beautiful, but she's a good friend and an enormously talented actress. She's a woman with a soul, who loves a man without one. Neil could never get over the fact that Sam's arrogant artiste shit worked so well on women. The black clothes, the fakola creative moods. When the guy is six-foot-two and good-looking, why did he bother to use a shtick to get laid?

Neil had seen a dozen guys just like Sam Shields. Guys who'd gone to an Ivy school but pretended to be from the streets. Guys who wrote plays about blue-collar characters, but who wrote dialogue with words like 'plethora' and 'facetious' and 'cosmology.' Neil *was* a street guy – his dad had been a minor capo in one of the New York families – and he hated the suckfaces from places like Exeter who liked to talk 'dese,' 'dems,' and 'dose.' Neil watched Sam pull his tough-guy act out of his ass, and watched the women fall over and spread their thighs. It made you lose respect for them.

For a short, skinny, homely guy, Neil had managed to joke his share of women into bed, but he could never treat them cruelly enough to make them love him. And because he loved Mary Jane, he could never treat her cruelly at all.

Hey, he told himself. None of that self pity, now. Neil stood up abruptly, went into the tiny bedroom, and began to toss the contents of bureau drawers into an empty packing box. Mary Jane was the one bridge he was *not* going to burn, he thought, and went to the phone to leave a funny message on her machine. Maybe this last humiliation in front of the troupe would be enough. Maybe Mary Jane would finally wake up and smell the Sanka.

7

Sharleen was happy, happier than she ever had been. Going out – well, 'sneaking out' would be closer to it – with Boyd was real nice, and they'd been dating for almost a month now. Just like a normal girl. Just like they showed on TV. And he was nice. Real nice. Just sitting beside him here in his red Trans Am convertible felt good. Then the car crunched along the stony dirt road and, when the lights picked out the outline of the trailer ahead, Sharleen felt the feeling fade. She reached across Boyd and turned off the lights, then put her finger to her lips. He stopped the engine, and the silence of the Texas night fell around them. Sharleen laid her head back on the seat and looked directly up at the star-filled sky, stretching like a blanket from horizon to horizon. What was it she had felt? Different? Special. She felt special.

Since Sharleen had begun dating Boyd, she'd started to see just how special she was to him. She saw it in his eyes, which reflected her own face back at her.

They sat in comfortable silence for a moment. Sharleen was grateful that Boyd didn't start pawing her the moment he turned off the engine. That was one of the things that made him different from the other boys at school. He was such a gentleman at the party tonight. The other boys seemed so childish in comparison to Boyd.

'Did you have a good time, Sharleen?' he asked.

She turned her head so she could see his profile in the dim light. 'Oh, yes, Boyd, I sure did. I had a wonderful time. Thank you.'

And she had. She held in her arms the stuffed animal he had won for her in the dunking-for-apples game. When he handed it to her, a fuzzy poodle-dog, she knew what it was about him that made him special, too. He said, 'I remember you said you once had a puppy that died.' Boyd *listened* to what she said.

'Sharleen, you're the prettiest girl in the school, you know that?' he asked now. Sharleen blushed with pleasure, then became uncomfortable at what might be coming next.

'And you write the prettiest poetry. That poem in the school paper was good. It really was.' He turned sideways to face her. Sharleen tensed at the movement. 'You're not like other girls. You're . . .' He paused.

'Sharleen,' he said softly, 'would you be my steady?' She turned her head to face him and studied him closely. Boyd was the richest boy at Regional, the only boy who had a new car, not a secondhand. He was a senior, but had a very boyish face, kinda like Dean's. But he made her feel two years older instead of two years younger. Sex with him was something different, scary but good in a way. She reached out her fingers and touched the outline of his square jaw. She could manage one night out with him each week, but more and Daddy would surely find out. Plus, Dean would be alone so much. But how could she explain any of it to Boyd?

'Boyd, I don't want to go steady with nobody. It's not that I don't like you, Boyd. I really do. But I can't go steady with anyone right now.' She felt his hurt and disappointment and rushed to relieve it. 'Couldn't we just be friends for a while, Boyd? You know, just do things together? I mean, like go for rides and talk? Once in a while. Without all the fuss? I surely do like you.'

If she went steady with him, she'd have to wear his ring. Word would get out. And her daddy might make trouble. Dean would feel left out, or maybe even jealous. She leaned forward and kissed Boyd on the lips, barely brushing them. She lingered there, her lips against Boyd's, not moving, not touching anyplace else. Then, gently, she pulled away.

'Sharleen, I love you. I'll do whatever you want. I just want to be with you,' Boyd said, and he seemed relieved at last to be saying these words to her.

She heard the whoosh of the falling wood first, then the thud of the bat on the back of Boyd's head. She saw him then, stumbling around to her side of the car, the baseball bat still grasped in his hand. Boyd slumped forward, his head bumping against the wheel. There was blood, a lot of blood. In a moment, the seat was covered with it.

'You filthy bitch,' her father snarled. 'Giving it away to strangers. Get out of the car, you whore.'

Sharleen's wide-eyed gaze fell first on the bloody head of Boyd lying against the steering wheel, then back to her father as he grabbed crazily at the door of the car, not able to open it in his frenzy. She threw herself back, trying to clear the car by scampering over the seat, then over the far side, but he jumped across the back fender and his hand fell on her ankle, pulling her with such force that she lost her breath. The scream died in her throat; her breath gasped from her. Instinctively, she knew that he had gone over the edge: she was going to die.

Her daddy's grip left her ankle while he tried to get a hold of her arm. She used her last moment of freedom to kick out with both legs, succeeding in knocking him off balance. She got down off the car trunk and ran towards the trailer.

'Dean! Dean!' she screamed. 'Help me, Dean, help.' Then her father was on her in a leap, forcing her to the ground.

'You little cunt! Just like your mother. Slut! I'll show you. Fuck every boy that comes walking by.' He wrenched her over, straddling her at her waist, then slapped her hard across the face, stunning her. She knew he would kill her now, or worse.

'Deannnnnn! Help meeeee!' she screamed as loud as she could, and, with that gigantic effort, slackened her body. He used the moment, and quickly had her skirt up and blouse ripped open, his body pressing the breath out of her lungs.

'The Lord is my shepherd; I shall not want,' she began to pray. 'He maketh me to lie down in green pastures.' It was going to happen, like she always knew it would. Like she'd always been afraid of. She closed her eyes and felt his rank breath against her face. She heard the sound of his fly being unzipped. 'Yea, though I walk through the valley of the shadow of death, I will fear no evil,' she whispered.

She didn't see the bat, or Dean holding it, or the arc it made before it connected with her father's skull. But she heard the sickening crunch, felt him tumble off her, and heard her father's last fluid gurgle. Not until she opened her eyes, managed to scramble up from the dirt, and saw him lying there, his blood spreading over the ground, did she realize he was lifeless. And she was glad.

She pulled down her skirt, looked at Dean, who now seemed paralyzed, then ran to Boyd. She didn't have to touch him to know that the blow from the baseball bat had killed him. His face was calm and serene, in spite of the mass of red-and-white pulp strewn on the seat of the car. He never knew what hit him.

She turned back to Dean and put her arms around him. 'Dean, thank you. You saved my life. He would have killed me.'

Dean was still staring at the body of their father. Dean didn't move, didn't blink, didn't even seem to hear her.

His stillness frightened Sharleen, forcing her to take command. 'Dean, listen to me. He killed Boyd. Look, Dean.' She forced him to the driver's side of the car. 'He bashed in Boyd's head with the baseball bat, Dean. He was going to kill me, too.' She stood very close to him, circling him with the warmth of her arms, reviving him, a frightened animal, with her closeness and the familiarity of her smell.

'You saved my life, Dean. Now, listen to me, and I'll take care of both of us.'

He nodded, then looked at her. 'He killed our puppy, Sharleen. He hit Momma. He was hurting you, Sharleen. He was hurting you.'

'I know. But I'm okay now. You have to be okay, too.'

He dropped his head on her shoulder and began to cry. 'I'm okay, Sharleen. I'm okay. I didn't want to do that. I didn't. But I'll never let anyone hurt you. Not ever.'

8

Mary Jane sat swirling her coffee cup in circles on the Formica table in the kitchen. Through the small, grimy window facing the airshaft, she was able to see that the sun was out only when she craned her neck with her cheek on the pane. She took a spoonful of plain yogurt, wishing it had strawberry preserves in it, then pushed the container away.

Holding the mug in both hands and blowing across the top, she sipped mindlessly, and stiffened as she heard Sam in the next room: he often mumbled in his sleep, and now he cried out, then sighed deeply. She listened as he coughed once, then heard the bed creak as he turned over.

Mary Jane relaxed in relief. I can't talk to him yet, she thought. I've got to figure out last night first. What to say. How to say it. Where to draw the line, the line she would have to draw to preserve her self-respect. He really hurt me, she thought. And he did it in front of Molly and Neil and Chuck. In front of all of them.

As always, she found herself backing off from the confrontation, beginning to formulate excuses. Well, they *had* been going through a hard time lately. Guilt, shame, and anger – now, there was a nice pot of emotions to stew in. And though they'd talked about it – endlessly, it seemed – there was really nothing that could be changed. Sam had to take this shot and do the movie, she'd feel lost out there, and neither of them could force Hollywood to change. She just couldn't stand the thought of being without him.

But she couldn't stand the thought of going with him as nothing more than his unemployed girlfriend, either.

She knew he was angry at her for that – for not wanting to go. For abandoning him when he was so nervous about his first film. Maybe *that* was why he'd staged that humiliation last night. To 'get her back' for not coming with him to L.A. Mary Jane shook her head. Whatever the reason, he was way out of line.

But perhaps it was more. Wasn't it Freud who'd said there were no jokes? Maybe the gag last night was Sam's way of transforming her. Maybe he wanted someone who looked like Bethanie Lake. Or maybe he wanted Bethanie herself; she certainly wanted him.

Mary Jane got up, walked across the tiny kitchen, stood in the doorway to the narrow bedroom. Sam lay, his hair spread out on the pillow, his long arm over the side of the bed. Just looking at the long, lean arm, the bulge of the muscle above the elbow, the downy hair on the forearm, made her weak, gave her pleasure. With his dark, shoulder-length hair and tomahawk nose, he reminded her of a sleeping brave.

Since *Jack and Jill and Compromise* was sold, after she was passed over, it seemed as if Sam was angry – angry not at International Studios; not at Seymore LeVine, who had promised Mary Jane the role; but at Mary Jane herself. He couldn't bear her grief – 'moping,' he called it. He'd become impatient, easily irritated. And he took it out on everyone. On her, on Neil, on Molly, on everyone. The scene last night had just been his most extreme way of showing it.

So he was going out to L.A. Big deal, she told herself. It was only for one film, *his* script. Sam had always said he wasn't interested in Hollywood – he was a Broadway gypsy, too. Maybe he was frightened about going. Still, it was no excuse for last night.

She sipped at her coffee and then sighed. Her mind kept running in circles, like a rat in a trap. Well, she felt trapped. Last night especially. She had lasted through the rehearsal, then avoided coffee with him and the others, come straight home, gone to bed, and pretended to be asleep when he came in, much, much later.

She picked up her coffee mug, pulled her old terrycloth bathrobe around herself, and went into the living room. She put a disc on the CD – a recording of the sounds of the rain forest – and sat in the recliner, closing her eyes. To the sounds of a brook and bird calls, Mary Jane took the deep breaths she had learned in yoga class. I can't let this get out of hand, she thought. Not like the other times. I must be clear about what happened, and how I feel.

As always, she felt a part of herself wanting to let it go, to chalk last night up to his enthusiasm for the show, a momentary lapse of taste, *anything*, so long as she didn't have to confront him. But the hurt had been so blatant. The looks of pity on Molly's and Bethanie's faces flashed again before her eyes. And again she thought, How could he? Tears began to sting her eyelids. No, she *had* to confront him.

Sam's voice from the bedroom broke into her thoughts. 'Any coffee, babe?'

'In the coffee pot,' she called back. Let him get his own fucking coffee, she thought. I've spoiled him by bringing his coffee to him in bed every morning. I'm so pathetically grateful for his attentions that I serve him like a faithful dog. Not today, she told herself, and she wiped the tears away quickly. Then a thought came to her. Maybe he would apologize. All on his own. Blame stress, blame jet lag. Give her a good, contrite act of repentance and save the day.

Sam came into the living room. 'Can I get you a refill?' he asked. Oh, he knew he was in trouble. Otherwise he'd never have noticed her empty cup. As Sam placed his mug down on the scratched old coffee table in front of the Salvation Army sofa, she could feel his uneasiness. Well, at least he had the decency to feel some remorse. He reached over to lift her cup.

'No thanks. I don't want any,' she told him. Sure, she told herself. Try a little passive aggression; that's right up your alley.

She watched him attempt to be casual. Well, clearly there would be no apology; she would have to begin. She reminded herself not to lash out at him, to talk calmly about her feelings. She didn't want this to deteriorate into a shouting match. She hated arguments. They'd had only a few, but those had been whoppers. Each time he slammed out the door, she feared she'd never see him again. She watched him now as he picked up the newspaper.

'Sam, I need to talk about last night.'

'What about last night?' His eyes didn't leave yesterday's *Post*, which, she noted, he was reading as if it were tomorrow's.

'C'mon, Sam. About the magic act. Jesus, that was mean. You hurt me.'

Sam looked up, his face a blank. Oh, Jesus, she thought, not the little-boy-lost routine. 'Hurt you? What are you talking about? What does hurt have to do with casting? I'm trying to do a show.'

Christ. He was defensive already. She sighed. Why did otherwise normal men find it impossible to admit they were wrong? Why did they have to get so blind and stubborn? 'But to hold me up to ridicule and humiliation that way . . . that was so unnecessary. Were you *trying* to hurt me?'

Sam placed his mug down with a thud. 'Now, wait a minute, Mary Jane. What I did was try to put together a skit for a show. It was a funny bit. If you don't like your part, I'll recast it. You're blowing this all out of proportion. *I* didn't humiliate you.'

She couldn't believe that he was going to try and stonewall. It made her even more angry, as if he were ignoring an elephant in the room with them. 'I was held up to ridicule because of my looks. Tell me that's not what happened. And tell me it's not humiliating.' His face remained blank. He's not going to cop to this, she thought, a sick feeling in her stomach. And if he doesn't, we'll have to break up.

'Mary Jane, get a grip. I needed to cast a 'Before' and an 'After.' It was a classic old gag. And you were there, could do for the 'Before.' Hey, this is no discovery. You weren't passed over for Jill because you resemble Michelle Pfeiffer.'

Mary Jane felt her stomach cramp — as if she'd been punched in the gut. Sam picked up the paper again. 'I don't want to have to take the rap for your feeling bad about your appearance. I've told you, you look fine to me. We've been through it a hundred times. Own up to your own feelings, and don't project them on to me.' Sam got up and went to the kitchen. She heard him pour himself more coffee but could barely look up as he returned to his spot on the couch. She took a deep, shaky breath.

'I'm not *projecting*, Sam. I'm hurt. Everyone there last night either laughed at me or pitied me. And I can't stand either.' But that was nothing compared with this. Compared with his pretending it hadn't happened, and throwing the blame back on her. She felt her eyes fill, her throat close. She wouldn't allow herself to cry. Not now.

Sam stood in the doorway, looking in at her. 'You know your problem? You're paranoid,' he said, and walked to the bedroom.

She got up and followed him. 'Paranoid? What are you saying, Sam? That you *weren't* insensitive? That I *wasn't* hurt?' Mary Jane was raising her voice, her anger pushing back the lurking tears.

Sam turned to her, standing in the doorway, and looked up at the cracked plaster ceiling. 'Okay, Mary Jane. Now you're not paranoid. *Now* you're getting hysterical. I can't talk to you when you're like this.' Calmly he pulled on a pair of socks and struggled into the black sweater that lay on a chair next to the bed. 'I'm going out until you've cooled down.' He tucked his T-shirt into his jeans, and pushed into his cowboy boots. Grabbing his black leather jacket from the closet, he turned back to her. 'And don't play the misunderstood martyr, Mary Jane. That doesn't work anymore.'

'Sam, don't go. Not till we've sorted this out,' she said, her voice raised.

Sam strode to the door and put his hand on the knob. 'It's not my issue. *You* do the sorting. Then stop screaming like a banshee,' he told her.

'You bastard!' Mary Jane cried. 'You always do this. How did it start out being a discussion about my *feelings*, and wind up with me being the shrew who chases you out of the house?'

'Maybe because I have feelings, too,' he said calmly.

'And you're not understood here, so you're going to take them to Bethanie, right?'

Sam stopped, stock-still, at the door, his hand still on the knob.

'That does it, Mary Jane. Now you've gone too far. You *are* a fucking paranoid.' He went through the door and slammed it behind him.

Mary Jane stared at the back of the chipped old fire door, the Fox police lock jerked out of its slot on the floor by the violence of Sam's slam. 'Oh, shit,' she wept, her voice too low for anyone else to hear.

9

Lila opened her eyes, straining to see the clock in the gloom of the heavily draped guest room. The small green number said 11:17. She squinted and saw the even smaller 'A.M.' She couldn't have known that, because the fabric over the windows shut out the light. The entire room was swathed in silk, and looked like some kind of tent from the Arabian Nights, complete with camel saddles and brass lamps.

She lay still, trying to get it together. The dream lurked behind her eyes. She strained for a moment to bring the images back, but could only feel the horror, so she willed the pictures away.

The days and nights had merged into one long searing burn, broken only by the blessed blackness of sleep. It was when she first moved her head that she realized the pillow was damp. She must have been crying in her sleep, she thought. She turned her head to avoid the clammy spot, as she raised her hand to her forehead.

What day was it? Tuesday? Wednesday? How long had she been here?

Seven, maybe eight — no, nine days. Nine days ago, she had come running here to Aunt Robbie's from her mother's house. The picture of Kevin bent over the potting table snapped into place. The headache sprung full-grown again. The memory of the animal sounds curling from his lips accompanied the picture. The scene brought spasms of nausea to her stomach. She swallowed hard against the urge to retch.

A low whirring sound came from the other end of the one-level contemporary house Aunt Robbie had built in Benedict Canyon. The sound, familiar to her, grew louder as it neared. Then it stopped, and Lila heard Aunt Robbie fiddle with the door handle before swinging it in. It had to be Robbie. José, Aunt Robbie's houseboy, normally left her breakfast tray outside the door.

'"Suffering was the only thing made me feel I was alive."' The words were sung by Rob's deep basso voice as he rolled into the room, Chinese-red lacquer breakfast tray held chest-high before him. Aunt Robbie came to an abrupt stop at the low hammered-brass table. He put the tray down and reached up to pull the drapes back from the windows, suddenly flooding the room in a bath of sunlight. Again he sang Carly Simon's line from the song: '"Suffering was the only thing made me feel I was alive."'

'Shut up an' go away,' Lila growled.

'Come on, Sister Miserere — novena's over. Nine days of pissing and moaning over a man is all the good Lord allows.' With surprising grace, Robbie sat down on the camel saddle, his mauve-trimmed flowered satin caftan billowing around his feet, hiding the roller blades he wore. 'Makes me feel light on my feet,' he had once explained to Lila. Now he grinned. 'Come on, I had José make this especially for you.' Robbie poured thick black coffee from a small antique Russian samovar he swore had been given to him by his first john — who was most assuredly one of the deposed Romanoffs.

'Lila?' he asked, and paused. When, after a few moments, there was no response, he leaned over and picked up a mallet and banged the brass temple-gong to which it was attached. She jumped. 'Listen, girlfriend, get the fuck over here this minute.' He slapped the filled Limoges coffee cup onto the brass tray.

Her head ached with the echoes of the gong. 'Don't do this to me, Aunt Robbie. Please,' Lila begged.

'Now, now. No whining. It's time you and I had a little chat.' He patted a stack of cushions beside him. Robbie's voice softened. 'Come sit next to your old but ever-so-attractive auntie.'

Lila sighed, sat up, and moved with effort to the cushions. It was exhausting, so she dropped down, then put her face in her hands and began to cry. 'Robbie, I can't bear it another minute.' She cried soundlessly, and he let her until she wiped her eyes with the sleeve of the peignoir he had given her the day she arrived. After a few more minutes, she looked up and took a sip of the coffee Robbie handed her. 'What am I going to do?' she asked for the thousandth time in nine days.

'What do you *want* to do?' he asked. Aunt Robbie reached across the table and touched Lila's chin with his stubby, crimson-nail-tipped fingers. Lila knew that he loved her as much as he had loved her father, though she shrank from his – or anyone's – touch. Still, his gentleness and soft voice showed his concern.

'Honey-girl, I know how hard this is on you, how confusing. But you can't let yourself just melt away. I'm serious, now – nine days *is* long enough.' Robbie stood up and rolled again to the window, touching Lila's arm lightly as he passed. 'You haven't been out of this room since you got here.'

'I hate her,' Lila said.

Robbie turned from the window and faced her.

'She was the one who set up the marriage. My own mother. She said he'd never bother me. But she didn't tell me *why*. *I* didn't know until I walked in on them that he was . . .' Lila's voice trailed off. She didn't want to offend Aunt Robbie, although she knew she could always be honest with him. 'Well, *you* know,' she continued. 'Not only was it *disgusting*, it was *deceitful*. He said he loved *me*.'

'Well, maybe he does. There are different kinds of love, you know.' Robbie was standing at the full-length mirror now, patting his red-dyed hair in place. 'If I curled up in bed every time one of *my* boyfriends dipped his wick in another inkwell, I'd be a fat mental case by now.' He made a full spin on his skates, then considered his reflection once again. Actually, I *am* a fat mental case now, but you get my point.'

Lila got up from the low cushions with what felt like an immense effort and sat on the chair in front of the vanity table. She stared into the triple mirrors. She picked up the Victorian silver-backed brush, and began to run it through the accumulation of knots at the back of her usually silky red hair. 'What I don't understand,' she said, as she strained against a tangle, 'is how my own mother could have absolutely no regard for my feelings. She manipulated me into this engagement, but she didn't do it for *me*.' Lila dropped the brush, helpless against the snarls, and turned to Aunt Robbie, who was now sitting on the end of the bed, legs crossed, one skated foot swinging slowly.

'It's called narcissism!' Robbie said. 'I've known your mother a long time and I love her, but I can't say I've always liked her. Still, Lila, you have to try to remember there are reasons why people are the way they are.' Rob's foot stopped moving. 'Do you know anything about her childhood?' he asked.

'Oh, give me a break! Are we going to start that bit about how she went to her first audition in L.A. through the snow without shoes?' Lila snapped.

'You know, Lila, the only training for *being* a good parent is *having* a good parent. She didn't, so she raised you the same way she developed a career – by the seat of her pants.' Lila angrily stood up and started walking towards the door. 'No, wait, you've got to hear this,' Robbie continued. 'Do you think you could do any better raising a child than she did, Lila? Given the way *you* were raised?'

'*I'm* not having children.'

'But if you did?'

'I'd like to think I would do better,' Lila said.

'That's my point. So did Theresa. And she *did* do better than her folks did to her.' Robbie got up.

They both stood in silence for a moment; then Aunt Robbie skated back over to the open window. He looked out at his lover, Ken, who was cleaning the pool wearing only a tiny chartreuse Speedo swimsuit. Suddenly Robbie shouted to Ken: 'Mary, what did I tell you about wearing that marble bag? You look ridiculous!' He turned back to Lila as if there had been no interruption.

Lila had to smile and look, too. She could see Ken moving the pole of the pool vacuum slowly up and down on the sides of the pool, as if he hadn't even heard Robbie's voice. Someone else was with him, she could see.

'Look at this, Lila.'

'Like I haven't seen Ken in his bathing suit before,' Lila said, more grumpily than she felt. 'Why don't you leave him alone?

You know he never listens to you.' Lila paused, looked at Robbie's getup, and then laughed. 'And how can you say *he* looks ridiculous?'

'No, I don't mean Ken. Do you see that girl sitting on the chaise longue talking to Ken?'

'You mean the little black kid?' Lila asked.

'That's Simone Duchesne, the star of the TV show *Opposites Attract*. And she's no kid. She's twenty-two.'

'*That's* Simone Duchesne? But I thought Simone was the same age as her character – about six or seven.'

'Yeah,' sighed Robbie. 'So does everyone else. She only looks like a kid. She has a benign tumour on her adrenal gland. It stunted her growth. It *could* have been removed by simple surgery when it was first discovered, but her parents – who, by the way, managed her – decided against it. Now it's too late.'

'Why?' Lila asked, though the feeling in the pit of her stomach told her she already knew.

'They say they were too poor. But, hey, if she'd grown normally, she would have outgrown the TV role. The parents chose the money instead.'

'Poor kid. I mean, woman,' Lila said and shivered. 'So is she after Ken?' she asked.

'Oh, no, she's asexual,' Robbie said. 'Her parents robbed her of that, too, when they wouldn't allow the surgery. No, she's just become attached to Ken, follows him around like a puppy dog. You know what a good listener Ken is. They met on the show. Ken did the lighting for it.' Robbie came away from the window. 'She'll never get hired for anything else. What a life, huh, Lila?'

Lila couldn't answer, allowing the silence to speak for her.

'Some things are worse than being the child of a star. Like *being* a child star. Robbed of her stature *and* sex life *and* money by her greedy parents. Ken tells me Simone sees a shrink five days a week, and has started a lawsuit against them. But, no matter how the lawsuit turns out, she'll still wind up the loser.'

'I know how she must feel,' Lila whispered.

'Tsk, tsk. Do you, Miss Self-Pity? Look in the mirror. I don't mean at the puffy eyes and pale face – that'll go away in a couple of hours. I mean, look at *you*. What do you see? Not a black female midget.'

Lila studied her reflection for a moment. 'I know I'm beautiful, Aunt Robbie, and that men want me. But *I* don't want *them*. Then my mother picks the only man that doesn't want *me*. And I don't really want *him*, either.'

'Do you want girls, then?' Robbie asked, gently.

Lila shuddered and turned her head quickly, as if slapped. 'No! I *hate* women.'

Robbie tsked again. 'Doesn't leave much choice, do it? Well, if it's any consolation to you, you come from a family with a long line of gender confusion. Your father was the only man I ever loved – nothing personal against Ken – but your father didn't know if he was coming or going. He spilled his seed all over Hollywood. "Boys and girls together, me and Mamie O'Rourke," Aunt Robbie sang. 'Theresa was the one who wore the pants in the family. You might take a lesson from her. As fucked up as she is, she *did* make one good decision in her life, once she realized that he would always make her unhappy. I don't like what that decision did to you, but it saved her sanity. She decided, since her love life wasn't going to be her career, then she would make her career her love life.' He paused. 'That was what she wanted, and she went for it. What about you, Lila? What do *you* want?'

Lila stared at her reflection in the mirror for a long while before she spoke. Without taking her eyes off herself, she said, 'I want everyone to love me – but always from a distance.'

10

Seven and a half miles outside Fort Dram, Texas, Sharleen stood at the side of Interstate 10, the white-hot glare of the sun beating down on her head, the steam of the blacktop burning through the thin soles of her sandals. She knew it was seven and a half miles, because she had walked every flat sizzling inch of them. So had Dean, and he had carried their bag as well. When they had first begun to walk, it seemed like the best thing to do. After only three miles of their last ride, Sharleen had begun to suspect that maybe the truck driver was being too friendly to her. They'd gotten out fast. Maybe he meant no harm, and maybe she had been too quick to get Dean away from the guy, but when the trucker had taken her hand and asked if she wanted a chance to steer, she'd become afraid that somebody might get hurt.

Yes, it was the right thing to do, she reasoned. It's what Momma would have told her to do, if Momma had been there. But even with her momma so long gone, Sharleen would still never want to do anything that might bring shame down on her momma's head. All those things her daddy had said were a lie. She made a silent prayer: Thank you, Lord, for getting us out of Lamson and to Fort Dram, and for getting us out of that truck and on this here road that's burning my feet, instead of staying in the truck and maybe ending up burning in Hell. The thought that maybe Dean and she would go to Hell for what they had done to her daddy came to her. But surely Jesus would understand. 'Dear Jesus, forgive us. It won't happen again,' she said.

Dean was struggling along beside her, sweat rolling off his forehead and down his face, his white T-shirt now grey against his muscular chest, damp both from walking and carrying the one suitcase they had between them. He had broken at least two of the Ten Commandments, but Sharleen couldn't see Jesus not forgiving Dean. And if Jesus sent Dean to Hell, Sharleen was surely going to beg to go right with him. Not, she thought, that Hell could be too much hotter than Interstate 10 outside Fort Dram, Texas. A white Chevy sped by, its wake more like a gust from an open oven door than a breeze.

'Sharleen!' Dean called out. 'That was a New Hampshire tag! Ain't never seen one of them! What does it mean — "Live Free or Die"?'

'Means they don't cut you no slack in New Hampshire, I guess,' Sharleen told him. Since Dean was a little boy, he had sat beside the highway, watching for out-of-state tags. Dean's ambition was to see all fifty licence plates. At home, he'd sit beside the highway for hours, though not much passed but local Texas plates, and the others often flew by too fast to decipher. Still, Dean was real patient.

'Now I got me fifteen, Sharleen: Texas, Arkansas, Oklahoma, Florida, New Mexico, Arizona, New York, Ohio, Colorado, Indiana, California, Tennessee, Mississippi, Louisiana, *and* New Hampshire!'

'That's real good, Dean.' She wondered how far it was to the next town, and how far that town was from the one after that. She couldn't remember how many miles across Texas it was to the border. For a moment, she felt so overwhelmed by fatigue that she wasn't sure she could take another step.

But she had to. And she had to risk taking another ride. Because they had to get out of Texas, and maybe even out of the country.

And if a trooper or even a local sheriff drove by, she was sure that she and Dean would be in a world of trouble.

They had carried their father's body over to Boyd's Trans Am along with the bat, then pushed the car behind the dumpster. Sharleen said a prayer, best she could, and asked God to accept the two souls. But she didn't imagine even Jesus could forgive her daddy, and she knew she never could. Then she and Dean lit out, stopping only to take Momma's Bible, some clothes, and the few bills and change that they had saved in the place under kitchen cabinet. They'd walked all night, gotten a ride to Fort Dram, slept all the next day in a park next to the post office, then caught another ride, the ride that hadn't worked out. Sharleen knew she had to make a plan, a good plan, but all she kept thinking, over and over with each step, was 'Father, forgive them; for they know not what they do.'

She heard it long before she saw it. The car's engine sounded strong and sure as she squinted against the light to catch a first glimpse. Out of the waves of heat rising from the road they had just walked, Sharleen could make out a silvery glint. Before she realized it, it was near, the first car they had seen all afternoon that wasn't going so fast it was almost a blur.

Without a word, the two of them got into their positions. Dean stood at the edge of the road, one thumb out in the air, the other thumb tucked passively onto a belt loop. Sharleen sat on the suitcase, shaded slightly by Dean's shadow, and slumped down, elbows on knees, to hide the obvious curves of her body.

It was a Pontiac, she could see. A big car, tinted windows shut tight against the heat of the day. Sharleen caught a glimpse of the driver as he came to a stop just beyond where they stood. Old guy, maybe fifty or sixty. Another plus. And he had a dog with him. Would a pervert have a dog? She hoped not. They both rushed up to the lowering window on the passenger side and peered in.

'Where you headed?' the old guy asked.

'Montana,' said Dean.

'California,' said Sharleen. They had answered together.

The driver laughed. 'Confused, ain't you?' he asked, smiling.

'No, we know where we're going,' Sharleen spoke up. 'First we're going to California, then, later, to Montana. Where are you headed?' she added, deciding that this ride might be okay. She saw Dean reach out to the dog, a big black Lab.

'To California and beyond. Hop on in,' he said, and reached

64

across the seat to open the front passenger door. Sharleen eyed Dean, then opened the rear door and sat in the back. Dean pushed the bag onto the seat next to her and got in the front beside the dog, just like she had told him to. With the doors closed, it became immediately, blessedly cool.

Sharleen looked around and noticed the driver's large satchel on the floor at her feet, along with a beat-up five-gallon can. Overflow from the trunk, she thought. Must be going to be away a long time to have this much luggage. She leaned her head back on the soft headrest and felt herself sink into the plush upholstered seat. The cool breeze from the air conditioner came wafting back to her, drying the sweat from her damp shirt, the chill making her nipples hard. Dean turned back to her for a moment and grinned.

'What's your names?' the driver asked as the car gathered speed.

'I'm Sharleen, and this here's my brother, Dean,' Sharleen answered, touching her brother gently on the shoulder with one hand while straightening her messy hair with the other. 'What's yours?'

'Dobe Samuels is as good a name as any, I figure. Named the dog Oprah 'cause she's fat and black and smart. No disrespect intended.'

They rode in silence, Dean petting Oprah, Sharleen lulled by the air conditioning and the motion of the car. Blessed relief, she thought as she thanked the Lord for their good fortune. She noticed the back of Dobe's neck and saw that he had a fresh haircut. The collar of his cotton shirt was clean and pressed. Sharleen checked the rearview mirror to see if he was eyeing her and was satisfied to see he wasn't but seemed instead to be staring at the long stretch of road before them.

Hanging from the mirror was a small plastic-coated sign that said, 'My boss is a Jewish carpenter,' written in a sort of churchy print. Who's his boss? she wondered, then realized what it meant. He's a Christian, she said to herself, and felt the last of the tension leave her body with a sigh. Thank You for this message, she prayed.

Then a car pulled up behind them, real close, almost like it was following them. She felt her stomach lurch, just like it did when David Janssen was almost caught on each episode of *The Fugitive*. Sharleen turned around, looked, and was grateful to see it wasn't a cop car. But maybe it was *plainclothes* police: she felt her heart begin to pound.

'I'm doing sixty-five and the guy is on my tail,' complained Dobe.

'The dirty dog,' Dean agreed, then looked at Oprah. 'No disrespect intended,' he added.

Dobe laughed. 'Oh, she don't take offence easy.' Dobe patted Oprah, and her heavy tail thumped. 'Guess a dog is the only thing that loves you more than you love yourself.' The car behind them pulled ahead to pass, and kept right on going. Slowly, Sharleen's heart stopped pounding.

They drove for a long time, the Pontiac easily eating up the miles that Sharleen had dreaded walking. They were far from Lamson. They looked like a family on a vacation drive. And maybe no police would notice them now. They'd be out of Texas in no time. Maybe it would all be okay.

Dobe was the first to break the long silence. 'Need to stop at that station up ahead,' he said, as he slowed to turn into the isolated filling station.

Sharleen became immediately alert. 'Are you going to get gas?' she asked. Did he expect us to pitch in for it? she thought. With only sixty dollars between them, Sharleen and Dean could not afford gas, and only an occasional something to eat.

'Well, you'll see,' Dobe answered. He drove the car past the single, rusting pump and came to a stop. He got out of the car and greeted the figure of a young man almost obscured by the shadows on the porch.

'Howdy,' Dobe called, then opened the rear door to the car, reached in, and took out the gallon can that was beside Sharleen. Dobe left the door open, told Oprah to stay, and took two steps towards the young man on the porch. He was sitting on a straight chair, tilted back, his feet on the railing. Sharleen noticed that the guy, who was wearing coveralls, hadn't said anything.

'Could I trouble you for some water?' Dobe called out, holding up the empty can so the man on the porch could see it.

'What about gas?' the man asked.

'Don't need none. Just water.'

'I *sell* gas.'

'I don't need gas, young feller. Just water.' Dobe smiled broadly, takin' no offence, even if some was intended.

Sharleen then got out of the car and stood with her hands tucked into the back pockets of her jeans. 'We'd be much obliged,' she called out. In the many towns they'd lived in, she had known a lot of ornery backcountry trash. She didn't want no scene now.

The man on the porch put the chair right and placed both

feet on the floor. A shaft of sunlight caught his long, horselike face, and she watched as his small eyes opened wider.

'Sure thing, ma'am,' he said. ''Round the side. He'p yourse'f.'

Dean jumped out and went with Dobe. 'What do you need water for, Mr. Samuels? The car's not overheating.' Dean was almost as good with motors as he was with animals.

Dobe reached down and picked up the brass spigot of the hose, turned on the water, and placed the spigot in the can. 'Son, you're about to see a miracle of modern science,' Dobe told Dean as his eyes watched the water climb to the top.

'What kinda miracle?'

'I'm going to pour this here water into my gas tank, then drop in a magic tablet, and I'll have instant gasoline.'

'You can do that?' Dean asked, his voice gone high with amazement.

'Sure. Just watch.'

Dean called over to Sharleen. 'Hey, Sharleen! Dobe's gonna make his car run on water. He got a special pill.' Dean was wearing a grin as wide as a wave on a slop bucket and watching Dobe's every move.

Sharleen eyed Dobe as he started walking back to the car, straining to carry the gallon of water. What kind of foolishness is this? Sharleen wondered. Is Dobe one of them guys that make themselves look smart by teasing Dean? There were enough of them back in Lamson. She'd play along, but try also, as she always did, to protect Dean's feelings. Still, she felt disappointment in Dobe, funning Dean like that. 'Why, sure he can, Dean. And he's the only one in the world can do it, too.' Sharleen didn't show any surprise until Dobe actually began opening the gas tank.

'Mister,' the man in the coveralls said, as he came down the two steps from the porch. 'If'n you mix water in with yer gas, you ain't driving this car out a' here. I bet you five dollars you cain't do such of a thing.' He stood with his hands in his pockets, grinning for the first time since they pulled up.

'That wouldn't be a wager, young feller. That would be pure theft,' Dobe said as he tilted the water can into the gas tank. Dean and the coveralls man both gasped.

'Whoa, don't do that, mister! You're going to ruin your car.'

Dobe ignored the stranger's protest and finished pouring in the water, then called out to Dean: 'Son, get me the box of tablets out of the glove box, would you?'

Dean nodded eagerly, ducked into the car, and carried a box to Dobe, who placed it on the hood and opened it. Both Dean and the good ole boy drew closer, eyeing the array of red, horse-sized capsules. Dobe took one out and held it up to the sun, then slowly, as if performing a ritual, dropped the capsule into the gas tank and shut it.

Dobe leaned towards Dean and tossed him the car keys. 'Start'er up, son, while I get us a couple of Dr. Peppers.' He walked past the yokel towards the soda machine just as the engine coughed into a roar.

Sharleen looked back at the idling car, then towards Dobe. She wasn't sure what was happening. What was in them pills?

'Where'd you get them pills, mister?' The gas jockey's voice was filled with awe. He was as surprised as Sharleen herself.

'I made 'em,' Dobe said, walking back towards the car with four cold Dr. Peppers in his hands. 'I invented a way to make gas out of water.' Dobe passed two bottles of pop to Sharleen and Dean, then gave a third to the gas pumper.

'My name's Samuels – Dobe Samuels,' he said, also offering the man his hand. 'What's yours?'

The young man accepted the pop and the hand. 'Eb Cloon.' Eb walked over to the car. 'How many miles to the gallon can you get on it?'

Dobe took a long drink of pop, then said, 'Ain't quite like gas that way. One gallon of water and one of these pills is the same as three or four tanks of gas.'

'Three or four *tanks?*'

'Sharleen, have we stopped for water before today?' Dobe asked.

'No, this is the first time,' she answered.

Dean was excited. 'Sure didn't,' he said proudly.

'And this mornin' I started in San Antonio.'

'What's they made of?'

'That's the funny thing, Eb. If I may call you Eb?' Eb Cloon nodded. 'Made from stuff around the house. Nothing you ain't got in your kitchen cupboards right now. But I sure ain't gonna tell you any more than that. Lots of folks purty interested, I can tell you.'

'How much do them pills cost, anyway?' Eb asked.

'They're not for sale, young feller. I'm on my way to show my invention to one of them big oil companies.' He took another gulp of soda and turned to walk back to replace the empty. 'Can't say more, but they're mighty interested, I can tell you that.'

'I'd buy me a couple of them pills, if the price was right,' Eb offered.

Sharleen watched Dobe rack the empty bottle and then raise his head skywards as if considering. 'Will you promise not to try and copy the recipe?' Dobe asked. Eb nodded agreement.

'Well, I *could* let you have a few at five dollars apiece, but you can only have ten of 'em. We got to get to California, then on to Montana,' he said, and turned and smiled at Sharleen. He had a nice, friendly smile. 'That's if you let me have some more water for my dog. She's gettin' powerful thirsty.'

'Well, sir, I'll take them,' Eb said, and turned and almost ran back to the house to get the cash. 'Take all the water you want,' he shouted as an afterthought.

'Now, remember,' Dobe said after he gave a pan of water to Oprah, watched her lap it up, and handed Eb ten red capsules, pocketing the crumbled wad of dirty bills that made up the fifty dollars. 'One gallon of water and one of these pills will last you as long as *three* tanks of gas. Mebbe four, but I ain't makin' no exaggerated claim.' Eb nodded. 'Wouldn't want you to be disappointed.'

Dobe told Oprah to get back into the car and sat down in the driver's seat, vacated by Dean; and Sharleen again slipped into the back. Dobe started the motor, lowered his window, and extended his hand. Eb took it. 'I'm sure you'll get what you deserve,' he told Eb.

'Mr. Samuels, I sure do thank you. Wait'll Pa sees this,' Eb said, and stepped back, grinning.

'Don't mention it,' Dobe said. 'I only wish I had more to give you.' He put the car into gear and pulled out, waving friendlylike at Eb as he did.

Dean was only silent for a little while. 'Mr. Samuels,' Dean said when they returned to the highway, 'you're going to be rich when you get to California.'

Sharleen caught Dobe looking at her in the rearview mirror. 'I'm already rich enough, son,' he said, patted Oprah, and winked at Sharleen.

Sharleen woke early, while Dean slept on beside her in the single bed they had shared, leaving the second bed untouched. She got up slowly, so as not to wake him, and went into the tiny bathroom of the motel cabin. The crisp, clean sheets on the bed when they got in last night had felt so good that she had moaned with pleasure as she slid between them. Tired, full, and happy, both Sharleen and Dean fell immediately to sleep, Dean's arm wrapped protectively around her. She touched the green-plaid bedspread on the bed as she passed, wishing she had had one as nice as that when she was a little girl. The solid-green drapes with the green-plaid pullbacks framed the light coming in the window. The grey hooked rug felt soft and warm under her feet as she padded barefoot to the bathroom. All of it was so nice and clean – jest like a room in the Sears Catalogue. It was the nicest room she'd ever been in. This was the fourth motel they'd stayed in, after almost a week on the road with Dobe, and Sharleen still couldn't figure out the danger. The Lord had surely provided. And, as if it were a sign, Sharleen had found a Bible at each of the motel rooms.

They'd travelled more than a thousand miles, Sharleen figured, and they'd finally left Texas yesterday. Dobe stuck to small roads, and sometimes he doubled back a bit. He also stopped for water three or four times a day – because he was experimenting on mileage, he said. And at each stop he topped off the tank with water and sold some of his pills. It seemed so easy that Sharleen had come to accept Dobe's offers of meals and a place to stay – and he hadn't tried to touch her or nothin'.

Sitting on the bathroom stool, Sharleen looked around the tiny, spotless white-tiled room. There were two towels for each of them, also two new, tiny, wrapped pieces of soap. They were really nice, and it seemed such a waste to use 'em just once and leave them. She longed for the neatly wrapped little soaps, but she wouldn't steal nothin'. She finished, flushed the toilet, then stepped back with a giggle as it made a strong woosh noise, then went silent.

She pulled back the white shower curtain and turned on the water, amazed at how powerful the spray was compared with the trickle she was used to in the trailer back in Lamson. There were two *more* tiny bars of sweet-smelling soap here, *and* a little bottle of shampoo. Dobe had told her they came with the room and she could keep them, but still she hadn't liked to. Just in case.

This place must be very expensive, she thought, but she couldn't tell. She had never been in a motel before this week. This place seemed a little nicer than the other ones, but all of them were a treat to her. And Dean was in hog heaven.

Back in Lamson, Dean's biggest treat, aside from sightin' a new licence plate, was always watchin' the *Andy of Mayberry* show. He'd seen all of the episodes many times by now, but he was never bored by them. He loved Aunt Bea, laughed at Gomer, and got frustrated with Barney, the deputy. It seemed to Sharleen that Dean liked Opie most of all. Well, she figured, in a way he *was* Opie – a motherless country kid in a small town. 'Cept his daddy was no Andy Griffith. Now, on the road, more than anything else he was missing the nice Mayberry people. So, when they pulled in last night, and there was a TV running the episode of Aunt Bea's pickles, Dean was soothed and happy.

Before she fell to sleep last night, her thoughts were how lucky she and Dean were to have met Dobe, and to eat in nice restaurants and sleep in clean beds. Now she added having hot showers to the list. As she patted herself dry, she happened to look out the bathroom window in time to see Dobe Samuels walking back from the gas station across the highway. He was carrying two gas cans. Oprah followed behind him.

Sharleen watched from the steamy bathroom window as he went to his car, opened the trunk, and, after a quick look in both directions, emptied the gas from the cans right into the trunk of the car! Then he closed the trunk cover and walked around to the spot where he had poured in the water yesterday. He knelt down and looked under the fender, then pulled something. Water rushed out and made a puddle around his feet. Oprah licked at it. Dobe reached into his back pocket, pulled out a handkerchief, and wiped his hands. Then he turned and began to walk towards Sharleen and Dean's room.

She ducked back, away from the window. What had she just seen? Sharleen felt her hands begin to tremble. She wasn't positive, but something about it all sure didn't seem right. She quickly pulled on her jeans and T-shirt and tried to open the door before Dobe knocked. She didn't make it in time.

Dean stirred at the sound of the knock, and Sharleen gave him a poke as she passed, indicating the bathroom behind her. She had to squint to make out Dobe's face, because of the strong early-morning sun behind his head.

'You kids ready for some breakfast?' he asked.

'I sure am,' Dean called out, still shaking the sleep from his head as he walked towards the bathroom.

'Then meet me in the coffee shop in ten minutes,' Dobe told them cheerfully, and turned back to the main building.

Sharleen waved at him as she closed the door, then yelled in to

Dean, 'Ten minutes, Dean. Make it snappy.' While he washed and dressed, she neatly made the bed, dusted the room, and folded the towels.

The coffee shop was almost empty as she and Dean entered, except for a few truckers at the counter. Sharleen led Dean to the booth where Dobe already sat waiting for them, reading a paper. She slid into the seat opposite Dobe, and Dean sat beside her, his long legs sticking out into the aisle. The waitress came over, poured them each a cup of coffee, and freshened Dobe's.

'What would you like, kids? Anything you want, remember. It's on me,' Dobe said, pushing aside the menu without opening it.

Dean suddenly came to life, brought around by either the coffee or the offer of food. 'Steak and eggs,' he said. 'And grits. And pancakes on the side – *with* syrup.'

Dobe laughed. 'That's what I like to see, a man with no fear of cholesterol.' He looked at Sharleen. 'And a woman, too. Oh, and, miss?' he asked the waitress. 'Could I have a side order of bacon to go? Seems my dog gets surly if she don't get her breakfast bacon. She likes it crispy.'

Restaurant bacon, just for a dog? Sharleen was awed. But then the scene at the trunk of the car came back to her. Maybe for Dobe money was easy come and easy go.

They ate in silence, the forks and coffee cups the only sounds at the table. Dean was finished first. He dropped his fork noisily, leaned back, and patted his stomach with two hands. 'I'm full as a goose in a corn crib. I better walk around for a minute. I'll take the bacon out to Oprah for you, Mr. Samuels, if'n that's all right.' Dobe nodded. 'Sharleen, I'll be outside,' Dean promised, and headed for the door.

Sharleen sipped her coffee, then placed it gently on the saucer. 'Mr. Samuels,' she began.

'"Mister?"' Dobe asked, his brows raised. He smiled and put down his paper. 'I think this is going to be serious.'

'Dobe,' Sharleen corrected herself. She would give him a chance to explain. 'I know you're a very smart and kind man, but, well, with that gas pill, I can't help feeling there's something I just don't understand.' Sharleen hesitated, not wanting to offend the man but also, if there was something not . . . well, not *right* about what he was doing, she had to know. She and Dean were in enough trouble already.

'What don't you understand, Sharleen?' Dobe asked.

It was best to tell him what she'd seen, she reckoned. 'I saw you pouring gasoline into the trunk of your car this morning, and now I'm confused.' Sharleen added quickly, 'Not that I'm judging you or nothin', Dobe. It's not for me to judge anyone. But, you know . . .'

'I see,' he said. Dobe's voice lowered, and he leaned forward and looked directly into Sharleen's eyes. 'I respect you, young lady.' He paused for a few moments, as if he was thinking of how to say something, then continued. 'I can tell when people are in trouble, and I can see you and Dean — well, let's just say you might need a friend. And I see how you watch out for that boy, and how he looks out for you. It's nice. Real nice.' He paused. 'You know, God gave me a certain talent, and I use that talent to make money. I don't know why he didn't give the talent to everybody. And I never do evil to those that do good. You watch, and you can see that. You do, don't you?'

She thought of Eb Cloon, of the other men, of their meanness. She nodded. 'I do understand — but maybe me and Dean better move on.'

Dobe looked at her, it seemed sadly.

'Well, I sure would hate that. I got this gift, and the least I can do is share some of the Lord's bounty. Plus, sure is lonely on the road. Even with Oprah. So's I'm asking if you would be kind enough to let me take care of you and Dean as far as California. I can see Dean needs some taking care of.'

Sharleen thought about how good it felt to have the comfort of a ride, good food, good beds. But Dobe was telling her that he *was* doing something wrong. Get thee behind me, Satan, she thought. But Dobe, with his kind face and crinkled eyes, didn't *look* like Satan. Was he lookin' for somethin' else from her?

'Dobe, you know me and Dean don't have no money. There's nothing we can do for you other than help with the driving. Nothin' more I'm goin' to do for you.' There, she'd said it.

Dobe continued to look into Sharleen's eyes. 'I respect that. You don't owe me nothing, Sharleen. I appreciate the way you get out of the car when we stop at a service station. You pretty up the scenery. That really helps me out. Without you, sometimes I don't think I would have even gotten the water. Or the attention. These ole boys can be right mean. All's I'm asking is that, when we stop someplace, you get out of the car again, like you been doing.

73

Sometimes it takes a pretty face to get what a good Christian should offer by nature.'

Sharleen lowered her eyes.

'Dobe, those pills don't work, do they?'

'They work for me, Sharleen. And I never sell too many. It isn't a big sting. Only people who want something for nothing buy them. I'll never ask you to lie – all you do is stand beside the car. I'm not putting you on the grift. I'll never ask you or Dean a question you can't answer honestly.' He paused for a moment, then went on: 'I'll get you both to California – and to Montana, if you want – well fed and well rested.'

Sharleen sat for a long, silent moment, her hands clenched in her lap. 'Okay, Dobe. Just so long as I don't have to lie, or do anything else that's wrong, we'll go.'

Dobe offered his hand across the table and gave Sharleen's a firm shake. 'You do me a great favour, ma'am,' he said, then tipped an imaginary hat.

Dobe leaned back against the restaurant banquette and stretched, then smiled. 'You know, I'm a lot older than you, and take kindly to women. I'd politely ask for your favours, but I know how it is between you and Dean. You're safe with me. Anyway, the last few years I've switched my affection from women to dogs. You can make a real fool of yourself with a dog, and she won't lose respect for you – in fact, she'll make a fool of herself, too.' Dobe joined Sharleen in a laugh. Then he got a serious look on his face. 'See, I have a practical problem. Never did like any woman on the grift. Con them, con me, I always found. But good women are too dependent and too shockable. Either don't want nothing to do with me or want what I got but don't want to know how I got it. Makes for a lonely life.' He paused. They sat there together, the sun pouring in through the diner's window, in a friendly silence and a pool of sunlight.

Then Dobe leaned towards her. 'Sharleen, when I went to wake you up this morning, I saw that you only used one bed last night. And that's your business. Just let me give you a little advice. What you do *ain't* nobody's business. But a lot of people you'll meet will think it *is*, so I don't think you should call Dean your brother no more. Sharleen, tell people he's your boyfriend. That's what people want to hear, so it makes it easier on you.'

Sharleen blushed deeply, and her mind began to race. What was he talking about? But she knew, of course. All these years of being so close to Dean, their warm times in bed, the comfort they took from one another. But never was it ever spoken out loud by either of them or anyone else until this moment. She pushed the shock of it from her mind. But she had to say something.

'He *is* my boyfriend,' she said, returning Dobe's steady gaze as she felt the blood still rushing to her face. 'I only say "brother" so's people don't think we're living in sin.' The lie felt heavy on her tongue. Now she'd broken another commandment.

Dobe sat back in his chair. 'Sorry for the misunderstanding,' he said, and lowered his eyes. Then Dean returned to the table, and Dobe stood up and stretched. 'Time for us to hit the road. Let's have us some adventures.' He clapped Dean on the shoulder, and Sharleen could see how the fatherly gesture pleased Dean. Their daddy had only touched Dean when he meant him harm.

As Dean walked ahead of them in the parking lot, Dobe leaned towards Sharleen and said, 'He's a real enthusiastic boy, Dean is. And good-natured. I'd sure hate to see him ever lose that.' He looked sideways at Sharleen.

'So would I,' Sharleen agreed. Then all three of them got into the car.

11

Mary Jane sobbed herself into a light sleep. It had been four days without a word from Sam. She alternated between being frantic with worry and livid with rage. She ate two bags of Pepperidge Farm Milano cookies. She drank the end of a bottle of Jack Daniel's and started a new one. She passed out, woke up hung over, showered, drank, and slept again. She couldn't leave the apartment for fear he'd call and she'd miss him. Anyway, she had no place to go. She had Chinese food delivered – vile sweet-and-sour pork and moo-shu chicken – and ate it for lunch and dinner. Now, in their big bed alone, she tossed in her sleep. The ringing telephone roused her, and she rushed to it. Sam, she thought. Oh, thank God!

She made herself stand beside the battered black phone and

wait one more ring before lifting the receiver. 'Hello.' Not too breathless, not too pathetically eager, she hoped.

'Hi, Mary Jane. It's Neil. Are you okay?'

'Oh, Neil.' It felt as if all the air was sucked out of her lungs. 'No, no, I'm not okay. I feel terrible, as a matter of fact.'

'Well,' Neil said, 'you know what Confucius says: "Shit happens."'

'Yeah, well, Protestants say, "If shit happens, you deserve it."'

'More Sam crap?'

'No less. He's gone walkabout. I haven't heard from him.'

'You want to talk about it?'

'Spare me! Just cheer me up.'

'I think I got just the prescription. You didn't forget I'm breaking in the new material at the Comedy Club tonight, did you? My last gig before the big time.'

Oh, damn, Mary Jane thought. Of course she had. Jesus, she didn't even know what day it was. 'No, Neil, how could I forget?' she lied.

'So you'll be there? I reserved a table right up front for you and the shmuck.'

'Oh, I'll be there.' She knew how Neil felt about Sam in general, how he'd feel about the argument, and she didn't want to go into it all with him. She sighed, miserable but loyal. She added quickly, 'What time's the show?'

One more thing to do that she didn't feel like doing, she thought as she hung up. Midnight, her fat white Persian cat, jumped up onto the counter and pressed himself up against her, his squashed-in face expectantly looking towards her own. She opened the cheap, scratched metal kitchen cabinets. No more Tender Vittles. She searched the shelves until she found a can of tuna stuffed behind a box of stone-hard brown sugar. 'Here,' she told the cat as she opened the can, 'knock yourself out.'

She stumbled into the bathroom and turned on the shower, making it almost hotter than she could stand. She had just finished the first shampoo of her thick, heavy dark hair when the phone rang. She flung open the curtain, leaving the water running, and ran down the narrow hall, trailing soapy footprints. She slipped when she stepped into the kitchen, caught herself at the edge of the table, twisting her ankle, and lunged for the phone.

'Hello,' she panted.

'Hi.' Sam's voice was dead, cold, the way it always was after a fight, but it *was* Sam's voice.

'Hi.' Well, Christ, *that* was stupid. 'Are you okay?' she asked. Fuck. That was *pathetic*.

'Yeah. What about you?'

'I've been better.'

'Listen, M.J., I'm sorry about the other night. I didn't think. You know. Coming back from L.A., and the negotiations. There's been a lot of pressure on me lately and . . .'

Oh, sweet Jesus! He'd apologized. Tears filled her eyes. 'Hey . . .' she interrupted. 'I understand. I do. And I've been thinking.' She paused now, took a deep breath. It would be all right. He'd said he was sorry. She'd go with him to L.A. He'd still love her. And she could still love him. 'I want to go with you,' she said. 'The part doesn't matter. *We* matter. I'll get my shot later. I'll just wrap up a few odds and ends here, stick Midnight in a box, and hop a flight to L.A.'

There was silence at the other end of the phone. A long silence. 'Sam?' she asked. 'Are you still there?'

'Sure. Sure. I'm . . . I'm just surprised, is all. But that's fine. That's great. I'm just, well, surprised.' He paused. 'Look, we have to talk, M.J. Maybe I can come over tonight and . . .'

'I have to go see Neil,' she interrupted. 'It's his last gig.'

'Oh, fuck Neil!' There, he was irritated again. 'The guy's animus is scary.'

She sighed. 'I'd rather fuck you. Baby, it's been a long time to do without you. Listen, I *have* to go, but the show's at ten; I'll be home by midnight. How 'bout if we make up then?' She packed all the warmth into her voice that she could manage.

'Yeah. Fine,' he said, and hung up.

She did, too, and as she turned she caught her own reflection, her hair full of lather, her body naked and wet. She forced herself to look. Her breasts hung, like sagging water balloons, to the place on her rib cage where a small roll of fat had developed. It, in turn, rested on the swell of her round belly. Her *fat* belly, she corrected herself, which protruded over her pubic hair. Her hips were another monument to fat, the saddlebags visibly divided into three small but distinct ripples. Cottage-cheese thighs. Even her knees were ugly. She had let herself go and become a rounded, disgusting fertility figure. Even her thick, long hair, her one beauty, was starting to show grey streaks. She'd let herself go, something no actress could afford to do. No wonder Sam didn't sound happy on the phone, or eager to make love. Oh, God, how could anyone love me? she wondered. She was so very, very lucky to have Sam.

At a quarter to ten that evening, Neil saw Mary Jane come through the door of the club and try to adjust her eyes to the dark interior. He rushed over to her, hugged her, and cried, 'Mary Jane, thanks for coming. Christ, I'm nervous. All the guys are here, waiting to tear me apart. Feeding time at the zoo. Jesus, they're so jealous that I've had to hire a food taster. Hey, you look great. Very Mildred Pierce-ish. When she's on the decline.'

He was so kind. Even in the midst of his spritz, he took the time to notice. Mary Jane had been collecting vintage clothes for years. Neil always managed a riff based on the film or actress she dressed as. He always said she looked great, and Mary Jane always ignored it. But she didn't usually look as wrecked as this. Well, she'd done the best she could. He took her coat as he led her toward the small room at the rear. 'This place is larger than I thought, Neil,' Mary Jane said. 'How many people does it seat?'

'Seat? Forget about seats. We got *standees* here tonight. The entire bridge-and-tunnel crowd, plus every out-of-work stand-up motherfucker in the city. Them alone would fill Shea Stadium.' Indicating the one unoccupied table in the front, he added, 'The publicity about my pilot is paying off. But there's always room for you, Mildred. Boy, what a crowd!'

Bending to kiss her, Neil whispered, 'Wish me what I need, Mary Jane.'

Mary Jane patted Neil's cheek. 'I do, Jughead. Break a leg. Now, get started, funny-man, and make me laugh.' She followed the waiter to her table.

Neil was a good friend, and the crowd looked good, too. Hell, everything was rosy to her now that she knew Sam was waiting for her at home. After all, he had apologized. She shifted in her seat. The crowd was noisy tonight. It was the short break before the headliner, her pal Jughead.

For years, since they'd discovered that, among other shared tastes, as kids they both had read and collected Archie and Veronica comics, she had called Neil Jughead, and he'd called her Veronica. Now, with any luck at all, her pal would kill 'em. She felt her stomach tighten in nervous anticipation. He's good, she reminded herself. It will go well.

Neil had taken the three steps up to the stage and walked off into the wings. Now, after a rave introduction, he returned with a hand-held microphone, entering to a roaring welcome. He looked at her. 'Hello, Veronica,' he said. She smiled, and he was off on his spritz.

'Evening, folks. Good crowd. You all look very prosperous. You, sir' – pointing to a well-dressed man in the front row – 'you look like you do all right. What do you do for a living?'

What was this? Mary Jane knew that Neil never stooped to working the crowd for his act. It was for hacks and amateurs, he said. Now he watched his mark in the audience, and so did everyone else. Mary Jane shifted, uncomfortable in her seat. Was Neil going to embarrass the poor guy?

'I'm an investment banker.' The guy sounded wary but self-satisfied.

'You are?' said Neil. 'And what did your father do?'

'My father?' The guy paused. Not so self-satisfied now. Embarrassed. Mary Jane hunched her shoulders. 'My father was a school custodian.' There were a few titters.

'School custodian?' said Neil. 'You mean a janitor, right?' Someone actually laughed, but the rest of the audience was silent. What's he doing? Mary Jane wondered. That's nothing to mock. He's shaming the mark. He'll lose the crowd.

The guy adjusted himself in his seat and after a pause finally said, 'Yeah, you're right. He's a janitor,' and managed to laugh himself.

'And did he get you your job?' The audience tittered, but more out of confusion, than embarrassment. They were definitely uncomfortable. Where was this going? Mary Jane again asked herself nervously.

'How could he get me my job? I told you, he's a *janitor*. I got my own job.'

'Me, too,' Neil agreed. 'We got something in common. I got my own job, too, which is weird, 'cause that doesn't happen much in show business anymore. I mean it. Like now there's a new generation of Fondas making it in the movies. Henry's *grandchildren*. Can you believe this shit?

'As far as I'm concerned, the *first* fucking generation of those bastards was more than enough. Then we had to have Jane and Peter. He was a fuck-up, and, let's face it, Jane was a dog.' Some shocked laughter. 'You think she got parts based on her looks or her

79

talent? Get the fuck out of here! Even with her father's connections, she had to settle for *Barefoot in the Park*. And she had to marry Vadim to get cast in *Barbarella*. You think there aren't ten girls in the room right now better-looking and more talented than she was? But, hey, let's talk about Peter, a *true* no-talent degenerate. What the hell did he ever do? Now we got *his* kid, and we're going to have to watch *her* for another generation?

'They call them show-business dynasties. Get the fuck out of here! That isn't a dynasty. That *legitimizes* the no-talent dog shit. It ain't a *dynasty*, it's a *conspiracy*. This country is supposed to be a democracy, but we're fighting nepotism.'

He paused and looked around the audience. 'See, America was supposed to be a meritocracy. It was what you *did*, not who you *knew*, remember? And it sure wasn't who your father was. Who the fuck was Thomas Jefferson's dad? Or George Washington's? The trick is, this isn't private enterprise. Hey, you want your son to join you in your plumbing business – aces with me. But this is *broadcasting*. This is television, radio. Airwaves that are owned by us all. But these fuckers have a lock on 'em. Nothin' left for us.

'See, show biz has lost that grand American ideal of rewards based on talent, a combination of hard work and talent. Tell me that Talia Shire was the best Connie that her brother Francis Coppola could buy. Well, maybe not, but his daughter was *perfect* as Mary in *Godfather III*, right? Get the fuck out of here!' The audience laughed. 'Hey,' Neil continued, 'there were entire theatres that cheered when that bitch got shot down. Did anyone count the number of Coppolas in that movie? Of course not, because no one can count that high. You know, Coppola won a special lifetime-achievement award for putting more family members in a single movie than anyone else. And he had stiff competition in that category. Let me tell you about Anjelica Huston. No, *you* tell *me*. A big, ugly girl who can't act. John Huston put her in all his later films, 'cause Nicholson wouldn't marry her and she needed an income.

'What I love is when these bastards say they had to audition for the part, just like everybody else. We know how she had to audition for Nicholson. What I don't want to think about is how she auditioned for her father! Don't ask.'

The audience was rolling now. Mary Jane saw heads nodding, the laughs were building. And the janitor's son shouted 'Right on.'

'I'm a working actor, and what burns me up is how rarely I get to work. Then you hear these assholes on TV telling Arsenio or

Jay Leno how much harder it is being Debbie Reynolds' daughter, because people expect so much more from you. Get the fuck out of here!

'Hey, don't get me wrong. I have compassion. Being rich and having famous, powerful parents in the Industry *can* be a liability. And I'm sure Arsenio will schedule me as a guest so I can explain how being Nunzio Morelli's son made it *easier* for me, since people expected so little.'

There was a true explosion of laughter, and Mary Jane sighed with relief. Despite the bitterness, the hostility, in the routine, the crowd was going for it.

'Of course, in the music industry it's different. Wilson Phillips were a different story. I mean, even if they hadn't been the children of multi-millionaire, drug-addicted, degenerate recording artists, I really do believe they'd probably be the same dog shit they are today.'

The audience was rolling with shock and laughter now. But Neil had no mercy. 'Or the Nelsons. Oh, excuse me. Just 'Nelson.' Get the fuck out of here! They're the California white-bread visual equivalent of Milli Vanilli. But, hey, Grandma Harriet says they're her pride and joy. Well, that makes it all right for the rest of us, right? Shit, even *Ricky* was a lousy musician.

'Okay. So you're mad, too, but you say there's nothing you can do. You say the abuse is too rampant. You say you're just another man on the street. Get the fuck out of here! The solution to the problem, as I see it, is taking a simple action. Like the Boston Tea Party. Join the Neil Morelli Antinepotism League. You *can* make a difference. I say a few acts of terrorism could liberate the airwaves.'

Oh, sweet Jesus. He's gone too far now, Mary Jane thought. Some people in the audience 'ooooh'ed.

'Oh, you think that's too extreme, huh?' Neil said, voicing her thought. 'Well, let me just say one word to convince you: Sheen. Am I right? Marty, then Charlie and Emilio. *He* said he didn't want to use his dad's name to get ahead. Right! He must have used it to get an ass – that fat ass had to come from *somewhere*. So they make every movie a family affair, to keep it a secret. Get the fuck out of here! Waste 'em. The world will thank us, I promise you. Think of the alternative: Emilio might reproduce.'

The crowd was whooping now, and Neil, his hostile energy aflame, was playing them, pacing across the stage, punctuating his gestures with a Mick Jagger strut. Then he stopped dead and turned to the crowd, still.

'But one more thing. We can't be accused of sentimentality or favouritism. There are a *few* talented children of the stars. Think of the Bridges boys. Still, we gotta be fair. Waste 'em. And then there are the old standbys. Oh, I know. You'll beg for them. But hey, if we spare Liza Minnelli, we have to pass over Laura Dern or Tori Spelling, Melanie Griffith or Nicholas Cage. Of course, *he's* a special case. He's getting by on his good looks.' He paused, got his laugh, and went for his tag line. 'Get the fuck out of here!' he cried.

It went on and on. He killed them. Mary Jane looked over to the corner tables, where Belzer, Leary, Barry Sobol, and half a dozen other stand-ups watched. Even *they* were laughing. At the end of the set, Mary Jane rose while Neil was still getting his ovation and made her way back to the crowded, tiny area that passed for a combination dressing room and green room backstage.

Now Mary Jane waited while Neil accepted congratulations, drank down a Scotch, joshed with the guys, and greeted the heavyset woman that Mary Jane knew was his sister, Brenda. At last he noticed her. He moved towards her and planted a kiss on her lips. He smelled of sweat and alcohol. Neil rarely drank and could never hold his liquor; the adrenaline from the set, plus the Scotch, had made him high. But he was still sharp.

'You must be one of the Aristocrats,' she said, quoting the old vaudeville joke, too dirty to repeat.

'Yeah,' he said, getting the reference, 'I've been fucking everyone onstage,' he laughed.

'You're stinko,' she told him. 'In both senses of the word.'

'*In vino veritas.* And in humour, too. That's why they laughed. Because it's true.'

'But too much. Too mean. It's . . .' she paused.

'Bad taste? Mean-spirited? Provocative? Uh-oh. You know what happens to comics who err in that direction?' He took a beat. 'They fill Madison Square Garden!' Neil took the towel from around his neck and patted down his sweating forehead. He stopped smiling, and, for a moment, his thin, almost weasel-like face looked sad. 'You didn't like it?'

'I did, Neil. I did. But I just worry. People might take you at your word. It won't endear you to Hollywood.'

'Who cares about Hollywood? There isn't going to be one person in L.A. that I respect.'

'Neil, *I'm* going to L.A.'

He paused, shook his wet head like a spaniel, then recovered. For a moment, he looked serious, and tired. 'Great news for me. Great news for Sam. Great news for you?'

She shrugged. Neil smiled at her, his burning energy surging again.

'Hey, we'll grab the bitch goddess by both teats, huh? We'll hang on hard and squeeze.'

'Yeah, a regular Hollywood Romulus and Remus,' she said drily.

'Weren't *they* with the Aristocrats?' Neil asked. 'Oh, no, excuse me. They were that dog-and-parrot act.'

'Was Romulus the dog or the parrot?'

'I don't remember, but I know Remus was the uncle.'

She laughed. She couldn't help it. He *was* funny, and he was her friend. He smiled, his weasel face lit up by the grin, his eyes narrowing. He put out both arms to her.

'We'll slay 'em, Veronica,' he said. And he was half right.

'I worry about you, out there with those . . . those . . . Americans.'

'Ah, fuck 'em if they can't take a joke. Anyway, I don't have to do sets anymore. I got a sitcom now. Let the *writers* sweat their guts out over the yocks.' He paused, his toughness draining out of him like dirty water down a sink. 'But you liked it, didn't you? You laughed?' He looked at her, needing her benediction. 'I was funny, wasn't I?'

'Neil, you were a fucking riot.'

Mary Jane left as soon as she could and splurged on a cab to get her back to the apartment and Sam as fast as possible. Aside from the debacle at the rehearsal and the fight that followed it, they hadn't been together since he got back from L.A. His body against hers was almost all she could think about. Just in time, she remembered the cat, though, and stopped the cab at the corner bodega to pick up Tender Vittles and a bottle of wine. What the hell.

She ran the three flights up the cold stairway, but when she got to her apartment, no light showed under the door. Midnight met her, his fluffy white coat silken smooth as he moved in figure eights against her legs. She scooped him up, flicked on the light, and called out to Sam. Had he fallen asleep? Had he not come? Her stomach tightened in fear.

She walked through the kitchen clutching Midnight to her, peeked into the empty living room, and then continued down the hall to the tiny bedroom. Maybe, she thought desperately, maybe he's asleep.

Sam was stretched out on the bed. And he seemed to be sleeping. Well, with jet lag and all, it was understandable. As always, Mary Jane was moved by his grace — his long body stretched diagonally across the bed, his feet relaxed over one corner, an arm thrown negligently over his head reaching the other corner. It was his length and leanness more than anything that attracted her, she thought. She longed for Sam's arms, for the comfort of his body pushing against hers. But he was tired. She'd let him sleep. There was always tomorrow. She began to undress in the dark.

But when she climbed into bed beside him, as quietly as she could manage, he turned to her. He buried his head in the soft flesh of her neck. 'I'm sorry,' he whispered. 'I'm so sorry.'

And all at once she *could* forgive him. Completely. His voice, husky with sorrow and maybe with lust, released her from her anger, from her pain. He was in pain, too, and she could free him. All it took was his apology, her acceptance of him.

Because she loved him so much. 'That's all right,' she told him. 'It's all right.'

'You love me?' he asked, his mouth close against her ear, his deliciously warm breath tickling her. She felt her body warm to him.

'Of course.'

'I need you, Mary Jane.'

She pressed herself against him, her softness against his hard flesh. Pressing him at the shoulder, at the chest, belly to belly, thigh to thigh, she still couldn't get close enough, be close enough to him. Then his hands were on her breasts, and his mouth was on her mouth, and his body rolled onto her body. She felt his erection, and tears sprang to her eyes: tears of gratitude and pleasure. She had the power to excite him, and he loved her. He *needed* her. He had said so. And she needed his love, needed him so desperately that she was almost afraid to let her neediness show.

'Sam. Oh, Sam,' she whispered.

'Promise you'll forgive me.'

'I do, Sam.'

'No, promise that you'll *always* forgive me. I need you to.' In the dark, his voice sounded as desperate as she felt.

'Yes. Yes, I promise. I forgive you.'

With a groan of relief or pain, he slid inside her. She shuddered, but he remained still, cradling her in his arms. Yet it was she, she felt, who was giving comfort, giving absolution.

'I love you,' she said.

'I know,' he told her, and it was only much later that she realized he had not told her he loved her, too.

The next morning, she awakened with a smile, reached across the bed, but found that Sam was already up. Quickly she rose, shrugged into her chenille robe, and walked out, barefoot, looking for him. Midnight, nestled at the foot of the bed, stretched and followed.

Sam wasn't in the bathroom, or in the living room. She didn't smell coffee brewing, but he must be in the kitchen, making it.

He wasn't. But there was a note propped on the old, scarred Formica table. He had gone! Fearfully, she sank onto the sofa and unfolded the paper.

> M.J., First of all, your grandmother called while I was here last night. She's real sick and wants you to go upstate.
>
> Also, I've given a lot of thought to what went down and I guess I feel that I was way out of line. I'm sorry.
>
> I'm also sorry that I don't think it's a good idea for you to come out to L.A. You know how very, very special it was for us with *Jack and Jill* and how good things had been. I always told you that I wasn't the kind of person who compromised. Something's lost and I think it best not to go on without it.
>
> > My silks and fine array,
> > My smiles and languish'd air,
> > By love are driv'n away;
> > And mournful lean Despair
> > Brings me yew to deck my grave:
> > Such end true lovers have.

Then he'd signed his name and had added, 'Try not to hate me.'

Mary Jane stood there in the bleak little room, staring at the note. He fucks me, quotes Blake to me, and blows me off! she had time to think before the tears began.

12

The strangest interview I ever did was a brunch with Theresa O'Donnell out at her Bel Air mansion more than a dozen years ago. I showed up with a photographer for an 'at home' shoot. It was the first time I had been to Theresa's home and the first time I met Lila Kyle.

Theresa was decked out in one of those lacy bed jackets and silky pj's. The kid was in a matching outfit. But so were Candy and Skinny, the two dummies that were featured on Theresa's TV show at the time. And the luncheon table was set for five. Cute gag, huh? Except the dummies were served, too. And they spoke up throughout the meal. Theresa was a fairly good ventriloquist, but it was Lila I watched. The kid – she was five or six then – acted as if this were the most natural thing in the world. She called her mother 'Lovely Mummie' and had perfect table manners. Meanwhile Candy picked on her. So did Skinny. And Theresa intervened when it got too rough.

I can't remember what provoked the final incident – I think Lila didn't want to finish her fruit cup. Theresa said she had to. Lila pointed out that Candy and Skinny hadn't eaten theirs. Theresa smiled, overly sweetly, and said it was too bad. Lila would still have to. So Lila dumped her fruit cup on Skinny's lap.

And Skinny called the child 'a little cunt.'

I often wondered what the rest of life was like for that little girl in that big house. But I didn't see her again until her birthday party almost five years later.

Lila remembered the party. It was a turning point in her life. And now, in the quiet of Aunt Robbie's house as she faced the question of what she wanted, the party kept coming back to her.

Lila had given it a lot of thought. At least for her it was a lot. And when she tried, really tried, to think about what she wanted, what she wanted more than anything, it was to be a star. A powerful, important star. A star a lot bigger than her mother, or even her father, had ever been.

She wasn't sure if she could act – she didn't even care. She knew that what she could do was get people to look at her, to want to know her, to be interested in – no, fascinated by – her. It had happened to her before – she knew she could hold a room. She remembered her moment onstage, in the room full of stars at that party, when she sang 'The Loveliest Girl in the World.' She remembered the feeling in the room. Everyone stopped. They only wanted to watch *her*.

She shivered. Her mother's theme song gave her the creeps. She hated it. Lila Kyle knew that she was born to Hollywood royalty. But, like Princess Anne, or Margaret, or even poor Queen Elizabeth herself, Lila also knew that lineage didn't ensure happiness. Still, she wasn't going to wind up like Nancy Sinatra or her brother Frank, like Julian Lennon, or even Jane Fonda, who had never exceeded the reputation of her father. She, Lila Kyle, would be important in her own right.

Years ago, she recalled, she had sat before the mirror at the vanity table in her bedroom, watching Estrella's reflection as the woman stood behind her, when their eyes met. Perhaps they hadn't looked one another in the eye since then. 'It's your *tenth* birthday, that's all I know,' Estrella had said, in answer to Lila's question. 'That's what your mother say.' Estrella had turned Lila around while she inspected her from head to toe.

'But it's my *eleventh*,' Lila remembered she had continued to insist. 'I was ten *last* year.' Lila wanted to cry but was afraid to ruin her makeup. Aunt Robbie had warned her about that all week, when they were rehearsing. 'And eleven is too old for bows in my hair,' she told Estrella once again. The woman shrugged. At times like that, Estrella still pretended she couldn't understand English.

Lila had been sure – *positive* – that she had been ten years old on her *last* birthday, the year *before*. Why were Lovely Mummie and Estrella saying she was only ten years old *this* year? Lila *remembered* her other tenth birthday. She remembered it so clearly. Unlike this birthday, there had been no big birthday party, only birthday cake with Aunt Robbie and Estrella, because Lovely Mummie and the girls had been too busy working.

But that was before Mummie's TV show was cancelled, which must be a terrible thing, because Mummie had yelled all the time since then, and it was getting harder to understand when she spoke, even in her normal tones. Lila didn't know what 'cancelled' meant, but it sounded worse than sickness, or even death. And Mummie and Aunt Robbie acted as if it was. And so did the girls at Westlake. 'Your mom's show was *cancelled*,' sneered Lauren Caldwell. 'Some big star.'

Estrella tightened the bow in Lila's hair and gave her a gentle prod. 'Now,' she said, 'perfect.' Estrella placed the brush back on the blue-mirrored vanity table and waddled to the door. Before she closed it behind her, she said, 'Lila. Listen to Estrella. For the last time, you're *ten* years old, and your mother say you got to have a big bow in your hair. Please,' she added, 'don't ask questions. Promise?'

Lila had considered Estrella's request, then nodded in agreement as she always did. Even though Lila didn't really like Estrella, they both wanted the same thing: to keep Lovely Mummie happy.

Alone, Lila ran to her bedroom window and stood on tiptoe looking out, hoping that it wouldn't put cracks across the front of her new black patent-leather shoes. She strained to see the occupants of each of the limousines as they were pulling up at the door of her mother's house. As the cars disgorged their well-dressed occupants, Lila practised naming the famous persons she recognized: 'Miss Taylor, Mr. Stewart, Mr. Peck,' she murmured. Her mother insisted she be polite and greet every one of the party guests by name. Some were famous, and she knew them from movies or TV, but the others were harder. And even more important. She had to get them all right. Mr. Sagarian, Lovely Mummie's agent. Mr. Wagner from CBS. And her business manager. And lots of fat, bald guys. All grown-ups, she thought. Lila didn't really have any friends at school, but, still, since it was her birthday, she wished some kids were here.

For Lila, it was a relief that there weren't as many parties as there used to be, back when Lovely Mummie was working. Lila could remember how she used to long to be with her mummie and Candy and Skinny on TV. Every Friday night, Lila would sit before the TV, watching her mother's show. She often played at being Cinderella: she had two mean stepsisters and a wicked mother who wouldn't let her go to the ball. *Theresa O'Donnell Presents 'The Candy Floss and Skinny Malink Show.'* Why couldn't she be on television with them? The Theresa and Lila show. Without stupid Candy and Skinny. Lovely Mummie might let her, *if* she was very, very good tonight, and if they got another show.

Except Lila wasn't so sure she wanted to anymore. Mummie was home all the time, and sometimes Lila wished she weren't.

It wasn't so much fun to be with her mummie. Maybe it would be different, though, when they got their new TV show.

'This is important,' Theresa had said to her, over and over, as Theresa made the party preparations while rehearsing Lila. 'If we can get Jack Wagner or one of those rat bastards interested, I'll just move to CBS and start over. Update the concept. Cut back on Candy and Skinny. More skits. Less singing. And bring you on. Wholesome. A family show. Like the Osmonds. No one wants these cops and westerns for their kids.'

Lila liked the idea of cutting out Candy and Skinny. She hated the two puppets. When she'd been a little girl, Lovely Mummie had told her they were real – her real sisters. Now Lila knew they were only puppets, that Mummie made them speak, but even now, at eleven – she was sure she was *eleven* – she sometimes wasn't certain that the two were not alive. Still, she had done all she could in rehearsing and rehearsing with Mummie and Aunt Robbie to try to take their place, and that night she would do it.

Though all of it happened years ago, Lila would never forget a moment of it. She had left the window and run to the guest room, on the other side of the house, to look out once again at the decorations around the pool. Japanese lanterns were strung between trees, gently swinging in the warm evening breeze. The surface of the pool was dotted with cork disks holding lighted candles in clear glass containers, with scented gardenias floating among them. White-jacketed waiters were already moving through the colourfully dressed crowd. The sound of their chatter urged Lila down the stairs to join the fun, but, instead, she returned to her room to wait to be summoned, as she had been told.

She sat down in her rocker, and looked over at Candy Floss and Skinny Malink sitting at their usual seats at the tea table, both of them smiling like they didn't have a care in the world. Easy for you, she thought. 'I'm the one that's got to be good tonight,' she told them, part proud, part frightened.

The dummies' heads were tilted slightly, and Lila could see the place where her mother's hands went behind the dolls to manipulate their mouths and extremities. She'd never noticed that when she was little. Before, when she was little and stupid, she used to think they were real, that they were really her sisters. But that had been a big fat lie. A joke her mother called it. Ha ha.

Candy Floss and Skinny Malink had been part of her mother's

life long before she had been. 'I love these two as much as I love you,' she'd say.

Lila sat and rocked, closed her eyes and tried to remember her lines and the movements her mother and Aunt Robbie had gone to so much trouble to teach her. She was sure she had everything right. She leaned across and arranged Skinny's and Candy's dresses just so, then fluffed her pink dress around her, taking care not to lean back too far for fear of crushing the big bow at the rear.

She jumped as she heard her mother, coming down the hall to her room, calling her name. 'I'm here,' Lila called.

'Girls, I've come to take you down to entertain our guests. Oh, how pretty my little babies look.' Was Lovely Mummie slurring her words again? It made Lila shiver. Mummie patted both dolls' heads, then turned to Lila. 'Let me look at you,' she said, and frowned. Theresa O'Donnell watched as Lila turned slowly in front of her, waiting uneasily for her mother's comments.

'Lovely, just lovely,' Theresa finally said, her frown dissolving into her TV smile. Lila breathed out and smiled, too. 'How do you like my hair, Mummie?' Maybe she could take the stupid bow out. 'Estrella put a big bow in it.'

'Perfect,' her mother said, 'Exactly the right touch. Now, if only you weren't so goddamn tall.'

Mummie looked more closely. 'But what's that?' she asked, pointing to a locket. 'A necklace? Take it off. Candy and Skinny don't have necklaces, so that's not very fair, is it?' Theresa stood and reached over to pat the dummies. 'Don't mind,' she told them. 'Lila's taking it off now. Aren't you?'

Lila bit the inside of her cheek as she unclasped the locket Aunt Robbie had given her for luck. She put it safely in the top drawer of the bureau. Oh, God, why did Mummie still talk to the dummies? Why did she still pretend like this?

'Lila,' her mother said, becoming very serious. 'There are a lot of people here who are *very* important to me. I want you to make Mother proud of her little girl.' Turning to the dummies, she hummed, 'And my other two little babies *always* make me proud.' She kissed each doll on its painted wooden cheek and demanded of Lila, 'You *are* going to be perfect, aren't you?' Lila saw her mother take Candy's hair in her fist and pull very hard, while keeping her eyes on Lila. She could almost feel how that must hurt. For once, Lila felt sorry for Candy, and, unconsciously, she reached up to her own hair. Lila whispered, 'Yes, Lovely Mummie.'

Then Theresa released Candy's hair, and gently patted it back into place.

'Smile, girls, we're on now,' Theresa said as she took the dummies, each in the crook of an arm, and walked very carefully down the stairs, Lila trailing behind. Please, Mummie, don't trip again, she thought.

'I hate these fucking stairs,' Lila had heard her mother mutter. 'Elegant, my sweet Irish ass. Cross of Christ!'

As they reached the main floor, Theresa paused and took a moment to command the attention of the crowd. 'Hi, everyone. Tonight I'd like you all to meet my other little girl, Lila, who will be making her debut right here with us.'

Candy leaned forward and said, 'Her debut and retirement in one performance.'

'Candy, that's not nice,' Theresa scolded the puppet.

'Not nice but true, it seems to me,' said Skinny on the other hand. The crowd laughed, and Lila's heart quickened at the sharp barbs from the two. This hadn't been in the rehearsals. She wanted to tell them to shut up, but then she remembered that it was her mother who'd said those things. And it was her mother who'd told her over and over: 'Don't be mean to your sisters, they're your bread and butter.'

'She wouldn't be Theresa O'Donnell's daughter if she couldn't sing and dance with dummies, would she?' Mummie said. Everyone laughed again and looked at Aunt Robbie Lymon, Mummie's stooge on the TV show. 'No, no, everyone, not *that* dummy,' she laughed. 'Now, please, come with us into the ballroom.'

Lila walked up to the raised platform at one end of the room and was helped up by Aunt Robbie, who whispered to her: 'Hey, kid, don't worry about anything. Just do it like we rehearsed.'

Sitting on a small chair next to her mother, Lila waited until Aunt Robbie finished playing the introduction. Candy and Skinny each sat on one of her mother's knees, their heads turning, scanning the crowd. The music stopped, and Theresa spoke.

'Skinny, Candy, who's that other pretty little girl sitting on the stage? Is she with you?'

Skinny and Candy looked at each other and shrugged their shoulders. 'I don't see any pretty girl on the stage,' Candy said. 'Do you, Skinny?'

'Nope,' Skinny said. 'I just see you and me pretty little girls, but I don't see no *other* pretty little girl.'

Lila's toes tingled cold in her shoes. This wasn't the opening to the act. Mummie had forgotten the opening. Oh, no. Oh, my God. Aunt Robbie had told her what to do if her mother forgot her lines.

'Well,' Lila said, 'I see *one* pretty little girl and *two* dummies.'

Both of the dolls turned their heads to Theresa at the same time, then towards Lila. She was aware of the laughter from the audience and was surprised at how good that made her feel. She noticed how her voice sounded in the big room, and made a point of remembering to speak to the back of the crowd, just like Aunt Robbie had taught her.

'Excuse her, folks,' said Skinny. '*She's* hoping for a notice in *Variety*.'

'*I'm* not the one whose acting is wooden,' said Lila. The crowd laughed again. Lila preened. But Lovely Mummie looked flustered.

As the routine continued, more or less according to the script, her mother forgot some lines, but Lila filled in. She got caught up in her interchange with Candy and Skinny. She remembered to hold her head just like dolls did, just as she had imitated so many times while sitting in front of the television set. She moved her jaw just like Candy, and kept her arms immobile like Skinny, while reciting her lines. Then, at last, it was over, and all she had to do was sit there while her mother sang her famous song.

When Aunt Robbie began to play the music for Mummie's song, Mummie just kept on smiling. It was a strange smile. The audience murmured, a sound like wind in the orange trees. Why wasn't Mummie singing? She was supposed to sing her song, 'The Loveliest Girl in the World.' Aunt Robbie began the intro again, and Lila understood what he was trying to say to her. So, desperate, Lila began to sing her mother's closing song. She sang so hard, she didn't notice that the whole room had grown quiet, and every face was on her, even her mother's. She sang with all her heart the famous final words of the song. Lila had never rehearsed it, but she had watched her mom's movie *Birth of a Star* so many, many times that she knew it perfectly. When it came time for the last bar, for the high note, she closed her eyes and made it easily.

When she opened her eyes and looked at Aunt Robbie, he was standing at the piano, applauding. The audience suddenly came alive, shouting, clapping, and whistling. I did it! she thought. I remembered every word and motion and then, when I had to, I even remembered Lovely Mummie's song. And they like me.

She looked towards her mother, a smile of achievement on her face. Her mother looked back at her without expression, holding Candy and Skinny down by her sides . . . like dolls. She *never* did that. Lila was confused, but continued to bow to the audience and accept their applause.

Then, at last, Mummie stepped forward, stood next to Lila, smiled broadly, and bowed. She led Lila off the stage, turned, and took the last bow alone, holding Candy and Skinny in her arms like infants. Ignoring the cries of the crowd for an encore, she said, 'Thank you, everyone. It's past the girls' bedtime. But you will be seeing us again.' Floating on a cloud, Lila waved as her mother led the way through the crowd.

Mr. Wagner put his hand on Theresa's arm as she was passing, and the audience stopped chattering to listen. 'Jack, darling, how nice of you to come,' Lovely Mummie said so everyone could hear, kissing him on the cheek. 'What did you think of our little family entertainment?'

'A perfect performance. It gives me an idea for a TV show. Interested?'

Theresa smiled broadly at Mr. Wagner. 'We're always interested in television, Jack. We'd love to do another show, wouldn't we, girls?'

Lila's heart jumped. Did he mean *her*, too?

'I mean Lila, Theresa. The kid's a natural. We'd start her with a half-hour after school, see where it goes.' He leaned down towards Lila. 'How about it, kid? Want to have a television show?'

'Oh, yes, Mr. Wagner' — remembering to say his name. Then she saw the expression on Lovely Mummie's face, and knew that something was wrong. 'I mean, I don't know. I'll have to ask my mother.' She just knew that she had better get away from Mr. Wagner, and not hear any more about a television show. She could tell that Lovely Mummie didn't think it was such a good idea.

Her mother closed the door of Lila's room behind her and leaned against it, Candy and Skinny dropped in a heap like dirty laundry at her feet. Lila looked at her, apprehensive.

'Just who do you think you are?' Lovely Mummie growled.

'What do you mean, Mummie?'

'You humiliated me tonight, before everyone who means anything in this town. And in front of Mr. Wagner, of all people. "Oh, yes, Mr. Wagner,"' she mimicked. Stepping closer to Lila, she screamed, 'You humiliated me,' and swung her open hand across Lila's face. Lila fell against the puppets. She was stunned, both by the blow and by the words.

'Mummie,' she sobbed, 'what did I do wrong? I remembered the words when you forgot, Mummie. And I was good, wasn't I? Mr. Wagner said so.' Lila was confused.

'Shut up, you little traitor. I didn't forget my lines. I never do.' Lila saw the spit spray from her mother's mouth as she yelled. 'You deliberately stole my song.' Theresa grabbed a handful of Lila's hair and pulled her towards her. Lila, sobbing, pleaded with her mother to tell her what she had done wrong.

'Everyone was laughing at me, you little brat. You couldn't wait to humiliate me, could you? You must really hate me, to deliberately steal the scene, making me look like a fool.' She was screaming, in a frenzy. 'I'll never be able to get a contract now, because *you* fucked it up. Wagner would have asked me if it wasn't for you.'

Theresa picked up the two dummies and shook them in Lila's face. 'Are you trying to take their place on television? Do you think you can make their money?' Mummie didn't wait for an answer. 'No, you can't, and you never will. Just remember this, *I* got the talent. Not *you*, Lila. *Me.*' Her mother swung a hand at her face again, but Lila pulled away with a sudden effort.

Lila shrank back into the corner of the room. Her mother, breathless, paused. Then she brushed her hair out of her face, and her breath came more slowly. She went to the vanity mirror and fussed with her hair, patted down her gown. 'I'm going to return to my guests now. I'm going to look those people in the eyes and pretend that my daughter didn't humiliate me in my own home. You're to stay in your room until I tell you you can come out. And I want you to think about how you've ruined my career tonight.'

Then Theresa had turned and left the room, a doll in each arm, shutting the door behind her with a crash. Lila had slumped to the floor and let the tears flow. What did I do? What happened?

She wasn't sure of anything, except that she would never sing again.

And since that night, Lila never had. There was something else about that night, though. It was the first time Lila had known it was the Puppet Mistress who had made the mistakes, not her. But still, she was punished. I did it *right*, Lila had told herself after her sobs subsided. They *liked* me. They applauded. The audience liked *me*, not Theresa O'Donnell. Mr. Wagner liked *me*. And despite her burning cheek, despite her tearing eyes, that had felt very, very good.

Lila put her hand up to her cheek now. She could still feel her mother's slap. She'd never sung since then, but now she knew what she wanted. She wanted that audience, and she'd have to get it. The first step was getting some money. The Puppet Mistress was not going to give her any, or help her move forward in her career.

So after eleven days in the darkness of Robbie's guest room, here she was at Moody, Shlom, and Stone. Her dead father's lawyers. Because, even if he was dead, her father could help. He had left her money, and through these lawyers she could get it. Still Lila was intimidated, and Lila wasn't intimidated by much. Never having been to a lawyer's office, she wasn't prepared for the size or the sumptuous furnishings. Whenever there had been any business about her father's estate, Mr. Shlom had come to the Puppet Mistress's house.

Now Mr. Moody came out to the reception area himself, and seemed genuinely glad to see her. 'Lila Kyle. Bart Moody.' He shook her hand. 'I've met you before, but there's no way you would remember,' he chuckled. 'You were two months old, I think.' He led her into a corner office, decorated like something out of some corny *Masterpiece Theatre*. She sat on the leather club chair opposite his desk, crossed her legs after hiking up her skirt, and smiled across at her father's lawyer.

'You'll forgive me,' the old man said with a laugh, 'but you've certainly grown since the last time I saw you.'

Lila laughed, and faked a rearrangement of her skirt, as if demurely trying to cover too much exposed thigh. It worked. She noticed him looking at her legs. Well, it couldn't hurt, she thought. 'And *you* haven't changed a bit,' she giggled.

He blushed. 'I see you've inherited Kerry's Irish blarney. And the combined good looks of him *and* Theresa.' The lawyer paused, and in that moment remembered himself. He cleared his throat. 'But enough of that. What can I do for you?'

'As I told your secretary yesterday, I wanted to talk about the current state and provisions of my trust fund. The one my father set up for me.'

'Yes, your father was very specific; although not exactly a prudent

95

man in many things, he made sure you would be provided for.'

'Yes, Mother told me all about that.' Screw him, talking about her father. Her father had been a fuckin' *star*, not a fat-ass lawyer. Well, she'd keep it together. 'That brings me to the reason I came to see you. I feel that I can't be a drain on Mother any longer. I need to be independent, and to devote my energies to acting. I've decided that's what I really want to do. But I understand that I can't get an income from my trust fund until I'm twenty-one.'

Mr. Moody, the jerk, shook his head.

'Well, I thought, maybe, you might be able to make an exception for me, since I am doing *exactly* what my father wanted for me – and my mother, by the way. So could you, you know, let me have money now?'

The jerk smiled at her, but it wasn't a nice smile. It was an aren't-you-pretty-for-a-stupid-girl smile, and Lila wished she could reach across the desk and kick the old bastard in the nuts. 'I'm sorry, but the terms of the trust are very specific, and I'm bound by law to adhere to them.' He put on reading glasses and looked down at a file of notes. 'I'm afraid that my late partner Bernie Shlom used to handle this, and I'm not quite filled in yet. How old are you now, my dear?' he asked, when he looked up.

'Eighteen,' she lied. Well, close enough.

'Ah. Time flies. I hadn't realized. Well, there *is* a provision, for you to receive income from the trust after your eighteenth birthday.'

Lila smiled. Thank God. Maybe the old wrinkle bunny wasn't so bad after all. 'Yes? When can it start? Right away?'

He reached into a side drawer of his desk and took out a yellow legal pad. Looking across the desk at Lila, he said, 'I *could* draft a request form asking that you receive benefits immediately.'

Lila gave him her sunniest smile, then grabbed the paper and pen from Moody's hand and scribbled her signature. This was easier than she had thought. 'There!' she said. 'Could you fill that in and do it?'

Again he gave her that annoying grin. 'Well,' he said, 'first we'd have to petition your father's executor to give you your benefits now.'

'And who is the executor?' Lila sighed. What bullshit.

'Well, here,' Moody said, and handed her a paper. Lila looked down at the paper, then up at Bart Moody's face. She was trembling, but was determined not to lose it. 'My mother? Why does she have to give her permission?'

'It's a provision of the trust. If you would like to receive income before your twenty-first birthday, your marriage or your mother's permission is necessary.'

Lila sank back into the chair, her arms folded across her chest. How could her father have done this to her? Withhold her *own* money, and give *Theresa* power over it – and her. Why, he hadn't even *liked* Theresa!

Lila leaned forward, one hand on her hip. 'Let's forget about Theresa for a minute, Mr. Moody. What about getting a loan – like an advance on it, then? Can you do *that* much for me?'

The old man shook his head, looking forlorn. 'The only one who can help you is your mother,' he said. 'I'm afraid we couldn't touch the fund without her permission.'

Lila jumped up. 'My mother can't even help *herself*. Have you seen her in the last ten years? She's a drunk. A crazy, booze-soaked, washed-up nut case. She's not going to give me permission for *anything*. I need that money to get away from her.'

'Now, Lila, you're only eighteen. The legal age of inheritance is just three years away. Then you . . .'

Lila leaned over Bart Moody's desk, and stared into his face. 'Three years? Do you know what L.A. can do to a woman in three years? I'm new *now*. I could be hot. I can be someone. I could be dead in three years, for chrissakes. I need the money *now*.'

Bart Moody stood up and walked to the door. With his hand on the doorknob, he said, 'Then I suggest you have this conversation with the only person who can get that money to you now.' He opened the door. 'Good day,' he said.

She was so angry, so frustrated, that she walked down the stairs rather than wait for the elevator. Now what? What the fuck *can* I do? It's not like Westlake gave any career counselling to their students. That would have been ludicrous. Most of the school's graduates were going to walk into jobs their parents got for them, if they were going to work at all. And even if they had job counselling, how did you counsel someone on how to become a star?

She had to have money. She needed a good car, manicures, facials, clothes, a decent place to live. Lila reached the parking lot, and stopped. It was going to have to be Aunt Robbie. How long can I stand him? she wondered. How long will I be able to beg money from him? He wasn't a rich man, and certainly couldn't afford to keep Lila in clothes.

Well, she'd have to economize. Right. Facials only once a month. She'd do her own pedicures. Ask for a comp on her haircuts. Get an allowance from Robbie, promise to pay him back, and live within a budget.

It was that or crawl back to the Puppet Mistress.

No fucking way!

13

'What time is your flight?' Mary Jane had asked Neil to be polite. She couldn't stand to talk to him, or Molly, or anyone. Sam was gone. Flown to LALA Land. Her life felt unliveable. It wasn't quite bad enough for suicide, she thought dully. Only bad enough to wish you'd never been born. She hadn't bathed or changed or cleaned the place since Sam left. Perhaps she'd leave it just as it had been then. Stop the clocks. The whole Miss Havisham bit. Neil was calling from some other century.

But Neil, with all his hustle and excitement, meant well, so she pretended to be interested. With Sam gone, Neil leaving, and a trip up to her grandmother's to look forward to, Mary Jane felt like death on toast.

'Nine A.M., from Kennedy,' Neil had said when she asked. 'Will you come see me off?'

Mary Jane hesitated. She had been afraid of this. It would be the fourth send-off of friends in a year, all going to L.A., all with contracts tucked under their arms. And she'd heard through the grapevine that Bethanie had gone off tucked under Sam's arm.

Had he known when he made love to her that he was leaving her? Or had that only come to him afterwards? Or had he meant only to say goodbye, then rolled into her arms as a knee-jerk reaction? Had Sam met someone in L.A.? If so, why was he taking Bethanie with him? Did he simply need someone, anyone? Had her initial refusal soured him? Did he love her? Had he ever loved her?

They were unanswerable questions. Perhaps Sam himself could not have told her. But that didn't stop her from asking herself, over and over, why. Why? Why?

Now she had to cope with Neil's departure. Mary Jane hated airport goodbyes, hated the interminable subway-and-bus ride, the cheapest transportation back to the city. An hour and a half, at least, wasted, when she could be home, lying in bed, eating Entenmann's chocolate doughnuts and watching videos. God, she couldn't disappoint Neil, though. Well, she'd bring some doughnuts and a book with her. Or maybe splurge and take the Carey bus back to town. 'Sure, Neil,' she'd said. 'What time are you going to catch the bus?'

'The good news is: no bus. Hey, the producer's paying my way by limo. The bad news is the time. Pick-up at seven in the morning,' Neil had told her. Mary Jane moaned audibly, then Neil quickly continued, 'We'll have breakfast at the airport after I check in.' She had heard the gratitude in Neil's voice when she agreed. Aside from his sister, who did he have to see him off? 'Thanks, Mary Jane,' he had said just before he hung up.

But that was yesterday. Commitments look different at ten after six on a Sunday morning. She yearned to get back into bed, to become once again oblivious to everything. To avoid the temptation, Mary Jane sat on the tattered sofa in her living room, sipping a steaming mug of coffee, conscious of the total stillness in the apartment. She'd never felt so tired or so alone.

Mary Jane hadn't thought about it till now, but she had been the only handkerchief-waver each of those other three times friends went off to succeed, and she was sure she would be the only one today, too. It couldn't be she was the only friend that all these people had. That was true of Neil, of course – he was much too angry a loner to have many friends – but the others had been outgoing, popular types on the theatre circuit in New York. Maybe other friends hated goodbyes more than she. Or maybe, she realized with a jolt, other people were too lazy, too self-involved, and too goddamn envious to share in their friends' good fortune. Maybe she, too, was envious, she thought.

She dressed slowly, forcing the good cheer she didn't feel. It was Neil's triumph today, she thought. She wasn't going to let her feelings about her own career interfere with Neil's success. Maybe she *had* driven Sam away. Tears began to fill her eyes. 'Oh, Christ!' she told herself, standing up and almost spilling the coffee. 'Get on with it.'

Mary Jane was down at the door in front of her building at seven on the nose. While she waited, she studied herself in the reflection of the glass entrance door, and ran her fingers through her thick, almost black hair. At least her hair was nice. But she had to do something about the grey. The denim wraparound skirt made her hips look even bigger, but Neil had commented once on how much he liked her in it. It made her look exactly like Veronica in the Archie comics, he had said. Veronica had given him his first hard-on. So Veronica was who he was getting today, Mary Jane thought, and tried to smile to herself.

She also had on a Laura Ashley print shirt, cream-coloured with tiny pink rosebuds and a Peter Pan collar that she had found in a thrift shop on Third Avenue uptown. Very Veronica. On one collar tab she wore a small gold circle pin, and a ridiculous charm bracelet on her wrist, both plastic, both from Woolworth's. Plus, a school cardigan with a letter on it. Penny loafers completed the costume. Now Mary Jane smiled at herself again.

She had just switched her bag to the crook of her elbow, like schoolbooks, when she saw the dark blue Tel Aviv sedan turn the corner from Tenth Avenue onto Fifty-fourth Street. Neil was at the open window as the car came to a stop, and yelled out, 'Veronica!'

'Jughead,' she called back, and did a tiny pirouette to give Neil the full effect before she got into the car.

'You're crazy, Mary Jane,' Neil said, laughing, as the car pulled away from the kerb. 'That's why I love you.'

'*I'm* crazy,' Mary Jane said in mock surprise. '*You're* the one with the Veronica fetish. I never knew anyone who was in love with a comic-book character before.'

'What I felt had nothing to do with love,' Neil leered. 'I wanted to get her into the back booth at Pop Tate's and do the horizontal boogaloo.'

'Other boys jerked off to *Playboy*. You always had to be different,' she laughed. She turned and eyed Neil from head to toe as they sped downtown along the East River Drive to the Midtown Tunnel. Pink rawsilk shirt, the top three buttons open, white slacks, white Gucci loafers, no socks. On someone else it would look good. 'Looks like I'm not the only one who visited Wardrobe,' she said. 'Let me guess. You're going to a party costumed as Robert Evans.'

'Hollywood *is* a costume party,' Neil said, and laughed. 'So what do you think? Will I fit in?'

'Just a minute,' she said, and began to rummage through her handbag. 'You're missing something.' She extended a small, gaily wrapped gift box. 'Bon voyage,' she told him, and handed it over.

Neil opened the wrappings roughly, then shrieked with laughter as he held up the wide fake gold chain with the huge Capricorn medallion suspended from it.

'*Now* you'll fit in,' Mary Jane said, and secured the garish chain around his neck. She patted the medallion so it nestled against Neil's exposed skinny chest and sparse chest hairs. '*So* L.A.'

'Actually, I think they're now into the fake cowboy stuff again, mixed with wire-rimmed glasses. But, hey, I'm a traditionalist.' Neil laughed.

At the terminal, Mary Jane watched from the sidewalk as the driver pulled Neil's bags from the car trunk. Neil's usual angry frown was gone, and he had a smile on his too-wide mouth. His ferretlike profile would put Jamie Farr to shame, she thought, but, God, she was going to miss him. 'Let me help you,' she offered.

'Nothing doing,' he said. 'Stars never carry their own luggage.' He signalled to a skycap, who was able to check him in and tell him the gate number for his flight. Once inside, Mary Jane let Neil take her arm and lead her across the near-empty waiting area to the coffee shop.

The waitress poured coffee for them, then took their breakfast order. 'And two Bloody Marys, doubles,' Neil added before she walked away.

'Why, Jughead, what would Pop Tate say? Are you trying to get me drunk?' Mary Jane asked coquettishly.

Neil leaned across the table and took Mary Jane's hand. 'Come with me, Mary Jane,' he said softly, his voice serious.

Oh, not this, she thought. Not now. I have no strength to be brave. I used it all up being a good sport. Mary Jane tried to keep her tone light. 'Sure, that's just what Hollywood needs: a fat, ugly broad who can't get a job, because the beauties can't get them, either.' The waitress came and placed their drinks in front of them. It was the distraction she needed. 'Here's to you, Neil, and your success.' She clicked her glass against his and took a sip.

Neil took a gulp, then put his glass back down. 'I mean it, Mary Jane. Come with me now. I could buy a ticket on my credit card, and we'll be gone. Just do it.'

Mary Jane shifted in her seat. 'I can't do it, Neil. You know that.'

'I love you,' Neil said. 'Now that you've split from Sam, I can say so. I love you. I dream of you almost every night. I want to touch you all the time. I want to take care of you.'

Mary Jane felt the tightening in her chest. Oh, good Christ, it was too much. It was impossible. And, in a way, insulting. A cosmic message: Sam was too good for you; this clown is all you get. But Neil wasn't just a clown. He was her friend. She looked over at him and saw his pain. 'Neil, I thought ... I thought we were just good friends. I didn't know.' She began to cry. 'I'm so sorry, Neil.'

'If you won't do it for me,' Neil said, 'then do it for yourself. You have a unique talent, Mary Jane. You could get work out there.'

She tried to get control of herself, mopping her eyes with the damp cocktail napkin. 'Neil, if I didn't get cast in the movie version of *Jack and Jill and Compromise* when I'd originated the role on the stage, I'm never going to get a role in the movies. *Jack and Jill and Compromise* was my only chance. I know that now.' She saw Neil's face fall, the dejection causing his eyes to turn down at the corners. His sadness was more than she could bear. She didn't want him to leave New York so glum. And she prayed he didn't feel about her what she felt for Sam. 'Hey, Neil,' Mary Jane said. 'What time is it when your best friend dresses like your fantasy?'

Neil tried to smile, but didn't answer.

'Time to get out of town,' Mary Jane said, and patted his hand.

Neil sighed. 'Okay,' he said. 'So I get out of town. What about you?'

'What about me?' Mary Jane asked. 'I have the theatre group, I have friends. I don't know, maybe one of these days I'll even get another successful play. And when Sam comes back . . .'

'Forget Sam.'

'Don't, Neil. I've asked you before.' Mary Jane felt her colour rise. They paused, looking intently at each other as they listened to the boarding announcement on the public-address system. 'That's your flight,' she said, and was grateful that this scene was ending.

Neil picked up his carry-on bag from the seat next to him. Without looking up, he said, 'Forget Sam, Mary Jane. He was never good enough for you. He was just a nice tall body and perhaps a dick the size of his ego. And he stuck it into anything that walked.'

Mary Jane got up quickly. 'This isn't the time or the place, Neil. I didn't want to hear this.' She began to walk towards the exit.

'I'm sorry, Mary Jane.' Neil said as he caught up to her. They stood in silence next to the security desk leading to the boarding gates. Neil dropped his bag and turned Mary Jane around by the arms to face him. 'I *do* love you, Mary Jane. But I wouldn't be a friend if I didn't tell you what I think. I don't dislike Sam because he's with you. I dislike him because he uses people, and he's used you. His play would have folded in a minute, just like his other plays, if your talent hadn't held it together. And I think, Mary Jane, that you just fell for a pretty face. Don't be shallow. I'm not so great to look at, but I think you ought to look twice.'

'I wish you hadn't said that.' Mary Jane looked intently into Neil's eyes. 'Goodbye, Neil, and good luck.' Mary Jane turned and began to walk away, choking back the tears of sadness and anger.

But Neil pulled Mary Jane towards him again and hugged her. 'I won't ever forget you, Mary Jane,' he said, then kissed her on the lips. It was a real kiss, his tongue darting into her mouth, his lips wet against her dry ones.

Mary Jane froze.

Neil let her go, then picked up his bag. 'Am I still a frog, or have you turned me into a prince?' he asked, his voice hard.

'You've always been a prince to me,' she told him.

'That's the first lie you ever told me,' he said. 'You know what? I'm tired of playing a supporting role in your life. I'm ready for the lead. Why is it that I called you "Veronica" but you never once called me "Archie"? It was always "Jughead." Sure, Jughead had the lines, but Archie got the girls. I could see you as Veronica, Mary Jane, but not once, not once could you look past the surface and see me as Archie. Every time you called me "Jughead," it hurt. Every single time. Well, I'm sick of that role. I'm trying out for Archie's part. And if I've failed the audition, fuck you!' Then he turned, walked up to the security desk and dropped his bag on the conveyor belt, moving through the security check. He didn't look back.

In just another moment, he was gone.

Mary Jane stood at the kerb outside the terminal, waiting for the Carey bus that would take her back to the city. She dabbed at her eyes with a tattered tissue, then dropped it into the trash barrel beside her. She looked up and saw the bus pull into the pick-up lane. She turned back to the trash barrel, took off the stupid charm bracelet and pin, and dropped them in, too, then boarded the bus without looking back.

When she got back to her apartment, Midnight greeted her, along with a yellow Western Union envelope. What fresh hell is this?

she wondered, and tore it open. Am I being evicted, or has the IRS decided to audit penniless actresses this week? She pulled out the message.

> YOUR GRANDMOTHER DIED THIS A.M. PLEASE COME TO ELMIRA NO LATER THAN TOMORROW TO MAKE ARRANGEMENTS. PLEASE CALL ASAP. EDWARD ROBINSON. ROBINSON'S FUNERAL HOME.

Mary Jane stared at the message. Her grandmother was dead. After all those false alarms and miserable complaints, when Mary Jane had finally decided to ignore the old woman just for once, then the old woman dies. Tearless, profoundly tired, Mary Jane stared at the slip of paper. Her grandmother was dead.

And, with a pull deep in her gut, Mary Jane realized that she envied her.

14

Sharleen's fear had begun to recede, lulled by the comforts of Dobe's car and the easy living. And, she thought, if the police were looking for her and Dean, they wouldn't be lookin' for a family. Together, the three of them did look like a family. It was pleasant in the car. Dobe told funny stories, and Dean kept them busy with licence plates. 'Look! There's an Oklahoma. "Oklahoma is O.K.,"' he read off the tag.

'Never struck *me* that way,' Sharleen said.

'Well, at least they're not making exaggerated claims,' Dobe said mildly. 'Not like Louisiana.'

'Sportsman's paradise!' Dean told him proudly.

'Depends on what you consider sport,' Dobe said grimly.

They stopped in gas stations, and each time Dobe filled up with water, sold a dozen pills or so, and they moved on. They spent more than a week in Arizona, then moved up to Nevada. And at each state line they crossed, Sharleen said a prayer and drew a deeper breath than she'd been able to breathe before.

That night, in yet another motel, this one outside Carson City, Nevada, Sharleen knelt in prayer and thanked the Lord for all the blessings He sent her way, and for His help in taking care of her and Dean. And she thanked Him again for Dobe, who was a gentleman and a Christian. As always, she prayed for the souls of Boyd and her daddy then. Sharleen stood up and walked to the night table, opening the drawer. Again there was a Bible. God *must* be leading them. But she was starting to think there might be a Bible in every motel room, just like there were towels and soap. She walked to the bathroom door, knocked, and called in to Dean.

'They got another Bible here, Dean. Almost ready?'

'What are you going to read tonight?' Dean asked from behind the door.

Sharleen took the black-covered book and put it aside. 'I like reading from Momma's,' she said, as she placed the motel's Bible back into the drawer of the nightstand, picking up their mother's tattered copy instead. 'I don't know just yet, Dean. You know I like to open it without any plan, and just let the Lord and Momma give us their message.'

From the time Dobe had spoken to her about Dean, she had been mulling over what he had said. The lie that Dean wasn't her brother troubled her, but not as much as the fact that he *was* her boyfriend. And her half-brother. It all seemed so complicated. Dean in many ways was like a child, but he also was her protector. She took care of him, but she needed him, too. He was her family. At home in Lamson, she could keep the problem out of her mind. On the road, their relationship troubled her far more.

Dean came out of the bathroom. 'Read me the one about Daniel with the lion again, Sharleen. I like that part. I don't understand some of the other stuff.'

Sharleen sat at the edge of the bed. Dean was sprawled the length of it, wearing only his jockey shorts. He had his eyes closed, his hands behind his head, and a small, peaceful smile on his lips. Sharleen looked down at him, marvelling as usual at his beauty and the perfection of his body. He reminded her of an angel, a frightened, gentle, loving angel, and it was her responsibility to take care of him, to see that his gentleness and beauty would not be destroyed by the harshness of life. Sharleen knew she wasn't too smart herself, but at least *she* was smart enough to make sure that they both got along without getting in too much trouble with some of the wicked people that roam the earth.

Sharleen flipped the pages of their mother's dog-eared Bible, then stopped and opened to a page. 'Tonight's reading, Dean, is from Deuteronomy, chapter ten, verse nine. This is in the Old Testament, Dean, before Jesus was born.' Sharleen looked closer at the passage, and saw that the scripture she had chosen had been marked in pencil by their mother, as many had. 'Dean, guess what! Momma liked this passage, too, and marked it. So let's see what she's telling us from the Lord.'

Sharleen leaned back on the bed's headboard, the Bible opened on her lap. As she settled in, Dean turned his face towards her, rested his forehead against her thigh, and threw one hand across her legs. He kept his eyes closed.

'This is the place Momma marked,' Sharleen told Dean. '"Wherefore Levi hath no part nor inheritance with his brethren; the Lord is his inheritance, according as the Lord thy God promised him."'

Sharleen closed the book slowly, holding a finger in it to keep her place. 'Levi hath no part . . . with his brethren.' She thought of Dobe's advice to her about Dean, of her shame, and she got gooseflesh all up her arms.

'Go on, Sharleen. It sounds real pretty.'

'Dean,' she said very gently. 'This is a message from Momma.'

'She says things in her book so pretty, Sharleen.'

'Momma is telling us something, Dean. Sit up and listen.'

Dean opened his eyes and pulled himself up to a sitting position, also using the headboard for support. 'I can't understand what Momma tells us in the book, Sharleen. She don't talk like she used to back home.'

'These aren't Momma's words exactly, Dean. These are the words of God. Momma just tells us where to look in the book. And tonight she told us to look at these words because they tell us something. Something very important. It says Levi has no part with his brother.'

'Only Levi I know is dungarees. What do you mean, Sharleen? Who's Levi?' Dean asked.

'It don't matter who *he* is. He just ain't supposed to have no part of his brother.' Dean looked at her, and slowly, very slowly, she saw the fear come into his clear blue eyes.

Sharleen put her arm around Dean's shoulder and stroked his white-blond hair, so like her own. 'Dean, Momma is telling us we got to sleep in separate beds from now on. Now that we're growed, it's time we slept alone.'

'But why? *Your* name ain't Levi. It don't say *Sharleen* don't have no part with her brother. And why should Momma want us to sleep alone now? She always tucked us in together back home. Why's she saying now we got to sleep separate?' He sounded petulant, almost on the verge of tears.

'Because we don't just sleep. And it ain't right, what we do. Brothers and sisters ain't supposed to share the same bed. They ain't supposed to touch each other like we do.'

Dean's face crumpled. It pained Sharleen, right to her heart. 'You mean we can't be close and feel good no more?'

'That's right, Dean. We can be close friends, but we can't make each other happy in that way no more.' Sharleen thought again of Dobe's comment. About seeing how things were between her and Dean. Before he had warned her, she had tried real hard not to think too much about it, it had felt so natural at night to be close to Dean, safe and happy. Why, they had always been close like that. She couldn't sleep any other way. It was their secret. But Dobe was a good man, and smart, and now Momma sent this word from the Bible. That's twice now she had been warned.

Sharleen rose from the bed and pulled the covers over Dean's body. She noticed the bulge in his briefs, and quickly covered it.

Dean continued to cry. 'But the dreams, Sharleen. I get so scared. I can't go to sleep without you holding me, Sharleen. I never had to before.'

Sharleen thought of her own, more recent bad dreams, but bent over him and kissed him on the forehead. 'I'll be right here in the other bed, right beside you. Nothing bad's going to happen to you, not as long as we do what God wants us to do.' She pulled back the covers of the other twin bed and slid in, then turned off the light, leaving her mother's Bible on the table between them. 'Now, just say your prayers and go to sleep. The Good Lord will watch over us. And don't forget to pray for Boyd and Daddy, and especially for Momma, and thank her for her guidance.'

Dean sniffled. 'Okay, Sharleen. I will, if that's what you want.'

They lay in silence for a long while. Sharleen knew she would not be able to sleep, but hoped that Dean would finally drift off. And she prayed he wouldn't dream. Not one of the real bad ones anyway. She continued to lie there, wide awake, as Dean's breathing slowed. She missed his warmth beside her, but now she knew what

Dobe had meant. Still, it was hard to relax without Dean next to her. Silly, because their daddy couldn't hurt them now. It mustn't be right to be with Dean. Hadn't Momma's message practically said that exactly?

Eventually, she heard Dean's breathing even out into sleep. She tried to sleep herself, and dozed a little, but just as she became aware of the first streak of light on the horizon outside her window, she heard him.

Dean had started to thrash in bed, whimpering. 'No,' he moaned. 'No, please!' Sharleen couldn't bear it, but forced herself to stay in her own bed. It will pass, she thought.

But Dean's cries grew louder, and his movements in the bed more violent. 'No! Daddy! Please!' he cried out. She knew he was having one of the bad ones, but she was resolved to do the will of God. It was torture, though. Dean writhed, groaning. She picked up Momma's Bible on the nightstand, hoping to find words of comfort. She clicked on the small light over her bed, and ran through the pages of the Bible. Dean quieted down, but he still wept in his sleep. Sharleen closed her eyes and prayed. 'Oh, Lord, please help me do the right thing, and give Dean peace in his sleep. Momma, help me.' She, too, began to cry softly, and once again opened the Good Book, to Psalms, her favourite. But once again Dean moaned, a deep, pained cry.

She flipped a page or two and stopped at Psalm 133. 'Behold,' she read in the dim light, 'how good and how pleasant it is for brethren to dwell together in unity!'

She stared at the page, running her finger over the text, over and over. Then Sharleen put the book back on the night table and said in a whisper, 'Thank you, Lord.' She got out of bed and went over to Dean. She touched him gently to make room for herself, and got in next to him. She put her arms around him and whispered in his ear, 'I'm here, Dean. Everything is going to be all right now.'

Dean had wakened as Sharleen came into his bed. Without opening his eyes, he nuzzled deeply into Sharleen and said, 'Don't never leave me alone, Sharleen.'

Sharleen rocked him gently in her arms. 'No, Dean,' she promised, 'I never will.'

15

Mary Jane was suddenly and completely awake, but she knew the effort of opening her eyes was beyond her for the moment. She lay there, her body fitting into the familiar depression of the lumpy mattress. Her skin quickened from the cold in the damp, unheated room.

She allowed her eyes to flicker open for a moment, saw as much as she could bear, then shut them again. Oh, God! No. She hadn't meant to wake up. At least not here. Couldn't she do *anything* right? She was a nurse, for chrissakes. She was lying on the bedspread, no blanket, still wearing the black dress she had worn to the funeral yesterday, now twisted about her body. One black pump lay on its side at the bottom of the bed.

The funeral. I came back here after the funeral yesterday. And then . . .? And then I had a drink, she remembered. And that was as far as she could go for the moment. Another chill ran through her body, this one forcing her to sit up, the sudden movement making her lightheaded. She turned to the edge of her bed, very slowly now, and lowered her feet. She sat there for a moment, gathering her resources for the next movement. And then, without warning, she vomited.

When she was done, Mary Jane looked around the sparsely furnished, unadorned room, feeling like an intruder, even though this was the bedroom in which she had grown up. Hell, she'd felt like an intruder *then*! Her eyes fell on the closet door, knowing the remains of her childhood were in cartons in there. The smell of mildew mixed with the smell of her vomit. Slowly, she stood, tottered over to the bureau, and wiped up the mess with an old tattered towel. She opened the half-rotted window sash and dumped the fetid rag outside.

Even after all these years, it still hurt that her grandmother had packed all her belongings into boxes the week she went away to nursing school. Mary Jane could never bring herself to go through

109

the boxes of old clothes, clippings, yearbooks, and memories, but she still resented her grandmother for erasing all signs of her presence. The resentment lingered now, even after the old woman was dead.

Mary Jane wrapped her robe around herself for warmth, closed the bedroom door behind her, and walked down the worn wooden stairs, her stockinged feet making shushing sounds as she moved. For a moment, in the silence between steps, she could almost hear Snowball, her old black cat, walking at her side, thumping down the steps to join her at her lonely breakfast, his tail swishing back and forth in excitement. That cat – long dead – had been her only comfort growing up. Now Midnight was her only friend back in New York. Well, she told herself, not much has changed.

She walked into the kitchen and looked around at the chaos, resenting her grandmother even more for her slovenly ways than for the poverty of spirit that engendered them.

She picked up the coffeepot from the stove, filled it with cold water and coffee, and placed it on the flame. She waited for it to percolate while she recovered from the effort, seated at the stained white-enamel table, her chin in her hands. Her eyes swept the mean room, coming to rest on the stack of empty soup cans off in one corner. The shelf over the cracked porcelain sink held a few chipped plates and mugs from the five-and-ten; the wallpaper was faded and bulging in spots, probably from the many leaks the house regularly sprung each spring. The green-and-brown-enamelled stove stood on six metal legs, the surface dark from layers of grease untouched for years. The linoleum was worn through before the sink and the stove, exposing older, tattered linoleum and the grey splintering wood underneath.

She looked out the grimy window at the steel-grey day, and the other pieces of the day before began to slip into her consciousness. The funeral, the burial. The few people in the church were there out of neighbourliness, even though Mary Jane's grandmother had been anything but neighbourly. Only one other person made it to the grave, Mrs. Willis, Grandma's closest neighbour, who lived a mile away.

After hearing the first thud of dirt from the shovel hit the cheap, unfinished pine box, Mary Jane had settled the bill with Mr. Robinson and gotten back in the rental car she couldn't afford. She drove Mrs. Willis back home. Then she returned to the desolate farmhouse. Yes, and had a drink.

And another. And another. And cried. At least I cried, she thought, as she poured out the coffee. But I didn't cry for my grandmother. I cried for me. And then, she admitted, she'd walked into her grandmother's room and taken every pill on the nightstand, washing the whole collection down with the Chivas she'd brought with her from New York. She planned never to wake up, never to face another bleak morning. Because at thirty-four she knew she had had her shot – an important part, a special man – and it was over. If a fat, plain actress couldn't make it by thirty-four, should she expect it would be better at forty-six? At fifty? I've ended my great expectations, she thought.

But her suicide obviously hadn't worked. The irony of it – a nurse who couldn't find the right prescription for suicide! There had been a lot of pills, then the rest of the Chivas. Then, at last, blessed unconsciousness, unconsciousness that she hoped was permanent.

But she'd awoken to this: the ugliness and filth of herself and her surroundings. *This* is what I came from, and, despite all my work, *this* is all I am. Trash from trash.

There wouldn't be another Sam, or another part like Jill, or another friend like Neil, or another theatre group like the troupe. She sat at the table, too sick, too tired even to cry. She remembered the Dorothy Parker suicide poem and added a stanza of her own:

> Pills taste awful;
> Vomit stinks;
> But I've had a crawful –
> The suicide thinks.

The coffeepot began to bubble as she walked into the pantry to look for something she could eat to calm her sick stomach. Saltines, maybe. She surveyed the contents of the shelves, mostly squat mason jars containing the dried peas and beans and preserved vegetables her grandmother had religiously put up every year but never used. Rows and rows of aged tomatoes and carrots and string beans. The short wall of the room held perishables, each tightly enclosed in a baggie with a red wire twist at its neck. Her eyes fell on some crackers; she knew that this was the only solid food she could manage. She took the plastic-bagged box from the shelf, untwisting the tie as she walked back to the littered kitchen table.

She poured a cup of the coffee, reached into the box of crackers, and removed the opened portion. She bit into one tentatively, tasted its mustiness, spat it out, and pulled out one of the other waxed-paper sleeves. She was about to open it when she noticed it was already unsealed at the wrong end. Through the opaque wrapper, she saw something. Something greyish-green.

A mouse? She almost dropped the packet, but it didn't move, and she looked more closely. No. Not a mouse. Mary Jane tore open the wrapping and sucked in her breath. A rubber-band-wrapped bundle rolled onto the table. Mary Jane stared down at it for a moment before she croaked the word out loud.

'Money!'

The bills had been so tightly rolled, it took her some time to get them unfurled and laid out in denominations on the table: all $637. The shock of the discovery forced her to sit back in the creaking chair. Where had this come from? For an instant, she wished her grandmother had known about the money, then realized the truth . . . her grandmother had put it there!

Oh, no, Grandma, she thought. Why? What did you hope to do with this money? Then, at last, Mary Jane cried for the crazy old woman, mourning her grandmother's missed opportunity of spending this money, which Mary Jane guessed must have taken a lifetime to save.

As her tears abated, she sipped her now lukewarm coffee, trying to think. How long had it taken the old woman to save over six hundred dollars on her egg money, her vegetable sales, her Social Security? Mary Jane wondered.

She realized she had never thought about her grandmother's finances before. She'd always accepted the fact that they were dirt-poor. Grandma had told her over and over how she, Mary Jane, lived out of Grandma's charity — 'when I haven't even enough for myself.' But was that the truth? Surely her grandmother had received Aid to Families with Dependent Children after Mary Jane's mother had been killed and her father incapacitated. And hadn't her grandfather, long dead, been with the railroad? Had there been a pension? What about the V.A. Was there a pension from the army for her dad? It also had never occurred to her that her grandmother had made extra money from leasing out her grazing land to farmers. The belief was always that that rent was barely enough to pay the mortgage, but could there be more? And had the mortgage been paid off? Like a dreamer, waking up, she shook her head. It was probably a crazy idea, but Mary Jane stood, dropping the opened crackers to the floor. She walked to the pantry.

Mary Jane ripped open the other package of crackers. Nothing. Of course not; silly idea. Look at this place. Worse than Miss Havisham's. Dust and cobwebs everywhere. Grandma was dirt-poor. But what if there *is* more? she thought. What else is in the pantry? In the house?

Trembling, she began to pick up each mason jar of vegetables, to study their contents through the dusty glass. Halfway down the row, the heft of one of the jars in the back was different. She returned to the kitchen, washed off the dirt, and looked. Hurriedly, she released the vacuum seal with effort, reached in, and removed a plastic-wrapped bundle: another roll of bills. Her heart thumping in her chest, her hands shaking, she counted out the money. Almost two thousand dollars.

She poured a fresh cup of coffee and slumped into the chair, her heart still pounding. More than two thousand dollars! And if there was this much, there was more.

Looking down at the growing stack of bills, Mary Jane knew with certainty: My grandmother never loved me. She took me in when my mother died and my father went into the V.A. She was the only family I knew, but she never loved me. No wonder I always felt like a burden. She remembered, as a child, when she asked for something, as children do – money for the movies, candy, a toy – the words of her grandmother's refusal. 'No, can't afford it, not now that there's two mouths to feed. Now that I'm saddled with you.'

So she had soon stopped asking, and even stopped expecting. She expected nothing, and felt everyone was 'saddled' with her, as if she were some unspeakable burden. And when she lost her scholarship because she'd had to take a night job while going to nursing school fulltime during the day and her grades had dropped to B's, she accepted without questioning what her grandmother had said: 'Can't help you out. I can barely feed myself.'

Mary Jane crashed her fist down on the table. The old woman had lied. Where had this money come from? What if there's more? She stood up and looked around the room, at the ridiculous stack of empty soup cans that had been washed out and saved for no discernible purpose. She kicked at the pile, sending them clanking across the floor, kicking at each one, bouncing them off the walls, stomping on some as they rolled along the floor.

Goddamn you, Grandma. How could you? I was a good girl. How could you have withheld this money? How could you not have loved me, not even a little?

Mary Jane's eyes fell to a bubble in the faded wallpaper over the sink. She reached out and felt a bulge and, now with purpose, took a knife and cut out the square. She peeled back the paper and exposed sheets of the kind of plastic found in photo albums. Through the shiny surface, Mary Jane saw the certificates. Bearer bonds. Old ones. She counted them. Eleven thousand dollars' worth of bearer bonds!

She tore the house apart. It took her hours. The backs of pictures, the lining of upholstery, the floorboards, the rest of the preserves. In the freezer she found almost four thousand dollars frozen in an ice block. In the bathroom there was $760 in an old – a very old – Modess box. As she tore and smashed and cried, as she searched every inch of the filthy, nasty little shack she'd been forced to grow up in, she sobbed.

That night, Mary Jane picked up the bundle of cash and bonds, over sixty-seven thousand dollars' worth, and started upstairs to her room. Her step was slowed by exhaustion from the search, from the anger, and from the tears. As she passed the thermostat at the foot of the stairs, she looked at the setting: sixty-five degrees, the highest her grandmother ever allowed it to be set. With a snap she pushed up the setting to seventy-five, and continued upstairs with her bundle, knowing that now, at least, she would be warm.

16

In twenty-five years of covering the Hollywood waterfront, I – Laura Richie – have learned one thing for sure: There are faces that the camera loves, personalities that come alive, project, expand under attention. It isn't simply a question of looks, although being photogenic helps. But it's much more than that, much rarer than that: Sophia Loren had it, Gina Lollobrigida did not. Gary Cooper had it, Gregory Peck did not. Burt Reynolds had it, Tom Selleck does not.

You can't learn it, or practise it. It's just there, like your breath.

People want to watch you. You have an intrinsically riveting persona that plays on screen. How? Why? Nobody knows.

And it isn't acting. There are some great actors who didn't have it. Back in the thirties, the Schencks and Goldwyns and Warners called it 'star quality.' It's as good a term as any. And believe me, dear Reader, it's as rare as, and more valuable than, a black diamond.

Lila pulled her old Mustang convertible into the parking space behind the low grey building in West Hollywood. She jumped out and, throwing her bag over her shoulder, walked quickly to the side entrance and up the flight of stairs, her red hair flowing in the breeze behind her. She could tell from the chattering voices that the door to the classroom was still open. I'm on time, she thought. Lila hated to be late for acting class. George Getz took perverse pleasure in singling out late arrivals and haranguing them about their responsibility to the 'company,' as he called his pretty little collection of wannabes. Not that he could ever succeed in making Lila feel uncomfortable. On the contrary. George was usually so busy fawning over the daughter of Theresa O'Donnell, that Lila felt like she might lose her lunch.

She looked around the cavernous, windowless room, at the grey-tweed carpeting that went halfway up three walls. Several stacks of putty-grey folding chairs were piled to one side. Next to them were mounds of soft cushions. One wall was entirely mirrored. Lila walked past a knot of young women who greeted her by name as she sailed by. Just like Westlake. She was still the popular girl, and it was still because she didn't give a shit. She didn't look in their direction, but gave a general hello as she opened the door to the ladies' room. Inside, she pulled a brush through her silky red hair to get out the tangles caused by the wind lashing around her as she drove her convertible with the top down. Well, Ken's convertible, actually. Aunt Robbie had talked Ken into lending it to her. She actually hated the Ford, and the maroon colour clashed with her hair, but beggars couldn't be choosy, so they said.

The door opened behind her and, in the mirror, she could see one of the young blonde women rush in. Bandie something, Lila thought, and turned her attention back to her own hair. She was friendly; they were all friendly, because once they had watched her mother and Candy and Skinny. Now they felt they knew her, and that maybe the famous Theresa O'Donnell would help them. Yeah, like she could help herself! Or her own flesh and blood!

'Oh, hi, Lila,' Bandie cooed as she dropped her bag on the table in front of the mirror and began to rifle through it. 'Guess what,' she said. Not waiting for Lila's reply, she continued, 'I got a commercial. A *national* commercial!' Bandie applied the melon-coloured lipstick she'd finally found. 'I can't believe it,' Bandie said. 'There were sixteen callbacks, and *I* got it.'

'Congratulations,' Lila said. Even though money was a problem for her, she'd *never* do a commercial. Yet she knew that for one of her classmates to get a commercial was a big coup. The income from a national ad could go a long way towards easing the financial strain brought on by acting classes, elocution lessons, singing lessons, and dance classes. Not to mention clothes, cars, personal grooming, personal trainers, orthodontists, hair colouring, colonics, and a touch of the surgeon's knife from time to time. But Bandie, like so many of the others, actually considered commercials real acting jobs. For most, Lila knew, it would be the closest thing to performing before the public that they would ever get. Lila shuddered. *She'd* never sell floor wax or douches on TV.

Lila remembered when her mother was asked to endorse some crap – a detergent or something – on television, with Candy and Skinny. Theresa had gone apeshit. 'Stars don't do laundry *or* TV commercials,' she had screamed at Ara Sagarian, her agent. Lila had heard many of Mother's definitions of stars through the years, and filed all of them away. The Puppet Mistress was a manipulating bitch, a drunk, a pain in the ass, and a total nutcake, but she *had* been a star. And that is what Lila wanted to be, a *star*, someone who never carries cash; always arrives by limousine; never opens a door; doesn't smoke in public; never refuses a request for an autograph; remembers everyone's name; never wears a gown publicly more than once; addresses her directors as 'Mister,' encourages others to address her as 'Miss'; does not socialize with the technical crew; never makes her own reservations; shakes hands in greeting instead of kissing; calls her *producers* by their first names; has a secretary; never drives her own car unless it's a fun one; has favourite charities; attends other stars' performances; knows how to turn a man down without rejecting him; arrives late and leaves early; sits in the best seat at a party and waits for *them* to come to *her*; does not serve herself from a buffet table; knows how to read a contract; and is never offstage.

And that is what she aimed to be: a bigger star than her mother. So no fucking commercials.

She turned to Bandie. 'What's the product?' Lila asked pleasantly, like she cared.

'A premium bathroom tissue,' Bandie said with a look of triumph.

Deliver me, Lila thought. 'Congratulations,' she said politely, and put her brush back in her bag.

'I called Mr. Getz immediately. He's *so* proud of me.'

Great. Their acting coach was proud his student was selling ass-wipe. Lila sighed. Robbie had *sworn* that Getz had connections, and Lila had to start someplace. She went back out into the open room and dropped down onto one of the cushions. She looked around at the other participants and was struck once again by the number of beautiful men and women in the room. It was an L.A. cliché. They were a plague, these perfect-looking mannequins. Here assembled in one room was the handsomest boy from Debbins, South Dakota; Lake Winesha, Wisconsin; Portland Bay, Oregon; Charleston, West Virginia; Cudahy, Iowa; Woodbridge, Massachusetts; and Shreveport, Louisiana; as well as the most beautiful girl from Shadley, Mississippi; Goochland, Virginia; Barre, Vermont; Standish, Rhode Island; Black Springs, Ohio; and Enid, Oklahoma. Their looks had made them special, had been a passport out of the backwaters they'd crawled away from, but here in Hollywood even the best looks only guaranteed a waitressing job, a parking-valet job, a blow job. Lila shook her head.

A door opened at the end of the room and a paunchy man in his fifties entered, his long, grey hair pulled back into a pony tail. There was some hesitant clapping from a few of the recent enrollees, then silence as George Getz plopped heavily down on a cushion one of the students had brought for him. The semicircle re-formed around him. Only Lila didn't move. Lila studied George as he sat cross-legged, poring over some notes. His paunch rested on his legs; his white, scrawny legs were like matchsticks extending out of his khaki safari shorts; black leather sandals shod his feet. He was wearing a faded, white 'Save the Whales' T-shirt, which stretched across a distended stomach. His rimless glasses were thick, so his small eyes appeared open in amazement all the time.

Well, it was Aunt Robbie who had suggested George Getz. Robbie's opinion about acting teachers was well known. He felt that either you could act or you couldn't. If you couldn't, no one could teach you how; if you could, all you needed was someone to show you a few of the tricks to develop your craft, and George,

117

he felt, was at least capable of *that*. Plus, he was still plugged in to a few of the older producers and directors.

Now George looked up, calling the class to order by letting his eyes drift over the faces in the room. Lila could feel the tension in the stillness. Everyone was here to learn from this man, but they all knew that there was a high price to pay, besides the tuition. George rarely praised anyone's efforts, and took great delight in humiliating the youngsters' least competent attempts.

'Everyone, spread out on the floor . . . get rid of the cushions . . . make sure you have a large space around you. . . . This is going to be a group effort. Bring your focus within, close your eyes, do your breathing exercises.' The class responded to his instruction, the only sound the hypnotic breathing of the group. Personally, Lila thought it was a load of crap. 'Now sit up, keeping the eyes closed. Bring your legs to your chest, hugging them. Breathe. Breathe. Now, focus. I want you to convince me that you are vanilla ice cream melting in the sun. I want you to *be* vanilla ice cream melting in the sun. Forget about time. I will tell you when to stop. Begin.'

Lila slowed her breathing. What an absolute pile of dog shit! Lila supposed that good acting came from the ability to visualize and then represent an intense inner experience of a character, but ice cream? Anyway, she wasn't planning to be an actress. She was planning to be a star.

The silence was broken by George's voice. 'Corey,' he said, 'continue with the exercise, but don't open your eyes. Class, open your eyes and look at Corey.'

Lila did, then sighed. She knew what was coming, and resented the ridiculous interruption just to satisfy George's egotistical rants.

'What do you see, class? Keep studying Corey. Do you see vanilla ice cream melting in the sun? NO!' he suddenly shouted. The class jumped. 'He looks like a mound of mashed potatoes. And mashed potatoes don't melt, do they, Corey?'

Corey opened his eyes and gave George an apologetic smile; then his face coloured as he saw the entire class looking at him.

'So that, boys and girls, is an example of how it's *not* done.' George looked around. The others looked away, but Lila boldly returned his stare. 'Ah, Lila, would you come up to the front? I want *you* to demonstrate how you did it. Watch *her*,' George said, and stepped back.

Lila had become used to being singled out by George in this way. But what the hell was this ice-cream-cone dreck? Instinctively,

Lila knew how to centre attention on herself. She pushed conscious thought from her mind, and slipped easily into the mood. As a sop to George, she relaxed, first her neck, then her shoulders, then her arms. All eyes were riveted on her. And she could keep them there by force of will. Moments passed; then she became aware of George's voice breaking the silence. 'That's vanilla ice cream melting in the sun,' he said, turning to the class, then turned to her once again. 'Lila, have you worked on Portia's soliloquy yet?'

'Of course, George.' It had been their assignment last week.

'Then do it for us now, if you will, Lila. I have need of some *real* acting today.' George leaned back against the wall and closed his eyes. Lila's classmates shifted their positions to get comfortable, as if another body angle could make their envy stop hurting.

Lila rose, ran the first couple of lines in her head, and then flipped the internal switch on, the switch that made her a magnet for the eyes. She hadn't understood much of the monologue, but Robbie had coached her, and the direction was etched into her brain. She had performed the scene for Ken, and he'd loved it. Now, without hesitation, Lila became a Shakespearean heroine, the strange words and their melody welling up out of her. She was a good mimic and remembered where Robbie had dipped his voice and caught his breath. But it was her energy that mattered. She turned it on, a lantern of glowing energy. For a moment, she noticed the faces of some of the people in the audience. They were mouthing her lines, eyes turned up to her in envy and adoration. In that instant, Lila loved them all, these desperate, sad, pretty, lost little people, and poured out that love in every word and gesture. She wanted to give them a piece of herself, to give them something they did not have, could not have, would never have, so she reached across the open space and drew them into her heart. She spoke the words not to the group, but to each individual. Admiration was good, but only when she was safely up onstage.

When at last the final lines came, the room was silent. Then, as she came out of character, they burst into applause and shouts. Lila smiled dryly, bowed deeply once, then returned to her seat, avoiding the eyes of her classmates. The good feeling ended. She felt almost empty – no, dead – inside. Bandie, sitting beside her, reached over and patted Lila's hand in congratulations. Lila snatched back her hand and touched her throat to hold back the disgust that bubbled up in her mouth like bile. Contempt popped up goose bumps on her forearms.

George praised her. 'Only four months with me, and see how she's applied herself. You should all learn from her example. That's the Getz method.' After his plug, he moved to another topic, his voice droning on. She looked at the class out of the corners of her eyes while they now paid rapt attention to George. As if they could learn to be what she was. She almost laughed. They were all beautiful, she thought, but she knew that *she* was the best in the room. She also knew that looks alone would not make her a star. Nor her connections through Theresa, *if* she could somehow manage to use them, nor Aunt Robbie, nor poor George. And talent wasn't enough. Deep, deep inside, Lila knew she had something special, something that drew the attention, the interest of others. But that something had to be showcased. Sitting in this class week after week was not going to do it, either. Half the room hoped that Sy Ortis would suddenly walk in the door one day and discover them. Well, she had news for them; he wouldn't. So now the only thing she had to figure out was the same trick these lamebrains were working on.

How to make it happen.

17

Mary Jane left her grandmother's the next day, and stopped at Mr. Slater's, an Elmira lawyer, to discuss selling the house and its contents. She had her grandmother's will – she'd been left the house, but in trust for her father. Her father, the man whose drunken driving had killed Mary Jane's mother and turned himself into a vegetable! She told Slater to probate the will and sell the place off as soon as possible. Then she drove across the state line, into Massachusetts, and called in the bearer bonds. Finally, she began the long drive back to New York. How could $67,411 (all of it undeclared and tax-free) make her life worth living?

What did she want? It wasn't enough money to buy a house in the Hamptons, or even a co-op in New York. It couldn't buy her a business, and anyway, she didn't want one. She could use the money to live on, but what would happen when it ran out? Back to Elmira, the Chivas, and a handful of pills?

In her whole life, it seemed to Mary Jane, she had wanted only two things: Sam, and a career as an actress. Well, the money wouldn't bring Sam back. And it wouldn't buy her a theatre. She kept on driving down the Thruway, the radio playing some stupid seventies disco music. She stopped for coffee at a disgusting roadside rest stop, sat down at a table, and thought some more. And then it came to her. What she wanted, what she truly wanted and needed.

She needed to be beautiful.

Why hadn't she thought of it before? She had the talent to succeed as an actress – her reviews for *Jack and Jill* proved that – and she had the love to succeed with a man. After all, despite her looks, Sam had wanted her. It was only her outer self, her mortal coil, that offended, that limited her, that ruined her. She had tried to kill it, but with it would have gone all the rest – her talent, her ability to befriend, to love.

As she sat at the orange Formica table, while the cars flew by on the Thruway, she felt her hands on the Styrofoam coffee cup begin to tremble.

Why couldn't she use the sixty-seven thousand dollars that lay in the bag beside her to buy a new face and body? Become a new person, at least on the outside? Throughout all of history, men had had the money and could buy women's beauty. A Nell Gwyn could move up from the streets and trade beauty for wealth. Now, for the first time, a woman could buy beauty for herself. She, Mary Jane Moran, had the money to buy a new face, perhaps even a streamlined, perfect body. She knew the technology was there. It could be done.

She felt the trembling move from her hands up her arms to her whole body. She tried to breathe deeply, and hoped no one would notice, but the fat, distracted mother with three cranky children at the next table, and the old man with what looked like a wife with Alzheimer's across the aisle, had other things to do. She pushed away the coffee cup and closed her eyes for a moment. Could this thing be done? Did she have the courage to do it?

The trip to New York passed in a blur. She shut off the radio, put the pedal to the metal, and sank into a strange state, between fear and elation. She hadn't been a nurse all those years for nothing. So, when she got back to New York, with the sixty-seven thousand dollars in cash, wrapped in plastic, stuffed into a canvas Channel 13 tote and hidden safely in the back of her closet, she began her research. She knew about Dr. Walden at Doctors Hospital, of course, and John Armstrong at Columbia Presbyterian. They were the Park Avenue plastic surgeons that the *beau monde* employed for the subtle but critically important nips and tucks they all required. They had great reputations, but Mary Jane required a lot more than that.

She told no one about the money or her plan – if it was a plan. In fact, she didn't see any of her friends. She'd have to do some research first. She called Nancy Norton, an old classmate, now a nurse at the Mount Sinai Burn Pavilion. After burns, major reconstruction was often necessary. She also spoke to Bobby Watkins, a black actor who moonlighted as an emergency-room nurse and saw lots of trauma cases – smashed up from accidents. She sat for hours in the library at Cornell Medical Center, poring through *The Lancet*, *The Journal of the American Medical Association*, and the specialized plastic-surgery bulletins. She cross-referenced all that with research in the AMA's who's who.

It came down to four men: Robert Ducker of Miami, who had developed dozens of innovative techniques when he worked in Haiti and the Dominican Republic, on poor patients, who couldn't afford to sue; William Reed, who practiced out in L.A. and was purported to be the best nose man in the business; John Collins, a Park Avenue type; and Brewster Moore, chief of plastic surgery at Cosmopolitan Hospital in New York. He'd been an army doctor, worked on Vietnam vets, and had been chief plastic surgeon at the hospital for close to a dozen years. But he was the only one without an extensive private practice. He was known in the medical profession as 'the doctors' doctor,' and the word was that he corrected the errors other plastic surgeons made.

Mary Jane lay in bed – her bed, which was now so big, so empty, with Sam gone – and stared at the ceiling as she thought it out. Midnight kneaded her stomach, purring deeply with satisfaction, and she stroked him as her mind turned her plan over and over. Was it really possible to stop being plain old Mary Jane, her talent hidden under a bushel of body, and emerge as someone not just better-looking, not even just pretty, but beautiful? Was it possible that now, at thirty-four, she could belatedly join that sisterhood of women who turned men's heads when they walked down the street, who entered a room and caused a stir, or even a momentary silence, who inspired lustful dreams, romantic fantasies, simply with a look, a smile, a toss of the head?

What would it feel like not to always have to compensate for her looks, not to have to work against her formless cheeks, her big nose, her absent chin? Never again to see the wince when she walked into a casting call, met a director, was introduced to a man? What would it be like to play the ingenue, to be sought after by men, not to be invisible, as she so often felt, but to be undressed by their eyes, the way they did Bethanie and those other beauties?

Was it possible? How much art and science would it take to sculpt her formless putty into a classically chiselled profile, to raise her pendulous breasts, thin her thunder thighs, flatten her wattled stomach, remake her into the image that men called beautiful? How much would it cost? How long would it take? How much would it hurt? Could it even be done?

Her medical background gave her a basic understanding of the names and techniques for most of the procedures she'd need. But would a surgeon be willing to perform them all? And she knew that it had to be not just a surgeon but an artist, willing to work for months, maybe longer, willing to take her seriously, willing to undertake a transformation, a reconstruction, but on someone undamaged by burns or disease, functionally adequate but needing to be beautiful.

They might think she was frivolous, or a nut. She knew she wasn't the former, but she wasn't sure about the latter. Maybe she was crazy. Still, she had decided. What else could promise so much possibility for the better? The money, Grandma's money, wasn't enough to fix her life in any other real way. Sure, she could pay off all her charge cards, take a trip with it, but then she'd come back to this life. And she wouldn't live this life, the one she'd been dealt.

Since she was in New York, she'd start by making appointments with both Collins and Moore. Her hands actually shook as she dialled the old rotary phone – probably the last one in Manhattan – she still had and made the appointments. It wasn't easy. She had to use the name of a hospital administrator she knew to get an early appointment with Collins. First Collins, then Moore. Then she'd see.

Dr. Collins' office was in a very impressive building on Park Avenue at Sixty-fourth Street. The lobby was marble-floored in that patrician pattern of checkerboard black and white squares that ran diagonally. The floor shone so that it looked wet, and the brass buttons of the doorman were as shiny as the polished nameplate on the office door. Intimidated, Mary Jane walked in, ashamed of her lumpy down coat and her bulging black bag.

The secretary-receptionist didn't make her feel any more comfortable. The woman was thin, blonde, and beautiful, her hair done up in one of those complicated French braids that Mary Jane could never get her own hair to hold. She wondered if the woman had been worked on by Dr. Collins. If not, he was guilty of false advertising.

She waited almost half an hour, filling in the usual forms. Her hands were shaking. At last, the woman led her down a long, thickly carpeted hall to Collins' inner sanctum. He rose when she entered, seeming to take her in from top to toe.

'Well, Miss Moran, how can I help you?'

Mary Jane cleared her throat. 'I'm an actress,' she said.

'Really?' Did his voice rise at the end of the word, almost as if he didn't believe her? Quickly she outlined some of her credits. 'The problem is, I can't get work. Because of how I look,' she told him. God, this was hard. She looked at him. His face was impassive; his eyes were attentive but cold. She couldn't go on.

'You were thinking of surgery?' he prompted.

'Yes.'

'How old are you?'

'Thirty-four. Almost thirty-five,' she admitted.

'What exactly did you have in mind?'

'Everything. Whatever it would take!' she burst out.

'I don't understand. Rhinoplasty? Or . . .'

'Whatever it would take to make me beautiful,' she cried.

The man looked at her and sighed. 'I am a doctor, Miss Moran, not a magician.'

She spent two days in bed, and very nearly didn't go to the appointment with Dr. Moore. But she decided, in the end, she could manage one more humiliation before killing herself.

Dr. Moore's nurse, Miss Hennessey, was one of those battle-axes that Mary Jane had seen in hospitals for years. A commuter from Queens, no doubt, and a real yenta. 'The doctor doesn't do body work. Exactly what are you thinking of? Procedure-wise?' she had asked over the phone.

'Seeing the doctor,' Mary Jane had told her, and it shut the woman up, even if it put a sour tone to her voice. When Mary Jane showed up at the office the sourness had moved up to Miss Hennessey's face. She silently ushered Mary Jane into the Spartan office. Brewster Moore was a small, dark man, no taller than five six. She noticed his hands – very small and soft-looking – before she sat down. His skin was pale but healthy, with a pink glow, set off by his black hair and dark-brown eyes. He was wearing a dark suit with a white shirt and blue tie. She'd never seen anyone who looked as clean as he did.

She looked up at him, a slight man with a receding hairline and a cool, blank, professional manner.

She sat before Dr. Moore, her eyes downcast, her hands dangling in her lap, feeling worse than she had felt at Dr. Collins', more nervous than she'd ever been before any audition. Christ, what were the lines that would get her this part? What would win a surgeon's empathy and compassion? If any surgeons had either.

'How can I help you?' he asked, and, to her complete surprise and shame, she burst into tears.

She cried for a long time, while he sat silently and still, except for pushing a box of tissues toward her. At last, after gasps and nose blows and eye wiping, she finally looked up, her shame washed away by her flood.

'I'm an actress,' she said.

He nodded, attentive. There was no wince, but no other expression, either.

'I'm very good.' She reached into her coat pocket, took out a now crumpled résumé. 'You have to believe that,' she added.

He looked the résumé over, then looked back at her. 'Many of my patients are very courageous, Miss Moran. It takes a lot to walk in these doors. Why don't you tell me what you want?'

So she did. Calmly. In as professional a manner as she could. She ended with the disappointment over *Jack and Jill and Compromise*. 'So, you see, I need surgery. I need a lot of it. For my business. But I don't know what's possible, and I don't know what it will cost.'

He looked at her, as he had throughout. At last he spoke. 'I understand your problem, Miss Moran.' He stood up, walked around the table he used as a desk. Gently, he touched her under the chin, raised her head, turned it, first left, then right.

'Flesh isn't stone, Miss Moran. It's not predictable. It moves, it drapes, it scars. Your face lacks definition. There are no planes here' – he touched her cheeks – 'and here' – he placed his finger under her nose – 'there is no decisiveness. Your brow is too protruding. Your chin is weak. Your nose joins your upper lip without the recess we define as beautiful. Of course, the chin and nose present few real problems, but surgery can't really alter the shape of the face, or the head itself. And beauty depends on the relationship of so many of these separate parts.' He paused. 'Certainly I can make improvements. But I'm not sure I can promise you beauty. And I'd caution you to avoid any surgeon who tells you otherwise.'

She thought of Collins' words, licked her lips, took a breath, and spoke. 'Doctor, I'm not looking for a magician, but I'm also not here for a little profile-contouring. I don't want a cute little snub nose. I don't just want some "improvement." I'm looking for an artist. I've heard about you. I've seen your work. I think you can do what I want.'

'Thank you. I've seen your work, too. You were brilliant in *Jack and Jill* and *Compromise*. You *are* very good.'

'But can I *look* good?'

'There is a very narrow standard of beauty in the commercial sense,' Brewster said, looking out the grey window at the grey day beyond it. 'There is an aesthetic intolerance in this country for the ethnic, for the imperfect, for the unusual. Although, of course, beauty actually is unusual. That is why we venerate it, I suppose.' He sighed, as if he were tired of thinking about a very old problem, one he had reviewed a thousand times before. He turned back to her. 'I worked with cadavers all through my internship and residency. I dissected almost four hundred noses, trying to determine what the magic formula was. What made a nose beautiful? What magic proportion, what relationship to the rest of the face, what line, what curve was responsible? Then I reconstructed each one, striving to achieve that perfection.'

Had he achieved it? She wanted to ask him, but she was far too afraid to, afraid that she'd hear that he had failed.

He turned back from the window. 'In my opinion, society is sick. They have created a false, an almost impossible vision of female beauty and then induced women to attempt to achieve it. All of them fail. I have some of the most beautiful women in the world in this office, and they're frightened because they feel they aren't quite beautiful enough.'

126

'That's hardly my situation,' Mary Jane said drily.

'No, it isn't,' he agreed bluntly. 'But most plastic surgeons feed off this sick society. Women who have been made neurotic, who feel their breasts should be bigger, their noses smaller. Or who have husbands that believe that. Or who *want* husbands who believe that. The medical profession's fed off the illness of society for years: we are banishing the natural, creating the supernatural.'

'Why do you do it, then?'

'Well, it isn't my main practice. Mostly I do reconstruction. But there *is* a fascination in the work. I'd lie if I said there wasn't. And, of course, the money is very, very good. I can charge what I like. It is, after all, elective.'

'For some people,' Mary Jane said flatly.

'Well, for my face-lift clients, for example. Seven thousand dollars, and I can do it in under two hours. That might buy faces for two of my clinic kids. Or a new operating room for our little Honduran hospital.'

'You work in Honduras?'

'Yes. Lots of gunshot wounds. I prefer impoverished, under-developed countries. No face lifts in Honduras. There, living long gains you respect, and surgery is only for important issues, not breast enlargement and nipple placement.'

'No silicone-breast cancer cases?' Mary Jane asked.

Brewster Moore shook his head. 'Dow has always been an enemy of the people. Clearly disturbing data on silicone implants were already published in 1979. But it appears that women in America would rather risk cancer than live with small breasts. And doctors would rather collect fees than be scrupulous. The deadly search for beauty.'

'All right, doctor,' she said looking directly at him. 'Now we both understand the situation. So. What would it take to make me truly beautiful?'

The doctor looked out the window. 'There would be a great deal of surgery involved,' he began. He turned back again and looked at her. 'And there would be body scars. Scars that would never fade and couldn't be disguised. Keloids might form and disfigure you. I don't do body work, but I can recommend those who do.' He paused. 'And there would be discomfort. No, pain. Real pain. Undeniably. And it would take time. Time for multiple procedures, and healing in between. There are no guarantees. Work on this scale is difficult. And costly.'

'But you could do it?' she asked. 'It would be possible?' Her voice caught for a moment. She stopped there, took a breath, and continued. 'They all told me you were the one. That you work miracles. You can make me beautiful?'

The doctor folded his hands over the file on the otherwise barren desk. 'Too soon to tell. I need to see preliminary X-rays and the results of a complete workup.' Gently he touched her head, moved it left to right, right to left. 'But it may be possible.'

She sighed, then drew her breath again. 'Would it take more than two years and sixty-seven thousand dollars?' she asked.

'I'm not sure. Perhaps. That's assuming, of course, that it can be done at all. Why do you ask?'

'Because that's how much time and money I've got,' she said, and pushed her purse across the desk to him. He looked at the battered bag. Then back at her. For the first time in the interview, he almost smiled.

'I'm glad you have the money, though it's a bit premature. I don't consider this frivolous surgery, Miss Moran, but the clinic would never underwrite it. And it *will* be expensive. *And* you will be incapacitated for periods after the procedures. You certainly couldn't work.'

Mary Jane laughed. 'I don't get to work now.' The laugh sounded almost as bitter as she felt. 'But it won't cost more than I have?'

'Perhaps. I don't know. But we can cross that bridge when we come to it. For now, I'd like a series of detailed X-rays, as well as your dental records. And I'd like you to think about the seriousness of what you're proposing. Then we can meet again.'

'Yes, yes. Thank you. Thank you, doctor.'

'You're welcome, Miss Moran.'

'So, you want a deposit? I mean, should I give you a cheque or something?'

He looked across the table at her, another appraising look. 'Give me forty pounds,' he said, and for a moment she thought he was talking about English money. For the first time in the interview, Mary Jane felt the colour rush to her cheeks as she blushed hotly. 'We can't even see what we're working with until you lose that weight,' Dr. Moore told her. 'Then we'll get a better idea.'

Forty pounds! She knew she had always been chunky, thick through the waist, fat thighs – but forty pounds! She'd really let herself go. The misery over losing the part, over losing Sam. Forty pounds! That would bring her down to about 115. She hadn't weighed that even back in high school in Scuderstown. Christ, it was hard to face ten – how would she lose forty?

Still, if that's what it took, she'd do it. She'd quit eating, she'd exercise, she'd fast if she had to. She'd show her commitment. She was going to change herself, her life. She nodded, and rose from the chair.

'Forty pounds, Miss Moran. Then we'll be able to see what you're made of.'

Mary Jane nodded again, and managed to stumble out of his office.

18

'Where're we going?' Dean asked, excited by the surprise Dobe said he wanted to show them.

'You'll see, young feller. It's just a few miles more.'

Sharleen sat forward, leaning both arms on the back of Dean's seat. 'Now, what do you and Oprah have up your sleeve today, Dobe?' she asked, and smiled. She was sad that she and Dean would be going their own way tomorrow, when they got to Bakersfield. Dobe had been a perfect gentleman for the whole trip, and never once asked her to lie or behaved improperly towards her. But Sharleen knew that what Dobe did wasn't right, and, anyway, it was time she and Dean stood on their own two feet. She wasn't sure how they were going to do that exactly, but the good Lord would provide. Hadn't He gotten them to California?

Of course, they were sinners. They'd broken two commandments that Sharleen knew of for sure, and she prayed to Jesus every night that they'd be forgiven. But she also remembered her momma's last words – and she had to take care of Dean.

She didn't know how she would have managed without Dobe. He'd broken a few of the commandments himself, she felt sure. She thought of the story of the traveller who fell among thieves and was rescued by the Good Samaritan. But what did the Bible say when the Samaritan and the thief was the same person?

'Up my sleeve?' Dobe was asking her now with exaggerated surprise. 'Why, young lady, would you think I have something up my sleeve?' he asked, looking at her in the rearview mirror, his eyes wide.

'Sharleen, that ain't right. Now, you apologize to Dobe. He's been mighty good to us,' Dean said, half-turning in his seat. 'Anyway, Oprah don't have no sleeves, do she, Dobe?'

'I'm sorry if I hurt your feelings, Dobe,' Sharleen said. She patted Dean's shoulder and smiled. Dobe brought his eyes back to the road and slowed down. 'Here we are,' he said.

'Look at all them cars!' Dean cried out. The glittery sign over the building read 'Honest Abe's – Ten Acres of Used Cars.' Dean jumped out of the car after Dobe, and Sharleen followed.

Dobe waved to a man behind the picture window and started to walk down the long rows of cars, the multicoloured pendants flapping in the warm California breeze over their heads. Dobe came to a stop in front of a car that had 'Special – $1,999' scrawled in white paint on the left side of the windshield. 'Seems it's time to buy a car,' Dobe said. 'This looks like a California model.' It was sporty – a Datsun 280Z, and it was silver.

Sharleen stood by Dobe's side as he and Dean studied the car. Dean walked around it in circles, patting the roof, kicking the tyres.

'It's a beauty, Dobe,' Dean said. 'And it's silver. Like your car. Like the Lone Ranger's horse.'

'It sure is pretty,' Sharleen said. 'It's one of them foreign cars, isn't it?'

'But what do you want with another car, Dobe?' Dean asked. 'The one you've got is real good. There wouldn't be much room for more'n you and Oprah in there.'

'It's not for me. I was thinking maybe you would like it.'

Dean's eyes opened wide. 'Me?'

'Sure, why not? Oprah and I wanted to get something for you and Sharleen here as a going-away present, seeing as how you been good enough to keep an old man company.' Dobe turned to Sharleen. 'And you'll be needing a car in California. I hear they arrest people out here that don't own one.'

Before she could speak, before she could refuse, 'Welcome to Honest Abe's,' they heard a voice behind them say, and they turned to see a short, pudgy man with a big belly walking towards them, wearin' a Abe Lincoln stovepipe hat on his head. 'If I can't help you, I won't hurt you. Oh, it's you again, Mr. Samuels. And is this the son you were telling me about?' Honest Abe asked Dobe, pulling his eyes away from Sharleen.

Sharleen went over to Dobe and touched his shoulder. 'You've been so good to us already, Dobe,' she said softly. 'We've been living like rich folk since we met you, and eating better than at a country funeral. And you've been a perfect gentleman. You don't need to give us no present. You give us enough already.'

Dobe looked down at his boots. 'It would make me very happy, Sharleen,' he said. 'This has been a real nice time for me. It's like you're my own kids. And you've been a big help. You earned the money.'

'Sharleen,' Dean said, 'this here car's a beauty. You know, I could put her into top shape if anything goes wrong.' She could hear the yearning in his voice.

'But if I'm overstepping my bounds,' Dobe continued, 'just say so, and no hard feelings.'

Tears filled Sharleen's eyes. Not since Momma left, not for such a long time, had anyone been this good to her, taken care of her. After a moment, Sharleen said, 'Thank you, Dobe. We'd be grateful. And we'll pay you back someday.'

Dobe turned back to Abe. 'This could be the one,' Dobe said, as he took Abe by the arm and walked him away from them, talking into Abe's ear as they strolled.

When he came back, he tossed the keys to Dean and said, 'Well, son, let's take her for a ride.' Dobe opened the front passenger door for Sharleen, then got in the tiny back seat with Oprah and leaned forward. 'How's she feel?' Dobe asked Dean as they turned onto the main drag.

Dean floored the accelerator, then let up. 'She's a beauty, Dobe. Great pick-up.'

'And she's all yours now, kids. Makes sayin' goodbye a bit more cheerful.'

Sharleen wondered if they did some kind of police check when you bought a car. She wondered if the Lamson sheriff had put their names in one of them computers, the kind that tracked you down. But as Abe went over the car with Dean, Dobe took her aside.

'Seems to me, Sharleen, from the first time I saw the two of you, that you was on the run.' He put his hand up. 'I don't know nothin' and I don't want to know. But I know how it feels. I truly do. Anyway,' he continued, 'I put the car in my name. Well – in

131

the name Dobe Samuels. Clean as a whistle. Consider it a loan. Someday I may ask you for a favour. I'm sure you'd do it for me. And keep your own nose clean, huh?'

Sharleen swallowed and nodded silently. Then she leaned over and gave Dobe a big kiss on his sunburned cheek.

When they got back to the motel, Sharleen and Dean loaded their suitcase into the back seat of the Datsun. Dobe stood with his hands in his back pockets, while Dean fussed over the car, proud as a coon with a catfish.

'Sharleen, could I give you a little more advice?' Dobe asked, his voice quiet so it wouldn't carry.

'Why, sure, Dobe. You're a smart man. And a good one, too.'

'Well, you're more than pretty, Sharleen. You're beautiful. And life can either be too easy or too hard for a beautiful girl. Now, you ain't the type to make it too easy for yourself. But don't make it too hard, neither.' Dobe looked into Sharleen's eyes. 'If you got to say yes to somebody someday, Sharleen, just make sure it's for the right reasons.'

Sharleen nodded, not quite sure what Dobe meant, but figuring that, like some of the Bible's meaning, it would come to her later. She stepped on tiptoes and kissed Dobe again on the cheek, then hugged him tight. 'Thank you, Dobe, for being so good to us.'

Dean came over and put his arms around Dobe. 'I'm sure going to miss you. Now I got no one but Sharleen to talk about licence plates with. And thank you for the car, Dobe. And for the food. And the beds.' Dean's face got red, and he knelt down to Oprah and put his arms around the big dog. 'You take care, hear?' he told her. She licked his face.

Then Dobe called to the dog, and she got into his car next to him. Dean shut the door, and Dobe turned the big silver Pontiac out of the motel parking lot onto the street. Sharleen turned around and waved a kiss to him. Dean blew his nose.

'He been real good to us, Sharleen,' Dean said. 'I was going to ask for some pills for the gas tank, but since he never offered, I thought it would be greedy. Right, Sharleen?'

'Right, honey,' she told him, and put her arm around his shoulders.

Mary Jane sat at the battered desk before her front window, looking out onto West Fifty-fourth Street. Since she had met Dr. Moore, two days ago, she had hardly managed five hours of sleep. She had unplugged her answering machine and had spent the time both pacing and lying flat across the old double bed in the back bedroom, staring at the cracked plaster of the ceiling.

How, she kept asking herself, how could she do this thing? That she *would* do it, or die in the attempt, she knew. But how could she manage to survive the transformation she was contemplating? And not just the physical one. Plain, almost homely, all her life, how could she learn to act the part of a beautiful woman? For without action, she knew, no role could be successfully played. How many pretty girls had she seen who never believed in their own beauty, and couldn't make anyone else believe in it, either? And how many unextraordinary women had she seen who could project an aura of beauty despite only average looks? It wasn't enough to get the exterior right, the costumes, makeup, and posture. She would have to perfect the persona of a beautiful woman. How could she, a female who had had absolutely zero faith in her looks, act the part of a beauty? Would she be ridiculous? Would she fail? Once again she stood up and paced the tiny front room. What misgivings did a fat old caterpillar have as it started to close itself into its cocoon? Did it have a genetic script for its upcoming role as a butterfly, or did it ad lib? Well, she had no script, and since she'd never been good at improvs, she'd have to create one.

She walked back to the desk and stared down at the spiral-bound notebook in front of her. On the first page she had written four headings: 'Financial Plan,' 'Social Plan,' 'Career Plan,' and 'Physical Plan.' She had determined that she wouldn't leave the dark apartment until she had considered all the problems of each category and come up with solutions. She had always been good at observation and imitation, the tools of an actor's craft. And she would use visualization, the tricks she had learned in therapy, to feel her way to her new role. But how you went about becoming a new, successful, beautiful person when you were an almost middle-aged, unattractive failure wasn't going to be so easy to visualize.

One thing she knew: she couldn't go through the process in front of her friends (or her enemies). If all the world was about to become her stage, she knew that she couldn't undermine her new role by letting people peek into her dressing room. Molly, for instance, would tell her that she was wonderful just the way she was. If Bethanie had been around, she would, no doubt, have felt superior and acted supportive. It made Mary Jane's skin crawl to think of that. Father Damien would suggest the power of prayer, or maybe some Prozac, which had helped him out of a depression. Chuck would probably suggest primal therapy. Neil, if he had forgiven her and if she could reach him out on the coast, would just crack wise and make her laugh. But Mary Jane knew that all the affection of friends and primal screams in the world wouldn't change how she looked or give her what she wanted. Unless she took this drastic step and succeeded, she'd never get a leading role again. Sam or any other man worth having would never love her as she was. Her friends were wrong when they told her otherwise, and their kindnesses or lies were useless. The Mary Jane that her friends knew had died alone in that grim farmhouse in upstate New York.

She jumped up from the desk again and recommenced her pacing. If there weren't already holes in the old tweed carpet, she would be making them now. She wrapped her arms around herself and continued walking to and fro. She would have to disappear, she decided. It wouldn't be all that hard: just move and leave no forwarding address. New York was a big city. After all, she had no family that would try to reach her. The fight with Neil would be a good excuse not to keep in touch. Who knows, perhaps he never meant to call her again anyway. Sam, obviously, had no plans to try to see her. So all she needed was a relatively believable pretext for disappearing. Well, she'd always been a theatre gypsy, as they all were. She could simply tell Molly, Chuck, and her other friends that she'd gotten a job doing stock, then go away and not return. Perhaps, afterward, when she was out of the chrysalis and knew that she could fly, she could call them up, explain everything, and see them again. But not now. If they judged her or dissuaded her, she wouldn't have the courage to go on, and if she didn't make this change, she didn't want to live anymore.

God, it all sounded so melodramatic! She had to smile to herself, but it was a grim ghost of a smile. She walked to the mirror, the small, scratched one that hung over the bookshelf, and stared into her own dark eyes, her pale, shapeless face. She shivered. She felt as if she were staring at the head of a corpse.

She turned away and moved back to the window, then reached into the top drawer of her desk and scrabbled around for her cheque-book. If she was going to do this, she had better figure ways and means. The torn blue plastic cheque cover had her name stamped on it in faded gold. She'd paid four bucks extra for that. Well, she wouldn't have four bucks extra for a long, long time to come, *and* she'd need a new name. She threw the cover into the wastepaper basket. She opened the ledger side and looked at it. She had a balance of $1,471. She also had her old passbook savings account. She opened the book to the last entry: $3,054. Plus whatever the interest was, not that it was ever much.

Of course, that wasn't counting her grandmother's money. That she had already put in a safety-deposit box at the Bowery Bank. She would need it for the operations, and she was determined not to touch it for anything else. But since she didn't want to have to work during the next year or so (and probably wouldn't be able to during recovery), she would need a lot more than the cash in her two accounts to live off of, no matter how cheaply she lived.

Well, she could start with a tag sale. Of course, since she'd mostly always been broke, she had decorated the apartment with Salvation Army purchases, thrift-shop finds, and discarded furniture from off the street. She couldn't raise anything on that stuff. But she could sell her books and her record albums. She would get rid of her stereo, and her TV. That would bring in a few hundred. And her vintage clothes would have to go.

For a moment, she felt a pang. Over the years, she'd collected the old silk dresses, the alligator bags, the taffeta petticoats by relentlessly searching out quality among the crap at flea markets and auctions and thrift stores. She'd lovingly hand-washed and pressed them all, stitched up seams, and mended tears. But hadn't she collected and worn it all to distract attention from her appearance? Hadn't it been a pathetic ploy? See my clothes, don't see me. Some of her stuff was worth money. Well, she wouldn't need the clothes now, she told herself. She'd give Molly the cashmere forties jacket that Molly had coveted, and bring the rest of it down to a dealer she knew in SoHo. It would give her another few thousand at least.

And she could sublet the apartment and get key money up front. There were hundreds of kids in the theatre district who would want it. She'd guarantee them two years, but they'd actually be getting it free and clear. She picked up her pen. Under 'Financial Plan' she wrote:

1) Have tag sale
2) Sell books/records/clothes to dealers
3) Put up flyers/run ads for sublet

She did a quick calculation. That would give her perhaps a total of eleven thousand dollars. But she owed some money, too. She added to her list:

4) Pay off MasterCard balance
5) Pay off Nurses' Credit Union

The only other asset she had was her IRAs. She looked in the bottom drawer of her desk for the Merrill Lynch statement. She had a total of just under eight thousand dollars salted away, but if she cashed them in there'd be tax to pay. And then she wouldn't have a dime of retirement money. Oh well. What the hell good would eight thousand bucks be when she was sixty-five? Probably wouldn't pay for a month in a nice rest home by then. And who would want to live this life up to retirement age? She was gambling for high stakes, so she'd better ante up everything, or give up now. She picked up her pen again.

6) Cash in IRAs
7) Close bank accounts. Open new ones.

Since the tellers knew her at her branch, she didn't want them to comment on her changing looks, bruised eyes, or bandages.

8) Set a daily budget for food, carfare, etc.
9) Stick to the budget
10) Don't buy anything
11) Find cheap weekly hotel rental

She'd thought it out. A shared apartment, maybe up around Columbia, would be cheapest, and she wasn't likely to run into her old friends up there, but she didn't want the hassle of room-mates with their questions and curiosity. Still, she needed people around, just in case there was a medical emergency. A single-room-occupancy hotel would do the job: transients wouldn't notice her, and the desk would ask no questions as long as they were paid. Maybe there was something out in Brooklyn or Queens that would be a few steps up from a welfare hotel. If, in the end, she had to work a little, she'd see if she could do night shift. She'd cross that bridge when she got to it.

Under 'Physical Plan' she wrote:

1) Lose weight
2) Exercise

She stopped and had to smile. Well. Easier said than done. But she'd live in a place without a kitchen. There would be no temp-tation to cook up a pot of pasta with a little garlic, basil, and olive oil. No sneaking Mounds bars. And this, meeting Dr. Moore's first specification, would be her only job right now. With the pressures of her work and the relationship off, all she had to do was focus on this.

She'd been fifteen pounds overweight her whole life, always fighting it, losing it, and gaining it back. She'd been a size ten when she should have been an eight. Then, in the last year or so, the pounds had really started to creep up. But forty pounds! How long would it take to blitz that off?

In the margin of her notebook, she used some of her mathematics from nursing school. There were about thirty-five hundred calories in a pound. If she lost two pounds a week, took in seven thousand calories less than she expended, it would take twenty weeks before she could see Dr. Moore again! But if she went down to a lot fewer calories than that, she knew she'd be constantly hungry, and prob-ably binge.

She would have to make it up in activity. But she hated exercise classes, and she couldn't afford a health club now anyway. She would simply have to walk the weight off. Walking was aerobic, she liked it, and it didn't cost anything. It also kept you out of trouble, as long as you didn't eat éclairs as you walked. She crossed number '2 Exercise' off her list and replaced it with

2) Walk a minimum of 10 miles per day

At twenty city blocks per mile, that was two hundred blocks! Almost from the George Washington Bridge to Greenwich Village! Well, she could work up to it, and she could walk a different route every day. With determination, she could lose the weight in four months. As a nurse, she knew that any faster wouldn't be safe or lasting.

She also knew that she would have to be as concrete and specific as possible in writing her plans. Otherwise, she might as well simply write down 'Become a famous great actress and win the love of a wonderful man' and be done with it. She picked up her pen again and added

> 3) Plan each day's meals in advance
> 4) Write down everything eaten
> 5) Keep no food at home

Under 'Career Plan' she had quite a bit to put down. But, then, she had done all of this once before.

> 1) Create new résumé
> 2) Write to West Coast repertory companies
> 3) After surgery get new head shots
> 4) Choose new name

If she changed her name, created a new identity, she'd have to give up her Equity card. She had worked so hard to get one, and it had been such a validation of her that it seemed, of everything so far, perhaps the hardest thing she'd have to relinquish. It was the big question that separated the pros from the tyros: 'Are you Equity?' She thought of all the audition notices that stated 'Equity Only.' She shrugged. Well, so it goes. Equity membership hadn't gotten her where she wanted to be. Putting together a phony résumé was nothing. She knew enough defunct theatrical endeavours, and could drop enough names, to make anyone believe she had played Eliza Doolittle in the Oak Bluff, Missouri, Dinner Theater revival of *Pygmalion*. Or Emily in *Our Town*. Or Laura in *The Glass Menagerie*. Too bad she'd never gotten a chance to play those roles: always the character actress, never the ingenue, she reminded herself bitterly. But now that would change.

Of course, she'd have to leave off her triumph: creating the role of Jill. And she'd have to drop off mention of her equally precious

Obie. But she could bring her talent along. That and good looks should be enough to justify one more assault on the mountain.

But she would also have to work on creating herself anew. She would have to study up on how to play the part of a beautiful, hopeful, successful young woman. Well, she'd read interviews with them, and she'd watch films with those kinds of characters. She knew how to do research for a role; this would be her greatest challenge, more difficult than playing fat, frumpy Jill.

Mary Jane stretched her back against the oak mission chair, then stood up. Outside, dusk was beginning to fall, and people had begun to troop by, all of them coming from the east and walking west from the subway exit towards their homes. Would they have a family waiting? Would there be a nice hot meal, a hug, and maybe a few laughs after a day of hard work? For a moment, she felt self-pity begin to settle on her like a wet, cold mantle. Courage, she told herself. But what if she couldn't lose the weight that imprisoned her, holding her tighter than a shroud? What if Dr. Moore wouldn't take her on? Or what if he did but failed?

She *would* lose the weight, Dr. Moore *would* take her on, and, if he didn't, some other doctor would. But what if you simply fail again, and this time without the excuse of your looks to blame everything on? After all, who do you think you are? How many pretty girls try to make it and wind up waiting tables in San Diego? How many job openings are there for new stars? Who do you think you are?

And there, in the deepening dusk, she heard her grandmother's voice. 'Want a part in the senior play? Who do you think you are? Auditioning for drama school? Do you think you're Sarah Bernhardt? Who do you think you are? Who do you think you are? Who do you think you are?'

She held her hands up to her ears, her grandmother's voice too loud to block out. 'I don't know who I am, or who I'm going to be, but I'm not who I was!' she shouted. 'I'm not who I was!'

The afternoon sun cast long shadows across the verandah that encircled Aunt Robbie's pool. Lila was on her stomach on a chaise longue, her bikini top open so she could get the full warmth of the sun, though she was so covered in sunscreen that a hydrogen-bomb explosion probably wouldn't even pinken her. She wasn't turning into some lizard-woman. Her silken red hair, coated with a thick layer of conditioner, was wrapped in a towel. And soon José would bring her a huge frosty glass of lemonade, made from real lemons and diet sweetener. He even put a leaf of real mint in it. Heaven. Staying here at Robbie's, though it was a drag in both senses of the word, definitely had some benefits. And Aunt Robbie was as gung-ho about her career as she was. 'Decide what you want, then grab it by its nuts,' he had delicately said. So she'd have to start doing some nut-grabbing soon.

There was no longer any doubt what she wanted. She needed a movie, a movie more wonderful than anything her mother had been in. A vehicle to catapult her into the public eye. Lila heard the soft padding of someone walking towards her. She opened her eyes in a squint and saw Aunt Robbie, sans roller blades, a huge, floppy straw hat on his head. It was odd to see him waddle instead of glide.

'Why, Aunt Robbie,' Lila asked in her best Southern accent, peering down at the bare feet that stuck out from beneath the hem of his aquamarine-and-pink caftan, 'whatever has become of your skates?'

Aunt Robbie dropped heavily down onto the chaise next to her. 'That bitch José. He hid them on me, I'm sure of it.'

'Why would he do that?' Lila asked. She had become used to the daily battles between the two of them. In fact, she occasionally even enjoyed listening to the two queens snap at each other.

'He hates the skates. He says he's embarrassed for me. Can you believe that?' Rob tugged the caftan skirt down around his legs. 'So

I said, "Honey, if *I'm* not embarrassed, why should *you* be? After all, this is *Hollywood*."' Robbie laughed, extending his flabby arms to the air in general. Then he lowered his eyebrows and tried to make his pudgy face menacing. He called out in a theatrically loud voice, 'If he doesn't get them back to me today, I swear, I'm calling Immigration,' then leaned his head back on the chaise, adjusting the rim of the hat to shade his eyes.

'And what, may I ask, are you doing out here broiling?' Robbie said, looking over at Lila's near-nude figure slick with suntan oil. 'Don't you know about the holes in the ozone layer? You'll get skin cancer. If you up and die on me, I'll kill you. Keep that in mind. And no mourning. I look like shit in black.'

'I need to work on my tan.'

'You need to work on your judgement, it looks like.'

'This is *Hollywood*,' Lila mimicked. 'And this is what people do in Hollywood.'

'No, my dear, they do more than that. They also try to build careers.' Robbie turned his head toward the house and roared, 'José!'

The small, dark-skinned man came out of the kitchen door, wiping his hands on a frilly apron while mincing towards them. He stopped in front of Robbie and put one hand on his hip.

'Wha' chu want, Miss Thing?'

Robbie ignored José's attitude and said brightly, 'I'd like a frozen margarita, José, please, and bring another diet lemonade for my date here.' Then Robbie flicked his hand, and José turned and sashayed back to the house.

'Now, it's time we did some more career planning. Aunt Robbie has been thinking a lot about your future, Lila, and I have a couple of ideas.'

Lila had heard all this before from Robbie. He meant well, but so far his ideas hadn't panned out to anything. He was out of touch in a business that didn't want to hear about yesterday's news. Much less, news from the fifties. 'A film?' she asked in mock excitement. 'Is one of your friends doing a film?'

'Give me a break, girlfriend. You'd be very lucky to do television.'

'I'm not doing television,' Lila grumbled, and sat up, allowing the top to fall from her perfect breasts. Robbie certainly didn't care. 'I want to do a movie. Television brings you too close to the public. There are no real stars on television. Just celebrities.'

141

'My goodness, what a pair of knockers!' Aunt Robbie said. 'A little decorum, please.'

'Look who's talking!' she snapped, but turned away for a moment, then made a face at Robbie and tied her top behind her. 'You've said television is second-rate yourself. You always say so to Ken,' she added.

'That's because Ken *works* in television. But I'm only suggesting television as a starting point. A lot of stars got their start on TV.'

'Name one.'

Robbie thought for a moment. 'Rob Reiner.'

'He's not a *star* – he's a director, for chrissakes,' Lila said. 'So is Ron Howard. Anyway, name a *woman*.' She paused. 'Don't even bother racking your brain, Aunt Robbie. There are just no stars on television.'

'Carol Burnett.'

'She's not a star, she's a has-been. And no one ever paid to see her in the movies.'

'Shelley Long.'

'Who?'

'The blonde from *Cheers*.'

'Exactly. Name one of her *films*. Forget it!'

'Sally Field.'

'Oh, my God. Gidget goes to work in a factory. She *never* had any draw. Aunt Robbie, these women have no glamour. They aren't anything. I've got to get a *film*. A major one.'

'Mary Tyler Moore.'

'Oh, fine. What has she done? *Ordinary Movie*? If Redford hadn't directed it, it would have died like a dog. No. No TV!' Lila was beginning to lose her patience. 'Come on, Robbie. I want to be like my mother was. I want to be *bigger* than my mother was. You know exactly what I mean.'

José returned with their drinks and a bowl of macadamia nuts. 'Well, we're jumping ahead of ourselves, Lila. You've got to have an agent first,' Robbie said, popping a handful of nuts into his mouth.

'Who do you suggest, Robbie? One of your little friends? First assistant to the first assistant of something? Spare me, Robbie. I'm thinking bigger than that.'

'All your thinking hasn't done you shit, has it, honey? It's time to stop thinking and start *doing*. I happen to know just the man for you, and he's a big thinker, just what you want.'

Lila paused, then said, 'Wait. I know what you're going to say.'

'No, you don't.'

'Yes, I do. Don't suggest Ara. He's my mother's agent, he's a hundred and four, and he has the breath of a sick dog. Plus, he'll never see me because Theresa wouldn't stand for it. Anyway, he's got a foot in the grave.'

'I swear, it's morbid how paranoid you are about your mother. If she were so goddamn powerful, don't you think she would have scared up a part for herself by now? She's not going to stop you. And Ara is only eighty-one, and if he has one foot in the grave, then the other foot is firmly planted on Hollywood and Vine. Ara Sagarian is so well connected that he'll be getting work for his people even *after* he's dead.'

'But I hate him,' Lila said.

'Of course you do,' Robbie said with exaggerated patience. 'He's an *agent*. But he's handled Jimmy Stewart, Frank Sinatra, Joan Crawford, *and* your mother, of course. And he still has lots of biggies. Hagman and Michael Keaton, I think. Lots of others.'

'Oh. J.R. and Bat bore. *Now* I'm impressed.'

'Well, laugh if you want to, but Ara Sagarian is very big on television these days. Says it's what the studios were like in the forties. And I don't see anything else on your horizon, Miss Thing. I can get you in. Then you just charm him.'

'Well, maybe I could go talk to him,' Lila conceded. Then she laughed. 'Should I just walk in and tell him I want a starring role in something? That I won't take television, but that I really want to be a movie star?' Even though she was the daughter of Theresa O'Donnell, the old man wasn't going to be exactly thrilled at another Beverly Hills brat knocking on his door. Still, if he *would* see her . . . Lila hated to admit it, but Robbie might have something here. And if Robbie could guarantee getting her in . . . Ara *was* big. The biggest contact Robbie had suggested so far. 'You're certain he'll see me? I mean, not just a courtesy call.'

'Oh, don't worry about that,' Robbie said. 'Ara's my godfather in the gay Hollywood mafia. He'd do *anything* for me. If you agree, I'll talk to him, just feel him out.' Robbie leaned over the arm of his chaise and looked into Lila's eyes. 'Just say you're willing to do some TV and I'll make the call.'

Lila sipped her lemonade, then said, 'Okay, Robbie, but only a miniseries and a starring role, even if it *is* my first shot out of the box. No crappy sitcom, no guest shots. I mean it.'

'Jesus, Miss Thing! Aren't we the choosy one?' Robbie said, and rolled his eyes.

'Hi,' Lila heard Ken call as he walked towards them from the garage. 'I'm slaving under hot klieg lights all day, and you two are out here taking it easy?'

Robbie looked at his watch. 'I didn't realize it was so late, Ward,' Robbie said in his best June Cleaver voice. 'It was just that the Beaver here was giving me trouble. Maybe you two can talk!' He turned and sashayed towards the house again, and was about to yell out for José when he saw the little man coming towards them, a frozen margarita for Ken on a silver tray before him. Robbie waddled back to his chaise.

'Well, it's about time, Maria. Ken, sit here and have a drinky.' Robbie pulled up his fat legs to make room for Ken at the foot of the chaise.

'So what were you two up to?' Ken asked, after taking a sip of the iced drink.

Lila smiled at him. 'I've been getting skin cancer and some career advice from my auntie, here,' she said. 'Both unwelcome.'

'He usually gives good advice. Not very good head, but good advice.'

'Oooh! Aren't you a little kiss-and-tell!' Robbie cried, and the two began to bicker.

Meanwhile, Lila decided. She would see Ara. After all, what did she have to lose? 'Okay, Robbie,' she said. 'Set it up. But no assistant shit. With Ara. Himself.'

21

Mary Jane gave herself a budget: nine hundred calories and nine dollars a day for food for the next three months. She spent the first two days of her new regime in bed, mostly sleeping, but once her exhaustion began to pass she knew that would never work. Home, in bed, was where she ate. She had to be out. She needed the exercise to drop the weight. And she had to lose the weight before she made another appointment with Dr. Moore or

Miss Hennessey, his dragon lady. She needed some results to show him.

So on Wednesday, exactly two weeks after her grandmother's funeral, she bundled into her old dun-coloured down coat and trundled heavily out the door, after a breakfast of one poached egg, two pieces of (dry) melba toast, and a small glass of tomato juice. It was a cool March day, but at least there isn't a cutting wind, she thought, and began walking east. West Fifty-fourth Street wasn't beautiful at any time of day, but it was particularly unlovely in the morning. Eleventh Avenue was still streaming with trucks, a few patches of filthy snow, covered completely in black soot, and littered with dog droppings, making nasty detours for pedestrians. She walked over to Tenth, past the dank tenement houses, then Ninth, with its bodegas and liquor stores, past the piles of restaurant garbage, to Eighth Avenue, and then over to Broadway. Christ, it was even worse here, she thought. The guys in straight business suits rushed by, clutching attachés, their faces grim, their eyes averted from the tawdry posters outside the grind houses and porno-book shops. Mary Jane wasn't sure who depressed her more: the civilians in their commuter ruts or the degenerates already clustering at the shop gates, waiting to get their sex fix for the morning. Jesus, imagine a porn-film audience at 9.00 A.M.! Who *were* those guys? She shuddered and headed south, moving quickly because she didn't want to find out.

She was getting cold, so she stopped at Seventh Avenue and Thirty-eighth Street, the heart of the fashion industry, for a cup of coffee – using up a dollar of her precious hoard, but at least not adding any calories. There was a tabloid newspaper at the counter that some garmento had left behind, and she thumbed through it. The usual stabbings, shootings, and child abuse. She turned to the gossip columns. They contained the typical mix of New York theatrical, society, and Hollywood names. Shirley MacLaine was apparently writing yet another book on yet one more of her past lives, while her brother was making the most of this one by sleeping with yet another starlet.

Then she saw it. '*Crystal Plenum loves her work so much that she's taking it home with her. Rewrites have started on the script of* Jack and Jill and Compromise, *a real hot property. Apparently so is Sam Shields, the writer-director. Crystal and Shields have been seen at Spago, Mr. Chow's, and were even making nice over breakfast at the Polo Lounge.*'

She felt herself flush, then go cold. She was afraid for a moment that she would fall off the stool at the counter. She felt dizzy, as if she'd been spinning on it as she had when she was a child. It was strange, she thought, as she threw the dollar and assorted change on the counter and stumbled out onto the street. *He was my life for more than three years, and now he's gone.* She looked at her watch. *Right this minute he's probably lying in bed, asleep beside Crystal Plenum, who's got my part.* She didn't know which hurt more, that the woman had her role, her precious role as Jill, or that she had Sam.

She cried all through the garment centre, down to Twenty-fourth Street. She kept walking, and finally paused long enough to go the bathroom and wash her face in the ladies' room at the Chelsea Hotel. The hip, tatty place which artists and writers had been checking in and out of for decades was grim as ever. 'Well,' she told herself, looking into the old, cracked mirror over the sink, 'if Dr. Moore won't take your case, or the plan doesn't work, you can always come back here to the Roach Motel. Perfect for a successful suicide.' She wouldn't be the first. It was the only thought that comforted her.

She walked down Seventh Avenue to Eighth Street, stopped in a used-book store, and browsed distractedly for an hour. She would learn not to think of Sam; she'd train herself starting now. She wandered over to Hudson Street. Then she had half a cantaloupe at a Greek joint (no cottage cheese – only forty calories, but an outrageous $3.50) and made her way down the Avenue of the Americas to Houston Street. There the marquee over Film Forum attracted her. It was a Mai Von Trilling double feature – both of which she had seen countless times before. Still, she loved those German movies of the early thirties, and Mai was surely one of the most beautiful actresses of all time. Mary Jane lined up along with the other losers who make up the crowd for the first show at art theatres. Still, for six bucks she'd buy four hours of forgetfulness, see some *real* acting, then walk all the way home and chew on some salad before she hit the sheets. And she wouldn't let herself think about Sam.

So her pattern was set: out of the house by nine, walking for almost eight hours, with a movie break and a cup of coffee (black) when absolutely necessary. She didn't call anyone, didn't return any calls, not even Molly's. After a week, she disconnected her answering machine. She found two kids to take the apartment, sold off her stuff, and found a cheap place to stay on East Nineteenth Street. But they wouldn't take cats. So she made one last visit to Molly, with the cashmere jacket in one hand and Midnight howling in his travel box. Oddly enough, it was giving up Midnight that made her more lonely than anything else.

Mary Jane walked, hungry, up and down Manhattan, without the courage to weigh herself, or to read another newspaper. Her room was grim. No place to hang out. She avoided mirrors and haunted public libraries, bookstores, and the shops with theatre and film memorabilia. She splurged and bought a few cheap stills, black-and-white glossies of the faces she'd loved on the luminous screen. Could I get Jeanne Moreau's mouth? Garbo's chin? Mai Von Trilling's nose? Cheekbones like Hepburn – either Katharine *or* Audrey. She wasn't particular. But mainly she walked. And when she was too tired to walk anymore, she rested at Grand Central Station, or Penn Station, or any one of the lesser hotel lobbies – temporary homes of the displaced person in Manhattan.

As she walked, memories came back to her. Memories of her grandmother, of Scuderstown, of nursing school. But mostly she remembered Sam. Whole conversations they had had. The night they got locked out of her apartment. The day he cast her as Jill. The surprise birthday party she threw for him. The way he made love to her. Sometimes she walked with tears running down her cheeks. Luckily, it was New York, and no one even noticed.

And she discovered something: if you only had one purpose, it wasn't so hard to achieve it. When she had to cinch her jeans in three notches on her belt, she decided to call the Hennessey witch at Dr. Moore's. She'd show him the photos she'd collected, she'd get weighed by Yenta, his nurse. But had she lost enough? she wondered. Would it prove her commitment? Would he take her really seriously?

When she called, Miss Hennessey was cool, but without argument she made the appointment for a week later. For six days, Mary Jane really starved herself. Would he not see her again, not move her on for more X-rays if she hadn't shown enough will power and commitment? She showed up almost an hour early, and paced the hospital lobby. At last, she had the courage to take the elevator up.

Stripped to a hospital gown, she stood barefoot on the scale while the nurse weighed her. Miss Hennessey fumbled, looked at Mary Jane's chart, and then moved the weights again.

'Can this be right?' she asked Mary Jane. 'In seven weeks, you've lost twenty-one and a half pounds?'

'Have I?' Mary Jane said, and wondered if it would be enough.

When Mary Jane passed Miss Hennessey's desk and entered Dr. Moore's office, she felt as if she might pass out. By now he'd seen the preliminary X-rays. What if he told her that he couldn't give her the results she wanted? What if Dr. Moore said it was possible but chancy? Would she risk it? And what if he simply said he could do it? What then? She was determined to move forward, but she was, she had to admit, petrified.

Dr. Moore was standing before a light screen, looking at cranial X-rays. He looked up as she came in, and gestured at the pictures. 'The face is endlessly fascinating,' he said. 'When I was looking for a surgical speciality, I had every intention of becoming a cardiac surgeon. It was where the hottest, smartest surgeons gravitated. But I found out there was a glut of them, and that I'd probably wind up practising in Idaho. Then I was stuck, because, aside from the heart, I couldn't think of an area where I could make a living but that would never get boring. Until I talked to a plastic surgeon, and I was hooked.' He looked back at the X-rays.

'Are those mine?' she asked. He nodded.

'Come over and take a look.'

She moved to his side, surprised to find she was taller than he was. Wordlessly, she looked at the dark shadows on the film. She could not bear to have to ask him again, to form the words, to beg. As if he could read her mind, he answered without taking his eyes off the screen.

'Yes, I think I can make you beautiful. You're one of the lucky ones. For you, all it will take is time and money. Of course, there are no guarantees, and I need you to understand that and the extensiveness and risks of the programme I'd outline.'

She nodded, feeling as if she hadn't enough breath to speak. She was immensely grateful, not only for his answer but for the privacy that his averted face gave her. He was very close to her. He smelled of disinfectant soap and a very slight underscent – was it vanilla?

'I'd propose that we'd begin by working on the skeletal altera-tions: the bony superorbital ridge, which would have to be shaved down; the cheekbones, which require implantations; and the work on your chin to bring about a better proportion and relationship to the facial planes themselves.' As he spoke, he touched the X-rays of her jutting brow and her cheeks, and moved his hands finally to her chin. Only then did he look at her, and she nodded her agreement. She still couldn't speak. 'The skeletal work would take six months to a year, depending on your rate of recovery. Then we would move on to the soft-tissue work.'

'What's that?' she managed to croak.

'The movement and realignment of your skin on your new skeletal frame. Blepharoplasty, for one thing, though I would propose only a modified eye-lift. You don't have bags under your eyes, just some sagging on top. We only need to melt the fat that is deposited above, at your eyelids, and we can do that with a procedure I invented. I'll insert a needle here' – he touched her eyelid very gently, but she winced – 'and heat it, melting the fat away. That will give you a very clean, well-defined upper eyelid. And almost no incision, so no visible scars.'

He touched her neck, gently fingering the skin. 'We'll need liposuction here, and then we'll do a fairly aggressive lift. I'm not talking about simply stretching the facial skin, but actually separating the skin from the fascia all the way down to about here' – he moved his hand to her breast bone – 'then peeling it back, pulling it taut, and excising the excess before reattaching it.'

'That leaves scars,' she said.

'None that you will see. I reattach the skin *above* the hairline, into the scalp, so that natural hair growth will cover almost all of it.'

'Then you'll have to shave my head?' she asked, horrified. Her thick mane of hair was the only naturally beautiful thing about her. Sam had loved her hair.

'No. We succeed in sterilizing it. I've never had infections at the scalp.'

He moved to his desk and indicated a chair. 'I'm glad you've already done so well on the weight reduction. It demonstrates to me not only the resilience of your tissue but also your motivation.' He peered at her. She tried not to squirm under his gaze, wondering what imperfect feature he was assessing. But at the same time she felt grateful, and also close to him in a strange way. Finally, here was one man from whom she had nothing to hide.

Once again, as if he could read her thoughts as well as her bone structure, he spoke. 'You know, there is a great intimacy in a project like this. In a way, it is a mutual seduction, and then a marriage. We will work together: a great deal will depend on your tissue, your ability to communicate what you want, to follow a regimen, and to heal; the rest will depend on me and my talent. Facial surgery is a gift. Beyond technique, there has to be a vision, and an ability to see the possibilities. And for me to do my best work, I have to be in love with the project.'

'And are you?' she asked. Outside, the rain was pouring down, and the only noises were the heavy dripping at an outside eave and the humming vibration of the frame of the light board against the clip that held her X-ray.

'Yes,' he said, and she felt a tightness in her chest. 'It's a challenging, fascinating project.' He came closer to her, very close. 'Have you ever smoked?'

'No.'

'Good. Now you never will. Also, no sun. None at all. Never. Sunscreen at all times.'

She looked out at the freezing rain and the overcast day. 'At all times, doctor?'

He smiled. 'Well, not at night. Also, no alcohol.'

'Not even wine?'

'Not even beer. Well, let me put it this way: I know you will, so be very moderate. It's not good for your skin. I can see you've lost weight, and the sun has done little damage to you so far.'

'I never could afford a vacation, and tar beach didn't appeal.'

'Well, *that* was good luck.' He paused. He took her hand in his and for a moment, she thought he was going to get personal, to give her a kind word. Instead, he pinched the back of her hand, then watched as the little ridge of skin he had made resolved itself back into the relative smoothness of her wrist. 'You still have remarkable elasticity for a woman your age. That helps. What's your diet like?'

She told him.

'Fine. But I want you to eat more raw vegetables. A lot more water, too. Hydration is critical for skin. And to keep this some-what unnatural weight and the benefits of surgery, you can only eat two spare meals a day from now on. You are trying to attain an unnatural ideal, one that is almost impossible for a woman to maintain beyond adolescence. Now that large breasts have been added to the lanky, extremely thin model that's been in vogue for years, almost no woman naturally has that shape to begin with.'

150

'Do you give young, thin models those breasts if they want them?' she asked.

'I don't do body work. Only facial surgery. And I don't know any male surgeon who does a good job on breasts. I recommend a woman doctor: Sylvia Wright. It makes sense that a woman would have a better feel for breasts than a man.' He smiled. 'But Wright won't do implants. Nine years ago, reputable journals were reporting problems with silicone. Anyway, you won't need implants. Yours would only require a restructuring and lift.'

She looked down at her drooping chest. Despite the weight loss, or because of it, her breasts looked worse than ever. Well, she told herself, one thing at a time. The important thing was, he would take her case. And that she believed he could work miracles.

22

Sharleen pulled the Datsun that Dobe had bought for her and Dean onto the gravel parking lot in front of the aluminium-sided diner there on Ming Avenue and braked to a halt alongside a row of battered cars, pickups, and semis with trailers. She sat in the car, the *Bakersfield Times* in her hand folded open to the want ads, and thought about what she was going to say.

Darn, she thought, they all said 'experienced.' Eight diners today said 'experienced only.' Then each of the disgusting diner owners had made her a proposition, if she really wanted the job. She thought of Dobe, of what he told her about being beautiful. Maybe she could have handled the men, but she didn't want to get into another situation with Dean.

Anyhow, how much experience do you need to serve eggs and hash in a truckers' diner, for heaven's sake? I've eaten in enough of these places to do the job in my sleep, she told herself. But she hadn't been sleeping. No work, no money equalled no sleep. What could she do? Unless she let these guys touch her, or told a lie, she didn't know what she'd do. If only she had experience that wasn't a lie.

151

She snapped her fingers. That's it, she thought. I've had experience *eating* in them for months; maybe that's enough experience for anyone.

Sharleen strained to look at her face reflected in the grimy rearview mirror. She pinched her cheeks the way she remembered her mother doing when she couldn't afford makeup. It brought a bright-pink glow to her face.

Sharleen squeezed her lips together, bruising them to a cherry red. She felt along the top edge of her white Mexican blouse, and gave a tug to pull it up; it did keep falling off one shoulder.

'Oh, Lord, help me with this,' she prayed.

She sprang out of the car, locked the door, and gave her cowgirl belt a cinch to pull it tighter. Sharleen sucked in her breath and encircled her small waist with her hands. Just right, she thought.

She rubbed the front of her high-heeled sandals against the backs of her tightly blue-jeaned legs and, deciding she was ready, walked resolutely towards the front door. She swung her hips and her straw bag just a little, in case the boss was watching her approach. Might as well walk like she felt good, even if she didn't.

Before she could put her hand on the knob, the screen door swung open, and the fattest man she had ever seen stood before her.

'I've been expecting you,' he said. 'Or I should say, I've been praying for you.' He stepped aside, holding the door open to let Sharleen squeeze past. She paused, then shrugged and walked into the cool, noisy interior. She saw that all the men plus both women customers and the waitress had turned to look at her. So she *had* been noticed as she came up the walk, she thought.

'My name's Jake and this is my place. Jake's Place. Get it?' he asked as he led her past the few occupied tables to the semiprivacy of a rear booth.

Sharleen couldn't keep from smiling. 'Sure thing, Jake. And I bet you guessed I'm here about the . . .'

'You're hired. Now, get rid of that newspaper and have a cup of coffee with me and tell me all about yourself.' He walked behind the counter and came back with two white mugs of coffee and a tray of doughnuts.

'Wait a minute, Jake. What do you mean, I'm hired? You haven't asked me if I had any experience yet. Your ad said "experienced."' Maybe she wouldn't have to lie, or flirt, she thought with relief. A

152

man as fat as Jake wouldn't be chasin' her around counters.

Jake leaned his huge, beefy arms on the table between them and smiled. 'Lady, I could see you was experienced the moment you started to walk towards the place. Hell, everybody in here could see it.' Sharleen could feel her face flush. Anyone could see she was embarrassed. But Jake didn't. He just looked down at his coffee, reached over to pick up a doughnut, and continued. 'And everybody in here said you was hired before you got to the door.'

He indicated the few businessmen at the tables and booths, and the truckers lined up at the counter. 'They're my regulars, and I like to keep them happy.' He took half the doughnut into his mouth and mumbled, 'So, you're on. What's your name?'

Sharleen sat back and laughed. The Lord sure did work in mysterious ways. She looked around the place.

There were rows of wire-stemmed white plastic flowers, now grey from dust and grease, along the bottom of the front window. The tables in the middle of the floor had flowered oilcloth covers, with a fake potted plant in the centre of each, surrounded by the sugar pourer, salt and pepper shakers, napkin dispenser, and a bottle of barbecue sauce. The booths along the walls were high-backed and deep. The seats were upholstered in orange vinyl, broken in spots, their stuffing pushed back in with silver-grey duct tape. The jutting tables were blue Formica, chipped here and there. Each booth had a miniature juke box with a flip-card selection of records, a mixture of country-and-western and fifties hits, Sharleen was sure.

Her eyes went to the long blue counter that seemed to join both sides of the room. Big trucker butts hung over the stools, the bodies above them huddled over bottomless coffee cups. The noise level was high; the topics of conversation were baseball, road conditions and hunting. The two women customers in the place talked only to each other.

A stocky woman in a pink polyester waitress uniform plodded back and forth to the kitchen, carrying armloads of meat-and-gravy dishes and pie, all the while shouting orders to the Mexican cook dripping sweat in the tiny kitchen. An open slot in the wall held the waiting meals under hot lights.

Well, Sharleen thought, it's better than McDonald's. At least there'll be tips. Now Jake wiped the doughnut crumbs off his rubbery mouth with the back of his hand. 'What's your name?' he repeated.

'Sharleen, Jake. And when do I start?'

COSMOPOLITAN HOSPITAL

Patient:	Mary Jane Moran	Insurance:	None
Age:	Thirty-four	Address:	749 East 19th
D.O.B.	Sept. 22, 1958		New York, NY

Date:	July 22, 199-		
Procedure:	Abdominoplasty		
Physician:	Silverman	Cost:	$ 7,425.00

Date:	Oct. 18, 199-		
Procedure:	Face lift & submental lipectomy		
Physician:	B. Moore	Cost:	$ 4,300.00

Date:	Jan. 11, 199-		
Procedure:	Buttocklift, flankresection		
Physician:	Silverman	Cost:	$ 3,830.00

Date:	April 21, 199-		
Procedure:	Blepharoplasty		
Physician:	B. Moore	Cost:	$ 1,540.00

Date:	Sept. 28, 199-		
Procedure:	Lipectomy—batwingarms		
Physician:	Silverman	Cost:	$ 1,950.00

Date:	Feb. 28, 199-		
Procedure:	Mastopexy		
Physician:	Wright	Cost:	$ 4,300.00

Date:	April 1, 199-		
Procedure:	Dermabrasion		
Physician:	B. Moore	Cost:	$ 1,750.00

Date:	June 3, 199-		
Procedure:	Rhinoplasty		
Physician:	Moore	Cost:	$ 4,100.00

— From the files of Laura Richie

After all the preliminary workups had been finished, Brewster Moore set up a schedule for her. He suggested other surgeons for the tummy tuck, the breast lift, and the liposuction. He would supervise their work carefully. Many of them worked with him at the clinic he had founded for indigent children.

'Isn't that work depressing?' Mary Jane asked.

'Less depressing than talking to a socialite begging for her third face lift,' Brewster Moore snapped. 'Would you like to see my other work?'

She felt properly chastised, and accepted his invitation. It was the only time in the weeks since she'd met him that he had offered anything about himself or his interests. She'd grown used to surgeons and their coldness, but he was unlike them – he had the surgeon's sureness, but beyond that he possessed an odd combination of formality, detachment and compassion.

She discovered his secret on the tour. His clinic was his passion. There, from all over the world, were children who had been born with deformities so frightening, so monstrous, that many of them had been abandoned or left for dead. 'Well, you can understand it,' Brewster Moore told her matter-of-factly. 'We are conditioned to respond to a baby's smile. Some of these children didn't have a mouth to smile with. Even educated parents have problems accepting this,' Brewster explained. 'Imagine what it was like for a peon in Peru.'

He introduced her to Winthrop, a Canadian boy whose parents had died in a private-plane crash which he had survived, though he was burned beyond recognition. Now he had a new face, constructed from skin grafted from his back and thighs.

And Hilda, a blonde three-year-old who had been left at a Bremen church a day after her birth. In the year since she'd arrived, her harelip had been corrected, but she still required a nose.

And Raoul, a twelve-year-old from Honduras whose bright eyes and clever little drawings were his only means of communication, since he was born without a tongue or a lower jaw.

The ward and private rooms were cheerful, the equipment up-to-date, and the operating theatre the most advanced in the country. 'How do you pay for all this?' she asked as she looked around at the facility and the bustling staff.

155

Dr. Moore shrugged. 'A bit of government funding, lots of private donations, and the rest comes from my fees. I do cosmetic work for some very wealthy and influential people.' He smiled. 'They support a lot of this.'

'It makes me feel even more petty,' Mary Jane said.

He stopped there in the hall and turned to her. 'It shouldn't,' he told her. 'Don't buy that Puritan idea of predestination, or some outdated morality that says appearance is nothing but vanity. Some things have not changed since the beginning of time. Your face is your fortune. These children could attest to that.'

She trusted him completely. So it was silly, really, she told herself. After all, she was a nurse and had been in hospitals for years. Still, hospitals made her nervous. And she was more than nervous before the first 'procedure,' as Miss Hennessey kept calling it.

Because, after all, she'd never been a patient before. 'Healthy as a horse,' she used to say, and slap her own wide flank.

The first surgery was a horror. The long ride on the gurney, through the hospital corridors and on the elevator used by visitors, flower-delivery guys, and employees, had been humiliating. The orderly who wheeled her along pushed her as if she were a supermarket basket, and he must have been running for mayor of the hospital — he stopped and talked to everyone he passed. She actually was relieved when she finally got to the operating room.

Perhaps if it hadn't been *elective* surgery, perhaps if it had been life-saving, she wouldn't have felt the contempt that seemed to roll off the orderlies as they dragged her, one more piece of meat, under the knife. Plastic surgery, they seemed to sneer. Self-indulgent. Neurotic. Selfish.

She had lost thirty-eight pounds and her stomach had receded, but instead of being flat, it hung in a nasty pouch of stretched skin. That would be neatly stretched in the abdominoplasty. It was a fairly serious operation, but Dr. Moore wanted it first, to give her time to recuperate.

The abdominal surgery — both liposuction and a 'tummy tuck' — was a major procedure.

'You've lost about as much weight as you need to,' Brewster Moore told her. 'But you'll have to keep it off.'

'But I still look awful!' She raised her arms and swung them. Excess flesh waved back and forth.

'Batwing arms. Typical.'

'Is that what it's called?'

'Yep. Descriptive, huh? Dieting won't help them. The rest is exercise, liposuction, and surgery. But your stomach muscles need to be tightened. So we'll actually cut and shorten the muscles and reattach them, slice off excess skin, and stretch the rest down.'

'What happens to my belly button?'

'Well, it will be excised. Don't worry. I'll supervise everything. And Silverman will make you a very nice new one.'

'A new one? How is it done?'

'It's just a staple from inside. Unless, of course, you want an "outie" instead of an "innie." But that will cost extra.'

Her eyes opened wide, until she realized that he was teasing her.

Despite being considered cosmetic, it was major surgery, with a seven-to-ten day hospital recuperation, and was scheduled for seven-thirty on a grey Thursday morning. The night before, an aide had come in to – of all things – shave her pudenda. 'All skin exposed to incision and its environs must be shaved, to reduce the chance of infection, and to make the removal of surgical tape and staples easier later on,' the bored orderly droned. Her only comfort was that, at least for this one, she'd be unconscious.

The standard joke is that in a hospital they'll wake you up to give you a sleeping pill, but on the morning of the abdominal surgery Mary Jane was awoken at five-thirty and given an injection to relax her. The hypo worked, and she felt as if she were floating as she was lifted onto the stretcher for her ride to surgery. Oddly enough, the shot did little to ease her embarrassment at being in the elevator lying down while people in street clothes stood around her, pretending she wasn't there. No one looked her in the eye, and she had trouble stifling her laughter at how ludicrous the situation was.

Dr. Moore didn't do the surgery, though he had selected the doctor who would. Still, he came to visit her the evening before, and she was touched by his gesture. 'Bob Silverman is a good man. You've got good tissue, and there should be little scarring. But for the mastopexy I've lined up Sylvia Wright. She has a feeling for breasts that no man I know has.'

Mary Jane had giggled at his phraseology. And Dr. Moore actually coloured. He was a very formal man, but Mary Jane was getting to know him and see the humour behind his formality. Dr. Moore smiled. He had a very nice smile. 'You know what I meant,' he said.

On the way in to the abdominoplasty, Mary Jane kept her eyes on the ceiling, following the overhead lights as she was wheeled along the halls. She knew she should be nervous, but, with the injection she had received finally kicking in, she at last lost all guilt, all shame, all nerves. She really couldn't care less. The orderly parked her outside the operating room, in what felt like an alcove, but since she was disinclined to turn her head, she couldn't really tell. Time passed. She had no idea how long. Minutes? Hours? she asked herself. Or is it over? A nurse approached her and said her name, while inserting an IV in her arm. 'We're going in now, Miss Moran,' she said, and pushed the stretcher through swinging doors, into a pale-green room with huge, blinding lights overhead.

She was aware of a group of people in what looked to be camouflage, which she was able to remind herself was surgical green. They seemed to be standing around a table that wasn't there; then, suddenly, *she* was the table, and they were all looking down at her.

'Hello, Mary Jane,' Dr. Moore's voice said from somewhere. 'Are you comfortable?' She didn't expect him to be there at all.

'I'm very relaxed,' she murmured.

'Count backward,' the masked gas-passer told her. 'Start at one hundred.'

She tried to think of a joke, a wisecrack, but could barely manage the count. 'One hundred. Ninety-nine.' And then she couldn't remember the next number . . .

Blessedly, it was over. 'You can go to sleep now,' the nurse said. Mary Jane started to say thank you, but never got it out.

She opened her eyes again later, but couldn't move. Her mouth was so dry that her tongue felt like sandpaper. The pain was worse than the worst stomach ache she had ever had. It felt as if she'd been stabbed. Mary Jane tried to call out to someone, but no sound came. She started to cry to herself, but the slightest movement increased the pain, so she began to whimper instead. The incision across her entire pelvis felt like a fiery slashed wound, and her whole midsection was knotted, as if she'd been kicked in the gut a million times. Then nothingness again.

She was aware she had slept. Or had blacked out. She opened her eyes once again, and now knew she was in her hospital bed. The pain was still there, but she knew that someone would do something about that soon, just as soon as she let them know she was awake. But she couldn't. She couldn't move a muscle. Not yet.

A hand touched her shoulder gently. 'Hi, you want to wake up now? Come on, Mary Jane, wake up. How are you feeling?' The voice kept talking; she was being called to arousal, the nurse intent on getting her fully out of the anesthesia. Mary Jane tried to cooperate. 'Water,' was all she could manage to say. She also wanted to say 'pain,' but could only squeeze her eyes closed. The nurse understood, and Mary Jane blessed her as she felt a prick in her side and then – slowly, slowly – the pain ebbed. And Mary Jane felt fine. Her last thought, before she was gone again, was that she'd got one down and only eight more operations to go.

The incisions itched like crazy. But when the bandages came off, Mary Jane had a stomach as flat as a teenager's. She stared at it, fascinated. Was that her flesh? So smooth, so tight, so taut? She forgot about the pain, the cost, the knowledge that her excess flesh had been cut off and discarded somewhere.

Instead she simply contemplated her own brand-new navel.

The breast lift and reduction – mastopexy – seemed the worst, though actually Brewster Moore assured her that the pain in healing would be far less than the abdominal incisions had caused. 'We're not cutting muscle, only fat. You have plenty of breast tissue; it is simply attached too low to your chest wall.'

'I find this talk very titillating. Get it?'

Dr. Moore groaned. 'Mary Jane, that is the most obvious pun I ever heard. Now, tomorrow Dr. Wright will make a new pocket of skin, higher up, fill it with tissue, and reattach the nipples centrally . . .'

'Reattach the nipples? You mean you *cut off my nipples*?'

'Yes. I thought you understood that. From the material that Dr. Wright reviewed with you.' Dr. Moore sighed. 'She should have told you. But the scars are almost completely hidden in the areolae . . .'

Mary Jane felt a wave of nausea. 'But when they reattach them, do they work? I mean . . .' She stopped, embarrassed. 'Will I be able to *feel* anything?'

'Well, you certainly won't be able to nurse, but sensation sometimes returns. But in my opinion the nerves do not regenerate. It's an important consideration. I thought you understood about it. Of course, you must decide if the sacrifice is worth it. And some women have reported *increased* sexual pleasure after the operation, because, I think, of their increased pride in their appearance. You know, the mind is the most important sexual organ.'

'It's not my *mind* you're operating on, doctor.'

'I know that. And I hope you know that I do appreciate how . . . courageous you've been.'

'Hey, it's the kids like Raoul and Winthrop, or the ones who've lost half a face to cancer, who are courageous. But I appreciate the thought. And I'll make you a deal: Dr. Wright can cut off my nipples if she gives me perfect breasts and you'll give me a nose like Mai Von Trilling's.'

'You drive a hard bargain, Mary Jane,' he laughed. 'I'll see what I can do.' He turned to leave.

'Oh, and doctor? About those nipples.' He turned to her, his face concerned as always. 'You *will* be sure that Dr. Wright remembers to put them back, won't you?'

24

Hi there, Laura Richie here. While Mary Jane was struggling through her pain in New York, I bet you forgot all about me, back in Hollywood. No surprise. Hollywood is used to short memories. Nothing ever stands still. In this town, everyone in the business is either on the way up or on the way down. Like sharks swimming through the ocean, none can afford to stop. And, like sharks, all of them operate on hunger and fear. Hunger and fear are the fuels that generate the Hollywood agent-client relationship. The young up-and-coming starlets covet and fear agents as if they were gods in the pantheon known as Hollywood. Agents can make or break careers.

But fear is a two-way street. Once they have become established as talents and celebrities, stars have been known to drop their agents in favour of even more powerful brokers. Every agent fears being dropped.

Lila could smell that fear in Ara Sagarian's reception room, and hoped that it was not hers. There were half a dozen other young people scattered around the room, one more beautiful than the other, each clasping a portfolio while thumbing through the latest issues of *Variety*. Only losers had to wait, and she hated waiting. But Lila was sure none of them had appointments with Ara. She guessed, too, that these were the flotsam and jetsam of the Industry, who regularly made the rounds of agents' offices, hoping each time for that brief five-minute interview that could result in an acting job, a walk-on role, or even that coveted prize: representation.

Because in Hollywood an actor without an agent is an actor without a chance.

'Miss Kyle?' the young secretary said, as every head in the room turned to Lila. 'Mr. Sagarian will see you now. Will you follow me, please?'

Lila smiled, as if she expected to be treated specially, and picked up her bag from the floor next to her chair. She tossed it over her shoulder as she followed the woman down the long, deeply carpeted hall. The walls on either side were lined with scores of framed, signed photographs. As Lila glided by, she was able to pick out Frank Sinatra, Sammy Davis, Jr., Lucille Ball, Duke Wayne, Joan Crawford, and a dozen others. 'To Ara,' began each autograph.

'There's your mother's picture, Miss Kyle. It was a promo shot for *Birth of a Star*.' Lila recognized the shot. She had seen it dozens of times before, in her mother's house. That and hundreds of others of her mother papered the walls of the Puppet Mistress's library and den. 'This is Mr. Sagarian's suite,' the secretary said, and rapped gently on the rosewood door.

Lila was nervous, but reminded herself that Ara Sagarian was not what he had been. He wasn't representing Sinatra or Davis or Wayne or Crawford or Ball now. Some of his clients were retired, and the other half were dead. He needed fresh blood, but not the blood of those losers waiting in the lobby. He needed a Madonna, a Tom Cruise, a Lila Kyle. A superstar, or someone with the potential to be one. He needed Lila Kyle. At least that's what she told herself.

'Come in, come in,' Ara called out, as the door was opened and Lila stepped through it. How long had it been since she had last seen him? Five years? Ten? She wasn't prepared for the figure that came limping towards her. Once tall, even powerful, Ara Sagarian now was stooped and shorter. His left arm hung loosely by his side; his left leg dragged after his right. The left side of his mouth was partially paralyzed, and the words of his greeting sounded muffled. Everything about him seemed reduced from what Lila remembered.

Of course, I was young then, and maybe he wasn't as big and as strong as I remember. But he'd certainly shrunk. And it looked like he'd had a major stroke.

'Mr. Sagarian, how kind of you to see me. I know how busy you are.' Lila walked briskly towards him, her hand extended.

Ara shook her hand, then dabbed a linen handkerchief at the trail of drool that escaped from his mouth. His pencil-thin moustache was wet, too. 'Not at all, my dear. I'm delighted to see you again. I haven't laid eyes on you since, let me see, you must have been seven or eight years old, and you performed a skit with your mother and her puppets at a party at her home.' He looked at her appreciatively. 'You've been busy growing up since then,' he said. 'Come sit over here.' Ara indicated a seat on the loosely cushioned sectional sofa, and settled himself back into the plush down pillows.

'How is your charming mother?'

'She's very well, Mr. Sagarian. She sends you her love, of course. She's *so* grateful that you should take the time to talk to me about my career. As Mother says, if you can't get Mr. Sagarian to represent you, you're not in show business.'

'Please, call me Ara. We're practically family. Now, what career is it that I'm to help with?' he asked, and wiped his mouth again.

'I'm an actress,' she said, and suddenly felt very young. God, she *had* to make this happen. 'That is, Mother tells me I'm a born talent, and has been pushing me for years to get into the business.' Lila patted her skirt nervously in place and continued. 'So I finally gave in. And here I am. Lila flashed her brightest smile.

'Here you are, indeed. And very beautiful, I might add. Now, what would you like me to do for you, my dear?' Ara asked.

Lila faltered. All the bravado she had felt on her way over here was slipping away. He was, despite his stroke, despite his age, so, so . . . so sure of himself. So courtly. She wasn't prepared to have to spell it out for him. He had to know what she wanted, and it certainly wasn't a date. Was he playing with her? She felt a flash of anger, but tried to stay calm.

'Well, I . . . I wanted to ask you if you would take me on as a client. You see, I was thinking of starting in television, but really I'm more interested in a career in movies.' She rattled off a list of fake credits, though she'd never spent a minute before the camera.

Ara knitted his brows. 'I'm so sorry to have wasted your time, Lila. I'm not taking on any new talent. This is nothing personal. I haven't in years, in fact. Had I known that was the purpose of your visit, I could have saved you the trip. But perhaps I could help you in another way. Maybe I could refer you to another agent?'

Lila was near panic. This was not going as she had planned. And she didn't want a referral to some has-been or wannabe agent out of the William Morris mailroom who had no more contacts than she did. Maybe flattery would work. 'But I don't *want* another agent, Ara. I want *you*. Mother always said you understood the artistic temperament better than anyone else in town, better than any director.' Lila dropped her eyes, as if to keep him from seeing her tears of frustration and disappointment. 'I want to work with *you*, Mr. Sagarian.'

'I'm sure you've given this a great deal of thought,' Ara said, 'and that your mother has prepared you for some of the pitfalls to such a career. But let me give you the history of an acting career in Hollywood. It goes like this: "Who is Glenn Ford?" "Get me Glenn Ford." "Get me a Glenn Ford type." "Get me a young Glenn Ford." And then, "Who is Glenn Ford?" I know that sounds a little cynical, but that's the way of this world.' Ara wiped his drooling lips once again. 'You've seen what your mother had to do to get on top and stay there as long as she did – as long as she has. Surely you don't want to have to go through that for the rest of your life?'

Oh, Christ, he wasn't going to start with fatherly advice now, was he? Why couldn't he just shut up, wipe his mouth, and send her over to Spielberg or Frears or even Robert Altman, for God's sake? She took a deep breath. She'd just have to lie. 'It seems my mother has wanted this for me long before I wanted it for myself. I've been trained for the life by the mistress of the business.'

'So, your mother is completely behind you on this?' Ara asked, raising his brows. 'She's convinced you have the talent and the perseverance to handle such work?' Ara used his handkerchief once again before continuing. 'Funny, I don't remember. But my memory isn't what it was. You see, I have great respect for Theresa's opinion. In the old days, she could pick talent like no one else. I have her to thank for the discovery of several very important talents I handle. It was Theresa who sent Marilyn to me, *and* James Dean. So, if Theresa thinks you have it, I would reconsider my decision. Of course, she must show a mother's favouritism, but she's no dummy. I'm old, and I haven't been well, and I've considered retirement. But perhaps, just one more time . . .' He paused.

Lila began to relax. What the hell. He was buying the lie, and she knew, if he sent her out for just one go-see, she could get a part, a foothold. She smiled. 'Mother is one hundred and fifty per cent behind me on this. We've spent many hours discussing the pros and cons of my decision, and she has been uncommonly candid with me about the business.'

'Then excuse me while I make a quick phone call, Lila,' Ara said, as he reached for the telephone on the coffee table in front of them.

Lila's heart jumped in her chest. Jesus Christ, could it really be this easy? she thought. He'll make one phone call, and I'm on my way? Who will he call? Coppola? Sherry Lansing? Barry Levinson? Lila thanked all the gods of fortune and fame that she felt lurking over her shoulder, and stifled a smile of triumph.

Then she heard him speak. 'Good morning, Estrella. Ara Sagarian here. May I speak to Miss O'Donnell?' He looked over at Lila and smiled a tiny, tilted smile, then wiped at the corner of his mouth once again with the handkerchief.

Lila stopped breathing for a brief moment. Oh, shit!

'Theresa, darling. How are you? I haven't seen you since my unfortunate hospitalization. It was so nice of you to come to visit. No. No. Not at all. But guess who I have sitting next to me at this moment, thanks to you.' Ara listened for a moment, then continued. 'Why, Lila, your daughter. Thank you for sending her to me, darling. I think I can help her.'

Lila watched as Ara's expression changed while he listened intently to Theresa's side of the conversation, his expression becoming grave. Lila felt the blood rush to her face and her stomach tighten. Oh, God! What was the Puppet Mistress saying? She shouldn't have come here. She shouldn't have listened to Robbie!

'I'm sorry to have bothered you my dear. I must have misunderstood. By the way, I will be seeing you at my Emmy party, won't I?' He paused again, nodded. 'Good. It wouldn't be a party without you.'

Ara hung up the phone and got to his feet. He stumbled over to his desk and opened the top drawer, removed a small vial, and took out a pill. He poured himself a glass of water from the silver carafe on his desk and swallowed the pill. Then he turned to Lila and finally looked her in the eyes.

'It should be very clear to you, Miss Kyle, that I was not born yesterday. You almost sent me up shit river without a paddle. Not only did your mother *not* send you to me, but she is decidedly *against* your choice of careers.' Ara walked slowly around his desk to his chair and sat down. 'She also believes that you have problems of an emotional nature that would prohibit you from ever living a public life. And that you don't have a shred of talent, and no experience. That she has begged you to go on to college, to pick some other career. But, frankly, none of that bothers me as much as the fact that you lied to me.'

'Ara, Mr. Sagarian, please, let me explain.' Lila's voice was tight with panic.

'There is no need to explain. I understand completely. But I will not help you, for two reasons. One, you jeopardized a very old, very lucrative relationship I have with one of my major stars, and, two, you underestimated me.' Ara now held the handkerchief to his mouth as the drooling seemed to increase. 'And for those reasons, Miss Kyle, consider yourself lucky that I'm only throwing you out of my office, and not out of the business.' Ara pressed a button on his desk, and his office door was opened immediately. 'Miss Bradley, please escort Miss Kyle to the elevator. And, Miss Bradley, Miss Kyle will *not* be making any further appointments to see me. Our business together is finished.'

Ara Sagarian swung around in his chair and faced the window, picking up the phone as he did so.

Lila followed Miss Bradley, this time in silence. When they came to the elevator bank, the door opened to an elevator and Lila got in. 'I'm so sorry, Miss Kyle,' Miss Bradley said. 'I always loved your mother.' Then the door shut between them.

In the isolation of the swiftly moving elevator, Lila Kyle covered her face and cried.

25

If you have to pick a city to get lost in, you can't do better than New York. Mary Jane found it surprisingly easy to disappear, to melt out of her previous life and turn into a ghost. She spent almost all of her time alone. Those days of endless walking, spending nothing, eating nothing, speaking to no one, with no place to go but the room that she could not bear to call 'home,' seemed emptier than any life could sustain. But you have to make space if you want something new, she told herself, over and over. Since when is giving birth easy? Or being born?

And her memories kept her company. Memories of laughing with Neil, shopping with Molly, and hanging out with the troupe, and memories of Sam.

She couldn't forget him. In fact, it seemed that the longer the separation, the more often she thought of him. How he had cast her for *Jack and Jill*, the rehearsals, the start of their affair. What he said, how he looked. Perhaps it was because she was so lonely, but his memory did not fade. It got stronger.

Starving herself, exercising, undergoing surgery and recuperation were lonely occupations almost beyond bearing. But Mary Jane learned from it. She learned that she could survive almost anything, and that she could accomplish almost anything she wanted, if she kept to a single goal: she didn't think about meeting a man, making friends, getting a part, choosing what she would wear, buying a new book, or even eating a good meal. She focused only on the perfecting of her body, and the study of this new persona she hoped to become: a beautiful woman. And if the loneliness sometimes seemed almost to suffocate her with its blanket of New York isolation, at least, wrapped in it, she was safe from distraction.

By the third operation, she was more relaxed. She had seen the implants that would be inserted into her cheeks and chin. Dr. Moore showed her how they would be placed and where the incision scars would be hidden. She wasn't as fearful before the surgery, but the bruising and swelling afterwards were so horrendous that she swore off mirrors for the duration. It was too frightening.

And, of course, she had to be conscious. It helped the surgeon better understand how the skin draped over her face. Brewster Moore had told her that, and she knew it, but she hadn't known how much it would bother her – seeing the gowned, masked faces, hearing the scraping of the bone as he worked on the ridge under her brows, hearing the drill that Dr. Moore used to cut away at her. But she was determined to move ahead with this plan, and she could see some signs of progress. She could easily wear size six now, and her breasts, though scarred, pointed up perkily under her blouse.

Well, she reminded herself, the oral surgery had been much worse. *That* wasn't any goddamn discomfort, and she'd demanded Percodan and gotten it. Eight teeth pulled – four wisdom teeth, four of the perfectly healthy molars beside them – so that there was room in her mouth for the others to straighten out. 'It's not that your teeth are too big,' Dr. Kleinman told her, 'it's that your mouth is too small.'

'I wish my grandmother could hear you say that,' Mary Jane muttered, remembering all the times she'd been called a big mouth.

Her teeth had ached. Her jaw had been broken and realigned by Dr. Moore; then Kleinman, the master orthodontist, had begun his work. At least she hadn't been able to eat for weeks, and she'd dropped another nine pounds. When she had nothing better to do, she could now count all her ribs when she held her breath.

So she'd pop a Percodan, crawl onto the lumpy cot in her hotel room, and stroke her ribs like a washboard until the pain let up and she fell into a sleep too drugged for 'discomfort.'

But worse than the tooth pain had been the electrolysis. A Frenchwoman, Michelle, had worked over her hairline and eyebrows, following Dr. Moore's template, burning out hair follicles with a tiny needle inserted into her forehead. It was agony, and the smell made her want to gag.

'Easier to raise your hairline than surgically build you more forehead,' Dr. Moore said. 'And your hair *is* beautiful.' It was the first time he had complimented her, and she felt herself flush with pleasure.

'My grandmother called it "Indian hair." It's so thick and heavy that I was ashamed of it.'

'Medically speaking, your grandmother sounds like an asshole,' Dr. Moore told her, and she had laughed despite the 'discomfort.'

She liked him. She liked him very much. And throughout the long, painful, boring hospitalizations, during the examinations in his spare office, even in phone calls to her, he treated her . . . kindly. With compassion. As if she was as serious a patient as Raoul or Winthrop, or the little girl who'd had her face burned off in a car accident, or the teenager who'd been kept in the basement by his parents, or some of the other horrors who waited in his office, hoping for a human face, a face he could give them to end their shame and isolation.

Still, even the steeliest determination has to grapple with financial realities. After eleven 'procedures,' Mary Jane had to face the fact that she was close to broke. She hadn't worked in almost twenty-two months, the longest 'vacation' in her life. Not that all the surgery had been a day at the beach. Brewster had called her lucky – he said all she needed was money and time. Well, she'd certainly run out of the latter because now her money was just about gone. The only asset she had left was the farm up in Scuderstown, but in the more than two years since her grandmother's death it had been immersed in the legal tangle left by the old woman. Her grandmother had stubbornly left it to her son, Mary Jane's father, although he had been *non compos mentis* and hooked to machines at the V.A. for more than thirty years. Mary Jane had counted on that money's coming through by now. Leave it to Grandma to ruin my plans, even when she's dead, Mary Jane thought.

Slater, the Albany lawyer, was still trying to clear probate, but it was taking a long time, and his fees would probably eat into what little the farm would bring. By the time the money came through, Mary Jane, like her grandma, would also be dead of old age.

She tried to live on even less, and sold the engagement ring she'd had from her mother. But the four hundred dollars she got for it wouldn't last long. When she was down to her last thousand dollars, she had no choice – she went to Dr. Moore to tell him.

Mary Jane sat across from him, once more, in that austere office. 'I have to stop the surgery for now,' she said. She tried not to let her lip tremble, or show any emotion. She remembered the breakdown she'd had in this same chair the first time they spoke. 'I mean to go on. It will just have to wait for a while.'

'Why?' he asked.

'Personal reasons,' she said. She really liked Dr. Moore, and she'd come to understand the compassion that he contained behind his formality, but she didn't want to discuss her problems with him.

'Well, I know this is a difficult thing that you are going through. Identity, self-worth, aesthetics, pain, anxiety, fear, scarring. It's a great deal that you are asking of yourself. If there is any way that I or the team can provide more assistance . . .'

She could see his concern. That he had done wrong. God, he must think she was having second thoughts! 'I've run out of money,' Mary Jane mumbled.

'What?'

'I've run out of money.' She said it more loudly, more angrily than she meant to. They were silent for a moment. Brewster Moore blinked.

'Is that all? Jesus, I thought you were having regrets or some kind of mental problem. It's just the money?'

'*Just?*'

168

'Well, what I mean to say is that, as long as it's only financial, I think we could work something out.'

'But I have to get a job. I'm really down to the bottom of my savings. And working isn't going to make me enough to pay my rent *and* surgical fees. I'll have to put everything off until my grandmother's estate comes through. If it comes through.' Tears filled her eyes. She'd put her life on hold for so long. How much more delay and disappointment could she take?

But Dr. Moore seemed unfazed. 'Didn't you used to be a nurse?' he asked. 'You could work for me now.'

'With Miss Hennessey? No thanks.' The nurse still gave her the creeps. And she felt the woman resented her growing relationship with Dr. Moore. Not that it was anything more than professional. Once or twice, Mary Jane wondered if she herself wished it *were* more. And if Nurse Hennessey had a yen for the doctor, too.

'Oh, she's not so bad.'

'You say that because she worships you.'

'Well, it's nice to have someone admire you, even if it's only Miss Hennessey.' He laughed. 'No, I was thinking perhaps you could work at the clinic with the children.'

'Raoul and the others?'

'Yes.'

She felt her stomach tighten. 'I don't think so.'

'I think you'd be good for them. I want them to see people who go through successful surgery. Of course, yours isn't as extreme as theirs, but, as a role model, you'll do. And they'd be good for you. Plus, I need the help and you need the rhinoplasty. A good exchange for everyone.'

'But it will still take a long time to save up the fees.'

'Tell you what. We continue with the procedures now, and you pay me out of your inheritance or future earnings. Meanwhile, if you're a clinic employee, I think I can get the hospital to waive its fees.'

She felt tears come to her eyes again. He was being so kind. Was it just pity and charity on his part? Or professional pride in a project he wanted to see completed? She decided not to question it too deeply and simply be grateful.

And so they made the deal.

Now Mary Jane sat in a back booth at a Chinese restaurant, eating the dull steamed-vegetable dish before her. Even Buddha couldn't delight in this, she thought. She pushed the plate aside. Brewster Moore had explained it clearly – 'to keep this somewhat unnatural weight and the benefits of surgery, you can only eat two spare meals a day.' She was going in this afternoon for her first job at Brewster's clinic, and she was nervous. She knew that there he dealt with the most severe types of facial deformity. What would those poor, freakish patients feel if they knew that she, normal as she was, was also going through a series of surgeries?

She looked down at her plate. Eating had always been her solution to anxiety, but no more. Now it was steamed vegetables and a little brown rice, even under stress.

The placemat had the Chinese horoscope on it. She was born under the sign of the Dog – 'Generous and loyal, you have the ability to work well with others. Compatible with the Horse and Tiger. Your opposite is the Dragon. 1910, 1922, 1934, 1946, 1958, 1970, 1982, 1994.' She had been born in 1958. Well, she was generous and loyal, and she did work well with others – with Brewster, anyway, if not jealous Miss Hennessey. She looked up Sam's birth year, 1952. Yes, there he was – a Dragon. So, the Chinese knew their relationship was doomed from the start. It said he was robust and passionate, his life filled with complexity. He was compatible with the Monkey.

Despite the long months, despite the separation, despite the pain of what she was going through alone, she still thought of him. His smile. His long, slow hands on her body. His laugh, and the way he shook his head over a joke. Despite everything, she still missed him as badly as she had the first day he left her. Did he ever miss her?

She wondered what year Crystal Plenum was born. Monkeys were 1944, 1956, 1968. Was the bitch two years older than she, or ten years younger? What surgery had *she* had? What lies did she tell?

Well, Mary Jane decided, even if she did change her age, she was going to stay a Dog, if not in looks, then in Chinese horoscopes. But she wouldn't be a 1958 dog, she'd be a 1970 one. She thought she could pass for twelve years younger – the eye job and radical face lift seemed to have eliminated all wrinkles, and her skin's elasticity was such that she didn't have the stretched look that she had been afraid of.

It was the nose that still troubled her. She hated, as she always had, to look in the mirror. Now the fine cheekbones and the delicate chin that had emerged from under Brewster's scalpel seemed to mock the pendulous nose that still hung in the centre of her face. In a way, she was uglier than she had ever been. She avoided all mirrors. There was a wall of them on the other side of the restaurant, facing her banquette, but she kept her head averted.

Dr. Moore had insisted that the rhinoplasty come last, after all the other work had settled. She trusted him, but, despite the lithe body that now looked good in tight jeans, despite the more feminine brow, the cheekbones, the improved hairline, the dental work, and even the coloured contact lenses, the face that she glanced away from was barely attractive. Could the rhinoplasty fix all that?

Well, she sighed, the work on the ward should give her a sense of proportion.

And by the end of the first week, she realized it had. Brewster had asked her to come on as night nurse. There were few medical requirements – she simply administered painkillers to those children out of recent surgery and comforted all the children who were too frightened or restless to sleep. Brewster said they needed conversation and attention as much as anything else. 'And they need to be looked at. So many people avert their eyes. Look at them. Not to stare. Just give them the gift of being seen.'

'The gift of being seen.' Yes, it was a gift, to be looked at approvingly. With her newly emerged slim body, Mary Jane had received wolf whistles. Only from behind, and only from some gross construction workers, but she'd be lying if she said she hadn't been thrilled. How long had she gone unnoticed? Thirty-six years seemed too long. She would look at the children and give them the gift of being seen, and she swore to herself she wouldn't wince.

There were dozens of kids, and all of them, beneath the frightening failures of their faces, had the gift that children have: they were innocent and vulnerable and curious and alive. She had her favourites right away, of course. Sally, who was fourteen, and a victim of craniosynostosis: her skull had prematurely fused. She had undergone more than a dozen operations already to correct a frighteningly deformed head and jaw. And Jennifer, a three-year-old black girl whose brachycephaly gave her the pop eyes of a Crouzon's disease sufferer. But of all of them, from the first night on, it was Raoul who drew her. Raoul, with eyes that had done all his speaking for twelve years. Raoul, born in South America without a tongue or lower jaw, unable to nurse, since there was no suction his poor deformed mouth could manage. Raoul, abandoned after his birth, who now tried, with a new mouth and tongue, to learn a new language. And Raoul, who made her laugh.

Raoul was twelve, and an active kid. He'd already had six major operations on his mouth and tongue, and was in for a seventh. He'd spent his first three years in a hospital, then his next two in an orphanage. But, despite all that, he had a strong spark of life and love. Raoul couldn't say much, but he could write and draw almost anything. Mary Jane played endless games of tic-tac-toe with him, and bought him a connect-the-dots book which so enchanted him that he designed his own. During her second week there, he gave her a picture to connect the dots on.

She picked up her pencil and followed his numbers. It was a nurse, complete, as she was, with comfortable shoes and a name tag. But when she got to the dots of the face, she realized it was a portrait of her, with her delicate cheekbones, almond eyes, and her awful, ridiculous nose. She nodded and tried to smile, then Raoul took the pencil. 'LINDA MARY JANE,' he wrote, and looked up at her with a face full of affection. She was confused for a moment, until she remembered that *linda* was Spanish for 'pretty.' She looked down at his ruin of a face. There was no irony there. He was the first male who had ever called her that.

Don't feel so sorry for yourself, she said. Look at Raoul. And she did. Night after night. And in no time at all, his ghastly grin seemed normal to her. Normal and welcoming.

Often, in the early evening, Brewster Moore stopped by, visited with the children and the frightened, overwhelmed parents who came. He spent extra time with Raoul. Then he usually had a cup of coffee with her. She came to look forward to it. On the nights he didn't, she felt a strange disappointment. Oh, fine, she thought. My life has become so small that I am obsessed with my nose and in love with my surgeon. Perfect. Nothing wrong with that. But maybe I should think about getting a life.

Because she was, for the first time, drawn to nursing, to Dr. Moore, and to these children. The idea of abandoning them, as everyone else had, troubled her. Better move on before you get trapped, she told herself. Better move on before you lose your nerve.

So she decided, one night: after this surgery, it was California. However she came out, it was time to move on. For two years her life had gotten smaller and smaller. Now it was time to expand.

She'd need a new name. Her new age was twenty-four; she

was still born in a year of the Dog, but it was a different year. And though she'd keep the same career, she certainly hoped that she'd be more successful than she'd been before, in her first incarnation. She was, of course, afraid she'd fail again, but it was time, she knew, to get on with it.

Once, of course, she had the new nose.

'Ever consider surgical improvement? I think if you had asked me that when I was twenty,' she says, *'I might have said yes, but after seeing such bad facelifts, no.'* Emma Samms was being quoted in an interview in *People* magazine. Mary Jane threw the magazine down on the floor. She was sick to death of reading about how naturally beautiful women kept themselves so. 'Drink lots of bottled water,' 'Never eat red meat,' 'Simple yoga exercises and meditation to help you project your *inner* beauty!' Fuck the inner beauty. It had never gotten her a date *or* a part. And it was a load of crap anyway. As if Perrier would alter your bone structure or clear up your skin! That new ingenue, Phoebe Van Gelder, had sworn she stuck to a macrobiotic diet, but Mary Jane knew through Neil, the skinny bitch was on drugs most of the time, and had had a major nasal reconstruction. Sure, the Phoebe Van Gelder New Age diet: carrots and cocaine.

Over the last months, doing her research on beauty, she'd read all of the bullshit: 'How to Lose Five Pounds This Weekend!,' 'Ten Tricks to Prevent Ageing,' 'Top Models' Secret Makeup Tips for You.' Yeah, the real tip was 'Be young and tall and gorgeous with a perfect bone structure.' Well, Mary Jane knew the real secret to beauty now for the average woman. Beauty meant pain, expense, surgery, and almost full-time maintenance. It sure didn't leave time for the day job.

God, she was cranky, she admitted to herself. She glanced briefly into the tiny mirror she now kept in her purse. The bruising under her eyes was just about gone. She averted her face. It had been weeks now since the nasal surgery. She still wasn't pretty. If anything, her nose loomed even more hideously on her face. But Dr. Moore had explained it would take some time for the swelling to go down. Now there was only the final rhinoplasty left – the 'refining,' as Dr. Moore called it, that remained to be done on the nose. She noticed that Dr. Moore never referred to 'your nose,' only 'the nose.'

'Most cosmetic surgery needs to be done in multiple stages,' he had explained. 'For financial reasons – and emotional ones – most surgeons to the middle class don't bother. After all,' he mimicked, "Missy does look *so* much better now, with that big bump gone." But nasal tissue swells, and it sometimes takes months for the swelling to go down. Most surgeons are butchers. They break the nasal cartilage. It causes all kinds of temporary swelling. The only way to see the actual contour, to see both how the tissue, takes to the cartilage armature and how the skin drapes the tissues, is to wait. And then "refine." Which often means a second operation. But most women don't want to undergo another procedure. Ergo, the instant nose. Now, with your face, on the other hand . . .'

Brewster explained that he had perfected a rhinoplasty procedure that didn't require the breaking of the nose. 'And that means less swelling, no discoloration at all. But I didn't want to work on the nose until the rest of the armature was completed. And I want to wait for a second chance to work on the tip.'

She'd been through the swelling, the taste of blood always in the back of her throat, the difficulty sleeping. 'Refinement'? She laughed to herself, but even smiling hurt. Oh, no, she remembered. It didn't hurt. It caused 'discomfort.'

The last operation was surprisingly quick, less than an hour. Mary Jane got up off the table with little more than wooziness and a neat white pad of gauze taped over the new tip of her nose. After a night of restless sleep, she spent the next day packing her few belongings and telling the hotel she'd be leaving. Not that the ever-changing front desk staff cared. She worked her last week at the clinic, and said goodbye to the children. She did everything she could do to prepare for her departure, except take off the gauze.

Now the months of pain and waiting and Dr. Moore's kindness were over. Now she'd see the best he could do. The face she would live with. And she was afraid. So afraid that she couldn't do it alone. She left on the bandage, and avoided reflections in plate-glass windows; she'd long ago covered the medicine-cabinet mirror at the hotel. She simply had to trust this little man, the doctor, her only friend, and see what he had wrought. She made the appointment with the ever-cold Miss Hennessey for her final visit.

Now, at last, here in his office, the time had come for revelation. She was so nervous, she wanted to ask to hold his hand, but she was far too shy. As if he knew what she felt, Dr. Moore came up close behind her. He put his hands on her shoulders and walked her to the corner of the room. He had her face the wall mirror, and he lifted the last bandage from her nose.

She stared into the mirror.

A perfect stranger stared out at her. A perfect stranger. An oval face, with just a touch of squareness, firmness at the sides of the jaw. A broad, smooth forehead, thin, tapering brows, cheekbones that wouldn't quit. And the nose. The nose! It was long, but perfectly so, straight and long, with a thin bridge and wonderful sharpness where it met her upper lip. It was beautiful. It was all changed and beautiful. *She* was beautiful! All changed, except for her eyes.

Then, for a moment, she had the panicky feeling that her own eyes were staring out at her, trapped in a strange, lovely face, while her own, *her* face, on this side of the mirror, hadn't changed. Involuntarily she lifted her hands, and blinked as her fingers touched *her*, yet moved over the stranger's perfect face in the mirror. It was eerie, but it convinced her this perfect face was really hers.

He gave her plenty of time. She looked and looked, and was surprisingly unselfconscious in front of him, perhaps because he was staring as hard as she was. At last he broke the silence. 'Are you satisfied?' Dr. Moore asked softly.

With difficulty, Mary Jane pulled her eyes away from the mirror and looked at him. 'Thank you,' she said. 'Thank you more than I can ever say.' She stared back at the mirror, the mirror that was now her friend. Gently she touched her face, her own face, again. Then she held out her hand to him. 'You've given me a new life. Now I can leave. You've given me a second chance. I'll never be able to thank you.'

He looked away; maybe she'd embarrassed him. But he turned back quickly and smiled. 'Are you prepared for a new life?'

She nodded, proudly. 'I've got it all planned. Even a new name.'

He raised his eyebrows. 'Galatea?' he asked.

It was her turn to smile, and she shook her head. 'Jahne,' she said. 'I've always hated "Mary," but I was afraid to be plain Jane before. Now it will be J-A-H-N-E. Not plain at all.'

'So, Jahne Moran . . .'

She shook her head again. 'Not Moran,' she said. 'I'd prefer a new name. But with the same initial. I'd like to use "Moore." I mean . . .' She blushed. '. . . if it's all right with you.'

'I'd be delighted. Truly. Quite a compliment.'

175

'Something else, Dr. Moore.' She paused. 'Could I write to you? And Raoul? I mean just occasionally. I know how busy you are. You wouldn't have to write back.'

'I'd be delighted. And I *would* write back.' The little man smiled.

Jahne stood up. She found it was harder to say goodbye than she'd expected. She had a lot of feeling for this artist, this healer, this good doctor.

'I'm going to make one last visit to Raoul.'

'He'll appreciate that.'

'I hope that he recognizes me without the bandage.'

'He's an artist. He can see deeply. He'll know you. But no one else will.'

'Are you sure? Certain?'

'Mary Jane, you look twenty-four and magnificent. You have a flat stomach, thin legs, high breasts, and a perfect face. Not to mention Mai Von Trilling's nose. Who is going to recognize you?'

'No one,' she agreed, and smiled.

'M.J., M.J.,' Raoul yelled as he saw her from a distance moving through the ward. They were special friends. He drew her wonderful pictures, and she brought him little treats. She would miss him very much. His speech had improved a lot since she'd started working with him. As she got closer to him his face changed. The sparkle left his brown eyes, the smile slipped from the wreck of his mouth.

'*Buenos dias*, Raoul,' she said. 'What's the matter?' For a moment, her stomach knotted. Perhaps she wasn't what she thought. Maybe he was disappointed with her looks.

'What is it, Raoul?'

'Did the doctor do this to you?' the boy asked. It was still difficult to understand him, but she had learned to. Now she nodded. Oh, God. Maybe Brewster had lied to her. Perhaps she didn't look as good as she thought. Raoul turned away.

'What is it?'

'You'll go now.'

'How do you know?'

'Because now you are so beautiful,' he said, and tears welled up in his eyes.

'Oh, Raoul,' she breathed, and hugged him.

Mary Jane waited, listening as the phone up in Albany rang.

Finally, Mr. Slater picked it up. 'Mr. Slater, this is Mary Jane Moran.'

'I'm sorry, Miss Moran, I've been meaning to call you. But there has been no progress on the probate. I was thinking perhaps that we could simply probate your father as the heir and get you both executor and power of attorney. That would . . .'

'Mr. Slater,' Mary Jane interrupted, 'I have a proposal for you. When the will is finally probated and the farm is sold, how much do you think it'll be worth?'

'Well, the market isn't good, but perhaps forty or fifty thousand dollars. Maybe less.'

'Would you be prepared to take the estate in lieu of fees, and simply send me a cheque for ten thousand?'

She listened for a moment to the silence at the end of the line. Greed fighting with morality? 'Well, that's quite irregular, and there is no telling when this might be settled and the farm sold. . . .'

'I know. That's why I'm willing to take so little. Is it a risk that you are willing to take?' She knew she had him hooked; she could tell by the tightness in his voice. All these small-town lawyers were alike. Now that it was in his interest to do so, he'd have the whole business cleared up in a week. Still, she needed the money now, to finance her new life. She held her breath.

'Well, I think I could see my way clear to do that.'

Yes! 'One more thing, Mr. Slater. I also need you to do a legal name change for me. It's important for my career.'

'That's no problem, as long as you're unmarried. I'll need your birth certificate and a few other documents, though.'

'I have them, and I'll get them in the mail to you today, but I expect my cheque in today's mail as well.'

'No problem,' he told her.

And now there wasn't any.

Jahne walked up First Avenue, the sunshine glinting off her glossy hair, her stride long, a tilt to her pelvis that ensured an alluring twitch to her walk. I'll have to practise this, she thought. She might not have been born sexy or beautiful, but she *was* an actress, and she'd been watching the Bethanies of the world for half a lifetime. She might not *know* beautiful, but she could *play* beautiful, and now her old frame and face wouldn't make the portrayal laughable.

She stopped at the bank machine at Sixty-fourth Street, pulled out her card, and got on the short line of people already impatiently waiting. A plump, youngish man was about to pull out his wallet as she joined the line behind him. He stopped, his hand poised on his back pocket, and looked at her. Just looked. Then, 'Please,' he said, and indicated with his other hand that she should move ahead of him.

'Oh, no. That's all right.'

'Please,' he said again, and then coloured to his receding hairline.

She glided ahead of him, accepting the tribute due to the lovely from the unlovely. She inserted her card and punched in her code, asking for her balance. Green numerals appeared on the screen: $694.18. She withdrew twenty dollars, then collected her card.

'Thanks,' she said to the plump guy.

'Thank *you*,' he breathed. She twitched by him, playing it, and walked up a block to Liberty Travel. The place was empty, just a single reservation agent at a middle desk. The agent was blonde and pretty in an obvious, big-hair way. Jahne walked up to her.

'Can I help you?' the woman asked, and gave her the head-to-toe once-over that attractive females reserve for the competition.

'Yes, please. My name is Jahne Moore: That's Jahne with an "h" in the middle and an "e" at the end of Moore. And I'd like a one-way ticket to L.A.'

Discovery

When love and skill work together, expect a masterpiece.
John Ruskin

In Hollywood 'breakfast' means maybe we'll do business, 'lunch' means yes, and 'dinner' means we're in bed.
Richard Rouilard

1

By now, unless you have spent the last two years as a hostage in some hostile third-world country, you know why three women as disparate as Lila, Sharleen, and Jahne came together. But even you, hip Reader, don't know how.

Remember that I told you it was all because of a lipstick? An oversimplification, perhaps, but still the truth. It was, more accurately, an argument over a lipstick that set the wheels in motion.

For what seemed like a thousand years (but was really only a few decades), Hyram Flanders had to take back seat to his mother, Monica. Monica was the queen of cosmetics, the chairman of the board of Flanders Cosmetics Inc., and Hyram's boss as well as his mother. No wonder Hyram hated strong women.

Since he had taken over – at last – as president and CEO, Hyram had been searching. Not, as his mother had, for a new beauty product. After all, he knew all the crap they sold was basically the same. He was searching for a way to cut the advertising budget. Because beauty is sold through advertising, and if he could keep selling current volumes but cut the astronomical ad budget, he'd be a hero to everyone.

Well, to everyone but his mother. Monica said no to every proposal to cut advertising spending. It was as if she, too, believed in the ads, the way the consumer did. And Hyram had watched as the cost-of-sale grew and grew, while the market segmented into more and more pieces. Flanders carried twenty-three separate lines to appeal to the young, the very young, the not-quite-so-young, the middle-aged who didn't perceive themselves as such, the middle-aged who did. . . . Well, the list was endless.

It was Hyram who first talked to Les Merchant, head of the Network, about sponsoring a show that would appeal to multigenerational women viewers. TV, unlike the movies, targets female audiences. Hyram and his advertising-agency rep, Brian O'Malley of Banion O'Malley, played with the idea. And Les Merchant, panicked at the Network's dwindling Nielsens, took the idea up with Sy Ortis, one of the hottest agents and packagers in Hollywood. Sy in turn reluctantly brought it to Marty DiGennaro, the director who could do no wrong (and who also never did TV).

Well, Reader, you certainly aren't surprised to hear that most, if not all, of what is broadcast on TV is spawned to sell you something. Perhaps you aren't old enough to remember the early days, when television-set manufacturers sponsored programmes simply so there would be something to watch? Or after that, when shows were called by their sponsor's name? The Campbell's Soup Hour? The Hallmark Hall of Fame?

It still happens. It's just a little less obvious. Or sometimes more so. Plugs, endorsements, 'infomercials,' and all the rest. So, when Monica Flanders told Hyram, her son, that it was impossible to sell more than one consumer sector at a time, Hyram was convinced he had to find a way to do it. 'Don't waste my time,' his mother sniffed. 'No woman will wear the same lipstick as her mother.'

Which brings us to Sy Ortis. It is the agents who run Hollywood today. Agents control the stars, and put them together with the directors and screenwriters (also clients of the agents) in 'packages' that they try to sell to the studios. Agents with a powerful stable of stars are the most envied, sought-after, and hated people in L.A. And among all the agents, Sy Ortis was the most envied, sought after and hated.

Sy Ortis stretched his little body, his feet lifted off the floor, his back arched against the black leather of the swivel chair that, with its eleven identical brothers, surrounded the electric-blue lacquer conference table. He turned from the glossy photographs laid on its shiny surface and the anxious faces that watched him. He stood up, walked to the window that overlooked La Cienega Boulevard, and sighed. Christ, he was sick of incompetent assholes! And it wasn't as if Weinberg and Glick didn't know better. They were one of the two best casting agencies in L.A. He turned to Milton Glick.

'Let me explain it again, shmuck,' he said to Glick. He spoke slowly, his high-pitched voice almost a whine. 'Marty is a genius. And Marty wants three blank slates. New pennies. Fresh meat. Don't show me these twenty-six-year-old twats who've been selling it up and down Hollywood Boulevard for the last decade. Marty wants new. And what *Marty* wants, *I* want.'

Glick licked his thin lips and nodded nervously, running his fingers through his equally thin hair, obviously replanted with even little tufts of curls that were plugged into his scalp. Sy turned away, not from any delicacy over Milton's discomfort, but, rather, at a queasiness that had always made his stomach reactive. Jesus, where did those hair plugs come from? he wondered. Milt's back? His armpits? His pubic hair? Why didn't the guy cover himself with a hat, so decent people didn't need to puke when they looked at him?

The room was silent. All of the young, trendy California go-go staffers looked down at their laps. As if, Sy thought, they had the answer in their crotches instead of their heads. Then Milton cleared his throat. 'I think we can do it, Sy.'

'Not if this shit is any indication,' Sy snapped, and swept his arm across the table, dumping several dozen perfect, smiling, beautiful eight-by-ten faces onto the floor, decimating as many hopes with the gesture. None of the trendies moved.

Sy Ortis was, arguably, the most powerful agent in Hollywood, and one of the five most powerful men in the Industry. He'd scrabbled up the heap, he'd worked like an animal, he'd bled, and he'd performed bloodlettings. Most people in Hollywood would do anything he asked, just as a favour, gratis. And now he sat here in front of a bunch of morons he was paying to help him and got *nada*.

'Look,' he said again slowly, as if each of them was mildly brain damaged. 'Marty DiGennaro has never done television before. This is going to be the biggest show, the biggest trend since spandex. He's creating something totally new. He calls it a "content-free show." And the network has given him carte blanche. *Carte blanche, for chrissakes!*' His face was red, his voice strangled. He'd negotiated the deal between DiGennaro and the network, and it was unbelievable, unprecedented. But Marty had insisted on total secrecy, so – irritatingly – nobody could admire Sy's handiwork. No one ever really appreciated what he did. They called him 'the most powerful man behind the scenes,' and with secretive, paranoid clients like Marty, he'd had to stay there.

Sy now swept the worried faces quickly with a frustrated look. He'd try again. 'So we're trying to do a *new* thing. Get it? That means no sitcom hacks, no refugees from Budweiser commercials, no rat-burgers from slice-and-dice flicks. This is Marty DiGennaro we're talking about, not Roger Corman. Marty wants fresh blood, and you've been given the exclusive to get it for him. Do you understand what that means?'

The little man was breathing hard, his voice rising almost to a scream. Christ, he couldn't breathe! He reached into his jacket pocket and pulled out his inhaler, thrust it up against his mouth, and sucked on it like a greedy infant at the breast. Not another asthma attack! *Madre de Dios*, it's the pressure, he told himself. And the smog in the Valley today didn't help. City of Angels, my butt hole! he thought angrily. With this air quality, it was only the Angel of Death who worked here. But, this was where the business was, and Sy hadn't become the most influential agent in the Industry by breathing calmly in Scottsdale, Arizona.

It wasn't just Milton and the shitty job he'd done, Sy admitted to himself as he gasped for breath. It was this whole new Marty DiGennaro project. Marty was, maybe, the most prestigious big-money film director in Hollywood; he was class *and* cash, and then he gets this crazy yen to stoop to television. *Television*. The ghetto of the entertainment industry, with the Kmart of plots and the Walmart of actors. But Marty wanted TV. And with this nutsy idea: an MTV-type, hip, freewheeling show about three girls hitchhiking across America. What the fuck? Marty was a genius, and Sy's most powerful client, but the thing made Sy nervous. 'I want freedom from plots,' Marty had said. 'I'm so goddamn sick of telling a story. Let's forget stories. Let's do something new.'

New! NEW! Christ, why not just say 'dangerous,' 'risky,' 'a moneyloser.' If DiGennaro got his kicks from losing big at the high rollers' table in Vegas, that was all right with Sy; why the fuck did Marty have to pull this gambling shit with his career? Talent! Go figure. Talent loved to fuck with your head.

Then, to make things worse, Marty wouldn't use any of Sy's clients. An entire stable of stars, all of them willing to stoop to TV just to work with Marty, and Marty says no. A whole show to be cast, deals to be made, favours to extend, percentages to collect, and Marty says, 'Bring me someone new.' Sy was ready to suck his own dick over this one. So here he was, in the offices of Weinberg and Glick, pulling on his inhaler and looking for an unopened can. 'Cause if he didn't cast it soon, Marty would go to the outside, and Sy would lose control of the casting. Just the thought of losing control made Sy suck a little harder.

At last, his breathing calmed. The frozen trendies still sat there, useless as tits on a monitor. He turned to Milton, still nervously licking his lips. 'Milton,' he said. 'These girls are gonna be big. Enormous. They'll be on the cover of *TV Guide* and *People*, they'll be on *Tonight* and *Arsenio* and *Letterman*. They'll host *Saturday Night Live*. And that's just for starters. If everything goes right, they're going to be a fuckin' industry. So I want them new and fresh. No nudes in *Penthouse*. No past jobs as weather girls in Kankakee. No porno, no agents, no bounced cheques, no husbands, no *problems*. New and clean, so we can tie 'em up nice and neat. So, Milt, don't insult my intelligence. Don't piss up my back and tell me I'm sweating. Get me some new faces.'

Sy turned and walked to the door, then spun on his neat little foot at the doorway. 'Because, if *you* don't, Milt, Paul Grasso *will*.' Sy saw Milt wince at the mention of his ex-partner, now his bitter enemy. 'You've got till Tuesday.'

'I'll do it,' Milt assured him, but Sy was already down the hall.

If Sy Ortis had been the bully of the meeting at Glick's casting office, he knew he was about to be bullied at his next one. But in a lineup that included Les Merchant, the head of the Network; Brian O'Malley of Banion O'Malley, the largest advertising firm in the world; and Monica Flanders and her son, Hyram, he knew he was the smallest fish. He shrugged. One could do worse than be a guppy in *that* pond. There would not be a person in the room whose net worth was under fifty million dollars.

And there was nothing Sy respected as much as money. Thinking of the raw power of – say – fifty million dollars made him almost weak in the knees. Someday he'd have a net worth of that, and then he wouldn't take shit from anyone. Not that he had to take much now.

Sy, as usual, was on time, but, surprisingly, so was everyone else. The difference between big business and show business: big business had the discipline to keep to schedule. Sy smiled as he shook hands around the table. No one smiled back. Another difference.

The meeting was being held at the L.A. conference room of Banion O'Malley, and Sy was there to represent his client Marty DiGennaro. Both had decided it was best this way. After all, the deal had been consummated, but it was best to keep both the sponsor and the Network happy for as long as possible. Anyway, today the pressure was off Sy. It was Merchant's and O'Malley's dicks on the table. Sy almost smiled at the thought as he took his seat.

'Well, gentlemen. And Madame Flanders, of course,' Brian O'Malley began. He was a big Irishman, his bulk carefully disguised by a Savile Row suit, his chins almost camouflaged by the Turnbull and Asser shirt he wore. Monica Flanders, the object of the meeting, who must be in her eighties, made a dismissive gesture. O'Malley nodded. 'I think you're going to like what you see.'

'We better,' Monica Flanders said, and looked to her son,

the president of her international cosmetics firm. He nodded. Les Merchant, a tall man with a huge head of white hair, cleared his throat. Sy had been told that today was only a formality, that Flanders Cosmetics was in, and that Hyram had sign-off power. But he could see everyone sweating, in case the old *puta* didn't approve.

'Well, you know the demographics,' O'Malley continued, and as he spoke a wall behind him lit up, as if from within, and a bar graph in glowing neon colours was projected onto it from some invisible source. 'We are looking at a more and more fragmented female market, with the largest segment the ageing baby boomers, flanked by two smaller segments of makeup-buying women: the menopausal and older, and the younger, teen-to-thirties segment.'

He turned himself to look at the chart, and as he did so, the 'menopausal and older' bar disappeared. 'Discounting the older women, who are largely either brand-loyal, limited by shrinking purchasing power, or taken out of the consumer market by disease and death, we have the lion's share in the other two segments.'

Sy noticed Monica Flanders wince when O'Malley mentioned death. Now her son spoke. 'Brian, the lion's share means everything, not the biggest piece. Anyway, we know all this.'

'Yes. But the point is that the ageing-boomer market has been lagging in its purchase of cosmetics, although their spending has increased somewhat on anti-ageing-care products. While the youth market has simply not had the purchasing power of the boomers at their age. This has spawned the need for narrow, expensive, targeted print and television campaigns, increasing per product-line cost-of-sale.'

'Brian, may I remind you that narrowly focused campaigns were something *you* sold us almost a decade ago?' Monica Flanders said.

'And for a good reason. There was no alternative. But what if I told you there was a way to reach forty or fifty million women, week by week, in both the youth and boomer markets, with a single campaign?'

Monica Flanders wrinkled up her face in impatience and disgust. 'I would say you were crazy. DAUGHTERS DON'T BUY THE SAME LIPSTICK AS THEIR MOTHERS.'

'But what if I told you they would?'

'Gentlemen, I'm an old woman, but I know my business. Brian, how many shades of lipstick does Revlon produce?' The man paused, then shrugged. 'One hundred and seventy. Their best seller is Wine With Everything. Estée does ninety-five. Their best seller is Starlit Pink, but ten years ago it was Rosewood and fifteen years ago it was Frosted Apricot. Even Chanel has to make sixty-eight colours. Because the nature of the market is fragmented. AND DAUGHTERS DON'T BUY THE SAME LIPSTICK AS THEIR MOTHERS.' Monica Flanders stood up. 'Hyram, would you call for the car?'

'Mother, wait just a moment more. Please.'

Monica looked at her balding, paunchy, sixty-two-year-old son and shrugged. Silently she sat down again.

'Mrs. Flanders, what if there was a show, a weekly television programme, that attracted a huge female audience of both young females and the ageing boomers? What if we could put together a programme whose demographics guaranteed *both* groups?'

'If wishes were horses, most people would be buried in horseshit,' she said. 'The youth market watches young people. *90210*. And the older market watches movies of the week. Or *fortysomething*. Or the fat housewife.' She shuddered at the thought of Roseanne Arnold, pulling her aristocratic shoulders together around her ears like the ends of an ermine stole.

'What if there was a show that featured young women . . .'

'Boomers wouldn't watch it,' she said flatly.

'But what if it were set in the sixties, when the boomers also were young?'

She sat, still and silent for a moment. For almost half a century, Monica Flanders had been selling beauty to American women. She had started by cooking creams in her own kitchen and now had a lock on almost a third of the market. She knew what worked, what didn't, and still had the best ear for naming new products in the business.

For the first time, Les Merchant spoke. His Network had been losing audience to cable and Fox for the last ten years. But in this project he saw a resurgence for the Network. He was ready to gamble everything on it. Still, for something of this size he needed a powerful partner. Hyram had already agreed, in principle, to sponsor the show, but Les was no fool, and he knew he needed Monica's full support. 'Monica, think of it. A quality project, with beautiful young girls. To make the older women long for their youth, and the younger ones long for beauty. Exquisite girls, irresistible girls, Monica.'

She hated to be wrong, but she hadn't gotten this rich by being stupid. She sat, silent and still, the only movement in the whole room the blink of her eyes. She sat for a minute – then two. Then three. No one spoke. Probably they didn't dare to breathe. 'It could work,' Monica acknowledged, dipping her ancient head. Despite the surgeon's art and the expert maquillage, she resembled nothing so much as a tiny painted monkey. A very powerful painted monkey. O'Malley smiled, and Les Merchant continued.

'We have an exclusive. Marty DiGennaro will direct. A million and a half budgeted for each episode. And new talent.'

'How many girls?'

'Three. They are hitchhiking cross-country.'

'I want a blonde, a brunette, and a redhead. I want exclusive three-year contracts with each for print ads. They model the new line. We won't pay more than five hundred thou for each modelling contract, but we add smoke so we can tout them as million-dollar deals. We do a new line. We include both makeup and skin care. The girls wear nothing else, on camera or off. And no hitchhiking. It's trashy. Put them on motorcycles. That's sexy. Plus, we get the male audience. We sell them the fragrances for their girlfriends at Christmas.'

'What fragrances, Mother?' Hyram asked.

'The new fragrances. Named for the three characters. What the hell are their names?'

'Cara, Crimson, and Clover,' Sy volunteered.

'Perfect.' Monica grinned.

'But, Mother! The cost! Developing and launching three new scents in a year! I never planned . . .'

'If *you* don't have the time, Hyram, *I'll* do it,' Monica snapped.

Les smiled at Brian O'Banion. 'Shall we show you some storyboards?'

'Show Hyram. I'm tired.' Once again she stood up. She began to push away from the table, her age-spotted left hand clutching her gold-topped cane. But she stopped for a moment and turned back to them. 'We have approval on the leads. No drug addicts. No whores. Clean. Get them from Canada if you have to. I understand they still have some virgins up there.'

Then she turned her Chanel-clad tiny back on the men and left the room.

2

After Jahne picked her one suitcase from the luggage carousel at LAX, she headed towards the rental-car counters. In her purse she had a little less than six thousand dollars of the money she had received from Albany. May as well get the cheapest deal I can, she thought. In New York, a car was an expensive luxury, and in her years there, she had gotten out of the habit of owning one. But she knew, here in L.A., it was a requirement. She moved towards the group of businessmen standing at the Budget counter.

'Here, let me help you with that.' A tall, grey-haired man in a blue suit and a deep tan moved to help her with her bag.

'Thank you,' she said, and she flashed the smile that she found now worked so well.

'Bob,' the executive said to his companion, ahead of them in line, 'let the lady through.'

'Oh, it's really not necessary.' She played it as Audrey Hepburn had in *Breakfast at Tiffany's* – ladylike but knowing. A woman stood in front of her, also waiting for the attention of the rental-car clerk. She was a dumpy woman, stuffed into a size-fourteen sage-green suit. It was not a good colour for her.

'Can I help you?' the man behind the counter asked Jahne.

The dumpy woman whined. '*I* was here first,' she said, and shot a look of deep dislike at Jahne.

'Yes, she was,' Jahne agreed.

Reluctantly the clerk turned to the piqued woman. 'Have you a reservation?' he asked.

'No.'

'Then I'm afraid I can't help you,' he said smugly. 'We're all out of cars except for customers with confirmed reservations.' The woman stomped away to another counter.

Then, with a smile of relief, the clerk turned back to Jahne. 'Now, how can I help *you*?' he asked her with a smile.

189

'I guess you can't,' Jahne said. 'I wanted a car, but I don't have a reservation, either.'

'What kind of car did you want?' he asked.

'The least expensive,' she admitted.

'Well, for you I just may be able to find one of our specials. How long will you need it?'

'Two weeks would be fine,' Jahne said, and despite her guilt, she flashed him another Audrey Hepburn smile.

The Star Drop Inn had only two advantages: the room was clean, and it was only $286 weekly, paid in advance. It was one of those modular buildings that looked as if it had been dropped onto the black tarmac that surrounded it. The grey-haired old woman at the front desk had told Jahne it was a no-frills kind of place, and she certainly had not been lying. Jahne's room, number 29, was ten feet by nine feet, with room for two twin beds, a built-in shelf for a nightstand between them, a hanging rack in the wall across the way, and a television riveted to a bracket that was chained to the wall. There was also a fibreglass bathroom not much bigger than an unopened coffin. But it was clean and it did have double locks on the door. It seemed to cater to transients and tourist families mostly, but there were no fights and not much noise at night. Also, she had noticed a nice-looking, long-haired blond guy that lived in Room 28. She could do worse, she supposed.

Jahne lay on one bed, the other one covered with copies of *Daily Variety*, *The Hollywood Reporter*, *Weekly Variety*, and several other trades. She sat with a pen and legal pad that she had bought for $1.29 at the Jiffy Mart on the corner; on one side of the page she listed every audition, open call, or look-see; on the other she wrote notes to herself about what they were looking for. It was odd, after all her years of reading the trades, to be focusing now on those casting notices looking for young, attractive ingenues.

It was thirsty work, and she longed for a cold soda or beer, but there wasn't even a vending machine at the Star Drop Inn. She'd walk across the hot parking lot to the convenience store in a minute. The page was almost full, although Jahne expected little from cattle calls and the like. Still, she had carefully arranged a pile of head shots and attached résumés to the back of each. Before she left New York, she had spent almost two thousand dollars of the precious Albany money on a photographer, and she had to admit he had done a brilliant job that justified every penny. Her mane of dark hair emerged from a backlit drop behind her; her face appeared perfect. Even now she stared, mesmerized by the picture. If she couldn't get in to see people, at least she could leave this calling card behind.

She turned the page of *The Hollywood Reporter*. Ratings for all the season's new television shows were listed. Quickly, she looked up *All the President's Chakras*, Neil's show. Once again, it lagged at the bottom of the long list. She sighed. She'd watched it a few times, but it was almost too awful; she could see the desperation in Neil's eyes during each close-up. It was ironic that he and Sam were the only two people she knew out here, and it was impossible to call either of them – one because he loved her, and the other because he didn't.

There was a knock at the door, and she jumped. She looked quickly to see if the chain lock was up. It was, and she went to it, grateful for the protection. She opened the door slowly. Outside, the tall, blond man from next door stood awkwardly leaning against the wall. 'Hi, I'm Pete Warren,' he told her. He held up a beer. 'Want one?'

'No thanks.' He looked like a nice kid, twenty-two or -three, with the kind of beautiful teeth you seemed to see only in California.

'Hey, no strings attached. It's just an extra beer,' he said. He handed it in through the crack and turned away. 'See ya,' he said. His shoulders were broad, and she could see his back muscles move under the T-shirt he wore.

'Thanks,' she remembered to shout at his back, then shut the door. Gratefully swigging the Coors, she wondered if Pete Warren ever would have noticed Mary Jane. Certainly not, she decided. The beer was a good omen. But being pretty and young-looking might only be enough to get a cheap car rental and a free beer. Drinking again from the bottle, she wondered if any of the casting agents and assistant producers would notice her on her rounds. She patted the head shots for luck and hoped so.

If the last two years – and all that had preceded it – had been like a nightmare, this felt like a dream. L.A. was so sunny after the darkness of New York – the beach, and the boardwalk in Venice, and the nonstop sun. But the main difference was her. She was so L.A. – with her heels on she was tall and slim and perfect, except for a few grey hairs. Just waking up felt great. Getting dressed felt great. Putting on her makeup felt great. Aside from the occasional itching of her scars, she felt wonderful. Hopeful.

And that, really, was the difference. In L.A. there was hope.

Jahne established a kind of pattern to her days. Each morning, she drove to the track at the junior high school and ran three miles, then came back to the Star Drop, showered, threw a banana, skim milk, and brewer's yeast into her blender, and drank it while she applied her makeup. Then she dressed and spent the morning following up every lead she could. At one o'clock, she'd either go to Dim Sum and eat the lunch special at the outdoor café, or she'd stop at Chin Chin and have their shredded chicken salad. And in both places she only had to wait ten minutes or less. Men would come to sit beside her. They'd make her offers: offers to buy her lunch, to take her out to dinner, to introduce her to their agent. They'd offer to show her Malibu Colony or their condo or a part of their anatomy. In a way, their offers shocked her. Not because she was a prude. It was simply getting used to all the attention. Although she had always presumed that her looks had affected her life, she knew now that they had ruined it. When you were young and beautiful, everything was easy. For the next ten years, at least, she would never have to eat another meal or have another drink alone.

All she had to do was do her face, find a crowd, sit down, pick out a man, and stare at him till she caught his eye. With eight out of ten, she noticed, all it took was a smile to get them to come to her. She perfected a look: a sort of pouty 'You-know-what-I'm-thinking-about' expression that hooked them like trout. Then there was one out of the ten who needed a serious look, not a smile. She started to be able to pick them out. They usually wore black.

There was the one man in ten who didn't respond at all, but she figured there had to be a few gays and honest married men in the crowd. She didn't take it personally. After all, after years of starvation, L.A. was a feast!

It all got her hormones running. How long had it been since she'd been with Sam? Since any man had touched her?

But even though she was horny and she looked twenty-four, she was thirty-six, and the lines that men threw at her almost made her laugh out loud. They were 'producers' or 'good friends of producers' or 'working for an independent production company' at some undisclosed job. No one was in insurance or data processing or banking. Everyone was 'in the Industry.' She talked and laughed and flirted. She considered it good rehearsal time, but she made no friends and she didn't give out her number. She could tell that none were for real. And it was too much of a strain to act the part of a beauty by day and also in the evening. At night, she needed to recuperate.

Pete Warren, her neighbour at the Star Drop, continued to stop by. He was twenty-four, from Encino, and working as an assistant cameraman. His dad was a projectionist at one of the studios and had gotten him his union card. He was sweet – very Californian and very, *very* young. He came over most evenings, and they drank a beer or two and watched some TV. He was only at the Star Drop until the sublet he had arranged while he was off on location ended.

It was easy to be with him, but it was odd. Pete presumed she was his age, and she did not tell him otherwise. But she had forgotten the differences between twenty-four and thirty-six, between New York and California mentality. He struck her as a child, although a sexy one.

It was Pete who told her about the Melrose Playhouse – a hip theatre group in West Hollywood. His sister was a lighting designer there and could get Jahne an audition, if she wanted one. She did.

So she spent her days making the rounds, dropping off her head shot, begging to be seen. She actually got an appointment for an audition at the Melrose Playhouse, and a callback from one cattle call she'd shown up for. She wound up as background in some beer ad they shot on Venice Beach, but it was something. It encouraged her.

So did Pete. He became her friend. At the end of the day, she looked forward to telling him her adventures. He was optimistic and supportive. He was sure she'd get a part eventually. And he didn't hustle her or crowd her like all the other men who hit on her daily.

Finally, Pete tried to kiss her, and she pushed him away. He didn't come back the next night, and she was sorry. His absence made her realize that she was lonely, and that his strong arms and big hands curled around the beer bottle had been a pleasure to look at. All of him was a pleasure to look at. When he knocked on her door two nights later, she gave him her best smile.

'How ya doin'?' Pete asked.

'Fine,' she told him.

And he walked in, handing her the obligatory bottle of Coors. He sat on the edge of her spare bed. 'Jahne, can I ask you something?'

She nodded.

'Don't you want to sleep with me?' he asked.

She smiled. 'I don't think so,' she said.

'You're not goin' out with anyone else. Don't you like me?'

'Sure I do, Pete. But not enough to sleep with you.'

'How much more would you have to like me?' he asked. He wasn't belligerent. He didn't sound angry. Just confused.

She laughed. 'I'm not sure.'

'Jahne, I really like you. I thought maybe you'd like to move into my place when I go back there.'

'Oh, Pete, I hardly know you. And you don't know me.'

'Well, it would be a good way to get to know each other.' He stood up and gently put his long arm around her shoulder. He bent down and kissed her. She felt a pulse of excitement. His arm felt so good, so warm, across her back. It had been so long. He kissed her again, and even though she knew she shouldn't, she kissed him back. It was irresistible. His flesh under his T-shirt felt warm and smelled young. For a moment, but only for a moment, she thought of Sam. Then she let Pete push her back gently onto the other twin bed.

3

After more than a week of sulking and licking her wounds in silence, Lila was speaking to Robbie again. Well, arguing and screaming more than speaking, but at least they were communicating.

'I've never been so humiliated in my whole life!' Lila was yelling.

'Oh, *sure* you have,' Robbie said. 'You just don't want to remember when.'

Lila narrowed her gorgeous eyes. 'I could *kill* you! You act so important, so sure. As if you know people. As if you can open doors. Yeah! George *Getz*! Or the *exit* door at Ara Sagarian's! That's all you can do for me.'

'Lila, calm down!' Robbie snapped. 'How was *I* supposed to know that Ara was going to call Theresa? *I* didn't tell you to lie. That was what screwed it up. He might have taken you on if you hadn't lied to him. *My* advice was good.'

'Don't you blame me for this! It was *your* plan, and a really stupid one. My mother is still Ara's pet. You're a fat, faggot has-been. No. A never-was. You just hang on to anyone who *was* famous. Like my mother.' A terrible thought occurred to her. 'I know you still see her.' Lila stopped yelling for a moment. Perhaps Robbie was scheming with the Puppet Mistress! Maybe they both set her up. For a moment Lila felt sick and dizzy. She clutched the edge of the mirrored coffee table in front of her.

'Lila, I see your mother because she is my friend, and she needs me. You need me, too.'

'I don't need anyone,' Lila spat.

Ken walked into the living room, a pained expression on his face. 'I wish you'd stop it, the two of you.'

'Look, I have a new idea,' Robbie said, ignoring Ken. 'We forget agents for a minute. We focus on getting you a part. The right part. Then you'll have your pick of agents. Even Ara Sagarian.'

'I'd ice-pick Ara,' Lila said. 'But someday I'll see him crawl.'

'Hey, maybe by next week. He can hardly walk now,' Ken joked.

Robbie shrugged, as if Ken were a bothersome insect. 'I want Lila to start her acting career in television. I'm sure we can find her a little *something*.' Robbie turned to his lover. 'Tell her to listen to me, Ken. That's where she'll get the most exposure, but *she* says stars don't do TV. Like she's a star!'

Lila gave Robbie a murderous look. To defuse the bomb, Ken broke in. 'Why not, Lila? If Marty DiGennaro would consider doing television, so should you.' Lila and Robbie looked at Ken in silence.

'Marty DiGennaro doesn't do television,' Lila said.

'He does now,' Ken said smugly.

'Marty DiGennaro would do television?' Robbie asked.

Ken nodded.

'How do *you* know?' Lila demanded.

'Don't you keep up on the business end of the business?' Ken asked. 'In an interview in *Variety* last month, he said he sees television as a whole new medium. The way he envisions it, television since the cable revolution is more exciting than film, with more creative possibilities.'

'Why would one of the top movie directors consider doing TV?' Lila asked.

'Search me. But he is. I know it for a fact. He's talking to a network, and Marty DiGennaro has his fingers on the pulse of the Industry.'

'God, what I wouldn't give to work with him,' Lila breathed.

'Does he actually have a show lined up? Scripts? Actors?' Robbie asked.

'Must have. They are lining up technicians. He asked me.'

'Marty DiGennaro asked *you* to work on his TV show?'

'Well, not *him*. Dino, his AD, asked me.'

'I'm impressed.' Robbie whistled. He looked at Lila, made an I-told-you-so moue, then lay back down on the sofa, pulling the broad brim of his hat down over his eyes. 'I rest my case,' he said. 'For a fat faggot has-been without connections, I guess I have a few tricks left.' He lay there in silence. Then he had pity on her. 'Maybe we could get you in front of him. Through Paulie Grasso. Or maybe through Dino or another of those Italians of his. And I know a typist over at Zeller, Mossbacher. They handle DiGennaro's legal affairs. Maybe we could check out his contract. And I once had a fling with a guy over at Ortis' office. He's Marty's agent. Maybe I could confirm this with him.'

Lila didn't say anything for a moment. What the fuck. And maybe television might work. It all depended on how she was positioned on it, but maybe.

'Christ, what I wouldn't give to work with him,' Lila repeated.

'What's the show?' Robbie asked.

'Oh, it's all top secret. Something about three girls travelling across the States together.'

'*Three* girls?' Lila asked, and for no reason at all she thought of Skinny and Candy.

Paul Grasso wearily looked up from the restaurant table, across at the still-talking director. Yahta, yahta, yahta. Christ, he wished it was back in the days of silent movies, just so he didn't have to listen to this whiny little Jewboy. Well, he guessed, even then the people *in* the Industry talked. It was only that the *audience* didn't have to hear them. Sure. He'd be willing to pay not to hear this

196

strunz. Paul sighed. No such luck. He was paid to listen to A. Joel Grossman. Well, he might be paid.

'We need someone absolutely fresh. *Totally* exciting. But not in the expected way. There's a look – a vision, almost – that I'm trying to capture, an innocence that's *so* knowing, a purity that *understands* defilement . . .'

Paul tuned him out again. Yahta, yahta, yahta. Like everyone else, this A. Joel Grossman wanted fresh, beautiful cooze to sell his product. Why didn't he just say so? And why was his name A. Joel? And why did the guy talk in *italics*, for chrissake? With all that *emphasis* he sounded like a fuckin' faggot. All these fuckin' stupid commercial directors were the same: couldn't just *do* the fuckin' job, had to act as if it was art, as if the shit that sold Buicks and shave cream and, in this case, denim jeans was actually important. Christ, didn't they know that no one gave a rat's ass? The biggest acting jobs in Hollywood were those performed by directors like this one. Paul couldn't believe he was reduced to buying the little fuck an overstuffed sandwich here at Geller's deli.

Christ, the whole Industry was overrun with annoying little Jews. Spielberg, Ovitz, Zeller, Ortman. April Irons, and Paul's own ex-partner, Milton Glick. You couldn't buy a property, draw up a contract, cast a movie, or sell the distribution without a Jew involved.

Okay, he was bitter. He'd admit it. But just because he was bitter didn't mean that he wasn't also right. There had been a time, back when he was working with Milton, when he had been an insider. When they were riding high, and when casting the next big picture seemed to matter. But that was long ago. Milt and his prissy Jewboy ways. Nervous in the service about the gambling, as if I'd ever welshed on a bet. Paul Grasso's marker was still good all over town. But he pushed me out. Christ, then Milton and all of them just closed ranks and hung together. Clannish.

Well, Milt was a pussy, and this little director was a pussy. They were all pussies. He didn't know a single Jew who could take a punch, except maybe Jimmy Caan, and he was so weird, maybe he didn't count. Paul looked across at the kid director, who was still talking. Yahta, yahta, yahta.

'. . . and the campaign is *based* on that. The essential female. We need to cast this with great sensitivity. There must be a sense of *responsibility* here. The *image*, if you will, is more than an image. It bespeaks . . .'

Holy shit. Did the guy actually say 'bespeaks'? What the fuck was with him? Thinks he's the fuckin' Sir Ralph Richardson of commercials, or what? No, probably wants to be the next Spielberg. Wake up and smell the coffee, jerkoff. There was room for one skinny, nerdy Jewish director of TV commercials to become a giant, but the job's been filled. Go back to Jamaica Estates or wherever the fuck back east you came from. In Grasso's opinion, these guys were always bragging about their contribution to the arts and sciences. Hype and bullshit. Aside from agents and lawyers, the twin scourges of the earth, he felt their biggest hit was pastrami. He bit into his deli sandwich appreciatively.

'. . . subliminally. Because this is really more than just a commercial. We're saying a lot not only about the *product*, but about *ourselves*.'

Paul stuffed the last bit of his pastrami sandwich into his mouth and nodded. Let the jerkoff ramble. But the jerkoff had stopped. He was looking at Paul. Now, *now*, when his mouth was crammed with pastrami and rye, the miserable little Hebe motherfucker wanted a response. Paul gulped. Christ, the hard edge of the rye crust was going to choke him. His eyes watered.

The guy reached out and patted his hand. Paul managed to swallow down the mouthful. Jesus, *was* this kid an actual faggot or something? Paul needed the work, but not that badly.

'Thank you for sharing my vision,' the kid said. 'I can really appreciate an honest reaction like that. And it means a lot that you can still cry over something that to others may seem jejune.'

What the fuck was the little bastard talking about? Holy shit! Did he think I, Paul Grasso, was crying over his conception of a designer-jeans commercial? Paul looked around the restaurant. Who else was going to witness his humiliation? It was too much. Paul took a deep breath and stood up. If he hadn't blown every available dime he had on his last junket, he would tell this A. Joel to fuck himself. That was absolutely his last visit to Vegas. Absolutely.

He tried to smile at the kid director. 'I think I know what you're looking for. Let's go look at the girl,' he managed to choke.

Paul Grasso looked over the pink message slips scattered across his desk. Mostly creditors, and an ominous message from Benny Eggs, a 'creditor' who broke legs. Nothing else, except for this one from Robbie Lymon. Paul wondered what that old queen wanted.

198

A favour, no doubt. A. Joel cleared his throat, restive. Paul turned to the overweight woman in toeless high-heeled sandals who stood at the door of the Grasso and Associates conference room, tapping her foot nervously. 'She's in the can,' she explained to Paul, gestured towards the bathroom, and then shrugged. Paul looked down and noticed the chipped magenta nail polish on her big toe peeking out of the shoe, and the horny, yellowish toenail, complete with a visible sliver of dirt. He shuddered. What a pig. But he'd seen the girl, and she was a honey. Maybe the solution to young Eisenstein's problems. He looked back at A. Joel, kid director.

'I think you'll like her. She's got something undefinable.' Yeah, the best ass and the flattest stomach in Los Angeles. Plus a perky pair of tatas. Face was okay. Only so-so, really. Pretty enough to get her voted prom queen, but less than average out here. Still, for a jeans commercial with no closeups, it was ass that sold. And for this soft-core crap that was passing as an ad, she'd be perfect. Too bad the little bitch was only fifteen. Or maybe less. The mother had the girl's birth certificate, but Paul had been through *that* shit before. When they were underage, it made all kinds of problems with the L.A. County Bureau of Child Welfare. Try to arrange a tutor for a two-day shoot! Still, for this ad it was probably worth it. Anything to get the kid director, this A. Joel Whatever, off his back. Also get Benny Eggs off his back. And put a few bucks in the bank.

The girl walked in. She hung her head, but despite the lousy posture Paul couldn't help but again notice the ass, the long legs, the nice pair of jugs. She had to have an eighteen-inch waist – nineteen tops. And this kid wasn't fifteen yet. He prayed she was already fourteen. He shot a look at his client. At last, the little cocksucker was silent, staring. Grasso smiled to himself. Well, this would make a nice little fee. Yeah, he hadn't lost his touch yet.

'Could I have a right profile?' he asked, and the girl slowly turned. Her hair, a medium brown, obscured her face, but the angle revealed the soft curve of her buttocks, emphasized by the taut stomach.

'So, Adrienne, could you look this way?' The girl said nothing, but she raised her head.

'Mrs. Godowski, I'm going to have to ask Adrienne to take off her shirt and slacks.' He'd informed the mother from the get-go.

'She'll do anything you need her to, Mr. Grasso,' the woman told him in liquid tones, then turned to the girl. 'You heard the man, Adrienne.'

Very nice, very maternal, Mrs. Godowski, Grasso thought, while Adrienne began unbuttoning her blouse. It was a cheap blue thing with a line of limp ruffles down the front. She shrugged out of it, letting it fall to the ground in a heap. She was wearing a red lace bra, an underwired job that served her tits up like grapefruits on a platter. Grasso eyed his client. So far, so good.

The girl kicked off her shoes with a practised movement and put her hands up to the zipper of her tight white jeans. She pulled, and the only sound in the room was the metal noise of her fly opening. She began, ungracefully, to struggle out of them, but the zipper must have caught her underpants, for they slid off as well. From the waist down she was bare. There in the conference room, leaning with one hand against a file cabinet, she seemed unfazed, uncaring, revealed: her perfect flesh rose up in a white fountain from the jeans crumpled at her feet. There wasn't a mar or a ripple to spoil the perfection of her ass, her thighs, her belly.

This was what size fourteens in Tenafly, New Jersey, dreamed of looking like. *This* is what sold jeans. The girl looked blankly at the two men. Paul Grasso turned expectantly to his client, the kid director.

'She's too old,' A. Joel Grossman said.

4

Sharleen juggled the plates along one arm down to her palm and grabbed the coffeepot with the other hand. She rushed from behind the counter towards the three police officers in the corner booth, her heart pounding.

'Okay, boys,' she said with forced cheerfulness, 'pot roast and mashed for you, chili and onions here, and chicken-fried steak for the good-lookin' one in the corner.' She placed the dishes all around and poured coffee, trying not to make eye contact. The men began to rearrange their mismatched orders without correcting her. Sharleen hoped that Jake didn't notice she got the orders wrong again. North, south, east, west. Well, she'd never been good with maps. 'Sorry, fellas,' she said quietly. Police just frightened her. She was as rattled as a china cup in a buckboard.

The young officer in the corner was staring at her, she realized. She ducked her head back down, but she knew he could still see her face.

'Haven't I seen you someplace before?' he asked. She kept her hand from shaking and filled the last cup with coffee, then tried quickly to clean up the spill she made.

'You sure have, every time you been in here,' she joked.

'No, I mean before, outside of here.'

Sharleen felt her face go white, but dared herself to raise her eyes and look directly at him. Now she needed to spread a little grease to move him right along to another idea. 'No, handsome, I don't think so. I'd remember *you*.'

The other man at the table whistled and one stomped his feet. She turned to go, but the cop reached over and held her round her wrist. 'Yeah, I seen you before. You're wanted by every police officer in the state.'

Sharleen felt her hand turn cold. She tugged it away. 'Me?' she said weakly. 'I think you're thinking of someone else.'

'No, I'm not, honey, I'm thinking of you. All the time. And so are all the other cops in Bakersfield. We all want you.' The other two officers began to laugh.

'He's in love, honey,' the fat one told her. 'Can't you tell?'

Sharleen let her breath out. 'Well, then, fellas, that makes two of us. I'm in love with my husband,' she said, and walked through the swinging doors to the back.

She leaned against the greasy wall inside the overheated kitchen. Carlos, the cook, looked up at her, raised his eyebrows, then looked away. She went to the sink, poured a glass of water, and drank it in a gulp. Get a hold of yourself, she thought. Forget about Lamson. It was already a long time ago and far away.

She walked back through the swinging door, pushing her damp hair up off her neck, and picked up a napkin at the counter to wipe away the perspiration, unaware that her upraised arms lifted her breasts and pushed them invitingly forward. As she lowered her arms, she noticed a man at the end of the counter staring at her. Oh, Lord, no more today, she prayed. Why am I such a target for trouble? She sighed, dropped her eyes, picked up a menu, and walked towards him.

She saw that he watched her as she approached. But he's not like the other guys that come in here, she thought. This one was fifty, plain, with little eyes behind thick glasses, but he didn't look used up the way most men his age did. Thinning hair combed straight back, deep, cultivated tan, a white linen jacket crumpled loosely over a grey silk T-shirt, white pants. He wasn't a businessman, and he wasn't a salesman. Sharleen couldn't describe *what* the guy was, but she knew he was not your run-of-the-mill Bakersfield truck driver.

'Menu?'

'No thanks, I know what I want. Two scrambled eggs, no toast, no potatoes, sliced tomatoes on the side, black coffee.'

'Sure,' she said, and began to walk back to the grill to give Carlos the order. But she'd already forgotten it. She turned back to the guy quickly and noticed his eyes still on her. 'How did you say you wanted your eggs?' she asked. With a tremor, she heard Jake sigh from behind the register. Jesus, in your mercy, make me a better waitress, she prayed.

When Sharleen had placed the food down before the new guy, she turned to filling the sugar pourers now that the diner had started to quiet down. The guy ate quickly and called out for more coffee. While she was pouring it, she noticed him reading the nameplate on her breast.

'Sharleen,' he said. 'Pretty name. You an actress, Sharleen?'

Sharleen half-turned to him. She laughed. 'Actress? Oh, no, not me. I'm just a waitress.' She put the coffeepot down on the counter and went on. 'But I've worked in the rodeo once. Went all over the South—west. That's kinda like show business, isn't it?'

The guy laughed, but not unkindly. 'Yes, I suppose it is. But I meant, have you ever acted on the stage?'

She laughed again and turned back towards the kitchen. 'Nope.'

'Never made a commercial, been in a movie?'

'Dream on.'

'Never even had your picture in a magazine?'

'Once some guy at the rodeo took my picture, but he never sent me one. I never done nothing like that.'

'Would you like to, Sharleen?'

Sharleen paused. She didn't want Jake to get on her again about how she talked too much and didn't pay enough attention to her job, but this guy was interesting. He was different. He talked different. Soft, like he was a money person. But best to be careful.

'What are you doing in Bakersfield?' she asked him. 'Out looking for actresses?'

'As a matter of fact, I was, but I had car trouble. I'm waiting for a tow.' He turned, and she saw a white Mercedes convertible, one that Dean would give ten bucks just to touch, parked out in the dust. 'But this must be your lucky day.'

'Yeah?'

'My name is Milton Glick, and I'm trying to cast actresses for a TV show. I think you might be right for a part. Interested?' He waited for it to sink in.

He must think she was dumber than Dean. Next he'd tell her he'd make her rich. 'How much does it pay?' she asked.

Milton leaned back, but almost slipped off the stool. He seemed to be enjoying himself. 'A lot,' he said. 'More than you ever dreamed of.'

Sharleen stepped closer to him. 'What do I have to do to get this job?' she asked, her head tilted slightly to the side, her arms crossed over her chest.

'Nothing,' he said, moving away from her, standing up to pay his bill. 'All you have to do is come to this casting office next week and meet some people for an interview.' He continued placing bills down on the counter from his wallet. 'No guarantees, but you really could get a part on a TV show.'

He handed Sharleen his card and said, 'This is for real, Sharleen. And there are no strings attached.'

She accepted the engraved card and said, 'Okay, Mr. Glick. If I decide I want to be a TV actress, I'll give you a call.' She walked away quickly as Jake, frowning, started over to her.

'Do it, Sharleen,' Glick said to her retreating back, 'if you want to be very, very rich.'

5

Jahne moved out of the Star Drop Inn with Pete's help. Not into his place, though. She'd found an apartment to share with two girls. It had been a tiring move, and after she and he got her new bed in place and made up, she fell into it gratefully. She slept – alone, for Pete had an early call the next morning – the sleep of the justly tired.

The next morning Jahne opened her eyes, stared at the sunny, cracked blue ceiling, and smiled. Oh, yes. California. Her new place, off Melrose Avenue, to be precise. And the room in the apartment she was sharing with the two other actresses in the troupe.

It had all been so easy, but it was so very odd: everyone's birthright on the whole planet since time began was a face, a body, and a name. She had changed all three. In a way that could never have been done before. It was audacious, painful, risky. But it had already paid off.

She smiled and stretched. *Everything* was different now. Not just her name and her face and her body, but everything. Each morning, she woke up with a smile on her pretty face. She jumped out of bed. Dressing was a pleasure. Everything, anything looked good on a beautiful girl who was five foot six and weighed 121 pounds. Jeans slid over her thin, long thighs. T-shirts clung to her perfectly rounded breasts. Looking in the mirror was a gas, but being looked at was even better.

Men stared at her. Her every movement seemed to fascinate and delight them. She'd taken to tossing her head, arching her back in a stretch, all those bits of body language that she used to despise in other, pretty women. But it was irresistible now. It got such a reaction, how could she refrain from crossing her legs and pointing the toe, enhancing the leg line? Or just licking her now beautifully pouty lips? She knew how to play sexy. And she knew that now it played.

She also knew that women watched her. Not so directly, but they watched her just the same. Now she was actually in the contest, not just an observer. In fact, she might be a major contender, and they sized her up out of the corners of their eyes. Better hair, better nose, better breasts. She could feel their cataloguing, weighing, judging.

Always before, the Bethanies of the world had simply written her off, choosing to ignore her or befriend her, but in either case the choice was a condescension. Jahne didn't mind if now some of the women hated her for no reason other than the potent one of her appearance. She felt it was an honour, an acknowledgment, and she'd live with it.

Because, for a woman, being beautiful – a real knockout, which she was – opened more doors than Aladdin's lamp or a trust fund the size of Onassis'. Look at poor Christina, for chrissakes. Killed by her homeliness and her father's and the world's view of it. Too bad *she* hadn't met Dr. Moore.

Best of all, the audition Pete's sister had gotten her had been worth the trouble. It was a bit dicey, she knew, to bother with stage acting here in L.A., where the camera was king. But the Melrose Playhouse in West Hollywood was hip enough to have an audience that included agents, casting directors, and even a few producers and directors. And what could be better for her, a stage actress, than a Hollywood debut on stage? It wasn't as if anything else had come her way.

And she'd easily gotten the part. It was the lead in a revamped version of *A Doll's House*. The characters had been updated to a successful Hollywood producer and his dependent starlet wife. Oddly enough, Ibsen's old themes of male domination and female dependency still worked. Sad, really.

The irony was that she, a woman who had never had the luxury of depending on a man, would get to play Nora. Well, it was a part to kill for, and she was delighted that she had snagged it, even if it only paid 175 bucks a week. Less than New York unemployment. But if she was lucky, it could bring her to the attention of people who mattered.

Jahne stood, throwing off the crumpled sheet. She slept in a long, shapeless white cotton nightgown, and had a cheap white terry robe that she used as a bath towel as well. The one thing she was having trouble adjusting to was the scars, and she intended neither to expose them nor to look at them much herself. In the shower, she simply faced into the spray, and the rest of the time she kept clothed. She continued putting on the vitamin E and was grateful that she'd never developed keloids. But even now the scars itched. Sometimes she felt they must glow in the dark. She always kept the lights off with Pete, and if she ever wanted to sleep with another man, she'd figure out how to cross that bridge when she got to it. But it didn't seem likely. Because right now she was, despite her thirty-six years, behaving like an adolescent. She liked the game far more than the scoring.

Hector, the artistic director of the playhouse, was gay, thank God, and not the slightest bit interested in her except professionally. But he appreciated her, and not just her looks. She'd been cast after her first audition. Hector was *not* a genius, and listening to his lame stage direction was painful – it made her miss Sam.

Well, to be honest, everything made her miss Sam. That was the only other fly in the ointment: the memories, the things they had done together, came back, replaying like an endless loop in her head. Weirder than that, now that she was here in California, where he was, new things made her miss him. She shook her head. Here is an orange tree. I'm standing under it, and I could pick one right off that branch. Maybe, right now, Sam is standing under an orange tree. Those were the stupid kind of thoughts that ran through her mind continually. She had to laugh at herself. Yeah, and I hope an orange the weight of a cannonball falls on his head. But she did miss him, and the idea that they'd never stand under an orange tree together brought tears to her eyes.

'God, I am an incorrigible masochist,' she said aloud.

The thought that plagued her most was ... Well, she hated to think about it. If she'd looked then as she did now, would Sam have left her? If he wouldn't have, does that mean that he'd still love her? Or, since he left her, did it mean that he never had? What would he think of her looks now? Was her beauty enough to keep him from wandering, to keep him forever satisfied? Would he even know her?

Oh, it was ridiculous to think about! Yet the thought kept coming back. And behind it another, even more insidious one: When people liked her now, when Pete pulled her to him, when other men smiled, and women submitted to her beauty, did they want Mary Jane Moran or Jahne Moore? If the world hadn't liked her before, should she like it back when it responded now? She groaned, and pushed the thoughts from her mind. She'd gotten exactly what she wanted, but she still knew how to make herself miserable!

She finished dressing and, now clothed, looked in the mirror. Her new looks stared back at her – long, lithe, perfect. She was smart enough to know that she didn't know how to dress – after all, when had she the time, money, or motivation to learn? – so she kept it simple. Her wardrobe consisted of three pairs of long-legged, slim-cut Levi's and a few white shirts, a couple of turtlenecks, and a great hot-pink cashmere sweater. It and her boots had been her only splurge. She'd bought the softest, most supple pair of brown, tall leather boots, with three-inch heels. When she slipped those on, she got the perfect height and tilt. She buckled a brown leather belt around her waist and was ready for makeup. Not that she really needed it. But she wore it, always, because looking her best was part of her role, and she was always onstage. She was playing the part of a beautiful young girl, and she never stepped out of character.

Only at night, after she made love with Pete and lay quietly in his arms, could she, just before she fell asleep, relax. Their lovemaking was athletic. Pete lacked the subtleties of an older, more experienced lover. He rammed himself into her, and didn't really seem aware of what a woman needed. But he made up for his gaucherie with his enthusiasm. After the first orgasm, he'd get hard again quickly, and then he gave her all the time she needed. She rode him to exhaustion. There, in the dark, with his delicious young body beside hers, she could wonder at who she was, and where unhappy Mary Jane had gone.

In the daylight, she had no time for that. She'd developed a simple, easy-to-apply face, as well as theatre makeup and some more extreme maquillage for evenings or events. Not that she had anyplace to go. She found the crowd at the playhouse both dull and clannish. But, after all, they were all fifteen years younger than she; though she looked the same, she was not what she appeared. She watched the pretty girls date the wrong guys, do the wrong things, set the wrong goals.

She knew now what she'd needed to know then. She could see through the bullshit the way a thirty-six-year-old in sheep's clothing could.

6

Sam looked up from the storyboards that were splayed across his desk. It was dark. The L.A. twilight had quickly turned an inky, smoggy mauve. His light was probably the only one on in the long, low building.

Seymore LeVine, one of April's flunkies, had given him this production office and Rita, his secretary. While he worked on the picture, this little bit of Hollywood real estate was his. He looked around at the low ceiling, the whitewashed wooden walls. Once this had been the Writers' Wing at International Studios, back in the days when dozens of writers had been employed turning out three films a week. Who had worked here? Benchley? Agee? Had Bill Faulkner dropped by for a sip of bourbon and branch? What had been written in this room, and, more to the point, would *he* ever write anything here?

Sam shook his head, trying to concentrate. Only halfway into production of his first film, and he was already worried about his next job. That way madness lies, Sam told himself, but he couldn't help but worry. He had already pitched two of his plays to April, and she had passed on both of them. Sam could see what happened to a director and a producer here at the studio after their job was through: they gave up their offices, the parking spots with their names stenciled on, they packed up their tent and moved on.

But Sam didn't want to move on. In the almost two years he had spent getting *Jack and Jill* through development hell and into production, he had come to want to be a part of this town. And what was there to go back to? The thought of New York, its coldness, its greyness, chilled him. The pretensions of the troupe, his little off-off-Broadway productions. Could he settle down to that very small life, writing alone in a dark room for hours every day? What would he write about? The story of a neophyte in Hollywood, in over his head?

Sam Shields knew he was in over his head. Even though he finally had the screenplay for *Jack and Jill* under control, and even though he was doing the best he could to learn the technical part of movie producing, he was. And it wasn't just the film. Women were driving him crazy, and he wasn't coping well.

The fact was that he was more than scared. He was terrified. Since they'd begun principal photography on *Jack and Jill*, there hadn't been a night when he could sleep without waking up at three-fifteen, in the morning darkness, fear gripping his belly. He had been running over budget and behind schedule almost since the first week, and April had twice come down on him fast and hard.

Her first angry phone call had shocked him. After all, they had been, briefly, lovers. But then he had started sleeping with Crystal, during the first week of rehearsals. When April called, he expected a scene over that, not the budget.

'What the fuck do you think you're doing?' April's voice had asked coldly. Sam was ready with his excuses: he and April had no commitment; this new affair had simply happened, a chemical thing between him and the actress; he was wrong and he would apologize. April Irons was not a woman to offend. In fact, Sam could admit to himself that he was afraid of her.

'I'm sorry. I didn't mean to hurt you, April. This thing just happened.' It sounded lame, even to him. He'd have to try harder, to . . .

'What the fuck are you talking about?' she demanded.

Was it possible she didn't *know* about the affair? Sam was not that naïve. Everyone on the set except Crystal's husband knew, and April never missed a trick. And if she had missed this, Seymore LeVine would be sure to fill her in. Seymore was officially associate producer, but 'corporate snitch' would be a more accurate title. His father was chairman of International, and April's boss. April *had* to know about him and Crystal. Wasn't that what this call was about? But perhaps she wanted a confession. Some women were like that.

'Crystal and I, . . . Well, it just happened.'

'Oh, Christ! That! She sleeps with all her directors. Who cares? But why the fuck are you two days behind schedule already? Do you know what that costs? We haven't even begun location shooting yet. Seymore figures we'll be delayed at least a week.'

Sam tried to recover and switch gears. 'Take it out of my salary,' he told her.

'Nice offer, but it's already twice your entire salary,' she retorted. 'Don't you know what a day of studio time costs? Those union cocksuckers will eat us alive if you let them. *No* overtime. I mean it. What the fuck do we need rehearsal time for anyway? This isn't Broadway.'

'Mike Nichols always rehearses on the set. As an actress, Crystal needs to . . .'

'You, Sam, are no Mike Nichols. And Crystal is no actress. Just get the shit on film, okay?'

She'd hung up.

Since then, terrified, he had barely managed to keep to the budget. He might or might not be a Mike Nichols, but April was right that Crystal Plenum was no actress. She was a star, which, Sam was only now beginning to appreciate, was something different. She had fought him every step of the way as he tried to coax an actual performance out of her. She wanted to play the part of Jill in full Hollywood makeup, with perfectly manicured hands and good clothes and soft focus. She'd begged for the role, she'd fought for it, but then she wanted to change it, make it over into another Crystal Plenum vehicle.

But one that would surely fail, and take him down with her. It was only now, when he had something to lose, that a paralyzing fear of failing, of fucking it up, came over him. Crystal and all the rest of it seemed overpowering. It was only in bed that he could master her, calm her, coax her into giving it up, letting it go. He'd hold her, caress her, and tell her over and over and over again how she could do it, how great she could be. Night after night, in bed, he would convince her to be the role, to play the loser, to go it straight, that she had the talent, that she could act.

And then, each morning on the set, her hairdresser, her makeup man, and her costumer would begin again. Decked out for the part, she'd refuse to be filmed. 'Jesus, I look like shit,' she'd say, staring, almost mesmerized, into the mirror.

'You look exactly like Jill,' Sam told her.

'I look *old*,' she retorted.

'You look perfect. You're tired. You're lonely. Your life isn't working. That's how you look.'

'We should use a wig.' She tugged at the dark roots of her blonde hair. 'It's so thin. I knew I shouldn't do this with my hair.'

'Crystal, no wig. This is really perfect.' He put a hand on either side of her face and forced her to look away from the mirror, away from herself, and at him. 'This is really perfect. You're going to wow them all. You're going to give the performance of a lifetime.'

'Really?' Sometimes, when she looked at him this way, asking a question, he could see the child there, the little girl who had always been so pretty, who counted on being pretty. Who felt she had nothing but pretty to give.

'Really,' he told her, and tried not to think of the half-hour that had been wasted.

When Crystal had seen the first dailies, there had been a crisis that lasted two days: she had cried so hard that night and the next day that they couldn't shoot anything then, or even the following day, until the swelling around her eyes and nose had gone down. 'God, I look so old. I look so awful,' she kept moaning.

'You look like a normal middle-aged woman,' Sam had told her, but she had cried harder.

'I'm *not* middle-aged!' she almost screamed.

'No, but Jill *is*,' he reminded her.

'I can't do this!' she had cried. 'This shit works for Farrah

Fawcett, but I don't want to spend the rest of my career playing beaten women in made-for-TV movies. Oh, God!'

So he calmed her, he loved her, and then he made a new rule: no one saw the dailies except Seymore, Sam, and the cinematographer. He closed the set. He watched the budget. And he made love to Crystal twice a night. It was a vigorous schedule, but he managed to do it.

And, despite all the pressure, all the problems, all his fear, he felt that, at last, he was in the centre of things. That here, now, he was converting his vision into something that millions, not just hundreds, would share. And that this vision would last as long as celluloid. In a small way, he was becoming immortal.

New York seemed long ago and far away. He still became uncomfortable when he thought of his promise to return. But the idea of a ragtag bunch of actors in a basement no longer had any appeal. He'd put off returning calls to Chuck until the calls had almost stopped coming. They would feel betrayed, they would say he had sold out, but they were losers who had never gotten a shot at this. If they had, they, too, would grab it.

Because now he was a player. At least for now, he possessed an office at International Studios. He possessed a secretary, and he had taken Crystal Plenum, the movie star, as his lover. He possessed her, too. It was still hard to believe. It still bothered him that she was married. But Crystal had explained that the marriage was over in all but name, and it did not seem to complicate their affair. Nor did her four-year-old daughter.

It meant, of course, that he'd had to unload Bethanie, but that had been a mistake from the beginning. After all, he'd promised her nothing, and she'd gotten herself a ticket to L.A. and a place to stay. She'd even snagged a small continuing part on *Houston*, one of those dying primetime soaps. She should have no complaints. But of course she did. They always did.

Except Mary Jane. She flickered across his mind's eye again. In all the time since he left New York, guilt and something else had stopped him from calling her. What's gone is gone, as his father used to say. But after all this time, it surprised him how he still thought of her, missed her. They would have had a lot of laughs over the ridiculousness of L.A. And somehow all the other women in his life seemed to drain him. Only Mary Jane had filled him with confidence, and more. She had comforted him.

But it was just as well he hadn't contacted her. Not now, with this thing with Crystal going on. It was too much to run on the side; it had become a full-time thing. The film and Crystal's performance had become his whole life; the set and locations and cast and crew were their world. During the months of preproduction and the last two months of shooting, he hadn't known any other.

Yes, the pressure was intense, but the reward, he hoped, would be worth it. He was eking out a performance from Crystal that would startle. Her name would ensure box office, his direction would do the rest. His work would be seen. And now, if he could just find the time to write, he'd be all right.

7

Jahne left the stage of the Melrose Playhouse after her final curtain call, the applause still echoing in her ears. The adrenaline from her performance made her almost skip backstage, passing Beverly, the stage manager, who thrust a newspaper under Jahne's arm as she passed. 'A review on page thirty-six. Read it and cheep, Jahne. You should be happy as a lark.'

Jahne closed the door to her dressing room and leaned against it, trying to catch her breath. Really, what she wanted to do was laugh out loud. Today was her fifteenth performance as Nora in *Doll's House*. Each night, her curtain calls had increased. Tonight she'd had eight – count 'em, Jahne – *eight* curtain calls, and she was delirious with joy. This was what it was all about, after all, she told herself. The applause, and the love and respect of the audience. And so what if it was only a West Hollywood theatre with an audience who couldn't tell Ibsen from Ionesco. She hugged herself to keep from crying out with joy.

She got undressed and stood in front of the full-length dressing-room mirror. She placed her hands on her hips, and turned first one way, then the other. Her once low, pendulous breasts were reduced and high, her nipples pointing to the ceiling. Funny to think they had been cut off and placed there, giving the illusion of an even perkier bustline. Catching sight of some of the scars, she quickly jumped to check that her door was locked. She had made

212

it a point to lock it whenever she was dressing or undressing, and found that, of course, it was. She didn't take any chances.

The incision line across her lower abdomen had already begun to fade, from angry red to a light-brown line just above her pubic hair. But the two scars that cut down the centre of her breasts, from the nipples to the rib cage, were still an angry pink. She put vitamin E on them all every day, but they still glowed. The lines around her nipples were hard to see, but when she lifted her arms, the scars from elbow to armpit were obvious. So were the ones on the insides of her thighs, and the ones below her buttocks. No one except Pete ever saw her naked and she still insisted they do it in total darkness.

Dr. Moore had said she had 'good tissue,' and he was right. All the incisions had healed quickly, and the scars were fading. But they would always be there. They reminded her of New York, of what she had been, and of what her life had been like. She hated to look at them.

She put on a cotton kimono, dimmed the rheostat, and continued to study herself. You're beautiful, she told her image. Beautiful and talented. Finally, both. She dropped down into the battered chaise longue provided only for the star and snapped open the newspaper Beverly had given her. The paper was folded to the theatre section, and Blitstein's review jumped out at her. 'The history of the Melrose Playhouse,' he wrote, 'is, for all intents and purposes, the history of theatre on the West Coast. And while it isn't the Lunt-Fontanne or the Winter Garden on Broadway – Melrose can boast many consistent successes. And all can envy the discovery of great talent that has been the design – not luck, you will note – of this great Western American theatre. Once again the MPH makes history, not only in its courageously updated production of *A Doll's House*, a play without peer, but also in its choice of leading lady. Jahne Moore is the consummate actress, and beautiful beyond words. As a Hollywood wife, trapped by the Beverly Hills life-style but longing for freedom from her gilded L.A. cage, she evokes pathos and compassion – a difficult trick since she is so lovely and her life so enviable. But Moore's talent overcomes the obstacle and, while the adaptation of the play is flawed, her performance is flawless.'

Jahne read on, feeling her jaw drop, in spite of the fact that the review was so similar to the others she had received since the play opened. In fact, some of the others had not been as positive about the play as this, but all agreed, that Jahne Moore was a major acting talent. This, however, was Blitstein in the *L.A. Times*. It would draw the Hollywood crowd.

She crushed the paper to her in a burst of intensity, then immediately unfolded it and straightened out the kinks. This was going in her scrapbook.

The crackling noise of the paper covered the light tapping at the door. She stopped, and heard the noise. The knock was gentle, but nonetheless it startled her. She jumped for her longer dressing gown and called out, 'Who is it?'

'It's Marty,' a voice said. 'Marty DiGennaro.'

Jahne smiled to herself and opened the door. The cast had taken to teasing her about her success, and had been playing a series of practical jokes on her. 'I never heard of any Marty DiGe . . .' She stopped, the doorknob in her hand. He stood, a small man, outside the half-open door. Holy shit! 'Mr. DiGennaro, I'm so sorry,' she said. 'I thought one of the guys was playing . . . You know how the crew gets when we're working on a hit. I mean, of course *you* do.' She almost giggled now. If Marty DiGennaro didn't know about hits, who did?

'May I come in?' he asked, his eyes crinkled into a smile. He was small, ethnic, a real New York Italian. He walked across the room and slid into a straightback chair, not saying anything, simply looking at her. Jahne didn't have a clue what to do, so she looked back. The silence stretched out.

'Mr. DiGennaro, please excuse me but I feel like Fanny Brice did when she opened her dressing room door and found Nicky Arnstein. I'm a little giddy. Can I get you something to drink? Anything?'

'No, nothing, Jahne. And please call me Marty. I had to come back to see you . . . to tell you what a wonderful performance you gave tonight. I have to admit, I didn't want to come to the theatre – I was dragged here by friends who raved about you. It's been my experience that when friends say, "You must see so-and-so, she's great" . . . well, I've been disappointed so often.' He paused, continuing to look at her, his dark eyes so intense she almost felt they were piercing her flesh. She thought of Superman's X-ray vision. Could he see the scars under her wrapper? The director smiled. 'Tonight, I wasn't disappointed. You're as talented as everyone is saying you are.' He chuckled. 'I agree with the theatre critics one hundred per cent, for a change. What an honour to see you perform.'

He began to rise, and Jahne found her voice. 'I don't know

what to say. I mean, thank you, of course. But you must know what this means to me. More than anyone, you're the person in the business whose opinion I respect. To have *you* say those things . . .' She paused. 'Thank you.' She laughed; then her voice lowered, and she grew mock-serious. 'You really *are* Marty DiGennaro, aren't you? Not some celebrity look-alike. This isn't a practical joke?'

'Hey, who'd want to admit they looked like me?' Marty laughed, stepped through the door, almost out of Jahne's life. But he hesitated, turned around for a moment, reached into his pocket, took out a business card, and handed it to her. 'Call me tomorrow. My private-line number is written on the back. I'd like to work with you.' Then he was gone.

Jahne stood at the open door for a moment, watching Marty's back as he walked away. 'Hey, Susan,' she called to the stagehand; then she yelled to Pete's sister and the rest of them. 'Beverly, anybody. Listen!' Several of the cast stopped what they were doing and looked towards her. Pete's sister, Mary, came rushing over. 'Listen,' she announced to everyone, waving the business card in the air. 'Marty DiGennaro just told me he'd like to work with me.'

Beverly's face broke into a grin as she turned to the rest of the crew and winked. 'So who's Marty DiGennaro?'

After the performance, Jahne usually spent her evenings alone, except for the once or twice a week that she went over to Pete's place. They had fallen into a pattern: he'd make a couple of burritos, they'd drink a beer, watch the late news, and then make love. His body was strong, his face was handsome, and he was both enthusiastic and gentle. He never spoke while they made love, and he never protested over Jahne's insistence that they kept all the lights off. If he felt any of her scars in the dark, he never mentioned them.

But tonight, after the visit from Marty DiGennaro, she insisted they go out to dinner: her treat. 'After all, it's through you that I found out about the auditions.'

They went to a cheap Italian joint on Melrose. As a celebration, she ordered a bottle of Chianti.

'What's that?' Pete asked.

'Italian wine,' she told him, and nearly sighed. Well, after all, he *was* young and Californian. How could she expect him to know about European wine? Bistros with candles stuck in Chianti bottles? Still, his youth and inexperience sometimes made her lonely.

'Do you think he really meant it?' she asked him, both playing the coquette and also truly frightened about it. 'Does he have a part in mind for me? Will I get it?'

'Sure you will,' he told her.

His certainty would have reassured her if she could have trusted what he based it on. 'Why?' she asked. She wanted his dissection of her strengths and weaknesses. She wanted his analysis of the Industry, and of Marty DiGennaro specficially. 'Why?' she repeated.

'Because you're so pretty and so smart,' he said simply. She felt her mood begin to slip. He hadn't reassured her.

They ordered dinner, and she tried to keep the conversation going, but she felt her excitement draining out of her, slowly. She kept drinking the Chianti, annoyed that his glass remained full.

'Don't you like it?' she asked.

'Not much,' he admitted.

'Well, then, order a Corona, for God's sakes!' No wonder she never went out with him, she thought. He was impossible. She wondered how long this relationship could last. And she wondered if she could do without his comforting physical presence. She looked across the table at him. 'What's wrong?' she asked.

'Nothing,' he said, and shrugged his wide shoulders.

'Oh, come on,' she pushed.

'It's going to be like my sister told me: you are going to get real successful and then you're going to drop me.'

She was stung by the accusation. And the fact that she had just been thinking of breaking it off made it worse. She had always been a loyal person, the type who was left, not the type who left others. To her own surprise, she felt tears spring to her eyes. Pete had been kind to her, but his fear of losing her was the first sign of deeper affection that he had shown. Like a sweet and friendly big dog, Pete had kept her company. Now he expected to be forgotten.

'Maybe they'll need a cameraman,' she said softly. 'I could talk to Marty, if he hires me.'

'Oh, he'll hire you,' Pete said sadly, but he smiled. And, smiling, he reminded Jahne of a grinning golden Lab, or some other slow but affectionate puppy.

Paul Grasso sat in the grimness that was his office. The open pages of his desktop appointment calendar flipped back through the printed months, stirred by the sudden breeze that fluttered through the semi-functional air conditioner below the dusty window. The motion brought Paul's eyes down from the ceiling, where they had been searching the cracks for solutions. He took his hands from behind his head, brought his reclining chair back up to a sitting position, and began to rearrange the pages, grateful for any activity. But the emptiness of his daily booking sheets reproached him, proving the validity of the worries that had been occupying him.

Nothing! _Nada_! Not a fucking thing new in months. Okay, to be honest, in almost a year. Thirty years in the business, but that counted for shit. You're only as good as your last deal, and that one was too long ago. Christ, he hated the Industry!

At least he did at times like this, when he was scrambling like a wetback for every scrap of work he could get, just to keep his head above water. It hadn't always been this way, of course. He used to be the best. He and Milton Glick, his ex-partner, were _the_ casting house for quality television, movies, you name it. No bullshit commercials, no exploitation flicks then. Then there was a different babe every night. An office with a view. And the high-roller suite in the Sands, where he could really let himself go.

Hey, he'd _been_ a high roller. Paul Grasso. Rolling in it. Christ, he was good. _Was_? The word chilled him. Was he himself talking in the past tense already? Holy shit, he couldn't let it get to him. Because, despite the split-up with Milton, despite his current lousy business, he wasn't a has-been. He'd told Milton, the day he walked out the door, that Milton would run back to _him_. Milton cried, said he, Paul, was running him into the ground, but Paul was sure Milt would come back. He needed _me_ to make it rain. To bring in the really big ones. 'What are a few gambling debts?' he'd asked. 'C'mon. Loosen up, Milt. Without me you'll sink.'

Except Glick didn't sink. He kept on swimming, hooked up with that fat prick Weinberg, and now Weinberg and Glick Casting, Inc. were centre stage. You needed to cast a quality movie, call Weinberg and Glick. That was the word on the boulevard. You need to cast a shit jeans commercial, call Grasso, then blow him off. It was Paul Grasso who had sunk.

So here he was, back to nickel-and-diming. It wasn't that he wasn't making some money; that wasn't it. But what he made just covered the vig. And he hadn't made one of those big hits on a really big deal like he used to. But he'd close on one of them soon, he told himself, then pay off Benny Eggs and the other sharks and be back on the comp list. Christ, he *had* to close on something big soon. Because, if word got out that Paul Grasso had lost it, then it would be all over for him. The sharks would close in for a feeding frenzy. And he couldn't let that happen. Not for himself, but also so that stiff Milton Glick would never be in the position of laughing at Paul Grasso. *No one* laughed at Paul Grasso.

His secretary buzzed him to announce that Lila Kyle was here, his two o'clock. 'Tell her to wait.' This is how it's been going. People asking for favours, useless dreck kids of stars hoping for a bit part, or producers wanting freebees.

Now he'd have to waste time and bullshit Theresa O'Donnell's kid. Well, he couldn't turn Robbie Lymon down. Theresa and he had a lot of history.

He was also mildly curious to see what the child of beauty Theresa O'Donnell and swashbuckling grade-B movie hero Kerry Kyle – more handsome, some say, than Tyrone Power, and a hell of a bigger swish – looked like as an adult.

He buzzed his secretary to show Lila in, reminding his girl to buzz him again in exactly fifteen minutes. She knew the drill. He had decided that fifteen minutes would be polite enough. Jesus, even if the kid was Julia Roberts, he had nothing for her. As the door opened and Lila walked in, it took Paul a moment to get to his feet. He shook her hand, then gestured to a chair in front of his desk. Jesus Christ! What a beauty. Tits out to here, legs down to there, and a cascade of red hair that ended at her perfect butt. And none of the sloppiness, the casualness of the kids of today. This girl was turned out. She was finished, with the high gloss of a pageant winner.

'Lila. Lila Kyle. I didn't know that was your name. I always thought your name was O'Donnell until Robbie finally told my secretary the other day. Lila Kyle. I'm speechless. You sure have grown up. How old are you now? Twenty-one, -two?' He laughed at how ridiculous that sounded. 'Jeez, you're beautiful, Lila.'

'Thanks, Paul. You haven't changed much. Still smoking smelly cigars, a little wider around the waist, but still a fine specimen of a man.' Lila smiled and crossed her sheer-stockinged legs.

Yahta, yahta, yahta. Flash a little cooze. Not that it will help. Well, turn up the heat so she doesn't get pissed or tell her mom I molested her. 'Lila, I always knew that you would wind up more beautiful than your mother and father. And just call me "Uncle" Paul!' Jeez, maybe he shouldn't mention the fairy. Never know how much these Hollywood kids knew. He sat forward, elbows resting on his desk. 'You were a gorgeous little kid, but, well, pudgy, not filled out, no height, you know? But, hey' – he opened his hands at the evidence sitting before him – 'a raving beauty.'

He thought of Kerry Kyle, a raver, and smiled again as he watched Lila's expression at the compliments. Not a blink. Listening politely, but she already knows all this shit. Okay. Move on to the family yahta yahta.

'How's your mother, by the way?'

'I'm not here to take a stroll down memory lane with you, Paul. Neither of us is the type, so I'll get right to the point. I have a business proposition that will be good for me *and* for you.'

He sat back and lit the cold stub of a cigar that had been resting on the edge of a chipped Steuben ashtray. Christmas gift from Milt. He needed the activity to give him a second to think. This was not coming off as your average Bel Air brat looking for a job. She'd read too many detective novels. Who'd she think she was, Mary Astor? He released a mouthful of smoke and said, 'Okay, what can you do for my business?'

'First get me in front of Marty DiGennaro.'

Paul smiled broadly, and crossed his hands on his belly. Same old yahta yahta after all. He knew his ground again. Was she in love, or did she want DiGennaro to make her a star, or both? 'And how's that supposed to help *me*?'

Lila sat forward in her chair. 'Marty DiGennaro is going to be making a TV series, and he's looking for new talent. Old-fashioned, virgin talent.'

Paul laughed out loud. 'My ass, you should excuse the expression.

You got him confused with Barry Levinson. Marty DiGennaro does not do *television series*.' He said the last words as if they were street smut. The kid had shit for brains.

As if she could read his mind, her face changed. 'I haven't tried for three weeks to get an appointment with you so Paul Grasso can treat me like I have shit for brains. If you listen to me, you might learn something – okay, *Uncle* Paul? Marty DiGennaro *is* going to do a TV series; he has the story, the concept, the network, everything – except the leads. I *saw* the contract. You doubt me?'

He nodded. You could keep a secret in this town, but not a big one. And this would be *very* big. The girl flushed, bent down, and rooted around in her big white leather bag.

'Here,' she said, and dropped papers on his desk. She sat back and waited for Grasso to look it over.

It *was* a contract. It looked in order. What a deal! Paul realized he was losing face, but she had him pinned. Christ, he'd played cards with Marty once a month for years, with Johnny the Jump and the other guys from back home. They used to let go in Vegas together regularly, though not for a while now. Was this legit? And how did *she* know, how did *she* have the motherfucking contract, while *he* was in the dark?

'If Marty was going to do television, he'd have come to me, Lila. No way he's having someone else do the casting. And no way I don't know everything he does. Him and me, we go way back.'

'Right, Paul, except Marty DiGennaro doesn't look back, he looks forward. He needs three leads. New faces. All new.' She pointed to the wall of mostly black-and-white head shots of actors Grasso had gotten roles for. And not one of those pictures was less than three years old. 'Why would Marty come to you for casting? What have you got that's hot? Why should he?'

Paul's intercom buzzed, and he snapped into the speaker, 'I don't want to be disturbed.' He was about to go bananas. Either this broad knew what she was talking about, or she was nuts and making a fool outa him. She sat waiting for him to say something, not dropping her gaze. No, she's not nuts, he decided.

'Okay, *if* this is true, and *if* I get you an intro to Marty, and *if* he likes you, and *if* you get cast, how's that gonna help me?'

'Right now,' Lila went on, 'your old pal Milton Glick has got the exclusive for casting the series. Ortis gave them the shot. Anyhow, the word is Weinberg and Glick showed up at a meeting with Sy

Ortis last week with nothing but their dicks in their hands, and Ortis goes apeshit. He threw every résumé and picture and video in the garbage. Things got tense.' She smiled, licked her lips, and recrossed her legs. Paul was beginning to see Lila in a new light. She was tougher than Mary Astor. And the mention of Milton's name threw Paul into a real slow burn.

'So now,' she continued, 'they're standing knee-deep in dog caa-caa, and unless they come up with some girls, they can kiss this deal goodbye. You know, it's not a good idea to fail Sy Ortis.' Lila put an exaggerated frown on her face, taunting. 'But *you* should already know all this, Paul, shouldn't you? I mean, you *are* tight with Marty DiGennaro.' Lila waited.

Grasso's mind was working quickly now. She wanted tough? He'd play tough. 'How am I supposed to get you to him? I mean, every cousin is trying to get Marty to meet some chick or other. And what if I do? You're nice pussy, Lila, but Marty has it thrown at him from cars. What have you got?'

'I've read every word ever written on Marty DiGennaro, genius director. He grew up living in the world of old movies and movie stars. You know what his personal collection of first-print classics is like? Probably the finest in the world. And guess which one is his favourite, Paul?'

Paul shrugged his shoulders, pretending it wasn't important, but knew it was. Why don't I know what Marty's favourite old movie is? he thought.

'Does *Birth of a Star* ring a bell?'

Right! She was right. Marty *had* talked about it. He loved Theresa O'Donnell's first big hit. Yeah, Paul remembered now. Marty had once said he had seen *Birth of a Star* fifty-two times, or some crazy-ass number like that. Because of *Theresa O'Donnell*! Said she was one of the last natural beauties with talent in Hollywood. Yahta, yahta, yahta. Paul never listened to that movies-as-art bull-shit. But it rang Marty's chimes. And here was her kid – a natural beauty – sitting across from him.

Now the kid stood up and leaned over Paul's desk, looking down at him. 'All I need is to see him over dinner. An hour with him. Make it happen, Paul. You're not slipping, are you?'

Paul was beginning to feel the old feeling again. This had dropped in his lap. But I *could* make this happen, he thought. 'So I get you in front of Marty. Then what?'

Lila's tone turned patient. 'Then leave the rest to me, Paul. I'm a

221

big girl now. And, believe me, when we pull this off, Marty will be very grateful to you for doing what Milton couldn't. *Very* grateful. The show will need lots of cast. A weekly series. An hour. Think of it.' Paul did, and licked his lips. 'So call Marty DiGennaro, invite him out to dinner, with me as your date. Just one thing. Don't tell him who my parents are. Not one word. That's a must.'

'You crazy? That's your draw.'

'Listen to me: don't you dare mention my name. I'm a woman you're dating. Tell him I *hate* to talk business, and that you just want to fuck me. I'm another Beverly Hills Industry brat who hates the business. No ambition, no talent, no illusions. Got it?'

'Sure, but why?'

'It's important for *Marty* to discover *me*. He might not even look at me if he thought you were pushing me or I was hungry. I'm with you because you're trying to get into my pants. And you can't. Okay?'

'Sure. Okay.'

She started to exit, then paused and returned to Paul, who was still sitting at his desk. She bent over and kissed him on the top of his head, then walked back to the door. As she opened it, she said, 'Nobody keeps head shots on their walls anymore, Paul. They date you. Get rid of them. You're getting yourself a second chance.'

Paul stared at the closed door for moments, then looked at the phone. Make it happen, he said to himself. Shit, make it happen, he ordered, and picked up the receiver. He punched in Marty DiGennaro's private number from memory.

9

Sharleen lay on the lumpy bed, listening to the sounds of Dean's breathing beside her. It was usually comforting to hear him so close in the night when she couldn't sleep, but tonight it was driving her crazy. She didn't want to put on the light. When she did yesterday morning, she saw the cockroaches scampering for safety. She wished she could put off tomorrow forever. The red neon haze from the motel sign pushed in through the holes in the torn shade. Sharleen knew that soon it would be replaced by the red light of dawn, the dawn of another bleak day.

She got out of bed and tiptoed into the bathroom, closed the door, and sat down on the covered toilet seat. The odour of mildew stung her nostrils, so she shook a cigarette loose from the pack on the vanity, lit it, and leaned back, releasing the smoke in one long, white trail. That skunk, she thought. Jake didn't have to fire me. I wasn't as good a waitress as Thelma, but he hardly gave me any time. It was only a month, for Lord's sake.

It was Thelma, she knew. Jake said as much. Sharleen sighed. Women seemed to hate her, no matter how nice she was to them. The same thing had gotten them fired from the rodeo. But she'd been nice to Thelma. It hadn't worked. She was afraid I would take her fat husband from her, Sharleen thought with wonder. If only Thelma had known how repulsive Jake looked to her. But if she'd told Thelma that, Thelma would have been offended. Sharleen sighed, dragged again on the cigarette, and coughed. She didn't really smoke. She'd only bought them because she was worried, and her momma always said that they soothed. Well, they were makin' Sharleen sick as a cat.

She and Dean had toured with the rodeo. Dean was great with the animals and the motors, but when guys came on to her – and they always did – Dean got into fights. So they'd had to leave. She'd worked in Burger Kings, and once, for over a month, they'd been so broke that they lived out of their car. They'd been tired and hungry and dirty when she got this job at Jake's, and now she'd lost it. She took another drag on the cigarette and choked.

Well, never mind; now what do I do? No job, Dean earning two eighty-five an hour pumping gas. Lord, show me the way. Sharleen continued to smoke while looking up at the ceiling.

It was disrespectful to the Lord to smoke and pray at the same time, she thought, so she stubbed the cigarette out carefully, threw it into the uncovered toilet tank, and then knelt on the dirty linoleum floor, her head bowed over the seat.

Oh, Lord, I know we have sinned, and I know you have sent us into the desert, she began. But, please, dear Jesus, I am so very tired. Tired of the dirt, tired of runnin', tired of these old clothes, tired of bein' afraid, tired of the nasty motels, the torn towels, the greasy food.

Tears began to form on the lower lids of her beautiful azure eyes, pearling up and rolling down her perfect cheek, beside her lovely nose, landing on her pink, plump upper lip. Like a child, she licked them away and continued.

Oh, please, dear Jesus. Show me the way. She reached for her mother's Bible, which she kept in the medicine chest, then sat back on the toilet with the book on her lap. I'll open it and it will tell me what to do, she told herself. She wiped her face with the back of her hand, wiped her nose, too, then sniffed and took a deep breath.

With a swift motion, she inserted a fingernail into the Good Book and opened the binding. It flipped open to the New Testament, first page of the book of Acts.

She stared at the large-print heading on the page. Acts. Acting. She looked up to the flaking thin ceiling of the bathroom.

What had that guy Milton said last week? I could get a job on TV and make a lot of money? But it couldn't be for real. She stood up and quietly made her way out to the dresser in the bedroom, picked up her straw bag, and crept back into the john. Rummaging around, she found the little bit of paper she was looking for. 'Milton Glick, Weinberg and Glick Casting, 25550 La Cienega Boulevard, Hollywood, California.'

'The Lord works in mysterious ways,' she murmured.

It wasn't a comfortable drive from Bakersfield to L.A. for Sharleen. The Datsun's air conditioning wasn't working right, and she and Dean got lost twice. When she'd called, Mr. Glick had given her directions, but they didn't make sense, and she'd never been a good map reader. Plus, Los Angeles was so much busier and bigger than Bakersfield.

They got lost in a section of town that looked pretty rough. When they finally got on La Cienega, she sighed with relief. She had gotten all dressed up – a nice skirt from J C Penney, with a new blue blouse that had white lace with silver spangles on the cuffs and neckline. She had her old white pumps, but she'd covered the scuffs with the shoe polish she had used on her waitress shoes at Jake's. She thought she looked nice, but when she got out of the car she nearly cried. The skirt was all rucked up, and the wrinkles wouldn't smooth, while the blouse was wet up her back and under her arms. Her face was flushed with the heat, and her hair was lank from the humidity.

'Dean, you wait here, now, okay?'

'Sure, Sharleen. You gonna get another job?'

What if this guy was a crook? What if he was lying, and he tried to rape her? What if they were Mafia or worse? Her hands shook as she closed the car door and looked in at Dean. 'I hope so, honey.'

She walked towards the office-building door. It looked big, and new, with marble floors and glittery metal edges on everything that wasn't glass or mirror. The chilled air hit her with a blast as she moved through the revolving doors. She felt goose pimples raise on her flesh. Well, she was nervous. What would they do if she didn't get this job? She clutched her patent-leather purse. She had only seventy-six dollars and some change from tips left.

What if Mr. Glick was like them other men? Just makin' come-ons to her, lookin' for trouble? She remembered Dobe's words of warning. As she stepped onto the elevator, punching the button for the twelfth floor, she prayed that she'd get some honest work.

'Do I have to pray to Yaweh to get some honest work out of you?' Sy Ortis was asking Milton Glick.

'Sy, I know you're going to like this girl.'

'I better. And Marty better. Because otherwise he's casting that nasty New York twat, and you are shit out of luck.' Sy was furious about Bethanie Lake, a nobody from the East Coast that Marty was considering. She was already represented by Judy Priestly, so Sy would be cut out. And if *he* was cut out, Milton would be, too. He could guarantee that.

Sometimes desperation can alter perception. Even if Sharleen Smith had not been one of the most beautiful young women on the face of the planet, she might have been perceived as such by these two desperate men. But as she was ushered into the conference room, she had never looked lovelier. The cheap clothes, the messy hair, the flush all contributed to an air of irresistible youth and sensuality.

'Mr. Glick?' she asked. 'Remember me? Sharleen, from Bakersfield.'

'Not originally from Bakersfield,' Sy Ortis replied. 'Unless that's a fake accent.'

'Do I have an accent?' The men laughed.

Sy Ortis stood up and walked over to her. No one had offered Sharleen a seat, so she stood there. Sy walked around the girl, then looked over at Milton.

'Almost white-blonde. And no roots. Monica Flanders will like this one. Well, this is at least a possibility,' he said to Milton. 'The hair. It's your hair, Sharleen from Bakersfield?'

'Well, of course it's my hair.' Except she pronounced it 'hay-er.'

'Give her a script,' Ortis ordered Glick, and Milton rejoiced. He handed the girl a blue-covered binder, showed her where to read.

'We'll run some lines, okay? You read the part of Clover.'

'Okay,' agreed Sharleen, but it sounded to them like 'Oh-ky.' Milton read a line, and Sharleen stumbled through the next one. Then Milton read again.

Sy barely listened. He knew that Marty primarily cared about the way things looked, and this looked good. Was the kid wearing any makeup? It didn't matter. He could see this one would put lip gloss on her butt to please. He could draw up the Flanders contract and probably get her to sign for less than a hundred thousand dollars. Perhaps he could charge her an equal amount in finder's fees.

Excited but too experienced to show it, Sy picked up the phone and punched in some numbers. He stared blankly into space as he listened to the car phone at the other end ring, then be picked up. He said 'hello,' then punched them onto the speakerphone and put the receiver down.

'Marty?'

'What, Sy?'

'Marty, do you want to say hello to your new Clover?'

'Sure.'

Sy motioned to Sharleen with an uplifted hand. 'Say hello to Mr. DiGennaro,' he told her.

'Hello, Mr. DiGennaro.'

Marty snorted, the noise accompanied by crackles of transmission friction. 'Where did you get that phony corn pone from?' he asked.

'From the mouth of the most beautiful virgin you'll ever meet.' Then it hit him. Were they playing with jailbait here? A greedy parent could fuck up any deal. *Madre di Dios!* He turned to Sharleen. 'How old are you?'

'Nineteen,' she said, but to all three men it sounded like 'Nan teen.' On the speakerphone, Marty laughed again.

'You're pulling my thing.'

'Get over here and take a look for yourself,' Sy told him. 'Let her pull it.' Milton Glick smiled for the first time that month.

'Sy, I'll personally kill you if I have to get on the freeway at this hour for nothing,' Marty threatened.

'This isn't nothing,' Sy promised.

They spent the next hour running the lines with her. Sharleen began to worry about Dean, but she was afraid to ask them if she could go. They wanted her address, to know how long she'd lived in Bakersfield, where she was from, if she had representation, and if she was married. Lots more questions, too. Sharleen thought of Lamson and lied. Talked about Arkansas and Oklahoma. She prayed she was saying the right thing. She had been standing in the shabby white high heels now for over an hour. Her calves were aching.

'Please,' she finally asked, 'kin I sit down?'

'Certainly,' said Milton Glick.

Sy Ortis realized the girl had been afraid to ask to sit down until now. He took a deep breath. 'Milton' Sy said, 'she's perfect.'

By the time the third man arrived, Sharleen was worn out. She was afraid to ask if she had the job, what it paid, and if it would last for more than a week or two. She read the lines as she had been instructed and tried not to be put off by Mr. DiGennaro, who prowled around her, sometimes close, sometimes farther away, occasionally crouching, once even pulling up a chair, jumping onto it, and staring down at her.

'Incredible,' he said at last. 'She doesn't have a bad angle. You know how easy that will make shooting her?'

Sharleen heard the word 'shooting' and took a step backward. Maybe these guys *were* mobsters. After all, 'DiGennaro' sounded like a Mafia name. She licked her lips, gathered her courage, and finally asked a question.

'So do I get this job or not?' she asked.

'Oh, I think you do. I truly think you do,' Mr. DiGennaro said.

10

By now you've probably forgotten Neil Morelli. Why not? So did several million people who tuned him in for the brief time that he starred in All the President's Chakras.

I – Laura Richie – had interviewed Neil back before the show came out. He was as high on his success and as cocky as any actor I've ever met. He talked about how he was 'gonna kick Seinfeld's ass.' He was driving a fancy car. He was dating his costar, a blonde bombshell who needed a reading for every line she had to deliver. It wasn't a pretty picture.

It wasn't that the concept of the show wasn't funny. It was. It was about a loony astrologer who had the President's ear and had been named to the newly created Cabinet post of 'secretary of astrology.' The show, All The President's Chakras, could be really wacky, if only the writers could write jokes. But they couldn't. What can you expect from guys whose writing credits included Charles in Charge? Neil knew he could do better. In fact, he had, but no one would even read his suggested changes, never mind admit that the lines weren't working. It was a script from Ortis' group of hacks, and they were losers, skidders, and bums. But Ortis represented him, too. So what the fuck was up?

Neil had gone to the producer over the director's head and shown him some of his proposed changes to the script. Okay, maybe he hadn't been diplomatic. Maybe he had tried to push his bantam weight around, but the guy had overreacted.

'Get the fuck out of my office,' Lenny Hartley had yelled, throwing the script back at him. 'And you're off the lot for the rest of the day,' he screamed. 'I make the decisions around here, not you. You guys are a dime a dozen, so, if you can't do what you're told today, don't come back tomorrow.'

That was the part that really frightened Neil. He was supposed to be the star of this little piece of shit. So where was the star treatment? He thought he had made it, that he'd finally gotten to a point where he'd get some respect. Some power. Wrong again, bean head. As he drove out through the gates of the lot he shivered, thinking about not being able to come back there. He had finally arrived, finally made it to Hollywood, burned all his bridges. There was no turning back.

But the script was lousy, and the President was an empty suit of an actor, while the other lead, the First Lady, was played by a dumb bitch who had fucked her way into the part. In fact, she'd fucked Neil. If she didn't make it on this show, she could always arrange to get another shot the way she had gotten this one. But what about him? If it flopped, where could he go? And as it looked now, there was no way that this bird would get picked up for the entire season.

Neil knew that it was make-it-or-break-it time for him. Maybe he shouldn't have screamed like a maniac at Sy Ortis' secretary; maybe he should have spoken again to the guy, the mini-agent in Sy's office, Brad or Tad or Todd or Ted, who had been assigned to him. But that guy was another know-nothing, do-nothing, a schmuck in Armani who specialized in taking meetings and fucking the dumb broads banging down his door.

I did a bit in the column about the trouble. But, hey, that's nothing new. There are over four hundred pilots shot each year. Only about two dozen of them make series. Of those, only one or two go on for more than a year. Not great odds. Neil was just a statistical probability.

Change is a bitch. Not all change, of course. Let's face it, it's not so tough getting used to living in a beach house, driving a BMW, having a cleaning woman who does your laundry and cooks your meals and irons your clothes. It's not so hard to take, after a lifetime of deprivation. Accepting those changes hadn't been a problem for Neil Morelli. The house in Malibu and the BMW, the pretty girlfriend, the sex in a hot tub – and the cleaning woman – it was like he was born to them. No, they weren't the changes Neil hadn't adjusted to.

It was the new changes he'd had to deal with the last few months, since his series was cancelled that were the bitch. Getting used, once again, to a crummy apartment in Encino, dirty laundry that didn't get washed by itself, and working a day job.

Fucking *working* again, like a slave, for fucking assholes. For tips! Neil Morelli returned home from his gig exhausted and miserable. When *All the President's Chakras* was cancelled, Neil wasn't surprised, since he had known almost from the beginning that the scripts were crap, that the writers were fourth-rate. In fact, he had prophesied that it would be a catastrophe, unless major revamping was done.

But knowing the show was going to flop sometime in the future was no preparation for the devastation when it was actually cancelled. For the first few weeks after the cancellation, he spent his time on the phone with anyone at Ortis' office who would listen. Todd, Tad, Brad, et al. After a while, Sy Ortis' office said the inevitable: 'Don't call us, we'll call you.' And the great man didn't talk to him at all. Not once. That was something out of a thirties movie, for chrissakes. Who the fuck was Sy Ortis anyhow?

He tried, as he always did, to joke himself out of it. Remember, he told himself, what the Muslims say: if shit happens, it's the will of Allah. He also remembered Woody Allen's line about Hollywood: 'It's worse than dog eat dog: it's dog doesn't return other dog's phone call.' But jokes didn't help. There was no Mary Jane or anyone else to laugh with him. Then the isolation and inertia set in. He knew he needed to do something. His money was running out, he had no plans, his agent had dropped him, and he couldn't – wouldn't – go back to New York with his tail between his legs. So he did the only thing he knew how to do. He continued to work on his routine. He wrote and rewrote. But writing funny when you feel like used cat litter isn't easy. The routines weren't coming, and when they did they didn't work.

Overnight, it seemed, he had gone from Malibu to Encino, from a leased BMW to a used Honda, from starring in a TV series to working as a waiter in a comedy club. It was like getting broadsided by a car. The months had passed, and all he could say was 'What happened?'

Shit happened is what happened, he thought. Or, as the Hindus say, this shit all happened before. Problem was, he was no Hindu.

Neil tossed his white shirt and black bow tie on the pile of clothes next to the convertible sofa that he never bothered to close and fell across the bare mattress. While he lay on his stomach, he kicked off his scuffed, black Gucci loafers with the holes in the soles and heard them thunk onto the pile of dirty clothes beneath them. He welcomed the sound – the only sound at four in the morning.

The musty odour of the mattress filled his nostrils, forcing him to turn on his back. There was no one he could share this with, no one who wouldn't gloat. Even his sister, Brenda, would just offer him some money and sympathy, tell him to come home. Christ! He felt as shamed as a beaten dog. As he lay in the silence of the night, he thought, as he often had, of Mary Jane. *She* was the only one who would understand, who could comfort him. There wasn't anyone else who understood him, or whom he understood. If she still did, he thought, after all this time.

But when he had tried to telephone, only a few months after he arrived in L.A., he found her phone had been shut off. The couple of cards he sent her had been returned. She'd moved and left no forwarding address. Neil still missed her. Missed her more, in his failure, than before, in his success.

He got up and unbuckled his trousers, let them drop to the floor, kicked them to the far wall, then tossed along his shorts. He plodded into the bathroom, turned on the hot water, and went back outside to the joke his landlord called a kitchenette, took a beer out of the refrigerator, and waited the ten minutes it took for the shower water to begin to run hot. He pushed the collection of old newspapers off the only chair in the room and flopped down, stretching his feet out before him. He was relieved that it was night, still not dawn. He hoped he would be asleep before the daylight crept into the room and illuminated all the nastiness that was now mercifully hidden. Hidden, but lurking.

He knew the hole worn in the acrylic carpet was still there, just inside the front door, something Neil had thought was a scientific impossibility – to wear out an acrylic carpet. And there in the darkness was the crack in the wall over the kitchen sink that had been caused by a leak from upstairs. And the grease on the stove burners. And the penetrating smell of decay everywhere. That even the darkness couldn't hide, but the malty aroma of the beer he held just below his nostrils covered it. Thank God.

He went back into the bathroom, turned on the overhead light, and tested the water. Hot; it took exactly ten minutes, the only reliable thing in his life. He adjusted the temperature slightly, then pulled back the sticky, stiff shower curtain and stepped in. He reached for the soap, and cursed when he realized he was down to a sliver. The shampoo would be almost gone, too, he knew, so he washed quickly and got out of the soap-filmed stall. The towel he plucked from the back of the door smelled, but at least it was *his* smell. He rubbed himself roughly, tossed the towel onto the damp stack on the floor, and went back to the other room.

He reached into the fridge for another beer, but was greeted only by a Diet Coke and a rotting apple. Neil slammed the door and flopped back down on his bed. He closed his eyes and prayed that tonight he would be left alone. But he knew he wouldn't be.

He breathed quietly for a while; then, just as he was beginning to drowse, he heard it. The words seemed to come in through his left ear, piercing his brain and shocking his spinal cord. It was him doing his comedy routine at the club tonight, and he would have to relive it even if he didn't want to.

It had been like this for several months now. Every evening, he went to work and waited tables, waiting for his spot in the last of the three nightly shows. Then it was back here, shower, go to bed, and, before he could sleep, listen to the routine all over again. He always used to record it, but he didn't need to now. It ran in his head, over and over. Some nights, it was fairly good, and Neil slept relatively peacefully. Other nights – most nights – he had to scream out that it was all wrong, then get up and write and rewrite the routine until he got it better, adding here, deleting there. Then back to sleep, maybe, for a few hours, until it was time to report to the club to wait tables and do the rewritten routine.

Finally, home again for the private reviews, as he began to call them.

At least tonight's review was good. He listened to the piece he had added about Hollywood agents, and he could hear the crowd laughing. Yes, this bit wasn't bad. After a drought for months, he was onto something. This was good and I'll make it better. I'm going to get my second chance, he thought. He stretched out, exhausted, on the nightmare of a mattress. I'm not always going to live in a dump in Encino, he told himself. Someday, he thought . . . someday . . . I must do my laundry.

And he slept.

11

Jahne tried to keep calm as she drove over to the television studios. Her Toyota was vetted by the guard at the entrance, who checked her name off of a list.

What do you do to prepare for the chance of a lifetime? She'd gone to the best hairdresser in L.A. Viendra was a man who wore a tight little red dress and size-eleven slingback pumps. He'd looked at Jahne's heavy hair. 'What have we here?' he'd simpered. 'How about a crew cut? You've got the face for it.'

'No cut. Can you just cover the grey?' she asked. The white strands stood out against the darkness of the rest of her head.

'Hmm.' He considered, did a tiny dance around her chair, and shook his head. 'No. It would dull the rest of it. Nothing worse than dyed black hair. I have a better idea. We highlight it with blue.'

'Blue?' she asked, and her voice must have quavered, but he explained it all calmly. The blue would make the black look darker and yet give a lustre to the whole mane. She agreed to try.

Now she tossed her hair in front of the rent-a-cop. It did shine beautifully. 'Go right into Building Three,' he told her. She drove across the lot. Once the place had been Desilu, the soundstages where *I Love Lucy* and so many pioneering TV shows had been filmed. Before that it had been Selznick International Pictures. Jahne turned a corner and there, in front of her,

232

was Tara, the plantation house from Selznick's *Gone With the Wind*. She gaped like a Hollywood tourist, but then she saw the sign — Building 3. She remembered now that Selznick had used the building as his offices. *She* was going in there. Not like a tourist, but as a working actress, the way Ingrid Bergman and Olivia de Havilland and Vivien Leigh had done. She pulled the rented Toyota over and took a few deep breaths. Her hands were shaking. Playing this part was a lot harder than she expected. She pulled down the vanity mirror in the car visor and stared at her reflection. She *was* beautiful, if a little pale. Her hair glistened like a raven's wing. She thought of Pete's voice whispering in her ear — 'You're so beautiful. You're just so beautiful.' And certainly Marty DiGennaro wouldn't have invited her here if she wasn't.

'You *are* beautiful,' she whispered to her reflection. 'You *are* beautiful. And you *are* talented. Go show him that. Go show him how pretty and how talented you are.' Her hands still trembled. 'Don't be afraid,' she told herself. 'This is an adventure.' She took a deep breath. Her own voice didn't help her much, but the echo of Pete's came back to her again: 'You're so beautiful.' She could believe *that* voice.

She got out of the car and walked up the path to Building 3, then followed the receptionist's directions to the suite where Marty's offices were. A pretty woman with a crew cut met her outside the door. Did *she* go to Viendra?

'Jahne?' she asked. 'Marty's waiting for you.'

Wordlessly, Jahne followed her down a long hallway where dozens, hundreds, even thousands of actors had walked before. You are Jahne Moore and you are talented and beautiful, she had time to tell herself fiercely, and then was ushered into his office.

Marty DiGennaro was crouched on a big leather sofa, surrounded by a tangle of cables and cameras and lights. As she entered the room, he leapt up and took her hand. He was so nervous and small and wiry, he reminded her of a whippet as he bounded off the sofa, across the room, and then onto an ottoman.

'Sit down, Jahne.'

She slid into the low beige leather chair across from him. He made a gesture with his hands to the several people crouching amidst the tangle of equipment. 'This is Bill, Steve, and Dino,

233

Jahne. If you don't mind, we're just going to talk, and they're going to tape us.'

Oh, fine, Jahne thought to herself. She wondered what he would do if she said she did mind, but that was not in the cards. She felt her hands and armpits go clammy with sweat. She knew she could impress him at an audition, or even a cold reading, but playing Jahne Moore was not so easy for her. She tossed her head, shrugged, and smiled. 'You're the boss,' she said.

He laughed, a high-pitched giggle. Since the time he'd had two movies that were each grossing ten million a day, he'd been called 'the Boss' by much of Hollywood.

'What do you know about the sixties, Jahne?' Marty asked her.

'You mean hippies and flower-power kind of stuff?' she asked.

'Exactly!' he said with such a high level of enthusiasm that she figured that it had to be faked.

'Well,' she continued, 'I guess it was the Beatles era.' She quickly calculated how much it was likely a twenty-four-year-old would know about the period. And how to play a little with Marty's head. 'Wasn't Paul McCartney a Beatle before he was in Wings?' she asked innocently.

'Ouch!' Marty yelped, and one of the guys behind the camera groaned. 'Makes you feel old, doesn't it, Dino?' Marty asked. 'What else do you remember, Jahne?'

'Well,' she said, another punch line prepared, 'Bobby Kennedy was president until he was shot.' She smiled into the camera and licked her lower lip. 'And wasn't there a war someplace?'

It took them a minute to see that she was putting them on. Then belly laughs from the guys, that giggle from Marty. 'Okay, okay. Very cute.' Marty smiled at her. He stood up and walked to her left, over to the window. She turned her head to look at him, but the camera remained on her. Well, if this was her screen test, she could play to a camera as well as to an audience at the Melrose Playhouse.

'Jahne, I am a child of the sixties, and I am obsessed with it. But I think other people are, too. Baby boomers who lived through the sixties, and the younger generation that wishes it had. Do you know what a PIQ is?'

'No,' she admitted.

'It stands for Programme Idea Quotient. Every year the HTI – the

234

Home Testing Institute – asks television viewers to rate programme ideas. The networks use the results to make forecasts of audience levels. My idea for a sixties show was tested. It scored the highest possible points, both with the sixteen-to-twenty-five-year-old group and the thirty-five-to-fifty-year-olds. *That* never happened before. I want to do a show that is set during that era. I can exploit the music and the style of the time, and I can bring in the political upheaval as well. This is Clinton country. There's a lot of opportunity for nostalgia, but it is more than that. There are a lot of parallels to today, and I think I can bring those out.' He moved back to the seat across from her. She nodded, tossed her head, and watched the camera pan as she turned her head to follow him.

'You ever see *Easy Rider*?' he asked.

'Sure. That was Jack Nicholson's first movie, wasn't it?'

'Yeah. Well, I want this project to be a new take on that kind of pilgrimage: finding oneself; finding America. And I want three girls to do it. Three girls on motorcycles.'

'Sounds interesting,' she said. Jesus, she had never been on anything bigger than Neil's motorbike. She crossed her legs, smiled at the camera, and said, 'I wish I had worn my colours.'

Marty smiled. 'I have a lot of ideas. I want this show to look different than anything else. We'll use a single camera and film it – no videotape at all. And we'll use a lot of locations. These girls will cross America. I'll use smears and sneaks and follow focus. It's not going to look like any other TV show. I have some of the best technicians in the business already signed up.'

Jahne nodded, although she didn't have a clue what a sneak or a smear was.

'What kind of makeup do you wear?'

She blinked, paused. Why? Did she have a visible scar? Was there something he, a great director, saw on her face that others didn't? 'Just some regular base. Lancôme, I think. And blusher . . .'

'Any objection to signing an exclusive with a makeup company to only wear theirs?'

'No.' She tried not to show even a flicker of her relief.

'Hey, Dino,' Marty said. 'How are we looking?'

'Looking good, boss,' Dino told him.

Jahne flashed the camera another smile. 'So what next?' she asked.

Marty handed her a dozen unbound pages. 'How about reading this? The part of Cara.'

She picked up the script. A young girl talking to another one about her ex-boyfriend, about her parents, about society, about life. Kind of cornball, but sweet. Over it all, that veneer of toughness that a kid needs to protect herself from being thought a kid.

She looked up. 'Okay. Who reads with me?'

'I'll feed you the cues off camera,' Marty said.

So she began. She pitched her voice a little higher than usual, to get the youth, but it made her tough act so much more poignant. And she took the monologue about her father really fast – almost gabbled it – as if she had to say it aloud but didn't want it heard. She ended the scene – where she asks, 'Do you know what I mean?' – with a whisper and a look right into the camera. She knew it was a good reading. A real good reading.

But was it good enough?

Dear Dr. Moore,

Well, you were a great doctor to my now great body, but how will you do as a psychiatrist? I have so much news that I don't know exactly where to start.

I'm glad you got the clippings – I try not to care too much about what critics say – but the one in the *Times* brought in a lot of L.A. people, including Marty DiGennaro! No, I am not making that up. He came backstage to compliment me, but that was only the beginning! He asked me to do a test, and, yesterday, he asked me to be one of the stars in his new television show.

Okay; I know what you're going to say: did I go through all that agony and you do all that work merely so I could become the next Vanna White? But, Dr. Moore – Brewster – *this is Marty DiGennaro*. And the series is truly innovative. It's called *Three for the Road* and I've seen the first couple of scripts. It's wacky! Three girls (yes, I'm passing for a girl!) go cross-country together by motorcycle. The trick, though, is the terrific dialogue and the wonderful visual concepts – great crosscuts, fades, camera angles. It's evocative more than linear.

Oh, Jesus, I just reread that. Do I sound like I've gone Valley girl on you? Listen, I am very excited, but it's not a done deal yet. Marty (that's me, calling Marty DiGennaro 'Marty'!) has said he needs to cast all three of the leads to see how we play off one another, but I should get my agent to begin working on the contract! When I told him I didn't have an agent, he nearly plotzed! (How many exclamation points have I already used in this letter? I'm afraid more than my quota.) Anyway, he said he'd set me up with Sy Ortis, his agent. *Sy Ortis*! (Absolutely my *last* exclamation point.) Only the most powerful agent in the business.

Anyway, I've also heard that Ortis is a lying scumbag, and that he dumps anyone who doesn't regularly deliver. Not your Mister Rogers type. But, then, the neighbourhood isn't much like Mister Rogers'.

Speaking of neighbourhoods, I've been looking for a place of my own – just to rent, of course – and Roxanne Greely (the real estate agent to the stars) has shown me a really adorable two-bedroom bungalow overlooking the water. She got my name from Marty. All these famous people seem to know each other. I won't tell you the rent, because you'd kill me, but I'm not signing any lease until my contract is signed first.

And talk about money – I can't even imagine it. They're talking $33,000 per episode, and the contract is for eighteen of them! I can't multiply that high. The first cheque I'll write, though, will be one to finish paying off your fees, and I want to thank you again for waiting and believing in me.

There is one fly in the ointment. I have to sign a contract with Flanders cosmetics to be their spokesperson. I hate the idea of selling anything, but I have to to get the job – well, they do promise me a quarter of a million dollars to do it!

Dr. Moore – Brewster – you know that I owe all this to you. You know who I really am – fat, plain, old Mary Jane Moran – and so you know all that I owe you. I can never thank you enough.

Right now, the really strangest thing is how this being beautiful works: it's like having a superpower. Just because of how I look, I'm able to melt barriers, draw people to me, and leap buildings with a single bound. All right, I can't do that last one, but I sure can do the others. It's wild.

How is Raoul? Has the reconstruction around his nose worked? The gifts inside are for him. Send him my love. Save some for yourself, and say hello to the other kids for me, too.

Anyway, I feel like a kid – but a happy one – in a candy store. Write!

Love,
Jahne

There are a few restaurants in the studio zone of L.A. that are more theatre than the Melrose Playhouse ever was. One, of course, is Morton's, where the star-makers dine. Word is that Peter Morton loses money on the place, but keeps it running so he can be part of the scene. Then there's Le Dôme, known to the hipper crowd as 'Le Dump.' Very much the centre of the gay mafia. The young stars eat at The Ivy – all salads and little vegetarian crêpes at fifty bucks per head for brunch on a Sunday. And then, of course, there's Spago.

Tourists are always disappointed by it. After all, it looks a lot like a suburban carpet store from the outside. But inside, the stars do twinkle. And it was where Marty chose to meet Paul Grasso for dinner.

Marty sat down at the banquette as the headwaiter pushed the best table in Spago back into place. After making the obligatory stops at stars' and star-makers' tables, Marty had managed a Hollywood hug for Wolfgang, the owner, and graciously stood until the maître d' had seated Marty's date, Bethanie. Only then could he turn his attention to her. 'Sorry for the delay, but you know how it is here.' He scanned her perfect face, her shapely shoulders, her deep cleavage, her baby-fresh skin, all lightly, evenly tanned.

'You look beautiful tonight, Bethanie,' he said automatically, thinking once again that they all looked alike, the California wannabes. He was considering her for *Three for the Road*, but he had his doubts. She was pretty, even beautiful, but there was nothing *unique* about Bethanie. He'd just found the blonde – well, Sy and Milton had found her – an incredibly fresh girl, Sharleen Something, and *so* fresh she'd be fabulous. With Jahne Moore virtually signed up and vetted by the Flanders and Banion O'Malley crew, he had a brunette already. *She* was intense and brilliant; she'd be good contrast to Sharleen. Was Bethanie the last member of this trinity? He needed a redhead, and Bethanie was a blonde – but Bethanie would be more than willing to dye her hair another shade. Hell, she'd be willing to *shave* her head if it got her the spot. But she was no virgin in any sense of the word; she had been on several crappy television shows, and he really couldn't call her a new face anymore. Casting would be everything on this project, and he had to decide, because time *was* running out.

He removed a silver cigarette case, the one actually used by Cary Grant in *The Philadelphia Story*, took out a Dunhill, tamped it on the antique cover, and placed it between his lips. Marty didn't actually smoke, never inhaled, but he'd always loved props. A flame appeared at the cigarette's tip, held by the lurking captain, and he pulled at the end enough to light it.

Tonight was going to be quick and easy, for old time's sake. It might even be fun. He made it a point to keep up his old friendships – no one would ever be able to say that Marty DiGennaro had forgotten his old pals – but lately he preferred not being around Paul Grasso. Paul's gambling had gone too far, it had begun to show on him, the way an alcoholic's drinking inevitably became apparent. Marty had seen enough, in this town of swingers on the decline from too much drugs, sex, money, and the wrong people in their lives, not to be surprised by anyone's skid. But with Paul, it was different. He had known him from the old neighbourhood, back when they were kids. So he tried a little harder with Paul, although he knew from experience that no one could stop a skidder.

Paulie could still make Marty laugh, however. That was the one thing that Paul consistently gave Marty: funny stories, and hilarious memories. And since Paul hadn't asked him for anything on the phone when he'd called, Marty was going to assume the best: Paul just wanted a night out with an old friend. Paul had never begged Marty for work. He had too much pride, and he knew the risk he ran if he tried that.

Also, Paul had reassured Marty that Paul's date was not a wannabe. Paul raved about her beauty but emphasized that the kid was wealthy in her own right and, being from some family in the Industry, hated the business. Paul just wanted to get in her pants. Typical Paulie Grasso. If she's as beautiful as Paul says she is, he should be peddling her to every producer in town instead of spending all his energy trying to fuck her.

Bethanie broke into Marty's thoughts. 'Who else is coming, Marty? Anyone I know?' What that translated into was 'Anyone who can help me? Anyone I can use?' But Marty could be tolerant of a woman, as long as she was beautiful. And Bethanie *was* beautiful.

239

'No, I don't think you know him. An old friend, Paul Grasso, and his date.' You wouldn't know him, Bethanie, because he hasn't done anything for anyone for a long time.

Marty looked at the old gold Philippe Pattek watch, the one he'd bought at the Errol Flynn estate sale. On the back was engraved 'To E.F. from his S.T.' He'd often wondered who the S.T. was. His most amusing conjecture was Shirley Temple. As he looked up, his attention was drawn to the entrance to the room, the direction, he noticed, in which the other diners were also looking.

A woman – a very beautiful woman – was standing alone, her small black silk bag held in two hands in front of the skirt of her black chiffon dress. She at first appeared to be all magnificent legs, the illusion, to his trained eye, created by the shortness of the dress, the subtly shaded sheer black hose, and the dyed-to-match black *peau de soie* shoes. But she was also tall – god, so tall she made him hard! The top of her dress had a tight, low bodice, held up by the flimsiest spaghetti straps, straining at the fullness of the breasts. And, God, she was tall! Six foot, maybe, but a lot taller in those shoes. And what colour would you call that hair? Not red, not *just* red. Her hair was deeply toned, but much more alive than any auburn. Her only apparent jewellery was a single diamond on her neck, and sparkling diamond earrings. In a town where beautiful women were a dime a dozen, where every waitress had been a Miss Tennessee runner-up, where perfection was ordinary, she was a knock-out, a heart stopper. There was also something familiar about her, something that he knew. Had they met? Surely not – Marty never forgot a face. And certainly not one sculpted as cleanly, as precisely, as that.

Though he could see she was completely aware of the attention she was getting from the room, he could also see that, unlike the beautiful women he had known and observed, she truly seemed not to care about it. There was a calm – no, an aloofness – that held her apart. Then a man turned away from the maître d's desk and took the woman by the elbow as they were led into the room.

Holy shit! The man, Marty realized, was Paul Grasso. *She's* with Paul Grasso? Marty laughed quietly to himself, keeping his eyes on them as they came towards him. Why, that old son-of-a-bitch! This one was definitely *not* Paul's usual – typically, a Las Vegas showgirl or a tart just off the bus from somewhere. Paul's definitely in over his head. And as Marty stared, once again came that nagging familiarity. I know her *somehow*, he thought, or maybe I just want to.

Bethanie, along with every other pretty woman in the room, had watched the spectacular entrance. Now she was talking to him. Babbling on and on.

'What?' Marty asked.

'I *said*, "Who are those people who just came in?"' Bethanie knew she couldn't afford to whine, but she almost was. After being dumped by that bastard Sam Shields, she had no intention of letting Marty get away. She knew the rule of Hollywood survival — 'fuck upward.' Only someone as powerful as Marty could afford to fuck someone beneath him. She and Sam, just breaking through, needed more powerful partners, like Crystal Plenum and Marty DiGennaro. What she didn't need was competition from this Amazon.

'Why don't I introduce you?' Marty stood, extended his hand to Paul, and kept looking at the young woman who reminded him of someone. 'Paul, good to see you. This is Bethanie Lake, Paul Grasso. He's one of my oldest friends.'

Paul's handshake was vigorous, his good mood apparent. 'Marty DiGennaro, Lila, and Bethanie . . . Lake, right?'

'Yes,' Bethanie answered, but her displeasure was evident in the way she bit the word off. Shit! Who needed a bitch who looked like this one sitting across from Marty all night? she asked herself. Why was she so unlucky?

The maître d' had pulled out the chair for Lila opposite Marty, and she smoothly slid into it.

'I have to apologize for making Paul late, Mr. DiGennaro.' She turned her eyes to Bethanie, then Marty, and smiled.

'Marty. Please call me Marty, Lila. And it's very nice of you to take the responsibility for Paul's lateness. Except I expect him to be late.' Looking at Paul, smiling, he added, 'Paul and I go back a long time.'

Marty noticed Lila looking intently at Bethanie, who was now sitting up stiffly on the banquette. 'Bethanie Lake. Didn't you create the role of Leora in *Houston* last season?' Bethanie nodded, perhaps a bit defensively. 'You left that show just in time,' Lila continued. 'After that, the writing went downhill.'

Marty noticed Bethanie relax slightly beside him, but he kept his eyes on Lila. In fact, he couldn't take them off her. Gracious, very gracious, he thought. Everyone knew that it was the stupidest move Bethanie could have made, to leave a successful TV series to try to do a mediocre movie that fell apart. Her agent and manager tried to talk her out of it, advising her to wait another year. But she wouldn't listen. A standard case of biting off more than you can chew. Bethanie *wasn't* ready, and it had really fucked up her career. Unless he gave her another shot. As he looked at the divine redhead, he suspected Lila knew that, too.

Marty forced himself to speak. 'I've ordered a California merlot, if that's okay with everyone,' he told them, as the waiter poured.

Lila held her hand over her glass. 'Actually, I'd prefer a Manhattan, if it's all the same to you.' She turned to the waiter and said, 'Straight up, with a twist,' then dropped her eyes and snapped her purse open. Marty nodded to the waiter, then noticed the cigarette Lila held to her bow-shaped lips in the long fingers of her left hand. Nobody smoked in California anymore! She was a trip. He immediately pulled out his rarely-used Dunhill lighter, and beat the waiter's hand to Lila's cigarette.

She inhaled deeply, holding her cigarette hand straight up with its elbow cupped in her other. Where had he seen that gesture? God, it was driving him nuts! She raised her face to the ceiling and released a long, slow stream of white smoke, then dropped her head and stated to no one in particular, 'I hope no one minds if I smoke.'

He knew her, he was *sure* he knew her. Her gestures, her voice. It was maddening really, the familiarity of her, mixed with the utter strangeness. Yet how would he have forgotten her? He hated to stoop to the oldest line in the book, but he felt compelled. 'I seem to know you from somewhere,' Marty said, 'but have we met before? You look very familiar.'

Bethanie, her wineglass to her lips, choked, put down the glass, nearly spilling it, and coughed to clear her throat.

'Something tough to swallow?' Paul asked her, and gave her a smack on her back.

Lila smiled, raised her lovely brows at Marty, allowing the gesture to speak for itself. 'Westlake School for Girls?' she asked. She looked away as if bored. 'No, I'm sorry to say. We've never met.' Then, looking back at him, she added, as if she had almost forgotten her manners, 'But you're very nice to ask.' Oh, Christ, Marty thought wryly, you can take the nerd out to Hollywood but . . . He watched her as she sipped her drink, holding the glass by its stem. It accentuated the length of her fingers, and he felt a tingle in his groin at the thought of those same fingers wrapped around another stem. But he was still perplexed.

'Do you act? I'm sure I've seen you in something.' She was just so familiar . . . yet so distinctive.

'The one thing I do *not* do is act. My mother tried to push me into the business, but I won.'

'Hey, I thought we weren't talking business tonight, *gumba*,' Paul reminded Marty. He picked up his menu. 'So, Beth, what's good?'

Bethanie looked away, but only for a moment, from Marty and Lila. She knew she couldn't afford to. Marty studied Lila some more, ignoring both Paul and Bethanie. 'What did your mother do, Lila?'

'About what?' she purred.

He laughed. He was enjoying this woman, and he could see that she seemed to make Paul more like his old self. Only Bethanie was definitely not at ease tonight. She was way out of her league. Well, he thought, almost sympathetically, she *was* losing the chance of a lifetime. That could make *anyone* uneasy.

Marty smiled at Lila, and returned the conversational ball over the net. 'About life, liberty, and the pursuit of happiness. And about a paycheque – or perhaps she was born rich?'

'She was born poor and made herself rich. And I was born rich and intend to stay that way. I just haven't yet figured out a way to do it. My mother had talent. I just resemble her.' With a dip of her head, she indicated to the waiter she wanted a refill. Marty marvelled at the familiarity of the gesture, sinuous, almost dramatic, yet still natural. Lila looked at him. 'Now, *you* were born poor and became rich, and *Paul* was born poor and became rich, and then poor, and then rich again,' she said, poking Paul gently in his side. She laughed, the noise a deep purr.

'You could act, Lila, I keep telling you,' Paul said. 'Your mother wasn't wrong about everything, remember? I knew her when. You're just like her. Even when she was on the balls of her ass, I had to sell roles to *her* harder than I had to sell her to the *producers*.'

Then the light dawned. Of course! The resemblance was there, not only to her mother but to her fabulous father, too, a guy who had always been too beautiful to be a man. Marty smiled, placed his wineglass on the table, and said, 'Theresa O'Donnell's daughter.' He was almost embarrassed, but it would have been a lot easier if Lila had cooperated. She obviously was not the typical 'my mom's a star' kid.

'I'd prefer that people say *she's* Lila Kyle's mother, but I haven't yet figured out how to make that happen. Anyway, I'm Kerry

Kyle's daughter, too.' Looking around the table, she said to no one in particular, 'I'm famished. Would someone slaughter me a fatted calf?'

'*Days and Knights*, 1949,' Marty said. It was a great old line from Theresa's first movie. She'd played a vaudeville hoofer.

'Nineteen forty-eight,' Lila corrected. 'But how did you know that? It's a little obscure for someone who's as current as yourself.' He saw the surprise in Lila's face.

'It was *shot* in 1948, but it wasn't *released* until 1949.'

'Well, I'll be damned,' Lila said, obviously impressed.

'And I believe it was in that movie that she first met Kerry Kyle.' He watched Lila sit back in her chair, her surprise growing. Picking up the menu, he looked over the selections and said, '"I believe there are no more calves, my dear. Would a thigh do?"'

Lila's small shriek of delight pleased him. He knew not only Theresa's line, but also Kerry Kyle's response. Now Lila leaned over the table, took his face in both her hands, and kissed him on the forehead. The skin where she had brushed it tingled. 'Oh, thank you!' she cried. Bethanie made a noise that sounded to Marty like a snort.

'I used to watch it whenever it came on television,' Lila was saying. 'It's how I got to know my father. He died when I was little. And I watched all my mother's films, over and over. I think it made me miss her less when she was away. But how do *you* know those lines?'

The waiter, who had been discreetly standing at the table for some time, finally cleared his throat. They ordered, the appetizers were served, and they ate and chatted. Or, rather, they ate while *he* chatted. About every film, about the fifties and sixties in Hollywood. Marty finally paused as their meals were placed before them. 'It's sad, you know, that that era has passed. But I'm so grateful that I have some of the original prints from those times.' He chewed and thought for a moment more. 'Ted Turner, of course, should be horsewhipped.'

Paul, who was never very interested in anything except gambling – who was playing the main rooms in Vegas, and how could he make some fast money – asked, 'Why, what did Ted Turner ever do to you?'

Lila became indignant. 'Ted Turner took Gainsborough's *Blue Boy* and had someone change the colour to green!'

'So what?' Paul shrugged. Marty looked at him and shuddered.

Watching Paul eat was a lot like watching a horror movie: you wanted to cover your eyes, but you couldn't look away. Marty tried to explain. 'Eh, *gumba*, what Lila means is, you don't change a work of art once it's been created. Turner is taking hundreds of classic black-and-white films and putting colour into them with the use of computers. That's *batz, capisce*?'

'Yeah, sure, Marty; okay, it's crazy. But, you know, I'm not so sure. I can't remember wanting to watch too many black-and-white movies lately. *Shadows and Fog* didn't pack 'em in.'

Marty and Lila laughed. Bethanie jumped in to join them. But her laugh sounded more like a death rattle, Marty thought. He could feel her urgency to join the conversation somehow.

'So, Lila, what was it like growing up the child of Theresa O'Donnell and Kerry Kyle?' Bethanie asked. 'You must have received a lot of special treatment.'

'Well, to be honest, when I was a kid, I didn't think I was different from anyone else, really. I was alone a lot. And when I was old enough to go to school, I was going to school with other kids like myself – you know, Tori Spelling, the Nelson boys, Cary Grant's daughter – so I still was like everyone else.' Marty watched Lila break a roll in half and butter a small piece.

'High school was the same. Well, not really; by then I was reading more about life outside the Hollywood ghetto, but, still, none of it seemed very real to me. I guess I was too sheltered,' she said, and nibbled at the roll. 'But I also took a lot for granted. I *do* remember a couple of really exciting times.' Marty saw her look around the table to be sure everyone really was interested. 'Once, Uncle Cary played Santa at my house and I sat on his lap. I knew *immediately* he was Cary Grant. My mother had every one of his movies at home, and every movie magazine had pictures and stories of Cary Grant. He had silver hair, he wasn't young anymore, but he was still gorgeous. Still, I was so disappointed, because in *that* role I wanted the real thing, not any old actor. I cried and said, "You're not Santa Claus, you're just Uncle Cary." I got off his lap and wouldn't return. I couldn't understand then why all the women laughed so hard.'

Bethanie said it for everybody. 'Cary Grant came to *your* house and played *Santa Claus* for you?' After a pause, however, she laughed a forced, throaty laugh, said, 'Oh, come on, Lila,' then took a dismissive sip of her drink.

Lila appeared almost embarrassed, her translucent white skin momentarily flushed pink. Her beauty was not lost on Marty's professional eye; for most of the evening, he had been looking at her as if through a camera's lens. She's more beautiful than her mother, has the eyes of her father, skin like Merle Oberon, a voice like Lauren Bacall, and the body of Ann-Margret, except taller. What a package!

Lila shrugged one shoulder. It was an elegant movement. 'That's what happens when I talk about my childhood. People get jealous.'

Bethanie suddenly wasn't laughing. 'Jealous? I'm not *jealous*. I just don't believe you. I can't picture Cary Grant putting on a Santa Claus beard and having some snotty Beverly Hills kid sit on his knee. Why would Cary Grant do that?'

'Because he wanted to fuck my mother. And that was the deal,' Lila said. 'Anyway, that wasn't so much. When one of the Mankiewicz kids locked himself in the bathroom, *they* got the Three Stooges to do a show on the lawn so he'd come out. Of course, they worked cheap by then.'

Marty gave up on Bethanie at that moment. He found himself staring intently at Lila. What he saw was more than beauty. She had poise, intelligence, and – instinct told him – talent. Plus a face that could move through a camera lens and be welcomed in every living room in America. And every bedroom. He wondered if she and Paul had set him up for this, with the reluctant-virgin bullshit. But what if they had? Selznick had never complained when his brother shlepped Vivien Leigh over the night that shooting for *Gone With the Wind* began. Marty could take a lucky break however it came. 'Lila, I think Paul's right. I'd suggest you think seriously about acting on TV.'

'But TV is crap,' she said.

'Not when *I* do it.'

'*You* don't do TV.'

'I do now. And I'm going to change it for all time.'

Marty watched as Lila, keeping her eyes on his face, put down her fork and stared. Finally, she spoke. 'You're not kidding, are you?'

'No, I'm not. And in fact, if you give me a call tomorrow, I might even have an idea for you.'

Lila put her hand to her throat and tilted her head back, letting her long, red hair cascade over the back of the chair. She seemed to be searching the ceiling of Spago for words.

Paul Grasso, quiet too long, said, 'For chrissakes, Lila, just say

"Thank you, Mr. DiGennaro" and then kiss my ass for taking you out to dinner.'

Lila smiled and said, 'Thank you, Marty. I'll give you *my* number.' Then she turned to Paul Grasso. 'But it's a little too soon for any ass-kissing, Paul. After all, I haven't even had dessert yet.'

13

After the *Jack and Jill* wrap party, Sam Shields drove home from the studio alone. He was exultant, because he knew the picture in the can was good, and had the potential to be great. He had the wonderful feeling of all creators when they look upon their work and find it good. His words had been made flesh, and the flesh was delicious.

Of course, it hadn't been accomplished without a certain amount of pain and suffering. And compromise. Well, that was appropriate for a work titled *Jack and Jill and Compromise*, he told himself. All of life was a compromise, after all. Wasn't that the home truth he was trying to express? And also trying to live?

For a moment, only for a moment, he thought of Mary Jane Moran's transfiguring performance as Jill. Filming the part she had created had brought her image back to him over and over again. There had been times in New York when he had felt that her face, her plain muffin of a face, had actually lit the stage. Well, he had managed to coax a good performance out of Crystal Plenum. It might not be as intense, as sensitive as Mary Jane's, but it was good. Crystal had never worked as a stage actress; it was only now that she was in her thirties and off a long string of ingenue roles in films that she wanted to try *acting*. And, Sam told himself proudly, he *had* gotten her to act.

He smiled as he drove the BMW onto the expressway. Even now, months later, when he was a soon-to-be-successful director, he was surprised that he, Sam Shields, was sleeping with a movie star. Crystal Plenum.

And, he had to admit, it was a thrill to look down at that perfectly exquisite face as he made love to her. It was a face he had already seen in ecstasy on the screen as Mel Gibson, Warren Beatty, Kevin Costner, and other stars had made love to her. Now he was doing it in real life. Her silken skin, her perfect breasts, her long legs – all for him. It certainly enhanced his pleasure, knowing that she was probably one of the three most beautiful, most desired stars in the country, maybe in the world. And *he* possessed her.

He possessed her and her image in the cans of film. Immortality in tin. There was still so much to do, and to learn. There was the cutting and editing, the soundtrack had to be laid down, the final looping done. Even the credits had to be designed and laid in. And it would be a lot easier to learn the next batch of tricks of the trade without the entire cast and crew as his audience. From now until release date, he and a handful of pros would work without witnesses to any foolish question he asked or mistake he made.

And then – the release. He caught a glimpse of his reflection in the rearview mirror, and the stupid smile of triumph was still on his face. Well, why not? He had done well, and he was almost sure he'd get another shot at directing. For a moment, he felt a small shiver of anxiety tarnish his day: he had no other vehicle that he felt he could sell as a film.

The fact that he hadn't written a word since he came out to L.A. shouldn't worry him. After all, working on *Jack and Jill* had been a full-time job. But the idea of finishing this film and retiring to a quiet corner of his rented house and writing alone for a year did not excite him. Well, he'd cross that bridge later. Meanwhile, he had a triumph to prepare for.

And he had to admit that showing the film to his mother and father would be a sweet part of it. They had never been much interested in his stage career: to them, theatrical success meant Broadway. Now they were impressed. He'd had them flown up from Florida for a week during the shoot. They'd stayed at his Laurel Canyon house, swum in his pool, come down to the studio, watched him direct on the soundstage. His mother, perfect and immaculate as ever, still more than pretty despite her age and the toll that drinking took, surveyed it all coolly. He longed for some warmth, some sign of approval: a hug, a kiss, a loving look. Finally, at the airport, his mother had looked up at him with tears in her eyes and a tremor in her voice and said, 'You're not like your father.' It was hardly an embrace, but Sam took it as a benediction.

His father had taken his hand and, out of earshot of his mother, had simply gestured at his son's linen suit, the L.A. sunshine, the palm trees, the limo they had taken to the airport, and said, 'Don't fuck this up for yourself.' Not exactly a vote of confidence, but an acknowledgment, of sorts.

And if there was one thing Sam was determined not to do, it was fuck this up for himself. It was a funny thing: the higher he rose out of the muck of oblivion into the sunshine of L.A. success, the more determined he was not to sink back even half a step. He wanted not only success but all its trappings: the right table at the Polo Lounge, a house account at Morton's, people to take his calls immediately. He didn't care too much about the money – that was nice – but he did want the power and all that came with it.

Now Sam drove along the winding road to Laurel Canyon. His own driveway was hidden by the scruffy undergrowth and pine trees that passed as naturalized landscape out here. His leased house was small but choice, cream-coloured adobe outside, and inside decorated in the Santa Fe style, complete with Indian artifacts, colourful serapes and rugs, big unglazed pottery. Giant stands of cattails and reeds grew around the tiled patios and pool area. He passed by them now, walked into the living room through the glass doors facing the sapphire-blue tiled pool, and threw his jacket onto the sofa. As always, he headed straight for the bar but stopped, as always, to turn on the answering machine. He listened as he poured out an Absolut, threw in a few ice cubes, and sat down to enjoy his two fixes of the day: his single drink and his messages.

The tape rewound, making its usual beeps and squeaks. Then it clicked into forward. 'Hi, Sam. It's Bethanie. I've got a real shot at a Marty DiGennaro project, but I've run into a little snag, and I wondered if I could use your name? Look, could you please call me at . . .'

Sam, with his remote, fast-forwarded to the next message. He'd broken that off long ago and could smell a ploy for a get-together a mile off. But what if it was true? Sam admired Marty DiGennaro more than any other American director. Well, Bethanie knew that, was using that. It was bullshit. He'd forget it.

'April Irons' office. Could you please call her back at seven this evening at . . .'

Sam jotted down the number quickly. He had planned to spend the evening with Crystal, celebrating the wrap, but he could call April on his way over.

'Sam, it's Molly. I haven't spoken to you lately, and I just

249

wondered if you're all right and if by any chance you've heard from Mary Jane . . . .'

Sam sighed and fast-forwarded over the rest of the message. The hell with her. Molly and Chuck had been guilt-inducing and tiresome, resenting him for leaving them behind, a reminder of how small his life had once been.

Another beep. 'Sam, it's Crystal. I won't be able to make it tonight, I'm afraid. Some other time.'

For a moment, he felt a stab of disappointment. Disappointment and something else. Was it fear? But Crystal had a complicated life: a kid, a husband. She had cancelled at short notice before. Still, he backed up the tape and replayed the message.

'Sam, it's Crystal. I won't be able to make it tonight, I'm afraid. Some other time.'

It made him uneasy. After all, he *knew* dialogue. He was a playwright, for God's sake. There was something about the line. It was formal, too formal. And the 'some other time' – it sounded so perfunctory.

He played the message yet again. Goddamn it, it *wasn't* his imagination. He could *tell* when something was wrong. He was intuitive. That's what made him such a good director. He lifted up the phone receiver and dialled Crystal's number. Her au pair answered and tried to blow him off, but he managed at last to have Inga put him through.

'Crystal, about tonight,' he began quickly. 'April just called and I've got to see her. Could we cancel, or could you come over later?'

'Didn't you get my message?'

'No. I just walked in.'

'Well, I said I couldn't make it.'

'Great. That's convenient. I'll call tomorrow.'

There was a pause. 'I don't think it's a good idea, Sam.'

He felt his palm go wet, making the receiver slippery to hold. For a crazy moment, his mother's face, as he'd last seen her at the airport, flashed before his eyes. He literally shook his head to rid himself of the image, to hear Crystal's voice clearly. 'Listen, Sam, it's been great, but I think it's run its course, don't you?' he heard her say. 'I mean, it's silly to beat around the bush, isn't it?'

His mouth was as dry as his palm was wet, but he managed, calmly, even rather coldly, to ask one question. 'Just like that, Crystal?'

'Well,' she said, her voice tight with impatience, 'after all, the shoot *is* finished. The movie wrapped, Sam, didn't it?'

14

Lila awakened early the morning after she'd signed the contract to play Crimson along with the exclusive Flanders Cosmetics deal. Her picture, along with those of the other two bimbos, had made the third page of *Daily Variety* and Army Archerd ran an item. She poured a glass of orange juice and, carrying the cordless phone, took it out to the verandah. The money from the cosmetics company would come in handy. Of course, she didn't plan for a minute to wear that cheap crap, but so what? Anyone who knew anything wore MAC and she'd keep wearing it. But she'd use the money. She'd get a good car, some new clothes, *and* a place of her own. Plus, she would start her payback plan. And she knew who she'd start with. She reached over to the Princess phone beside her bed and dialled the number. 'Ara Sagarian, please. This is Lila Kyle.'

After a pause, Lila said, 'I *know* what Ara said, Miss Bradley. But if you let him know that I'm calling him because I have to make a decision about representation, I think he'll talk to me. No, I'll wait.'

Lila didn't have to wait long. 'Good morning, Lila. I'm a little surprised to hear from you again.'

'Mr. Sagarian, I've presumed terribly on you and I'm very sorry. I'd like to make it up to you. I'm not going to ask any favours, except for advice. You know I got the part in Marty DiGennaro's new TV show? Well, I've practically signed with Sy Ortis, but I was hoping that you would approve before I did. There's a million dollar contract involved. Is it the right thing to do?'

Lila listened to Ara breathing at the other end. It was a long moment. Would he take the bait? 'You don't owe me anything, Lila. This is show business. I'm just happy for you that you got the part, and that you have such prestigious representation in Mr. Ortis.'

'You're a real gentleman, Ara.' She just let the hook dangle. He bit and asked the question. She smiled. 'No, I still haven't signed with Sy.'

'Lila, this is an important step. Let me take you to lunch today, you know, to make up for the way I treated you. Can we say the Polo Lounge at one?'

'Great. I'll see you then,' she said, and hung up smiling.

For years, the Polo Lounge had been the place for power-broking breakfasts and lunches. But when the Beverly Hills Hotel closed for renovations, others had abandoned it, even after it reopened, refurbished. Ara Sagarian had not. Ara prided himself on his loyalty to anything excellent.

Ara was seated at what was once the most sought-after corner table when Lila arrived at ten after one. He stood with great effort to greet her, and Lila graciously kissed his deflated cheek.

'Thank you *so* much for the invitation, Ara. I was afraid I had really alienated you.' She leaned forward. 'I couldn't bear that. I think too highly of you.'

Ara smiled. But he was too curious for chitchat. 'Lila, how did you get Marty DiGennaro to give you the part in his new series?'

She threw back her head and laughed. 'Blood will tell, Ara,' she said.

After a moment, Ara joined her in laughing. 'Well, it looks like you have done very well on your own. It hardly seems as if you need representation at all.'

'Except, as you know, there's a lot more to be done. I'm certain Marty's series will be a major hit, and that will bring in endorsements, movie deals, licensing – millions, I'm told. It's not just a new series, Ara. It could be an industry. Les Merchant at the Network is really throwing everything into this. I need someone I can *rely* on. Someone I can be *sure* would watch out for my best interests. The way you did for my mother.' Lila lowered her eyes. 'Is Sy Ortis the man, Ara?'

He reached out an ancient claw and took her hand in his. 'I'd be afraid to tell you yes, my dear,' he said.

Lila fluttered her lashes.

'I was afraid of that! You know, I didn't like what you did to me at first, but after my ego repaired, well, I respect the loyalty you showed my mother. Even though she doesn't bring you in much money anymore, you still stood up for your client.' Lila looked directly into Ara's eyes and added, 'I like that.' Lila watched as Ara adjusted himself in his chair. He took up a spotless linen handkerchief and delicately dabbed at his mouth, wiping the spittle away. The next move was his, and she could see he knew it.

'I'm not sure you can expect the same commitment from Sy Ortis,' he told her gently. 'But you say you haven't signed with him yet?'

'No, I haven't,' Lila said blandly, and picked at her salad.

'Well, then . . .' Ara faltered. Lila remained silent. She wouldn't want to make this one bit easier for him.

'Well,' Ara began again. He licked his lips. Yes, Lila thought. *Yes.* The old bastard is going to go for it. He's not so old or so sick that he can pass up the action. When was the last time he signed on a *new*, hot talent? 'Since you haven't yet signed with Sy Ortis, perhaps it's time *we* talked about a relationship.' Ara dipped a spoon into his gazpacho and brought it unsteadily to his mouth. 'Let's see, there are the endorsements, as you say, and future movie projects. There's already a lot of buzz on this project. We should start putting out feelers for something for you to do during your first hiatus. And there'll be contracts, contracts, contracts. Oh, the list is interminable. By the way, has anyone read your contract with Marty yet? You should have all sorts of options in it. There are a number of "what-if" situations that one couldn't possibly anticipate, unless, of course, one had been through it with others for years and years.'

'Unless one was someone like you?' Lila asked, just to set the hook firmly before she began reeling him in.

'Not someone *like* me, my dear. *Me!*' Ara said, and dabbed at the corner of his mouth.

'But I thought Mother wouldn't let you take me on. She'd be furious,' Lila said.

'*I'll* handle Theresa,' Ara told her. 'After all, she's not so active now, and there would be no conflict.'

'I'm afraid it would come down to an "It's her or me," Ara.' Lila said, and she felt a delicious thrill. Would it really be this easy?

'Theresa would never be so foolish as to force my hand in that way.'

'I'm not talking about Theresa, Ara. I'm talking about myself. If you were to be my agent, you would have to drop Theresa O'Donnell.'

Ara put his spoon down and held the linen napkin to his mouth. He stared at Lila. For the briefest, most horrible moment, she felt the line go slack between them. But the bait was too rich, the hook too deeply set. Ara, the dying old shark, had smelled fresh

253

blood in the water. Lila almost laughed out loud as she watched him struggle and then succumb. 'I understand, Lila. Of course, I'll do it as delicately as possible.'

Lila gave Ara a brilliant smile, then turned in her seat and called over a hovering waiter. 'Bring Mr. Sagarian a telephone.' Lila continued to look at him as the phone was jacked in and placed at his good right side. 'I'm not particularly concerned with the delicacy, Ara, but rather the timing. I'd like you to show me some loyalty. Now, Ara. Call her *now*. You know her number.'

Ara, staring at Lila almost mesmerized, picked up the receiver, dialled the number, then reached into his pocket and pulled out yet another pristine handkerchief to wipe the drool from the corner of his mouth. At last he tore his eyes away. Had she actually seen shame in them? Lila sat back and listened, the smile still on her face. 'Theresa, please,' he almost whispered, and Lila imagined Estrella going to the Puppet Mistress with the phone. 'Theresa,' he asked. 'It's Ara. And I'm afraid I have some bad news.' Lila listened to Ara's side of the conversation as if it were a wonderful dream. It was a more sumptuous sweet than the Polo Lounge's famous white-chocolate mousse.

When Ara had finished and hung up, Lila leaned over to him and patted his good cheek. 'Now, that's taken care of,' she said with satisfaction. 'What would *you* like for dessert?'

15

It was a rat race, Sy Ortis thought as he drove his Bentley Turbo R out of the canyon. And there were a lot of different kinds of rats. Sy always thought of 'RAT' as an acronym for 'Regulars,' 'Assholes,' and 'Talents.' It was his little code, his theory of life, almost.

The Regulars were in the vast majority – all the poor nine-to-five working stiffs, all the guys in dull businesses, the insurance agents, the waitresses and waiters, the IBM salesmen, the guys who worked in tool and die shops – all of them were Regulars: consumers of the dream machine that Ortis helped to create. Regulars watched other people's dreams and nightmares on big screens and small ones while they lived their boring lives, too unimaginative even for good dreams of their own. In Hollywood, they were called 'the flyovers,' – the masses between the coasts.

'Talents' were Ortis' clients. The special people, the ones who dreamed big enough to entrance the Regulars. So many Regulars, so few Talents. Christ, how boring was it when most people started in with 'I had the most interesting dream last night.'? Balls. It was only the Talents, with their weirdnesses, their visions, their little streaks of eccentricity, that really *were* interesting. Ortis worked with the most interesting people in the world. Writers who wrote down great dreams, actors and actresses who looked like great dreams, directors who could put the two together and create great dreams.

Yeah, sometimes the Talents were difficult, sometimes they got fucked up on coke, into bad debt with the IRS, into trouble with their marriages, but, hey, they *produced*. Sy knew how to handle Talents. And he had almost nothing to do with Regulars.

It was the Assholes in the middle that gave him trouble. The ones who *thought* they were Talents and wouldn't fuckin' let up on you until you had to crush them and wipe them off your shoe bottom like the dog shit they were. Sy's biggest problem was unloading an Asshole he'd mistaken for a Talent, and his worst nightmare was the revenge of a Talent he'd treated like an Asshole.

That Morelli character was giving him trouble now. A definite Asshole. Got the pilot, fucked it up, couldn't go the distance. So why didn't he just crawl back into the hole that he'd crawled out of? Instead of fuckin' driving Sy crazy with his phone calls and his crazy letters and his ambushes outside the office. Him and every other Asshole.

But Morelli wasn't *really* a problem. Sy was virtually certain the guy was a true Asshole. As long as the fucker didn't have a gun, Sy could give two shits what the little weasel thought or said.

April Irons, on the other hand, *she* was a Talent. A big Talent. So big that now she almost ran International Studios, one of the last big ones in the movie business. And Sy, to his eternal shame and grief, had mistaken her for an Asshole. He'd fucked her bad on a Marty DiGennaro deal, back in the days when you could fuck April over and live, and the bitch would never forget it. Christ, back then how was he supposed to know that gashes could run studios?

So, though he would go to a screening of Crystal Plenum's latest movie, produced by April, he knew he'd be seated back with the dog shit. That was despite being Crystal's agent and, he reminded himself, the most powerful man-behind-the-scenes in all of Hollywood. It was just that April was powerful in front of the scenes, too, and the bitch never forgave, never forgot.

Of course, neither did Sy. But he was at the mercy of his Talents. It was an agent's lot in life. And it pissed him off big-time that Marty, his guy, his resident genius director, was not only doing this stupid television gig, but had gone out and hired one of the little bitches for the goddamn thing without even consulting him. Marty's latest 'find,' was already represented by that dying old dragon lady Ara Sagarian, or so he had heard. Ara had represented her mother. Now there was nothing Sy could do about it, except suck his own dick. Instead, he reached for the inhaler on the seat beside him. He'd make Milton Glick pay for this. Okay, Milt had brought in the blonde and they'd tied her up, but Marty himself had also found the other actress, the Melrose one. Sy absolutely *had* to sign *her*: two out of three would give him the majority of representation, if not the unanimity he had craved.

Well, at least Glick *had* come through with that hillbilly. It had been and, he saw, would continue to be, easy as pie with her. Sign here, do this, move there, smile nice. Why couldn't it always be so easy?

The phone in his car rang and he winced, reached over, and lifted it from the receiver. Jesus, he hated to talk on the phone and drive at the same time. It made him nervous, and that made the asthma kick in worse. He sighed. 'Hello?'

'Mr. Ortis? It's Michael McLain on the line,' his own secretary's voice told him. 'Can I patch him through?'

'Yes.' There were a series of clicks and squawks. Sy almost went up on the divider at the Burbank exit. *Jesu Cristos!*

'Mr. Ortis? Michael McLain is on the line.' This time, it was Michael's secretary. Michael still made *you* hold for *him*. Well, those days will be ending soon if he makes another goddamn flop like *Akkbar*.

'I know that, goddamn it!'

'Hey, you old Spanish son-of-a-bitch. How goes it?' Sy swerved to avoid a Toyota Tercel that nearly cut him off. Sure. He was driving a nine thousand dollar piece of shit. What did he care. Sy almost dropped the phone, recovered it, and tried to inhale.

'What's up, Mike?' he asked. He knew that Michael hated to be called Mike.

'Listen, I wondered about what was going down with Addison and that script I liked.'

Sy sighed. No way that Rex Addison was going to star Michael in his next action picture. For chrissake, Rex was only twenty-eight. He *grew up* watching Michael McLain movies. To Rex, Michael was an old fart. And the bullshit about Michael always doing his own stunts was bought by the civilians, but Rex was savvy.

'Jeez, I think we can do much better than *that*,' Sy said. 'The script has no style, no cachet.'

'Fuck the cachet. Addison's last three had *legs*. I can give it the style.

In a pig's ass. 'Listen, Mike, I have something much better. A buddy flick. Something I saw this week that's perfect.'

'And who's my buddy?' Michael asked, suspiciously.

'Ricky Dunn.'

'Who?'

Michael knew perfectly well who Ricky Dunn was. He'd had two unbelievable big ones. *People* magazine had voted him 'the sexiest man alive.' Sy slowed to avoid an old man just in time. 'He's signed to play a rookie architect in that new Benson thing.'

'Great. And I'm the geezer who shows him how to build a skyscraper? Fuck that.'

'Michael, there comes a point in a man's career when he has to broaden . . .'

'I get top billing. My name alone over the title.'

Sy knew it was impossible. Hell, Michael probably knew it was impossible. Although you never could tell: these guys' egos were so big they often lost touch with reality. Sy reached for his inhaler. 'Listen, *compadre*, why would you want to cut off your nose that way? Might as well bring in all the Ricky Dunn fans, too.' Sy knew that there was no way that Ricky would give up top billing. Why should he? Michael, on the other hand, hadn't had a solid hit in three years. He should be grateful for a chance like this. Sy knew he had to move him in that direction. Because if he could sell Michael on this, he could make a fortune off of packaging the deal – he also represented his client Benson and the crappy script.

'Mike,' he began in a reasonable tone, 'this is a real opportunity. Bob Redford asked to see the script.'

'Look, don't start to tell me that playing second banana to a new kid on the block is *broadening*,' Michael screamed.

'Look at Paul Newman,' Sy began again.

'Paul Newman is almost seventy fucking years old. I'm forty-six.'

'Michael, you're fifty-three, and everyone knows it but you.'

'Look, I still act as well as I ever did. I still fuck as well. *Better* even.'

'I, thank God, would have no way of knowing that,' Sy said. He slammed on the brakes, nearly hitting his head on the windshield and almost rear-ending the motherfucker in the Benz in front of him. *Madre di Dios*, the roads had been taken over by assholes! And he was driving a car that cost more than most people's homes. He sighed. 'Listen, just do me a favour. *Think* about the Ricky Dunn movie. It's just what you need now.'

'Fuck you!' Michael screamed, and hung up on him. *Sangre de los Santos*, did it have to be this hard? Michael had been in a slump lately, and he was ageing, but he was still important, and Sy wanted him as a client, at least for another year or two. Sy felt himself begin to gasp for air and reached across the seat again to his inhaler. Okay, he admitted to himself. He was upset. Normally he didn't let little things like this bother him. After all, he was riding high. He was the consummate deal-maker in Hollywood. April Irons might be powerful, and very visible, but she wasn't in his league. No one was.

Back in the twenties, it was men like Lasky and Mayer who ran the Industry: the big studio bosses were sultans, with the power of screen life or death over their stable of performers. Then, in the late forties, things began to change. The stars began going independent, and the studio system began breaking down. But no star, no matter how popular, had overwhelming power. It was only by controlling dozens of them that Warner or Mayer had stayed on top, and none of the studios today could afford to pay dozens of big stars.

But agents didn't pay stars. They were paid *by* them. It was a perfect setup. The more talent you represented, the more power you had, and the more money you made. So a series of superagents arose. In the forties, it was Lew Wasserman and Leland Hayward, in the fifties and sixties, it was Lew Wasserman and Ara Sagarian; in the seventies, it was Lew Wasserman and Sue Mengers; in the eighties it was Mike Ovitz. Now, Sy thought with a smile, laying down his inhaler, now, it's me. The next Lew Wasserman.

He told himself he should be happy. More than happy. Rich. Because Sy Ortis had a secret. Well, he had many of them, but he had one very big secret. It was that he had also kept the bodega, as his grandma used to tell him.

When he was little, it was his grandmother who had raised him and his five sisters. Tía María, as everyone in the neighbourhood called her, ran the local bodega, and the rest of the neighbourhood. And it was his grandmother who had taught him more about business than Wharton ever could have.

'*Pepito*, if I was Rockefeller,' she'd say, staring deep into Sy's eyes, 'I would be richer than Rockefeller. You know why?'

He shook his head.

'Because I'd also keep the bodega.'

Now Sy, on his way to being as rich as Rockefeller, had come up with a bodega of his own. It was too hard to make a living simply by peddling bodies to producers and taking his percentage while they got rich. Sure, when it worked, it worked big. But Sy understood from the very beginning that he should also try to keep the bodega.

So he did. He had started a dummy corporation – two, actually. One of them sold scripts – all bought cheap, mostly useless – to many of his stars' development companies and to studios. The other bought up merchandising rights from his clients for as little as one dollar, and sold them for a hell of lot more. A conflict of interests? Perhaps. But very, very profitable. And nothing had ever been as big as the potential on this deal with Flanders Cosmetics. The girls signed up for *Three for the Road* were going to be pitched like a product to America, and unless he was *loco en la cabeza* they were going to be bought faster than condoms in a whorehouse.

Now Sy was only a few blocks from his office. He sailed through a red light and turned onto the wide avenue. He sighed with relief. Well, sometimes it was easy. At least that cornpone blonde had been signed easily, and could be big. Real big. Sharleen Smith. She was an extraordinary-looking girl. Glick had pulled that one out of his ass.

But it was still a constant struggle to stay on top of the slippery pile. Sy mourned the fact that he'd lost the redhead. He tried to take a deep breath. One step at a time. All he had to do today was sign this New York actress of Marty's, convince Michael McLain to do the Ricky Dunn movie, and then eat April Irons' dirt at the premiere. That, and manage to breathe.

Jahne sat across the desk from Sy Ortis, watching him while he talked on the phone. Christ, she hated these smarmy bastards. Flesh peddlers, she thought. Pimps. An evil in the Industry, but, she admitted reluctantly, a necessary evil. She didn't want to be here.

But Marty had suggested she see Ortis. And what Marty suggested, Jahne would do. On the set, off the set, anything Marty said, she did. Well, *almost* anything.

'That was Michael McLain,' he said. No apology for keeping her waiting, as if the name alone was explanation enough. 'Now, where was I?' he asked.

'You were telling me what you would be able to do for me if you were my agent.' Jahne paused. 'Let me ask, how long have you worked for Michael McLain?'

'*With* Michael,' Sy corrected. 'Maybe ten, twelve years. Why?'

'That means he came to you as a big star already. You didn't discover him, make his career. It was already on track.' She watched Sy adjust the sleeves of his shirt under the Armani jacket. Although Sy's firm was called Early Artist Recognition Ltd., they didn't usually spot new stars. They exploited the hell out of established ones. Some people said Sy had insisted on the name so he could call himself the duke of Earl.

'He was working, if that's what you mean. But he wasn't rich, which is where I come in. He could have made a good living for life without me, don't get me wrong. But rich?' Sy chuckled to himself. 'Nah, that was *me*.' He looked into her eyes. 'And I could do that for *you*, too – may I call you Jahne? Rich *and* famous.' He kept his eyes on her, and a smile on his face.

Jahne knew that he was right. He *had* made Michael richer and more famous. And other people as well. And wasn't that what she wanted, after all? Money and fame? Those gave you power to get the roles you wanted. 'The money is, of course, important. Enough to make me independent. But fame? Well, I'd like to have enough of a reputation as an actress to be able to pick and choose my roles, take only the ones I want. *That* would make me happy.'

'You mean like Meryl Streep?'

Was that a sneer Sy had on his lips? 'Exactly. Like Meryl Streep,' Jahne said.

Sy got up from behind the desk and came around in front, then sat with one buttock on the corner, his hands folded in front of him. 'Except, Jahne, no one ever really gets to that point. Not even Meryl Streep. She has choice among some roles, but, nevertheless, she took the part in *She-Devil*. You remember that big bomb? And *Death Becomes Her*? Worse. Now, why would a talented, established actress take a role like that, risk her box office?' Sy leaned forward. 'Let me esplain.' For a moment, his accent slipped. 'An agent is more than a contract negotiator. He should be a career maker. Someone advised Meryl wrong, and, talented as she is, she still didn't have the objectivity to really know a hit when she saw it. Someone like Meryl will bounce back. But maybe not quite so high as before.'

Jahne was beginning to see his point. It was, after all, pretty much the point Marty had made when he suggested she see Sy. 'So that's where a good agent comes in?' she asked, saving Sy from having to point out the obvious.

'Exactly. And not just a good agent. A good *businessman*. Someone who can see the big picture, who has enough of an overview of the Industry to know where the placement should be, and with whom, and when. And someone who can read the fine print of a contract. Protect your interests. And that's me. That's what I do. That's what I do for Michael McLain and all the others.' He swept his hand across a wall of pictures of famous people. 'And that's what I will do for you. Just say the word,' he said, his hands open, waiting for Jahne's answer.

Jahne was committed to acting, but she was no fool. She put aside her prejudices and extended her hand to Sy. 'It's a deal,' she said.

'Michael McLain on line one, Mr. Ortis,' his receptionist said over the intercom.

Sy kept his hand on the phone for a moment before picking it up. Shit, he thought, this is all I need. *Now* what the fuck does he want? Although the meeting with Jahne Moore had, in the end, gone very well, and he now had her as a client, he was pissed. It always got him pissed, pitching a new client. And she'd been uppity. She needed to be brought down a notch or two. By the time they agreed to sign on the bottom line, she had pushed his ass as far as it could go, taking all the fun out of the triumph. Now Michael would drive him nuts. He sighed and lifted the receiver.

'Michael, you're calling to say you're going to do the Ricky Dunn movie, right?'

'Maybe. I just thought of something we haven't discussed yet. Okay?'

Sy leaned his head on one hand, suddenly feeling tired. 'Do you want me to guess, or are you going to tell me?'

'I get the girl. Not Dunn. *Me. And* my name above the title? Right?'

Now Sy's head fell forward onto his hands. This guy is going to fuckin' kill me. 'I'll have to talk to his people.'

'You *are* his people! Anyway, I get top billing *and* I get the girl. Then I'll consider it.'

'Michael, it's a very special screenplay. You won't be the main love interest, you understand? We can't have the Olivier of the screen making love to a nineteen-year-old. It would be *ludicrous*. Your fans expect someone more sophisticated for you.' Sy felt his wheeze coming on. Now he was really winging it. 'You know,' he continued, 'the name above the title is usually for the guy who gets the girl. But your name will be bigger – way *bigger* – than his.'

'What the fuck do you mean, "ludicrous"? I fuck nineteen-year-olds all the time, Sy. You should know that. I got them coming out of the woodwork, for chrissakes. Ludicrous!'

Sy was feeling pushed. Normally, no matter how much he wanted to push back, he was usually able to control it. But not today. Maybe if that little bitch Jahne Moore hadn't just sat there, forcing *him* – Sy Ortis – to make a sales pitch, like a fuckin' new kid on the block. Jesus, twenty years in the business and a snot-nose like her can sit there and interview *him*. But for Michael he needed patience.

'It's ludicrous when there's a thirty-four-year age difference. It would be like watching Sean Connery fuck Drew Barrymore, Michael.'

'*I* fucked her,' Michael said.

Jesus, Sy thought to himself. Was it true? And who cares? 'You did, huh? You're *amazing*, Michael. Think you can fuck anyone you want, right?'

Michael laughed.

'How about a real challenge, Michael? I bet you can't fuck all three costars in DiGennaro's TV show. They're all kids – maybe nineteen, twenty – but I bet you can't.'

'And when I do? What do I get?'

'I'll guarantee your name above the title in this project.'

'And if I don't? . . .'

Sy laughed for the first time during the conversation. 'You do *this* movie without top billing, *and* the next two I tell you to.'

Michael paused.

'Hey, what's the matter, Michael? There isn't any real problem for you here, is there? Not Michael McLain, questioning his prowess?'

'You got a deal, you prick. All three.'

'Right you are! But I want proof, Michael. Not just war stories.

262

Proof!' Sy hung up. If Michael McLain made Jahne another notch on his belt, it should take her down a notch or two. And if he didn't, well, he'd have to make Sy's movies. Sy breathed deeply for the first time that day. *Now* he felt better.

16

Hollywood, like Dante's hell, has many levels. And rarely, if ever, do they mix, except at work. I – Laura Richie – have been on stage sets, TV sets, movie sets, and location shoots, and, believe me, that is one thing that never changes.

The technical staff, the boom operators, the other sound men, the camera crews, the lighting designers, the gaffers and best boys and grips all belong to one level. The suits, those businessmen in charge of production, budgets, the front office, publicity, marketing, and the like, all belong on another.

Then there are the extras: part of the talent, but not really belonging to it. They play the small roles, the crowd scenes, the background, the colour.

And there are the stars. On a successful TV show, the set is built for them, the schedule is designed for them, the catering caters to them. Well, everyone caters to them.

Lastly, there is the director. Even on the shows where stars actually rule, the director is still on the highest level. But remember: that it is only the highest level of hell.

The hell is trying to take three hundred people and get them to the right location with the right clothes and the appropriate weather to have the right light, the right script, the right performances, to ensure that whatever is being taped or filmed or (God forbid!) performed live gets performed according to the director's vision. At least that's the theory. And on the soundstage of Three for The Road, *Marty DiGennaro was going to ensure that that theory was put into practice. He was going to create a show, a wonderful show, that transcended anything that had been done on television before. And to do it, he had only to concentrate on that one thing. Wasn't it Lanford Wilson who had said that style was nothin' but always concentrating on one thing?*

Marty had the vehicle for a hit. He had the first three scripts, the cast and the crew. The only thing, the one thing he might lack, just a little, was concentration.

Because, since he had met Lila Kyle, it seemed he couldn't get her out of his mind.

Marty DiGennaro looked across the bustling soundstage, his laboratory for dream-making. Even now, after all his years of success, it was hard to believe all these toys were his. A funny-looking little Italian kid, growing up in Queens, he'd been too puny to play with the tough kids of his neighbourhood. And he'd been lousy in school, a failure with girls, bad at sports, even bad with his hands. He'd escaped, whenever he could, to the safety of the darkness of the movies. The Roxy, the Corona, the Flushing Loews. They'd been his haven, his home, and it was a daily miracle to him that they'd given him this life, this almost perfect life.

The success, the money, the perks, the opportunity to make movies of his own. All unbelievably lucky. It was only in his private life that things weren't absolutely perfect. Because it was hard, maybe even impossible, to know who his friends were. Even Joanie, his soon-to-be-ex-wife, had benefited from him, had built her career on his contacts. He hadn't minded that, but then, when he wanted the child, and wanted her to stay home with Sacha, she left him.

Now women, other women, virtually *any* woman, were more than available. Eager, even. Too eager. Because, despite his success, his power, his enormous wealth, his contacts, he knew he was still Marty DiGennaro, a skinny, funny-looking Italian kid who was bad with his hands. He suspected all those women were disappointed in his sexual performance, all merely faking their response. Love-making was, too often, a burden. And the parade of anonymous lovelies that he'd started seeing since his marriage broke up were rarely asked to return or spend the night. Work, work, and more work was all there was for him. For, just like back in Queens, the only place he was comfortable was in the movies – on a set or a soundstage, except instead of watching magic, now he made it happen.

Go know.

This was Marty's mantra in show business. It was the punch line from an old borscht-belt joke. A guy goes to the doctor for a complete physical. After a thorough exam, the doctor, an old Jewish type with an accent, says, 'Mister, you are in top condition for a man of your age. Lungs, heart, colon, all in great shape. You're a lucky man, in peak physical condition. You could live another hundred years!' The guy thanks the doctor, gets dressed, walks out the door, and drops dead of a thrombosis on the doorstep. The doctor looks at the corpse, shrugs, and says, 'Go know.'

Go know.

Hollywood marvelled at Marty's unbroken string of hits. They wondered what the secret was to his magic formula for picking them. Marty knew the secret.

There was no magic formula.

If bankers wanted to believe this wasn't the biggest crapshoot on the face of the earth, let them. But Marty knew how dangerous a game it was. Still, no matter how dangerous, he was getting tired of it. He'd always been a thrill seeker, and putting out another movie, getting another Oscar nomination, or even winning one was beginning to pall. So he'd started gambling in Vegas. But that thrill had died, too.

So then he'd thought of TV. The vast wasteland. The thing called a medium because everything on it was so very average or below. Yet watched. Watched and watched. What if he, single-handedly, could help one of the dying networks, the dinosaurs that were having the living shit kicked out of them by MTV, by cable, by home videos? He could be a hero to Les Merchant, but, more importantly, he could have autonomy and a vehicle that didn't have to prove itself every fucking time it came out of the gate. He could take hours developing characters over seasons, instead of minutes in that precious 120. What if he put together something that had never been seen, never been done before?

The idea had intrigued him, and when he ran across the remaindered copy of *Three for the Road* by that obscure woman Grace Weber from Jersey, he knew he had his stepping-off point. He'd bought it for a song, and now, for the first time in years, he was excited by a project. Excited and scared.

He reminded himself that all he had to do was concentrate. He had the scripts, the cast, the crew. Still, he was frightened. Because, if he fell flat on his face, all the jealous bastards in town (and they were *all* jealous bastards in this town) would dance on his grave. But frightened felt alive; he was in the game.

He reminded himself that he had everything he needed for another huge hit. And then he reminded himself of his mantra.

Go know.

Jahne and Pete arrived at the studio separately. He had been grateful for the job, and accepted her explanation that it was best to be discreet about their relationship because Marty seemed concerned.

But was that really her reason? she wondered. With excitement and nerves churning her stomach, she knew that having Pete on the set was just an extra complication, one she wished she did not have to consider. Her relationship with him was BTN – better than nothing – but little more than that. He was a warm body in the dark, a generous sex partner, a nice kid, but no one who could ever know her.

In a way, now, the relationship made her more lonely than if she had been alone. Because how could she explain how she felt? How could a young kid like Pete, honest and clean and simple, understand what she was going through? There was no way to explain it to him. To be honest, she could barely explain it to herself. There were so many feelings that swirled through her, minute by minute, that she couldn't keep up.

Right now, on the first day on the set, she knew what she felt. It was a single feeling, strong and deep, and it left a metallic taste at the back of her tongue.

She had never been so frightened in her life.

Sharleen stepped out of the trailer she had been assigned as her dressing room and placed her hand on the director's chair that had her name stencilled across the back; her other hand held her mother's small Bible. Until this moment, none of it had been real to her: the contract, the publicity-photo sessions, meeting all those important people. Not even the dressing room. But *this* was real. She tried to remember; no, she had never seen her full name printed out, except in her own handwriting. She wished Dean could see it, but she couldn't have him come to the set. She'd have so much to tell him about tonight.

'Miss Smith,' the man with the headphone said. 'Mr. DiGennaro would like to see you at the cast meeting.'

She realized she was being spoken to. 'Oh, am I late?' she asked, jumping up.

'No, Miss Smith. Miss Kyle hasn't gotten here.'

Sharleen walked gingerly across the floor, stepping over lighting cables and electrical tape, afraid to put her feet down for fear of upsetting something. There was a lot of bustling, and people with clipboards, and other people with headsets on, but they weren't listening to Walkmen. Everything looked confusing to her, but she was sure it made sense to *somebody*.

'Sharleen,' Mr. DiGennaro said, coming towards her. 'I'm sorry we kept you waiting. I'd like to introduce you to everyone.'

'Oh, that's all right. I was just sittin' back, like a hog on a barrel, looking around. It's kind of like a circus I seen back home once. Everything happenin' at once. 'Cept in the circus, at least they had a ringmaster keeping that organized.' She turned back to the chaos she had just passed through. 'Does everyone know what they's supposed to do?' she asked.

Marty laughed. 'Yes, that's *my* job. I'm the director – a lot like a ringmaster – and I'd *better* know what everyone's supposed to do, or I'm out on my ass. This is Ted Singleton, he's in charge of special effects; that's Dino, my right-hand man; and Bob Burton from Wardrobe; Jim Sperlman, lighting technician; the tubby one is my new AD, Barry Tilden; over that side, Charley Bradford, technical consultant from Harley-Davidson . . .'

'Whee, Mr. DiGennaro, please! Give me a minute to catch my breath. I don't know what any of them jobs is, so, if it's okay with y'all, I'll just try to memorize your names for now. Heck,' she said with a laugh, 'I don't even know what *my* job is yet, but I'm here to learn. I'm Sharleen,' she said to the group, and took a seat at the conference table. 'Howdy.' She wondered why Lila and Jahne weren't here yet. She had met them already, of course, but she was a little afraid of seeing them again today. *They* were *really* beautiful. Lord, she asked herself, how have I been picked to stand beside *them*? Sharleen looked around at the sea of faces and smiled. She was very pleased to see them all smile back. They're all so nice over here in Hollywood, Sharleen thought. Much nicer than in Bakersfield.

Jahne Moore didn't have to be called to the opening meeting twice. She knew that today's first impression was very important. It would set the tone with Marty, with the other two leads, and for how she would be treated by the crew for the duration of the show. Marty was already there, and, Jahne was sure, so were all the other departments, but the last people to arrive at these meetings were usually the stars. Costars, she corrected herself. Jahne wondered about Sharleen Smith and Lila Kyle. She hadn't seen either of the girls since they had met at the publicity party that announced their signing. She had liked Sharleen, and knew instinctively that Sharleen was no threat. Lila, she was afraid, might be another story. But maybe I should wait and see, she told herself, before I form *any* opinions.

The meeting was held on Soundstage 14. Marty DiGennaro met her halfway across the floor of the huge hangarlike space, took her by the arm, and escorted her to the table. 'Sharleen, you've met Jahne Moore, your costar?' Then he introduced her to the rest of the crew, and Jahne made it a point to shake each one's hand. She knew how much any production was a team effort. And how much she'd depend on them. She might be a costar, but if *these* people didn't do their jobs right, *no one* looked good. Pete was there, sitting behind Jim Bert, head cameraman. He smiled at her, but was discreet enough not to do more.

Jahne joined the group at the meeting. 'Hi, Sharleen,' she said, sitting next to her. 'How are you doing?'

'Jahne,' Sharleen leaned to her and whispered, '*how* I'm doin' ain't the question. The question is, *what* am I doin'? And *here*? Don't tell anyone, but I think I'm asleep and dreaming this.'

Jahne laughed and touched Sharleen's arm. Yes, she liked Sharleen. *If* she was sincere. Sincere or not, she was breathtakingly beautiful. She was to play Clover, the Texan, to Jahne's Cara, a New Yorker. Jahne listened to Sharleen chattering comfortably away to a couple of the lighting guys, as if she'd known them all her life. I just hope she keeps that innocence, Jahne thought, then laughed to herself. Fat chance. This is Hollywood. The girl was going to need more than the little book she was clutching to protect herself. Especially with *that* body.

Jahne looked over at the only empty chair at the table and saw who it was everyone was waiting for. Lila Kyle. She still hadn't come out of her dressing room. Jahne had heard Lila arrive on the set, but where *was* she? It's not as if there were costumes and makeup today. It was just a preliminary meeting, to get to know everybody. She saw Marty lean towards his assistant and whisper something to her. Clare nodded her head, stood up, and walked in the direction of the dressing rooms. Give me a break, Jahne thought. Lila isn't playing 'star,' is she? Not this soon? And not with Marty DiGennaro?

More than anything, Jahne was a professional. In the past, someone might criticize her talent, her appearance, her interpretation of a role, but *never* her commitment to a project. She prided herself on always being on time, knowing her lines and her blocking, and believing that the director had the final word.

The murmuring died down slightly, and Jahne looked towards the approaching figure. Lila Kyle was walking slowly across the set, through the taped-down cables and lighting apparatus, every movement choreographed, Jahne could tell. Lila wore tight black leather pants, black high-heeled boots, and a black leather jacket with zippers and enormous shoulders. The boots and the shoulder pads didn't seem excessive on Lila's six-foot frame. On the contrary, in a strange way, Jahne felt that Lila's height and bone structure demanded them. And she was certainly in character for her role: Crimson, the runaway rich girl from San Francisco.

Lila came to a stop at the end of the big table as Marty stood to greet her. Before he could make any introductions, she kissed him on the cheek and turned to the rest of the crowd. 'Hello. I'm Lila Kyle,' she said, her voice resonant. She paused and took a beat. Jahne looked around. Every man had stood. Well, I'll be damned, Jahne thought. Now, how did she get them to do that?

Lila sat down, her mother's favourite famous movie line echoing in her ears: 'Don't fuck with me, boys.' Okay, they got *that* straight, she thought, watching the men take their seats. It was one of the tricks she had learned from Theresa, coming to the sets with her when Lila was a child: how to make an entrance. Be the last to arrive. And let them know you're a lady. It makes them drop their guard. And their jaws.

Marty was introducing everyone at the table by name. Lila didn't look around, just kept a small smile on her lips. She had met Sharleen and Jahne before, but hadn't seen them in street clothes. Lila let her eyes fall on Jahne, who was sitting on one side of her, listening to Marty like he was God. She knew Jahne had real New York acting experience behind her, but, besides her looks, nothing else. And she was short – despite those boots she wasn't more than five six or seven. The *blonde* didn't even *have* acting experience. A waitress, for chrissakes, but definitely another beauty.

I don't have anything to worry about, Lila assured herself. Because while Marty insisted they were three *costars*, Lila intended there to be only one *star*, no matter *what* Marty DiGennaro said.

Lila felt Sharleen's hand on her arm, and turned, coolly, to look at her. 'Those pants are beautiful. Where'd you get them?' Sharleen asked.

'I had them made. They're from Florence,' Lila said. It didn't hurt to be a *little* friendly.

'Maybe you'll give me Florence's phone number,' Sharleen said. 'I'd like her to make me a pair, too.'

Lila blinked, then forced a smile. This one's too good to be true, she thought. Her eyes fell to the Bible on the table in front of Sharleen. Puh-leeze.

'Florence, *Italy*,' she said, and Sharleen blushed. Lila looked around at the table. 'What do you call three blondes sitting in a circle?' she asked. All the faces looked at hers expectantly. 'A dope ring,' she told them, and was rewarded with a big laugh.

Only Jahne Moore didn't join in. She turned to Sharleen. 'Florence, Italy, is a city that's famous for its leather,' she explained to the blushing girl. 'But most people pronounce it the Italian way: Firenze.'

Well, fuck her, Lila thought.

Marty DiGennaro sat back and looked around the table. The meeting was going very well, very well indeed. He smiled to himself. Everyone he talked to in the business tried to give him advice. The biggest problem he was going to have, they said, was trying to direct three gorgeous women who had never worked television before. There was no way, they said, he was going to be able to maintain the right balance that would keep them all happy. Now he chuckled. He wondered if they had said the same thing back in the thirties to George Cukor when he was filming *The Women*. If Cukor could direct Joan Crawford, Paulette Goddard, Rosalind Russell, *and* Majorie Main in the same film, for chrissakes, he knew he could direct these three.

All of them were gorgeous, and all of them would look great on screen. But he also knew that one of them was born for the camera, not only because of her beauty, but also because of that certain way she looked back at it. Monroe had had it; she could look into a camera and into the eyes behind it, into the eyes staring back at her on the screen. She saw into the future and men's souls at the same time. And didn't seem aware of the gift.

Marty looked at Lila now. *She* had the gift, but, unlike Monroe, she knew it. Which made her dangerous, and probably difficult to control. But oh so exciting.

Cukor controlled his brood mares. Kept them in line, had them pulling as a team, but each stepping to her own beat at the same time. Like Clydesdales. And he had pulled off the coup of a lifetime. An all-female movie.

And Marty would prove he could do it, too. After all, he *was* Marty DiGennaro, and this *was* only television.

17

After work, Jahne went home exhausted. Most nights, Pete called and asked to come over. Jahne hoped it wasn't just snobbery that kept her from revealing their relationship, but, to be honest, there wasn't much of a relationship. He was kind and cooperative. He made love to her and he held her close, and she needed that, but they shared very litte else. Pete's idea of conversation was to comment on the television shows that he always switched on for background noise. He was as comfortable as a warm bath, and about as stimulating. So different from Sam.

She pulled her mind away from the subject. It was madness, an obsession with her. The fact was, she had slept with Pete for all the wrong reasons: out of boredom, loneliness, horniness, and need. She'd behaved the way men do, and now she had to make it right. Poor Pete would pay the price.

When the phone rang, Jahne sighed. She knew it would be Pete. She hated to put him off another night.

'Jahne?'

'Uh-huh.' She tried not to sigh into the receiver.

'Can I come over?'

'I'm awfully tired, Pete.'

'Me, too. Those tracking shots really take it outa ya. But I only want to see you for a minute. I think we have to talk.'

It was such an unusual request from him that she agreed, and in less than ten minutes he was at her door. She moved to the sofa but, instead of following her lead, he continued standing, though he leaned against the wall. 'Jahne, I'm no Einstein, but I think I got the picture. You don't want to talk to me on the set,

271

and I understood that. I'm grateful for the job, too. But my dad explained how it is. You're going to be a big success with *Three for the Road* and you don't need a techie hanging around your neck. You can date whoever you want now, and I can tell you don't want me.'

Jahne stood there, silent. He was goodhearted and sexy and kind to her. How could she tell him that it wasn't his job but his age that made him inappropriate? And how, in good conscience, could she string him along for her own convenience?

For the first time it occurred to her that, in his inarticulate, young, California way, he loved her. It had been so long since anyone had that it was hard for her to consider it. But who, exactly, did he love? A reconstructed body? A beautifully designed face? Certainly he did not know who she was in any deeper way.

'Maybe you're right,' she said, and she let him go.

Jahne had never thought much about money. Of course, she had never had much to think about, until after her grandmother's death, and then all of that had been carefully earmarked for Dr. Moore, the hospital, and other expenses. She had worked in the theatre, both for pay and for free, and had managed to eke out whatever else she required from nursing, when she had to.

Back in New York, she'd always kept her expenses low: a rent-stabilized walk-up, Con Ed, the phone and answering service. She'd had a virtually empty savings account, a MasterCard she'd gotten when she'd opened her first account at Chemical Bank, but she'd never had binges on credit. She'd lived frugally, even marginally, and imagined it was fine, a part of *la vie bohème*. After all, she'd never known anything else.

Now, for Jahne Moore, the money was rolling in in swells, each wave larger than the previous one. First the Flanders Cosmetics cheque had come. Jahne still felt uncomfortable about plugging a product, but she'd had to sign to get the part though she'd only agreed to one year, not the three they wanted. And the money was glorious! She'd sent off what she owed to Dr. Moore, and, despite taxes, Sy's agency and finder's fees, and legal expenses, she'd had over ninety thousand left!

Then, when Jahne got her first paycheque – almost fifty thousand dollars – and realized there would be another one in two weeks' time, she was staggered. When she had signed the contract with Sy, she had seen that she was paid thirty-three thousand dollars an episode, but somehow, in the excitement, she hadn't had time really to focus on it. She'd just opened an account at California National and deposited it and the Flanders cheque. But as cheque after cheque came rolling in, she began to feel uneasy.

Now she stared at the bank balance on the latest monthly statement. Two hundred and seventeen thousand six hundred and sixty-three dollars and forty-seven cents! It was unbelievable. And, Jahne knew, it was only a start. Even though the series hadn't yet begun running on the network, Sy Ortis had already forwarded her several new scripts for future consideration: they were lousy made-for-television quickies, but not one of them paid less than $250,000. A quarter of a million dollars for five weeks of work! She shook her head. With all of her New York scrambling, Mary Jane had never made more than thirty-five thousand dollars in any year of her life.

Ortis also wanted to talk to her about authorizing a line of leather goods, jeans, and wallpaper, of all things, along with *Three for the Road* dolls – sort of biker Barbies, as she understood the deal. All of it, tawdry and ridiculous as it was, meant a lot more money. And though she had no intention of doing *any* of this proposed crap, she understood that she had fallen – or climbed – into a money stream that wouldn't stop flowing for some time. Look at Jaclyn Smith or Kate Jackson – since their first TV hit, they'd always had at least a TV-movie-of-the-week or a sitcom gig. Even Suzanne Somers and Farrah Fawcett at least had exercise-equipment ads to fall back on. What had Mary Jane ever had to fall back on but bedpans? And both nursing and New York acting had been hard work. This stuff was insultingly easy. And lucrative.

It was all unreal to her: just as she had felt the unfairness of never being able to live off her craft in New York, she felt the unfairness of receiving the gigantic amounts of cash for very little craft here in L.A. Was it simply her looks that had entitled her to this enormous windfall? It was ironic that she had bought them for about 15 per cent of her income so far. Not a bad return on investment, she thought, smiling to herself.

Well, at least I'm not burdened by much financial guilt, she thought. After all those years of famine, she supposed she could deal with some years of fat, although not of the physical kind.

But what must it be like for those actors who never went through the struggle she had? Those who hit it big, fast, and early. No wonder they so often drifted into drugs, excess, and bankruptcy. The guilt would be difficult, the burden of responsibility too unmanageable. Even she, with years of experience, stared at her bank balance now, feeling both helpless and exalted, and wondered what she would do with all the money.

Of course, she could simply blow some of the money. She could finally afford nice clothes and had the body to wear them well. She could have another spending spree. But was that what she wanted to do? She probably would need to find a nicer place to live. But she didn't want to *buy* a place out here, and she wouldn't spend a lot on a rental. She stared again at the bank balance. Maybe she should give some to charity, or use some of it to help actors and playwrights? But how could she do that? I mean, you just don't send a cheque in the mail to Molly and Chuck or the latest off-off-Broadway writer.

Well, she could send a cheque to Father Damien. His church had given shelter and an outlet to a lot of New York actors. And ten thousand dollars would mean a lot to him and almost nothing to her. She decided she'd do it. But should she give money to individuals? Endow the arts? As she continued to stare at the bank statement, she realized that, though she had suffered when she chose to live that way herself, she had *chosen* to live that way, and it made all the difference. As Mary Jane, she had never much felt that state-supported arts programmes and private grants were good things. No, she wouldn't become a philanthropist to culture. What she *would* do, she decided, was find herself a pleasant little bungalow in Birdland. The Hollywood Hills was an area where the streets were named for birds – Oriole Drive, Robin Lane – and since a lot of gays had moved there it had another nickname, the Swish Alps. They had converted middle-class two-bedroom houses into chic, tiny shangri-las. She'd rent one, furnished. For her it would be total luxury. And let's face it – things with her two roommates were getting tense. Although both girls spoke only of their pride and happiness for her, both had also already asked for loans *and* guest shots on the show. She felt that each one looked at her and asked herself, Why her and not me? She felt she was a constant goad to them, and she knew resentments would flare at any moment.

She put down the bank statement. That was it, then. She'd get a nice place of her own. And she'd put some of the money into a money market – nice and safe. But what about the rest?

Then she thought, unbidden, of what she could do, what she had to do.

She remembered her own agony at her adolescent reflection back in Scuderstown. And she'd been normal, if unlovely. But all that was coming her way now was coming because she was beautiful. What must it be like, how deeply damaging, to be born deformed? It was unimaginable, yet tears sprang to Jahne's eyes as she felt herself an imperfect infant in Lima, Peru, or a monster-faced toddler in Guatemala. Well, then, this was something she could do.

She stood, walked to the desk, and pulled out writing paper. The burden of the money had lifted. She took out her cheque-book, and scrawled a cheque for one hundred thousand dollars. 'Dear Dr. Moore,' she wrote, and smiled as she added the dash and 'Brewster.'

I remember you once estimated that $20,000 was the cost for a mobile Interplast unit for a month. I enclose five units, which I hope gives, by my reasoning, about fifty kids their faces back. Try not to make them all look like me.

Your grateful friend,
Jahne Moore

18

Sharleen looked down at the light-green cheque in her hands and blinked. She had to be careful counting all these numbers. It was hard to imagine how much was hers. She looked up at Mr. Ortis. 'Just for wearing some lipstick? What do I do with it?' she asked.

'Put it in the bank.'

'Which bank?' she asked.

'Your bank,' Sy Ortis answered.

Sharleen laughed. 'Mr. Ortis, I don't have no bank.'

She and Dean had moved around so much, and they'd never had much money. Banks and schools and police stations – official places like that – made her nervous. She kept their money tucked in Momma's Bible.

She noticed Mr. Ortis lean back in his swivel chair, his eyes on her, then lean forward again and lift the phone.

'Tell Lenny to come into my office.' He hung up and looked at her. 'Honey, we're going to fix you up. I got a guy who's going to take care of everything – bills, investments, taxes – everything.'

There was a polite knock at the door; then a tall, thin man with a serious face came in. He looked over at Sharleen, and his face didn't move a muscle. Sharleen smiled anyway. 'Sharleen, this is Lenny Farmer. I'm making him your business manager.' Sy looked up at Lenny and indicated the cheque in Sharleen's hand. 'Set up a business account for Ms. Smith and draw up the necessary papers. Get power of attorney. And have Anita give her a cash advance.' Sy turned to Sharleen and smiled. 'So you can do some shopping for yourself today,' he explained. 'And now that the money is coming in, we'll find you a house, lease you a car, set up charge accounts at some of the better stores, arrange for credit cards. Whatever you need. You tell Lenny. You won't have to give another thought to money. All you have to do is spend it.'

It was a load off her mind. For a moment, Sharleen wondered if it was really okay to trust Lenny Farmer – or anyone – with all that money. But, after all, there would be more paycheques. More than she and Dean could spend!

Sharleen walked out the door of Mr. Ortis' office building and across the parking lot towards Dean, who waited patiently in their Datsun. The brown manila envelope that Anita, the bookkeeper, had given her felt heavy in her hand as she swung herself in next to Dean. Before speaking, she broke the seal on the envelope and looked inside. 'My, my, my,' she murmured.

'What's the matter, Sharleen?' Dean asked. Sharleen had already explained to Dean how she was making a television show, just like Andy Griffith. She was never sure just how much Dean understood about what she told him. Of course, Sharleen was not understanding much of this herself, she admitted.

'What's the matter?' Dean asked again.

'Nothin', honey. Not one dang thing.' Sharleen patted Dean on the shoulder and smiled. 'I just got myself my first couple of paycheques, so let's go shopping. It's a lot of money, Dean. So what would you like more than anything else in the world?' She sat facing Dean, watching him search for an answer to her question.

'I don't know, Sharleen. I don't want anything. I got you, and a car, and we got a real nice apartment now. And I ain't hungry no more.' He paused. 'I don't know, Sharleen, I guess I don't want nothin'.'

276

Sharleen urged him on. 'Sure you do. I know there's something you've been wanting for a long time. Think, Dean.'

Dean's brow knitted in thought. 'Well, I always wanted a dog. A puppy. You know, a Lab. Maybe like Dobe's.'

They had gotten a cat – a fat black stray that Dean had already named Oprah – but Sharleen wasn't sure about a dog. Still, why not? 'Well, let's go then. What are you waiting for?' she asked, waving them forward with her hand.

Dean's eyes opened wide. 'You mean it? We got *that* much money?'

'Dean, since I started playin' this part of Clover, we got more money than the richest man in Lamson.'

Dean stepped on the gas and screeched out of the parking lot. 'Wheeoo!' he screamed, as the sudden acceleration pulled them back into the bucket seats, the squeal of the tyres quickly fading in the wind behind them.

The pet shop was not unusual for Los Angeles, Sharleen realized. *Everything* in this city was the best. The salesman – dressed in a grey suit, a white coat like a doctor, sleeves rucked up to his elbows, shirt collar buttoned, no tie – came from behind the desk. 'What may I show you today?' he asked.

'We'd like to get a puppy,' Dean blurted out.

'We'd like to see maybe a black Lab, if you got any.' Sharleen looked around the showroom as she spoke. Nothing in here except those pictures on the walls of dogs all brushed up. Bet they even smell pretty, she thought. 'Where do you keep the dogs?' she asked.

'You're in luck. Our collection is usually shown by appointment, but since we had a last-minute cancellation, we can present several to choose from today.' He pushed a button on the desk telephone. 'Lisa, please bring in the black Lab we were going to show Mary Tyler Moore.' He looked at Sharleen appraisingly. 'And also the setter, and the golden retriever,' he added, *sotto voce*.

Moments later, a young woman in another spotless white doctor's coat opened the door and pushed in a cart holding a basket of three puppies. Good Lord, Sharleen thought as she noticed the huge blue satin bows on each of them.

Dean hunkered down beside them. She watched him as he breathed carefully on the face of each puppy, closing his eyes as they licked at his mouth and cheeks. 'Please, mister, take them bows off them. That ain't natural,' he said. 'Kin I touch them?' he asked.

'Sure!'

He dipped his hands into the basket. 'Hey, Sharleen, look at these guys. They're all beauts.' He looked up at her wordlessly. 'I can't chose one and leave the others.'

'Oh, Lord,' Sharleen said to the salesman. 'Why did you have to bring out all three?' She patted her purse crammed now with her mom's Bible and the manila envelope of money. It felt good, reassuring, and Mr. Ortis had promised her another one, just as big, next week. She looked down at Dean, who had the setter on his lap and was holding the lab, while the retriever was on the floor, pulling at his sleeve. Dean laughed. 'We'll take *all* of 'em,' she said, and took the manila envelope from her bag.

'*All* of 'em, Sharleen? Can we? Really?'

'Surely can. But what will we name 'em, Dean?' She looked at his face, so happy. It made her want to cry. Neither of them spoke about the pup their daddy had killed.

'Can't name her Oprah now,' Dean said, patting the black Lab. 'But let's name the blonde one Clover!'

'That's it, Dean,' Sharleen said, and began to laugh. 'She's Clover, the black one is Cara, and the red one is Crimson. Just like on the show!'

Back in the car, Sharleen spoke over the yapping coming from the boxes in the back seat. 'We got one more thing to do, Dean. Let's go to the supermarket, get some puppy chow, and fill that fridge and freezer at home. What do you say?'

The store was almost the size of the football fields they'd seen on TV. 'Where do we begin?' Dean asked, bewildered.

'With an empty basket,' she said. 'Then we go up and down the rows and take anything – you hear me, Dean? – *anything* – we want from the shelves, as much as we want. Like that TV show where contestants have to fill their baskets in five minutes, and the one with the most wins? Let's do it like that. I'll take one and start at that end. You take the other and start here. I'll meet you in the middle. Okay?'

'Okay!'

'Ready, set, GO!'

Dean won. He was in the middle first, with the most. He had three baskets in tow. He even had stuff crammed *under* the baskets on the frame. 'Sharleen, I never knew supermarkets could be so much fun. It was hard work, but let's do it again.' He was puffing, trying to catch his breath.

'Sure thing, honey. Tomorrow, if you like. But that's not all yet. Now comes the real easy part. Paying for it.'

19

Hollywood has always been a town where PR rules, where even the slickest operators will sometimes buy not only their own PR but the PR of others. I – Laura Richie – certainly know it and benefit from it every day: invitations to parties, press junkets, gifts, and even the always-tempting 'consulting assignment' – just a legal bribe to help in the successful launching of a bum movie or a new TV show. Most publicity is bought, one way or another.

The strangest thing about the way Hollywood operates is perhaps the way PR (which everyone buys whenever they can) is so often believed by Industry suits and producers when it's bought by someone else. Once there is buzz about a film or an actor, the buzz seems to take on a life of its own. It is sometimes strong enough to create a success. Is it because the suits have no judgement? Is it because everyone is always desperate for a success? To steal the mantra of Marty DiGennaro, go know.

There was certainly the beginning of buzz about DiGennaro's Three for the Road, or 3/4 as it was being called by the insiders. Of course there were a lot of angles: three fresh faces, the revival of the sixties, and, most importantly, DiGennaro's debut on television. Twenty years in Hollywood had led me to believe that in this case the buzz was the real thing: not purchased PR but real excitement over something that could become the biggest hit of the season or any season. And that Lila Kyle, Sharleen Smith, and Jahne Moore were stars in the making.

Making a TV show was hard work. Jahne thought she knew about hard, from her off-Broadway and repertory work, where she'd sometimes been her own wardrobe mistress, run lights, and even had to move scenery from time to time. But this weekly TV show had a killing pace that made off-Broadway look like a day at the beach.

The weeks took on a pattern. She got her script only the night before taping began, read it, and began learning lines. The next day, she was on the set and in makeup by 6.00 A.M. Then Marty liked a run-through, and scenes were blocked, but there was almost no time for rehearsals. By the evening of the first day, a few scenes had actually been shot. She had to know her lines, make her marks exactly, know where the camera was; then, and only then, if she had any energy left, she could act. By seven each evening, she was wrung out, exhausted, and grateful for the limo and driver that got her home most nights by eight. Then she had a little (*very* little) something to eat, worked out, and fell into bed, only to start again the next morning. Each week, it went on for six days straight. On Sunday, she collapsed to rest, but Sunday evening she had to learn the new script. Try emoting after a couple of weeks of that schedule! Jahne had a new respect for the TV actors she and Molly and the gang at St. Malachy's used to mock.

She still saw Pete on the set, and he seemed to have become like all the other crew members: helpful and pleasant but standoffish. Well, she told herself, she couldn't have it both ways: to use him for affection when she wanted it, and to keep him in the background all the rest of the time. She supposed it was just as well that they had split: she had no energy except what she marshalled for work. In the evenings, she lived like a nun, and if she was often bored and lonely on the set, his presence there would not have helped that.

Then, one evening, she turned on *Entertainment Tonight*. They were doing a segment on *3/4*. But before it came on, they led off with a shot of Crystal Plenum and Sam Shields. She sat, paralyzed. *Jack and Jill* was on location. She sat, and watched them interviewed. She sat, and gaped as Crystal Plenum played Jill in a clip from the movie.

And it was as if a vacuum opened up in her. A vacuum that sucked all she had gained right through her and left nothing: nothing but jealousy and emptiness.

In the vacuum, dreams and memories of Sam continued to haunt her. He rejected you, she told herself. He lied to you. He broke promises. But though all that was true, he had been passionate, fascinating, intense. He had really listened to her, really looked at her, really *known* her. He'd been capable of producing art, of discussing acting, theatre, films, and of making her laugh. When she had free moments – on the set, or at home – the thought of Sam's laughter, *their* laughter and jokes, crept up on her. It robbed her of her concentration. It distracted her. But thoughts of Sam kept her company.

Because working on the TV programme was a little like what the army must be like – all 'hurry up and wait.' It was exhausting always to be on call, always to have to be ready, waiting to go, and then at last actually to begin shooting, only to be told that a light needed adjustment, or a boom was down, or continuity had forgotten a prop, or a shadow had changed. A minute of screen time could take an hour to film, sometimes more. It was backbreaking, serious work.

In fact, on the set, the only laughing was done at Sharleen.

Jahne and Sharleen were poised on their bikes before one of the cycloramas used on the soundstage for *3/4*. As usual, there had been a lighting problem, and now that it had been fixed, as usual, Lila was making them wait. Jahne felt her makeup running, her forehead beginning to shine. At last, Lila sashayed out, without an apology.

'Lights up,' Dino shouted, and the spots they had been setting were switched on.

'Hey, guys,' Lila called out to the crew. 'Do you know how a blonde turns on the light after sex?' There was an attentive silence from the fellows behind the lights and camera. 'She opens the car door,' Lila said, and smiled only slightly at the laughter that gusted out from the dark.

Sharleen blushed to her hairline. Jahne felt sorry for her. 'Are you about ready now?' Jahne snapped at Lila. 'Or do we have more stand-up to listen to?'

'*I* won't blow my lines eight times,' Lila said, another dig at Sharleen. It was true. Sharleen got flustered and blew her lines fairly often. Jahne knew the girl must feel in over her head. Lila's hostility didn't help.

'Come on, now. Settle down,' Marty told them as he replaced Dino on the set. Lila looked him over coolly, then threw an incredibly long leg over her Triumph. Once Lila had learned that the other two characters had Harleys, she had insisted her character would have the only Triumph.

Marty DiGennaro was no dummy, and even though he wasn't asking for much in the way of performances, Jahne could see that he had something simply in the juxtaposition of the three of them, so similar and yet so different from one another. It was the undeniable sexy and visually interesting combo of the motorcycles and the women, the hardness of steel and chrome, the softness of the three girls. After working with him for a couple of months now, she didn't actually like or trust Marty, or even knew what he was doing, but she respected his talent and shrewdness.

Talking of shrewdness, Lila Kyle was one cute cookie. Jahne had seen the type over and over in New York, the steal-the-scene-at-any-price ambitious starlet, but California seemed to raise these traits to the tenth power. Maybe it was the fault line, or the plethora of crystals, or just what Californians still seemed to call 'vibes,' but it was clear that Lila, totally beautiful, was also a total narcissist; no one else existed on the set, unless he or she was there to do something for her. Yet the crew loved her. And Lila had certainly seemed to win most-favoured-nation status from Marty. Even when she wasn't being filmed, Marty's eyes followed her wherever she went. Jahne wondered if the two of them were playing hide-the-salami together.

Sharleen was the opposite. If Lila acted as if everyone was there to do as she wished, Jahne noticed that Sharleen would do what virtually anyone told her to. Even the grips and gofers bossed her. She called them all 'Mister' and seemed absurdly grateful for the smallest thing – Jahne heard her thank the makeup man three times when he powdered her just before shooting started. Jahne still hadn't decided: was Sharleen for real, or was it the most complete hokum Jahne had yet seen? And what was it with that Bible? Sharleen sat there, in between takes, with it in her lap. Was she a born-again starlet?

Jahne felt she herself was fitting in nicely. Her character, Cara, was the smart one, the most cerebral of the trio, and the rest of the cast seemed to accept that about her, Jahne, because she played Cara. The crew seemed to like and respect her already, and she had established an easy, bantering relationship with Marty. She noticed, though, that he became irritated if she asked too many questions about what was going on. Discussions about motivation, or even the point of a script, were not welcome. Marty was a control freak. He had pictures in his head that he wanted to get on film. Her job was to do as he said. It was a far cry from her days with Sam and *Jack and Jill*. Marty said 'Jump,' they all asked 'Where?' and then jumped. Except Lila, who sometimes felt the need to make a scene. Jahne found it all exhausting. She, after all, wasn't really twenty-four, despite her unlined face and what it said on her bio.

But, to be honest with herself, she was starting to feel disappointed. She had hoped that, with Marty at the helm, they would have an exciting ensemble, and a new kind of television. Certainly on the first score she was disappointed: Marty was the Boss, and only interested in moving them across the sets and locations in response to some internal vision that he never shared. But perhaps it *was* art they were making – art that would also be a commercial success.

In the few episodes they'd already taped there wasn't much *acting*, Jahne thought ruefully. Just as well, because neither Lila Kyle nor Sharleen Smith appeared to be an actress. They did each have something, though, Jahne readily admitted that. The camera loved them, and both had a naturalness that played. Jahne was afraid she, a more traditional actress, actually might not play as well, and that she didn't have the stamina to keep it up.

More than the demands of the script, the camera, and Marty, Jahne was afraid of Wardrobe. For the first fitting, she had been terrified of entering the room. How much would she have to expose? How much of her body scarring would show? She wore her usual Gap outfit – slim jeans and a white shirt, cowboy boots, and under her clothes a thin Lycra jumpsuit. It masked everything, a bit. But if they looked for them, the scars would show. Would they ask her to strip? Hesitantly, Jahne had walked in. She'd already met Bob Burton, head of wardrobe, and his assistant, an older woman whose name she'd forgotten. He did ask her to take off the clothes. She kicked off her boots, slipped out of her jeans, and shrugged the soft shirt from her shoulders. She stood, exposed like a silvery eel, wearing the smooth body stocking. She held her breath. Would she have to go further? What then?

'I've got the stuff laid out. Why don't you and Mai start on this?' Bob asked, lifting up a pair of bell bottoms, and left the room.

Mai, the old woman who was wardrobe mistress, turned away from the cluttered table that also served as her desk and came towards Jahne, measuring tape in hand.

'Some numbers for designer,' she said, in a heavy accent that reminded Jahne of the cartoon character Natasha from the old Rocky and Bullwinkle shows. If she hadn't been so nervous, Jahne might have been tempted to giggle.

'First here,' Mai said, rolling the 'r,' and encircled Jahne under her arms with the tape. The old woman then had to hold the tape at arm's length, her finger marking the spot. She nodded, made a mark on her pad, and next circled Jahne around the bust line. Then she stopped, looked at Jahne. 'You are sveating,' she said, bluntly.

Jahne was, like a horse, from nervousness. She shrugged. 'The lights,' she said.

'Bad for costumes,' Mai said, then only shrugged again. She continued her measuring, while Jahne continued to perspire. 'Vat you vould like?' Mai asked. 'A towel, or I should put up air conditioner?'

'Please, yes, put up the air conditioner.' Jahne knew that it wasn't the heat of the room that was causing her to perspire. But maybe the air conditioning would help. The old woman continued measuring and making notes. So far, she hadn't asked Jahne to strip, and perhaps she wouldn't. Jahne finally broke the silence, to take her mind off the process. 'What are the costumes like? Have you seen any of the sketches?'

'Humph,' Mai snorted. 'Costumes? Cheans! Cheans and T-shirts, that's the costume. For this they need a designer?' She shook her head.

Cheans? Jeans! Jahne laughed. 'But I bet they're beautiful jeans. Marty DiGennaro wants everything perfect.'

'Oh, yah, they are beautiful. And the shirts. Silk. And *your* colour vill be blue. Best colour for television camera. Vhite no good – drains face,' Mai confided, then stood back from Jahne and asked, 'That's good, no? You are definitely blue.'

Jahne thought about it for a moment. Mary Jane had never worn blue. It somehow looked wrong on her. But now, with her hair high-lights and her coloured contact lenses, Jahne Moore's best colour *was* blue, she suddenly realized. She smiled down at Mai. 'Yes, blue *is* my colour.'

Mai smiled. 'You are perfect veight. Not fat. But camera makes ten pounds fat, so ve must compensate. But don't be too thin. Like the redhead. Unnatural. The blonde will go soon to fat. But you vork hard to keep so, Mai can tell.'

Mai couldn't tell *how* hard, Jahne thought. And so far, Mai wasn't able to tell what else Jahne had done to get this body. She thought back to New York, not only the operations, but the starvation diet she had placed herself on. The one she was *still* on. To those long, lonely afternoons in New York, going to cheap movies, trying to keep her mind off food. Eating nothing, or almost nothing, walking, walking, walking in the cold, in the rain even, afraid to go home, afraid to eat, afraid to rest. Her only interests were in losing the weight and watching old movies. Here, in sunny

California, where everyone was thin and tan and happy, it was hard to connect with that other world, that other life. But even here she was afraid to eat. Coffee and fruit for breakfast, cottage cheese and salad for lunch, a small piece of chicken and a steamed vegetable for dinner. Or, if she had a beer, no dinner at all.

Jahne didn't like to think of those New York days, but something about the woman now kneeling at her feet nagged at her and brought New York back. Something about the movies. What was it? Certainly there were a lot of lonely old immigrant women in the movie theatres she had frequented, though this one, Jahne could see, had once been beautiful. Despite the wrinkles, despite the sunken cheeks, the bones of her face were still there. And the nose, the cheekbones, were still . . .

Jahne looked more closely.

Here, in the Wardrobe Department, looking down at the old woman's face, Jahne made the association. She remembered not the old women in the art-theatre *audience*, but the young woman on the *screen*, the painfully beautiful star, the one who had starred in those prewar von Sternbergs, the only woman of the time who could compete with Dietriech, the woman who was, in Jahne's opinion, more beautiful than Dietriech.

'My God! You are Mai Von Trilling!' Jahne cried.

The woman shook her head and smiled, a small, polite smile. 'No, no,' she corrected. 'I *vas* Mai Von Trilling.'

20

April waited for her latest secretary to usher in the moronic journalist from the *L.A. Times* who was doing some puff piece on her. She had no time for this bullshit, but after she was featured on the cover of *West Coast* as the winner of the world's worst-employer contest, scoring lower even than the South African diamond mines, Public Relations had suggested this as a counter. So she'd waste a valuable forty minutes with a jerk from the press.

April Irons was her own greatest invention, and, like any great invention, she worked well. In fact, some people said that work was all she did, but she didn't give a rat's ass what people said. You didn't get to run a major movie studio by caring about what a bunch of hard-ons said.

Running production at International Studios made her the *capo de tutti capi*. She got to green-light all the other producers' projects, as well as produce a few of her own. She had power: power over them, and power to do what she wanted, as long as the bottom line looked good to Bob LeVine and the International stockholders.

At forty-four (though all the publicity put her three years younger), April Irons could, at last, *do* what she wanted and *be* what she wanted. After all those rocky years, hustling for a few dollars to produce some book or play that she'd managed to option for a buck three-eighty, she'd finally gotten a few credits under her belt. Not that any of the sons-of-bitches in the Industry had helped her. She'd spent four years working at Warner's, doing coverages of every piece of shit that came in the mail sacks, trying desperately to get the ear of someone, anyone that mattered. She'd begged for a job with Ray Stark, with John Huston. And she got them: carrying bags. *Nona: A Life* had been the low-budget hit that was her breakthrough, and she'd done it without anyone's goddamn help. She'd used all her savings, the sixty thousand dollars her grandfather had left her and the money from a second mortgage that her mom took out on her house in Brookline, Massachusetts. When April finally got distribution from an independent, she was down to paying for prints with her MasterCard advances. But the critics ate it up, and it had legs: first the young and the hip, then the suburban intelligentsia. Finally, Orion picked it up, and even the mall rats got to see it. Then she'd followed it up with *Request*. She'd gotten Angela Blake to do her first nude scene. April had been able to get good distribution for it. *It had done eight million its first weekend, and the fucker only cost four.*

And that, my dear, was the trick. She'd gotten out of independent producing and into a studio, working with other people's money — money she didn't have to raise. And she had the formula. Be very smart, be brave, work your balls off, and never let the motherfuckers tell you no.

Now she looked at the journalist sitting across the coffee table from her. They came in three varieties: overly ambitious ass-kissers who wanted a job as a *quid pro quo* for good press; normally ambitious ass-kissers who simply wanted access and to get to do another story again someday; and, lastly, the bitter ass-kissers who would grill you and misquote you just to get a byline, a few bucks, and some mindless spleen vented.

All Hollywood called her the Iron Maiden. The real joke was that half of them also called her a nympho, while the other half called her a dyke. Which doubled her chances of getting laid, but *that* was *never* a problem. Certainly not now that she had so much power.

The reporter, a rumpled-looking kid in his late twenties, shambled in and nervously took his seat. She made an attempt at a smile, asked the girl to bring them some coffee, and looked at him attentively. They began with the usual half-assed questions: was it hard to be a woman in this business, what accomplishment was she proudest of, what trends did she see? She answered, her mind going over her afternoon. She wanted to freshen up before lunch, when she was meeting Sam Shields. It looked like *Jack and Jill* would work, and she was considering signing him up for another movie.

She was also considering him for a more personal job: her consort. She was sick of the pathetic men she'd been seeing: the ones outside the Industry bored her, the ones inside took advantage. But Sam Shields had amused her. He had a detachment that attracted her, a stupid East Coast snobbery that she found naïve and old-fashioned. Plus, he was a man who actually liked women, and there were few enough heterosexual men who loved females around.

Maybe Sam did not love them exactly – what man ever *really* loves a woman? – but he liked those things about women that women like about themselves. Softness, gentleness, complimentary colours. Femininity. Femaleness. April had enjoyed their brief affair. Of course, then Sam had gone after Crystal Plenum, like . . . like every man had gone after Crystal. And, as usual, Crystal had reciprocated. April expected it, knew Crystal had fucked every director she'd ever worked with. And April didn't really give a shit. Hey, whatever was good for the project.

But now the picture was over, and, as she knew so well, so was the love affair. Crystal would be reconciling with her husband/manager and then moving on to her next affair. And Sam would be ready for something new. April decided that something would be her. He looked right, he might be the new, hot *auteur*, and they would make a good team. Maybe even a marriage. Because, at forty-four, it was time.

April decided to give the kid with the pencil another three

minutes. Then it was off to lunch with Sam at The Grill. 'Any more questions?' she asked him brightly, pulling out her dark-red lipstick to freshen her immaculate makeup.

'Well, actually, I read recently that, before you fired your last secretary, you spent a month calling her 'Bitch' instead of her name. Is that true?'

April stopped, her hand with the lipstick frozen in midair. Hadn't anyone briefed the little putz that there would be no questions of this nature?

She turned her grey eyes on him coldly. 'Get this straight,' she told him. 'I *never* called that cunt a bitch.' She stood up. 'You can go now,' she said.

The drive to The Grill was taken up with a call to Public Relations to deal with the *L.A. Times*, so she had only a moment or two to prepare herself for Sam. He sat, waiting at the bar, his long body curved into a sulking question mark. Well, Sam was definitely the dark type. It was why she liked him. She was sick of California sunshine and businessmen.

'Postpartum blues?' she asked Sam as she approached the bar. One of the independent producers who had recently pitched her was sitting on the stool next to Sam, and he immediately vacated it for April. She took it without acknowledgment, and waited for Sam's answer.

'Isn't that what women get after giving birth to a baby?'

'Yeah, but directors get it, too, after they've given birth to their baby.' Sam didn't answer, just stared sullenly ahead. 'If I have to get my own drink, then what the fuck am I sitting here with you for?' she asked sweetly.

Sam tried to shake himself out of his blue mood. 'I'm sorry, April. What would you like?'

'To drink?'

Sam looked at her. 'Yes. Or whatever.'

'Get me a Stoli iced. Then get yourself a real drink instead of beer, for chrissakes, and let's sit over there, at my table.' April walked away from the bar, and Sam followed with the drinks, his now a vodka also.

'So, are you taking me to the premiere?' she asked. She tried to sound casual.

'If I have to go, there's no one I'd rather go with than you.'

'Of course you have to go. And it's for a good cause.'

'You mean the kids' charity it benefits?'

She laughed. 'No. I mean International's stockholders.'

'Just tell me one thing: are you *always* thinking about the business?'

'Let me tell you a couple of things. One of them I already did: Directors get depressed when their movie is finished. It's natural. Everyone gets depressed when the shoot's finished. That's why we have wrap parties, to try to soften the blow.' April took a sip of her drink. 'The other thing, Mr. Broadway, is, every director fucks his star, and every star fucks her director. It's never love, and rarely even respect. It happens because it gives a level to the communication between director and actress that they wouldn't have without it. Sometimes it shows on the screen. It's good for the picture.'

Sam grinned and shook his head. 'You're a real piece of work, April. I appreciate your loving concern, but how come you're so worried about me? I'm a big boy, I can take care of myself. If I'm down, I'll get back up. And one actress doesn't a love affair make. Don't have any illusions, April. A good fuck is a good fuck. And when it's over, it's over.'

April was surprised by how much she liked this guy. This was almost fun. 'So why the doom and gloom?'

Sam paused, sipped his drink, put it down on the table, and looked directly at her. 'I have some decisions to make. I have to decide on my next job, whether I'm going to stay out here or go back to New York. . . . I have a lot on my mind.'

'Well, let me give you some more to chew on. How would you like to do another movie for me?'

'You rejected my plays.'

'I didn't say your *plays*. I said a movie.'

'What movie?'

'Forget about that, and just answer the question. How would you like to work with me again?'

Sam let a grin cross his face. 'I'd rather eat broken glass,' he said, still smiling.

'I don't know how to take that. It means yes if you like eating broken glass, and no if you don't. So which is it?' She was smiling back at him now.

'I've got to give you this, April. You *do* know how to get things done. I've never worked with anyone who was so on top of things. Seymore was a shmuck. But getting a decision out of you is a pleasure. Watching you arrive at one is also a pleasure.'

'So I'll take that as a yes. And I've made one of my famous decisions. I want to do a remake of *Birth of a Star*. I managed to snag the rights to it. I'd like you to direct it.'

Sam stopped smiling, looked away, and shook his head. 'I don't do remakes.'

'Did you ever see the original?'

'No,' he admitted, a little sheepishly.

'Good. So for you it won't be a remake. It'll be original. Now, will you do it?'

'You have a script?'

'You want to write it?'

'I swore I would never work on someone else's story.'

'You changed your mind. Hey, it's a classic. Guy on the way down falls for girl on the way up. Love affair. Disaster. But we set it all modern. Liberated. Nineties.'

'Who for the male lead?'

'Michael McLain.'

'Michael McLain? Jesus Christ, April, the guy is over the hill.'

'Exactly. It's called typecasting, and a brilliant stroke of genius, if I do say so myself. Plus, he's cheaper than he used to be, and reliable. I hear there's trouble on his latest deal, a Ricky Dunn movie that might not happen. After *Akkbar*, if it falls through, he's got to give this everything he's got or he's out of the arena.'

Sam thought for a moment. 'Who for the female lead?'

'Suggest someone.'

'Don't know. But if we're getting McLain 'cause he's really on the slide, let's get someone really on the way up. Cinéma vérité.'

'Like who?'

'Maybe Phoebe Van Gelder. Or the girl who was featured in that last Redford thing.'

'It's a possibility.'

'Or how about one of the girls from the Marty DiGennaro thing? They're getting beaucoup publicity, and I think they're going to be hot now.'

April looked at him, nodding in thought. Wasn't one of them the daughter of Theresa O'Donnell? She'd starred in the other *Birth of a Star*. That would be good for lots of press coverage. 'I don't know. Television isn't the movies.'

'Only movies are the movies. But the casting would be *perfect*. They're new, they're fresh, and any one of them would be great juxtaposed against the old harlot Michael McLain.'

'Plus, it doesn't hurt that they're gorgeous and very fuckable, right? But can they act?' April laughed. 'I'd rather go with a movie neophyte than a TV star.'

'But one of them might be able to make the transition easily.'

'Sure, that's what they said about Tony Geary.'

'Who?'

'My point. The balding guy from *General Hospital*. Luke of Luke and Laura. Tried the big screen.'

'I never saw him.'

'Neither did anyone else.'

Sam sighed. 'Well, there's a lot of talk about the show and them now. Wouldn't it be a good thing to check it out?'

'Talk is cheap, especially talk *before* the show is out. But if you're interested, I could get an advance copy and we could screen it.'

'Come on. No one can even get in there. DiGennaro is a nut about secrecy.'

'I can get it.'

It might even be interesting, she thought. And if it pissed off Marty, it might be worth it. Yes. Yes, it certainly might be.

Sam turned his body towards April, and looked at her. 'Do you know everyone and everything?' he asked.

'Everyone and everything worth knowing,' she told him, and slowly licked her blood-red lips.

21

Lila came back to Robbie's house from a long day of househunting with a dreadful headache. She climbed into bed and prayed he wouldn't bother her. She rubbed her forehead and tried to adjust the pillow so that her neck was supported. The Malibu sunlight had made her eyes water and intensified the pain at her temples. But now, at least, she knew her stay here was ending. She'd have the chance to get away from Robbie and his constant prying and badgering. She'd rent the Nadia Negron house – the home of the silent-film star who had played the lead in the very first *Birth of a Star*. It was more than a coincidence – she was destined to live there.

Because she needed a place of her own. Marty DiGennaro and 3/4 were only a stepping-stone to the larger career she wanted. It was nerve-racking not knowing if the show was any good or not. If it came out and flopped, she knew that the Puppet Mistress would do a victory dance. And that Ara would dump her. Even Robbie would be disappointed in her.

Well, if she had her own place, she could have more privacy, more control. And maybe, just maybe, she could bear to let Marty DiGennaro touch her, if that was what he wanted. But first she had to make sure he wanted her badly. Really, really badly. And she knew how to do that.

There was a knock at the door, that annoying whisper of a knock Robbie used when he wasn't supposed to be knocking at all.

'What is it?' Lila asked, exasperated.

Robbie rolled in, the cordless phone in one hand, his face an exaggerated moue of excitement.

'It's your director,' he whispered.

Inwardly, Lila smiled. But she only winced before Robbie. 'Oh, God. Not again. Why didn't you say I was out?'

'Because it's Marty DiGennaro, the biggest director in Hollywood and your boss. That's why. Can't you make an effort, for heaven's sake?'

Angrily, she reached out for the receiver. She wondered what pretext he would use now. A private screening? An extra run-through? Since shooting started, Lila felt that Marty had become more and more insistent on seeing her outside of work. But she had to make sure it was only her that he wanted. Not just any of the three of them.

'What is it?' she asked into the receiver.

'What's the matter, Lila? You sound ill.'

'I have a headache.'

'I'm sorry. I wouldn't have bothered you if I'd known.'

'That's all right. What is it?' she repeated, but she did feel a little better.

'I wanted to know if you could have dinner with me. But not if you don't feel well.'

'Call Jahne or the dumb one. You could eat with them.'

'Oh, come on. Are you really sick? Would you like me to bring over anything? Advil or chicken soup?'

'No thanks, Marty, I'll be fine. I'll see you tomorrow.'

'Okay. But I hope you feel better soon.'

'I doubt it,' she told him.

But by the time she'd hung up and Robbie left her, Lila found her headache had gone away.

22

The uncharitable in Hollywood would call Michael McLain a pimp, but they would do so quietly. He was too powerful and well connected to insult to his ageing, pretty-boy face. If you asked for Laura Richie's opinion – and why shouldn't you? – I would agree, but I would add that he was a dual career pimp. Like Sy Ortis, Michael McLain had decided to try and keep the bodega. As a young actor, he had foreseen that the tides of stardom did not flow predictably. If he could have a fallback position, something that kept him in the public eye for those times when his current movie did not, he would be far better positioned to weather the storm.

And what better position than a recumbent one? Michael's policy was to bed the hottest Hollywood newcomer. If his first career was being a movie star, his second career was making love to, and headlines with, the most beautiful, wanted women on the planet. Nice work if you could get it, but work it was. Michael had schooled himself not only in his sexual techniques but also in those dozens of small wooing gestures and comments that made him irresistible and indispensable to the girls who became the Hollywood flavours-of-the-month.

And if, when the flavour lost its tang, he moved on, who could blame him? Everyone else did the same. That was the nature of a flavour-of-the-month. After all, who wants a steady diet of Pecan-Walnut Fudge? Certainly not Americans. They want their Cherry Garcia to be followed by Cashew Rocky Road, and after an addiction to Rain Forest Crunch, a switch to French-Mocha Praline is not only pleasant but necessary. After all, he never promised them forever. In fact, Michael McLain was very careful; he never promised them anything.

Michael now lay on the portable massage table that his therapist had set up for their weekly session. Clear plastic tubes lay on the table beside them. 'Roll over,' Marcia told him. Each week, she administered a high colonic to Michael, as well as another two dozen stars and spouses of stars. Michael insisted on the clear tubing, to be sure that she flushed out enough material. 'A clean colon is a healthy colon,' he always repeated. His crazy sister had turned him on to Marcia, and for once she made sense. The time he spent on the table was the time he used for thinking, and he found that, despite the discomfort of Marcia's hose pushed up his butt, the satisfaction in watching those toxins flushed past his line of sight soothed him. He did his best thinking then.

Now he was considering how he might proceed. There was no doubt in his mind that he could win the bet with Sy and have all three of the girls from the new show. To accomplish it would not be easy. Still, Michael was a veteran of difficult campaigns and almost never took no for an answer. Plus, the prize was so alluring. Not the women – long ago, Michael had begun considering them more work than treats – but star billing over that little prick Ricky Dunn. The kid was as hot as Michael had been twenty years ago. Everything Ricky touched turned to box-office gold. If Michael could maintain star billing over Ricky and also get fresh exposure to that sixteen-to-twenty-one-year-old crowd, he knew that he could really score.

So how could he score with the three new TV pussies? He felt a sudden cramping in his gut as Marcia turned on the water. 'Hey, watch it,' he told her sharply.

'Sorry, Michael.'

He shifted on his knees, his butt still raised high in the air. He felt the pressure as the water continued to press up into his intestine. 'Ouch,' he cried, and looked towards the plastic to see if more than the usual feces was breaking away.

'Sorry, Michael. Have you been eating red meat?'

'No, goddamn it.' He was sick of being blamed for her incompetence. He hadn't eaten red meat since 1981, for God's sake. A lot of other therapists would die for the chance to do *his* colonics. 'Watch it,' he told her, and tucked his knees tighter under his chest.

He considered the girls. He had seen that Sharleen, the blonde, would be no problem. He'd done some checking, and it seemed that she was living with some kid, but that didn't trouble him much. After all, he didn't want a *relationship* with her. With the right setup, it seemed like it wouldn't take more than a couple of dates to be photographed together. Trash like that would probably be willing to do it in the limo. That would give him a witness for Sy Ortis, in case he needed one.

Jahne Moore, the dark-haired one, seemed a little more problematic. Word on the set was that she and Lila Kyle did not get along. Should he let her and Lila know that he was pursuing both of them? Let them do the work of pursuing *him*? If they didn't like each other much, did they dislike one another enough to be jealous? Would they compete for him the way they competed on the set?

He grunted as the suction in his gut intensified. Nah, he didn't think that approach would work. Jahne Moore was a New Yorker, playing at the serious-actor bit. Maybe he could work on that. After all, when he first came to Hollywood, he had made some arty-farty films. But had little Jahne Moore ever heard of them? They were two decades old now, probably older than she was.

Of the three, it was Lila Kyle who troubled him most. He doubted she could be easily impressed with the star razzmatazz. Of course, with only an unaired TV show to her credit, she was not a star yet. But, she'd watched that game her whole life. He had heard not only about her bratty behaviour but about how Marty DiGennaro had begun to cater to it. If so, Michael would have to come up with something even more attractive than copping all the close-ups on your television show. That was a tall order. Michael smiled. Maybe Lila would like the part of the female lead in the movie with Ricky Dunn. Of the three, Michael figured Lila was the only one worth pursuing into a relationship. Yes. If he made a film where Ricky got the girl, but *he* got her in real life . . . She would be striking in photographs, of course, but, more important, even if the TV show went down in flames, she was the newest generation of Hollywood royalty. Pictures of him with Lila would help him stay forever young. Michael smiled. More than twenty years ago, he had had a brief fling with Theresa O'Donnell – it was his older-woman phase. She'd been a maniac in bed. Like mother, like daughter, Michael thought.

The noise of the colonic device subsided. 'All finished?' he asked.

'Clean as a whistle,' Marcia told him.

Sharleen heard the baseball bat as it connected with her father's skull. Thunk. Thunk. She shut her eyes and turned away and heard a siren. No, it was a phone. She was dreaming that a telephone was ringing. The sound of the phone pushed through the haze of sleep, until she realized that she was awake, and the ringing telephone was the one on the floor next to their bed. She turned towards the sound, and saw the green illuminated dial of the clock: 8.53 P.M. She and Dean were in bed by eight most nights. After all, she had to be up by five. The three puppies at the foot of the bed snuggled more deeply into the blanket. She moved Dean's paint-splattered arm from across her waist and placed it gently by his side, then leaned over the side of the bed and picked up the phone in mid-ring. 'Hello?' she muttered, then cleared her throat.

'Hi, is this Sharleen?'

'Yes,' she said, sleepily. Who was it? Only Sy Ortis, Mr. DiGennaro, and Lenny, her business manager, had her new, unlisted number. Oh, and Dobe, if he was picking up his mail. This voice wasn't any of theirs, and Sharleen didn't know anyone else that might call her. But the voice *was* familiar. She pushed her fuzzy brain to try and think.

'This is Michael McLain. Did I get you at a bad time?'

'Oh, *come on*.' Had one of the guys on the set gotten her number? Barry Tilden, the new assistant director, was always teasing her. '*Sure* it is,' she added, sarcastically. After all, she wasn't a fool. Then she heard the laugh at the other end of the phone. Oh, Lord, it did *sound* like Michael McLain – just like in that scene in his movie *The Last Stranger*, where he's challenged by the bad cop and, even though he knows he's going to lose, he laughs.

'If I'm getting you at a bad time, please . . .' His voice trailed off.

'How did you get my number?' And, more to the point, why would Michael McLain – if it *was* Michael McLain – be calling me? she thought.

'Sy gave it to me. Sy Ortis. He's my agent, too. I know it must be an intrusion,' he said, but it didn't sound like he meant it. There was a slight pause; then he added, his voice lower, 'Do you mind?'

'Are you *really* Michael McLain?' Sharleen asked. He laughed again. There was no mistaking it. Sharleen sat up, her back against the bare wall. Dean continued sleeping, unaware. 'Mr. McLain, why, no, I don't mind. But are you sure you got the right person?'

'If you're the Sharleen Smith that's the star of Marty DiGennaro's new TV show, I do.' Then that laugh again.

'Costar,' she corrected. She wanted to be fair. 'There is no star.' Dean stirred in his sleep next to her in the bed. He was exhausted from painting their new house all day, he had collapsed into bed before eight, too tired to eat anything more than the Big Mac she'd brought home for him. And Sharleen was happy to join him. She was tuckered out each night, too. She'd finished six straight days of shooting, but thank the Lord tomorrow was her day off.

'Mr. McLain, could you hold on a minute?'

'Sure,' he said.

Sharleen laid the receiver down and slipped out of bed. They were so rich now, she had a phone in the living room, the kitchen, and even the bathroom. Turning around, she pulled the sheet up over Dean's back, then tiptoed over the plastic throw-cloths scattered around, hoping the crackling sound wouldn't wake him. She walked into the bare living room, closed the bedroom door behind her, snapped on the wall switch, wincing as the six bare bulbs in the light fixture hanging from the ceiling cast a harsh light, and sat cross-legged on the floor next to the extension phone, her shorty pajamas leaving her behind bare against the cold floor. Was Michael McLain really on the phone, or was this a joke or even a dream? She rapped her knuckles sharply on the phone. Her knuckles hurt. It was no dream. Picking up the receiver, she said, 'Thanks for waiting, Mr. McLain. I just needed to get comfortable.' She put her sore knuckles in her mouth.

'Michael, please. Are you alone?'

Sharleen looked around the large, empty room. 'As a matter of fact, I am,' she said. Well, Dean *was* sleeping in the bedroom, wasn't he? He wasn't there, so she was alone, she told herself. Anyway, this must be business.

'Good. Then how about having dinner with me?'

'Dinner? *You* want to have dinner with *me*?' If this *was* Barry Tilden with another one of his gags, boy, she'd sure look foolish. 'I mean, sure. When?'

'How about tonight?'

Sharleen looked down at her shorty pajamas. 'But I already ate,' she said. Anyway, it was nine o'clock. Normal people ate at five or six. She didn't mean to turn Mr. McLain down or be rude. Could she go out and leave Dean? But could she say no to Michael McLain, if it really *was* him? Well, she had said no, she realized, and sighed.

'Okay, how about a drink, then?'

'I don't drink, neither.' Sharleen paused. 'But, if you like, maybe we could have some coffee.'

'Great idea,' Michael said. 'I'll pick you up in twenty minutes. You're over in the Valley, right?'

'Yes. But maybe you should make it thirty minutes, if you don't mind,' Sharleen said. 'I need to change what I'm wearing.'

Sharleen hung up, then sat motionless for a moment, her hand still on the receiver. This couldn't be happening to me, she thought. Michael McLain just doesn't call up strange girls out of the blue and ask them out. But this was Hollywood, and she was going to be a television star once the series came out, she reminded herself again. And *nothing* can be stranger than that. She jumped up quickly and ran across the shiny wood floor to the bedroom. She wasn't so careful not to make noise now; she had to find something to wear. She pulled the plastic off the floor lamp, and turned it on. Looking around the room at the boxes and suitcases through the opaque covering, she decided to start with the big brown suitcase she had bought on a shopping trip with Dean, and filled the same day. She pulled it out and began to go through the mass of new clothes, finally settling on a powder-blue silk shirt and a pair of white jeans.

Sharleen dressed quickly, then went into the bathroom and washed her face. She applied the liquid-base makeup the way Marcel on the set had shown her. Then the smallest amount of blusher, right above her cheekbone. She brushed her hair quickly, pulled it back in a pony tail, and tied it with a blue scarf.

As she walked through the bedroom again, Dean just barely raised his head. 'What are you doing up, Sharleen?' His voice was groggy with sleep.

'Go back to sleep, honey. I have to go out for a while. It's business.'

'You work too much,' Dean mumbled, and his head dropped back onto the pillow. She stroked his back, then, seeing that he was breathing deeply again, walked quietly out of the room, switched off the light, and closed the door. In the living room, she put on the strappy sandals she'd held dangling from her hand, and left the house. She'd wait out in front for Michael, to avoid having Dean disturbed by the car's engine or a honk. It reminded her of those nights she'd waited for Boyd Jamison. Standing there in the dark California-soft night, Sharleen felt a momentary thrill. This was their property now, a nice house of their own, with a garden and a pool. And, Momma, she thought to herself, I even got a date with your favourite movie star.

Sharleen sat on a chair just inside the wrought-iron gate that looked out onto the curving driveway. Lenny had found them the house, and it was real nice, plus Dean loved the yard. She waved at Bert, the security guard in the development, but kept herself from blurting out that she was waiting for Michael McLain. Glaring headlights caused her to close her eyes for a moment; when she opened them, she saw the most beautiful limousine pulling up at the front door, black and shiny with chrome that shone like silver. It wasn't a regular limo – it was some kind of English car or something. Maybe it *was* silver, she thought. For a moment, she wished Dean were here to see it. But, she reminded herself, that could lead to trouble.

She saw Bert approach the car and lean into the driver's door even before it hardly stopped, taking off his cap as he did. Meanwhile, from the back, a man got out and turned towards the front door, and Sharleen felt her hands get cold. Michael McLain. It really was him. Then he was standing in front of her, smiling. Sharleen finally spoke. 'You *are* Michael McLain,' she said.

Michael took her hand in both of his, as if to warm her, laughed, and said, 'And *you're* Sharleen Smith.'

Sharleen giggled, and took her hand back from him to cover her mouth. 'Of course you are. We are. I mean . . .' She stood up, still looking up into his famous blue eyes. 'They *are* real blue,' she said.

'Everything about me is real,' Michael said, and took her by the elbow to lead her to the car. Bert held the passenger door open as Michael handed her in; then Michael crossed in the headlights, and his driver held open his door. Then the driver pulled the car out onto the boulevard.

'Where are we going?' she asked. Not that it mattered – she'd go anywhere with Michael McLain.

'Wherever you want,' he said. 'Still want a coffee?'

'Sure. Do you know a place?'

'I know just the one. West Hollywood. Around La Brea?'

'Never been there.'

She saw Michael look at her again. 'You *are* new in town, aren't you?' Without waiting for an answer, he continued, 'The shops on Melrose Avenue are different from any of the other places in L.A. Most of them will be closed, but we can walk around and look in the windows. Everybody does.'

'What's it like?' she asked. And what will it be like walking on the street – in public – with Michael McLain? Sharleen felt giddy.

'They have the hottest shops in town. You'll see some of the prettiest boutiques, and *the* latest designs. Not that you need them. You're perfect just as you are.'

She blinked at the compliment, flustered.

Then he began asking questions. Questions about the show, about her costars, about her life before. It was real nice, if only she hadn't been nervous not to mention Dean, or her daddy or Lamson. But he made it easy. He seemed so interested. Slowing down after turning onto La Brea, Michael said, 'Here we are. Let's park and walk.'

Sharleen had never seen anything like it. Even on Rodeo Drive. There was a shop all filled with leather – even a leather bikini. Maxwell's had clothes by Japanese designers. Sharleen felt like she was in a new world.

'I have to bring you back here when they're open,' Michael said, as they passed a store with a sign outside that read 'Twist.' Sharleen looked in the windows and agreed. The clothes were all tight and flouncy, both at the same time. 'No one over twenty should wear this stuff. It's scary on them. But they'd be great for you,' he added.

Sharleen felt her face begin to flush, and spoke before the blush became noticeable. 'Look at the name of *that* store,' she said quickly. '"Wacko"! I like that.'

Michael slowed down, looked over at the sign and laughed with her. 'Let's go to Jackson's Place and have some cappuccino,' he said, and took her elbow in the palm of his hand. There was something about the way he held her, something hard. For a moment, Michael's touch made Sharleen feel that old fear. Then she quickly reminded herself that this was Michael McLain, and not some trucker on a back road in Texas.

'Jackson? Not *Michael* Jackson? We're going to his place for coffee?'

Michael laughed, not unkindly, she noticed. 'Well, no, it's just a café. But it's a nice one. And they know me there.'

Sharleen laughed out loud. 'People know you *anywhere*.'

Michael greeted the hostess by name as they made their way from the main entrance to the corner table in the rear of the restaurant. Once seated, Michael ordered cappuccino for them both, then looked directly at Sharleen. She didn't know what the stuff was, but she'd drink it. Embarrassed, she looked around the glittering café. 'Everyone in here is staring at you,' she said.

'No, Sharleen. I'm old news. They're staring at *you*,' Michael told her.

Sharleen shifted in her chair slightly, and was grateful for the arrival of the waitress with the coffee. 'Excuse me just a minute,' he said, as the coffee was being served, and walked out of the restaurant. Oh, Lord, had she been so dull that he was going to leave without her? What would she do? Well, she could call a taxi, or if she had to she could call Dean. But then, in only a few moments, he returned to their table. 'I'm sorry, I had to take care of something.'

'I just can't get over you calling me up,' Sharleen said after he sat down. 'Did Mr. Ortis ask you to? He's afraid I don't get out enough, but, between work, and my new place, and memorizing scripts, I just don't . . .' She realized she was talking too much, and took a sip of cappuccino. 'I sure do love this coffee. I never knew coffee could taste so good.'

Michael smiled, reached into his jacket pocket, and pulled out a little box, all wrapped in pretty blue paper with a white ribbon. He handed her the present, all dressed out so nice.

Sharleen was confused. 'What is it?' she asked, not reaching for the box.

'It's a little present from me to you. To welcome you to town. Go ahead, open it.'

Sharleen untied the bow and lifted the cover from the box. She pushed the tissue paper aside, then cried, 'Oh, Michael.' It was a necklace. She took the delicate chain out. Three stars were suspended from it, and it looked like there was a diamond in the centre one. Sharleen had never had a diamond. She held it up to her face, as if looking into the stone. 'It's beautiful,' she said softly, then looked up to Michael. 'But I can't keep this!' Still, her heart cried out for it.

'You'll hurt me if you don't keep it. And I can't take it back. Keep it.'

'Thank you,' Sharleen said, her eyes moist. 'I never had nothin' like it before.'

Michael was smiling broadly. 'Of course not. I had it made for you.'

'You did? But why?' Sharleen asked as she cradled the necklace in her hand.

'Because you're a star. One of three, but from what I hear *you're* the only diamond.'

'Really?' Sharleen asked. 'Oh, no!' But she blushed with pleasure. She had so far felt she was the least of the three. But she was the one Michael McLain had called.

'Wear it for luck,' he said. 'I think you're a very lucky girl.' He smiled and helped her clasp it around her neck. 'Now, how about finishing your coffee? I want to show you something else.'

'I'm ready,' Sharleen said, and jumped up. She was having such a good time.

Michael paid the bill, and followed Sharleen to the door. As they walked around the tables, she saw that people *were* looking at her, too. But that was because she was with *him*, she was sure.

Then there were lights – two or maybe three flashes. She winced and jumped in surprise. 'It's nothing,' Michael told her. 'Just reporters. You'll be in all the papers tomorrow.'

When they got into the car and pulled out, Sharleen turned towards Michael and asked, 'Why are you being so nice to me?'

Michael smiled. 'Because you're new in town, and probably could use a friend to show you the ropes.' Then he put his hand gently on her knee for a moment and looked at her. 'And because you're very easy to be nice to.'

This was *too* easy, Michael told himself, partly satisfied and partly bored. She's either real smart or real dumb, and he figured it was the latter. She wouldn't last in this town. Meanwhile, he already had pictures of the two of them together, the necklace round her neck. It would probably be enough for Sy, but Michael felt he might as well do the thing. After all, she *was* attractive.

He checked the ice bucket at the side of the console. The Moët was chilled. Jim knew his job and did it well. For six years now, he'd driven Michael around in this Rolls, kept it in immaculate condition, and discreetly assisted in the seduction of the moment. Without a word spoken, he knew to drive up to the hills, to the spot Michael had used so often before. It happened to be right where Monty Clift had cracked up his car and his face.

'It's so pretty in the moonlight. I've never been up in these hills before,' Sharleen said. 'Can we stop somewhere for a while?' she asked. 'I want to see the lights.'

'Good idea,' Michael said. 'I'll have Jim pull over to a little place at the top of this hill. Wait until you see the view.'

It was spectacular. Even after all the years of bringing woman after woman up here, it still impressed him. His town. Tinseltown.

All of it stretched out before them, little lights twinkling. 'Oh. It's beautiful,' the girl gasped, right on cue. Jim pulled over.

'Let's go out to that rock,' Michael suggested. 'That's the best view.' He took out the bottle of Moët. Then he grabbed two champagne flutes off the hanging rack and led the way.

Sharleen followed. The night air, for once, was clear, and scented with the pungent smell of eucalyptus and brush. Below them lay the entire city of Los Angeles. She walked to the cliff side and stepped out onto the rock there, the lights of the city flickering beneath her like an inverted starry sky. 'Oh my!' was all she said. 'Oh my,' she repeated, and hugged herself.

Behind her, Michael opened the bottle with a pop, then stood next to her and handed her one of the filled glasses. 'It's champagne,' he told her. 'You said you don't drink, but this isn't like liquor. It's like drinking moonlight. It's always to celebrate something important. Like our friendship. Try it,' he urged, and knew she could see his most winning smile.

Sharleen sipped the cool drink, then wrinkled her nose. 'So this is champagne?' she asked. 'I don't know what they make such a big fuss about it for. It just tastes like a real sour ginger ale.'

Michael laughed. 'It kind of grows on you,' he said. 'Come sit over here. This is the best spot.'

Wordlessly, Jim had set out the rug and pillows from the Rolls, then returned to it. Sharleen sat down on the soft cushions and took another sip. She stared out at the glittering grid beneath them, and dreamily she said, 'You know, you see this kind of thing in the movies, but you never believe that it really exists, or that *you* can ever be part of it. And here I am.'

She really was lovely, he thought, warming to his work. 'Here's to you, Sharleen,' Michael said, raising his glass to click hers in a toast. 'A part of Hollywood.'

Sharleen clicked her glass back, and, following his lead, took another sip of wine. She stretched, leaned her back against the pillows, and said, 'I feel very happy.'

'That's why people like champagne,' Michael told her. 'It helps them feel happy.' He poured more into his glass, then nodded to Sharleen's. 'Have some more. I'll just top it off for you.'

Sharleen took another quick two swallows, then coughed. Michael tapped her gently on the back. 'Go down the wrong way, Sharleen?' he asked, smiling in the faint light.

'I'm okay. I just drank it too quickly.'

303

'Better take another sip. It will help clear your throat.'

'It doesn't make you drunk?' she murmured.

'Only if you drink lots of it. We're only sharing this one bottle,' Michael reassured her, and he poured more into her glass. She had to take another big gulp to keep the champagne from spilling. He himself had better lay off, he realized. He couldn't drink and perform the way he had a decade ago.

'Oooh. I feel so good. Like I can reach right up and pluck one of them stars right out of the sky.' Her voice was blurred. Time for his move, he thought. 'They all look like diamonds,' she murmured.

Michael reached over and gently touched the one around her neck. She lifted her hand to it as well, and their fingers touched. He leaned across her, and brought his face very close to hers. 'I've never known anyone like you,' he said. Then, looking into her eyes, he kissed her, sweetly, lightly, on the lips. He saw her draw back, and he touched the back of her head with his free hand. Slowly, now, he told himself. Slowly.

'You're very beautiful,' he said. 'Much more beautiful than the other girls. And sweeter, too.' Then he pulled back. Not too fast, he thought again. He drained his almost empty glass, and indicated for Sharleen to do the same with her full one. Then he refilled both their glasses, and touched his to hers once again. 'Here's to your success. I *know* you're going to be a *very* big star.'

'Thank you,' she said, and he recognized the glazed look that Moët, gifts, and the Michael McLain charm induced. She looked a little like a blonde bunny trapped in the headlights of a car. But she was a very beautiful bunny. 'I'll help you any way I can. Let me. I can teach you a lot of secrets.' He leaned forward. This time, she didn't pull away. He took the glass from her hand, and held her in his arms. Slowly, ever so slowly, he stretched out next to her on the blanket. 'Let me love you, Sharleen,' he said, and rolled his body onto hers.

Sharleen looked up at Michael, unable to see anything in the dark except the starry sky. A star, he had said. A big star. How could that be? she thought. She didn't even want that, but that's what Michael McLain had said. Maybe she didn't have to be so afraid anymore. Afraid of losing her job; afraid of Lila, who was mean; afraid of Jahne, who was smart; afraid of the police, of her dreams of Lamson; afraid that she and Dean would be found out. She felt

Michael's warm hand touch her shirt, and stroke her through the soft fabric. It felt different, so different from Dean's touch. This must be what movie stars did, she thought fuzzily. She felt Michael's lips on hers again, and tasted the champagne as she opened her mouth to him. Michael slipped his hand under her loose blouse, and placed the palm of his hand on her skin. Then he pulled back from her slowly, and laid his face against her bare stomach, kissing her navel, and the spot right under it. Then right on her belly button again. She almost laughed! Then he kissed below it. She heard a zipper opening in the dark, and realized it was hers.

'No,' she said, starting to struggle up from the cushions. She felt as if the noise had awakened her from a dream. She hadn't meant for this to be – well, for them to go so far. It was like a dream. But this was real. Oh, God, how had this happened? She hadn't meant to give the wrong idea. 'No,' she said.

'Yes,' he whispered, and one hand was on her head, the other pushing her shoulder back, back down into the cushion.

'Don't you like me, baby?' he asked her.

'Yes. Yes, but . . .' His mouth covered hers again.

'Just yes. Yes,' he murmured. God, she didn't want to hurt his feelings. Had she led him on? She hadn't meant to. She didn't hardly know him. He moved his head down to her breast, his lips on her nipples, on her belly. She tried to stop him, but she was falling into the dream again. The stars spun over her head. She felt as if she were floating over the city.

Michael tugged at her pants, bringing them down over her buttocks. Oh, God, what was he doing? His head was still down there, his lips now moving lower, lower down, down. Sharleen felt her nipples harden, released from her shirt, exposed to the air. Michael reached up and pinched each slightly, so gently that the pleasure made her move her hips.

Sharleen closed her eyes briefly. She felt tears well up in them and spill onto her cheeks. What was she doing? What was he doing to her? Everything continued to spin. She opened her lids and saw Michael stand, silhouetted in the starlight. He dropped his pants, then pulled off his shirt in a slick, single movement. He didn't mean to do it – to do *that* – right out here? She had to tell him to stop.

'The driver. Jim. He can see us. Stop. Please.'

Michael said quietly, 'No one can see.' Then he was on her again, moving her legs apart, already moving his hips rhythmically.

'No,' she said, 'please.' But it was too late.

'No one can see anything,' Michael told her, just as Jim silently pulled the infra-red camera from the glove box of the Rolls.

23

Parties may just be parties in other places, but in Hollywood – or Holmby Hills, to be exact – a party is never just a party. It's a place to see and be seen, a place to make contacts, make deals, and make out. And if Hollywood has always been famous for its parties, the choicest, the fanciest, the most exclusive, was Ara Sagarian's Emmy party, held on the night of the annual television awards. Originally, it had been a party where the most select movie actors and actresses hooted with derision at the doings on the small screen. But for years now, the small screen had been too important to hoot at. Still, this party was the place where Hollywood let its hair down, so exclusive that no journalists were ever allowed. It was the hot ticket, and no one who was anyone ever admitted to being in town and not invited. It was the only important party that I, Laura Richie, was never invited to.

Ara, despite his courtly manners and exquisite politesse, winnowed the guest list mercilessly. Joan Collins had been dropped long before Dynasty was. Burt Reynolds was no longer invited. After all, an A-list party only remained A-list if no one but the crème de la crème attended.

But like all rules, Ara broke this one for the singular exception of Theresa O'Donnell. For twenty-two years, as long as he had hosted Emmy parties, Theresa had been invited. Because although her star had waxed, waned, and then waxed and waned again, she had been Ara's first big star. And despite the booze, the pills, and the paranoia, she was still a legend. She was his talisman, his good-luck charm, and she showed the world (and his clients and potential clients) that Ara Sagarian was loyal to his clients. But now that he was no longer representing her and not inviting her he felt guilty – terribly, terribly guilty. Ara based lots of his self-worth on knowing he was both a gentleman and loyal in a land of locusts.

But he had, at last, been disloyal to Theresa. That was undeniable. His only excuse was that, despite his age, despite the stroke, despite the disability, Ara still wanted to play – he still wanted to be not just in the pack but in the lead. Still throwing the most exclusive parties, still representing the biggest stars. And he knew he had been slipping. His stable was ageing. He felt he'd had to take the chance with Lila Kyle.

Neil Morelli lifted the last of the trays of canapés from the caterer's van and brought them into the kitchen. The fat guy in charge kept referring to a clipboard and barking orders to the swarm of waiters and chefs. All the asshole needed was a fucking whistle, Neil thought. Neil resented having to take this job, not that he didn't need it. Since the show had been cancelled, he'd lived hand-to-mouth, using up his last few dollars licking his wounds. Now, totally broke, he had to take whatever he could get. Because Sy Ortis wasn't getting him anything else in the Industry; Christ, Sy still wasn't even getting his fucking calls, or at least he wasn't answering them. So Neil threw himself back on the old survival jobs of all players who are 'at leisure': driving a cab, waiting tables, and trying again.

This one, working for Table d'Hôte, wasn't the worst. At least he wasn't slinging hash in some public place, making himself a spectacle, humiliating himself in front of everyone. These were private parties: rich orthodontists, corporate lawyers, and the usual crowd of Orange County Reaganites. Stiffs.

It wasn't until the caterer had pulled the van full of waiters into the driveway of this one that the honcho told them whose house they would be working tonight. Ara Sagarian's Emmy party. Jesus. Tears nearly filled Neil's eyes. He'd been reading about this party in the columns since he was a kid. He used to gobble down the pictures of celebrities around the pool – all laughing, all perfect. His dream was to join them. Join them as an equal. He – Neil Morelli – should be on the other side of the table. That's what he had come to this town for, to be waited on, not to be a waiter. He stood at the kitchen door, paralyzed, not sure he could force his legs to cross the back-door threshold.

'Hey. You with the nose. Move it. Grab a tray,' the fat guy yelled.

When Sy Ortis called Jahne and invited her to Ara Sagarian's Emmy party, she'd been surprised. 'Strictly business,' he quickly explained. 'You got to be out and about now.' Jahne was being talked about, but she was still an unknown to everyone outside the Industry and many inside it, too. So she said yes, though she could barely stand Sy. Sy might be handy for introducing her around, but it was clear that he also had disadvantages as an escort. Ara had been polite but cool to him. Of course, who *could* like Sy Ortis?

She was nervous about this, her debut in the Hollywood social scene. But Sy insisted, and he promised they'd come late and leave early. Now, with butterflies in her stomach, she turned to him. 'Who would you like to meet?' he asked her smoothly. 'Cher? Keanu Reeve? Hey, Michael Keaton is over there by the bar. He hasn't come to a party since Batman returned.' Jahne smiled. 'No? How about Crystal Plenum?' Jahne's smile disappeared. Take it easy she told herself.

'No thanks,' she said

'So who, then?' Sy asked.

Jahne looked around. An enormous man, at least six and a half feet tall and well over three hundred pounds, stood at poolside. It must be Marvin Davis. Jeff Katzenberg stood at the bar, a circle of people around him.

And was that tall old man David Lean? No, wasn't David Lean dead? Jahne's head spun. Before Jahne had a chance to answer, Sy took her arm. 'Oh, here's somebody you *must* get to know.' Sy walked up to a tall back and tapped the man's elbow. 'Michael, say hello.'

The man turned, and Jahne found herself looking into the blue, blue eyes of Michael McLain. He smiled at her, and she couldn't help smiling back. 'Any friend of Sy's is someone I'd better watch out for,' Michael said. Then he extended his hand to hers. 'Hi. I'm Michael McLain,' he said.

'This is Jahne Moore. She's doing the new Marty DiGennaro show that premieres this coming season.'

'Oh? Is Marty doing a TV show? What is it about?' Michael asked her.

She began to explain, and found him surprisingly easy to talk to, after she got over the undeniable weirdness of standing beside a man-sized Michael McLain. Not that he was exactly tall. With her highest heels on Michael McLain only reached to her ear. After years of seeing him only in ten-foot-high close-ups on the screen, it was a difficult adjustment. No wonder people always thought movie stars were shorter in 'real life' than they were on the screen. Still, other than his height, Michael McLain stood up fairly well. He was still very handsome, and if his neck was a little crepey and his eyes set in a few lines, it didn't bother her one bit. They chatted pleasantly for a few minutes.

'I was sure the two of you would get along,' Sy said as he drifted away. 'But watch out for him, Jahne. He eats girls like you for breakfast.'

'Only if they *want* to be eaten, Sy.' Michael smiled, though this time the smile didn't move up to those incredible blue eyes.

Crystal Plenum adjusted the fall of her signature white wrap on her equally white shoulders and walked into the big room ahead of her husband. That was part of their understanding. Entrances were *always* made alone, just as exits *never* were. She heard the stir she made, the slight pause and then the increase in the ambient noise, and smiled as her husband came up behind her. 'Wayne,' she said softly as he approached, 'don't leave my side for *one minute*. And make sure and say everybody's name. You know how I get.' Crystal was terrible with names, but knew how important it was in this town to be able to put a name with a face. People liked to be recognized, no matter who they were – or weren't. And they really liked to be recognized by a star. Plus, it kept her from wasting time on the unimportant people at parties. Although, Crystal knew, there were *no* unimportant people at *this* party. Except, of course, for the spouses.

Last year, Ara had neglected to send her an invitation. She'd told everyone she was going to be in New York, and then holed up at the Hotel Bel-Air instead. But now *Jack and Jill* had been lauded by the critics and was doing good box office for a woman's picture. She was up for a New York Film Critics *and* a Golden Globe. There was definite Oscar talk. The gamble she'd taken – playing her age, looking like shit, and trying to act – had paid off. Everyone would be kissing her cellulite-free ass tonight! She was on top again.

And she'd have to keep Wayne a while longer. Right now, she had to focus on prolonging the roll and starting her next film before she cooled off. A divorce, especially from a husband who was also her business manager, would be costly and distracting. She wondered if she'd get a *People* cover the way Joan Lunden did, because Wayne would sure stick her for a pile of alimony. She should never have let him manage her in the first place. Well, if it came to that, she never should have married him. There would be time for a divorce later.

'Crystal,' Ara said, limping towards them, dragging his stroke leg, his hand extended to her, 'how kind of you to come.'

'Ara Sagarian,' Wayne said quickly in a whisper.

'*Him* I know, Wayne,' she told her husband, annoyed. Maybe she *could* afford a divorce this year.

Turning to the approaching small man, she said, 'Thank you for having me. I'm honoured to be here, Ara. I couldn't be more pleased if I were winning an award *myself* tonight. Except not a *television* award, of course.' They both laughed.

Paul Grasso hunched in the dark in the back seat of the taxi. Across the way, the drive to Ara Sagarian's house was lit by tiny twinkling lights and peopled by parking valets and the beautiful invited guests. He looked down at his tux, wrinkling into a pathetic mess as he sat and sweated in the warm darkness.

'Pathetic' was definitely the word for him. Pathetic that, after thirty years in this town, twenty years as a *player*, he was passed over by an old, half-crippled queer. What was Ara saying? That Paul Grasso was no longer worthy of an invite?

Paul knew that if his access to the people that matter was cut off, he could fold his tents and go home. And he had no intention of folding anything. If any folding was going to go down, Ara could take his invitations, fold them five ways, and put them where the moon don't shine.

But now the moon *was* shining. Just one more thing against him. Because Paul knew he *had* to be at the party. He owed too much money and needed work too bad to risk letting the word get out that he had been overlooked.

He watched and waited for his opportunity. The underbrush at the Fred Wiseman house was thick – more a jungle than a garden. Well, he'd have to use it to his advantage. Because the Wisemans' property was next to Ara Sagarian's. He hoped it wasn't patrolled by dogs.

Cautiously, he got out of the taxi and dismissed the driver. He didn't know how he'd get home, but he'd cross that bridge when he came to it. Stealthily, he moved into the underbrush that ran along the dividing line of the two properties.

Paul Grasso was not the only bitter, excluded person left in the darkness that night. In Bel Air, Theresa O'Donnell sat in the musty bedroom that was reserved for Candy and Skinny. She didn't speak to them or for them, but merely sat, motionless as the two puppets, and as empty.

April Irons wordlessly handed her empty glass to Sam Shields, and looked around Ara's vast, crowded living room while her escort went to fetch her a fresh one. They were negotiating on the new film she was producing, the remake of *Birth of a Star*. Wait until Marty DiGennaro found out! She knew he loved the thing. Maybe she'd introduce Sam Shields, as the director of the remake, to Marty. He'd eat his liver! But Sam would probably ass-kiss. April didn't feel the need to give her protégé entrée to absolutely everyone.

Her eyes stopped when, across the crowded room, she spotted a handsome man with Kikki Mansard, the new girl in town, on his arm. When his own eyes met hers, she beckoned with an exaggerated motion of her index finger for him to come.

He pointed to himself and mouthed, 'Me?' April nodded her head up and down, deliberately. The man began to walk towards her, his hand on Kikki's back, guiding her. April shook her head and watched the man whisper to his date, then continue towards her, alone.

'April, you flatter me,' Michael McLain said, and raised the tips of his fingers to his lips. 'But don't you want to meet Kikki? She's doing the Dino De Laurentiis thing.'

'No thanks. I had dog meat for dinner. This is business. You were supposed to call me about that script,' April said.

'That's not a pout, is it? On April Irons?' Michael asked, his eyes twinkling. Jesus, these actors, she thought. They never turn it off.

'I'm ten years past pouting, you big prick. You *begged* me to see the script, I sent it over. Then nothing. What am I supposed to do? Chase you around town to get you to take a part that every male star would give his left testicle for? I'm not one of your twenty-year-old chippies.'

He leaned into her ear. 'Oh, yes, you are,' he whispered, using the voice that makes America's women wet. April shrugged, though actually she always enjoyed sparring with Michael McLain.

'That does it,' she said, but she smiled. 'I've got to move on. Beatty wants the part. And I have to work the room. So either you call me – soon – or I'm going to pass it around town that Michael McLain can't get it up.'

Michael made a look of mock horror. 'Please don't do that! I won't be able to get a night's sleep for months. Women all over this town would take that as their biggest challenge.'

Sam Shields stood by the bar, nervously swirling the vodka in his highball glass. He had not been invited to this party. When he got the call from April to come as her escort, he had been surprised. He wasn't sure if this was business or pleasure, and though he wanted to work with April again, he wasn't so sure he wanted to sleep with her. She was a demanding mistress, and there was something more than intimidating about her. To be blunt, he felt that she used men the same way most men use women. It made him nervous.

So did gatherings like this one. Sam liked to think of himself as a player, but when he was surrounded by these heavy hitters, he felt damn insecure. Nobody had sought him out, and he wasn't very good at 'working the room.' He wished he could go home. To kill time, he watched the guests milling about. He tried to identify them. The stars, of course, were easy. It was the power brokers and studio suits he worked on. Mike Eisner. Michael Medavoy. Michael Ovitz. Was 'Mike' a prerequisite to success out here?

Then he saw the redhead. She was with DiGennaro. In fact, that was Marty DiGennaro surgically attached to her arm. She might be good for *Birth of a Star*. She looked young and hot.

He looked over at April. She had been talking to a series of movers and shakers, the last being Michael McLain. Now, seeing her 'between engagements,' he crossed to her side. Perhaps she'd introduce him to DiGennaro. Perhaps he'd get a shot at the redhead perhaps . . .

'I have had about enough of this,' April said to him. 'Let me just talk to a few more of these guys, and then what do you say we go back to my place and fuck?'

Jahne stood at the side of the pool, the lights threaded through all the palms twinkling like tiny stars. Big stars and big movers and shakers stood around the pool. No one knew who she was, and in the shadows she had a moment of privacy.

At a party like this, just being beautiful was not enough to draw interest. You had to be beautiful, successful, *and* famous. Because this was a party of the most beautiful, successful, and famous people in the world. And she, Jahne Moore, was there.

Well, she reflected, I must have arrived. How else could I be here? She smiled. This unreal scene was her reality. But the reality she was living was becoming more and more unreal. She breathed in the fragrance of night-blooming jasmine, mixed with just the slightest scent of chlorine from the pool. Essence of Hollywood.

Then, as she watched, a man climbed out of the shrubbery in the darkness. He was short, and almost as dark as the shadows he had hidden in. He looked up at her. 'Hi,' he said nonchalantly, and brushed off his crumpled dinner jacket. 'I was looking for my wallet,' he explained, and strolled off into the crowd. She shook her head.

Behind her, two society women began to gossip. They were older matrons, clearly married to Industry heavies. One looked up. 'Oh. Oh! Look!' she cried. 'It's Mary Jane.'

Jahne felt a tug in her stomach. She felt herself almost dissolve, and instantly a film of sweat broke out all over her. God! Were they from New York? How had they . . . Then another older woman walked up to the group. 'Mary Jane Wick, meet my friend Esther Goodbody,' the matron said. Her voice faded.

Jahne could only hear the buzzing in her ears. She tried to take a deep breath, one that moved all the way down to her solar plexus. She took another wobbling step forward on her very high heels and almost slipped but caught herself just in time. Get a grip, Jahne, she told herself sternly, and then she looked up. There, across the pool, she saw him. He was wearing black and white, like all the men. She could hardly believe her eyes. It had been such a long time since she'd last seen him in New York. 'Oh, my God!' she said out loud.

No, she told herself. She was merely shaken by the women and the mention of her old name. She turned her eyes away, blinked, took a few more deep breaths, and told herself to be calm. Now I'll look, she said to herself. Now I'll look, and find I am mistaken. But as she raised her eyes and looked across the tiny lights floating like lotus blossoms in the pool, she knew it was he.

It was Neil, and he was dressed as a waiter, serving canapés to the party guests.

Paul Grasso stood with a drink in his hand, moved slightly back and forth from heel to toe, rocking where he stood, and shook his leg. Yahta, yahta, yahta. He hated these fuckin' Industry soirées. But it was his shot to get to Marty, and he'd managed to corner his prey at last. You would think it would be easier, since Marty was there with Lila Kyle, who looked gorgeous as ever but not one bit grateful. But Paul knew there was no gratitude in this town. Paul thought of the Italian proverb that asked, 'Why does she hate me so? I never did anything for her.' Because Lila clearly hated him. She'd gotten the part but never delivered on the casting job she promised him. The job he was desperate for. Anyway, she never took his calls. Now she stood beside Marty, obviously gorgeous and obviously bored.

'Nice tux,' Marty DiGennaro commented, his sarcasm heavy. Paul ignored him. He needed to pick up some work, but nothing was lower than asking for it here, at a party like this. Still, it wasn't like he was begging. Hey, he was *owed* it.

'So what you been up to? Make it over to Vegas lately?'

'Nah,' Marty said. 'Too busy.'

'How's the show going? I haven't heard.' Paul felt sweat bead his upper lip.

'Real well.'

Well, he'd have to do it. 'Got any casting trouble? Maybe I could help?'

'You mean maybe *I* could help. You looking for work, Paulie?'

'I wouldn't mind the casting for this new project,' he admitted, and held his breath. Marty paused. It wasn't the pause that refreshes. It was the one that ended a friendship and turned it strictly business.

'Call my office tomorrow,' he said, and Paulie knew he'd cashed in his last chip but that he was back in the game.

Lila cleared her throat and shifted from one leg to the other. It made her boredom more than apparent. Ara had invited her, since she was his client, but Marty had an invitation for two in his own right. She had refused to come with him, however, and told him she would meet him at the party. Now she was regretting her decision. This was all so dull. And Paul Grasso looked like he wanted to play 'I've Got A Secret' with her. She'd blow them both off. 'I'm going inside,' she told Marty, and without a goodbye or acknowledgment she walked across the deck and through the open French doors to the huge tiled living room. Near the centre of the room, a mammoth chair stood, surrounded by a gaggle of morons. Lila did not want to look too interested, but she floated towards them. Lots of power there: Don Simpson and Joel Schulmacher. *Days of Thunder* meets *Peter Pan*. When would *she* be the centre of attention, she wondered? As she came up to the group, not one of them turned to look at her.

At the centre a tall, dark woman was talking to an equally tall, dark man. He smiled at her. She smiled back. From the corner of her eye, she saw Marty approach.

314

'Miss Kyle?' the tall man asked. She nodded. 'I'm Sam Shields. And this is April Irons.'

Lila gave April a big smile. April Irons meant features. First-class features. Marty joined them.

'Hello, April,' he said, and took Lila's arm. Lila felt her annoyance build. He didn't own her. She took her arm back.

'So, what are you up to, April?'

'Oh, a new little project. Sam here is directing. Just getting some pointers from Don.'

'Really?' Marty smiled stiffly. 'Got a working title?' he asked idly, obviously bored.

'It's called *Birth of a Star*,' April cooed.

Neil stood on the back porch, sucking on a cigarette, his hands trembling. Sam Shields. Fucking Sam Shields! Neil had been passing a tray of caviar and had turned to offer some to a small group. He recognized Michael Douglas, Kevin Costner, Richard Gere, Marty DiGennaro, and Crystal Plenum. He served Michelle Pfeiffer, Phoebe Van Gelder, Kirk Kirkorian. And that producer bitch, April Irons. Then the guy in front of him had leaned into the bowl of Beluga, scarfing it up. Neil almost dropped the tray when he saw it was Sam Shields. His first instinct had been to push the fucking bowl of fish eggs into Sam Shields' face; then he realized he had to get away.

The humiliation was stinging. It was both a relief and an insult that Sam didn't even recognize him, hadn't even looked at who was serving him. All the bastard could see was free four-hundred-dollar fish eggs.

'I told you, Nose, there are no breaks.' The fat guy again, now standing at the kitchen door, warned him.

'You're telling me!' Neil said, flicked his cigarette into the Beluga and began to walk down the driveway, unclipping his stupid black bow tie.

'Where you going, Nose? You got a job to do.'

'Yeah, fat boy, you got that right. But it's not *this* one.'

Where the fuck did the caviar go? Sy Ortis thought, looking around the room. Another waiter passed at that moment, and he grabbed him before he got away. But he was only carrying skewered vegetables on a bed of kale. Even in Mexico, we threw that crap out. But he was hungry – nerves always made him eat

– so he took four of them. These guys disappear so fast, Sy didn't want to take a chance on *this* one's getting away.

'I'd like to have ten per cent of everyone in this room.'

Sy looked up from the skewers to find Milton Glick at his elbow. 'Yeah, well, you'd have to be a faggot to get it,' he said, indicating with his head Ara standing with a group of young men. Then he looked Milton up and down. '*And* a hell of a lot prettier than *you* are.'

'I've already gotten fucked up the ass in this town. I guess it won't hurt to suck some dick.' Milton shrugged.

'Who did you come with?' Sy asked.

'My wife. She's over there, talking to Mary Jane Wick about some charity ball. Who are you with?'

Sy shrugged. 'Jahne Moore. The client Marty had to find on his own. The client from hell. Because *you* didn't get me two Sharleen Smiths.'

'Nobody is perfect, Sy. Except you, of course.'

Neil stood at the bottom of the driveway. *Now* what the fuck do I do, he thought? I can't thumb a ride. Not in Holmby Hills. And no money for a cab. There once had been buses in this town but they must have ended in the tar pits with the hairy mammoths. He turned at the sound of the beeping horn. A car was parked across the road from Ara's driveway, and a woman was leaning out its window, beckoning to him. He walked over slowly; blessing his luck. He had never been picked up in this town – in any town, for that matter. Maybe his luck *was* changing for the better.

The woman stepped out of the car as he approached. She was not pretty, he could see. Shit, she was ugly. And old – well, middle-aged. But what the fuck? He was no Miss America, and was stuck here without transportation.

'Hi,' she called out as he approached. 'Working the party?' she asked, nodding towards Ara's house.

'Yeah. I should say, was. I just quit.'

'I'll give you a hundred bucks for your waiter's outfit,' she said.

Neil didn't answer for a moment. I should have known. 'A crasher, huh? I guess people would do anything to be seen at Ara's party. A hundred, huh?' he asked. 'John Ritter would give me a thousand.'

I shrugged. Yes, it was me, Laura Richie. And Laura Richie has stooped

to lower than this to get a hot flash. For you, gentle Reader. All for you.
'Maybe you should be talking to John Ritter, then.'

'And what am I supposed to wear home? Your dress?'

I opened the back door of the car and reached in. I came out with
a pair of black trousers. 'I have the pants; all I need is your shirt and
jacket. And tie. I'll let you have my leather bomber jacket along with the
hundred. That should get you home.'

'Throw in twenty bucks more for a cab and it's all yours,' he said,
unbuttoning his shirt and pulling it out of his pants.

24

'Did you get that tape?' Sam Shields asked as they sat down on the
bed. He was exhausted from the strain of Ara's party, and the idea
of athletic sex with April was not, at that moment, number one on
his hit parade. He began to unbutton his shirt as April stripped her
own blouse off. 'Could you get the ¾ tape' he repeated.

'Of course. Why?' she asked.

'I'd like to take a look at it,' he said, and reached across
the bed for the remote control and clicked on the TV.

He guessed they were celebrating the deal they had just made:
he agreed to the drafting of a new script for *Birth of a Star* and
directing it. He'd get half a million bucks – twice what he'd gotten
for *Jack and Jill* – if the picture actually went into production. He
could hardly believe it.

'Sam, what are you doing?' April asked, making no attempt
to mask the irritation in her voice. 'Turn the fucking television
off. Now is *not* the time.'

'I know, I know,' Sam said, trying to calm her. 'But now
that I've seen Lila Kyle, I just want to see the show for a minute.
Everyone is talking about the thing. Where's the tape?'

'In my briefcase, over there.' It hadn't been easy to smuggle
out a copy of *Three for the Road*, not even for April Irons. Marty
DiGennaro was running a closed set and didn't want a knockoff
of his stuff to appear the same season his show debuted. But in
the end she'd managed.

She watched as Sam crossed the room, naked except that his cute buns were encased in those cute blue boxer shorts. He crouched, retrieved the tape, and popped it into the VCR. His eyes were glued to the screen, watching the opening credits. 'I just want to see what Marty DiGennaro can do.'

After the great critical reception of *Jack and Jill*, April was ready to move ahead with Sam on another picture. And Sam was glad April had made the offer; since he hadn't written anything else in the last two years, it might be what he needed.

April was certainly what he needed. After all, she was powerful. She'd never mentioned Crystal and seemed not at all bitter over his affair with the actress. After all, Sam figured the performance he had gotten out of Crystal had sweetened April's bottom line. So now they were talking preproduction. Costs, casting, above the line, below the line, the whole ball of wax. This was a big one. April was going to trust him.

Now he looked up. April had left the room.

'Wait. Where did you go?' Sam called out to her. 'Come on back. I want you to see something . . . a genius at work.'

'That would be a nice change,' she snapped from the doorway, but her curiosity was piqued. Know your enemies better than your friends, her father used to tell her. And she hated Marty DiGennaro. She hoped the show died like a dog. There'd already been so much buzz: new techniques, feuds on the set, enormous budgets. Maybe it would bring that self-important little prick down. Might as well see what all the talk is about, she decided. She sat down on a far corner of the bed.

He patted the place by his side. 'Come on, it's business,' he said in a coaxing voice.

April leaned back against Sam's chest and took a deep breath. She had taken out her contacts, expecting to get right into bed with Sam and now she couldn't see the screen too well. But that was all right, she thought. It's only TV. They watched in silence for a few minutes; then April sat up and leaned forward, squinting. This was *not* your usual Sunday-night television fare. But, then, she thought, how could it be, with Marty DiGennaro behind it? He was a prick, but he was a talented prick. This was *good*. More like the big screen than television. But different from both.

'Sam, hand me my glasses. They're in the drawer of the night table,' she said, not taking her eyes off the monitor.

She watched carefully. He'd used every trick in the book, but all in new ways and to great effect. He had the wiggle and the jiggle, but the women were tough, liberated, almost androgynous. He had nostalgia, but his cuts and fades and smears, his matching shots, were startlingly different. Better, hotter, newer than MTV.

And maybe, just maybe, there was a lead here for *Birth of a Star*.

'What do you think of the redhead?' Sam asked, reading her mind. 'We saw her at the party.'

April watched the girl. There was the angle that her mother, Theresa O'Donnell, had starred in the last reincarnation of *Birth of a Star*. That would be good for some free publicity. She was gorgeous, and sly, but ... Anyway, April didn't want this film to look like nothing more than a shlocky parlour trick, a shtick remake. No.

'Too obvious. And the blonde is doing a Vanna White impersonation.'

Sam kept staring at the screen. 'Yeah, but watch the other one. The dark one.'

April did. The girl was undeniably beautiful, but she had something else. Her voice, her movements were so ... natural. The girl could act.

'Not bad,' she admitted.

'We need a new face for the part.'

'Well, she's a possibility.'

They fast-forwarded through much of it. It was fascinating. The show ended, credits rolled. She looked over at Sam, his hard-on obvious through the sheet. 'Is that for her or for me?' she asked him.

'For you,' he said, reaching out and cupping her left breast in his hand. 'But let's audition *her*.'

'Sam, it's unlikely we can afford to use a television star, even if we yoke her with Michael McLain the way I want to do. We need a *movie* person.'

'Yeah, so get me Kikki Mansard. She's hot. Or how about Julia Roberts.'

'Come on. The Hermit of Hollywood? Unavailable, *and* her people insist on a big position. I don't give six per cent of the gross to *anyone*. Bear that in mind, Sam: I don't give head, I don't give percentage of gross, and I don't give final cut.'

She had signed him for a hundred thousand for a first draft and one set of revisions against four hundred thousand if they went into principal photography with him directing. He'd come cheap – his pussy agent had folded when April threatened to walk away. Sam didn't know she'd had another quarter of a million she was willing to throw below the line for it. Well, she told herself, she'd use the money to fix up a nice trailer for Michael McLain. It would come in handy.

'Please can I have final cut?' he asked in a wheedling voice. They had been arguing about it for days.

'Since *Heaven's Gate, no* director gets final cut.'

'Woody Allen gets final cut.'

She raised an eyebrow and looked at him. 'To paraphrase Senator Bentsen; "You, Sam, are no Woody Allen."'

'But I give better head.'

'I wouldn't be so sure of that,' she told him. 'Now, what else? Or can we just call it a deal and go fuck?'

'I shouldn't mix business with pleasure,' he said, grinning at her now.

'You shouldn't, but you do. Just don't right now.' She reached out for his crotch with one hand and flicked off the TV with the other.

25

Since seeing Neil at Ara's party, Jahne had been searching for him. Discreetly, of course. She began by calling Directory Assistance, but they had no listing. Then she looked him up in the white pages. When they yielded no listing, she stopped at the L.A. Central Library and looked for Morellis in last year's L.A. phone book, and in Orange County and all the surrounding areas for the last two years. There was nothing. Could he have an unlisted number? Or, worse, did he have no number at all? An out-of-work actor without a phone number was an ex-actor. Had Neil given up?

Next Jahne began calling answering services, trying to leave a message for Neil Morelli. But each night, as she worked her way through a dozen or so of the hundreds listed, she felt her hopes fade. It was tiring, depressing, to come up empty again and again.

She missed Neil, and she worried about him. But what would she do if she found him, she wondered. Would she reveal herself? She didn't think she could. Not yet, but maybe she could help him indirectly: send him some money, or ask Marty to use him in a small role on 3/4.

She wished she could have a friend like Neil. Pete had been kind, but they'd had so little in common. He was still friendly, but not a friend. Sharleen had been friendly, but Sharleen was too limited. Jahne realized she was lonely. Jahne missed the fun of Neil's sharp rants, of the heart-to-hearts she'd had with Molly, the deep conversations she and Sam had shared.

Of course, the thrill of the show's coming together was fun. But her life, aside from work, was nonexistent. Now that she was getting into the rhythm of it, putting out the show was becoming, if not easy, at least routine for Jahne. She looked good on the screen, even in close-ups. She'd tested her face for still photography back in New York, but stills and film were completely different, one was a cool medium, the other hot. She agonized over it. It was the lights that had scared her the most at first. She hadn't thought about it until she was under them. Television lighting was brighter than theatre lighting. It shone on every pore, making them look cavernous if the skin were not made up properly. Onstage, lighting was more highlighting and spotlighting. And there were no close-ups, no dense light. On the television soundstage, however, its purpose seemed to be to bring the sun right onto the set. Jahne would sometimes walk under the lights and know, just *know*, that what were tiny, hairline scars in the lighting at home in her bedroom turned here into deep, red gashes. Hester's scarlet letter. But it wouldn't be an 'A'. Perhaps 'F' for fake. Or 'I' for imposter. She would hold her breath as the cameramen did run-throughs, waiting for the inevitable cry of discovery. That they never came didn't lessen Jahne's vigilance. Even if there was nothing she could do about the lighting except submit to it.

Makeup, however, was one area where she could exercise some control. Her concerns for her makeup went beyond a professional's concern for perfection. For Jahne, it had become an obsession. She had made a point of becoming friendly with the makeup guy. Both agreed that the Flanders stuff didn't hold up. He smuggled in MAC and some stuff of his own, despite the contract. And since he would stand back every day and look at her face as if he had created the

Mona Lisa, Jahne was more relaxed with that part of her preparation for the camera.

But all in all, going before the camera on this show wasn't the exciting opportunity Jahne had at first believed it would be. Marty DiGennaro was directing. She had assumed that meant the show would be above average in every way – camera work, writing, costumes. Unfortunately for Jahne, she became too painfully aware how limited a director's control could be. The writing seemed to her atrocious. A team of writers created dialogue like a 'David Mamet-does-Huey-Dewey-and-Louie.' It was stunted, unbalanced, hard to develop timing with. She started a sentence and Sharleen interrupted, only to have Lila finish it. So much for art, Jahne had thought after their first script run-through. Well, maybe on the air, finished, it would work.

Meanwhile, the persona of the three characters on the show seemed to have flowed over to the set itself. Jahne was perceived as the smart one, Lila the sexy one, and Sharleen the dumb one. They were being forced to play their roles in real life. Jahne knew she was smart. Or, more accurately, experienced. Because of her perceived age, it came across as smart. And Lila was sexy. Not sexual, really, Jahne could tell. But sexy. And there was poor Sharleen. She wasn't dumb, exactly. Just never exposed to much. And the mistake that the jaded almost always made was that 'ignorant' meant stupid. Jahne was sure that that was not the case with Sharleen.

But of the three of them, it was Lila who was smart enough to have ingratiated herself with Marty. Now that she'd seen the first six shows, Jahne could see that Lila had somehow managed to get more close-ups, better lines. And 'smart' Jahne was looking less and less directly into the camera, and getting fewer and fewer lines. Of course, all the lines were crap, but still. She laughed to herself. She was reminded of the joke about the two old women who met in the lobby of a Catskills hotel after dinner. The first woman said, 'The food is terrible.' The second woman added, 'Yes, and the portions are so small.' So Jahne's portion of bad lines was decreasing. Silly as they were, she admitted she would have liked to have more.

None of it was what she had imagined. It was only when Jahne was with Mai Von Trilling that she was able to feel she was really in show business. During the long waits on the set, she spent hours talking to Mai, hearing the stories of her life. And her loves. Jahne never tired of listening, and Mai seemed to take as much pleasure in telling them. Mai was a survivor of the earliest days of Hollywood.

Now Jahne was in Wardrobe, working on next week's costumes, hanging on Mai's every word. She looked down at Mai, who was managing to tuck a seam, hold her beer glass, talk, and keep the spare pins in her mouth, all at the same time. 'So I left him, my dear. Vat else vas I to do? He vould alvays be jealous of my success. It vas poisoning him. After a time, he vould no longer haff luffed me anyvay.'

'But you loved him?' Jahne asked.

'Huff course. He vas the vun great luff I had. For he truly luffed *me*. Not the image on the scrin. Alvays I could see the others, later on, seeing not me, but my image from the scrin. Or, vat vas verse, comparing me to it. You know. You vill see it. "Oh, she's not as tall as I thought. Her teeth are not as good. She is thinner, smaller. Not as *much* as I thought."' Mai laughed, but there was no humour in it.

It seemed so cruel, watching this wrinkled old woman as she knelt at the hem, remembering her glory years, how she'd been one of the world's first screen idols and how even then she had not been beautiful enough. What was it like *now*, when no one looked at her, at least not as a woman? When she couldn't trade on her face, or her body? And she *had* been stunning. One of the most beautiful. What was it like for her now? Jahne had neither the courage nor cruelty to ask. She looked down again to see Mai staring up at her.

'You are a strange one,' Mai said. 'Your eyes are too old for your face.' She took the last pin out of her mouth and thrust it hard through the tough denim fabric. Jahne felt the hairs on the back of her neck rise. Could this old woman see through her? 'You are alvays thinkink,' Mai said. 'As if you are in danger. But vat does such a pretty girl have to think about? I never thought until I vas forty.'

'Just a habit.' Jahne smiled at her as she stepped off the little platform before the mirror.

'No. You are strange.'

'How?' Jahne tried to sound casual. But she was frightened. Did she give herself away?

'Vell, you let me say somesink like that. This is unusual. And you come here, not make *me* come to *you*. . . .'

'But this is a favour you're doing for me! It was the least I could do.'

'Silly girl. A favour for the star is a pleasure. It is money in the bank, a paid insurance premium, my dear.'

'What kind of insurance?' Jahne asked, confused.

'Unemployment insurance,' Mai said, and laughed as she stood up, slowly and stiffly. 'Now, vith luck, you von't let me get fired.'

'Oh, Mai! No one would do that! Bob loves you. You're fabulous.'

'Fabulous today, unemployed tomorrow.' Mai shrugged. She looked into the three-way mirror before them at Jahne's reflection. 'You like?' she asked.

Jahne looked. Mai *was* miraculous. She had taken apart the jeans that the costume designer had provided and restructured them completely. Before, despite all the diet and surgery, Jahne simply wasn't as slim as the other two girls. Well, she was shorter and older. Now her stomach was flat as a pancake. 'Oh, Mai. They're fabulous. Really. How did you do it?'

'A few tricks. A Lycra panel in the front, behind the fly. And those side seams. Reinforced that vay, they von't vrinkle to show a bulge at the saddlebags. But no sittink in these. For these, standink scenes only. And use a slant board to rest in. I am vorking on a pair for the motorcycle shots. For sittink only. They'll have a bigger seat, but still make your legs longer, thinner-looking.'

'A sitting pair of pants and a standing one? It's so unfair!' Jahne laughed. 'Women at home don't have you.'

'No, and they vill never understand vy their jeans don't fit like yours.' Mai smiled. 'The magic of Hollywood,' she said, and shrugged as she began to pick up the shears, snippets of cloth, and stray pins from off the floor.

'No, here. Let me do that,' Jahne said, and began to help the old woman. Mai looked at her again.

'You see? This is strange. To be pickink up. Not just for a new star. Many are polite at first. No, but for a natural beauty like you it is very odd. And you took it as a compliment before ven I said you vere pretty. Beautiful girls don't like to be called that. Just like pretty girls don't like to be called "attractive." It is beneath them.' She looked at Jahne appraisingly. 'Maybe you vere blind as a child?' she asked. Then she laughed. 'Ach, now you see how I could be fired. I think too much, too.' She looked down at her empty glass. 'That vas good beer. For me, good beer is better than champagne. Vich is just as vell, since I hafn't got a champagne purse. You vould like another glass?' she asked Jahne.

Jahne wanted to, but she couldn't afford the calories, not with tomorrow's shoot. 'I'd better not,' she said reluctantly.

'Some vater, then?' Mai said, as if reading her mind.

'Yes. I'd like that,' Jahne said, and smiled.

'Then sit down. But first, first take off those pants.'

When Jahne got home that evening, exhausted by the ten hours of filming at the dusty San Clemente location, she was so tired she could barely lift her arms to the mailbox at the gate to her drive. There was never much waiting there anyway. No packages from home, no cards from friends. Every now and then, a letter from Dr. Moore or a drawing from Raoul. She hoped the boy liked the roller blades and paint set she'd sent. Well, that was why she stopped now, tired as she was. It might not be much, but it was all that she had for a private life.

That was by her choice, she reminded herself grimly. But she admitted to herself that she missed Neil, her New York friends, the quick meetings in Greek coffee shops, the cheap pasta dinners. Most of all, she still missed Sam. More than anything, she still missed beautiful, brilliant Sam. But she reminded herself, for the hundredth time, how badly all that had ended.

Would all this, too, end badly? she wondered. What if the series didn't do well? What if it faded quickly once this early fanfare died down? What if it faded *slowly*, and for three seasons she was stuck in television hell – a show that ranked sixty-seven in the Nielsens and was neither popular nor cancelled? Would she then be an actress who wasn't ever going to get choice roles? A Meredith Baxter-Birney – a good actress who graduated from ingenue only to be Michael J. Fox's mom and, when she was lucky, to have the disease of the week in a minor TV movie? An Elinor Donahue, who outgrew *Father Knows Best* to grow into a brief stint on *The Andy Griffith Show*, then played Felix's girlfriend on *The Odd Couple*, and finally wound up as Chris Elliott's mom on *Get a Life*. Had Elinor Donahue wanted a serious acting career? Had she had great expectations?

Sometimes, with her new face, her new body, her new life, Jahne seemed to herself invincible – all this was a bold gamble she'd taken and won. And other times – times like now – it seemed as if it might only be another false promise. Just as *Jack and Jill* and Sam had been. Her stomach tightened with fear. She was too old and too tired to try again.

God, she was morbid! It came from the unknowns in her life right now, and from being so much alone and tired. Well, she couldn't control the unknowns, and she was too tired and frightened to make friends at the moment. Her work exhausted her, and 'playing' Jahne Moore was a constant drain. She had a correspondence with her surgeon, was pleasantly friendly with the crew on the set, spoke to Mai, but other than that had to marshal her energy to manage to survive her long days.

With a sigh, she pulled out the little door of the mailbox and emptied its contents onto the seat of the newly leased racing-green Mazda Miata. It was the usual, she thought, disappointed. No letter from Dr. Moore. A couple of bills, two catalogues, and some circulars addressed to 'Occupant.' But there was also a large cream-coloured pasteboard envelope. And it was addressed to her, written in black ink in an Italianate hand. Postmarked L.A. If it was advertising the opening of a new boutique, it was a very expensive one, she thought.

Once through the gates and into the bungalow, she dropped her script, the catalogues, and junk mail onto a chair and opened the big envelope.

April Irons
requests
the very great pleasure
of your company
Tuesday, sunset
Drinks and dinner

Above the address, scrawled in an unfamiliar handwriting, it said, 'Love to see you. Bring a friend. April.'

April? April *Irons*? The most powerful woman in Hollywood was sending *her* invitations and signing them herself? *Love* to see you? She, Jahne Moore, was invited by a complete stranger — albeit a famous one — and the stranger would 'love to see her?'

Jahne shrugged. Well, this *was* Hollywood, after all, and she *was* living a fairy tale. Hadn't she just wished she weren't so alone? Her wish was granted: she had an invitation to the ball. But now that Cinderella knew about the party, where would she find a fairy godmother to supply the gown, the glass slippers, the carriage, and, most important, the prince?

The idea of appearing as Jahne Moore, up-and-coming, young,

beautiful actress, in front of all of social Hollywood was more than daunting. She had hated the party at Ara Sagarian's. But didn't she need to get out, meet people, build a life? She felt herself break into a sweat. Who would talk to her? What would she talk about? Who would care? And what would she wear? She had to smile at that. Well, she could ask Mai how to dress – maybe even borrow something through Bob at Wardrobe. Or go shopping – shopping with Mai! That was it. And after all, it wouldn't be Loehman's budget dresses, and she was no size sixteen anymore. It could, actually, be fun! But how to behave? And who to bring?

There was Pete, but they'd broken up, and anyway she couldn't imagine Pete talking to April Irons. How embarrassing. They'd both look stupid. God, she'd hate that.

Well, she'd call Sy Ortis. He'd probably know what to do about 'a friend.' And he'd be pleased that she had such an important event to go to. He was always pushing her to 'be seen.' Hell, for all she knew, maybe he had set it up.

Jahne ran a bath, poured herself a glass of Beaujolais, and turned down the rheostat (even in the bathroom!) so the lights were low. Ah, the warm water felt delicious! She set the pasteboard invitation on the tile surround propped against a bottle of shampoo, sipped her wine, and stared at it. This was, perhaps, the *real* beginning for her.

'First of all, what do you wanna go to April Irons' for anyway? She's a world-class bitch.'

'I want to go. Should I go alone?'

'*Madre di Dios!* Forget it. I'll set you up with someone appropriate.'

'A blind date? I hate blind dates.'

'Jahne. This is Hollywood. Only Stevie Wonder has blind dates. Do you think Michael Jackson and Madonna went to the Oscars together because they were *dating?* I'll set you up with someone, for business, that can do your career some good. At least someone who won't humiliate you.'

Jahne sighed. 'All right,' she agreed.

Getting the dress was easy. Mai brought three things over; they picked one, and it was a knockout: a long, blue-black silk taffeta that started at her cleavage and then fell in perfect, clinging waves to the floor.

'So, it is beginning for you,' Mai said with satisfaction.

'I'm so frightened I could die,' Jahne admitted. 'What if no one talks to me, or if I say something stupid or . . .'

'Ccht! Cht!' Mai made a clicking noise with her tongue and teeth. 'Men vill *alvays* talk to you – vell, for the next ten years or so, anyvay. Und you should vorry about findink somevun who doesn't talk stupid, not vorry about vat *you* say. You are doomed to be bored a lot more than you vill be borink. See if I am not right.'

Sy sat at his desk, his feet up on the credenza. More trouble. Jahne Moore troubled him. And Jahne Moore and April Irons were double trouble. Sy would not say he hated women: not women like his mother or his wife, who knew their place. Sy only hated *pushy* women. Like Jahne. And April herself. So, what if *he* escorted Jahne Moore to April's dinner party? That would piss Miss Irons off. It would start any relationship between them on the wrong foot. And he could keep an eye on both of them – excellent plan. Sy smiled and put down his inhaler.

But perhaps he could go one better. He still had to get Michael McLain to agree to let Ricky's name be billed alone over the title. The bet he had made with Michael was stupid. He'd regretted it immediately. Then Michael had informed him he'd already bedded Sharleen. *Putana.* Clients were nothing but trouble. But now maybe he could kill two birds with one rock. He would let Michael McLain take Jahne. That woman was not so easy as Sharleen. And after Michael struck out, he, Sy, could negotiate the Ricky Dunn deal.

Sy lifted up the phone and smiled.

Jahne was nervous, but, even so, she couldn't help taking in the scene before her. 'I'm here, and I'll never forget this,' she told herself. She was on the threshold, looking in. Michael McLain stood beside her, his arm locked around hers. The house was perfect – totally elegant in its simplicity, a big English Tudor. The huge double front doors opened into a reception gallery that was big enough to hold an L.A. Rams game, Jahne thought to herself. The sunken living room was an expanse of ivory upholstery and dark wood antiques, and candles – hundreds of them – illuminated the room. Beyond it, the dining room was inviting, the table draped with gleaming ivory linen napery and tall candelabra. Ivory orchids in moss-covered pots were everywhere. Some plants were six feet high. There was enough room for a hundred people, Jahne thought. But this party was intimate, with only a dozen guests.

Two waiters, balancing silver trays that reflected the candle glow onto the cut-crystal glasses, passed among them, delivering an astonishing array of hors d'ouevres and drinks. Jahne stepped down the three steps into the living room and was greeted by a dark, painfully thin woman in an ivory satin dress – April Irons, Jahne was sure. 'Jahne, I'm so glad you could come,' April said, extending her hand. Jahne smiled, thanked her, and turned to introduce Michael McLain.

'Mike. Nice to see you. Didn't take you long to find new talent,' April said. Michael smiled.

'If you don't mind, we're going to go in to dinner right away. I have a film to screen afterwards that I think you'll like. Is that okay?' April asked.

'Of course,' Michael said, and turned to Jahne. 'All right?' he asked.

'Wonderful,' Jahne agreed, and the three of them crossed the polished floor to the dining room. Michael helped her into her seat. April began to make introductions. Not that the guests needed them. All were world famous. Jahne almost had to pinch herself to be sure she wasn't dreaming.

Then she saw him.

He had arrived late, took the three steps down to the living room in one bound of his long legs, and moved easily, graceful as ever, to the single empty seat.

Jahne didn't drop her glass, or her jaw. But she stared. She stared at Sam, *her* Sam, drinking him in. And it was as if there had been no time, no pain, no operations, no new name, no new career, no triumph at the Melrose, no Marty DiGennaro, no television show. It was as if time had stood still.

And she wanted him as badly as ever.

Fame

Remember when Pinocchio goes to Stromboli, and Stromboli convinces him to be an actor? And Pinocchio performs a little bit, and Stromboli puts him in a cage? Well, that's a lot like what it's like. You want to do this, and you're completely fascinated by the dream. And you get there. And suddenly you're in a cage.

Bette Midler

There are photographers who sit in their cars outside my house all day long who frighten me.

Julia Roberts

1

Haven't we all wondered what it would be like to take our place among the stars? Not just as an observer, the way I, Laura Richie, have, but actually as one of them. Not to be tolerated, as a reporter is, or condescended to as a fan, but to be welcomed as an equal.

What does it feel like to sit down to dinner with a dozen of the most famous and most beautiful and most talented people in the world? What is it like to have Elizabeth Taylor – never 'Liz' – call you by your first name, to have Cher ask you to pass the butter, to have Warren Beatty smile at you and ask about your work as if he's really interested? Before, Jahne was on the fringe. Tonight she was at the epicentre.

Jahne experienced it all for the first time, but she couldn't focus on any of it. Instead, she focused on trying not to make a fool of herself over Sam Shields. She kept her eyes away from his, she kept her head turned the other way, towards Michael McLain, and Elizabeth and Larry, and April Irons.

What if Sam recognized her? Of course, she was completely different now – not just her looks, but the mannerisms she'd adopted, the way she moved. She was certain that she played the part of Jahne Moore well. But no one had ever known her as well as Sam. Surely he could see through her performance, and what if he did? Would he give her away? Would he despise her?

Her heart was beating so hard, so fast, that she was sure Michael, at her left, could hear it. It was almost all that she could hear, the pounding of her heart in her ears. Her flesh had gone clammy, and she felt herself begin to sweat.

She tried to lift the crystal goblet of water by its stem, but her hands were shaking too hard. She glanced around the table to see if anyone had noticed, and clasped both of her hands in her lap. Only April was looking at her, but April just smiled and nodded her head. 'Where are you living, Jahne?' she asked.

'Birdland,' she explained. 'Off Oriole.'

'Have you bought that place?' Michael asked.

'No. I'm only renting,' she managed to say.

'Is security good there?' Goldie asked.

They began to talk about security – and the relative benefits of Malibu versus Bel Air versus Holmby Hills. Jahne listened as they complained about costs; she wondered if any of them had bodyguards. 'Well, I was always happy at the Beverly Wilshire,' Michael said. 'I let the hotel worry about security. Best in the world.'

'That doesn't work with children,' someone said drily. 'A hotel suite isn't a home.'

'It was for me for ten years.'

'You needed the revolving door,' someone cracked, and they all laughed. For a moment, Jahne wondered if they were laughing also at her – she must look like Michael's latest conquest. Well, she supposed that was better than looking like the professional fix-up they actually were. She looked around and saw that Sam Shields had his eyes on her. She turned away.

'You need a gated community,' April was saying. 'To be safe, and especially if you have kids.'

'Oh, isn't that a bit paranoid?' Sam asked. His voice sounded better than ever – rich and deep, with that New York sharpness. 'I mean, after New York, this is child's play. I'm in the canyon, and I love it.'

'Isn't that what Sharon Tate said?' Michael asked.

'It *isn't* paranoid,' April said. 'Now, Barry Diller had a twenty-four-hour security guard watching his parking space at Fox. *That* was paranoid.'

The conversation went on around Jahne. She could barely manage a bite of her shrimp-mousse starter, and did little better over the Dover sole and asparagus. For once, she wouldn't have to worry about her diet: she'd choke on a crumb. The plates were beautifully, artfully arranged, the fish set in a frame of asparagus, the gold rim of the dish sparkling along with the gold rim of the crystal goblets, of the gold-chased sterling candelabra. She stared at the plate, trying to listen to the conversation as it ebbed and flowed. They'll think I'm mute, she told herself. I must say *something*.

She lifted her head. The talk had gone from security to real estate and then back to security again.

'Since I moved out of the Beverly Wilshire, I use La Brecque,' Michael was saying.

'He's expensive,' one of the others murmured.

'Yeah, but he's the best. And we *are* talking about our lives,' Michael said.

'Isn't that a bit melodramatic?' Jahne heard Sam say. She still didn't dare to look at him, only in his general direction.

'You want to talk melodrama?' Michael asked. 'I've had a guy in prison writing me death threats for seven years. He blames me for breaking up his first marriage: his wife was a fan. Since he killed his wife and was sentenced to twenty years, he swears he's going to get me. Shouldn't I be nervous?'

All of the people at the table murmured sympathetically. Sam cleared his throat. 'I guess as long as he's in prison you're fine.'

'Well, he was almost paroled last year. La Brecque keeps stuff like that under control. He presented the letters to the parole board. He had other testimony, too. He neutralizes things. As much as he can. Anyway, writers and directors don't know about this stuff – it's only us actors on the front lines who know.' Michael turned to Jahne. '*Is* your place secure?'

'I don't know,' she admitted. 'Nobody has ever bothered me.'

'Well, I hope that never changes, but I wouldn't count on it. When does your show premiere?'

'Next Sunday.'

'How exciting for you!' Elizabeth said kindly.

'How has it been going?' April asked.

'Well, I don't have anything to compare it to,' Jahne admitted, 'but I think it's going well.' God, couldn't she say something clever? Couldn't she be witty, if not charming? Well, at least she *did* sound like an authentic twenty-four-year-old ingenue, she realized.

'I'm sure you'll be a big success.' Kurt smiled, and Goldie nodded.

'All of the key indicators are there – after all, Michael is dating you,' April added. There was another murmur of laughter, and Jahne felt confused again. Annette nudged Warren and they both giggled. But Jahne could see no malice onthese faces. Though they were joking, it was not at her expense. They were complimenting her, including her. She smiled.

Dessert was a lemon-and-mint sorbet. The conversation turned to the next AIDS benefit, and then the guests stood to take coffee in the living room. But Jahne needed a moment to herself. She headed out to the terrace. As she walked through the living room towards the open arches, she felt her legs tremble. The dress, its raven-blue-and-black taffeta falling so beautifully to the ground, rustled.

'Masterful.'

It was Sam's voice, a low murmur at her shoulder. Jahne felt herself pale. She turned to look at him. Was he talking about her new incarnation? Had he seen through her already?

'Masterful,' he repeated. 'The dress and your hair. A perfect match. Both so simple and exquisite.'

He was close to her. She could smell the clove of his aftershave and that sweet, warm scent his breath always had when he drank wine. It was hard to believe that here, in this warm night air beside her, stood the man she'd last seen more than three years ago in the dank, grey winter of New York. Here he was, the man she'd thought of, dreamed of, longed for, and tried to forget. Here he was, and he had followed her, sought her out, was standing at her side. She felt herself tremble. Was it with rage, or desire, or fear? It was dark on the veranda, and he stood very close. How much of her could he see?

'So, you live in Birdland' he said. She remained silent. 'I always thought of myself more as the Benedict type.'

'Arnold or Canyon?' she asked sweetly.

Jahne heard laughter in the living room, and Michael's voice protesting. 'We'd better join them,' she said, and took a step towards the light.

'Have you ever thought about films?' Sam asked her.

She stopped and turned to him. How could she tell him that she used to, before she spent all her time thinking about him? She looked away, across the terrace, to the exquisite espaliered fruit trees in the garden. The balcony railing had ivy tied to it with raffia training cords, as if it were playing some sort of vegetable bondage game.

'Someday, perhaps,' she told him. A breeze began to rustle the trees. She felt it raise her flesh into goose pimples, and waken the whispers of Mai's wonderful dress.

'There's a part I'm casting in a movie that you might be right for.'

She laughed out loud. She couldn't help it. Was that the line he'd used on Bethanie and all the others? Well, hadn't he cast Mary Jane before he bedded her?

'Yes, and I am Marie of Roumania,' she said, quoting Dorothy Parker.

He laughed in turn. 'I know it sounds like the oldest line in Hollywood, but it's true.'

'I'm very involved with Marty DiGennaro right now,' she said.

'*And* with Michael McLain?' he asked.

God, what was going on? He was flirting with her. And now what would she do? How many times would she let herself be hurt by this man? There was no way this was a good idea. She heard more laughter coming from the brightly lit room where the others had gathered. She could see the sparkle of crystal and the light of the chandelier reflected in the pool. Sam stood beside her, his own face obscured by the darkness.

Get away now, she told herself sternly. Get away and stay away. This time, don't let anything start; stop the damage before it begins.

'That's really none of your business,' she told him, and she left him there in the dark.

Michael McLain helped her into his car, deftly sweeping her trailing hem into the sedan before he slammed the door. He'd obviously had lots of practice. Then he circled to his side and got in.

Now that the ordeal of the party was over, Jahne felt as if she were waking from a dream, the very best dream of her life. But now her beauty, her achievement, her future weren't going to dissolve with her awakening. She was desirable, she was successful, and she could control her destiny. What could be better than this – having blown off the man who hurt you, and now sitting beside this idol, this movie star, driving through the Hollywood Hills in a Rolls convertible? Jahne took a deep breath. She hadn't just survived. She'd triumphed. She felt intoxicated, higher than she had ever been on wine or grass.

'Thank you for taking me,' she said to Michael. 'It was kind of you.'

He laughed. 'My pleasure,' he said. 'But you must be new in town to be so polite.'

'Well, I know Sy asked you to do this, and I . . .'

'I owe him. Which, by the way, is just how Sy likes it.'

She smiled.

'So, how's it going for you. Are you exhausted?'

'Yes!'

'Typical. Marty will work you to death, he's such a perfectionist. And Sy will keep throwing supermarket openings at you if you'll do them.'

Jahne laughed. 'Well, I hate to say no right now. I mean, a year ago at this time, I couldn't get arrested.'

'Oh, yeah. The good old days.' He took his eyes off the road and smiled at her. He had a nice smile.

'It's really the Flanders Cosmetics stuff I hate,' she admitted. 'I'm an actress, not a model or a saleswoman. But I couldn't get the part without agreeing to the hookup.' She sighed. 'The sessions take hours. I pose till I hurt.'

'I'm sure the money doesn't hurt,' Michael said. 'Don't be too hard on yourself. We all had to struggle to survive. Even Elizabeth sells perfume.'

When they pulled up to the house, she found herself inviting him in. He shrugged, nodded, and took her hand as they walked to her door. She felt almost stunned by the feel of his hand in hers. She opened the door, then switched on lights.

'Sit down. I'll get a bottle of something,' she said.

'Don't take too long. I like looking at you,' he told her.

She felt attracted to him, undeniably. The cute smile wrinkles around his eyes, the long lines that made a parenthesis around his full, sensuous mouth. Well, he was a grown-up, not a boy like Pete. And certainly in Sam's league. Maybe way past it. He was age-appropriate. Despite her streamlined exterior, she was, after all, approaching forty. And he must be over fifty. He had been a movie star she'd always had a crush on, and now he was sitting on her sofa, desiring her. He was Hollywood royalty – he was accepted in the highest circles by everyone.

'I like you,' Michael said simply, echoing her thought. 'You're nice. I'll bet you could be very nice.'

She felt the compliment. Michael McLain had had every beautiful woman in Hollywood for the last two decades. Hadn't they joked about that over dinner? And now he wanted her. In a way, it was almost like an invitation into a very exclusive sorority: the beautiful women's club.

She took out the chilled bottle of white wine she kept for guests, grabbed two glasses, and joined Michael on the sofa. Her ego was dancing the tango, but she was also aroused and curious. His hand had been so warm, and his skin looked as if it had more blood flowing under it than other people's did: it was a delicious flushed brown colour. What did it feel like to make love with Michael McLain? Wouldn't it be the perfect antidote to Sam? Because she was determined not to fall under Sam's spell again. She had spent more than three years banishing thoughts of him, not allowing herself to daydream of him. She would not weaken now. She looked at Michael and imagined his lips on hers.

But then reason, or morality, or fear intervened. Are you going crazy? she asked herself. She didn't even *know* him. What about AIDS? There was no such thing as casual sex anymore. This was the nineties. And Michael had been far from discreet in the past. Did she want her private life smeared across the tabloids? Worst of all, what about her scars? Making love with Pete, in complete darkness, was one thing, but Michael wouldn't settle for that. What was she thinking of?

'What are you thinking of?' he asked her, and she found herself blushing.

'I was thinking how comfortable it feels to sit here with you,' she lied, because she felt a lot of things – excited, sexy, nervous, titillated, flattered, unreal – but none of them were 'comfortable.'

'Women say that to me all the time,' he laughed. 'I think it's because they've seen me on the screen, so they're used to looking at me.'

She laughed. 'Is that true?'

'I'm not joking,' he laughed back. 'You'll see. Once *your* show comes out, people will feel that they know you personally. They'll come up to you on the street and call you by name. They'll get your private phone number. They'll write to you. They'll dream of you.'

'That's a spooky idea,' she agreed. She felt the hair on her arms raise with gooseflesh. 'But I've always felt that, despite the disadvantages, fame is a valuable commodity – something you could use as a chip. Trade it for power and control over your life. Once I've risen out of obscurity, I hope I can use it to get some feature work. To get some really good parts.'

'You've already got some good parts,' he said, with a joking Groucho Marx leer. She laughed and felt another wave of gooseflesh. Surely this was an invitation. Oh, God! She felt like a schoolgirl.

She rose and walked to the window, looking down on the sparkling lights. 'Isn't this view beautiful?' she asked, as she watched the lights of the city glow like a carpet of giant fireflies.

Michael came up behind her, but he didn't touch her, he didn't push. 'You like it, it's yours,' he joked.

'No, it's nobody's,' Jahne said, still peering out at the lights. 'This town is like water. You can hold on to it only so long; then it drips right through your fingers.'

Michael turned her gently so that she faced him. 'A little cynical for someone so young, and so new to Hollywood. There was a time starlets trembled at this sight. Like it was a dream come true.' He sipped some of her wine and made a face. It wasn't very good. 'Are you a cynic, Jahne? Or are you very wise?'

Jahne thought about it for a moment. The air was electric between them, but they were talking like a bad movie script. 'A little of both, probably,' she said. 'What about you? Do you still tremble? Or are you wise?'

He put his hand on her arm. It was warm, so warm, and she could feel him tremble. God, Michael McLain was trembling for her! For *her*. Surely he couldn't fake that. She didn't move away. 'The trappings of stardom don't make me tremble anymore. No, what turns me on is talent. Raw, driven talent. Like yours.'

'You know,' Jahne said, looking into Michael's eyes, 'I want to believe that Michael McLain thinks I'm talented. That here I am, of all the girls in town, and Michael McLain is telling *me* I'm talented. And that it turns him on.' Jahne shrugged and took a step away, breaking the current between them. 'It's nice to hear and all that, but, come on, I'm not the first starry-eyed new-girl-in-town you've said this to. And you've never even seen my work. So how would you know?'

'I never lie about talent,' Michael said. 'Why would I? To get a woman to sleep with me? I don't need to lie for that.'

Jahne thought of Sam and his line about getting her a part in his movie. She shivered.

Michael kept looking into Jahne's eyes. 'You're one of three truly talented women that I have met in twelve years. I won't name the other two – chivalry forbids it – but, trust me, Jahne, you have talent. I saw you at the Melrose Playhouse.' He leaned forward and whispered in her ear, 'A *unique* talent. And a very old soul.'

'Michael,' Jahne chided, moving her head away. 'Next you'll be telling me we knew each other in a previous life.' But she was touched that he'd actually seen her perform.

Michael laughed, his charming, deep, baritone laugh. 'I guess I mean you're very mature. Special.' There was a silence between them for a moment; then Michael leaned across and kissed her. Jahne didn't respond, except to run her tongue gently along her lips afterwards at the sensation that lingered when he moved away. This was fun. Maybe dangerous, but fun! It had been so long since she could talk, really talk, to a man. Since Sam, she realized. Too long.

Jahne knew then that she had already made the decision to sleep with Michael. He seemed considerate, and gentle, and interesting. And he kissed nice. But what about the scars? Would he be repulsed? Just how sophisticated was he?

Jahne lifted her hand and placed it behind Michael's head, drawing him closer. This time, she kissed him, first gently, then more insistently. He responded, holding her hard against his chest. Slowly, his hand moved down her back, dipping into her dress.

She pushed him away, very gently. 'Michael, wait. I've been in an accident. I have some . . . well, some scars.'

He laughed. 'Who doesn't have scars in this town?' he asked, and drew her back towards the sofa. 'You're very beautiful. No scar can mar that beauty,' he whispered as he began to undress her.

The dress, Mai's beautiful creation, fell to the floor in an inky black cloud. Jahne took a deep breath and then, in the gentle but frightening light of the living room, she began to peel off the bodysuit. She was ungraceful, she knew, but Michael was fumbling with his own clothes. Only then did he turn to her. What would he say?

He said nothing. He simply reached across the gulf between them and ran his fingers lightly over the scar at her groin, then to the two that ran up the centre of her breasts. His touch was as light as a breeze. She wondered if he could yet see the scars under her arms, or what he would say about the ones under her buttocks and along her inner thighs. No one could mistake them for accident scars: they were too symmetrical, too perfect. She trembled, waiting for his reaction.

But he merely took her hand and drew her to the sofa. He paused and took out a condom, slipped it on, then pulled her onto the couch, covering her with his own warm body.

As she lay naked beneath him, she began to shiver. 'Please, this is the first time anyone has seen me since . . .' she whispered, and paused. How could she ever explain? She took a breath and it sounded like a sob. 'I'm afraid about how I look.'

Michael raised himself on his elbows and looked down, scanning her breasts again with his eyes, tracing the thin scars, from nipple to chest wall, with the tip of one finger. He finally looked in her eyes, after examining her. 'Beautiful,' he said. 'You look beautiful.'

2

A television premiere is nothing like a movie premiere, Jahne thought as she slipped into her old terry robe and padded barefoot to the TV. For her network premiere tonight, there was no dressing up, no theatre with spotlights searching the sky, no arrival of stars, directors, producers, agents. There was no live coverage by reporters. Just as well, Jahne thought. As it was she was nervous enough. Because this, tonight, would determine her future just as surely as Dr. Moore's scalpels had.

Tonight, for the first time, all of America was going to get a chance to tune in to *Three for the Road*, and all the time and money, all the effort, imagination, sweat, technical tricks, the hours of waiting, the moments of acting, all the makeup, the lighting, the musical scoring, all the stitches made by Mai, all the stunts – all the work was going to be applauded or rejected by the public.

Some of the crew, she knew, were getting together to watch. But she had not been invited. Was it because she had broken up with Pete? Was there resentment that she had dumped one of their own? Or was it simply that the Hollywood caste system was taking hold? Had anyone already heard she was dating Michael McLain? Did they think she was acting like a starlet? Did they feel that she thought of them as nothing more than techs? She felt – she hoped – that she had never been a snob, that she liked and respected the crew. But did they like and respect her? She couldn't be sure. All she knew was that, the closer the show came to its debut, the more distant the crew had become.

Except for Mai Von Trilling. Thank God for Mai. Jahne felt Mai was her only friend in Hollywood. Well, in the whole world right now, except perhaps for Dr. Moore and little Raoul. The old woman had a way about her that charmed Jahne. Tonight, Mai had suggested that she join Jahne to watch the show, and Jahne had gratefully accepted. Somehow, watching her television premiere all alone with ten or even twenty million people had seemed unbearably lonely.

There was a knock at the door, and Jahne jumped up to get it. Mai stood on the doorstep, a brown paper bag in her arms. She looked Jahne over, taking in the old robe and still-wet hair. 'I didn't know ve vere goink formal,' she said drily, and walked past Jahne into the living room. As always, she wore the white sweatshirt and soft black cotton pants that seemed, with her immaculate white Keds, to be her trademark.

She set the bag down on a low table and pulled out a bottle of Veuve Cliquot. 'Napoleon and Josephine liked this. Of course, I am only speakink from hearsay. Even I am not *that* old.' She looked about the room. 'I don't suppose you have champagne flutes?' she asked. Jahne shook her head. 'Just as vell I brought these, then.' Mai smiled and pulled out a pair of impossibly graceful blown-glass flutes. 'But an ice bucket? This even you must have.'

'*Even* me?' Jahne asked, smiling as she went to get the Lucite ice bucket and filled it with cubes. 'Am I such a barbarian?'

'Everyvun under forty is a barbarian. I vas, too.' Mai pulled a second bottle of the champagne out of the bag. 'Do you think I grew up drinking vintage French vines? I, the daughter of a tailor? It vas my beauty that let me into the club, und then it took a decade or two to learn vat vas vat. Vell, at least *I* learned. Gloria Svanson vas *alvays* a barbarian.'

Jahne had to giggle at the disapproval. But 'Two bottles, Mai?' she asked. 'Very extravagant!' How much did vintage Veuve Cliquot cost? she wondered. Could Mai afford it? She knew she could not offer to pay for one: Mai was proud.

'Vell, how often do you make your national debut? Next time, ve'll be more conservative.' Mai sat down stiffly while Jahne put one bottle into the refrigerator and the other into the ice bucket. Carefully, she peeled off the lead seal, exposing the cork.

'Shall I open it now?' she asked. Mai looked at her watch and nodded. 'Ve haff six minutes before the show starts. Shall ve drink a toast?'

Shyly, Jahne nodded. She twisted the wire basket off the cork slowly. The cork released with a low pop, the bottle smoking from the top. Mai held the two glasses while Jahne filled them quickly, before a drop was spilled.

'Neatly done,' Mai complimented her. 'But I alvays think it is sad ven vimmen must open their own champagne. Don't you?'

Jahne nodded, and couldn't help thinking of Michael. It would have been nice if he could have come over, but since Wednesday he hadn't called. She felt both excited by and ashamed of her night with him. Had she just been another conquest? Or did he mean it when he said he'd call? He had seemed so warm, so sincere. She wasn't sure how she felt about *him*, but she knew she wanted him to like *her*.

She turned to Mai, who seemed settled and ready, watching a commercial for the new Buick Skylark, with a minute to go. If the show worked, if it was good, Jahne might yet get to have the career she dreamed of, a worthwhile career. If not . . . she shook her head.

'It starts!' Mai hissed, and the screen went dark. The music began: heavy bass back beat, and then Martha and the Vandellas beginning the first verse of 'Dancing in the Street.' A red thread snaked across the screen, moving to the music, followed by a dozen, and then a hundred more. Then a white thread joined, also pulsing to the driving beat. It, too, was followed by hundreds of other, white threads. Superimposed over that came an image of a woman rider on a motorcycle. Then another joined her. Finally, there were three. Behind them, the threads now covered the screen, and it became clearer now: they made the alternating stripes of the flag, red and white, with a blue-black patch in the upper left hand corner. Then the camera moved out, focusing first on Lila, then Jahne, and lastly Sharleen. Crimson, Cara, and Clover. Their names appeared under their faces. Now, though the flag remained in the background, it became clear that it was hair, the mingled hair of the three girls, blowing and twisting, incredibly long, dancing to the Motown music. Then the title appeared, THREE FOR THE ROAD, spelled in tiny white stars.

The programme opened with noise, with quick cuts of chaos. It was the antiwar-demonstration sequence they had shot in Bakersfield. Marty had made sure everything was perfect, and it did look almost like documentary footage to Jahne, until she herself appeared on the screen. But Marty used the cuts, and then a sort of psychedelic smear where one cut bled into another, so that it looked like no documentary Jahne had ever seen. It was sixties content with a nineties edge. Jahne watched as her character, Cara, met Crimson for the first time, on the steps of the courthouse. Then they were confronted by the cops and dragged off to jail. Their dialogue came off well, she thought. Next there was a black-and-white montage, the fingerprinting, the I.D. photos. It reminded her a little of *A Hard Day's Night*, but, once again, with an updated edge. The show had its own style. It was unique.

'It's good,' Mai said at the first commercial break.

'I think so,' Jahne agreed. Was it good enough to be popular? Was it *too* good? Would it go over the heads of the audience? She could see how Marty was making a serious statement about a better, more hopeful era, and yet simultaneously exploiting their looks, youth, and sex appeal. She and Mai watched in silence.

Using a single camera to shoot, shooting film, not video, working mostly on location rather than in the studio, focusing on the stunts, the fabulous special effects, it all seemed right. Jahne knew that each episode cost over a million dollars. They already had the first eleven done.

Well, she had nothing to be ashamed of. The show had quality. But it did feel kind of sad, just she and Mai sitting there in the dark. She wondered if anyone she knew would watch the show; if people in New York, or even high school classmates from Scudersville, would tune in.

The phone rang. She looked at Mai. 'No one has my home number,' she said. It wasn't exactly true: Michael McLain did, and so did Sy and Marty. Mai shrugged. The phone trilled again. Jahne reached for it.

'You are great. So is the show. But you are the best thing on it.' It was Sam's voice. Jahne felt her hand, holding the receiver, begin to shake.

'Thank you,' she managed to say.

'This is Sam Shields. I hope I'm the first to congratulate you, and also the first to offer you a new job.'

Jahne looked over at Mai. Could Mai see how disturbed she was? She took a deep breath. Had he been serious, back on the terrace at April's? Or was this just another stupid come-on?

'Are you interested?' he asked. 'It's for a remake of *Birth of a Star*. I think you'd be perfect for the female lead. Would you consider it?'

'Call my agent, Sy Ortis,' Jahne managed to tell him. 'Let me take a look at the script, and then we'll let you know.'

'Spoken like a true star!' Sam laughed. 'I'll have a treatment over to him in the morning. Bear in mind, it's only in first draft. I can do better. I'm always better the second time out.'

'I'll bear that in mind,' she said, and dropped the receiver into the cradle.

Lila sat in the darkness of her beach house, in the empty room on the second floor that looked out over the Pacific. The room that had once been Nadia's bedroom. The room Nadia had died in. Nadia Negron, who had starred in the first *Birth of a Star*. Well, the room wasn't totally empty. All around its edges, Lila had ranged candles – black candles – of almost every size and thickness. All of them now were lit. Since Ara's party, Lila had a single obsession, a single desire, a single goal. This was how she'd reach it. An offering. A twofold offering. Because Lila wanted – needed – to get to play Nadia's part, Theresa's part, in *Birth of a Star*.

On the wall, a single shelf held a sort of altar that Lila had created in the otherwise empty space. On it was a picture of Nadia, two more candles in silver candlesticks, a dish of smoking incense, and the video cassette of Theresa's *Birth of a Star*. Since she had heard about the remake, she had had no other goal.

Lila stood up and bowed to the picture of Nadia. Then she lit a candle, lifted it off the altar, and went around the room lighting one taper after another. Tonight, she had a lot to ask of Nadia. She needed her mother, the Puppet Mistress, to watch *3/4* and feel envy. She needed the premiere of *3/4* to rack up great ratings. She needed April Irons to watch it. But most of all, she needed Sam Shields to cast her in *Birth of a Star*.

Lila lay flat on the floor, her face against the bare tile, her arms spread. She said aloud the only prayer she ever said: 'Whatever it takes. Whatever it takes.'

Sharleen switched off the set and turned to Dean, who sat beside her on the floor, finishing the last of the popcorn. 'Well, what did you think?'

'You're good, Sharleen. Real good,' he said.

'Really? You *really* think so?'

'Sure.' She could see his hesitation.

'But . . .'

'Well . . .'

'Tell me.'

'Well, the show sure isn't as good as *Andy Griffith*.'

Flanders Fields was the largest single piece of property in Bel Air. Inside it, in the master suite Monica Flanders sat beside her Pekingese in her satin-brocade upholstered canopy bed. And not just *any* canopy bed, mind you, but the one that once belonged to Josephine, back in the days when she was a simple island girl from the West Indies. Of course she, Monica, had had it completely redone, but the provenance still mattered to her. It was the bed of a woman of no special beauty, whose charm and brains had raised her to empress. A woman not unlike herself.

'Will there be anything else, Madame?' her maid asked. Her *Irish* maid, not a *schvartzer* as so many women her age had to put up with. No. Monica Flanders was called the Queen of Cosmetics, and she lived like a queen. All the other great ones were retired, gone, dead. Helena Rubinstein. Elizabeth Arden. Coco Chanel. Now the business was ruled by corporations; heartless, mindless entities that lived and sold by statistics, by studies, by market share and focus-group results. Men like her son, Hyram. A good boy, perhaps, and a good father to his children, but a bit soulless, no?

What could those men in control know about a woman's needs? For half a century Monica had been selling women a dream: the dream of beauty and perfectibility. Perhaps a new face cream, a different colour eye shadow, would do the trick: make them beautiful, make them loved, make them happy. That it never worked seemed not to matter; hope was what she sold and it simply kept most of them restlessly looking for the right product – the one that *would* work.

She had started by listening to their laments in the little beauty parlour in lower Manhattan: a husband who cheated, an engagement that was broken off, an empty marriage, insecurity, unhappiness, discontent. And to each she had nodded, clicked her teeth in sympathy, let her eyes fill with a sheen of tears. She understood them. And then 'Try this,' she would say. 'Try this and things will change. You'll feel younger, you'll glow. People will notice a new you. A better you. Softer. Dewy. New. Young.'

Since then, little had changed but the size of her market. Tonight, Monica felt that she had perfected her pitch. Tonight a million, ten million, perhaps even fifty million women would watch the new show that she had caused to happen. And each one, no matter her age, no matter her appearance, would look at the screen and envy the images she had put there. It was like an hour-long commercial. Maybe better. And she had the products ready, the advertisements that would tell these yearning, envious women what they could do to look like those three beautiful, perfect girls on their screens.

'Put on the television for me and bring me the remote and

my glasses,' she told her maid. 'I have something to watch on television.' Monica had bet millions that this show would succeed.

And, as always, she was right.

In Bakersfield, Jake's diner was closed on Sunday nights. It was the one night a week that he could spend alone, without Thelma, watching TV. First *911*, then *Rescue Squad*, followed by reruns on cable. He stretched his feet out on the footrest and pushed the recliner until he was almost supine. As his hands scrambled in the seat beneath him, he yelled out, 'Thelma.' After no response, he yelled it again. Ah, she'd left. He settled back, sighed, ready for a pleasant evening.

Then, out of the blue, Thelma waltzed into the family room, kicked off her floppy rubber sandals, and dropped her large form down onto the plaid Herculon-covered sofa.

'What's the matter, Jake?' she asked, like she didn't know, and she placed a bowl of microwaved popcorn between them on the table, along with two beers she snapped open. Then, most shocking of all, *she* picked up the remote control.

'Hey!' he said. '*911* is coming on.'

Thelma reached into the pocket of her housedress, took out a Kleenex, wiped her nose, and then calmly looked at him. 'Not tonight it ain't,' she said, and clicked a button. The twenty-seven-inch RCA screen instantly burst into colour.

'What are you talking about, Thelma? You don't watch television Sunday nights. I thought you go play bingo over to the Bakersfield Rotary?' He couldn't keep the disappointment from his voice.

'Bingo ain't on Sundays no more. Don't you remember? They changed it to Mondays now. 'Cause of the TV show.'

What show? he thought. Not the one she tried to get him to watch *last* week. Jesus, now he thought of it, she'd come in then, too. He'd had to go back to the diner and watch his shows on the black-and-white he had in the kitchen. Oh, shit. 'I thought that was only a made-for-TV movie, or something like that. You mean to tell me it's on *every* Sunday night now?'

'Where you been? This show's the most-watched TV show in America,' she said. 'Where's your patriotism?' The television went silent during the opening credits. 'Anyway, I got something I want to show you. A surprise I figured out.'

Jake sat back, his arms folded across his chest. He was mad. Another woman's piece of shit, some *Designing Women* garbage or something, with the actresses in frilly clothes and crazy hairstyles. He looked over at the screen: a desert in Utah or somewhere, with Eagle Rock or one of them tall buttes. As the camera got closer, he saw three motorcycles, a woman in full leather on each bike, jackets open revealing full breasts under tight T-shirts. Nice tits. Well, so what?

'I'm going over to the diner.'

'No, you're not. You're stayin' right here. Look carefully. Look at them girls.'

Thelma was letting him look at tits? This was a new one. On the screen, each of the girls pulled up in a sharp gravel-spattering stop for a close-up.

'Remember I said last week that I'd seen that blonde somewhere before?' Thelma asked. 'Well, I have. And so have you. Look at her close, now.'

Jake squinted at the screen. Thelma was right – there was something about her that was familiar. 'Maybe. What of it?'

'Jake, I think we just got on the map.' Thelma held up a piece of cardboard with hand-lettering. 'Jake's Place. Home of *Three for the Road's* Clover.'

The camera moved closer, and Jake's face lit up. There she was, big as life. Sharleen! 'You mean that blonde waitress we had working for us? That's her? Goddamn, Thelma. You're right. Holy shit, we had us a real star at the diner! But you fired her.'

'Good thing I did. Otherwise you'da made a fool a yourself and she wouldn't be on TV!'

In Manhattan's East Village, what was left of the St. Malachy rep company's Movable Feast had moved from Saturday night to Sunday night. The tiny living room of the tenement apartment had people sitting all over – on the secondhand sofa from the Salvation Army, the stacks of Woolworth's cushions, even on the bare linoleum floor. The actors used to eat at makeshift tables, but that was before *Three for the Road* had become the focus of their weekly meals together. Now the meal was buffet-style, set up on the cover of the bathtub in the kitchen that doubled on these nights as a side-board. Everybody watched *Three for the Road*.

'Anyone need anything?' Molly called out from the kitchen. 'I'm not getting up again after the show starts, so let me know now.'

The television had been on for several minutes, but with the sound off. 'Here it is,' Chuck, Sam's replacement as director of the group, said, and turned up the volume. The teaser began. Molly wiped her hands on the dish towel. The dialogue had already started. 'Clover! Wow, man! That's psychedelic!' Then another voice spoke. 'Groovy! I can't take it.'

Molly blinked. For a moment, the voice had sounded exactly like her old friend Mary Jane. Had Mary Jane gotten a bit part out on the coast? Molly rushed to the doorway. But it was only Jahne Moore, one of the three stars, speaking. Molly sighed. Since Mary Jane disappeared without a trace, Molly had 'seen' her on subways, on buses, in museums, and once on the down escalator at Bloomingdale's. But, like this time, she'd been wrong. Mary Jane had disappeared.

A close-up of each of the three actresses flashed on the screen with the opening credits. 'They *are* beautiful women,' Molly sighed, '*really* beautiful.' And young, she thought. Very, very young.

'That's all it takes out there,' another woman, Sharon Malone, said. 'That's why I'm sticking with the stage. You can get by on just talent here,' she said, the sarcasm heavy in her voice.

'Now, let's not be catty,' Molly called out in a singsong voice.

'That's right, sometimes they *can* act. Look at Jahne Moore. I read she was discovered in some Ibsen play at the Melrose Playhouse. Not *too* shabby,' Chuck reminded them.

'Still *reading* those *People* magazines, eh, Chuck?' someone joshed.

'See her, the tallest one, Lila Kyle?' Sharon asked. 'Well, I read in *TV Guide* that it was hard for her to get taken seriously as an actress, since both her parents were so famous and all.'

'Wait a minute; can you believe this shit? Remember what Neil Morelli used to say? Poor little rich girl? Come off it. Lila Kyle wasn't discovered while working in some hash joint. She was "discovered" by Marty DiGennaro himself, *while they were having dinner, for chrissakes*. When was the last time *you* had dinner with Marty?' Harvey Jewett asked sarcastically.

'Sounds like I'm not the only one scarfing up *People*,' Chuck laughed. 'Try not to sound too bitter, Harvey.'

'Hey, I could do an hour of material on that, but Neil would do it better,' Harvey said. 'Where's Neil Morelli, now that we really need him?' Harvey shook his head, his eyes glued to the screen.

'Where *is* Neil Morelli?' Molly asked, not for the first time. 'Anyone hear from him?'

'Speaking of the lost and deported, do you think Sam Shields has put the wood to any of those honeys?' Harvey asked. 'Maybe he's gotten real lucky. You know how he was in New York.'

'Harve,' Craig, another of the out-of-work actor, said, 'even Sam would be out of his league. These girls are working with Marty DiGennaro; Sam doesn't have a chance.'

Then the programme started again, and they were silent, drinking up the fast cuts, the dissolves, the weird, innovative camera angles, the quirky dialogue. And the youth and beauty of the three girls. Too soon, the show ended. Sighs went round the circle. They would all have to go back to their day jobs tomorrow.

In Los Angeles, George Getz sat down in his easy chair and clicked on the TV he had recently bought. George, child of the sixties, hated television. He was a movie person. But then he found out, a little late, what all the students in his classes were talking about with such excitement. *Three for the Road* was on its way to becoming the phenomenon of the decade. It wasn't until he heard the names of the costars that he reacted. Lila Kyle, his former pupil, was in a Marty DiGennaro series.

That hadn't hurt business, either, he thought. Now his classes were doubled in size and had waiting lists, for chrissakes. And he was, at last, happy. It was the money, he told himself. No, it was the money and the recognition he had been robbed of for so long.

He watched tonight's show with intensity. It was, as they would have said in the sixties, psychedelic. And all style, no substance, if you asked his opinion. But on a medium that usually had neither, it was a major breakthrough. Tonight's show gave Lila more close-ups and lines than the other weeks, he noticed. Leave it to Lila, he thought. She always knew how to draw attention to herself! As the closing credits rolled across the screen, George rolled himself another joint and lifted it in a silent toast to the screen.

'Taught her everything she knows,' he said out loud to the empty room, and pulled the sweet smoke deep into his lungs.

Theresa O'Donnell squinted at the screen in the sitting room adjoining her bedroom, trying to make the double images converge into one. She reached for the glass of lukewarm vodka, neat, that sat at her elbow on the low table next to her chaise longue. Kevin entered the room, looked at the clear liquid in the glass, and was about to say something. 'Sit down and shut up,' Theresa growled

351

before he could open his mouth. Since Kevin had been dumped by Lila, Theresa had inherited him. He lived there, kept her glass full and kept her company, much to the disgust of both Robbie and Estrella. Well, Theresa had no choice about keeping Kevin on. After all, he knew her secrets. Fuck Estrella. It didn't matter even if Estrella left. She'd still have her two little girls.

She turned to the wooden figure beside her on the sofa. 'Do we have to do this?' Candy asked.

'It's *so* boring!' Skinny chimed in.

'Oh, now, you sound jealous!' Theresa admonished, but she smiled. 'After all, she *is* your sister.'

'She's a coldhearted bitch!' muttered Skinny.

'Language, please! Unless you like the taste of soap.' Still, Theresa smiled, until the show began and Lila's face appeared. Then the smile disappeared.

Theresa stared at Lila's image on the screen for the third week in a row. Lila, a star. This was not good news, not good news at all. It made her look old – it could make her look bad. *Now* what's going to happen to me? she wondered. Doesn't the little bitch think about anyone but herself? Who's going to hire me now, when it has become so public that I have a daughter Lila's age?

Jesus, and on television. Television was over, finished. Everyone knew that, except maybe Marty DiGennaro. And Lila. It would *never* be the same again, not like it was in the days of Theresa's show, and *Lucy* and *The Honeymooners* and *Ed Sullivan*. Theresa marked the death of the medium from the day she and Ed had left the tube. It was downhill from there – a vast wasteland of no-talent trash. Trash and PR.

The build on this show had been ridiculous. In a place famous for hype, they had outdone themselves. Mother of God, there wasn't a magazine or newspaper that wasn't running some story or other. And not wholesome pieces, either. Not ones like she used to do.

'She looks like a tramp,' Skinny said.

'So do the other two,' Theresa agreed.

'But they're famous tramps,' Candy taunted.

'If I hear another nasty word like that from you, I'm calling in Mr. Woodpecker!' Theresa threatened. But what Candy said was true. Lila was famous. So were the other tramps, who costarred. And when the fame became so big that every little detail of their lives would become public, what was Lila going to do then?

'I told her to stay out of the business. I told her, but she didn't listen.' Theresa looked over at Kevin, who returned her look, then shrugged, as if reading her mind. Theresa drained her glass and held it out to him. Wordlessly, Kevin stood up and took it, refilled it from the bottle on the dresser, and returned it to Theresa.

'They're calling her one of the three most beautiful women in the world,' he said to Theresa.

'Sweet St. Joseph! She'll be America's sweetheart. They'll be saying that next. The loveliest girl in the world.' Like mother, like daughter, Theresa thought, and laughed bitterly at her private joke, then almost choked on her drink. Perhaps she was being too harsh, too bitter. There must be a way she could use this to her advantage.

Maybe that's it, she thought. Ride her wave. Maybe a mother-daughter show. Perfect! This show can't last. There's nothing to it. No singing, no dancing. After she bombs in this, I'll help pull her back up on top, rescue her with *our* show.

'Don't worry, girls,' she told Candy and Skinny. 'This won't last. And I have a plan.'

They could begin rehearsing tomorrow, brush up a few old routines, maybe develop some new ones. She could get Robbie to choreograph a dance routine or two.

'Forget about plans,' said Kevin bitterly. 'She don't need you no more.'

'Shut the fuck up!' Theresa snapped. 'She'll come crawling when she realizes she can't get through this without me.'

'She will!' Candy shouted.

'Kevin, get out of here,' Skinny added. 'We want to watch this alone.' The man rose and, shaking his head, slowly left the room.

Theresa settled back to observe the rest of the show. Maybe things would work out for the best after all.

Dobe sat in the television lounge of the Wayfarer Hotel in Edmund, Minnesota, watching the screen in silence. Sitting next to him was a John Deere salesman from St. Paul. The front-desk clerk, leaning against the door jamb so he could hear the phones if they rang, was engrossed in the show unfolding on the TV.

Dobe put his fingers to his lips, afraid that his delight would cause him to smile, and cause people to ask what he was grinning at. When you were on the grift, it was best not to call attention to yourself. But it was hard not to grin back at the pretty blonde on the screen. Sharleen was radiant, lighting up the room, making him feel young again. He was as happy as a father could be for his daughter. Good girl, he said to himself. You done it. I'm proud of you, kid.

The salesman leaned towards Dobe and whispered, 'Look at the tits on that blonde.'

Dobe looked him straight in the face; his smile faded. 'Watch out, mister. You're talking about a lady,' he said. Then Dobe turned his eyes back to the screen.

Brewster Moore sat across from the television, its screen flickering in front of him. The three women were incredibly beautiful, picked for their looks more than for their talent. But Dr. Moore knew that Mary Jane had always had talent. Now, thanks to him, she had beauty as well.

He watched her image on the screen closely. Was it professional or personal? he wondered. Her letters to him seemed excited, but they also had an edge of sadness, telling not only of her success but also of her loneliness in her new life. And Brewster Moore, divorced now five years, knew something about the loneliness Mary Jane wrote about. Like her, he had his work, but, unlike her, he knew his work would never quite be enough.

He had to force himself not to write too often to Mary Jane. That would not be right. He had created her looks; now it was up to her to create her new life. And he could not play a part in both. People wanted to forget his work once it was done. She didn't owe him anything, and she wouldn't want to be reminded of his services. Patients rarely did. But at least he had her letters.

Now he couldn't take his eyes off Mary Jane Moran – Jahne Moore, he corrected himself. My handiwork, he thought. My Galatea. *I* made her, not God. Of course, he could never say those words out loud to anyone. His triumph was a lonely pleasure. But delicious nonetheless.

After all the reconstructions of burn victims, of the children with nature's defects, of faces that, despite all his skill, would never even approximate the norm; after all the Park Avenue matrons insisting on premature face lifts, after the models with perfect noses who wanted them to be a bit *more* perfect – Jahne Moore was unique. An achievement of perfection, appropriate and complete. Beautiful. Rewarding. Brave.

A woman he could love.

Neil Morelli owned nothing except the clothes in the closet and the thirteen-inch colour TV he had bought from a guy at the club who was selling hot Korean TVs for fifty bucks. Well, he hadn't actually bought it yet, since he still owed the guy twenty dollars.

He had no money, no car, no friends, and nowhere to go. He had a stinking job driving a cab. But he had his television, and while that was on, Neil could feel he was still connected to the world. It was Sunday night, but it could have been any night in the week. The calendar didn't mean much to him anymore. All he needed to know was when *Sienfield*, *Evening at The Improv*, and that show with Paul Provenza were on. So he could envy and hate them. But tonight he was making a special effort to watch the show all the assholes at the club had been carrying on about for weeks. He would never admit it to anyone tomorrow, but tonight he was going to watch *Three for the Road* for the first time. Just to see what the fuck everyone was going nuts over, the guys at the taxi garage especially.

Not that it was a hard show to watch, Neil soon saw. Three gorgeous girls, all with great tits and legs, romping around right before his eyes. And all that sixties shit. Love beads. Bell bottoms. Moby Grape. He was lying on his open sofa-bed, and had the television on a chair next to him. For this show, he had pulled the set up real close to his face, so that he wouldn't miss anything. Actually, this was the closest thing to a date that Neil had had in a long time. He felt his dick get hard as the show progressed, and he tried to fantasize which one he would fuck, if he gave them the chance.

He still hadn't decided by the end of the show, although he had begun to stroke himself, and was close to climaxing. Then the credits began to roll. Neil always was on the lookout for newcomers. Three kids had managed, against the odds, to break into the business big time. Well, good for them. He watched their names roll. Sharleen Smith, Jahne Moore, Lila Kyle.

Wait a minute. Lila Kyle? Neil knew who she was; he had researched her for his routine. She was the double-dynasty kid, *both* parents stars. He felt his dick grow limp in his hand, his frustration now fuelling his rage at another Nepotism Squad target. She must have got the job through connections. Her mother got it for her. She got a free ride; he, Neil Morelli, got nothing.

You fucking cunt, he thought. I could kill you.

3

If politics makes strange bedfellows, just think of the couplings Hollywood creates. Doris Day and Rock Hudson. Madonna and Michael Jackson. Michael Jackson and Brooke Shields. Madonna and Warren Beatty. Michael Jackson and Diana Ross. Madonna and everyone else.

On the surface, Marty DiGennaro and Lila Kyle would seem as unlikely and ridiculous. But given their backgrounds, there was a certain symmetry to it. Both were loners. Both had spent their childhoods in darkened rooms staring at movies. In fact, both had stared at some of the same movies. Both Lila and Marty loved Birth of a Star, *and if one had a mother who had been featured in it, it enhanced everything for the other.*

So despite Marty's plain face and unimpressive build and Lila's glamour and leggy height, the two shared more than most odd couples in L.A.

And when did a beautiful woman on the arm of an ugly, shorter, older but powerful man ever look out of place in Hollywood?

Marty DiGennaro sat back in his limousine, his feet up on the folded seat in front of him, savouring the moment. Everything was better than good. The reception of 3/4 was great. He'd just heard that the network was renewing for the next thirteen episodes. Monica Flanders was ecstatic. Their new cosmetics line was already profitable. And, on top of it all, Lila Kyle had accepted his invitation to dinner. In fact, she had accepted so unexpectedly that he hadn't had time to really plan. Unusual for a control freak like Marty. How many times had he asked her out? It seemed like every day since they'd started shooting the series, and always the answer was the same. A frigid 'No, thank you.' Then, just like that, she accepts. Go know.

Maybe it had just sunk in that he had done what he said he'd do: he'd made her a star. In just a month, the show had captured an unprecedented audience. You couldn't go by a magazine stand or a variety store without seeing the girls' pictures everywhere. So why question his luck? Or her motivations? He was too excited. Excited like he used to be as a little kid waiting for the Joan

Crawford movie to begin. Or Myrna Loy. Or Merle Oberon. The other kids watched TV on Saturday for the cartoons. Not Marty. He was into beauty. He couldn't wait for his star of the moment to light up the old Dumont television screen as the *Early Show* began.

His star of the moment was definitely Lila Kyle. Only she was *real* – flesh and blood – not some colour emulsion on celluloid. From the moment he met her, he knew she was different, special. She was Hollywood royalty, after all. A combination of the grandeur of the old stars and something altogether new and contemporary. At the end of the day's shoot, he couldn't get her out of his mind: her smouldering red hair, her narrow waist, the long, long legs that seem to start at her neck. He would catch himself staring at her while he was setting up a shot of Jahne or Sharleen, when his attention should have been on them. And the craziest part of it all was, she didn't seem to care that he – Marty DiGennaro – was paying so much attention to her. In fact, she didn't even seem to notice. Not that he needed that, but, let's face it, when you offer an unknown a chance of a lifetime, you expect a little something, a little appreciation. Not a fuck, necessarily. He wasn't into power fucking. But gratitude, respect, friendship, warmth. Lila gave him zip.

And the most amazing part was, he didn't think it was an act. She wasn't playing coy, hard to get, as his first wife had. Lila was simply cool. Cool as they come.

She hadn't seen him, except on the set. Tonight, she had agreed to have dinner with him, just the two of them, but then she asked that they not go out. She had smiled warmly; she hated crowds she said. She just wanted to talk. Every other chick he knew, when he took her out, wanted not only the hottest spot in town, but also the hottest *table* in that hottest spot. Women wanted to be *seen* with Marty DiGennaro. One bitch had even brought her own photographer to the restaurant to record the momentous occasion. But not Lila. He couldn't figure her out. And that gave Marty DiGennaro a hard-on.

He had one now, as he finalized plans for the evening. He had his office on the phone. Staci, his secretary, had taken care of most of the details, in her usual unflappable way, but Marty wanted to do *something*, put his own imprint on the evening, as it were. This wasn't just another date with just another starlet. He gave Staci a few comments, then hung up, but he was too restless to do nothing. Instead, he picked up the car phone and began to dial numbers. The first was to his florist.

'This is Marty DiGennaro,' he said into the phone, and waited while the salesperson at the other end went into the usual fawning tizzy. Tonight, he allowed it. Everyone should get what they need tonight. He finally had a dinner date with Lila Kyle, and could afford to be magnanimous. 'Brian usually does my house every week, but tonight is special. I need crimson gladioli.' He had read in some stupid interview that that was Lila's favourite flower. 'Dozens of them. Tell Brian I want at least four dozen each in the bedroom, dining room, living room, and two or three dozen in baskets around the pool. And make sure they're crimson, not that red-orange shit. And I need them delivered and set up no later than seven-thirty.' He paused. '*Of course* tonight.'

He planned social events of importance the way he planned his movies. He wanted every detail perfect. Next the caterers. Again, he wanted to check, although Staci had already made the call. He went over the schedule in his mind. Drinks and hors d'oeuvres at eight. Dinner at nine. Bed at ten? Marty wondered. After all, she'd *asked* not to go out. Marty thought about her smooth skin, her long, shining red hair. How would it feel to have that hair draped across his chest, his belly? He grunted.

'Sally,' Marty said into the intercom to his driver.

'Yes, Mr. D.?'

'I want you to pick up Miss Kyle at seven-forty-five. Exactly.'

'Got it, Mr. D. Seven-forty-five on the nose.'

'And I want you to put on your white jacket and serve drinks, then disappear when dinner's served. But don't go anywhere tonight. I might need you later, so hang around the pool house. Watch some TV. No drinking, and no nose candy, *capisce*? You're on duty until I tell you different.'

'Don't worry about me, boss. I'll be available for as long as you want, same as usual. You can depend on me, Mr. D.'

And Marty knew he could. He had known Sally since his earliest days in L.A. Sally was a gift he had inherited, more or less, from a capo in New York, someone who wanted Marty 'treated right.' And Sally had been just the man. He seemed to have no life of his own, just vicariously enjoying the life Marty had made for himself. But, then, Marty always saw to it that Sally got taken care of, too. Always had women, a little coke – only the best – now and then, a comfortable apartment over the pool house. And Sally was justifiably grateful. The last job he'd had was for an ex-wise guy who had been on edge twenty-four hours a day, a guy who had been shot at more than once. Sally felt his life had been spared when the guy died in his sleep. No more sweats when he turned the guy's ignition key, praying there wasn't a bomb wired to it. Working for Marty was like living in Disneyland.

Lila knew how to make good out of bad. After all, growing up with Theresa O'Donnell had taught her *something*. So, when an old fart in love with himself like Michael McLain called her and asked her out for dinner, she turned him down. Not because he was an over-the-hill playboy – which he was, in her opinion – and not even because she didn't think she could get through the evening without dropping her pants, which she knew she could. She just didn't want to date anyone. And she certainly didn't want to date a man who had once fucked her mother. Theresa bragged about all the men in her life, and Michael McLain had been on the top of her list at one time, when he was younger and Theresa was only a little older. It gave Lila the creeps. Michael was one of those guys who dated older women when he was young and younger ones when he was old. He made her sick.

But he *was* important. He still knew everyone that counted. No sense getting him angry. So she had to think fast when he asked. 'I'm sorry, I'm involved with my director. Maybe another time.' She hadn't wanted to alienate Michael, just to get him the fuck off her back. Marty would be a good cover; plus, now that she thought about it, it might even be the time to lean on him a little to see if he could get her the part in *Birth of a Star*.

So now, after a long day on location, she was getting dressed and putting makeup on yet again. She leaned back from the vanity mirror in her dressing room at home, and blinked her eyes. Perfect, she thought, as she always did after expertly applying mascara. She'd been taught makeup by Theresa when she was nine, and sometimes she even thought of herself as one of those Kabuki dancers in Japan who develop all their feminine wiles before puberty. Now that she thought of it, weren't they all men? But perfect in their female role, with nothing to learn. There was very little left for Lila to learn, either. From now on, it was performance time. Her years of understudying Theresa would pay off. She would take over Theresa's role and outdo her at it.

But could she get April Irons to give her the part in *Birth of a Star*? And could she get Marty to help her? It would kill Theresa, Lila knew, and she smiled. Marty's already so crazy for me, he would do backward somersaults. Lila was aware – very aware – of how he followed her with his eyes wherever she went on the set. She pretended not to notice, but she did. Every time. And that's just the way she wanted it.

Well, she had tried to avoid it, but perhaps dating him was inevitable. The idea of dating frightened her, since Kevin. But she was feeling a lot better now, even about spending the evening with a man. Marty was one man she could handle. And he had more influence in Hollywood than any other man she knew. Certainly more than Michael McLain. She stood at her three-sided mirror and did a series of poses, liking what she saw. Tonight is going to be very good for me, she told herself, and smiled at her image.

The doorbell rang, and Lila jumped. Who the fuck would come up to the door of her house and ring the bell? She lived in Malibu Colony just to be sure that didn't happen. Who had gotten past security, and how? She walked down the curving stairs, and peeked out the peephole. Marty's guy – what's his name, Sally – was standing there, holding his cap in his hand. Lila flung open the door. 'What are you doing here, Sally?' she asked. 'Got lost?'

'No, Miss Kyle. Mr. D., he said I should pick you up at seven-forty-five.' He indicated his watch. 'It's seven-forty-five,' he added, and smiled.

'I drive myself, Sally. Take the night off.' She slammed the door and went back up the stairs to her dressing room. What was that all about? She didn't like the idea of being trapped without a car at Marty's place. She ran the brush through her hair for the last time, straightened the seams in her stockings (she figured Marty would *love* seamed stockings), put a black lace mantilla over her hair, and ran down the stairs, car keys in hand. She opened the door, and Sally was still there, practically in the same position she had left him in minutes ago. 'What are *you* still doing here?' she snapped, as she walked towards her black Land Rover.

'Miss Kyle, I promised Mr. D. I'd see you to his house. Why not ride with me? I promise I'll drive slow, and bring you home anytime you want. Come on, Miss Kyle, Mr. D. made me promise.'

'What you promise Mr. DiGennaro has nothing to do with me. I feel like driving myself, so that's what I'm going to do.' She hiked her blue suede skirt up and got up into the driver's seat, pulling the mantilla around her head to keep her hair in place. She put the car in reverse, then first, and squealed out the drive, watching Sally, in her rearview mirror, scamper into the limousine to follow her. She paused at the entrance ramp to the coast highway, then squeezed into a spot that opened between two cars, making it impossible for Sally to follow. But when she checked the rearview, he was just one car behind her. She accelerated, weaving in and out of traffic lanes, and arrived at Marty's house breathless but with a smile on her face. Marty himself answered the door. Well, she could surprise him.

'Where's Sally? Where's my car? Who's jeep is that?' The questions came out one right after the other, without pauses for answers.

'And how nice to see you, too, Mr. DiGennaro. Thank you for the compliments. I paid particular attention to my hair this evening.' Lila let her voice drip sarcasm. 'And may I come in, or is this as far as I'm getting this evening?' Just then Marty's limousine sped up the driveway, and Sally was out of the car almost before the engine turned off. 'I'm sorry, Mr. D. She wouldn't come in the car, Mr. D. She insisted on taking hers.'

'Fine, Sally,' Marty said. 'Come in, Lila.'

But Sally wouldn't quit.

'I tried to keep up with her, Mr. D., but she drove like a man. I mean, no woman drives that good. No offence, Miss Kyle. Jeez, I'm sorry, Mr. D.' He had his hat in his hands in front of him.

Marty looked at Lila, who was smiling a broad, innocent smile. 'Don't be a chauvinist, Sal. I should have known better. Thanks for trying. Come on in the house and make us a couple of drinks, then take the rest of the night off.'

'What can I get you to drink?' Sal asked Lila.

'Chardonnay?' Lila asked sweetly, still standing on the steps outside.

Marty jumped. 'Lila, I'm sorry. Where are my manners? Come on in. I thought we'd have drinks on the lanai first. Would that be all right with you?'

They walked in, crossed the vast marble foyer with the grand staircase, and stepped out onto the marble-paved lanai. Sally joined them, placed the wine cooler next to Marty's elbow after pouring two glasses of the white wine, and went inside.

'What should we drink to, Lila? I feel that this is such an important occasion, we should formalize it with a toast. Should we drink to the success of the show, or is that old news already?'

'How about, to everyone getting what he – and she – wants.' She clicked his glass and took a long sip.

'Well, I feel like I already have everything I want. A hit TV show, a nice home, and the most beautiful woman in America sitting opposite me. What else is there?'

'For me? *Stardom.*'

'You already have that. You'll be on every magazine cover in the country, and most of Europe. Even South Africa. What are you getting in fan mail already? Five to six thousand pieces every week? Shall I go on?'

'That's celebrity, Marty. Not real fame. Fame comes with doing something that lasts, something like your first picture, that made everything else possible for you. *Back Streets* made you famous. *Three for the Road* makes me a celebrity. Celebrities are just famous for being famous. See the difference?'

'You'll get your shot at fame, then. Just hang on. Don't be so impatient. You're very young. Enjoy this, and then move on. Something will come along, the perfect piece, the thing that cries out for you and only you.'

Lila leaned forward, her elbow on her knee. 'Something has. And I want your opinion about it. And your help in getting it.'

She could see she had piqued Marty's curiosity. 'What's that?' he asked, his brow furrowed.

'*Birth of a Star,*' Lila said, and sat back to watch his expression.

There was no movie that Marty loved more than *Birth of a Star*. Years ago, he'd tried to get an option on a remake. He was bitter that now it had gone to someone else. And not just anyone, but his old *bête noire*. Well, she'd fuck it up for sure. Wasn't it she who'd done the remake of *The Front Page* with Burt Reynolds and Kathleen Turner? A sacrilege. God, he'd love to do *Birth of a Star*. How had April gotten a hold of it?

Still, he couldn't show this loss of face, this loss of control, to Lila. Lila whose mother had starred in the film.

'*Birth of a Star?* Are you crazy? That's a remake of a movie that wasn't very good to begin with. The only thing that movie had going for it was Theresa O'Donnell, and at that point in her career, *anything* she did would have gotten raves.'

'I want to do the same thing to the remake,' Lila said, keeping her voice low and steady.

'Remakes suck, Lila. I know that, you know that, the public knows that, for chrissakes. They are worse than sequels. The only one who doesn't know it is April Irons, and she's got her head up her ass. *Birth* is going to bomb, trust me. Now I remember what I heard: it's a so-so script, and its timeliness is over. It's passé. You want to make a movie so bad, let *me* direct you.'

'I'd love for you to direct me. But first I want to do *Birth*.'

Marty stood up and began to pace the length of the veranda. This was not what he'd expected. Where was her excitement over *3/4*? Where was her gratitude? Where was her respect? 'Lila, listen to me. You're the hottest property in the United States at the moment. For your first film, you can name your own price, pick any script you want. Why would you fuck up your career to do that piece of shit? It would be like tossing all your opportunity down the toilet.'

'So you won't help me get it?' she asked, allowing her anxiety to show for the first time this evening.

'Help you? I'll do everything I can to *stop* you. I won't let you throw away something you've worked so hard to achieve. Something *I've* worked so hard to achieve. I have approval of your movie roles while you're on *3/4*. That's in your contract. I won't let you do it, Lila.' He swallowed the last of the wine from his glass, and walked over to refill it. 'And that's that.'

Lila stood up, shrugged the mantilla up from her shoulders to her head, and turned to Marty. 'You can't stop me. No one can, Marty. I want that part, and I'm going to get it.' She turned and began to walk the outside path towards her Land Rover. 'And if I have the celebrity you say I have, I'm *going* to get it.'

Lila wasn't exactly surprised when she got another call from Michael McLain. It was Robbie who danced around the room like a deranged, obese ballerina on skates.

'Michael McLain! Michael McLain!' he carolled. 'He's *sooo-oo* cute.'

'He's *sooo-oo* old,' Lila said, reaching for the little slip with his number. She knew from her mom's life how this stuff worked. If things went well, soon *everyone* would be calling her.

'Billy over at Sy Ortis' office said he might star in something with Ricky Dunn.'

Lila stopped in her walk to her bedroom. 'Really?' she asked. Ricky was hot. 'Well, maybe I'll call him back.'

'Maybe? *Maybe.*'

God, she hated how Robbie was down on her all the time. He wanted a full description of each day at the studio, of each bit of gossip he could milk and retell to his friends. She sighed.

'I said *maybe?*'

'Call him now. Let me listen on the extension.'

'Forget about it.' Lila sighed again. God, she felt totally smoth-ered. Now that she was living in Nadia's house, she'd hoped for some privacy, but Robbie was *always* there.

'You wouldn't be so quick to blow him off if *you* knew what *I* know.'

'What's that?' she asked, her voice nasty. He was always pre-tending to have some inside scoop, but she could see now that Robbie was just a small-time guy who got his inside tips from gay waiters and faggot secretaries living at the edge of the Industry.

'Well, I guess you're not interested in *Birth of a Star* casting,' he said, and began to waltz out of the room.

'What are you talking about?' she snapped.

'I heard that April Irons wants Michael McLain for *Birth of a Star*.'

'Get out of here!' she cried. 'He's ancient.'

'Not too ancient for that. Or to star with Ricky Dunn,' Robbie sneered. 'You should be so lucky.'

Lila tried not to react. She wouldn't give Robbie the satisfaction of showing any interest. 'Who cares?' she sneered. But she knew that she did.

The next day, from her trailer at the studio, she called the number that Robbie had copied down. It must have been McLain's private line, because he answered the phone himself, his voice husky. Was it with sleep, or some stupid sex appeal he was trying? Well, it didn't hurt to be nice, and even if it did, she could take the pain if it would get her the lead in *Birth*.

'This is Lila Kyle. I think you called me.'

'I couldn't help myself.'

Give me a break, she thought. 'I don't really know you,' she said, and wondered if he remembered the last time they'd met.

'Would you like to?' he asked, his voice suggestive. 'I hear you broke up with your director friend.'

Christ, gossip travelled faster than the speed of light in this town. But how could she find out if Robbie's rumour was true? She couldn't just come out and ask McLain what his two next vehicles were and whether she could be in them. Well, she'd just have to see him.

'I wouldn't like to,' she said, 'I'd *love* to.'

4

With the relentless 3/4 shooting schedule, the publicity work for
Flanders Cosmetics, the brutal exercise and self-maintenance drills,
and her occasional secretive dates with Michael McLain, Jahne had
succeeded in keeping herself too busy to focus on Sam Shields. Until
Sam had called her. Since then, it had been hard to keep him out
of her mind. Somehow, somehow, always in the background was
a thread of awareness, an almost animal instinct that Sam existed:
since he'd called after her debut, she'd waited to hear whether a
script had been submitted to her agent. Jahne was not completely
surprised when she got the call from Sy Ortis.

'I got a ring from April Irons' office. They're interested in casting
you for some remake they're about to do. You interested in going
over there for a look-see?'

She felt her heart beat faster but she knew how to play casual.
'Why not?' she asked.

'I say it's beneath your dignity. A look-see. Like you're not
the hottest kid in town.' Sy snorted. 'Anyway, she's someone to
avoid. A real shark. And I hear they want to use that guy Shields
as director. He's the one who made Crystal look like shit in her last
film.'

'But I heard it was an acting triumph for her. She got good
reviews.'

'Fuck reviews. He made her look like a hag. She hasn't gotten
a decent script since.'

'Well, it can't hurt if I go; I need the experience,' Jahne told him.

'I got other deals I like better. And I hear they're having trouble
with the script. They only sent a treatment.'

'Well, what can it hurt?' she repeated. And, really, what could
it hurt? she asked herself. She would see Sam, and if she got the
part she could turn down his job offer. It was an ironic little joke
she could play, after he had rejected her so completely. And the
beauty of it was that he would never know. It was the reward,

the gift, she could give to poor Mary Jane Moran. She'd had to play poor Miss Havisham but now Jahne could play Estella. Yes! She'd have the chance to be both the disappointed, rejected lover and the cold-hearted avenger.

But the truth was, she could not resist seeing Sam at least one more time. And if she was seeing him through new eyes, so much the better.

She stood at the maître d's desk at Chasen's, where the Hollywood establishment ate. Henri immediately approached her. Though she'd never been here before, he knew her by name. 'Miss Moore, how nice to see you. Miss Irons is waiting for you. Please follow me.' He led her to a centre table that could seat six, and she carefully made eye contact first with April Irons, and only then with Sam. Once again, she wondered exactly what their relationship was.

'Thank you for meeting with us, Jahne,' April said, after the pleasantries were exchanged and the drink orders taken. 'I know how busy you must be with the series, and all the other demands on you. You seem to be holding up remarkably well. Are you?'

'I have my moments,' she said, then bit the inside of her lip. I used to say that all the time in New York, she thought. Before leaving home today, she had talked to herself in the mirror, reminding herself that this was the supreme test. If Sam didn't figure anything out after today's lunch, he never would. Watch your speech patterns, she'd told herself. That's the only way Mary Jane Moran could be uncovered. Now she added quickly, 'But, actually, overall, it's been fan-*tas*-tic.' There, just enough L.A. And definitely *not* Mary Jane Moran.

Jahne scanned the oversized menu and realized she was very hungry. Nerves always did that to her. But she'd been dieting again for weeks. Of course, she couldn't eat. It was almost impossible to keep her weight at 109. She certainly wouldn't blow it for Sam. 'I'm starving,' she said. 'So I think I'll have a large salad, with the house dressing on the side.' April ordered a salad also, but Sam asked for very rare filet mignon with Béarnaise sauce. Some things didn't change. Jahne smiled to herself at the memory of Sam's unfashionable love for beef. Her big splurge one year for his birthday had been at the Old Homestead back in New York, where the steaks were so large they flopped over the edges of the plates.

Sam had greeted her, but April did all the talking about the movie. Jahne knew all about *Birth of a Star*, of course. She'd seen the classic with Theresa O'Donnell. But she had only glanced at Sam's treatment. Apparently, there was no script yet. She asked why.

'Sam, tell Jahne – may I call you Jahne? – tell Jahne your ideas about the project.' April sat erect, her hands steepled in front of her, looking intently at Sam as he spoke.

'Have you ever seen *Birth of a Star*, Jahne?' Sam asked.

'Yes, and I loved it.' She had rented the video only last week and run it three or four times. Old-fashioned and melodramatic. She took the plunge. 'But I don't know if I'm the right age for Theresa O'Donnell's part. She was about, what, thirty-five, thirty-six when she played the role?' Jahne felt a scar tighten on her inner thigh – it felt like a caterpillar moving on her flesh – and slowly crossed her legs under the table. It began to itch. 'What age do *you* see the character as?' she asked.

Sam spoke quickly. 'Your age, Jahne. Theresa was really too old at that point in her career to play the ingenue. But she had the drawing power, and good skin, so she got the part.' He chewed a bit of his steak, and wiped the corner of his mouth with his napkin.

April agreed, and they talked some more about it. How to update the story, how to make it work. Jahne picked at her salad and tried to appear intelligent.

But in reality Jahne was there simply to look at Sam. She watched him throughout the meal, one part of her present for the conversation and involved with the details of the script. Well, she *was* very interested, despite what Sy had said. But there was another part of Jahne, the voyeur, who sat there all the while and peeked into Sam's private self without his knowing. It was like standing outside his house, peering at him through his window, watching him eat. He was, if anything, better-looking than she had remembered. California clearly agreed with him. He was wearing a pair of black linen pants, and when she peeked down to the end of one long, ever-so-long leg, she saw that his narrow feet were sockless and tanned, slipped into casual but obviously expensive loafers. He was tanned, and the white shirt he wore made his teeth and the whites of his eyes seem to glisten. That was new, Sam in white. The only other change she could see was that his hair, still sleeked back into a pony tail, had begun to go salt-and-pepper. Even the grey looked good on Sam.

Watching him like this made her feel odd – half hot, half a voyeur. But it also gave her a perspective on Sam she had never had before. She had always believed that Sam was his own person, that he didn't kowtow to anyone. Now, though, he deferred to April. Even the simple act of delicately wiping the corners of his mouth with the edge of his napkin was so telling. Jahne remembered Sam's movements as being big. He'd never dabbed at the corners of his mouth. It was such a studied movement for Sam.

Sam was self-conscious, she realized, and seemed concerned with making an impression. But on whom? On Jahne Moore? That made her almost giddy. On April Irons? Of course, he *was* playing to April as well as to Jahne. What *was* their relationship?

She shook herself, almost physically, and realized their coffee had arrived. 'So, Jahne,' Sam asked, looking directly into her eyes. 'Will you audition? Can I hope that we might be working together?'

Jahne smiled, first at April, then at Sam. The meal had progressed so quickly, and it appeared that she'd been a success. Her most important role ever: Jahne Moore. 'It's certainly a possibility,' she said. 'There's a first time for everything.'

She looked down at her almost empty coffee cup and saw that Sam was leaning on the table. April was busying herself with a lipstick and a gold Dior mirror she was peering into. Jahne looked away and felt a tingle in her right hand. It was his hand – Sam's hand – touching hers. Just the edge of his pinkie against the side of hers, but she remembered – oh, she remembered *everything* – and she remembered how very tentative he'd always been, half teasing, half waiting for her response. To avoid rejection and ensure success.

Now, once again, his hand just brushed hers. And it felt as good as it had back then – maybe even better. Because it had been so long and she'd missed him so much. And because she knew what that hand could do to her.

The hairs on her arm lifted, and she told herself no. It was too much. What had happened to her resolve? She was already involved with Michael. Was she becoming a slut? Had she always been faithful simply out of lack of options? What a horrible thought! And what if she slept with Sam? Surely then he'd realize who she was. What if she slept with him and he didn't? Jahne didn't know which was more unthinkable. And then it came to her: that which was really unthinkable.

And that was not sleeping with him at all.

5

Sharleen sat with the phone pressed tightly against her ear, listening, trying not to get angry with Sy Ortis, who was breathing heavily on the other end. He was just trying to do right by her, she told herself. He was teaching her manners and all. But somehow it didn't seem right.

'Stars don't *go* to crew parties. It's just *not done*,' she heard him say again.

Sharleen sighed. 'But why not? I been goin' to 'em all along. And I always had a good time. What's changed?'

'Everything! Do the crew get their pictures on the cover of *TV Guide?* Are they going to make a million bucks this year? Sharleen, you need to see and be seen with people on your *level*. Stars. Say, did Michael McLain ever get together with you? He called for your number.' Sharleen blushed. She was glad she was not seeing Mr. Ortis in person, because she thought she could remember that night, though she didn't like to. It confused her, shamed her. The fun of going out with a movie star, Mr. McLain's kindness, his gift, his prediction about her career. But then there had been the drinks, the dizziness, and that time on the hill, when he . . . when it had happened like it did.

She wasn't surprised that she had never heard from him again, that he had never called. She'd behaved like a tramp. He'd lost respect. Well, she was sorry and ashamed. She felt dirty, so she tried not to think of it at all. 'He called once. But not since then,' she told Mr. Ortis. Probably he was seeing some other, nicer girl by now. She put her hand up to her neck, the necklace still hanging there, just over her breastbone. It had hurt when she hadn't heard from Michael McLain, but she hadn't been surprised. 'So, now I'm a star? And everything is changed?'

'Exactly. Now, honey, you're big. Too big to go to some West Hollywood stuntman's parties.' Sy paused. 'Sharleen? Think of security. Those parties are open, no security check as you go

369

in. If word got out that you were showing up – and it would, believe me – the party would turn into a riot. And no one could protect you. Don't put the guy in that position. They're good folk, and they really like you. But, you know, you can't just call up and invite yourself along. *They* know what the deal is. And they wouldn't say no to you.'

'I used to make the potato salad for those things, for crying out loud.' And Sharleen did feel like crying out loud, although she wasn't going to on the phone with Mr. Ortis. 'And the guys used to call me Shar. Now they call me Miss Smith. That don't feel so good, you know? I miss them.'

Sy's voice lowered. 'I know you do, honey. But you can make other friends. Maybe Michael. Or someone else. Want me to ask someone to call you?'

'No!' Sharleen said quickly. What had happened with Mr. McLain was too scary, too much. She didn't want *that* again.

'You like Jahne Moore, don't you?'

'Sure I do. I like her fine. But we're not friends.' Sharleen sighed. 'I'd jest like to go out to a party again. All I do is work and take lessons. Singin' and dancin' and all that other stuff you lined up. And the exercise classes! Mr. Ortis, I'm so sore and tired. I'd like some fun. I mean just a *party*. At someone's house. Someone normal, you know?'

'Well, don't worry, you will. Listen, Sharleen, what do you think about that recording idea?'

Not again! She was tired of all this. 'Oh, Mr. Ortis, I can't really sing.'

'Sure you can. And there's a lot of people who'll buy the album.'

'I'd feel stupid. It's bad enough bein' an actress that can't act. But also being a singer who can't sing? I . . .'

She could sense the loneliness fill up her chest once again, but tried not to feel it. It only made her want to cry, and what did she have to cry about, after all? She had Dean, and her new house, and every room furnished just the way they wanted from the old Sears catalogue. Funny that now they had money to buy stuff, the catalogue goes out of business! But one of Mr. Ortis' people got everything for them, jest like they picked. It had been fun, going through the catalogue with Dean in the evenings, after work, choosing whatever they wanted, then having the lady in Mr. Ortis' office arrange for the delivery, and getting some decorator to come in and put it all in place, make it look just like the catalogue pictures. But then, after buying everything they needed – everything they *wanted*, she corrected herself – they were left with evenings to fill, with no place to go and no one to see.

It wasn't so bad for Dean. During the day, he at least could go out wherever *he* wanted without worrying about getting trampled by a mob of people at the supermarket who recognized him because of the show, or from the pictures spread all over those magazines they sell at supermarket lines. So Dean went to places like Tail O' the Pup and the pizza joint without her, and he did the shopping and always came home with twice as much as they needed.

Anyway, even if she wasn't recognized, she couldn't go out much, 'cause she was booked up with these lessons. And posing for Flanders Cosmetics ads *and* publicity pictures, and goin' to those appearances Mr. Ortis' office set up, *and* bein' interviewed. She looked at her watch. 'I gotta go. I got my voice lesson in about six minutes. And Miss Cardoza is real strict.'

'Good girl. So you'll do the album, and you won't bother the crew anymore. Right, Sharleen?'

'Well, we'll see. I don't want to go where I ain't welcome. I sure don't want to give none of them a hard time. It's just that I feel like . . . like a prisoner.' She hated the whining sound in her voice, but couldn't stop herself, now that she was saying what needed to be said. 'Mr. Ortis, I have to have my private telephone number changed every week. I never give my number out, just to you and Mr. DiGennaro. But the calls – you should hear some of them. I can't answer the phone no more. Things sure have changed.' Sharleen began to laugh. 'There was a time I couldn't afford to make a local call at a pay phone. Now I have phones in every room of the house – oh, Lord, including the bathroom – and I can't answer them. And who'm I gonna call? It's kind of funny, isn't it?'

'Yes and no, Sharleen,' Mr. Ortis said. 'It might not be so good for you right now, but wait. After you get used to it, you'll be able to handle it.'

'Will I ever be able to shop in a supermarket again?'

She heard Mr. Ortis laugh. 'I sure hope not, honey.'

Sharleen hung up and looked around the large room of their new house. They had to get out of that really nice one-bedroom apartment in town – people would sit in the lobby all day waiting for her. Lenny from Mr. Ortis' office found this big house for them, way out, almost in the Valley, with lots of land and trees around.

And a high fence with a big gate. Mr. Ortis had hired security guards to sit at the gate and patrol the grounds twenty-four hours a day. And even *they* would go out of their way to peek at her whenever she walked on the lawn, or sat in the sun. It gave her the creeps, but she had to agree with Mr. Ortis. What else was she going to do?

She knew what she'd *like* to do. She'd like to walk down the street somewhere, and look in store windows, try on some clothes, maybe buy some shoes, have a hamburger at McDonald's, sit in a movie show. All the things she *longed* to do back in Texas. All the things she *could* do, now that she was making all this money. More money than she could *think* about. More money in one week than Mr. Hardiman, the richest man in Lamson, would make in a *year*. In *ten* years.

But Sharleen couldn't go to McDonald's. Sure, she could get a twelve-dollar hamburger at one of them fancy restaurants that she'd been to since she made money. But make reservations to have a *hamburger*? And then the hassle of getting dressed up fancy and getting a limo and driver. Dean didn't like to put on a tie, and he didn't feel right in those places. And even there, in those fancy restaurants where they only have celebrities, even there she was ogled, and approached. And bothered. Mr. Ortis had said it was time to get a personal bodyguard, but Sharleen drew the line there. 'I'm not the President, Mr. Ortis. No FBI,' she had said.

But there was *nothing* like a Big Mac. So Dean would go for her, bring her one home with a vanilla shake, but it wasn't the same. It wasn't normal. She picked up another of them catalogues Mr. Ortis' secretary had sent over when Sharleen told her how she couldn't go out no more. Her money manager had told her to order whatever she wanted. *Everything* she wanted. He would tell her when she was spending over her budget. He hadn't said anything yet, and she still had stuff being delivered every day, some in boxes still unopened. Sharleen knew she had to leave for her voice lesson, but she still sat there and flipped through the glossy pages, the colour photos blurring before her eyes. Shopping from catalogues instead of in stores. Ordering food from outside to be delivered to the security guard instead of going out to dinner. Watching movies on the VCR and the thirty-five-inch Japanese TV, instead of going out to a show. It all would have sounded like heaven to her, once. But that was before she knew what fame was *really* like. Well, she better get a move on. She'd already missed ten minutes of her class.

Sharleen heard the front door slam in the distance. Slowly, she forced herself to get up and go down the hall to Dean. 'Howdy,' she said. 'What did you get for tonight?'

'*Top Gun*,' he said, 'and *Terminator 2*. It's about this guy . . .'

Sharleen sighed. 'Dean, didn't we see them before?'

'Yeah, but they're real good,' Dean said as he made his way into the TV room and opened the cabinet. 'Oh, and, yeah. I got us a paperoney pizza, just like you like it, Sharleen.'

Sharleen groaned.

'What's the matter, Sharleen?'

Dean got that worried look on his face he got whenever he thought she was unhappy. 'Nothing,' she said, with a big sigh. 'Except I'm tired. I wish I didn't have to go to voice. And then I got to go to exercise.'

'Oh, why don't you cut?' Dean asked.

'Hey, we *pay* for them classes.'

'So what?'

The idea of simply not showing up was so sweet, so irresistible to Sharleen that she smiled for the first time that day.

'I don't have to be at work until the day after tomorrow. But even if I cut, I can't go nowhere, do nothing. What could we do that's fun?' She flopped onto the long Early American sofa.

'I can show you something great,' Dean said. He whistled, and the three dogs all sat down. 'Say your prayers,' he told them, and, one by one, the dogs stood on their hind legs, crossed their paws, and put their heads down.

Sharleen had to laugh. 'How did you get 'em to do that?' she asked.

'Oh, I don't know. Jest practised them. It's not a sin, is it?'

'Surely not. It's great, Dean.' She hugged him.

'Hey, I got an idea,' Dean said, suddenly eager. 'Want to play Parcheesi? This time I'll let *you* win,' he said with a grin.

'Dean, honey,' Sharleen said, very patiently. 'I've read every magazine, seen every movie, played every game. I even went through all those new catalogues. There is nothing I want to do except get out and go for a walk. Nothing. And we both know I can't do that.'

'We could get that nice guy with the long limousine. He could drive us around awhile. How 'bout that?' he asked, hopefully.

Sharleen didn't want to upset him, and she could see she was. She forced a smile. 'No, honey, I'll be all right. Put on *Top Gun* first.'

As he popped the cassette into the VCR, the phone rang, and Dean answered. 'What?' she heard him say. Then, 'You little piece of worm dirt. If I get my hands on you, I'll cut . . .' He slammed down the phone.

'Dean, don't go getting yourself all upset. I'll just unplug all the phones tonight. Now, let's relax and enjoy ourselves, okay?'

'Sure, Sharleen,' he said, but his face was red, and his eyes had teared up. 'How come people are just so mean and dirty? I can't believe what that guy just said about you. I tell you, Sharleen, something's wrong when you can't be left alone in your own home.' He flicked the switch of the remote control, and the screen lit up. Sharleen sat down beside him and stroked his soft, white-blond hair. It was funny: she should be happy, because she had everything she'd dreamed of: a nice house, a new TV, lots of clothes, and good stuff to eat. The Lord had provided for them. She should be grateful.

Oh, Lord, Sharleen thought to herself. I should have been more careful about what I asked for. I guess I didn't really believe You'd give it to me.

6

The traffic slowed suddenly as it came around the bend of the freeway. Probably an accident, Jahne thought, as she settled into the new pace. The drivers in the cars on each side of her seemed to be straining to look ahead, but Jahne could see no obstruction. Up ahead, the four lanes of traffic were moving, no stalled or wrecked cars in any one. What the hell was the problem? She had a meeting with Sy Ortis in only half an hour, and she didn't want to be late.

Jahne followed the craning heads of the other drivers, and observed that the slowdown stretched across all eight lanes of the freeway. Then she saw it. The billboard was at least four stories high, and displayed the three women from the show, standing next to each other, elbow to elbow, hair flying, arms akimbo, legs parted in a defiant stance. Their black leather jackets were open, revealing deep cleavages; in fact, the jackets barely covered their nipples. The only words on the billboard were: 'SUNDAY NIGHT.'

Jahne pulled the Miata over to the shoulder of the road, stopping on the dry brown grass, and got out of the car. She stared at the giant figures, at the massive sign that at one time would have been considered one of the seven wonders of the world for its size alone. That's me, she thought to herself. That's Jahne Moore. Or me, Mary Jane Moran. Whoever I am. It's *me*. She wanted to say it out loud to someone, but no one was there. Just the faces in the slow-moving cars staring at the three beautiful women on the billboard. It was hard to take it in. It was hard to breathe. For a moment, she felt faint, and bent over a bit to bring the blood to her head.

She had done it. If she never did anything in her life before or after, she had, at least, accomplished this. She was there, fifty times bigger than life, over the freeway. And once a week, she was being watched by fifty million people.

Her will, her pain, her work, her courage had brought her to this. Unlike the other two girls, she'd had no natural beauty or family ties to help her. And even though it wasn't Shakespeare, even though it was only television, she had risen up out of the swamp of greyness to this.

'Miss?' a voice said behind her. She nearly jumped, then turned and saw a California Highway Patrol officer standing next to his scooter. 'Are you in trouble?'

Jahne shook her head, then began to laugh. Realizing that she must seem like a crazy person, she tried to stop. 'No,' she said. 'I'm just looking at the picture.'

'Lady,' the cop said, walking cautiously towards her. '*Everyone's* looking at the goddamn picture. You better get back in your car and get on your way. It's a little too dangerous to be standing out here.' Then he stopped, looked at her again, stared at her face, looked up at the billboard. The light dawned. 'Hey, you're the smart one!'

Jahne giggled, and nodded her head. 'I'll say,' she told him, and got back into her car.

Jesse Helms' Anti-'Three' Rally Complete Bust

Winston-Salem, North Carolina.
The much-publicized rally organized by Jesse Helms and the Christian Family Network to protest the airing of 'Three for the Road' was the biggest non-event of this senator's eventful public life of protestations against what he calls attacks on family values. The rally was scheduled for nine o'clock Sunday night, but, unfortunately for him and CFN, only a handful of his most ardent followers showed up. Helms, reached at his Washington, D.C., office today, was unable to explain the lack of numbers in support of what he calls massive resistance to the show. He wouldn't comment on this reporter's speculation that perhaps everyone stayed home to watch the show instead.

Harold from the mailroom knocked on Lila's dressing-room door, then entered when she answered. Lila was very clear about that: no one was to be in her dressing room without her, and it was kept locked at all times. 'Miss Kyle, where do you want your mail?' he asked. He wanted to get away from her as fast as possible. Everyone at the studio knew she could be dangerous, even without provocation. He was the one in the mailroom who had lost the draw, so here he was.

Lila didn't turn around to look at him. 'Where the fuck do you think I want my mail? On the desk!'

'But, Miss Kyle . . .'

Lila turned to him. 'Don't make a major production out of it. Just put the fucking mail on the fucking desk down at the end, where I told you to. And get out.'

He watched her go back to brushing her long hair, shrugged his shoulders, and stepped outside. He lifted a large mailbag from the cart, and walked back in. 'And take it out of the bag,' she yelled at him. Harold lifted the bag and dumped the contents on the desk. He went back outside, and brought the other two bags inside, emptying each on the now buried desk. Bitch wants it out of the bag, bitch goin' get it out of the bag.

He closed the door quietly after him, and had begun to push the empty mail cart back to the mailroom when he heard Lila shriek.

Then the door to her dressing room slammed open, and she stood screaming at him. 'You asshole, get back here. I didn't know there was so much. I can't even walk! Get back here and put all that mail back in the bags. Every piece, do you hear?'

Harold sighed, moved back into Lila's trailer, then began scooping up the fan mail and stuffing it back into the sacks. The bitch looked up at him.

'How many sacks did it come to?' Lila asked him.

'Seven, Miss Kyle. There's four more I couldn't fit on the handtruck.'

She paused for a moment. Then she frowned.

'How many did Smith and Moore get?' she asked.

What's On . . .

SUNDAY
8.00 p.m. – **Star Search Famous Look-Alikes**. Tonight, Ivana Trump.
9.00 p.m. – **Three for the Road**. In San Francisco Cara meets and becomes romantically involved with a Tim Leary follower. Crimson, Cara, and Clover try LSD. Cameo appearances by Leary and Donovan.

Paul Grasso leaned back in his swivel chair and stretched as he listened to the harangue coming out of the phone earpiece. Yahta, yahta, yahta. 'Mel, listen, I'm sorry, but we're booked till February. Ya wanna talk about then, maybe we could . . .' More Australian-accented yahta yahta yahta. 'Look, I understand you'll be on location then, but that's the slot we got. Everyone and their bookie wants a guest shot. No, no, Bob definitely couldn't reschedule. I mean it, man. Look, I'm sorry. Maybe first episode next year. Sure. I know it's perfect. The girl road warriors meet the original. Right. Listen, here's what I'll do: I'll talk to Marty tomorrow, and his people will call your people, all right? Maybe *they* can find a slot. Right. You, too, babe.'

Grasso hung up the phone and rubbed his eyes. He felt the stubble on his upper cheeks. Shit. He'd been out late last night,

378

at a poker game with a few buddies, and he'd woken up so late this morning he hadn't had time to shave. He reached into the side drawer of his desk and pulled out the Braun electric razor he stored there, switched it on, and began to run it over the left side of his jaw. He didn't even need to use the mirror, which was just as well, since he must look like death on a bender after nine hours at the card table. He felt the smooth side of his jaw. You had to hand it to those Nazis. They knew how to build the shit out of anything. He moved the razor to the other side of his face. Then the buzzer began again.

'Yeah?' Christ, this business would kill him. One day you can't cast a fuckin' jeans commercial, and the next day you're the gateway to the hottest show in the country. 'Whataya want, Patty?'

'It's another one.'

'I'm out,' he told her. 'You handle it.'

'I don't think so.'

'I'm *out*,' he repeated. Patty was smart – shit, she could run the fuckin' place without him – but she was sometimes a pushy bitch.

'It's Brando,' Patty said.

It was hard to hear her over the buzzing Braun. 'Brandon Tartikoff?' he asked. 'What the fuck does *he* want?'

'Not Bran*don*. Bran*do*,' Patty yelled.

'Holy shit!' Paul Grasso said. '*He* wants a cameo?'

'Apparently.'

Paul Grasso laughed and turned off the razor. 'Hey, Patty. Ya think the wild one can still ride a motorcycle?'

Jahne clutched her hands nervously behind her. The two other people in the green room – her publicist and some nerdy stand-up – stared at the screen where Arsenio was busy rapping with some black dancer. Jahne wished she hadn't agreed to do this. She was an actress, not a personality. This was the kind of stuff Neil used to want to do. How would he handle it? The butterflies in her stomach were as large as barn swallows. Then the assistant producer was there, leading her through the dark hall and leaving her to enter into the glaring light. Arsenio, now in person, stood up and extended his hand. She took it, smiled, and sat down. The chat began.

'So, are you as political in life as you are on the show, Jahne?'

'Not really.' She knew she should say more, sparkle, be funny or sexy or something, but she was only an actress, and she had no lines.

'So, you've got no position on stuff.'

'Well, women's rights . . .'

'Like abortion?'

'Yeah. I feel strongly that no women should be given abortions.' She felt Arsenio stiffen, and heard a hiss from the audience. 'Unless, of course, they're pregnant,' she finished, and after a beat she got her big laugh. Thank you, Neil Morelli, she thought, and the interview continued, smooth as silk.

What's On . . .

SUNDAY

8.00 p.m. – **Star Search Famous Look-Alikes**. Tonight, Larry Fortensky.

9.00 p.m. – **Three for the Road**. Crimson and Clover and Cara go to Woodstock, N.Y., for the concert. Bob Dylan and Neil Young guest star.

It was her day off, and Jahne was exhausted. Who'd ever imagine that success could be so tiring? Already Sy had let her know that movie offers were pouring in – they were mostly jiggle-in-leather scripts, but better things would surely follow. The Arsenio gig had gone surprisingly well; after her initial stage fright, she'd loosened up and been tough and funny. Now Sy was pushing more appearances. She stared at the pile of movie treatments, her next week's scripts, memos and pictures to autograph, and sighed. No, today she would simply rest. She'd bought an Anne Tyler book, and she'd stretch out by the pool, ready to enjoy it. But first she picked up the copy of *Vogue*. It opened to the two-page spread of the three of them. Gorgeous black and white photos. They all looked beautiful. Only the three of them knew the hours and hours they'd spent under the hot lights to get that perfection, dozens of specialists huddling over them constantly to create the illusion of perfection. But my, she looked fabulous. She stared and stared.

Dr. Moore had warned her about the sun, so she was prepared. 'Sun is bad for everyone, but it would be murder on you,' he had reminded her in his last letter. 'I've been able to get such good results because you never tanned, so your skin, despite ageing, has retained a lot of its flexibility. But in the future, no sun – ever.' She'd laughed, and written him back to say he made her sound like a vampire, and that the only reason she hadn't tanned before was that she could never afford to go away to a beach. Now she had her own private lap pool. But she'd rubbed SPF number fifteen all over herself half an hour ago, she'd poured half a jar of conditioner on her hair, swathed it in a towel, and was wearing huge sunglasses. To stay cool, she had a long, white cotton robe, a wonderful, fine Egyptian cotton, smoother than silk. And the houseman had fixed her a pitcher of iced tea. Now, for the very first time, she was going to spend the whole morning just quietly enjoying the warmth, the pool, the vista. Then, later, she'd do her laps, work out with her trainer and, at two, a masseuse that Mai had recommended was coming over to work on her back and legs. Jahne stretched out luxuriously, opened to the first page of *Saint Maybe*, and took a deep breath.

She heard it before she saw it. There was a grinding of gears out front that sounded as if an eighteen-wheeler was making it up the hill in front of the house, and then a loud radio or something. Did politicians drive around the Swish Alps making announcements? Then she heard it more clearly.

'. . . ACTUAL PRIVATE HOME OF JAHNE MOORE, BETTER KNOWN AS "CARA" IN *THREE FOR THE ROAD*. THE ACTRESS LIVES HERE ALONE IN A TWO-BEDROOM BUNGALOW COMPLETE WITH POOL AND POOL HOUSE. SHE MAY EVEN BE AT HOME RIGHT NOW.'

Jahne jumped up, her heart pounding, and turned. She could glimpse the top of the smoked windows of the bus from where she stood. Did that mean they could see her? She scuttled closer to the fence and peeped through a crack in the weathered grey boards. 'See the Stars' was painted in rainbow colours across the side of the bus. 'Tours of the Hollywood Homes of Your Favourite TV and Movie Stars,' it said on a raised panel along the roofline.

Not sure whether she wanted to laugh or cry, Jahne turned and walked, quickly as she could, back into the house, leaving her book unread and the tea untouched beside it.

FLANDERS COSMETICS
GO THROUGH ROOF

In perhaps the most successful launch in the industry, Flanders
Cosmetics has pulled off a coup historic both in conception and
implementation. Tying in their new integrated line of treatment
and makeup products with the hot new *Three for the Road* TV
show has been a masterful stroke of market savvy and just plain
hard work.

'I envisioned it and I made it happen,' says Monica Flanders.
Banion O'Malley, the agency that handled the project, echoes
her . . .

'T-shirts only, Phil. We're doing a separate deal on posters and
the rest.' Sy looked across at the man who had waited three weeks
for an appointment with him.

'Sy, please, this is just the tip of the fuckin' iceberg. . . . Sorry,
Miss Smith. But, listen, you give us the T-shirts *and* the posters,
and we'll keep our profit to five per cent an item. What do you
say?' He was begging Sy, but looking at Sharleen.

Sy was shaking his head. 'We got the posters lined up already,
Phil. I could have the T-shirts done by the same guys, but I wanted
to give you a break, you know, a piece of what's happening. I
don't forget my friends, but don't go greedy on me. T-shirts, that's
it. And you still keep your share of the net only to five per cent.'
Sy waited for Phil to respond; then, when he nodded his head yes,
Sy signed the sheaf of papers and passed them to Sharleen. After
she scrawled her signature, he handed them to Phil. 'Have my
girl make copies of these on your way out.'

When the door closed behind Phil, Sharleen finally spoke. 'Only
five per cent? How's the poor man going to make any money?'

Sy grinned. 'At five per cent, honey, the guy's going to be
able to retire. Do you know how many of those T-shirts we're
going to sell? Over five million the first month on sale. *Five
million T-shirts!* He'll make six figures the first month alone.'

Sharleen shook her head, as if trying to understand. 'And we
get money on each shirt?'

Sy nodded, waiting to see if Sharleen would calculate her share.
But she didn't. Sy almost laughed. This hillbilly was a pleasure. It
was such a nice change to meet a beautiful woman who didn't have
a computer for a heart. It made running his bodega so much easier.

'That's right, honey. And we haven't even figured in the posters, stationery, line of clothes, endorsements, pens, leather jackets, shoulder bags, lunch boxes. . . . Honey, we're talking millions here. Millions.'

'Millions? For just my picture on things? Mr. Ortis, are you *sure* you got this right?'

Sy laughed. 'Sharleen, about this stuff I don't make a mistake. I said millions, and I mean millions.'

What's On . . .

SUNDAY
8.00 p.m. – **Star Search Famous Look-Alikes**. Tonight, Milli Vanilli.
9.00 p.m. – **Three for the Road**. Clover meets the Merry Pranksters and she, Cara, and Crimson 'get on the bus' and tour San Francisco. Michelle Pfeiffer and Marlon Brando guest star.

THE MEDIA . . .

A three-character nostalgic TV series is hardly a phenomenon in these times of imitation and reproduction.

But this season's 'Three for the Road' – yes, another three-character nostalgic TV show – is special. Directed by film great Marty DiGennaro ('A Woman Matters,' 'Back Streets,' 'Trouble in the Tower'), the heir-apparent to George Cukor as a woman's director, the show has captured the style and the angst of the nineties, while delving into the fun and psychic scars of the sixties at the same time. DiGennaro, the Sultan of Style, has given us more form than function, but what forms! The three co-stars – Sharleen Smith, Jahne Moore and Lila Kyle (SEE: Personalities, this issue) – popped up out of nowhere, and, under DiGennaro's aegis, have developed into the personification of all that was good and beautiful in America. Great? Far from it. But a phenomenon in the impact it has made on the psyche of the television viewing public (now greatly expanded because of this show). Quirkier than 'Northern Exposure,' more stylish than David Lynch at his weirdest, hotter than 'Miami Vice' ever was, 'Three for the Road' has got legs – six of them. At a cost of more than a million dollars an episode, the shows are a pastiche of actual archive clips, new footage, and special effects. Like a gripping miniseries, the show has garnered a weekly audience that few specials can boast – and it goes on, week after week. While some critics carp that it trivializes it's time – one asked what it would do next? Have Cara date Martin Luther King – its popularity has revived the lagging Network.

Without question, the repercussions of this programme, not only on future programming, but also on how television programming is conceived, will be felt at studio city in the very highest echelons in the lofty aeries of Executiveville.

Time magazine

MEMORANDUM

TO: Ara Sagarian
FROM: Lila Kyle
SUBJECT: See Attached

Ara, what the fuck is going on? I got this fan letter and, as you can see, Sharleen Smith and Jahne Moore fans are getting silk-screened T-shirts. All Sy Ortis' work, apparently. I thought you had it all worked out with the Network? Are your people in Publicity on the same planet?

I don't want to have to go directly to Selma Gold on this myself. So, Ara, get them shaped up! I'm busting my ass here day after day, and then I find out Publicity is playing favourites. I want to get shirts, signed pictures, pins, medals, membership kits – the whole works. Have Gold put this on the priority list. She's as important to me as the fucking assholes at *Time* magazine.

Do I have to think of everything? Stay on top of this, Ara. Sy Ortis is fucking you over – and me. What's he got going with Gold? Get back to me.

L.K.

Jahne was standing on the express checkout line at Mrs. Gooches, where celebrities did their fancy grocery shopping. The place was fabulous: all the fruit and vegetables were displayed like jewels and cost almost as much. She had a wig pulled down low over her forehead, and a large straw hat sitting on top of it. She wore an old, thin trench coat, although it was hot out, and a pair of tattered Reeboks. She felt like an escapee from someplace, incognito, taking a chance on getting mobbed because it was better than hiding behind locked doors another minute. It would have made her smile, but she didn't want to attract any unnecessary attention to herself. Going to the market had suddenly become a daring treat.

She placed her basket on the edge of the counter, waiting her turn at the cashier. The magazines were screaming her name and her face at her. She picked up the first one at hand. 'Three Beauty Secrets from Three Beauties,' read the blurb on the front cover. Jahne flipped through the pages until she came to the article. 'Jahne Moore, the brunette star of "Three for the Road," uses only ...' Yeah, she thought. She uses only the finest plastic surgeon. So much bullshit. She was replacing the magazine on the rack when the woman behind her spoke up.

'Can you believe those three?' she said, indicating the picture of the costars of *Three for the Road* on one of the magazine covers.

Jahne smiled and nodded.

'They really piss me off, you know? How are any of us supposed to get to look like them? I mean, what am I supposed to do? You think eating carrots and doing fifty thousand sit-ups will make a goddamn bit of difference? Look, I always say, if God didn't give it to you, you can't get it. So I make do.'

Jahne's turn at the register came up just then. 'I know what you mean,' she said, as she picked up the brown bag and walked out the door.

TO: Sharleen Smith and Jahne Moore
FROM: Sy Ortis
SUBJECT: Sports Illustrated write-up, attached

Have you seen this?

Just received a call from Bill Gottlieb from *Sports Illustrated*. How about doing their annual Bathing Suit issue? Have already discussed this with Marty and he's all for it.

Let's talk.

S.O.

LILA KYLE

YOU ARE MERELY A PRODUCT OF HOLLYWOOD NEPOTISM. I WOULDN'T FUCK YOU WITH SOMEONE ELSE'S DICK.
    JUGHEAD
    President
    National Anti-Nepotism League

Marty DiGennaro's secretary, Staci, opened the door and rolled her eyes. 'Unbelievable!' she said. 'If this shit keeps up, I quit!'

Marty looked up from his messy desk. 'What? Come in. Sit down. I'll get you some coffee. What is it?'

'What is it? They're driving me nuts. Every asshole in Hollywood – no, in California – no, maybe in the whole *country* – is trying to bullshit me to get to you. The girls are going crazy. Just this morning, we had three calls from your "brothers," a call from your "doctor" about the "test results," a hysterical call from "Joanie" about your son. . . .'

'Is anything wrong with Sacha?'

'Yeah, he's got a madman for a daddy. They weren't your brother, your doctor, or Joanie. They were assholes. And gifts – how about a diamond-and-gold Rolex that's already engraved "To my friend Marty from his friend Larry."?'

'Who's Larry?'

'Another asshole. Some producer out in East Bumfuck who

wants to talk to you about a movie deal. He needs two of the three girls, but he writes, and I quote, "I don't care which two, and if you prefer we can cut the lesbian scenes with the full frontal nudity." He enclosed the screenplay from hell.'

Marty laughed. 'Come on, Staci. This isn't the first hit you've been through with me. You sound like a kid out of Katie Gibbs. You've handled worse.'

'Yeah, but not for so long. I mean, *week* after *week* after *week*. A movie comes out, it hits, we react, then it's over. This is relentless. Marty, you never heard me complain before, right? Well, I'm exhausted. I don't know if I can keep up with you on this one.' Staci sat back, her fatigue showing in the dark shadows around her eyes.

'Okay, get yourself a secretary.'

'But *I'm* a secretary.'

'Not anymore. You are now my executive assistant. With a raise. So hire yourself a secretary – right away – give her a week's training, then take a week off at the Hotel del Mar in San Diego. My treat.' Marty smiled at the surprise on Staci's face. 'Then get back here rested up and get back to work.'

'Marty, thanks. Hey, I didn't mean it seriously. I just like to bitch. I don't know. . . . I wasn't coming in here to hold you up. . . . I just wanted to get this stuff off my . . . Thanks, Marty.' She leaned over the desk and kissed him on the forehead. 'But what about you? You need a rest, too. To get away.'

'Get away? I've worked all my life to get *here*. And I'm staying for as long as I can.'

What's On. . .

SUNDAY
8.00 p.m. – **Star Search Famous Look-Alikes**. Tonight, Shirley MacLaine.
9.00 p.m. – **Three for the Road.** Cara helps an old boyfriend avoid the draft. Crimson and Clover stage a diversion and he escapes to Canada. Ricky Dunn guest stars.

'Sickos,' 'Beggars,' 'Negative,' and 'Real Fans.' The signs were lettered over the empty boxes, and Lila was explaining how she wanted her fan mail stacked each day to the secretary and clerk she had hired for the job. Lila knew from her mother that fan mail was an important indicator of how marketable one was. 'The sick shit I want delivered to the head of studio security every day. Keep a record of names, addresses, and phone numbers that are on any of them, but usually they write anonymously. Staple the envelope they came in to the letter, in case there's someone who's scary enough to have to track down.' The secretary, Myra, an older black woman, nodded. She'd been through most of this bullshit before.

'Beggars are sent my picture, the standard sympathy bullshit letter, plus a list of charitable resources they can write to. I'm not the fucking Red Cross.' Lila twisted a lipstick up out of the tube and smoothed it over her pouty lips. The secretary noticed it was MAC, not the Flanders brand.

Lila continued. 'Now, never show me the negative mail, but keep it in case I might want to go through it one day. The positive stuff – the stuff that seems to be coming from real fans – I want to see every one of them. Every one. Do you have that, now?' she asked.

Myra nodded. Poor sick bitch didn't have much of a home life if she cared about this.

7

Jahne was still surprised by how much she liked L.A. Back on the East Coast, Sam and her New York friends had always spoken about it with derision, contempt, and bitterness. But it *was* pretty. And it was easy. So much easier than New York. What had Bertolucci called it? 'The big nipple.' Yes. In some ways, it was as easy as that.

Jahne loved the little house she'd rented in the Hollywood Hills; it was only two tiny bedrooms and a big living room, but it had a deck with a view and the small lap pool. It even came complete with a part-time houseboy, and oranges on the orange trees!

Of course, at first Jahne had had to adjust. Being alone in a house was so different from being stuck in a dark fourth-floor walk-up on Fifty-fourth Street. Not that she got to spend much time here: with work and the dozens of business appointments, her hairdressing, facials and manicures, costume fittings, and the Flanders Cosmetics photo sessions, she wasn't home much. But when she was, the hours felt lonely. So Jahne got a cat — a sweet black Persian. In a typical burst of perversity, she named him Snowball, in honour of the cat she'd had as a girl in Scuderstown, and thought also of poor Midnight, her white cat left back in New York.

She thought of Midnight, and a lot more from her past. In fact, since she'd seen Sam at the Chasen's look-see, she couldn't seem to stop thinking of all her friends back home. She hoped that they, like Midnight, would get what they needed. What would they say if they could see her now? A TV star, with a great place to live, money in the bank, and an affair with Michael McLain.

It still amazed her that a star as big as he was interested in her. He had been so kind about the scars. He listened to her problems on the set, gave good advice, and even ran lines with her. If his performance in bed seemed a little bit — well — like a performance, she guessed it was a small price to pay. He was good company, and a wonderful listener.

But she still missed her old friends. She had never thought it was a mistake back then simply to drop out of their lives: not when she was so miserably a failure. Even now, she could easily conjure up Molly's look of pity for her and feel almost physically sick. She'd gotten so tired of the role of fat, plain, goodhearted, and pitiable Mary Jane that she didn't, couldn't, have anything to do with those who'd known her and expected her to play that role.

And now, even if she wanted to, it would be more than a little awkward to call up Molly or Chuck or Neil or any of them and say, 'Hi! Sorry I disappeared like that, but now I'm famous, beautiful, and rich. I got my own TV show. How *you* doing?'

With her cute house, her new face, her perfect body, her cute kitten, her new romance, and a career that was taking off, Jahne figured she had nothing to complain about. If it was a bit shallow, so be it. She had her weekly letters to Dr. Moore, working now in a plastic-surgery mobile camp in Honduras somewhere. It was ironic that her best friend, the only person who knew her, was in another world. But he had taken the time last week to write her a long letter.

Somehow, though, none of it was enough to banish thoughts of the past. Thoughts of Sam.

She knew that the answer was to make new friends. But it was harder than she'd expected. Perhaps she could build some sort of relationship with Sharleen. And she *was* becoming friends with Mai. The rest would just take time. Slowly, she knew, her world would expand, and as she met more people, tested their loyalty, she would build a new community. Transitions were hard, she reminded herself, and thought of nursing school, of her first auditions, of the New York cattle calls, her first summer-stock job. She'd been alone then, and it was only natural to be alone now.

But since she'd seen Sam, something had changed. The loneliness she'd tried to assuage first with Pete and now with Michael seemed to grow: it was palpable, a real feeling in her chest. During the day, the busy, frenzied workday, she was all right, but in the evenings she found herself reliving those moments with Sam at the party and the lunch at Chasen's, trying to read their meaning.

He had seen her but not known her. In a way, it was a graduation: her transformation was complete. She was the consummate actress. If no one knew, it should be enough that she did. And now she should forget him. But the feeling of his hand against hers, or their brief conversation on April's terrace, came back to her again and again.

She was proud of her performances: *I* walked away from *him*, she told herself. I haven't called them back about the audition. But she thought of his after-shave, and the warm scent of his breath. 'That way madness lies,' she murmured, and tried not to remember how he had looked at her, the approval in his eyes as he had complimented her hair, her dress. Twice since then, she had slipped into it again and stared at herself in the mirror, looked at what he had looked at. He had flirted with her. He had been attracted to her, had singled her out. Could she work with him? What would she do if he ever called her about the film? What would she do if he asked her out?

Maybe I could see him, she thought. Maybe I could try to make him love me, and then leave him. The ultimate revenge. She almost smiled, then shook her head. She had schooled herself to play the *belle dame sans merci*, the *femme fatale*, but could she really do it? Could she be the victimizer, not the victim? What would it be like to make him want her, love her, and then reject him? Sam deserved it, but could she trust herself to stay uninvolved? Perhaps the worst part of all this was how guilty it made her feel about Michael. Here she was, thinking about Sam, and she had a date with Michael McLain tonight! He was kind to her, but she knew she was using him. I'm acting the way men do! she thought. They are the ones who sleep with a substitute when they can't get the real thing. Oh, she was confused, but she had to admit it was a heady, exciting confusion.

Right now, however, there was no time for it. She sat, her legs up on the low deck railing, and waited for Laura Richie. She was going to be interviewed! And not just for a silly squib in *TV Guide*, but for a *Vanity Fair* cover story. Me and Demi Moore, she grinned to herself. And I'm not pregnant or naked. Of course, it made her nervous, even though she had been interviewed alone before.

How the interview with Laura Richie would go was anyone's guess, but the one thing Jahne *did* know was that she was not going be so relaxed with Laura. Richie had a reputation for both looking for the dirt and then getting you to spill it. On her televised interviews, she pushed and probed for the soft white underbelly. It was said that she hated to air one if the subject didn't cry. Jahne knew it was a fine line she was going to have to walk today: to seem open and interesting enough to keep Richie interested, yet not so stupid as to let her catch wind of what the story *really* was.

Network Publicity had offered to have a representative present, to field those questions that interviewers had the habit of dropping like bombs. But Jahne had decided that one-to-one was better. She didn't want to have to divide her attention.

And Publicity did tell her a little about Laura Richie. Not enough for Jahne to feel completely comfortable, but enough for her to know that Laura could be a tricky interviewer. So ground rules were set. The focus of the interview was *Three for the Road*, not just Jahne Moore, so that would keep some of the pressure off Jahne.

She'd decided that limited truth was the best approach. Small-town life. Upstate New York. Keep the dates blurry. Year of the Dog. If pushed, she'd tell about the car accident, though she could barely remember it. And she'd say both parents had died. She'd play the orphan; God knows she had always felt like one. She closed her eyes for a moment, visualizing the role she was about to play, as she often did before going out onstage or before the camera. 'Hi, I'm Jahne Moore,' she said to herself, and waited while the words sunk in.

When she opened her eyes, a car was pulling into her driveway. Jahne got up and walked through the house to the front door, and had it open before Laura Richie reached the top step. 'Hi,' she said. 'I'm Jahne Moore.'

That was the first time I met Jahne Moore. I stood outside the door of that little tarted-up bungalow in Birdland and I wondered how long it would take her to move to Laurel Canyon. She opened the door herself, dressed in white slacks and a deep-blue silk T-shirt. She invited me in, took me through to the kitchen, and indicated a stool at the breakfast counter. She poured the coffee and took out a tray of finger sandwiches the Network caterer had probably dropped off that morning, along with a small selection of petits fours. Of course, now I'd like to say that somehow I knew I was on the edge of the showbiz scoop of the decade, but it wouldn't be true. To me, this was just a routine profile, and I hoped it wouldn't take too long. I mean, how interesting can a twenty-four-year-old TV star be?

As Marty DiGennaro might have said: 'Go know.'

'So you cook,' I commented, watching Jahne move gracefully around the kitchen. If she lied straight off about making the sandwiches, I would know where I stood.

Jahne paused, and tried to figure out if I was making a joke or not.
She laughed. 'No, I just heat, or reheat. I used to cook a lot, but now,
with my schedule . . .' She let her explanation trail off.

Well, she passed the first test. 'What a lovely little house, Miss Moore.'
I like to start off formal, see if they want the 'Miss' stuff, see what they
call me. Hollywood is an informal town, but it's best to know your place
before someone puts you in it.

'Please, just "Jahne." If I can call you "Laura."' Well, she passed
the second test. She seemed like a nice kid. 'I like the house a lot,' she
agreed. 'It's just the right size, too. Manageable.' Jahne picked up the tray
of coffee and snacks and started to walk to the living room. 'Would inside
be okay?' she asked. 'I'm still not used to so much sun all the time.' That
was certainly true. Her skin was pale. She took me into the living room.
It was furnished charmingly – big Mickey Mouse armchairs in old faded
florals, a few cute chotchkes here and there. Jahne had the white drapes
drawn, softening the light. Maybe so I couldn't examine her too closely?
But I didn't note it at the time.

I sat on the sofa and peered around the room. 'You've done quite
a lot in such a short time. I take it you did it yourself?'

'Well, it's only a furnished rental. But some things I already had.
And I've picked up some others since I came here. Somehow, it all feels
like home to me.'

I shook my head. 'I don't know. I see something in the store, I think
it's pretty, I bring it home. I stare at it for a few days, then wonder where
I got my taste. It always looks like shit, and never feels comfortable. I've
got to get some professional help. You're very lucky. You have a wonderful
touch.'

Jahne looked over at me and shrugged. I liked her. She looked
like she didn't bullshit anyone, herself included. Go know.

'That's a gorgeous suit, Laura. At least you have good taste in
clothes. I hate to shop, and I never shop for clothes alone.'

I sat forward, ignoring the compliment. After all, we weren't there
to talk about me, and the suit ought to be nice – twenty-six hundred
bucks at Escada bought nice. 'Can we consider this the beginning of the
interview?' I asked. 'That's something I know readers are interested in.
How you choose your clothes, how your house is decorated. All that good
stuff. Have you ever been interviewed before?' I took a small black cassette
recorder out of my bag and set it on the table between us, clicking it on.

'I'm going to consider this interview with you to be my first real
interview. You certainly must have some clout if you were able to be
the first person to interview all three of us.'

'Nah, it's not clout, honey, it's persistence. Keep your finger on the doorbell, I always say. Like a vacuum-cleaner salesman. Pretty soon, someone will open the door just to get you to go away.' I put down my coffee cup on the table in front of her, picked up my notebook, and opened to a clean page. 'So just a little background. How did you get to where you are today?' Sometimes that corny question is all I have to ask to keep them going for hours. All actors are narcissists.

But Jahne just shrugged. 'I've been asking myself the same question. At first I told myself it was talent – that always surfaces, like cream rising to the top. Then I thought, my looks didn't hurt. Then, well, I figured it was my time. Now' – she shrugged again – 'all I can say is, it's a confluence of influences. Nothing more.'

'That's very grounded of you, Jahne. But certainly your time practising your craft paid off. You were discovered at the Melrose Playhouse, weren't you? Tell me how you got that part.'

Jahne laughed and started talking. The usual kid-comes-to-L.A.-scrabbles-around-for-work-and-gets-lucky saga.

I asked a little about her background. I've gone over the tape now a dozen times, but there really wasn't any clue that what she seemed was not what she was. Except perhaps for the momentary pause that stretched out when I asked her if she'd always been so pretty. Now it seems to me her voice was strained when she asked, 'What do you mean?' but I didn't notice it then.

'Were you an ugly duckling? Did you go through a rough adolescence? Or were you always a prom queen?' I asked. It's a funny thing. Almost every beauty I've ever interviewed likes to tell me how plain she was as a kid. Like they feel guilty about their looks. And a lot of them try to tell me how they're not really pretty now.

But Jahne just laughed. It was a bit more sustained than the question warranted. 'I guess I was always nice-looking,' was all she said.

'Any men in your life?' I made sure that that came out of nowhere. Inevitable, but sudden. Sometimes it surprises them into honesty. And I'd heard a rumour about her and a certain much older Lothario-about-town. Plus, I'd seen her talking to Michael at Ara's party. But she was cool. 'Not at the moment, but in the past, and, hopefully, in the future. Right now all I can do is work and sleep. I'm in love with my job.'

Just before I got up to leave, I turned to her and said, 'You're remarkably mature for someone so young. I wish I had been as smart as you at your age. Good luck, Jahne.' I leaned forward and kissed her lightly on the cheek. 'Don't take any wooden condoms,' I told her, and waved goodbye.

Out on the street, I threw my notebook onto the car seat. A pretty girl who got lucky. A real dull but pleasant enough interview. Nothing new there.

So much for Laura Richie's nose for news, right?

Jahne needed a little time to get herself together after the interview. The woman had eyes like gimlets, she thought. And that question had, unexpectedly, completely unnerved her. *Had she always been so pretty?* Jahne didn't know if she should laugh or cry.

She bathed and laid out her clothes for the evening: her first public Hollywood date. Her first date as a celebrity.

Celebrity was like a club, Jahne was finding out. And if there was someone else in the club you wanted to meet, you only had to ask another member. That's how Sam Shields and Michael McLain got Jahne's telephone number. She was now a member of that club.

She'd probably agreed to go public out of guilt. At first she and Michael had agreed to keep the thing private, but what was there to hide? If Michael was going to use her for publicity, she'd benefit, too. After all, wasn't she using Michael to try and keep her growing obsession with Sam under control? She liked Michael, but he was no Einstein. Still, she enjoyed his company.

And she had to admit, tonight would be a kind of threshold, another peak she had reached. There was a certain thrill that she – plain Mary Jane Moran – was now one of the starlets she used to read about. Michael McLain, whose performances in movies had been lacklustre for the last decade, seemed always able to sweep down on the latest really hot starlet and score. It made her a little uncomfortable that she'd once mocked those starlets. Now it seemed different. Now she could empathize with them. Because, for her, dating Michael McLain was really a rite of passage, an announcement that she, too, had arrived. If it helped her career, she couldn't afford to ignore that possibility.

Earlier that day, the doorbell had rung, and Jahne had found herself facing a tall bunch of flowers hiding a short delivery man. 'For Ms. Jahne Moore,' he said, and grinned at her in recognition as she handed him a twenty. When you were a celebrity, you had to tip generously, Sy had cautioned. The flowers were roses, three dozen of the palest-pink roses Jahne had ever seen. The card said, 'Your beauty makes white roses blush. Michael.' It was the corniest shit she had ever heard, but the roses *were* breathtaking. And it was sweet of him.

Now she lifted the flowers in their vase and held them in front of her like a Miss America Pageant winner, while watching herself in the full-length dressing mirror. She was wearing a simple A-line dress that Mai had sewn. The underlayer was black silk jersey, overlaid with sheer blue organza. Another Mai masterpiece of simplicity. Jahne pressed her face into the abundant blossoms and took a long, heady whiff of the bouquet. She now understood what the word 'swoon' meant. It was hard to believe her life was real, and not some silly Danielle Steel novel being televised. There was only one person she could share her feelings about this moment with, who would understand. She *must* write to Dr. Moore, first thing in the morning.

Michael picked her up himself. No limo. That was nice. Just the two of them in that luxurious Rolls. The interior was like a leather-lined velvet jewel case. It made her feel pampered, as if she herself were a jewel. And when they arrived at the restaurant, Jahne was delighted Michael had been so original in his choice. She had assumed that they would be going to one of the big name spots, and had dressed accordingly. But this elegant little Thai restaurant was perfect for the occasion. It was furnished with rattan, and there must have been three hundred pots of orchids, all as purple as the walls. As if reading her mind, Michael spoke.

'Every Thai place I've ever been to is painted this colour. I think it's a patriotic thing,' he said. 'But I wouldn't have taken you here if your outfit clashed with the decor.' Jahne smiled.

'It was nice of you to send me the flowers,' she said. 'I really appreciated it.'

'My pleasure. Wasn't it nice of Sy to set us up? Sy rarely has such pleasant suggestions. Sy and a lot of people don't really get along.'

'Really? Like who?'

'Oh, like April Irons. She doesn't like him.'

'Neither do I.'

Michael laughed. 'A point in your favour,' he said.

'I don't know what to order. It all sounds great. I'm torn between the red curry or the noodles in peanut sauce.'

'Don't tell me you need a Thai breaker,' he said and she groaned at the pun.

The meal was excellent. And Michael couldn't have been more gentlemanly. After their arrival, Jahne had felt herself begin to relax. It was the first time she'd been out, doing something normal, in months. She began to talk to him about work, as she always did. In fact, he almost seemed more interested in her work and her career than in her body.

'What are you going to do when the season ends?' he asked her.

'I was thinking about taking a part in a movie during the hiatus.'

'Good idea. Can you fit it in?'

She nodded. She felt too guilty to mention Sam or *Birth of a Star*. 'Of course, I have the Flanders cosmetics commitment. God, I hate doing that stuff. I never meant to be a model.'

'Good exposure. I saw them in *Vogue* and *Harpers*. They're very classy.'

'Oh, they're just ads. I hate them. It's degrading. Don't you think?'

'It is for an artist,' Michael said.

Jahne smiled, pleased that he took her seriously, and as she did she realized she could sit here talking with Michael for three more hours but there was nothing more she could manage to eat. And three cups of tea were more than enough to counter the effects of the champagne the very grateful owners presented to them with their meal. Jahne was impressed that Michael paid the bill, instead of pulling the bit that she had heard so many of the other actors did: 'My presence alone pays for the meal. Here's an autographed photo, signed "to my dear friends at Siam House."' He paid in cash, she noticed. *And* left a huge tip for the waitress. Jahne was having such a good time that she didn't want the evening to end. So what if paparazzi photographed them leaving the place? She hoped they would make the papers. She was delighted when Michael suggested they go on to a club. 'It's a real dive,' he explained, 'but lately it's become hip to be seen at the late show. Guaranteed to show in Army Archerd's column. We'll see some of my friends there.'

There was a huge crowd outside the place, but after the paparazzi had again blinded them with strobes, the doorman waved Michael and Jahne through. Some of the women in the line started calling Michael's name, but Jahne was surprised to see that people also paid as much attention to her as to Michael. Once inside, she saw that the club was bigger than she'd expected, and it looked as if every table was taken. The maître d' led them to the front of the room, however, and a small table with chairs seemed to appear out of thin air, and was placed in front of the tiny stage for them.

'Kevin Lear's here,' Michael said, after he waved to the handsome actor across the room. 'He's with his latest fiancée, Phoebe Van Gelder.'

'And Crystal Plenum is also right up front,' Jahne said, nodding her head in the actress's direction. Her stomach did a little dance as she saw the woman who had played Jill.

'Do you know them? Want me to introduce you?'

Jahne shook her head no casually, making an effort not to show discomfort. She wouldn't mind meeting Kevin Lear, but she definitely *did not* want to meet Crystal Plenum. I have a successful career of my own, she reminded herself, but she still felt cheated.

'This club is the lowest rung on the comedy-club-circuit ladder,' Michael was explaining to Jahne. 'Only the really new kids work here. The ones without any following, no experience. After a while, they get to work other clubs, but here they have to be willing to work as waiters, too, and in return, they can get the mike two or three times during the night. I like to look in here a couple of times a month. Usually the routines aren't very good, and I've seen people booed right off the stage. But every now and then, you find a real comer. There's a crazy guy who does a real mean monologue. Mean, but funny.'

Jahne had been through it all dozens of times, back in New York with Neil. She just smiled, and sat through two painfully unfunny routines, noticing that it was getting late. Talking with Michael had been fun, but just sitting through this was hardly bearable. The audience seemed to be there as much for the comics' humiliation as for entertainment. Perhaps that *was* the entertainment. These guys were so bad, she ached for them.

Once again, Michael seemed perfectly attuned to her mood. 'There's one more scheduled; then we can go. He's the one people are talking about, the one I brought you to see.'

The emcee – one of the waiters, actually – came up to the stage to announce the next performer. Even though the emcee must have said his name, it wasn't until Jahne saw him bounding across the floor and jumping up on the stage that it hit her.

Neil. Neil Morelli! Jahne tried to make sense of it, but Neil was already beginning his routine. Oh, my God! Neil in a bottom-of-the-food-chain L.A. club like this! And as a waiter! A waiter who has to wait until the last spot to get up and perform. Yet, despite her horror, she began to tune in to his routine.

Neil was already talking, his delivery even faster, if possible, than it had been back in New York. 'A couple of celebrities here tonight.' Neil cupped his hand over his eyes and squinted out into the darkness. 'Kevin Lear, ladies and gentlemen. I've had the pleasure of waiting on him this evening. Thanks for the buck, Kevin. Now, if my mother lived in L.A., I could afford to call her.'

The audience laughed, but Jahne felt frozen. Neil looked around the room, then stopped suddenly, as if overcome with surprise. 'Oh, my God, it's Michael McLain. And – get this – he's with a starlet! That's right, who would ever believe it? He's here with the costar of *Three for the Road*, Jahne Moore.' Jahne wasn't prepared, in her shock at finding Neil in this place, to be identified as Jahne Moore. It took her a couple of seconds and a tug from Michael to stand up; then she quickly sank back into her seat, her legs shaking. 'Everyone knows about Michael's interest in riding. Motorcycles, that is.' Mild titters from the audience. Jahne felt numb. Neil working the audience? Stupid smutty jokes? It wasn't his style.

'Okay, did I miss anyone?' Neil paused. 'Any Fondas here? No? How about any Coppolas? *They're* everywhere. Are you sure? Look around you, folks. Be very sure, because I have something very important to say, but first I have to be certain these people are not here.' He was almost whispering into the mike, his voice urgent.

'Any Carradines? Bridgeses? Arnazes? Okay, lastly, is Tori Spelling in the audience?' When no one responded, Neil began to speak in a different tone, slightly louder but more conspiratorial. 'Someone watch the door and let me know if any of those people come in.' Neil looked around the room for a few minutes, then let his eyes stop at Jahne. He looked thinner than ever – gaunt, almost – and his eyes had a paranoid gleam.

'Miss Moore, forgive me, but what did your father do?'

Jahne felt her skin turn to ice. 'My father worked for the government.'

'A diplomat?'

'No, a mailman,' she lied.

Neil laughed at that. 'Just wanted to make sure. Not like your costar, Lila Kyle, right? *Her* mother is Theresa O'Donnell, and *her* father was Kerry Kyle. Now, tell me, Miss Moore, exactly how hard did Lila Kyle have to work to get her part? Did she have to work as hard as you? Do you suppose the fact that your father was a mailman, and Lila's father was a swashbuckling matinee idol, made any difference to the producers of your show? No, no, don't answer, I don't mean to put you on the spot.' Neil started working the other side of the room. 'Oh, coincidentally, Lila Kyle went to the Westlake School with Tori Spelling. About a hundred in the entire student body. Let's see,' Neil said, pretending he was trying to figure something out. 'In my high school, Evander Childs back in the Bronx, there were four hundred graduates my year, and not one, *not one*, got on a major television show. Isn't that hard to believe? What a bunch of losers, huh? And Westlake produces *two*. Must have a great curriculum, huh? Plus, it don't hurt that all the girls' mummies and daddies own the Industry,' Neil said, and shook his head. There was some laughter. 'You see, folks, it's becoming clearer every day that the only way to make it in this business is to be a member of a show-business family, a dynasty.' He looked wild; nasty and bitter and intense. He went through the old New York routine Jahne had heard, but there was more. And it was all meaner.

Jahne couldn't take her eyes off him.

'I'm not talking about the brother-and-sister acts. Like Penny Marshall and Garry Marshall, and Randy and Dennis Quaid.' By now Neil was talking louder and louder. Yelling, almost. 'No, siblings helping siblings, that's okay. Hey, I help out my sister, Brenda. But what I resent,' Neil began to scream, 'what I resent is Tori fucking Spelling just fucking *happening* to get the lead on that TV show. The show that her father just *happens* to produce. And what's the show about, boys and girls? It's about a rich Beverly Hills brat in high school. Now, that's not really acting, is it, Tori?' The audience laughed. 'She's going to be the next Sigourney Weaver. What, you don't know?' Neil asked, looking at the audience, surprised. 'Yeah, Sigourney's father was a network heavy. You didn't know that? How the fuck did you think she got her jobs? Sigourney's what I call a Hidden. They're the ones whose family connections aren't easily known, the way the Sheens and the Fondas are. I just heard that Seymore LeVine, Bob LeVine's son – you know, the guy's the head of International Studios – was just made an associate producer. How many people here know what the fuck an associate producer *does*? I'll tell you what Fred Allen said: "An associate producer is the only person in Hollywood who would *associate* with a producer."'

The rest of Neil's routine was pretty much as Jahne remembered it, from back in New York, except it had become sharper, harder, more nasty and desperate. Oh, Neil, she thought, what has happened to you? He'd always been extreme, but now he was scary.

'But blood is thicker than talent,' he was saying. 'I stole that line from someone else. But, what the fuck, these bastards are stealing my *parts*.' Neil was winding down. 'You know the only people in this town who have made it on their own? The car thieves and the whores.'

Finally, it was over, blessedly over. But before he walked off, Neil did his usual call for the formation of an antinepotism league, with the purpose of going out and killing all the Toris and Lilas in the business. Jahne felt sick. 'Can we go home, Michael?' she asked, her voice small.

Back in the car, she felt sicker — almost dizzy. Neil seemed vicious and mad — like a dog that's been beaten. A terrible feeling of loneliness flooded her again. 'I guess you didn't like it,' Michael said as they drove down La Cienega. 'I'm sorry. Maybe this will make it up to you.'

He pulled the Rolls over to the side of the street and reached into the glove box, withdrawing a wrapped present. He extended his hand. 'For you.' Jahne took a moment to collect herself, then, looking up at Michael, took the present and unwrapped it. Michael sat still in his seat next to her while she did. She snapped open the black velvet box. She paused for a moment, then reached into the satin lining and took out the necklace. It was three gold stars, with a diamond in the centre one, all hanging from a gossamer gold chain.

'It's very beautiful,' she said. 'How can I accept this, Michael?'

'Simple,' he said, taking the necklace from her hand and fastening it around her throat. He looked at her face. 'You just did.'

Jahne was touched. At this moment, when she had felt so alone, so bereft, he had offered this gift of kindness, of generosity. She had never received an expensive present from a man before. Never owned a diamond, although now she could afford to buy one. All the emptiness she had been feeling earlier that day, all the horror at Neil's demise, seemed to loosen in her. Her eyes filled with tears, and the pain washed away in an instant. This man, how could he have touched me so? she thought.

But he had. Touched her, and made her happy.

'The star speaks for itself, Jahne. You're on your way, big-time. One day, when you're way up there, will you think of me, and this night, and touch the star around your neck? I hope so.'

And all at once she was flooded with such gratitude, such pleasure in his warmth, his approval. They went back to his place. He ran a bath, helped bathe her as if she were a very young child. It was as if he knew how needy, how upset she had been. Then he wrapped her in a towel and carried her into his bedroom. Michael

401

lifted her, lightly and easily, as if all her weight were nothing – she was, as the old clichéd song lyric went, 'a feather in his arms.'

And making love was such a release. She didn't think, she only responded. After the kissing and the back rub, after she felt hot and hungry for him, he held her by her shoulders above him, suspending her effortlessly. He teased her, lowering her face to kiss her and then pushing her away. Then, at last, he placed her on his dick, pushed her down, and lifted her, over and over, again making it effortless, making it fun.

He made her feel light, and small, and feminine. He moved her with grace and strength and skill. 'Thank you,' she murmured. 'Thank you.' She felt the necklace circling her throat. She moaned with pleasure. It didn't take long for her to come.

Afterwards, as she lay beside him, she wondered at his stamina and asked, 'How do you do that?'

'It takes a lot of push-ups, but it makes them all worthwhile,' Michael said, grinning.

'It reminds me of that old biblical question: "How many angels can dance on the head of a pin?"' She giggled.

'Hey – that's no pin!' he protested.

'Well, I'm no angel,' she told him, and moved to cover his mouth with her own. Her blood hummed in her ears. Which was just as well, because it kept her from hearing the tiny whir of the concealed video camera.

8

While Neil Morelli was unwinding after his monologue and Jahne slept in Michael's arms, Sam Shields paced back and forth across the speckled tile floor of his office. Surrounding him were dozens of sheets of balled-up, discarded pages. He wasn't making any goddamned progress with the script. Maybe because it was a dated, hopeless melodrama, or maybe because he was a dated, hopeless melodramatic screenwriter, but, for whatever reason, it wasn't coming together. And while Hollywood had seduced him, there was still enough of the old Sam left to believe passionately that the story mattered, that the characters had to make sense, and that the unities should be followed.

He ran his fingers from his forehead down through his tangle of hair, which had come undone from the lacing that he used to pony-tail it. He caught a glimpse of himself in the mirror that hung on the back of his office door. He looked like a madman. Well, he *was* a madman. *Cinéma vérité*. He went back to the desk and peered at the screen of his laptop word processor. God, it was worse than he'd thought! Still, he printed it out to see it in black and white. Jesus! It was even worse on paper! He crushed the page and threw it down among the flotsam and jetsam already at his feet.

He was choking. Like Kareem Abdul-Jabbar, who could make any kind of action shot but could rarely sink a basket from the foul line when the crowd was watching. Too much pressure. But who was watching him? Sam had found it easier to be brave when he'd had almost nothing to lose. Now he was no longer a neophyte director with a low-budget first offer. Now he was Sam Shields, the successful director of *Jack and Jill*, and instead of it bolstering his confidence, he felt that he had something to risk.

How could it be that he had never noticed the number of danger points that stood in his path to continued success? If April didn't like the script, he was done for. If Bob LeVine didn't green light it, he'd be done for. If they went into production and he fell behind budget, or if April didn't like the dailies, he was done for. And if he managed to finish the script, cast the movie, get it shot on budget, and released, but the audience didn't come to it, he was done for. So many chances to fail, and such a slim hope for success – no wonder he wasn't sleeping.

He thought of his father's words of advice, 'Don't fuck this up for yourself.' Well, Dad, I'm trying not to. But you and Mom didn't seem to give me a base of confidence to work from. Couldn't you have picked some up for me on one of your trips to the liquor store?

Sam kicked viciously at the tide of discarded paper around him. He had better clean all this up, because, worst of all, he had to put a good face on everything. This was Hollywood. Never admit that you are hungry, angry, lonely, or tired. And never, ever, admit that you're afraid. On the evenings he saw April, he exhausted himself with fake passion and fake assurances to her that things were going well. If only he could level with her, talk through his problems and fears, he might be able to move forward, but April was no Mary Jane Moran.

Sam sighed, and thought of the days when Mary Jane would listen while he poured out all his insecurities and problems. She knew when to help with suggestions and when simply to listen and let him work things out on his own. Perhaps the work he did with her had come out so well because of her collaboration.

Collaboration? Well, that was going too far. His work belonged to him. She had merely been a good listener.

He knew what he needed. He needed the relaxation of a sexual relationship where he wasn't always on the line. He thought of the lunch with Jahne Moore. *That* was something he'd like to try on for size. She seemed to Sam to be more than just a pretty girl. He had thought about her a lot. She seemed to draw him to her, as if her warmth were a magnet and he a mere iron filing. She seemed so young, so fresh. And she had that hunger, that actor's need to perform, that so excited him. He felt that she would be a good listener. Well, he'd push April to try again to get the girl to audition.

Now he needed a good listener. He needed to throw his ideas at somebody who would neither belittle his suggestions nor cheapen them. Because Sam was saddled with a project that was, he saw now, a dog. How do you take a dated but revered classic film and update it to something relevant and real without turning off the old audience, while attracting the new?

He threw himself onto the lumpy sofa. There was a story line buried in the script that still made sense: the successful man who watches his woman surpass him as his sun sets. Themes of rivalry, jealousy, and love. But how the hell do you dramatize it?

Sam jumped up and began his pacing. There was a meeting to start on storyboards at the end of the week, and he was not going to hand in this piece of shit. With a sigh that seemed to come from somewhere deeper than his liver, Sam sat down at the desk. 'Come on, get with it,' he said aloud. 'Don't fuck this up for yourself.'

9

They were running late tonight on the 3/4 location, and no one was in a good humour. Oddly enough, the early success of the show had not made the set more relaxed and jovial, as success usually did. Instead, it seemed ever more tense. I had heard about nothing but trouble, and I had three crew people who fed me the dirt. I was there just to get a bit of colour for the Vanity Fair *piece. Now they were trying to get a complicated Steadycam shot in the can. Some poor bastard cameraman was rigged up with this ninety-pound monster, following the three costars down the stairs of the building that was doubling for the scene of the Chicago convention centre. It was, as they say, a tough act to follow – the three costars had such specific marks to hit that their progress down the steps was almost choreographed, while the camera operator skipped backward in front of them.*

This was the sixth take. The problem was that Lila kept hogging the shot. It reminded me of the old rumour that, during the filming of Wizard of Oz, *both the Lion and the Tin Man kept crowding Dorothy off the yellow brick road. Poor little Judy. Now Sharleen kept blowing her lines. In addition, they were losing the light. And if that wasn't enough, everyone – from the crafts-services staff to the Flanders Cosmetics representative – wanted to leave and go home. But Marty had to get this shot – this great, fluid shot – right.*

'Okay, let's take it from the top,' Marty said, and tried to smile as he indicated the top of the steps. The Steadycam guy once again climbed up, slowly, with his extra burden, uncomplaining. After all, he was a specialist, paid by the hour. What did he care? Marty had thirty-five thousand dollars sunk into this sequence already – he'd have their faces, their hair, their breasts floating down the stairs, the violence of the convention behind them. Soft against hard. Two minutes on the screen. Maybe only ninety seconds. And already thirty-five thousand bucks.

Now, before he started the action, he had to straighten Lila out. He walked wearily up the stairs to her. 'I already have you in the centre,' he said to her. 'I have you ahead of the other two. But I can't have you alone. You are the centre of the wedge, but I need you to let them be in frame. Please, Lila!'

Lila tossed her hair. Since their aborted dinner, she'd been particularly cool to him. 'I'm not cutting them out,' she huffed. 'Can I help it if they can't keep up with me?'

He sighed. She was an enormous pain sometimes, but here – at the improbable setting of the Pasadena Library at the end of the day during the time of special light they call 'magic hour' – she was breathtakingly beautiful.

He looked over to Jahne and Sharleen, both being powdered by Makeup. 'You ready?' he asked. Sharleen nodded, but he could see she was rattled. He sighed again. Marty needed to get the shot tonight – he was already over budget and couldn't afford the ungodly expensive Steadycam for another day.

'You look great, Sharleen. Now, just come down the stairs, and when you get to the bottom, turn to me and give the line. Okay?'

Sharleen nodded, silently.

Lila looked at the director with annoyance. What was he babying Sharleen for? Marty was one of *Lila's* assets, although sometimes Marty lost his focus, gave too much camera time to Jahne or Sharleen, or too much attention. Since their dinner, Lila knew she would have to put things into balance again. Give Marty a threat or a promise of something, a jerk on the leash. Marty had been too patient with Sharleen as she flubbed her lines through the multiple takes. Lila needed to let Marty know she was someone to be dealt with. Remind him what he just might get from her in return for his . . . devotion? Well, attention, at least.

'How many times does the hillbilly have to blow a line before we're allowed to go home?' Lila asked, loudly. 'I have a date.' Let Marty chew on that for a while.

'Just hit your marks, okay?' Marty asked wearily, without admonishing Lila.

'Sharleen isn't just a dumb blonde,' Lila said, emboldened. 'If she dyed her hair brown, you know what they'd call it?'

The rest of the crew had gotten tired of Lila's relentless put-downs of her costar. But the Steadycam operator, new to the set, fell for it. He looked at Lila questioningly.

'Artificial intelligence,' Lila said, and laughed.

*

Now that the day's shooting was, at last, finished, Lila flounced to her car. Sharleen had, predictably, blown her line one last time; they'd lost the light and had to wrap for the day. Lila smiled. She didn't look forward to her long drive from Pasadena to Malibu, or her date tonight. But she had to do it. She knew word of *who* she was dating would get back to Marty. This was the way to treat a man. At least, she thought it was.

Lila didn't really like to think about it, but when she did she recognized that most of the men that she had grown up around were homosexuals. Her father was, or was bisexual – or probably omnisexual, if there was such a thing. Apparently his rule was, if it moved, fuck it. She knew about the famous statutory-rape case with the thirteen-year-old. Of course, that had been before she was born, but she'd seen Aunt Robbie's scrapbooks, and the clippings were as complete as only a compulsive Virgo queen could make them.

Not that she'd spent much time around her father. He and the Puppet Mistress had divorced when she was a newborn. He'd shown up every now and then, but the PMS had custody, of course. Anyway, Lila hadn't really known him, homo or not.

But she *had* known Robbie, and all those other gay men who hung around the PMS. There was her hairdresser, Jerry, and for a long time there was Theresa's business manager, Sammy Bradkin, and then Bobby Meiser, her second business manager, and there was Ron Woodrow, her *third* business manager (the PMS had trouble with business), and Alain Something-or-Other, that totally hopeless, lisping cameraman, and the photographer whose name Lila couldn't remember but whose idea of a hot time was to sit up all night and watch the PMS cry. And of course there had been Kevin. Disgusting, lying Kevin. He was still hanging out at her mother's, Robbie said. Lila shuddered. Well, she was sick of them all.

But she had inherited one. Now it seemed that Robbie himself was switching his attention from Theresa to Lila. Where the action was. He was nothing but a fame junkie, totally beat, and Lila knew it. Almost as bad as Kevin, and always snooping. She could barely manage to keep him out of her shrine room. He had taken to saying 'we' when talking about how Lila had gotten on the show. As if *he* had done something. Other than give her a bed, what had he done for her career? Sending her to George, for God's sake? Humiliating her at Ara's? What the fuck had he done? Nothing. Not a goddamn thing. She had done all her own work. Aunt Robbie was getting confused. *And* getting to be a pain in her ass. If Lila weren't sure that Robbie would go running back to the PMS the minute she sent him packing, she would have shut the door on him months ago. But she wouldn't give the PMS the satisfaction.

So, anyway, Lila admitted, she had grown up around a bunch of queers. And all of them were 'Uncle' Jerry, or 'Uncle' Bobby or 'Uncle' Somebody-or-Other — except, of course, for 'Aunt' Robbie, who was way too much of a queen to allow himself to be called 'uncle.' It wasn't surprising that those were the men that she was most comfortable with. She supposed that's why she said yes to Kevin: on some level, she *knew*.

Not that she approved. The thing about gays was that they were always thinking and talking about sex. It was so *boring*, for God's sake. Sex was something she didn't like to think about, much less talk about. Lila thought it was all mildly repulsive as well as ridiculous. Think about it: putting a flesh tube from one body into a flesh canal of another. She shuddered. Lila knew that *more* than almost anything she wanted to be sexy, but that *less* than almost anything she wanted to have sex. And with gays it seemed as if having sex was the main thing in life — like 90 per cent — and they fit the rest into the 10 per cent they had left over.

Of course, she realized, her perception could be a little, well, *skewed* or something, because of all the nutsiness with the PMS. And she'd been to shrinks since she was eleven; so it wasn't as if she were *stupid*. She had hoped everything would change, once she grew up and had a place of her own. But now being on the set, in real life around heterosexual men, didn't really seem that different from being with the gays. Well, they *acted* different, of course, but they all just wanted to fuck. It was only that now they wanted to fuck *her*.

She could see it in their eyes. Lila divided heterosexual men into two categories. One was the men like Marty and Michael McLain, who loved women so much, and wanted to be with them, and noticed everything about them. How they dressed, how they smelled, how they moved, even how they thought. That type might as well *be* homo, as far as Lila was concerned. They made her sick. Then there was the other type, the guys like Sy Ortis and that fat worm Paul Grasso, who talked about tits and beaver but really only liked making deals and hanging around with a bunch of guys. Come to think of it, that type was like homos, too. They were *all* homos.

The whole thing gave her a headache, one of those sick migraines, if she thought about it too much. So she didn't, because all she had to know was one basic fact: men were generally useless, and she hated them. She hated the gays and the straights, she hated how they talked, how they walked. She hated how they were hairy, how they thought they owned the whole fucking world, how they blotted her out, how, even when they wanted her, they made her feel like nothing. She didn't trust one of them. She feared them all. And she hated them all, even Robbie, even Marty. *Especially* Marty. There was no doubt in her mind: Lila hated men.

The thing was, no matter how much she hated men, Lila knew she hated women more.

Her mother most of all, of course. That went without saying. But now, on the set, Lila's hatred had taken on a broader focus, you should excuse the pun. Working with Jahne and Sharleen had given her daily practice in woman-hating. Up until this show, Lila had never had much contact with women. Theresa wasn't exactly what you would call a *woman's* woman: she had no 'girlfriends.' Nor was she a *man's* woman, considering the males she surrounded herself with.

So, it wasn't difficult for Lila to understand how she'd gotten to be this way. Weird. A loner. It was realistic, really. Why have *anyone* close enough to compete? Only Candy and Skinny, and Lila *still* hated them. Estrella had been the only real female around when Lila was growing up and living in the Puppet Mistress's house, but she didn't count. A Mexican, *and* a servant.

Now Lila had two women, her own age, beautiful, very close: too close for comfort. She wasn't used to the smell of women, seeing their beauty every day, right there, in her face. It made her nervous. It made her angry. Because Jahne and Sharleen – while no competition – *were* a presence. A presence that others saw, considered, sought opinions of, fawned over. Not Marty so much – right now Marty was the only one who counted on the set, after Lila – but the others.

Thank God, Marty was giving Lila all kinds of special attention. Well, that was the way it *should* be. As far as she was concerned, the other two dummies could look out for themselves.

For most of Lila's solo scenes, she knew all eyes were on her. But for the group scenes, when all three women were in front of the camera, Lila felt – almost heard – the clicking of eyes and camera as they went back and forth from Lila to Skinny to Candy, back and forth, as if there weren't enough to look at. As if Lila weren't enough.

So Marty, as director, was the key. Lila couldn't control what people did with their eyes, but she could control what the camera lens focused on. She could control that by controlling Marty.

Lila had known, since the night she'd met him with Paul Grasso, what drove Marty. Beauty, of course. And talent, but not as much as beauty. What tipped the scales for Marty – *compelled* Marty – and what Lila traded on – was elusiveness: being always just a little out of reach, promising but unattainable. Wasn't that the essence of beauty? She had the mystery that Sharleen and Jahne lacked. It was the tantalizing that Marty – and so many men like him – relished. Merle Oberon, and all the other old-time actresses that Lila knew Marty worshipped. Jennifer Jones. Paulette Goddard. And Theresa O'Donnell. Lila knew what they all had in common.

They could not be possessed. They teased. As she would tease. For Lila, it was easy. She had no intention of delivering anything of herself, except on camera. And she had *every* intention of making Marty believe otherwise. Lila had perfected that talent, that magic. She'd watched her mother, and her mother's old films. She was smart enough to know that she should use every asset she was given. In that respect, she knew she was smarter than the other two. They were so middle-class, so open, giving too much. *They* didn't understand how to hold something back. She would be the one who succeeded, big-time.

Now she wondered if Robbie's stupid gossip was, for once, trustworthy. If it was true that Michael McLain was doing a Ricky Dunn film, and that he also was being considered for the lead in *Birth of a Star*. Well, she'd find out over dinner with him tonight. Her earlier refusals just made him try harder. And if seeing her name linked with Michael's made Marty try harder, all would be well.

Michael McLain sat across from Lila in the vast, high-ceilinged dining room of the Beverly Wilshire and smiled. Lila noticed the tiny wrinkles at the corners of his eyes, which spread, weblike, into his temples. His skin was still good – well, it *would* be, since she knew for a fact he has two facials a week from Gydia – but she wondered how much longer it could hold out. Jesus, how old was he, anyway? She imagined having to kiss him on camera and felt her stomach turn. But maybe the part was for *Ricky Dunn's* girlfriend. At least *he* was no wrinkle-bunny. Well, even if it wasn't, it wouldn't hurt her to costar with Michael. After all, she was savvy enough to appreciate the benefits of a slip yoke like this one. He had been a great star of the past, and she planned to be a great star in the future. If kissing him was a necessary rung on the ladder, she'd kiss him.

'My, my, my. You're a big girl now, Lila. How long has it been since I saw you last?'

Oh, Christ, was this going to be another one of those old Hollywood walks down memory lane? A remember-the-party-at-the-Nivens'-that-Christmas bullshit rap? She didn't mind pulling out the nostalgia for Marty, but with Michael she had expected something a little hipper. She reminded herself that he could help her cross over from TV to features, and flashed him her biggest smile. 'Not since I was six, or maybe seven. It was my birthday party, I think.'

'Really?' She could see him back off that. She had to hide her own smile. Like Theresa, he was one of those Hollywood mummies who wanted to exploit old times and connections while denying how very old they were. Well, Lila knew how *that* game was played. Just be positive about the connection, but hazy about the time. So she smiled at him. 'You used to come over to our place a lot,' she purred. 'I really missed you when you stopped coming around.'

'Your mom still live in Bel Air?'

Christ, everyone knew she did. The estate was still the hottest piece of property in town, even if the house was a tear-down. 'Like she'd ever leave, except feet first. No, Theresa's still there, but *I'm* in Malibu. I live in Nadia Negron's house. She starred in the silent-film version of *Birth of a Star*.' Let's get the subject back on track, she figured.

'Really? Where? I lived in Malibu for a while.' And before she had a chance to get him onto the subject of *Birth*, he launched into some long story about the seventies, Steve McQueen, some grotty house party and mescaline on the beach. Real old-fashioned stuff. Mega-lame. She tried to nod at the right places. She knew that, if she blinked a lot, it kept her eyes wet and made them shine. That usually helped. Finally, it was over.

'I guess those were the days.'

Michael cleared his throat. Shit! She'd made him feel old again. Well, Jesus, he *was*. She smiled, then ran her tongue over her teeth. She would have to do some make up time here. Get

Michael all comfy again. The waiter brought their blackened fish and twinkled confidentially at both of them, like he wouldn't be feeding any conversation he overheard to the columns tomorrow. Still, Lila smiled.

'So, you really knew Steve McQueen?' she asked, opening her eyes wide.

10

'You think I don't know people are laughin' at me? 'Cause I don't know how to talk and I don't know how to dress or anything like that?' Sharleen asked, teary-eyed. 'I *know* they are. but I just try to ignore it. It's what my mother told me to do when the girls in school made fun of me.'

Jahne nodded, handing Sharleen another tissue. Out of pity, she had followed her back to her trailer after the Steadycam sequence finally wrapped. It was the first time they'd spent any time together alone.

'You know, it might be easier for you if we could run lines together.'

'Run lines? You mean practise? Just us two?'

Jahne smiled at the girl. 'Not practise, Sharleen. *Rehearse.* Actors call it "rehearsal," but if you are only rehearsing the dialogue, then we call it "running lines."'

'Would you do that for me? But no. That would be too much trouble for you.'

'I'd love to, Sharleen. I could use the rehearsal myself,' Jahne lied. 'Anyway, who else makes fun of you?' She was feeling guilty for her own private jokes about Sharleen.

'Well, Lila, of course. Look what she did back there. She gets me all flustered. I know she don't mean nothin', that she's just nervous herself, but I get upset over it. I try so hard. Every night, I read my lines over and over. I practise them out loud, too. Dean helps me. I know he's slow, but I guess I'm almost as dumb as he is. I know everyone on the crew hates to do it again and again, but I get so confused. And I'm so tired. It seems like I'm workin' or takin' lessons all the time I ain't sleeping. It don't help when Lila rags me.'

'Yes.' Jahne nodded grimly. 'She does make fun. But she hates both of us. Try not to take it personally. Who else bothers you?'

'Well, Mr. Tilden, the assistant director, he called me "Elly May Clampett" the other day. Made all the crew laugh.'

'I don't get it.'

'From *The Beverly Hillbillies*. Remember her?'

Jahne nodded. Of course. Barry Tilden was a bitter, funny, middle-aged gay guy. But he shouldn't have mocked Sharleen before the crew. She *was* becoming the scapegoat.

'I know people think I'm ignorant, and I am. But I'm not deaf, dumb, and blind,' she sniffed.

'No, you're not,' Jahne agreed, handing her another Kleenex. 'And you're not seven years old anymore, either. You've got some *power*. Do you know, if Barry Tilden insults you, you could get him fired?'

Sharleen lifted her head up, the long, lovely fringe of silvery blond hair falling away from her face like a white wimple. Despite her reddened eyes and her tears, Sharleen's face was still beautiful. Jesus, Jahne thought, she's even gorgeous when she cries. 'Oh, I could never do that!' Sharleen said. 'He's a wage earner. Why, he might have children to feed.'

'Two Shih Tzus, more likely,' Jahne said dryly. 'Anyway, the point is not that you *would* get him fired, but that you *could* if you wanted to. You're important to this production. All the cast and crew's jobs count on you and me and Lila. So no one should be making fun of you. You really *could* get them fired, just by telling Marty or Sy that you want them off the set.'

'Have *you* ever been fired?' Sharleen asked, her voice lower, calmer, and almost ominous.

Jahne, lying, shook her head.

'Well, *I* surely have. And nothin' feels worse than losing a job when you got rent to pay and groceries to buy.'

Jahne smiled at Sharleen. 'You're a very nice person,' she said. 'But, now, I'm not saying you *should* get Barry fired. Just let *him* know you know you could do it.'

Sharleen seemed to let that sink in. 'Well, what should I do?'

'Just look at him like this and say, "Don't speak to me that way *ever again*." He's a bitch, but he's not stupid. He'll stop on a dime.'

'Well, maybe for you and Lila, but not for me.'

Jahne stared at her. Boy, oh, boy, the nice-girl, modest-little-home-spun act was wearing pretty thin. Then Jahne looked at Sharleen more closely. Was she kidding? This hillbilly bit was unbelievable, but could it possibly be true?

'Sharleen, don't you know?' Jahne asked her gently.

'Know what?'

'Know that you're the biggest sensation since talkies. You're *it!* Right this minute, there are girls cutting their hair like yours, trying to buy a jacket like yours. Women are naming their babies Sharleen after you. Don't you get it?'

'Oh, come on.'

'Well, they are.' Jahne took a breath. 'Don't you read the newspapers? "Sharleen's Three Beauty Tips for Teens." "Sharleen Smith models a dazzling new wardrobe!" "How to be like Sharleen Smith." Don't you see the magazines? Sharleen, you're about as hot as a star could get right now.'

'Well, me and Dean don't get out much, and neither of us is much of a reader.'

'Sharleen, I think you should know what's happening. We're a phenomenon. Like Garbo.'

'Who's he?'

'*You don't know Garbo?*'

'Don't think I recollect him. Was he one of the Marx Brothers?'

Jahne laughed out loud. 'How old *are* you?'

'Nineteen.'

Jahne sighed. 'Sharleen, you're very, very popular now. And people already want to know *everything* about you. Like the Laura Richie woman. All the columnists. The woman's magazines. *People. Entertainment Weekly.* They want to eat you up. What you have for breakfast, how much you weigh, where you shop, what your favourite colour is.'

'But why?'

'That, my dear, is the riddle. Maybe people are lonely, or bored, and we give them something to do. Or maybe we seem like their neighbours, their community, if they have none. Some people just need to look up to someone. Be interested in someone. Maybe they hope for our good luck. And other people just need to look down on someone. Maybe they feel superior when we have bad luck. So, for whatever reason, a lot of people are really interested in you. They see you on TV, they like how you look and what you say, and they want to know more.'

Sharleen looked upset. 'But what I say on TV ain't *my* words. The script says them.'

'I know, but people who watch don't always make the distinction.'

'But I don't want people messin' around trying to find out everything about me!' Sharleen cried.

'Well, you can't have everything. You got money and fame. You can't have privacy as well.'

Jahne saw the colour drain from Sharleen's perfect face, and something very much like terror welled up in her eyes. The poor kid really had no defences. For a moment, Jahne felt enormous pity for the girl. After all, if this had happened to *you* fifteen years ago, she told herself, *you* wouldn't have known how to handle it, either; maybe you don't now.

'Sharleen, it's not so bad. You just have to be careful in interviews and be sure to be discreet in your private life.'

'Like what do you mean?' Sharleen raised a hand to her forehead for a moment, almost as if warding off a blow, and Jahne saw that the hand was shaking. Jesus, what could a simple kid her age have to hide?

'Well, be careful whom you trust. Be really careful with journalists like that Laura Richie. Don't tell your secrets to just anyone on the set. Be careful whom you sleep with. Don't pick someone who might sell his story to the press for a thousand dollars. Don't keep a diary, don't trust waiters or hairdressers or your cleaning person. Things like that. They could be reporters.'

'What if I already haven't been so careful?' Sharleen asked.

That night, after her talk with Sharleen and the long drive home from Pasadena, Jahne had trouble sleeping. But it was a relief to be alone. Sleeping with Michael, like sleeping with Pete, wasn't really working. Despite his kindness to her, and his gift, she had to admit that she didn't feel deeply about him. Plus, she didn't really have time for a sex life *and* a career. The irony of it was not lost on her: now that she was at last desirable, she had no time for it. Between her evenings with Michael, her thoughts about Sam Shields, and her tension from the set, Jahne hadn't slept well for several nights. And she couldn't afford to miss sleep, to look haggard. But since seeing Neil Morelli waiting tables, waiting for his turn at the mike, she just hadn't been sleeping.

Seeing Neil had been awful. She wanted to run up to her old friend and put her arms around him, comfort him, and tell him how wonderful life had become for her – which, as Jahne Moore, she couldn't do. But she also wanted to run from the place, hide under a blanket, shut it all out, as if that would make it less humiliating for Neil. Of course, she had read about the cancellation of his pilot in the trades, and she'd seen him working Ara's party, but when she couldn't track him down she'd assumed he had returned to New York and picked up where he'd left off. To be honest, she'd *hoped* he had gone back, so neither of them would have to be going through what she was going through now. Feeling helpless, and sad. And very worried about her old friend.

Neil was no good at handling adversity. And he had already had plenty in his life. But seeing him made her realize that, for Neil, there could be no going back. He had always been a bridge-burner, while she'd been conservative, an appeaser. Of course she'd burned her bridges since then. Well, now, she thought, we have more in common.

She tossed and turned for several hours. She knew what she had to do – the idea had come to her sometime before dawn – and now that it was morning, she was dialling Sy Ortis' office. 'It's Jahne Moore. Can I speak to him?' she asked politely.

She didn't have to wait. 'Hi there. All set for your *Birth of a Star* screen test? They want to see you. But I still say it's a waste of time. I have at least three better scripts right here.'

She felt her stomach flutter. So, April had given her a callback! She felt herself flush with pride, followed by nerves. Well, she'd have time to get herself together. 'Yes, but . . .'

'I don't know why you're interested. It's a nothing. You know that?'

'Of course. But, Sy, right now I'm calling because I need a favour.'

'Just name it,' Sy Ortis said, as she knew he would. The show, she and Lila and Sharleen, all were hot right now. Now, when she didn't really need favours, she had only to ask.

'There's a guy in town, a stand-up comic. I saw him, and I think he's got a lot of talent. I'd like you to get him a guest shot on *Three for the Road*, Sy. He's *really* good.'

'I'll give it my best shot, Jahne. What's his name?'

'Neil Morelli,' she said, and listened to the silence at the other

416

end of the phone. It was a long silence. 'Sy, what's the matter? Ever hear of him?'

Sy found his voice. 'Yeah, I've heard of him.' Sy paused again. 'In fact, my office represents him. Or we used to. And, to tell you the truth, Jahne, I don't know if getting him a job is the right thing to do. He's more trouble than he's worth. Temperamental, or maybe just mental, you know? A real asshole. He made himself a few enemies from *Chakras*.'

Jahne wasn't surprised. 'Just do this for me, will you?'

'I don't know, Jahne. It's not like I'm the casting director. Grasso is in charge. Maybe they won't want him.'

What bullshit! Jahne thought. As if Sy couldn't push his weight around. She hated to act like a pushy brat, but she'd obviously have to. 'Sy, listen to me. I had a very bad night last night, and I need to be at my best for my screen test. Now, you represent two of the three costars on ¾. I say that gives you a little clout with Grasso. All I want is for Neil Morelli to get a spot on the show, maybe even a continuing. I'm not saying big. And as soon as possible. Make me happy, Sy.' Jahne hated pushing people around almost as much as she hated being pushed, but it seemed to be the only way to get things done out here.

'Let me ask you, Jahne. Who's this guy to you anyway?'

Jahne had been afraid of this question, had even prepared an answer. 'He's a friend of someone I used to know. I owe her.'

'Like I said, I'll give it my . . .'

Jahne was losing patience. 'Like the Nike ad says, Sy: Just *do it*. This is the only favour I've asked of you since you landed me in your stable. Remember you said representation was a two-way street? Well, now it's coming your way.' She went to hang up the phone, then thought better of it and added, 'Thank you.'

Jahne leaned back in the armchair and took a deep breath. Why the fuck did everything have to be so difficult in this town? Such a big goddamned deal? Well, she'd done a favour for a friend. And she had her first screen test coming up. What did she have to bitch about? Things could be a lot worse.

The next afternoon, still on location in Pasadena, Sharleen was scheduled for shooting a small scene with Lila. Thank the Lord the Steadycam shot was in the can at last! Since Sharleen's talk with Jahne the night before, she was feeling a little better about herself and her work. Rehearsing with Jahne was just what she needed.

417

Meanwhile, she only hoped that Lila was in a better mood than she had been in yesterday.

Sharleen was walking to her trailer to get dressed when she saw an assistant come running up to Lila with one of the ubiquitous mobile phones that everyone used on location. 'Miss Kyle,' he shouted breathlessly, 'it's Michael McLain!'

Lila turned and grabbed the phone out of his hand, motioning the kid away.

Sharleen froze in her steps. Michael McLain calling *Lila*? What could he possibly want with *her*? Sharleen walked up to Lila, who was hunched over a slant board, restlessly playing with a long twist of her hair. She heard Lila say something about taking a ride to a canyon. Sharleen gasped. He wouldn't be mentioning how he took *me* to the canyon, would he? Sharleen's mind was whirling. Or is he planning to do the same thing to Lila that he did to me?

She felt sick. Lila had been unkind to her, but not even Lila deserved this. As a Christian, what should Sharleen do? Sharleen moved in front of Lila. Lila looked up, then turned around, surprised to see Sharleen standing there. Everyone knew Lila was a nut about privacy, and no one went near her or her trailer without an invitation. 'Excuse me for a minute, Michael,' Lila said with exaggerated patience.

Lila glared at Sharleen. 'Just who do you think you are, standing there, listening to my telephone conversation?'

'Lila, I have to tell you . . .'

'You don't have to tell me anything. Just get out of here and mind your own business. Go get ready for the shoot, and don't screw up your lines like you did yesterday.'

Sharleen tried to speak again, but Lila turned away and, with the telephone glued to her ear she walked to her own trailer. All Sharleen could hear as she disappeared inside of it was Lila's low-pitched laugh as she continued to talk to Michael.

Please, God, Sharleen prayed, don't let him mention me to Lila, and don't let him do anything to hurt her.

11

Hitchcock said it best: All actors are cattle. Ara Sagarian knew that, and over the fifty-one years of his career, it had helped him to deal with all of them, from an hysterical Claudette Colbert, to a raging Joan Crawford, to the tantrums of Sean Penn. The one thing he observed that all his clients had in common was that they all wanted what they couldn't have. '*Ahmon!*' Ara sighed, mouthing the Armenian equivalent of 'Oy vey.'

Look at Lila Kyle. Posters of her in every shop across the country, her face on half the women's magazines and on all of the men's. Truckloads of scripts, a whole department in Ara's agency devoted to handling Lila's endorsements alone, national *and* foreign interviews, even an invitation to the White House. Everything except a mention in Geraldo Rivera's book, which she could have had and did not want, and a shot at April Irons' remake of *Birth of a Star*. So of course it was the part in *Birth* that Lila wanted – and couldn't have. Never enough! Ara was tired of the demands, and the demanding. *Bagos* – crazy. They were all *bagos*.

He lowered himself onto the downy cushions of the sofa in his office, sat with effort, and punched the speakerphone on the coffee table. 'Put her through, Miss Bradley,' he said, and leaned back with a sigh, pulling his legs up to stretch out full-length. 'Lila, my dear, how are you?'

'Did you get her?' Lila snapped. Lila had eliminated the courtesy of a greeting dozens of phone calls ago. For the past week, Lila had been relentless. All her calls to Ara – and there had been many, every day – were about one thing, and one thing only: her desperation for the part in the remake of *Birth*.

'She's been in New York, Lila. I told you. When she comes back, she *will* call me. Rest assured, child.' He smoothed his tiny moustache against the edge of the phone.

'I'm not your child!' the girl snapped. 'Call *her* in New York, then. I mean, I can't understand why she hasn't called *you*. It's

419

not like there are no *phones* there, Ara. Doesn't she *know* who you *are*? Maybe she never got . . .'

What, now Lila was going to teach him how to play the phone tag game? Ara had *invented* it. He could hear no more today. 'Lila, darling, April is due into the office this afternoon. If I don't hear from her by three, I *will* call her back. Now, be a good girl and keep yourself occupied till *I* call *you*. And think instead about the Ricky Dunn movie. *That* I like.'

'You're not purposely fucking this up for me, are you, Ara? I don't give a fuck whether you think it's right for me or not. I want to see April Irons. I want that part.' Ara could picture Lila saying those words through clenched teeth. Tsk, tsk. Amazing that her enamel had not melted. He shook his head.

Ara knew what Lila *really* wanted. She wanted to have everything her mother had. Including him. Ara thought maybe Lila wanted to *be* her mother. 'We'll speak after three,' he said as gently as possible, more gently than he felt, and punched the speakerphone off.

Despite Lila's desperation, or perhaps because of it, Ara had to stop himself from smiling. It reminded him of one of the oldest of Hollywood jokes – the starlet who begs and pleads and grovels for a part to no avail. At last, she promises the heartless agent that, if only she gets the audition, she'll take his cock in her mouth and suck on it for as long and as hard as she can. 'Yeah, but what's in it for me?' he asks her. Ara had to laugh.

But it wasn't a laughing matter: this girl couldn't act. Surely she knew that. It wasn't a tragedy. It wasn't even necessary. Lila was beautiful, no doubt about it, and, more than that, she attracted attention. She had that undefinable something that made people want to watch her, to know more about her. She was like Elizabeth Taylor. All she had to do was pick the right vehicles and be there. It was enough.

But they never knew what was enough.

'It's Miss Irons, Mr. Sagarian,' Miss Bradley's voice came through the intercom a few moments later. Ara was still on the sofa. *'Ench bede nem?'* he murmured in Armenian to himself. What to do?

He punched on the speakerphone. 'April, how was the Big Apple?' Ara asked.

'Like the Marine who went AWOL, it was rotten to the core.'

Ara chuckled. 'I'll forgive you that, April, if we can have a meeting of minds today. You know why I've called you – I

420

outlined it in my fax. *Birth of a Star*. Lila Kyle.' Ara paused, and used the opportunity to wipe his mouth and moustache with his linen handkerchief. He'd had to use it less and less frequently now, thanks to the therapy he had been receiving at Cedars since his stroke.

'Oh, Ara. I hate to tell you this, but the part has just about been cast. We're about to test the girl, and she looks good. Sam Shields is sold on her.' Ara could hear the regret in April's voice. And why not? He had helped her in small but important ways on her rise. And in a couple of big ways, too. He had no reason to disbelieve April. *Ench bede nem*? What to do?

Well, there was still hope. 'Just about' left some room. 'That does put me in a bit of a spot, April. It seems Miss Kyle believes that all she has to do is meet with you and you will jump to offer her the part. Seems to think it's such a natural for her . . . and you. I can't say I entirely disagree with her reasoning, since her mother *did* do the original.' He wiped his mouth again out of habit, even though it didn't need it. 'Who have you picked?'

'Funnily enough, it's a co-worker, Ara. Jahne Moore. You know, her costar on *Three for the Road*.'

Ara muffled his groan with the handkerchief. 'And who for the James Mason part?'

'Michael McLain may sign.'

'I see what you're doing. You're taking a star on the decline, and someone on the way up. Nice yoking. So that it looks like you have *two* stars, right, April? But you only pay half for each.'

'I *hope* it looks that way,' she said with a chuckle.

'Then, my dear, why *not* consider Lila if you're going with an unknown? What possible difference could it make *who* the unknown is? I mean, the publicity angle *alone* of casting Lila, the last star's daughter, will be enough to ensure some box office.'

'Ara, honey, listen to me. I want *seichel*, not kitsch. There's a rumour going around that Jahne Moore can actually act. We don't want a *personality*, Ara, we want an *actress*.'

Ara sighed. 'Of course, you're absolutely right. But, as a favour to me, would you at least meet with Lila as if you *were* considering her? She has become so obsessed with this that I can't get her to see how ill-suited for the role she may be. I need to get her focused in other directions, and she won't take no from me.' Ara hated to do it, but he was tired. If he didn't get Lila before the producer, then it would be *his* failure. But if he got her before the producer and she

421

was rejected, then it was *her* failure. Ara usually tried to protect his people from that very thing, but he couldn't protect Lila any longer. Maybe she needed a little rejection. Some humility. And maybe he was getting too old and too tired to keep up this charade.

April wasn't stupid. She knew the game. 'Ara, please don't ask me to do this. Not that I mind being the bad guy, but I'm up to my eyeballs in shit right now.'

'Let's go down memory lane, April. Remember how I bailed you out of that Stallone thing? I was the genius who suggested a way to get both Newman *and* Redford. Right? And that time . . .'

'I give up, you old bastard.' April was laughing. 'Give me her fucking number.'

Ara Sagarian was not the only agent in Hollywood having a bad week. Sy Ortis was also miserable. Maybe he shouldn't have laughed when CAA used a Chinese feng-shui master to guarantee 'good vibrations' before *they* built *their* new offices on Wilshire. Maybe Early Artists should have done that too. Because all Sy had was bad vibrations.

Michael McLain was a thorn in Sy Ortis' side. And a bug up his ass, a boil on his dick, a toothache, a blackhead, a pubic hair in his coffee, genital herpes, an ingrown toenail, haemorrhoids – every fucking little thing that could make your life miserable, minute by fucking minute. Michael was like Chinese water torture, peeling one cell off Sy's body at a time, until he got down to bone. Sy looked down at the veal on his plate. Delicately sliced piccata. Michael was having osso bucco, and having trouble cutting it.

But now Michael had finally reached bone.

'Don't tell me anything more about Ricky Dunn. Jesus, Sy, whose side are you on? *You* work for *me*, right? So forget Ricky Dunn, for Christ's sake, and listen. I am *not* doing the Ricky Dunn piece of turd. Understand? Unless I have top billing, and maybe not even then. Do you want me to say it in Spanish, too? *Mi non esta* making Ricky Dunn's *muy stupido* fucking movie-o. *Comprende, amigo?*'

Sy was past reacting. This wasn't the first time he had gone round and round with McLain about a part. It was the ritual, in fact. Sy would come up with an offer for Michael, review it, study it, sleep and eat the idea. If it stuck in his mind after a few days of chewing on it, if it began to feel right, then he would go to Michael with it.

And every time – *every fucking time* – Michael said no. Then Sy would tell Michael why he should do it. And Michael would still say no. And Sy would do the dance. About why it was right. About why Michael needed to do it. About why it was a great shot for Michael. And, finally, after the dance, and the ass-kissing, and the begging, Michael would reluctantly agree. And – this was the part that really pissed Sy off – after a while, it would be like Michael had come up with the part *himself*, and had to talk Sy into it.

Usually Sy didn't give a shit. 'Just give me the fucking money' was the mantra he would recite when he felt he was getting too emotionally involved. But now Sy wasn't going for it.

And why should he? He was sitting on top of the world. His merchandising company was projecting a banner year. It was bringing in more net than his agenting did! Plus, there were all the undeclared cash 'gifts' he received from manufacturers who wanted either movie placements of their product or permission to merchandise one of his stars. He had indeed kept the bodega. Gone were the days of nickel-and-diming. So what if Michael had been the first big star he'd coaxed away from CMI? Sy now had a stable, a fucking ranch of money-making talent. And the two girls from *Three for the Road* would make him another bonanza. Plus a hell of a lot more independent.

'Now that that's settled, let's get back to the good news. I am considering doing *Birth of a Star*,' Michael said. 'That might be the vehicle for me. Irons has the financing, lined up an amazing young director. It's a go, Sy.'

What was it with this *Birth of a Star* thing? First Jahne Moore, then Michael. Was April doing this just to piss him off? Did Michael know Jahne was interested? Did he care? But, to keep everything to himself, Sy had been going around about this with Michael for weeks. 'And that's your final decision?' Sy asked. 'No matter what I think, you're going to do it? I must say, I'm surprised.'

'Surprised about what?'

'Well, about you being a welsher.'

'A welsher. Since when? What are you talking about?'

'About our little bet. That you could fuck all three of the *Road* girls.'

'Yeah?'

'So?'

'What do you mean, "so"?' It was a vamp for time. Michael knew he couldn't lie outright – it was too risky – and he certainly

423

wasn't going to tell the truth. He hadn't been able to nail Lila. At least, not yet. When he had tried to kiss her, she'd laughed. The thought of Lila Kyle's beautiful face wrinkling into incredulity and disgust was too painful to remember, much less to discuss with Sy Ortis.

'So did you put the wood to all of them?'

'You want pictures?'

Sy nodded. Michael pulled out a Polaroid from his pocket. Sy picked it up.

'My God!' he said, staring at the shot of Sharleen. 'She's a natural blonde!' Michael threw another few photos on the table. Sy shuffled through the pictures hungrily. Michael looked down at his meat. There was something gross about Sy's curiosity. I mean, how often did a lizard like him get laid? Michael wondered. Michael knew he had a Mexican wife stashed somewhere, but Sy never took her out in public. Now he grinned over the pictures of Sharleen. 'What about Jahne Moore?' he asked greedily.

'You're getting me top billing, right?'

'Right.' Sy felt breathless. He loved the idea of the snotty Jahne being taken down a peg or two.

'No photos. But I've got videotape.'

'A video?' Sy laughed aloud. 'I *gotta* see this.'

'You know, Sy, I've been thinking. This has been like taking candy from babies, and I'm coming around to feeling that it's ungentlemanly to kiss and tell.'

'Bullshit. Did you do Lila Kyle, too?'

Best to distract him with a joke.

'Hey, Sy, what's the difference between a blimp and 365 blow jobs?'

Sy shrugged.

'It's the difference, Sy, between a Goodyear and a great year.'

'Oh yeah? Well, you may have had a thousand blow jobs, but you haven't had a good year since *Akkbar*. Did you do Lila or not?'

'Forget it, Sy.'

'So you couldn't nail her! Do you think Marty has?'

'I didn't say I couldn't, or that I didn't. I just said that I don't think I want to talk about it. I think we should drop the whole bet.'

Sy stared at him for a moment. Michael tried to look morally superior, giving him the look he had used on Rod Steiger in

Corruption, after he discovered that Steiger had stolen from the pension fund. He used the same concentration, the unblinking stare, the whole bit, but, after a moment, Sy lifted up his pointy chin and just laughed. His laugh had the bark of a hyena in it.

'Not bad, Mike. For a moment, I thought maybe you had gone gaga on her, like Marty. But you haven't, and you haven't fucked her, either. So don't pull your dying-days-of-the-Actors-Studio routine with me. I'm not some shmuck from William Morris.' Sy stood up and walked over to the restaurant railing. 'What is it with that bitch?' he murmured. 'Is she a professional virgin or something? Or a rug muncher, maybe? But when did *that* stop an ambitious dyke from going down on a director? Is she smart enough to play *that* hard to get? I could understand if she didn't do him or you 'cause she was boffing Brad Dillon or Ricky Dunn or some other young piece of meat, but we checked it out. *Nada*. I swear to god, she's Marty's obsession. He'll have to start going to Al-Anon meetings if he doesn't straighten out soon.' Sy shook his head and sighed.

'Well, speaking of Ricky Dunn, it seems as if you owe me a meeting with *that* gentleman.'

'Sy, I said I wanted to drop the bet. It's . . .'

'You can't drop the bet, 'cause you *lost* the bet. You told me you'd put it to all three for the road, or else you'd do the Dunn movie without top billing. Don't bullshit a bullshitter, Mike. You're starting to slip. Losing the touch, huh? It's time to settle up.'

Michael couldn't take it. 'I've done all three!' he snarled. 'I'll send over the video and the other photos this afternoon. Now *you* owe me a meeting. *And* top billing, Sy. My name over the title. And if you can't deliver, I'm going to call Mike Ovityz'

Sy went back to his office feeling both angry and out of control. If what Michael said was true, he, Sy, would have to try to convince Ricky Dunn to give Michael top billing. Almost an impossibility! He reached for his inhaler. He would lose face if he couldn't deliver, and he wasn't sure he could. He was Dunn's agent, but Dunn was no fool. Why should he give up top and only? How could Sy convince him to?

As always when Sy was rattled, he began to think of ways to increase his take. After all, money was power. He needed some other means of making more money on these clients of his. He was sitting on two of the hottest new stars since Julia Roberts, and realizing *nada* on them, aside from the extra fees he'd created out of the Flanders Cosmetics deal. He couldn't count on Jahne Moore to do any other commercials, advertising for bathing suits, or practically any other publicity. Sure, she was going to screen-test for *Birth of a Star*, but he knew that it wasn't going to make any money for him: April was cheap and smart, and even if she gave points, remakes never make any profit.

So how about Sharleen Smith? At least *she* was easy. He'd have to force her into the recording contract. Yes. Hal King was pushing for the deal. Her face alone would sell half a million copies. She couldn't sing? So what? If the little redneck only showed up and barked like a dog, they could always overdub her. Now all that was needed was a little influence. Because Hal King had promised Sy seventy-thousand dollars in cash, in a bag, if Sy could deliver the kid to the studio. If Hal King can push for a deal, Sy Ortis can push even harder, he thought as he reached for the receiver.

Sy had had this conversation twenty times with Sharleen. This time, he'd have to get her to do it. Sy tapped his fingers on his desk impatiently. 'Come on and pick up the ... Hello? Dean? May I speak to Sharleen, please?' The guy was even slower than Sharleen was. Who was he? Her boyfriend? Her husband? Thank God, she kept him out of sight. That they had found one another was proof there was a God.

'Hello, Sharleen, Sy Ortis here. Sorry to bother you, but I have to get your go-ahead on the recording.'

'Well, I . . .'

'So what do you say I call a studio and we set it up in ... oh, a couple of days?'

'A couple of days? I don't know if I can do this, Mr. Ortis, I mean, I just haven't had enough lessons and . . .'

'Now, Sharleen, I just know you'll be fine. You're doing so well with the TV show that I know you can do just as well making a record.'

'I just don't know,' Sharleen muttered.

'Look,' Sy said with a little growl in his voice, 'just come to the recording studio and give it a try. If you don't like the way it sounds, we can drop the whole thing.'

'Oh, I don't think . . .'

Sy was searching his desk. 'Where the hell is my inhaler?' he muttered. He choked once, sputtered, and grabbed for it.

'Mr. Ortis, are you okay? I don't mean to make you upset,

Mr. Ortis. If you really think it will work, I guess I can do it. It's just that I'm so tired all the time . . .'

Sy took a deep breath on his inhaler, and with a sigh of relief said, 'Great, Sharleen. You'll be thanking me all the way to the bank.'

'The bank? I can't go now, Mr. Ortis. It's after five.'

Sy laughed, 'Don't worry about it. I'll see you in a couple of days, Sharleen.'

Sy hung up the phone, sat back in his leather-upholstered chair, and put his feet up on the corner of his desk. That was seventy big ones in the bag. He smiled, looking at his inhaler. *Madre de Dios*, if all he had to do was have an asthma attack to get a client to give in, he'd have to try it on Michael McLain – if, as he suspected, he couldn't get Ricky Dunn to give Mike top billing.

12

Jahne had kept her promise. Now, after running lines for more than an hour, Sharleen seemed better, and more confident. 'This really helps,' she said cheerfully. 'Thanks so much, Jahne.'

They were at Jahne's place. Jahne had noticed one thing the two seemed to have in common: like Jahne, Sharleen didn't ask people home or seem ever to mention her past or her private life. But now that their rehearsal was over, Sharleen seemed to want to talk. She stood up, stretched out her arms, and shook out her incredible hair. Then she walked over to the fireplace.

'Remember what you said the other day, about bein' discreet?'

'Uh-huh.'

'Well, I don't think I been discreet.'

Jahne smiled. 'Unless you were shoplifting or recently slept with a married man, I don't think you'll wind up on the front page of the *Enquirer* or the *Informer*.'

Sharleen picked up an ashtray off the mantel and fingered it absently. 'Michael McLain isn't married, is he?' Sharleen asked.

Michael's name and the *non sequitur* hit Jahne almost as hard as a slap. How does Sharleen know about my affair with Michael?

Had pictures of their single public date already hit the papers? She felt her own stomach tighten. Was he putting her name all around town? Was he talking about her? More important, was he talking about her scars?

Jahne, scared and shocked, looked across the room to see Sharleen watching her closely, her perfect mouth slightly open, her eyes wondering. 'He fucked you, too?' Sharleen asked. 'Oh, excuse me,' she added, beginning to blush. 'I don't usually use cuss words. I was just surprised, is all.'

Jahne could hardly take it all in. '*You've* slept with Michael McLain?'

Sharleen nodded. Jahne couldn't even manage to be polite. 'When?' was all she asked.

'Not so long ago. He called and asked me out. To dinner. At nine o'clock at night! We didn't eat, I just went out for coffee. And he was nice. Really nice. I shouldn't a done it, but he was so kind, like, and he was so interested in me. And he really listened to me. He gave some real good advice.'

That sounded like Michael, Jahne admitted. She felt her stomach turn over. 'So you've been dating?'

'No. Only that once. And then . . .' She paused and took a deep breath. 'He took me in his car up a canyon road and we had champagne and . . . well, like they say, he didn't call me the next mornin'!'

Jahne was reeling. Was he seeing Sharleen right about the time he took her, Jahne, to April's party? Well, she told herself fiercely, he never said he was a virgin. Or that he was seeing her, Jahne, exclusively. So, he saw Sharleen, and took her out once. So what?

'He gave me this,' Sharleen said shyly, and Jahne saw the twin of her own necklace hanging beneath the turtleneck Sharleen wore. But all at once, Sharleen began to sob. 'It wasn't nice, what we did. It wasn't right,' she said. Then Sharleen told the muddled story of what actually happened.

Jahne could hardly believe it! Was this the same man who'd been so forgiving of her own imperfections? He'd gotten Sharleen drunk and taken her against her will? Jahne felt her stomach turn. 'Sharleen, that's date rape.'

'What?'

'Date rape, Sharleen. He forced himself on you when you didn't want him to.' Jahne shivered. Hard to believe that the gentle lover

428

Michael seemed to be was capable of that. But Jahne knew one thing: Sharleen was incapable of lying.

Sharleen shrugged, ruefully. 'I got what I deserved, cheatin' on Dean. Made me feel small.' She looked up at Jahne. 'Guess I shoulda known I wasn't smart enough for him.' She paused, and wiped her eyes. 'He really likes you, huh? You like him, too?'

'Well, I did.' Jahne sighed. 'Sharleen, he doesn't like me, either. But he didn't rape me. And it wasn't your fault he did it to you.'

Oh, how could she, Jahne, be so stupid? She'd actually fallen for his bullshit, the old hambone. He'd never mentioned Sharleen. But he must run the same routine all the time. The advice, the necklace. Yes, Jahne thought wryly, and *you* thought you were special. She looked at Sharleen. The kid is for real, she decided. And he suckered her. Poor thing. Jahne would admit the truth to Sharleen, but not the whole truth. Not that she was *still* involved. Well, she wouldn't be for long. 'I slept with him,' Jahne acknowledged. 'Not that we did much sleeping,' she added.

Sharleen paused and considered for a moment. 'Did *you* like it?'

Jahne was surprised by the blunt question. 'Well . . .' Jahne thought about it. 'I liked the *idea* of it. I liked the idea that it was famous Michael McLain who was doing those things with me, but if I close my eyes I can't say it was much fun. I kept getting the feeling that the whole thing was choreographed.'

'What's "corey-oh-graft"?'

'Like he'd done it all a hundred times before – like all his moves were rehearsed.'

'Yeah, I know what you mean. Like there was no one home.'

'Well put. He did all the right moves, but I couldn't *feel* him.'

'Yeah. Like that Yule log that they show, Christmastimes, burning on TV. It looks like a fire, but you can't get no heat.'

Jahne laughed. 'Exactly.'

'I didn't want to do it with him, and I don't remember that much. Still, I really liked him,' Sharleen admitted. 'But then he didn't call. I guess he was like some of the boys in high school.' Sharleen thought for a moment of Boyd, and of that terrible night, but pushed the thoughts from her mind. She looked at Jahne. 'But he must have liked *you*.'

Jahne laughed. 'No, I don't think so.' Jesus Christ, she told herself. Thirty-seven years old and still falling for an actor's bullshit. Wouldn't she ever learn? How soon would Michael drop her? Well, she decided, not quite as soon as *she'd* drop *him*. It was over. She

429

leaned towards Sharleen. 'But I didn't know that you were involved, or that you cared about him. I wouldn't have dated him if I'd known. I'm so sorry if it hurt you. I'd never do that to a friend. I've had it done to me, and I know it hurts.'

'Oh, Jahne! What woman could take a man from you? You're so gorgeous and so talented and so smart.'

Jahne just smiled. 'I had my ugly-duckling phase,' she said.

Sharleen nodded, serious. 'You'd have had to, because if you'd always been so pretty you'd have no charity for plain girls. Did you have a dumb phase, too?'

Jahne laughed again. 'No, I think I'm having that *now*,' she told Sharleen.

'Jahne, it ain't none of my business, but I just want to tell you that Michael McLain called Lila yesterday.'

'*Lila?*'

'Remember she told Marty she had a date? I think it was with him.'

'How do you know?' Jahne asked sharply. She felt her stomach go queasy, her hands clammy.

Sharleen explained what she'd overheard. Jahne did not know what to think. What kind of game was Michael playing? And just how dumb had she been? 'I can't believe I've been so stupid,' Sharleen said.

'So, speaking of stupid, do you think you've ruined it with Dean?'

Sharleen shook her head. 'He don't know. But I feel *so* bad. Maybe I should tell him. Oh, I don't know what to do. Dean ain't smart. Lord, Jahne, he's way loads dumber than *me*. But he's got totally good feelings, you know what I mean? He don't never do anything mean or bad out of orneriness. Kind of like a hound, you know?'

Jahne nodded.

'I'm afraid to tell him, but I hate to be lyin' to him.'

'Want my advice?'

'Well, I most surely do.'

'Don't tell, and don't dwell on it, Sharleen. It wasn't your fault. Meanwhile, something real weird and real big has happened to us. It's like Cinderella. One day we were sweeping up the hearth, and the next day we're princesses. And you don't always know who's the prince and who's the frog.' She thought again of Michael. A real frog. 'It's a lot for anyone to adjust to. So we both went a little crazy. Let's just forgive ourselves, and promise each other we won't let it happen again.' She held her hand out to shake.

430

'You mean it?' Sharleen asked. Jahne nodded. Sharleen took her hand and shook it enthusiastically. 'It's a deal,' she said. They were both silent for a moment. 'You know, Sy Ortis wants me to do a record album.'

'I didn't know you could sing.'

'I cain't. But he says it will make a lot of money. And he wants me to. Think I should?'

'Sharleen, I don't know. If you want to, maybe. Sy Ortis doesn't want me to take a screen test for a movie, but I'm going to do it tomorrow anyway.'

'Good for you! You nervous?'

'A little. Well, a lot, really.'

'Kin I ask you somethin' else?'

Jahne nodded again.

'Did you mean it when you said you wouldn't do somethin' bad to a friend?' She paused, shy. 'Do you mean that *I* was your friend?' she asked.

'I most surely do,' Jahne said in a perfect imitation of the girl. Sharleen laughed.

'Hey, we better go,' she said, and gathered up her bag. 'I got to go to the recording studio.' She sighed.

Jahne walked with her to their cars. And then, both tentative, both shy, they hugged each other. But as Sharleen got into her car, Jahne thought of something. 'How did Michael get your number?' she called.

'Mr. Ortis gave it to him.'

Jahne stood very still. Sy had also set up the first date between her and Michael.

Sharleen and Dean pulled up into the circular driveway at the recording studio. Before the limousine came to a full stop, the rear door was pulled open by a young woman. 'Miss Smith, I'm *so* happy to finally meet you,' she said, extending her right hand. 'It's *such* an honour.' The girl was wearing a full cotton skirt, a Mexican blouse, and sandals, which Sharleen thought made her look like a poor Mexican, except this one was blonde and was wearing about ten thousand dollars' worth of jewellery. 'My name is Sandra,' the young girl said. 'I'm your personal assistant while you're here at the recording studio, so, if there is anything I can do for you to make you comfortable, *anything*, why, you just let me know.'

Sy Ortis moved between them then, coming out from a dark

limo that had been parked beside the entrance. He shooed Sandra back, took Sharleen's arm, and led her up the steps to the entrance door. Dean bounded up the stairs ahead of them, his tight, faded jeans straining at his rounded buttocks with each step, his black silver-tipped boots making clicking sounds on the concrete steps.

The cowboy hat Sy Ortis had given Sharleen just this morning sat forward on her head, like a hen on a fence post, casting a shadow across her eyes. It was uncomfortable, but Mr. Ortis had insisted she wear it.

Sharleen felt at home in her faded jeans and a man's unironed white shirt, tied in a knot beneath her breasts, but the cowboy hat felt awkward on her head, so now, thinking of what Jahne had said, she took it off and carried it in her hand by the string. Hell, she hadn't worn one back in Texas, why start now. Her feet in the new boots felt as cramped as a muskrat in a rabbit's hole, but she tried not to let the discomfort show. The whole outfit had been Sy's idea. 'These people are used to working with all the C&W greats. Hal King has personally produced Crystal Gayle, Roy Acuff, and all the hit albums of the New Ozark Boys. He'll be more confident if he sees you're for real, Sharleen. Let him see your Texan side. It'll help set the mood for the recording session.' Even though Sharleen knew there was no other side to her *but* the Texan side, as Sy called it, she decided to go along with his idea. So far, he'd been right about the endorsements and the other business deals he had arranged. And she sure didn't know cactus juice from cattle piss when it came to business contracts. So she smiled gratefully at Sandra and followed Mr. Ortis.

Sharleen felt a little nervous about bringing Dean, but she couldn't always leave him back home alone. It wasn't right. But she hoped he'd be – as Jahne had cautioned her – 'discreet.'

The glass door swung open as they reached it. A short, barrel-chested man stepped out and spoke in a deep drawl. 'Why, howdy, young lady. I been wanting to meet you since the first day I set eyes on you on my television set. My name's Hal King,' he said, and extended a huge paw of a hand, which Sharleen took and released quickly.

'And you must be Dean, Sharleen's friend. Any friend of Sharleen's is a friend of mine,' he said, and shook Dean's hand vigorously.

Sy Ortis didn't wait. 'Is there someplace where she can freshen up? It's been a long trip.'

Hal jumped back and reopened the doors. 'Why, of course! What could I have been thinking of?' he said. He turned to Sandra, who had scampered in just as the doors were closing. 'Sandra, you take Miss Smith to the star's suite, and see that she gets everything she needs. Curtis,' he said to a young man who had been standing by, 'why don't you show Dean around a bit. Make sure he sees the recording studio Miss Smith will be using, and show him around the electronics board.'

As if Dean would know the difference between a mike and an amp! Not that Sharleen knew much more. She nervously watched as Dean walked away. Then she and Mr. Ortis followed Hal King down the corridor of offices, the doors open onto each, secretaries peeking out, trying to catch a glimpse of Sharleen as she passed by. They finally came to a thick steel door, over which a sign said 'Recording Studio. Do not enter when red light is on.' Hal pushed it forward, and beckoned for them to follow. He opened another door, on the right, and Sharleen was immediately transported to someone's living room. The only indication that it was a recording studio was the four huge audio speakers placed expertly around the room at ceiling level.

'I hope you like it, Miss Smith,' Sandra said in a reverential whisper.

'Oh, of course I do. It's real cosy.' Sharleen turned to Mr. Ortis. 'I'd like a few minutes to rest and have a cola first; is that okay with you, Mr. King?'

'It would be more than all right. But you must do me the favour of calling me Hal. Everyone else does.' He turned the door handle and said over his shoulder, 'Just buzz me on the intercom on the phone when you're ready. Now, you just take your time. Sandra, anything Miss Smith wants,' he added, and opened the door.

'Hal,' Sharleen called out, 'call me Sharleen, would you? And would you kindly send in Dean as soon as he's finished with his tour?'

When she and Mr. Ortis were alone, Sharleen sat down and struggled out of her cowboy boots. 'I swear, my feet haven't hurt this bad since I walked home from school barefoot on the gravel road when I was a kid. Now, don't you ask me to put these on again, Mr. Ortis, 'cause I ain't going to do it.' She massaged her feet in silence for a moment. Why had she ever agreed to do this? Despite the voice lessons, Sharleen knew she couldn't sing. Not one song through without flatting.

Sharleen sat back with her feet dangling over the padded arm of the sofa, swinging them so the breeze would cool them off. She laughed and slapped her thigh. 'Why, if the kids back in high school heard I was going to record a country-and-western album, they would die laughing. I tried out for the glee club, but was hooted out of the room. I never *could* sing.'

'All you got to do, Sharleen, is what you did on the set a couple of months ago. Remember the scene Marty was directing you in? You were repairing a broken motorcycle, and he suggested you sing something to yourself while you were making the repairs. Remember that?'

'Well, sure, but I wasn't really singing. I was just imitating Patsy Cline.'

'That's what you think, kid, but that day the crew went crazy when they heard your voice. That's where I got the idea for you to record an album.'

Sharleen looked at him doubtfully. No one had said a word about her singing that day. Was Mr. Ortis telling the truth? 'Even though I'm just imitating somebody? It doesn't seem right to make money just by imitating other people.'

'Let's not go through all that again, okay, Sharleen? *You* say you're just imitating Loretta and Patsy, but that's not what's coming out. Trust me, Sharleen. You got a great voice all its own. Wait until you hear the playbacks today. You'll know what I mean.'

The door flung open, and Dean burst into the room, as excited as a kid at a state fair. 'Sharleen, I swear, they have every kind of gizmo and gadget out there. I bet Nashville ain't got nothing better. Curtis showed me all them colour-TV screens. He can write music on them, and they can play the music back without any instruments. And Sandra tole me about her job. You know, she's got to pick all the green M and M's out of the bowl because they upset Loretta Lynn. No, maybe it was Garth that hates 'em.' He paused, confused.

Sy looked over at Dean. 'Dean, can Sharleen here sing?'

'Sing? I guess so. Sometimes she sings.'

'See, Sharleen? Even Dean thinks you can sing.'

'Oh, but she don't sound too good,' Dean said.

'See? Even Dean don't think I'm any good. Doesn't that prove anything?'

'It proves you have another way of making money, Sharleen,' Sy answered. 'And you keep saying that's what you're looking for.'

'Right. Okay, I'm ready,' she said, and ran her fingers through her hair.

When she and Dean got home that night, Sharleen was well and truly exhausted. She had tried all day to sing a few tunes and knew how awful she sounded. She was embarrassed and ashamed, and wished she'd never have to go back there again.

Then, just as she was about to collapse onto the sofa, the phone rang. She groaned. There was no one – not even Jahne – that she wanted to hear from now. She was just too tuckered out.

'Sharleen, can you get that? I need to take the dogs out,' Dean shouted.

'Okay. But I just hope it's not a crank call.' She reached for the receiver. 'Hello,' she said.

'Hello yourself, young lady. How's my girl?'

'Dobe?' Sharleen almost looked at the receiver for confirmation.

'The one and only, young lady. Dobe Samuels, alive and well. So how are you and Dean?' he asked, his voice sounding friendly and cheerful.

'Dobe! Dobe, I can hardly believe it.' She struggled to sit up. 'Where are you? How did you know how to find me?' Sharleen was beside herself with joy. 'We moved since I sent you our last address. And this is an unlisted number.'

'I got my ways, you should know that by now, young lady.'

'Can you come on by?'

She heard his warm laugh. 'Not right now. I'm in Oregon.'

'What are you doing there?' she asked. She wanted to ask him to come to L.A. Lord, it felt so good to hear his voice!

'I'm working on a deal, honey-chile, and I can't get away. But, Sharleen, I need to ask you for a favour.'

Sharleen paused. As fast as it had come, that good feeling ebbed away. She should have known. That was the way it had been going since she started doing the TV shows. Everyone wanted her to do something for them. But very few thought about what *she* might need. She shrugged off her disappointment. Well, if there was anyone she *owed* a favour to, she and Dean sure owed one to Dobe Samuels. She'd be happy to do Dobe a favour, she told herself, but, before she could say so, Dobe said, 'Now, honey, if you're too busy, why, old Dobe would understand. I don't want you taking on too much.'

435

'Oh, no, Dobe. It wouldn't be too much. I'd be happy to do you a good turn.'

'That's my girl,' Dobe said, his voice friendly as usual again. 'Now, this is what I need you to do. There's a United States Customs auction in three weeks, at the Federal Building in downtown L.A. I need you to go to the auction and place a bid on something for me. I need you to bid on – now, write this down – I need you to bid on Lot Number 604. Can you do that, Sharleen? It starts at nine in the morning, and it will take a while for Lot 604 to come up, but it's *real* important to me. Of course, I'll pay you whatever you spend, but the most you'll have to bid is fifty dollars. Tops, seventy-five.'

Sharleen was busily writing on a scrap of paper. Why did Dobe want this? Was it some kind of scam? 'Now, wait a minute. What is it I'm bidding on, Dobe? Exactly. Is it them red pills? It's not drugs or anything like that, is it?'

'Sharleen, this is one-hundred-per-cent certified legal. It's doing business with the federal government, and I don't mess with them G-men in their mirror sunglasses.'

'Okay. So, in three weeks, I go to the auction and bid on this lot number. Then what?'

Dobe outlined the registering and payment methods for buying from a U.S. Customs auction. Then he gave her a number to call him at when she got finished with the auction, so he could arrange for pick-up. 'Got all that, kid?'

'Sure, Dobe. You can count on me,' she sighed. 'Are we gonna see you again?'

'I'll be in town to see you next month, Sharleen. And we're going to go out for a nice sit-down, you and Dean and me, and you're going to tell me all about how it feels to be a rich Hollywood star.'

'Dobe,' she said, in a whisper, 'It don't feel that good. In fact, it feels real lonely.' To her horror, she began to cry.

'Ah, there, there. Poor little girl. I told you, Sharleen. It ain't easy being a beautiful woman, especially a rich beautiful woman. But, now, honey, you hold on to them tears for a little while. Dobe'll be there next month to take care of both of you.'

'Dobe, I miss you,' she whispered, and wasn't sure if he'd heard her say it before he'd hung up the phone.

13

Pity the poor exposé writer. That's me, Laura Richie. Because you're only as good as your last scandalous book. And there aren't that many scandals to go around. Well, that may not be true: there are plenty of medium-grade, medium-weight, middle-class scandals, but they are not enough to make a best seller. So we are left with the scandals of the legends or the legends of the scandals, and everyone has done those. Between me and Kitty Litter (oh, Reader, you know who I mean), we have covered the waterfront. After her books about Ol'Blue Eyes and Nancy and that poor English dysfunctional family, and mine about Christina Onassis and the Cher book, there wasn't much left on the grand opera scale. So I was casting about me at this time for a new subject.

Because, let's face it: in gossip, people want the best. Sodomy and embezzlement barely raise an eyebrow unless the organs and amounts are the largest ever. And even then, the scandal palls quickly unless it's someone famous or who is attached to them. A story about a secret transvestite is only kind of sordid and pathetic, unless the guy is dressing up in famous underpants. And with all the stuff going on out there, there isn't much left that's shocking anymore. Look at poor Madonna. She has to stoop to photographing herself having sex with a dog to keep in the public eye.

My publisher was pressuring me. I was deciding between a Woody/Mia tell-all and a Michael McLain unauthorized but I was afraid that Woody was too New York Jewish for a broad appeal. And Michael had been around since the year of the flood. Plus, women were the ones who bought gossip books and they prefered gossip about women. My secretary was pushing for a triple biography of the 3/4 girls. But despite the absolutely massive wave of publicity they'd received, I felt they didn't have enough history to make more than a quick paperback out of. And I did only quality hardback gossip.

If only I'd known.

After Jahne heard Sharleen's revelation about Michael, and thought about the painful talk with Sharleen that had led up to it, Jahne rehearsed

the ways in which she'd tell him off. At best he was a sexaholic who was
out of control as well as a liar. At worst, well, it didn't bear thinking
about. Jahne rehearsed in her mind what she would say to him when
he called her. The accusations and names came easily. But each time she
got rolling she remembered not only how kind he had been to her about
her scars, but also how much he now knew. Was it safe to make him an
enemy? she wondered.

It was a question she did not have to answer. Michael McLain
never called her again.

It took more than a week for Jahne to realize Michael McLain had
dropped her. It reminded her a bit of that old punch line: You can't
fire me – I quit! But even if she didn't call him, she felt she had to
do *something* to exorcise his memory. One afternoon, driving down
Wilshire Boulevard, she passed Rancho La Brea and pulled over to
the side of the road. One of the stranger juxtapositions of Hollywood
was the La Brea Tar Pits, filled with prehistoric slime, sitting there
next to the movie and television studios, business towers, and the
Los Angeles County Museum of Art. There was symbolism there you
didn't have to reach hard for. Jahne got out of her Miata and walked
over to the cyclone fence that surrounded the pits. An appropriate
resting place for Michael's gift, she thought, and took the diamond
necklace on the thin gold chain out of her pocket. It was the first
piece of jewellery a man had ever given her. She shook her head,
and wondered if Michael got a quantity discount.

But, despite her joke, she was hurt. Not that she had loved
Michael, or that they had been committed to one another. She had
simply liked him, and she had believed that he had liked her, that
he had understood her. Well, she'd been wrong. Now she looked
down at the three stars in her palm. She hated the necklace, and,
with all the force she could, she threw it into the air. The sun glinted
on the diamond for a moment before it hit the viscous black of the
pit. She only wished it was Micheal, that old dinosaur himself, that
she was flinging away. The necklace sank without a trace. Let the
archaeologists of the future figure that one out, she thought, and
turned back to her car. Then she drove home to prepare for her
screen test.

If Jahne thought that TV had prepared her for movies, that
the small screen was like the big one, she found out she was
wrong. Makeup, for example, was a whole other reality. Bill
Wougle the makeup artist seemed to paint another face over her

own for the test. And the lights took more than an hour to adjust. Jahne nervously fondled the few sheets of script she'd been given. They didn't read like much. It was a fight scene between her and the male lead.

She was ushered onto the soundstage and was surprised – no, shocked – to see nothing but a fully made-up bed there, under the spotlight. She scanned the space, looking for Sam, and cleared her throat nervously. Was she expected to do this scene in bed? Then, from the corner of her eye, she saw him. Dressed in black, as usual, and striding towards her from behind the cyclorama. He tossed his head, swinging the pony tail from off his shoulder, a movement she remembered as habitual. 'Jahne!' he called, in what seemed a cheery voice. She felt anything but. He approached her. She felt his presence moving towards her almost as if a wall of energy were coming at her. She tingled.

'What's this?' she asked, nodding at the bed, trying to keep the question casual.

He smiled. 'Jahne, would you mind if I pulled the rug out from under you? You have every right to say no. But I'm not happy with the script I sent you. Not yet, anyway. Instead of lumbering you with it, I thought it might be better if we worked with something that wouldn't distract me. Something I'm familiar with.' He handed her a script.

She looked down at the cover. *Jack and Jill and Compromise*, it read. Despite the incredible brightness of the lights, Jahne felt her vision darken for a moment. 'I'm not prepared,' she said, and she felt that it might be the understatement of the nineties.

'I know. It's a lot to ask. Will you be a trouper?'

Quickly, she ran through her options. She could turn him down, but then he would believe her to be afraid of cold readings. And he might just ask her to prepare this for later, or he might decide not to work with her at all. If she said yes, she certainly would know this material better than anyone else. She could probably blow him away with it. But wouldn't he recognize her, and could she stand to tear her heart out in front of him this way? Could she bear being filmed in the role she'd lost forever? 'Give me a minute,' she told him.

'Of course,' he agreed, and walked her over to a chair in the corner. 'Take your time,' he said. 'I've marked the monologue I would like you to try.'

She waited until he left, joining the cameraman and boom

operator. But she already knew. Of course. It was the 'I've never been loved' aria. She'd recited it every night and twice on Wednesdays and Sundays for 426 performances. Back then she had thought that she was loved. She had thought that she was loved, at last, by Sam. She had had the strength to deliver it as a wounded bird, but what would she do now? She opened the script. She felt sweat trickle down her scalp and run to the back of her neck. The scars on her breasts began to itch. Her armpits were clammy; Bill's makeup must be running down her face; what could she do? What would she do?

Her eyes swept the script, and then the inspiration came. Not pathetic. Angry. Not sad and vulnerable because she'd never been loved, but enraged over it. She scanned the text. It would work. It would work *better*. She went through it, the whole thing, in her mind. She stood up and strode over to Sam. 'I can do this,' she said.

Jahne pulled the Miata onto the freeway, and released a long, noisy breath. I got it, she thought! I took my first screen test and I blew him away.

Of course, she couldn't be sure of anything. But she had taken his monologue, *her* monologue, and put a whole new spin on it. Instead of the pathetic cry 'I've never been loved,' it became one of rage. She delivered the whole thing with the passion of anger, of rage at the waste, the unfairness. And when she cried over the last words, they'd been tears of rage.

The crew had applauded. Jahne knew enough to know how rare *that* was, and if Jahne still knew Sam at all, she knew when he was interested in working with someone. And Sam was *definitely* interested in working with *her*.

Jahne wanted to be out of the car, physically moving, walking. The waiting for the callback was going to be tough. In the old days, she would have bought herself a good meal, or, better yet, a really sinful cake and some Ben & Jerry's ice cream. But now she couldn't afford to gain an ounce. Well, when the going gets tough, the tough go shopping, she thought, and groaned to herself at the silly expression.

Still, it would make a good release, a nice reward. She pulled her car into the underground parking at the huge shopping centre on the west side of Century City. Riding up the escalator to the main floor in the mall, she became aware of the looks and the whispers of people as they were going down. Damn, she thought, I forgot my sunglasses. Well, she'd just have to keep her eyes down. But as she scanned the displays in a store window, a teenage girl and her mother rushed up to her. 'Aren't you Jahne Moore?' the girl asked. 'May I have your autograph?' She thrust a crumpled Kleenex and pen out at Jahne, who signed it quickly while eyeing the entrance to the store. She'd better move into it. But, faster than she could get away, another woman came up behind the first two, and said, 'Mine, too, Miss Moore?' It took a moment for Jahne to realize, but suddenly a crowd had formed around her. And then almost in an instant the crowd grew. 'Me next,' someone yelled, and two women began pushing. 'Jahne Moore!' someone yelled. 'Cara!' yelled another. The crowd pushed. She was being pushed. The space around her disappeared. Then someone actually screamed.

Jahne fought the panic closing up her throat. Over the tops of the heads of the throng, Jahne noticed a tall, black security guard coming out of the store, and begin to push through the crowd. She felt elbows in her back, and the bodies pressed in around her. Then someone pulled at her hair. There were more screams, and her name was being shouted over and over. She felt as if she were drowning. 'This way, Miss Moore,' the guard said when he finally reached her, and extended his hand. Jahne took it, and let the man propel her through the crowd, blindly pushing aside arms holding paper and pens as he pulled her along.

'Miss Moore, please, for my little girl,' one woman said. Jahne hurriedly took the paper, signed it while she moved, and handed it back in the general direction of the woman. Another hand grabbed at it, but a new voice started screaming, 'That's mine, give that to me.' Jahne caught a glimpse of two women struggling, and, for the first time, she actually began to fear for her safety.

'Give me one, Cara! You gave one to that bitch, why not me?' a woman was screeching at her, as the guard pulled on the shop door to open it against the mob.

'No more autographs today!' the guard shouted.

'Too good for us, Jahne?' a fat, middle-aged woman shouted. She kept her head down. 'Fuck you! We made you, you bitch.' That last remark would have frozen her to the floor if the guard hadn't given her arm a final tug, pulling her to safety on the other side of the doors, which he then locked behind them. He led her to the back of the store. Jahne, feeling dizzy and almost faint, heard the security guard calling the police on his walkie-talkie, leaving the crowd to swirl behind the glass like aquarium sharks in a feeding frenzy.

Jahne didn't have to look in the mirror as she slumped onto the little office sofa. She knew she was pale.

'Drink this,' a woman in a security uniform said, handing her a cup of water.

She gulped it, just to do something. But it did make her feel better. 'What happened?' she asked.

'What happened?' the guard repeated. '*You're* what happened.'

'I . . . I had no idea. I mean, I've never seen this before.'

Two policemen came hurrying into the office from the rear delivery door. 'Follow me, Miss Moore,' one of them snapped. 'We'll go out through the trucking bay and drive you to your car. Then we'll follow you in the squad car until you're safely home.'

'Thank you, I can't tell you how . . .'

'Don't thank me. Just don't do this again. Next time, bring your own security, like all the others.'

It was surprisingly difficult for Jahne to get an appointment with Gerald La Brecque. She resented it. Perhaps she was simply getting used to the star treatment she thought she deplored, Jahne told herself grimly as she waited for the man to arrive. Both Michael McLain and someone at Marty's office had recommended him, but, despite her calls, it had taken almost two weeks to get this home visit. Two weeks during which she had not heard a word from Sam Shields.

At two-thirty – *exactly* two-thirty, Jahne noticed – her buzzer rang. Not bad-looking, she thought as she opened the door. Oh, fine, she told herself. How desperate are we? Next we'll be looking over UPS men and personal trainers as potential dates.

The audition, seeing Sam, and the mini-riot had unsettled her, no doubt about it. Funny how being mobbed had made her feel lonely. It took the riot to make her believe that she was different now. Special and alone. Then she hadn't heard from Sam. Could he have recognized her? Could he have simply rejected her performance? For two weeks, she'd been obsessed with the question. No wonder she was looking for love in all the wrong places. She smiled politely at the security consultant.

But La Brecque really wasn't bad-looking. Average height, dark, with a neat moustache that looked very soft, although the rest of him looked anything but. He eyed her very directly – his eyes were a strange, very light grey that made them seem almost colourless – and accepted her offer of a seat but not a drink.

'Sorry about the delay in setting this up, Miss Moore, but we've been swamped just now.'

'That's all right,' she found herself saying, and meaning it, though she'd resented him two minutes before. He seemed so, well, so very *real*. God, when was the last time she'd dealt with anyone outside the Industry? she wondered. No time during the last five months. Even her houseboy was an unemployed actor.

He looked across the coffee table at her. 'So,' he began. 'Why don't you brief me on the current situation . . .?' His sentence trailed off with such a slight inflection that she barely recognized it as a question. It was more of a directive.

'Well, it's really an issue of security. I mean, of course it would be or I wouldn't call you. Security here and when I'm out. I mean, I don't want a bodyguard or anything. Probably I'm overreacting, but there have been a few . . . incidents. And fan letters.' It was the letters from prisoners that really bothered her the most. She'd read the first one with compassion and a vague sense of obligation. Then the next. She got so that she could pick them out in the piles, the number at the upper left-hand side, the prison franking instead of a stamp. Some were almost all right, others merely obscene, but the worst were the fifty-page dedications, complete with drawings and/or poetry. Lots of them were worse, but the letters from men in prison really frightened her. 'They make me nervous. But it's probably nothing. Religious nuts, or teenage pranks. You know the sort of thing. . . .'

But instead of smiling at her reassuringly, he only put his hand to his cheek and rubbed, a sort of assessment movement. 'Have you saved them?' he asked.

For the very briefest moment, she thought he was talking as Sharleen might, in the religious sense. Then, stupidly, she asked, 'The letters? No. They're horrible. Why would I save them?'

'To save yourself.'

'Save myself from what?' she asked, fright rising, and with it anger. Jesus! She had waited to see this guy and used up a precious free afternoon to be reassured. Now was he going to try to scare her out of her wits? Is that how he earned his living? By increasing the ever-growing paranoia of the Hollywood crowd? 'Are you saying this is a matter for the police?'

La Brecque rubbed his cheek again. 'I'm afraid not. They only intervene *after* something happens. Before that, it's up to you, me, and the courts.'

'But they're just the usual crank letters. You know.'

'Well, I don't, because I haven't seen them. And probably most of them are. But there are others that are more indicative of possible deranged behaviour. And we keep a computerised file of the dangerous ones we know about, try to be aware of their whereabouts. We keep adding to our data base. It's important to save them.'

'I get a lot of mail from prisoners. They scare me,' she finally admitted.

'Well, those are the ones behind bars. It's the *others* I worry about. Rebecca Schaeffer. And that sniper shooting of Genny Logan, for example. Right in her living room. That one hasn't been solved. She wasn't a client of mine.' He looked around. 'If you don't mind my saying so, Miss Moore, you are being very cavalier about your safety. Anyone could get in here if they wanted to. And you couldn't stop them if you didn't want to.' He paused. 'Do you own this place?'

'No.'

'Good. Because it can't be secured. Not here in Birdland, and on a public road. They call this part of the Hollywood Hills the Swish Alps. Lots of gays. Nothing wrong with them, but lots of possibility of street hustlers.'

'So what can I do?'

'You can move. Buy a place. We'll have to seal your property tax records so no one can access your home address. And we'll check any place out that you consider buying to ensure its safety. But you've got to get out of here.'

'But I just rented it!' She'd barely settled in here, was just starting to feel comfortable, *plus* she had a lease she couldn't break.

'Miss Moore, this is really a matter of life and death we're talking about.'

Jahne looked at him, expecting a smile at the hyperbole. But there was none. 'You ever hear of Robert Bardo?'

'No.'

'He walked up to Rebecca Schaeffer's door. She was starring in a sitcom. Lived in a place a lot like this. Never met Bardo. Didn't know him. Opened the door. Gave him an autograph. She was nice, pleasant, to him. It wasn't enough. He came back. He killed her.' Jahne shivered.

'I'll do whatever you say.'

'We'd need quite a bit of information to start.'

'Such as?'

'Names of friends, past lovers, any enemies. Professional jealousies, past and current employees, that sort of thing. Relatives, their addresses, current relationships.'

Jahne felt a moment of panic. Should she disclose her past, or pretend she had none? Tell him about Sam, about Michael, about Michael and Sharleen, about Michael and Lila? Oh, Jesus, her life was becoming unmanageable!

'Of course,' he told her, 'all of this will be totally confidential. There has never, ever been a leak from my organization.'

'And how much will all this cost?'

'Quite a lot, I'm afraid. For the time being I'll put staff on per diem. Then what I'll do is put together a proposal along with a fee quote. There will be an initial fee, and then a monthly retainer. A year will run in the mid-five figures.'

She sat there, stunned, and just looked at him. Mid-five figures. Like fifty thousand dollars? She could take care of a lot of Dr. Moore's patients for that! And buy a few Donna Karan outfits as well. She sighed.

'It might make it easier if you think of it as part of the cost of doing business,' he said gently. It was the gentleness of his tone, combined with the glint of his wedding band as it rubbed his cheek, that brought tears to her eyes. Because, all at once, she wanted him to rub his hand across her own cheek, to tell her that it would be all right. To take care of her.

Jahne spent the evening throwing a few things in a bag and calling hotels. She didn't know what she would do. In the meantime, she called Mai and slept at her house.

The next day, back to pick up more of her stuff, Jahne was still reeling from La Brecque's security evaluation. How vulnerable he said she was, how she would have to move to another place, how much it would cost, how she would have to watch her movements in public. It was all so depressing, so limiting.

And lonely. She almost blushed at remembering how she had reacted to the sight of La Brecque, as if she hadn't been with a man in years. As if she were desperate. He didn't catch any of it, of course. Nor the expression on her face when she noticed his wedding ring. At least she hoped not.

Jahne walked over to her desk, which, now she knew, dangerously exposed her to the sights of possible snipers from outside. She sat at it nonetheless, took out a piece of her new stationery – with her address here, which would be useless now – and began to write to the only friend she felt she had in the world.

> Dear Brewster,
>   Thanks for the picture from Raoul. He's getting good. I'm glad to hear about the speech improvement. Who cares if all he wants to say are swear words, as long as they are well articulated. I guess his speech therapy is working. I miss him and I miss you.

Could she write that? Wasn't it too personal? She'd sound pathetic, and give him the wrong idea.

The phone rang, and Jahne put down her pen and walked over to answer it. Anything was a relief right now, though she couldn't imagine who had her number except Sy and some other Industry types she didn't want to hear from. She sighed. 'Jahne, it's April Irons. Have I caught you at a bad time?'

'Not at all. In fact, I was just sitting here, staring out at my view, feeling how wonderful it was to be in California. How are you, April?'

'Couldn't be better. And neither will you be after I tell you why I'm calling. Sam and I *love* you. We've screened the test a dozen times already. We feel you're *perfect* for the part of Judy in *Birth of a Star*.'

Jahne felt her heart surge in her chest. She was right! She had blown Sam away! 'You *have* made me happy, April. *Very* happy. Thank you.' But what was flooding her? It wasn't joy or triumph or even relief that she had 'passed' her screen test. It focused on the 'we': April said 'Sam and I.' April referred to them as 'we.' And why hadn't Sam called her?

'Of course, we'll work out the details with your agent, but I wanted to be the one to tell you personally. By the way, is your agent *still* Sy Ortis?'

Still? Jahne caught the inflection. 'Yes, he is.'

April sighed. 'Fine. We'll talk to him, then. But I *know* we'll work everything out. I *know* you're going to be just fabulous.'

'Well, thank you. Really. Thank you,' she mumbled. God! She'd done it. She'd be in a movie. No, she'd *star* in a movie. If she wanted to. But Sy would be furious. He'd told her over and over that it was a stupid concept. Well, it was her career, her decision, not Sy's. 'April, send the contract to me first. I'd like to think it over. And I'd like to give it to Sy.'

'Fine. And congratulations, Jahne.'

Jahne put the phone down and threw her arms around herself. She couldn't believe it! Even though she'd thought she'd been good at the screen test, even though she'd been confident, she hadn't really believed this could happen: that she could be cast in an important feature, that she could be a star, a *movie* star, and that she could work again with Sam!

She waltzed herself around the room, and then she stopped again at the phone. My God, she'd have to tell someone! Who could she call? Mai! And she'd get Mai a job on the picture, doing her wardrobe! It would be good news for both of them!

'Hooray for Hollywood,' she said out loud, and drew the curtains so the snipers might miss.

14

Lila felt as if there wasn't anyone in her life who didn't want something from her. Marty wanted her gratitude, Michael wanted her body, Robbie wanted her fame, and every asshole out there wanted her autograph. This afternoon, all she wanted was to spend some time alone, but no one would let her.

Aunt Robbie had called and asked to come over. This wasn't going to be just a friendly visit, Lila was sure of it. His tone told her something was up. But, whatever it was, Lila didn't give a shit.

Lila stretched out on the lounge, her body glistening under the sleek film of oil. Beyond her, Malibu Beach also stretched out, glaring white in the sun, while the waves rolled relentlessly. She felt the knots of stress begin to uncurl, and willed the muscles in her body to soften. She heard the clomping on the steps to the deck, then opened her eyes to see Aunt Robbie's huge form lurching around the corner of the house. 'Where're your skates?'

she called out to him as she settled back and closed her eyes again. 'Let me guess. José?'

Lila heard Rob waddle over to the other chaise and flop down with a grunt. 'That queen Krazy-Glued the fucking wheels. Tight as a frog's ass.'

Lila opened her eyes and sat up, pulling the backrest of the chaise into a sitting position. She picked up the towel at her feet and dabbed at the perspiration on her forehead. 'If you want something to drink, you'll have to get it yourself,' she said. '*And* bring me a Diet Coke,' she added, as if she'd just thought of it.

'Where's Yolanda?'

'Catch up, Robbie. Yolanda was three or four wetbacks ago. I fired the latest lazy bitch this morning. Carmen or Carmela, or whatever.'

'Why? Caught her trying on your crown or something?' Robbie snapped as he went in to pour their drinks.

That had a little too much edge to it to suit Lila. She felt her muscles tensing up again. She'd just have to get rid of him. She waited until Robbie returned. 'I just like my privacy. If I tell them not to go into a room, they go into it. If I lock a drawer, they want to find out why.' Lila sighed. 'So, Robbie if you have something on your mind, just spit it out, for chrissakes. I hate those sideways jabs you give. It reminds me too much of someone I used to know.' She watched Robbie's expression change from feigned surprise to resignation.

'Okay', he said, and took a sip of his vodka Collins, as if to lubricate his vocal cords. Lila waited.

'I saw your mother,' he said, and paused, as if Lila gave a shit.

'She's not dead yet?' Lila asked.

'She's in a bad way, Lila. She's fallen apart.'

'So's the Soviet Union. I could care less about either of them.'

Robbie got up and came and sat at the foot of Lila's chair. 'Lila, I need your help in pulling her together. She's killing herself, and Kevin is helping. Please Lila. It's not like you didn't have something to do with the fall.' He took another sip of his drink, then held the frosty glass out in front of him, looking at it. 'And, after all, you *are* her *daughter*.'

Lila didn't have to stop to think about it. She raised both feet and kicked Robbie hard enough to knock him off the lounge chair, right on his fat ass on the wooden deck. She couldn't see the shock in his face; she could only feel her own. 'You fucking hypocrite,' she screamed, now standing over him. 'You are just jealous that she spends more time with Kevin than with you and then you have the balls to pull the oldest guilt trip on the planet on me? Like your own fucking mother isn't living on welfare somewhere in Minnesota – you don't even *know* where – and you have the nerve to tell *me* what my responsibility is? Well, I'm not her daughter. You get that? I'm not and I never was!'

Robbie struggled to his feet while Lila strode over to the gate. But he still whined. 'I can't take it alone, Lila. She needs help, and there's no one to help her except you and me. Ken won't go near her, won't have her in the house anymore. You've got to . . .'

'I don't got to do shit, Robbie. Do you hear me? Not *shit*. She's your friend, not mine.' Lila whirled around and through the door into the house, Robbie on her heels.

'If you don't do something . . .'

'What? If I don't do something, *what*, Robbie? What could possibly happen to Lila Kyle if I don't do something for Theresa O'Donnell?'

Robbie was rubbing his ass where he had fallen. 'See her, Lila. Make contact with her. She loves you, Lila, in her own way. And she misses you.'

Lila was suddenly very calm. She had thought Robbie understood, but she could see now he didn't, never had. He'd been on Theresa's side all along. He was nice to Lila, just to be close to the action, to be able to do what he was trying to do today: get Lila back under Theresa's talons. 'She doesn't love me or anyone. She just wants a piece of the action. She just wants back into Hollywood. She misses an audience, not a daughter. Go back to the cunt and tell her I said she should die. And while you're at it, die with her, you traitor.'

Lila walked calmly to the staircase to her bedroom, then turned. 'Now get out, Robbie, and don't come near me again. I don't want to see you here again, ever. You're toxic, just like she is.' Lila walked up the stairs, knowing, even before she reached the top, that she was alone in the house.

15

There may be one thing worse than having a TV show that bombs as big as Neil Morelli's did: having a hit. If Hollywood hates a loser — and trust me, it does — it hates and envies a winner even more.

Marty DiGennaro had been big and commercial before, but now he was big, commercial, and had to produce a constant string of toppers. Whereas he was used to producing one movie every two years, TV was forcing him to produce the equivalent of a movie every two weeks.

There were problems with the writers, problems with the locations, problems with the setups, problems with the sponsor, and problems with the suits from the Network.

Marty was used to dealing with problems, but he had never dealt with such a fast, massive buildup of interest in a project that he was still working on. Usually the media, the publicists, the critics, the money men started in on his work when it was done. Now they were all over him *while he still had a goddamn hour to film every goddamn week*! No wonder David had given up on *Twin Peaks*.

There was so much goddamn interest in the show, he knew he couldn't top it. And now he'd managed to script an end-of-season cliffhanger that would have them screaming for more. But so what? Then he was going to have to follow it up with next season's opening show.

He'd hoped for a hit. He'd gotten it. He'd hoped to change the look of TV, to revolutionize it. He had. He wanted carte blanche, to write his own ticket. He had that. And the pressure was killing him.

Go know.

Worst of all was the situation with Lila. He, Marty DiGennaro, had leverage. He'd already had a string of Oscars, and now, after taking a risk, he's actually created a *succès d'estime* and an incredible money-spinner for TV, yet he had abso-fucking-lutely *no* leverage with Lila Kyle, the star he'd made, the woman he'd not only cast out of nowhere but given all the best lines, the best shots. Since their first and last date, nothing.

When she raised an objection, he folded. When she asked, he gave. Her picture on every goddamn magazine in the country, more film and public-appearance offers than she and a twin could handle, and she had Marty to thank for that. But she didn't.

She wouldn't sleep with him. No, it was worse than that! She wouldn't even date him!

It's not like there was anyone else. Sally had checked that out for him. Marty could at least understand if there were. Not *like* it, but understand. A date with Michael McLain. It ended early. Nothing else. Sally followed her everywhere for more than two weeks. *Nada.* Then, relieved at first, Marty thought, maybe she's gay? But she didn't even have any girlfriends. Sally had told him that Lila had *no* friends, at least none who visited her at her house in Malibu. *Marty* had never even been in her goddamn house. Just that crazy old swish, Robbie What's-His-Name. He was the only one, came and went as if he lived there. But, then, there wasn't a starlet in the Valley who didn't have a pet queer.

Maybe Lila was just single-minded, put all her energy into her career, had none left over for anything or anyone. Marty tried to remember some of the other actresses he had worked with. *All* of them had one-track minds, for chrissakes, but he had slept with most of them, at least the ones he wanted. Actually, the ambitious ones were the easiest to lay. So why not Lila?

A religious nut? No way. Lila didn't have a spiritual bone in her body. Marty knew that much. What, then – celibacy? Fear of AIDS? Coldness? What the fuck *was* it? I'm not *that* ugly, he thought. I have money, I keep my body in fairly good condition, I'm sensitive, unselfish in bed – generous, even. Hey, I'm a fucking Boy Scout.

Once, long ago, Marty had been a nerd kid from Queens, a kid who couldn't get laid. But that was very long ago. And Marty didn't like, even now, to remember how it felt to be an awkward, lame outsider with fantasies that would never be fulfilled. Lila made him remember, though. Doesn't the bitch know I could still make or break her?

But, of course, Lila did. And it was almost like she didn't care. She even had told him that she was going all out for that April Irons *Birth* remake. And then she had the nerve to ask him to coach her. No other actress had ever treated him like this. They all had responded to his overtures; it was expected in the business. Actresses slept with directors, that was the Hollywood Law. Long ago, Marty had decided not to question actresses' motives, but to happily accept their attentions. And he got plenty of attention.

But not from Lila. And *that* only made Marty want her even more.

16

The pressure of a weekly TV taping schedule is beyond the imagination of the everyday TV viewer (what Sy Ortis would call 'The Regulars'). The stars and crew spend a lot more time with each other than they do with their own families. Most of their waking hours are spent in each other's presence. And all the fear and competition, jealousy, insecurity, pettiness – all the ugliness of people under pressure – gets magnified and exaggerated. The behaviour on the set almost makes the U. S. Senate look mature.

Of course, feuds break out despite the work of publicists, and word often leaks to civilians about the bad behaviour of the stars on the set. And there's plenty of it. The women act like children and the men act like babies. But in my experience, when there's fighting between women, it gets a lot more media attention. Catfights make better news. Hey, who said life was fair? My readers keep reading me, and that's what counts.

Sometimes, keeping the peace is easy: Just meet the star's demands. When there is only one big star, cave in or dump 'em to keep the peace. On Dallas, *Larry Hagman had the biggest stick. On* Dynasty, *only Joan Collins played prima donna. And on* Designing Women, *Delta Burke was, in the end, expendable. But on* Three for the Road, *all the girls were necessary, and each, in her way, was difficult.*

Never did bad blood run thicker, never did the competition get sharper, never were the stakes as high as on Three for the Road. *Back in the days of* Charlie's Angels *cast and crew alike were calling one of those stars Hate Jackson. But the nicknames on the 3/4 set were unprintable. And by the closing episode of the season, the bile flowed like wine. That was the scene a disintegrating Neil Morelli was so cheerfully walking into.*

Neil stepped off the bus and walked the two blocks to the studio entrance. If he'd still had a car, the trip would have taken only twenty minutes. But by bus, transferring, stopping, and starting, it took almost an hour. The geriatric local. Where do all these old ladies come from? Neil wondered. Are they sent to California by the government when they reach a certain age? There ought to be a law. If it takes more than five minutes to climb onto a bus, you don't ride.

'Neil Morelli,' he said to the guard, who looked him up and down before peering at his clipboard. 'My car's been seized by DEA agents,' he explained with a smile, while standing in the driveway next to the security booth.

The guard looked up and, now also smiling, said, 'Oh, yes, Mr. Morelli. You're expected. Lot Five. Take a left at the main building.' He tipped his hat as Neil mimed starting a car engine, shifting gears, and, making motor noises with his mouth, driving away, turning an imaginary steering wheel.

This is more like it, he thought as he approached the lot. Back where I belong. Neil had been surprised – no, stunned – when Sy Ortis' office tracked him down and told him about this gig. He didn't speak to Sy himself, but maybe the guy *wasn't* a complete piece of shit. Maybe he was all right. I gotta call him later and let him know all is forgiven, Neil reminded himself. Some of those notes I sent him were pretty rough. But it just goes to show you, you gotta stay on these bastards' asses to get what you want. Perseverance pays off, especially when you don't have connections.

The large steel door was open, so Neil walked into the hangar-like building and looked around. The buzz of activity sent adrenaline shooting through his body, almost causing him to walk on tiptoe, he felt so high. 'Where's the second-unit AD?' he asked a technician who was walking past, carrying a roll of cable. The guy motioned with his head and kept walking.

Neil approached the second-unit assistant director, who was wearing a sweatshirt and jeans, and holding a clipboard. She was in charge of shooting pickup shots, backgrounds, and some of the extras' scenes, but she reminded him of a camp counsellor. All she needed was a whistle on a cord around her neck. She was standing in a semicircle of what appeared to be Hell's Angels, but were readily identifiable to Neil as actors in costume. Except for one guy who was more interested in his nails than what the AD was saying, everyone stared passively at the woman as she ran off a list of instructions.

When she dismissed the actors, Neil turned on his best smile. 'Hi, I'm Neil Morelli.'

'Yes,' she said, as she continued to walk away, absorbed in whatever was written on her yellow pad. Probably the list of those who were to be shot at dawn.

'I'm in the show. There was some mix-up, and I haven't gotten a script. But I'm a quick study.'

She stopped and looked at him, consulted her list, nodded, then made a check-mark on the pad. 'I'm Ronnie Wagner, AD. Pick up your script at that table over there,' she said, pointing, 'and read your part through; we'll start blocking in an hour.' She started to walk away.

'What *is* my part?' he asked, hoping she would stand still long enough to answer.

She did, but impatiently. 'I don't know. A waiter or something.'

'Not a continuing character?' he asked, trying to keep the panic from sounding in his voice.

Ronnie looked at him and began to rattle off the specs of the job. 'You're a bit, not a character. Four lines or under, used on an as-needed basis, no contract. Didn't whoever got you the job explain all this to you?'

He didn't like her tone, or her attitude. Whoever got me the job? He felt his anger boil up in him. 'Hey, bitch,' he said, 'my *talent* gets me jobs. My *agent* arranges details. My *agent* is Sy Ortis. And I haven't gotten all the details from him yet. We'll be having a meeting after the shoot today. And I'll mention your name. So thanks,' he said, and walked away.

He grabbed his script from the table, and began to look for his part. Whale shit. Once again he was playing a part as low as whale shit was on the bottom of the ocean. 'FIRST WAITER' was yellow-highlighted. Jesus, who the fuck is *Second* Waiter? he asked himself. Whoever is is lower than whale shit, he answered. Not that that made him feel any better. The bitch was right, he thought as he finished looking over his lines. Under four. Well, at least that means no agent's commission. But if Sy doesn't even get a piece of this, why did he bother? What the fuck is going on? He looked over the part. The lines aren't even *funny*.

'How're you doing?' a voice said from behind him. 'I'm Todd Shanley, Second Waiter.' A big smile on his too-broad, too-tanned face. 'I'm a friend of Ronnie's from school. Northwestern.'

For Chrissakes, doesn't *anyone* in this town fill out an application for a job and take a test? No, he told himself, nobody does. Not even secretaries. 'Nice to have pull,' Neil said to the kid. 'Who do you have to blow to get *five* lines?'

'Who do *you* blow?' Todd tossed back, still smiling.

Neil felt his scalp tingle, constricting under the mounting anger. 'I been fucking Ronnie Wagner three, four times a week for a couple of years now. If I get real good at it, she said she's gonna get me an even *bigger* part *next* season.' Neil pushed away from the wall, and began to walk towards the public phone, ignoring Todd's dropped jaw.

He dialled the now unfamiliar number of Sy's office. But the still-familiar secretary-from-hell spoke first. 'Hey, Laura, let me speak to him. I want to thank him for getting me this job.' Neil forced himself to smile. Amazingly, without a wait, he was put through. He spoke into the phone again. 'Sy, hey, thanks for the gig, man. I really appreciate it. No, really, I know I've been a ball-buster . . . okay, a prick . . . but I just wanted to tell you, I really appreciate this chance.' Neil paused. 'Especially since you don't get a piece of it, since it's a four-and-under.'

Neil waited for Sy to say something, but he didn't. 'I'll make it up to you, Sy. Just wait. I promise. I'll turn this bit into a continuing character in three episodes, mark my words. But, Sy, tell me, is there anyone else I should thank? I mean, how did you get the spot for me? I don't want to appear ungrateful to anyone, you know, so how did it come about?' He paused, and listened while Sy both wheezed asthmatically and sucked on his medicine. What was he mumbling?

'Marty DiGennaro? Shit, if I had known *he* was in the audience, I would have been *good*. But that's great to hear. The director liked my bit at the club. Except, if I was so good, I mean . . .' He paused again. '. . . how come he didn't give me any funny lines?' Sy mumbled something else, warning him to take it slow, to behave. The usual bullshit.

'Sure, sure. You're right. I can be as patient as the next guy. And thanks again, Sy.'

Ronnie, the AD with attitude, called everyone together on the set, the interior of a hippie restaurant. Neil's heart started pounding as he saw the three stars of the show cross the floor from their dressing rooms to the set. He wasn't a fan type, but they really were spectacular. Neil hadn't been prepared for this reaction. He had made it a point *not* to watch the most-watched show in America,

455

just because it was, and also because the dynasty-kid was on it, Lila Kyle. But when he got the gig, one of the guys he worked with had provided Neil with the tapes of every show since day one, and Neil had spent a brain-numbing twenty-four hours watching them on a borrowed VCR. He would have assumed that he had been desensitized to the three beauties, but instead he found himself gaping. He hated to admit it, but Lila was even more beautiful in person than on-screen. And the other two weren't chopped liver.

Marty DiGennaro joined them, and immediately got down to work. Neil hardly had time to be impressed by the guy, who was almost as short and skinny as he was. Neil started to relax. When there was a moment's silence, he even filled it with a little joke. The blocking was going well until Lila finally looked at his face. 'Wait a minute,' she said, stopping rehearsal. 'Don't I know you?'

'I've never had the pleasure, Ms. Kyle. I'm Neil Morelli,' he said, smiling, holding out his hand, then dropping it to his side. His face coloured. Everyone on the set was looking. But, hey, she *was* gorgeous.

'That's what I thought. I heard about you. You're the guy that has a lot to say about families in the business. It's nice to see you're not too righteous to make money off them, though.'

Neil noticed Sharleen Smith wince and avert her eyes and fold her arms across her chest, and Jahne Moore take a tentative step forward, then stop. 'I work when I can, Ms. Kyle.'

Sharleen came over and introduced herself. 'Glad to have you on board, Neil. I heard you're very funny.' Jahne Moore was right behind her. She patted him quickly on the shoulder, then moved away.

The tension on the set was real. And Neil became more and more agitated the closer he got to doing his bit. In the first take, Lila stepped on his lines, then glared at him like *he* made the mistake. Then, for the second take, she jostled him with her elbow, and accused him of being off *his* mark. Neil wanted to strangle the bitch. He was so on edge, he was sure he was going to make a real mistake now. This witch was working on him.

They tried a third take, then a fourth – too many tries for a simple line. Neil started sweating, certain this was going to do him in. Sure enough, 'I want a conference, Marty,' she said, as she walked over to him. Neil heard Lila say, as he was meant to, 'Get this guy off the set.' But, this time, Marty shook his head, and walked away. Jesus, what do I do now? Neil knew that everyone's eyes would be on him, his every move scrutinized. And right there he made a vow to himself. Someday, he'd kill Lila Kyle. But in the meantime, he'd save face.

He tried to lighten the tension, and leaned over to Sharleen. 'Was Lila ever a nun? She reminds me of my third-grade teacher.'

'Oh, no,' Sharleen said, without the slightest glimmer of a smile 'She's been in show business all her life.'

'It's not enough I have the *Birth of a Star* audition today, but now I have to put up with that asshole? Marty, I'm a nervous wreck. I can't work with him here. I'm too upset.' She held her forehead in one hand, as if she had a bad headache.

'Fine. Let's finish the take so you can prepare yourself for your audition. Forget about the guy, Lila.'

'I *can't* forget about him, for Christ's sake, Marty. He's the bastard who puts me down, compares me to Tori Spelling! He's upsetting everyone. Look at the expression on Jahne's face.'

She saw Marty turn to Jahne, then back to her. 'You're right, Lila. Okay? Now, go along with me on this one. Then I'll even help you with your script for the audition.'

'Get him off the set,' she said, making sure her voice was loud enough to carry. She wanted the worm to know, when he got canned, who was responsible.

Marty shook his head. 'I can't, Lila. I owe someone. I have to keep him for one episode, at least.' Then he turned from her and rejoined the cast.

Lila felt humiliated. Everyone had heard her demand the guy be kicked off. And now everyone knew Marty had said no to her. He didn't usually do that, but this time was more than she could tolerate. To take this guy's side over her! This little weasel, this ferret! Everyone knew what his comedy routine was. Lila had heard the crew snicker over some of the lines from Neil's act. She cursed Neil, and cursed Marty.

She pushed it from her mind. I've got other things I have to handle today, she thought. The big part, my chance of a lifetime. A part in *Birth of a Star*. Time enough to deal with the Neil Morellis of the world. After today, when she got the part. After today, when she would be more famous than her mother. Wait until April Irons sees me. Marty says I can be good. But *I* know I will be *great*. Then, *then* I'll step on the cockroaches. Lila flounced off to her trailer and jerked open the door.

It was comparatively dark inside, and she didn't bother to turn on the light. The darkness and the coolness were a relief after the hot lights. She began to tear off her sweaty blouse and underwire brassiere. The goddamn thing felt as if it was cutting holes in her rib cage. Then she unzipped the buckskin jeans that she wore and let them drop to the floor.

'Excuse me . . .' a heavily accented voice said out of the darkness. 'I vas just leaving your new costume. . . .'

Lila clutched at herself, bending over and trying to hide her body. She scrabbled in the dim light for a towel, a robe, anything to cover herself with. What the fuck was anyone doing in her trailer?

Mai Von Trilling handed her a cotton cover-up from the hook next to her dressing table. Lila snatched it from her hand and struggled into it, tearing a sleeve as she viciously pushed her arm through the armhole. 'What the fuck are you doing here?' she screamed. 'Who gave you permission to spy on me?'

'I'm very sorry, I vas only . . .'

'You were only snooping. Did Jahne tell you to look through my things? Have you taken anything?' The skinny old bitch was backing out the door. Did she think that was it? Did she think she was going to get away with this? Did *everybody* think they could treat Lila Kyle like shit and get away with it? Lila followed her to the door and began calling for Marty.

'That's it! THAT'S IT! I want this bitch fired! I mean it, Marty.'

The crew all turned to see the commotion. Jahne, Marty, and a few others ran towards the door. By now, Jahne could see that Lila was out of control. She was raving. 'Goddamn it! How many times do I have to tell the old cunt that I want some fucking privacy?' Lila was screaming. 'Tell the wrinkled bitch to keep her fucking nose out of my ass!'

Mai's face was pale, and Jahne could see tiny beads of sweat on her forehead and under her nose. 'My God, and she eats vith that mouth!' Mai said, and, for a moment, Jahne had to smile.

17

Michael McLain had already given the photos of Sharleen to Sy. Next he sent over the video of Jahne Moore and himself. But either he had to bed Lila or fake a photo of it to save face and get top billing from Ricky Dunn.

Well, he figured, the other two proofs were legit; so what if he had to fabricate the third? Any tall, young hooker with a long red wig and a fuzzy focus ought to be enough. After all, how much could Sy expect? Close-ups?

But, somehow, this whole adventure left a bad taste in his mouth. It wasn't that he cared about that bitch Lila, or Sharleen. He had actually liked Jahne – she was smart and funny – but had sensed that she wasn't either smitten with him or overeager to please. And Michael liked his women to be both. Plus, there were those scars. Unsightly, almost ghoulish, but so secretive as to be almost erotic. And Michael didn't believe for a moment that they were from an accident. For one thing, they were too symmetrical. For another, what kind of accident causes incisions on the *inside* of thighs, or across the pelvic girdle, or under each buttock? Clearly, she had had plastic surgery, but how much could she have had? After all, a girl her age is too young for most of those operations.

He wrinkled his brow, then reminded himself to stop. After all, it wasn't worth a collagen treatment to him. Well, he could give up Jahne Moore. No problem. And, despite her bitchiness, he'd concentrate on Lila. Let word get back to Sy that they were an item. He smoothed his forehead and then dialled Lila's number.

She was weird. She certainly didn't seem to desire him. But she did seem, in some ways, eager to please. Michael knew her type: she wanted his help, his influence, but she didn't seem willing to come across with the standard *quid pro quo*. Michael was tempting her with two apples: a part in *Birth*, or in the Ricky Dunn thing. She seemed eager for either. And if he got her in on the Dunn thing, it would be one more person on his side. Then she'd have to come across.

Occasionally, just for a change of pace, Michael enjoyed fucking a woman who didn't want to fuck him. It added spice to a sex life that could otherwise be compared to shooting ducks in a barrel. Having a young and reluctant woman go down on him had a distinctive pleasure all its own. The last time he had done it – aside from the little dust-up with Sharleen Smith – had been when he promised a small part in a film to his friend Bob's fiancée in return for a blow job on the morning of her wedding. She didn't want to, but he knew how much she wanted the part. After she'd serviced him, he'd stood over her and asked if she'd liked it.

'No.' she said, wiping her mouth, tears filling her eyes.

'Well. You weren't supposed to,' he told her and, shrugging, zippered his fly.

So perhaps Lila would, in the end, reluctantly, coldly, come across. And maybe Michael would really enjoy that most of all. He'd promise her a part in the Ricky Dunn movie and make it clear how the deal stood.

Jahne sat in the big, overstuffed chair in her suite at the Regent Beverly Wilshire Hotel. She was camped there temporarily until she found a new place to live and had it vetted by La Brecque. It was very luxurious camping. The phone that rang at her elbow was one of six in the two vast rooms: there was another on the desk, one on each of the two bedside tables, and extensions beside the bathtub shower and toilet. Jahne wondered who actually talked to friends or business associates as they washed their armpits or relieved themselves. The bathroom itself was splendid, and larger than her whole New York apartment had been. It was white marble, and in addition to two sinks, the loo, and the deep, almost pool-sized tub, there was a separate steam-and-shower stall with more jets than she could count, a makeup table that looked like something out of a Jean Harlow movie, and a dressing area complete with walk-in closets, three-way mirrors, and a white chaise longue.

'The nominations are in,' Sy announced over the phone, a trace of triumph in his voice.

Jahne remembered that the Emmy nominations, formally known as the awards of the Academy of Television Arts and Sciences, were being announced this week. 'So, how did we do?' she asked. Although by now she had little regard for Industry awards, the cast and crew of *Three for the Road* had worked so hard. It wasn't what she had hoped it would be, but the show deserved *something*.

460

'You mean you haven't heard yet? You got it.'

'*I* got it? Well, I'll be damned.' Jahne thought back to her days off-Broadway, to *Jack and Jill* and the Obie award she had received for her performance. Her friends at St. Malachy's had rejoiced, and she had, too. And Sam. Back then, everyone was forecasting a rosy future for her.

'But what about the show? What about the rest of the cast?' she asked again.

'Forget about the show for a minute, Jahne. Forget about the others. *You* have been nominated for an award – an *Emmy* Award. What, six months in television? Do you realize what that does for your career? With your talent *and* an Emmy nomination? Maybe even the award itself? Vaboom, kid. We'll be flooded with offers.' Jahne winced. She had told Sy about the audition for *Birth*. And the offer. But not that she was determined to do it. He would only try to talk her out of it.

'Sy, I'm grateful for the recognition, I really am. But, you know, "you're only as good as your last, etcetera."' She laughed. 'In a year or two, if I come begging you to get me a part somewhere – and I *might* be begging, you know that, too – I want you to remember this conversation. And when I say, "After all, I've had an Emmy nomination," I don't want you to tell me, "Yeah, but what have you done lately?" Okay, Sy?'

Now it was Sy's turn to laugh. 'You're very cynical for such a young woman.'

'I prefer to think that I keep things in perspective.'

'Well, I hope Sharleen keeps it in perspective. She's been nominated, too.'

'Both of us? No kidding.'

'No kidding. And Lila, too.'

'All *three* of us have been nominated?' Typical. Just in case there weren't already enough stories about the competition between the three of them. Jesus! Hollywood! This would not lessen tensions on the set.

'Listen, Sy, did you go over the contract for *Birth of a Star*?'

'Listen, yourself: I have three better offers for you.'

'Forget it, Sy. Do you have the contract?'

'Yes.'

'Great. That's all I care about. Because I'm going to do the film. Don't say one more word about it. So, are you going to call Sharleen with the good news?'

461

'Yes.' She could hear his silent fuming.

'Great. I'll call to congratulate her, too.' But before she could, the phone shrilled again. She lifted it to her ear, and almost dropped it when she heard Sam Shields' voice.

'Congratulations.'

'Good news travels fast!' She laughed.

'How are you going to celebrate?'

'I'm not sure.'

'How about lunch with your director on Friday?'

'No,' she teased. 'I hate eating with Marty.'

He laughed. 'Your *film* director. Have you signed the contract?'

'I will by then,' she promised.

'Great! Then we have two things to celebrate! Friday at the Getty Museum? One o'clock?'

Back in New York, Sam often made dates to meet in the museum cafeterias. Inexpensive and usually beautiful, although the food was rarely artful. The more things change, the more they remain the same, she thought. 'One o'clock,' she agreed, and held the phone to her ear long after he had hung up.

Sharleen hung up her phone and turned to Dean.

'What's the matter, Sharleen? You look like something's wrong.'

Dean was watching *The Andy Griffith Show*, the episode where Aunt Bea enters her pickles in the contest. Sharleen knew he'd seen it a thousand times, that he knew that Andy and Opie hated her pickles and had replaced them with store-bought, and that, when Aunt Bea won the contest, they'd have to tell her. Dean knew all that, too, but he was watching as if for the first time. Sharleen sighed.

She sat in the armchair across from Dean and flicked her fingers in a motion for him to switch off the VCR. The room became suddenly quiet. 'No, nothing's wrong, Dean. In fact, everything's right. I just got an acting nomination. An Emmy nomination.'

'Uh-huh,' he said, waiting for her to continue.

'I wish Momma could know about this,' Sharleen said. 'She'd be real pleased, I think.'

Dean nodded, then whistled, and Cara, Crimson, and Clover came over and sat down. 'Sharleen won a prize,' he said, and made a clapping noise. The three dogs began to tap their front paws together, like applause. A new trick. Sharleen smiled. Dean always had a way to cheer her up.

'It's not a prize yet. But Sy says this could help me get my next job.'

'Your *next* job? I thought you said we have so much money now that you'll never have to work again?'

Sharleen thought for a moment. 'Not how Mr. Ortis explained it. There's taxes and fees and all kinds of stuff. Anyway, let's say I *did* want another job after this, Sy says the nomination would help.'

'What's a nomination?'

Sharleen tried to sort it out for herself while she explained it to Dean. 'All the people in the television business write in to say who they think is the best actress on TV. From those, some people are picked to be nominated for the award. "Nominated" means "considered." Then they take another vote for only those people, and the one that wins that vote gets the award.'

'So you got an award, Sharleen?' She could see Dean struggling to understand. How could he, when *she* didn't understand so well?

'No, I'm one of the people that got picked for the semifinals, like . . . you know, like in football.'

'Does that mean that you got to go to playoffs?'

'No, honey. There's nothing more I can do to get the award. The committee is going to vote on past performance.'

'Seems silly to judge people like they're judging Aunt Bea's pickles,' Dean said. 'People ain't pickles. But, hey, if there's nothing more you can do, why do you look so worried?'

And Sharleen agreed, and didn't know why.

'Who am I up against?' Lila snapped into the phone to Ara. When he didn't answer right away, she asked again, 'Who, Ara? Tell me.'

'Lila, that's not really important right now, is it? After all, *you've* been nominated for an Emmy,' Ara said.

'It's only a nomination, Ara.' What was it her mother used to say about nominations? They were like the last ten seconds in a game, the score tied. But only the final score mattered.

Ara didn't try to stifle the sigh that he now released. 'Sharleen Smith and Jahne Moore.'

'You've got to be fucking kidding me, Ara. Those two bimbos? Those nobodies? They're just supporting players. Dummies. Candy and Skinny. I'm competing with them?' Lila was screaming now.

'Don't be what we Armenians would call an *"ashek."* A jackass.

There is no competition, Lila,' Ara said gently. 'You can see how it would be a very difficult decision for the Academy to pick one of you out of the three, considering the distribution of the three characters throughout the script.'

'I can see no such fucking thing, Ara. I've busted my ass to be an actress. It hasn't been easy getting work, being the daughter of a star. I've had to work twice as hard as anyone else to get where I got. Those two bitches pop up out of nowhere and get made overnight. It just isn't fair, Ara. And what about *Birth of a Star*? Still no word?'

'I hear that it's deep in development hell, Lila. New trouble with the script. You gave a good audition. Now there is nothing more about the Emmys or *Birth* that you can do.'

Lila slammed down the phone.

She bit the skin on her knuckle. There's got to be something I can do. *Something.* For the first time in her new house, Lila felt lonely. She had no one to tell about the nomination, no one to plot with, no one to praise her or admire her.

Lila let her gaze move beyond the glass doors of her house to the ocean beyond. What had she said the day she decided to buy this house? When she'd found it was Nadia Negron's house. It's going to bring me luck? Where's my luck now, Nadia?

Nadia had won one of the first Oscars for her performance in *Birth of a Star*. Lila had read up on her since she bought this house. But there was something about the award. The other nominees died? No, there was scandal. Gigantic, humongous scandal. It destroyed the other nominees, and ensured Nadia her Oscar.

Now Lila remembered. Nadia Negron had been behind the scandal-mongering, it had been rumoured for years. And Lila believed it. Nadia Negron had been powerful. She didn't just sit and wait. Maybe Nadia could help me. Maybe she would help me.

'I'm going to try to contact Nadia,' she said aloud, as she walked upstairs.

18

Michael McLain literally dragged his feet down the hallway of the Château Martine, doing no good to the seventeen-hundred-dollar Tony Lama hand-painted snakeskin boots he was wearing, for this preliminary meeting with Sy, Lila Kyle, and that little prick Ricky Dunn. No other agent, no lawyers. A family get-together.

He was late, and he didn't give a fuck. After all, *he* was the one who had already paid his dues. When this little twenty-three-year-old dickhead manages to stay on top of the slippery pile called Hollywood for twenty years, then he'll deserve respect. Michael had decided to do the fuckin' movie – after all, he hadn't stayed on top this long by being stupid – but the kid would simply have to give him top billing. Like Newman and Cruise in *The Colour of Money*. It was a sign of deference, of respect, and it had done good box office. So he'd do the movie, and Sy would get him top billing. And if playing the mentor instead of the hero made him look old, he'd fix that by having the character he played get the girl. Lila Kyle was wild for the part.

Sy had seen the video of Jahne and the faked Lila photo, and he had been forced to set this meeting up to go over the deal, to allow them all to meet face to face. But already Michael was annoyed. Why the fuck was it held here, instead of Sy's office, or the production company? The Martine gave him the willies. It was the West Coast equivalent of New York's Hotel Chelsea: where the hip went to die of overdoses. It was expensive, exclusive, and seedy, and it made Michael very uncomfortable.

He had driven over himself, left the Testarossa with the valet, who looked as if he would immediately fence it off to some East Hollywood chop shop, and now Michael stood outside of Room 711. A lucky number. He straightened himself to his full height, sucked in his gut, and knocked.

Sy opened the door. Weird, but if Sy wanted to play hostess that was up to him.

'Michael!' Sy said, as if he were surprised and deeply pleased to see him. Michael didn't answer, just kept his gut in and entered.

The room was as shabby as the valet and hallway had been. Limp blue drapes hung a good four inches above the floor; the carpet was blue tweed, one of those speckled jobs erroneously touted not to show the dirt. It did, along with the cigarette burns on the side of the bureaus, the cheap glass ashtrays on the coffee table, and the sofa that looked as if it were covered in Herculon. Other than the sordid furnishings, the room was empty.

'Where the fuck is the little son-of-a-bitch? And where's Lila?'

'Michael, he called. There was a problem. Something about some looping that wasn't on target. He'll be here any minute.'

'He's late? *He's* late for the meeting *he* set up?' Michael knew he himself was late by almost twenty minutes. That meant the little fuck was going to be half an hour late, or more. 'Did he think I was sitting here with my dick in my hands, just praying for his arrival? Did you tell him *I* was late, too?'

Just then Lila Kyle walked out of the bathroom. Oh, great, now she was witness to his humiliation. Fuck! Michael grimaced. Ortis sighed. 'Michael, please. This is no way to begin a picture. He'll be here any minute. Just . . .'

Lila smiled at him. 'Don't you want to talk to *me*?' she asked.

'Not unless you're looking for top billing,' Michael snarled.

'Top billing? I'd be happy to be in *anything* with you,' she cooed. Christ, he didn't know when she was worse: when she was doing her fake worship act or exposing her real piranha personality. Well, he wasn't there to get her a part *or* make more points for Sy Ortis.

'Michael, this meeting is very important,' Sy said. 'Lila wants to meet Ricky, he wants to meet you, and all of us need to talk about a few things. We still have to straighten out the billing. . . .'

'Sy, this is starting to make a deal with Scott Rudin look good,' Michael sneered.

'You know, maybe I should have brought Ara,' Lila said.

'No. No. Not at all. He's an old man. A sick man. We'll wait until we have some of this ironed out.'

Michael snorted. Yeah, like when Sy has ironed out a contract to represent Lila. Jesus. Anyway, what needed to be straightened out?

'Straighten it out? I thought you straightened it out already?'

'Well, partly. But there are some issues, valid issues, and this meeting . . .'

'Just shove this meeting up your ass!' Michael cried, and had begun to walk to the door when it swung open. A tall, cadaverous man, the palest, thinnest guy Michael had ever seen, walked into the room. He was dressed all in black. If Morticia Addams has an anorectic younger brother, this was the guy. Behind him was the little prick, Ricky Dunn, who, Michael noticed immediately, was not so little. The kid was taller than Michael by a good two inches.

Dunn was dressed in a pair of torn and filthy jeans, some kind of T-shirt that looked like camouflage or something, and an oiled canvas duster that must have been out of Wardrobe, used for some stupid Australian-outback movie. The Mickey Rourke look, but clean. He also had on a pair of wraparound sunglasses with mirrored lenses. He didn't take them off, though the room was dim.

'I'm Shay Wright,' the cadaver said, holding out his hand to Sy, who obviously already knew him but shook it. Michael didn't make a move, and Shay dropped his skeletal arm. 'And this,' he added, 'is Ricky Dunn.'

Shay nodded to Ortis and Lila, but Ricky acknowledged none of them. The two of them moved to the sofa and sat down so close together that they looked as if they were joined at the hip. Sy moved an armchair out for Michael and, unwillingly, Michael sat down. Lila smiled at Ricky. Michael noticed that she both licked her lips *and* tossed her head before crossing her long legs in front of them all. Christ, why didn't she just spread-eagle?

'We're sorry we're late,' Shay said.

'No problem,' Lila purred.

'I just got here myself,' Michael told them. Fuckers.

'Fine, fine,' Sy said. 'So, Ricky, everything just about wrapped on *Zoom?*'

Ricky turned to Shay, bent even closer, and whispered something into his ear. 'Mr. Dunn says he's very pleased with the rough cut.'

Michael couldn't believe his eyes – or his ears, for that matter. Before he could say anything, Sy continued. 'Did you enjoy working with Carpenter? I hear he's a hell of a director.'

Again, Ricky leaned over and murmured something inaudible into Shay's ear. Shay nodded. 'With all due respect, Mr. Dunn says that Bill Carpenter is a fucking bag of shit who couldn't direct traffic with a stoplight to help him.'

Sy blinked. Michael definitely saw him blink, but he recovered without a whimper. What a reptile! 'Have they picked a release date?'

This time, Shay answered without any tutelage. 'Christmas Day.'

Sy nodded. 'So, we just love the script for *Scraper*; don't we, Michael?'

Michael hunched over to Sy and whispered, 'What the fuck is going on?' Lila, still smiling, was following all this with eyes that looked as old as those of the Sphinx.

Sy only shrugged. 'We did have a few questions about Buck, the character Michael will play.'

'*Might* play,' Michael corrected. He was sick of this charade. Why not get to the point? 'But, more important than that, we need to talk about the billing.'

'That might be premature,' Sy said, and cleared his throat. What the fuck was *that* supposed to mean? Michael flipped Sy a look.

'I'd expect top billing,' Michael said.

Ricky remained expressionless, as did Shay, but Ricky, once again, began his inaudible murmuring. When he was done, it was Shay's turn to clear his throat. 'Meaning no offence, Mr. Dunn says he would rather fuck Michael Jackson up the ass than take second billing to Mr. McLain. Understand that I'm only speaking for Mr. Dunn when I say that. . . .'

Michael scrambled to his feet, knocking over the coffee table. 'Hold it! Hold it. If Mr. Dunn wants to say something, he can fucking well say it for himself. If I hear one more word out of you, you fucking bloodless cadaver, I'll break you into pieces. . . .'

'No need for that kind of talk,' Sy began. 'We're reasonable people and . . .'

Without a word from Ricky Dunn, Shay bent forward. 'With all due respect, Mr. Dunn says he'll let you have top billing when you grow tits and fly away.'

'That's it!' Michael McLain yelled. 'I'm fuckin' out-of-here.' He kicked the table out of his way and walked to the door.

'And fuck you, too,' Shay said sweetly.

Lila ran down out the door of the Martine after Michael. 'I guess this means no part for me,' she said, almost breathless when she caught up with him. 'Look, I never thought Ricky Dunn was worth shit. But you and me in *Birth of a Star* . . .'

Michael handed his claim check to the valet and only then turned to look at her.

'Forget about it,' he said.

She stood, silent for a moment. Then she tossed her long red hair. Like that would help her. Michael snorted.

'Look,' she said, 'I thought we had an understanding. We had a deal.'

The Testarossa pulled up, and Michael nearly dragged the valet out of it in his hurry to get in. Only then did he look up at Lila, looming over the low-slung car. 'Hey, babe, it was only a verbal. It's not like I balled you,' he said, and, putting his foot on the gas, he peeled out.

Sy Ortis raised his head and stared at Jahne. 'Are you crazy?' he asked, his voice low. 'Are you?' he repeated.

He had already tried every rational reason he could think of to dissuade her. Faxed her half a dozen times, both on the set and at the hotel. Harangued her on the phone. Called her into his office for this special meeting. But she wouldn't listen, wouldn't cooperate. First Michael blows the meeting with Ricky. Then, in desperation, he wants to do this retread piece of shit for – of all people – April Irons, and now, *now*, this one, this one he made himself, waltzes in, cool as a frozen daiquiri, and tells him – *tells* him, mind you, not asks – that *she's* going to costar in *Birth*. Without a preliminary goddamned word to him. He gets the contracts from April, and the whole thing is a *fait accompli*. Only he looks like an asshole. Well, he'd eat Michael's shit and Ricky's, too, if he had to, but he wasn't going to eat Jahne's and April's for dessert.

He reached for his empty inhaler and fondled it as if it were some magic amulet that would make Jahne Moore disappear. 'So, are you crazy, or what?' There was only one thing to do. He'd have to scare her. Then, maybe, she'd behave.

She stared back at him, insolently. She *was* an insolent bitch. Had been from the very beginning. 'I don't think so,' she said.

Sy laughed. 'No, I guess you don't. I guess you think you're smart, or talented, or some other grandiose, self-inflated horseshit. The next Sarah Bernhardt. Better watch out you don't become the next *Sandra* Bernhard.' Sy was so angry, so outraged, that he even slipped, his accent showing. 'Well, let me esplain something to you. You aren't here because you're talented, or smart, or hardworking, or any of that crap. That doesn't esplain why you're here. What you are is *lucky*. Right now you might be one of the three luckiest bitches on the face of the planet. And you're too fucking stupid to realize it.'

'I guess that means that you don't think *Birth of a Star* is a good idea,' she said coolly.

'Very good. Nice use of sarcasm. Maybe you're not so stupid.' Sy felt his chest tightening. Hold on there, he told himself. You're losing control. You got to scare them, but not scare them *away*. Still, this was outrageous. Sy Ortis, the ultimate deal-maker, cut out of the negotiations, not even consulted. Left out of the deal. By not one but *two* of his clients. April must be laughing like a hyena in a fun house. Which just about described both her *and* International Studios. The thought of April Irons was like a band tightening around his chest. When would his secretary get back with his inhaler? Jesus, these bitches!

'Sy, it's a good deal. They've offered me points. Five points is very good.'

'Five points of the *net*. There's never any *net*! Those are monkey points. Even *Batman* never made a *net* profit. You want gross points, and on this deal you want *nada*. You want out.'

'Why?'

'It will stay in development hell forever. There still isn't a shooting script. And you have only ten weeks' hiatus. This will take twice as long to film, if it ever gets made. Plus, it's just not right for you.'

He tried to calm himself. 'Listen, Jahne,' he said with a wheeze. 'I'm talking to you the way I would to my own daughter. You can't have your cake and eat it, too. And the show is the biggest thing on TV. It's the biggest thing that's *ever* been on TV. It may save a fucking network. You're at the very best place you could possibly be. So why risk *Birth*? There isn't even a decent script!' he repeated. 'How could you commit to something without even seeing a finished script? Has everyone gone crazy? What if it's *muy malo* – big-time bad? Why give up a gold mine for a bird in the bushes?'

The bitch smiled. Good, he'd won her over. But, *Madre de Jesus*, these women would kill him!

'I don't see it that way.'

He couldn't believe it. 'What?' he asked, his voice reduced to a rasp. When she had called him and told him she wanted to talk, he hadn't been prepared for this. Who would be? But she sprung the idea of doing the April Irons film on her hiatus from *Three for the Road* – and then added she'd need four *extra* weeks off from 3/4. Like the show could wait. Like Marty wouldn't mind. Like the network wouldn't go loco. Like it was nothing. She was sitting on top of the world, and now, behind his back, she wants to go film some stinking remake with a pup director instead of keeping her sure thing.

'The reality is, Sy, I get the time off or I quit.'

'What?' he whispered.

'Listen, the way I see it, it's all got to be downhill from here. What the show has going for it is novelty. That will wear off next season. And the imitations will start. If I leave now, it will be big news. Leave at the peak. Anyway, this show was *not* what I want to do. It was only a stepping-stone. And the Huey, Dewey, and Louey dialogue is really getting me down. I want to do some serious work.'

'Since when is a potboiler like *Birth of a Star* considered serious? It's not *Hedda Gabler*, for chrissakes.'

'It's better than the crap I'm doing now. And it's a *film*. I hate TV. Wasn't it Gailbraith who said nobody could compete with us in producing morally depraved TV programmes? I want out of the Flanders Cosmetics deal, and I don't want to do the show at all.'

It was unbelievable. Women all over the country would give their left tit to be in those ads, and she wanted out? And out of the *show*?

'Wait a minute. Now you're not talking about an extension of the hiatus, you're actually talking about leaving the show altogether?'

'Well, why not? I only signed the one-year contract.'

'Why not? Why not? *Sangra de Cristos*! Because they'll replace your ass so fast that no one will remember your name one year from now. You'll become an answer in trivia games.'

'Maybe. But I could use a lot less fame than I've got now. And if you don't agree, perhaps I ought to leave the agency.'

Sy got up from his desk, walked over to the window, and looked out on the glare and dust of the L.A. freeway. Holy jumping Jesus. It wasn't the Assholes or the Regulars. It was the Talent that would kill him in the end. He began to truly fight for breath. How many times would one of them crucify him, castrate him? Crystal Plenum insisted on doing that *Jack and Jill* bullshit that ruined her career. She was becoming the Zsa Zsa of her generation. Michael makes an ass out of himself and Sy in front of Ricky and Lila Kyle. And now this! Marty would kill him if he lost Jahne. Jahne would leave the agency if she couldn't do April Irons' movie. And April would bust his chops over Jahne's stupid contract.

He was one of the most powerful men in the goddamn Industry, and these empty-headed, loco *putas* tried to tell him that they were smarter. They were always smarter. Until they became yesterday's news. He turned to Jahne.

'Now, you listen to me. You want to become the Art Garfunkel of the television industry? Never quit a winner. This town eats up pretty girls faster than reporters chew up free lunches. You get your shot, you're hot, you can make any deal for any money; then along comes someone younger, a different type, and you're history. You can't get a fuckin' guest shot on *L.A. Law*. You'll be happy to make an appearance on *Hollywood Squares*. And you won't even get called on by the contestants.'

'Oh, come on. The first film I do is important, but it *is* just one film. I mean, it doesn't make or break a career. Who was ever ruined by one bad choice?'

'The list is long and distinguished. Suzanne Somers. Sexpot. Beautiful. Quit TV. Couldn't get a supermarket opening for a decade. Shelley Long. Walked off *Cheers*. Name one of her films. Or Farrah Fawcett. Hottest girl of her decade. One season, leaves TV. *No one* pays to see one of her movies, *ever*, except maybe Ryan O'Neal. Movies are riskier. People pay cash to see movies. Not like a TV series, where people get it free and want to see you every week. Even for a features actress, it's riskly. One bad movie, two the most, and . . . Look at Michelle Pfeiffer. Ellen Barkin. Or Melanie Griffith, Kathleen Turner. Holly Hunter. They each got to be the hot girl. For a year. Where are they now?'

'They work, Sy. They all work.'

He looked at her, disgust plainly written on his simian face. 'You don't get it, do you? You just don't get it. Right now you got *heat*. They want you. *Everybody* wants you. You can go anywhere. You can meet anyone. It doesn't last long, not without good management and luck. And once it's gone, baby, it's gone.'

'I'm not your baby,' Jahne said coldly.

Sy stopped. He looked at her directly. And in that moment of silence, Jahne knew how much he disliked, even hated her. She shivered.

Is it because I'm a client or because I'm a woman that he condescends so? she wondered. Would it be any better with another agent? 'Sy, I know this won't really mean much to you, but I'm not doing what I don't want to do. The show is crap. Stylish, sometimes even funny, but it's crap. I want some work that's important. Work that I can respect. That *others* will respect.'

Sy let out a small noise, a kind of sigh, as if this was childish and he'd heard it all before. Well, he probably has, Jahne acknowledged. His job is to turn people into deals and money machines; mine is to control that. Sy licked his lips, picked up what was left of his asthma spray, and began talking very slowly. 'Listen to me. Things are different now: The networks are desperate. Television is still lucrative, but more competitive; they have to have hits or they'll go the way of the old studio system. With a hit show, even a small hit, a network can schedule something before and after you, they can spin you off. They can build a lineup. They can attract new viewers. And hold them. And they can attract sponsors. A show like yours is a godsend to Les Merchant. They'll put *everything* into getting you the Emmy. You'll probably win. You can propose a television movie. They'll back it. You'll *have* respect. They'll respect the *shit* out of you.'

'Thanks, Sy. But shit is not what I want.'

'Look, just tell me what is so respectable about a tired old melodrama, a *puta* that's going to be directed by a newcomer and produced by a shark. Why, why would you want to do this to yourself?'

Jahne paused. She had known, clearly, before she walked in, what she wanted to do, but now she was uncertain, even a little scared. Could he be right? Could she wind up another out-of-work actress? 'All right.' she said at last. 'All right. I'm doing the film, but I won't quit the show. I'll do one more season. And I'll make a deal with you: you arrange to get me enough shooting time with Marty. If *Birth of a Star* flops, then I'll stay. But if it's a hit, I quit the show.'

19

Sharleen was stretched out on the couch in her 3/4 dressing room, trying to rest before her next camera call. Sy Ortis was on the chair next to her, handing her documents to sign as they talked.

'Listen, it's the end of the season, and with the Emmy nomination you're hot. I got a great job for your hiatus. A movie deal,' Sy said, as he reached over and took a bunch of signed papers from her. 'It's light. Fun. It's called *Buffy the Cowgirl*.'

'*Another* job? Mr. Ortis, I'm tired. I don't *want* another job.' She wasn't sure she could finish this one, even though there were only two more episodes to go before the season ended. Thank the Lord. 'What happened to what you told me when I took *this* job – that this one would make me so rich, I'd never have to work again?'

Sy laughed. 'Well, it might take a little longer, what with taxes and agent's fees and lawyers and all. And, to tell the truth, I never figured you'd get so famous, Sharleen. You gotta strike while the iron is hot. You're in demand, and this movie would be great for your career.'

'I don't want no *career*, Mr. Ortis. I just have a *job*. And I think what you told me back then was right. With what I've made on this show, I'll never have to work again.'

'Only if you don't want to live like a queen,' Sy added quickly. 'This picture deal could do that for you, you know. Make you richer than your wildest dreams.'

'I'm *already* richer than my wildest dreams.' She finished signing the last paper and, with a sigh, thrust the stack of them towards Sy. 'No more today, Mr. Ortis. I'm tired. I'm *really* tired.'

Sy stood up. 'That's okay, Sharleen. It'll cost me money, and you might regret it later, but you do what you think is best. I'll send your lawyer over tomorrow with the rest of this stuff. You just take it easy for a while before they call you.'

Sharleen closed her eyes and let her hand touch Sy's arm as he moved away. 'Thanks, Mr. Ortis. You've been good to me.'

The door clicked closed behind him, leaving her alone with the hum of the air conditioning in the darkness. She didn't want to think about how disappointed Mr. Ortis was that she wasn't going to work during her vacation. And she knew he was. But there was no way she *could* work. Sharleen had been working six days a week, twelve hours a day for months. Always nervous, always messing up. It was a little easier now that Jahne was helping her run lines, but still a strain. And I used to say *waitressing* was hard, she thought, as she slipped into a light sleep.

The hands felt real, but Sharleen knew she was dreaming. All those hands, pulling, grabbing, palms up. But this hand . . .

'Miss Smith, you're wanted on the set in twenty minutes.'

Sharleen opened her eyes and saw Ronnie Wagner, the new second-unit AD, shaking her gently. 'Boy, I must have been dreaming.'

'Is there anything I can get for you? Cappuccino?' Ronnie asked. Sharleen liked Ronnie. Ronnie made a point of having fresh cappuccino available on the set when she heard Sharleen liked it.

'Yes, that would be nice.' Sharleen sat up and put her feet on the floor, then pushed herself off the couch with a low groan.

'You okay, Miss Smith?'

'Oh, yeah. I'm fine. Just a little tired.'

Ronnie was about to say something else, then hesitated.

'What is it?'

'Well, the president of one of your fan clubs is out there to see you. And this one's a beaut. Ordinarily, I'd suggest you meet with her, but since you're so tired, maybe . . .'

Sharleen shook her head. From the beginning, she had decided that this went with the territory. She could never get used to the concept of fan clubs – as Dean said, 'It ain't like you're Lucy Ball' – but she was overpowered by the sheer numbers in the groups that came from time to time. Mostly teenagers and young women, they all treated Sharleen both like a goddess and like they had known her all their lives. But to Sharleen they were still strangers. Strangers she tried to be sweet to. 'Oh, no, Ronnie. I'll talk to her on my way out to the shoot. Maybe I could ask her to stay and watch. Would that be okay?'

'Sure, whatever you want, Miss Smith.'

Ronnie let the man from Makeup in as she was leaving. While he retouched her face, Sharleen thought about the fan-club president again. She felt even less like seeing this one after Ronnie's comment. She hoped she was at least young, like most of the others. The older women frightened her. They all seemed so poor, so desperate. Sharleen could understand a young girl getting all excited at television people. She knew that for most of them it was a phase they'd outgrow. Jahne had explained all this to Sharleen. But the older ones, the ones in the pants suits and the high-piled hair, they upset Sharleen. Somehow, they reminded her of the desperation of Lamson. The crew made jokes about these women. 'Get a life,' they would mutter under their breaths. But Sharleen knew how impossible it was for most of them ever to have anything of their own. She remembered herself back in Lamson, and shuddered. For most of her fans, this was all the life they were ever going to have, and that made Sharleen sad. She thought of Proverbs 6:25 – Lust not after her beauty in thine heart. But the poor women did.

Sharleen never had to be called to the set a second time; she knew what was expected of her. She let the door to her dressing trailer clink shut as she scanned the set for her visitor. She caught the eye of Ronnie, who pointed towards the waiting woman. Then she noticed Ronnie raise her eyes to heaven. Sharleen nodded a thanks as she followed Ronnie's gaze.

Oh, Lord, she thought. The woman was not only one of the older ones, but also loudly, though shabbily dressed. She waved to Sharleen as Sharleen walked across the floor, and seemed to be standing on tiptoe in anticipation. Looking at her more closely, Sharleen could see that the woman was very different from the others. Down and out. Drawing nearer, Sharleen was surprised to see that the woman also looked worse than loud. She looked, well, cheap. She had dyed yellow hair which fell in tight greasy curls to her shoulders. She wore a pink sleeveless blouse, too tight across her sagging chest. One of the buttons had popped open. Her too-small yellow skirt had a tear along one seam, and her large belly strained against the fabric. She had no eyebrows, just half-circles of dark pencil lines in their place. A smear of red rouge on her cheeks was exaggerated by the thick gash of red-orange lipstick. Tangee for sure. Sharleen stopped in front of the woman, who was gripping a tattered Mexican straw bag in both hands in front of her, her eyes wide in anticipation, a hint of panic suddenly sweeping across her face.

Sharleen blinked once or twice and stared. The woman took a step forward. 'Hello, baby,' the woman called out. After a moment, Sharleen answered.

'Hello, Momma,' she said.

Sharleen sat with the Bible opened on her lap, reading the psalms of praise. Who would have dreamed two years ago that she would be on TV, that Dean and she would get a wonderful home, and that they would find their momma? God was good!

She had begged her momma to come home with her, but Flora Lee had refused. 'In these rags? Why, girl, I know how I look. Like hell in a nightie. Before I see my boy, I want to look right.' So instead, they had agreed that Momma would freshen up in the trailer for now, and just the two of them would go out for dinner.

Sharleen had ached to call Dean with the great news, but perhaps this was best. Sharleen would have a chance to get reacquainted with Flora Lee, then tell her about Dean being . . . well, the way he was. Lovable and all, but maybe not so smart. But should she tell Flora Lee about what had happened back in Lamson? What if Momma felt it was their duty to go to the police? Sharleen never talked about it to anyone, and had cautioned Dean over and over not to. But would he talk to Momma about it?

Sharleen sighed, some of the happiness draining out. It was taking Momma a long time. She looked down again at the Bible. She was sure that God would forgive Dean. She thought about Flora Lee. Surely she was kind, and generous, and understanding. She saw the next line below her fingers: 'The ungodly are not so but are like the chaff which the wind driveth away.' What did that mean? she wondered.

When Momma came unsteadily out of the trailer, they drove to the Sheraton. It was a big hotel but not too fancy. Sharleen wore a baggy old dress she had borrowed from Mai, and a big hat, along with sunglasses. She had her hair tucked up, covered with a scarf. She hoped no one would recognize her.

'Where should we go to sit down?'

'Here's as good as anywhere, honey,' Momma said, ready to dump herself down in the lobby.

'Well, maybe not here.' Sharleen looked around. 'Let's go somewhere quieter.'

'Why, how about the bar?'

'The bar?' Sharleen never went to bars. Did her momma?

'It's dark and quiet,' Flora Lee reminded her.

So they went to the bar. And Sharleen began with all the questions she wanted to ask. 'What happened to you right after you left, Momma?'

'I got as far as El Paso. Thought I might settle there. Heal up a bit. Nice town, El Paso. Got a job at a truck stop. Got a place. But then I met a trucker. Should have known better, but after your daddy, well, any man looked good. He left me in Salem, Oregon. Stranded without a penny.' Flora Lee emptied the nut dish out and called out to the waitress. 'Honey, could we get some almonds and some service over here?' she called.

The waitress came to them and forced a smile. 'What will you be having?' she asked.

'Ginger ale,' Sharleen said.

'A beer, please. A Bud.' Flora Lee turned to Sharleen. 'Those nuts can make you powerfully thirsty.'

Sharleen smiled at her mother, and now she felt her own smile was forced. Did Momma drink? She never used to. Well, she'd be entitled to a beer at the end of a day like this one. 'What did you do then?' Sharleen asked.

'Oh, I spent a long time getting out of Oregon. Wanted to go to hairdressin' school, and the Department of Welfare was going to pay for it. But then I met a feller who worked for Chrysler – he travelled through the whole Northwest training their service mechanics. Took me down as far as Sacramento. We set up house there. Right nice, too. Till I found out he had a wife and four kids up in Olympia, Washington.'

'Oh, Momma!' Sharleen said, and pulled the hat farther down on her head. The waitress brought over the soda pop and the beer. Flora Lee drank hers down in two or three gulps while Sharleen toyed with her own glass. Somehow, her happy feeling from earlier in the day was disappearing just like the bubbles that were leaving the glass.

Don't you be judging your momma, she told herself harshly. She wasn't even kin, and she raised you. And who are you to judge? You remember what you done with Boyd, and what that led to. And how Mr. McLain got you drunk. Momma was beaten and alone, without her children, and she must have been powerfully lonely.

Flora Lee rambled on, about more men and more towns. She beckoned again to the waitress. 'You want to freshen that up?' she asked Sharleen. Sharleen shook her head.

'Well, I'll have another beer,' Flora Lee paused. 'Make that a beer and a ball,' she said. The waitress nodded. Sharleen wondered what that was, but it wasn't until the waitress returned and put the beer and shot glass side by side that she opened her eyes wide. If Flora Lee noticed, she pretended not to. She picked up the shot glass and threw the whisky back down her throat.

Well, Sharleen told herself, if she takes a drink, it don't mean she's evil. Tears filled her eyes. Poor Momma, all alone and turning to whisky.

Flora Lee told a lot more of her story, but after another beer and whisky, it, or Sharleen, or Flora Lee, or maybe all three became real confused.

'So you see,' Flora Lee finally said, 'so you see why, if I just had a little money for beauty school, and could set me up a shop, I know I could make a real killing. Why, Mrs. Ramirez, the woman who lives down my hallway, she asked me to do her hair just the other day. I didn't charge her or nothin'. I don't have my licence, and I wouldn't want to get reported to the state, but that's just an example.' She looked at Sharleen, expectant. Sharleen nodded, helpful. Then Flora Lee turned her head. 'Where's that waitress got to?' she asked.

20

After weeks of Lila's calling Ara to nag him about the *Birth of a Star* audition, he had at last suggested to her that she come in, and she knew – she just knew – that her time had come. All the candles and other offerings to Nadia had paid off. Lila knew she was born to play this part.

Lila dressed carefully for her meeting with Ara. You never knew who you might run into at his office. She slipped her legs into tall, electric-blue pantyhose. Naked now, except for the smooth blue legs, she looked into the full-length mirror that covered the wall of her dressing room. She had legs that just wouldn't quit. At five foot twelve, as she had told the reporters coyly, at least half of her height was legs. She smiled at her reflection and undid the towel that turbaned her hair. Still damp, it fell in a flaming cascade, the red more vivid against the blue of her stockings. Her white skin accentuated the strawberry of her tiny nipples. She looked at her breasts appraisingly. Her breasts were perfect, but not really large. Big, really big breasts were the style. But there were far too many complications to having surgery now that she was famous. She'd surely find herself on the cover of all the tabloids if she tried to. She put a hand over each breast and pinched her nipples to redden them. Yes, she looked like a perfect female, she thought. This would have to do. She sighed and turned away.

Surveying the room full of clothes, she picked out a simple white silk T-shirt and a butter-soft bright-yellow leather miniskirt. She surveyed row upon row of shoes, each pair nestled into a specially built compartment that housed them. Smiling, she chose the electric-blue spike heels made of dyed snakeskin. They added three and a half inches to her height and cantilevered her forward in such a way that her tits jutted out and her calves were emphasized. She slipped them on. They were a bitch to walk in, but so was the skirt. Well, she wasn't running any marathon, so let's give the men what they want, she thought, and smiled. If I don't know, who does? she told herself.

She went into the bathroom to comb out her still-damp hair. Never brush it wet, Theresa had taught her, because brushing breaks wet hair. Carefully, Lila pulled the comb through, stopped for a moment or two under the amber heat lamps that dried the last bit of moisture without damaging the long strands. She tossed her head and approved. This was definitely a good hair day. Finally, she snapped open her jewellery case. She took out the lapis-lazuli cross that Aunt Robbie had given her, and fastened it around her neck. Just a touch of Madonna trash. She looked up at the picture of Nadia and smiled.

'You're going to be a big star,' Ara smiled. He was seated at his desk as Lila was escorted into his office. 'You are already a big name. But you'll be more. A star.'

Lila grunted a laugh. 'You'll excuse me, but I already know *that*, Ara. I hope that's not news to you. I thought you said you have good *news*. Now, tell me.'

'Lila, where is your sense of values? You come in here, sit down, and start with the questions, always the questions. Why can't you be a little sociable? Have a cup of coffee with me, a glass of wine, talk a little?'

'Ara, this is show business. Like something could be more important than that? Your health? The weather? Give me a break, Ara. Now, do you have good news for me or not?' Lila couldn't stand waiting another minute. Ara was totally lame.

'I do have good news. I've gotten you *the* lead in *the* movie of the year.'

She knew it! She knew it! Oh thank you, Nadia! She smiled at Ara. 'That *is* good news. Now, isn't that more important than the weather? The lead, right, Ara?' Lila could hardly contain her delight.

'The lead. And the movie is going to be the biggest hit. *Princess of Thyme*.'

Lila suddenly sat up very straight in her chair, but it seemed

480

the whole room had tilted. '*Princess of Thyme*? I thought you were talking about *Birth of a Star*?'

'Lila, how many times in the last months have I told you, forget about that remake. It wouldn't have been right for you. Just as well you didn't get it. Now you can do *Princess of Thyme*. It'll make you bigger than big.'

'I didn't get it?' For a moment she didn't recognize her own voice: it sounded like a very young child's. 'I didn't get it?' she asked again.

'No, Lila,' Ara said gently. 'But I promise you this is a better movie. A more important one.'

'Who got the part, Ara?' Lila asked, her voice very low.

'Don't do this to yourself, Lila. You're not the girl for the part, believe me.'

'Don't call me that again. Now, who got the part?'

'If it matters, I think it went to Jahne Moore. And let her have it. You're meant for greater things.'

'Jahne Moore! Jahne Moore!' Lila could hardly believe it. 'You useless old bastard!' Lila whispered, the rage rising in her and almost strangling her with its intensity. 'Robbie was right. You're over the hill. You've lost it. I should have signed with Ortis. I could have that part now; instead, that insufferable, condescending bitch walks off with it!'

'There is the lead in *Princess of Thyme*, Lila. The title role. It will be bigger than *Star Wars*. And Lucas wants you. It's all lined up.'

'A cartoon? With spaceships and Ewoks and crap! Are you nuts? I wanted to do the remake of *Birth of a Star*. I wanted *that* part.' How long had he been keeping this news from her? How long? She'd like to pull his old, bald, drooling face apart, peel off his stupid moustache, kick his leathery football head into pieces. He wasn't taking care of her. He was killing her, suffocating her, using her. The prick. The goddamn cocksucking prick. It was him and her mother. Lila caught her breath.

'*When* did Jahne get the part, Ara?' She already knew, suddenly and clearly. She watched carefully, noticed Ara's mouth twitch. He paused, looking at her for a long time. Lila didn't drop her eyes, just sat there waiting.

'I'm not sure,' he finally mumbled.

'Guess!' Lila demanded.

'Look, Lila, I got you the audition. And it didn't work out. What

481

difference does it make when they made their decision? Decisions are made and unmade. I was hoping that, once they saw you, they might rethink . . .'

'They'd already picked Jahne when I auditioned! She already had it, didn't she? It was bullshit about script troubles. I see her on the set, she knows, everyone knows except me! This was just a plot to humiliate me. You did it just to shut me up, placate me like I was a little girl. Theresa made you do this, didn't she? You and Theresa worked this out. What do you think I am, a dummy?'

'No, Lila. Not at all . . .'

'Balls! She was jealous. She couldn't let me have the part that she once had. She couldn't stand to see me in the spotlight. So she gave the part to Candy. Candy gets the part, and I get nothing.'

'Not Candy, Lila. Jahne Moore.'

For a moment Lila stopped. 'That's what I said. Jahne Moore.' But that wasn't what she'd said. She'd said 'Candy,' hadn't she? Jesus Christ, she was losing it, and she was losing it here, in front of Ara Sagarian. Christ, now both of us are senile!

He was picking up a handkerchief to wipe his wet mouth. She turned away, suddenly nauseous. He was disgusting, a nasty, slimy, drooling, leather lizard of a man.

'Lila, I can see you're very upset, but you have to understand that was not the only part for you. It's not even the best one. The director is untried, and I think the thing is too big for him. Remakes are always dicey, at best, and remakes of classics are even more risky. *Old Acquaintance*. Bette Davis and Miriam Hopkins. Remade into that dreck with Jackie Bisset and Candice Bergen. Into the toilet. Then *Robin Hood*. Look what happened even to Costner when he tried to replace Errol Flynn.'

'Yeah. He made fifty million dollars.' She began to tremble, and couldn't stop. Nadia has been wrong. Jesus! She turned back to look at Ara. The spittle-face. She was born to have her triumph over Theresa, her freedom from Ara, from Robbie, from all of them. But Ara and her mother had conspired. *That* she was sure of. And maybe with Robbie's help. He'd do anything Theresa wanted, even befriend Lila in the pretence of helping her, but all the while plotting with the Puppet Mistress against her. They had lost her the part.

'What did my mother tell you about me?' she asked. 'What did you tell April about me?'

'Nothing, Lila. Please, you must . . .'

'What did she tell you?' Lila asked again, her voice rising.

'Lila, it had nothing to do with Theresa or me. It was your audition. They hated it. It was your audition, not anything I did . . . .'

Lila was across the desk in a moment, her hands around his throat. Her long legs scrabbled for purchase on the shiny desk surface, her skirt rucked up, her feet pushed off papers and mementos. Lila began to squeeze, her big hands reaching deep into the folds of Ara's leathery turkey wattles. 'What did she tell you about me?' she screamed, as she cut off the air in Ara's windpipe. 'What did she tell you?'

Ara spent the rest of the morning trying to recover. After his secretary and two agents had pulled Lila off him, after the security men had escorted her off the premises, after Ara had taken a few pills and managed to coax a glass of sweet tea down his bruised throat, he had asked not to be disturbed. He lay down on the big blue sofa in his office and found he was trembling. God, the woman was *bagos*. Worse than a Turk! He lifted one hand to his throat and shook his head. She was strong as an ox, too, and dangerous. He shook his head again. *Ench bede nem*? he asked himself. What to do?

Ara was no longer young, and just now he felt every one of his eighty-four years. Maybe his doctor was right. Maybe it was time to retire, to move down to his place in Palm Springs. He was too old, too tired to deal with the craziness anymore. He had, perhaps, another decade left. He could sit in the sun, a survivor of the Armenian holocaust, a survivor of Hollywood, and enjoy life. Play a few rounds of golf. See Frank, and Johnny, and all his cronies.

Just the thought of giving it all up, of stepping out of the action, made him almost dizzy with dismay. For over fifty years, he had lived to make deals. He had survived while the studios died. He had managed not to dwindle but to gain power. Lately, he had lost a few clients, perhaps, to the sharks like Ortis, but he was still respected, still a *player*, and he still revelled in the action.

But this scene with Lila Kyle had been too much. He had made a mistake with the girl. She was crazy. Worse than Crawford had been. And he'd betrayed Theresa, an old client, for this one. Worse yet, once he signed Lila, he hadn't been able to manage her. He shouldn't have gotten her the fake audition for *Birth*. He shouldn't have tried to soothe her into forgetting about it. She, like so many of their new stars, was empty of everything but ego and ambition. And now, without the studios, without any real control, chaos reigned.

He thought of Louis B. Mayer's reaction when he'd heard that Chaplin and Pickford had formed their own movie company – 'The lunatics have taken over the asylum,' he'd said. And United Artists *had* been a madhouse. Artists needed businessmen to help them, and businessmen needed artists to create a product. Ara had spent more than five decades trying to make that marriage work, but things were worse than ever.

Well, it was time. The party was over. In a way, he should thank the child for showing him the light. He would retire. He would enjoy life. He would rest. Not without regret, but with relief.

The telephone buzzed. He lifted it. Who would Helen put through now? he wondered. 'Ara, I'm sorry to bother you. But it seems very important. It's Michael McLain. He's very upset. He says he must see you as soon as you can. About a possible change in his representation.'

Ara blinked, and wiped his mouth. Michael had been his star, his protégé, his success story. But Michael had left him nine years ago, at the height of his success, to go to Sy Ortis. Lately, Ara had heard rumours that all was not well between them. Could it be that the prodigal son was returning to the fold? Signing Michael McLain! Stealing him back from Sy Ortis! That would show everyone that Ara Sagarian was still a player. Ara sighed. *Ashek* – jackass – he told himself. You would be better off in Palm Springs. Can't you give this up? It will kill you, he told himself.

He stared for a moment, unseeing. *Ench bede nem?*

Then he smiled into the phone. 'Tell him to come around,' he told his secretary. 'It would be a pleasure to see him.'

21

'I'm as tired as a duck in a hailstorm,' Sharleen complained as they walked off the set together.

Jahne laughed. 'Me, too.' She shrugged off the makeup man and picked up her jacket, putting it on herself.

'Jahne, kin I talk to you for a minute?' Sharleen asked. It was the end of the day's shooting, and Jahne was bone tired.

Well, Sharleen looked even more tired than she was. This wasn't like Sharleen. Something was obviously bothering her.

'Sure. Let's go to my trailer.' They walked to it and sat in the cramped 'lounge area.'

'Is some of all this startin' to git you down?' Sharleen asked, waving her hand around them.

'You mean the show?'

Sharleen nodded. 'The show, the crowds, fans, bein' like a prisoner in my own home. All of it.'

Jahne knew what Sharleen meant. 'Sure. A few weeks ago, before I moved into the hotel, I was sitting at my pool when I heard a voice over a loudspeaker. A tour bus, for God's sake. With a tour guide showing them where I live. I had to run inside, I became so paranoid. I didn't know if those ladies with blue hair were going to come over the hedge or not.' Jahne looked at Sharleen. 'Is that the kind of stuff you mean?'

Sharleen paused. 'Kinda. People you don't know wanting to know you. Relatives you ain't seen in years showing up. Friends askin' for favours. And about not being able to have any friends. I mean, I have you and all, and Mr. Ortis. He's good to me. But the crew all act all different, like I became queen of England overnight. I did like you said with Barry, and it worked. But I'm not comfortable. I mean, they worked all their lives in television. Don't they know this is all make-believe? Lordy, if *they* don't know, sometimes I'm afraid I'll get to believin' maybe I *am* queen of England or somethin'.'

Jahne laughed at Sharleen's observation. She was right. If the people in the Industry took it all so seriously, then why was everyone surprised that the public did? But Jahne wasn't upset. She had lunch Friday with Sam. She had something to look forward to.

"'Member the impersonations Phil Straub used to do? He was so funny. He used to do Marty DiGennaro perfect – better than Marty hisself.' Sharleen laughed at the memory. 'Now Phil calls me "Miss Smith." All the fun's gone.' She shrugged her shoulders. 'Well, anyhow, I got you, and Dean. And the dogs. So, it can't be all that bad. 'Cept we can't go to malls and stuff. 'Member what happened to you?'

Jahne shuddered at the memory. Sharleen seemed really sad. Was something else bothering her? 'But maybe, Sharleen, we could go shopping together. We both have security staff now. But no malls,' Jahne laughed.

'Right. 'Cept we'd both have to take them FBI men with us,'

Sharleen reminded her. She sighed. 'I got all the trouble of bein' a star but none of the fun.' She thought about her momma showing up, and how it didn't seem as good as she had dreamed. How could she tell Jahne about that? She couldn't, she realized.

For a moment, Jahne was filled with sympathy for the girl. 'Why don't we just have fun like stars tomorrow?' Jahne asked. 'With bodyguards, in an expensive restaurant, after we shop in expensive stores? Like good little stars should.'

They sat down in the back, though Jahne would have preferred one of the charming window tables that looked onto Melrose. But by now, after the briefings that Gerald La Brecque had put her through, she knew that was only asking for trouble. So the two of them parked their shopping loot on the banquettes and took seats that discreetly faced away from the rest of the restaurant.

Jahne was tired, and hungry, and thirsty. She'd have a beer, despite the calories. 'I'll have a Beck's,' she told the waiter, a gorgeous blond Adonis. His eyes registered recognition, but then he pulled down the shade of discretion necessary to be cool in L.A.

'Yes, ma'am,' he drawled, and turned to Sharleen. 'And for you, Miss Smith?' he asked.

'I'll have what she has,' Sharleen told him. She was thrilled with their shopping, and glowed with excitement. 'Oh, Jahne, I don't believe I ever saw such things. How did you find these places? Wasn't that pink outfit cute? And the leather shop! I loved that purple fringed-leather bikini. And Planet Alice. Wasn't that stuff wild? I never saw elephant bell bottoms before.'

Jahne, who remembered the seventies disco scene, and had almost been old enough to be part of it, smiled. 'Yeah, it's all updated L.A. versions of Carnaby Street, as if Carnaby Street the first time wasn't enough. Well, they didn't have Lycra then. It makes all the difference.'

'But you didn't buy hardly anything.' Jahne had seen lots of things, but she felt most comfortable when Mai dressed her. In fact, she had an appointment with Mai this afternoon for a fitting.

'Well, mostly I like Donna Karan. Anyway, there's nothing I need.'

'Jahne Moore, when did shoppin' have to do with what you *need*? Even when I was dirt poor, I knew *that*. We just used to look over the Sears catalogue and dream on what we *wanted*.'

'Well, I don't want much. And I feel like all this clothing and makeup is so confusing. It seems like I never have the right things. You need the right dress shoes, the right casual shoes, the right sports shoes. And they have to be the right colour for the dress or the skirt or the slacks or the shorts or the gown. And then you need the right sweater or wrap or jacket. And the belt and the purse, and that's not mentioning jewellery or makeup. Don't wear salmon lipstick with pink earrings. I don't know what I'd do without Mai. She's a pro. God, it gets me confused.'

'You, too?' Sharleen sounded shocked. 'But you always look so great.'

'Do I?' Jahne asked, surprised. She knew she owed it to Mai. 'I just keep it real simple,' she told Sharleen.

'Well, Lila isn't simple. She does it every day, and she does it perfectly. How do you think *she* does it?'

'Maybe it's in her genes.'

'But she don't hardly wear jeans.'

'No. I mean genetics. Maybe she gets it from her mother. After all, her mom was a movie star, so maybe Theresa O'Donnell taught her some tricks.'

'Did your mom teach you any?'

Jahne winced. 'No. She died in a car accident when I was very young.'

'Oh, I'm so sorry. My mom left home when I was nine, but I'm so happy for those years and all she taught me.' For a moment, Sharleen paused, and Jahne thought again that Sharleen was upset about something. Well, it must be hard to have a mother run out on you, Jahne thought. Maybe worse than having a mother die.

'My mom taught me a little poem. "I desire to leave Elmira!"' Jahne smiled at the vague memory.

'What's Elmira?'

'A really dreary town in upstate New York. I grew up there with my grandmother.'

'Well, I guess you listened to your momma, though.' Sharleen turned and surveyed the glitzy restaurant, which was decorated as an Italian spa, complete with *trompe l'oeil* pool on the ceiling and crumbling pillars along one wall. The gaily-striped chairs and awnings indoors sparkled, as did all the cerulean-blue china and glassware on the marble table. 'This,' Sharleen said, 'sure ain't Elmira.' They both laughed.

When the waiter returned with their drinks, they both ordered salads. After he nodded conspiratorially and left, Sharleen turned to Jahne.

'Kin I ask you a question?'

'You surely can,' Jahne said, and Sharleen giggled.

'Do you worry about how you look? I mean, Lila is so beautiful and all, but seems as like she worries a heap about it.'

Jahne almost laughed out loud.

'Sure, I worry.'

'You do, too?'

Jahne took a deep breath. 'Wait a minute? You mean *you* worry, Sharleen? But you're gorgeous. I mean, I can understand worrying about what you wear, or makeup, or something, but you're perfect – your skin, your hair, your eyes. Everything. Sharleen, you're absolutely gorgeous.'

The colour rose in Sharleen's perfect face. 'Oh, no. I ain't – I mean I'm not – nowhere as pretty as you or Lila. I mean, the two of you is about as beautiful as movie stars. I just look nice.'

Jahne stared. Then a wave of a kind of sick horror hit her. Here they were, by luck, by genetics, and by surgery, maybe the three loveliest and most desirable women in the country, perhaps the world, and two of the three, at least, didn't even believe in their own beauty. For her, of course, there was the contrived nature of her looks. But Sharleen was clearly a natural beauty and had always been, yet she, too, felt imperfect. And, in a moment of almost frightening clarity, Jahne bet that Lila, perhaps the most beautiful of all, was the most insecure. Out of nowhere, tears flooded her eyes.

'What is it?' Sharleen asked, her voice full of concern.

Jahne made a noise, nearly a groan. 'Oh, it's just so very sad. If *you* don't think *you're* pretty, and if *I* don't think *I'm* pretty, how do those poor women in America watching us feel?'

'Pretty bad, I guess. If they care.'

'Oh, Sharleen, every woman cares. They make us care.'

'Jahne, do you feel bad about them makeup ads? All them tricks and mirrors and lights?'

Jahne nodded. She thought of poor Mary Jane Moran. 'It doesn't do what it promises, does it? It doesn't make any of us beautiful, unless we already are.'

They were silent for a while. Jahne looked over at her companion. She realized how much she really liked her. She'd miss her over the hiatus. 'How is the album coming?' she asked kindly.

'Well, everyone thinks I kin sing 'ceptin' me. I guess it's okay. At least it's almost done, and then I'm takin' a long rest. Me an' Dean is going to get us a truck and go up to Yellowstone, or maybe Montana. Take the dogs, and the FBI, too, I guess. What about you?'

'I'm thinking of doing that movie.'

'*Workin'* on your vacation?' Sharleen could hardly believe it. 'Mr. Ortis wanted me to do a movie, but I said, 'Heck no!' Ain't you dog tired?'

'Yes, but I really want to do this movie.'

'Boy, with a movie and a TV show, then you'll *really* be famous.'

Jahne laughed. 'I don't think we could get more famous than this. But if the movie works, maybe I won't come back to *Three for the Road*.'

Sharleen's face dropped. 'Not really! Oh, Jahne, you wouldn't just leave me alone with Lila? She'd eat me up.'

'Oh, come on. You've got to get tougher than that. Just tell her to fuck off.'

Sharleen blushed and giggled. 'Oh, I could *never* do that.'

'Sure you could. Try it now. Practise on me.'

'But it's not religious.'

'Sharleen, where in the Bible does it say, "Thou shalt not use the word 'fuck'"?'

Sharleen giggled again. 'I don't know. Nowheres, I guess. It's just that nice girls didn't . . .'

'Sharleen, nice girls were all *doing* it but not *saying* it. So just stop being a girl altogether. Practise now. You're a woman. Tell Lila to fuck off.'

Sharleen looked at Jahne, thought for a moment, then nodded. 'Okay, I'll try, but I don't know if I can.'

'Try it.'

Sharleen pursed her lovely, soft pink lips. She took a deep breath through her perfect nose. 'Okay.' She paused. 'Eff you.'

'Oh, come on! That was pathetic. Tell the nasty piece of work to fuck off.'

'All right,' she paused. 'Lila, you just . . .' Her voice was sweet as ever.

'Come *on*. Be angry. She's so awful to you. And to me. And the crew. And she makes Marty be mean, too. Come *on*, Sharleen. Don't be such a little wimp!'

'Oh, fuck off!' Sharleen burst out.

The people at the next table turned to look at them. Sharleen's face grew rosy, and she covered her cheeks with her hands.

'Bravo!' Jahne told her. 'You've broken the "eff" barrier. Now you can live in Hollywood.'

After lunch with Sharleen, Jahne dismissed La Breque's guard and drove over to Mai's apartment on Cahuenga to discuss an outfit for tomorrow. It was easy to slip in – there was no gated security, just a pleasant but shabby U-shaped two-storey stucco apartment building with dark-green shutters. She knocked at Mai's door.

Mai was wearing all white – as she almost always did. White, or the same silver-grey as her hair. Today she had on a sweatshirt made of some kind of stretch terrycloth, with a strip of it wrapping up her head in an impromptu turban. Her face lit as she greeted Jahne.

'So, you are vell? You look so.'

'Yes,' Jahne said, and realized she was. It seemed that, perhaps, at last, the loneliness was lifting. She'd enjoyed her lunch with Sharleen, and she had a feeling that she'd enjoy this time with Mai. She was making friends. And she had her lunch with Sam to look forward to.

'Sit down,' Mai said, indicating a chair. Jahne, who'd been here before, wondered at the apartment. It was only three big rooms, but all three were immaculate, and painted white from floor to ceiling. All the furniture – not that there was much – was slipcovered in white cotton. There was a lot of sunlight filtered through the green-black shutters, and, other than one large fern in a white tub, no decor at all: nothing hung on the walls, no knick-knacks on the table. But somehow, with the sunshine and shadow, with the cleanliness and the whiteness, the rooms seemed filled, not empty.

'This place is so . . . original, Mai. Like you.'

Mai shrugged, and took two glasses out of a cabinet. 'Ven you are young, you are original. Ven old, you are only veird. But this suits me. I love colour and paintings and *objects*. But now I look at them in museums. It is a relief to have so little to care for.' She poured half a beer into one glass and was about to fill the second.

'None for me,' Jahne reminded her. I have to lose weight, not gain it.'

Mai sighed and brought out a bottle of spring water. 'For tvelve years, I ate the same dinner every night: a small steak and a salad

490

vith no dressing. Think of all those meals I missed! If you vant diet help, call Nikki Haskell. She is Liz Taylor's guru.' She looked up at Jahne. 'So, is it vorth it, being famous?'

Jahne sat on the sofa and put down the glass of water. 'Not if this is all there is,' she told Mai.

'Vat more do you vant? You are famous und vill be very rich, und you are young and healthy.'

'I never wanted fame, and the money wasn't the main thing. I wanted, I still want, to make films – to be in good films and do good work in them. To build up a body of work, something I can be proud of.'

Mai shrugged. 'You may be too famous for that now,' she said.

'What do you mean?' Jahne asked. She felt a moment of panic, a flutter against her rib cage.

'A famous and beautiful voman becomes a . . . a special kind of force. You cannot do normal things. You do not have normal friends. You are a target of many. You are loved by strangers, but you sometimes have no friends. And often, just as you adjust to being a goddess, you are finished, or they are finished with you. Think of how many are chosen and burn bright, but only burn out: so many new girls, so many girls of the moment, so many. But think of how few *vimmen* have lasting careers. Can you name five, even? Five who have built up a body of vork?'

'Yes. Of course. Susan Sarandon.'

Mai nodded. 'Who else?'

'Meryl Streep.'

'Of course. But vat has she done lately? Und who else?'

'There *are* women who have done it.'

'Yes. But, as hard as it is to become famous, it is a hundred times harder to stay so. To stay "hot." Use this time vell, Jahne. It may not last for long.'

22

Jahne had asked Mai for help in dressing for her lunch date with Sam. 'I want to be casual, but also look really good.' She giggled.

She'd finally signed the contract for *Birth* and, despite Sy Ortis, she felt as if she were five years old and on her way to a birthday party. 'You understand, Mai. Understated devastation.'

'Of course.' Mai had smiled. 'Like you just threw on your clothes and took no trouble, when you have really vorked on yourself for hours. That is the trick. The study of naturalness. But, my dear, haven't you already gotten this part?'

'Yes, but . . .'

'But maybe there is another part you are auditioning for? Is that it?'

Jahne just laughed. 'What do you think? Slacks or a skirt? Slacks look more casual, but I can show more leg with a skirt.'

'Vere are you lunching?'

'Over at the Getty Museum.'

Mai made a face. 'Vell, he is maybe cultured, but has bad taste in food.' She regarded Jahne for a moment. 'I think maybe a low-cut tank top vith a matching long jacket. Quvilted silk for the jacket. Lined. Blue linink. Black jacket, and the blouse in the blue of the linink.'

'Really? But I'd feel too dressed up in a jacket.'

'Not if you vore it with jeans,' Mai told her. 'Perfect, no?'

'Perfect, yes. But could you get it done in time?'

'Ven is this lunch?'

'Tomorrow,' Jahne admitted guiltily.

Mai had laughed. 'Who am I to hold up progress? But I'll have to leave right now to shop for fabric.'

'Yes, of course.'

Sometimes Jahne wondered if Mai tried so hard to please her because she had saved Mai's job when Lila had gone ballistic and tried to fire her. Or because Mai needed the extra income. Or because Jahne had secured her a job on the *Birth of a Star* project. Or because Jahne was the star. Would Mai pretend to like me if she didn't really? Jahne wondered. But Mai never seemed to show any special fondness for Sharleen, or, of course, for Lila. Yet they could be helpful to her career.

I have to believe she really does like me, and if it means another movie job for her, or some money on the side, or someone to stand up for her when Lila goes nuts or Bob is abusive, so what? Isn't that what friends are for? Jahne asked herself. I have to be sure not to ask for too much, and not to take her for granted or underpay her.

Still, it made Jahne a little uncomfortable to think that the woman she was closest to was paid to be with her. She pushed the thought from her mind. Instead, she tried to imagine the quilted silk jacket. She'd be gorgeous in it. Sam, always sensitive to such things, would be impressed.

Everything in Los Angeles was different from New York. Even the museums, Jahne thought with a laugh.

The Getty was located just off the Pacific Coast Highway. And, believe it or not, you had to call ahead to make a reservation. Not to see the collection, but to park your car! So-o-o L.A.! She laughed to herself.

Of course, she hadn't known that until the parking-garage attendant asked her for her reservation number. She thought he was joking. But then he explained how the museum had been built by J. Paul Getty in a residential neighbourhood, and the neighbours in Brentwood, Pacific Palisades, Los Flores, and Topanga had enough muscle to ensure that no one would park on *their* streets.

Luckily, the guard recognized her and made an exception. 'We always keep a few spots for celebrities, Miss Moore,' he told her confidentially. She hated to take advantage, but she was so pumped up for her lunch with Sam that she simply thanked the guard and parked.

A narrow staircase led up to a wide garden carved out of the cliff face. And there, in a perfect Hollywood style, was a *faux* Pompeian villa, complete with not only Doric but Ionic *and* Corinthian columns. Typical Hollywood: If one was good, why not have all three? Authenticity be damned. Blazing bright wall murals, complete with more columns, this time *trompe l'oeil*, lined the porches of the two colonnades which enclosed the Peristyle Garden, the centre of which sported a gigantic turquoise pool. Jahne put on her sunglasses to avoid squinting at the bright reflection. She wandered down the South Porch, gliding over the inlaid-marble floor. The Tea Room was in the West Garden, and before she went to it she stopped in the ladies' to check herself out and calm herself down.

She was alone there. She smiled at her reflection. Mai's jacket fitted like a supple skin, and the blouse showed just the right amount of cleavage. She took out the pink Flanders Cosmetics lipstick that she wore and carefully reapplied it. She had spent fifty minutes on her eye makeup: carefully lining her lids with a subtle blue-black and then building layer upon layer of matching mascara. She wore matching contact lenses, and only a smudge of eye shadow, buried in the crease at the outer edges of her eyes. But it did the job. When she took off her sunglasses, her eyes looked enormous. She knew she was beautiful, and, smiling at herself, she felt confident. If Sam came on to her at lunch, she could handle it. And she was certain that he would be mesmerized.

He rose as he saw her crossing the formal garden. The Tea House itself was casual. She took the chair opposite his, pleased that it was in the shade.

'Quite a venue,' she said.

'Do you know much about art?' he asked.

'Oh, I know my Jan van Huysums from my Jan Vermeers,' she said airily.

'Speaking of van Huysums, they have *two* here.'

'I'll look forward to seeing them.' She smiled sweetly.

They ordered iced teas and salads. Sam congratulated her again on the Emmy nomination, and they talked desultorily. She had a chance to really look at him.

He hadn't changed much. If anything, he was a little thinner. His dark hair was pulled back, but the pony tail had been trimmed to a discreet George Washington. He was tanned, though, and his brown hand, lying beside hers on the table, looked beautiful, lean and long and sensitive as ever.

He caught her eye and looked down to the table, too. But he noticed her hand, and picked it up in his own.

'You're so cold!' he exclaimed.

'So many men have said that,' Jahne intoned, 'but I thought with you, with you it would be different.'

He stared at her for a moment, recognizing the dialogue from *Jack and Jill*, and then she laughed, and then he did, too. His teeth, always good, white and strong, looked better than ever against his tan. The sinews in his throat moved as he swallowed the last of his laughter.

'I was blown away by your screen test,' he said. 'It was . . . novel. But more. It was intelligent. And heartfelt.' She felt herself start to blush. She murmured her thanks. 'I must have watched it a hundred times. And it was uncanny. You reminded me of someone. I'm not sure. It was so evocative.'

She had to change the subject. 'I look forward to playing Judy. So, how's the script coming?' she asked. She wondered again, for a moment, if Sy could be right. He might be a chauvinist pig, but he did know the business.

Sam stopped smiling, then recovered himself. 'Well, it's coming. It's a great theme: Does a woman love a man for his success or for who he is? And can a man love himself if he fails?'

'Funny, but I always thought the movie was about envy – Judy loved James and never envied his success. But when *she* succeeds, he envies her so much that he ceases to love her, if he ever really did.'

'Interesting view,' he said, and he looked at her, this time with a deeper, more quizzical look. 'Are you an envious person?' he asked.

'No. Not really.' She was surprised by the question, and by her answer, but she was aware it was the truth. She wondered why. 'Maybe it was because I had such low expectations. I never imagined myself a candidate for other people's success.'

'Really?' he asked. 'I'm the opposite. If I read about *any* director's triumph, my first thought is why *I* didn't do that or get that or present that.'

'It must make life very uncomfortable for you.' Jahne took a sip of her iced tea, watching him over the rim of her glass. This was going well, very well. She was succeeding in being both seductive and distant – a deadly combination. She smiled. What if he fell in love with her? What if he did, and she could spurn him? She almost giggled.

'You are so incredibly beautiful,' he said. 'That's the smile that played so well in your screen test.'

Jahne blinked. Was he being personal or professional?

'I was nervous,' she told him.

'Didn't show,' he said. 'April and I were both fascinated. She said . . .'

Jahne felt her smile slip. There it was again. Was it her imagination, that he and April had more than a working relationship? He went on talking while she wondered. Why had he invited her out? Was it a professional courtesy, a business lunch, or was it more? She tried to focus on what he was saying.

'They're talking about this as this year's *Pretty Woman*.'

'Well, I hope not. I mean, that was a film about a prostitute who got lucky. I hope there will be more content than that.'

Sam looked uncomfortable 'You do take yourself seriously.'

'So who are you going to cast opposite me?' she asked him.

495

'We were thinking of Michael Douglas, but he's not quite old enough.'

'But he's such a great actor! I'd love to work with him!'

'What do you think of Newman?'

'*Paul Newman*?' she could hardly believe it.

'April thinks he's maybe too old, but she thinks she can get him interested.'

'Oh, God, that would be wonderful!'

'You think you could play a convincing love scene with him?'

She laughed. 'Just try me.'

'I'd like to!' he said, and smiled. Jahne felt the heat. He *was* interested in her. 'I tell you the one reservation I have,' he confided. 'I don't see Judy as a beautiful woman. I felt maybe you couldn't be convincing as a plain girl.'

She began to laugh. And, for a frightening moment it seemed as if she might not be able to stop. 'I'll research it' she said at last.

'Great. Glad I entertained you.' Then he looked down at his watch, which, she noticed, was a gold Rolex. 'This has all been great,' he told her, 'but I've got a script to write. Can I walk you to your car?'

She declined. She needed a few moments alone. 'No, I'd like to take a look at the collection.'

'Oh, yeah. The van Huysums.' He grinned at her. 'Maybe you want to drop by my office this evening. Run a few lines.' He looked at her.

'No.' She smiled. 'I think there's been enough lines thrown out already.'

He laughed, leaned over to her, and gave her hand a squeeze. 'Forgive me,' he said. 'I can't help myself.' Then he picked up her hand, kissed the palm, and strode away.

It took her a moment to control her voice. 'Good luck with the script,' she called.

After he'd left her, she sat for a few moments alone. The lunch had been interesting, to say the least. But was Sam simply being a professional flirt? Could she keep her cool if only this much attention from him excited her so?

She freshened her lipstick, then wandered over to the galleries. She picked up a brochure and found there were indeed two van Huysums. 'What the hell,' she murmured to herself, and went in search of them.

They were magnificent: one a floral still life and the other a bounty of fruit. Both were in the jewel colours of a thousand Persian carpets. She knew it had taken years for the artist to paint each one, applying layer after layer of transparent pigment, building the depth of colour and shading before her. Years and years to create beauty almost everlasting. And for close to four hundred years, art lovers had admired the flowers and fruit at their ripest moment of perfection. She stared at the visual feast, but her mind was on other things.

After the hard years in New York, after the surgery, after the fiasco with Pete and the nasty affair with Michael McLain, after taking this job more than anything to get to work with Sam, it seemed that Sam and April were still a 'we.' And that Sam was as flirtatious as ever. But he probably had no interest in her, except as a co-worker. Well, she told herself, it's just as well.

Her life was no longer empty and grey, she reminded herself. It was a colourful abundance, like the van Huysum paintings. But, like them, it was unrealistic, chaotic, and perhaps even wasteful. All that fruit, about to rot, all those out-of-season cut flowers, about to wilt. Wasn't she like that? A perfect bloom that would go unsavoured until she wilted?

Hooray for Hollywood, she murmured again, and walked down to the garage to get her car.

23

Nothing was easy, Sharleen told herself. She had to get up, out from their warm bed, while it was still dark, so she forced herself up and began to gather her clothes to creep into the bathroom to get ready. She was so tired, it was hard not to resent Dean, lying there asleep, looking so angelic and so at peace.

Well, I'm not at peace, and that's for danged sure, Sharleen told herself, and patted Clover, who raised her head off the bed, but then snorted and turned over. All the dogs slept on the bed. So did the cat, and Dean. It was only she, Sharleen, who couldn't sleep. She had too many worries — worries that started up just as she closed her eyes for sleep and then continued all night.

She was still afraid, still dreaming about her daddy's death, and about the police comin' to look for her and Dean. She was worried about rememberin' her lines, about not makin' a fool of herself or gettin' fired. She was worried about the stupid record album, lookin' like a fool when it came out. She was worried most, maybe, about her momma. She hadn't yet told Dean a word about her. The funny thing was, she'd prayed and prayed to get to be with her stepmomma again, to help share the good luck and part of the burden of Dean, to be reunited, protected, comforted.

Well, be careful what you pray for, or you just might git it, she told herself again, and looked grimly into the mirror. She looked awful. The sleepless nights sure were showing in her face, and she already knew that the camera was merciless. Talking to Jahne would have been a comfort, and she was tempted to tell her everything, but she was too ashamed. Sharleen almost cried, but that would make her face worse. Instead, she filled the sink with icy water and, taking a deep breath, submerged her face in it.

It was terrible. Like dying by drowning in a freezing lake. But it would bring down the swelling under her eyes, reduce the puffiness, restore a little natural colour to her paleness. She counted – fast – to fifty, then came up for air.

It wasn't good enough, so she got two trays of ice, threw the cubes into the sink, and swished it around with her hand. Lord, it was cold! But, though she hated to do it, another look at her face forced her to. Lord, she looked old – maybe thirty!

Her face pushed again into the ice water, she tried to distract herself from the thought of Flora Lee. Why did she have to be a drunk? Because she was one, and Sharleen knew it. If there was a single thing her daddy had learned her, it was all about drunks. Flora Lee had left them with her daddy, and she didn't get no job to help them or try to find them. She just got herself drunk.

It hurt Sharleen right in her heart. And not only for herself but for Dean. Dean was Flora Lee's baby, and sweet as sugar. How could she just up and leave him and never try to help him at all? And though he wasn't so smart, Sharleen knew that Dean would wonder, too.

She pulled her face up out of the ice water. Then she remembered. For Lord's sake, today she wasn't shooting! Today was one of the few days she had off, but it was also the day she had to do that business for Dobe! Her face burned and tingled. All that ice water wasted!

With all the worries Sharleen had about her momma, the police, and the show, she had nearly forgotten about Dobe's date for the Customs auction. It wasn't easy to get time off when you were a TV star. Lucky it had come out this way. Sharleen told Dean not to tell anyone who called where she was going, just that she was going out.

She dressed quickly now. Her car and driver were right on time; it was only a green Plymouth sedan, not a limousine, and she'd ordered it not from the studio but from the car service that drove her cleaning ladies home. She looked at herself in the hall mirror before going out the kitchen door. Everything was right, she thought. The long black wig under the floral-print kerchief tied under her chin, the oversized Jackie O. sunglasses, the plain, tattered trench coat she had borrowed from Mai in Wardrobe covering the two bulky sweaters to make her look fat, along with a pair of baggy slacks of Dean's. Just right. Not even he would recognize her.

'Federal Building,' she said to the driver when she got in. She noticed him glancing in the rearview mirror. She read the address off the paper Dobe had sent her.

'Do you work for her?' the driver asked as they drove away.

'Who?' His question had taken Sharleen by surprise.

'Sharleen Smith. That's her house you came out of, right? What's she like?'

Sharleen relaxed a little, then smiled to herself. 'Yes, I do. She's a right nice person.' Well, that was all true, Lord, she told God. I do work for myself – and Dean, and now maybe Momma – and I am right nice. But, she realized, she hadn't disguised her voice, so she'd better shut up. She didn't know who might be watchin' her or followin'. She just prayed Dobe wasn't sending her into trouble.

Because now it wasn't just Dean, it was her momma who needed her, too, at least for a while. Sharleen had already given her money to move, and money to register in hairdressers' school, and some more money for some nice clothes. She couldn't afford to get in trouble over this Dobe business.

At the Federal Building, Sharleen followed the directions to the auction room the man at the front desk had mumbled to her without giving her a second glance. A quick look around the spacious lobby told her there were no reporters, something she had come to expect whenever she left the house. Her disguise had worked.

She walked into the crowded auction room, and was suddenly caught up in the commotion and din. She registered under a fake name at the desk, just as Dobe had told her to, although Sharleen wasn't sure if that was legal or not. The woman handed her a sheet of paper with instructions on how to bid, and a catalogue with descriptions of the lots. 'Lots,' Sharleen thought, confusedly, were property. Dobe had wanted her to buy him property, hadn't he? Sharleen found a seat in the last row and waited for the right number to be called, then flipped through the booklet, looking for Lot 604. She had to know what she was getting into.

As she skimmed through the pages of the inch-thick catalogue, she felt her heart racing. What was she bidding on? It wasn't land. They called everything 'lots.' But here was all kinds of stuff being sold.

Maybe she was bidding on something illegal. She liked Dobe, but she knew he wasn't completely honest in business. Still, Sharleen trusted Dobe, she really did. If he said there was nothing for her to worry about, she believed him. But Dobe was nervy, she knew that.

Drugs? No, not Dobe. He was a good Christian, he'd never do that. But what? And was it illegal? Oh, Lord, she prayed, I hope not. Sweat broke out on her forehead and upper lip. She hadn't really stopped to think this all out before she left the house.

Could I be arrested? Sharleen thought, glancing at the uniformed security guards stationed around the auditorium. That would be terrible. They'd find out about Texas, about Dean and her. About their daddy. Panic began to well up in her throat, so she said the Lord's Prayer, as she did whenever she was frightened. Then Psalm 23 for good measure, and, with a deep sigh of resignation, she returned to the catalogue.

She hadn't yet found the lot description in the booklet when she heard the auctioneer call out 'Lot Number 604,' and ask for an opening bid of one hundred dollars. Sharleen froze in her seat. She didn't know what to do, so did nothing, since Dobe had said she probably wouldn't have to pay more than seventy-five dollars.

When there were no bids from the floor, Sharleen heard the auctioneer drop the opening bid to fifty dollars. Well, she'd done the right thing. She felt her palm wet and hot on the handle of the paddle. This was when she was supposed to raise it, she knew, but the pounding of her heart was making her breathe too fast. She felt dizzy. The security men around the room scanned the seats.

Sharleen pulled the kerchief forward on her face and raised the paddle in the air, then quickly pulled it back down.

The auctioneer nodded in her direction and took her bid, but then he didn't seem to stop talking. He kept droning on, and Sharleen grew panicky. Torn between the fear of being pounced on by the guards or the police, and the need to get the bid in for Dobe, Sharleen felt her shakes increasing. If there's dope in them packages, Dobe Samuels, and I go to prison, I'm goin' be mighty mad. Here goes, she thought. Sharleen raised her paddle again.

'Sold! Lot Number 604 for sixty dollars to Bidder 123.'

Sharleen looked at her paddle number, just to be sure, then looked cautiously around the room. That was her number, all right. But no one was paying her any attention. The auctioneer was already going on to another lot. She took a few minutes to calm down, then stood up gingerly and walked back to the payment desk. She handed the bored-looking woman the money, got the receipt and instructions on when to pick up the lot, and where.

As she walked away from the desk, she tensed, waiting for a voice to scream out behind her, but none did. She got into a waiting elevator, and as the doors closed after her, she took her first breath in what felt like hours. She looked at the receipt for her purchase, which she still grasped in her hand, read the description of what she had just bought for Dobe, and gasped.

Why would anyone in their right mind buy 837 shoes – all for left feet only?

24

Neil Morelli dropped his fare in the box and walked down the aisle of the bus as it lurched into the traffic. He took the only single seat available, relieved that he didn't have to stand all the way to the garage. Either a seat alone or stand – that's the way it had to be for Neil. The thought of touching elbows or shoulders with these other people could make him gag right now. He screwed up his long, long nose at the odour. Neil had forgotten that people who rode buses and subways smelled.

When he'd left New York, he'd thought he would never be riding public transportation again.

But that was then. Now, since the dynasty-bitch got him kicked off his gig on *Three for the Road* – his last hope – Neil was back riding buses. And *driving* cabs, not taking them.

It wasn't even limos, with maybe some hotshot sitting back there, waiting to discover talent, someone who could give him a boost, someone who would take Neil's résumé and head shot and maybe – just *maybe* – give him another chance. No, Neil was reduced to pushing cabs around the streets of Los Angeles. Okay, at least it was dispatch cabs, not cruising for fares. But, still, most of his work was hustling Vietnamese home after their office-cleaning jobs were finished for the night. The companies paid the tab. Or picking up a guy too drunk to drive himself.

And lots of runs to East Los Angeles, where Neil had to keep his eyes open, be on the lookout every minute he was on those streets. He never knew where it was going to come from. He hadn't been held up yet, but the other guys in the garage – mostly Mexicans and Iranians – had warned him to be careful. Told him horror stories of how they had been ripped off for a couple of bucks and a pack of cigarettes. How a couple of the guys had resisted and were shot – in the head.

Neil took those stories seriously. He knew how dangerous the town could be. Even where he had spent most of his time since coming to the city, he knew how you could be robbed and no one would come to help. Robbed of your dignity, have your job stolen from you. Your livelihood. These wetbacks weren't telling Neil something he didn't know.

He thought again of how Sy Ortis had betrayed him, of how Lila Kyle had ruined his last shot, a good shot, at getting a continuing part on *3/4*. No, the cabbies couldn't tell him anything about getting ripped off that he didn't already know about.

But they did tell him something he hadn't thought of. Since the riots, all those guys had access to guns – handguns, rifles, whatever. And some of them carried while driving. Neil didn't like the idea of carrying a gun, but he had begun to think about it.

And the more Neil thought about guns, the safer he began to feel. He reminded himself to ask Roger about that tonight. *If* Roger got in contact with him.

The trip to the garage was only a little more than ten miles, but with waiting time it took almost an hour, on the slowest bus system in the country. Why should it be efficient? It was only for the illegals, and the other poor. The people who worked for hourly wages if they were lucky to work at all. Neil looked around at the fat women and shifty-eyed men. No one was happy to be here, Neil could see. So how bad must it have been where they came from?

Living hell, he thought. He felt for them, but he had his own problems. And one of them was now approaching. His stop came, and he got out of the bus to walk the three long blocks to the garage, where he had a twelve-hour shift coming up. He'd worked for the last three nights without one word from Roger. After his initial contact, Roger had stopped calling. Neil wasn't sure why. He knew why Roger had started to call him, but now he couldn't understand why he had stopped. Two nights in a row, he'd gotten Roger's messages, coming in over the dispatch radio in Roger's best newscaster voice.

Of course, at first Neil had been surprised. He didn't think Roger Mudd even knew who he was. But Neil guessed Roger had heard how Neil had respected the man, how he'd handled his career and all. And when Roger had radioed him privately, coming through on Neil's own radio that night, and told Neil not to get down on himself, that he, Roger Mudd, was going to contact Neil again, and tell him how to handle this mess, how to get out of it, Neil began to feel better.

So Neil waited. He *knew* Roger was going to call again. He just knew it. But he was afraid. Because, without Roger, he didn't know how he'd get along. Then it hit him. Maybe, Neil thought, maybe Roger meant I should radio *him*. Neil stopped on the sidewalk. He thought about that for a minute, then continued to walk towards the garage, now looming in the darkness at the corner.

But how do I get him? I don't know how. Neil decided that he could figure it out. There had to be a way. After all, Roger Mudd had found *him*.

The cab smelled of some goddamn foreign food, not Mexican or anything from the Western Hemisphere. This smell came from like out of a desert tent, like rancid cabbage cooked over camel dung. Neil wondered how these fucking Arabs were able to get camel dung in this country. Maybe way down in the San Diego Zoo? I'd walk a mile for a camel turd.

He rolled down the window, trying to get some air circulating in the car, but he knew from other nights that the smell was here to

503

stay. It gets in the fucking vinyl and wraps itself around the vinyl molecules, and combines with them, becomes a new substance, a new chemical. One that would never go away. Like the smell of dog shit on the bottom of a shoe. Once you know you've stepped in dog shit, you always smell it whenever you wear those shoes again, no matter how you cleaned them.

Fucking Arabs. They should stick to international terrorism. They're better at that than cooking, for chrissakes.

His dispatch radio scratched into voice, startling Neil. He reached for the volume button as he rolled along Santa Monica Boulevard, adjusting it to a bearable level. The guy that was driving the car just before Neil must have been deaf. Or had his burnoose tied too tight.

Neil radioed in his position, then pulled into Century City, where he was supposed to sit and wait for his first call. He waited and waited. He turned off the engine, then put his head back. It was going to be a long, slow night, Neil decided. There hadn't been one call since he got in, except for the location call. And Neil was tenth on line. He would have been twenty-second, but he had figured out the scam. If he paid off the dispatcher, he got moved up. So he had, but, still, he only had number ten. The fucking Iranians must have dropped a lot of rials tonight, to get so far ahead of Neil. Dollars aren't what they used to be.

He wasn't sleeping, Neil knew that. He had his eyes closed, and his chin had dropped to his chest. There was a short rivulet of drool out of the corner of his mouth. But he hadn't fallen asleep. The voice from the radio was familiar.

'Roger, I hear you, go ahead,' Neil said into the air instead of the hand-held mike. Neil listened, while Roger told him the whole story. How he had been passed over and didn't get the national anchor spat, just because he had the wrong family tree. His great, great granduncle had been the doctor who treated John Wilkes Booth. How Roger didn't have the right connections. Neil had read a little bit about it in the newspapers when it happened, he was sure, but now Roger was giving him the inside dope. Why he understood what Neil was going through. How the assholes of the world have a private club that gives them special membership discounts on bullshit. How the rich and connected were going to do away with all the little guys that wouldn't allow themselves to be pushed around. Roger talked about Lila Kyle, and the other two. All the pretty women who had laughed at Neil, rejected him.

504

Neil listened, not opening his eyes. Then Roger explained everything. About how unless your father owned the network, how unless you had connections or were very good-looking, you got fucked over. But Roger was now going to be Neil's connection. Roger would take care of everything.

It wasn't till Roger told him what to do – *exactly* – that Neil opened his eyes. He jumped for the mike. He *had* to talk to Roger. Just to be sure he'd gotten the instructions right. He blurted into the mike, calling Roger's name, but got no response. He began to play with the dials of the two-way radio, all the time screaming into the mike. *He had to get back to Roger.* 'What's the frequency, Roger?' he kept screaming over and over.

'Hey, Car Forty, leave the radio alone. What you doin' to it, man? You screaming over there. Leave it alone!'

Neil put back the microphone on the stand, his hand trembling. Could Roger really have meant it? Neil thought for a moment. Yeah, Roger meant exactly what he said. No two ways about it. Neil made a mental note to talk to the guy in the garage that could get things. Neil needed something. Real bad.

And now Neil didn't feel alone anymore.

25

When the phone rang, Lila wasn't surprised to hear Aunt Robbie's voice at the other end. She just hadn't thought it would be so soon. 'Don't hang up,' he said when she answered. Lila had no intention of doing that. To tell the truth, she was bored and needed some diversion. And if *she* was bored, think how bored Robbie had to be – he who'd put up with years of abuse from Theresa just so he could be the lackey of a star, so that he could be a witness to the action.

'Are you there, Lila?' Robbie asked sheepishly.

'Where the fuck did you think I was?' But the fact was that, just as Robbie needed to be a party to the fame and the action and the success, Lila needed him – or someone – to witness it. All the interviews, all the fan mail, all the offers, the invitations, the publicity – none of it seemed to be really happening to her if someone else wasn't there to be excited and impressed by it. She would not hang up. Keep the line open, but don't make it too easy for him. After all, she had to get him to agree to her plan. Her new perfect plan.

'I was thinking, Lila . . .'

'Uh-huh,' she said, examining her manicure.

'I was thinking . . . I mean, we've been friends for years, since you were what? A baby? It's silly for us to quarrel, Lila. I'm not mad at you.'

'What does that have to do with anything, whether *you're* mad at me or not?'

'Well, I mean, after our fight and all. I mean, I have no hard feelings.'

'Why should you?' she asked, letting the wonder roll over the telephone lines.

'Well, you kicked me, but . . .'

'You asked for that, Robbie.'

He didn't say anything for a minute. 'Well, I admit I shouldn't have brought up the subject of your mother, but, well, your reaction was a little extreme.'

'I'm confused. Why are you calling me? To tell me I was wrong? That doesn't seem very sensible, does it? I mean, Robbie, come on. It wasn't *me* that was in the wrong.' Either he was going to crawl or he wasn't. Lila wasn't going to play this game much longer, so she decided to listen to one more sentence from Robbie. If he didn't know how to do it, she was going to hang up on him. Not a loud crash, like he was important to her or anything. Just that low click that would make him think – but only for a minute – that they had been disconnected by accident.

Robbie was getting it. 'Look, I'm sorry, Lila,' he said.

'For what, Robbie?' Like Theresa used to make Lila do when she was a kid and had been naughty. Make her apologise to the two dummies. Rub her face in it.

'Lila, this is very difficult.'

'Then maybe you should send a candygram or something, Robbie. If you're having trouble finding the words.'

She waited while Robbie took a deep breath; then the words began tumbling out. 'I'm sorry I overstepped my bounds, Lila. I shouldn't have tried to manipulate you like that. You're right. Theresa did it to herself, I see that now.' Then he paused. 'Forgive your old auntie?' he asked, in that fucking baby-talk voice that put her teeth on edge.

Now Lila imitated it. 'But Auntie's been a naughty auntie. She should be punished, shouldn't she, Robbie? She's been a naughty, naughty girl.'

'Aunt Robbie should be punished, Lila. What can she do?'

There was a pause, and when he spoke again Robbie's voice had an edge of panic in it, as he realized they weren't just playing games. 'What, then? What do you want, Lila?'

'Candy,' she said.

Robbie laughed, relieved, 'Oh, sure, I'll get a box of Godivas – a five-pound box. We can sit up all night and eat chocolates.'

'No, Robbie. I mean Candy . . . and Skinny.' Lila paused, feeling her breath quicken. 'A kidnapping. You know where they are, Robbie. This is something only you can do.'

'No, Lila. Your mother would . . .'

'Fuck her!'

'Lila, please.'

'I mean it, Robbie.'

'But why, Lila?' Robbie's voice had tears in it. 'What do you want *them* for? You know what that will do to . . .' He stopped himself from saying Theresa's name. She heard the realization hit, and the acceptance. 'Okay. I'll do it.'

'That's the good auntie,' Lila said, in her baby voice once again.

'Lila, now I need a favour,' Robbie said.

Jesus. He simply didn't get it, did he? '*No, no, no*. That's not the way it's done, Aunt Robbie. *First* the tribute, then *maybe* a favour. Ta-ta,' she said, and hung up.

It would be a good punishment, and would keep him in his place. It would also be certain to put him on Theresa's permanent shit list. There's only one way to deal with traitors, Lila thought to herself sternly. And she realized she was smiling for the first time that day.

26

Bouncing back from the shit meeting with Ricky Dunn, Michael McLain had decided he had to take an action and take it fast. So he'd signed the contract with April Irons for *Birth of a Star*. He signed it, and *then* he sent it over to Sy's office. Sy would be furious, but fuck him. Michael would leave him for CAA or William Morris or even for Ara if Sy gave him any more shit. April knew her stuff, the old film had been a classic, she was willing to pay top dollar, *and* she was getting Julia Roberts for the female lead. Michael signed, despite not having a finished script, despite Sy's warnings.

Now he was feeling actor's remorse. He threw the script that had just been messengered over across the room, its pages fluttering like the feathers of a dirty pigeon. He'd read crap. He'd watched crap. Hell, he'd even *been* in crap. But he'd never had anything to do with crap as bad as this. *Birth of a Star* should be called *Death of a Star*, he thought angrily. *This* star. Me. It will pull me lower than Redford after *Havana*. Christ, it's worse than *Akkbar*. And nobody, not any star in Hollywood, could afford *two* Akkbars. In his heart, he knew he should have followed Sy's advice on the fucking Ricky Dunn movie. Eaten crow, given up on the billing issue. But screw it. He wasn't ready to play sidekicks yet.

Still, after this dreck, he might not get the option to.

He almost shivered, then pulled himself together. All right, so the screenplay is shit. That's a definite. He didn't have to think anymore about that right now. If that was all that was wrong with this movie, then he wasn't going to worry. Not just yet, anyhow. Scripts could be fixed.

Michael always did this final analysis of a project perhaps a bit too late: after the contracts were signed, the dates set. Then, because there was no way out, his denial would break, and in fear and loathing he would let himself see the negative side. Up till now, when he was still pushing for the job, he would only consider the good aspects. In this case, one was the money, *lots* of money. And work, for the first time in over a year and a half. With the Dunn project blown, he needed a movie right away.

Point two: the director. April had told him about Sam Shields, praising him to the skies, but Michael was definitely not impressed when they met. The guy had been an off-Broadway director in New York, not exactly an exclusive club. Then, somehow, he got himself hooked up with April and did *Jack and Jill* with her. Got good reviews, made some money, and even got Sam mentioned seriously in some Hollywood circles. But let's face it, the guy had only busted his cherry: that didn't make him a director. *Jack and Jill* had been a small movie. This was a big one. A *real* big one.

Lousy script, half-assed director. Now he was down to one out of three. At least the stars would be top drawer – him and Julia Roberts. Her comeback, and his. And if this May–September romance was a bit too much like *Pretty Woman* – well, the public had loved *Pretty Woman*. And it wasn't as if she – or Michael – needed a lot of directing. All Julia ever had to do was walk in front of a camera and people fell in love with her. Luckily for her and everyone else, she could act and carry a project. So, while Sam Shields was no hotshot director, Michael was certain that he and Julia would be able to pull off *Birth of a Star*, given a few changes in the script. With his talent, and Julia's star quality and likability, and considering that April, who was no fool, seemed to be able to lead Shields around by the gonads, this might not be so bad.

Michael started feeling better. He went over and picked up the script again, flipping through the pages where he had earlier made margin notations in red. He picked up the phone and called April at home. He knew how to work as a team player. He'd call the coach and give *her* a pep talk.

April answered her private line. Michael dropped his voice to his deepest baritone. He took an audible breath, then said teasingly to April, 'Talk down and dirty to me. Say something that will make my blood froth over.'

'You're a lousy actor, Michael,' she said. 'Is that down and dirty enough for you?' Without waiting for an answer, she continued, 'Come on, what do you want, Michael? I was just about to brush my teeth.'

'I thought you had them sent out. *Both* of them.'

'I know you have something on your mind when you call all cutesy, Michael. What's up?'

'Julia Roberts. She's signed for *Birth*, too, right?'

'I never said she was *signed*, Michael. I only said we were talking.'

'Talking? Listen, principal photography is supposed to start in two weeks, and you haven't signed her?'

'Actually, Michael, we decided you're such a strong presence that Julia would be overkill. We needed someone newer, someone who would be a perfect counterweight to you.'

He knew it. Goddamn it, he knew it! After over twenty years in the business, Michael McLain had a built-in shit detector. And he was waist-deep now, and sinking. 'Uh-huh. Like who?' Michael said.

'You're going to love this, Michael. Jahne Moore.'

Michael didn't say anything for a long moment. It was too fucking much. Starring him with that TV tramp! 'You're wrong, April. I don't love it.' In fact, he hated it. And he hated the bait and switch. He was too old to fall for it, but he had. 'Jahne Moore is a nothing,' he said.

'A nothing? I was sure you would be ecstatic. She's the flavour of the fucking month! She's beautiful, relatively unknown – in the movies, I mean – and you two have . . .'

'She's a lightweight, April. Television. It'll all be on my shoulders. New director . . .'

'Hardly new, Michael. He's made me a lot of money on *Jack and Jill*.'

'You made a lot of money on that because you had a nothing budget. *Shields* didn't make it for you, the *accountants* did. And now you're giving him – what? – a forty-million-dollar budget? And a dumb bitch from the Melrose Playhouse as my costar?'

Michael couldn't hold it in any longer. He was screaming now. 'I see the plot. A real-life drama. Fading movie star. Young TV nothing. A slip yoke. Perfect for you, April. But I'm not carrying the weight for the whole fucking movie, April. I'm not fucking doing it!'

'You don't have to, Michael. All you have to do is show up every day and take direction. This movie is my responsibility; let's be very clear about it. *I'm* the producer, and *you're* the actor. And your contract is airtight. No costar approval. So you show up next Friday or prepare to meet with our lawyers. Okay?'

April hung up before he could say another word.

Sy Ortis and Michael McLain sat at the best table at Via Veneto. Michael was getting loud. A lot too loud for this place, where the big money, the real heavy hitters, ate.

Michael had been ranting for the last twenty minutes about his *Birth* deal. How April had baited him with Julia Roberts and switched him to Jahne Moore, how the script sucked, how he hated the director already, how he – Sy – had to find a way to get Michael out of the contract.

Sy simply listened. He had known for over a month about Jahne's role. If only Michael had not kept his talks with April secret from Sy. This served him right.

'So, you got to get me out of it. Just get me out of it. I can't do this piece of shit. I won't.'

Typical. Like a child. 'I'm afraid you'll have to. A lot of money is tied up in this, and if you back out now, it will cost.'

'Tell them I'm sick.'

'*If* they believe it, it will be around the Industry in an hour. Remember what those rumours did to Burt Reynolds' career? What did Sydney Pollack say in *The Player*? How rumours were always true? And it won't be so easy to get insured on the next one. If there *is* a next one.'

'What's that supposed to mean?'

'Michael, you made your bed. You'll have to lie in it. I told you not to do this movie. I begged you. Just like I told you not to insist on top billing with Ricky Dunn.'

'Okay. Get me out of this piece of shit and I'll do the Dunn thing.'

'Too late. Eastwood signed on.'

'Goddamn it, Sy! You better take care of this. Find a solution. I mean it.'

'Is that a threat, Michael? A threat that you'll leave the agency? That you'll fire me?'

'You got that right. And if you don't like it, Sy, you know where the door is.'

Sy had been waiting for Michael to say this. Michael always said it at the end of one of his tirades. Usually Sy would just switch to another tack, wait for another time. But not today.

Sy put down his fork, swallowed the last of the veal piccata, wiped his mouth with the oversized linen napkin, and looked across the restaurant table at Michael. 'It's been a pleasure, Michael. Sorry it couldn't have worked out between us, but I respect your judgement.' Sy pushed back his chair and stood up.

Michael looked up at Sy, his eyes wide. 'What? Where are you going?' Michael still had a forkful of food dangling in the air, halfway toward his mouth.

'The door. I finally figured out how to get there, after all these years of you telling me I knew where it was.' Sy motioned with his hand. 'So, *muchos gracias* for firing me, Michael. It saves my having to quit. And *adios, amigo*!'

27

When Jahne received the revised *Birth of a Star* script, messengered to her at the Beverly Wilshire Hotel, she was disappointed to find no note from Sam included. What did you expect? she asked herself crankily. A marriage proposal?

She *was* cranky. She'd spent the day in the seemingly endless round of upkeep and grooming appointments that filled so much of her spare time: first a facial, then three hours at Antonio's, having the grey covered and streaking the black and blue and other shaded highlights into her hair. That was always a trial, because of the face-lift scars buried in her hair. Viendra looked at them, looked at her, and winked. She tipped him a hundred bucks and hoped he'd keep his mouth shut. Then two gruelling hours with Arna, her trainer, who didn't believe he'd really worked you unless you were doing dry heaves by the end of it. Even now her legs were shaking. And she still had to change, do a quick interview with Melinda Bargreen a journalist from Seattle, and then look for a place to live: at $480 a day, the hotel was a high price to pay for security.

She got through the interview, and then spent three exhausting hours touring with Roxanne Greely, house broker to the stars. She came back to the hotel exhausted and depressed. Roxanne had explained that she might be able to find something for $750,000, but that anything nice was over two million! Jahne knew that the world out here was nuts, but this proved it.

It wasn't until that evening, back at the Beverly Wilshire that she got to relax. She ran a bath, a rare luxury. Brewster Moore had cautioned her that more than three minutes of immersion in water was injurious to the dermal layers, but tonight she didn't care. She threw in a generous handful of Flanders bath salts (another Brewster no-no) and slipped, with a sigh, into the huge, deep, sparkling tub. Then she opened the *Birth of a Star* script and started to read.

She was on page 37 when the tub-side phone trilled. She reached for it, wondering if she could be electrocuted by a phone call. She could just see the headlines: 'CARA DIES IN BATHTUB TRAGEDY.' The *National Enquirer* would have a field day.

She picked up the phone.

'What do you think?' Sam's voice asked.

As if it were the most natural thing in the world, she answered, 'I'm only up to page thirty-seven, but I like what I've read so far. That opening is visually brilliant.'

'Goes along with the rest of me,' he said. 'How about a drink?'

'Tonight? Sorry, I'm bushed. I've spent the whole evening looking for a place to live. I'm looking forward to crawling into bed with your script.'

'Lucky script. So, did you find a place?'

'I saw something I could maybe lease in Bel Air. Expensive, and it's a bit pretentious, but La Brecque tells me it's secure as Fort Knox.'

'So, how 'bout dinner tomorrow night?'

Dinner instead of lunch. This was an upgrade.

'I can't make it until Thursday,' she purred. 'And not until about nine,' she told him. Then she regretted it. She was still playing too easy, making the same mistake Mary Jane used to make. She should have just told him no.

'Fine. I'll pick you up at the hotel.' Why was she doing this? she wondered. It was ridiculous. If you wanted to work with Sam, you are, she told herself fiercely. That does not include visits to art museums and dinners alone.

Or would they be alone? It hadn't occurred to her to ask. But maybe this was to be a working dinner. She and April and Sam and God knows who else. Michael Douglas? Paul Newman?

Jahne was up to the second act of the new *Birth of a Star* script when she got to the love scene.

FADE UP with a POP DISSOLVE:
                [James]
PULL BACK to reveal James, his face a mask of desire.
Judy, you know how I feel, don't you?
                [Judy]
PULL BACK. Judy in bed, holding sheet.

Yes. I think I do.

[James]

WIDER
But show me how you feel.

[Judy]

I feel bared before you. Like this . . .

[Slowly, she slips out of her robe. She is awkward with love.
Under it, she has on only a plain man's pajama top. She slips
it off and stands revealed before him, naked and in a state of
grace.]

[James]

FOLLOW his eyes.
You're so beautiful!

A nude scene! And from there, on pages 50 and 51, they make
love. Well, of course Judy and James were lovers, but in the first
version she'd read it was not as explicit as it was now. Jahne read
now and groaned. '*Close-up. He cups her breast. Long shot – his hand
moving from her ankle to her knee, from there to her thigh.*'

Oh, God! She should have known! She felt herself break into
a sweat. She was too upset to judge whether or not it was a good
scene, or justified. All she knew was that she couldn't do it. Not
with her body. Not with her scars.

Well, she'd talk to Sam. She'd get him to change it. He'd
have to. She'd insist.

Certainly she wasn't the first actress to resist nudity. Many
actresses did. They were embarrassed by nudity, or felt exploited.
No women wanted to do it, except for the few exhibitionists. Well,
it was not in her contract, and she wouldn't do it.

She read the rest of the script numbly. She couldn't judge it,
couldn't be intelligent. She just prepared for her battle Thursday
night.

Thursday came quickly. The restaurant was a hip L.A. version
of a sushi bar – very white walls, black tables and chairs, and a
long black counter with the sushi chefs on one side, diners on the
other. As if in unspoken agreement, most of the patrons wore either
black or white clothes. They were a mixed bag: some young, dressed
almost sloppy-casual, and others, older, who looked like Industry
suits in their linen Armanis. The place was crowded, and the tables
were close together, the noise level high. Along the walls, shadow
silhouettes were painted: a pony-tailed man holding chopsticks, a
woman with a hat on. They were clever and disconcerting: at one

514

table a small, birdlike woman appeared to be casting the painted shadow of a big man with an Afro.

In case Jahne had any question of the hipness of the place, Sam pointed out Barry Diller, a small bald guy who sat with an entourage of young men. 'Past chairman of Fox,' Sam told her. 'Just up and quit one day. People say he got tired of the game. Now he's into home shopping.'

They were taken to a table by Yoshi, the owner, who welcomed Sam by name. There was a stir, the usual moment when the conversation silenced as she entered a room; then the buzz continued, a little louder than before. Fame. She wondered if she would ever get used to it.

Sam ordered saki, but she only tasted from the tiny black pottery cup she was offered. She played with the cup nervously. She didn't care for saki, but she loved Japanese beer. And a beer would calm her down right now. Too bad it was as fattening as American beer. Well, she'd call Nikki in the morning.

She looked up from the menu to see Sam staring at her.

'Is something wrong?' she asked.

'You remind me of someone,' he said, and continued staring.

She stopped breathing, and then reminded herself that she had to take another breath. 'Really?' she managed to ask, and lowered her head, letting a black wing of hair fall forward.

'No,' he said. 'Don't do that.' He reached across the table and brushed back the hair. 'Let me look at you.' She surveyed him from under her eyelashes, everything stilled for what might have been half a minute but felt like hours. Now he sees, she thought. At last, he'll know me. And what will happen?

'I know!' he said triumphantly. 'The young Vivien Leigh!'

She breathed again. But her body felt loose, as if she'd been working out too hard all day. She was frightened. Frightened and weak and fascinated.

'So, what did you think of the script? I'm dying to know.'

'Well . . .' She'd have to talk about the nude scenes.

'You hate it. God, you hate it!'

'No. No. I just . . . I have some reservations.'

'Look. It hasn't been easy, updating this. I mean, essentially it's the story of a sadistic man and a masochistic woman – old-fashioned melodrama.'

'Is that old-fashioned? I think it's pretty current.'

'Oh. The old "Women Who Love Too Much" and "Men Who

515

Make Hitler Look Good" scenario. Well, I didn't want to write some codependency screenplay.'

'Look, I don't think that's the problem. It's . . .' she paused.

'You're killing me. First Michael McLain, then you.'

'Michael McLain? What about him?'

'He complained, too. Says he doesn't want to be typecast as a degenerate fucked-out star. So why did he take the part?'

'Michael?' Jahne asked. What was Sam talking about?

'Well, yes, Michael McLain. He's costarring with you. Didn't April tell you?'

'Tell me? Last I heard, you were considering Paul Newman for the part.'

'Oh, no, not really.' Sam lowered his voice to a throaty whisper. 'April wanted Michael, I wanted Newman. So she gave me you, and I gave her McLain.' Sam paused, then asked, 'You *are* excited about working with Michael, aren't you? He's perfect for the part of James. It seems that the two of you are already close. I thought you'd be jumping with joy.'

Well, of course. He had seen her with Michael. He thought they were still an item. Maybe that was why he wasn't being more aggressive with her personally. One thing she knew about Sam was that he didn't like to compete with another man to get a woman.

Should she tell him that she and Michael were – well, estranged? That the way was open for him? And that she didn't want to work with Michael – didn't even want to see him?

But it was none of his business, or if it was, he'd find out for himself. This time, she wasn't going to grovel or pave the way.

But, God, what would it be like if she had to work with Michael? And if she had to watch Sam nuzzle April Irons right in front of her? She wasn't sure she could take it. Jahne caught herself. Well, if it wasn't definite, there was a chance it wouldn't happen. She would have to hope not. 'I'm just so surprised, so . . . overcome. Me working with you *and* with Michael McLain! It's like a dream come true. I'm delighted, Sam, and really very honoured.'

He seemed not to notice how shaken she really was. Well, she reminded herself, when he was wrapped up in a project, he never did notice anything else.

'But listen. We do have a problem. I can't do the sex scenes,' she blurted. 'I can't.'

He stopped, smiled, and looked at her. Then he laughed. 'Is that all this is about?' he asked. 'The nude scenes?'

'I don't consider that "all,"' she said stiffly.

'Oh, look, if you don't want to strip, we get you a body double. No problem. I can fake the frontal shot. Cut from your face to her body. No problem.'

'Why have it at all? Why *show* it?'

'It's a love story.'

'But it's not a sex story.'

'Oh, come on. *Basic Instinct. Damage.* Modern times. A necessity.'

'But it isn't necessary to show a nude Michael McLain. Isn't *that* modern?'

'I'd guess it was late-middle-aged,' Sam smirked. 'But *you* ought to know.'

'You know what I mean. Why is it necessary?'

'Oh, you know the answers as well as I do. Because men like to see it. Because women don't mind. Because men *don't* like to see nude males. . . .'

'Why not?'

Sam shrugged. 'I don't know. Ask Neil Jordan. Don't want themselves compared to someone else. Are afraid of their own homosexual feelings. Or feel degraded by the sight . . .'

'What if women feel degraded by all the female nudity? And no matching male?'

'Oh, come *on*. I didn't invent the world. This is the way it is. A naked female is beautiful. A naked male is offensive.'

'I think it goes deeper than that,' she said. 'I think it's a way to control women. To show them how perfect they are supposed to be. To use their bodies to sell something – a product, a film, an idea. And to teach them to sell themselves, the way you want me to.'

He reached his hand out to her and covered hers with his. She pulled away.

'I can see you like me, Jahnie. You don't want to, but you do.'

'Of course I like you. You're my director.'

'No, I don't mean that you like me professionally. I mean you like *me*. And I'm very impressed with you. You have integrity. You're a very unusual woman. Not just beautiful, but really focused, really intelligent. And we can work this out. I understand your concerns. But like me. Work with me. Trust me.'

She looked into his long, tanned, and handsome face. He was

still the best-looking man she'd ever known. And the blend of his intelligence, his drive, and his 'Hey, I'm one of the good guys' attitude was as seductive as ever. She felt herself blush, and glanced down at the tabletop. She couldn't help noticing his lap. Was that sashimi in his pocket, or was he really glad to see her? She looked away. Despite the restaurant noise, she could hear him breathing, and she could hear her own breathing as well. God, if just for an hour they could lie down together and comfort one another, be truly together even if only for a little while.

He reached for her hand again, and this time she let him hold it. 'I'll protect you,' he said. 'Just let me in. Let me try. I'm a good director. I love my actors, Jahne. Trust me.'

'I'll try,' she promised.

28

Sharleen had the maid service make a special trip to clean the house for Momma's arrival. Now it was spotless, except for the boxes that Sharleen had bid on for Dobe. Just what is he going to do with all of these left shoes? she wondered for about the thousandth time. Could he be coming up with another scam like he did with the gas tablets? Dobe, you better not be makin' me store somethin' that's against the law, Sharleen thought to herself. Just what would she say to Momma when she got here and saw all these cartons? If Momma ever did get here.

Sharleen sat in the big living room, flipping through a catalogue and out of the corner of her eye watching Dean playing with the dogs. Then her eyes flicked to her watch once again. Sharleen had arranged for a car to pick up Momma and bring her here at seven. It was almost eight o'clock. The food had already arrived and was getting cold. An hour late; Sharleen was worried. Tonight, Dean was going to see Momma for the first time. Sharleen didn't want anything to go wrong.

But so much had already gone wrong: Flora Lee had taken the money to move, but she hadn't moved – she was still in the bad place in East Los Angeles. And they'd made two dates for her to come over, and both times she hadn't come at all. Then, the next day, she'd called Sharleen and cried, telling her she was too ashamed to see her baby.

Dean had been upset.

Now Dean broke into her thoughts. 'Do you think Momma will know me?'

Before Sharleen could answer, the security guard at the gate buzzed and admitted Flora Lee's car. Thank the Lord! 'Of course she will,' Sharleen reassured him. Together, they opened the front door and stepped outside, standing on the top step as the car pulled into the driveway. Flora Lee got out and, with the driver's help, was able to steady herself on her feet. Flora Lee looked up and saw Sharleen and squealed, then began to run up the stairs to her, her arms open. 'My little girl,' she said, as if she hadn't seen Sharleen since Lamson. Then she slipped. Sharleen reached out and broke her fall. Flora Lee righted herself as if nothing had happened. Sharleen's heart dropped to the pit of her stomach. Flora Lee had been drinking. That's why she was late.

'Now, where's my little baby boy?' she yelled, as she walked unsteadily into the house, straight past Dean. He followed her. 'I'm right here, Momma,' he said to the woman who was moving around the living room in a crooked line. She turned to him and flung her arms out.

Dean took an involuntary step backwards.

Sharleen watched Dean as he looked his momma up and down. Then she took a look at Flora Lee's attempts to make herself look special for this reunion. They had made her look ridiculous. Especially ridiculous to Dean, a boy who was only six when he'd last seen his momma. Flora Lee's hair was fairly neat, but way too yellow. The lime-green dress had too many flounces at the neck and shoulders. There was way too much jewellery, and Sharleen could smell the perfume all the way over on this side of the room. And the shiny yellow high-heel shoes didn't help her studied attempts to walk normally.

Flora Lee was all over Dean before Sharleen could say anything. 'My little boy, my baby.' Flora Lee had her arms around Dean's shoulders, and her face on his neck, crying. 'You got so big I didn't know you! Momma's home, baby. Momma's home.'

Dean didn't move, but his eyes found Sharleen's and locked on them. Sharleen met his gaze, for a moment. 'Momma, why don't you come sit over here?' She guided Flora Lee to the end of the sofa, and eased her gently onto the cushions. 'Now, if you just sit a bit, Dean and I will get things ready in the kitchen. We'll be right back, okay?'

'Don't you think this calls for a drink? It's a celebration, ain't it?' Flora Lee suggested.

'Okay, Momma,' Sharleen said, guiding Dean through the kitchen door before her.

'That ain't Momma,' Dean said, the moment the kitchen door closed behind them.

'What do you mean, Dean? 'Course it is.' But Sharleen felt her stomach sink.

Dean shook his head. 'No, it ain't. I remember how Momma smells, and she don't smell like Momma.'

'Well, people change. She ain't so young as she was. Remember when you were a little boy, and Momma took you to school your first day? Remember? You told me the other day you did.'

'Yeah, I remember that. Momma was pretty and not fat, and had brown hair. And she didn't wear no makeup, or smell like Daddy.'

'You kids comin' out?' Flora Lee yelled from the living room 'We got to have a drink together, remember?'

'Dean, just give her a chance. You'll remember more in a little while.'

When they got back to her, Flora Lee was sitting on the sofa, the Bible open on her lap. She looked up at them, her painted face crumpled in surprise. 'Why, you kept my Bible the whole time since I saw you.'

'We try to live by the Good Book, just like our momma taught us,' Dean said, and he took the Bible out of her hands before he handed Flora Lee a glass of vodka and ginger ale. 'Ain't that right, Sharleen?'

'Yes,' she said. 'Just like *you* taught us, Momma.'

Holding up her glass, Flora Lee said, 'Now, what should we drink to?'

Dean stared at Flora Lee for a long moment. Flora Lee saw the scrutiny, and reluctantly lowered her glass. 'Well,' she said. 'Maybe I'm jumpin' the gun. Maybe you all aren't as happy to see me as I am to see you.'

'Of course we're glad to see you,' Sharleen said, and hugged the woman. 'Aren't we, Dean?'

Dean stood there, still holding the battered white Bible in one hand. He didn't say anything.

'I've got a nice supper for us,' Sharleen said. 'Why don't we eat it?'

Over fried chicken and slaw and biscuits, Flora Lee did most of the talking. She wanted to know all the details about TV, about how Sharleen got the job, about what her costars were like. She complimented Sharleen on her dress, on the cooking, on the house, and she complimented Dean on his suit and the behaviour of the dogs. Then she pushed away her plate and asked for another 'teeny-tiny drink' and a tour of the house.

Reluctantly, Sharleen led her around, through the big dining room to the even bigger kitchen and den, then upstairs to the three empty spare bedrooms and the room she and Dean shared. Flora Lee stopped on the threshold. 'You *both* sleep here?' she asked. She looked over at Sharleen, who felt herself blushing.

'Dean's still afraid of the dark,' she told her momma.

Flora Lee raised her eyebrows. 'Ain't we all?' she asked.

'You got plenty of room here,' Flora Lee remarked as they trooped back downstairs. 'Empty rooms. Why, you should see my teeny-tiny place. You could put it in a corner of your bedroom.'

'Maybe you want to live here, Momma,' Sharleen offered. She felt Dean stiffen beside her.

'Well, that's a right nice offer, dear,' Flora Lee said. 'But I might bother you with my guests.' They had walked into the living room. 'But do *you* want me to, Dean? Do *you* want your momma back?'

'Why did you leave us, Momma?' Dean asked.

Sharleen watched as the expression on Flora Lee's face changed. The smile, along with the rest of her face, seemed to disintegrate. For a moment, Sharleen thought she glimpsed the other face of Momma, the face she had back in Lamson. 'Honey, I had to. If I had stayed, your daddy would have killed me. I needed to get away . . . to find us a safe place, get a job and all. *Then* I was going to get you both.' Flora Lee eyed the almost empty drink in her hand.

Dean lowered his head. 'Then why didn't you come back for us?'

Sharleen was aware of the silence that fell over the room. She, too, waited for the answer to that question, although, to be honest, she could never have brought herself to ask it. Finally, Flora Lee spoke.

'Honey, things were very bad out there. A lot worse than I thought they was going to be. I couldn't keep a job long enough to settle down. I was laid off so many times, I finally lost count.

And when I was working, I couldn't hardly make enough to live on myself, never mind support two children. And, after all, only one of you was mine.' Flora Lee paused, then forced a small smile. 'Honestly, you was better off with your daddy. At least he could give you a place to live.'

'But you said you was coming back for us. We waited for you. Waited and waited.'

'I know, baby.' Now her smile was back, broader than ever, but her face still had the collapsed look of an empty paper sack. 'But Momma's back now, so let's drink to our all being together finally. Like I promised.'

Sharleen felt stung, but also sorry for Flora Lee. 'Sure. And soon Momma's going to have a job as a hairdresser, just like she always wanted. She's going to school and everything. Right, Momma?'

'Well, I don't really think that place was for me, Sharleen,' Flora Lee said. 'They started at eight A.M. Now, who comes in at that time for beauty appointments? Got angry if I wasn't there. Chewed my ass in front of those little snot girls. I don't want to waste my time on an amateurish place like that.'

'Oh,' was all Sharleen could say.

'But let's have a drink' – Flora Lee raised her glass – 'to a happy reunion.'

'We don't drink,' Dean said, and walked out of the room, calling his dogs after him.

Sharleen had sent Flora Lee home, and it had taken the better part of two days to stop Dean from cryin' and mopin' around the house. And it was real hard to do, because Sharleen felt like mopin' and cryin' herself.

And then, in the mail, she'd gotten a package that she thought might help. She coaxed Dean out of the bedroom and sat him on the sofa. 'I got a real nice surprise for you,' she said, and slipped the CD out.

At the studio, Sharleen had been amazed at the sound of her voice they had recorded. In fact, she couldn't believe it *was* her voice, but Mr. Ortis and the others insisted it was, that with modern electronics they could do anything. Well, they'd done a good job of making her sound like a real singer. Sharleen was impressed. Still found it hard to believe, but impressive. She guessed that all those exhausting lessons had paid off.

'Dean, listen to this.' Sharleen inserted the new CD and pushed 'play.' She sat back, and watched Dean's face as the music began to fill the room. 'What do you think?' she asked him.

'That sure is pretty, Sharleen. I like it.'

'See, you said I could sing and you were right,' Sharleen chided, smiling.

'Sure you can. But who is *that* singing?'

Sharleen grew serious. 'Dean, that's me. That's my new album. Mr. Ortis sent it over. Remember, I made a record?'

'Sure I remember, but that ain't it.' He paused for a moment more, listening to the voice more closely. 'Sharleen, that ain't you. I don't care what you say, or what Mr. Ortis says. I know how you sound, and you don't sound like that. You can sing all right. But, Sharleen, don't let anyone tell you that that there is your voice, 'cause it ain't.'

Sharleen stared at Dean, the chill of the truth creeping up her spine. 'What makes you so sure, Dean? I mean, I trust you and all, but why are you so sure?'

'Why? Sharleen, you could *never* sing that high. Remember how we used to laugh when you tried to sing the "Star Spangling" song before baseball games? You could only go so high, and no higher. This gal can go way up there, and more. Nope, it ain't you.' Dean paused, and continued to listen to the music. 'But, hey, it sure is pretty,' he said.

29

Sam Shields was working feverishly on *Birth*, both the script and preproduction work. He was also sleeping with April. And he was thinking more and more about Jahne Moore. Surely these were four full-time jobs. No wonder he was tired.

Principal photography began in only a week, and there were still several smaller parts to cast, a body double to locate, a Northern California location to finalize, and lots of rewrites to be done. Sam sighed and looked over at April. If he had to cut something or someone from his overcrowded life, it would be his affair with her, but he knew that wasn't possible. She had allowed and forgiven the dalliance with Crystal Plenum, but she'd made it clear that Sam was not to stray like that again or she'd take it personally. The spectre of a vengeful April Irons was not a pretty thought.

Now he needed help, and was casting about for an assistant. Sam knew that an assistant director was a necessary evil, although he wasn't completely convinced, even after *Jack and Jill*. He had barely consulted the AD on that one, and wouldn't hire the same guy again. But that, April kept reminding him, was a *small* movie.

On the stage, there was no AD. Only in the movies, where many sets, and location and studio shots were called for, was it necessary. The AD could save time and money by shooting exteriors, location shots without the actors, or establishing shots – those quick cuts to street signs or skylines that told the audience where you were.

Casting for AD was going to be easy. Since Sam wasn't looking for someone with creative ability, just a gofer mentality, the field was wide open. He supposed that A. Joel Grossman was as good as anyone. But he didn't say that right away.

'What do you think?' April asked, after the interview was done and Joel walked out of the room.

'He hasn't had very much experience,' Sam said.

'But he comes well recommended.'

'He's your boss's secretary's son. What kind of a recommendation is that?'

April dismissed Sam's question with a shake of her head. 'He's done those jeans ads. They were hot. And about a thousand other commercials. And he's been on enough sets to know how to handle himself. He's dependable. And I think he can be inventive, if not creative. You'll get your money's worth, Sam. Trust me on this.'

That was the whole point: Sam trusted no one. But he did think A. Joel would work out, just because he had little experience, and had artistic pretensions. If he could shoot those jeans ads, he could walk around behind Sam carrying a clipboard. This guy wanted a job in features, any job. 'Okay,' Sam finally said. 'But I hope it doesn't come back to bite me on the ass. And you owe me.' Sam looked down at his list of actresses scheduled for readings today. 'Who's next?' he asked.

April raised her empty coffee cup in the air without looking up from the script notes in front of her, and the cup was immediately taken by an unobtrusive hand. When a refill was placed in front of her, she took a sip, then suddenly spit it out on the floor. 'Who the fuck did this? Goddamn it, Melanie, this has Equal in it.'

The young woman came running up to her. 'I'm so sorry, Miss Irons. . . .

'Sweet 'n' Low – how many times do I have to tell you?' Melanie ran off to get a fresh cup. 'Christ!' April said to Sam on her right at the table. 'Where do these people *come* from? Can't even remember how I take my coffee.' April pushed the script aside, along with a stack of rejected résumés. 'And I can't get an actress to read a few lousy lines through without a flub. *Read* them, for chrissakes. Not memorize and *act* them, just fucking *read* them.'

Sam thought of Jahne Moore and how she'd blown him away with her audition monologue. At night, alone, he ran the film of it over and over. Sam brushed his dark hair back on his head, then let his forehead rest on his palm. He was tired. They'd been at the casting table since eight this morning. It was now almost four. Seventeen readings, and not one even adequate, let alone good enough for a screen test. It was going to be a long night. 'I got better reads from the kids trying out for my group in New York. At least they could read. Hollywood,' he said, shaking his head. He'd better stop there. Sam knew April didn't want to hear another attack on Hollywood by 'Mr. Off-Broadway,' her derisive nickname for him. But now, apropos of nothing, Sam remembered Mary Jane Moran, and the time she had come for that first cold reading of *Jack and Jill*. She had been one of a slew of actresses, all good. Except she was the best. By far the best. Why couldn't there be another Mary Jane in this town?

He realized that lately what he missed the most was playing mentor. Mary Jane had been a wounded bird who had blossomed under his direction. And she had also bloomed in their personal relationship. Why did he so like the role of director, of Pygmalion to Galatea? He enjoyed being needed, being wiser, being more experienced, more in control. Was it a power trip? Yes. Was it because he was insecure? He didn't think so. What was so wrong about wanting to teach someone, wanting to help someone? How would he find that fulfilment? Where was another pupil for him?

Well, perhaps, in a way, there was. Jahne Moore, Sam knew, had already memorized the entire new script, and they weren't even in rehearsal yet. She was intelligent, hard working, and she was good. He was sure of it. But she was young, and needed direction. He had been working with her for a little over two weeks, every day, and was amazed at what a quick study she was. He knew filming *Birth of a Star* was going to be a breeze with her. He'd calmed her down about the nudity, and he enjoyed their give-and-take. Jahne was professional, refreshing, beautiful, and funny. Yet not hardened, the way April was. A dynamic woman, he thought. Yet still vulnerable.

Sam had been impressed first with Jahne's looks, then her talent, and now by her brains and professionalism. He found that, more than any other part of his job, directing Jahne was what he most looked forward to. It would be . . . satisfying. There was something special about Jahne Moore.

But now April was talking. 'You're wasting our time, here, Sam. And time is money. You have to change the way you motivate actors, Sam. Movies are different than plays. I've been telling you that. You've got to approach movie actors in a different way. They're used to a scene-by-scene prep. You're giving them the script overview. Just do the moment. Don't waste your time. Or mine.'

'Look, that's just not the way I work.'

April looked at him coolly. 'Well, this isn't working. We haven't cast one more part.' She paused. 'Maybe it's not the direction, Sam. Maybe it's the script. Try using the word "abandonment" in a sentence. It can't be done. But this character has to say the word *three times* in a page and a half of dialogue.'

Of course she was right. No one had ever accused April of being stupid. His script was rough – very rough. And Sam was, he had to admit to himself, scared. And he didn't like the feeling. Always before, he'd been the most powerful person in any group. Back on off-Broadway, at St. Malachy's, even on *Jack and Jill*. He hadn't just been the shmuck writer, he'd also been the director; it was *his* movie. The line producer Seymore LeVine was a nothing, the son of Bob (International Studios) LeVine, and Sam had bedded Crystal Plenum right away. Although *she'd* been the real star of the movie, once he'd slept with her, *he* had the power.

Of course, he told himself, he hadn't slept with her for the power. Who wouldn't sleep with her, if they could? An entire nation of men wanted to sleep with her. And they'd had a good time, until the end of the picture. Then he had started up again with April. . . . Well, being with April was a whole other scene.

Sam knew the world of acting, of directing. Hell, he'd been at it all his life. But April seemed to know *everything*. Including that grown-up world of money, deals, and percentages of the gross. She was as smart and as tough as any of the men, and as sexy as any of the women. And he liked that. With

April, he felt like he was with the very best, the Rolls-Royce of women.

It was only that with April he sometimes felt different about himself, almost, well, inadequate. It wasn't the way it had been with the other women. When he slept with April, instead of gaining her power, it was as if *she'd* stolen *his*. Not sexually. She was a tigress, but he could keep up with her. And it wasn't anything she said or did. It was just that he didn't feel any submission from her. Not that he asked for any. Certainly not. And he knew she liked him. But with other women he had felt his leaving them would matter. With April, he knew she would continue, as seamlessly as before.

It unnerved him, and on top of that there was the problem of Michael McLain. Let's face it, I hate the prick and he hates me, Sam told himself. The guy was a coaster — he'd coasted through on his good looks and his reputation as a womanizer, not as an actor. Perhaps April was right. That as a guy on the slippery slope down, he'd be perfect.

But the problem was that the prick had accepted the role and now didn't want to play it. Christ, the guy couldn't act, but if he simply *read* these lines he'd get an Oscar on this one. This part *was* Michael McLain. All he had to do was show up. But now he wanted to 'improve' on it, to sweeten it. He wanted the character to have an upbeat, charming slide, not a desperate one. He'd actually suggested that, instead of a suicide in the sea, James should die saving Judy from drowning! What bullshit!

So the son-of-a-bitch was taking every cheap shot he could at the script to try to get his way. His way, which would weaken or kill the goddamn thing.

Sam didn't have to tell April there were problems with the script. Act two was weak as hell. She knew it, and had said as much this morning, both to him and to Michael. But she'd stuck up for me, Sam thought. 'James is a suicide,' she told Michael. 'He has to be.' But what, Sam thought with a little chill, what if she hadn't sided with me? Because that was the least of Michael's script suggestions. The script had already gone through five revisions even before this casting call. Sam looked over at April. How long would she side with him, and what would happen when she didn't? She looked at him now, with that unnerving look, as if she were reading his mind and found it amusing.

'Get them to *act*, Sam. We can always fix the script later. Okay? Ready?'

Sam nodded.

'Send in the next bimbo, Melanie,' April called out, and leaned back in her chair, her arms securely folded.

30

After Lila had been pulled off Ara, she managed to get herself home. Then she spent three days licking her wounds and regrouping.

She'd lost *Birth*, and there was nothing she could do about it. All she could do was focus on her future, a future that had to be bigger and better than Jahne Moore's. There were three things she could do: First, get Marty to direct her in a film, a major feature. Second, be sure that it was her, not Sharleen, and certainly not Jahne, who won the Emmy. Lastly, get Sy Ortis to represent her.

She handled the first part of her campaign with a phone call to Marty, setting up dinner. If he was surprised by her invitation, he didn't show it. Then she called Sy Ortis' office for an appointment at the end of the week. Only then did she get dressed and leave the house.

Lila drove to the right address and stood looking at the facade of the two-storey building in front of her. It was far from the typical excessive Malibu and Beverly Hills real estate she was used to, in one of the seedier sections of Los Angeles, an area not well known to the Hollywood crowd, unless their business was of the nature of Lila's.

Lila figured this was one way she could help herself win the Emmy. And Nadia had shown her how. Not with the stupid candles and incenses. That was beat. But Nadia had won an award. And, by thinking it out carefully, Lila realized what she needed. Lila Kyle needed a private detective.

The requirements for the job were basic enough: a nose for digging up dirt and a love for money, whatever its source. Lila looked down at the card in her hand, the one Aunt Robbie had once given her. 'Minos Paige, Private Investigator.' Lila had learned from Aunt Robbie that Minos Paige's expertise was used from time to time by the national tabloids. This was the guy who got the picture of Jimmy Swaggart coming out of a motel room with a prostitute. And she'd heard from Robbie that Minos was the one who tipped Mia about Woody's affair. Lila wanted no less from Minos Paige. It was time to get the upper hand again.

Since the word had got out that she hadn't got the part in *Birth of a Star*, Lila had felt her upper hand lowering. And now that they were in hiatus, she felt she was losing the publicity edge she had on the show. *TV Views* had run a story about trouble on the set, blaming her. Suddenly Jahne Moore was getting the professional respect Lila had been demanding, and Sharleen Smith had become everyone's darling, thanks to the album publicity and the poor-little-Texan act she was able to pull off. It was clearly time for action.

Lila pushed through the glass door at the entrance to the building and walked up the flight of stairs to the second floor. Paige's office was one of four on the floor, the last one at the end of the corridor. She knocked loudly, then opened the door without waiting for a reply. Instead of the reception area she anticipated, Lila found herself in a room hardly bigger than a closet, facing a large desk, behind which sat a small man in a grey polyester suit. He had on a dull-white shirt and a Godawful orange rayon tie. She could see the pilling along the suit sleeves from here. His shirt collar was a size too big, making him look even smaller.

'Minos Paige?' she asked.

'What does Lila Kyle want with Minos Paige?' the figure asked, not having moved a muscle since she opened the door.

'That's only your business if *you're* Minos Paige,' she snapped, staring down at the pale-faced man. He blinked, nodded, then indicated a seat in the corner of the room.

'What can I do for you?' he asked, now leaning back in his creaking chair.

'I need someone investigated. Two people, actually. I understand that's your line of work.'

He nodded his head imperceptibly, almost without moving. 'Who?' he asked.

Lila took in a breath. 'Jahne Moore and Sharleen Smith.'

Minos didn't react. That was something he knew: don't react no matter what you hear. He, like Lila, also knew that most people had more to hide than they would like to admit.

Lila reached into her bag, then handed Minos two sheets of yellow legal paper. 'These are the details of their present lives – addresses, where they eat, where they shop, recording dates, and their shooting schedules.' Lila placed the sheets on the desk in front of Minos when he didn't reach out to take them. 'I've also included some of the facts about their pasts that I've dug up on my own. Not the publicity stuff – facts. Things I got directly from them, in casual conversations.'

Minos didn't say anything, just peered down at the notes in Lila's plain block print. 'Those details would be the starting point. Like' – she leaned over and pointed to a line on the page – 'what did Jahne Moore do before the Melrose Playhouse? How did she get that part? Not much is known about that.'

Paige continued to look at her.

'And Sharleen Smith. Supposedly, she came from some town in Texas. What about her family? High school?'

Minos Paige finally spoke. 'What do you want this information for, Miss Kyle?'

Lila thought of telling him it was none of his business, but could see that that was not the way to get this guy motivated. 'I like to know who I'm working with. I don't like secrets, and I think both of these bitches have secrets.'

'And what's *your* secret?'

Lila didn't flinch. 'I have no secrets, Mr. Paige. That's the point. My life is an open book, the legacy of being the child of two celebrities. What you see is what you get. So you can understand when I say I'm at a disadvantage. They know everything about me, but I know next to nothing about them. And, frankly, that makes me nervous.' She thought she saw the slightest hint of a curl to his lip, but chose to ignore it. 'Are you interested in the job?'

'Let me make sure I understand exactly what the job is.' Minos tucked a finger in his loose collar and tugged at it slightly, as if it were too tight. 'You want all the dirty little secrets of their lives, like who they slept with, and if they did it for money. Any porno movies, scandal. Family background, legitimacy, money problems, prison records, sexual tastes, any illegitimate children, abortions, drug history, shoplifting, felonies, homosexuality, bestiality, necrophilia . . .'

Lila smiled for the first time since meeting Minos Paige. 'I think you got the general drift, Mr. Paige. What will it cost?'

'A ten-thousand-dollar retainer. To start. Expenses billed separately. There will, no doubt, be some travel involved. I'll keep you posted on that.'

'Fine. When can you start?'

He cleared his throat. 'The minute your cheque clears.' He shrugged apologetically. 'It's company policy.'

Lila opened her bag, took out her chequebook, and began writing the cheque. 'By the way,' she said as she scribbled in the little details on the cheque, 'I have one other minor situation. It's not a problem really.' She handed Minos the cheque. 'It – I think it can be covered by the extra amount I've included in your retainer.'

Lila opened her bag again, replaced the chequebook, and took out a small packet of letters, held together with a rubber band. 'I've received these lately. I get a lot of crazy stuff in the mail, you must know that. But these are a little over-the-top. They're written by a member of some league or something. A guy named Jughead signs them. Could you look into these for me also?' Lila stood and handed Minos the bundle.

Minos opened the first of the envelopes and took out one sheet of paper. 'LATEST BULLETIN FROM THE ANTI-NEPOTISM LEAGUE,' he read. 'DEATH TO LILA KYLE. Guess which famous Hollywood star's daughter got a part on *Three for the Road*? Lila Kyle, of course. And she claims, in a recent interview in *People* magazine, that it was really harder for her to get seen as an individual in her own right, that she had to work harder. . . .'

Minos refolded the paper and put it back into its envelope. 'Surely you get a lot of these. Hate mail. Goes with the territory.'

'There are a lot like that. Crazy. But I just don't like the idea of any *league* of crazies. And this is delivered to my door. Not by mail. It just shows up. Individual nuts I can deal with. This bothers me.'

Minos Paige nodded. 'Don't worry about a thing. I'll look into it. Like I say, the minute the cheque clears.'

Sy Ortis laughed with true delight. He'd done it! He hung up the phone and for a moment he thought he might dance around the room like a demented, loco little Hispanic leprechaun. And why not? He'd won the biggest poker game of his career so far! He was signing Lila Kyle, and what sweetened it all was that she was leaving Ara Sagarian to come to him – Sy Ortis, the wetback, the spic, the Johnny-come-lately. He held three queens against Ara's empty hand! Ha! The courtly old *maricón* would have a stroke on his right side to match the one on his left after this. Then he'd have to carry *two* fuckin' handkerchiefs!

Of course, he had reservations: his film clients didn't like him to represent TV. And Lila would be a handful – a true bitch. But she was a thoroughbred, an AKC-registered bitch with the right bloodlines, not some little mutt from nowhere. Lila's grandeur was born, not delusionary, like most of the *nouveaux* Sy dealt with. And if he could handle Crystal Plenum and that *puta de diablo* Jahne Moore, then he could handle Lila, too. Because Lila had it – the star quality that most of these girls lacked, that secret magic *something* that went beyond looks or talent, that power that compelled you to watch her.

Sy walked to his office window and laughed. Wait until all the agents in town heard about this!

31

Birth of A Star would be filming in Northern California for nine weeks. Jahne was flown up in the International Studios corporate 727, and when they landed at Oakland Airport a limo was waiting to take her to the Cupertino hotel the crew and cast were put up in for the duration. The next morning, she was whisked down to the first location and shown her dressing room, where Mai was already waiting.

Jahne stared into the mirror in the plush trailer. It was far more luxurious than the utilitarian tin box she was assigned for *Three for the Road*. Everything about an April Irons production was first-class. The trailer had a bevelled and highlighted mirror, a built-in mahogany makeup table beneath it, a tiled bathroom, a tastefully furnished flowered-chintz sitting area, complete with crystal-and-brass lamps, and a separate bedroom – with a four-poster bed! Not for her to spend the night in, of course. Just in case she wanted a nap! Jahne felt like a star. Flowers splayed from a Baccarat crystal vase – a gift from April Irons.

But did she look like a star? Anxiously, she began, once again, to search the flawless face before her in the mirror. Even the return of Mai, lugging another huge garment bag, didn't break her concentration, or her fear. But she was too self-conscious to study herself that way for long in front of another person, even someone she felt as comfortable with as Mai.

The night before, she had had a terrifying dream: she was onstage, doing a nude scene before a full theatre. The scene was serious, moving; and then, she felt first one thigh, then the other bulge out. There was a titter in the audience. Then her stomach bulged. Next a breast expanded, and hung to her waist. The audience began to laugh. She threw her hands up to her face, only to find her old nose, her old weak chin. The audience roared. She woke up in a sweat.

She was sweating now as she turned back to the huge mirror, catching Mai's eye. 'Did you *always* think you were beautiful?'

'Neffer.'

'Never?' Jahne spun around. '*Never?* Mai, you were the most beautiful woman of your time. You *never* thought you were?'

'Now I know I vas. *Now* I can see it – in the old movies, in the stills from that time. But then – no. I vas alvays vorried dat someting, some imperfection, vould show. My mouth – too big. My eyes, too round. I vas alvays comparing myself – first to other girls, then to other vimmen. And ven I came here! Hollyvood! Theda Bara! You can't imagine! And Nadia Negron. And, of course, Garbo. The Face of All Faces. I vas never goot enough. Not goot enough for me, or for the camera. Or for the men. All of the time I vas beautiful, vasted.'

Jahne watched Mai in the mirror, then flashed her eyes back to her own face. Still retaining its elegant bone structure, Mai's face was a ruin of wrinkles, sags, and age spots. Jahne's was young, fresh. How long would it stay that way? And was it beautiful enough? Beautiful enough to fill a thirty-by-fifteen-foot screen at the Triplex Odeon? She certainly was not as lovely as Mai had been. And she had thought she focused on her imperfections because of her past – because of the face she once had had. But Mai had done it, too. And Sharleen had told her she didn't feel as pretty as Lila or Jahne herself. And Lila . . . well, Lila was a freak. No one was ever allowed to photograph her without her approval of the prints.

Now, faced with the terror of the big screen, Jahne found herself afraid and almost obsessed with her looks. And it wasn't only her:

533

Jerry, the makeup guy; Laslo, the principal cinematographer; Bob the cameraman – all of them were fixated, it seemed, on how she would look. Jahne bit her lips and looked over at Mai, who, once, long ago, had been through all this.

'Oh, darlink, are you vorried about photography? You vill be lufly. Listen, ve vill do some tests and find all your best angles. Ve vill make you perfect.'

'I was hoping I already was.'

Mai laughed. 'My dear, so silly! Vy, Jean Arthur – she had only vun side. *Alvays* her left. Whole sets built so she could enter from the right and never show her right profile. Everyone knew it. Capra never minded. And Claudette Colbert also. Very French, very chic, but a face like a – vat you call dem – pumpkin. Special lighting to give her cheeks. Even Elizabeth Taylor. Shadow on her upper lip. *Alvays* must be covered. So vat, darlink, is your problem?' Mai laughed.

Her problem, Jahne decided, was threefold: One, she was scared of how she'd look on screen. Two, she was scared of what was going to happen with Sam, and, three, she realized with surprise, she was angry.

'Why all the tricks?' she asked Mai, though she didn't really expect an answer. 'Knowing our good side, lighting, retouching. Why aren't we good enough as we are?'

'Because, my darlink, as ve are is not the vay men dream of us. You know the story of John Ruskin?' Jahne knew of the English Victorian art critic, but when Mai said the name she made it sound like some Russian count. Jahne shook her head.

'He vas London art critic. No: even more. He vas journalist who made the taste of that time. He told people vat to like, vat vas beautiful, vat vas ugly. Very important man in arts in London. Maybe most important.'

'Yes,' Jahne said. 'Now I remember his name.'

'Vell, he married. Beautiful young girl. He vorshipped her. Until after ceremony. Und ven she undressed on vedding night, he vas sicken. You know vy?'

Jahne shook her head.

'He saw her pubic hair! It made him sick. Alvays he had been looking at statues of vimmen. Alvays they had been hairless. His real, beautiful vife disgusted him!' Mai laughed. 'This is how it is for vimmen, alvays. This is the joke the gods play on us. Ve are of the stars but also of the earth. Ve are closest to perfection, but

534

neffer perfect enough.' She paused. 'Is a funny thing, really. All the aesthetics in America are on the decline: only think of art and architecture. Only female beauty obsesses us. And alvays more perfect. Ah, the tyranny of beauty.'

'That's so sad. Is it all true?'

'About Ruskin or life?'

'Both.'

'Vell, it is true for both. Marilyn Monroe, I worked on her costume alterations for *Misfits* – that is vere I learn about jeans. She throws up before every take, afraid she is not pretty enough. Vell, and again; Garbo *is* perfect voman. At thirty-five, sees a few lines on her face on the screen, she cries for three days, they must stop filming. People say she didn't care about her looks! She cared so much she spent the rest of her life hiding! Can you imagine? If ve are imperfect, ve are scorned and hate ourselves. If ve are perfect, ve age und *then* are scorned and hate ourselves. You know, ven Greer Garson vas big star, they alvays used her favourite cameraman, Joe Ruttenberg. He vas genius. But after a long vile, she vas unhappy. She called him in for talk. "You know, Joe," she said, "you're not photographing me as vell as you used to." He said, "I'm sorry, Greer, but I'm ten years older." Poor Greer. Dead now.' Mai sighed.

'Men make these dreams, men run the studios. Alvays the studio says, "Somethink is wrong. You are not perfect enough for our dreams," and alvays ve believe them.'

'But why do they do it?' Jahne cried.

Mai shrugged. 'To control us. Because they are afraid of our power. So they make *us* afraid.'

Jahne sat, feeling very small suddenly, her knees tucked under her. 'What happened to Ruskin's wife?' Jahne asked.

'She stayed virgin for long time. Then, finally, she ran off vith artist. A real man. First he used her as a model. To him, at least, she vas perfection. Hunt, I think, vas the artist, but maybe Millais. She had his baby in the end. You know vat is moral of story?'

Jahne shook her head.

'Stick vith the artists, not the critics,' Mai smiled.

Mai helped Jahne prepare for all the wardrobe tests – preliminary filming of her in costume to see how they, and she, looked on the screen. Usually these were done before principal photography began, but everything seemed to be running late on this film, and the tests had just started. Sam had been remote, distracted, and –

thank God – Michael wasn't due to show up for another three days.

It was late, past seven, when Mai helped her change and waited while she took off her makeup. And Jahne was bone weary. 'I vill go back vith you to the hotel, if you like,' Mai offered.

'Yes. Let's have a late dinner together,' Jahne suggested.

'A beer. All I vant is a beer,' Mai sighed.

They were driven back to Cupertino in silence. Even Danny, the driver who would actually get a screen credit for this job, was tired. And in the darkness of the back seat of the limo, Jahne wondered at who she had become and what she was doing here, in a town she'd never seen, working on a film she didn't really like from a script that wasn't finished. Beside her was the latest draft, the new version photocopied on pink pages. Each version was on a new colour, to prevent confusion. How many colours had she already seen? Light-yellow, dark-yellow, green, lavender, blue. Had there been a white version? A grey? She couldn't remember anymore. What happened when they ran out of colours? Well, she reminded herself, Michael Curtiz filmed *Casablanca* without a finished script. The actors didn't know the end until the day they shot it. She wondered again if she was making a mistake. With the choices she had, why this film?

It was Sam, of course. Like a moth to a flame. She sighed. And, like a moth, would she wind up burned? Hadn't she gone through her transformation so that *she* could be the flame, the centre of attraction? Well, her flesh had changed, but her centre had not been altered.

Suddenly, there in the back seat of the lush limo, a wave of terrible loneliness and despair rolled over her. She felt overcome, a million miles away from Mai, sitting there beside her in the dark. If I died right now, she thought, who would know me? Who would really know me? What am I doing in this place? She shivered, though it wasn't cold. She felt so truly miserable that only a groan or a wail could relieve her. What would Danny and Mai think of that? For a few more exquisitely painful moments, she restrained herself as they rode along in silence, Jahne crushed by the immense burden of her loneliness. Then they arrived at the hotel.

She was so tired when she got upstairs that she suggested room service to Mai, who cheerfully agreed. Then Jahne showered and got into a robe. Under the hot water, she felt a little bit better, but she also knew she could not go on this way: having more nightmares, sitting through other panic attacks. So, there in the shower stall in that Cupertino hotel, Jahne came to a decision.

When she emerged from the steaming bathroom, Mai had already dismissed the room-service waiter, and dinner was set, waiting, on a rolling table pulled over to the window. They sat down together, the white linen and sparkling silver between them. Jahne sipped at the hot consommé, and then they began on the mesquite-grilled chicken paillard.

'Mai, I want to tell you something.'

Mai put down her pilsner glass and looked up, expectant.

'I feel as if I have to tell someone or I'll die,' Jahne said, and then she began.

Mai was a good listener. She let Jahne cry, and she waited, silent, during the long pauses while Jahne fought for the words and the courage to continue her story. Mai didn't interrupt, and asked only one question – exactly how Jahne had found Brewster Moore – but she responded through the long tale with little nods and sympathetic sounds. Jahne finally finished, and the two of them sat beside the window, the suburban lights of Cupertino twinkling beneath them. Then Mai sighed, and pushed her chair away from the table. She stood up, walked to the window.

'Vat ve do to ourselves! Vat they do to us!' she whispered. Then she turned and looked at Jahne. Her face showed no shock, no disgust, but only love and sympathy. 'My dear, I am so sorry,' was all she said.

Jahne actually slept through the night, better than she had slept for a long while. The next morning, Mai was already in the living room of the suite, waiting for her.

'My dear, I vould like very much to talk to you,' she said. Jahne nodded. 'I haff been up all night thinking of this, of your story. And I must tell you, I think you are in grave danger.'

Jahne sat down on the sofa, her heart beating fast. 'What do you mean?' she asked.

'When God gives great beauty, he also gives us time to learn what it is useful for. For beauty is power in this vorld. Men haff made it so. And it can be a veapon or a tool. Most of us haff the luxury of time, first to see our power grow, then to test our powers, and at last to see them decline slowly. A few unlucky vimmen vere given great beauty vithout the knowledge that they had it. It kills them. Alvays. Jean Harlow. Marilyn Monroe. Jean Seberg. You know the list.'

Mai paused. 'I am speaking to you as one who knows. I vas vonce beautiful. But you, my dear . . . You are beautiful outside, but you haff not come to terms vith your power. I have noticed all the strange lapses. You are shy to look at yourself in front of others. Beauties never are. You are pleased ven someone calls you "pretty." That is an insult to a beautiful voman. There are many small signs I vondered at.' She sighed.

'But you need your power. You need to use it, to acknowledge it deeply. Because, if you don't, the veapon vill turn against you.'

'Oh, Mai! You're scaring me. What can I do?'

'I don't know. This is indeed a new vonder of science. But I vill help you any vay I can. Maybe I can teach you. If you vant.'

Jahne felt her eyes fill with tears. 'Thank you,' she said.

32

Marty watched Lila as she talked, her hands moving like Japanese fans, her elegant red nails punctuating the air. They were sitting together on the sofa in Marty's living room, and Lila had just finished telling him about the role she had turned down in the movie, *Princess of Thyme*. Then she began to talk about Ara Sagarian, what a disappointment he was. Her eyes, he saw, were wide with excitement; her skin had a rosy cast under her golden tan. All this about a part in a movie. How much more passionate would she be in bed?

Marty had almost given up on Lila. And then, once again, she had called him. This time, Marty was determined that nothing would go wrong. He had sent Sally into town, he'd underplayed everything. No gladioli, no catered dinner. And things were going well. This was simply going to take patience. There was going to come a time when he would have her. Somehow, some way, Marty was going to make love to Lila Kyle. Up to now he had accepted her distance as a temporary thing. But till now it never seemed to waver. Still, *she* had called *him* and she now seemed ready for a friendship, at least. Why now? Go know.

Marty was a lot of things – short, skinny, stoop-shouldered, pock-marked, maybe even ugly – but one thing he wasn't was a shmuck. Lila had almost made a shmuck out of him. Yet now, tonight, he wanted her more than ever. He would have to get the upper hand. Perhaps advice and avuncular patience were the answer.

'Ara is just too old, Lila. Family loyalty is nice and all; you need someone like Sy Ortis to manage you.'

'Really, Marty?' she asked. Marty felt a small thrill. He liked it when she listened to his opinions.

'Would you like me to call him and set something up? I'm sure he'd love to talk with you.'

'Sure. Great idea.' Lila wondered if he'd find out she'd *already* called. Well, she'd tell Ortis' secretary that Marty had told her to.

So, what else could he do to help her, to move the friendship forward? Marty wondered. 'Do you want to hear my idea for next year's first episode?' Marty asked. May as well dangle the bait now, he figured.

Lila curled her feet up under her. 'Sure. What's your idea?'

'I thought I might have the opening episode with only one girl. Let the other two be flashbacks, or sidebars, maybe not even refer to them. I don't know yet.' He didn't have to look at Lila's face to know what she was thinking.

'It might be interesting,' she said cautiously. 'It might work, depending.'

'Depending on what?' he asked, egging her on, getting her into position.

'Well, to be very honest, Marty, its success or failure would depend completely on which girl was being spotlighted. Like, she'd have to be strong enough to carry that kind of weight, but also . . .'

'I've already decided.'

He watched Lila, sensing, almost hearing, her brain whirring. 'Yes?' was all she said.

'Uh-huh. You.'

Lila shrieked and threw her arms around his neck and hugged him. Touched him for the first time. Marty felt himself tremble. He hoped Lila didn't notice. 'Me? Oh, Marty, that's wonderful. You're brilliant. A genius.' She sat back. 'Tell me more. What's the story line? What's the setting?'

She settled back in the sofa, curled up like a cat on a fireplace cushion, ready to listen to every word, to soak up every gesture.

'It's you leaving home, showing why you've taken to the road.'

'Great idea. I love it.'

'You'll be walking out on a privileged life: wealth, huge house, cars, servants, absent father, domineering mother . . . everything. Use the Beatles as background. You know, "She's leaving home after living alone for so many years." It's been a living hell, and now you're leaving. Sort of a sixties thing, but relevant to the nineties, turning against the eighties.'

'I like it, Marty. It's perfect.'

'You walk out, leaving all this behind you, to get away from your mother. . . .'

Lila was nodding, her face lit up with anticipation and maybe something else.

It may have been hiatus for Lila, Sharleen, and Jahne, but not for Marty and the production crew of 3/4. Things were going well with Lila, but Marty had to top last year's ratings. And deal with the problem of Jahne Moore's schedule. Today the production meeting would be brief, and to the point.

'Just keep on doing what you're doing, folks,' George Young, the producer said as he said at every production meeting. 'I'm not going to fuck with a winning formula.' Not that he could. Sy's contract was ironclad. They couldn't change a hair in the girls' coiffures, even if the show took a nosedive. It was all in Marty's control.

'But there is one thing we hadn't considered, George.' Now the guy from publicity was about to come up with another lamebrain idea. Marty sighed. So much for not fucking with a winning formula. Still, he'd sit through the meeting and then try to brainstorm a few more ideas for next season.

'I'm getting calls, lots of calls. Everyone and her sister wants an appearance or a continuing part on this show. Even Katharine Hepburn, can you believe that? Her agent says Kate sees this as *the* woman's TV format for the nineties.'

Marty spoke softly. 'Fine for a cameo, but not a continuing character. From the beginning, I told you I want unknowns on the show. Only unknowns. And aside from cameos, that's what we got, and that's what's working. Now, with what I've achieved with them, you want to undermine it with Katharine Hepburn, for chrissakes? There's no justification for Hepburn on the show. We look like a documentary. She'll look like an actress, for chrissakes. It's an obvious manipulation.' Marty kept his voice from rising. 'No way.' He looked directly at George Young.

George shook his head. 'Except, the opening episode this season has got to really make a statement. It has to say the second season will be better than the first, no matter how good the first was. And we don't want to lose even a tenth of a point, even if *every* other show does that week. In fact, we want to *gain* points. That *hasn't* been done before, and I think this show, of any show, can do it. We need a gimmick, and – quite frankly, Marty – I think a superstar might be just the thing.'

Marty made it a point to appear to consider every suggestion a producer made before commenting on it. Even though they were almost always empty, stupid windbags, as George certainly was, he pretended to consider. He did that now. But the silence of the room was broken by George's production assistant, a young girl too young and too pretty to have been hired for her knowledge of the business.

'How about Theresa O'Donnell instead of Hepburn?' the girl asked.

No one said anything. Finally, George said, 'Lila Kyle's mother?'

'Yeah, sure. I mean she's both. She was a superstar and she's Lila's real mother. Documentary. You know? Have Lila's mother play her mother.'

Marty smiled at the young woman. Theresa O'Donnell! What Marty wouldn't give to work with Theresa O'Donnell! The kid was right. The tie-in was perfect – real, commercial but not overpowering. But would she do it? Theresa O'Donnell hadn't done anything in years. But now, with her daughter on the show . . . Marty was sure Theresa would see both the artistic and the commercial value in it. 'What's your name?'

'Leslie Snow,' she said.

'I'll consider it, Leslie. Okay boys and girls. Let's strap on our steel jockstraps and fight the good fight.'

33

Sharleen had been calling the telephone number Dobe had given her for two weeks, but hadn't been able to reach him. She was more than a little concerned: she still had his cartons all over the house, and she wasn't sure what she should do if she didn't hear from him. Should I have it picked up and stored somewhere? What might be in those shoes? Well, with all her other worries, she didn't have to think about that now, she decided. She'd give him two more weeks. But still, she'd keep trying.

Sharleen picked up the phone once again and dialled Dobe's number, as she'd done every day since the auction.

This time, though, after two rings, Sharleen heard Dobe at the other end. 'Hello.' His voice was cheery.

'Dobe Samuels, you got some explaining to do! I've been calling you every day. Where have you been? And what in Sam Hill are you going to do with a hundred dozen women's left shoes?' she asked.

'Sharleen, honey. You did it! How much?' he asked.

'Sixty dollars. Now, you goin' to answer my questions?'

Dobe's voice got serious. 'I'm sorry, Sharleen. I had to go out of town on business. I should have called you before.'

'What kind of business? Dobe, what do you need those sneakers for?' She tried to sound strict. But Sharleen couldn't stay mad with Dobe. She was just so glad to hear his voice again.

'Not sneakers, honey. The best aerobic shoes money can buy. See, I'm in the import-export business now.' Dobe began. 'And I needed to get those "sneakers" for a customer of mine. But the import duty on *pairs* of shoes is so high, I'd never make any money, so I had the shoes shipped in two separate shipments, one shipment of left feet to Los Angeles, one shipment of right feet to Portland.' Dobe paused to chuckle to himself. Sharleen joined him, the idea sounded so silly. 'And when no one came forward to claim them and pay the duty, I knew they would go on auction, and that no one would want *left* shoes only, or *right* shoes only. So I get the whole shipment without paying duty, and saved a lot of thousands of dollars. Sweet, ain't it?'

Sharleen didn't say anything for a minute. He was slicker than a greased goose. 'Dobe, now you tell me. Was there anythin' in the heels of them shoes? You know, like dope or somethin' like that? Now, tell me true, Dobe Samuels.'

Dobe's voice got very serious. 'Sharleen, I told you once I would never hurt you. And I won't. I would never – *never*, young lady – do anything to harm *you* or *Dean* in *any* way. It's like . . . it's like you're family, Sharleen. Okay? I need you to trust me.'

'Dobe, I do. I honestly do. It's just that I read the other day a guy got off a plane in Miami and got arrested for smugglin' dope. He had it in the heels of his shoes! So I guess I just got a little scared.' Now she laughed. 'Dobe, you still making them water-into-gas pills?'

Dobe's laugh came back to her over the miles. 'I'll tell you all about it when I see you tonight.'

'Tonight?' Sharleen asked. 'You're going to be here *tonight*?' Lord, her momma was coming over tonight, too! But Dobe would be welcome. Maybe he could even give her advice about Momma. 'How long are you going to stay? You're coming to stay for a while, right? Dobe, we got a big house. Wait until you see it. And wait till I tell Dean.' She gave him directions to the house, and told him about the security guard outside.

'Sounds like you're in a safe neighbourhood, girl. Makes me feel a lot better about you being in that city.'

'Dobe, it's more like a prison.' She didn't stop to explain. She wanted to get home and get everything ready. And tell Dean. 'Dinner'll be ready, Dobe. And we'll be waitin' for you.'

Sharleen hadn't felt this happy since . . . Funny, she couldn't remember feeling this happy – ever.

Filled with new energy, Sharleen went to look for Dean. She walked through the living room, past the dining room and pantry, then into the huge kitchen she was usually too tired to use. 'Dean,' she called out again, as she walked past the gleaming, untouched stove to the back door, where she peered out the window to the hedge-and-brick-enclosed garden. She knew she would find Dean out there, either working on the flower beds or playing with the dogs. Or both.

Dean had taken the overgrown back yard and transformed it

into a garden like you would see in the garden magazines he would look at over and over. Here, in what Sharleen was told was the most expensive four acres of property in America, Dean had created the equivalent of a perfect tiny farm.

Dean knew the name of every single thing he had growing, could even identify the occasional weed that had somehow missed his eye. He had talked to her so often about them, *she* now knew them all by heart. There was a small stand of fruit trees – a mini-orchard, really. Two peaches, four apples, and three pears. And a vegetable garden filled with beefsteak and plum tomatoes, three kinds of lettuce, scallions and onions, cabbage, broccoli, cauliflower, green and yellow beans, carrots, and okra. He even had peas growing up some teepee he'd built of sticks. Beyond the vegetables, there was a small pond stocked with fish – carp, she thought – that Dean fed by hand from the little wooden bridge he'd built across the pond.

Prettiest of all to Sharleen were the flowers. Alongside one brick wall, extending maybe thirty, forty feet, was a perennial bed. He had planted all the old-fashioned flowers that he loved so much, and, in less than a year, he had made them bloom. There were peonies especially for Sharleen, because she favoured them, and also larkspur, hollyhocks, and fox-glove. There was a stand of delphiniums almost as tall as she was, but Dean considered them a cheat, since he'd bought them potted and blooming and only transplanted them. Still, they were gorgeous.

Beyond the perennials, around the lawn, he had annuals bedded out – pansies, johnny-jump-ups, lots of zinnias, their colours sweeping the rainbow, strong-smelling marigolds, and nasturtiums. The grass was trimmed perfectly; he did it himself. And a rose garden, his pride and joy, had centre place. But despite his garden, Dean was glum. Sharleen could tell.

Well, she knew what they'd do to cheer him up. They'd have a barbecue for Dobe and Momma. She saw him romping with the three pups on the emerald lawn. 'Howdy,' she called to him as she walked across the grass towards him. 'Whatcha doin'? Teaching the girls new tricks?'

'Yeah, and watch this, Sharleen.' He was like a little boy. Whenever he got the three dogs to do somethin' new, he always presented the trick to her like a bouquet of flowers. Just as well, because Dean hated to cut the flowers out of the beds. 'They're dead once you do that,' he'd explained. And to Sharleen, the dog tricks were just as good, if not better than a bouquet. She liked to see him happy, and she knew she had news for him that would really get him goin'. But she decided to wait a little bit before she told him who was comin' tonight. He'd be pesterin' her the rest of the day if she told him now.

Dean called the three dogs and made them sit in a row. It took some coordinatin', but they finally were all sittin' at the same time, their eyes turned up adoringly at Dean. He stood back and took a ball from his pocket and called out, 'Cara, go git it, girl,' and Cara ran and jumped into the air and grabbed the ball in her teeth. 'Now, give it to Clover; good girl.' And Cara walked over to Clover and dropped the ball in front of the other puppy.

'Clover, give the ball to Crimson,' he instructed, and Clover picked up the ball in her mouth and walked to Crimson and dropped the ball, then walked back to her place. After their performance, he was beaming, and gave each of them treats from his pocket.

'That sure is something, Dean. How long did it take you to teach them that?'

Dean was stroking the dogs. 'Just a few days. Ain't they smart, Sharleen? Now they know eight tricks. Smart dogs,' he said to them, then stood up and looked at Sharleen. 'You tired, Sharleen? Let's go inside, I'll get you a pop.'

Sharleen sat at the kitchen table sipping the cold soda from the can. She could see something was botherin' Dean, and considered telling Dean the surprise she had for him. But first she wanted to know what was wrong.

'Momma was here yesterday, while you were out,' he said, as if answering her unasked question.

'I forgot to tell you she was comin'. I left an envelope for her on the table. She run short,' Sharleen explained. 'Was she . . . okay?'

'Yeah, she was, but not for long, I could tell. All she wanted was to get the envelope and leave. And she asked a lot of questions about. . .' He paused. 'Well – about stuff. Like how we slept together.' Dean paused, then looked directly at Sharleen. 'Sharleen, it ain't like I thought it was goin' be, having Momma back. Like bein' a family. It's like she's someone different. I don't remember her like this. She's old, and smells like whisky all the time. It's like she ain't *our* momma, you know?'

Sharleen did know. She *wasn't* like their momma. Not the momma she had known when she was a kid. *Before* she left

545

them. All these years, Sharleen and Dean had believed that their momma was going to get them some help or something, and even when she didn't come back, they kept believing.

Now it was hard to believe anything good about Momma. She was a drunk, and only thought about herself. She'd quit beauty school, and it looked like she was planning to live off of them. Sharleen remembered what Jahne had told her about not trusting *anybody*. Would Momma talk to newspapers about Dean and her? What a terrible thought! Well, Sharleen wasn't exactly sure why, but she didn't trust her momma. She did trust Dean. And Dobe.

'Dean, honey, have I got good news for you,' Sharleen suddenly said, then sat back and crossed her arms, a teasing smile on her face.

Dean opened his eyes wider. 'What, Sharleen?'

Sharleen stood up and started to leave the kitchen. 'Oh, I think I changed my mind. I don't think I'll tell you about the surprise. About who's coming tonight.'

'Momma?' Dean asked, his face dark.

'Momma and someone else,' Sharleen sang out, teasing, 'Me to know, you to find out.'

Dean smiled and jumped up and ran after her, and grabbed her around the waist as she got to the stairs. Sharleen shrieked and squirmed her way out of Dean's grasp and ran up the steps. 'No, Dean, I ain't telling you,' she yelled, and continued to run. Dean grabbed her by one foot and got her down.

'Oh, yes, you are,' he said, now straddling Sharleen, 'or I'm goin' tickle you to death.' He held one hand up, squiggling his fingers threateningly.

Sharleen shrieked again, and begged Dean not to do it to her. 'Okay, then, you gotta tell me the surprise.' He loosened his grip, but didn't let Sharleen stand.

She gave up. 'But first take one guess. And it ain't only one person. It's two.' Dean looked perplexed. 'What two people would you want to see more than anyone else in the whole world if you had your wish?'

Dean's eyes squinted as he tried to think. 'Oprah and Dobe?' he finally asked, his question spoken softly.

'Right, honey. Oprah and Dobe are coming here to visit. Tonight!'

Dean scooped Sharleen up in his big arms, and ran up the stairs with her, two at a time. He was yelling like a hound dog in the bayou. 'Sharleen, wait till I show Dobe the dogs! And all the tricks they know. Oprah, she's going to love them, even if they're only babies.' He kicked open their bedroom door and dropped her on the huge bed. 'Yippee!' he screeched.

That night, the four of them sat around the dining-room table, the first time since Momma's dinner that they had laid out a spread like this. Left on the table were remains of the fried chicken, ribs, and fixings Sharleen had had prepared, along with the fresh vegetables from Dean's garden. Dobe was sitting back, wiping his fingers on a wet towel Sharleen had given him. Momma seemed to be staring at Dobe, a big smile on her face. Sharleen wondered how much she'd had to drink. 'You are one hell of a man, Mr. Dobe Samuels. I bet you've put a smile on a lot of ladies' faces.' Flora Lee smirked. All through dinner she kept laughin' at his jokes and sayin' how smart he was. Dean hadn't noticed, thank the Lord, because he had Oprah's head on his lap the entire meal, and was feeding her a piece of food for every bite he took.

'Did you get enough for the guys at the gate?' Dean asked Sharleen. Usually he made sure before he started eating that the security guards got food also, but tonight, with Momma and Oprah and Dobe here, he'd been so excited, he forgot until now.

'Sure did, Dean. I got something for them, too. Just like you told me.' Sharleen looked over at Dobe and saw him smiling.

'Well, I've got to go to the little girls' room,' Flora Lee declared, and left the table, her walk affected by all that she had drunk.

Dean got up and began to gather the rib bones. Oprah began dancing around him, and the three pups joined her. 'Let's go, girls. Let's go out,' he coaxed. 'When I come back after taking them for a walk, you all want to watch *The Andy Griffith Show* with me, Dobe? I got practically all of them on tape, if you want to start from the beginning.'

'Sure. I love that show. I love what's-his-name – the barber. Floyd.' Dean was rushed out the door by the pack of dogs, who knew they were going to have fun. 'He's one sweet boy,' Dobe said. 'And it looks like you got one sweet life, from what I see and read.'

Sharleen looked at Dobe. 'Dobe, it ain't how it looks.' She had to tell him, had to tell *someone*, what it was really like. She didn't want to complain. But Dobe was the only person who would understand that just because things got better didn't mean that things got good.

Sharleen told him the whole story. How she got the job as an actress on TV, and what it had been like since. Not all the good stuff — that he already knew — but what she had lost when she gained so much. She never thought that the success, the money, would be a trade-off, a phrase Jahne had once used that Sharleen now understood all too well. If she had been asked back then, when she was offered the job, she would have said that she had nothing to give up in return for great fame and wealth.

Now she knew different. She had lost her freedom. 'I can't go out by myself. I can't go to a movie like other people. I can't go into a supermarket, even though I can afford to buy the whole store. I have to go everywhere in a car with a driver and a security guy. A *bodyguard*, for goodness' sakes, Dobe. *I* need a *bodyguard*!' Sharleen wasn't concerned whether she was sounding ungrateful or not, or whining. Dobe understood. 'When I'm workin', I'm tired all the time. Men are always hittin' on me. Worse than ever. And I have no one to talk to.'

'What about your momma, Sharleen? Now that you found her. Can't you talk to her?'

Sharleen wiped tears from her eyes on the linen napkin and grunted a laugh. '*We* didn't find *her*. *She* found *us*. I never thought we was goin' to see her again, although we wanted to. Then, one day, she shows up at the studio. At first, I was real happy. Now? Now she's never sober long enough to hold a conversation with. She just comes by for her money, then goes back to the bars, where she throws it all around. Dean don't like her. I know it's a sin, Dobe, but I can't blame him. 'Cause she don't want to be nice. She don't, Dobe. I give her lots of money. But it seems there's never enough. She keeps coming back for more and more. And she's started askin' questions. Nosy, like. And it upsets Dean. He still remembers her as our momma, but now . . . well, he don't like her. Momma ain't Momma no more.' A tear rolled down Sharleen's cheek. 'I wish she'd never found us.'

Dobe stood up and went over to Sharleen. He pulled her out of her chair, put her head on his shoulder and his arms around her. Sharleen felt herself grow limp in Dobe's arms, and she cried like she hadn't cried since she was a little girl. Since then, she'd always had to be strong, to take care of herself and of Dean.

'Your momma's had a little too much to drink. Why don't I just take her home and make sure she don't get into any trouble.'

548

Mutely, Sharleen nodded. Somehow, she already felt much better.

34

I have never had the advantage of beauty. Somehow, you're not sur-prised, right? Who ever heard of a beautiful writer? Writing – even the kind I do – is hard and lonely work. Who'd do it when they could be out getting laid? Not that I haven't had my share of men. A bad first marriage (that's where I got Richie as a last name) and then several bad affairs. But beauty wouldn't have ensured any better men. Just different ones. I figure it like this: Beautiful women have a better early life. Then they have to suffer more later. Us plain ones have a tougher beginning – you know, no date for the prom, and the usual heartbreak – but if we work at it, life does get better. Maybe.

Hollywood has made it worse for all of us women: the expectations are higher and more unrealistic than ever while the 'life expectancy' of an actress is shorter. Female stars used to reign for a long time. A decade was a short career. Now a year is. Men want novelty. Younger, fresher, newer. And there is always some kid ready to fill the void.

There aren't any women – with the notable exception of Barbra – who can open a movie. The days of the Crawfords, the Hayworths, the Grables and Hepburns and the like are not just over, they are almost forgotten. And the women on our screens today most often play whores or victims or sluts or long-suffering secondary roles. Dehumanized, turned into a body or a stereotype, a simpleton or a cliché; the actresses are angry and sad. And none of them are bankable.

But the saddest ones are not the ever-more-quickly fading stars. The saddest are the body doubles. The girls who are not quite good enough all over for a part, but whose breasts or stomachs or asses or legs get to star in a feature. Each time they get called in by the director for the close-up of their navel, there are a hundred technicians and movie people glorifying a piece of them and insulting their face and talent. Think about it. Would you like to play Julia Roberts's belly in Pretty Woman *or Jane Fonda's breasts in* Klute?

Most body doubles are paid very little and have to sign an agreement swearing them to secrecy. After all, none of the stars want to publicly admit their bellies and breasts aren't good enough. Spoils the illusion. The illusion that you, dear Reader, buy.

Anyway, there's an old adage in Hollywood: the director gets to fuck the star; the AD only gets the body double. And Birth of a Star *would be no exception to that rule.*

A. Joel Grossman was more than eager to do what he could for Sam. But it wasn't as easy as he had expected to curry favour on the *Birth* shoot. He'd been lucky to get the job, which so often went to the director's sidekick or his long-time bag man. Walking into an assistant directorship on an important film like this one was sheer luck, made possible only because Sam was such a loner and had no sidekicks or pals. That was the problem now. Sam gave him little to do, barely talked to him, didn't seem to trust him. Oh, Christ, let's face it, Sam didn't trust anyone.

And things weren't going so well. In his opinion, Michael McLain was a putz, and a washed-up old has-been. Plus, the rumour was that he had been shtupping Jahne Moore, but now it looked like Sam was interested. Although the rumour was that Sam had been shtupping April Irons as well. Or perhaps that was before he was shtupping Jahne Moore. Joel sighed and shook his head. How did these men let a little thing like sex get in the way of their careers? He couldn't understand it. Anyway, something was making the shoot go particularly slowly and be as difficult as hell. There wasn't one take in ten with any warmth or feeling. But Sam, of course, wasn't asking for his help, though Joel would have been happy to give it.

So, when the call came, Sam sounding so urgent about the need for a body double, Joel felt it was a godsend, his chance to do something, anything, that would give him a shot at the next job, through either Sam or the studio. Sam had asked for his help in casting the body double, something he could do. 'Total security on this,' Sam had insisted. 'No middlemen, no publicity. I mean it. Can you do it?' 'A mere bagatelle,' he'd answered. Now he was desperately going through his messy pile of cards and torn bits of paper, looking for the girl's name. The one that Paul Grasso had brought over that time. The one with the so-so face and the body that would melt molybdinum. He hadn't used her, but he knew that in Hollywood she couldn't afford to hold that against him.

There it was! Adrienne Godowski. Jesus, what a name! He picked up the telephone and stepped out onto the veranda overlooking the little sapphire-blue pool. He punched Adrienne's number into the receiver.

'Hullo?' a voice said. Christ, it sounded like she'd just woken up. What time was it? He looked at his Oyster Rolex.

'This is Joel Grossman. Adrienne Godowski, please.'

'Who's this?' It was a woman, but the voice was so gravelly, it was hard to tell at first. Christ, was she drunk? Or dying?

'Joel Grossman. I interviewed Adrienne once, through Paul Grasso. Is this Mrs. Godowski?'

There was a pause, then a deep cough. 'Oh, yes, Mr. Grossman.' The woman's voice sounded like it was an effort to speak. 'What can I do for you?'

'I have a part in a movie, small part, no lines, and I wanted to see Adrienne for it. Can she come over right away?' He gave her the address.

'I'll put her in a cab. I got a very bad virus or I'd bring her myself.' The woman coughed again, as if to prove the fact. 'She'll be there in twenty minutes,' she slurred.

Fifteen minutes was more like it. 'My mother said you would pay the cab. She didn't have any change,' Adrienne announced, as she stood on the front steps looking at him. Joel went out and paid the driver in the beat-up Chevy.

Adrienne was still standing outside the door when he returned. 'Let's go inside,' he said. 'Got your résumé with you?'

Adrienne dug into the large, beaten-up leather bag, pulled a dog-eared sheet of paper out, and handed it to him. He looked at her résumé. Jesus. L.A. was the kind of place where an actress would put a CAT scan down as a film credit, but this was ridiculous. What the hell was 'lead . . . *Girls in White Satin*' supposed to mean? If it was a lead role, why didn't it have a name? He looked at the misspellings and the ragged margin.

'You need a manager,' he said.

'I got one. My mother.' Her tone was flat, affectless.

'No, I mean a professional,' he told her, though he knew it was useless.

'No one could be more loyal than a girl's mother,' Adrienne said, but she said it in the same dead tone, as if she were merely parroting something repeated to her a million times. Was she all right in the head? She gave him the impression of being hypnotized, or mildly retarded, or both. And it gave him the oddest reaction: he could feel the boner growing against his pants.

551

He decided it was best to ignore both her answer and his hard-on and just get on with it. 'So, we need a body double for Jahne Moore, and when the director asked me, I said you'd be perfect for it.' What the hell, build it up a little. 'He had someone else in mind, but I'm pretty sure I can get it for you. I need some pictures, though.' He stopped.

'I got these,' she said, and handed over a messy pile. He riffled through them.

'No, no. I mean some special pictures. Ones where we'll have to show all of your body. Because you'll be a body double. You'll do all the love scenes. And some other stuff.' He stopped, waiting for a reaction, but there was none. 'So is it okay?' he asked.

'I have to ask my mother,' Adrienne told him, and walked across the room to the phone. Her legs moved so smoothly that, from behind, it was almost like watching the ocean recede. If her face and brain left something to be desired, that perfect ass, those lean, coltish legs, those incredibly slender ankles left him with nothing but desire. He licked his lips nervously. When the dick stands up, the brains go into the ground, he told himself, but his dick didn't seem to be listening.

She was only on the phone briefly, then turned back to him. 'Okay,' she said. 'My mom says it's okay.' And then she reached up and began to unbutton her shirt.

'Uh, listen. Let's do it out on the deck,' he said. 'I need the light.' And some air. And the *camera*, he reminded himself, and went into the hall closet to get it.

When he returned, she was standing in the middle of the living room, her clothes in a pile on the chair beside her. The only thing she was wearing was those cheap, scuffed white shoes, the pointed toes curling up, showing a bit of the sole. Her body was perfect, and its whiteness glowed in the centre of the almost empty room. 'Where do you want me?' she asked him.

'Outside,' he answered, not surprised to hear the hoarseness in his voice. She turned, and he followed that perfect ass out onto the deck. It was the contradiction of her body that created the tension he felt when he looked at her: she was lean yet curved, toned yet soft, long yet round.

He posed her on a wooden chaise longue. He had no cushions for it, but her white body against the rough wood stirred him deeply, and he figured it had to work on Sam, unless the guy was made of concrete. He shot a roll, thirty-six exposures. He had her stretch out

552

with her arms over her head; then he asked her to hold a breast in each hand, then to sit up. He tried to keep her face out of most of the shots. 'Sit at the edge of the chaise now,' he suggested. 'Put both arms behind you.'

She did as she was told. He wondered how far her docility would go. She looked at him mildly, her face registering neither disapproval nor pleasure. 'Hook your legs under each leg of the chaise,' he told her.

'Like this?' she asked, as she spread her knees.

'Yes,' he said, and squatted down, angling the camera up. A beaver shot. What was possessing him? He could never show *this* to Sam.

He felt as if he had been privy to a secret, a great mystery, and by exposing it to the sun, to his eyes, to his lens, he was desecrating it at the same time as he worshipped it.

'Look, I want to splash some water on you? Okay? There is a scene in the water.'

'Okay,' she agreed, 'but it's kinda cool. I don't want to get sick, like my ma.'

'Don't worry. We're almost done.' He went to the hose beside the house, shut the nozzle, but turned on the faucet. He approached her, the hose dragging behind him, a long tail. He pointed the nozzle at her belly and pressed the trigger down hard.

The jet of cold water arched up into the sun and gushed down onto her flat white belly. It contracted, and the water splashed up to her perfect pointy tits, the doll-pink nipples immediately hardening, one pointing to downtown L.A., the other directly at Joel. 'Oh!' she gasped, and he released his grip on the nozzle and threw it aside. He watched as the water ran down her belly, glistening on the soft brown patch of hair, wetting her between her legs. His penis pressed so hard against his zipper that he felt dizzy.

You are taking your life in your hands, he told himself, sounding like his own grandma. You French-kiss her and you may wind up with French foreign lesions. Before you put that in your mouth, do you know where it's been?

'Come inside,' he said, against all his better instincts. 'Come inside. I want to fuck you,' he groaned. As he knew she would, she stood up and began to follow him. He stumbled through the open door, through the living room into the bedroom. He walked around the unmade bed to the side table, opened the drawer. Thank God. Four condoms. He grasped at one, turned, but she wasn't behind him.

Had he misunderstood? Wasn't she coming? He walked back out to the living room just in time to see her hanging up the phone. Christ! Had she called for a cab? Had she called the cops?

She was just hanging up the phone. She looked up at him. 'My mother says as long as I got the job it's okay,' Adrienne said, and began to walk towards him.

35

Jahne sat, protected from the lights both by a creme block and the white canvas umbrella, staring at the script. Her heart was pounding in her chest. Today was the first day of shooting with Michael McLain, and she was nervous. Nervous about seeing him, about April Irons' visit today, about the script that still wasn't working. Sy Ortis had been at least partly right. The working script for *Birth of a Star* wasn't awful, only pedestrian, but Jahne hadn't been prepared for the rewrites. Each day, new versions were distributed, and each one worse.

While the story hadn't changed, the settings and style had. And now there were three — count 'em, *three* — scenes with nudity. She put her hand to her chest, as if it would do any good to cover her breasts now. Well, at least she wouldn't be the one who had to expose herself in front of a couple of hundred strangers. Sy and her contract had seen to that. But she felt sorry for the poor, anonymous girl who would.

The San Francisco soundstage, large as an airplane hangar, was chaotic. Cables crossed the floor in a demented roadmap. Equipment of every conceivable sort was heaped about. Grips called out to one another, barely audible over the noise of hammering and rendered invisible by the shower of sparks from arc welding that fell in a bright cascade from somewhere on a catwalk overhead.

Mai had told Jahne how different movies were from television, but she couldn't have imagined the scale without seeing it. From the lushness of her trailer to the vastness of the soundstage to the numbers of crew, the enterprise was intimidating. Jahne thought of the little band of players in St. Malachy's basement, and of the cast of two in the original production of *Jack and Jill*. How had Sam learned to handle so much so soon? And could he handle it? Jahne had always admired him as a director, but this was too much for anyone to manage.

She made her way through the maze of workers and crates and props and lights, the little AD at her side. Jahne, always polite, remembered that his name was Joel Something. She turned to him. 'Joel, who will attend this meeting?'

'Oh, Sam, April, Michael, Bob, and Samantha Reiger.'

'April Irons will be there?'

'Yeah. It's unusual, but this is such a big-budget baby that I guess she wants to see it off on the right foot.' He flashed an ingratiating grin at her. 'Not that it won't be a huge success with you in it,' he told her. 'I really admire your work.'

Jahne nearly laughed. After almost a year, she still couldn't get used to the L.A. crowd's talking seriously about dreck like *Three for the Road*. And sometimes it was hard to figure if they, too, knew it was dreck, in which case they were toadies, or if they actually did admire it, in which case they were subliterate. Joel, she could see, was a toady. That made it easy for her. She didn't have to feel sorry for him or like him.

She sighed. 'Tired?' he asked. Christ, the little worm was right in her face! Jahne knew the biggest job of an AD was babysitting the stars. Well, she didn't need a sitter. What she did need was a little more confidence in her judgement and fewer butterflies in her stomach. Her fear was that Sy might – just possibly – be right: that *Birth of a Star* was nothing but a potboiler. And Sy called her every other day to remind her over and over how important her first picture was. 'If this goes down the toilet, you'll be a TV queen forever,' he had said. 'Totally ABC's *Movie of the Week*. Coming down with the newest disease or vamping through some stupid romance. Strictly Jane Seymour territory.' Involuntarily, Jahne put her hand to her stomach.

'You okay?' Joel asked.

'Fine,' she told him, and her annoyance showed in her tone of voice.

But she wasn't fine. Because she had worked so hard, had suffered such pain, had been so brave, all so that she could get here. Here. On this set. And, if she was really honest with herself, she knew she hadn't made the best choice. If this movie bombed, she'd gone through the surgery, the humiliation, the loneliness, the fear . . . for nothing. She'd never get to play any of the great roles. She'd wind up nothing more than a TV whore, which, in her cosmology, was several steps lower than a Broadway gypsy. And she'd picked this role, against the advice of her TV director and her agent, for one reason.

So she could be with Sam, the man who had betrayed her once already.

She felt the butterflies dance in her stomach. Why should she be nervous, seeing Michael? *He* was the one who had behaved like a dog, not her. And if he had never called her, she certainly hadn't wanted to be called. So why, now, did *she* feel almost – well – ashamed?

Ridiculous! she told herself, but the butterflies didn't go away. Nor did the curiosity about April Irons and Sam. What *was* their relationship? If she watched them, wouldn't she know? Couldn't she tell who Sam slept with, after all this time?

Sam looked good on the set. Even leaner, his mouth more deeply parenthesized by the long dimples on either side, his jaw sharper. He was still tanned, and it still suited him, but it didn't cover the darkness under his eyes.

Jahne wondered if he actually sat beside some pool, his face turned to the sun, Bain de Soleil with an SPF of 8 slathered on his face. Somehow, it put her off, thinking of him indulging in the most ordinary of Hollywood cosmetic improvements. As if *she* were in a position to judge anyone else's vanity. She almost sighed again but caught herself before Joel had a chance to inquire about her health, digestion, bowel movements, or the state of her spiritual life.

Sam looked up from the conversation he was having with the best boy and a grip. He didn't smile. Instead, he did that thing where his mouth stayed still but his eyes warmed. Jahne felt as if she could be tanned by the warmth. Oh, Christ! she told herself. Don't be a fool.

She walked up to the group that sat under one of the location tents, slightly removed from the hive of activity. There was April, looking cool and elegant as ever, plus two other actors, and Michael. As she approached, Michael turned and looked up at her.

'Jahne!' he said, and stood up. 'Jahne!' And before she could move, before she could react, he had his arms around her, and his mouth on her mouth! She was surprised into speechlessness.

Michael kept one arm on her back and walked her over to the group. She joined them and couldn't help noticing April's satisfied smile and Sam's eyes on her. She couldn't help it – under his scrutiny she blushed like a schoolgirl.

'Sit here, next to me,' Michael cooed, and laid his arm proprietarily across the back of her chair. Jahne sat down, conscious of all of them watching her.

Blessedly, the AD came over with a question for Sam. In that moment, Bob Grantly and Samantha Reiger, two supporting cast members, introduced themselves and said hello. Then the meeting began.

Jahne could barely keep her eyes on the script. Michael seemed to think that nothing had changed between them, or that, if she was upset by his disappearance, she would completely forget it now that he was back! Of course, he didn't know that she knew about Sharleen, the matching necklaces, the calls to Lila – and perhaps a necklace for Lila as well. Well, Jahne didn't care who Michael fucked as long as he kept his hands off her and didn't rape her friends. She sat there, longing to wipe the feeling of his lips off of hers, so angry that the script in her hands trembled. The meeting seemed interminable.

At last, they were through. April wished them luck and left to fly back to L.A. It was then that Michael turned to her.

'How have you been?'

'Just fine. How about you? And Sharleen? And Lila?' she asked, her voice as cold and hard as she knew how to make it.

He had the grace to pause, at least for a moment, the smile gone from his face. Then he sighed and shook his head. 'What's that line?' he asked. 'Hell hath no fury . . .' he murmured, and his smile turned to a smirk.

'"Hell hath no fury like a woman raped," Michael? Is that the quote you're looking for?'

His world-famous blue eyes grew cold as the north Pacific. 'What are you talking about?'

'Sharleen Smith. Drunk and struggling.'

Michael barked out a laugh. 'Come off it, Jahne. I dated her once. The little Okie *begged* me for it.'

Jahne blinked. For a moment – half a moment – she wondered if perhaps Sharleen had exaggerated or misunderstood. Then, disgusted with him and herself, she looked him in the eye. 'You're a pig!' she said.

'You're a slut,' he answered, and began to turn away.

All at once, her fury at him, at all men who did what they wanted with women and then walked away, seemed to rise up in her. Before he'd taken three steps, she was beside him and had grabbed at his shoulder. He turned, surprised, and she lifted her right arm, swung it back, and then slapped him, as hard as she could, across his world-famous left profile. The sound her hand made as it connected was loud and frightening. All of the crew stopped what they were doing. Silence fell over the place. Michael, stunned, lifted both hands to his face and stifled a groan.

Without a word, Jahne turned and walked off to her trailer.

'Jesus Christ!' Sam cried. And ran over to Michael's side.

The pandemonium had calmed down. Sam had run back and forth, between a raging Michael and a frigid Jahne, until one had been soothed with both an ice pack and an apology, and the other bribed with a promise that she didn't have to see Michael anywhere except on the set. And an invitation to dinner with her director.

The crew had been buzzing all afternoon, but now, as evening came on, the scandal was calming down. Sam sighed, flipped the visor on the car to block the rays of the setting sun, and turned to Jahne.

'Couldn't you wait until after the wrap to hit him?' Sam asked plaintively, but then he had to laugh. 'Not that he doesn't deserve it, but it could make filming rather – how you say – *difficile*?'

Jahne shrugged. For once, she'd behaved badly, and this trip was her reward. She had actually seen nothing of California in the year since she had relocated. She'd arrived in L.A., got the Melrose job and then *Three for the Road*. She'd been on back lots and gritty locations like Louisiana and Idaho for *3/4*, but had seen nothing of the Golden State. Now she would see something, if she could keep her eyes off Sam. He was taking her out, going to show her around, he said, before dinner. It was supposed to be a meeting to calm her down, to discuss the script, he said. Now that Michael's face had been packed in ice and Sam had spoken to him, it was her turn. She smiled. She actually felt good. She'd never in her life acted like a prima donna, she'd never caused a scandal. And now she wasn't being punished for it, she was being 'handled.' She smiled and looked at Sam again. It's probably just business, she told herself, but he *had* asked her out. He had. And, like a teenager waiting for her first date, she wondered if he liked her. But that's the old Mary Jane. I should only be worrying about whether *I* like *him*.

Sam had picked her up a few minutes early, as if he couldn't wait to be with her. Stop reading into things, she'd told herself sternly. Just stop. But she couldn't. She slid into the low seat of his rented Nissan 300ZX Turbo and breathed the same air he had been breathing. Her lungs hurt. *Eine kleine Nachtmusik* was playing on the sound system, filling the car. Sam had stepped around to the driver's side and folded his lanky frame into the black leather seat. As he accelerated away from the hotel, she felt herself pushed back into the seat, almost as if his weight were already on her.

'I'd thought we'd go to Santa Cruz for dinner,' he said now. 'Have you ever been?'

'No,' she told him. 'I don't know Northern California at all.'

'Never been to Muir Woods? Never been to the wine country? No? I'll have to take you. It's wonderful.'

She tried to remember if he used to say 'wonderful,' back in New York. She didn't think so. But then, not much had been wonderful. Except maybe *Jack and Jill*. Except maybe their time together. And, then, she thought, maybe it had only been wonderful for *her*. Hadn't he just said something about taking her someplace? He meant to see her again. He *assumed* he would. And she felt both angry and breathless.

Well, of course he'll see me. Why shouldn't he? I'm the star of his latest production. He's a star fucker. And I'm pretty. I'm sixty-seven thousand dollars' worth of pretty. Why shouldn't he expect to see me again? And why should it make me happy that he does? I ought to learn to take this stuff for granted, as Mai told me to. She sighed.

'Well, that doesn't sound like a delighted response,' Sam said dryly.

'No, I guess not. But I *am* delighted. I'd love to see Napasono-mamendocino, or whatever the place is.'

Sam laughed. 'Those are *three* places, and the third one is the prettiest. I know a little inn at a small winery there. It's just great. A sort of merging of all that's best in Europe and California.'

Jahne wondered if April Irons had introduced him to it. And if it was before or after he had agreed to cast Crystal Plenum in the role of Jill.

'You know, Jahne, your conduct on the set today won't make this production any easier to get off the ground.'

'He's an animal.'

'It wasn't very professional,' he admonished.

'It wasn't very professional for him to grab me and tongue-kiss me. We broke it off months ago. He's a pig. And I don't want to talk about it anymore.'

The car took a sharp curve, and Jahne felt Sam's shoulder brush against hers. The soft leather of his jacket was warm against her bare skin. She felt a chill run up her back.

Something had changed in the air between them. Somehow, she *knew* that he was interested in her – that he wanted her. Was it her slap at Michael that had done it? Was it because she'd acted like a brat? Or like a woman? She didn't know. But something *had* changed.

Well, this time, she swore, whatever happened, it would be different. As the French put it, this time she would be the one who was kissed, not the one who did the kissing. This time, Sam would love her more than she'd ever let herself love him. She'd no longer play Miss Havisham. It was Estella all the way.

They broke free of the traffic and moved onto the coast road. Jahne marvelled at the dry brown hills – austere but beautiful in their way. The wind from the Pacific rippled the long grasses as Jahne had always imagined wheat fields to ripple, a beautiful undulation, a sexual wave that fascinated her.

'Where exactly are we going?' she forced herself to ask, but she didn't really care. Cupped in the comfort of the car, the Mozart rippling around her, Sam beside her at last, she only wanted this moment, this final reward, to continue forever. Her great expectations were at last coming true. Let me remember this, she told herself. Let me remember it and know that once I was perfectly content.

'I'm taking you to a restaurant in Santa Cruz,' he said as the sportscar effortlessly crested each hill. 'It's sort of the end of the line, the last stop on the train for all the wanderers and frontiersmen and westward-ho-ers. When they got to Santa Cruz, there was nowhere farther west to go but into the ocean.'

'Did some of them drop into it like lemmings?' she asked.

'Probably the better genetic stock started swimming for Asia. The chickens stayed behind.'

'So Santa Cruz is based on chicken stock, like a good cassoulet?' she asked.

He laughed. 'You're a little too clever, aren't you? Santa Cruz is the end of the road, kind of like Key West. Ever been there?'

She'd been there with Sam, on the one and only vacation they'd ever taken together. All at once, she was flooded with the memory of their walk down Duval Street, the beer in Sloppy Joe's, their visit to Hemingway's house. That was a time when she thought he'd loved her. For no reason, tears filled her eyes. She'd been through a lot today. She was not handling this as easily as she had planned. She turned her head towards the sere hills and blinked the tears away.

'Yes. Route One ends there,' she managed.

'Well, so do a lot of people's dreams. Santa Cruz is like that. And it's been the location of a lot of films – they did the last *Dirty Harry* here, and then *The Lost Boys*.'

'It sounds kind of gruesome.'

'No. It's got a real down-at-the-heels charm. Rather like my own.' He smiled.

She could almost feel his warmth, his seductive 'like-me-even-though-I'm-trouble' come-on envelop her. His profile, hawk-nosed and as clean as a paper silhouette, was dark against the sunset behind him. In the ruddy light, his skin glowed. She wondered how it felt. She'd have loved to reach out and stroke his face, feel his cheek under her palm, run a finger across his wide mouth. She clutched her hands together in her lap and looked away from him.

The Mozart CD ended, and Sam slid in a new disk. Tom Waits' raspy voice filled the car. Sam had introduced her to Waits' clever lyrics and almost unbearable vocals years ago.

'Ever heard Tom Waits?' he asked now.

How many women had he asked that question of? she wondered. Had Crystal Plenum liked Tom Waits? Had April Irons? Oh, God, she thought. I'm going to drive myself crazy if I keep this up. Just let it alone, Jahne. Tell him no.

But she couldn't stop herself. 'Yes,' she said. 'And the piano sounds drunk,' she added, misquoting a lyric.

Sam smiled in delight. Her friend Molly used to call this 'the Seiko phenomenon' – when two people met and discovered the mundane things they had in common, they all seemed to be pre-ordained and of earthshaking significance. 'You use Paul Mitchell shampoo? I do, too! *You* wear a Seiko? *I* wear a Seiko!' She laughed at the thought.

'What's so funny?' he asked.

'Nothing.'

561

He looked at her. 'Mysteries, mysteries,' he muttered, a line from *Jack and Jill*.

'I liked your play,' she told him.

'You saw it?' he asked. 'The play, not the film?'

'I never saw the film, only the play. I loved it.'

'I'll get you the tape of the movie. Maybe we could . . .'

'I'd rather not,' she said quickly. *That* would be more than she could bear. She moved on to another subject, any subject. 'Is this Santa Cruz?' she asked, as they finally topped the last of the seemingly innumerable hills and looked down on a collection of brightly coloured lights, like the contents of a little girl's jewellery box spilled along the coastline. Sam nodded.

'I remember the opening of *Lost Boys* now. I think they used a long shot like this,' she said.

'Great opening,' Sam agreed. 'It was shot from the ocean side, though. Too bad the rest of the movie didn't live up to it.'

She nodded. 'What other openings did you think were great?' she asked.

'*Once Upon a Time in America*. It had that opium dream. . . .'

'With the phone ringing!' she continued.

'Yeah, that was masterful. What ones did you like?'

'*The Pope of Greenwich Village*,' she told him.

'"Summer Wind"! Frank Sinatra singing and Mickey Rourke shooting his cuffs. Great opening!' he agreed approvingly. 'So, what movies did you hate?'

'*Internal Affairs*. Every man was brutal, and every woman was a whore. Richard Gere hit seven actresses, and Andy Garcia, playing the good guy, beat up his wife.'

Sam nodded. 'Realistic, though,' he said.

'Oh, come on. All the cops' wives were a size six. Tell me *that's* realistic.'

Sam laughed. 'Okay, okay.' He looked at her, his eyes warm. 'You've got good instincts,' he smiled, and she was angry to find how much his approval pleased her.

He pulled the car into a parking spot, and stilled the engine. Then he turned to look at her again, deeply and carefully, with his director's eye. She remembered him looking at her this way, so very deeply, almost *through* her, just before he cast her as Jill. She tried not to cringe, but now surely, *surely* he'd recognize her. Now he'd know, and it would all come tumbling out; for good or ill, it would all be told.

'You're a deep one, Jahne,' was all he said, and he slid out of the car, coming around to help her out.

Santa Cruz was diverting, a sort of decadent playland, a scenic board-walk nestled on the ocean, with just that undercurrent of carny danger. Sam took her to an indifferent Italian restaurant where they split a bottle of indifferent wine, ate pasta, and shared the breathtaking view of the white-frothed combers pounding in from the night-black sea and sky. Then they walked the boardwalk and tried a few games of chance, where chance seemed to have little to do with the inevitable outcome. Sam seemed undismayed that he didn't win her even a tiny stuffed snake, the lowest possible prize. The snakes were made of ugly plush, with eyes of glued felt, bedraggled ribbons around their necks, if snakes had necks.

'You don't want one of those, do you?' he asked. 'Obvious phallic displacement.'

'No,' she told him, and laughed, but she found she did. She desperately wanted something he would give to her, win for her, that would remind her of this night.

'Athletics are not my strongest suit.'

'And what is?' she heard herself ask in a smoky voice. She couldn't believe she'd thrown out a *double entendre*, especially when she was determined *not* to sleep with him.

'Would you like to find out?' he asked, looking at her directly. Then he placed his hand, his long, lean, tanned hand, under her chin, and tipped her head up to his face. He bent his head down to hers, and then his lips were on her lips, his tongue in her mouth, his delicious breath mingling with hers. She had never been kissed like this. It was Sam, and he wanted her, he was kissing her, and she could feel his heat, she could feel his desire. Her whole body felt alive, vibrating. He wants me, she thought. He really does!

He lifted his mouth off of hers. 'Would you like to find out?' he asked again.

She caught her breath. 'If I do, I'll ask April,' she told him. 'Now I'd like to go home.'

36

Marty hung up the phone and smiled. Normally he was too big-spirited to wish ill on anyone. But after April taunting him about her option on it, after all the trouble with Jahne Moore, with the concession of time off and the schedule for the taping of next season's show completely revamped because of her, and then the total shit storm that caused with Lila – both personally and professionally – well, he couldn't help but smile to hear the *Birth of a Star* shooting was in trouble. She'd need another two weeks, and he'd grant it. What the hell. He already had his season's first two shows scripted, and neither included her.

It wasn't just that she'd caused him trouble. Also, he admitted, he simply couldn't wish April Irons well. It was like that old showbiz saying – 'Why does he hate me so? I never did anything for him' – but with a new twist. He had backed out of an agreement, an early one, with April, and it had hurt her badly. Marty knew himself – too many years of therapy to deny that – and he knew that he felt himself to be an inherently good guy. That's why he worked with Sy, for example. Sy was born to be the bad cop. But Marty had been bad to April, and it made him feel guilty, even now, years later. So he couldn't like her or wish her well. Then, when he heard she'd gotten the option on *Birth*, one of his favourite old films, well, he'd resented it. But, as much as he resented April, he knew she resented him more.

Anyway, she knew vendetta as well as any Sicilian, and played it better than most. Casting Jahne Moore had made nothing but headaches for him. But he'd endured to triumph. The first two shows of the new season would feature Lila. And her mother. Paulie Grasso was setting it up. Because Jahne wasn't available, and it could be done partly as back-story: why Lila had left home, and then the return of the prodigal son. Well, daughter. The scripts sang, and the visuals would be unbelievable. Because, Marty acknowledged, he was obsessed with Lila. And a season premiere that starred her and brought in her mama would also bring in the ratings. He owned the youth audience on Sunday night, but Theresa O'Donnell would bring in the heavy-furniture crowd, too. He'd kill them. The Network might even set up a St. Marty of the Road shrine and begin worshipping there. Not that they weren't already kissing his skinny Italian ass. But a killer rating for the first two shows of the season, which starred Lila, and which brought in the older audience, would give Marty leverage in about twenty-three directions at once. And if Lila had a few objections, that was just as well. But for once, he'd get his way. Because he knew there was no love lost between Lila and her mom.

So, it seemed he had all kinds of bases covered. And just to be safe, he'd throw in a few long shots of Sharleen and Jahne in the beginning and the end, when Lila rejoined them – Clover, Crimson, and Cara on the road again. It would be a blockbuster. It might even exceed that 'Who shot J.R.?' episode. Then again, departing from the formula might bring down the wrath of God.

Go know.

Theresa O'Donnell hadn't been as excited about a job since she'd had her own show with Skinny and Candy. Paul Grasso had told her the part on *Three for the Road* was 'significant, integral to the story,' but she hadn't yet seen the script. In fact, she was supposed to have received it first thing this morning, and here it was almost three, and the assholes at Grasso's office hadn't followed through.

Theresa sighed and reached over to the white table by the pool, picked up her drink, and sipped. Well, she could wait. It wasn't like she ever needed more than a day to memorize her part. She was a quick study. Always had been. Had to be, to keep up with the younger tramps that were creeping up behind her.

Like Lila. Theresa laughed, picturing Lila's face when she was told her mother, Theresa O'Donnell, was going to play the part of her mother on *Three*. In fact, she threw her head back and laughed out loud. The bitch. It serves her right. Fuck with me. I'm *good*, she thought. *Real* good. And they couldn't ignore that fact. I have a strong following, and the powers that be know that. It was Lila who didn't.

Or maybe she did; that's why she hates me so much. She may be young, she may be pretty, but I still have drawing power, stamina, after all these years in the business. And Lila is afraid – deep down inside – that she wouldn't be able to maintain her edge. Not like I have.

Well, maybe I have slipped a little, Theresa admitted to herself. She hadn't done a movie or TV show in . . . well, a long time. But she didn't *like* the movies they were making now. And she'd done a guest shot, well, last year. No, the year before.

Paul Grasso, the guy Marty had given the casting job for *Three* to, had caught her off guard when he called to offer her the part. 'I tried to reach you through Ara, your agent, but he tells me he doesn't represent you anymore.'

'Mr. Grasso,' she had almost stammered, 'I no longer *need* representation.' And, of course, Mr. Grasso had agreed. She'd put the word out that *she'd* dumped Ara, the old fairy.

Now she picked up the portable phone from the corner of the chaise while taking another sip of her drink. She looked down at her personal telephone book, lying open on her lap. Who's next? she wondered. She'd been on the phone all day, letting the right people know that she was going to be on television again.

Of course, she had to play the game a bit. She had implied rather than stated some out-and-out lies. Like that her part would be a permanent character on the series. That Lila was as excited as she at the thought of working together. That Theresa might have a picture deal with Marty DiGennaro. How absolutely thrilled Theresa was to be able to work with a director of Mr. DiGennaro's stature.

But, she thought to herself as she began to punch in yet another telephone number, this is the way the game is played.

Then a shadow fell across her. She looked up. It was Kevin, unshaved, drunk and dishevelled. 'No script yet?' he asked, his voice nasty.

'It's on its way,' she said, but the fear sounded in her voice. She was paying him over a thousand a week now, but he got worse and worse.

'So, you'll get to see our little girl,' he sneered. 'That is, if they do wheel you out for the part.'

'I'll get the script.'

'Yeah. And I'll get married.'

37

Nothing is like a movie shooting on location. It is its own little world, where a group of highly trained, highly paid, and usually highly sexed professionals come together under enormous tension to try and create. Freed from their families, alternately bored and overworked, separated from the world of the Regulars and the Assholes, the 'Talents' find themselves tired, lonely, and frustrated. Little wonder that such close friendships, so many intense affairs spring up on location. And both the friendships and the affairs generate lots of gossip.

The gossip takes on a life of its own. That's where I, Laura Richie, come in. I seek it out, publish it, and it affects both the people on location and the folks they've left at home. Sometimes the gossip lives on longer than the people gossiped about. But one of the secrets of Hollywood is that, after a movie has wrapped, none of the friendships and few of the affairs continue.

Of course, Jahne's slap was heard round the world. Michael's swollen face was fine by the following day, but his ego was more than bruised. If it hadn't been difficult to hit Michael, it was difficult to work with him, Jahne had to acknowledge. 'Ach! He iss a child!' hissed Mai, and she was closest to right: Michael was behaving as only destructive, angry children do. He had temper tantrums when he had to wait for anything – and Jahne had already learned that the movie business was all about 'hurry up and wait' – and he sulked when they had to do take after take, even if it was he who had blown a line.

They spoke, but only when necessary, and neither was civil. Jahne was afraid Michael made jokes to the crew at her expense.

He seemed to feel perfectly comfortable making the meanest personal comments, and they were always true, or true enough to cause alarm. If Jahne missed a mark and ruined a careful setup, he sneered and called her 'the movie virgin.' When the unfortunately rabbitlike continuity girl forgot to put his tie back on for a shot and the entire scene had to be done over the following day, he called her an 'airhead with an overbite' and ripped her apart verbally in front of a dozen people.

'*Ach*, he is disgusting. And a bully. I can't understand such a man. He iss still so angry because you give him a little slap and von't sleep vis him? Ridiculous! Didn't any vimmen say no before?' Mai, who had been virtually remaking all of Jahne's costumes, looked up from her sewing and rubbed at her temples. 'He even giffs *me* a headache. Surely ozzer vimmen haff told him that?'

Apparently very few had, but Jahne knew it was more than her rejection that rankled. Like a pig trained to hunt truffles, Michael McLain was a specialist in detecting the scent of sexual tension in the air. She watched him watch her and Sam. And since he wasn't the object of the passion, he was enraged.

Because it was, of course, she and Sam generating the heat.

She constantly thought about her hunger for him. To be honest, she thought about very little else. She remembered everything she could about what it used to be like, what he did, what he said, how it felt. But what she remembered, felt, most about their sex was shame. Shame over the size of her thighs, shame at the stretch marks on her breasts, shame at the way her belly hung down when he rolled her on top. It wasn't sexual shame, not a feeling that sex was dirty. It was personal shame, a shame that she didn't look good enough, perfect enough. A shame that he wouldn't desire her sagging breasts, her wide hips.

Was she the only woman who felt that way? She had not always been overweight, but she'd always been shamed. Now that she was transformed and saw what it took, even in Hollywood, to get the right images on the screen, perhaps she could blame it on Hollywood. Every love scene she had ever seen had beautiful people in it. Ugly ones, fat ones, short ones were objects of fun or of scorn. Older people, wrinkled people, unlovely people didn't have sex, or if they did it was dreary and always shown offscreen. How could she blame herself, when all the images she had ever seen had been so much more beautiful than she?

And now wasn't she a participant in this scam that robbed people of their sexual comfort? Because the love scenes they were shooting were anything but real. With a body double, makeup, lighting, special diffusing lenses, and every other trick in the book, she'd be up on the screen making every woman in the audience feel inadequate.

She hadn't slept with Sam. And even though she wanted to,

wanted to so very badly that she found it hard to think of anything else, she wasn't sure that she would. What would he think of her scars? How would she explain? And, worse, once she had given herself to him, how would she control her feeling for him? How could she keep the upper hand? Continue the Estella role. Mai had given her advice – 'Don't ever be liking heem more than he is liking you!' It was advice Jahne planned to follow, but it was becoming difficult to resist him.

He was certainly attentive. In fact, it seemed as if he tracked her all day long, that every comment he made, each joke, each order, was also a secret message to her. Each evening, after work, he came to her suite, or sent a car to bring her to the house he had rented for the duration. They discussed the day, the difficulties with Michael, the problems with the crew, the script. She thought about telling him who she really was, toyed with the idea each evening, but never acted on it. They laughed a lot, ate together, and drank some wine – though Jahne was careful of the calories as well as its effect on her face and libido. She never talked about herself. And she tried to be as seductive as possible. Yes, she was making him crazy! But since the one kiss in Santa Cruz, she hadn't let him touch her. Except once. Yesterday, as she was leaving, he took her hand and held it up, flat, against his hard chest.

'Can you feel my heartbeat?' he asked.

'Yes.' She tried to keep the breathlessness out of her voice.

'You've kept my heart beating like that for weeks now. What is yours like?' He moved his hand, still on hers, to her own chest and pressed her hand against her own heart.

'It's quite steady,' she lied to him.

'Liar!' he said, and for a moment she thought he had read her mind. 'Liar!' he repeated and smiled. 'You're heartless. Heartless or sexless. One or the other.'

'Men's oldest incorrect assumption: that any woman who doesn't have sex with them doesn't have sex at all! I'm sexless. Just because I don't roll into bed with you?' she asked, trying to laugh.

'No,' he said, serious, his voice low. 'Because you don't love me back. Do you?'

She'd pulled away from him wordlessly and gone back to the hotel, to her empty bed, to another night of troubled sleep. When she awoke at 2.00 A.M., she felt so upset she almost called Mai. But Mai needed her rest. The old woman looked so drained and tired. Well, Jahne told herself, so will I if I don't get some shut-eye. Yet

569

she was as nervous as a cat. She had never in her life played hard to get. But was it morality and strength that kept her from sleeping with Sam, from loving him? Or was it simply fear that he'd be turned off by her scars, that he'd stay involved with April and reject her once again? Or worse, she asked herself. Worse, that he'd make love to her and realize who she was. Or, worst of all, that he wouldn't.

She laid her head against her rumpled pillow again. Did Sam love her? she asked herself. And if he did, who was it that he loved? Did he love who she had been, or only who she was? Had he only left Mary Jane because of his weakness for beauty, and now that she was beautiful, would he not leave her again? Or was he simply . . .

There was a knock on the door. It was soft, but it was unmistakably a knock. Jahne lay absolutely still. La Brecque's security people were on the job, as well as the movie security staff, and the hotel's. But the knock came again, this time with a whispered 'Jahne.'

Her heart jumped within her, but not in fear. She got out of bed, took a minute to turn on a low light and run to the mirror. Then she went to the door.

'Yes?' she asked. 'Who is it?' But she knew.

'Please,' he said, and she opened the door. Sam made no move to come in. He simply stood there, his face wet with tears. 'I've never felt like this,' he whispered. 'Never.'

She looked at his long, lean face, the shadow of his dark beard on his cheeks, the wrinkles at the corners of his deep-set eyes, eyes wet with tears, tears shed for her. Surely this was proof. No man had ever cried for her before.

'What about April?' she asked.

'Forget her! I have. It will probably ruin my career, but I have. And you don't care.'

'I care,' she told him. Taking his hand, she drew him into her room and into her bed.

38

Sam's long body lay beside Jahne, his right arm over her shoulder and just barely touching her back. She was having trouble breathing, and she couldn't swallow. Her hip bone was pressed against him, her left foot just brushing his. And all those places where they touched – her back, her hip, her foot – felt as if they were burning.

She would have him at last! And have him on *her* terms. Have a man – not just *any* man, but Sam Shields – have him love her. Adore her. Have him lusting after her. Wild for her. Crying for her.

But the excitement, the thrill, was almost too painful. She wanted to tear off her bra, her panties, rip off his blue boxer shorts, and fuck him to death. She wanted to ride him, to swallow him inside her and rock away this unbearable tension. She could hardly control herself. And I must tell him, she reminded herself. I must tell him who I am, now, before it's too late.

His face was inches away from hers. In the semidarkness, she could see his eyes gleaming. He, too, was breathless with desire. Looking deeper into his eyes, she saw two tiny reflections of her own face. What was he seeing in *her* eyes? Surely the ghost of Mary Jane?

He began to move, only the slightest bit, and now her nipples were just brushing his bare chest and she could feel the head of his penis – through his shorts – pressing against her thigh. His shorts were wet there, and the wetness echoed her own. He lifted his hand from her back and gently, ever so gently, ran it all along her side, from her shoulder to her knee and back. She shivered.

'Cold?' he teased, and his voice was almost unrecognizable, it was so gritty with desire. She couldn't speak at all, she only shook her head. He reached over to her face then and held her head still, his long hand cupping her chin. His hand on her face felt so good – she could only think of Snowball and the way the cat pressed itself against her hand, pushing the caress. She, Jahne, wanted to rub every part of herself against him, like a cat pushing on a rubbing post. Then, still holding her face, Sam kissed her, and she stopped thinking of anything.

His lips against hers were so hot that they sent another shiver down her back. But his other hand was there to draw her closer against him. He held her face to his as if her mouth were a fruit that he was eating. His tongue moved slowly around her mouth, tasting each cheek and under her tongue and behind her upper lip. Then, gently, ever so gently, he took her full lower lip between his teeth and slowly – ever so slowly – bit her.

She groaned, and he let go just at the second the sensation moved from pleasure to pain.

'I want to eat every bit of you,' he whispered. 'You're delicious. I want to love you with my hands and my mouth and my dick.' He unhooked her bra and effortlessly freed her from it. Oh! The heat of his chest on her breasts was exquisite, and she felt her nipples tingle. Yes! She had sensation there. They tingled. She took a deep breath, and it pushed them even harder up against him.

He took her hand, and moved it down, to his penis, still clothed in his boxers. It almost burned her hand. It was hard, and she let the head press against her palm. It was slick with his fluid. 'That's for you,' he told her. 'All for you.'

He moved his own hand and put it down the waistband of her panties. He pressed it against her flat stomach, the very tips of his fingers just touching her pubic hair. She groaned again, and he moved his fingers – not any lower – he simply drummed them gently for a moment there. She shuddered, and he laughed and kissed her again, this time only lip to lip. But she wanted his tongue, wanted his hand, wanted his cock. Still, he pulled back, and began to kiss her cheek, then her neck, then, slowly, her upper breast. His left hand remained on her mons, but he moved his other to cup her breast to his mouth. 'Oh, God, yes!' she whispered, but instead of taking it in his mouth he only held it to his face, and then, gently, breathed on it. And her nipple felt every breath.

She was crazy with desire for him. And she felt his desire, but also his control. He isn't like Pete – all humping and no technique. And he's not like Michael, who was all technique and no passion. Sam had the control and subtlety to choreograph his lovemaking, but he also had the passion and energy to make it so much more than a horizontal dance.

Her body had never felt so alive. The slightest touch, the least change in pressure or position, made her tingle. Now, at last, he put both of his hands on her breasts, covering them completely. He put his mouth against her ear. 'Hold me tighter,' he told her, and he squeezed her breasts gently in his big hands. 'Hold me like that,' he said, and she felt his penis jerk in her hand. She closed her fingers around it and echoed his kneading. He moaned, and she felt a surge of power and lust that was electric. *She* had made him sound like that. She tightened her fingers around him again, and again he moaned.

She used her other hand and pulled down his shorts. Then she took him in her hand again and rubbed his cock slowly against her belly. 'Oh, yes,' he groaned. She felt the trail of wetness it left. She put both hands around it and squeezed hard. He had his tongue in her ear, and what he was doing felt so good, so wild, that she had to let go of him. She felt as if there were no time, no place, only the waves of feeling from her ear to her neck to her nipples to her pussy.

'Don't let go,' he begged, and moved a hand down to hers, pulling it back to his penis and pushing himself against her palm. 'Don't ever let go of me,' he begged, and kissed her, deeply and hard. He rolled on top of her and his weight was perfect. Face to face, chest to chest, belly to belly, thigh to thigh, they lay for a moment.

'Let me come inside you,' he whispered, and, when she nodded, he reached for a condom and slipped into it. It gave her a moment to breathe. What am I doing? she asked herself. This wasn't what I planned. Not to sleep with him. Not to keep in the dark about who I really am. I *have* to tell him now. It's my last chance.

But he moved his hand down, again to her panties, and then, quick as a fish, slid his hand under them to the slickness between her legs. 'Ah. Yes,' he sighed.

She felt him slip a finger inside her. She arched her back and pushed against his hand. 'Does that feel good?' he asked, his voice a thick whisper. He began to stroke her, and she thought she'd die from the pure pleasure. 'Do you feel good?'

'Yes,' she whispered back. 'But I want more.'

He pulled her panties down to her knees. She started to wiggle out of them, but he stopped her. 'No, let me look at them there. Let me look at you exposed.' He got up on one elbow, eyeing her. 'Open your legs a little wider,' he said. The panties pulled at her knees, but she spread them as far as she could, conscious of him staring. 'Ah,' he sighed. 'That's how I've pictured you a hundred times. It's such a wanton look. Let me put on the light.'

'No!' she cried. 'No. Not now.'

He shrugged. And reached over and put his hand back on her, opening her first with two fingers, then a third. She had to thrash her head back and forth on the pillow, her pleasure was so intense. 'Oh, God,' he groaned. 'You're so beautiful. I don't know if I want to watch you or fuck you.'

He pulled his hand away from her, and she opened her eyes. He was rubbing her wetness on his cock, covered as it was by the condom. Then he tore off her panties and spread her legs wider, positioning himself between her knees. He bent over, kissed her belly, and moved his mouth up to her breasts, her neck, and then covered her own mouth with his.

'Now?' he whispered. 'Can I have you now?'

'Oh, yes!' she nearly screamed, as she felt him slip just the head of his penis inside her. He didn't move for a moment, but her urgency had her shivering and almost bucking underneath him. 'Slow down,' he whispered. 'You've got me so nuts I'll come in a second if you move.'

She stopped, trembling. Slowly, bit by bit, he slid the entire length of him into her until she felt so full that she almost clawed his back. 'There. Is that what you wanted?' he asked, and she felt tears spring to her eyes.

'Yes. That's what I wanted,' she confessed.

'Me too. Me too,' he whispered.

He began then to move on her, slowly and smoothly, entering her over and over and over. 'Oh, you're so good. It's so good,' she wept.

'It's all for you, baby. All for you.' She felt the waves of pleasure overtaking her then, and knew she was about to come. 'Ah,' he cried. 'Give it up. Give it up, baby,' he told her, and she did.

Jahne sat the next morning, smiling and humming, in front of the makeup vanity. 'Are you likink him more than he iss likink you?' Mai asked.

'No. No. Not at all.'

'I think this is qvite dangerous,' Mai warned. 'He is critic, not artist, don't you think? You give all to him. Vat does he give you?'

'His love,' Jahne said, simply.

'How do you know?' Mai asked.

Jahne turned to her, serene. She had proof. She almost shivered as she remembered Sam's passion in the dark the night before. And the tears that had coursed down his face. 'Because he cried over me,' she told Mai, turning back to her own reflection in the mirror.

'Phaw! Men *alvays* cried over me. They cry over beautiful vimmen every day. Vat else?'

And Jahne watched the smile disappear off her own beautiful face. Because she didn't have an answer.

39

Lila was beginning to look forward to her time with Marty. At first, when his attention to her on the set became obvious, Lila had accepted it as both a tribute to her beauty, and a stroke of good luck. But beauty is an abstract, and an abstraction isn't human. Marty craved glamour and glamour was remote. If she warmed to him, would he still worship at her shrine? No one in Lila's life had ever given so generously of his time to her. No one had ever really listened. At first, she was like a caged animal suddenly let loose in the jungle. She had pushed and criticized, obstructed Marty in every way. And Marty had hung on. Until she began to trust. Now he listened to her all the time, and she even occasionally listened to him. He knew stuff. He was really smart.

Trust was new to her. How could she ever really trust anyone? Not the PMS, that was for sure. Not Kevin. And not Aunt Robbie, she had gradually come to learn. Not that she believed that Aunt Robbie would deliberately hurt her, as she believed her mother had and would, but Robbie was a little too far out for anyone to consider dependable. Since Lila had laid out her terms of forgiveness, she hadn't seen Robbie, and she knew why: he was afraid to burn his bridges with Theresa by bringing Lila her 'sisters.' Fine. He'd made his choice.

She was spending all her free time with Marty, and she found that she didn't need anyone else. At first, being seen with Marty in public was enough of an incentive. The man had a presence, a persona, that seemed to appeal to everyone, men *and* women. It wasn't the allure of sexuality, nor the macho attitude that some men projected. Marty was different.

For one thing, when they were out in a restaurant, or at one of the A-list parties, Marty never took her elbow to steer her around. Lila appreciated that. She hated to be touched, and led around like a dog on a leash. Marty seemed intuitively to know that, and to respect her separateness. As a result, when she walked into a crowded room with him, she felt she walked in with him as an equal, not as a prized possession.

And the more Marty's attentions to her became known, the more everyone on the set treated Lila special, with a heightened awareness of her presence, of her unspoken needs. She knew that, of the three costars, she was the one that was feared. And the fear made Lila feel secure, because she knew that there had to be something to keep people in line, and fear was the basis for power.

Except Marty didn't use fear to project his strength. It puzzled her.

While Marty was single-minded in his work, he also knew how to spend his free time, the little he had. Marty loved opera, so they went up to San Francisco. And symphonies, ballets, art shows. And theatre, although there was less of that in L.A. than one might imagine. Marty seemed to take pleasure in exposing Lila to those things that, despite her privileged background, she had not experienced before. Marty was knowledgeable. And very patient. He was making the down time of the hiatus fun for her. And the publicity of their dates wouldn't hurt her Emmy chance at all.

Meanwhile, he hadn't tried to touch her. They spent an evening at her place, sitting on the deck, overlooking the Pacific. Marty had been in production meetings all day, and now he was talking about the new opening for the season. Lila was staring at the water, mesmerized by the spectacle of the sunset over the waves. He droned on while she nodded.

'And we'll have Theresa play your mother,' Marty said casually.

For a moment, Lila's expression didn't change, as if she hadn't heard what he had said. Then, suddenly, her face was ashen. 'What?' she asked.

'Theresa has agreed to play your mother.'

Lila couldn't believe what she was hearing. 'No, Marty. Not my mother.' Lila finally croaked out a hoarse whisper.

Marty didn't know very much about Lila's relationship with Theresa, but he knew that it wasn't very good, and that Lila had very little to do with her. Still, he hadn't thought she *hated* her mother. But the look on Lila's face was unmistakable. Lila *did* hate her mother. In that instant, Marty knew that he now had the upper hand.

'Why not? It's a natural, Lila. Think this through.'

'I won't work with my mother.' She folded her arms across her chest.

'Come on. Don't be so quick to make up your mind. Don't you realize what this could do for your career? This could give you an incredible boost, and it certainly would help the show's ratings. You'll need those rating points, don't forget, when it's Emmy time, and also when you negotiate your next contract.'

'Fuck the points. I said no!'

Marty wasn't Italian for nothing. And Machiavelli had nothing on him. At last! The worm has turned, he thought to himself. Marty smiled at Lila. 'You have nothing to say about it, Lila. I'm only telling you this as a courtesy, as a director to an actress. I'm not asking your permission.'

She should have known! She should have known not to trust him, not to trust anybody! 'Who the fuck are you? God? You're not God, Marty, you're just a director.'

'And you're just an actress, Lila. I *made* you an actress, remember that.' Marty stood up, feeling in control for the first time since he had met Lila. He spoke more casually then he felt. Now he could practise diplomacy, and wind up getting them both what they wanted. 'Anyhow,' he said, walking to the edge of the deck, 'I haven't made my final decision yet.'

'About casting my mother?' she asked. Marty could see the hope rising in her eyes.

Marty turned to the sunset for a moment, then turned back and looked directly at Lila. 'Listen, I've committed to *her*, but we could make a change.'

'Get rid of her?'

'No. We could feature Sharleen. Have Theresa play *her* mother.'

Lila sank onto a chaise, as if his implied threat had a physical impact on her.

'But you said I have the lead.' Her wail of betrayal sounded almost childish.

Marty stood up and shrugged. 'That was my scenario. But you don't seem to like it. And we have a play-or-pay contract with Theresa: she's paid if we use her or not.'

Lila, he could see, was near tears.

'I'm sorry, Lila. I didn't know you felt this way. You never told me.' He finally had his advantage, and now he was going to push it home. She had had him spinning since they met. Now it was *her* turn. She wanted something from him? This time, *this* time, Lila was going to have to negotiate.

She remained seated. 'Please, Marty, couldn't we talk this out? Why my mother? I mean, the idea of the rich girl leaving home is perfect. Sharleen can't play that. But you want an old bag like Theresa for the show? There must be a million others who'd jump at the chance. Let's think of someone else. How about Debbie Reynolds? Or Dina Merrill?' A forced smile strained Lila's face.

Marty almost felt uneasy at Lila's desperation; almost, but not quite. The taste of his own recent desperation was still fresh. Only last night, he had dreamt about her, had fantasized watching her undress in front of him, seeing her lying next to him, her long, slim body stretched out, waiting for him, her legs open, inviting, then accepting.

'You're a very beautiful woman, Lila.' He looked directly into her eyes.

Lila stared up at him, then dropped her eyes. 'I know you're attracted to me, Marty. But . . .' She stopped.

Marty didn't say anything. He knew his time had come. She spoke again. 'It's not you.' She paused. 'I'm . . . I don't enjoy sex, Marty. I mean, I never had sex. I'm still a virgin.'

Marty wasn't buying that virgin bullshit. Anyhow, he wasn't one of those men that worshipped at the altar of virginity. 'You don't owe me anything, Lila. I don't want you to feel that you *have* to do anything. My decisions are based on artistic considerations.'

Lila reached up and took Marty's hand, pulling him gently back down to the chaise. 'But isn't there something I *can* do? I mean, Marty, I *can't* work with my mother. You have no idea what she's done. What it's like between us. I *hate* her, Marty. I *despise* her. Please, don't use her, Marty. Please, *please*.'

He felt her free hand touch the zipper of his pants, and he

immediately grew hard in reaction. He smiled. 'Don't, Lila. You're a virgin, remember?'

But she didn't listen. Or didn't hear him. She had the zipper down, and his penis between her perfect lips before he even knew what she was doing. Right there, on the deck, in the fading pink light of the sunset. Oh, God, he thought, as the warmth of her mouth enveloped him. He looked down to see her beautiful head moving at his crotch. A beautiful head giving beautiful head. He swelled in her mouth. This wasn't exactly what he'd had in mind, what he had dreamed about, but it was a good place to start.

The phone beside Theresa rang. She turned to Kevin. 'Be a dear and answer it for me, will you? I'm hoarse.'

Reluctantly, Kevin did, then handed the phone to Theresa, knowing she would want to take this call. 'It's Paul Grasso.'

Theresa smiled brightly, as if it were a camera, not a phone, she was speaking into. 'Paul, darling. How are you?'

'One minute for Mr. Grasso, please.' Then Theresa was put on hold.

Christ, she hated that! Put on hold by a secretary! 'Am I old-fashioned, or doesn't anyone dial their own phones in this town anymore?' she asked aloud as she held for Paul. Then he was on the other end.

'Yes, Paul. How nice to hear from you. Where's the script?'

As she listened to him, both the colour and the smile drained from her face. No. It wasn't possible. No fuckin' way. Theresa tried not to let her feelings show in her voice, but the effort was too great. 'What do you mean, *they've* gone with someone else? *Who's* gone with someone? You mean *you've* gone with someone else. *You're* the casting director, for chrissakes, aren't you? Why? I demand to know. I *wanted* that part. That's *my* part. I have the right to know.'

Theresa was now sitting up on the edge of her chair. Grasso, the goddamn cocksucking dago prick. It was him. Him and Lila. By the Virgin's Holy Blood, she wouldn't stand for this! 'Lila made you do this, didn't she?'

Theresa understood now. He mumbled something. 'Out of your hands!' she cried. 'Out of your hands! And right up your ass. You and Lila! Both of you together! She was jealous. She couldn't let me be on the same show with her. She's afraid I'd walk away with the spotlight. She couldn't *stand* to see *me* in the spotlight. So she gets *her* way, and I get *nothing*.'

At the other end of the phone Grasso was yammering. Across the room, Kevin sneered. 'Fuck the money. It's not the money I care about!' Theresa stopped for a moment, trying to catch her breath. She felt like she was losing it – in front of Kevin, but, worse, in front of Paul Grasso. A nobody. A nothing. He disgusted her, a nasty wop toad of a man. She mustn't let him hear how desperate she was for the part. How desperate she was to prove to everyone – to Lila – that she was still on top. How desperate she was to work, to get before the public again.

She forced her voice to frigid normalcy. Icy calm. 'Well, Mr. Paul Grasso, I can see we have nothing else to say to each other. Of course, you realize, you *will* be hearing from my attorney.' She paused. 'I don't care that I get paid anyway. I want that part!' She slammed the receiver down, then flung the phone across the pool, where it clanged against the stone garden wall.

She looked over at Kevin, who, up to this moment, had said nothing, hadn't even moved. 'I guess you heard all that,' Theresa said to her old friend.

Kevin leaned back on his hands and crossed his legs. 'You were heard on Capistrano. Killed off a flock of swallows while you were at it.' Theresa was not in the mood for Kevin's so-called humour right now. 'Theresa, I am sorry. But perhaps it's for the best.'

Theresa snapped her head up, her eyes almost bulging in unconcealed rage. Perhaps she had to show some control in front of Paul Grasso, but not before this blackmailing bastard, 'For *whose* best? Lila's? Certainly not *mine*, Kevin.'

'I just mean that maybe you and Lila shouldn't be around each other, especially in a work situation. Let things continue to calm down. Wait until you both have had more time apart. You can both use a rest from each other. And then bring us together again. Give Lila what she needs.'

'How the fuck would you know what she needs?

'What did she say I did to her? What did Lila tell you?' Theresa's voice was now becoming shrill.

'Nothing, Theresa. Don't let your mind run . . .'

'What did she tell you?' Theresa shrieked at Kevin, now standing over him, her fists clenched by her side.

Kevin looked up into her face, the sun coming from behind Theresa causing him to squint. 'Nothing, Theresa. Only the usual rebellious-teenager stuff. You *know* that. Kevin put his hand across his eyes to shade them from the glare.

'Listen to me, you little hustler. I know that you're gloating over this. And that you still hope to cash in big time with Lila someday. But you can forget it! I wouldn't wish you on Saddam Hussein, much less my daughter.'

Kevin narrowed his eyes, turned abruptly and began to walk away.

'Where do you think you're going?' she screamed in panic.

'I've heard enough for one day, Theresa. I'll be back when you calm down.'

40

Flora Lee opened her eyes to the pounding at her front door, and, in the darkness that now surrounded her, she couldn't find the light switch. She heaved herself upright on the edge of the bed, and became aware of the weight in the bed next to her. Dobe. He was still asleep. What time is it? She made out the green figures on the clock on the table next to her bed. Four-thirty-three. A.M. She could remember flirting with him over dinner at Sharleen and Dean's, and then Dobe had offered to take her home. She'd just known he'd be a wild man in bed, but they'd stopped at a bar, and then another, and – well, she often didn't remember the rest of her evenings.

The pounding took on a new intensity, so she struggled upright, and began to feel her way out of the room towards the front door. 'Who is it?' she croaked to it.

'Police.'

Holy Jesus! What were they doing here? 'What do you mean, the police? How do I know you're the police?'

She peered through the peephole and saw the badge being held up in front of it. She looked down at her nakedness and said, 'Just a minute till I get some clothes on.' She snapped on the living-room light, and looked around at the empty glasses and bottles on the coffee table in front of the sofa. Flora Lee closed her eyes for a moment, trying to remember, then pushed open the door to the bedroom, the light from the living room coming in over her shoulder.

What she saw in the bed was so frightening, she couldn't scream, or even move. The pounding at the door was harder now. Flora Lee put her hands to her mouth to keep from shrieking. What had happened? Why was Dobe lying in her bed with her kitchen knife sticking out of his chest? What had she done? Jumping Jesus Christ!

She grabbed her coat and rushed to the door, grateful the police were here. Her hand was on the doorknob when it hit her. They're going to think *I* did it, she thought. She stifled a sob, but since the pounding continued, there was nothing to do but open the door to let them in.

There was only one cop, and he was in plainclothes. He flipped open his wallet and showed his badge and ID to her. He stepped into the room warily, and looked around. 'We have a complaint of a fight, screaming coming from this apartment. Are you all right, ma'am?'

It wasn't the first time the neighbours had called the cops. Probably Mrs. Ramirez, the bitch. But she couldn't remember no yelling. Flora Lee slumped down on the sofa. The plainclothes cop looked at her, then moved over and put the coffee table right. 'What's wrong, miss? What happened?' He sat down on the sofa next to her.

He seemed very nice. Flora Lee didn't know what to do, but she knew she had to tell the policeman about the dead man in her bed. 'I been drinking. I didn't know nothing till I heard you at the door. . . .' Flora Lee began to cry. She wished she were sober enough to think.

'Go ahead, tell me,' the cop said, very gently.

Flora Lee tried to stop sobbing, and pointed her finger towards the bedroom door. The cop stood up quickly and walked into the bedroom, was in there for what seemed like a long while. Maybe he's not dead, Flora Lee thought. Maybe Dobe's still alive. As she was about to get up to go in the bedroom, the policeman came back into the room, closing the door behind him. 'Lady,' he said, taking a small card from his pocket, 'I got to read you your rights. I'm arresting you for murder. "You have the right to remain silent. . . ."'

'Wait, wait,' she wailed. 'I didn't murder *nobody*. We were just having drinks, and, the next thing I know, I'm waking up next to him dead and you're pounding at the door.'

'Let me finish reading you your rights. "You have the right to an attorney. . . ."'

'*Listen to me,*' she nearly screamed. 'I didn't do it. It must have been a heart attack, or a burglar. It couldn't have been me.'

'Why not?' the cop asked.

'Because I never hurt nobody in my life. And he was a real nice man, real nice to me. He's a friend of my kids. A gentleman.' She began to sob. 'I don't know how this could happen. Dear God, on my word as a Christian, I didn't hurt him.'

'You're a Christian?' the cop asked. He sighed. He was a nice-looking guy, about fifty-five maybe, tanned, wrinkled face, brown hair. Maybe now he'd be a little more on her side. He sat back down on the sofa next to her. 'Is there anyone you can call? Someone who can come to the jail right away? I'm not supposed to do this; I'm supposed to wait for you to make your call from jail, but, seeing's how you and I are both Christians, well, maybe, just this once . . .'

Flora Lee looked up; the first glimmer of hope passed over her since she had flipped on the light and looked at her bed – only moments ago, but it seemed like years. Would a blow job help, too? No, she figured, murder was more serious than that. 'Oh, yes. I got a son and a daughter. Maybe you know her. Sharleen Smith? I could call her. She'd take care of everything. She's got lawyers, and money and . . .'

'Sharleen Smith? You don't mean that actress on television, do you? *That* Sharleen Smith? She's *your* daughter? *You're* Sharleen Smith's mother?'

Flora Lee nodded, animated. Maybe she could get out of this mess after all. Who would believe that the mother of a famous star would *kill* someone? 'Yes,' she said, as she reached for the framed picture on the end table and handed it to the cop. 'See? That's my baby.'

The cop studied the picture for a moment, then handed it back to Flora Lee. 'Anyone can have a picture of a star. I have a picture of Sharleen Smith at home myself. A fine woman, and a good Christian.'

'But, see, it says "To Momma, Love from your daughter, Sharleen." That's me. Momma.' She waited while he mulled it over. Then he stood up, and began to pace back and forth. Flora Lee watched him, her eyes eager. Finally, he stopped pacing and stood in front of her. 'If she's your daughter, you have her private number, right? Let me have it.'

Flora Lee ran to her pocketbook and took out the card with the number on it. The number she was never supposed to share with *anyone*. 'Here it is. I always carry it with me, 'cause I can't remember numbers.'

The cop took the card and sat in a chair next to the phone. 'Okay, lady, I'm going to give you a chance. Because, in this town, television is important and we don't want to mess up the Industry. But if you're lying, and this isn't Sharleen Smith, or she don't know you, you're in big trouble. Murder One gets the death sentence in this state. Now, what's your name?'

'Flora Lee. Smith.' Well, maybe she better not lie. 'Flora Lee Deluce.' She began to explain. 'See, I wasn't actually married to Sharleen's daddy. I'd been married, but Deluce ran off. Me and Dean Smith Senior had been together, oh, seven, eight years. Dean Smith was her daddy. My husband. Well, let me explain.' Flora Lee talked about those days back in Arkansas, and then the move to Texas, and desperation, and about Dean Sr., and Dean Jr., and all what happened. But then, after a few questions, the cop stopped her.

'Now, is this all the truth?' he asked. 'You got birth certificates and all?'

'Well, I don't no more. But they have 'em at the hospital. See, I had another baby there, too.' She was about to launch into the story.

'And what was your maiden name before Texas, back in Arkansas?' He was busy taking notes, which made her nervous. He stared at her now. 'If you're lying now, Mrs. Deluce, you're going to fry.'

'I'm not lying,' she whispered.

'Okay, Mrs. Deluce. I want you to go into the bathroom and take yourself a hot bath. Wash off all that blood. And clean out the tub. Real thorough. Don't come out till I call you. Understand?' He picked up the phone and placed it on his lap.

'Could I . . .? I mean, I'm awful shook up. Look, I'm trembling. Could I take a drink before I go in? For my nerves?'

'Take the whole bottle in with you, I don't care. Wash up real good, but don't try to get away. I already checked the window.'

Flora Lee closed the bathroom door behind her, turned on the taps, then quickly unscrewed the top of the vodka bottle, and took three long pulls on it before coming up for air. Then she took three more. She placed the bottle on the edge of the tub and sat on the commode, waiting for the alcohol to hit.

How in the name of a bad bull's balls did I get into this? she thought. What happened? Did someone come in and kill Dobe while I was passed out? Maybe he killed hisself. No, the knife was in the middle of his chest. Christ Almighty! Could I have done it? In a blackout? Flora Lee knew all about blackouts. She was used to drinking and then finding herself in dingy rooms with dirty men she didn't know. But she had never hurt nobody before while she was in a blackout.

But that she couldn't know for sure. Maybe she did and couldn't remember. Oh, sweet Jesus, get me out of this. I don't want to die. I'll stop drinking if You just help me. For the first time in almost a dozen years, Flora Lee dropped to her knees for something other than a blow job. Oh, please, sweet Lamb of God, please help me, she prayed.

Flora Lee stood up and turned off the water, then took a couple more pulls on the vodka bottle. She stepped into the tub and began to wash her body roughly with a washcloth. She was out of the bath and onto the bottle of vodka again when she heard the policeman call to her. He still held the phone to his ear.

Flora Lee opened the door to the bathroom and cautiously came back into the living room, her robe pulled tight around her. She was feeling a little better, but she still knew she had a problem. Still, he was such a nice man. He seemed to be on hold, only listening. 'Would you like a drink, officer?' she asked quietly.

'Mrs. Deluce, I'm on duty. Just sit down.'

She took a seat at the edge of the sofa.

'I just got finished talking to your daughter. You're who you say you are, all right. Now, let me tell you, I don't like this situation any better than you, but for Sharleen Smith I'd do anything. The Department and the studios don't like this kind of thing, either. Bad for everyone. The guy was just a drifter. No one will miss him. And I'm too close to retirement to have this ruin me now.'

Flora Lee felt some of the tension leave her body, but she still remained perched on the edge of her seat. Had God listened to her prayer? 'What is she going to do for me?'

'You're going to get dressed, pack a suitcase, get a cab to the airport, and be on the first flight to New Orleans this morning. In New Orleans, you're going to call this man,' he handed her a piece of paper with a name and a phone number. 'He'll set you up with a place to stay. Miss Smith was shocked, but she was kind enough to say that she would continue your allowance, but only through this man. He'll see you get a cheque each month.'

Flora Lee started to cry. 'I knew it. I just knew my baby girl would help me. And thank you, sir.' The sobs started to rack her body again.

'Hold up, lady. There's more. If I let you go tonight, you're never to contact Sharleen or Dean again. You're *never* to mention your relationship with them, tell *anyone* you know about them. Nothing. This means you'll never see your kids again. But that's the only way I'm going to let you out of this without at least a life jail sentence, and a short life it might be.'

Flora Lee didn't take a moment. 'Sharleen said she'd keep sending the money?'

The cop nodded his head. 'Yeah, but you gotta watch that mouth of yours. You tell anyone, and the FBI gets involved. Then you're in the chair for sure.'

'Well, she got nothing to worry about from me. I'd never hurt either one of them. It ain't like I raised them or nothing.' Flora Lee nodded her head. 'I'll go to New Orleans, and you kin tell her, starting tomorrow, I'll never drink again. I just promised the Lord that in the bathtub.' She dabbed at her eyes with the edge of her robe, then stood up.

'I have to pack my bag ... in there.' She pointed to the bedroom where the murdered man still lay.

'Make it fast. I got some more work to do tonight before this whole mess is over. And two other cops are coming. I want you outa here before they get here.'

She didn't have to be told twice to rush. Flora Lee grabbed a couple of pants suits, some underwear, and as much of her makeup as she could squeeze into the brand-new suitcase Sharleen had given her. She was dressed and back in the living room in less than five minutes, and hadn't once looked at Dobe in the bed.

The cop had money in his open hand, which he was thrusting towards Flora Lee. 'This will be enough to get you to New Orleans. You'll get more when you arrive and call the number I gave you.' Flora Lee reached for the money with one hand, grasping the handle of the suitcase with the other. 'There's just one more thing you got to do before you go.'

Flora Lee looked up at him with renewed alarm. Was he going to make her sign a confession or something? 'You got to write this note in your own handwriting before you leave.' He handed her a piece of paper.

'*Dear Sharleen and Dean,*' she copied. '*In case I don't never see you again, thanks for everything. I feel like a burden to you, nothing I aimed to be. I won't be coming back, so don't expect me.*' She signed it, '*Love, Momma.*'

Flora Lee jumped up as she heard a horn blast. 'That's your taxi. I called it for you. Here's your money.'

Flora Lee grabbed it and stuffed it into her pocketbook. 'I'm told they're bringing back death by hanging. It's a terrible way to die, Mrs. Deluce. Understand?'

Flora Lee nodded her head, grabbed her suitcase and the bottle of vodka and ran out the door.

The cop stood at the window and watched her scuttle away. He sat down and dialled the phone. While he was on the phone, the door to the bedroom opened slowly, and Dobe came through it, the blade of the knife still protruding from his chest. The cop turned to look at him and smiled.

'Goddamn it, Barney, it took you long enough. I've had to take a piss for the last hour,' Dobe said, as he opened his shirt and removed the trick half-knife.

'You did an excellent job – for an amateur,' Barney said with a nod of approval.

Dobe moved into the bathroom now, where he made sounds of relief. When he came back out to the living room, he slumped into a chair, and Barney handed him a double vodka from another bottle he'd found in the kitchen. 'Well, Barney, that was probably the easiest thousand dollars you ever earned in all your years in acting.' Dobe smiled. 'Thanks for making the riff work.'

'No problem. How'd you like it when I told her hanging was coming back?'

'Ad libs were never your strongest suit, Barney. Now, give me all them notes on the birth certificates, and let's get out of here.'

41

'Darling, wonderful lunch, but I simply have *got* to run,' Crystal Plenum told Sy Ortis as she slid out of the booth, then bent to kiss him on both cheeks. 'Being on time is my Hercules heel.'

'Achilles heel, Crystal.'

'Whatever!'

Her two camp followers, Crystal's constant companions – her 'people,' for chrissakes – hovered before and behind her, as they made tracks to the exit. Sy watched as Crystal stopped occasionally, air-kissed somebody while her 'people' stood waiting, then, finally, made it to the door.

Sy let out a sigh of relief as the door shut behind Crystal. There were two kinds of lunches: the hard and the soft. Sy found the soft ones more difficult. This lunch, a soft, had no purpose – no immediate purpose, that is – except to keep Crystal warm, tell her how beautiful and talented she still was, and what great properties he was looking over for her. All lies, as it happened. A sort of aborted jerkoff: a lot of stroking but no climax. Ass-kissing, it would be called in any other line of business. The part Sy hated most about the way he made money. These stroking parties left him feeling more like the puppet than the puppeteer.

Crystal was sinking, and both she and Sy knew it. Since *Jack and Jill*, there had not been a decent lead offered her. Of course, there were never many leading parts for women approaching thirty-five, but she'd been big box office up till *Jack and Jill*. That film had changed the public's perception of her. Now she couldn't play young anymore.

Sy sipped the last of his coffee, and didn't have to beckon to a waiter for a refill. It appeared before him, before even *he* knew he wanted a second cup. But, then, this *is* the Polo Lounge, and I *am* known here, he thought. If I can't get it here, where would I get it?

He was startled for a moment by the presence of a small,

impeccably dressed man, standing at his table. It took him a minute. 'Ara Sagarian,' Sy finally said, and just looked at him. Ara was obviously on his way to his own table. 'Mind if I join you?' Ara asked. The waiter hovered, waiting for Sy's decision.

'Well, I'm on my way out. Just had lunch with Crystal. My last espresso,' he added.

Ara sat down opposite Sy, not accepting the brush-off, and the waiter hurried to set his place. Sy grimaced, not giving a shit whether Ara noticed or not. Sy could see that Ara obviously had something on his mind, but at Ara's age, and with a stroke, it would probably take a little time for him to get it out. Sy wasn't in a very patient mood.

'I don't know if you've heard,' Ara said, coming surprisingly quickly to the point, 'but I wanted you to hear it from me.' Sy watched Ara meticulously wipe the corner of his mouth. 'I've signed Michael McLain. I didn't solicit him, I want you to know. He came to me.'

So that was it. The old Armenian *maricón* wanted to lord it over him. Sy leaned over towards Ara. '*You* know who I got in my stable. And, the way I see it, three queens beat a pair. Michael McLain for Lila Kyle isn't exactly the trade of the century. I wouldn't brag about it if I were you.'

'I'm not telling you to brag. I'm simply extending you the courtesy of hearing it from me.'

'I think you confuse me with someone who gives a shit,' Sy snapped. He stared into Ara's rheumy eyes.

'Let me tell you something, son,' Ara began. 'In this town, in this Industry, it's best to be nice to everyone. On your way up especially, because you might need them to be nice to you, on the way down.'

Sy watched Ara as he ministered to the drool on his mouth, then picked up a fork to begin to eat his salad. Sy's lunch was now grinding away at his intestines. How dare this old *maricón* give him advice! All the bile from his lunch with Crystal, from all the ass-kissing he'd had to do, rose into his throat. 'You fucking old has-been. Who the fuck are you?'

Sy saw Ara blink. Then the old man struggled visibly for control. 'Let me tell you a story, Sy.'

Sy held up one hand to hold off Ara for a moment, beckoning for a waiter at the same time with his other. The waiter was at the table in a second. 'Do something for me,' Sy said to the waiter.

'Listen to this pathetic old guy's story, will you? I have something more important to do.'

Sy stood up, walked passed the maître d's desk, stopped to sign his tab, then went through the open door out to the parking valet.

With all his aggravation that afternoon, it was just as well that he didn't see Neil Morelli, lurking near the entrance to the car park, his hand in his jacket pocket, holding an ominous bulge.

42

Marty DiGennaro, famous director, conqueror of the film world, recipient of four Oscars, winner of a contest of wills with Bob LeVine, television's new prince, the most powerful creative man in Hollywood, lay tied to the four corners of his bed, spread out as flat as a road map and naked as a newt. He strained at the silken tasselled cords that wrapped around the mahogany bedposts and doubled back over his wrists. The knots were neat half-hitches, he noticed and, absurdly, he wondered if Lila had been in the Girl Scouts. Back in Queens, he'd made it all the way to Eagle Scout. Classic nerd. He still knew how to tie clove hitches, square knots, and sheepshanks. In the dark, he pulled against the taut restraints and grinned. As an Eagle Scout back in New York, even in his wildest masturbatory fantasies, he'd never imagined this.

The first time Lila had tied him up, roping him to the bed, he'd been shocked, but not because he was a prude. It was just that she was so, so, well, *reluctant* to have sex at all that he assumed her to be, if not the virgin she claimed, then at least inexperienced. Or perhaps damaged in some way.

So, when she raised a perfectly arched eyebrow and slowly began to pull the silk rope out of an Hermès bag, he had been nonplussed. And, to be honest, turned off by the idea. He had, of course, done a little roleplaying – his ex-wife had liked spankings from time to time – and he'd had more than any man's fair share of kinky starlets who demanded everything from golden showers to letting their dog participate.

But being tied up himself, being vulnerable, immobilized, pinned to the bed, didn't seem desirable. Still, for Lila to suggest anything, to allow anything, was such a surprise that he had agreed. Without a smile or a giggle, with utmost concentration, she had wrapped his wrists and ankles in businesslike knots. Then she'd lowered the lights and left him alone, tied down.

The strangest thing to Marty was that *that* was when his erection began. There, powerless and naked in the dark, he felt the anticipatory tingling, the excitement that he hadn't felt since the old days at the Flushing Loew's movie house. He smiled at the unlikely association. So much in life – well at least in *his* life – had been more exciting in the anticipation than the acquisition. The movies he ran in his head were almost invariably better than the ones he made. He sighed. He supposed that was what made him so successful as a director.

But, once tied to the bed, he was the director of nothing. Lila had reemerged, her long hair loose and bright as a flame, even in the dimness. She wore a kind of corset or something – Marty didn't know exactly what to call it – a bronze-coloured bustier without cups. Her breasts, so full, so perfect, rode over the top of the thing, her waist even more compressed by the lacing. And she wore a matching lace G-string, a sort of high-cut triangle in the front, but when she turned around, all there was in the back was a silken cord that slid up between her perfect ass cheeks to hook on the bottom of the corset. Marty tried to take a breath, but it was hard; his chest hurt him so. Aside from a few blow jobs, he hadn't had sex with her, and he'd never seen her naked. Her incredible long legs, her perfect ass, her tits, so swollen, so round, so perfect, all moved him. His penis strained towards her, but it was the only appendage he could move.

'Pretty?' Lila asked.

'Beautiful,' he gasped.

'Want to touch?'

'Yes.' His hands pulled against the rope. 'Untie me,' he said.

'Oh, no. Where's the fun in that?' she asked, her voice husky. She sashayed over to him and bent from the waist until her right breast, her perfect right breast, just barely brushed his outstretched left hand. He tried to close his fingers around her softness, but with a smile she pulled away. 'Oh, no,' she said again. Her voice was a throaty whisper. 'First you have to kiss it.'

He smiled back at her. 'My pleasure,' he whispered. 'Untie me. Please.'

'Oh, no,' she demurred. Instead, she moved to the foot of the bed. Then, in a single graceful movement, she stood on the bed, over him, a foot planted on either side of his waist. He could feel her slim ankles against his hips. Looking up, he saw her breasts over him, her cool, perfect face, her hair hanging down like a velvety curtain. She straddled him, careful not to touch his swollen penis, and sat on his chest.

'Kiss it,' she told him, and slowly, ever so slowly, she lowered her breast towards him. Hungrily he strained his head up towards her, but the ropes held him firmly, and she stopped just short of his mouth.

'Say "please,"' she told him.

'Please,' he begged.

'Please what?' she asked.

'Please . . . please, may I kiss your breast?' His voice was a croak. His testicles felt as tight and as hard as summer plums in their skin. He groaned.

Lila smiled. She bent lower, her tiny coppery nipple suspended a half-inch above his pursed and open mouth. 'Here,' she said, and let the nipple just brush against his lips. It was hot as a flame against his dry tongue. He groaned again, her weight heavy on his chest.

'More,' he pleaded.

Then Lila slid off the bed and stood beside it. She lit a candle and in the flickering glow she stood, displaying her perfection. She was, he thought, the most exquisite woman ever created. Her flawless skin gleamed. Her hair, so thick, so glossy, so long, was like the tail of the most perfect thoroughbred. Her teeth, her eyes, her lips reflected back the light. Tears filled his eyes.

'Want to touch me?' she asked.

Marty could only nod.

Lila cupped both her long, slim hands under her full breasts. He could see the shapely nails of her perfect manicure sink into the milky flesh near her nipple. 'Want to touch me here?' she asked, a little breathless. He nodded again. She smiled, and slowly, ever so slowly, squeezed her breasts harder, lifting them up like offerings. Then, with thumb and forefingers, she pinched each nipple, first the left, then the right. She closed her eyes. 'Oooh,' she moaned. 'It feels so good. Do you want to do this?'

Marty couldn't even nod.

Lila ran her hands along her waist, down her thighs, up over her belly, touching, stroking, pinching her own flesh, while Marty lay there, powerless to do anything but watch, his penis engorged and throbbing, throbbing in a way he had never felt before. She turned her back towards him, and he felt a pang at losing sight of her wonderful tits, but Lila again began to run her own hands over her back and then down to her rounded, perfect ass, her fingers kneading her own flesh until he almost cried out that she must be bruising herself.

She turned to him. 'Do you want me to touch you?' she asked.

'Oh, yes. Please,' he said. She smiled, and slowly moved her lovely long hands towards him. Lightly as a butterfly, barely touching, she ran her fingers over his bony chest, then down to his flat belly. His penis twitched up at her. He could see a bead of clear liquid at its head. 'Yes,' he moaned, but her hands moved up, away, up to his chest, to his own nipples, then over his face, his eyes, across his mouth. He kissed her fingers then, and they stopped for a moment in their movement to explore his burning lips, his mouth, his tongue. Slowly, Lila inserted a finger into his mouth, and hungrily, eagerly, he sucked at it. Then another finger, and another, until his mouth was stuffed full of her hand. Gratefully, he held her in his mouth with his lips, his tongue, even his teeth. He held a part of her, but too soon, too soon, she withdrew and moved her hand again across his hairless chest, over to a nipple, which she idly tweaked with a fingernail, then drew her nails down, down, but once again past his loins, past his aching joint, not touching his straining testicles, down his thighs, raking his calves, not stopping until she was at the foot of the bed, holding his feet. Gently but firmly, she cupped his feet in her hands and then carefully, deliberately, she began to rub her breasts against them.

The heat shot through him like an electrical charge. His feet were connected, directly connected, to his penis. He'd never known that before. Through his bare soles he felt Lila's hard nipples moving back and forth. He strained again, uselessly, against the ropes that held him. He had never know such heights of sexual frenzy, of utter frustration. Hopelessly, he arched his feet against the heat and softness of her breast. And then he began to cry.

The sobs, small at first, began to rack him. He pulled against the cords and shook as the crying – deep, deep sobbing – welled up from somewhere in the very centre of him. Tears ran down from the sides of his eyes, wetting the sheet. He turned his head to one side, his silent sobs continuing.

And then Lila was on him, her face beside his, her hair cascading over his eyes, his nose, his mouth. 'Ooh, baby. Oooh, no. No, baby,' she crooned. She wiped his face with her silken hair. 'No, baby. No,' she said, gently as a loving mother, and kissed his lips, his eyelids, his still-wet cheeks. 'Here, here, baby,' she said, and lifted her heavy breast into Marty's mouth. 'Here. Here,' she told him. He suckled, too crazed, too frenzied to be embarrassed. And then she crouched over him, her back to him, and bent over his cock, her soft, hot, perfect mouth kissing him there, her hands stroking him, her fingers loving his balls, his ass, his cock. Through his tears he could see her move her G-string to the side, watched her as she mounted him, feeling the head of his penis push against her, into her. At last. At last. He was surprised but he was beyond questioning, beyond judgement, beyond words, and she was in control; she pressed her perfect flesh down onto him, impaling herself slowly, so slowly, on his throbbing dick. Moving up and down, using her knees, in an atavistic crouch, she slid up and down on his cock, whimpering.

Marty made no sound. But it felt as if his whole being, the whole universe, was centred in his loins, an inferno of pressure that pushed and throbbed into Lila's silky flesh. It was agony, and yet it was the best, absolutely the best that Marty had ever had. He came at last, and he sobbed as he did, gasping with each endless spasm, filling her to overflowing, emptying and cleansing himself.

And so it went. The ritual changed slightly, and it was only once a week, or maybe less, but each time Lila brought out the silken ropes, Marty was more and more inclined, more hungry, more grateful.

And it was strange. Because it wasn't worrying him that he was drawn into this utterly powerless, passive sex. Instead, he found it a huge relief. He realized that all his life had been spent striving to please demanding, difficult women. First his mother, then his professor, then his wife, and a host of beautiful, spoiled Hollywood actresses. He was, he knew, simply a small, skinny, bright, hard-working, overcompensating kid who had been trying to satisfy the goddesses' demands. At thirty-seven, he was still the strike-out kid from Queens, desperate to score, to please his lovers, to perform and be liked.

Now, with Lila, he was relieved of all the burden. The director finally became the directed. And the relief was so enormous that each and every time it brought tears to his eyes. He was no longer responsible for the timing, for the choreography, for the sexual etiquette. Lila chose to perform for him, to be in charge, and if that made her more comfortable, if she needed to be in control so as not to be frightened, it was more than fine with Marty. In fact, Marty was pathetically grateful. For once in his clever, hard-working, overcompensating life, Marty didn't have to work to please a woman. Lila pleased herself, and he took his pleasure like a precious gift.

Once again, he lay in the darkness, one of the most powerful men in the Industry, tied to the bed, flat as a roadmap, naked as a newt. Who would image this? Who, in this morass of climbing, backbiting Hollywood serpents, could picture the sex life of one of their most powerful directors and one of their most popular stars? Marty smiled in the darkness. Go know, he thought, and pulled against the tightness of the cords at his wrists and ankles.

43

Jahne lay in the circle of Sam's arms, alternately watching his face while he slept and the face of her watch. These moments were so precious to her, but, no matter how much time they spent together, she was left hungry, ravenous, for more. And soon, too soon, they'd have to be up, preparing for the difficult shoot on the beach.

This was what she had always wanted! And now, at last, it was hers. Sam loved her. She knew it! By his touch, by his gaze, and by the way he made love to her. His passion was so strong that both of them were dizzy, even exhausted by it. All she wanted was him, more of him. And all he needed was her. If only they weren't forced to work on this stupid film together.

He had told her how unsure of it he was. She comforted him. And she told him how afraid she was as well. They gave one another comfort. In bed together, nothing else mattered. The world went away.

Jahne sighed. Neither she nor Sam had said so out loud, but the film was not going well. Michael was almost impossible to deal with. During her big breakdown scene, he'd left his fly undone – an accident, he claimed – and the whole thing had had to be reshot the next day. That wasn't all. Jahne had seen the dailies, and she looked wooden. Beautiful, but wooden. Her new face didn't react in the same way as her old, and on a big screen it looked lovely but almost . . . bland. She'd have to learn to exaggerate her reactions, but it was already too late for the half of the script that was in the can. And it was exhausting to hold the youthful posture she'd created. She projected her chest always forward, her shoulders back; she stood swaybacked to give the illusion of youth. But it was agony to hold. And day after day, it drained her. Of course, Michael and his hammy performance didn't help. Every day was a torture. It was only this time, the time in the dark with Sam, that mattered; it was all she cared about.

After making love that first time in the dark, in her hotel suite, she had had to tell him about the scars. She had been frightened of his disgust or censure or even mere distaste. But he had only looked at her and asked, 'Don't you understand? I don't care about your looks. I don't care about that. I love *you*.' Then they'd made love again, even more hungrily than before. And she seemed to be fed by his words. 'I love *you*. Only *you*.'

And it seemed that he did. Each evening, they lost themselves in one another's arms, in one another's bodies. She kissed him all over, tears in her eyes, so happy to have his flesh returned to her. And he caressed every part of her, made love to her so completely, his love burning like a fever under his skin.

'I love you,' he murmured as he kissed her neck, her hair. 'I love you. I love you.' And she, Jahne, believed him as Mary Jane never had.

But what would happen if he found out the truth? She could never tell him now. Once, she'd planned all this as revenge. Now it seemed a punishment for her. She had everything she had ever wanted from him. Why was it, then, she wondered, as she watched his face and the clock's, why was it that she was so sad?

Michael McLain hated Northern California, he hated filming on location, he hated Sam, he hated April, he hated this script, and he hated this movie, which was a definite *pièce du merde*. Most of all, he hated Jahne Moore, and, he realized with a start of surprise, he hated acting. Not just acting in this dog-meat production, but in *any* production. Christ, it was foolish and wimpy and childish. It was boring. And if, at his level, it paid well, that had long become irrelevant, because he already had all the money he'd ever need.

Still, he couldn't give it up, because, aside from this, he couldn't think of anything else to do. What the fuck else was there? He'd always liked being a star and fucking beautiful women. But now both had become tiresome.

He was too young to retire, and business had never been interesting to him. Somehow, starting a popcorn or a spaghetti-sauce company, or, worse, opening a chain of restaurants, didn't seem attractive. Because, whatever his next venture would be, he knew two things about it: it would have to be on a grand scale, and he'd have to be number one.

Of course, one natural next step was directing and producing. Everyone wanted to direct. But Michael had tried it once, on *Cliffhanger*, and he didn't want to do it again. The pressure was crippling. You were number one, but only until the picture came out. Then they ate you alive.

He could try to pull off some kind of Sundance bullshit, but, let's face it: Redford had already done it, and Michael really didn't have that much interest in sitting around listening to asshole students from Chicago explain their views on 'the cinema'.

Politics was an option. But not if he had to do it on some local scale, like that putz Sonny Bono. National politics was far more intriguing. He'd done a lot of fund-raising, he was plugged into his party. But where was the niche? Senator? Could he beat the incumbent? And then wouldn't he just be one of all those senators?

'Ready for you, Mr. McLain!' one of the assistants called to him from outside the trailer. Michael clenched his fist, banging it down onto the table before him.

Christ, he thought. Sometimes life was so unfair! He was not only better-looking than Ronald Reagan had ever been, he was also a better actor. How come Ronnie had gotten the good part?

They were losing the light for the beach shot, and the crew was scrambling to beat the clouds. They could cheat, to a certain extent, with kliegs, but without that natural light the film came out looking like videotape. After trouble with a cable (don't mix electricity and water, something almost inevitable on a beach), and then trouble with a lens (don't mix sand and cameras, either), they were finally ready. It was a long panning shot, ending with a swooping close-up of an embrace and kiss. Jahne, jittery enough at the thought of the upcoming scene with Michael, felt just about crazy from the delays. Now, at last, they were ready.

She turned to Mai, to take her sweater and to replace it with the deceptively simple white shirt she would wear for the shot. Of course, the shirt was far from simple. It looked like a man's, was in fact supposed to be Michael's shirt that she'd put on for this walk after their lovemaking, but it was fashioned out of the finest cotton cambric, softer and more sheer than any man's shirt. And, to heighten its ability to reveal her, it was dampened, so that it turned semi-transparent, moulded itself to her breasts, and clung.

Jahne had wanted them to use the body double for this shot, but Sam had begged her to do it. 'It would be hard to fake convincingly, and your breasts *are* lovely,' he'd murmured, burying his face against them as they lay in bed. Jahne had argued, but he had prevailed. 'Trust me. The scars won't show.'

Now she turned to Mai, both for the shirt and for the reassurance that the old woman gave her. When it came to Jahne's appearance, Mai was the only one Jahne trusted. God knows how she could have made it through the filming if it hadn't been for Mai.

'It is all in the skin, my dear,' Mai told her. 'Notice how disappointing stars look in person?'

Jahne nodded. They had looked unspectacular.

'It is the skin. Always it is uneven. Splotchy. Or else makeup is obvious. But on the screen, makeup disappears. On the screen, more than anything, it is the flawless skin that creates the illusion of beauty. We must make you up to create the illusion.'

'Even my cleavage?'

'Especially your cleavage. We all like smooth. It is primal, infantile. The full breast. Not empty, withered dugs like these.' Mai patted her own chest and laughed.

But now, as she turned to the old woman, it was Mai's appearance that startled Jahne. God, Mai looked old! Her face was paper-white, and it seemed to Jahne that every line, each wrinkle was etched deeper than ever before. Is making this movie as awful for Mai as it is for me? Jahne wondered. 'Are you all right?' she asked.

'A headache,' Mai said, and winced, but that was all Jahne had time for before Joel hustled her out. The wardrobe mistress began misting her shirt some more, while the hairdresser sprayed some artfully tousled strands across her face.

'Watch out for my makeup,' Jerry Detria warned him. Jerry crossed his arms, his brush ready to correct any flaws. Jahne almost smiled. Jerry was so protective that, when he finished with her, he'd tell her to 'be careful of my face.' Now he looked her over minutely, nodding his approval, and Joel moved her to her place. Her stand-in, a nice woman named Dorothy, smiled and stepped out of the way. Jahne took her spot. Then she waited.

And waited. And waited. At last, after perspiration had begun to trickle down her side despite the cool wind whipping at her wet blouse, Michael stepped onto the set. Without a greeting, without even a look at her, he turned to the camera and the place where Sam was ensconced with the cinematographer and the best boy. 'Ready,' he told them, through tight lips.

There was another pause, and then: 'All right, ready, action.' There was a pause. 'Rolling!' Michael took her in his arms, and the long shot began, the camera circling them from a distance as they embraced, beginning the long dolly ending with her close-up. Michael nuzzled her neck. He smelled good, a vague mixture of English soap and some mild spice.

'Like it?' he asked, holding her tighter. It wasn't scripted; there was no dialogue in the scene, so they weren't miked. 'Like it?' he asked again.

To be polite, she made a 'mmmm' sound.

'I know you like it, you little slut. But do you like it better from Sam or from me?' Michael said, still hugging her tight, the camera moving in for her close-up, only to catch her face frozen in a grimace of distaste.

'Okay. Cut!' Sam yelled. He stepped from behind the cameras and lights. 'I know it's a lot to ask, Jahne,' he said, 'but can you *try* to act as if it's not disgusting to be held by that man?'

Jahne broke out of Michael's grasp. 'You ruined that shot!' she yelled at him.

'What did I do?' Michael asked, an exaggerated innocence playing on his face.

'Oh, Jesus! Would the two of you stop bickering?' Sam asked. 'We're losing the light! Jerry, could you fix her face? Laslo, we'll back it up and try once more. . . .' There was a loud murmur behind him, somewhere. It simply wasn't done when the director was issuing orders. 'Could I have your attention?' Sam asked, annoyed. But the noise didn't stop. It grew.

'Get the nurse. Someone call an ambulance!' Joel yelled. Jahne moved, along with everyone else, towards the ruckus. A group was already huddled near her chair. Because she was the star, or for some other reason, it parted for her and she moved through them, as if in a dream. At the centre of the group was a small clearing, where Dorothy, her stand-in, sat on the ground, Mai's head in her lap. Even from where she was standing, Jahne could see the thin stream of blood at the corner of Mai's mouth.

'Oh, God!' she cried, and crouched beside them. 'Get a doctor!' she screamed.

'It's too late,' Dorothy told her.

44

Sam entered the darkened bedroom quietly. Jahne lay, exhausted and sedated, asleep under the top sheet. Only her dark hair and one hand were exposed, her hand flung over her head and now lying limp and all but lifeless on the pillow, an abandoned leaf. The room had become too warm, almost stuffy, since he and the doctor had put her to bed and turned up the thermostat to help stop her shivering. Now he turned it down a bit and went to check on her. Jesus, he didn't need this! Another delay. April was already on his back. How soon could he expect Jahne to recuperate? And why was she taking the death of the old lady so hard? She was a very sensitive girl. Gently he lifted the sheet away from her face. Jahne was so pale she was almost luminous, dewed with a light film of perspiration. He carefully lowered the sheet. She was bare, and he pulled the cover down as far as her waist. Jahne murmured, moved her head to the left, but continued sleeping heavily.

Standing beside the bed, he watched her. She was so beautiful to look at. Her perfect face was partly obscured by her hair, but her neck, her arms, and her breasts were revealed to him. From this angle, he could not see the slight scars on the underside of them. She looked perfect, but, beautiful as she was, she reminded him of nothing so much as a wounded bird – his dove.

Sam felt a stirring in his chest and and in his groin. He knew that he had never felt this before. There had been women – lots of women – that he had felt desire for, and he had felt a tenderness this strong for Mary Jane, back in New York. But now, for Jahne Moore he felt a welling up of tenderness that almost brought tears to his eyes, along with a desire so intense that even now he felt a tug at his crotch. Unlike April, Jahne was beautiful *and* vulnerable. Unlike Mary Jane, Jahne was vulnerable *and* beautiful. How had it happened that he was finally granted this woman?

And now, after the death of Mai, Jahne needed him.

He slipped out of his jeans and into the bed beside her. He would hold her until she woke up. What could be more comforting after a shock than that? He would hold her and comfort her for as long as she needed it. To hell with the shooting schedule.

Her body was voluptuously warm against his. He put his chest to her back and fitted his body to hers so that they curved against one another like two spoons in a drawer. She fitted him perfectly, and he felt a wave of such tenderness, mixed with such passion, that he couldn't resist putting an arm around her and cupping her left breast in his hand. The heaviness of her flesh and her unconsciousness made the moment intensely erotic and private. He felt almost as if he could possess her more now than he ever had. He also felt his erection bump up against the soft curve of Jahne's buttocks.

Perhaps she felt it, too, for she stirred a little and murmured in her sleep. Oh, how he longed to enter her now, to lie beside her, inside her, until she woke. But was that for her or for him? Wasn't it selfish, even masturbatory, to consider it at a time like this? He wasn't the kind of man who had ever enjoyed taking advantage of a drunken date. He didn't like them passive. But, somehow, his feelings for Jahne were so strong, and at the same time so insecure, that the more often he had her the less he actually felt he possessed her. The public, the media, the Industry owned her. Would she leave him, in the end, the way the other beauties had left him. Was she gone when the picture wrapped?

He pulled her closer against him. This time, in this relationship, he felt her warmth, he felt her sincerity. Was it because he had gotten her while she was young and inexperienced? But what would time and fame do? She was hot, and this film would probably make her hotter. She could negotiate any deal she wanted. She could also take any man she wanted. Would she keep wanting him, or was this merely an adventure? And was she old enough to know?

He ran his hand along the sensuous curve of her side, letting it rest on her hip. His hand was trembling, so filled with desire that it seemed to have taken on a life of its own. It ran over the smooth skin of her behind, and then slipped between her legs. He buried his fingers in her pubic hair and cupped her sex in his hand. Holding her there, his palm at the mouth of her femaleness, both soothed and further aroused him.

Then he felt her wake. 'Oh, Sam!' she breathed, her voice thick with sorrow, sleep, and drugs. He nuzzled into her neck and kissed her there. He felt her move her head. Was it towards his caress or away?

'Oh, Sam! Mai. She's dead, Sam. I'm all alone again.'

His own voice seemed husky with his restrained lust. 'You're not alone. I'm with you now. I'm with you, and I'll never leave you.' He rose on his elbows and covered her mouth with his own. She tasted of tears, and the metallic tang of the sedative. He couldn't bear to take his mouth off hers, or to wait a minute more. He'd never felt this for a woman, any woman, ever. He could hardly stand it. He spread her legs and entered her swiftly, then held still, his body shielding hers.

'I'll never leave you,' he promised.

45

'I can't believe she just disappeared!' Sharleen said to Dobe. 'I mean, I just can't.' Sharleen was seated at the redwood picnic table in her backyard. Flora Lee's letter was before her. She looked up. Dobe was preparing to barbecue ribs. Sharleen watched as he turned a slab of ribs over in the marinade with the long-handled fork. Then he sat down at the table opposite Sharleen.

'It's for the best, Sharleen,' he told her, his voice serious and low. 'We had a long talk. She was ashamed of what she was, and of being a burden on you. She thought this was best.'

Sharleen shook her head, indicating that Dobe shouldn't speak in front of her brother. 'I don't know what he'll think,' she said softly to Dobe. Dean was sitting on the grass, tossing balls, to the dogs, who chased them across the lawn. Oprah sat upright at Dean's side, unmoving.

Sharleen smiled at the picture Dean and the little herd of dogs made, then looked at Dobe. 'We're goin' to miss her, Dobe,' she said.

'I ain't,' Dean said, not looking at anyone. 'Not Flora Lee. *She* wasn't my momma. I'd know Momma in a Texas minute, and that weren't her.'

'What makes you say that, Dean?' Dobe asked.

''Cause of the way she smelled. Like my daddy used to. But Momma, she used to smell different than him. All sweet, like clean laundry.'

Sharleen knew that in a way Dean was right. Their momma *had* always smelled good. She remembered it, too. Momma was always washing herself, her clothes, her hair. Sharleen remembered how she used to brush her momma's hair, after it was washed, for what seemed like hours, and her momma would nod off to sleep while Sharleen brushed.

'No,' Dean said, 'I'm glad Flora Lee's gone. Now I can go back to rememberin' my momma. That was better than having Flora Lee here.' He stood up, and all four dogs jumped to follow him. 'I'm goin' to do their tricks one more time with them, make sure they got it right, then I'm goin' to come back and show you all. All four of them. How much longer for the ribs, Dobe?' Dean grinned. 'I could eat a calf and a half.'

'You got time enough to play with the dogs. But the hot dogs is done. Help yourself. They'll hold you for a while.'

They watched Dean walk away, the dogs bounding around him, each trying to get the hot-dog bits that Dean began tossing at them.

'I'm surprised he said that, Dobe. I guess most folks would say Dean is simple, but it seems to me he gets most things right. Still, I feel scared about Flora Lee. Should we do somethin'?'

'Sharleen, I'm here to tell you some home truths, unless you don't care to hear 'em.'

Sharleen looked at him silently, then visibly took a breath, but said nothing.

'Sharleen,' Dobe continued, 'your momma, who *ain't* your momma anyhow, is – excuse my language now – nothin' but a whore, and maybe a little bit worse.'

Sharleen winced, but she continued sitting, silent and still, except for a tear that flooded over her lower left eyelid and began a slow course down her cheek. 'I don't say this to hurt you, girl. I say it to clean out an infected wound. I know it pains you, but you gotta know.'

'Didn't you think I did?' Sharleen asked quietly.

Shamed, Dobe looked away. He had underestimated her. 'I had to be sure you knew. 'Cause she's gone away and she won't be back. She's taken care of — least as well as she can be, till someone puts an end to her, or she puts an end to herself. And there ain't nothin' you can do to change that, Sharleen. Not one damn thing.'

'I know that, too,' Sharleen said. 'I watched my daddy dyin' for years. But Momma — Flora Lee — well, maybe she wasn't my blood kin. But she was good to me. And she is my family.'

'Family ain't what you inherit, girl, it's what you make with those you love who love you back.'

Sharleen thought about that for a while as the ribs sizzled on the grill. 'I wanted to be a good daughter,' she said. 'Maybe, if I'd done better, she could have . . .'

'Ain't no one can be a good daughter to a bad mother,' Dobe interrupted. There was silence between them for a long while.

'I'll tell you what's funny,' Sharleen said. 'Seems like I lost my real mother early but I was given Flora Lee. She *was* a good stepmomma, Dobe. Honest she was. She treated me good as her own child. Never made no difference between me and Dean. I never blamed her for leavin'. My daddy would have killed her. But I did sorely miss her, all them years. Then we found her. And here's the funny thing: I missed my momma most, right here in L.A., after she came to us. It was like I'd lost not only her but her good memory, too.'

'I know how that can be, Sharleen,' Dobe said. 'I was married once.' He stepped away from the grill, wincing at the smoke. 'Sharleen,' he said, 'I want to give you this.' He handed her a key.

'What is it to?'

'A safety-deposit box at California Central Bank. It has important papers there. Papers from your momma. I want you to have the key for safe keeping. Go look at 'em someday.'

The phone rang inside. 'I'll get it,' Dean said, and jumped up. He returned with a portable phone, and handed it to Sharleen. 'It's Mr. Ortis,' he said. Dean made it his job to answer the phone, to make sure Sharleen didn't get any of them dirty calls.

'Hey, Mr. Ortis. What're you doin' workin' on Sunday afternoon?' But Sharleen knew that Mr. Ortis always worked, and always called her with more work for her to do. Sharleen listened to his excited voice.

'I'm not doing it no more,' she insisted. 'No more albums. It ain't right. It ain't me singing, no matter what you say. No. No. I mean it.' She hung up the phone.

Dobe raised his eyebrows as she'd raised her voice. 'Another problem, Sharleen? Sounds as if you do got a lot of troubles.' His eyes wrinkled in a smile. 'It's 'cause you're such an important person.'

'It's a good thing you know me, Dobe. 'Cause sometimes I begin to wonder about that. But then I look at you or Dean, and I know. I'm just regular folk.'

'Well, it seems you're folk that can sing.'

'Dobe, I ain't kiddin'. I *can't* sing.'

'Well, you could have fooled me. I heard that record. They're playin' it on the radio night and day, and, Sharleen, you *can* sing, girl.'

'That's just it, Dobe. That don't even sound like me. Sy says they can fix your voice with all that technology they got. I mean, you sing any old way, but they can do lots of things with all that stuff, make you sound different. But I think they just called in another girl. One who can sing but ain't famous like me. Somehow, it don't seem fair, do it?'

Dobe chuckled, then looked at her troubled face and shook his head while he took the ribs off the grill. 'Ever hear of con games, Sharleen? Almost anyone can play 'em.'

46

'Miss Irons?'

If she heard her name one more time today, she would cut someone's throat. She answered the steward without looking up from her notes. 'What?'

'The captain asked me to tell you we'll be landing in Oakland in fifteen minutes. Is there anything I can get for you?'

'No,' she snapped. 'Just make sure my car is waiting.'

'I've already called ahead. It'll be on the apron as you deplane.'

April waved the steward away, made a few last entries on the page, and closed the leather-bound book. She looked around the cabin of the Cessna Citation to the only other person on board and beckoned to her. The woman came immediately and stood beside April. 'Yes?' she said, simply. No 'Miss Irons,' April noticed. At least this one was learning. 'Did you get him?'

'No. I left three messages that you wanted to speak to him, but he hasn't returned your calls. His secretary said Mr. Shields was working on a scene with Miss Moore and wasn't to be disturbed.'

'Does he know I'm coming?'

'Yes, since yesterday.'

April shook her head, then handed her secretary the notebook and snapped, 'Type this. I want it by the time we get to the set.' She watched the woman move forward, sit down at the word processor, and begin to type. A hundred words per minute, but what the fuck was her name? she thought. April had been through three or four of these bitches in six months and couldn't remember one from another. A thousand bucks a week to type and place phone calls, and they couldn't take the heat. Not one of them. Well, the next one's going to be a man, she told herself. Like the old queen Samuel Mayer had. In his fifties, on top of everything, and loyal to a fault. Except they don't make executive assistants like that anymore.

April looked down onto the Pacific coastline, and saw the waves pounding the nearly empty beaches. Somewhere down there, on one of those beaches, was the cast and crew of *Birth of a Star*. Fucked up and out of control. All of them, bending under the pressure.

Michael had been whining to her on the phone all week. 'I'm not going to take a dive on this one, April. I can't even get to see the dailies. No one can, for the last three weeks. Sam has that flunky kid leaving the set every night with them and a fucking security guard. They've started to call the kid "Tsar of All the Rushes," security's so tight.'

She knew that. Sam had stopped sending them to her, too. And she was the fucking producer! 'What's your read on this, Michael?' she had asked.

'What's *my* read? Jesus Christ, April, you have a director just out of the gate who's taking a week to set up a two-character beach scene – the fucking beach is *already there*, and he's three weeks behind schedule. *And* over-budget. Performances suck, morale is worse. And *no one* gets to see the dailies. Plus, he's holed up all the time with the dumb bitch. What's that tell you? If this film goes down the tubes, I'm fucked!'

Everything had gone wrong. Michael fucking Jahne. Sam fucking me. Sam fucking Jahne. Michael giving it to Sam for fucking Jahne. Christ, they were all skittish. Michael was the bankable star; the movie rode on his back. Also, he had to be asking himself, Is this my last romantic lead, or only my second to last, or third to last?

And Jahne Moore, nervous as a cat. Well, of course. Her *first* film. Would the transition from the little box to the silver screen work? April had seen personal lives fuck up her deals before, from the Julia Roberts-Kiefer Sutherland breakup to getting caught with a Madonna-Sean Penn deal on the table. But she'd never had a film where the female costar had fucked the male lead *and* the director. And certainly not when she, April, had *also* been fucking the director.

She gritted her teeth. Sam Shields and she had come to an understanding: she had forgiven the dalliance with Crystal Plenum, but before she signed him to direct this turkey, she had made it clear that from that point on she expected loyalty and continuity.

Now the shmuck was sleeping with Jahne Moore, and April would lose face. Not to mention money. Sam had dipped his wick and lost control. Control of himself, the crew, the project, the budget.

April was coming to fix all that. Everyone would be punished.

The plane banked to the right, and the seat-belt sign came on. April noticed that her secretary fastened hers but kept typing. Now, if she could just get that kind of work out of the artistic assholes she was on her way to see, she'd have a movie. Maybe not a box-office smash, but at least respectable return on investment.

They taxied to a stop outside the private terminal. April stood up, smoothed her skirt, and motioned for her secretary to pick up her briefcase. She walked down the lowered steps to see the black stretch limo pulling up. The back door opened, and a young man stepped out, holding the door for her. It wasn't Sam. She couldn't believe it. April strode over to the door and looked at him. He smiled, a light mist of perspiration forming on his upper lip. 'Good afternoon, Miss Irons,' he said, as she was about to lean forward and step into the car.

When he made a move to follow her into the back seat, she paused, turned, and looked him over from head to toe. 'Who the fuck are you?' she snarled.

The skinny kid jumped back. 'Joel Grossman, Miss Irons.' He spoke quickly. 'Sam's assistant director, Miss Irons. We met in L.A. I mean, I was at the meeting when Sam hired me and I saw you, Miss Irons.'

This was as good a place as any to start meting out the punishment, she thought. 'What do you keep saying my name for? Afraid you're going to forget it?' She ducked into the car and sat, not moving over to make room for him.

'May I join you, Miss ... I mean, do you want me to ride in the front?'

'Am *I* supposed to move?' she asked. He didn't answer. Instead, he closed her door and ran around to get in the other side. The secretary got in the front, next to the driver.

'Okay,' she said, when he'd got in and closed the door, not looking at him. 'What are the problems, and what are the solutions? In twenty-five words or less.'

'No problems, no problems,' he hurried to explain. 'We're just a little bit behind because of the weather. Other than that ...'

'You got ten more words left. Better talk to me straight.' *Just as I thought. This asshole is going to try to make a fool out of me.*

'Well, Miss Irons,' he said, really getting into it now, 'you know what an artist Sam is. Everything has to be perfect. In that way, he's a lot like Oliver Stone — he's dragging it out of himself, relying on personal experience....'

Oliver Stone! Why not quote Oliver Hardy? She held up her hand. 'Just tell me one thing. Was it your idea for you to meet me today, or was it Sam's?'

The kid's face dropped. 'It was, uh, Sam's, Miss Irons.'

She flicked the switch on the intercom to the driver. 'Pull over. Right now.'

The long black car came to a quick halt on the shoulder of the highway back to town. April turned to the kid. 'Get out,' she said, looking into his eyes. 'And tell Sam he should never send a boy to do a man's job.'

'But, Miss Irons, we're on a highway! It's three, four miles to the next exit.' She saw his lower lip begin to quiver.

'You're an AD. Be resourceful. Now get the fuck out of this

608

car,' she told him. She hated it when they made her have to do this. But, goddamn it, I got forty million bucks riding on my ass, she reminded herself, and this little shithead is going to fuck with my head? 'Out!' she repeated.

Joel stumbled out, his face imploring her.

'Shut the goddamned door. I'm in a hurry.'

The set on the otherwise deserted beach was chaotic. Goddammit, the set costs were astronomical. And what for? They were shooting the ocean, not some dotty Ferdinando Scarfiotti folly. Klieg lights were on all over, but no cameras were running. How much was *that* costing her? Another indication that this film was getting away from Sam. If he couldn't keep the crew running smoothly, he wasn't going to be able to make a film.

Where was he? Busy playing with Jahne Moore's clit? The movie was the only important thing right now, she reminded herself. Not Sam, not who was fucking who. Just the movie, and her forty mil. Well, not *hers*, but gotten on her name from the sons-of-bitches at American National Bank and Trust. She thought of Sam, wasting her money and gritted her teeth again. She would *never* allow her credibility to be undermined by *anyone*, whether she was fucking him or not.

She sat in the car for a few minutes, waiting for the location manager to notice the only goddamned limousine on the beach and come to her. Finally, he did. 'Get Sam,' she spat through the open window, then rolled it up in his face as the old guy started talking.

Another ten minutes; then Sam knocked on the door. This was the part she hated the most – wiping asses. She didn't mind it so much with actors. They approached life events as if they were movie roles. They were like troublesome children. But directors – they believed that *life* was a fucking movie. 'Get in,' she said, not bothering with preliminaries. 'I haven't been getting dailies lately, and you haven't returned my calls.' She watched as Sam brought back his head and stared for a moment at the ceiling of the car. 'No bullshit, now, Sam. I mean it.'

Sam began to shake his head. 'I don't know, April. It's just not coming together.'

'Well, *make* it come together,' she snapped, forcing herself not to speak through clenched teeth. 'If I had been getting the dailies, I might have been able to help you sooner.' And saved us all time

609

and money, for chrissakes. 'Why haven't you been sending me the dailies?'

Sam put his intense look on, the artistic-fucking-New York-theatre-turned-Hollywood-director look that she was beginning to despise. They forget that this is a *business*. The *movie* business. It's not art. It's money. 'Jahne's not coming across on the screen. I've been working with her – really hard – and she puts out a lot of energy, but . . .'

April dropped the sympathetic-ear shit. 'I already know she puts out. If you can get her to do that, then, goddamn it, get her to come across.'

'April, don't think I don't have total commitment to this project. Jahne and I . . .'

'Let's get this straight. I'm your producer, no matter how well we fuck. Do you get that? I'm your *boss*, and right now I don't give a shit what you do with your dick except when it interferes with my money. Your spot in bed can be filled with just a phone call. So don't talk to me about total commitment. You know, when Barbet Schroeder's movie was about to go into turnaround at Cannon, he showed up at his boss's office and threatened to cut off a finger with a jigsaw. They let him continue. Are *you* that committed? Me, I'd *help* you cut off body parts, and not just fingers. As your boss, I'm telling you that your job and your future can be taken care of that easily too. So don't get confused. You're working now. For me.' She allowed her voice to return to normal. 'Why are you three weeks behind schedule and two point six over budget?'

'Mostly the weather. We haven't had sun in seven days. I was hoping we'd get some sun this afternoon, but it doesn't look like it.'

'Then what?'

'Then . . .' Sam shrugged his shoulders.

April felt like choking him. He had no plan B? Why had she let him talk her into filming this on location? 'You wanted to play God, so you became a movie director. But this isn't a stage, Mr. Off-Broadway. This is the movies – the great outdoors. So, when you can't shoot outside, shoot interiors. Christ, do I have to tell you *everything*? Okay, make sun. You have fucking kliegs on, and you're not even shooting. You're over budget and you're going to tell me about *sunlight*?'

'Wait, it's not only that. Michael's been giving me a lot of shit. He's playing temperamental.'

'You're fucking his snatch. What the hell do you expect?'

'Jahne and I . . .'

'I told you, *I don't give a fuck*. Except it's costing *me* money. Now, what's the holdup on shooting this beach scene? It's James and Judy walking on the beach together, the next-to-last scene in the movie. What's the *problem*?'

'Michael is only five four.'

'So was Alan Ladd. So what?'

'But Jahne is five six. Plus heels. Plus hair.'

'Yeah, so?'

'Well, we needed time to come up with a solution that would allow us to shoot long shots front and rear. We finally got it. We had a ramp built the length of the beach. I think it's going to work.'

'I'll go you one better, Sam. It had fucking *better* work, because all you've got is tomorrow.' She pointed to the door, dismissing him. 'I'll be here at six in the morning, rain or fucking shine, Sam.' She paused, turned to him, and looked him in the eye. 'Oh, and Sam: another thing. You had best show up in my hotel room tonight. I don't care if you can't get it up, but I won't be left looking as if you prefer some television starlet to me.'

On the way back to the hotel, she laid her head on the cushioned headrest. Another migraine. The doctor said it was stress-related. Fucking shmuck. *Life* is stress-related. She wondered for the millionth time why she hadn't picked Bo Goldman for the project right after he came off *Scent of A Woman*. She had barely got into the hotel room when the phone began ringing.

'April, I heard you were on the set, but you didn't come to see me.' It was Michael. This one was hurt Michael. Well, *you* didn't come to see *me*, she thought. And *I* sign the cheques. Instead, she just sighed.

'I have a lot on my mind, Michael. And a major migraine. I had to get back here and lie down.'

'Migraine? I know an ancient Chinese cure for migraines. Want me to come over and show it to you?' His voice was syrupy.

'This is a forty-million-dollar headache, Michael. I don't think the ancient Chinese had a cure for anything that expensive. I'll see you on the set in the morning. That's six A.M., Michael. We're doing that scene, sun or no sun.' She thought of the six million bucks he was getting for this and gritted her teeth again.

'Of course I'll be there. I've been there every day, ready, willing,

611

and able.' His voice dropped, sexy. 'But, hey, April, this is *Michael*. I can cure *anything*. And I happen to be free tonight.'

'You've *never* been free,' she said, and hung up.

The next morning, April was on the set before Michael, Sam, or Jahne. She spoke to the lighting director, who then pulled in more lights, and had reflector boards positioned around the beach. Sam was the first one on the set. 'I see you've taken to directing?' he said.

'You sound surprised, Sam. As if it's a rare talent or something.' She turned to him before he could respond. 'Let me put it straight to you. You're not doing your job, so someone's got to do it. Either you do what I tell you today, or I'm going to get someone who will. Do you understand me?' He paled, nodded, and began to walk away.

'And, Sam,' she said, still not finished with him. 'What's with Jahne and all that makeup on her legs? Is she trying to cover leprosy, for chrissakes?' She saw Sam look over at Jahne's trailer, where the actress was walking towards them, her leg makeup thicker by inches than the rest of the body makeup.

'She's nervous about this scene. She wants to look right, so I gave her permission to do the makeup her way. I think it calls for it.'

'I hope you're right, Sam. That one's a judgement call. And you're being paid for your judgement. I just hope that's not your dick talking.'

Michael was walking quickly towards them, his hands thrust deep into the pockets of his robe. April braced herself, but she was in no mood for his bullshit today. If he didn't like getting turned down last night, fuck him.

'What's the look for, Michael? You've got a face like a man who's found out he has something that can't be cured.' Let *him* start off on the defensive, she thought.

Michael ignored her, and walked up to Sam. 'What the fuck is that?' he asked, indicating the length of wooden boards running along the beach. 'Is that a fucking ramp?'

'Yes, Michael. It's the best way we could compensate for Jahne's excessive height.' April could see Sam sweat. Pussy. He'd never manage Michael *that* way.

'I'm not walking on any fucking ramp. You can forget about it.'

'We got the lighting just right, the crew and cast is ready to go. I want this scene shot today, Michael. We've lost too much time on it as it is.' April had moved to stand next to Sam in front of Michael.

'Fuck you,' Michael said, turning his attention to her for the first time today. '*I'm* the one that's carrying this dog on my back. And I'm not going to lose my dignity by subjecting myself to walking on any fucking ramp.'

April had a movie to make, and investors, and a forty-million-dollar budget that was getting out of hand. 'But, Michael, how do we do the long shots?'

He took a couple of steps back towards his trailer, then turned and looked at them. 'Dig the bitch a trench!'

47

Jahne sat in her trailer, waiting to be called for next take, writing to Dr. Moore. Because, after all, she had no one else to explain anything to. Mai's death had hit her harder than she could have imagined it would. She wasn't sleeping, and the resulting bags and swollenness were making photography a nightmare. And her almost constant crying wasn't helping.

> I know you're going to think that you told me so, but even if you did . . .

She paused. She had everything she'd ever wanted. A great career and the man she loved. But did she? It was still hard for her to believe that she had Sam now, again. That he loved her, held her, wanted her. She still felt his hands run over her body, caressing it. His mouth against hers, on her neck, her breasts, her shoulders, her belly and lower, even lower.

> He loves me, but it doesn't feel like I'm there. Or maybe it's more that he's not. When he touches my face, it's not *my* face. Well, what I mean is of course it's my face, but it's not the face I had before, when he didn't love me.

In a way, it felt as if each caress were a blow. Each time Sam stroked her face, he might as well have slapped it. Each time he traced her profile with a loving finger and marvelled at her perfection, she trembled under his hand as if he wielded a weapon. How could it be? she asked herself over and over. He *is* what I want. He is what I *always* wanted, and now I have him. At last, I am loved.

But, somehow, some part of her couldn't take the love he so openly offered. It was clear to her that Sam adored her. She saw, firsthand now, what she used to observe other women receiving. She remembered her New York friends Chuck and Molly, and how Chuck had been almost sick with love for Mol. She thought of all the pretty girls, the actresses and dancers she had known, and their ardent lovers, men who followed their women with hungry eyes, who seemed drawn to them like pins to a magnet, doting. And she remembered her envy, and how bitter it felt to know that she would never be in their sorority, that she had never inspired, and would never inspire, that kind of passion.

She thought, then, of Neil. Mary Jane's one conquest. Yet his desire had shamed her – even sickened her, in a way. She felt that he had only loved her out of desperation and loneliness. He had so few other options that being 'chosen' by Neil had felt to her like a condemnation, not a compliment. It was official acceptance into the Losers' Society. It was admitting that not only were you unlovely but you accepted the fact and would lie to yourself as you settled for another such as yourself, another awkward, funny-looking, unlovely person. Your lie would be that you truly loved one another, but the truth was that you had run out of choices, time, and hope.

But was that perception true? Or had it come from her own self-hate? Hadn't Neil been the man who truly knew her, who really approved of her? Who accepted her true self? *She* had been the snob, she had been the one afraid of a plain mate.

She had escaped that fate, she told herself fiercely. Mary Jane, that unlovely lump of a woman, was dead, and Jahne Moore should now lie beautifully, gracefully, beside her handsome, lanky, successful lover and luxuriate in his caresses. She was one of life's winners now, and if she had had to purchase the spoils, they still belonged to her, the victor. The past was dead, the present could be delightful, and the future even more promising. Why did it all feel so empty? She just had to get over Mai's death and her own morbid attitudes.

There was no doubt in her mind that she was having a breakdown of some sort. Too bad she couldn't do it in the privacy of her own home. Now over two hundred people depended on her mood, her looks, how she'd slept the night before. This morning, Jerry, in desperation, had daubed Preparation H under her eyes to reduce the swelling. Every one of her pores was discussed and examined, like NASA scientists studied moon craters. And Sam depended on her ability to concentrate, to emote. But she couldn't do it, for chrissake. She seemed almost paralyzed, split into two or more selves. Was this schizophrenia? Or, for a person who had been, still was, two people, was it normal? And what was any normal person's reaction to the pressures she was under?

Each night, when Sam made love to her, she'd cry. At first, he was touched, and tears came into his own eyes. But it had been over a week now, and her tears continued. Lovemaking, the only thing she had found comfort and release in, had become a nightmare of tears.

And Michael was making each take an absolute nightmare. It was becoming almost impossible to stand on her mark beside him, let alone act as if she worshipped him. She despised him. She'd never seen a man be so petty about a rejection. Of course, she reminded herself, she'd never had the luxury of rejecting a handsome man before. But his nastiness was way out of proportion. After all, it was *he* who had deceived *her*, *he* who had not told *her* about Sharleen, or Lila. Why should *he* hate *her*? He'd cheated on her, dropped her, and insulted *her*. Why had he been surprised by *her* slap?

Well, whatever his reason for hating her, he did, and it was scary. He did small things to trip her up, odd line readings that threw her off her cue, movements that prevented her from hitting her mark. And now that she was so fragile; now, since Mai's death, he was even more heartless. This morning, he had called her a 'puffball,' alluding to her swollen face.

But the scariest thing of all was this feeling she'd get with Sam. When he looked at her, when he'd reach out and stroke her. She'd look at his face – the very look she had longed for, that look of adoration, of love – and she'd feel . . . jealous. Then the tears would begin. It was crazy. She'd feel jealous of Sam's feelings for her, Jahne. Because now that she, Jahne, had his love, she still wanted it for Mary Jane.

God, it was crazy. Had Mai's death unleashed all this, or was it the pressure of the shoot, or was it the affair itself? Oh, God, whatever it was, it wouldn't let her sleep at night, wouldn't let her relax. It left her so tired that she could barely concentrate.

Jerry, her makeup man, was sitting in the alcove by the mirror, smoking a cigarette and waiting to do what he could for her. She put down the pen and picked up another Mounds bar. She had begun to have a craving for candy: this after almost four years of going without any desserts or sugar. But the craving was irresistible. Each bite seemed a comfort. Until, of course, she tried to struggle into one of the costumes that Mai had worked so hard on and found the zipper stuck. She knew she'd gained at least five pounds. It shouldn't matter – it wouldn't matter in normal life – but the camera was merciless, and every bulge, even the smallest, would show.

Mai had worked so hard on each piece, perfecting the lines of every one, camouflaging the tiniest imperfections. Now, Jahne realized she was ruining Mai's last work. Was she doing it because she was angry at Mai for dying? Or because she was so desperate for comfort? Whatever the reason, she was driving both Wardrobe and herself crazy.

She finished the last bit of the Mounds bar and licked the dark chocolate off her fingers. She picked up the letter to Brewster again.

> I've been so tempted to tell Sam everything, but I don't know that it would improve anything for me, and it might make things worse. I suppose what I want is not a change in Sam's present behaviour but a change in his past. I want him to have loved me then like he loves me now.
> Too bad you couldn't do surgery on the inside of me as successfully as you did on the outside.

Oh, it was impossible! Jahne crumpled up the letter, threw it in the wastebasket along with the envelope from Dr. Moore's last note. She'd write to him later, when it made more sense, when *she* made more sense.

There was a knock from outside the trailer. 'They're ready, Miss Moore,' Joel's annoying little voice called. Jahne walked out to Jerry.

'I'm ready for my close-up, Mr. DeMille,' she told him grimly.

Minos Paige stood outside the trailer. He was wearing a dark-blue jumpsuit. Over the left-hand pocket it read 'Cinema Sanitation' in orange chain stitch. He waited until Jahne Moore was called to the shoot, then knocked politely on the trailer door. 'Sanitation,' he said. 'Can I vacuum up now?'

The makeup guy let him in. Minos carefully began to Hoover down the rug, then wiped all the visible surfaces of the trailer. The silly-ass makeup pouf sat there the whole time. So Minos just emptied the wastepaper basket into his big plastic garbage bag and walked out the door.

Later, in the van, he had the time to go through the rumpled tissues, the candy wrappers, the unpleasant flotsam and distasteful jetsam, until he found the gold: the envelope, postmarked New York, return address Dr. Brewster Moore.

48

Lila snapped up the phone on the first ring. For the new season of *3/4*, she had not only snagged the lead, she had a new trailer with three phone lines. Phones that, unfortunately, never stopped ringing.

'Miss Kyle, I'm sorry to bother you, but you got a visitor out here.' It was Security, at the front gate of the lot.

She waited. 'And I'm supposed to guess who it is, right?'

'Oh, no, ma'am ... It's Minos Paige ... I woulda gone through your secretary, only the guy says I should call you direct. Seeing as how I seen him around before, I figured it was all right. I mean, he ain't no fan or wacko, you know? He says he got business ...'

'Send him to me,' she said, and slammed down the phone. She held her hand on it for a moment, trying not to get too excited. Paige knew not to come to the studio unless he had something really big. Otherwise, he was to send his reports to her at home. Lila sat down at the vanity table and began to brush her hair – long, slow strokes. She started to braid it, changed her mind, and disentangled it again, then resumed the methodical brushing.

'Yes,' she said to the knock on the door, and turned to face it when Minos walked in. He waved a manila envelope in his hand, and smiled. 'It took you long enough,' she said.

Minos dropped his hand and the smile. 'It's only been a little over a month, Miss Kyle.'

'I mean from the front gate. What did you do, go on the studio tour?' She held out her hand for the envelope, but Minos turned and sat down without being asked, holding the envelope on his lap. Okay, we're going to play some games now, Lila thought. She was in no mood, but thought again of the possible contents and smiled. Officially, she would be judged for the Emmy by last season's performances, but she knew everyone would see the new show before voting. And now, if there was some juicy stuff to take some of the shine off the other two . . . 'It's been a very long day, Mr. Paige. You must forgive me. Would you care for something to drink? Coffee? Perrier?'

'No, thank you. I figured you'd want to hear all this in person, so that's why I came to the studio. Don't worry. I haven't worked this lot in a while, so not very many people would recognize me. So few old-timers left.' He settled himself more comfortably in the chair.

This is where I get the bit about how hard he had to work, and how his fee barely covers it, Lila thought. Well, he better have something, or else this creep is out on his ass for wasting my time. Lila leaned forward, her elbows on her crossed legs. 'What have you got?' she asked, still smiling.

Minos smiled back, evidently very pleased with himself. 'What do you want first? The good news, or the very good news?'

Goddamn him! 'This isn't a surprise party, for chrissakes. Spit it out.'

Minos got the picture. 'Jahne Moore,' he said, looking down at a small notebook he'd flipped out of his pocket. 'Real name, Mary Jane Moran. Born in Scuderstown, New York, September 22, 1958. She was . . .'

'What? *When* was she born?'

Minos jerked his head up, then looked back at his notes. 'September 22, 1958. In Scuders –'

'Jesus Christ! That makes her . . .' Lila thought for a moment. 'That would make her almost *thirty-eight years old*. You got that all wrong.' Lila sat back, folding her arms across her chest. Minos said nothing, just opened the manila envelope, reached in, and took out a sheaf of papers. He handed Lila the first one. 'Exhibit A,' he said, a smug look on his face.

Lila took the photocopy from him. It was a birth certificate, all right. For Mary Jane Moran, born September 22, 1958, Scuders-town, New York. So what? 'But how do you know this is Jahne Moore?' she asked, handing back the photocopy.

Minos shook the rest of the typewritten papers in the air. 'High-school diploma, yearbook with picture, nursing-school diploma, unemployment book from New York City, depositions from kids she acted with in some church-basement theatre workshop . . .'

'For Mary Jane Moran. But what about Jahne Moore?' Lila was having a hard time holding in her excitement, and her fear. 'What do you have on *Jahne Moore*?'

'A legal name change and deposition from a lawyer in Albany. Pissed off over some probate deal that's soured on him. But wait; it gets better. Interview and files from a nurse in a plastic surgeon's office in New York. It seems our Jahne Moore is a real Cinderella. She got a hold of some money and had herself done over. The grandmother died just before this, so maybe from her. Had herself carved head to toe. Took two years. According to this nurse, she went from an ugly, overweight mouse, to a twenty-four-year-old sexy beauty. Money can do that for you.' Minos paused, his expression changing. 'Speaking a money, I've taken the liberty of promising this medical source a large payment. Seeing as how the *National Questioner* would outbid you if they knew about it, I put you out on the limb. Not by name of course.'

Lila snatched the nurse's deposition from his hand and scanned it hungrily. Medical records. Pictures! Befores and afters! It was all here. 'She went to this plastic surgeon, Dr. Moore? Was she related to this doctor?' Lila asked Minos.

'No. Nurse says she probably had the hots for him, though. Who knows, maybe they traded tit for tat, you should excuse the expression. He was her Henry Higgins. You know, like in *My Fair Lady*. Anyhow, the nurse showed me the records.' Minos kept talking while Lila devoured the typewritten pages. 'Made her appointments as Mary Jane Moran. That was her biggest mistake. She shoulda started with the alias *first*, *then* the surgery. Typical amateur. His records even show her present name and address right here in L.A.' Minos handed Lila a folder. 'So,' he said, 'that's the "good." Ready for the "very good"?'

Lila didn't have to answer, couldn't answer. There was something better, juicier than *this*? She tried to digest it all, but realized that she couldn't. Not right now, at least. Just take it all in for now, she told herself. Then decide what to do. Slow down.

Lila could smile without forcing it. 'Minos, I'm impressed. Now the "very good."' She settled back to listen, although she was sure he couldn't top this. Jahne Moore, carved like a duck out of a piece of soap. Soap melts, she thought, then brought her attention back to Minos' words, which now, strangely, had a very calming effect on her. This must be how alcoholics feel after their first drink in a long while: peaceful, like the world is really okay. 'I'm ready,' she told him.

Minos turned gleeful. 'You're not ready for this. Listen: Sharleen Smith, from Lamson, Texas. Has a brother, Dean. . . .'

'You mean a *boyfriend* Dean,' Lila asked, almost afraid to breathe. She'd heard about Dean.

'No, a *brother*, Dean Smith,' Minos said. 'Two years younger than her. They've been passing themselves off as boyfriend and girlfriend for the last few years. But the mother says no, they are her kids all right.'

'Their mother *admits* this? Where's the mother now? How do you know it's the truth?' Lila felt the words rushing out of her.

'I traced the mother to New Orleans. She's was a drunk and a whore before she started getting money from Sharleen. Now she's just a drunk. Sharleen keeps her out of sight. Packed her off to New Orleans for some mysterious reason.'

'You don't have to be a detective to figure out why she packed her away, for chrissakes, Minos. Her kids are fucking each other.'

'Yeah, I know, but that's not what I mean. There's more to the story, but I didn't have enough time to get into it that deep. I figured I'd get back here to give you what I found out so far.' Minos handed Lila two snapshots. 'Got these from the mother's house.'

Lila looked at the pictures. It was Sharleen all right. Maybe she was eight or nine years old. The little boy must be Dean. They were standing with some white-trash couple in front of a trailer.

'How's that so far?' Minos asked.

Lila sat back, the papers and snapshots on her lap. Unbelievable. Had any incest perpetrators ever won an Emmy? Lila smiled. 'You've done very well, Minos. I'll go over this all tonight, then call you tomorrow. I might want you to do some more for me, depending.' She stood up to let him know his time was up.

Minos didn't stand. 'And the money, to the nurse?'

Lila smiled. 'Worth every dime, Mr. Paige. Don't worry about a thing. We'll talk tomorrow.' She shook his hand, then closed the door behind him.

Lila stood there, all the power she needed in her hands. I did it, she thought. I finally did it. I got both of them. Now Lila knew the Emmy was hers. She went over to her dressing table and picked up the old sepia photograph she kept there in a silver frame. Thank you, Nadia, Lila said to herself. Thank you. Now I got both Candy and Skinny out of the way. It took a very long time, but they're both dead now. And I get my *own* show.

She'd been so pleased she'd forgotten to ask about Jughead and his threats.

Lila had just finished rereading the papers Minos had left her, savouring every word, and put them back in the envelope, when the door to her trailer banged open. She jumped up and stared at the figure in the doorway.

'What are *you* doing here? How did you get on the lot? I gave specific instructions . . .' Lila's voice trailed off as she picked up the phone to call Security and rip that guard out another asshole.

'Lila, Lila, Lila. Don't overact. I always told you, hold *something* back.' Theresa O'Donnell began pulling off her long white gloves, finger by finger, as she stepped into the room, then sat in the chair Lila had just vacated at her vanity table.

Gloves in California, Lila thought. Leave it to her mother to develop an affectation that other people *wouldn't* copy. Who was she playing today? Miss Piggy? Now that Lila was past her first shock, she could cope. 'Isn't it a little dangerous for you to be out of your coffin in daylight?' Lila asked, putting the phone down before Security answered.

Theresa turned to the mirror and began to examine her makeup. 'We take our chances, darling. *You* know that.'

'You've taken a big chance today, then, because I'm going to have you kicked out on your ass.' But Lila didn't pick up the phone again. And she wasn't sure why not.

She heard Theresa's throaty laugh. 'Lila, I *own* a piece of this lot. They don't kick stockholders off their own property. And *no one* kicks Theresa O'Donnell out of *anyplace*.' Theresa was still looking in the mirror, now considering her hair.

Lila took a step closer to her mother. 'What do you want?'

Theresa sighed and turned to face Lila. 'There's been a terrible misunderstanding that I need to clear up. I was offered a part on

Three for the Road, then had it suddenly pulled out from under me. Paul Grasso said it would present too many conflicts. I said to him that he *couldn't* mean with my *daughter* – she's such a *professional*. But he seemed to think that you didn't want me on the show.' Theresa slapped the long gloves against one hand. 'So, here I am, darling. You have *got* to clear up this misunderstanding with Marty, tell him you *do* want to work with me. I'm *so* looking forward to us working together, Lila. It's something I've always wanted. And you, too, of course. So, call Marty. I'll wait.'

Lila had feared this day, knowing that it would come, but not knowing when. 'Get out,' Lila simply said.

She watched Theresa's face tighten; then a smile returned once again. 'Jack Warner taught me something, once. I've never forgotten it, used it to negotiate every contract I ever signed. Never issue an ultimatum unless you hold all the aces.' Theresa leaned back on the table on one elbow, and crossed her legs at the knees. 'I see you had a visit from Minos Paige, Lila. What was that little creep doing here? You're not thinking of doing business with the worst piece of scum in Hollywood, are you? You'd want to think twice about that.'

Lila kept her eyes from falling on the envelope still resting on her vanity table, too close to Theresa for Lila's comfort. What was in there was for Lila only. The last person she wanted to share the dirt with was her mother. Because somehow, Lila knew, her mother would use it for her *own* benefit.

'How do *you* know Minos Paige?'

'I know everything. *Everything*, Lila. *Remember* that.' Theresa laughed again, like she didn't have a care in the world. That always made Lila nervous. That meant that Theresa *didn't* have a care in the world. 'Once, when he was very young Kerry found out some smarmy little jealous actor put a private detective on him. Your father was – how should I put it? – vulnerable in several areas, but not stupid. So Kerry got one of his friends and a couple of prostitutes: a sixteen-year-old male hustler who looked twelve, and a dead ringer for the young Shirley Temple. You couldn't fuck with Shirley Temple and get away with it.'

Lila could see Theresa was having a good time, going down memory lane. But Lila wasn't in the mood. 'If this is your way of saying goodbye, I'm bored already.'

Theresa ignored the remark. 'They got this guy with chloral hydrate in his drink, took him to a hotel, stripped him, and photographed him in every position imaginable with the two kids. The next day, Kerry had the pictures delivered to the guy's house, and left them in a sealed envelope with his wife. Then he called the guy and told him what he had done, and where the pictures were. The guy beat it home just in time. The wife had a letter opener at the flap as he walked in.'

'Why are you telling me all this?'

'Because it's important for you to know your heritage. And to remember that what you can do to someone else, they can do to you. Or anyone can. My point, Lila, is that two can play the game. You see, I think that, if you really thought about it, you'd see how it would make much better sense for you to have me as your co-worker, rather than your enemy.' Theresa motioned to the envelope on the table. 'I've got some of those at home. Dozens. And if I have nothing to lose, maybe . . . who knows? – maybe I'd even open them up and pass them around.'

Lila felt the chill run the length of her body. '*You're* in those envelopes at home, Mother. That stuff pertains to you, too.'

Theresa shrugged. 'Let's keep this short and sweet, Lila. You want to find out someone's secrets but keep your own? Here are my terms: I do the season-opening show *and* a miniseries with you.'

'Miniseries! I am not . . .'

'I'm not *asking* you, you ungrateful, malicious little bitch. I'm *telling* you. Get a deal out of Marty DiGennaro. You could if you tried. Whatever little secrets Minos is tracking down for you will look like nothing compared to yours.'

'They won't just crucify me, Mother. They'll crucify you, too.'

'Better public crucifixion than private oblivion. So, consider next week the deadline. Sign on the dotted line, bitch. Or I'll blow your whole scene wide open. And I have nothing to lose. No television show, no movies, no powerful man in my life.' Theresa paused. 'But *you*, you have lots to lose, don't you, Lila?' Lila watched her mother stand up and begin to pull her gloves on. 'You want that Emmy, don't you? Ask yourself that. And if the answer is yes, then call Marty DiGennaro. And tell him how much you love me.'

Theresa grasped the door handle in her hand. 'And if you decide you have nothing to lose, well, then it will be back to just you and me. And maybe Kevin. One happy family.' Then she walked out the door and closed it softly behind her.

Lila sat down before her knees buckled under her.

49

Now that Flora Lee was gone, Dobe was with them, and Sharleen didn't have to work on ¾, she was actually beginning to feel good. She spent long afternoons in the garden, weeding, and she put up tomatoes, canned some peaches, and made an unbeatable three-bean salad.

Dobe was going to have to leave again, but, though she'd miss him terribly, Sharleen was so grateful to him that she could hardly resent his going, or his need to live his own life. It was just that she felt he was the only person who she could lean on, and when he left, she knew she'd feel very alone.

Tonight they were having a goodbye dinner, and the talk was casual but fun. Dobe told them half a dozen funny stories, while Oprah sat, content as usual, superior to the gamboling puppies.

'Hey!' Dean spoke up. 'I saw a new licence plate today. North Carolina. First in Flight. Does that mean they're chicken? I wouldn't be proud of that.'

Dobe smiled and explained about Kitty Hawk. 'Good name for a cat,' Dean said.

After Dean helped Sharleen clear, Dobe stacked the dishwasher while Sharleen mopped down the table – she didn't like to leave a mess. Dean took all the dogs out back. It was then that Dobe started talking business – not his business, but hers.

'What are you investing in?' Dobe asked.

'I don't know,' Sharleen told him. 'Lenny takes care of all of that stuff.'

'Buying any land?'

She shrugged. 'We bought this place, but I don't think we bought any other land.' Somehow, she felt uncomfortable talking about this with Dobe, as if it were wrong, or maybe dangerous. 'You had enough to eat?' she asked, trying to change the subject.

'Sure did, and it was good, too. You're a good little cook, Sharleen. But let me ask you another question, Sharleen. You still got that idea of havin' a ranch someday?'

She didn't want to talk about this to Dobe. Somehow, she knew it would lead to trouble. 'Yeah,' she said reluctantly. 'Me and Dean would like that someday. When we got enough money.' It was once she said the word 'money' that she realized what felt wrong: talking to Dobe about money made her feel as if, maybe, he was talking to her the way he did to those people he sold the fake gas pills to. 'Let's go outside,' she said. And wandered out into the darkness. She hoped that would be enough to change the subject.

'You lookin' for a partner?' Dobe asked. For a moment, she didn't understand. 'A partner in your ranch?' he prompted. 'Someone to scout out the real estate, maybe to get it started for you till you come out later.'

'I don't know, Dobe,' she said, and felt her heart grow heavy in her chest. Oh, God, she should have known that Dobe's help would have a price. Like everyone else out here, he was looking to make some money off her. Somehow, Sharleen felt it would be easier if he just asked her for money instead of trying to scam her out of it.

'Listen to the way I see it, Sharleen,' he was saying. 'The longer you wait, the higher land out in Montana is going to cost. But I met a guy, got about four hundred acres that he'd sell to me for a hundred thousand dollars cash. And it's beautiful land. But after I finish this shoe deal, I only got about fifty. Now, if you go in as a partner, we could either split the land or live on it together. There's a river there, Sharleen, that's so beautiful you would hardly believe it. And a house. Needs some work – kind of rough, you know, like how a single man lives – but it's sound. And there's a view from the front porch that would just about break your heart.'

Sharleen felt as if she didn't need to have her heart broken – again. Her daddy had broken it, Flora Lee had broken it, and now Dobe was. Could you have a heart broken three times? Well, she knew how it felt: real bad, real sad, and real tired. It seemed like everyone but Dean expected nothin' but money or work out of her. Tears flooded her eyes, and she turned her head so Dobe couldn't see her in the darkness. The only light was from the dying coals of the barbecue. She stood there silently for another moment.

'Well, I guess it's not something you'd chose to do right now,' Dobe said, and she could hear the disappointment in his voice.

He had helped them, back when they needed help worse than they ever would again. She remembered standin' in the road, outside Lamson, scared and tired, afraid of the police and without a place to go. Even now, she could recall the comfort of sinking into the air-conditioned back seat of Dobe's big old sedan.

'Sure, Dobe,' she said quietly. 'Me and Dean would love to be partners with you, I'll ask Lenny for a cheque tomorrow.'

'You sure?' he asked.

'Sure I'm sure,' she said, but she knew her voice lacked conviction. Well, like Lila said, Sharleen knew she wasn't a very good actress.

If Dobe noticed, he didn't show it. He stuck his hand out, took her own, and pumped it. 'You won't regret it, partner,' he told her. 'I really think I got us a hell of a deal lined up. Uh, excusin' my French.'

She nodded. 'Great,' she said.

'So, mind if I tell Dean?' he asked. 'I didn't want to bring it up in front of him in case you didn't like the idea. But now that we're . . .'

'No, let's not tell him until the deal's all done,' she interrupted, looking out into the darkness for Dean and the dogs. 'He gets so excited, and so tired of waitin'. Let's just surprise him later.'

'Anything you say, partner,' Dobe smiled.

50

April Irons' visit had shaken up the crew, but it had shaken Jahne even more deeply. She knew there were problems with the film – maybe there were nothing but problems. Still, she only thought of April as Sam's ex-lover. He had explained there was no longer anything between them, but Jahne was not so sure.

And when, on the night of April's visit, for the first time in weeks, Sam didn't come to her room, she'd been hurt and suspicious. He told her it was only business, but she could tell from the looks of the crew that word was out. Mai would have told her the truth. No one else would. Had Sam spent the night with April?

Has it started again? she asked herself. I've gotten difficult and emotional. Is he going to cheat on me, lie to me, the way he lied to Mary Jane? I'm dependent on him, she thought. Exactly what Mai told me not to be. Is he with April? Does he care for her? Is he touching her?

That night she'd driven herself nearly crazy, and the fiasco on the beach the next day only made things worse. Sam took her aside and told her he'd worked all night. She chose to believe him, and after the crew dug a ditch in the sand, she walked through it and the scene as best she could.

That night, Sam had been even more passionate, and had promised her again and again that there was nothing between him and April.

'Jesus,' he finally moaned. 'I wish this shoot were wrapped. I want to go home.'

But Jahne, though she desperately wanted the movie to end, had no home to go to.

Jahne had always heard that wrap parties were wild, outrageous farewell bashes, but the party at the end of the *Birth of a Star* shoot wasn't even cheerful with relief that the pain was over. Michael's misbehaviour, Mai's death, and April's wrath had combined to make this a hell trip for everyone. Jahne had, as she knew she was expected to, bought gifts for all the crew: carryall's with *Birth of a Star* and 'Love and Thanks from Jahne' embroidered on them. Sam made a little speech, but Michael showed up only for a few moments, and April Irons, Seymore LeVine, and the suits didn't show up at all. That was a relief, but still, the party was an ordeal that was best when it was over and she and Sam were free to leave the nasty little world of gossip and tension that the set had become.

Before editing and looping began, Sam had decided to take a few days off and drive down the coast. Jahne wasn't expected back on the set of *Three for the Road* until the end of the next week, so they'd holiday a little. She'd never needed a rest so badly in her life. As he tossed her bags into the trunk of the 300ZX, she felt her spirits lift for the first time since Mai's death. They got into the car, waving goodbye to Jerry and the others who were still left at the hotel, and then Sam gunned the motor.

'Why,' he asked, 'why did I ever think I wanted to be a director when I grew up?'

'Oh, doesn't everyone?' Jahne replied. The famous joke around the Industry was the one about Mother Teresa dying and being received in heaven by God and a host of singing angels. 'You were so wonderful, so good, down on earth,' God says to her. 'I want especially to reward you. Isn't there anything you wanted to do that you never got a chance to?' She begs for no special treatment. But God is equally insistent. 'Name one thing you've always wanted,' he insists. 'Well,' Mother Teresa finally admits, 'I always wanted to direct.'

Now Jahne smiled at him. 'You and Mother Teresa.'

'Yeah. We have so much in common,' he laughed.

'Well, you were both christened.'

'How did you know that?' Jahne realized Sam had — back in New York — told her a long funny story about the ceremony. Something she, as Jahne, just couldn't know.

'Oh, I just assumed you were. Wasn't everyone?'

'Was your family religious?' he asked.

'Not really.' Whenever questions about her earlier life came up, Jahne reverted to the shortest casual answers. She certainly didn't want to seem secretive, but she was always afraid she'd be caught in a contradiction if she said much. As she had always done for her stage characters, she had imagined a past, complete with an army dad, a housewife mom, and a peripatetic youth. Not enough time at the various bases to put down roots or make lasting friends. And then there was the tragic car accident, so she didn't have to contend with questions about living family members today. In fact, since she was representing herself as in her twenties, she didn't have much of a past to account for. She smiled, remembering her New York friend Molly's take on why men preferred younger women: they didn't have as long a story.

The only problem was that she wasn't a stage character and this wasn't supposed to be acting. This was her real life today, and she had everything she wanted. Except, of course, for the irony that she could never *be* herself. A day, an hour didn't go by in which she wasn't tempted to tell Sam everything, but now she was in too deep. She had told so many lies. Wouldn't he hate her for lying? And wouldn't he feel a fool to have believed them? And maybe a cad to have put her in the position to lie?

So she did her best to ignore her feelings and keep up her charade. Beneath all that, though, wasn't she still hoping, waiting, for him finally to look at her and see her, *know* her? The Bible referred to carnal possession as a man 'knowing' a woman. Now that they were lovers, why didn't Sam know her?

'Did your folks make a big deal about Christmas? Mine didn't. I was always jealous of other kids for that.'

'No. Baptists don't, really.'

'I thought you said they were Methodists.'

She smiled, but her stomach tightened. 'Well, Dad was. But Mom was Baptist.' She paused, a bit unnerved. They really hadn't had long periods of time to talk, what with shootings all day and lovemaking all night. Suddenly the car felt confining, claustrophobic instead of cosy. 'What was the best Christmas gift you ever got?' she asked.

It was always surprisingly easy to turn the conversation back to Sam. He did love to talk. About himself, about movie-making, about the theatre, about books, about the difference between Jung and Freud, about, well, about everything. And it was almost always interesting. But, Jahne had to admit this time around, it was also narcissistic. Sometimes she had the feeling he appreciated her intelligence, her self, more as an audience, a vessel to understand him and be filled by him than as a discrete entity.

In fact, sometimes she saw him as a sculptor, a creator, always trying to mould. He had created plays, he now created movies. She had to admit, when she was Mary Jane he had done a lot to mould her taste, her opinions and views.

Jahne turned to enjoy the view from the coast road. It was, really, a breathtaking drive, and the day was a good one for it: sunny and mild, and because they'd gotten an early start they'd get to see the sunset before they found a place to stay that evening. Tomorrow they might get as far as San Simeon, Hearst's castle.

The weather was cool enough for her to wear one of the big Donna Karan sweaters she liked, a huge creamy-white turtleneck, and she had the matching cardigan thrown over her shoulders. It was too warm in L.A. to get to wear them much.

'Pretty sweater,' Sam said. 'It suits you.'

It pleased her that he noticed, but she no longer allowed men to affect her taste in clothes. Mai had taught her that. Poor Mai. Well, poor me. Jahne sighed.

'What is it?' Sam asked.

'Oh, I was thinking about L.A. I've gotten a new place there. A more secure one. La Brecque helped me pick it out. It may be safe, but I don't like it nearly as well as my old rental. It seems so

grown-up. I was hoping that Mai would move in there with me.'
She stopped, her lips trembling. No, no more tears today, she told
herself. Mai would want me finally to have some fun. 'It's too big
for one person. It's impersonal. It's cold.'

'I'll help you warm it up,' Sam offered, a wolfish grin on his face.

'You'll be my first guest,' Jahne told him.

He took his eyes off the road, surveying her warmly, then
reached across the gearshift and took her hand. 'I'm honoured,'
he said, and there was no humour in his voice, only passion. He
moved her hand to his cheek. She felt the thrill move down her
arm, across her chest, and down to her centre.

Mai was gone, Neil was gone, Molly was gone, her mother was
so long gone. There was only Sam to love, to be loved by. And at
that moment, she loved him so much it hurt.

51

I might as well be into fucking astrology, April thought bitterly to
herself as the limo pulled up to the nondescript brick building in
West L.A. where forty million dollars was, at that very moment,
about to be lost. She could predict the future. Not a horoscope:
a horrorscope. April and the stars. That was her life. Reading the
stars and trying to predict the future. This project hadn't been hard
to pitch to the suits. Remakes they understood. Top stars they
understood. It was forty-million-dollar failures they had trouble
understanding. And it didn't matter how many winners she'd
brought in. One fucking failure and the pricks would start in again
with how she didn't understand the realities of the marketplace, or
how as a woman she was only good on small pictures, soft pictures.
Well, fuck them! If the picture worked, every one of them would
be claiming credit, but if it failed, they'd all point to her and say,
'I told you so.'

April got out of the car and stared up, not to the stars but
to the second floor, where carnage was already taking place.

Up there it was like a confrontation between the Crips and the
Bloods — two of L.A.'s most vicious teenage gangs. Testosterone

amok. None of the stupid bastards knew what to do, and all of them so scared that the only position was a defensive one. April sighed.

When she opened the door to the conference room, it was much as she had expected: the half-empty paper coffee cups, the smoke, the yelling. Michael McLain held the floor.

'Well, what the fuck are you going to do – send it out for a week to Billy Joe's Pitcher Show in West Des Moines, then slap "Recent Theatrical Release" on the videos and sell them in Asia?' Michael turned to her as she entered, and under the rage she clearly saw the fear. She sighed. She would have to find a way to turn his desperation into part of her solution.

'Hello, gentlemen,' she said drily, and took a seat. Seymore LeVine looked at her, his eyes almost weepy. Afraid his daddy was going to yell at him. Michael sighed but nodded hello. But Sam could hardly bring himself to look at her. She felt his shame, but from long experience she knew it wasn't shame over the ridiculous bungle of this film. It was sexual shame – that 'Oops, you caught me' crap that some men do. What a shmuck! As if a couple of orgasms one way or the other mattered, compared to this forty-million-dollar mountain of shit. Jesus Christ, *she'd* sleep with Jahne Moore if it would fix the picture.

'What's going on?' was all she said.

'The end of our lives as we know them,' Seymore moaned.

'We are discussing how the genius director wasted a multi hundred thousand feet of film to take home movies of his girl-friend,' Michael spat out. 'A girlfriend, I might add, who can put out anywhere except on the screen.'

'She never put out for me,' Seymore mourned. Everyone ignored him.

'Michael has been impossible to direct.' Sam spoke for the first time, ignoring the other two. 'That, and a certain – well – woodenness in the way Jahne sometimes comes across, has . . .'

'Okay, never mind the "who shot Jahne,"' April said harshly. 'The point now isn't that it's shit, or why it's shit, or even whose fault it is that it's shit. The point *now* is how to save it.' April was calm. She was always at her calmest after everything was lost and her back was to the wall. It was the time *before* all was lost that was agonizing to her. Now she could take over.

'We have to save it,' she repeated.

'Impossible,' said Michael, and April could see Sam wince.

April sighed. Sam was like a spooked horse: his eyes were wide, showing too much white; he'd take off in any direction, just to get away. Michael was impossible. He was also scared, but angry, too. And even at his calmest, Michael was not what one could call a problem solver. And Seymore ... Well, he was just Seymore. Laslo, the cinematographer, and Bob, the editor, were along for the ride.

But there was a great deal that could be done in editing. The right music, some new dialogue looped in, a voice-over ... and, if worse came to worst, a few new scenes could be shot. It would be expensive, but perhaps ...

'We can turn this around,' April told them.

'Impossible!' Seymore repeated.

'Look, have a sense of proportion. Eliminating infant mortality in Calcutta is impossible. *This* is only fixing a movie.' She stood up, smoothing her leather slacks. Nineteen hundred dollars at North Beach Leather, and the sons-of-bitches rode up into her crotch.

'We'd have a better shot at infant mortality,' moaned Seymore. At the studio they called him 'Seymore problems.'

'Thanks for the backup,' she told him, then paced to the window and drew back the curtain. There was no view. 'Okay, there's no point to a remake of a great movie unless it *adds* something. I mean, look at *His Girl Friday* and *Front Page*. When Hildy became a woman, it *added* something to the remake.'

'Yeah. Sex. *And* Cary Grant. We got nothin',' Seymore sighed.

'You've got me,' Michael said.

'I repeat: we got nothin',' Seymore groaned.

'Well, Cary Grant is dead!' April reminded them.

Seymore rolled his eyes. 'Even Cary Grant couldn't save this one,' he said.

'Jesus Christ, Seymore, would you shut up!' Michael yelled. He looked over at Sam. 'Well, *you're* the genius writer-director. What next?'

'Tighter cutting will help,' Sam began. 'It's too slow. And if we refocus on the love story ...'

'Piss on the love story.' Adrenaline was pumping through April's body. She'd been in this spot before, but each time it felt new. Each time it felt as if this time, *this* time, she wouldn't be able to pull it out and she'd lose it all. Lose the money, lose the job, lose power, lose face. But, just as she had each time before, she felt the solution dangling only slightly out of reach. She only had to be smart enough not to blind herself to it, and to be brave enough, once she saw it, to try for it, and strong enough to make it happen. Goldwyn could do it. Selznick had done it again and again. Capra, despite that motherfucker Harry Cohn, had triumphed. Please, she prayed, more to that pantheon of those dead heroes than to some Yahweh Hebrew-school God, please, let me see the way.

'I want to see the dailies. Every one. Every take. I want to see the out-takes. I want to see every fucking millimetre of film you've shot, and I want to see it forwards and backwards. *Everything.*'

52

Jahne returned home – well, back to her empty house – alone after the long day of work. This season, 3/4 was not going to be a picnic. Jahne was overworked and lonely, and Sam was as busy as she was, wrapped up in postproduction. Apart all day, seeing him only at night, both of them exhausted – this was real life, but it felt more like a nightmare. Sam had told her to trust him – trust him about the script, about her performance, about his loyalty and love – but she seemed less and less able to do so. It felt as if each night was a trial, and each day she'd shift through the evidence and her suspicions.

Sam had promised tonight that he'd join her later. She set the table, and put out some of the dinner that her housekeeper had left.

She ate some salad and half a cup of cottage cheese, then showered and got into bed. She'd have the rest of her dinner later, when Sam got back. The cat curled up in her armpit, purring. 'You didn't have a good day, either?' she asked it, as it began to knead her arm, preparing to sleep. Jahne fell asleep to its soothing mechanical hum.

It was later, much later, when she awoke. She didn't have a watch on, and there wasn't a single clock in the new house, except for the one on the oven timer. Jahne pushed the cat aside, rose, and paced the empty, darkened living room, afraid to find out just how late Sam was. It was like the night on location when April had shown up and Sam had never come to her. This must be how it begins, she thought. The lateness, followed by the lies, followed by the arguments, followed by the accusations and the denials. She was stupid and childish to think that this time it could be different, that this time he would not only love her but be faithful. She had let this happen to herself. She had promised herself that she wouldn't trust him, that she wouldn't love him. She had promised Mai the same thing. Oh, if only she could talk to Mai!

But what good would that do? Mai had told her what kind of man Sam was and what kind of danger she was in. But she hadn't listened. She had chosen this foolish movie despite her agent's warnings. She had alienated Marty DiGennaro, as well as Monica Flanders and Sy Ortis. She had probably messed up her career.

She looked around her at the lofty, darkening room. It was like a tomb, and she hated it. Perhaps La Brecque and his people had vetted it, perhaps there was an alarm system and a patrol to check on her, but she felt like a target here, exposed and alone. Without Sam, she hated to be in the house. She passed by the dining room, saw the set table. By now the salad had wilted on the plates, and the ragout would be vile. She shivered and climbed up onto the sofa, wrapping herself in the throw that draped its back. Time seemed to crawl by. It must be past one. He hadn't called. Perhaps he simply wouldn't show up. Perhaps she'd never hear from him again. Like with Michael McLain. After all, the movie was finished, except for some looping. Maybe she was no longer necessary.

When she heard him at the security gate, she knew her anger was mixed pathetically with relief. Then there was the sound of his car on the gravel, his footsteps on the walk, his key in the lock. She sat, motionless, and listened as he called out her name softly and walked down the hall. He must have checked the bedroom, then the kitchen. At last, he stood in the archway to the living room, where she could see him.

'Oh, here you are. I'm sorry it went so long,' Sam said as he walked into the room. He seemed haggard, the circles under his eyes darker than ever. 'We just had a lot we had to go over.' He looked at Jahne and he winced. 'Why are you sitting in the dark? You're angry, aren't you?'

'You're hours late, you didn't call, and you ask me if I'm angry?'

'I'm sorry, babe. I forgot to call from the office, and then the goddamned car phone wouldn't work. It just kept cutting

out. I figured by then that I'd be here in a little while anyway.'

'There are pay phones.'

'Oh, Christ, Jahne! In L.A. no one but a junkie uses a pay
phone! Give me a break. I'm really getting crushed out there! I
have a lot on my mind. I admit it was rude and thoughtless, and
I'm sorry, but it's not like we were going out or anything.'

She stood up. 'No, we weren't going out. We were just going
to have dinner and make love. Nothing worth telephoning home
about. And now dinner is ruined.'

'Oh, that's all right. I had a quick bite with April.' She saw him
wince again as he realized that what he had said would worsen
her mood. He sighed. 'Jahne, you don't seem to understand the
pressure I'm under. It's not going to be easy to finish this movie
the way we both want it to be finished. I have to stay on good
terms with April. We simply had a lot to talk over, a lot of planning
to do.'

'What else did you do with April?' she asked. 'Let's just get the
cards laid out on the table. You're not playing solitaire, you know.
This is at least a two-person game. Or is it a *ménage à trois?*'

'Oh, for God's sake, Jahne. April is the *producer*. Don't you
understand that?'

'Don't you understand that I'm not stupid and I'm not blind?
This time, I won't close my eyes while you humiliate me in front
of . . .' She stopped and turned away from him, biting her tongue.
Sam had never humiliated Jahne Moore, she reminded herself. He
had humiliated Mary Jane Moran. She strode across the wide, empty
floor to the window, staring out into the darkness. She felt him come
up from behind her. She didn't turn to him.

'When have I ever lied to you?' he asked, his voice husky
with hurt. 'When did I ever humiliate you?'

She wheeled to look at him. 'Don't tell me that you haven't
slept with April Irons.'

'Jahne, I told you. That was long ago.'

'I want the details. When did it begin?'

'On my first trip out here. She was trying to buy *Jack and
Jill*, and I was holding out because I wanted to direct it.'

On his first trip out to L.A., she thought. He was sleeping with
Mary Jane — with me! — in New York, and April Irons in L.A. She
remembered his apologetic phone calls to her in that dingy New
York walk-up. Had he called her from April's bed?

'Well, it seems you didn't hold out for long.'

'It was a complicated situation, Jahne. I wanted to sell the play, but I also wanted to direct it and get a part in it for a friend. I had never negotiated for those stakes. I won a couple of hands, and I lost one. We sealed the deal in bed. It was all very heady. You know, the limos, the palm trees, the ass-kissing. Feeling that for the first time in your life you're at the very centre of the universe. For once, I was sought after; for once, I had the power. I don't know. Maybe I thought an affair would give me some leverage. It didn't.'

All that time he was commuting, she thought. Comforting me, fucking April Irons. Commiserating with me, but sealing his deal in bed with her. Using jet lag as an excuse not to make love. And at the time I blamed myself. She felt her face flush. She wanted to slap him, to hit his face over and over and over. But how could she ever explain?

'Get out,' she whispered. 'Get out right now.'

53

April spent most of two days and three nights watching all of the film. Calling it a bomb would be polite. If she had the choice between releasing *Birth of a Star* or *Hudson Hawk*, she'd go with the Willis movie. After all, *he* had a mother who would pay to see it. Both Jahne Moore's and Michael McLain's parents were dead. And so would she be, if something wasn't radically altered.

For a moment, only a moment, she thought of the great pleasure it would give Bob LeVine to fire her. She threatened him and his job security. He'd love to return her to the subworld of indie producers. She shivered. Christ, it did sound like the title of a horror movie.

Well, the hours of shit that she'd been watching was a horror all right. Michael's performance was angry, even when it shouldn't have been. And Jahne Moore was simply another beautiful face. She read her lines intelligently, but, somehow, the two together made nothing happen.

The film kept running, but April closed her tired eyes. She rubbed the lids, careful not to stretch the skin further. She'd had an eye job only two years ago, and didn't want to go through another for at least five more. In the darkness, with her eyes closed, she could hear both the dialogue and Seymore's snores.

Actually, the dialogue sounded pretty good, she thought. Then she opened her eyes, saw another take, and closed them again. But once again, the dialogue sounded good. It sounded . . . hot. Well, anger was as good a sexual fuel as any, and there had been plenty of anger on the set. Too bad they'd been filming a love story instead of a Schwarzenegger vehicle. What she needed was Mankiewicz to doctor this up. To keep the heat. Too bad he was dead.

She stopped, held herself absolutely still. What was it that Mankiewicz had said? Something about the first guy who found a way to show fucking on the screen would become a billionaire. Or was it Goldwyn? Well, it didn't matter. She kept her eyes closed and simply listened. And then the idea came, slipping in as if it had always been there. The little chill that accompanied it, the thrill, the metallic taste in her mouth. Yess!

Carefully, like tonguing a very sore tooth, she felt her way around it. There was risk. But they had always seen this film as a way to contemporize a great old love story. Well, they just hadn't gone far enough! This was the nineties, for God's sake. It was time. Let's show the world a tender love story – a violent, tragic one – and let's show the lovers on the screen. Not porno actors, but stars you knew, stars you loved, real stars making love on the screen. Not a slap and a tickle, a quick frontal shot, but the real thing. Okay, a little soft focus here and there, but let's give the people what they want. Let's have every woman in the audience wet, every man stiff as a board. And so what if Michael was getting old? They'd use a body double, they'd fake it, they'd cut and intercut.

And she thought they could get both audiences: the young ones that would go to a movie half a dozen times, *and* the ageing boomers. Yes. Kids, gonads pulsating, would take their dates. Twice. After all, Jahne Moore was their biggest wet dream. While the boomers would feel nostalgia. The women had made Michael a teen idol twenty years ago, and the men had watched him as a role model and had grown old with him. There was life in the old dog yet. And, by extension, in them. They'd eat this up. And everyone would go home and rip one off. Then, later, what would it do in home-video release? Oh, my God! What wouldn't it do?

It all worked. It sounded great! Of course, it required a certain amount of daring. Not since *Last Tango In Paris* had a major star done sex. Even Michael Douglas in *Basic Instinct* had held back more than a little. But McLain was desperate. And afraid he was losing it. It would have stud appeal. April knew she could sell it to him.

It was Jahne Moore who might prove a problem. April smiled. The body-double clause that had cost her so much legal time and effort! Sy Ortis' stupid clause! It would allow her to cut and splice anything she wanted to. Why, she could have the body double dress like a chicken and bark like a dog if she wanted. And if the close-ups showed Jahne Moore's face, well, that was the magic of Hollywood. Of course, it might upset Miss Moore, or Sy Ortis, or Marty DiGennaro. Maybe it would lose the bitch her Flanders Cosmetics contract. It might even upset Sam to see what looked like his girl spread-eagled on the screen. Good thing she, April, had retained final cut. Sam could take it or walk, she couldn't care less. Her smile broadened as she stood up.

'Gentlemen,' she said, 'I have an idea.'

54

After she threw him out, two days without Sam, two nights alone, were more than Jahne could bear. She walked through her days, an automaton and sat up for the nights. What had he done to her, and what had she done to him? She got a copy of *Great Expectations* and read again about the mad Miss Havisham and her heart-cold ward Estella. Then she lay in bed and sobbed. Who had she avenged? What had she proved? How and why had she done this to herself? At last, hopeless, she called him on Friday, and he asked her to come over to his place on Saturday night.

They spent the evening together, making love as if they'd been separated for years, not days.

She agreed that she'd been irrational, that what was in the past was over, and that she believed him when he told her there was nothing between him and April. She went to sleep in his arms, the only way she could sleep now without waking with nightmares, always of the past.

But, like a crusty scab, the past was something she could not stop herself from picking away at.

Now, this sunny Sunday morning, Sam lay stretched across his living-room sofa. He looked exhausted. She knew postproduction was not going smoothly. Still, they would have this quiet time together.

Sam put his hand into his pocket and held it out towards her. 'I have something for you' he said, and when she saw the glittering in her hand she thought, for a moment of Michael McLain's gift. But this was no diamond. It was a key, Sam's key.

'For you,' he said. 'Mi casa su casa.'

She took it. 'Does this mean we're pinned' she asked and laughed to hide the depth of her feelings.

'Do kids *still* use that expression?' He was reading the *L.A. Times* and sipping fresh-squeezed grapefruit juice that he had picked up at Mrs. Gooch's. As usual, he had opened first to the sports section. She watched him as he scanned the columns looking for his basketball fix. Jahne clutched the key. He had never given his key to Mary Jane. She stared at him. He must have felt her gaze, because he looked up. Another tribute that only an exquisite woman would receive from Sam: he'd even interrupt his fanatical sports-fan pursuits for her.

'You know how I know that I'll never be a real Angelino?' he asked. She shook her head. 'Because I could never, ever love the Lakers.' He turned back to the sports pages. 'You'd think, with all the displaced New Yorkers out here, they'd give better coverage to the Knicks,' he grumbled. He cocked an eyebrow at her. 'Did I tell you that you look better in my sweats than any woman I've ever known?'

Demurely, she tucked her legs up under herself and pulled the stretched-out grey shirtfront over her knees. 'And have a lot of women modelled your sweats?' she asked. She tried to sound casual, and succeeded, but she cursed herself for asking.

'I've had my share.' Sam smiled, looking over the scores. Don't start, she told herself. But she felt the wave of curiosity and rage grow. Where had he spent the last few nights? In whose bed?

'Sam, how many women have you really loved?' she asked.

He looked up from the paper. 'Uh-oh. Is this going to be an "I'll-show-you-mine-if-you-show-me-yours"? Because I don't play that game, Jahne. And if we did, I'd win, because I'm a lot older than you are.' He paused and looked her over appreciatively. 'Although I imagine there was a long and distinguished line of high-school boys who broke their hearts over you. Not that I want to hear about any of them. After all, I'm more than a decade past *my* sexual peak.'

'Not that I could tell.'

'Ah, you bring out the best in me.' He went back to the scores.

She should read the arts section, take a look at the book reviews, and give it up. Just leave it alone, she told herself, but she couldn't. It was as if all those years of unspoken jealousy, all those horrible years as Mary Jane, when she lived on crumbs and closed her eyes to everything she couldn't bear to see, couldn't afford to see, were spilling out now. 'I don't want to hear about your conquests. I just want to know who you *loved*.'

He frowned, lowering the newspaper. 'Now, at last, you're sounding your age.' He put down the sports section, got up, and came to her, seating himself on the arm of the big chair she was in. 'What do you want to know that for?' he asked her, his voice gentle. 'Isn't it enough to know that I love you? Jahne, I'm working so hard to make you look good in the movie. I'm championing you. Don't you know how I feel?'

'You were married,' she said. It sounded like an accusation, even to herself.

He rolled his eyes and sighed. 'Yes, I was married. I thought I loved her at the time, but now I realize that we were both too young to know who we were, let alone who we loved.'

What was she looking for? she asked herself. She didn't know, but she couldn't stop. 'How old were you?'

'Oh, about your age,' he laughed. 'But you have your head on a lot firmer than I ever did.' He reached over and stroked her hair. Then he put a hand on both sides of her face, turning her head gently back and forth. 'Yep, this head is definitely on firmly.'

But this wasn't enough. She had to know. She had to hear it. 'If you didn't love your wife, who did you love?' she went on, relentlessly.

'Jahne, there are questions I've never asked you. I felt you didn't want to talk about them. That was all right with me. Can't you feel the same?'

'You mean my scars?' she asked. 'That's different. They have nothing to do with you. But who you love, *how* you love, does have to do with me.'

Sam stood up, turned away, and reached for his glass of juice. He took a swallow, then wiped his mouth with the back of his long, graceful hand. She thought he was ignoring her question, closing the subject, and she felt both irritation and relief. Then he spoke. 'I once loved a woman named Nora. She was crazy, I was crazy, but I did love her.'

Jahne felt her heart begin to beat harder. Was that it, then? Had he *never* loved Mary Jane? 'Did she love you?'

'Who knows?' He shrugged. 'She said she did, but she left me for the producer of my first play. I guess she figured producers cast more often than playwrights.' He gave her a lopsided grin. 'She was right.'

She couldn't smile at the joke. 'Who else?' she asked. Please, God, she prayed silently, please, God, let him say he loved Mary Jane.

'I loved a woman in New York. Another actress.'

Thank you, God. Oh, thank you. But then it occurred to her that it might not be Mary Jane he was thinking of. It could have been anyone. Bethanie Lake, for all she knew. Jahne felt her heart flutter, then beat even harder. 'What was her name?'

'It's not important now.' He got off the sofa arm and knelt on the floor in front of her, putting his two hands on her shoulders. He looked deeply into her eyes. 'I can honestly say that I never loved anyone the way I love you. No contest. Nothing even close. I feel blessed to touch you.' He moved his hands up to her cheeks and lifted her face to his. 'Do you believe me?'

So, there it was. The Lord had given, and the Lord had taken away. If he had loved Mary Jane, he was negating it now, even as he told her that he loved her. Tears filled Jahne's eyes.

'Oh, Jahnie, don't cry. I knew I shouldn't have played your stupid twenty questions! I swear that I've forgotten every one of them. They don't matter. There's only you.' He drew her from the chair and circled her with his arms, rocking her as if she were a child. 'There's only you,' he said.

Jahne stood on the set of *3/4* with all the lights turned on her, Marty and the crew all staring, the cameras rolling. 'Perfect,' Marty was saying. 'You are perfect.' But then it was Sam's voice coming from the darkness behind the light. 'Perfect,' he said clearly. She was naked, but she stood there proudly, admired by all of them.

Then, 'Are you crazy?' Lila shrieked. 'Look at those scars! Look at them!' And as they looked, Jahne could feel the scars growing red, glowing. Then, in her shame and horror, she felt her breasts begin to sag, her thighs to bulge, her stomach to hang, her ass to droop, and the men, Lila, and the audience all began to laugh. Neil was there beside her, dressed as a magician. 'Ta-da!' he chortled, as he waved a magic wand. 'Before and after. After and before.'

Jahne woke from the nightmare in a sweat.

Sam slept beside her, but Jahne was terrified. Her breath came in gasps, but Sam didn't awaken. Quietly, so as not to disturb him, she got out of bed, left the room, and went into the cold white marble bathroom. It was enormous, vaster even than the one at the Beverly Wilshire, with a big jacuzzi, built-in makeup drawers, recessed lights, an enclosed toilet, and a bidet. Jahne shivered in its coldness.

Jahne flicked on the light, blinked, and saw herself, reflected in the floor-to-ceiling mirror. She approached it more closely, scrutinizing her face, the face she had bought. She stared into her eyes, her own, unaltered eyes. But in the light of the new bathroom, it seemed to her even her eyes had changed. She couldn't bear to look at them.

She flicked off the light and wandered into the high-ceilinged living room of her new house. It was impressive. The white tile floor seemed to stretch endlessly into the dining room, the long hall, and through to the kitchen. Jahne drifted towards the glass doors that led out to the pool and garden. The moonlight poured down, one of the few smog-free nights in L.A. Jahne stood and looked out to the perfect terrace, the perfect topiary trees, the perfect Roman pool, the perfect everything. And, La Brecque had assured her, all perfectly safe. Little or no chance of madmen intruders, fans breaching the walls, photographers telezooming in on her.

Too bad she didn't like the place. It had nothing to do with her, it had nothing to do with her taste, who she was, or the way she wanted to live. It was forced on her, like her fame, like her new life. And it was grand, but no place she wanted to be. She sighed. Her feet were very cold on the tiles of the floor.

Then Snowball, her sleek black cat, rubbed up against her leg. When they had arrived at the house after their trip, Sam had admired everything but Snowball. Back in New York, he had never really liked Midnight, either. The city cat used to pounce on his chest at night and wake him. 'Why do women have cats?' he'd grumbled. As if sensing that, Snowball had kept away, but now he nuzzled Jahne's left foot, as if that would warm her. She scooped him up gratefully and went back to the bedroom.

Sam was awake when she entered. 'Where were you?' he asked, out of the darkness.

'I had a dream. It woke me, so I just took a look around.'

He held his hand out to her, tried to pull her onto the bed. 'I had a dream, too. It was about you,' he murmured. He tugged at her and she stumbled, almost falling over him. Snowball jumped out of her arms, tried to gain a footing, and took off across Sam's chest. Sam shrieked with surprise and pain at the scratch.

'Oh, no, Midnight!' Jahne cried. 'I'm so sorry, Sam. I was holding the cat.'

Sam was silent for a moment, then longer. In the darkness, she became frightened. 'Are you all right?' she asked. He said nothing; then she heard him move, fumble for the light, and the room was ablaze. She blinked in the sudden glare, saw the scratches across his chest, the blood just beginning to ooze up. But it was his face that scared her.

'Not Midnight,' he said. 'That isn't the cat's name.'

'What did I call him?' Jahne asked. But she knew. The dark, her voice, the cat had all conspired at last to give her away.

'Black cats named Snowball, white ones named Midnight. Contrary Mary. Who are you?' he whispered.

She sat, frozen, at the side of the bed.

'Who are you?' he demanded again, and moved across to her, a hand gripping each of her shoulders. 'This has all happened before, hasn't it? A cat pouncing on me in bed. Except it wasn't a black cat named Snowball, it was a white one named Midnight. Who *are* you?'

His voice had risen now, and he stared deep, deep into her eyes. Eyes from which she'd removed her deep-blue contact lenses. 'Oh, my God,' he said, and she saw the recognition come to his face. But 'Who are you?' he asked again.

She felt as if her world were coming apart, as if she were spinning out of control. 'I don't know,' she whispered.

They sat opposite one another, on either side of the kitchen table, the overhead light unbelievably harsh. The clock ticked loudly. A quarter past three in the morning. Sam was pale, his mouth compressed to a colourless line.

'When did you decide to do this?' he asked again.

They had been going around and around. Jahne had never been so tired. She had tried to answer all his questions. Despite her rage, she felt, somehow, guilty. Well, she should have told him. She should have let him make the decision, not forced this on them. But she was tired of all his questions. She had told him the story, all of it, and now he was asking her to repeat, to clarify. Like he was a lawyer, or something. But she owed him at least this, she told herself, and took a deep breath. 'In the winter. After you left.'

'Hey, don't make it sound as if those things were related — our breakup and your surgery.'

'They were, though.'

'Jahne . . . Mary Jane . . . you made a decision to slice up your flesh, and you can't blame it on me!'

'Oh, can't I? Why not? Didn't you always let me know I wasn't pretty enough? Didn't you?'

'That's a complete lie! Goddamn it! I never said a word about your looks.'

'I didn't say that you *said* anything. But you let me know. You slept with all the pretty ones. Because I wasn't enough. Not the way I was. And then Hollywood agreed with you, and you left me. So I decided to change things. Don't you dare rebuke me for that.'

'It was all in your head. We broke up because it was over, that's all.'

Jahne stood up. She felt herself trembling all over, and a heat in her belly and chest that she recognized for the pure rage it was. 'Don't you dare lie to me about that!' she roared, and her own voice filled the kitchen. 'I've slept with you, and I know the truth. Mary Jane never got a word, never a goddamn word of praise. But Jahne . . .' She took a breath, lowered her voice and began to imitate his during lovemaking. 'You're so beautiful. Yes, Jahne, yes. God, I love your legs, your breasts. You're so perfect. You're . . .'

'Shut up!' he shouted. Her mimicry had been eerie. He jumped up, striding to the door.

'Where are you going? Don't you dare leave now.'

'Goddamn it! Don't tell me what to do!' He tripped over the chair at the counter, and it clattered to the floor. He continued to move towards the door. Jahne knew that if he walked out now she would kill him or she would die. She picked up the heavy pottery bowl from the centre of the table and hurled it at the door. It smashed against the wall, leaving a deep scar in the door frame.

The shards flew around the room and skittered on the floor. She hadn't missed his head by much. He turned back to her, blinking his eyes. Was that fear she saw there?

'Don't turn your back on me,' she warned him. 'Don't lie, and don't take me for granted. I'm not the same woman you abandoned in New York, you son-of-a-bitch.'

'You've lied to me. What do you want me to do, ignore it? I don't even know who the fuck you are. I can't ever trust you again.'

'Big fucking deal! Like you haven't lied to me daily. About the part in *Jack and Jill*, about Bethanie Lake, about April Irons, about who was going to play opposite me in *Birth*, about whether the script was any good . . .' Despite her determination not to, she began to cry. Because she knew that, in part, he was right. Who was she? The ageing, abandoned Miss Havisham, raging in her rotting bridal gown, or Estella, the cold revenge? It felt as if she was both, and couldn't contain them. It felt as if victimized Mary Jane and the new Jahne were tearing at her own guts. She moved to the counter, picked up the vase of anemones, and threw them across the floor. The release felt necessary. She wiped her arm across the counter, smashing the pitcher, the crystal glasses. Because either the glassware or she was going to be smashed. She turned to him. Sam still stood in the doorway, frozen by her outburst. He was not a violent man.

'What do you want from me, Jahne? What the hell do you want?'

'I want you to love me.'

'But I did love you! And you do this.'

'Well, see how it feels. I loved you more than anyone in my life. You weren't just a walk-on in a cast of thousands. You don't know what it felt like, loving you and knowing I wasn't enough. Not perfect enough. Not pretty enough. Not young enough.'

'So you decided to teach me a lesson? Jesus Christ, it's macabre. The Revenge of the Stepford Wife. That's not your nose, that's half of your ass, and that's a plastic chin. All the time we were together, you were laughing at me. I was grovelling at your feet, and you were laughing.'

She looked up at him. 'Laughing is the last thing I was doing,' she said.

Then, there, under the unforgiving glare, in the shambles that had been her kitchen, she realized the enormity of her problem: he was the only man who could heal her pain. If he could love

645

her now, knowing who she had been and what she had done, he could heal the split in her. His absolution, his understanding and acceptance, his love would be the blessing of total acceptance. If he forgave her, she could forgive herself. If he loved her, she could love herself.

And if he couldn't, she realized that all she had been would blow away, be gone forever. And she could never trust that any man who loved her new incarnation was not betraying her old one.

A fear, deeper and colder than any she had known, slipped like a knife into her belly and froze the anger. She shivered. Her future, her life, depended on Sam's seeing the truth, owning it, and being able to come through this with her. He had loved her, he did love her. He must continue to love her. If she stopped, right now, and made him realize that here, at last, their better selves could meet, there was a chance that both of them could win. 'Please, Sam. Please,' she began. 'I know you're hurt. I'm so sorry. But this is important. Really, really important.' She started walking towards him, her bare feet numb to the broken glass beneath her soles. Tears ran down her cheeks. 'Don't just blame, Sam. Because, if you do, I won't be able to forgive you.' Jahne continued to walk towards him and to sob, but Sam, pale as death didn't try to console her. He merely shook his head.

'How could you?' he asked. 'Mary Jane, how could you?'

Oh, God, it seemed hopeless. All at once, she felt the glass beneath her feet, and the pain that began to throb. She looked down. Blood was mixing with the glass shards on the white ceramic tile. It didn't matter. It wasn't important. What was important was getting him to understand. How could she explain the self-hate, the desperation, the ambition that had driven her? How could she defend having her flesh vacuumed, cut, and stapled, having her skin peeled from her tissue and relocated? How could she explain giving up sensation in her nipples for sensational breasts? How could she explain dropping her friends, her life, and doing all this? How could she explain, to the only person that she wanted – that she needed – to understand, how could she explain what it had felt like to be plain, ageing, an invisible, undesirable lump of a woman? How could she tell him? She must gain his compassion. How could she do this? she wondered. But also, how could she not?

Sam looked at her again, with horror and disgust. 'How could you do this to me?' he asked.

Infamy

I wouldn't do nudity in films.
To act with my clothes on is a performance; to act with my clothes off is a documentary.

Julia Roberts

Facing the press is more difficult than bathing a leper.

Mother Teresa

It's all fantasy that if you're considered attractive you have a perfect life and there's no dark side.

Michelle Pfeiffer

So, you hate Sam Shields, right? He's like all those bums you've had in your own life, all those men who left you, who lied, who weren't there for you in the end. But remember, like all those bums, Sam Shields feels like he's the one with an axe to grind, he's the one who's gotten a raw deal, the one who has been disappointed, the one who was betrayed.

After the scene in the kitchen, Sam reeled out of Jahne's house as if he were drunk. He could hardly believe that the woman he had loved, the woman he had risked his career for, had betrayed him in this way. Jahne was Mary Jane. It was unbelievable. It was ghoulish, a Stephen King horror. She had fooled him, made a fool of him. In a kind of sick fascination, he tried to remember conversations about their past. How often had she laughed at him, how often had she caught him in lies, evasions, and half-truths?

Inevitably, defensiveness set in. After all, he'd been caught posturing, foolish for months. But how much longer had she worked at setting him up for it? He was, perhaps, not all that he should be, but she, she was crazy and malevolent. What kind of woman would dream of such an act? And what kind would actually achieve it? Well, Reader, how would you answer that question?

Sam sat in the darkened screening room watching the new rough cut of *Birth of a Star*, squirming nervously in his seat. It worked. Well, it worked in a way. It certainly wasn't the movie he had envisioned *Birth of a Star* to be. It was more like *Blue Velvet* meets *Akkbar*. But it did work.

He and April, Laslo and Michael, along with the body doubles, had flown to Hong Kong to work for nineteen feverish days on the new scenes for the film. Joy Wah Studios – 'Where Hollywood Comes to Get Oriented' – was a film factory that turned out dozens of action and porn films for the Asian market each month. They had technicians and special-effects crews that worked fast and cheap. And now their efforts had transformed the movie.

Sam lifted one of his hands to his temple. He had had a

merciless headache for a week or maybe more. Nothing seemed to help. Perhaps it was the food or water in Hong Kong, maybe it was staring at the moviola editing screen for hours, but even the daily massages and the Chinese acupuncturist hadn't helped.

Sam had worked day and night to save the film. Well, to save his ass. After the new scenes had been written and shot, after the more difficult splicing had been done, only then could he leave the scene of the crime, return to L.A. with the rough cut and his headaches.

He hadn't sold out, he told himself fiercely. The film was different from what he'd intended, but not necessarily worse. In fact, the first version of the film, as he had originally envisioned it, was a failure, stillborn. He'd always had reservations about the stupid melodrama. He even now wasn't sure if it was his forced revisions, Michael's hostility, or Jahne's flat performance that had miscarried, but, whatever it was, the film as it had been was a certain failure. Now, with the music laid in and a little more tightening, this *Birth of a Star* had a chance. That it was the most costly sexually explicit mainstream film ever made, he had no doubt. That it would make back its cost, he was almost certain. But whether it was any good or not, he was still not sure.

He had left for Hong Kong furious with Jahne. He had not spoken to her before he left. But, in the few hours that he had to himself there, he stared out the floor-to-ceiling windows of the Regent Hotel at the magnificent view of the Hong Kong harbour and tried to fit pieces back together. He had loved Jahne – perhaps he still loved her – and now he knew why. She had been able to please his eye, as only a beautiful woman could, while caring for him in the way that Mary Jane had. She had the passion of the plain. Mary Jane had made him feel comfortable, and worshipped. He did not have to strive to please her. She had given him the acceptance of a mother, while Jahne had given him the sexual thrill of a girl the age of a daughter. Had he been judged harshly for wanting that? Wasn't that what all men craved? The security of unjudgemental love without the boredom? Sexual temptation without challenge or the threat of abandonment? Jahne had all the maturity of a forty-year-old woman in the body of a teen. And the vulnerability of both.

Back in New York, he had been ashamed of Mary Jane, and ashamed of his dependence on her, but he knew now that he *had* loved her. And if she was someone he would never have introduced to his parents, or felt comfortable with at a Hollywood party, that was human, wasn't it? Anyone could understand that. He shifted uncomfortably in his seat, the images on the screen torturing him. Jahne's face, Jahne's body looming up at him. Overpowering him.

He also knew that he had loved Jahne. *And* had been proud of her. Surely she could tell that, and she would have to be the first to admit that as Mary Jane she had not been a partner he could show off with pride. The knowledge felt like a weight in his gut, but it was the truth, for good or ill. He was ashamed, and the shame made him angry. Now he just had to decide what to do about it.

Had Jahne made him a laughing stock? Did jerks like Molly and Chuck and that little rat Neil know and laugh at him? At his shallowness, and his stupidity? Who else thought he was a fool? All of Hollywood? He sighed. Had she done it all in spite? Or had Jahne loved him? Surely M.J. had. Had she gone through this transformation out of love, or revenge? The fact was, despite this horrible trick, despite this betrayal, he did still love Jahne. And perhaps, just possibly, they could work something out. Later. After he had done what he could to salvage *Birth*.

Now, returned to L.A., he holed up in editing rooms and guarded the screenings. No one but Michael, Seymore, and April could gain entry. He'd keep coaxing it into shape. Only then would the suits get to see it. But it would all be kept under wraps. And he would not speak to Jahne or see her. He would let her sit this out alone. She'd caused him enough grief for right now.

In the meantime, word had already appeared in the trades that the movie was in trouble. April was furious. 'Those fuckers could bury us before we have a chance,' she screamed. 'We won't be able to get distributors to even *look* at it.' She'd ordered Marketing to move up the opening of the film and to have a quick roll-out to eleven hundred theatres. Jahne, Laslo, none of the others, not even little A. Joel Grossman would get to see it. Sam shook his aching head. Poor A. Joel. He was a lost man anyway since Adrienne had coupled up with Michael McLain. Losing a love could do that to a man. Sam had to smile, despite the pain in his head. The smile increased his pain, and he winced, staring at the scene on the screen. The scene was as intense as his headache.

He knew it was the pressure, the guilt, and the anger. But he also knew he wasn't doing this to Jahne, to Mary Jane, out of anger or revenge. Not that she didn't deserve it. But he was going to work that out between them. No, he was doing this to the movie because he had to, to keep control of the project. To keep his career viable. As April told him plainly, if he didn't, someone else would.

And, after all, he told himself, looking up at the screen, it wasn't so very bad, what he had done. Adrienne's body looked beautiful, and the cuts had been seamless: far more seamless than the work that had been done on Jahne's own torso. She would see herself as perfect. Everyone would see her as perfect.

After all, wasn't that what she and every woman really wanted?

Michael McLain leaned back into the softness of the sheets and smiled. And it wasn't even for the camera. Things had taken a definite turn for the better. Shooting had ended a week ago, and it had been, no doubt about it, a real pleasure. Although there had definitely been a certain – how shall we say – awkwardness about stepping out of the scene when his body double took over, Adrienne, the girl who was doubling for Jahne Moore, made it clear that she only had eyes for him. So, even if his stomach wasn't washboard-flat anymore, he still had what it takes. He reached out and patted Adrienne's bare ass, pushed against his back. She had stayed on with him to vacation for a week in Hong Kong. A week of shopping and sex. He loved doing both with her.

And he loved what he had seen in the dailies. The stuff wasn't just hot, it was beautiful and hot. In fact, it was *gorgeous* and *very* hot. The best stroke film ever made. Laslo and that shmuck Sam had figured out some clever angles and approaches. Not since *Don't Look Now*, when Donald Sutherland went down on Julie Christie, had sex looked this good on the screen.

And they had made it as easy for him at the studio as they could. They had a cadre of Oriental girls who powdered and massaged him, who sprayed him with glycerine to imitate sweat, who deferred, who bowed. They even had a 'fluffer,' the pretty, slender girl who ensured his erection.

Yes, it had worked, and it looked to him as if the rough cuts would work. It was risky, of course. But if Nicholson could have a career coup frugging as a fat Joker in *Batman*, and Lancaster and Kirk Douglas could get away with mooning the audience with their wrinkled old asses, surely Michael McLain could bow out as a leading man with lovemaking: bold, graphic lovemaking on the silver screen. And after that, he was history. He was going to get out of the picture business and into something with dignity.

Maybe he'd finally get married.

2

In her twenty years of life so far, there were a lot of things Lila had hated, but working with her mother definitely topped the list. She'd had to watch the old bitch arrive every morning as if *¾* were *her* show, greeting all the crew by name (how the fuck did she learn their names so *quickly*? Lila didn't know any of them after more than a year), seeing Theresa preen her pulled and lifted old face for the makeup man and consult with the boom operator. It all made Lila sick with rage.

Worst of all had been watching her with Marty. Marty had been surprised when Lila had told him she'd changed her mind, that she would allow her mother on the show, but he'd jumped at it. Lila watched him work with Theresa. Jesus, he didn't have to suck up to the Puppet Mistress. But he deferred to her, he laughed at her stupid jokes, he gave serious consideration to her suggestions about lighting and camera angles.

Lila had felt her rage boiling to the surface, but she swallowed it down over and over again, until she felt as if she might scream. Her mother had made the deal clear — she had made her devastating threat crystal-clear. So Lila raged in silence. And along with the rage, she felt something else. It was jealousy, she admitted. She was jealous when Marty paid attention to anyone else. All during the hiatus, she had had him to herself. She knew she would have to share him with the other two. Bad enough, but sharing him with Theresa was unbearable. She found herself watching them through narrowed eyes, biting the inside of her cheeks. After the first two days, her mouth had been a bloody mess.

The only comfort she had during all of it was the gossip that *Birth of a Star* was a shambles. Lila ploughed through the trades and the columns looking for the latest inside scoop. She had been delighted when Minos called and gave her a full report about the infighting between the director, the producer, and the stars. And she was even more pleased when Marty told her that he had heard it was a total bomb and being rushed into release before distributors could back out.

So, with her mother's segment almost finished and in the can, she could focus on the upcoming Emmys. She wasn't worried about Sharleen wresting an Emmy from her. It was only Jahne that Lila worried about. Well, a bomb at the box office shouldn't affect the Emmy award, but she knew it did. She smiled and prayed *Birth of a Star* would be released before the voting took place. It should have been the movie that made Lila a star, but if it was the one that brought Jahne Moore down, that would be some compensation.

It took almost two weeks, but at last the unbearable business with Theresa had ended. Going home that evening, for the first time Lila managed to smile at Marty's jokes. She'd agreed to have dinner with him, though not to stay over. She never slept at his house. Sally was getting used to the 2.00 A.M. drive back to Malibu.

'It wasn't so bad, was it, Lila?' Marty asked her, and she knew he was referring to the work with her mother. They had not spoken one word about it during the two weeks of shooting.

'Bad enough,' she told him curtly. 'Thank God the script didn't demand I had to act as if I loved her. If I could do *that*, I'd deserve an Oscar, not an Emmy.'

'First things first,' Marty told her. 'The Academy will see this show right before the voting. And you were good, Lila. Really good. It will help.' He smiled. 'I think we're going to break some records when this is televised. No one gets more than a thirty-per-cent share. Not even *Murphy Brown* after Dan Quayle's remark. But I think we'll top that.'

'What did *M*A*S*H*'s last episode pull?' she asked.

'Over eighty, but that was before cable fragmented the audience.'

'I want ninety.'

Marty laughed, until he looked at her and realized she wasn't joking. 'If we pulled ninety, Les Merchant and Hyram Flanders would pay whatever it took to have us both canonized. My mother would love it. A saint as a son. For a Catholic, that's better than a doctor.' Lila didn't smile. He decided to change the subject. 'Someone is having a birthday soon,' he said. 'And have I got a surprise for her.'

God, she hated it when he got cute. 'So what?' she asked.

'How do you want to celebrate it?' he asked. 'The town is yours.'

'I'd like to see a screening of *Birth of a Star*,' she told him.

654

He felt the cut. Jesus, she knew how to get to him. He still regretted that *he* hadn't gotten the rights, that a movie *he* should have made had fallen into the hands of barbarians. And he also knew how tight security would be over the prints. Lila had a knack for picking the only things he couldn't deliver as the only things she wanted. 'Why bother?' he asked, with a casualness he didn't feel. 'It stinks.'

'How do you know?' she asked. 'Have you seen it?'

'No, but . . .'

'I want to see it.' she told him. 'That's what I want for my birthday.'

Sally did it. How, Marty didn't even inquire. After all, Sally was still connected, and it was best not to delve too deep. Just appreciate that the cans of film, each marked *Birth of a Star*, were all ready for the private screening, along with the rest of the evening's props: the perfectly set dinner table, the gladioli, the candles, the fire that crackled in the fireplace and took the chill off the air conditioning, as well as the tiny velvet box that sat, waiting, on the mantel shelf.

Marty wasn't a vain man. Looking so ordinary – that's the most truthful he was capable of being about his looks – he usually dressed in a perfunctory way. But this evening, he was doing the full treatment. At Lila's insistence, he had started using a personal trainer, and had had a full, hard session with him today. He looked at himself in the mirror, naked after his shower, and was pleased with what he saw. Lila, it appeared more and more, was good for him. The training was beginning to pay off. Flat stomach, tighter skin. Even the slightest bulge of biceps on his skinny arm. Not bad.

The most difficult indulgence in vanity he had to accept was the hairdresser Lila had insisted he use tonight. If she had to put herself through such preparations, why should he be able to get away with less? she had asked. She was right again, although, with her beauty, any professional assistance she got was really only framing. The ministrations *he* needed came more in the category of camouflage.

But enough of that. He *was* happy. He turned from his full-length mirror, and held up the tux from Bijan Lila had bought him. He began to dress, each layer making him more excited, since everything he now wore was personally selected by Lila, including the silk underwear that brushed so gently against the head of his penis. The sensation was more than just pleasant. It was a taste of what was to follow, after the screening, during their oh-so-private party. Marty shivered. Scenes from their nights together flashed on him at all sorts of times during the day, leaving him sweaty and enervated. No woman had ever thrilled him, enthralled him like this. He was her slave. And tonight he would prove it.

He had come up with the perfect birthday gift. It sat wrapped with a crimson satin ribbon on the coffee table. And he knew it would make Lila happier than anything else would. It was a script – a script so perfect for her talents that she would have to love it. It would be his gift to her. And, after next season, they would make the movie together, even if it meant delaying 3/4. Even if it meant cancelling the fucker. He thought of Sy's screams, of the network's reaction, of Flanders Cosmetics going ballistic, but he only smiled. That's what Hollywood lawyers were for.

Lila looked down at the big box that Robbie had set on the table. She hadn't seen him for a long time, but he looked as pudgy and pathetic as ever. 'Well, happy birthday to me,' Lila said, smiling.

'I had to wait until she was on the set. Then Ken decoyed Kevin to get him out of there. There was no other way. I don't know what she's going to do when she finds out they're gone.' He was sweating, his bland, round face a mask of concern.

Lila just snorted. She had to get ready for her date with Marty – there were a lot of preparations for their evenings together – and she had no time for this wet, fat fuck. It had taken him months to bring over this tribute, so it might well take her that long to forgive him. But her eyes glistened as she looked at the box.

'Well, okay,' she told him curtly. 'But I've got things to do now. I'm going out.'

'Anyone I know?' Robbie asked brightly. Yeah, like I'm going to confide in you, she thought.

'Maybe,' she answered, as noncommittal as a confessional priest. She walked to the door and opened it. 'See you,' she said, indicating his way out.

'Don't you have time even for a coffee?' he asked. She hated how needy he sounded; it made her angry, not sympathetic.

Lila didn't have a lot of insights, but she knew she was the type who took advantage of and despised weakness.

'Not even a quick espresso!' she said brightly and shut the door on his hopeful face.

*

Lila settled back on the sofa of Marty's screening room. Dinner had been perfect, and now they'd screen the purloined copy of *Birth*. She knew she'd set him a challenge, and she knew he'd rise to it.

'Roll it, Sally,' Marty said into the intercom, and then dimmed the lights. The credits had not yet been cut into the beginning.

It began predictably. Michael McLain meets the bitch. He's successful. She's a nobody with talent. He helps her. He's on the slide, but she worships him. It was okay, but nothing special. She heard Marty shift restlessly in his seat. Good. He didn't like it.

Then Michael, up on the screen, bent in to Jahne. 'Prove that you trust me,' he said, and his eyes, for the first time, came alive. There was a quick cut to his hand on hers, then a dissolve, and his hand was now on hers again, but she was stretched across a bed, and he was holding her arms down as she gave him head! Lila gasped. You couldn't quite see everything, but the act was clearly implied. And then that close-up of her mouth and the cut to his thrusting hips from behind, and again her mouth.

Michael, on the screen, moaned, and Lila thought for a moment she heard Marty moan as well. Then Jahne's hands broke free and clutched at Michael's bare rump, as if she couldn't get enough of him.

'Jesus Christ!' Marty gasped.

'Worship me,' Michael was grunting, and the scene faded out.

The story unfolded, and there was another scene, now with both of them in a public doorway, Michael opening her buttons, pulling up her skirt, taunting her, and doing her from behind, oblivious of the occasional passersby. Then she turned to face him, wanting more. Jahne was gorgeous, her legs perfect, wrapped around him like a monkey. It was unbelievable. Her perfect breasts bobbed before his mouth and he gobbled at them.

Lila felt as if she were hypnotized. This stuff was porn – it was filth – but it was beautifully shot. And it was sexy. Very, very sexy. Wasn't it? Lila could never be sure. In the dark she quickly reached across to Marty and put her hand on his crotch. She pulled it away as if hot coals had burned her. 'You have an erection!' she cried, jumping up. It was a fact and an accusation.

'Lila, I . . .'

'You like her! You want her!'

'Lila, don't be silly. It's only a movie. It's a sexy movie. I . . .'

'Goddamn it!' she cried. 'You have a hard-on for her. You think she's more of a woman than I am, don't you?' Her voice had risen to a scream. Behind her, the images of Michael and Jahne continued to couple. 'You do, don't you?'

'Sally, please, turn it off,' Marty said into the intercom. 'Then you can go.' He turned the lights on and looked at Lila. It was the first time she'd ever appeared possessive. 'Lila, the hard-on was an automatic. Good porn will always get a rise out of me. I'm visual, Lila. But this is a desecration. *Birth of A Star* was a classic. It shocked me to see Jahne in a porn movie. I had no idea . . .'

'Do you want her?' Lila asked.

'I only want you. No one but you,' he said.

Lila collapsed onto the sofa and began to sob. 'She's going to get all the attention. She's going to get the Emmy and an Oscar.'

'Are you crazy? In this Puritan town? April must have been desperate. They'd never have gone for it otherwise. I mean, what kind of rating will it get? This is no PG-13. The Network will go nuts. They'll evoke the morals clause. And Flanders will go crazy. Jahne can kiss that contract goodbye.'

'Really?' Lila wiped her eyes. 'You think it won't go over well?'

'Jesus, Lila! One of America's sweethearts going down on Michael McLain?' Marty laughed. He walked to the console table at the side of the room and picked up a package. 'Not to worry, darling. She's history. Meanwhile, look what I got you for your birthday.' He handed her the script.

'What is it?' she asked, suspiciously.

'Just the best vehicle for a young actress that I've seen in ten years. And it's for you. We can film it before next season. I've got a green light from Paramount already.'

Lila jumped up off the couch and ran across the room to him. 'Yes!' she cried. 'Yes!' And she hugged him tightly.

'Happy birthday,' Marty told her.

'Oh, thank you!'

This was it! This was it! She'd be bigger than Jahne Moore and Sharleen Smith. That she could be certain of, even before this movie was shot. Marty had never done anything second-rate. It was Oscar-nomination stuff, for sure. And now, with the promise of this film and the Emmy all but guaranteed, now she *knew* she'd be the biggest thing to happen in this town in years. And, sweetest of all, she'd be bigger than her mother. Bigger than Theresa O'Donnell had *ever* been. She shivered to think she almost hadn't responded to Marty's advances, and almost turned down both him and the chance for this role. She reached out in the darkness and squeezed Marty's arm.

Only Marty was powerful enough to do this for her. Only Marty would care for her enough to do it. Perhaps their affair wasn't perfect. Perhaps he wasn't someone she even wanted to touch, but he was good to her.

He took care of her as no one ever had. Tears flooded her eyes. 'I love you,' she whispered.

'Good,' he said simply. He covered her hand with his own for a moment and then stood up and walked to the fireplace. 'There's something else here for you,' he said, and came to her with the little box. He held it out to her.

Lila took it and quickly flipped open the top. Inside, the white satin only enhanced the sparkle of a huge marquis-cut diamond.

'Twelve-carat. Perfect clarity. Perfect colour. Perfect. Just like you,' Marty said.

Lila stared at the ring. It caught the rays from the dying fire and refracted them in a thousand points of light across the ceiling and walls. The ring was so grown-up, so Republican, but so breathtaking. Lila could not take her eyes off it.

'You're going to marry me,' Marty told her.

3

Jahne couldn't eat, couldn't sleep. The scene with Sam had been awful, once he realized who she was. He had been more than angry, he had been enraged. And she had felt strangely guilty. Guilty for lying, guilty for loving him still, guilty for letting him love her. He had stormed out, shocked and hurt and angry, but he had called five days later, five long days later, during the day, when he knew she'd be out, and left a message. He said that he'd be working hard on the movie, that he'd have to go to Hong Kong for special effects and some reshooting and would be gone several weeks. But that he'd been doing a lot of thinking, that he wanted to see her and would call her as soon as he returned.

He still had not called. And she had been stupid enough to think that time would allow a healing, would allow him to join his love for Mary Jane to his love for her today. But did she want him to? Did she still want a man so selfish, so narcissistic, that he could only see her through himself? She thought again of his immense nerve, thinking that she had done all of this for him and to him. What an ass!

Yet a small doubt had entered her mind. She'd done it to grab a chance, a last chance to succeed on her own terms: to act, to pursue her career, her craft, her calling. Or had she?

Lying in bed, sleepless night after night, she was tortured by the idea. Had she done all this to get Sam back? Or to get back at Sam? Both ideas appalled her. She'd never imagined herself so needy, or so angry, that she'd go that far for either love or revenge. But maybe she had.

She roamed the big, empty house at night, lights off. The rooms felt empty, so empty. Tomblike. Oh, she could play Aida, bricked into the grave alone. That was how abandoned she felt. But abandoned by whom?

Over and over, she felt herself drawn to the mirrors in her dressing room. There, at the marble counters that were pristine and cold as a mortuary table, she stared at her own face, at the face she had bought. A face Sam said he had loved.

The face had given her power – power over Pete, and power enough to get the Melrose Playhouse part, power to be selected by Marty, power to entrance Sam. But what real kind of power was it, the power that these lips, this nose, the line of this jaw had given?

It was only clear to Jahne how very powerless she was after the breakup with Sam and the resumption of 3/4. It was clear that things had changed on the set. What little weight her opinion had earlier carried was now completely usurped by the new closeness between Lila and Marty and the ill will her absence for the beginning of the season had bred. As far as *Birth* went, since the scene with Sam, Jahne had clearly been cut out of the editing process. It wasn't only that her calls were not returned and her services no longer needed; Jahne Moore couldn't even seem to get a screening of her own film. It was incredible. The International offices informed her that both April Irons and Sam Shields were unavailable: both were out of the country. She called Seymore LeVine and got the same stonewalling, tried Sam's number at his house. No answer, no matter what time of day or night she called.

She left no message. What was the use? It was all out of her control.

Lila, on the other hand, appeared to be in complete control. Jahne's part was even stupider (and smaller) then before, while Lila stole almost every scene, got every punch line and every close-up. Sharleen walked through her part humbly, but Jahne found it humiliating. And Sy Ortis was no help. No help at all.

'What can I tell you?' he wheezed into the phone. 'You made your bed. Marty doesn't appreciate ingratitude. You screwed him with *Birth*, now he screws you. What can I tell you?'

'You can tell me how I can get a screening of *Birth of a Star*, for God sake!' Jahne snapped. 'I don't have a clue to what's happening.'

'You're not alone. Apparently it's in big trouble.' His voice was heavy with satisfaction; his silent 'I told you so' hung in the air. A part of Jahne knew that he was right, had been right all along, but for all the wrong reasons. I'll fire him, she thought, but the idea of getting a new agent when *Birth* bombed frightened her. No one but a hungry bum would want to pick her up then, and if Sy was also a bum, he was at least a well-connected, *powerful* bum.

'I guess you were right, Sy. Meanwhile, try and get me a screening,' was all she said before she hung up the phone.

Jahne felt as if she were falling apart. For once, she didn't have to worry about her diet: she couldn't eat. Slipping into her jeans, the ones Mai had sewn for her, she found they gapped at her waist. There were hollows beneath her cheekbones, and darkness under her eyes. And still she hadn't heard from Sam, had seen nothing of *Birth*.

On the set, Pete approached her one afternoon. 'Are you okay?' he asked. They hadn't spoken in months, except for 'hellos' and 'good nights'. She looked up at him from her folding canvas chair; he was as young and simple and straight as he'd always been. I must really look bad if he's noticed, she thought.

'Not so great.' She tried to smile, but it didn't work well.

'Can I do anything to help?' he asked. She had to turn her head away from the kindness.

'No. But thanks.' She watched as he started to walk away, and then it occurred to her. 'Pete. Wait. Isn't your dad a projectionist?' she asked. He nodded. 'Do you think he could get me a screening?'

You might say that Jahne Moore walked into the screening room for *Birth of a Star* a virgin. Two hours and ten minutes later, both her eyes and her cherry had been popped. She watched herself – or someone cut and pasted to appear to be her – fucked half a dozen times in as many positions and costumes by a younger, slimmer Michael McLain. She watched what appeared to be her right breast, ten feet wide on the screen, squeezed by his hands in close-up. She watched what appeared to be her nipples inflate, watched his lips surround them, watched her own face in close-up react to the sensation. She watched as she appeared to kneel to take it doggy style, her perfect ass a heart-shaped invitation. She watched as a leg – supposedly *her* leg – reached up around Michael's neck and caressed his cheek, only to be joined by her other, first framing his face with her calves, then opening wide as a protractor to accommodate him. She saw the sheen of sweat on her arms, her back, her thighs, the dampness on a perfect curl of what was represented as her pubic hair.

She sat beside Pete in the private screening room and she saw the film that *Birth of a Star* had become. It broke all the boundaries between 'popular entertainment' and 'soft porn.' And it wasn't soft at all. It was a film that she had not made, yet her face was up there, the illusion of her body was there for everyone to see: to see and watch her being made love to, watch her achieve orgasm, watch her be violated. Watch her capitulate. How had it happened? she wondered. How had it happened to *her*?

She felt actually dizzy. The beauty of Laslo's photography, the lush music, the perfect settings, all of it cushioned this violation. But a violation it was. How had they even managed to do it? It certainly wasn't either her own scarred body or Michael's ageing one up there. What tricks had April and Laslo and Sam resorted to?

Pete shifted uncomfortably in the seat beside her. He cleared his throat. Once he whispered, 'God!' Then he was silent. She wondered if he had an erection. She didn't want to know.

Then a small thrill of horror passed over her, like an exquisite chill. How many men would get a hard-on from this? How many men would jerk off to her image? How many strangers would fuck her in their minds, in the privacy of their own homes? One of La Brecque's warnings sounded in her ears: 'You can't seem accessible. It's the accessible ones who get killed.' Well, how accessible was a woman who was publicly fucked? And how would she get any respect in the community? How would she ever graduate to real acting jobs, the kind she craved? How would she even show her face? How had this happened?

She thought Sam had loved her. But this, this was not love. This was rage, betrayal, and rape. She stared at the moving images on the screen.

At last the horror ended. The credits rolled as Michael's character walked into the waves. Pete's father must have flicked on the lights from the control booth. Pete looked over at her, blinking in the glare.

Jahne stood up, reached for the arm of the chair, and vomited onto the vacant velvet seat before her.

'So what do you want to do?' Howard Taft asked Jahne. Howard was the best entertainment lawyer in L.A., and the most expensive.

'Sue them. Stop them. Get the film burned.'

'Fine. So what do you *really* want to do?'

'*Sue* them. *Stop* them. *Get the film burned.*'

'Miss Moore – Jahne – that's all well and good, and I know all about artistic differences, but we're talking International Studios here. We're talking April Irons. We're talking *Bob LeVine*. We're not talking about people who roll over nicely when hit with an injunction. Not that we could even *get* an injunction.'

'Why not? They . . .'

'Your contract clearly states that . . .'

'But I didn't know they would do *this*. Don't I have a right to control my own face, my body . . .?'

'Not according to your contract. You requested the body double. You insisted on secrecy and no credit for the body double. They're doing that. You can't sue them for keeping to your contract.'

'But then who *should* I sue?'

'Your agent, I would say. But not if you want to work again.' Howard took off his steel-rimmed glasses, removed a spotless white handkerchief from his breast pocket, and began to wipe the lenses carefully, his kind grey eyes watching her all the time. 'Listen, I'd love to take your money. And there might be some, some . . . *softening* of the final cut that I could wangle, but a suit, I promise you, would be costly, *and* disastrous to your career . . .'

'Fuck my career.'

He paused, shocked. And there was very little that shocked a Hollywood attorney. He licked his lips, clasped his hands together on his perfectly clear desk. 'Well, I can see you feel strongly now, but later your feelings may change. This suit would be longer and more costly than Cliff Robertson's. Worse than Art Buchwald's. The studios cannot afford to give up their right to use your image. You clearly signed the body-double agreement. And suing on this would end your options . . .'

'I don't need those kinds of options.'

'. . . and would ultimately accomplish nothing. April Irons and a squad of bankers put fifty million dollars into this film, and you can not stop it from . . .'

Tears rose in Jahne's eyes. The feeling of powerlessness that she had been trying to deny again swept over her, draining her energy, leaving her weak and helpless. She began to cry. 'Then there's nothing I can do?' she whispered.

'Here,' Howard said, extending his hand, his immaculate handkerchief still in it. 'You can wipe your nose.'

When Jahne left Howard Taft's office, she was too enraged to go home, too angry to stand still. She felt if she didn't keep moving she might hit something or break something, or even explode. Perhaps she had no legal options, but she had personal ones. She got in her car and began driving.

She was breathing hard by the time she reached the Canyon road. She snorted at herself. L.A. makes you soft, she thought, but she felt anything but. She felt harder than she had in her life, hard as steel, as a diamond, and just as ready to cut. If he was here in L.A., she'd find Sam. If he wasn't, she'd . . . She pulled into his driveway.

She found Sam's key, buried deep in her bag. Why did women, why did she, shlepp around so much crap? Makeup, hairbrush, comb, mirror. The burden of being a woman. She tried, quietly, to fit the key in the lock, but her hands shook. She took a deep breath, steadied herself, and, with both hands, managed to slide in the key, turn it, and open the door.

He was there, thank God, and he appeared to be alone. Not that she gave a rat's ass. He could be going down on April Irons while Crystal Plenum was giving him head and she wouldn't care. Not anymore. He was alone, though, lying on the sofa, a washcloth over his eyes, a script lying open on his chest. Some fresh hell of a movie for some new woman he would ruin.

'You lousy piece of shit!' Jahne screamed. He jumped up from the sofa, threw the script or whatever it was he was reading aside. 'Jesus! Oh, Jesus, Jahne. Mary Jane. Oh, Jesus. You frightened me! Listen, I know what you're going to say . . .' He was breathing like he'd run a marathon. Good. She'd scared him. Fine. She wanted him scared.

'No, you don't, you lying cocksucker.'

'Hey.' He stood there, breathing hard, his hands extended in a palmdown, Buddha-calming-the-waters gesture. 'No need for . . .'

'Don't you *dare* tell me what there's a need for *or* how to behave. You're a lying bastard.'

'You're the one who lied! I . . .'

'I've seen it.'

He had the grace to pause for a moment. She watched as he tried to slow his breathing. Old actor's trick. Fuck him and his tricks. 'Jahne, I had no choice. The film hadn't come together. I'd failed April. I failed *you*. This was the only way to get to roll the dice again. And it works, Jahne – Mary Jane –' He fumbled for a moment. 'Once you get over your, your . . .'

'Disgust?'

'Surprise. Once you get over your *surprise*, you'll *see* it works. The way I directed you . . .'

'Directed me? You *pimped* me. You pimped me as if I were a twenty-dollar whore. Now don't insult my intelligence by telling me I'm going to like it! And it wasn't *me* you were directing. I wasn't informed or involved with any of this. It was a couple of body doubles, Michael McLain, and a tube of K-Y Jelly!'

'What good would it have done to ask you? You wouldn't have agreed. And we were not exactly in the negotiating mode.'

'We aren't in that mode now, either.'

She had to pause for a moment as she felt her anger drain out of her. She dropped her bag to the floor and, in her weakness, would have sat down. But she didn't want to be weak in front of him. She wanted to be strong, angry, and scary. She narrowed her eyes and lowered her voice. She began to walk towards him, and was gratified to see him back away. 'You betrayed me, and, like a fool, I blamed myself. The first time, back in New York, I thought, if I'd been prettier, or kinder, or sexier, or more understanding, you wouldn't have run off with Bethanie, sold my part to the highest bidder, and never even bothered to speak to me again.' She had circled him around the sofa. He continued to back away. 'I blamed myself! But what's your excuse now? Now I *am* prettier and kinder and sexier. So what the fuck reason have you got for betraying me *this* time? You know I wanted to be a serious actress. You know how important this picture was to me, to my career. . . .'

Sam's back was against the adobe wall of the fireplace. 'Always you!' he yelled. 'Always you and what *you* want, how *you're* hurt, how *you* feel, what's important for *your* career. What about *me*? I thought you loved *me*. But you never even told me who you were. You tricked me into loving you, and it was *my* career on the line here. Think I'd get a shot at a lot more pictures if fifty million bucks went down the toilet on this one? Did you think about how *I* felt? *I* had to save the picture. And I have.'

'But at what cost, Sam?' She stared at him. Surely he'd admit what he had done.

'Look, *Last Tango In Paris* didn't hurt Brando's career.'

Oh, God. He was hopeless. 'No.' She laughed bitterly. 'Men gain status by fucking women on the screen. But how did Maria Schneider do? Didn't she wind up a suicide?' She turned, picked up her bag, and started to walk away, down the hall to the door.

'I love you, Jahne. I wanted to marry you.'

She stopped, her heart pounding. Then, slowly, she turned around.

'Well, this is a great time to tell me, and a great way for me to find out. Why does your proposal sound like a weapon?'

'Oh, don't give me any holier-than-thou shit, please. If your face wasn't like a blank billboard on the screen, I wouldn't've had to do this. Christ, I worked with what you had, limited as it was.'

'So, it *is* all my fault.'

'"Fault" is a word for children.'

'I'm hearing "fault" from you. And I'm not hearing an apology, or remorse, or even any guilt. Only that what you did was okay, was necessary. You're comfortable? You're glad you did this to me?'

It was the only moment when he paused. He had been looking at her, his eyes angry, opaque, and direct, but now, for the first time, he looked down, turning his head towards the bedroom, but not seeing the bed they had once shared. Then he looked back.

'I didn't betray you,' he said. 'I never told anyone about your scars.'

'Well, congratulations,' she told him, threw his key on the floor, and walked out.

Jahne stood there in the harsh sunlight outside Sam's stupid fake Santa Fe-adobe house and realized she had no place to go, no one to talk to, no one to tell about this horror.

If only Mai were alive. If only she could go to Mai's and have a glass of beer and cry and laugh with her. She got into the car and began to drive, accelerating until she was doing seventy on the Canyon road. Where could she go? Who could she go to? She knew that the mausoleum she now called home was impossible. She would die if she went home.

There was only one place left. She drove east, towards the Valley. After forty minutes, she pulled up to the gate, and the security guard recognized her. He greeted her, then buzzed the house while Jahne sat in the car and waited. Please, God. Please, let her be home, she prayed. The guard hung up the phone and told Jahne that Sharleen would meet her at the door.

Jahne drove up the driveway. Sharleen called out a greeting as she walked towards Jahne's car. She leaned onto the car door, smiling. 'Well, hi there. Good to see you.'

Jahne burst into tears, tears so violent she had to put her head down on the steering wheel, clutching the wheel tightly with both hands, just to keep from falling completely apart.

Sharleen was at Jahne's window. 'Why, Jahne, honey. What's happened?' Sharleen opened the car door for Jahne, but Jahne couldn't move. 'Come on, honey,' Sharleen said, gently tugging at Jahne's hands on the wheel. 'Get out of that car and come inside.'

But Jahne, at least for the moment, could only clutch the steering wheel, sit there, and shake and cry.

4

The bedroom was filled with sunlight when Jahne opened her eyes. It had been two, no, three days now that she had been staying quietly here at Sharleen's. Bless Sharleen's heart, and bless her boyfriend's heart, too, Jahne thought. Dean might not be real bright, but he was sweet as could be. It was relaxing just to sit beside him.

Sharleen had called Marty and the *Three for the Road* production manager for Jahne and reported Jahne sick. Then Sharleen had a doctor come in, 'jest to make it look kosher.' She left for work each day without even waking Jahne, who felt she could sleep for a month. It wasn't until about ten that Dean would knock timidly on the door each morning and bring in a glass of fresh juice and a cup of steaming coffee. After Jahne had drunk both, he'd bring the dogs in – Jahne laughed when she met Cara and the other namesakes, but she liked the golden retriever best.

'I don't have no favourites,' Dean told her. 'It wouldn't be right. They could tell, you know.' Then he lowered his voice. 'If I *did* have a favourite, it would be Oprah, my friend's Lab. But that's only right, 'cause I knew her the longest.'

After her juice, Dean would help Jahne establish herself under a tree in the garden, and he'd spend the rest of the morning working on the grounds, weeding the enormous vegetable garden, playing with the dogs, mowing the lawn on a tiny tractor, pruning back some fruit trees. Jahne just sat back on the lawn chair, at first too tired to read, too tired to think, too tired even to be sad.

The abundance of the garden reminded her of the van Huysums at the Getty. Abundance. But real and natural and in season. She shook her head. Her life so far had been the opposite: the meagreness of New York, the waste of her life in the theatre, the emptiness of her success out here in L.A. All of it had been a fruitless search for something she could not find: love, and warmth, and abundance.

She'd made a botch of it, there was no doubt. She'd picked a man to love who had no love to return. A shallow, selfish man. She'd abandoned her friends, she'd pursued the dictates of her own ego and vanity, and it had given her so little in return. Her face on magazine covers. Her image on a flickering TV screen. Money. Fame. But she'd never been to Europe, she'd never had a baby, she'd never ridden a horse, she couldn't speak another language. She'd never skied, or camped out in a wilderness, or taken a cruise, or gone to college. And she'd helped no one, not even herself.

God had given her talent, and Brewster Moore had given her beauty, and hadn't she been almost as blind and selfish as Sam Shields, wasting her gifts?

Sam. The thought of him was enough to make her cry, or laugh. Sam had never understood her, never truly tried. Both as Mary Jane and as Jahne, she had ignored that. He had taken comfort from her nurturing, he had been titillated by her beauty, but he had never known her. What had he given? A few words of praise. A hug. A caress. Crumbs. And she, always a fool, had accepted crumbs and thought they were a banquet.

Now, under the tree in Dean's garden, she had a horrible, chilling thought. Hadn't she, somehow, planned it all – the surgery, the success, the reunion with Sam – all in the hopes that he, alone of everyone – would see through her new flesh to her old heart, recognize her love, recognize and heal her? She thought again of the Bible, where the euphemism for sex was 'knowing.' 'And Abraham went with the woman and he "knew" her.' Sam had never known her at all. And wasn't that what she craved?

She understood his temptations now: ambition overcame his morality and judgement. Well, hadn't it overcome her own? She had wanted Sam, and agreed to make a bad movie to get him. And she had felt triumph at achieving her ambition: in luring Sam into her bed. At possessing him, the way a spider must gloat over its mummified prey. How often had she gloated over his sheet-wrapped form, sleeping in her bed? But had she known Sam? Clearly not.

A goal achieved is only admirable if it's a worthy goal. Who had said that to her? Mai? Brewster? Neil? Molly? Only the people who had a sense of values, who knew the difference between empty, selfish vanity and real achievement. But did *she* know the difference? It didn't appear that she did. She couldn't simply call herself a victim. She had been a willing victim, the wood that threw itself onto the fire. She'd given Sam warmth and it had consumed her, leaving nothing but ashes.

Sam had betrayed her, April Irons had manipulated her, Sy Ortis used her, Monica Flanders exploited her, but hadn't she allowed it? She'd used her beauty, flaunted it for money in the Flanders ads, used it to get work on a questionable show like 3/4, and agreed to bare it – or let another woman do it for her – in *Birth*. She'd sold herself like a commodity, so could she blame others for doing the same?

Jahne lay under the tree and thought difficult thoughts.

At noon, Dean came to interrupt her. They would have lunch together. Dean would bring in the salad fixings from the perfect rows of baby lettuce, tiny radishes, sugar peas, and miniature carrots. Jahne washed them and he'd chop them up, one day adding tuna and the next day pasta. Then they sat out on the patio and ate, drinking two or three fresh lemonades along with their meal. Yesterday Dean had turned to her and smiled. 'It's nice to have someone to eat lunch with,' he said.

'It is.'

'Guess you eat with Sharleen most days.'

'No. Usually I eat alone in my trailer. I can't afford to eat much. I used to eat with . . .' She swallowed. '. . . an old lady friend of mine, but she died.' Poor, dear Mai. Jahne missed her so.

'So how come you don't eat with Sharleen now?'

'Oh, we get too busy. Or we don't eat at the same time, because we're in different shots. Or she has other work. Or I do.' Or because I've been a condescending snob who didn't know who my friends were, Jahne told herself.

'You like your work?'

'No.'

'That's bad. It's really bad if you don't like your work. I worry 'cause I don't think Sharleen likes her job, neither. And I think it's too hard.'

'Well, they pay us a lot of money, so it should be hard, I guess.'

Dean shrugged. 'I don't think you should do it if it's too hard and you don't like it. I think that's probably why you're sad.'

'You're probably right,' Jahne told him.

The first night she was there, Jahne found herself waking from a horrible dream, Sharleen beside her, gently shaking her arm. 'Git up honey, it's just a nightmare, it ain't real.'

Jahne gasped for air. What had it been? The knives again? Or was it the one where she was on the set, naked, with the crew and the cast laughing and laughing and laughing? She pulled air into her lungs and felt her heart pushing against her chest. It felt as if it might tear out of her.

'It's okay, honey. It's okay,' Sharleen crooned. Grateful, Jahne reached for her hand.

'I'm sorry,' she whispered. 'You need your sleep. I'm sorry I woke you.'

'Want a glass of water? Or maybe I should get you some warm milk? When Dean has bad dreams, I make him some milk.'

'No, just stay with me.' Jahne felt as if she were five years old. She clung to Sharleen's hand, to Sharleen's warmth, as if she might drown or freeze without it. She shivered under the bedclothes. She couldn't bear to feel this lonely anymore. It was too big a burden to bear, having nobody know you at all. 'Sharleen,' she said, 'can I tell you something?'

Sharleen sat on the side of the bed and patted Jahne's hand. 'You surely can,' she said. And then Jahne poured out the whole sorry story about Sam and New York and *Jack and Jill* and Brewster and Pete and Mai and Michael and *Birth* and all of it. Sometimes she cried, and other times she could hardly bear to whisper it, but at last she finished.

Sharleen held her hand all through. She still did, and now she patted it. 'Why, you poor child. I think you must be even more lonely than I am.' And Sharleen bent towards Jahne, gathering her up in her arms. 'You poor, poor child,' she crooned, and rocked her friend until Jahne, at last, fell asleep.

Jahne felt better after that. She spent the morning with Dean and the afternoon alone in her room, avoiding the strong sun. But, though she felt better, she couldn't avoid her thoughts. She couldn't help replaying over and over again the images she had seen of herself flashing on the screen. And she replayed her relationship with Sam. All of it, from that first spring in New York when he cast her in *Jack and Jill* to the grimy winter he left her, to their time together on location. All of it.

And, while she was at it, she looked at the rest of her life. It didn't make sense, and now she was determined to figure out why. She'd accomplished what she had wanted to: she'd gone from a woman no one remembered to a girl impossible to forget, and she had all the money she needed, plus a lot more fame than she wanted.

But in the last three years, with few exceptions, she hadn't met anyone that she wanted to know. Now Mai was dead, Raoul was back home in South America, and Dr. Moore had his life in New York. She was totally alone, and, except for Sharleen and Dean, there was no one here she trusted, no one to be kind to her. And, in days or weeks, she'd become notorious. Maybe Sharleen and Dean would want nothing to do with her when this monstrous pornographic picture came out. Surely even unflappable Brewster would be shocked and disgusted, as she was.

She was relieved when Dean knocked on her door at the end of his day. In the evenings, the two of them made dinner and waited for Sharleen. Then they watched a video, or the two women talked while Dean watched a tape of *The Andy Griffith Show*. It was simple, and routine, and warm. Jahne began to rest, really to relax for the first time in longer than she could remember. It was like going home, home to a home she had never known.

And slowly, slowly, Jahne began to feel a little more human, as if maybe she could go back and face her life. Maybe.

But on Thursday evening, when Sharleen turned to her as they sat side by side on the sofa and said, 'I think you better come back soon,' tears unexpectedly filled Jahne's eyes. Suddenly she felt as if this place, this time, was the only bit of peace there was.

'Oh, honey. Don't cry. It's jest that Marty is shootin' so much around you, and he was already kinda mad about your takin' so long on the film . . . Well, and you know Lila. She don't miss a moment to blame you *or* me when *anything* goes wrong. When I blew a line today you know what she asked?' Jahne shook her head. 'She asked how come blondes can't make frozen orange juice. Because the can says 'concentrate.' They both laughed. Then Sharleen sighed, 'And Sy's callin' me three or four times a day.'

Jahne took a deep breath. 'I'm sorry I've been such a bother.'

'Hey, no bother at all. Me and Dean *like* havin' you. You're like family. Why don't you stay on with us instead of goin' home? We can go in to work together.'

'Yeah! Why don't you stay, Jahne? It would be great havin' two sisters, even if I can't have lunch with you no more. But, then, Sharleen can,' Dean said.

'Oh, could I? Just for a little while longer, until *Birth of a Star* opens? So I can weather that storm?'

'Well, of course you can!' Sharleen told her. 'And who knows? Maybe it won't be as bad as it seemed.' She smiled. 'Anyway, nothin' worse can happen to either of us!'

She was wrong.

The security phone rang, and Sharleen answered it. Both Jahne and Dean were out in the back, playing with the dogs.

'Security gate. There's a visitor here without an appointment. Should I send him up?'

'No. I'll speak to him.'

'Is Jahne Moore there?' a man's voice asked.

'Who is this?' she asked.

'Tell her Sam Shields is outside.'

Sharleen bristled. 'I don't think she wants to see you,' Sharleen told him.

'Who is this?' he asked.

'A friend of Jahne's. A true friend,' Sharleen said.

'Look, I'm in no mood for theatrics. Or moralizing. It took me a long time to track her down. I want to see her.'

'Look, yourself. I know how you treated Jahne, and I know the kind of man you are. Why, I've had men like you after me since I was eleven years old. Men who only cared about the outside, about how I looked, not who I was. You don't deserve a girl like Jahne.'

'Look, she's going to want to see me. Go ask her.'

Reluctantly, Sharleen put the phone down and went out to the yard. Jahne was running across the lawn, holding a rawhide bone, the three dogs chasing after her. Dean stood in the sunlight, laughing. 'Jahne,' Sharleen called. 'Jahne.' Her friend looked up. 'There's someone here to see you.'

Jahne squinted into the sun. She walked towards Sharleen. 'Who is it?' she asked.

'It's Sam.'

Jahne stopped. Sharleen looked deep into her eyes. Would she succumb? Would she fall again? Sharleen looked at her without saying a word. For a moment, the two of them stared at one another, silent. Then Jahne spoke.

'Tell him to go away,' she told her friend.

Later that night, Jahne wrote to Dr. Moore.

> I can't remember ever feeling as dependent as I do now. Not even on you, during that long, hard time in the hospital. Like Blanche DuBois, I am reduced to depending on the kindness of strangers. And I am afraid that even they and you will judge me harshly when you see that awful film I've made.
>
> I know it's a lot to ask, but if you could take some time off, could you come out for a visit? I'd come to N.Y. but I'm already in a lot of trouble on the set. I'll understand if you refuse, but I'd love to see you.

It was only after she had finished the letter and sealed it that she remembered something odd Dean had said that evening when he welcomed her to stay: something about how it would be great to have two sisters.

Had he said 'sisters'? she wondered as she turned off the lamp. How strange. And then she fell asleep.

Skin Flick Hits Big

DESPITE OR BECAUSE OF ITS GRAPHIC SEX, 'BIRTH' REVIVAL BREAKS BOX OFFICE RECORDS.

In a stunning exception to the old Hollywood rule that 'dirt doesn't pay', the Michael McLain–Jahne Moore remake of 'Birth of a Star' has drawn not only critical praise but also hordes of ticket buyers. An unexpected audience of ageing baby boomers, mixed with the teen and young-adult market hot for a romance flick with no holds barred, has exceeded all expectations. . . .

– Daily Variety

Lila crumpled the trade bible and threw it across the room. Damn! She picked up the *L.A. Times*.

'THE SEXIEST WOMAN IN THE WORLD!' screamed the banner headline across the top of the entertainment section. There wasn't even an interview to go along with pages of pictures of Jahne Moore, just the usual PR blather. The bitch was so smug she wasn't even doing publicity!

Somehow, in her mind, the success of Jahne Moore in *Birth* completely negated Lila. It was like she was back to square one. Despite its rating as an adult picture, it had opened to record box office and was now number two, with a good chance at being number one. It had done thirteen million last weekend. Worse, everyone was talking about it. How it had broken nearly every taboo, yet was also commercial. It brought every jealousy crashing back down around Lila's head. Just when she thought she had the Emmy in the little black velvet bag, tied up with gold braided tassel, this . . . this insult had to happen to *her*. It wasn't fair. *Something* had to be done.

She looked at another crumpled bit of newspaper. There, buried on a back page, was the announcement that should have been at the front of the whole damn newspaper:

DIRECTOR AND STAR ANNOUNCE UPCOMING NUPTIALS

Jesus, against all her better judgement, just to keep up with Jahne's newsworthiness, she'd told Marty yes, and *this* was the publicity it received? Aunt Robbie said he could guarantee great coverage. Well, buried on page 24 of the *L.A. Times* and getting a paragraph in *Milestones* was not coverage. It was a fucking insult. After all, *she* was Hollywood royalty. She was Kerry Kyle's daughter. And the daughter of the Puppet Mistress, who, for all her faults, at least had been a star.

The phone rang. Lila rarely answered it, letting the service do her screening, but she was expecting Marty's call. She lifted the receiver.

'Are you crazy?' the voice rasped. 'Are you completely fucking crazy?'

Lila considered, for a moment, hanging up on her mother, but the power of the Puppet Mistress held her on the line. 'Shut up,' she managed.

'I just read the *Times*. You can't get away with this, Lila. You've gone too far.'

'Just shut up. I can do what I want. And when I need your opinion, I'll send you a ballot.'

'Lila, *this* you can't do. Marty DiGennaro isn't Kevin. It will ruin us both.'

'Shut up! I gave you the goddamn show, didn't I? It airs next week. Now, keep the fuck away from me. That was our deal. Leave me alone, or I swear I'll get Marty to cancel the programme.' Lila was almost spitting with rage. She wished she could kill Theresa, once and for all.

'Lila, listen to me. You can fool some of the people all of the time, and all of the people some of the time . . .'

'Yeah, but I can't fool Mom. Right? Well, fuck you, Mom. Fuck you and Aunt Robbie and Kevin and Candy and Skinny and Estrella and all of you. You didn't worry about that twenty years ago, did you? Don't bother to worry about it now. I warn you: leave me alone!' She slammed the phone down onto the receiver. It took less than a moment for it to ring again. Lila snorted and looked away. It would be a cold day in Malibu before she answered it again. She stood up, shaking with anger. First Marty nags her into saying yes, then Jahne's movie is a hit, the season premiere is overshadowed, and her engagement gets no coverage. Now this!

She *had* to win that Emmy, and she had to show the Puppet Mistress once and for all that she, Lila Kyle, was not to be fucked with. She stood there, breathing hard, almost dizzy with rage, and considered her options. It was time for a no-holds-barred attack on all of them. She didn't need anyone but Marty. And she would marry him. She would.

She looked down at her hands to find they were shaking. She felt murderous. And then she thought of the box. The 'birthday present' peace offering that Robbie had brought. It still lay on the table, waiting for her. She smiled grimly, turned around, and went into the kitchen. She scrabbled through the utility drawers for a sharp knife. A very sharp knife.

Minos Paige couldn't exactly say he was surprised at receiving another call from Lila Kyle. Very little surprised Minos, certainly not the insatiable need of the denizens of this town to one-up each other. But he was surprised at Lila's carefully worded instructions. It was a good thing he hadn't been taken by surprise, because, if he had, he never would have worked out the fee that he did, the fee which was exactly quadruple that which he had originally gotten from Lila. But, then, this piece of work was at least four times as valuable to Lila as his original work had been. *That* he was sure of.

Minos didn't have to stop for a minute to think about how he was going to follow Lila's instructions. Minos had his priorities straight, knew just who to call and in what order. As he dialled the phone, he smiled to himself. The last job Lila had given him was for peanuts, took him all over and more than two months to finish. This assignment, for the most part, would take minutes, and would be done mostly by phone. Ah, fate.

When I answered the phone in my office, it was to hear a monotone

I knew too well. 'Guess who this is with some very good news,' he said playfully to me, Laura Richie, a woman who very few men played with.

'Kevin Costner, and you're having my baby.'

'Laura, it's better than that. And I swear, you are the first person I'm telling. I'm not doing this strictly for money, Laura. I'm doing this because you've been good to me in the past. So, get out a bunch of sharp pencils, and a long pad. All you gotta do is listen and write.'

The totally one-sided conversation with Minos took less than fifteen minutes. I have a tape of the whole thing. Every now and then, during his narrative, you can hear an uncharacteristic gasp come through the line from me, and once I say 'Holy shit!,' but, other than that, he did all the talking. I do repeat 'her brother?' parroting his words, but that's it. I asked only one question when he was finished. 'You got any paper on this, Minos?'

'It'll be coming over your fax machine in exactly five minutes.'

'Pictures of the surgery?'

He laughed. 'For that, you have to pay,' he said.

'How much for an exclusive?' I asked.

'More than you and Kitty Kelley combined could afford. No exclusives. I'm calling the Enquirer, *the* Observer, Entertainment Weekly, People *and* Time *in the next twenty minutes. But you are the first one to hear. Make hay while the sun shines.'*

Before he hung up, he did have to get in a commercial. 'Now, remember, Laura, you owe me. And you can't use my name in publication.'

'If you got the paper, I don't even want to know your name. But if I ain't paying for this, who is?'

'John Beresford Tipton,' Minos laughed, and hung up.

6

SHARLEEN SMITH IN INCEST NEST
The shocking story of the star who sleeps with her brother. Inside this issue of the National Observer

> THE SEXIEST WOMAN IN THE WORLD?
> WHO IS THE REAL JAHNE MOORE?
>
> PLASTIC TO THE MAX. THE FULL STORY OF JAHNE MOORE AND HER TOTAL FACIAL AND BODY SURGERY. A complete report by Laura Richie. IN THIS ISSUE OF ENTERTAINMENT WORLD. AVAILABLE AT NEWSSTANDS NOW.

The phone hadn't stopped ringing. Sam felt as if he'd kill himself if he heard one more 'b-b-b-r-r-i-i-i-n-g.' Every yellow journalist in the country wanted to interview Sam, wanted to know what it felt like to sleep with Jahne Moore. Yesterday, after lunch at Le Dôme, they shouted questions at him in the parking lot. 'Did she feel the same as she had before the surgery?' 'Did you do this as a publicity stunt?' 'How do you think this will affect *Birth of a Star* box office?'

His secretary was going crazy. Sam had disconnected his home phone. He'd been reamed already by Bob LeVine, who couldn't believe Sam had unknowingly cast a female Frankenstein in their sex film, and had threatened to sue. LeVine was ready to throw Sam off the lot. He'd heard from his agent, who couldn't believe he hadn't known all along, and who insisted Sam hire a PR firm for damage control. And now there was the inevitable phone call from April. He'd ducked two of them, but he knew he couldn't put it off indefinitely. Oh, Jesus! What would she say? What would April try to do to him? He lifted up the receiver.

'Hello, April.' He tried to keep his voice calm, his tone matter-of-fact, but he himself could hear the quaver. 'Sixteen million,' she said.

'What?'

'Sixteen million! We did sixteen million in box office this weekend. I just got the word. They had to run midnight shows of *Birth* to accommodate the crowds. Sixteen fucking million! It was a freak show.'

Sam, speechless, could only nod in agreement.

O'CONNOR ANNOUNCES TEN-CITY TOUR TO HEAL THE NATION; CALLS FOR FAMILY RESPONSE

New York, NY. Yesterday, in his Sunday sermon at St. Patrick's Cathedral, Cardinal O'Connor, the Archbishop of the Roman Catholic Archdiocese of New York, announced to his parishioners and the media reporters brought out by his press release that he denounced television and particularly *Three for the Road* as an example of what the worship of the golden calf of Hollywood had done to the country. After denouncing *Murphy Brown, Cheers,* and a host of other shows he went on to proclaim that his Christian Family Tour would heal the hurt caused the people of America by the charges of Sharleen Smith's incest and the sexually explicit new film starring Jahne Moore

that has rocked the nation. He asked the parish to join in his prayers for the costars of the popular program, then added that all three were guilty of 'provoking lustful thoughts.' The Cardinal invoked St. Joseph, the Patron Saint of the Family, to intercede in the country beset by confusion over lack of family values. 'What happened to Disney World?' the Cardinal asked in his heated oration. 'To *Mary Poppins?* Instead, today we have Hollywood, and Jahne Moore and Sharleen Smith. Something is very wrong in a nation that ignores all that is holy and beautiful in the example of the Blessed Virgin and turns instead to idols with feet of clay (CONT. ON PG. 6)

Jahne felt as if she was under siege. This is what it must have been like behind the walls of a medieval city during war. She had taken the phone off the hook, Gerry La Brecque had sent in three more security guards, and now the Beverly Hills police had stationed a cop car outside to try and control the traffic. She couldn't go out, she couldn't be seen, she couldn't go anywhere, and staying home was unbearable.

It was spooky. After only a couple of weeks of the media blitz following *Birth*'s release, this new exposure had come about, and the snowball had gathered enough momentum to become an avalanche. She felt flattened under the load. Who had leaked her medical history? Had Sam betrayed her in an even deeper way?

The irony that the nation's newest sex goddess was man-made wasn't lost on her or on the media. She didn't have the courage to read most of the trash that was being published, but she did tune in to *Entertainment Tonight*, only to see John Tesh interview Miss Hennessey, Dr. Moore's nurse. They had an old 'before' photo of her, a Polaroid that had been shot in Dr. Moore's office. She looked horrible.

'Oh, my God,' she moaned.

Then they began the exposé on Sharleen. It was awful. A sneering, smirking Jukes-and-Kallikaks-oh-those-hillbillies-can't-be-trusted number. Jahne felt sick. She remembered the slip that Dean had made: something about how he could have two sisters. Well, what if it was true? Who was she, Jahne, to judge? She picked up the phone, plugged it in, and dialled Sharleen's private number. Of course, she only got a busy signal. Well, she'd have to go over there. If Sharleen needed her, she owed it to Sharleen; and, anyway, she wanted to help. She's my friend, Jahne thought. They both are.

MEMORANDUM

TO: All Employees of Sy Ortis and Associates
FROM: Sy Ortis
SUBJECT: Press Leaks

Anyone discovered to have leaked any item about Sharleen Smith or Jahne Moore, or any item about *Three for the Road*, will be terminated immediately, and prosecuted for breaching client confidentiality.

If any part of this memo is unclear, please contact Miss Hancock in Public Relations for illumination.

S.O.

Jahne had managed to get through the barrage of press and over to Sharleen's. They sat now almost barricaded into the living room.

Sharleen looked even paler than usual, but otherwise seemed to be holding up. Jahne sat beside her on the sofa, her hand in Sharleen's. Two of the PR staff from Sy's office were buzzing around in the kitchen on the phones, and an attorney was screaming at his paralegal, both of whom seemed permanently camped out in the dining room.

'Jahne, are you mad at me?' Sharleen asked.

'Why would I be mad?'

'Because you told me about your secret, but I didn't say nothin' about mine.'

'Hey, Sharleen, it wasn't a trade. Friends don't work like that.'

'We're still friends?' Sharleen asked, a tear escaping from under a long eyelash and running down her pale cheek.

'Of course we are,' Jahne said, and squeezed Sharleen's hand.

'Well, it's a real hard feeling, knowing that everyone despises you.'

'It surely is,' Jahne said, and tried to smile. Her lip trembled, but she didn't cry. So what if everyone hated her. This was the risk you took. After all, she told herself, you didn't just want this, you *paid* for it. And it looks as if I'm going to keep on paying for it, she thought wryly. She also thought of Brewster Moore. In the maelstrom of all that had happened to her in the last months, she had come to realize that aside from Mai and Sharleen it was only Brewster's quiet talks at the hospital in the dead of night, only Brewster's letters, that seemed to have any substance. But she hadn't heard a word from him since her last letter. Surely *he* had not betrayed her. Was he being accosted by journalists even now? Would he despise her for the publicity and bother she had caused him? She shrank down onto the sofa. Somehow, the thought of being despised by Brewster was more than she could bear.

Sharleen Smith's Father Talks About His Years in Prison

By Clint Roper
Special to the Dallas Independent
Dean Smith, Sr., father of *Three for the Road* costar Sharleen Smith and her half brother, Dean Jr., met with this reporter and talked freely of Boyd Jamison, the boy the senior Smith has been found guilty of murdering outside the Smith trailer in Lamson, Texas, more than three years ago. He also confirmed reports of the incest between his son and daughter.

In the three-part series which begins this Monday, the Independent probes into Mr. Smith's allegations that Sharleen could have saved him if she had appeared at his trial, that he only killed the boy in self-defence while protecting his daughter from Boyd's sexual attack, and that he loves Sharleen despite her sins and begs her to contact him.

He hasn't heard from wife, son, or daughter since the time of the murder, and says he misses and loves them all. He claims that his drinking provoked him, but that he's cured of his habit, through the intervention of Christ. He has been sober since admission to prison. It is a tale that only a certain kind of Texan could love, a tale fit for a J. R. Ewing. In the annals of family dysfunction, the Smiths of Lamson, Texas, are one for the books. . . .

'I still can't believe Daddy is alive,' Sharleen murmured. She felt drained of all energy, as if she would never move off the Herculon-covered sofa again.

'We don't have to see him, though, do we?' Dean asked. His eyes were big, the way they got when he was scared. Funny how nothin' scared Dean exceptin' their daddy. Maybe his fright got all used up when we were kids, Sharleen thought.

'No. I guess we don't. But he's sayin' we're bad kids. And so's everyone else.'

'I don't understand,' Dean said, standing beside the sofa she was lying on. He held up one of the newspapers from the pile in front of him. 'I don't understand.'

'I know you don't, Dean, honey. I know.'

'But why are they so mad? I only hit him 'cause he was hittin' on you. And I'm glad he ain't dead, but I'd kill him again if he hit you.'

'That ain't why they're mad.'

'Why, then?'

'Because of what we do at night. Because of how we sleep together.'

'But we *always* sleep together,' Dean said. 'Why are they mad now?'

'Well, I guess they didn't know till now.'

'Does that mean you won't get the prize?'

For a moment, she didn't know what he was talking about. Then she remembered the Emmy. 'I guess it does, honey.' Dean hunkered down next to her. He dropped the paper and stared at her.

'Does that make you sad?'

Sharleen nodded. 'But I ain't so sad as I'm ashamed.' Though she tried to stop it, a tear escaped and slid down her cheek.

'Oh, Sharleen! Please. Don't be. It's like the time that Opie met the man who worked on the power lines. And he told everyone about it, but Andy thought he was makin' it all up. So he made Opie apologize for bein' wrong and lyin', even when he wasn't. But then Andy met the power-line man. So he came to see it Opie's way. We didn't do nothin' wrong, Sharleen. They'll come to see that.'

Sharleen took his hand and shook her head. 'I don't think so.'

'Why not?'

'Because that was Mayberry. This is Hollywood.'

FIRST PHOTOS:
JAHNE MOORE
Before and After

In this week's issue of the *National Questioner* are the exclusive photos of Jahne Moore's miracle surgery. See how surgery can take a woman from being a thirty-four-year-old, overweight, plain brown wren to a twenty-four-year-old beauty with the body of a goddess.
EXCLUSIVE!

'Jesus Christ!' Marty could hardly believe it! First there had been the rescheduling problems with Jahne Moore over *Birth*. Then the problems with Lila and Theresa. Then Jahne calls in sick for a week. Now both Sharleen and Jahne were in the epicentre of the biggest scandals since Fatty Arbuckle and the Coke bottle. Didn't they all understand he had a show to shoot?

He had suspended shooting for a week. Les Merchant was going nuts. It cost the Network almost the same amount not to shoot an episode as to shoot one. Meanwhile, Sy was constantly on the phone with new reports from the press, new outrage from the sponsors, and general fear and loathing.

Marty listened to the sound of phones going crazy and unanswered outside his office door. He lifted his hand to rub the bridge of his nose. He had a Headache from Hell, and he was afraid it wasn't going away anytime soon.

Sharleen Smith's Mother Busted for Prostitution

New Orleans, LA

Flora Lee Deluce, the mother of Sharleen Smith, costar of *Three for the Road*, was arrested last night for prostitution in a motel on Route 101, also known by the locals as 'Mattress Mile' because of the profusion of motels that rent rooms by the hour.

At first the police weren't aware that Mrs. Deluce was Ms. Smith's mother, and the booking was regarded as routine, the result of a regular stake-out by the police of the Sun Star Motel.

Mrs. Deluce, while declining to comment on her relationship with her daughter, did say the arrest 'was a frame-up. I didn't even have my teeth out when the cops crashed in the door.'

Sharleen Smith's meteoric career and the accusation of an incestuous relationship with her brother have cast the spotlight on all aspects of her life. Neither Miss Smith nor her spokesperson had any comment to make.

Arraignment is scheduled for 2:00 P.M. today in St. Charles Parish Courthouse. Fifty dollars bail was paid by an associate of Mrs. Deluce, who declined to be named or interviewed.

'What a family!' Sy Ortis screamed into his car phone. He could barely manage to get enough air into his lungs to do it. 'Is there one member of the Smith family who hasn't been jailed or broken a commandment today?'

Sharleen was sitting in the living room, hunched over, a blanket covering her shoulders. She heard his voice before she saw him, and turned around. 'Dobe!' she yelled, and jumped from the recliner, dropping the afghan. 'Dobe Samuels, what are you doing here? Why, you look better than a warm stove on a cold night.'

BIRTH TOPS IN BOX

Jahne Moore's *Birth of a Star* once
again topped all other releases in
box-office performance, bringing
in $83 million in the less than a
month since its release. . . .
— Hollywood Reporter

'And you look like something the cat dragged in,' Dobe told
Sharleen. 'What in the name of the living God got you tucked away
in this dark hole?'

'I told him you been sick, Sharleen,' Dean said. 'I told him
you were cryin' and all.'

'Well, what the hell have you got to cry about, I'd like to know?'

'Oh, Dobe. It's really been terrible. The newspapers and television people won't leave us alone, and then the news about Daddy
in prison. Dean and me both been sick about it. Plus Flora Lee's
been . . .'

'People make their bed, Sharleen. Only can do so much for
them. You, on the other hand, you never done nothing bad to
no one that I know about. So why are you holed up here like
some kind of outlaw on the lam?'

She only shrugged her shoulders. Dobe shook his head. 'Sit
down, you two,' he told them. Sharleen sank back down onto the
recliner. Dean took a seat on the floor with the dogs. 'Now, listen
up. Ain't no incest going on here. Never was, never will be. Flora

Lee ain't your mother . . .'

'I know that. Dean's only my *half*-brother, but . . . but that don't make it only half wrong.'

Dobe interrupted her with a brusque wave of his hand. 'Dean ain't your brother at all. Flora Lee told your daddy he was, but it wasn't so. And there's a birth certificate that proves it. Flora Lee was carrying Dean before she even met your daddy. He's a Deluce, her first husband's bay. Well, her only husband. She never even married your daddy. He was only a port in the storm.'

Sharleen sat there quiet for a minute. 'Dean wasn't my daddy's son?'

It was too much to grasp. All the secrets, all the shame, for so long. And for nothing. The surprise and the relief flooded her, and she began to sob. 'It's all been so hard. So hard. Lila bein' mean, and then Mr. McLain, and the album, with Mr. Ortis lyin' to me and makin' me a crook. And Marty so hard to work with now, and me so slow. Then this. I can't . . . Even if it ain't true, I just can't go to them Emmys and then to Ara Sagarian's party with all them people laughing at me, whispering about me and Dean behind my back.'

'What do you care what a bunch of misfits and perverts have to say about you? Why should you care what *anyone* thinks of you?'

'Did you read some of them stories? T·.ey would make you vomit. I wonder why Momma never told me this. Woulda saved a heap of worryin'. I hope Momma wasn't upset if she found out what they been saying, wherever she is. It would kill her dead, and that's the truth.'

'Don't you worry about your momma. Truth wasn't really her strong point, Sharleen.' He watched the tears course down her cheeks. Then he shook his head and sighed. 'Honey, I got something for you. But, before I give it to you, I gotta ask that you don't question me 'bout how I got it or nothin'. We got a deal?'

Mutely, Sharleen nodded.

'Okay, then, honey. You never told me much about your growin'-up years, but I got a powerful strong imagination, and I ain't stupid, neither. So I thought you might need these someday.' He went to his bag and took out an envelope of papers. He handed the sheaf to Sharleen.

'Your birth certificate. And Dean's. See, Sharleen, Dean's not your brother. Dean ain't your blood kin at all. These are just copies; you'll find the originals in the lockbox at the bank. You got the key I gave you.'

'But how . . .' she began, remembered her promise, and stopped, then abruptly sat down. 'Dobe, I just can't believe this. I just got to ask, is this for real? Not some fake papers, like a fake driver's licence?'

'No, this is strictly legit. And the newspapers will be gettin' a copy of this as soon as you want them to. Plus, you can sue 'em for slander.'

'Dobe, you got all the proof here I need?'

'Well, I think I got it all, Minos a Paige or two.' He chuckled.

'Where's the missing page?' Sharleen asked.

'Oh, probably in the hospital Minos a few teeth.' Dobe shook his head. 'Just a little joke. Now's not the time to go into it. You got everything you need here to disprove everything. Most important thing is, you know the truth now, and there isn't anyone out there

ROBOACTRESS?

The disclosure that Jahne Moore is the product of expert trans-formational surgery has hit Los Angeles, the entertainment capital of the world, like a ton of pâté de foie gras. In a town with the largest per-capita number of plastic surgeons – or 'transforma-tional specialists,' as some now prefer to be called – everyone is looking over her (and his) shoulder, waiting for another disgruntled nurse or lab technician of one of the multimillionaire surgeons to make public another list of names.

Many in the Hollywood community are considering going public about their cosmetic surgery before someone takes it into his (or her) mind to tell all. As names are being named, and reporters are being deflected from one big name to another, a small but radical group of surgery-philes have reacted to the public outcry against this type of elective surgery. Raquel Welch, the national spokesperson for the group known as America the Beautiful, asked, 'What's wrong with a nip and tuck? Or a full-body make-over, for that matter? I have nothing but respect for Jahne Moore. It's just like using any other cosmetic device. Men think nothing of using a blade every day to improve their looks, but as soon as a woman tries to do the same thing, she's branded a fake.'

Michael Jackson, Michelle Pfeiffer, and Cher have each called for a press conference to talk about the impact of the media's negative coverage of a private issue 'It's a form of rape,' Cher said.

who has the right to judge you. You go and marry Dean if you want to. I know you, Sharleen, and you're a real good girl. A fine girl. So stop your cryin'.'

'He's Not My Brother'

SHARLEEN SMITH ISSUES DENIAL.
In a new twist to the ongoing *Three for the Road* scandals, Sharleen Smith today in a public statement denied a blood relationship to Dean Deluce, known as Dean Smith, her alleged brother. She provided birth certificates and a written statement from Deluce, who declined to be interviewed.

Asked whether she would sue those publications that may have slandered her, Miss Smith told the assembled media, 'I think enough damage has been done.'

Lila rolled over onto her stomach. Around her, the stack of torn and wrinkled newspapers and magazines defaced the otherwise immaculate room. A breeze blew in at the window, riffling the neat pile of carefully scissored clippings before her. If she felt cheated out of publicity on her engagement, at least she was compensated by this avalanche of bad press burying Sharleen and Jahne.

Right now she was being cheated out of filming the next 3/4 episode. Marty and the Network had suspended filming for the next week while they decided what to do. If Marty knew it was Lila who had started this shit storm, would he be angry? She had sympathised with him, and then suggested that they fire and replace Sharleen and Jahne. He was going to take it up with Les Merchant at the meeting next week. Lila felt cheated that she couldn't go to that, either, but a girl could only do what a girl could do. She smiled to herself.

And she wouldn't be cheated out of the Emmy, that she was sure of. Voting was taking place next week, and no one in the Industry would vote for a monster or an incester. No matter, or because of, whatever monstrous surgery and incestuous secrets they had of their own. She had the Emmy for sure, and maybe *Three for the Road* would become her private show.

Since Dobe had appeared like an avenging angel with the good news, Sharleen had felt happier than she had in a long, long time. It wasn't just that she no longer had to be afraid of exposure. And it wasn't just that she no longer was a sinner. Dean wasn't a murderer, and while her daddy wasn't dead, it was good to know he was safely put away. And if having the spotlight of fame on them had given them this knowledge, it was almost worth it. And reading about Flora Lee's degradation was sad but not surprising. Sharleen would send her money, but make sure she didn't bother Dean again.

The best part of the news, she realized, was that she and Dean could be together. That there was nothing wrong about them loving each other the way they did.

The news was so good, so big, so *enormous* that it would take some getting used to. She had sat down with Dean and spent some time trying to make him understand. They sat outside, in the safety of the night darkness. Night was the only time they could go out into the yard without being photographed.

'Dean, I got some good news to tell you. You ain't my brother.'

He looked up at her with pained eyes. 'I ain't?'

'No. Momma lied to us and Daddy about it.'

'But I *want* to be your brother.'

'No, you don't, Dean. 'Cause brothers and sisters don't sleep together.' For a moment, Sharleen longed for some romance from Dean. For him to give a pretty speech about how he loved her, how he needed her, and for him to woo her with gifts and flowers. But Dean spoke only through his eyes. She could see how he felt. She sighed.

'Dean, you want to stay with me always?' she asked.

'Sure, Sharleen. You *know* that.'

'Well, I was thinking that we could get married. I could be

your wife instead of your sister.' Dean was silent for a moment.

'Can't you be both?'

'No. It don't work like that.'

'Well, then, let's get married.' It wasn't a romantic proposal, but it was real, and dependable.

'You mean it, Dean? You want to?'

'Sure do. We could still keep the dogs, right?'

Sharleen smiled and took his hand. 'We surely could.'

And there, in the dark behind their house, in the midst of their beautiful garden, she was flooded with such love for him, such a deep and full and pure swell of love, that she thought, for a moment, she might not be able to go on living. Her heart seemed so full it might burst, and she stood drinking in the fullness and the pain. Dean was imperfect: she knew he wasn't what most other women looked for in men. But he was what she loved and what she wanted. His goodness, his clarity and pureness were the most important thing in the world to her. He was her anchor and her compass, and he had always been the mechanism that helped her steer a clear path through dangerous waters.

Sharleen woke up on the day of the Emmy awards full of joy and gratitude. Copies of the birth certificates and appropriate statements had gone out to the press. And, inevitably, a new avalanche of publicity had started. The awards would still be a horrible ordeal. But, after breakfast, Dobe insisted that she should go – and go with Dean.

'But I *never* take him to business stuff.'

'No reason not to now.'

'But he'll hate it.'

'So do you. But he's a big boy.'

'Dobe Samuels, I don't want no award, and I don't want to go to no party where everybody will look at me like I'm a freak. All I want . . .' She paused, thinking her words out very carefully. '. . . is to live quiet, in the country like, on a ranch with horses for Dean, and a bunch of dogs, and lots of trees and open fields and lakes and hills. And kids running around, all over the place. They don't got to be mine. Just some kids got no place else to go. And *no* other people. Just you around, close by. And no fancy stores, or fancy parties, or gossipy magazines. I just want some peace and quiet for Dean and me. To be left alone, and never to have to wear a formal dress again.' She paused, imagining it. 'You ever been square dancin', Dobe?'

'No. Never stayed in one place long enough to learn how.'

'I'd like to learn. I always wanted to, but never got around to it. Now, if Dean and me had a nice country place, we could learn square dancing, and have some real fun. And maybe we can afford to do that soon.' She didn't want to make Dobe feel guilty about the money she had given him, so she shut up.

But Dobe didn't seem to even remember about the money. 'All that's possible, Sharleen. And sooner than you think. Now, all you've got to do is show up tonight like you own the world, and, believe you me, ninety per cent of them bastards – excuse me, honey – ninety per cent of them will actually believe you do. No matter what anybody's been saying or writing. 'Cause, to make it in this town, one of the things I learned, you act as if you don't give a rat's ass about nobody, and they eat it up.'

Sharleen was beginning to hear Dobe, and had to agree with him, for the most part. She usually did, because he usually was right. 'But I'll still feel like a freak in a sideshow.'

'Well, honey, to be really honest, that's exactly what you've been, since the first day you set foot in front of that there television camera. And so is every other one of them television and movie stars. All freaks. But you're also one of the sweetest and most beautiful women in America, and you can go anywhere and hold your head high. Most of them women gonna be there tonight would trade places with you in a Tennessee minute, publicity and all. Maybe even *because* of the publicity. Shows you how sick some of them really are. This ain't the real world, Sharleen. Don't make that mistake. It ain't even Planet Earth. We're on some separate planet that spins around the sun backwards, at ten times the normal speed. Hell, a woman gets old in this town in two or three years, instead of two or three decades. This is a town out of joint. Only you and I know that. Every one of them other jerks thinks this is heaven.' Dobe paused, seeing Sharleen was beginning to feel better. 'And not one of these Hollywood people could shine your boots, and that's the truth. Maybe Jahne Moore. Sounds like she got some backbone, but not one of them others. Remember that.'

Sharleen's eyes filled with tears. 'Dobe, you're one lovely man. You deserve the best there is in this life. But I'll only go on one condition: we get another ticket and you come, too. Okay?' She waited until he nodded. Was that a blush she saw? She rose, kissed him on the cheek, and started to leave the room, to go upstairs to get ready for the awards.

'Sharleen,' Dobe called, 'after tonight, after all this mess is over, you and me have to have a really good talk. I know some things that I think you're ready to hear, but we've talked serious enough for one day. You get ready now. I'll save the rest of it until all this is all over.'

Sharleen ran back to Dobe and kissed him. Perhaps Dobe had talked her out of some money, but it didn't matter now. He was a good friend, one who had proved his loyalty, and she loved him.

'Thank you for everything,' she said, and went to get dressed for the awards.

Jahne woke up on the morning of the Emmy awards with a bad case of the shakes. She'd taken two Xanax tablets the night before, but that didn't explain the tremors that shook her. And she simply wasn't able to get organized or to focus. She keyed in Sharleen's phone number, and her hand shook so badly that she misdialled twice. When Sharleen answered, Jahne just managed to croak out a 'hello.'

'Come on, Jahne. It ain't so bad,' Sharleen said. What? When they had last spoken, Sharleen had agreed that life was shit. What had cheered her up so?

'Are you going?' Jahne asked. She didn't need to explain. Sharleen knew what she was talking about.

'Yes. And I'm going with Dean. What about you, Jahne? Come with us. There was nothing wrong in what you did.'

'I don't know. Who would I go *with*? Sy said he could set something up, but I haven't agreed. And then Gerald La Brecque offered to take me. But that's too much – being so desperate that you have to go with your paid bodyguard.'

'Oh, Jahne. Come. Come with us. I'll ask Dobe to take you. He's a good friend. What do you say? We can't let Lila have *all* the glory.'

'I don't know. I'll call you back.' Jahne hung up and paced up and down the living room. She shivered. This house was always cold. She hated it.

Could she face the barracudas tonight? Could she afford not to? Lucky Sharleen, to be rescued. No one could rescue her. And what would she wear if she went tonight? It wasn't such a frivolous question as it sounded. The only point to showing up would be to demonstrate that she looked good, felt good, was good. But could she manage to *look* good? Without Mai, she had no guide and no confidence in her own choices. Let's face it, she told herself, when Mai died, you lost both your best friend *and* your sense of style.

It all seemed like so much trouble, too. Finding the right dress, getting her hair done, the manicure, the pedicure, the leg waxing, the makeup, the perfume, the jewellery, the whole thing. She was exhausted just thinking about it. And then, then, the ordeal began – being watched and judged by thirty or forty million people. She imagined the cameras closing in, the commentator recapping the scandal, the audience at home straining their eyes, looking for a telltale scar. And how the cameras would pan the audience, seeking close-ups of the losers when the winners' names were announced.

'No way,' she groaned, walked back to her bedroom, and threw herself back into bed. She shook two more Xanax into her palm and swallowed them dry.

It was more than an hour later when the phone rang. She picked it up, almost as if it were a snake that might bite. 'Hello,' she murmured, hesitant.

'Jahne? Thank God. It's Brewster.'

'Brewster? Oh, God, Brewster. It's so good to hear from you.' Warmth flooded her. It was a physical feeling. 'Brewster. Hello,' she repeated.

'Are you all right, Jahne?' he asked. The phone clicked and spit with static. He must be calling from far away. South America, she thought. Wasn't he making a clinic trip there? It was so good of him to call. 'Are you all right?' he repeated.

'I'm just so embarrassed, Brewster. It sounds stupid, but it feels terminal.'

'Which terminal?' he asked. 'Jahne, I can hardly hear you. What terminal did you say?'

'*Life* is terminal. Oh, Brewster, I feel so bad! Nothing has worked out the way I planned. I got a second chance and I wasted it. I simply couldn't swing it.' Her voice wavered. Even to her it seemed weak and far away.

'This connection is awful,' Brewster cried. 'It keeps cutting out on us. What did you say about swinging?'

'Brewster, aren't you ashamed of me? That horrible movie, and now this tabloid blitz. Are they driving you crazy at the office? Did I ruin your life?'

'More to the point, did I ruin yours? Are you okay, Jahne? You sound so far away.'

'Do you still like me, Brewster?' she asked.

'Of course I do. Jahne, I . . .' His voice faded out.

'Brewster? Brewster, are you there?' There was another wave of static, then the line was dead. Stupidly, she shook the phone in frustration. 'Brewster? Brewster?' she cried. But he was gone. She began to sob, but in the weak, disheartened way of a hopeless child. Oh, God, Brewster was gone. She couldn't talk to him. She sobbed on, her nose dripping, and picked up the quilt to wipe her face. Then the security buzzer sounded.

She lifted the intercom. 'Brewster Moore. Are you expecting him?' the voice asked. She shook her head to clear it. How had Brewster called on her security phone? 'Yes,' she mumbled, and hung on. Or should she hang up? Were they patching him through?

The doorbell rang. She reached for her robe and barely managed to struggle into it without dropping the phone. But Brewster didn't come onto the line. The doorbell rang again. 'One minute,' she yelled, but she knew that whoever it was couldn't hear. Could she put the phone down? Should she hang up? Would she lose Brewster's call?

She left the phone on the bed and tried to run to the door. But the pills affected her balance. She ran into the side of the night table and nearly fell. 'I'm coming,' she yelled, righted herself, and managed to get across the living room, down the gallery, and to the enormous front door. She threw it open.

Brewster Moore stood on the doorstep, a suitcase in his left hand, his raincoat bunched over his right arm. Brewster. Brewster was right there.

'Aren't you in Honduras?' she asked.

He stepped into the foyer. 'Aren't you in trouble?' he asked, and then he dropped his things and they hugged one another.

Later that day, after she had bathed, after Brewster had fed her lunch, after he had helped her wash her hair and she'd picked out a dress and managed to pull herself together – after all that, they sat side by side in the limo. 'There is no way,' Jahne said to Dr. Moore, 'that I could face any of this tonight without you. Thank you for coming all this way, just to take me to the awards and the party. If you couldn't make it, I wouldn't be going.'

'You'll excuse me, Jahne, but I wouldn't have missed it for the world. You don't know this, but there are a lot of people – men as well as women – who are going to be very nervous when they see me tonight. You won't believe who's been calling me in New York, since my name came out connected with you. Now that you've been "outed," everyone's afraid.'

Jahne looked at him. 'What do you mean?'

'Do you really think you're my *only* celebrity client? You weren't a celebrity then, of course. But, Jahne, I've spent years doing corrections of other surgeons' mistakes for some very rich, very famous people. It wouldn't have been ethical of me to have gone into it with you when we first developed our professional relationship. Or even now. But everyone will be afraid that I'm out here to do a book deal, or TV, or to somehow go public.' He took a sip of the white wine he had poured. 'And, considering what these bastards have done to you, and said about me, well, it's a very tempting idea. Do you know I've been approached – just in the last forty-eight hours – by Laura Richie, *and* every publisher in the English-speaking world, just to tell all? They're offering obscene amounts of money. Tempting, real tempting. The money would pay for the work on a lot of kids like Raoul. They'll be coming to you, too – don't be surprised.'

'Ha! I'll never talk to another bloodsucking journalist as long as I live. I wish I could just run away. Start over somewhere.' She laughed at herself. 'Does that sound familiar?'

'Yes, but it doesn't sound so stupid. Maybe you should do just that. Go back to New York.' He reached out and took her hand with his own. His hand was small, but warm and surprisingly comforting. She gripped it tightly.

'What for? To act? That's a laugh! Now the gape factor is high enough for me to star in some Broadway revival – people would come to stare and see if they could spot the scars. Might as well join a carnival sideshow. No, New York theatre is over – for good, I'm afraid. But I'll worry about my career dilemma later, when I have more time. Now I'd rather appreciate the moment – having you here.' Jahne managed a smile. 'But right now I have to face all those beautiful barracudas.'

Dr. Moore laughed. 'Some of whom once were *ugly* barracudas, before they came to me,' he pointed out. 'So what? And don't you think you're showing a lot of class and a certain *je ne sais quoi* by showing up with your surgeon? Sort of sticking it in their eye.'

Jahne laughed at that. 'But no one knows *that* about *them*, and now everyone knows everything about *me*. My age, my previous and present weight – they've seen my "before" pictures, interviewed girls I went to high school with, dragged out the affairs I had with Pete and Michael McLain. I'm humiliated.'

695

'Well, I'm no psychiatrist, but by now I think I know something about people. When they see who you're with tonight, they're going to treat you like Princess Diana. *Before her scandals*. Make no mistake, I know details of people's lives that make your puny little problems look like a pimple against their cancerous growths. And if it gets too bad for you, if you get the last-minute heeby-jeebies and don't want to get out of the limousine, I'm fully prepared to show you some of the pictures I brought along with me from New York. From my files. I know, it's unprofessional, but I hate hypocrites. Jahne, as I tell all my patients, it's only going to hurt a bit, then it's over.'

Lila stretched her arms above her head, her legs flexed down the length of the satin sheets, then reached to her face and removed the eyeshades. She winced as she opened her eyes to the harsh afternoon light. That was the bitch of a Malibu house – the harsh west light. Too much sun, even with the curtains drawn. Lila rang for the maid, had her bring fresh-squeezed orange juice, and slowly – very slowly – open the curtains. She didn't need any other help. As always, Lila would tend to her own toilette.

She lay motionless, sipping the iced juice intermittently, trying to figure out how she really felt about the night that lay ahead. The Emmy was *this close*. She could feel its heft in her hand, the coldness of the metal against her warm palm. Right now, squiggling her toes between the sheets, she felt delighted, as if she were Cinderella that first morning she'd awakened in the palace. After all, Marty *was* a prince in Hollywood, and she a princess. Their wedding and new movie together would mark the start of their reign.

Lila shifted a little in bed. Of course there would be a lot of risks, but they were worth it. She'd already told Marty that she insisted on her own room, her own bed, and privacy. Yet, if her antics could keep him satisfied, he had nothing to complain about.

And if she didn't marry Marty, what was there for her?

A chill wind blew in off the Pacific, turning her skin to gooseflesh. She felt the good mood begin to bleed away, as it did whenever she thought of marriage, but she refused to let it. She *would* be happy.

Lila knew there was a lot to do, but for the next few minutes she wasn't going to do anything but gloat about the waiting prize she would receive tonight, and what she would say in her acceptance speech. Maybe she would mention her costars, just for spite. She laughed.

Then the phone trilled by her bedside. She cursed the interruption, but answered anyway. 'Yes,' she simply said, her usual telephone greeting.

'Lila, darling, I'm so glad I caught you in.' It was me. 'Laura Richie here. I hope I didn't disturb you, but I wanted to be the very first to congratulate you on the Emmy. No one deserves it more.'

'Thank you, Laura. I'll always remember you for this. Congratulating me for something I haven't won yet. Now, that shows real confidence.'

I laughed. 'Nonsense, darling, what are friends for? Anyhow, it's in the bag. Why, anyone with half a brain knows you are a shoo-in. Everyone, my dear, is saying so. And I do mean everyone.' I was trying to get enough stuff to write tomorrow's column in advance. Tricky, because sometimes you have to tell a secret or get caught in a lie, but necessary when you have to be in three places at once.

'Laura, you'll have to excuse me, I must run. They're screaming for me downstairs. Photographers, network publicity people. The house is simply teeming. Of course, I won't tell them a thing. I'll save every detail just for you. After all, you're my oldest and dearest friend in Hollywood.'

Lila slung the manure just the way her mother did. 'I'm not so old, dearie, but thanks for the vote of confidence,' I said. 'Do you know who's presenting the award?'

'No. Do you?'

I ignored her. 'Are you going with Marty?'

'Of course.'

'And have you two set a date?'

'Not yet, but you'll be the first to know.'

It was the last time I ever spoke to Lila Kyle.

8

Michael McLain lay on the lounge at his pool, applying yet another layer of sun block. How to achieve that perfect colour of brown masculine health without destroying his skin's elasticity forever? Such a riddle. He hated to have to resort to bronzer, so he paid particular attention to the sun on his face today, changing his face's position every fifteen minutes to make sure the tan came out perfectly even.

Ara's party tonight would be both pleasure and torture – sort of like fucking a woman who had an exquisite body but an ordinary face. Which, in fact, was what he would be doing in a little while. His date tonight was, after all, Adrienne.

Birth of a Star had given him the boost that he had been needing for a while. It would prolong his life. He'd done it again! Still, he wasn't stupid or naïve. While it was by no means his swan song, he realized that this was the top of the crop of the older man parts he would be offered. He could see Stewart Granger-type made-for-TV-movie roles looming in his future, and he was not about to end his exceptional acting career playing old-but-still-attractive John Forsythe roles. Not Michael McLain.

No, it was time to move his public image to a whole new level. He liked being on the A list and wanted to stay there forever, the way Greg Peck and Jimmy Stewart had. So it was time, at last, for the inevitable. What was the one thing newsworthy Michael McLain had never done with a woman?

Marry one.

After all, it was the nineties. A time of family values. Hadn't Adrienne told him she'd missed a period? No D&C this time. He'd marry her. Have the baby. Be a dad. What a way to spend his sixth decade.

He shifted his face in the sun and stopped the smile from making dangerously ageing wrinkles. Yes. Right after the Emmys, he'd leak the info that Adrienne was the body in *Birth*. After she had a smidgen of facial work. Then announce that he was going to marry her. Wouldn't *that* make headlines?

Theresa O'Donnell walked out of the shower and wrapped a bath sheet around her sagging body. She couldn't be bothered putting on a robe. She was tired, and her evening's work had not even begun. She walked into the dressing room and picked up the Lycra body suit that Estrella had laid out for her. It was specially made for her in Paris and worked like a whole body girdle. She powdered herself down and began the arduous task of wriggling into it, a sausage struggling into its casing.

At last she finished and, exhausted, sat down at her mirrored vanity table. She very nearly groaned as she looked at the wreck that stared back at her. Vanity table, indeed! It was a holy crucifixion to look at the ruin that had been her face. The Loveliest Girl in the World! Well, once she had been.

Where once she had a chin she now had several. And the hollows under her eyes had long ago turned to bags. Well, she'd turned into a bag. Her hair, never her strongest suit, was thinner than ever. Forty years of colouring and perms had had their way. She snatched up a wig cap and stuffed the straggling grey ends into it, fastening the skintight nylon to her head by viciously stabbing in hair pins.

She began to coat her sallow skin with the Estée Lauder base she used. She daubed the natural sea sponge across the wrinkles on her forehead, the puffiness that had become her nose.

'Ah. Transformation Time,' Kevin said as he walked in with two glasses of gin. He looked over her shoulder into the mirror. There were no longer any secrets from Kevin. Now he was bitter because she was going to the Emmys and Ara's party with Robbie and not him. Because she'd be on TV presenting the Best Actress award while he was left home watching. She took the glass from his hand, drank it down and picked up the makeup sponge again.

'Can I get you a trowel?' he asked.

'Very clever. I told you, I'm not speaking to you until you return Candy and Skinny.'

'I don't have them. But I think I know where they are.'

Aunt Robbie arrived at Theresa's at four. 'Where is she?' he asked Kevin who nodded up the stairs to Theresa's bedroom, then shrugged his shoulders. 'Has she had anything to drink yet?' he asked.

'I don't know, and I don't give a shit.'

Robbie moved to the stairs. At Theresa's door, he stopped to knock, but, knowing he wasn't going to get an answer, opened the door and walked in.

'Jesus Christ,' he said to no one in particular. The room was in shambles. Even with the curtains drawn, the dim light showed piles of clothes heaped everywhere, the bed stripped of linen, a stained yellow pile on the floor, and a bloated, whitened heap of a human being stretched out full-length, as if dead, across the sill of the bathroom door. She was naked, and dirty, and her grey hair had the coated, greasy look of a street-woman's. This is what becomes of a legend most often, he thought. Robbie wouldn't let himself feel the sadness that throbbed in his chest. There was too much work to be done.

Robbie pulled back the curtains, and the room sprang into light. Theresa groaned and turned her head.

Robbie pulled Theresa off the floor. He called to Estrella. The maid arrived and gasped. 'Grab her black dress and iron it.

'Meanwhile, find a pair of her long white gloves, and shoes.' Estrella began to sort through the debris, mumbling to herself. Robbie called out to her, 'And thanks, Estrella. She's lucky to have you.'

'And you, too, Mr. Robbie. No one else would come to take her to a party anymore. You a good friend.'

'I have no friends,' Theresa cried. 'No one cares about me.'

'Goddamn it, Theresa! Pull yourself together!' Robbie grabbed her by the shoulders and shook her. 'You've got an appearance.'

'No. Not anymore. They'll find out. They'll all find out.' She mumbled. Robbie wondered what the hell she was going on about.

'Theresa, you've got to sober up, and you've got to go. If you don't show up, you're finished forever. This is live net. We are going tonight. You and I. Goddamn it, Theresa, I want to go to this party.'

'But, Robbie,' Theresa began to cry. 'I can't go. I'd be humiliated.'

'Not if you're sober you won't.'

'But Lila will be there,' Theresa wailed. 'With an Emmy.' Theresa stopped crying and looked around. 'She'll kill me, Robbie,' she whispered.

'Ridiculous! When has Lila or anybody scared you?'

'She was such a lovely baby, wasn't she? Kerry could never have raised a son. I didn't want a son. A daughter was just right.'

'Certainly. Perfect. Now, start to get ready for your hairdresser.'

'But she'll kill me. Like she killed Candy and Skinny.' She was wailing now.

Robbie had listened to the rambling, but didn't try to make much sense of it. Until she mentioned the dummies. He felt a tug of guilt. Well, it had been necessary to get this truce signed. Still, what was she talking about? The dummies were gone.

'What are you talking about, Theresa?' The star shrank into the middle of the big bed, and Robbie wasn't sure if she was shaking from alcohol withdrawal or fear.

'I did the right thing, didn't I, Robbie? I raised a girl. A lovely

700

girl. Only now she hates me. I should never have done it to her,'
Theresa whispered.

'What?' Robbie asked.

'The way I raised her. Then hating her because she was so
young, so beautiful. And that ghastly episode I shot with her. She
hates me for that. She wants to kill me. Like she killed Candy and
Skinny. She killed my other babies.'

'Theresa, what *are* you talking about?'

Slowly, as if each movement was painful, Theresa crawled to
the edge of the bed, then got off it, fell to her knees, and began
to scrabble about under it. Neither Robbie nor Miss Wholley had
had time to evacuate the horrors under there, and God knew the
last time Estrella had tried.

But instead of empty bottles, or old mateless shoes, Theresa
pulled out a long white box. A coffin, really. Then another. Two
actual coffins, perhaps for children's burials. Robbie shivered and
saw that Theresa was shivering, too. Whimpering, she flipped open
the lids.

Robbie looked inside. Skinny had been decapitated, her head
chopped to kindling. Candy had been defaced by a thousand vicious
stab wounds. Both dummies were nude, their bodies smeared with
paint, or maybe someone's blood. And each of them had perfect
little sets of male genitalia nailed to the appropriate parts on their
torsos.

Neil Morelli had not received an invitation to Ara's party. No
surprise. But he had been surprised to hear from Roger after so
long a silence. And to speak to him over the television set, not
the car radio, as he usually did. He, Neil, was getting closer to the
centre of things. Neil was very glad Roger had called. He needed to
ask him so much, needed to know so much. And, with failure and
humiliation weighing on him like a ton of bricks, Neil knew Roger
would understand – and help. Neil now knew who was to blame
for his failure – all those who traded on their celebrity names and
family connections.

He had at first been hesitant to tell Roger about whose ultimate
responsibility all this humiliation was, of his plan to go to the
Emmys, get into them somehow. But Roger had been so kind, so,
well, fatherly, he began to tell him everything, and, to Neil's great
relief and surprise, Roger not only agreed with Neil's appraisal, but
approved of Neil's plan, and gave him exact instructions on how to

carry it out. In fact, it was Roger who told him about the theatre manager who did the hiring of the ushers for the Emmy show. Neil had run off and applied for the job for the evening of the Emmys — for tonight — and gotten it, even though he'd had to lie and swear that he had a tuxedo. It was Roger's doing that he got the job, Neil was convinced, of course. Roger must have spoken to the manager on his behalf.

Roger also told him not to worry about the tux, and gave him the tip about the tuxedo department at Saks, and how easy it was to put one on under his regular clothes in the dressing room and walk out. The tuxedo department was the least busy department in the store, so there never were any salespersons or security guards lurking about. Walking out with the formal wear under his baggy jeans and windbreaker had been a breeze. Even the brazen act of grabbing a dress shirt and bow tie from a display near the door seemed easy, with Roger watching over him.

The other items Roger had told him to get were as easily acquired, some of them through the guys at the cab company. He wasn't exactly sure how or when he would use all this stuff, but Neil wasn't going to question any of Roger's directions. Because Roger told him that he — Neil Morelli — was going to host the awards show. Just like Billy Crystal did the Oscars. He, Neil, would be as famous, as admired, as loved. Roger had thought of everything so far, right down to the suspenders. This was a man on his side, probably the only man who had ever looked out for Neil in his life, and that included his degenerate gambler father. No, Neil was going to do everything Roger told him to do. Roger understood. Roger would help him set things right.

Neil adjusted his tie in the mirror of the bathroom, and wished he had a full-length mirror to admire the full effect of the tux. But wouldn't you know it? Roger called just then, and, as if he could read Neil's mind, told Neil how great he looked, and — this brought tears to Neil's eyes — how proud he was of him. Then Roger told him to sit down and go over the seating arrangement for the auditorium the manager had given each of the ushers, and told him to memorize where the key people were sitting. Roger also went over the physical plan of the theatre, and told him the exact spot where he should be standing, and the exact time, to get the best view of the award presentation.

Neil got it all, put the sheet of paper back into his inside pocket, spit on his hand and smoothed his hair, then opened the door and walked down the street towards the bus. On the way, he heard Roger's voice come from behind him, not through a radio or an amplifier like usual, but over his shoulder, like a guardian angel. 'Timing is everything,' Roger said. And Neil didn't have to turn around to know that Roger was with him and, as always, was absolutely right.

Sam Shields had definitely risen on Ara's Hollywood-heat barometer. This year, he had not only an invitation to go, once again, as April's escort, but his own invitation as well.

Since *Birth* had succeeded, he was a popular boy. No doubt about it. Two hits in a row. April wanted him to sign a three-picture deal, but so did Columbia. He had options now.

He also had a new Armani tux, and a Thai silk custom-made dress shirt. He slipped into the jacket and shot his cuffs. He'd look like a winner tonight.

But he'd see Mary Jane – Jahne – tonight, too. It was traditional for the Emmy winners to drop by after the award. Of course, he could leave early. But he *wanted* to see her. After thinking it over, Sam was ready to forgive her. He wanted her back. And being turned away at Sharleen's gate had only made him more eager.

And, after all, didn't she owe everything to him? Sam shook his head at the irony. Mary Jane couldn't get cast in a soap commercial, couldn't get a part off-off-off-Broadway, until he had given her the break in *Jack and Jill*. And she'd gone through the surgery for him. Because of that, now, tonight, Jahne Moore just might be walking away with an Emmy award. And perhaps an Oscar in the future. Sometimes Sam could see the amusement in the way things evolved in this town. Just as he could at this moment.

But he had his public persona to think about. Tonight, after the awards ceremony, if Jahne showed up at Ara's, Sam would be there. He couldn't – *wouldn't* – not be there; that was out of the question. How was he going to handle his encounter with Jahne, in front of the entire Industry, in front of all the media people? That's what he had to decide.

And how was *she* going to handle it? Sam hoped, for no other reason than that it would make things easier for him, that Jahne in fact did win the Emmy. At least she would be in a good – no, an elated – mood, and their connection could be swift and gay. Oh, he remembered all the things Mary Jane used to say about awards, and award shows, and award winners. But that was back before she had a spitting chance of getting nominated for one, never mind actually winning one. Would Jahne still be as equanimous as she once had been about these things, and not let her loss make her turn on him, bring unwanted attention? He doubted it.

But his final thought, the one that helped him get into the shower and ready for the night, was that Jahne Moore must have loved him a lot to go through all that she had for him. Even if she turned him away at Sharleen Smith's. Somehow, he was sure that they'd get back together. Because, really, who else had ever loved him like that?

Monica Flanders waited impatiently for Hyram to pick her up. Hyram's wife, Sylvia, still resented not being invited to Ara Sagarian's party. Or perhaps she resented Hyram's going with Monica. For the invitation was for Monica – always for Monica.

She took one last look at herself in the mirror. Tonight she would get more publicity and free advertising from the awards programme than ever before. Whoever won, they wore *her* makeup. And the commercial they were running would announce it. Just so long as it wasn't that surgery girl. She would be cancelled, but definitely. Unless, of course, she won.

Monica patted her wig into place and then clipped on her diamond earrings. They were so big – eight-carat emerald-cut perfect stones – that they hurt her ears, but pain was the price you paid for beauty.

Tonight one of her girls would win the prize. And she would win, too. Flanders Cosmetics was sponsoring the Emmy show. Sales would boom tomorrow. What an idea this whole *3/4* business had been! Despite the scandals or because of them. Best idea she'd ever come up with.

Paul Grasso took another sip of his vodka and tried for the third time to tie the fucking formal black bow tie. What's wrong with the clip-ons? he thought once again.

Tonight was a good night for Paul. He had finally made it, without Glick after all. He didn't like to remember last year: sneaking into Ara's party through the bushes. Tonight he was going to see his discovery Lila Kyle get an Emmy, then go on to Ara's Emmy party, where the real shakers were going to be, shoulder to shoulder. Like at the roulette tables at Vegas. Only the heavy hitters stood at the table. The little guys, the assholes with their twenty-dollar chips, stood around the outer edge. And not for very long, either. Either they made a hit the first time at the table, or they were on the move again, looking for the the next win. The whole secret was to stick with it, play it out, all night, if you had to. Like in this Hollywood game. Eventually, if you stayed with it, luck turned your way, and you were being back-slapped by the other heavy hitters.

Tonight Paul Grasso felt like a heavy hitter. And he was in the mood for some back-slapping. If only he could get this fucking tie tied.

It didn't seem right to Sy that he had all three Emmy nominees as his clients and not one of the bitches had asked him to escort her tonight. So he'd settled on Crystal, who was having a shit fit because she hadn't received her own invitation. Well, maybe they could use the party to jump-start her stalled career.

Of course, Sy didn't need any of the 3/4 girls to get into the awards ceremony or Ara Sagarian's party. This much he had done on his own. But it would have been a nice gesture on their part, considering. He was the one, after all, who got the three of them made into the hits they are. And stood behind them during the scandals. Only Sharleen had ever called him to thank him for the Emmy nomination. Jahne had written him a cool note. And Lila was out in fucking Siberia; he heard shit from her. Surprise.

But he could afford to put all that behind him. Tonight was a big night, probably the biggest night in his career. Tonight he owned everyone and everything, because all three of the big ones were in his stable. Tonight he even owned Ara Sagarian himself, not that he was such a prize. It's about time Ara moved over. Next year, Sy thought, I'm going to have an Emmy party at *my* house. *The* Emmy party. If I'm really bigger than Ara Sagarian ever was, and that's the word around town, then I might as well have the full coronation ceremony, and all the perks that go with it. So, next year it would be Sy Ortis' party, A list and then some.

Sy hadn't let on to anyone, of course, but all this tabloid stuff was turning out to be a boon to the reputation of his girls. Yeah, everyone's *cojones* were in an uproar, but he knew that the judgementalism over Sharleen and Jahne would pass, and in its place would come a torrent of new interest. And with that, of course, higher ratings.

So Sy wasn't ambivalent at all about showing up at the celebrations tonight. One of his girls was going to walk away with an Emmy, that much was guaranteed. He didn't really care which one, but kind of hoped that it would be Sharleen or Jahne – they could use the positive press and, in light of the tabloid mess, it would go a long way towards balancing things out.

But whoever got it would be Sy's. And that no one could take away from him.

The way Sy figured it, the only way he could lose tonight was if there was a nuclear holocaust. Other than that, he was already the winner. The very best, the absolute very best that could happen would be that there would be a three-way tie. Sy chuckled. About as much chance of that as a nuclear holocaust.

But he could hope, couldn't he?

April looked into the mirror and grimaced. Yes, lipstick *had* smeared onto her two front incisors, as it so often did. When she was a kid, some of the children at school had teased her, calling her 'werewolf girl.' Stubbornly, even now, she'd never had them filed down. They came in handy when she had to tear out the throat of her next victim.

Carefully she wiped off the offending makeup. Yes, she would do some throat-tearing tonight. Sy Ortis and Marty DiGennaro were about to participate in her favourite little game: retribution. Because, after all the chips she'd called in, it was certain that *Three for the Road* wasn't going to win a goddamn thing tonight. The bad publicity on the bitch Jahne hadn't hurt, nor had the exposé on that Jukes-and-Kallikaks brother-and-sister act, but she was pretty sure that she could have neutralized the thing anyway. Her pressure on Warren Lashbeck and the Industry censorship committee was tightening the pressure on Les Merchant, head of the Network. He might be pushed into cancelling the show. She couldn't trust anyone to do what they promised, of course. Still, if there was one thing she was dead certain of, it was this: that rats in Hollywood knew what to do about a sinking ship.

Tonight, after almost eleven years, she'd get to fuck up Marty DiGennaro and Sy Ortis as badly as they'd fucked her all that long time ago.

Marty DiGennaro hummed tonelessly to himself as he fitted the opal cabochon stud into his shirtfront. It was a habit that used to drive his ex-wife nuts, but he never thought about her anymore. He almost hoped that he would run into her this evening, with Lila clinging to his arm. His ex was petite and dark, not really an impressive woman. Lovely in her way, certainly, but not stunning. Not Lila. No one was like Lila.

He kept trying to push in the stud, but something wasn't working. Either the buttonhole was sewed closed or the damned stud was defective. Shit. Marty was a detail person, and he loved the detail of dressing. The opal shirt studs had once belonged to Gary Cooper. Marty had bought them, as discreetly as possible, from the estate of a past mistress of Coop. Sally had been upset, said that opals brought bad luck unless they were your birthstone, but Marty loved them. He was wearing them for the first time tonight.

Well, they were bringing bad luck now. He checked the time, then called to Sally for help. He would wear the opals, damn it. Because he was a man who had made all the good luck he'd ever need. He had a ravishing fiancée who never looked at another man, a string of Oscars a mile long, and a new, hot career in television, which he, single-handedly, was turning around.

'Sal!' he called, impatient. 'Hurry up and bring a scissors.'

As Sal walked into the room, Marty jerked at the stud. It spun out of his hand, arching across the room, and fell on the marble saddle at the bottom of his dressing-room door. As if in the slow motion of one of his films, Marty watched the opal shatter, sending gleams of iridescent colour across the floor.

'Goddamn it!' Marty cried.

'Maybe it can be fixed,' Sally said, and knelt to begin gathering the shards.

'Forget it!' Marty told him. 'Once it's broken, it's broken.'

Ara's guests began to arrive, and though he was tired – well, almost exhausted – from all the preparations, now it all seemed worth it. Not bad for an old man, he thought. Here he was, a man that should by all rights be dead, or at least retired and living in Palm Springs, here he was, giving yet another successful party, with only the *crème de la crème* of the Industry present.

He laughed at his little pretension. *Crème de la crème*, my wrinkled Armenian *vorick*, he thought to himself. Stars, star-makers, star-fuckers, and star-breakers – all grasping, back-stabbing cut-throats.

But, he reminded himself, most of the media clout in the

nation was gathered under one roof tonight. He was still a player. A major player. A man of power, surrounded by the tastemakers, the trendsetters, the wave-makers. All under one roof. *His* roof.

He smiled, nodded, and limped forward to greet his first guest.

'Don't forget who you're dealing with,' Theresa snapped at Robbie when she'd asked for a simple glass of sherry and he refused. 'I just need a little something to calm me down.'

'Theresa, right now you have enough Valium in you to float you higher than the Goodyear blimp. You don't need another thing.'

Theresa couldn't give up so easily. As if Valium could ever take the place of vodka. 'You don't seem to grasp one very important fact here. I'm under *incredible* pressure. In a little while I'll have to go out there and face her. And show myself to all those people. Live. Jesus. I haven't done live in a hundred years.'

'You'll be fine. It will all go fine,' he assured her and patted her shoulder.

'I was just saying to – who was it? Warren Beatty? No, it was Annette. No, April Irons! That's who it was, April.' Crystal Plenum almost had Ara by the lapels, standing very close. 'I was saying to April how Ara Sagarian never seems to age. What's your secret, Ara? You could make a fortune if you sold it.'

Crystal felt pretty desperate, and her desperation showed. She knew what it was like to enter a room and make an impression. And she knew that she had and hadn't.

Crystal's face hurt. If she had to smile at these fucking assholes, these insulting, insufferable assholes, for even ten more minutes, she would have facial spasms. Joel Silver was here. So was Larry Gordon. Dawn Steele looked great – where did she get that dress? God, Crystal was ready to stoop to being a Disney whore if she had to. They were famous for buying up fading stars cheap and resuscitating them. So smile nice at Dawn. She remembered what her first movie director had told her. He had said that some actors and directors thought the most difficult thing to do on cue was cry. He had disagreed and said it was laughter, not crying, that was the harder for actors to manage realistically. He was right. Laughing at people's little jokes at her expense was almost more than she could bear.

Then she saw him: the son-of-a-bitch! In tiny steps – all her dress would allow – she walked up to Sam Shields. He was surrounded by some of the powers in the Industry, but she ignored them.

'Aren't you going to say hello?' she asked.

He looked up and smiled — one of those useless polite smiles she'd been getting from people lately.

'Hello, Crystal.'

She looked him right in the face. 'I just wanted to say thank you. Thank you for ruining my career. And I wanted to give you this.' And then she spat at him.

Elizabeth wandered with Larry. Warren sat, laughing, beside Annette. Kevin Costner and Cindy chatted with Marvin Davis. Joe Pesci stood in a corner, sharing a bottle of Evian water with Jack Nicholson. Steven Seagal ate sushi beside one of the monitors. Scott Rudin threw a napkin at Paula Weinstein. Rob Reiner stood beside his wife, one of the famous Singer sisters.

Now the thirty-five-inch screens scattered around Ara's house were all forgotten, save one. The screen in Ara's library seemed to be the only one the guests were watching, as if sharing the one screen made them all feel more a part of the audience. Ara sat in the middle of the guests. On the screen, the emcee was introducing Theresa O'Donnell, who was smiling and opening the envelope. There wasn't a sound in the room, as if everyone had a personal stake in the outcome of the Emmys. Ara smiled to himself. He did, too. Yes, anyone, just so long as it wasn't Lila Kyle.

Theresa tore at the envelope, pretending she was having trouble getting it open, prolonging the tension. She opened the envelope, took out the card, and said, 'The winner is . . .'

9

Jahne had taken her place on an aisle seat, with Dr. Moore next to her. She had forced herself to sit back in her seat, and tried to breathe deeply. Brewster sat beside her, his hand holding hers tightly. And it was not just comforting, but a clever career move: it was as if she were laughing at the bad press, flaunting her doctor at them. She seemed unashamed.

As the evening wore on there were a lot more losers than winners. The audience was restive. Self-loathing and fear seemed like a palpable force. Winners glowed, but every loser had to sit in a pool of failure, everyone watching and judging. She told herself she could rise above it all.

But could she? It was hard to sit there, in this room filled with the best and the beautiful, and know that she was being watched and judged, perhaps most of all. Would she get the Emmy? Did she care? She was certain that neither Sharleen nor Lila could act. She was not so certain that the rest of her peers saw things that way. And she found that, oddly enough, she wanted to win tonight. Not because she thought these contests mattered, but because, right now, she needed a vote of approval.

When she arrived at the theatre, Sharleen had looked up to the monitor, only to see her own face turning from the camera. She had quickly looked away, back to Dean. On the other side of her sat Dobe — Sy had managed the extra ticket. 'I never been on live television before. Don't it make you nervous?' she asked him in a whisper, her throat dry.

'Sure do. Afraid some people we sold gas pills to might be tuned in.'

For a moment, she turned to him with frightened eyes. Then she saw he was jokin' with her.

'They never bother no one, Sharleen. They're too embarrassed by their own greed and stupidity. Now, hold your head up high, girl. You're on TV, and you got nothin' to be ashamed of.'

'I'm ashamed that I ever doubted you,' she admitted. 'I thought I'd never see you again after I gave you that money.'

'But you gave it to me anyway, didn't you? How come?'

'I couldn't say no to a friend, Dobe.'

'And I noticed you haven't asked me about our spread.'

'It's okay if you lost the money, Dobe. I just didn't want to lose *you*.'

'Lost the money? Well, hell, do you think I'm a dang fool? I didn't *lose* the money. But I didn't buy us any land in Montana.'

Oh, good. He was going to confess. Sharleen felt relieved. It was the one thing that had stood between them. 'That's all right, Dobe. It's water under the bridge.' He was welcome to the money. She just didn't want him to lie to her about it.

'Great. I'm glad you aren't disappointed. Montana was full of yuppies and Hollywood jerks. Turned the whole damned state into a fern bar.' She nodded. It was all right. She loved Dobe and she always would. As if he knew what she was thinking, he smiled back. 'Yep, Montana's been ruined. So I bought us the nicest piece a land in Wyoming that you ever laid eyes on!'

Her mouth opened in surprise. 'Did you really, Dobe?' She turned to him, her face shining. Happiness flooded her.

'Of course I did! You never doubted me, did you?' He grinned at her slyly. 'Got all the papers back at the house. Nine hundred acres. Not too shabby. Halfway between Daniel and Halfway.'

'Halfway?'

'No, not *in* Halfway. That's the town to the south. Daniel's to the north. We're halfway. Kind of like the who's on first joke. Anyway, I'll show you on the map tonight. Now, wave to the people at home, and then settle down and pay attention to the man onstage. They're announcing the Best Actress award. No matter what happens, I want you to keep that look on your face when the winner is announced.'

The master of ceremonies had gone through all the oddball categories, the ones only family and friends of the nominated sat at the edge of their seats for. He presented the penultimate award, for Best Actor in a Dramatic Series, then said, 'And now the one we've all been waiting for: Best Actress in a Dramatic Series. And to present it, someone who might have a preference. Ladies and gentleman, Theresa O'Donnell!

'The Loveliest Girl in the World' theme song began and Theresa tottered out. Was she drunk? She read the nominees' names from the cue screen, then the inevitable, 'The envelope, please.'

Lila felt paralyzed. The PMs here! To present the Emmy. No. No. She was totally prepared to win. But not for this. Oh God, not this!

And what if she lost? All at once, the possibility swept over her. She reached her hand out to Marty's beside her and almost crushed his in her clawlike grasp.

'Jesus, your hands are cold!' he said, and then the master of ceremonies, Johnny Burton, handed the envelope to her mother.

'And the winner is . . . Lila Kyle!'

10

The theatre audience gasped as if it were one person, then burst into applause. Hey, no one bought drama the way actors do. The camera picked up Lila's face as it broke into well-rehearsed surprise, then the broadest smile she had ever done, on- or offscreen. She kissed Marty sitting next to her, jumped up, and, holding up her long dress to ensure she wouldn't trip, ran up the aisle and to the podium. She felt the hammering of her heart, and the heat of the lights. She seemed to be moving as if through water, as if in a dream, all in slow motion: each step up to the platform, across the stage.

She faced her mother who clutched the Emmy in her own claws. Lila reached for the statuette. Theresa stared at her glassily. Lila pulled at the award. But Theresa didn't let go. Lila tugged. Theresa hung on. But Lila would have it. It was hers. Everything would be hers from now on. And, at last, her mother gave in. Lila held the award to her chest. The crowd went wild.

She had never stood before a crowd like this. Well, after all, she wasn't a stage actress. Now, standing in front of this audience, the *crème de la crème* of her world, she felt the applause, and she felt the love they had for her. Oh, it was indescribable, it was what she had dreamed of, night after night. Love. Pure love. Love that didn't sully, love that didn't touch her, but that surrounded her like a warm bath, like a mother's breast. She could feel the applause, she could feel it across her erect nipples, against her stomach, and lower, somewhere lower.

'Oh,' she gasped into the microphone. 'Oh. Thank you!' she managed to say, her prepared speech disappearing somewhere out of her head. 'Thank you all.' The audience, tired of the usual long-winded speeches and faked sincerity, responded to her pure feeling. The applause began again, building and swelling until it beat against her. And Lila felt something build and swell within. The applause seemed to carry her, the approval to build and to release her.

712

And, for the first and last time in her life, Lila felt the exquisite tingling that became a wave, a deep, powerful wave that made her shudder and brought her, right there on the stage at the podium, to orgasm.

It took a few minutes for the applause to die down, and, in those few minutes, Lila wept. From relief, from joy, but most of all because this was the first time since that party, so many years ago, that she had won applause from an audience. My mother hit me then. She was jealous then. Is she jealous now? Lila shivered in her triumph. Since then, before this magical night, Lila had only performed in front of a camera, cut off from reaction, from response, without the benefit of applause. Tonight she realized what she had been missing. And wanted more.

She gathered herself, though she still trembled. Then, carefully, ignoring Theresa she stepped from around the podium to take one more bow, to still the audience, yet at the same time to milk every glorious moment of it. Lila bowed and stood in place, the Emmy in her hands in front of her.

It was the happiest moment of her life. And the last.

11

The crack came from the back of the auditorium, and Lila pitched forward, the Emmy dropping from her hands and rolling several feet forward until it came to a stop, teetering just at the edge of the stage. It took the camera crew almost four seconds to realize something extraordinary had happened. Lila Kyle had dropped completely out of the frame. Mitch Goldman, the Emmy-show producer, who was back in the control booth, barked an order to Camera 1. 'Give me a long shot,' he yelled.

Lila was revealed, lying prone across the front of the stage. 'Is the bitch drunk like her mother?' Mitch asked. 'Did she trip? Get me a close-up, Bobby.' A dazed murmur had gone up from the crowd. Was this a gag? An accident?

Johnny Burton was the first one to Lila. He touched her, then looked at the red stain that had already begun to spread across the back of her dress to his hand.

'She's been shot,' he shouted. 'Get a doctor up here!'

'Fuck this live TV,' Mitch Goldman groaned.

Everyone surrounding Ara in his living room gasped as Lila fell. They all stood, paralyzed, as still as statues. No one even blinked, all eyes fixed to the screen. What was going on? Lila had just been named winner . . . was taking her bows . . . and suddenly keeled over. On the screen, Johnny Burton was leaning over her. His voice took over the room once again, breaking the silence. 'She's been shot.'

Ara's first thought was that it was shtick. Then, after the briefest silence, someone screamed.

'Oh, my God!' Michael McLain cried out. Several women screamed. 'Is she dead?' someone yelled. Everyone was up, pushing closer to one of the screens. Véronique Peck was sobbing. 'Hush! Quiet so we can hear!' Michael Douglas told the crowd. In the pandemonium, only Ara, unnoticed, continued to sit in his chair.

Sam had only just managed to come back from the men's room. He'd regained his composure after the incident with Crystal when he heard the commotion and looked up at the screen. He heard the announcement about Lila and gasped.

My God! Sam thought. What about Jahne? Is she safe? If she had won, would she have been shot?

And all at once a longing – the strongest feeling of his life – washed over him. My God, what if she were dead? What if I could never see her, never hold her, never love her again?

In that moment, he realized he would never love anyone but her.

Robbie couldn't think, couldn't put two words together, so he didn't try. He reacted instead, gathering up the collapsed form of Theresa and moving quickly out of the green room and to the auditorium exit. Lila! Was she really hurt? No, it's only television. It can't be real. Theresa's having an attack. Got to get her out of here. Jesus, where's the car? He screamed for the driver as he made it through the door. The driver was nowhere to be found. But somehow Robbie would get to the hospital, where both his girls needed help.

Sy Ortis stood in the middle of the room, the spot he had manoeuvred himself into, right next to Ara, so he could be where he belonged, in the centre of everything, ready to receive the congratulations. Now he didn't move, couldn't move. Lila's been shot? He put his hand on his chest for a moment, then dropped it to his pocket and his inhaler. But his breathing was fine. He looked at the screen. Lila's been shot. Jesus Christ! An Emmy, *and* national TV coverage of her shooting. Sy would never cease to be amazed by that woman. She must have set it up. He remembered what the bus crash had done for Gloria Estefan. If Lila survived this – and Sy didn't for a minute think she wouldn't somehow – she was going to be the hottest actress around for years to come. A definite cover next week on *People*. She'd own this fuckin' town.

The room was swirling now. There was no way Ara could stop it, even when he closed his eyes. When he opened them again, he saw everything through a rose light, like the jelly lights on a stage. Red. He knew it. He had felt it coming. The stab of pain, then the pain receding, giving him a moment to breathe. He tried to stand, to call out, but couldn't. Then the searing red-hot pain again, in his head, down the side of his body. Ara tried to open his mouth to call out for help, but all that came out was a long stream of drool. He fell back into the chair, grateful for the relief of the semiconsciousness that was falling over him.

Ara remained seated, with the crowd swirling around him, around and around like a merry-go-round. His head hurt. No, it was worse than 'hurt.' It felt as if his brain would split. He decided to sit there until everything stopped. And then, for him, it did.

'Oh, no, that poor girl.' The blonde starlet next to Paul Grasso was in tears, her head lowered to rest on Paul's shoulder. Paul shrugged it off.

Marty, he thought. What about Marty DiGennaro? They hadn't said anything about him. It seemed, as much as Paul could make out, that Lila was the only one hurt. The scene on the screen had already shifted to a newsroom set, and the newsman was speaking in a strained but clear voice. 'Word has just reached us that this was a terrorist act of the International Anti-Nepotism League. Police are still trying to identify the shooter. The FBI has been called in.'

Paul turned back to the blonde starlet, who now was only sniffling. 'I discovered Lila Kyle,' he told her.

'Wait a minute,' Michael McLain called out to the crowd. 'Shut up. Let's hear what they're saying,' he warned everyone, pointing to the TV monitor. Adrienne was by his side, as she had been all evening, only now she was clinging with both hands, bunches of his formal jacket in each of her fists. 'It's okay, honey,' he told her, charmed by her dependence. 'That's miles away. You're safe here.' Her belly was already protruding, making a pleasant mound that she now pushed against him. He patted it, then brought his attention back to the screen. It was Lila Kyle, he thought. Shot. Yes. It's been confirmed. What was this league? Christ, now the assassinations of movie stars would begin. He thought of the psychopath in prison who kept writing to him. The army of loners carrying copies of *Catcher in the Rye*. For him old threats would probably be joined with the threats of women fans once he announced his engagement to Adrienne. He turned to Adrienne to lead her out of the room. There was no sense staying here. Not with his fiancée in her delicate condition. As he led a grasping Adrienne to the door, he thought that it could have been worse. Lila could have been shot *before* the award. Then that bitch Jahne Moore might have won it by default.

Someone said, 'Who's Auntie Nepo . . . You know. That woman they said.'

'Nepotism,' came the answer, 'is when you get your job through family ties.'

'Holy shit,' Seymore LeVine yelled out. 'They're going to kill us all.'

12

Neil Morelli calmly turned away from the stage, not even waiting a moment to get a reaction. After all, Roger had told him what to do, and Roger had told him he wouldn't miss. When they hadn't

716

called Neil up to replace Johnny as master of ceremonies, Roger had calmed his rage, Roger had explained the change in plans. Neil let the gun hang loosely from his arm. He began calmly walking down the left aisle, towards the stage, towards the lights, towards Johnny, who was now holding the crumpled body of Lila Kyle in a sort of gender-reversed pietà. Calm. Neil felt perfectly calm, because now the worst was over.

The screams seemed distant. It wasn't that he didn't hear them. Half the auditorium was screaming, and the other half was either ducking under the seats or running for the exits. But the pandemonium seemed distant, unrelated to him.

He had gotten within fifteen feet of the stage before they tackled him. He felt the blow from behind, crumpled to his knees, and hit the floor, but there was no pain. Roger had told him there would be none. The gun was wrested from his hand, but Neil didn't need it anymore, anyway. What he needed was some air. His lungs felt curiously empty, with the pile of squirming bodies on top of him. It wasn't pain, exactly – Roger had promised no pain – but it was a lot of pressure. Then it lifted, and he felt the wrench as his arms were tugged together, behind him, but he was too busy trying to fill his lungs to mind the bite of the handcuffs on his thin wrists.

When he was jerked to his feet, the lights and cameras were there, as Roger had assured him they would be. Neil smiled. He *wasn't* a loser. Far from it. Now he'd be a star. The Deliverer. He would set everyone free from the wretched system. No more handing on from mother to daughter, father to son. And Roger had predicted all of this. Roger had chosen him. Neil had had his fears and doubts, but he had triumphed. He'd completed his mission, except for the speech.

People were shouting questions at him, at the five men who surrounded him. Neil just smiled. 'I represent the International Anti-Nepotism League,' he shouted. 'Death to those who defy us.' And then he launched into his comedy monologue.

13

The scoop of a lifetime comes only once to each of us, and then only if we're lucky. Did Woodward and Bernstein know what they had discovered as they checked out that break-in? I don't think so. I do know that the news of Lila's shooting was enough to make me bribe a rented-limo driver with $210 in cash and my Rolex to abandon his client at the Emmy awards and drive me to the hospital.

The streets around the hospital were mobbed, swarming with police black-and-whites. Their red bubble-gum lights spun eerily, bouncing off the strained faces of onlookers. The ambulance was losing precious moments, waiting for the police to clear a path. The police finally got the screaming ambulance through, and it pulled into the bay giving onto the emergency room. The back doors were pulled open, and medical personnel pulled the stretcher onto the walkway and ran it through the doors of the ER. I could just see Marty DiGennaro walking beside the gurney holding an IV bag aloft, the tubes a tangle.

The entrance to the emergency room at Cedars-Sinai was a madhouse. Another ambulance was pulling up. I didn't know it at the time, but in it rode the earthly remains of Ara Sagarian. From the midst of the growing throng, I could now see not only Marty DiGennaro but also Theresa O'Donnell at the head of the crush, pushing their way through the crowd of reporters and gawkers, trying to get in the doors of the hospital.

Theresa O'Donnell was behind the stretcher. I don't know where she'd come from. She stepped haltingly, her eyes scanning the watching faces. 'It's okay, Miss O'Donnell. Just police and hospital workers.' A police officer gallantly offered his hand, and she followed the stretcher through the doors, Robbie Lymon holding her by one arm. A woman in a business suit and an identification tag showing her to be a hospital employee, said to Theresa, 'Follow me, Miss O'Donnell.'

Another gurney came trundling down the pike. 'What you got?' one of the ER specialists called out.

'Stroke. DOA,' the paramedic yelled.

'Park 'im. We got a live one!' And that is how Ara Sagarian was left:

parked, dead, in the hallway of the ER for the next five hours, while the drama of the living played itself out around him.

The group surrounding Lila continued on, through a gauntlet of police holding back the throngs of people who, like maggots, came to feed on the flesh of the fallen. Camcorders whirled from behind the wall of police, and reporters screamed out questions. The last question Theresa heard through the noise and confusion, just before they turned down a corridor, was, 'Is she dead or alive, Miss O'Donnell?'

A nurse, her white uniform sharply contrasting with the black of Marty's tux, opened the door from inside and, while holding off the pushing crowd, pulled first Marty, then Theresa O'Donnell and Robbie into the lobby. By now my elbows had ensured that I was right behind those three, but I knew that, like the other media people, I would have to stand outside, my nose pressed to the glass of the doors, waiting like all the other newshounds and -hens for crumbs of information.

It was then that I got my lucky break. Literally. The door, pushed violently in, swung back, and bashed me in the nose. And I am an easy and copious bleeder.

Inside the hospital, it was still pandemonium, but the guard saw the blood and waved me in. Nurses and hospital personnel had already converged on Marty, Theresa, and Robbie, guiding them off to a quieter corner. 'I'm with their party,' I murmured to the charge nurse, and, checking out the jewellery and the blood in a single appraising glance, she seated me with them. I surreptitiously lowered my head between my legs to make sure the bleeding continued. It had already made dramatic smears on my yellow silk blouse ($316 at Giorgio's), and I made sure it was all over my face, too. The emergency room is no place for personal vanity.

The charge nurse had already begun ministering to Theresa, who was loudly moaning, clutching the Emmy statuette. Marty sat silent, his hands dangling emptily between his skinny legs. He looked catatonic. And Robbie Lymon was sobbing loudly.

A doctor came out through the double doors of the treatment area and asked for Lila Kyle's next of kin.

'Right here,' Theresa moaned.

'And I'm her aunt. Uh, uncle,' Robbie corrected himself.

'I'm her fiancé, doctor,' Marty DiGennaro said, standing up.

The doctor looked strangely at Marty. 'That patient in there cannot be your fiancé,' he said. To all of us he added, 'I need to speak to a blood relative or a legal spouse. Is there anyone here?'

Robbie spoke for Theresa, who was still moaning, held up on one *side by the nurse. 'This is the mother, doctor. Miss O'Donnell.'*

The doctor spoke directly to Theresa. 'Miss O'Donnell,' he said, 'we don't know exactly what's happened, but you needn't worry. The patient that was brought in is not your daughter. Of that I can assure you.'

Theresa went weak in the knees, and her collapsed hulk was beginning to slip out of Robbie's and the nurse's grasp, but I noticed she held onto the Emmy. 'Nurse,' the doctor barked, 'get Miss O'Donnell to one of the examining rooms.' A hospital suit came over and began to lead Theresa and the nurse away, though Robbie trailed after her, down the hall.

Marty, speechless up to now, at last found the words to speak to the doctor. 'What are you talking about? Of course that's my fiancée. I saw her shot. I came with her in the ambulance.'

'That's a physical impossibility,' the doctor snapped. 'It can't be Lila Kyle.'

'Why?' Marty snapped.

'Because the patient you brought in, the one with a gunshot wound, has a penis.'

14

The sign on the doors said 'No Admittance. Hospital Employees Only.' A lone hospital security guard stood in front of those doors, his hands behind his back, his stance military. The woman nodded to him as they passed through; Theresa and Robbie were finally shown into a secretary's office, then into a larger, tastefully decorated inner office, the nameplate on the door announcing ownership: 'Dr. Robert Stern, Chief Administrator.' Robbie didn't know what the hell was going on. What had the doctor meant, that Lila wasn't shot? That she had a . . . It was unthinkable. Robbie had seen her on the stretcher. Theresa seemed to have pulled herself together and had a whispered discussion with the doctor and an officious woman.

'I'm Ms. McElroy,' the woman who had guided them finally said, once they were safely in the office. 'Dr. Stern has been advised of the situation, and insists that you be given the privacy of his office for as

720

long as you wish to use it. A doctor from the emergency room will be in to speak with you as soon as the patient's situation has been completely appraised. Right now all I can report is that the patient is still alive. I'm sorry, Miss O'Donnell. I wish there was more I could tell you. But it won't be long now.'

She offered the usual refreshments, and gave Theresa a telephone number at which to call her directly if they needed anything, or had a question. She also opened the bottom drawer of Dr. Stern's desk and showed them the private telephone, the number only she and Dr. Stern would have. This was the only phone Theresa should answer. Ms. McElroy unplugged the desk model, and advised Theresa to replug this phone if she needed to make any outgoing calls. Only Dr. Stern's private phone was to be answered during this emergency.

When Ms. McElroy opened the door to leave, another security guard was standing there. As the door was closing behind her, Theresa could hear the efficient young woman giving him instructions.

As soon as the door closed behind them, Robbie threw himself down onto the leather chair, stunned into silence. Theresa began to walk around the room, opening and closing cabinet doors until she found the one she was looking for. She selected a bottle of excellent brandy from Dr. Stern's stock, then, with bottle and glasses in hand, flopped onto the leather sofa across from Robbie. She pulled off the bottle top, poured a full glass of brandy for herself, and, still with bottle in hand, drank hungrily from the glass until it was drained. She finally put the glasses and the bottle down on the coffee table, breathing as if she had been holding her breath under water.

'Keep it together, Theresa. And tell me what the hell is going on.'

'Don't say one fucking word to me, do you understand? I was a good little girl all night, and did exactly what you wanted me to do, right? Well, the party's over. I deserve a drink, under the circumstances. And I'd advise you to have one. You're as pale as a ghost. I don't need you fainting on me now, for chrissakes.'

Theresa poured herself another water tumbler of brandy, and began to sip this one. Her face was set in a grim but distant look. 'Well, there's no hope now.'

'You heard what Ms. McElroy said. Lila is still alive.'

Theresa shook her head, snapping out of her reverie. 'I'm not talking about Lila. Can't you think about *me* for one minute? What *I'm* going through? *Now* what happens to me? To my future?'

Robbie stared at Theresa for a moment, then there was a sudden, insistent knock on the door. Theresa could hear the security guard questioning someone, then the guard opened the door and let in a young doctor.

He was nervous *and* officious, as well as in a hurry. His white coat was bloodied, and he carried a sheaf of papers in his hands. He walked into the room and spoke directly to Theresa without preamble. 'I must talk to you – alone.' His tone was insistent.

'Is she alive?' Robbie asked.

'Yes,' he said to them both. Then, to Theresa, he repeated his demand: 'We must talk.'

Theresa let her breathing slow, then said to the doctor, 'You can discuss anything in front of Mr. Lymon. He's one of my oldest and dearest friends. What is it, doctor?' She asked as if she had no idea what was coming.

'Lila Kyle is *your* child? You are Lila Kyle's birth mother?'

'Yes,' Theresa answered.

'Then I have to ask you to sign the corrected permission-for-surgery sheet. Like the one you signed before, but this one states the gender correctly.'

The doctor paused again, this time to look at Robbie, then continued: 'You are, of course, aware of the genital sex of your child.'

Robbie could hardly believe his ears. 'What? What the hell is that supposed to mean, Theresa? What's he talking about?'

Theresa waved her hand to silence Robbie, then answered the doctor's question. 'Yes,' she said curtly.

'So you know that Lila Kyle is, in fact, a male, and not a female.'

'Yes,' she said again.

'What?' Robbie screeched, but they ignored him.

'Needless to say, that changes nothing in the approach we take to saving her – uh, his – life. But, for obvious legal reasons, we did need this clarified. Please sign the amended form, Miss O'Donnell. We have a lot of additional surgery to perform.'

Theresa scribbled her name at the bottom of the page. 'What are her chances?'

'That's too early to tell. I'm sorry. But we're doing everything we can. So far, it appears that it was only one bullet wound, but it has nicked the aorta. I have to be honest with you, Miss O'Donnell. It's touch and go, I'm afraid. I'm not going to offer you false hope, just my promise that we will do everything we can for him.'

'And, doctor, the . . . other information. How long will that remain confidential?'

He paused at the door. 'Any aspect of Miss Kyle's condition can only be made known by a hospital spokesperson, in this case Ms. McElroy. So, officially, there will be no press conference until we know something more. We will not mention the gender reidentification at this time. And until you have been advised.' He looked at Theresa directly now. 'Unofficially is another matter. This is a major piece of information. I can only say that I rely on the integrity of the staff, and hope that you can feel the same way. The mob of reporters and fans outside is overwhelming.' Then he left Robbie and Theresa alone.

Robbie, who had remained silent, pushed himself up from the sofa. 'What the fuck does he mean, "gender reidentification"?'

Theresa gulped from her glass. 'I always wanted a girl,' she murmured. She spoke as if to herself. 'There was no way I could have raised a boy.'

'Answer me,' Robbie demanded.

Theresa jerked her head erect. 'Don't take that tone with me. I've got enough to deal with now without having to deal with an outraged faggot.' Robbie didn't respond. 'The baby had a problem. A testicle hadn't descended. You know Kerry. He couldn't cope with being married, never mind playing the father to a son. Jesus, we only got legal for the publicity. The studio forced it. You know that better than anyone.'

'And?' Robbie asked.

'And what? We had our drunken nights together, I got pregnant, and Kerry returned to you, or whatever young man he was fucking at the time. When I told him I was pregnant, he laughed so hard I thought he was going to have a brain haemorrhage.' Theresa continued to drink from the glass of brandy, replenishing it even before the glass was empty. 'When he got used to the idea – when *we* got used to the idea – we began to talk about the little *girl* we were going to have. It was what we both wanted. We didn't even consider having a boy.'

'But you did,' Robbie said.

'Technically, yes.'

'Technically! *Technically*? What the hell do you mean? Was there a question?'

'Not actually. But with the testicle . . . Well, I tied a string around the other. It atrophied. No problem. And raised Lila as a girl.'

'So how did you ... Lila's birth certificate says "girl." I've seen it. How did you do that?'

'Oh, you remember Dr. Carlton. That old quack. He would do anything you told him to do. He got more people in Hollywood amphetamines or morphine than any drug dealer today could handle. He did abortions, which were illegal in those days, and even repaired bullet wounds that were never reported to the police. Anything. He was the Industry's very personal physician. He attended me at the Westlake Maternity Home. So, when he told me it was a boy, I simply told him he must be mistaken. I had a girl. And I expected the birth certificate to reflect that fact.'

'And Carlton did that for you? He had Lila registered as a girl?'

'Of course he did, for chrissakes. He tied off the testicle. And gave hormone treatments when the time came. And it cost me a bundle.'

'Jesus Christ! My God, Theresa! What did Kerry say about it?'

Theresa laughed. 'You might not know this, but the night Lila was born, Kerry was at one of Ara's all-night, all-boy sex orgies. He didn't show up at the hospital to see me or the baby until all this was taken care of.'

'But how could he never have known?'

'Why, would he have found out when he changed her diaper? Or gave her a bath? Don't be such an ass, Robbie. You knew Kerry better than I did. He wanted no part of me, or the baby, or a happy home life. He didn't even want any part of you, as I remember, when it looked like you wanted more than the occasional fuck. Kerry didn't want to be tied down. Not to anyone. So it became our secret. Lila's and mine.'

'But Estrella?'

'Estrella was bought and paid for. She knew what the deal was from day one. It was either live with it, and with all the comforts my life-style could provide her, or back she would go, to that thatched-roof *casa* in the desert of Mexico. What would *you* have chosen?'

The brandy was beginning to have its effects on Theresa. Her eyes filmed over. She sank into a low leather chair. 'She was such a pretty little girl. All round and soft, with beautiful eyes, and lovely hair.' Theresa seemed to get lost in the memory for the moment. 'We never thought about it again. When it came time, Carlton started her on hormones. He got her a breast implant in Mexico. She has a perfect set of tits. Lila never complained, never questioned any of it. She was happy as a little girl. The penis was tiny. Hardly noticeable. We forgot, most of the time, that she had been born male.'

'She wasn't very happy the day she moved in with me! Jesus Christ, Theresa, you robbed her of her sex. You neutered her! You crippled her. No wonder she hates you,' Robbie spat.

'This has nothing to do with that,' Theresa screamed. 'She hates me because I didn't help her career. But I knew something like this would happen. You can't have a private life, a secret, and be famous. Not anymore. I knew, somehow or other, she'd be exposed.'

'You mean that *you'd* be exposed. You're the author of this little tragedy.' Robbie took a gulp of his own drink. 'Theresa, you make Joan Crawford look like Mother Teresa.'

'How dare you! It's not like I beat her, or tied her to her bed. She had a perfectly wonderful life. Everything a child could want.'

'Except her identity.'

'Her identity? What about mine? What difference did it make to a squalling infant whether it wore a dress or pants? None. But it made all the difference to me, and my career.'

'Your career,' Robbie snarled.

'Yes, my career. Without it, there would be no pretty dresses, no big house, maids, private schools. None of it, without me. Then she had to go out and fuck it all up. With *your* help, I might add.'

'How did she fuck it all up?'

'She had to go and become an actress. She couldn't marry the guy I had picked out for her, make her life simple. No, she wanted to be a *star*. She only did it to compete with me. Since puberty. She's always wanted to compete. Except look what that has done to me. Now I'll have nothing. People will laugh. No one will understand. I'll never work again. I'll never be able to go to another party.'

'What about *Lila*? What's going to happen to *her*?'

'Nothing's going to happen. She still has Kerry's trust fund. And she's got the millions she'll make out of this series. And the Emmy. I hope they don't fuck up the Emmy for her. Isn't all that enough?'

The phone rang in the bottom drawer. Theresa looked at Robbie for him to answer it. He just shook his head. Theresa wobbled to her feet and lurched across the room.

'Yes? Certainly. I'll be waiting.' She turned to Robbie. 'That was Ms. McElroy. She just wanted to let me know the doctors are coming to give me a report, that I should let them in.'

The double rap was soft on the door. Theresa finished what was in her glass, then stood in the centre of the room. Robbie opened the door, and two doctors in surgical greens walked in.

'Miss O'Donnell,' the older doctor began. He took a step towards Theresa and reached for her hand. 'I'm afraid we have very bad news. I'm so sorry. We lost her.'

Theresa stood there silently for a moment. 'What do you mean, "lost?"'

'Lila Kyle is dead, Miss O'Donnell. He died during surgery.'

Robbie made a choking noise, but started walking towards the door as if to leave. Theresa screamed, 'Robbie, don't leave me. I need you.'

But Robbie didn't even slow his steps.

15

Jahne heard the shot, saw Lila crumple like a puppet with its strings cut, but it was the silence, that moment of eerie, terrible silence, that let her know something was horribly wrong. Then the screaming started.

Afterwards, Jahne wondered what she would have done without Brewster. He got her up and out of her seat; then, somehow, in all the screaming, pushing, hysterical crowd, he united her with Sharleen, Dean, and Dobe. 'Keep them here,' he told Dobe. 'I'm a doctor. I have to see if I can help.'

He made it up to the stage by walking on the seat backs. Dobe kept the three of them together, sheltered by a column. Jahne watched as celebrities tore at one another to get out the exit doors. Then Brewster was back, breathless but calm.

'He's been apprehended. It's all right. Some nut with a grudge, apparently. They've taken his gun. It's all right. We're all safe, as long as some actor doesn't kill us as he stampedes over us out the door.'

'Is Lila okay?' Sharleen asked.

'I don't think so. A chest wound. Serious, but maybe not fatal.'

'Oh, God! It could have been either of us!' Jahne shuddered. Sharleen began to cry.

Then, at last, Gerald La Brecque's staff reached them. There was a lot of talk then about security exits and conspiracies and snipers, but Jahne stopped listening. She had started to shake again, the way she had in the morning, except this time she couldn't stop. She wasn't afraid, not exactly, not of some sniper. She suddenly felt afraid of *everything*, the theatre, the stage, the security guards, the crowds, the lights, the noise. Her shaking got worse. She tried to say something, but found that she couldn't speak.

'Jahne's sick!' Dean said, and she felt a wash of gratitude that he had noticed. Then Brewster had his coat off, around her shoulders, and his arms made a safe circle for her. She closed her eyes, and he murmured something, and she kept her head down on his shoulder, and somehow they got out of the theatre and into a car and there was the noise of sirens, and lights flashing from the police cars, or cameras, she couldn't tell which, and then there was darkness.

Brewster stayed with her round the clock for the next two days. They were at the Beverly Wilshire, and in a corner suite. The house had been thought too dangerous, until the truth about the assassin became clear. Brewster talked to her and read to her, but mostly she napped. He kept the TV off and allowed her no calls or newspapers, but on the second day he told her all about Lila. Jahne listened, in shock and amazement, and cried.

'A man? She was a trans-sexual?'

'No. Not medically. She was still intact. Probably impotent. Asexual.'

She began to cry again. 'It's all so sad.' He held her hand until she fell asleep. Jahne felt she could sleep for a month.

Brewster didn't let her up out of bed except for trips to the bathroom. He called Room Service, let her speak to Sharleen, but he kept everyone else at bay. It was a relief.

Finally, she pushed herself up in bed and managed a smile. 'You're a wonderful doctor,' she said.

He shook his head. 'No, I'm a wonderful nurse. So are you, for that matter.'

Jahne thought back to how long ago it was since she'd been a nurse. It felt like decades.

'Are you feeling better?'

'Much better! I still can't believe it, but I'm okay. Really.'

'Well, there's someone who wants to see you. He's been camped outside in the hallway for two days. I didn't feel comfortable about sending him away.'

'Sam?' she asked, and felt herself blush. Brewster nodded.

'Do you want to see him, or should I send him away?'

Jahne sighed. 'I already sent him away once. I better see him. I'm sorry.'

'Don't be. It's your life, Jahne. You don't have to apologize. You don't owe me anything.' He turned and went to the door.

I must look like shit, Jahne thought, and then got angry at herself. Oh, God, who cared about looks? Sam? Well, he didn't matter to her anymore.

She looked up. Sam had silently entered the bedroom.

'You're all right? I couldn't believe it. I had to see you. You're all right?' She nodded. Sam approached the side of the bed. 'God, when I saw the murder on TV, I realized that it would kill me if anything happened to you. Mary Jane, I . . . I don't know what you need to hear to come back to me, I don't know what you want me to say, but I know that there is no one, absolutely no one on earth that I want to marry except you.'

'Marry?' She was speechless. 'Marry you? I never want to *see* you again.'

'Oh, I know you felt that way before *Birth* hit as big as it did. But surely now you see that it was necessary to . . .'

'Are you crazy?' she asked him. 'Have you gone completely crazy?'

'Listen, we've both done things we aren't proud of. But it's not too late . . .'

'That's where you are two hundred and ten per cent wrong. It's *years* too late,' she told him.

'Jahne, everything you said, every word, was true. I've been doing some thinking. Some real thinking. And I know what I want now. I want you. No one but you. Let's forget everything else.' He took her hand. 'Life's too short to waste.'

She looked at him. What had she loved about him? His looks? His selfishness? His easy, shallow style? His facile wit? How shallow had she been to care about this man?

'You're right,' she said at last. 'Life *is* too short to waste. That's why I won't spend another minute with you.'

It wasn't until the third day that Brewster let Jahne watch the news herself. There was a special segment of *Entertainment Tonight* that focused on the shooting. Jahne watched clips of herself and Lila and Sharleen arriving for the Emmy awards, then she saw the close-ups of them in the audience. It was macabre. Who would want to watch this awfulness play out? Why was the audience tuned in? To watch the death of an idol? A false idol? Poor, poor Lila. It made Jahne sick. Literally sick to her stomach. 'Well, as a doctor, I'll give you the remedy that my mother always suggested,' Brewster smiled. Then he called Room Service.

She was drinking from a glass of plain old ginger ale when she saw, for the first time, the apprehension of the gunman. And there, on the screen, was a close-up of Neil Morelli.

16

Jahne said goodbye to Brewster at her front door. The idea of an airport farewell reminded her too much of her last one, with Neil, back in New York. She shivered.

'Are you cold?' Brewster asked, and she smiled at his concern. It should be winter, after the killing frost that had descended upon them all, but Hollywood was heartless, and the air was balmy.

'No. I'm fine. I will be fine.' She stopped. She wasn't too certain of that, so why lie? 'Listen, Brewster, I don't know how I'm ever going to thank you . . .'

'Well, I think you just did.' He was looking down at his feet.

'No. You deserve something more than just words.'

'I *do* need these shoes resoled,' he said, then shrugged at his attempt at a joke. 'Hey, this is what friends are for,' he said. And he raised himself on his toes and kissed her, just once, and very gently, on the lips. Then he was gone.

Jahne went back into the house, her lips tingling. She hadn't kissed anyone since Sam, and it felt good. A tiny bit of the grimness lifted. But then she remembered Lila. Her lips were cold by now.

Jahne picked up her cat, settled herself on the sofa, and began to write a list. She had a lot to do.

When the phone rang, she couldn't decide whether to answer or not. But La Brecque's security guy did it for her. He stood at the door to the living room and called out to her, 'It's some guy called Sam. You want to take the call?'

Jahne sat, frozen. What in the world did he want now? She shook her head — not at the guard, but at herself. 'I'll take it,' she told him, and reached for the extension beside her.

'Mary Jane? Jahne? Is it you?'

'Yes. It's me.'

Sam was silent for a moment. 'Listen, this is business. I know how you feel about me, but I think we have a lot to talk about. Among other things, I'm just signing a three-picture deal with Paramount. And I want you for the lead in my first film for them.'

Now it was Jahne's turn to be silent. Hollywood! She almost snorted. It was the town where the devil disguised himself as a producer and offered a three-picture deal. Who *was* this guy at the other end of the line? Who had she thought he was, and who did he think she was? 'Sorry. Homey don't do that no more,' was all she said.

His voice deepened. She heard the actor bring in the strings. Was he acting, was he crazy, or was he just the most insensitive man in America? 'It can be the way it was. I'm working on the script, and it's good, Jahne. Really good. It's about a race-car driver who nearly loses the woman he loves because he can't give up racing.' He paused. She didn't say a word. 'Look, I know it sounds juvenile, but it doesn't play that way.' He stopped to take a breath. And, for the first time in this amazing conversation, Jahne thought she heard his true voice.

'We could be good together, Jahne,' he said.

Gently, she hung up the phone.

They wouldn't stop playing the goddamn song. Sy Ortis swerved, almost hitting a lamppost as he fumbled for the Blaupunkt radio dial, but it didn't matter what station he listened to. Since the shooting, they were *all* playing the Kinks' tribute to female impersonators. Next that stupid cocksucker Al Yankovic would do a parody actually called 'Lila.' But, really, there wasn't much that could be added to the original.

Not surprisingly, the Early Artists management offices were going batshit. Sponsors, the press, the studio – all of Hollywood, it seemed, wanted to cash in or cash out on *Three for the Road*. And that old *puta* Laura Bitchy had actually had the nerve to call him at home, at night, on his private number, to ask if he had ever seen either Jahne Moore or Lila in the nude.

When Sy Ortis reached Reception, the little fool at the desk had a copy of the *Informer* lying there, an obvious pastiche photo on the cover with a screaming red headline that said, 'The Scandal to End the Road Show.'

'What are you planning to do after you work here?' Sy asked the girl.

'I don't know,' she said, blinking.

'Too bad, because you don't work here anymore,' he told her. He grabbed the paper off her desk, then crumpled it and tore it to shreds before he threw it to the ground and walked over it. He slammed through the swinging glass doors on down the hall. His secretary stood waiting. 'Any word from Mr. DiGennaro?'

'No. He's still under sedation. But there was a call from the hospital. There's been a change in Miss . . . I mean, Mr. Kyle's condition.' She paused. 'I mean, the fact is, he's dead.'

'What the hell do I care?' barked Sy Ortis. 'The bitch – I mean the son-of-a-bitch – was as good as dead anyway.' Christ, he couldn't breathe! Sy got into his office and began to scrabble through his desk drawers, looking for another aspirator. His chest felt as if it would burst. If he wasn't careful, he'd wind up in the morgue at Cedars, next to that freak. He tried to count, just to get his breath. As he did, he saw the pile of pink message slips lying beside his multibutton phone. He rifled through them. All clients, soon to be ex-clients, he guessed. Of course, every one of the *niños de las putas* was calling in to 'discuss management issues.' Of course. There was no loyalty, no sense of history, with these children of pigs. They'd be calling Mike Ovitz, CMI and CAA and all the other agents so fast that phone lines would be melting.

Everything was falling apart! Marty was having some kind of breakdown, the Okie blonde was a pervert, Jahne Moore was a surgical trick, and fuckin' Lila Kyle was a man! Over at the Network, they were going crazy. Les Merchant was threatening to cancel the show. Hyram Flanders was homicidal, and all the other sponsors were bailing out. Christ, he'd be lucky if the merchandisers didn't sue his ass. Well, they probably would. This would cost him millions!

But it was worse than that! Hollywood was a town built on hype, but it was a town that believed its own. When you were hot you were hot, and when you were not you were frío to the max. Christ! Sy winced. What would those gringo cocksuckers at Morton's be saying about him this Monday night? He almost writhed in his chair as he thought about it. Their little grins as he walked by their tables, the concealed laughs. Jokes about wetbacks and chicano-ry! Oh, he could hear it all now.

Damage control was necessary. Lots of it, and fast. But wasn't it too late for the spin doctors? Well, he could salvage Jahne Moore. *Birth of a Star* was still a hit, a big one. She could eke out another major part. The curiosity factor was high on her. That TV script he'd read last month about the prostitute who adopts the two kids. It could work. Meanwhile, they'd sue the *Informer*, and that bitch Laura Richie. No, suits took too long and cost too much. He wrinkled his brow and took a prophylactic suck on the aspirator.

He had it! He'd call Hefner. This wasn't for Christie. He'd go right to the top. A centrefold. And not one of those soft-focus stills from the film. Fresh, hot meat. She'd show them *everything*. And then they'd put her, quick, into another TV film. The bitch would do what he told her now, if she wanted to survive. This shit worked for Madonna, didn't it? Then there was the Smith family. Apparently Dean wasn't the hillbilly's brother, so they would sue all those tabloids on Sharleen's behalf, and maybe she could get engaged – or, better yet, married. It should get the church and the

Moral Majority assholes off his back. That just left Lila. With her dead, maybe *Three for the Road* could go on, once Marty snapped out of it. Or even before, with another director. And the Kyle freak would be replaced. After all, finding fresh meat in Hollywood wasn't hard. Only a week ago, he'd decided to drop Sharleen and Jahne. Now he'd drop Lila and keep the other two. With two of the three in place, the show had a good chance of survival.

So, really, the only problem left was Marty. He was drooling and babbling, all right, but so what? A few weeks at the rest home and he'd be in the pink. And maybe, Sy Ortis thought, maybe even *Marty* can be replaced. Okay, the ideas, the format, all of it was his, but it was established now. Maybe that kid, the AD from *Birth* – what was his name? Joel Something. He could do it. After all, what was there to do?

For four more days, days of siege, Sy managed to hold Early Artists and himself together while they were buffeted by the media, by the Industry, and by the network and sponsors. Every bastard whom he had ever screwed felt it his duty to call in and be counted. Every son-of-a-bitch in the Industry had something smart to say. Well, fuck 'em all. The audience last night for *Three for the Road* had broken all records. As Sy had promised Hyram Flanders that it would. So now all Sy needed to do was find a way to replace Lila and Marty and keep, as they say, the show on the road.

The phone intercom buzzed. 'Miss Moore is here to see you.'

'Okay.' *Madre de Jesús*, he was in no mood for this twat who always had fuckin' opinions and attitudes. At least today she should be under control. He'd seen them, the Talents, when they first were hit with the realization that what the public giveth it could also take away. Look how humbled Crystal had become. And – he smiled to himself – he liked his Talents humbled; humbled and scared. It made them a lot more respectful. Until, of course, they were panicked, and then they'd turn on their own young and eat them alive.

Jahne Moore would be concerned but not panicked, he figured. She'd probably calmed down from the surprise of *Birth*, she'd realized by now he was right about it being a hit, and the opportunity to continue on *3/4* with, perhaps, an expanded part would keep her in line. Plus, the *Playboy* or *Penthouse* spread he'd just about lined up (with a bonus to him of course) would silence this plastic-surgery rumour. It was a good strategy. She'd finally appreciate him. Sy put down his respirator, ready to calm an upset and frightened Talent.

Except she didn't look upset or frightened. She looked beautiful as ever, but also calm. She was wearing a pair of those goddamn jeans with a plain white sweater, but he couldn't help thinking, for a moment, of what was under it. He smiled, but she didn't return it. What was wrong with this *puta*?

'Hello, Sy,' she said, and sat across from him. 'I'm here to exercise my option.'

'What option?'

'To drop out of *3/4*.'

'What?'

'I'm out, Sy. You put it in the contract. Now I'm using it.'

What the hell was this shit? Sy narrowed his eyes. 'I know you have a lot of other offers flowing in. In fact, I've read a few properties, possibilities, but let's not throw up the baby with the bathwater.'

'Out, Sy. Throw *out* the baby with the bathwater. But never mind. I'm quitting. Quitting *3/4*, movies, cosmetics ads, mall openings. I'm out of the business.'

Sy's secretary stuck her head inside the door, ignored Jahne, and said to Sy, 'Your wife's on the line.'

'Which one?' Sy snapped.

'Sandra.'

'Not which *wife!* Which *line?*'

He punched the blinking light the secretary indicated among the bank of other blinking lights. 'What?' he shouted. 'No! Don't you DARE GO TO THE CLUB. DON'T SPEAK TO ANYONE. NO. ESPECIALLY NOT ANNE.' Anne was his wife's friend, married to a reporter on the *L.A. Times*. 'So, *be* lonesome!' he told her, and hung up. He turned back to the Moore bitch.

'Listen,' he said as calmly as he could manage. 'You're still upset about *Birth*. About the violence. The death. You're overreacting. I understand. You're sensitive. You're an artist. But you must look at this as a challenge.'

'Forget it, Sy. I'm out of here.'

'Jahne. Listen. I have a great idea. A way to show them all. I've talked with Guccione. We'll show them that these rumours are all jealous lies. Exaggerations. We'll do a layout. Eight pages. Bob says he'll shoot it himself. And you'll be gorgeous. Spectacular. Bigger than ever. And you'll have your choice of parts.'

734

'Good. I'd like to do Cordelia.'

'What part was that? Did I see that script? What's the working title?'

'*King Lear*. We could pick up the option cheap.'

'Very funny. I've heard of *King Lear*. Shakespeare doesn't play. Except that Mel Gibson vehicle.'

'*Hamlet?*'

'Whatever. Anyway, Jahne, don't talk this way. We got a lot invested in you now, and I know this is just a stage you're going through. Bad publicity hurts. But you'll get over it. We'll just counter it with this layout.'

'Show them my goodies?' She laughed and shook her head. 'Forget it, Sy.'

'I'm not sure that you understand what I'm trying to say. Listen, *everyone* out here has had a little cosmetic work. It's nothing to be ashamed of. I realize you might not choose to do this normally. And normally I wouldn't recommend it. But we're talking about extreme damage to your career here. And a tastefully done layout in a fine magazine . . .'

'Sy, *Penthouse* isn't a "fine magazine," and Bob Guccione is the Antichrist.' Jahne paused, and then she smiled at him. 'Anyway, it wouldn't work. The scars are too obvious.'

'The scars? Wait. What are you telling me?' Sy Ortis cried, his hand clenching around the aspirator he clutched. 'Are you saying all this bullshit is *true?*'

Jahne looked at him directly. 'Yes,' she said. 'It is.'

'So you're scarred all over. Like a Frankenstein?' Sy Ortis asked, his high voice almost a shriek.

'I don't like to put it that way, but, yes, the scarring is extensive.'

'So, no *Penthouse*.'

'No *Penthouse*,' Jahne smiled.

'What the fuck are you smiling for?' Sy spat at her. 'The three of you were dream meat. God, now it's a nightmare! Do you know what this does to you?'

Jahne shrugged. 'Ends my career as a sexpot?' she asked, and giggled. The bitch *giggled*.

'How about ends your career completely? Don't you see? The illusion is gone. They'll look up at the screen and wonder, 'Where are the scars?' They'll be watching for clues. They'll be mesmerized. No producer, no director will want you.'

Jahne laughed.

'What the fuck are you *laughing* about?' Sy screamed.

'I think it's funny. A TV exploitation show that created the three sexiest women in America. What you so candidly call "dream meat." One is a Frankenstein, one sleeps with her brother, and the third one was a man. Not much left there to exploit, huh, Sy?'

18

There was never a funeral like it. Not Rudolph Valentino's, not Jean Harlow's, not even Marilyn Monroe's compared to the carnival-cum-media-orgy that Lila Kyle's funeral became.

There was no one to do it for her except poor, heartbroken Robbie Lymon. Theresa was drugged out, Sy Ortis was bummed out, Marty was freaked out, and Ara Sagarian was out-and-out dead. Loved by millions, reviled by millions more, Lila had no one to pick out her casket and arrange the memorial service but an old camp follower of her mother's.

Robbie had the body dressed in a lavender Bob Mackie dress – if she had chosen to be a girl in life, she'd also be one in death, he said – and a frightening picture of Lila in the casket, her red hair clashing with the lilac-coloured dress, was printed on the cover of half the magazines of the world. There were close to a thousand funeral wreaths and flower arrangements sent.

Thousands came to see her. 'They were her fans,' Robbie said, weeping. 'She loved them.' The problem was that not all of them loved her. One woman tried to wipe the makeup off her dead face. Another began speaking in tongues before the casket. The funeral home finally put Lila behind a glass viewing wall. It gave her a sort of Snow White-in-the-glass-coffin look.

Worse than the ones that reviled her, though, were the ones who came to worship at her shrine. Hundreds of young men (and some not so young) showed up in full Lila Kyle regalia, including high heels, makeup, and the de rigueur long red wig. Some screamed and fainted at the sight of her corpse. Others sobbed. Many had to be helped out. But, once they had viewed her, they raced to the end of the seven-block-long line to do it again.

Thousands of teenage girls showed up, too. Somehow, they didn't

736

*seem to mind the gender-bender revelation. Perhaps they even liked her
more for it. After all, David Bowie had dressed almost as extremely and
built a following twenty years before. And this was the nineties. The girls
wailed out their pain in a constant keen of adolescent screaming.*

*There were close to two hundred cars that tried to make the long run
to Forest Lawn. The scene at the gravesite was bedlam. And, with all the
people there, the only one who had actually known Lila in life was her
aunt Robbie, who had to be carried from the grave.*

19

Small things. If he kept his mind on small things, on tiny little
things, Marty knew he was okay. A patch of sunlight reflecting
off a wrinkle of the snow-white sheets. The shadow of the bedside
lampshade on the wall. The taste of the sliced banana on his corn
flakes.

Slowly, Marty, in bathrobe and slippers, moved to the window
that looked out over the beautifully manicured grounds. It must
be Japan, he thought. Everything was so perfect, so neat, it had
to be Japan. But then he remembered, and moved away from the
window.

He heard the now familiar key in the lock, and saw the nurse –
what was her name? – come through the door. 'Hi, how are you
doing today, Mr. DiGennaro?' She picked up his breakfast tray and
walked towards the door. 'You did very well today. Your appetite is
coming back.' She closed and locked the door behind her, leaving
him in the silence of his thoughts once again.

He sat in the reproduction-Queen Anne armchair that overlooked
the garden below his window. Oh, no. Now he was upset. Tears
filled his eyes, then slowly slid down his cheeks. He often sat here,
in this clean and quiet room, and cried. He still had not figured out
why, exactly, so he just let himself cry.

The hospital bed had been made earlier, the fake-Aubusson rug
vacuumed, and the Sheraton-style chest and bedside tables dusted.
All this while he was at water therapy, before breakfast. He was
impressed with the service here. A good hotel. No trouble in the

world couldn't be alleviated by a stay in a luxury hotel. Wherever it was. If it wasn't Japan, was it England? No. Too sunny for that.

He continued to sit on the brocade-upholstered chair and cry. Sometimes, every now and then, like now, just before medication time, a tiny window would open in his mind, and he'd remember. Lila. Lila was dead. And then he'd cry. Lila had lied to him, he remembered, the tears now flowing faster. And Lila was a man.

She didn't have to lie. He would have loved her anyway. But that made him a homosexual, and he was sure he wasn't that. Still, they could have found a way. They *did* find a way. It would have been okay, if only Lila hadn't lied. Lied and died. It made an ugly poem, buzzing in his head. She shouldn't have lied and died. They could have worked it out, just the two of them.

But now, Marty knew, it wasn't just the two of them. He was the laughingstock of Hollywood, and pitied by everyone. It was the pity that hurt the most. Or perhaps it was knowing he would never see Lila again. No, it was the fact that he could never work again, never create beauty on a screen again, that really hurt the most.

Lila lied to him. And now she was dead. Lied and died.

Soon the nurse would return with the pleated paper cup of pills and the glass of water. Soon, soon, and then the tears and memories would stop.

Usually Marty remembered none of this. Usually he couldn't pull up a past event, a memory. Not even when Sally came to visit. He knew he knew Sally, but he couldn't remember how, or from where.

And not remembering anything, not knowing what had brought him to this place where he lived behind a locked door, that was exactly the way Marty liked it.

20

Monica Flanders towered over the crouched form of her son, Hyram, who sat at his desk. At four feet eleven, it was not easy to tower, but Monica achieved the effect spectacularly well.

'First we find out the blonde is sleeping with her brother . . .'

'He wasn't really her brother, Ma,' Hyram began.

'Oh, excuse *me*,' Monica said icily. 'She recently found out he wasn't. I feel *so* much better. *Then* the world discovers that the brunette is a monster.' She took a deep breath. So did Hyram.

'Not a monster, Ma. Just a plastic-surgery patient. You yourself . . .'

'I myself never looked like she did,' Monica snapped. 'She was a nothing. A mess. *She* represents Flanders Cosmetics?' she snorted. 'And if that wasn't enough – a pervert and a lump – now we add a freak. A cross-dressing female-impersonator transvestite queer *faygele* to convince women to wear our lipstick. Perfect, Hyram. Perfect. Great idea you had.'

'Mother, the show this week got the highest rating *any* show ever got. It's . . .'

'It's a freak show, is what it is. And fuck the ratings. Fuck the *ratings*, Hyram. Tell me about *sales*.'

'Well, you have to expect a little dip . . .'

'Hyram, you really are an asshole. Even considering the possibility that you could take over for me is the only big error of judgement I ever made. Except, of course, for this fiasco. Don't you get it, Hyram? The line is over. Finished. No woman will ever buy that shit again. We sell dreams, Hyram, not nightmares. The party, as they say, is over.'

'But we have close to a hundred million dollars invested in that stuff.'

'Take your losses like a big boy, Hyram.'

'Mother, are you crazy? We'll get a replacement for Lila Kyle. We'll change the print-ad copy. We could even get rid of the other two. But we *have* to keep the line, Mother.'

'Pull our sponsorship. Cut our losses. Start over on this one, Hyram.'

He stood up. 'Forget it. I'm not going to eat this loss. Not in my first year as president. Mother, I mean it: I'll fight you on this. I'll take it to the board. I'll press the issue, Mother. They won't see it as you do.'

'Yes they will, Hyram. And they'll remember who brought this idea to them. Don't do it. You'll be sorry.'

But he did. And then he was.

21

Jahne sat on the verandah of Sharleen's house, among the wrapped furniture and crated kitchenware. The two friends had been silent for some time. The sun was setting over the smog of the Valley, creating a spectacular sunset.

'It's the pollution and dust that make the colours,' Jahne said.

'So, then, even dirt is good for something.'

'And I thought all that garbage written about us was useless.'

'Hell, no. We wrapped our dishes with a lot of it. And in Wyoming we'll use it for starting fires and mulching the garden.' Sharleen grinned. Then she looked back at the sunset. 'Sure is pretty. Nice to know there's a chance for one every night.' She sighed. 'I still can't believe that Lila is dead. She ain't gonna see another sunset. I mean, it's all so weird. I still can't believe she was a man.'

'Well, I guess she wasn't, really, was she? I mean, she had some of the equipment, but that didn't make her a fireman, if you know what I mean.'

'Speaking of mean, now we know why she was. I guess she was a really unhappy person.' Sharleen shook her head. 'What did her mother *do* to her?'

'I want to know what *Marty* did to her. I mean, she had to be pretty good at faking to make him think she was a woman. I've sometimes faked my orgasms, but not my gender.'

'Huh?'

Jahne looked at Sharleen. 'Haven't you ever faked an orgasm?'

'Uh-uh. Well, why would I do that?' Sharleen asked. 'What's the point?'

'Oh, to take the pressure off you, or him. To end it if it's boring. To, well, you know.' Jahne found herself looking into Sharleen's blank face.

'I surely don't. I haven't slept with many guys, but I never faked how I felt in my life. It would be like a lie, and at a very bad time to lie.'

'I think you're right, Sharleen, but I think most women do.'

Sharleen shook her head and shrugged. 'I don't understand about sex,' she said.

'Join the club.'

'I felt so ashamed about me and Dean for so long, it's hard to get used to it bein' okay. Plus, even when it wasn't supposed to be the right thing, it always *felt* like the right thing. Sometimes it was the *only* thing that was right.'

'You'll get over the guilt. Just keep telling yourself he's not your brother.'

'Well, even if he *isn't* my brother, he still *feels* like he is,' Sharleen said. 'That's what I like. That we're like blood kin, you know? We really *know* each other. But now I ain't ashamed. I know what other people still might say, and think, but I don't care. I really don't. Because I *ain't* shamed. What we done, what we are, felt right. It *is* right.' She looked up at Jahne.

'What *you* think is the most important thing, Sharleen,' Jahne said.

'Well, yes, but I'd like you to understand.' She paused. 'See, it's like this: Sex with men, with other men, always felt like there was two different kinds of us in bed. Their kind and our kind. Even with Boyd, and then with Michael McLain, it always felt like it was a kind of two-part contest.'

Jahne thought of Michael, of Sam, and nodded.

'Well, with Dean it don't feel like that. It don't feel like his turn and my turn. It don't feel like no contest. It's just *us* . . . We're *both* us, both the same. It ain't as excitin' as with Michael, I admit that. And for a while I got confused. But now I know one thing: it may not be the way sex is supposed to be, but the way it is with Dean is the way I like it.' Tears stood in Sharleen's perfect eyes as she searched Jahne's face.

And Jahne, all at once, was hit with such a strong wave of . . . of envy, she realized with a start of surprise. Because the strife, the battle, had always been there, between her and her lovers. The battle for possession, for dominance, for freedom. The battle of the sexes. And because always, following the excitement, there had been disappointment, loneliness, or betrayal. Always. They were never really on my side, she thought. Except maybe Neil. Neil was on my side, but he wasn't exciting enough, pretty enough for me. I never slept with him. And now it's probably too late for Neil. And maybe it's too late for me.

She looked at Sharleen, up front and beautiful as she'd always been, simple and straight and right as rain. She thought of all the advice she'd given Sharleen, of how she'd condescended to her, and she very nearly blushed.

'What are you going to do?' Jahne asked Sharleen.

'I reckon me and Dean are goin' to take up my friend's offer. We're goin' to move out to Wyoming with Dobe. He and us are partners on a big spread he bought out there. Dean and me'll get married later.'

'So, you'll just walk away without looking back?'

'Why, sure. And feel lucky. It could have been you or me got shot.'

'But won't you miss it? All the excitement, and the attention . . . and the money?'

'Oh, heck. It ain't ever the way it seems. *You* know that. Seems that there ain't much money. So much went in taxes and fees. And there's such a big mortgage on this place that lots went on interest and what all. Seems that only Mr. Ortis made money. I won't miss him. And I missed my stepmother more once I found her than I ever did when she was gone. I'll miss the *idea* of fame some. Wouldn't be human if I said I wouldn't. But I won't really miss any of this . . .' She turned to look out the window at the hills spread below them. Then she looked back at Jahne. 'I'll miss *you*,' she said, 'but I hope you'll come to visit.'

'I will,' Jahne promised.

'What about you? You stayin' on?'

'I have a few things I still have to take care of.'

'And then what?'

'Then I don't know.'

'You'd always be welcome on the ranch, Jahne.'

'Thanks.' Tears filled her eyes. She probably didn't deserve a friend as kind as Sharleen, but she was grateful she had her. She'd better lighten this up, or else she'd be sobbing all over the two of them. 'So,' she said, 'no more Crimson, Cara, and Clover.'

As if she sensed Jahne's mood, Sharleen tossed her head and whistled. 'Oh, hell, sure there is. We're takin' the three bitches with us!' She laughed, and turned to stroke the head of the first dog that ran to her side.

22

Jahne dressed carefully, as if for an important audition. But what role is it that you are trying out for? she asked herself. Good friend? A bit late for that. You haven't played that role opposite Neil in a long time. Lady Bountiful? Isn't that a laugh? You've never been a lady, and for the last year at least you've been spiritually and emotionally impoverished. What Neil must need is a real good psychiatrist and an even better lawyer, not some one-trick pony. Well, at least you can write a cheque. That might help him, though he may be beyond help now.

Probably Neil won't even have a clue as to who I am. He won't know that I'm Mary Jane. Well, that I *was*. And why should he when you don't? she asked herself. He might not even agree to see her. She surveyed herself in the full-length mirror of her marble bathroom. She wore a becomingly casual pair of the jeans Mai had made for her, and the big sweater that she had worn with Sam on their vacation in Northern California. She stared at her reflection in the mirror: tall, willowy, her perfect face a shining oval, her thick, lustrous black hair cascading down from her widow's peak, her lips full, her face a valentine. She still was amazed by her own looks. She looked like one of the people who'd always looked down on her. Back in New York, so many people had. Except Neil. She sighed.

Another one of the privileges of fame, Jahne thought as she walked down the green-tiled hallway of the Los Angeles County Jail. Only relatives and attorneys are allowed access to prisoners. And, of course, the occasional reporter willing to pay out a few bucks. Or a movie star.

'A close family friend' was how she had put it, and the prison official asked for nothing except the autographed photos she had been smart enough to bring, along with two tickets to a sneak preview of something or other that she'd received a week ago. He had looked her over carefully, and she was certain he was looking for the grisly scars. Well, he'd get a full report from the hefty female guard who'd searched her *very* thoroughly before she allowed Jahne to cross through the barred doors onto this corridor that led to the visiting room. Jahne had to announce herself as 'Jahne Moore,' of course. Would Neil even speak to her?

She left the security room, dressed neatly again, and began to walk down the hallway. She winced at the unbelievably harsh overhead lights, the green-checkered tile, the institutionally two-toned walls.

She entered the small, private room the guard pointed her to. It was almost completely filled by a scarred wooden table and four mismatched chairs. Neil was sitting in the fifth, his narrow back turned to the door, dressed in an orange jumpsuit. He turned to her, his face more feral than ever, his eyes more deeply sunk and hooded. He surveyed her, not moving a muscle of his body or face.

Then he stood. 'Veronica!' he said, and as he held his arms out to her his eyes filled with tears.

It was hard to believe that he recognized her so quickly, despite the surgery, the time, and the dislocation of this strange venue. But perhaps that was the magic of love. Neil had loved her, had known her, and he still did. She hugged him, then took a seat next to him at the table.

'I'm sorry that it took me so long to find you,' Jahne was explaining. 'I looked. I really did. But your number wasn't listed and I . . .'

'That's okay, Veronica,' Neil told her sweetly. 'I forgive you.'

He seemed normal, if a little subdued. How do you talk to an old friend who has become a murderer? Should she avoid the issue?

'What happened?' she asked gently.

'They made a mistake. It was all wrong.'

'What do you mean?' He'd been filmed by a dozen cameras doing the deed. Surely he wasn't going to claim innocence.

'I wasn't supposed to be Jughead. I was supposed to be *Archie*. The one everybody liked. That was the mistake. But it's fixed now. Roger fixed it. It wasn't my fault the girl was shot. Someone screwed up. Johnny Burton. He wasn't supposed to. I was. Master of ceremonies. Me. Forgive me, master.' He looked at her, his mad eyes glittering into hers.

'I'm sure you'll be forgiven,' she whispered.

'Great!' he shouted into the air. Then he turned to her again, a crafty look on his face. 'And then I'll get my show back? Because I can't take too much more of this shit. Not being recognized, getting no respect. I can't take too much more.' His voice had risen; now, abruptly he put his head down on his arms and began to weep. 'You don't know what it's like,' he cried. 'You don't know how it feels to be so close, so close to that love. And to lose it. To lose it all.'

'I do, Neil. I do.'

They sat together as he wept. She patted his shoulder as softly as she could.

'I'm so sorry. What do you need?' she asked. 'I'll get you anything they allow you to have.'

'I have everything I need.' He lifted his head from the table and wiped his eyes.

'What about a lawyer? I could help with . . .'

'My sister's girlfriend is a lawyer. Diana. And there's Roger. Roger will take care of everything.'

'Neil, I want to help. I . . .'

His face changed from a vacant, soggy smile to an animal snarl. 'Not Neil!' he yelled at her. 'Archie. I'm Archie now. Really popular. Everyone likes me.'

'Okay. Okay, Archie,' she said, to calm him down. His face had scared her. Was he crazy? Did he really recognize her? 'So, Archie, are you treated well here?'

'Treated well? Hey, I'm the most popular guy at Riverdale High. I was elected president of the senior class. Reggie ran against me, but *I* won. It was unanimous. Even Reggie voted for me in the end.'

Jahne tried to laugh at the feeble joke, but it wasn't easy. 'Archie, I'm just so sorry about everything. About your show getting cancelled, and about the . . .'

Neil sprang up, overturning the chair. Jahne jumped at the sudden movement, more startled than frightened. The door opened fast, and a big black male prison guard stood over them. Neil looked over at him. 'Hello, Veronica,' Neil said. Then he held out his arms, and his eyes filled with tears.

As Jahne walked down the corridor, away from Neil and his broken mumblings, she had to use all her acting strength not to sob out loud. He hadn't known her. He didn't know what day it was, or what had happened. Apparently he had started calling *everyone*

745

Veronica, or so the assistant warden said. He was locked into his own private prison of pain. His guilt was even worse than his madness, and, from time to time, when he came out of the paranoid fog of his delusions, the pain and terror in his eyes were worse than the ravings of his conspiracy theories. For the first time, Jahne could see why people sought the comfort of madness.

There in the prison corridor, the long enfilade of barred doors ahead of her, Jahne felt her own eyes fill with tears. How long would Neil be sentenced to a life behind bars? Or no life at all? She felt sick, and dizzy. Oh, God, it had all gone so wrong! She knew that Mary Jane and Neil had had a great deal in common: Both of us were born without the appropriate physical gifts. And both of us had the brains and sensitivity to know it. We've both spent half a lifetime overcompensating. But, in the end, Neil had failed, and he couldn't live with who he was. A skinny, funny, weasel-faced guy without an audience, without a friend. A murderer. Jahne took a shuddering breath. 'Oh, Neil, how could you?' she whispered.

But how close to her own murder had she been, back in Scuderstown? She wouldn't forget that time after her grandmother's funeral. After her own failures and rejections had made her almost as crazy as Neil had become from his. Neil, failing, had only been different in deciding to turn his anger outward, to kill another instead of himself. That was what men did. Women killed themselves. Which was the greater sin?

She stopped, leaned her long, slender body against the wall and felt herself trembling all over. Because, she realized all at once, she, too, was guilty of murder. She had killed Mary Jane Moran back in New York, more than two years ago. Mary Jane had died under Brewster's knife just as surely as Lila Kyle had died from a bullet. She had ended Mary Jane's life, sentencing her to death for not being pretty enough, successful enough, to live.

Poor, pathetic Neil. Poor, motherless, unloved Mary Jane.

23

Sam Shields slid into a seat on the aisle so that he could stretch out his legs. He'd forgotten just how uncomfortable regular movie-theatre seats could be. He only saw films at screenings or premieres now. When was the last time he'd actually paid to see a movie, the way civilians do? Certainly not since he'd moved here. Maybe not since New York, with Mary Jane.

His mind jumped away from the thought. He was getting good at that. Move on to the pleasant, to the present. *Birth* was in its seventh week of distribution, and it had already passed the hundred-million-dollar mark. He would make more than three million on it, and was moving out of the Canyon rental to his first real home: a soaring space tucked behind the Hotel Bel-Air. Meanwhile, he'd become the most popular boy in town. Everyone from everywhere was clamouring to have him direct their next film. He'd already met with Rob Reiner at Castle Rock, Mark Cannon from Columbia, and Stanley Jaffe at Paramount. It was nice to be popular.

The theatre darkened, and the trailer began. Sam watched the preview, until a couple stopped at his seat and asked to pass into the row. He stood up. He loomed over them. They were already chubbing up, the way middle-class Americans did. The two of them, in their late teens or early twenties, settled into seats only a short distance from him. Well, you wanted audience reaction, he reminded himself. Now you'll get it really close at hand. The guy offered his date some popcorn from a paper bucket the size of a snare drum. Sam turned back to the screen.

The music swelled, and the establishing shot with the LAX sign opened the film, *his* film. The audience, a pretty large one for an afternoon in Burbank, was still settling in, murmuring to one another and shifting in their seats. Then Jahne's image flashed on the screen, and that argument with the cabbie where Michael steps in and rescues her. It went fairly well. The audience laughed at Jahne's put-down, though he didn't get the second laugh out of them with the quick cut to the cabbie. April had been right about that.

April wanted him for another project. And why should he say no? So far, they were batting a thousand, and although she still wasn't giving him final cut, she was negotiating. In the wake of *Birth's* success, all the bad blood between them seemed to have washed away in the tide of cash. Offers from the other studios looked promising, but wasn't the devil you knew better than the one you didn't? Not that April was a devil, exactly. Where had that image come from? I have not made a deal with the devil, he told himself.

Birth was unfolding on the screen, and though he had seen it a hundred or five hundred or a thousand times, he was here to feel what it was like when it played to what Sy Ortis would call 'the Regulars.' And it seemed to be playing well. Jahne and Michael – Judy and James – had just kissed for the first time on the big screen. As James stripped off Judy's blouse, Sam heard the intake of breath from the crowd. Obliquely he glanced at the couple to his right. The guy had his mouth partly open, staring, mesmerized. Then his girlfriend reached over, took the hand that wasn't in the popcorn bucket, and placed it on her own breast. Sam felt a jolt. Did people – regular people – still neck in movies?

He turned back to the screen. Jahne *did* look beautiful. His own empty hand cupped, as if, just once more, he could circle it around her breast. He watched as the scene played. And he could feel it work its magic on the audience. The theatre was completely silent as James began his symbolic devouring of Judy.

It works because all my impotent love and rage is cut into it, Sam thought. I did love her. I do love her. And now, when I can have almost any woman I want, I'll never have another who loved me before I succeeded. Now they will always love what I can do for them, and what I have done as much as who I am. He looked over at the couple beside him. The guy had discarded his popcorn and was holding the hand of his girlfriend tight against the crotch of his jeans. Sam felt a stab of loneliness so acute that he almost lifted his own hand to his chest.

The love scene ended, and Sam watched the camera pan Adrienne's pale bare back and ass, Michael's tanned hand lying along the beautiful curve of her hips. The illusion was perfect: it was Jahne up there, Jahne exposed. And after the fight scene, in the drunken fuck, it was Jahne who was pinned, Jahne who was mauled. Sam

748

heard a guttural grunt from the guy beside him as, on the screen, Michael pulled off his trunks to ravage his target: a woman, any woman, Every Woman, who could serve as a receptacle for him.

Sam could feel the heat from the screen igniting the audience. 'Give it to her,' someone called out, and 'Fuck the bitch!' a deeper voice yelled, and there was a moment of silence, then a high-pitched giggle. Sam felt nausea sweep through him. Yes, he had meant to arouse them; yes, he had tapped his own anger; but what, exactly, had he done?

He watched the film, and he listened to the audience. He saw then how he'd used his own rage – at his mother, at his ex-wife, at Jahne, at April – and had used Michael's, to carry the movie. This was no love letter, he saw. The hot scenes were hot, all right, but the undercurrent was anger and fear. Oh, they were not love scenes. No. The drowning male character struck out at the female through sex. He didn't love her. He fucked her. Just as this film fucked Jahne.

Sam sat there, alone in the dark, and watched what he had done to Jahne, and then what that did to the audience.

24

Sharleen closed the door of the house behind her and jumped in the King Cab of Dobe's new truck. Dean was in the back seat with the four dogs, each of them fighting for his attention. She slammed the door of the cab and breathed in the delicious scent of new plastic, metal, and upholstery. 'Okay,' she nodded to Dobe, and they drove through the gates, Dean twisting in his seat to wave to the security guard looking after them as they drove away.

'You going to miss any of this, Dean?' Sharleen asked.

Dean was silent for a moment. 'Yes,' he said, the sadness causing him to speak softly. 'My garden.'

Dobe looked into the rearview mirror and caught Dean's eyes. 'How would you like a farm, not just a garden?'

'How big?' Dean asked for about the three hundredth time.

'Nine hundred and thirty-two acres.'

Sharleen laughed for the first time today. 'That's as big as some state parks,' she said.

'Not much compared to them big suckers' places. You know, Ted Turner and those types. But it's just about the prettiest land I ever saw.'

Dean was shaking his head. 'I don't know about them other farmers, but that's a big spread. I can't do it all myself. I'll need some help.'

Sharleen turned in her seat to face Dean. 'We'll help you, Dean. Right, Dobe?'

'Sure. That's why I'm going, to get out into the air, do some honest hard work.' He laughed, and Sharleen caught him looking at her out of the corner of his eye.

'It will be that, Dobe. Honest *and* hard.'

'Can't think of a better way to live, Sharleen. Honest and hard.'

'Does it have an orchard?' Dean asked.

'Not yet, but it will. If you want one.'

'And we'll get a horse,' Dean said. 'Are there trails?'

'We'll get *three* horses, and there's plenty of trails.'

Sharleen thought again about all that she was leaving behind and what she felt. Leaving this isn't hard, she thought, as the truck with the few belongings she cherished barrelled out of California to Wyoming. She now had everything she wanted. A ranch in Wyoming, Dean, Dobe, the dogs. There would be good, real work, and fun, too. And no people for miles around, Dobe had said.

No television. Or VCR. No interviews, no parties with dressed-up people who said they liked you when they really didn't. No newspapers, no magazines, no scandal sheets blaring out people's shame. No shame, no lies, no secrets. And not much money, either. Sy's accountant had explained about management fees, and legal fees, and taxes, and the agency's percentage. It didn't leave much. But they owned the land, and the furniture that would arrive in a day or two, and that was more than most people had. More than she'd ever expected to have. Leave all this to them as wants it, she thought, as they crossed the state line. It hadn't made her happy, only sad and lonely. And none of it was real, she thought. Except the pain.

'Look!' Dean called out.

'What?' Sharleen asked, bringing her thoughts back to the present.

'An *Idaho* licence plate. Guess what it says,' Dean said, his face bright with a grin. He couldn't wait to tell them. '"*Idaho*,"' Dean quoted. '"*Famous potatoes*."' Ain't that a funny tag?'

Dobe laughed. 'Sure 'nough is.'

'Famous potato,' Sharleen said through the ripples of laughter. 'Sounds like me.'

And then the only sound in the truck that was taking them away from Hollywood – the clothes and parties, the self-indulgence and fame, the security guards, the money, the special privilege, of having everything except privacy and peace of mind – the only sound, as the wheels of Dobe's new truck passed the state-line marker, was the sound of their laughter.

25

Giving it all up wouldn't be *too* hard, Jahne thought as she folded clothes into one of the suitcases that lay open on her bed. What was it she was losing? After all, she'd never, except for the time with *Jack and Jill*, gotten to play the parts she wanted. First it was all the 'character' parts, now it would be naked airheads. Moaning, jiggling, naked airheads. She threw a disgusted look at the pile of scripts that had been submitted to her. The women that Hollywood wanted: runaways, whores, victims; desperate, dependent women, and teenagers in trouble. The women that *America* seemed to want.

Yes, she could give it up. God, *why* had she wanted so much to be an actress anyway? That was a question with an answer too sad to ignore. She thought of Neil. Like him, she was a kid who had never had anyone's approval. And who had never had a family. I was a natural for it, she thought. The roar of the greasepaint, the smell of the crowd; the sense of family in a troupe, the attention of an audience, meagre as those sometimes were. All I really wanted was someone to look at me and approve. I was so tired of not being looked at. She shook her head and folded a white silk blouse, stuffed it into the suitcase, and shook her head again. No one had ever seen her, except perhaps Neil, and she hadn't believed *him*, hadn't cared enough about *his* good opinion. Would anyone's approval ever fill the void in her? Would more of Sam's love, more of the critics' raves, a larger audience's applause, would any of it have made her believe she was good enough? She doubted it.

With real pain, an actual hurt deep in her chest, she thought of all those kids back in New York, suffering to be seen, to be heard, to be *liked*. And the even more pathetic grovellers out here in L.A., desperate for a taste of fame, willing almost to die for a chance to be flavour of the month. Well, she'd had it, and someone else could have it now. She was sick of it. She had wasted herself, gone on a quest for a grail that was vulgar.

Still, it hadn't been all bad judgement on her part. Rather, it had been bad judgement foisted on her by every TV show, every magazine, every movie she'd ever seen. Be pretty, be popular, be attractive, be sexy, be wanted, to be desirable. Well, she thought grimly, she was desirable now. There wasn't a man in the country who couldn't jerk off to living, moving pictures of her imitation orgasms. And soon she'd go into international release. Today Scuderstown, tomorrow the world. She almost had to laugh at the irony. She had wanted to show them all. Show her grandmother, show the girls back at Scuderstown Regional High, show the casting agents and the producers in New York, show everyone how good, how very good she was. Well, her grandmother was dead, she couldn't remember the names of her high-school classmates, and New York never cared about anything.

Meanwhile, all she appeared to have shown was her genitalia, to any of the population on earth who could afford a VCR and a two-dollar rental. She had shown them how good she was at counterfeiting orgasms, a trait that almost every young girl would find useful, but hardly what she had originally had in mind. She shook her head at her own bitterness.

While she was facing home truths, she'd better face another one: Acting had also drawn her because she had been so afraid to live. Afraid of sinking into the day-to-day routine of a job, a husband, a family. She thought of Sharleen and her bravery: going out to Wyoming to live everyday life. Could Jahne do it? Playing a role was so much easier than living. Well, to hell with this idea of showing other people's feelings so that a numbed audience could have a few of their own. No, she'd *do* things from now on, not *act* them. Michael McLain had certainly taught her the difference between acting a hero and being a villain.

Villains. There were so many out here, all of them posing as heroes. Sy Ortis, Les Merchant, Hyram Flanders, Bob LeVine,

Michael McLain, Marty DiGennaro. And Sam, of course. All selling dream meat. She looked at the picture of her and Sam which still stood on the table beside the bed and shook her head again before she pitched it into the wastepaper basket, frame and all. It had been taken in Santa Cruz. That was only a few months ago. Back when she thought he could love her. Back when she thought he was worth loving.

One more home truth: Ridiculous as the charade had been, she was glad she'd gone through it. She'd longed for him, been rejected, and burned with her humiliation, a sort of culmination of all the humiliations of fat, sad, serious, smart, sensitive, plain girls. But, unlike them, at last, she'd had the chance to transform herself, and then to feel his longing for her. Still, the ending was the same. NOTHING HAD CHANGED. Beauty didn't protect you from betrayal. Hadn't Mai told her that? Hadn't Brewster Moore? Well, fuck it, then! Who needed beauty? It was only another trap for women. The silken trap, the desired trap, the exalted trap, but nothing more than a trap with trappings.

She stalked into the bathroom, ready to pack her toothbrush, deodorant, and that host of products that were lined up there, promising to make her more lovely, younger, softer; to bring out her hidden beauty or to hide her flaws. She looked up to the mirror, at her face: her sculpted, expensive, symmetrical, perfect face. And, once again, she saw her eyes, her old eyes, those eyes of a little girl left alone with her mother's blood in a hospital corridor. The eyes of a betrayed and abandoned child. They stared out at her, trapped behind the face that she now wore like a mask. Once again, she had hurt that little girl; once again, she had forced her to be hurt.

'I'm sorry,' she gasped, and found herself crying aloud. 'I'm so sorry about what I did to you.' The image in the mirror blurred through her tears but, desperate that she would lose touch with the child, her younger self, she rubbed the tears away.

'I'm sorry I hated you,' she choked. 'I'm sorry I caused you so much pain.' She thought of those years of rejection she'd forced herself to go through in New York, of rejection by directors who wouldn't cast her, by men who didn't want her, of starving herself, of the agony at the hospital. 'I'm sorry,' she gasped again. 'I believed them, not you.' She looked into her own eyes, warm, brown, unchanged, and still so sad, so frightened. 'I'll never do it again. I promise you. I'll never believe them again.'

She turned to the jars and bottles arranged along the vanity. She picked up a bottle of Visible Difference Night Repair. It was a pretty bottle, and fit smoothly, seductively, into the palm of her hand, like a pearl tucked in an oyster. But pearls were actually poison that the oyster had ingested, then coated with its own secretions.

'No more!' she said, and threw the little bottle against the marble floor. It smashed, sending tiny, diamond-bright shards across the floor. She picked up the one next to it. Système Anti-Age Crème de Jour. Where did they get these names? She flung it across the room, where it crashed against the marble baseboard and split open, its heavy white contents oozing onto the floor. She picked up the eye creams next, and the special hair conditioners, then the hand creams, the moisturizers, the makeup base, the blushers and their sable brushes, hurling them all across the room. She stamped on the blusher, crushing the colour into the white marble, pulverizing it. Then she broke open the eye-shadow colours, one after another. Glimmering Violet. Misty Mauve. Opalescent. She threw each one as if it were a grenade, breathing hard as they all smashed against the wall and fell to the floor. That wasn't enough. They had to be crushed for the lies they represented. 'Use me and you'll be beautiful.' 'Paint me on your eyelids and you'll be loved.' As she pulverized them, a bouquet began to blossom underfoot. 'Pretty poison,' she murmured and, lifting a bottle of Youth Dew Eye Make-Up Remover, poured its oily contents onto the floor. Then she smashed the empty bottle. She was out of breath, but she couldn't stop, didn't want to stop.

All her life, it seemed, she hadn't been pretty enough. She had lost jobs, men, and her self-esteem because she didn't look enough like the impossible pictures in the magazines, on the movie screen, on television. And even when she became pretty, even beautiful, even when she *became* one of the women on the screens, in the magazines, she had learned that *they* weren't perfect enough, that she still wasn't perfect enough, without special lenses, without careful makeup, without a full-time hairdresser, a stylist, a trainer, starvation diets, facials and manicures, an artful cameraman, a legion of specialists to perfect the illusion. No wonder there wasn't a single woman in America under forty who was satisfied with her looks. No wonder women were risking cancer to increase their breast size, no wonder they were anorectic, and bulimic, and crazy. Hollywood, Madison Avenue and the media, and men – all of them had conspired to make women hate themselves for not looking like Lila Kyle, a six-foot-tall post-adolescent boy with a huge pair of silicone knockers.

Jahne looked into the mirror again. Worst of all was that she had helped spread the lie. She'd had the surgery, she'd starved herself, she'd denied her appetites, her age, her face. I helped them, she thought. I helped Marty and Sy and Seymore and April. I helped them push product, push image. I helped Flanders Cosmetics with those endorsements; I helped to sell the lie. And I was loved for the lie. Which means I was never loved at all.

'No more,' she cried, and picked up a Chanel lipstick, Ultra Violet, and smeared it across the mirror. As she scrawled 'NO MORE,' the stick broke, and she threw it away from her, picked up another, and continued until it broke, too. Then another, and another, until the huge mirror was covered with 'NO MORE's in a rainbow of colours and the floor was littered with the broken remains of two dozen lipsticks. Jahne turned to the perfumes.

It wasn't enough to be ashamed of your looks. You also had to be ashamed of your smell. Don't smell like a woman. Smell like lilacs, or tuberoses and eucalyptus. Smell like citrus, or musk with a slight hint of lavender, or violet-scented talc. Put on deodorant, then perfume, then douche with the smell of country flowers, then slip in a perfumed panty liner and powder yourself fresh as a daisy, lovely as a lily bouquet.

With a single movement, she wiped the expensive perfume bottles off the counter and onto the floor. The crystal flagons crashed, then crunched noisily underfoot. The scent rose up, thick as a wall, and nearly sickened her. 'Yes!' she cried. It smelled like a whorehouse, and it should. It was appropriate. She had sold and been sold. Pimped by Hollywood, pimped by April, pimped by Sam, by Sy Ortis. 'But no more!' she cried, the smell clawing at her throat, nauseating her. She picked up the remaining face powder, the brushes, the cover sticks, the tweezers, the eyebrow pencils, the mascaras, the lip liners, the eyeliners. She broke what she could, scattered the rest, tore open the drawers, and found more: eyelash curlers, makeup sponges, rollers, mascara cakes and brushes, pancake lip glosses. She pulled out the entire drawer and emptied it onto the floor, smashing what she could.

By now it was a punishment to stay in the room: her eyes were stinging from the stink, and she was gagging. But she had to finish the job. She grabbed the next drawer, emptied it, and smashed the contents. There were the hot rollers, the hair gel, the mousses. There was the honey-almond facial scrub, the cucumber skin toner, the strawberry facial masque. Enough fruits and nuts and vegetables to feed a Honduran village for a week, enough alcohol to get them drunk for a month, enough cotton balls and pads to keep them clothed for a year.

She was taking her breaths in jagged, sickening gulps. She surveyed the filth of the ruined room. The desecration was complete: her pristine bathroom, that temple to feminine allure, was splashed with the muck that she and every other woman in America had been taught they needed. 'No more,' she said, and stepped backward, closing the door.

Jahne lay on the sofa in her huge, empty living room. Living room? This mausoleum? No, giving this up wouldn't be too hard. But what did she do next?

She thought back to New York, to the time before *Jack and Jill*, to her life with Sam, to the breakup. She thought about Molly and Chuck, about Neil before he lost it. And she thought about those two horrible, lonely years she'd spent getting cut and pasted back together.

Did she wish she'd never done it? Did she wish she'd maintained her identity as Mary Jane?

She couldn't say yes to that. She was glad she'd gone through it. Not for anyone else, but for *her*. Never having had beauty, she would have always craved it. She would not have known that no amount of it was ever enough. If she hadn't gone through with the surgery, she'd never have experienced all of this. She thought she'd known the differences in life for a beautiful woman and an ugly one, but she'd had to experience them. She was glad she had.

And now she was sick of the world that perpetuated those differences: that made the shape of an eye and the tip of a nose so much more than a genetic hat trick. She was sick of a culture that worshipped youth and beauty only so that it could humiliate, humble, and control all those without it. But Hollywood's mania, America's mania, was spreading all across the globe. America exported its vision of culture the way Japan exported televisions.

So where could she go? Where was safe? And what would she do once she got there?

Jahne could hear the phone ringing at the other end of the long-distance line. Please be home, doctor, she prayed. Please be home. She wondered what Brewster Moore's apartment was like. Did he sleep in a single bed, or a double, or even a king? Did he sleep alone? Please, God, she prayed, let him sleep alone.

'Hello?'

'Brewster? It's Mary Jane.' Thank God. It was a good connection. She could hear him take in his breath. 'Did I wake you? I'm sorry.'

'That's all right.' He paused. 'I haven't spoken to Mary Jane in a long time.'

'I know. Neither have I, really.' She stopped. How could she explain? How could anyone, even he, understand what had happened to her: who she had been and who she had tried to be and who she was now? 'Something has happened. I mean, I feel like I've changed, that . . .' She sounded ridiculous. She listened to the silence on the line and for a moment became afraid that he wasn't there. 'Brewster?' she asked.

'Yes, Mary Jane?'

'When do you go back to Honduras?'

'Not till next month.'

'Do you need a nurse?'

'Do you need a job?'

'No, but I want one. I want one very, very much.'

Was he going to laugh at her? Was he going to think she was a dilettante, a ditz with a new role to play? All at once, she felt this was the most important call she'd ever made, the most important audition of her life. She closed her eyes. 'I know it's kind of sudden,' she began 'but something has happened to me. I think I've been building up to this for a long time.'

'I think you have, too,' Brewster said.

'I think I could still nurse. I mean, I'd have to study. I've forgotten a lot. And I don't know any Spanish, except what Raoul taught me . . .'

'Wasn't that mostly curses?'

'Yes. I could call you a monkey's whore.'

'It may come in handy.'

She took a deep breath. 'I could help with the kids. I know I could. Not in surgery, maybe, but postop. And counselling, maybe. I could help the ones with no faces. I could look at them. I could *see* them, Brewster. I know I could. And that makes all the difference. Having just one person who can see who you really are.' Tears filled her eyes. 'Can I come, Brewster?' she whispered.

'Welcome aboard,' he said.

Obscurity II

Are you kidding? I would trade it all for anonymity again.
Kevin Costner

In the future everyone will be world-famous for fifteen minutes.
Andy Warhol

Fifteen minutes of that was more than enough.

Jahne Moore

1

Laura Richie here. Of course, I was there all along, reporting the facts, getting down each detail of the story. And what a story! I can't take the credit for making it up, but I can get the credit for writing it all down. Who could make something like this up? All of America worshipping at the shrine of the three false sex idols: one involved with her 'brother,' one a Frankenstein, and the last one a man! It was a story that used too many exclamation points, and I myself try to be sparing with them. Well, you know what they say: truth is stranger than fiction. You can't say that you didn't get good value for your twenty-three dollars. (Or six ninety-nine in paper.)

It has taken me more than three years to do the research and to fit all the pieces together. I don't suppose I'll get the Pulitzer, or a MacArthur grant, but it's a hell of a job of reporting, nonetheless. And if the critics, as they inevitably do, lambaste me as petty, small-minded, and vicious, I may shed a secret tear as I endorse my next royalty cheque. I already banked a seven-figure advance, and gave Nancy, my secretary, enough of a bonus for her to put down a large deposit on a nice little condo in San Diego. She's retiring next month. I tell her she won't be able to take doing nothing all day, but she just laughs and says she's going to try. She says she only wants to live through the typing of this final revision of this, my final book. I, too, am tired of the dirt, of the secrets, of the scandals that America loves to read about. Maybe, in my heart, I believe what my critics have said. Mine was a small and dirty contribution to literature.

But you, gentle Reader, you bought the book. Thank you. Perhaps you can explain to the critics and the reporters and sociologists this American fascination for gossip about the rich and famous. I don't have a clue. But I knew this story would sell like cellulite remover in the spring.

And don't think it was easy, ferreting all this out. Even for me, Laura Richie, gossip columnist extraordinaire. *Lila, of course, was dead, the poor thing. She or he wasn't talking to anyone. After that insane funeral, they had her cremated and the ashes interred at Forest Lawn, in the crypt with her father. Then I had to wait. And wait. Because, without Theresa, I didn't have Lila's story, and without that, I had nothing.*

Well, I admit it was a little ghoulish, but, see, I know celebrities. Once addicted to the hot white light of fame, they find it impossible to live in the darkness. In the end, bad publicity becomes better – much better – than none at all. Look at Zsa Zsa Gabor.

Theresa stayed in seclusion for months, but after the tabloids calmed down, after the worst of it blew away, after Robbie left and she had no one to perform for, no audience to watch her suffer, Theresa got bored. Very, very bored.

So, in the end, Theresa talked. A lot of what she said was lies and cover-up and garbage, but some of it was the truth. Then her maid, Estrella, for a price, told me what she knew. It was after that that Theresa finally went into the hospital. Not the Betty Ford – she was too far gone for that – but Cedars-Sinai. Cirrhosis. Terminal. She died last spring.

Robbie got himself into Al-anon and now runs a Twelve-Step bookstore in Aspen. He claims a celebrity clientele. And Kevin – well, once I found him, I couldn't stop him from talking.

Early Artists, of course, fell apart. Sy Ortis' three key clients had bitten the dust, Michael McLain was gone, and the others left in droves. So Sy took his money and went to that Valhalla of all ex-agents – Independent-producer status. His phone calls don't get returned.

Ara Sagarian, after he was found abandoned in the hallway of the hospital, was buried the same week Lila Kyle was. His obit was dwarfed by the media attention paid to Lila. In death, as in life, she crushed him.

It took a long time to track down Sharleen and Dean. They seemed, at first, to have disappeared off the planet. But we finally got a line on them by checking out her companion on TV at the Emmys. Once we got his name, Nancy and I did a lot of searching and found a real-estate transaction in the Butler County, Wyoming, records. Then I went out and spent four weeks in a deadly motel in the middle of nowhere to get a chance to talk with Sharleen. But that didn't help, because the locals didn't know her, or if they did, they wouldn't talk. The funny thing was, after the first couple of weeks of hating it, I started to like it out there. It wasn't like L.A. It was a clean place.

But I wasn't rich enough to take a permanent vacation. In fact, I was just about to give up on the story and start on the Douglas family when my own incompetence got me in the door. And it was through Dean that it happened. I took a drive out along the dirt track that led to their ranch. It was fenced at the entrance and there wasn't any way to get in. I knew that; I'd already been out there a dozen times, so I'd taken to driving by and up the mountain road, just for the view. It was beautiful, unspoiled country.

Well, the ruts got the tyre, and after a while I noticed I was driving on a flat. A real flat, on a mountain road, about twenty miles from nowhere. And I was in heels.

Let's face it, I'm not a wilderness kind of gal. Lucky for me, Dean found me. Sweet as ever, he took me home. I had lunch that day with the three of them on their ranch. In a month, I had their story.

With Minos, it was much easier. Money talks, nobody walks. I found out a lot of the basics from Minos, after a friend of mine at the LAPD placed a couple of calls. I got my info. Minos still has his licence. Everybody's happy.

Ricky Dunn's next movie bombed, and then he married Kiki Mansard, the new Crystal Plenum. When her career took off he was arrested twice for DWI and then for hitting Kiky. Shak, his P.A., apparently did not serve as his mouthpiece at the arraignment. Now Shay's working in the music industry. Ricky isn't working at all. So maybe Michael McLain's instincts on that were right.

But in other ways, Michael's instincts sucked. It took him more than fifty years to marry and to father a child, and he was had twice. Of course, before he got divorced, Michael McLain was claiming his wife Adrienne was a virgin he met at her convent-school graduation. I scouted down Mrs. Godowski, and a couple of six-packs unloaded a lot of resentments. We had the story on Mrs. McLain, but I never used it against Michael. It was only when Marvin Belli took on the case for Adrienne that Michael himself began squawking. Because, as I always say, community-property laws can surely make strange bedfellows. Michael needed everyone to know that his wife had been a whore before he met her. Even Michael McLain knows it's better to look like a woman's dupe than to be poor. It seems that Adrienne had an affair with A. Joel Grossman the whole time she was married to Michael. The child, apparently, was A. Joel's. Since the divorce, he and Adrienne are living together on Michael's money, and A. Joel is teaching film courses at Cal State.

Crystal Plenum dumped Sy. Then, by luck, she got a hot little script from some indie and her last picture, River Road, had legs as good as her own. She's back on top. They say she's a shoo-in for the Oscar.

Les Merchant watched his network slip back to number three; then he watched as the stockholders allowed him to be replaced. Bob LeVine was dumped from International, but his son, Seymore, was the money behind River Road, and he's moved into the big time on his own.

Success has many fathers, but failure is an orphan. There was no one connected with the Three for the Road debacle who was willing to admit it. And just last month poor Marty came out of the hospital, only to go into retirement.

Benny Eggs finally caught up with Paulie Grasso. Or perhaps I should say Paulie's gambling did. He's living in Seattle or a city a lot like it and was willing to talk to me for what he once would have called 'chump change.'

Monica Flanders died in her sleep, but not before a bitter proxy fight had ousted her son Hyram from Flanders Cosmetics. By the way, Monica looked terrific at her funeral.

April is doing fine. Anyone who reads the trades knows that. She gave me several interviews, now that she's the new queen of the studio. As the new president of International, she's redecorated Bob LeVine's old office in a masculine maroon colour.

And Sam Shields? What happened to him? Well, he made two flops, but it looks like his latest is going to be a hit. At least, that's the word on the street. And you've probably read that he and April are about to become engaged. A real love match.

Anyway, the last bits and pieces of the story I got from my husband. Yes, that is one more piece of gossip for you. Consider it a wedding gift from my new husband and me to you. Not that the public is very interested in the private life of writers, even one such as I. But I did get married, at this late date. When I met Dobe Samuels, I knew he was one of a kind. And so, in a way, am I. Reader, I married him. And he was worth waiting for. Sometime just before you read this, in a very private ceremony, I became Mrs. Dobe Samuels.

Brewster Moore and his wife attended. He has never spoken to me about any of this, and once the book is published I will welcome the opportunity to see if he has any comments to make. But his wife told me more than a few things. Mary Jane likes her privacy, and she says she has plenty of it in Honduras, except when her adopted son, Raoul, is home with his friends from school. But she was willing to talk, she said, to atone for her sins. And maybe because she had to talk to someone, just once, to make sense out of the whole thing.

She and Sharleen are still close friends, though they only get to spend part of their summers together on the ranch. Sharleen doesn't ever leave it. And I don't think I will, either. After this book sale, Dobe and I are buying another three thousand acres. He figures if we plant two thousand trees a year, we can add more ozone to the atmosphere than all that my books used up. Evening up our karma. He believes it isn't a bad way for me to spend my declining years and my increasing wealth. And he says three thousand acres ought to hold us all.

He also says he won't allow reporters or celebrities on any of it.

OLIVIA GOLDSMITH

The First Wives Club

When their best friend commits suicide over her divorce Elise, Brenda and Annie decide enough is enough. Each was crucial to her husband's career. But now the men are successful they've traded their first wives in for newer, blonder models.

Only Annie wanted reconciliation. That was until her husband, Aaron, humiliated her in front of his new wife-to-be – *her* therapist – and blew their disabled daughter's trust fund on an insider deal that went awry. Now, she wants retribution.

Over lunch one day they form the First Wives Club. But this is no support group. Painstakingly, they plan to turn each of their ex's neat little lives into a living hell.

SANDRA BROWN

Mirror Image

Imagine looking in the mirror one morning and seeing someone else's face . . .

Mistaken for a glamorous, selfish woman named Carole Rutledge after a tragic plane crash, the badly injured Avery finds that plastic surgery has given her Carole's face, a famous senatorial candidate, Tate Rutledge, for a husband, and a powerful Texas dynasty for inlaws. And as she lies helpless in the hospital, she makes a shattering discovery: someone close to Tate Rutledge plans to assassinate him.

TESS STIMSON

Hard News

Reporter Christie Bradley, beautiful and brave, is willing to take any risks for her job. It'll take a strong man to hold her. David Cameron has been INN's top war correspondent for ten years. He's survived bullets and bombs, but he's never met the right woman. Together, they discover that passion is the hottest story of all.

But love is dangerous in a world where sex is the ultimate weapon. Where the anchor position is more than just a job for newscaster Paragon Fairfax; where ruthless editor Ben Wordsworth would sell his soul for ratings. And where Sir Edward Penhaligon, seemingly INN's one voice of integrity, plans his own, shocking revenge.

LESLEY PEARSE

Georgia

From the seedy backstreets of London's Soho in the 60s to the tough, sexy world of international rock stardom in the 70s, Georgia sees it all . . .

When nine-year-old orphan Georgia James is unexpectedly fostered by the kindly Celia and her bankmanager husband she can hardly believe her luck. But then – on her fifteenth birthday – she suffers the cruellest betrayal of all at the hands of her foster father and is forced to run away, leaving everything she loves behind her.

Penniless, sleeping rough, Georgia is soon introduced to the sleazy Soho world of brassy strippers, sweat shops, camaraderie and hardship. Fired by a fierce ambition, blessed with an extraordinary voice, her long struggle for fame and fortune begins. But even when she reaches the top she finds that the scars of the past can open up to ruin her . . .

ROSE SHEPHERD

Too Rich Too Thin

Caroline Charteris has so very much. She wants for nothing – except a sense of self-worth. And a trim waistline. And the attentions of eligible young men. And the approval of her mother, the bored, beautiful, rapacious Laura.

Michele Fairchild has so little of anything. She has nothing – except the face of an angel. And a figure to die for. And the awesome secret which her grandmother has shared with her.

Nothing, for either of them, will ever be the same again . . .

'A stylish and touching comedy of manners . . . I loved it'

Penny Vincenzi

BARBARA DELINSKY

A Woman Betrayed

With a twenty-year marriage, two terrific kids, and a successful career, Laura Frye has everything she could ask for . . . until her husband Jeff mysteriously disappears.

Beside herself with worry, Laura maintains that the Jeff she knew would never leave voluntarily. But what about the Jeff she didn't know? As her husband's many secrets come to light, Laura is left with a shocking picture of the man she married – and a world that is falling apart . . .

'When you care enough to read the very best, the name of Barbara Delinsky should come immediately to mind'

Rave Reviews

A Selected List of Fiction Available from Mandarin

While every effort is made to keep prices low, it is sometimes necessary to increase prices at short notice. Mandarin Paperbacks reserves the right to show new retail prices on covers which may differ from those previously advertised in the text or elsewhere.

The prices shown below were correct at the time of going to press.

☐	7493 0576 2	**Tandia**	Bryce Courtenay	£4.99
☐	7493 0122 8	**Power of One**	Bryce Courtenay	£4.99
☐	7493 0581 9	**Daddy's Girls**	Zoe Fairbairns	£4.99
☐	7493 0942 3	**Silence of the Lambs**	Thomas Harris	£4.99
☐	7493 0530 4	**Armalite Maiden**	Jonathan Kebbe	£4.99
☐	7493 0134 1	**To Kill a Mockingbird**	Harper Lee	£3.99
☐	7493 1017 0	**War in 2020**	Ralph Peters	£4.99
☐	7493 0946 6	**Godfather**	Mario Puzo	£4.99
☐	7493 0381 6	**Loves & Journeys of Revolving Jones**	Leslie Thomas	£4.99
☐	7493 0381 6	**Rush**	Kim Wozencraft	£4.99

All these books are available at your bookshop or newsagent, or can be ordered direct from the publisher. Just tick the titles you want and fill in the form below.

Mandarin Paperbacks, Cash Sales Department, PO Box 11, Falmouth, Cornwall TR10 9EN.

Please send cheque or postal order, no currency, for purchase price quoted and allow the following for postage and packing:

UK including BFPO	£1.00 for the first book, 50p for the second and 30p for each additional book ordered to a maximum charge of £3.00.
Overseas including Eire	£2 for the first book, £1.00 for the second and 50p for each additional book thereafter.

NAME (Block letters) ....

ADDRESS...

....

☐ I enclose my remittance for ....

☐ I wish to pay by Access/Visa Card Number

Expiry Date

THE USURPER'S CROWN

Sarah Zettel was born in California in 1966. Since then she's lived in ten cities, four states and two countries. *The Usurper's Crown* is her second fantasy novel. She has also written four science fiction novels and many short stories in the sf, fantasy and horror genres. Her debut full-length work, *Reclamation*, won the Locus Award for Best First Novel. Sarah now lives in Michigan with her husband and their son.

'A tale that spins wonder with vivid and touching complexity – beautiful as a prism. Sarah Zettel has delivered a dazzling realm of amazement'
JANNY WURTS

'An absorbing yarn full of love, magic and treachery'
Starburst

'*The Usurper's Crown* has a sense of the price of everything and the moments of joy and victory that redeem tragedy; it is one of the most adult fantasies of the year'　ROZ KAVENEY, *Amazon*

'A rich and lively mix of fantasy and fairy tale elements'　　　　　　　　　　　　　*Locus*

Voyager

The Usurper's Crown

BOOK TWO OF
THE ISAVALTA TRILOGY

Sarah Zettel

HarperCollins*Publishers*

Voyager
An Imprint of HarperCollins*Publishers*
77–85 Fulham Palace Road,
Hammersmith, London W6 8JB

www.voyager-books.com

This paperback edition 2004
1 3 5 7 9 8 6 4 2

First published in Great Britain by *Voyager* 2002

ISBN 0 00 711402 8

Typeset in Bembo by Palimpsest Book Production Limited,
Polmont, Stirlingshire

Printed and bound in Great Britain by
Clays Limited, St Ives plc

This book is dedicated to my friend and
fellow practitioner of the writing arts, Karen Everson.

Acknowledgments

The author would like to once again thank the Untitled Writers Group for their honesty and support. Many thanks also to my editor James Frenkel and my agent Shawna McCarthy without whom this book and this series would not have seen the light of day.

In the lofty chamber, at the river mouth ... a fair maiden stands, stands and decks herself, commends herself to valorous folk, glories in deeds of war.

(*From* A RUSSIAN SPELL OF PROTECTION IN BATTLE)

Prologue

Medeoan will not yield.

Those words echoed inside Avanasy's head as he stood in the vestment room of the god house, one eye pressed against the rough, wooden door so that he might watch the wedding. Shame weighed on him. He had not found in himself the strength to leave while any chance remained for Medeoan to change her mind. Therefore, he must hide like a thief waiting for a household to settle into sleep. Avanasy was under sentence of banishment, and if he were found today within the borders of Isavalta he would be killed. So, where did he choose to harbor himself? In the heart of the Imperial Palace of Vyshtavos. Emperor Edemsko, Avanasy's patron, would have snorted at that, had he known, and pronounced it 'arrogance typical of a sorcerer.' Then, however much the Emperor might regret it, he would carry out the sentence his daughter Medeoan had laid down.

Medeoan will not yield.

A rush of air swirled the scents of incense and burning candles through the cracks in the door. By pressing his right cheek against the pitted surface, Avanasy could just barely see the tall, gilded portals open to let High Princess Medeoan pace gracefully but deliberately into the god house. As she glided

1

past his vantage point, he saw how the assured glow of a maiden's love had taken on a sharp edge in her face. This was her decision. Against counsel and advice, this love was all hers, and he could see clearly that she felt pride as well as joy in it. Her parents on the dais and the statues of the gods on their pedestal watched her approach with the same stately equanimity. Avanasy's jaw tightened as the courtiers' murmurs reached him. The poets and the gossips would doubtlessly set out a banquet of approved words to describe this sight. All those assembled in the god house would later be said to have noted how the color in the High Princess's cheeks rivaled the roses in her wedding crown and girdle for brightness. They would say her sapphire-blue eyes shimmered with joy the way the golden symbols of luck, happiness, and fertility embroidered on her blue gown shimmered with the light of braided candles set in every corner and cornice of the gilded room. Ballads and romantic themes would be composed on the heir of Isavalta and her great love.

Those themes would not last. Avanasy knew that fact as he knew that the sun would rise the next morning, and the knowledge burned his heart. The pain only grew sharper because he could do nothing. Finally, his restless, discontented student was happy. Finally, she was at peace with her place in the world.

That peace, however, rested on a carpet of lies. He had tried to tell her this hard news, but Medeoan had just stood before him, her jaw hanging loose in stunned disbelief.

'Why are you saying this, Avanasy?'

They had been in her private chamber, the only place he could possibly utter his accusations. They stood on opposite sides of the central fire pit so that he seemed to see her standing in a patch of flames. Beyond the princess, her waiting ladies sat in their alcove, her wedding veil stretched out between them so they could work on its embroidery. All of them bent studiously over their work, pretending very hard not to hear anything that was being said.

'Because it is the truth.' His voice had been soft, then. Anger would not serve. Medeoan had always looked to him for sympathy. He had to show her he felt that sympathy still. 'Kacha means to use you to gain Isavalta for himself.'

'He does not need to use me,' countered Medeoan doggedly. 'Once he becomes my consort, Isavalta passes to his heirs, our children. His blood line will have Isavalta.'

As it has been denied its native land of Hastinapura. Avanasy met her eyes, willing her to hear what he truly said. 'Medeoan, you are a sorceress. You may not conceive easily, and you will most certainly outlive Kacha.' He did not say: 'Why do you think your parents had to negotiate the marriage treaty so carefully?' He did not say: 'Why do you think those who sit on the Pearl Throne offered you the son of their Emperor's brother rather than their heir?' Medeoan already knew these things, however much she might wish not to. That knowledge hung in the air between them like the scent of the wood and charcoal burning in the fire.

He had expected anger from her. Indeed, he had hoped for it. Anger would mean that she had heard him, and that his words had reached beyond the walls she had erected in her heart and her mind. Instead, she drew herself up, her whole bearing showing an unfamiliar resolve. 'You think I do not know that my existence is shaped by politics? I know that as I know my name. The needs of the empire shape every single facet of my life but one; Kacha loves me.'

Kacha. Now, he waited for his bride beside Bakhar, the keeper of the god house. Kacha's narrow, rugged face was appropriately solemn as he watched Medeoan's approach. Like Medeoan, Kacha wore the Imperial blue, but his elegant kaftan was covered with a white coat embroidered with silver. He did not officially obtain Imperial rank until Medeoan accepted him before the gods. Then, that white coat would be removed, and his crown of white roses would be replaced with a crown of gold and sapphires, and he would have all that he wanted.

'Politics shapes your existence, yes.' Avanasy rounded the fire pit and stood directly in front of Medeoan. 'It also shapes Kacha's. His father should have been on the Pearl Throne, but he is not. It galls him. His son . . .'

'Is his route to empire,' Medeoan cut Avanasy off sharply. 'Why does that matter? I am marrying him. His father will have the empire he desires.' She turned from him then, gripping the back of a gilded chair. 'It is done. There is no need for this treachery you would dream up.'

'No need, perhaps,' said Avanasy to her back. 'But I fear that owning the future of Isavalta is not enough for them.'

Medeoan whirled around then, finally and truly angry. Avanasy suppressed a grim smile at that anger. At last, at last, she was beginning to hear him. 'How can you say such things?' Medeoan demanded. 'What proof have you?'

'You require proof?' Avanasy asked gently, taking another step forward. 'Answer me this question. Where is Kacha now?'

Medeoan frowned, her brows drawing together. 'He is meeting with the master of the treasury and the under-treasurers.'

Avanasy nodded. He had known the answer before he spoke. 'Were you not supposed to be in consultation with them?'

For the first time Medeoan hesitated, but she covered the pause with a dismissive wave. 'I must see to the wedding clothes. There are sigils that must be properly prepared.'

'I could do that with the aid of your mistress of the weaving sheds, as could any of the court sorcerers.' Avanasy spread his hands, encompassing the room and leaving her nowhere to turn. 'Why are you not in consultation with the men who will most likely be your ministers when you assume the throne?'

'Because I wish to be here.' Medeoan pronounced each word carefully and clearly, but her voice trembled all the same.

Forgive me, thought Avanasy silently, as he pressed on. 'Kacha said he would take care of these matters for you, did he not?'

Medeoan had a ready answer for that. Avanasy had known she would. 'I wish the Council of Lords to become used to him and his position of responsibility.'

'So it was your idea?' he asked, raising his eyebrows. 'He did not suggest to you that he sit through this dull meeting while you are more agreeably occupied?'

Medeoan stood silent.

'And how many other meetings in these past months has Kacha shouldered the burden for?'

Her fist knotted against the back of the chair. She was so young yet. She believed she had finally found the escape she had always sought, and it grieved him to force her to see the truth. But how could he be loyal and do otherwise? 'He is the first person who wished to make my life easier rather than more difficult.'

'He is the first person who wished to cut you off from the functions of the government that will be yours, or should be yours.'

That was his fatal miscalculation. It was those words that made Medeoan turn away.

There were those who heard of Avanasy's objections and cautions regarding the marriage and looked askance at him. They wondered if he had fallen in love with his Imperial student. He kept his silence at these whispers. They were not entirely wrong. He did love Medeoan. He loved her as a daughter or a sister. So he told himself, most days. He was too honest with himself not to admit that there were times, when they sat together in confidence, and she told him of her fears, that other loves were stirred in him. He loved the brilliance of her mind and of her magic, and he was by no means blind to her beauty. To see her so utterly overcome by treachery and flattery left him devastated.

As was required upon entering the god house, the High Princess Medeoan paused to kiss the robes of Vyshko and Vyshemir, the house gods of the Imperial family. Vyshko lifted his pike high, and Vyshemir spread her hands, offering her cup and knife to the assembly. Coins and velvets lay heaped at their feet, the gifts of the ones who stood before them. Silks and elaborately knotted carpets from Hastinapura had been carefully piled at the base of the pedestal. Those who were close enough, and those who knew Medeoan well, knew she did not observe the gods dressed in their finest indigo silk for this ceremony. Instead, she stole covert glances at her groom who had already marched in and honored the gods with treasures from his southern homeland. Now, he waited for Medeoan. Doubtlessly, she saw how fine his chiseled features were. In her memory she heard the sweet words of love and sympathy that he poured endlessly into her ears.

Perhaps they are right after all, the ones who call me a jealous fool. Avanasy bowed his forehead against the vestry door. *Perhaps she was right to exile me.*

'He's told you you'll be free, hasn't he?' he had said to Medeoan, his voice growing harder with each word, even though he knew it was a mistake. He knew he should stop, he must stop, or he would drive her away, but he could not stop. There had been then only himself and her, and the fire burning beside them, echoing the anger and fear burning in his veins. Nothing else registered in his mind. 'He has told you that you can have the one thing you have longed for, as long as you trust him.'

'He is helping me,' said Medeoan doggedly. 'Is that not what a husband and consort should do?' She walked up to him, slowly, deliberately, far too close for courtesy. 'Is that not what a teacher should do?'

'Is a consort supposed to bribe the treasury ministers?' shot back Avanasy.

Two bright spots of color appeared on Medeoan's cheeks. 'What?'

I'm sorry. I'm sorry. 'Your ministers have been the recipients of several small, but expensive gifts from the hand of your consort-to-be.'

Medeoan ducked her head, pretending to turn her attention to the ladies working so diligently on her veil. 'He is generous to all who serve well.'

'To all who serve *him* well,' Avanasy corrected her.

'I have heard nothing of this,' Medeoan said without looking back at him.

'No,' said Avanasy. 'Because you have ceased to attend meetings, and because Kacha has not told you.'

She whirled around then, and Avanasy saw fear behind the anger blazing in her eyes. She believed him, at least in part. She remembered that he had never lied to her, and so she must know that now he spoke the truth. Had not Kacha walked in at that moment, everything might have been different.

Avanasy heard the sound of something scrabbling against wood, and realized it was his own nails scraping against the door as his hand curled into a fist.

Kacha stood beside the keeper of the god house, waiting patiently while his bride poured a small heap of gold and sapphires out at the feet of the gods. He was handsome, for the most part. Although his face was narrow, the rest of him was broad and well sculpted. As suited a prince of the Pearl Throne, he had been well schooled in the arts of his homeland. He could read, and he could write several languages, which was more than most nobles of Isavalta could say. He could judge horse-flesh, cloth, and gems. He could dance, sing and play music, and write a letter that could singe a maiden's soul. He could speak politely but firmly in front of his elders, and he could weave a web of words to get what he desired. He had only two flaws. The flesh around his right eye was a network of white scars, and his right hand was twisted and withered like an old man's. A chariot accident, he had said. He had been thrown, but his hand had become entangled in the reins and then crushed when the car overturned. These outward signs that he had suffered in his life seemed only to draw Medeoan closer to him.

'Forgive me, Medeoan,' Kacha had said then, his gaze darting between Avanasy and his intended. 'I did not realize you were occupied.'

'No, come here Kacha.' Medeoan held out her hand. Kacha, his gaze fixed firmly on Avanasy, crossed the room in a swift stride to take her fresh, unlined hand in his withered one. 'What is being said here concerns you.'

Kacha's eyebrows lifted minutely. 'Then I am anxious to hear it.'

They did not look at each other. Both their gazes fixed on Avanasy, Kacha's with the mildest of curiosity, Medeoan's with cold anger. 'Avanasy, who has never lied to me, says you have been giving bribes to the treasury ministers.'

Kacha bowed with his palms pressed against his eyes, as was the fashion of his homeland. 'Avanasy does not lie.'

What little color she had left drained from Medeoan's face. 'Then it is true?' she breathed.

Kacha bowed again. 'It is true.' He spoke casually, and as he lifted his head, Avanasy saw how the prince's eyes shone.

Before either Medeoan or Avanasy could speak, Kacha asked, 'Did Avanasy tell you why I did such thing?'

Avanasy felt his heart go cold. 'Tell me why,' said Medeoan.

'Because your father's Lord Master of the treasury has been stealing.' Kacha held up his hand, forestalling protest. 'I have been reviewing the ledgers. I have some proof, but not enough. I needed spies.'

'And why did you not see fit to inform the Emperor of this?' asked Avanasy evenly. He must not accuse, not now. He must not lose hold of his anger.

'The Emperor is a sagacious man, he will require more than my word as a prince when I say that one of the high families of Isavalta harbors a thief,' countered Kacha. 'Which is why I needed proof.'

'And why did you not see fit to tell me?' asked Medeoan quietly.

Kacha dropped his eyes. 'I was afraid.'

'Of what?' Medeoan stepped closer to him. 'Of me?'

'No.' Kacha shook his head, and lifted his eyes, and stared straight at Avanasy.

It was a gesture Medeoan could not fail to miss. 'Of Avanasy?'

Kacha reached into the breast of his kaftan and brought out a tiny silver mirror. The surface had been carefully etched with a complex series of crosses and knots. A single human eye had been drawn in the center. 'My servant told me Avanasy had asked for this to be placed in my chamber. He was told it was an amulet of protection. There are books in the library that say otherwise.'

Kacha handed the mirror to Medeoan, and Avanasy knew the young prince, the would-be Emperor of Isavalta, had made his mistake.

'Highness, I swear on life, blood and soul that is no work of mine.' Avanasy stretched out his wrist. 'Take my blood, work your will, and see for yourself which of us lies.'

He hoped she would take his word, but knew she could not. Medeoan carried a knife with the small bundle of keys that hung from her girdle. She raised it now, and cut his palm, the swift, shallow slice he had taught her to make. Avanasy held himself completely steady. One, two, three drops of blood fell from his wound onto the mirror. Medeoan breathed deeply, calling up the magic that was part of her soul, part of her world. She traced her finger through the tiny puddle of blood drawing a new pattern, as complete and precise as any he himself could make. The air tingled cool and sharp against Avanasy's skin. It was a sensation Kacha could not feel. Medeoan shaped a spell of understanding. Had the watching mirror in truth been his, the blood would be absorbed into its surface. As it was, it would fall away like water, and Medeoan would know the truth. It was Kacha who lied to her, not he.

But the mirror drank in the blood until every trace of red was lost.

Avanasy's soul plummeted. Medeoan raised her face to his, and her skin had gone paper white. He saw the flash of triumph in Kacha's eyes, his scars standing out very white against his dark skin, and Avanasy felt the knowledge grow like a sickness in him – he was lost, and the fault for the loss was his own. He had grossly, stupidly, fatally, underestimated how well Kacha's father had prepared his son for the role he was to play.

'Get out.' Medeoan's voice shook with her fury. 'I ban you, I banish you. If I find you within my country again, you will be killed!'

'Medeoan . . .'

'Do not speak my name! Be grateful I do not have you killed here and now for the traitor you are! Get out!'

As the memory of her cry echoed in his mind, Avanasy

made himself watch Medeoan, trembling with excitement, complete the journey to her waiting husband. Part of him mused that this voyeurism must be his own punishment for his arrogance. This was how he sought to deepen his own guilt and at the same time justify his fatal boldness.

And it is just as useless. He watched the court, resplendent in its golds, silks, and velvets, reverence, bowing deeply from the waist with their hands crossed upon their breasts.

Medeoan will not yield.

Those words had been spoken by Edemsko, the Emperor of Isavalta, Medeoan's father, relieved that his only living child had finally ceased to sigh against the burdens her birth had placed on her. Avanasy had felt a traitor going to the Emperor in private to ask that Medeoan's order of exile be rescinded. But how could he not? Now that he had seen the depth to which Kacha had laid his plans, how could he abandon her?

But Emperor Edemsko was not one of those who believed the heir to the throne should be kept from power. Medeoan was never meant to be the heir. Her older brothers had been stout princes, but one had been thrown from his horse into a freezing canal, and the other had succumbed to fever, leaving only Medeoan to take the burden up. No effort of the court sorcerers could produce another living child from the Empress's womb. So, from her youth, the Emperor forced Medeoan to attend Council sessions. He had insisted she have practice in direct governance, knowing that she would rule when he was gone. Now that she had seen fit to give an order of her own, he would not override her, even when that order was to exile the teacher the Emperor had chosen for her.

Avanasy watched Keeper Bakhar gesture with one strong hand so that the court could rise and watch as he placed Kacha's mismatched hands into Medeoan's fair ones.

No, he said in the silence of his own mind. *No, Medeoan.*

Stop. His eyes turned involuntarily toward the Emperor and Empress. They sat on their thrones on the dais behind the keeper, laden with pride, sphere, scepter and crown. They glittered more brightly than even the gods. Today, the royal regalia seemed no burden as they watched their daughter tilt her happy face toward her husband. No doubt they were blessing fortune that political necessity could be married to happiness. Isavalta, fledgling Isavalta, Isavalta called eternal but really just a babe in its new borders, would be safe now. This union, this happy union, would assure it. There were plenty of other sorcerers at court. Kacha would be well watched, by them, and by the Emperor's own informants. Were it true that Medeoan was in danger, it would be seen, well before any plan could be completed. It might even come in useful in future negotiations with the Pearl Throne of Hastinapura.

'Now I do call on all those here assembled to bear witness.' Medeoan's voice rang strong and clear through the god house. 'High Princess Medeoan Edemskoidoch Nacheradavosh, being well pleased with the form and the offerings of Kacha *tya* Achin Ekulinjapad, does take his hands under the watchful eyes of Vyshko and Vyshemir, now and forever, as husband and consort, as Beloved Prince before the Pearl Throne of Hastinapura and High Prince of Eternal Isavalta.'

'Let Vyshko and Vyshemir hear,' intoned Keeper Bakhar. 'Let all pray to Vyshko and Vyshemir for their aid and blessing.'

Avanasy closed his eyes. He did not want to see the contentment glowing on Medeoan's face. He did not want to see the satisfaction of her parents.

Stop this. Stop her, he prayed, but whether he prayed to her mortal parents or immortal ones, he did not himself know.

No word broke the holy silence. There was only the rustle of cloth, the occasional sigh, and one badly suppressed cough. If the gods watched, they watched in silence.

'It is done, Avanasy,' said a quiet voice in his ear.

Avanasy stiffened. Slowly, refusing to betray any fear, he straightened and turned around. Behind him stood Captain Peshek Pachalkasyn Ursulvin, fresh and stern in his best uniform coat. Peshek's breastplate had been so brightly polished that Avanasy could see his own comical look of surprise in its surface. He gripped his poleax in one hand, and carried a bundle of cloth in the other.

No words came to Avanasy so he just spread his hands. In response, Peshek shook his head.

'Our good keeper thought you might need help getting out of here today.' He pressed the bundle into Avanasy's hands. 'Put this on.'

The bundle proved to be a guard's coat and helmet. Through the door, Avanasy heard Keeper Bakhar speaking again, extolling all the duties of a virtuous consort toward their sovereign. To be strong, to be constant, to bend mind and skill to the service of the sovereign, who in turn would shape them to work the good of Eternal Isavalta.

Yet, the solemn, celebratory words said to Avanasy only that all was done. No one mortal or divine had seen fit to intervene.

'You will be much more use to all of us alive,' said Peshek earnestly. 'You have friends enough, Avanasy. There are plenty among the high families who do not trust this treaty with Hastinapura. You can be well hidden.'

Avanasy shook his head. 'No. This is my fault. I accept my punishment.' He slung the coat on over his plain kaftan and pantaloons. Its hem brushed the top of his boots, hiding his everyday clothes. The helmet shadowed his face and Peshek passed him the pike to complete the hasty disguise.

'At least I will know you are alive somewhere, then,' muttered Peshek. 'Before you simply made a mistake. Now, you're playing the fool.'

As ever, there was too much truth in Peshek's words. 'Then let me play my role as I see fit.'

Peshek let out a derisive snort, but said nothing else. He held silent even as Avanasy turned back to his spy hole in the door and made himself look on Medeoan, his student, his responsibility, his sovereign, and his judge, one last time. A cluster of rose petals had fallen from her crown and lay like a puddle of blood beside the hem of her wedding gown. An omen? Avanasy did not know whether to wish it was so, or that it was not so. He only knew that he could stay no longer. Peshek, as he had been so many times before, was right in this. He should already have been gone, but he could not bear to leave while any hope remained. Now the choir raised its voice in song, and Medeoan stood on tiptoe to kiss Kacha full and warmly on the mouth. Now there would be prayers and more exhortations. Hours of ceremony were yet to come, and none of it meant anything. Medeoan had spoken her acceptance, and that was what mattered before the law and the gods.

Avanasy turned and nodded to Peshek. Peshek rolled his eyes heavenwards to say *finally*, but no word passed his lips. He simply led Avanasy through the vestry, silently opening the side door to the library and striding through. Peshek carried the authority of the House Guard in his straight back and measured gait. No door could be closed to him, especially today when it was so important that the palace be absolutely secure. Avanasy made himself copy Peshek's demeanor.

The library, with its long walls of books and windows, was deserted. Indeed, the whole palace was still. In the courtyard, the patrols of House Guards stood at attention. Even the servants had paused in their preparation of the feast so that their minds could be occupied in prayer and thanksgiving for the wedding they were not allowed to witness because there was no room left in the god house. None would stir until the bells rang. None but himself and Peshek, who would die as surely as Avanasy would if they were caught now. The realization that Peshek's safety hung in the balance put speed into Avanasy's steps. If he should die, that was one thing, but Peshek was loyal to Medeoan and Isavalta, and she was going to need such loyalty.

Outside, the spring sun was warm, but the breezes were chill. For all it was beginning to deck itself out in green and blossomed finery, the world still remembered winter. The canal that flowed past the marble steps of the palace had thawed, however, and it had been a full two weeks since word had come to him that the ice on the great river had cleared. That was all that mattered. He could leave now, leave Eternal Isavalta, leave the world and sail for the shores that waited beyond the Land of Death and Spirit. There he would never have to hear the name of Medeoan spoken. There, only memory would speak of how she had turned on him, or how he had turned on her, and memory would fade.

Chapter One

Sand Island, Wisconsin, 1872

The bed frame creaked, and Ingrid Loftfield instantly opened her eyes. Moonlight streamed in through the mended curtains laying a silver skin across the room's sparse furnishings. It was more than enough to show Ingrid the silhouette of her sister Grace climbing out of their sagging bed. Unblinking, Grace rounded the bed's foot. Ingrid held her breath. Grace's hand strayed out to pick up her knitted shawl from where it hung on the post, but her eyes did not turn to see what her hand did. All her attention remained fixed on the bedroom door as she padded across the bare boards and out into the hall.

Ingrid kicked back the quilt and jumped to her feet. She pulled off her nightgown to reveal her dark skirt and work shirt. Her jaw firmly set, she bent down to stuff her feet into her worn boots.

Tonight she would find out what ailed her sister.

'She just wants a good shaking,' their brother Leo had announced.

'You're too free with the girl.' Papa had glowered at Mama. 'You should not let her go galloping across to Bayfield whenever she pleases. It's some man, you see if it isn't.'

'You must watch her, Ingrid,' Mama had whispered in the

17

back kitchen as she banked the fire for the night. 'The Devil's finally got to her.'

Devil or man, I will have my answer. Stepping as lightly as she could, Ingrid followed Grace into the hallway. Her sister was already down the stairs. Grace did not look back once as she slipped soundlessly out the front door.

Ingrid herself was halfway down the stairs when a floor-board creaked behind her. She twisted to see back over her shoulder. Her mother stood at the top of the stairs, a candle in her hand, and her face pale with some emotion Ingrid found she could not name.

'What is it, Mother?' she heard Papa's gravelly voice call.

'Nothing,' Mama called back. 'Nothing at all.'

Ingrid swallowed hard, and hurried out after her sister into the chill of the summer night. The brisk wind smelled of pine resin and the ever-present cold of Lake Superior. Grace all but flew down the footpath toward the rutted track that served as Eastbay's main road. Gathering up her hems, Ingrid followed, her teeth gritted until they ached.

Tonight we put a stop to this.

The settlement of Eastbay popped up here and there out of Sand Island's wilderness like a cluster of spring mushrooms. It called itself a town, but it was little more than a scattering of dwellings connected by meandering dirt paths. Despite the fat, full moon that lit the night, the houses seemed blind and distant. Even the forge squatted darkly back in the woods. The trees loomed large and all the night noises – the rustling, hooting, rushing sounds – filled in the empty spaces, leaving Ingrid with the unaccustomed sensation of being a trespasser. *This is not your place,* the whole world seemed to say to her. *Go back to your bed until the daylight comes. Leave her to us.*

But Grace hurried on before her, a pale ghost in her flannel nightdress, and Ingrid could not even think of turning back.

Mama was trusting her to find out what was happening, and to do it quickly. If Papa found out Grace had gone out of sight of the house, unaccompanied, at night, Grace's life would be made unbearable, whatever the reason turned out to be.

Grace's illness had begun in May, just as the island's short, late spring was beginning to warm toward summer. Grace had been across on the mainland in Bayfield, earning a little extra by doing for Mrs Hofstetter who had just been delivered of twins. Papa had objected to her going, but Grace had simply faced him with her sunny smile and said: 'Well, Papa, you can lock me in the shed if you choose, but unless you do, I'm going.'

Grace could do that. Grace could smile, and laugh, and glide her way through any storm of shouts or tears. Sometimes it was maddening, but most of the time Ingrid clung to her sister like a sailor clinging to a lifeline. She willingly shouldered Grace's share of the work around house and field so that Grace might go to Bayfield. So that Grace might keep that easy smile.

Then, a squall had come up, suddenly, as they would in the spring, and Everett Lederle had burst into the back kitchen to tell Ingrid he had seen a great, gray wave swamp the small tug carrying Grace back home.

Ingrid had run then too, her skirts hiked about her knees so she could keep pace with her father and brother, sprinting through the driving rain down to the bay to help launch the boats and bend her back to row against the waves toward where the tug had last been sighted.

Lake Superior was the provider for everyone on the island, but it was also their mutual enemy. No one would be left to its mercy while there was any chance she might be saved.

They pulled Frank and Todd Johanssen out of the frigid, grasping waters, but although they strained their eyes and shouted until their voices were hoarse, there was no sign of Grace.

Ingrid was blind with tears and rain when her father ordered them back to shore. Shaking, she'd climbed over the gunwale onto the sand, brushing aside all the hands that reached out to help. She would have to be steady when they told the little ones. Fiercely, she'd knuckled the water from her eyes, just in time to see a white shape burst from the gray lake. Leo saw it as well and threw himself into the water, grasping Grace by her shoulders before she could disappear beneath the surface again. Amid the cheers of their neighbors, Leo had dragged Grace shivering to the shore. Coats and oilskins had been thrown over her, and her family had led her home to a bright fire and a warm, dry bed.

She'd been sick for a time after that, to no one's surprise. Mama had tended her with mustard baths for her feet and strong tea for her stomach. After three weeks, though, Papa began to ask what could possibly still ail the girl, and Mama urged Grace to come to the breakfast table. Leo and Papa frowned, sure she must be better by now, and equally sure she was lazing. But Ingrid looked at Grace's pale cheeks, and saw how listlessly she picked at her porridge, and knew in the depths of her heart something was still wrong.

The color in Grace's cheeks did not return, nor did the saucy light that used to dance in her eyes. Instead, her skin remained as white as if she had just been pulled from the lake. If left to herself, she would stand at the front window gazing across the tiny, weed-choked yard. Mama or Ingrid could nag or cajole her into lending a hand with the work, but they found they had to keep a sharp eye on her, or her mind would drift and the copper tub for the laundry would be overturned, or on baking day the fire would be built so unevenly the loaves came out charred lumps.

'What is the matter with you, Grace?' Ingrid finally demanded in exasperation.

'I don't know,' said Grace, tears brimming in her dimmed eyes. 'I don't know.'

Ingrid hugged her sister hard then, and let the matter drop.

After another two weeks of this, over even Papa's grim objections, Mama summoned the doctor from Bayfield. He could find no crack in Grace's skull, nor any irregularity in her eyes, heart, or breath. Nor did he find what Ingrid suspected was the greatest fear – that Grace was with child. He simply counseled patience and packed up his black bag.

But that same night, Grace began walking in her sleep. They found her first in the front room, kneeling on the horse-hair settee and staring out the window. On the next night, she was standing in the front yard, staring hungrily at the closed gate. On the next, she was halfway down the track toward the bay, for all Mama had locked and barred the doors for the night. When they questioned Grace afterward, she could give no answer, no hint of a reason for her behavior. In fact, she stopped talking at all. During the day, she would not get out of bed unless lifted bodily. She would not eat. Only Ingrid sleeping in a chair before the front door kept her inside at night.

It was desperation that had made Ingrid decide to follow Grace instead of barring her way tonight. Papa was talking about sending Grace away, and Mama's tears told Ingrid that she would wail about such action, but she would not stop it. Mama's tears only came when she was not going to take any other step.

Now, the darkness itself seemed to part for Grace's effortless, hurrying feet. All the purpose that had drained from her during the daylight had returned and even when she took a sharp right turn off the road, her gait was sure and unhesitating. Ingrid was left to stump behind her, blessing the full moon and cursing the brambles and tree branches snatching at her hems and elbows.

Where are you going? Ingrid thought, torn between frustration at her sister's silent purpose, and fear that her noise would wake Grace from her trance at any moment. If Grace woke, she might simply return to her stupor, leaving Ingrid still without answers. *Much further and you'll be in the lake.*

Indeed, the shore was in sight. Lake Superior spread out black and silver below the gentle rise which Grace had climbed. Ingrid ducked behind a wild blueberry bush, catching her breath and narrowing her eyes suspiciously. *Grace, if this truly is because you are meeting some fisherman, it's not Leo you'll be getting your shaking from.*

The water was calm tonight, Ingrid noted. The moonlight highlighted only the barest ripples in the night-darkened water. She could just hear the sound of water lapping at the stones under the whisper of the wind through the trees. Grace paused for a moment on the top of the short bluff. In the light of the moon and a million stars, Ingrid saw her sister scan the shore, searching for she knew not what.

Then, Grace began to run, down the slope, right down to the narrow strip of sand at the water's edge. Ingrid peered between the branches of the spindly shrub that sheltered her and watched Grace kneel beside what appeared to be a large stone.

'I came.' Grace's voice drifted up to Ingrid on the chill, steady wind blowing off the lake. 'I promised I would.'

'Cold,' answered a shivery man's voice. 'So cold.'

Ingrid shot up to her full height, uncertain which of the two on the shore she was going to murder first. But even her sudden motion and all the noise of it did not cause Grace to turn her attention from the man beside her. While Ingrid stormed down the hill, every fiber in her tight with fury, Grace just took off her shawl and draped it across the man's shoulders.

'Is that better?' asked Grace.

The man was little more than a collection of indistinct planes and angles in the moonlight, but Ingrid saw him reach out one hand to pull the shawl more tightly around himself. 'I never dreamed it would be so cold.'

'Let me help you,' urged Grace.

Which was all Ingrid could take.

'Grace Hulda Loftfield, what do you think you're doing!' she shouted as she strode onto the sand.

The sound of her full name seemed finally to reach Grace. She tore her attention from the man. Ingrid planted herself before her sister, hands on hips. Grace stood slowly, her own hands dangling at her sides.

'Ingrid . . .' she breathed weakly, as if the strength that had brought her here had all flowed away.

'The whole family has been in an uproar for weeks!' cried Ingrid, flinging her arms wide. 'I thought you were ill, and all the while you were just waiting to sneak out to meet some man! Papa will thrash you within an inch of your life!' Ingrid rounded on the man. 'As for you, Sir . . .' and her voice froze in her throat.

The man had also stood up. He was sopping wet. Water dripped from the bedraggled ends of his curling hair. It ran in rivulets down his naked shoulders and his sodden canvas trousers to puddle around his bare feet. Grace's shawl clung to his shoulders, soaking up quarts of water. His chest was so sunken that Ingrid could see his ribs.

But it was not this that robbed her of her voice, nor was it even his hollow eyes or his gray skin. It was the silver sand behind him. Ingrid could see Grace's moonlit shadow spreading clearly across that sand. Beside her, the man cast no shadow at all.

'What are you?' Ingrid croaked. 'Grace, come here.' She stretched out her hand. 'Come away.'

'Ingrid . . .' said Grace, but she did not move. She just swayed in place.

'No,' said the man, whatever he was. He knotted the end of Grace's shawl in his gray fingers. 'Don't leave me, Grace. I beg you.'

'Come here, Grace,' ordered Ingrid, fear and dawning comprehension giving her voice strength. 'Now!'

Grace slumped her shoulders. 'I can't.'

The drowned man – against all reason, Ingrid knew that was what he was – clutched Grace's shawl even tighter. 'You promised you would help me. You promised you would not leave me here.'

'I won't.' Grace lifted her foot to take a step toward the drowned man, but Ingrid dodged between them.

'Leave her alone!' she cried. Now that she stood before the ghost, she felt the cold. It rolled off him in waves and bit straight into Ingrid's bones. It was a cold beyond winter, beyond ice, beyond the waters of Lake Superior. It froze her blood in her veins and threatened to reach through to her soul. Ingrid staggered backward, trying to push Grace more fully behind her. Then, because she could think of nothing else that might help, she began: 'Our Father who art in Heaven, hallowed be thy name . . .'

At the sound of the prayer, the drowned man's face twisted into a horrible scowl and a light came into the hollows of his eyes that filled Ingrid's heart with fresh fear.

'No!' shouted the ghost, and his voice was like the winds of a winter storm. 'There is no God where I am! He left me there in the dark but I will not stay! I will not stay!'

Ingrid snatched at Grace's hand and turned to run, but her sister might have been a block of marble for all Ingrid could shift her. The ghost now gripped Grace's shawl in both fists. 'She promised,' he said grimly.

'I did.' Grace's voice was as pale as her cheeks. 'I promised. Under the water.'

'She's mine.' The ghost slid closer.

'No.' Ingrid stepped back between them, trying to stiffen her spine against the all-consuming cold. 'Jesus, Joseph, and Mother Mary, help me. You shall not have her.'

'She's mine by her own promise. We made a bargain. No name can keep her from me.'

The ghost reached out and Ingrid pressed back against her unmoving, unmovable sister. Her heart beat in wild terror at the idea that the apparition and all the cold he carried might reach straight through her and engulf Grace as if Ingrid were not even there.

A flash of movement caught Ingrid's eye. A fresh shadow dashed headlong down the beach. Moonlight glinted on metal as the new shape leapt forward. Ingrid opened her mouth to scream as the knife blade came down. With all her strength she threw herself backward, knocking Grace to the sand. The ghost's cold rushed over them, and for a time, Ingrid knew nothing more.

Ingrid woke to the scent and sound of a fire. She lay on her side, her back against the bracken-covered slope that led to the shore. A smoky blaze smelling of pine and moldering drift-wood burned on the sand and a man's form sat beside it. Stiff with cold and damp, Ingrid pushed herself upright immediately. As she did, she saw Grace, also lying on her side, her fair head pillowed by her own arm.

Ignoring the man, Ingrid crawled to her sister, laying an anxious hand on Grace's throat. Fresh relief washed through her as she felt the warmth of Grace's skin, the beat of her heart, and the slow draw of her breath. Only then did Ingrid lift her eyes to meet the gaze of the man beside them.

The moon had set, so she had only the fire to see him by. The resinous, red-gold light showed her a lined face with a hawk nose and deep-set eyes. She could not make out their color. The hair swept back under his fisherman's cap was a dark gold, and his hands, although tanned, showed themselves to be surprisingly long fingered and delicate as he reached for a fresh piece of driftwood. He broke the branch easily in two before tossing it onto the small fire and raising a fresh shower of sparks.

Ingrid was suddenly extremely conscious that she was rumpled, and half-covered in sand. In the next heartbeat, she cursed herself for such ridiculous vanity, especially at such a moment.

'Thank you for your help and company, Sir.' Ingrid attempted to gather her composure and her manners. 'My sister has not been well, and . . .' she dropped her gaze to the fire, intending to find some sort of lie to explain how two young women came to be out on the shore after dark. As she did, she saw the scraps of knitting among the ashes of the fire, and realized that they belonged to Grace's shawl.

The man followed her gaze with his own. He gave a tight smile that was at once amused and grim. Before Ingrid could recover herself, he asked, 'How long has this haunt plagued your sister?'

Ingrid opened her mouth and closed it again. She had absolutely no desire to speak of this to a total stranger. In truth, she had no desire even to remember it. She felt her mind scrabbling for rational explanations. She knew she could give in to them quite easily. There had been tricks of shadow and moonlight. Grace was simply more ill than anyone had realized. She needed the doctor again. She needed a rest. That was all.

The only problem with any of those thoughts was that Ingrid knew they were all lies.

'About two months,' she made herself say. 'Why did you burn her shawl?'

'The ghost touched it,' said the man as if it were the simplest reason in the world. 'If it was not destroyed, it could be used as a talisman against her.'

Ingrid felt her throat tighten. 'Grace touched the . . . ghost.' *Say it. Call it what it is. It is ridiculous. It is impossible. It is also the truth.*

The man nodded, all trace of the smile gone from his face. 'I thought she might have.'

Ingrid brushed Grace's hair back from her cheek. Grace did not stir at all, even as Ingrid stroked her shoulder and arm. 'Will she be all right now?'

'No,' said the man matter-of-factly. 'I am afraid after this she will be much worse.'

The answer sent a stab of anger through Ingrid, but she suppressed it. 'What must be done, then?'

The man turned his eyes from her, back toward the flames. 'I don't know,' he said. 'I wish very much that I did.'

'I see.'

They sat in silence for a moment. The man appeared to be ready to stare calmly into the fire until Kingdom Come, but Ingrid felt no such composure. Part of her was frightened and angry about this stranger and his pronouncements. Part of her was already shivering from imaginings of what Papa and Leo would do if Grace were caught out. Then there would be the scenes with Mama, and then if Grace got much sicker . . .

Mama might not send for the doctor again, not after last time.

Yet another part of her was still reeling with disbelief at all that had happened, and desperately seeking a way to deny it, but, here she was, in the slowly dying night, and here was Grace unconscious beside her. She knew a hundred ghost stories, of course. She had entertained all her siblings as they were growing up with stories of drowned men, sunken ships, strange lights, and seers who predicted disaster. She'd heard the men speak of mystic dreams, and of the Indians with their hosts of goblins, the Windego, the Bear Walker and Nanabush. These were part of her world, like Lake Superior surrounding her island home, but not this . . . this . . . thing that laid claim to her sister.

'Who are you?' she made herself ask the man. She had to root herself in the here and now. She could not let the coming daylight lull her into disbelief.

'My name is Avan.'

The name struck a chord with Ingrid. She had heard it from her father and Leo. He was a new man, come up for the fishing season. He was good with the boats. That brief statement from Papa was like a soliloquy of praise coming from another man. Leo had thought he was a Finn, although he had been vague about his origins. Papa had gone out with him two or three times now.

The realization should have been reassuring, but it was not.

'What brought you out so late?' asked Ingrid.

'Luck,' he said, poking at the ashes with a long stick, tucking the remains of Grace's shawl deeper into the coals. 'I could not sleep for too much thinking. I walked along the shore, and I saw you and your sister, and the ghost.' He paused, watching the sparks and smoke rise from the damp wood. 'That was brave, what you did. It should have worked, but I fear your sister has given this dead man too much.'

'But you were able to drive him . . . it . . . off. I saw a knife.'

'You did.' Avan reached inside his coat, and pulled out a short-bladed knife that glinted dully in the firelight. Ingrid stared, for she had never seen such a thing. The dark blade was not all of a piece. Instead, it was three separate strips of metal, braided together and twisted into a wicked-looking point.

'The blade is cold iron,' he said. 'Such is supposed to have power over spirits and haunts. I was glad . . .' he broke off the sentence, and began it again. 'I was glad to find out such sayings were true.'

'And is the haunt gone then?'

'Only for tonight. The iron tore your sister's shawl, which was holding him here despite your calling her and the holy names you invoked. But he himself is not injured, nor could he be by such means.' Avan looked at the blade with an expression of regret, and then tucked it back into his jacket.

'And how did you come to know so much?'

'I was well taught as a boy.'

Which was no answer, and Ingrid saw in his face that he was clearly aware of the fact.

Before she could ask another question, Grace stirred under her hand. She gasped once, sharply, as if in pain, and her eyelids flew open.

'Where . . .' Grace pushed herself upright. Ingrid expected her next words to be 'am I?' Instead, Grace stared wildly toward the lake. 'Where is he?'

Ingrid knelt down in front of her sister, putting her body between Grace and the water as she had put herself between Grace and the ghost. 'Who is he?' she demanded, grasping her sister's shoulders. 'What has he done to you?'

Grace's eyes searched Ingrid's face without recognition for a long, painful moment. 'He is cold,' she said. She spoke slowly, dragging each word from somewhere deep inside her. 'He saved me. I would have drowned, but he freed me from the water. I promised I would not leave him alone under there.'

'Ask her if he told her his name.'

Ingrid started, almost letting go of Grace. For a moment she had forgotten Avan. She frowned at him.

He had laid his stick across his knees. 'She will not be able to hear me. She is too far gone to hear any but those of her own blood.'

Ingrid nodded once, as if she understood what was happening. She tried to catch Grace's gaze again, but Grace was staring over her shoulder, searching for the ghost. Ingrid grasped her sister's chin as if she were still a child, and pulled it back down so that Grace would be forced to look at her.

'Grace, what is his name?'

Again, that heartbreaking pause while Grace came at least a small ways back to herself. 'I don't know. I just know I promised. He's alone. It's so cold.'

Grace began to tremble, and Ingrid's determination to find immediate answers melted away. She wrapped her arms around Grace's shoulder. 'This is no good. I have to get her home. Our family will be . . . frantic.'

'Yes.' Avan stood, still keeping hold of the stick. 'Can you manage her?'

'Since she was in diapers,' replied Ingrid. She stood, keeping a firm grip on Grace's shoulders. Grace struggled briefly, which Ingrid found she expected from the way Grace's gaze would not leave the shore. But Grace seemed to lack the will to fight for long, and sagged against Ingrid's chest. 'Although I wish this were as simple,' Ingrid breathed.

Ingrid found herself grateful that Avan pretended he did not hear that.

Avan let Ingrid lead the way, holding tight to Grace and pulling her forward one staggering step at a time. The further they moved from the shore, the weaker Grace seemed to become until Ingrid found herself supporting her sister's entire weight. She looked toward Avan, intending to ask for help, but then she saw the way he walked, stiff and alert, his arms ready at his side, clutching the stick the way he had clutched the knife. He walked like a soldier, she thought, as if he was expecting an ambush. Perhaps he was. The thought of that sent a fresh thrill of fear through her, and Ingrid kept her mouth closed.

She had no choice but to stick to the road, although dawn was turning the sky silvery gray and soon the men and boys would come trooping down the rutted track to the bay and the boats. They already thought Grace struck down by madness. They would stare, and they would talk.

Well, the Devil take them if they do. Ingrid found she felt far more worried about what she would tell their family. It was already too late to disguise the disappearance. If she told what had really happened, Mama would insist on a priest. Under the circumstances, there could be worse ideas. Papa, though . . . What would Papa think? He had been raised a strict Lutheran, and it came out of him at odd times. There would be words with Leo, no matter what happened. And what on earth would they tell the little ones?

'You must persuade your family not to try to send her away,' said Avan, as if reading Ingrid's thoughts.

'Why not? She's not safe . . .'

'I fear no boat with her aboard would make it across the lake.'

Ingrid felt her cheeks go pale. The words 'is that possible?' hovered on the tip of her tongue. Of course it was possible. If all the other things that had happened tonight were possible, so was this.

'But you don't know,' she said, cradling Grace's lolling head closer against her shoulder.

'I know she's being called. I know that in a moment of fearing for her life she bound herself to a dead man. I know that he will not let go that bond easily, and that he is restless under the water.'

'Then what are we to do? We cannot surrender her to this . . . thing.'

'No.' Avan hung his head and was silent for a long moment. Ingrid could not see his face well in the morning shadows, but she felt he was reaching some decision. 'Give me a day. I will find an answer.'

Ingrid looked down at her fainting sister. It wrenched at her heart to see Grace so worn down, and in such a way. Mama had spoken softly of her fear that Grace's boisterous nature might lead her astray, but this . . .

At the same time she distrusted the stranger. There should be a priest, there should be a doctor . . . but then again it was Avan who had banished the ghost.

'Ingrid? Ingrid!'

Papa's harsh voice called from the morning shadows, followed quickly by the sound of heavy boots pounding the dirt road.

'I will do what I can,' she breathed quickly.

Papa, Leo, pale Mama, and what seemed like all the men of Eastbay poured up the road.

'Och, Gott!' Papa cried, seeing Grace collapsed against Ingrid's shoulder. He swept his second daughter up in his strong arms as if she weighed nothing at all. Mama laid her hands on Grace's brow.

'No fever, but her breath's so shallow . . .'

'What happened, Ingrid?' demanded Leo. 'What did you see?'

Ingrid glanced at Avan, and she shouldn't have. Leo saw, and Leo, of course, jumped to the wrong conclusion. 'What've you to do with this?' he demanded, stalking up to Avan.

Avan looked down at Leo, and for one of the few times in her life, Ingrid saw her brother looking spindly. 'Your elder sister found your younger on the shore near the bay. She enlisted my help to bring her safe home.'

'If we find Grace's been meddled with . . .'

'Leo!' thundered Papa. 'Enough. Excuse him, Avan.'

Leo did not appear to wish to be excused, but he did keep his mouth shut.

'There's nothing to excuse.' Avan held his hand out, and waited. Leo, glowering still, shook it, and the tension in the air eased a little.

'What are you fools standing about in the damp for?' demanded Mama with unusual brusqueness. 'Is she not sick enough for you? Get inside, get inside, and you as well, Miss Ingrid.' Mama also had a hard glare for Avan, but it was plain to Ingrid it was not Grace she thought he might wish to meddle with.

Under the eyes of their neighbors, the Loftfields turned for home. Offers of assistance came, and were rebuffed by Mama and Papa.

'Thank you for your help, Mr Avan,' said Ingrid, careful not to look back at him as she followed her parents and brother. She realized absurdly that she did not know for certain if Avan was his Christian name, or his family name. One more small mystery of this long, strange night.

As they neared the yard, Grace moaned and stirred in her father's arms. When they were all inside the front room, Papa set her on her feet and Grace stood, swaying in place.

'Take her upstairs, Mother,' said Papa softly.

'I'll do it.' Ingrid moved forward.

'No, you will not.' Papa's cold words stopped her in her tracks.

Mama, her eyes already brimming with tears, took Grace's elbow. Grace offered no resistance as she was led away, but Ingrid thought she saw her sister's eyes flicker back, looking for her, pleading for help.

Ingrid swallowed and faced her father and brother. They were both square men, fair-skinned and auburn-haired, as she was. Hard men, shaped by labor and by the expectation of hard work and hard weather for the rest of their lives. The stubble on Papa's chin had gone gray, and his hands were thick with years of calluses.

Ingrid stiffened her spine, ready for whatever might come. It was then she saw the eyes of her two littlest sisters and their young brother peeping through the door to the back kitchen.

'Well there's a fine thing,' she said. 'All of you listening at doors when there's work to be done. The kindling is not gathering itself, nor are the hens going to give up their eggs without asking.'

'Out into the yard, all of you,' added Papa without taking his eyes off Ingrid.

The door swung shut as the children retreated.

'Now then, Miss,' began Papa. 'What do you have to say for yourself?'

'I thought to see where Grace was trying to go,' replied Ingrid steadily, folding her hands in front of herself like a child saying a lesson.

'You thought!' snorted Leo. 'You thought to humiliate us in front of all our neighbors. There won't be a man on the boats not asking me when you and Grace can come out again.'

'Such a trial for you,' snapped Ingrid. 'I am so sorry that your sister's illness has brought you to such grief.'

Leo took a step forward. 'If she were ill, I would grieve. But she is either shamming, or she is mad, and you had to make sure the whole of Eastbay knew it.'

Ingrid did not even blink. 'The whole of Eastbay does know it! What do we think we're hiding in here? They'd help us if we let them, but no, we have to stay shut up in our house and deny our neighbors' concern.'

'That's enough.' Papa dragged the words out through gritted teeth. 'You will tell me which of you the man Avan has to answer for.'

Ingrid said nothing. She had known the question would come, but now that it hung in the air, anger sealed her mouth.

Is that all you think of us? Of her? Is that what you think of any woman who smiles?

'Answer your father.' Mama stood at the foot of the stairs. She wore her black hair pulled into a severe bun, and at the moment her bright blue eyes were dim with disappointment and resignation. She had been an Irish beauty once, Ingrid was sure of it. What had happened? In her heart, she believed she knew, but she had never been able to speak the words aloud.

'Answer him!' Mama clenched her fists. 'Or has the Devil taken your tongue as well?'

Ingrid forced her chin up. She had only two choices now, she could either lie, or she could tell the ludicrous truth.

'It was a ghost,' Ingrid said. 'Grace is haunted.'

Leo threw up his hands. 'God in Heaven!' he cried to the ceiling. 'Are all the women in this family mad?'

'You asked what happened, and I've told you,' answered Ingrid, calmly and firmly. 'You can call me mad, or possessed, or any other name your stubborn mind can conjure up, Leonard Loftfield. It changes nothing, so you may as well save your breath.'

Hot, hard anger showed plain on Mama's face. She was going to start yelling in Irish and Papa would bellow back in German and Ingrid would have to shout at them both, or retreat with the little ones out back, when what she wanted was to go up to check on Grace.

But Mama did not yell. She just collapsed on the reed-bottomed rocker beside the fire, and hid her face in her apron. 'Mother Mary, help your daughter,' she whispered. 'Jesus, Mary and Joseph, help your child.'

'That's enough of that, Bridget Loftfield.' Papa walked up to Ingrid, and all at once, Ingrid was a little girl again and she had to work hard not to shrink in on herself. 'I've thought many things about my children, but I never thought you would be the liar.'

'You also can call me what you want. I've told you the truth.'

They stared at each other, neither one blinking, and Ingrid refusing to flinch. Behind them, she was aware of Mama in the rocker, her hands covering her face. Mama believed, and that was something. Surely that was something.

At last, Papa turned away. 'Get into the kitchen. There's work to be done. Leo, it's time we were gone.'

Ingrid turned and marched into the back kitchen. Once there, she gripped the edge of the table so hard she felt that it must break off in her fingers. She listened to the tramp of the men's boots as they marched out the front door. There was no other sound from inside the house, except the faint squeak of the rocker where Mama sat and wept her useless tears.

For a long moment, Ingrid let her anger burn. Then, at last, she willed it out of her, willed it through her hands down into the wood of the table, anything to get it away from her. It did her no good. It was as useless as Mama's tears. She had to think. She had to decide what to do.

A knock on the lintel made her jump. Her hand pressed against her chest, she looked up to see Everett Lederle standing at the threshold.

'Hello, Everett.'

'Hello, Ingrid,' he said, pulling off the battered, blue cap he'd worn since he'd come back from the war. 'I heard Grace had a rough night. I wanted to see if there was anything I could do.'

Hard labor and time had worked their way with Everett, like they had the men of her family, but with him it was different. Him, they had polished, like a stone on the shore, making him strong, patient, willing to let all the world flow around him and ever able to wait. He was certainly willing to wait for her. Everett loved her. She saw it in every look and heard it in every word. The shame of it was, she found herself unable to return that love.

'No, I'm afraid there's nothing to be done at present,' she told him. 'But I thank you for stopping in.'

'I'm glad to, Ingrid, you know that.'

And she looked at him, earnest, steady, strong and thoughtful, and for her lack of love of him she felt suddenly, deeply sorry. 'I do know, Everett, and as I said, I thank you for it.'

He waited a long moment for her to say something else, but she had no more words for him, at least, she had none he truly wanted to hear. But perhaps, after all, there was something he could do.

'Everett, there may be something.' *I should not do this. I should not use him so. It will give him false hope.* Ingrid could not love. To love would mean to leave Grace to be worn down by the burden of caring for their hard family. She'd thought of it, of course, she'd thought of it a hundred times. Everett would at least take her to another house, but to promise him love when she felt none, that would be so much worse than what she did now. 'I need you to speak with the fisherman Avan tomorrow. I need to know if he has any message or news for

me. He knows what ails Grace, and I would know if there was
. . . news.'

She saw the curiosity in Everett's face, and she saw disappointment. He did not want to be running errands to another man for her. But he said nothing of that. 'If that will help, that's what I'll do.'

For a moment, Ingrid thought to squeeze his hand in gratitude. But no, she knew how he would take that, and he would take it wrongly. 'It will. Thank you, Everett.'

Everett nodded, put his cap back on his dark head and stepped away across the yard. He was too late to catch the boats going out. He had lost himself today's work to come here to her.

Why do I not love him? Ingrid closed her eyes, and there in her private darkness, she saw Avan in the firelight, and she saw his long, graceful hands. Swiftly, she opened her eyes again, and went upstairs to Grace.

Grace lay still as a corpse under the faded quilts, her unbound hair spread out on the pillow showing the snarls the night wind had teased into it. Her eyes were opened, but Ingrid had no idea what she saw.

Ingrid sat on the edge of the bed and picked up the comb that lay on the chest. Slowly, gently, she began to run it through her sister's hair, singing softly.

'Hushaby, don't you cry.
'Go to sleepy, little baby.
'When you wake, you shall have,
'All the pretty little horses.'

'Ingrid?' Grace's voice was little more than a whisper.

'Yes, Grace. I'm here.'

'I didn't mean to . . . I was under the water. It was so heavy, I was so tired. I was afraid I would drown. My lungs were freezing. He held me. He told me he would keep me safe. I cried to go home. He said I could, but that I must promise to come back. He was so lonely. I promised.' She paused, and her chest heaved in a silent sob. 'I don't want to go, Ingrid.'

'You will not go.' Ingrid gently teased out one more snarl. 'I promise.'

'He calls me. He calls me by my promise and he is never quiet. I didn't know before, but I do now, and he calls . . .'

Ingrid gripped her sister's shoulder. 'Do not listen to him, Grace. He had no right to bind you so. You must not listen.'

'So cold.'

Ingrid bit her lip to hear how much her sister sounded like the ghost. She wrapped her arms around Grace and held her close, rocking gently back and forth. 'He will not have you, sister. I swear by God in Heaven he will not have you.'

Avanasy watched Ingrid Loftfield fall into step with her family, her back straight, and her hands gathering up her hems to keep them out of the way of her long, swinging stride. Her auburn hair had come loose during her night's adventures, and fell in dark curls down the back of her neck.

'Well, well, the one that got away, eh?' A hand slapped him hard on the shoulder. He turned his eyes from Ingrid to see Roman Thorfeld, a bony, blue-eyed man grinning at him, showing all his tobacco-stained teeth. Avanasy cursed himself for staring too long.

'I was just thinkin' about her poor sister,' he said mildly, falling into the low speech the fishermen favored. 'Gone right out of her head, I figger.'

'*Ja, ja.*' Thorfeld, like a number of the men grown up on the shores of Lake Superior seemed to speak a blend of three or four different languages. He was not a vicious man, just of a coarse upbringing, and now he shook his head heavily. "S a shame too.

They're good people, the Loftfields. 'S a sorry shame.'

'And we're doin' nuthin' 't all for 'em by standin' here,' announced Elias Ilkka, a squat, dark Finn, tough as tarred rope and the nominal leader of the itinerant fishermen who clung to the shore of Sand Island. 'Let's get to it, boys.'

The men voiced their agreement in their various tongues, and trooped to the docks in a mass. Avanasy stayed with them. It was not what he wanted, but he feared that if he begged off it would direct more talk at the Loftfields and plenty of that already swirled around him. Every incident, every encounter or interaction, especially involving the unfortunate Grace, was remembered, kicked over, examined and improved upon. It went on all through the day, even out on the gray waters with the sharp wind pouring over them and all the work of rope, sail, net and the great loads of silver-blue fish to attend to. Omens for the misbegotten voyage were remembered, and Grace's wild ways. Her mother was a Catholic, it was said repeatedly, with many a sagacious nod, and her sister, at twenty-four, showed no signs of marrying, even with Everett Lederle hanging about her door like a hungry dog.

With all this talk, all of it relishing, all of it wrong, Avanasy found it hard to lose himself in the work, as he usually did. By the time they came in at late afternoon, it was all he could do to make himself help with sluicing the decks and hanging the nets up to dry. As soon as he was able he retreated to the shack on the shore where he lived amidst a cluster of other fishers, each in their own summer dwelling. Come winter they would all head across to the mainland and turn to timbering for the season.

Come winter, what will you do? Avanasy dropped into his rough chair and stared at the banked coals in his tin stove.

After a time, he got up, poked the fire to life, put the remainder of the morning coffee on to heat, and lit his pipe with a splinter. He'd acquired the habit of both the brew and the bowl shortly after coming here, observing them to be the norm for the men around him, and he had to admit he found them both pleasant enough, if harsh. Like the back-breaking work on the boats, there was a rough enjoyment to be had in them, along with the singing, the gossip, the drink and the wild beauty of the islands. He'd thought himself content. Not comfortable, to be sure, and there were days when the easy familiarity of his fellow fishers could still slap up hard against his pride. But content. Content enough.

Until last night.

He'd lied when he told Ingrid he'd been awake for too much thinking. He'd woken because he'd felt a change in the air. Something unchancy, Roman Thorfeld would have called it, and that was as good a word as any. He'd felt such things before in this world on the far shore of the Land of Death and Spirit, but those sensations had been fleeting, momentary brushes with whatever spirit powers this world held. He'd felt nothing so strong and so steady since he'd left Isavalta. All his blood sang in his veins at the touch of power, real power, and he'd gone to meet it like a lover.

There he'd found Ingrid Loftfield facing down a dead man, and about to die herself for it.

He hadn't even thought. He'd drawn his knife, and charged. Thankfully, the ghost had with him something of the living world it was using as an anchor, or else Avanasy would have done little more with his blade than annoyed it.

Not that the burning of that shawl has driven it off for more than one night. Avanasy sucked on the stem of his pipe, noticing only absently that its fire had gone out.

He had not worked any magic since three days after he landed here. He'd woven himself a simple spell of under-standing that he might speak with the people who now surrounded him. At least, it should have been simple, requiring that he take pains and be precise in his workings, yes, but otherwise it should have been of no great moment. But the effort of it had laid him low for almost a whole day. Among the many strangenesses of this world was this truth – that the magic was buried deep in the fabric of soul and soil and it would be coaxed out only with great reluctance. So, Avanasy had abandoned the work of magic for the work of fishing. It had seemed no great sacrifice. He had believed that exile and Medeoan's turning away had left him with little desire to continue as a sorcerer.

But then had come that touch of the other world last night, the brush of power, and he'd woken hungry for it. No, ravenous. It could have been anything, any monster, any trickster, anything at all, and if Ingrid and Grace had not been there to bring his other instincts into play, he might have done anything at all to keep it by him, to feel that touch of power that his blood so missed.

'I spent my life telling Medeoan she could not change what she was,' he murmured to the fire. 'It seems I did not listen to my own good teachings.'

And I have given my word to help, he chewed on the stem of the pipe. He did not move to relight it. What did his word mean here? The word of a fisherman? The word of Avan? Nothing. He was no one in this place, with neither reputation nor honor to guard, and better off so. Power, and the revelation of power, could endanger him, forcing him further away into this world.

And the next time a power finds you? How much worse will it be next time?

Avanasy sighed. He removed his pipe from his mouth, knocked it out against the edge of the tin can he kept for the purpose, and stood. In the corner of his shack waited a heavy wooden chest which he kept locked with an iron lock, and which he now opened with an iron key he wore on a thong around his neck.

Inside lay his old clothes and boots, wrapped in oiled brown paper he'd purchased after his arrival, along with some gold stored up against emergencies, and three silken scarves, woven with his own hands, each of them tied with a different knot.

Avanasy chose the blue scarf, and tucked it into the pocket of his coat. After locking the chest again, he turned to consider the contents of his cabin. He really should have wine for this, but there was none. He set some fresh coffee on to brew, wrapped up a packet of tobacco and his spare pipe, and set out some bread and smoked fish on the least battered of his tin plates. Rough fare, but the best hospitality he had, and that was what would count.

As the coffee finished, he went outside and laid a fire on the sand, lighting it with kindling of pine needles and splintered driftwood. The night was silent, except for the noises of wind and water. The other huts were dark, the men within them snoring loudly in their sleep. Avanasy laid his offerings out on the far side of the blaze and drew the scarf from his pocket. He spat on the knot and breathed across it, and tossed the scarf into the fire.

For a moment the fire burned bright blue, and a shower of sapphire sparks rose from the flames, then it shone red, and then white, but gradually, the pure white light faded, and the fire glowed golden again, as if it were nothing more than a blaze of driftwood. Avan sat down on a stone, and waited.

The moon had worked its way another inch up the dome of the sky when the rabbit came hopping down the beach. Its round black eyes reflected the firelight as it advanced, hopping tentatively forward a few inches at a time, pausing to sniff the air. At last, it sat up on its haunches, combing its ears and twitching its whiskers.

Avanasy stood, and reverenced in his best courtly manner to the creature.

'I would be honored, Sir, on this chill night, if you would join me at my fire, and share my poor fare.'

The rabbit cocked its head to one side, considering. Then it hopped up to the plate bearing the smoked fish and bread. It used its teeth to drag one scrap of bread off the plate, and began to eat. It ate all that bread, and the next piece, and the next, and then all the fish.

Then, it ate the plate.

Avanasy held himself very still. The rabbit advanced on the tobacco snuffling it eagerly, drew a leaf out and ate that, and the paper it was wrapped in, and the pipe. Still, Avanasy did not blink, although he could not hold back some regret that he was about to lose his coffee pot. The rabbit stuffed its face into the coffee mug and drank it dry, swallowing the cup whole when it was finished. It knocked over the pot with one blow of its paw and crawled halfway inside, guzzling up the hot brew.

Then, to Avanasy's mild surprise, it withdrew its head, and sat up again on its haunches. And it was no longer a rabbit. Instead, it was a fat little man with copper skin and black hair bound in thongs hanging down past his shoulders. His ears were as long as his hair, and the lobes dangled down to his chest. His face was merry, and he smelled of sweat, tobacco, and coffee.

He belched loudly, the force of it shaking his long earlobes and making his round belly bounce. 'You're a long way from home, I think, Magician,' he said.

Avanasy bowed his head in acknowledgment. 'I am, Sir.'

'And why have you come so far to set out such a feast for

Nanabush, eh?' He leaned forward. 'Must want something, eh?'

Again, Avanasy bowed. 'I have heard it said it is ever the way with us.'

'Ha! Too true. Now, let me see if I can guess what ails you.' Nanabush tugged at one pendulous earlobe. 'There's a ghost, and there's a girl, and she's a fool and he's a bigger one, and you're the biggest fool of the three.'

Avanasy said nothing.

Nanabush spat in the fire. 'Knots and bindings, nets and weavings, that's your business, and you want Nanabush to tell you how to get yourself untangled.'

'Is there a way within my power to remove the haunting from the Loftfield family?'

'Nets and knots with you,' said Nanabush, picking up the coffee pot and squinting inside with one round eye to inspect the bottom for more liquid. 'Always nets and knots. Poor tangled magician.'

Avanasy reminded himself of the absolute need for patience. 'I believe I have had dealings with a relation of yours. She is Queen of the *lokai*, the fox spirits, in my homeland.'

'The Vixen. Yes.' Nanabush held the spout of the coffee pot over his wide open mouth and let the last drop of liquid fall in. 'She speaks of you.' He smacked his lips loudly and belched again.

'Of your courtesy, tender her my best respect.'

Nanabush stuffed his fist into the coffee pot, running one fat finger down along the bottom. 'She says if you stay here you will live longer.'

'I thank you for that news.'

'Poor tangled magician.' Nanabush sucked on his finger thoughtfully. 'You fish. I've seen you.'

Avanasy bowed. 'It allows me to earn my keep.'

'And it is not that different from shore to shore?'

'No, but one must know the waters.'

Nanabush raised his finger to make his point. 'And the fish themselves.'

He was getting close to an answer. Avanasy could feel it, but he must not appear too eager. 'I have heard, Sir, that you know the waters and the fish better than any.'

'Ha! It's true, it's true.' Nanabush tapped his finger on the edge of the coffee pot. 'These waters are deep, and they're dark. Many a soul is lost down there looking for the fish.'

'So I have heard,' said Avanasy gravely.

'But it's not just the soul that one must find.' Nanabush shook his head, his earlobes flapping and flopping against his chest. 'No. It's the bones. The bones of the fish that must be found and warmed. Bones bind as tight as any net.'

'There is great wisdom in what you say.'

'Ha! You will profit from listening to Nanabush.' He shook his ears, tossing his lobes over his shoulders. 'But others listen too. And others know things. The fish know that the dark of the moon is the time for fishermen, and they know that is the time for catching little fish, as well as big fish.'

'Things do not so much differ from shore to shore.'

'Not as much as some might think.' Nanabush contemplated the coffee pot one more time, then dropped it onto the sand and kicked it across to Avanasy. 'Nets and knots. Stay clear of the bindings and you'll live longer.' His eyes twinkled. 'Unless, of course, it is the bindings and their undoing that save your life.'

Then there was only the rabbit, hieing itself fast across the sand and disappearing into the brush. Then, there was only Avanasy and his fire, and his empty coffee pot.

Avanasy picked up the pot. Well now he knew. Perhaps he knew too much. That was the risk of calling upon the spirits. He knew he could save Grace Loftfield. He had to raise the bones of the ghost at the dark of the moon, the very night the ghost would call Grace to him for the final, fatal time.

But, he also knew that should he ever return to Isavalta he would die. Unless, of course, he should live.

Nets and knots. Poor tangled magician.

Chapter Two

Medeoan stood at her mother's bedside and willed her to keep breathing.

The Empress's private chamber was dark except for the light from the two braziers burning their pungent mixtures of charcoal and cleansing herbs which the physicians had prescribed as an attempt to clear the mucus from the Empress's lungs.

Without daylight, the rich apartment seemed as robbed of its vitality as the woman lying still and sallow under the layers of goose down and royal-blue velvet. The skin sagged around her throat and jowls, hanging in folds like the heavy curtains around her bed.

At least her eyes were still open, thought Medeoan as she reached out to try to smooth her mother's burning brow. At least some small sound still escaped her throat. Father lay in his own fever as if already dead. None of Medeoan's tears or pleading could rouse in him any sign of life.

The waiting ladies had all retreated to give Medeoan and Kacha a moment in relative privacy with her mother, and now those ladies stood in the shadows like ghosts waiting to come out and lay claim to the dying Empress. Medeoan remembered as a little girl being brought by her nurse before those five ladies, and not being sure which one she was supposed to reverence to and call Mother. She had burst into tears at her confusion. The closest, tallest lady, this lady who lay so slack in her bed, had come forward and taken her hand.

'There, there,' she'd said, smoothing Medeoan's fingers. 'Don't cry. A great prince never cries where others can see, and you, my daughter, will be a great prince.'

But not yet. Not yet. Medeoan's throat tightened, even as she forced herself to gently cradle her mother's hand. *I will save you. I promise.*

Normally, Medeoan's sorceries were kept out of sight. She was well-trained, yes, and well-read and she knew her own strength. But her actions were to be those of the mortal world whenever possible. No one, Father had said in a particularly blunt moment, wanted a ruler who appeared to strive for more than mortal greatness. But all that was laid aside for this. The court sorcerers had proven themselves useless in this matter. If there was to be magical aid for her languishing parents, the task fell to Medeoan. Already she had worn her fingers to the nub from two days of preparations while the others milled about trying to trap the life that spilled from the Imperial vessels.

You cannot die yet. I'm not ready. I will not permit it.

As Medeoan straightened up, Kacha pressed close behind her, reminding her of his warm presence, and trying to ease her shivering.

Medeoan kissed her mother's hand. The skin was far too hot against her dry lips. 'You must bear with this for a little while longer, Mother.' She tried to keep her voice steady. Mother's eyes were wide and shining with their fever. The Empress let her head fall sideways so that she could look at her daughter, but the only sound she could make was a rasping cough. The physics said that the fever had swollen her tongue so that speech was impossible.

Kacha held Medeoan close, without care for the eyes of the ladies who surely watched them from their places in the shadows. He lifted her hand from her mother's, his thoughts, as ever, all for her.

'You have cut yourself,' he said, looking at the delicate red lines that spread across her fingertips.

Medeoan only shook her head. 'The threads for the weaving. They wear on the skin after awhile.'

But Kacha would not let the subject be dismissed. 'You should rest before you go, Beloved. You are exhausted.' He touched her forehead, perhaps searching for some trace of the fever that racked her parents. As ever, the knowledge of his love sent a small thrill of delight through her heart.

Despite that, Medeoan shook her head. 'They are too ill. An hour could make all the difference.'

'Then do it here,' Kacha urged. 'Surely their home is a stronger place for them than the woodlands.'

'And if I draw out the sickness here, it stays here. I have to take it away from this house.' She smiled weakly and pressed her husband's hand. 'On these matters, I must ask you to trust me. I know how the magic must be worked.'

Kacha frowned down at their hands.

'What is it?' asked Medeoan.

He ran his thumb across her knuckles. 'You know what Avanasy thought best to teach you. I wish you had some other advisor for this part of your life.'

Medeoan sighed. Kacha could not forgive. She would have been well pleased never to hear her old teacher's name again, but Kacha could not bring himself to cease worrying about the wrongs Avanasy had committed, no matter how many assurances Medeoan gave him. 'It was not only Avanasy who taught me,' she assured him. 'Beloved, I ask you again, trust me in this. I will save them.'

'Of course, my heart,' he smiled. 'In this I am but a few months old, whereas you have a lifetime of knowledge. I will be quiet.'

No, Dearest, that will never do. 'You must always speak your fears to me, and your hopes. How else am I to know my whole mind and my whole heart?' She laid her hand on his chest. 'We are two halves of one being, after all.'

He gently kissed her wounded fingertips. 'Every time I look into your eyes, I am reminded of how much that means.' He released her. 'Go. The Lords can wait. I will sit vigil over your mother.'

'Thank you, Beloved. I will be back before nightfall.'

She kissed him then, allowing herself a moment to savor again the passion his touch sparked in her, and then she turned away. To look back would be to see Mother, her skin yellow and sagging against her bones. She could not carry that image with her into the woods. Her workings could not be tinged with despair. She must be all hope, all determination now.

Straightening her spine, Medeoan marched out of the sick room to join her escort.

Kacha watched his wife sweep out of the room. Truly, she was beautiful, and when she allowed herself to be, she was a power in her own right. What a consort she would have made. He shook his head. Well, the Mothers did not always place one to one's own advantage.

He felt the Empress's gaze upon him. Kacha turned to face her. Her eyes were little more than dark holes in her yellow skull, they had sunken so far back. Her hands, so tenderly cradled a moment before by her daughter, plucked nervously at the coverlet, one of them struggling to lift itself up, to make some sign or gesture.

'Now then, Mother,' said Kacha, stepping close to the bedside. 'Do not bestir yourself.' He leaned across her, hearing her breath rattle in her shriveled throat.

'The Empress is overheated,' he announced to her shadowed waiting ladies, as he straightened up. 'She asks for a bath. Let her physicians be advised to draw one,' he pointed to the first of the aging attendants. 'And you had best make sure her broth and milk are cooled before they are brought in,' he said to the second. 'And a change of clothing might be advised,' he added to the last two.

The women, one at a time, reverenced before his orders. Shortly after her mother had fallen prostrate to the fever, they had been scolded into obedience of his words by Medeoan's swift and accurate tongue. They removed themselves from the bed enclosure to go and pass the orders to their underlings, which gave him only a few bare moments of true privacy with his mother-in-law.

'Forgive me, my Mother Imperial,' he whispered. 'But this is necessary.'

From his kaftan, he drew out a kerchief, and then a velvet bag. Using the kerchief to shield his wizened hand, he pulled an amber bead about the size of his thumbnail from the pouch. The bead had been cunningly carved with delicate human hands, their fingers intertwined. If one looked closely, one could see how tightly those fingers gripped each other, as if they were the hands of corpses clenched in the rigor of death.

Kacha leaned once again over his mother-in-law. She shrank from him, burrowing as far as she could into her pillows and goose-down coverings. Her fingers stiffened all at once, as if they sought to scream for the woman who could no longer make any noise beyond a rasping cough.

'Now then, Mother,' said Kacha softly. 'It is but the work of a moment.'

Swiftly, he caught her behind the head. Her mouth opened to cry out, and he popped the bead inside it, pressing her dry tongue down so that the bead must roll back into her throat and then sealing her mouth shut with his other hand.

'Swallow, swallow, Mother,' he ordered her, massaging her throat with his free hand. 'Swallow, and it will all be over.'

Swallow, damn you, I have not much time.

She pressed feebly against his grip, trying to rise. Her hands flapped on the ends of her wrists, but, at last, he felt her throat convulse as she swallowed the bead, and the spell it had been fashioned to hold. He released her, and she fell back down on the pillow, her eyes wide, frightened, and accusing. At the sound of footsteps which signaled the return of the Empress's ladies, Kacha stepped away. Her first waiting lady rounded the edge of the screen, even as her Empress's eyes rolled up, and their lids drooped closed.

'No!' The woman screamed, grasping her mistress's hand and pressing it against her breast. 'Ofka, summon the doctors! She is in a stupor!'

Within moments, a flock of doctors and ladies surrounded the bed. Kacha stepped back, letting them near her. Two of the court sorcerers hurried in to join the throng, and only then did Kacha allow himself a moment's concern.

Yamuna, this had best be swift, or these fools will be able to hold her life until Medeoan does her work.

Kacha might find his bride naive in many ways, but he held her magical skill in great respect. It was that skill that made her dangerous. If her suspicions were ever roused such that she would choose to use it against him, the plans laid for her and for Isavalta would be at grave risk.

Be swift, Yamuna. Be sure.

With all eyes and minds directed toward the revival of the

Empress, Kacha walked out of her apartments unobserved, and strode quietly down the hall to look in on the Emperor.

Medeoan, High Princess of Eternal Isavalta, stood beside the mossy pool, several hours by canal from the palace of Vyshtavos, clad only in her shift, trying not to shiver.

You'll be warm enough soon, she told herself, as she watched Prathad, foremost among her waiting ladies, set the consecratory bowl down beside the pool. Beside it lay the cloth Mother had used to wipe Medeoan clean the day she was born, and next to that burned the stub of the candle Father had lit when she first drew breath.

Medeoan turned. Vladka, second among her ladies, held out the pillow upon which lay the girdle Medeoan had spent the last two days and nights weaving. The girdle's plait had been made up of silken threads twined with her hair, as well as that of her parents, and the blood and breath of all three of them tied together in the seven tassels that hung from its belt. She spat on the ends before she tied it around her waist.

Her parents were dying. The physics and the sorcerers turned their faces and said that Grandfather Death spoke to them, that he stood by the heads of their beds. Medeoan cursed them all. Her parents were not ready for death. She was not ready to surrender them. Not yet.

Prathad held out the silver knife with the golden hilt. It had been made over five hundred years ago by the first court sorcerer of Isavalta, when Isavalta was still merely one province among the northern countries. It was used only by the members of the royal family who were also born to magic.

Medeoan's was the first hand in four generations to hold it.

'Why are we born so?' she'd once asked Avanasy.

'None knows,' he'd answered, shaking his head. 'Perhaps because we are needed.'

Medeoan shut her mind against memories of Avanasy. Avanasy was a traitor. He was banished. He was nothing. If no other sorcerer could help, he could not have done anything had he been here. It was foolish to long after him. This was her work. She was the one who was needed.

Medeoan waved her hand. Prathad and Vladka stepped back. Medeoan stooped until the knife's tip was a bare finger's width above the ground. Schooling her mind, as Avanasy had taught her (no, no, don't think of him now), she reached down inside herself and reached outside to the world around. She touched the magic, pulling it in, drawing it out, and she walked in a circle around the bowl. The air grew heavy and hot around her. The weaving had begun. She continued the tracery around the candle, the bowl and the cloth, linking them all together with her pattern.

Medeoan knelt before the bowl, the cloth and the candle, holding palm and knife over them. 'I have gone into the deep country. I have stood beside the mossy pool. I have drawn the clean water. I have claimed the consecration cloth, the consecration candle and the consecration bowl. I have claimed the blood of my beloved parents and the blood of my own self.' She pressed the knife blade against her palm. 'I have drawn the transparent line, and in the open country I make a great cry. Over cloth, over water, over candle, over blood, I charm my beloved parents.' Hot. Hot. The air was on fire. Sweat beaded on her brow and trickled down her spine. So hot, hot with fever, burning, as her parents burned in their bed. *Good. Good. Let me summon the fever. Bring it to me.*

'I banish from you the fearful devil. I drive away the stormy whirlwind. I take you away from the one-eyed wood-goblin, from the alien house-goblin, from the evil water-sprite, from the outlaw witch and her sister, from twitchy-eyed mermaids, from the thrice-cursed Baba Yaga, from the dragon, the Vixen and all their works. I wave away Yvanka's children and the screeching raven. I protect you from the flood, the fire, the frost, the quaking ground, from the twelve fevers that clutch and burn, from the black magician, from the warlock, from the savage shaman, from the blind cunning-man.'

Pain now, running through her sinews. Her hands trembled, and the knife shook. She clamped her hand tighter and clenched her teeth.

Do not cry out. Do not break the weaving of words. This is their pain, you can hold it, they cannot.

Weak with pain and nearly blind with heat and effort, Medeoan took the knife in both hands and drove it straight into the ground.

'As the earth surrounds the blade of the knife, so shall my protection surround Edemsko and Kseniia.' She panted against the heat and groped for the bowl. Her hands grasped the edges and she struggled to lift it. 'As the pool swallows up the water,' she tipped the bowl over the pool's edge, her hands quivering to hold onto it, 'so will Edemsko and Kseniia's illness be swallowed.' Her fingers slid apart and the bowl thudded to the ground. 'As . . . as . . . as . . .'

Hold, hold. You can compass countries if you let yourself. Feel the words as you feel the threads on the loom, and the flames of the fire. The pain is nothing. It will be gone in a moment.

Avanasy's voice filled her. Avanasy exiled, traitor, and yet it was his words that rung around her head, that guided her groping hand to the candle, that allowed her to spit on her fingers, and pinch out the flame.

'As the flame is extinguished by my hand and spittle, so is Edemsko and Kseniia's illness extinguished.'

Medeoan forced herself to her feet. Her ears sang with the

effort it took to raise her arms. 'This is my word, blessed by Vyshko and Vyshemir, this is my wish, and this is my seal upon it. Be done! Be done! Be DONE!' She screamed the last word with all the force her heart held, and with that scream, the heat, the pain and all the summoned magic rushed through her body from her heart to the soles of her feet, and was gone.

Medeoan collapsed onto the ground. She heard Vladka gasp and start forward, then stop. Perhaps Prathad held her back. She was too numb to look up, too numb to do anything except lie on the cold ground and breathe.

Done, done, done, her last word echoed in her mind. *I am done, they are done, it is done, all done.*

But done, Granddaughter, too late.

Medeoan jerked her head up. There, across the pool stood a figure in black robes, its face indistinct, as if shrouded by shadow. It reached one fine, unmarked hand into the pool, and impossibly drew forth a wave of water.

'No,' gasped Medeoan, pushing herself to her knees. 'No, Grandfather, I beg you, it cannot be so.'

Grandfather Death stowed the wave in his deep sleeve and turned away.

'No!' Medeoan lunged after him, breaking her own, useless circle, running into the pool without even noticing.

'Highness!' shrieked Prathad. Hands grabbed her, hauling her backward out of the water.

The knife lay on the ground, and the candle burned beside it. Nothing. All for nothing.

'What is it, Highness? What has happened?'

'Ah!' cried Medeoan. 'Ah, they are dying. I failed. I failed and they are dying!' She buried her head in her hands. She felt Prathad hold her close, weeping her own hot tears. Distantly, she heard the murmuring of the guards who surrounded her working. Gone. The Emperor, the Empress, were dying. The High Princess had failed.

'Highness,' said Vladka in a tremulous voice. 'Highness, if it is as you say, you must return home, and quickly. You have . . .'

'I have nothing!' Medeoan snapped. She clenched her fists. 'What do I have?'

'A husband who waits to hear from you,' said Prathad. 'Let us take you to him.'

Kacha. She knotted her fingers in her hair, as if seeking to pull it out by the roots. How could she have forgotten even for a moment? She ached to feel his arms around her. Too late. Too late. But it could not be too late. Everything had worked, she had felt it. One or the other of them must still live. They were not both gone. She had not completely failed.

'Quickly,' she pulled away from her ladies.

They all but threw on her skirt, her sleeves, her bodice, knotting each lace as swiftly as possible, and tossing over all her outer coat, her veil and coronet. Prathad called out for little, pale Anka the page girl, who ran for the guard to form up the escort. Medeoan did not wait for the canopy to be raised over her. She strode down toward the river's edge where her barge waited. The guard followed in haste, reforming around her with the girl pages who all seemed as white as their kaftans. Let her ladies follow as they could. The captain would have left men behind to escort them. She had to get back to Vyshtavos. She had to know who lived and who died. She had to find Kacha. She had to know how she had failed.

But Vyshtavos and its parklands lay beyond the city of Makashev and although the captain sent the small barge ahead with a man to cry that the High Princess (just princess still, she had not completely failed) was on her way, it did little good. Barges and coracles, and rowing boats made a stew of the watercourse. The drawbridges were clogged with carts, and carriages, and old people on foot, and horses, donkeys, mules, dogs, all in the way, all streaming out of the streets between the wooden buildings with their peaked roofs and gilded spires and fat onion domes so that they could watch her pass. The river's breeze brought down the smell of the summer city — mud and garbage, smoke and cooking food — and Medeoan felt that with every passing moment her heart must burst for beating so hard as she clutched the rail of her bench and willed the oarsmen to pull faster, and faster yet.

The lock to the Imperial canal was at least open and the keepers reverenced as her men pulled them past. The buildings cramming themselves up to the shore gave way to willows, pines, and sloping, groomed banks planted with lilies and blue-bells, rare orange poppies and bleeding hearts. The air was fresh again, filled with the scents of the green and the growing. Birdsong replaced the endless gabble of people.

Which meant they were close, but not close enough.

Then the barge rounded the canal's great bend, and the trees parted to show the red-and-white granite of Vyshtavos, the palace built by her grandmother to show that Isavalta was a united and peaceful land, and that its rulers had no need to hide themselves behind castle walls. The Imperial dock was imported teak wood inlaid with ivory. More uniformed bargemen waited there to receive the ropes the oarsmen tossed them.

But Medeoan saw them only for an instant. Her gaze skimmed past them to the broad, white steps, where the Council of Lords stood, with Kacha before them.

Her mind went numb. She could not feel her body anymore. It was a paralysis even more profound than that which had taken hold after her failed spell. Her utterly failed spell. Prathad and Vladka had to grasp her arms and propel her forward before her feet would move. They had to walk along the dock and climb the steps, carrying her between them.

Kacha was the first to kneel. He would be. It was so very like him. The first to bow his head and murmur, 'Majesty Imperial.'

The first to catch her as she tumbled to the ground in a faint.

The next hours passed in a blur of moving color and the rustle of cloth. Crowds of people whose faces she could not make herself see kept on marching solemnly up to her to kneel and bow their heads and call her by her mother's title.

At last, her ladies took her back to her private rooms. She stood as still as a wooden doll while they removed her daytime finery and dressed her in her night clothes. They laid her in her bed and covered her over with velvet and eiderdown, and she still did not move. She lay staring up at the canopy, trying not to think of what had happened.

Mother and Father had tried so hard to prepare her for this time. She, in her turn, had tried so hard to hide from it. Her efforts were of no use, however. The moment had found her, and all her evasions had accomplished were to make sure that it had found her stubbornly unready.

'My heart?'

For once, Medeoan found herself with no answer for Kacha. She heard his soft step as he passed the screens. She felt the feather beds sink as he sat beside her. She rolled over, huddling like an infant before him. His warm and welcome hand laid itself on her head and stroked her hair.

'I thought there would be more time,' she whispered.

'I know,' he said simply. 'I believe everyone does.'

'I don't know what to do. They spent years teaching me, testing me, lecturing me, and now I don't know what to do.'

'That will come. What is important right now is that you realize you are not alone.' He grasped her shoulders and raised her up until she knelt on the bed before him. 'I am here with you. Together we will be the autocrat for Isavalta. You will be the flesh and blood, and the passionate heart. I will be the bone inside, supporting and binding.'

'Yes.' In the darkness, her mouth sought his to kiss him hard and desperately. The press of his body against hers held all the promise of life and the future. Together, as they were, they would know what to do. Together, hand to hand, skin to skin, and she would never be alone or confused again.

Some time later, Medeoan woke again to darkness. She lay for a time, listening to Kacha's breathing and feeling the warmth where his hand almost touched her shoulder. Beyond the curtains and screens that isolated them, she heard the soft rustles and sighs of her ladies asleep in their truckle beds. It was deep into the night, she felt that in her bones, and knew it by the sounds of sleeping around her.

Gently, Medeoan drew back the covers and slipped from the bed. Her black-and-gold mourning robe stood on its form waiting for her in the faint light of the brazier smoldering at the bedside. Before she could reach it, one of her ladies, in the dim light she was not sure which one, was there holding it out for her. She slipped into its warmth and let herself be buttoned in. Wrapping her sleeve around her hand, she gestured for a brazier's dish, which the anonymous lady passed to her so that she might have some light to see by. By its muted flames she could see it was Vladka who stood before her, ready to accompany her wherever she needed to go, and it was Vladka whom she waved back to her post as she made her way between her sleeping ladies to the chamber door. The soldiers of the House Guard and the young pages stationed there snapped to instant attention as she padded down the broad hall with its inlaid wood, its murals, and mosaics.

The god house lay down the south stairs and at the end of

the Gilded Corridor. Tonight, its wide doors stood open, releasing a flood of incense and candlelight. The double-wicked, braided candles that she had last seen at her wedding would be burning all night tonight. Those were the candles of Vyshko and Vyshemir, and their light called the gods to watch over the dead as well as the living. The court sorcerers and the keeper and his assistants moved about the room, shadows in all that gold and light, going through the forms of the ritual, keeping the vigils that were necessary to ensure that no ghost or goblin took advantage of the presence of death to make mischief.

Medeoan handed the brazier dish to one of the page girls and with a sharp gesture ordered her escort to stay outside.

The god house shone like a cave of jewels and fairy gold in a midwife's tale. The gods stood on their pedestal dressed in mourning black, and Medeoan imagined she could see tears shimmering in their glassy eyes. She looked up at them because she had no wish to look down to see the biers that flanked the gods' pedestal, piled high with flowers and green branches. Translucent white shrouds had been draped over her parents, so she could not see the yellow tint to their skin anymore. Those shrouds had been woven with care by the court sorcerers and contained spells as well as flaxen thread. Spells of peace, spells of protection, spells to keep the spirit from attempting to return to the flesh it had abandoned so that all things would remain in their proper orbits.

They would have fresh graves. The graves that had been dug in the case of Imperial deaths in winter were filled in when spring came. Medeoan had, more than once, walked through the cemetery with its stone monuments to see the gaping hole laid open for her, just in case she died while the ground was frozen hard. Every year it got a little bigger. There was a shroud for her too, somewhere.

So much laborious preparation for this ending. So much of life spent getting ready for death. This was what she had fought against since she had been old enough to fight, that her whole life was to lead up to this moment, to this end.

Well now the end had passed, and here she still stood.

'Majesty,' said Iakush Vtoroisyn Gabravin, Lord Sorcerer to her father, Lord Sorcerer to Isavalta until she said otherwise, as he stepped softly up beside her. 'It is not time for you to be here yet.'

Until she said otherwise. 'I have decided to be here,' she answered him. 'Therefore it is time.'

'You wish to speak to them,' said Lord Iakush with a sigh. 'You have something you want to say, or something you want to hear.'

Medeoan bit her lip, unable to answer. She had not thought her plan so evident.

'I stood beside my father's bier, just as you do, Majesty,' Lord Iakush said. 'I still remember the feel of his shroud under my fingertips. But my teacher was there with me.'

Medeoan swallowed. 'My teacher is a traitor.'

Iakush paused only a moment at that. 'Then I must ask you to hear me. It is a dangerous thing to call upon the newly dead. They remember too well the touch of this world, and if called back to this place they have loved, they may not wish to leave.'

'But the living are always stronger than the dead.' The words sounded hollow in her ears. She did not feel strong. She felt weak as water.

'Stronger, but sometimes not so desperate, nor so frightened, nor, at the worst, so angry,' Iakush told her gently. 'Your parents did not die easily. To call them back from the Land of Death and Spirit so soon will be to call them back to their hearts' best loves and worst fears. They may not be able to let go again.'

'If I bring them back, I can send them away again.' Medeoan did not look at the Lord Sorcerer. Her gaze remained fastened on the white-shrouded figures that were all that remained of her parents in the living world.

'It will be a struggle, Majesty Imperial. Would you wish on them more struggle now that they have gone to rest?'

'It is Vyshko and Vyshemir who are your living parents now.' Keeper Bakhar rounded the pedestal of the gods, coming to stand at her other side. 'They protect you, and expect your duty in return.'

Medeoan turned her gaze up to the gods in their black gowns, especially to Vyshemir with her cup and her dagger, the tools she had used to save Isavalta when Isavalta was only one city and Vyshemir was only a mortal woman. It was Vyshemir's sacrifice of her life that saved Isavalta from invasion by the barbarians of Tuukos, and blessed it so that it could grow into the empire that had been placed into Medeoan's hands.

Not so long ago she would have cried, 'But I do not want this duty!' She had, so many times, thrown herself prostrate at the foot of this pedestal, begging the gods for some way out. She was too small, she was too scared, she did not know enough, she did not want this duty. They had not listened. Instead, they had taken her parents and left her here.

'I know what you feel,' said the keeper gently. 'But if the gods trust you to rule their house, in their name, how can you fail to trust yourself?'

You are the heir of Vyshemir, her mother had told her long ago. *This is not a gift that can be returned. In the end you are the one who will decide how to make use of it.*

She had scorned those words then, and if she had not stormed out of the room on that occasion, she had on many others.

'I just wanted to tell them that I understand now,' she said, wondering at her own words, but knowing the truth of them.

'When death comes so close, we find we understand many things,' said Keeper Bakhar. 'Come, Majesty Imperial, let us not trouble your parents, but pray for their rest and comfort.'

So, for the first time, the new Empress of Isavalta allowed herself to be advised, and let the keeper of her god house lead her to the audience alcove so that she might speak to her parents properly, through the gods. So that she might say she would do her best.

So that she might say that she truly did understand.

Kacha lay in his wife's bed for a time after Medeoan left, listening to how, after a few dozen heartbeats, the rustlings of ladies disturbed by their mistress's passage faded once more into the sounds of gentle breathing and sleep.

The withered fingers of his right hand tapped restlessly on the covers. He could not be absent when Medeoan returned, nor could he risk one of those ladies waking up and finding him engaged in improper activities. His fingers tapped more urgently, reminding him that he had other concerns.

You will simply have to be quick. Kacha slipped from his wife's bed. The darkness confounded his left eye but made little difference to his right. He waved the attending lady away and moved surely across the dank stone chamber to the unprepossessing door that led to his own suite.

The room on the other side was also shrouded in darkness, and his own flock of attendants snored in their rude beds, except for the two on night duty who sprang to their feet as he entered. He waved them back and did not spare them any other thought. Many of these were men he had brought with him. Those who had been assigned to him by the Isavaltan court and could not be bribed, had long since been replaced by those who could. All of them knew better than to take any undue notice of what their master did after dark. Soon he would have to take similar measures with Medeoan's ladies.

The single advantage to the eternal cold and everlasting stone of this place was that there was always a fire burning somewhere. Kacha carried the smoldering brazier from his bedside behind a carved screen to the inlaid work desk where he wrote his letters. He set the brazier carefully in the waiting stand. He uncovered it with his right hand and blew gently on the coals to raise a cluster of delicate flames.

As the flames strengthened, Kacha felt a hunger seep into his mind. It flowed from his right eye and his right hand. Fire was gate and guardian. Fire was power and peace. These were truths he had not understood before his transformation, but now they were as much a part of him as his new eye and hand.

Prepared ink and paper waited for him on the desk. With his right hand, Kacha picked up the pen. He spat on the silver tip before dipping it into the thick black ink. Closing his left eye, he forced himself to relax and let his hand work. It was never easy, but it was necessary. Kacha knew himself to be a tool as well as a prince, and this was hard knowledge.

His hand worked busily at its task, sketching out particular sequences of letters, not to form words, but to form patterns, waves, tight, interlocking circles, and stars. His right eye saw the work, and it reached out to see beyond ink, spittle and paper to places Kacha's mind would never touch.

When eye saw that hand had finished, hand laid down the pen and picked up the paper. Sweat prickled Kacha's forehead and the strain of his spirit reaching outside his flesh made his temple throb. He turned to the brazier and laid the paper down atop the coals. With his right hand, he smoothed the flames over the page.

Pain flared down through his skin to the bone. Kacha clamped his jaw closed to keep from screaming.

It does not burn. It does not burn. He tried to fill his mind with that thought. He had done this before and he knew his skin would emerge whole. If he had been a sorcerer in whole rather than just in part, there would not even be any pain. But he could not stop his hand. He could not even pull it from the fire, so he must endure. Tool as well as prince. Conqueror and surrendered. But it hurt, by the names of the Seven Mothers, it hurt.

While the fire blazed and filled him with pain, to his eye it appeared to have lost the power to consume. Although his skin was surrounded by flame, it remained untouched. So too did the paper on the coals. Only the ink began to smoke. It bubbled as if boiling in a pot. Kacha's fingers stirred the flame. The ink sizzled and the smoke took on a bitter smell. At last, all the ink turned to black steam and drifted away.

Kacha's hand twitched the parchment out of the flames. The pain ceased at once and the chill air was like a blessing against his skin. Relief buckled Kacha's knees and he dropped to the floor. Tears of remembered pain and present relief mixed themselves with the sweat running down his face.

Kacha dashed the tears away impatiently with his left hand. His right hand smoothed the paper out against the floor. He peered at it closely and his right eye saw a series of faint, gray tracings, pale words that seemed to have been written with nothing but smoke.

I do not like that Medeoan has left your side now, read the words. *Keep close watch on her. It may be she has realized she can no longer play at being free from her birth. Concentrate your efforts on the Lord Sorcerer and the Mistress of the House. If we may secure those two, nothing may be done or said within the palace walls without we know of it.*

Soon it will be time to move to the summer palace. Before then, you must find your way down into the Isavaltan treasury. There you will be able to find the means to secure your wife should she begin to pull away from your side. Send word to me as soon as you gain access, and I will guide you further.

Kacha nodded in thoughtful silence at what he read. As usual, his father's sorcerer, *Agnidh* Yamuna, spoke with cogent understanding. Kacha allowed himself a moment to pity Medeoan. His child bride would lose her empire without ever having truly gained it. It would be sad to watch her when she realized what had happened.

Her death, when it came, would surely be a relief to her.

Chapter Three

'I'm taking the soup down to Mrs Whitkoff,' called Ingrid to her mother, bundling up the two crockery jars in the burlap satchel. 'Is there anything we need from the store?'

Mama remained bent over the washtub and shook her head. For once, Ingrid was glad of her mother's indifference. Since Mama stopped watching her, her task had become much easier, although her life had become that much lonelier.

For two weeks, Grace had languished in her bed. Ingrid had spooned broth, milk and beer down her, and she swallowed, but it brought her no strength. At least she had stopped her nocturnal roaming. Avan's advice had done that much already.

Everett had made good his promise the day after Ingrid had seen the ghost. He'd come to the kitchen door at dusk and stood there with his worn, blue cap in his hands. 'He said,' Everett did not bother to use Avan's name, 'that you should tie a piece of iron around her neck, and put another under her bed. This will keep her in the house. He has begun work on a stronger cure.'

Iron. Of course. When Ingrid was small, when Mama still felt inclined to tell fairy stories, she had told them that cold iron was proof against magic. Hadn't Avan said as much last night? 'Thank you, Everett.'

She expected him to bow his head bashfully then, as was his usual habit. Instead, he fixed her with a look of unusual determination. 'Ingrid, what is happening?'

Ingrid took a deep breath. He had earned the truth, but this time it was she who could not look directly at him. She watched her fingers pick at the edge of the kitchen table. 'Grace is haunted. Avan has knowledge of these things. We hope to lay the ghost to rest, and free her.'

'You believe this?' Incredulity filled Everett's voice. She could find no fault with that.

Ingrid nodded. 'I saw it.'

Silence stretched out long and tight between them until Ingrid saw Everett's shadow move across the table. She looked up. He had taken two steps inside the door, coming in just far enough to touch the tabletop, as if by touching the same surface she did he would be able to create some vibration of communion between them. 'Is . . . is there any way I can help?' He did not doubt her. He would not. Everett dealt honestly and expected honesty in return.

For the thousandth time Ingrid wondered why she looked at Everett without love. He would marry her in an instant. Papa and Mama would raise no objection. He would build a new house for her and they would live in it together. He would never raise his voice to her. He would never think of raising his hand to her or their children. It would be so easy. All she had to do was say yes to him.

Perhaps, after all, that was the reason. It would be too easy a release. She would never know if she went with Everett out of love, or out of a final need to escape her parents' house. Without that certainty, she would have to live with the fear of her heart's life washing out of her, as it had washed out of her mother. 'I will let you know, I promise.'

Her words caused a gentle grin to form on Everett's face.

'I'll hold you to that, Ingrid.' He started to turn away.

'Everett . . .' Ingrid raised her hand as if to snatch at him.

'Yes?' He looked back over his shoulder, his eyebrows arched.

'I can't . . . I don't . . .' Ingrid's voice shook, and her hand fell to her side.

But Everett spared her the necessity of finishing her sentence. 'I know.' He shrugged easily. 'It doesn't matter.'

But it does, she wanted to say. *You should love someone who is able to love you in return. You should be happy.* That, however, was not something Everett would want to hear, and she would not disgrace this moment he had given her by saying it. Instead, she said the only words left to her. 'You are a good man, Everett Lederle.'

He smiled. 'I am at that. I'll look in on you later, Ingrid.'

'Thank you, Everett.'

He waved his cap as a farewell before setting it back on his head.

So she had done what Avan said. She fetched a broken and rusted hinge from the shed and tied one half around Grace's neck on a piece of twine, and slid the other under her side of the bed. That night Grace had struggled, and she had cried out, but she had not risen.

'I hear him, Ingrid,' she whispered.

'I know.' Ingrid had tried to smooth out Grace's brow. 'But not for much longer.'

The Whitkoffs lived on the edge of Eastbay nearest the cove that gave the settlement its name. Mrs Whitkoff was down with the croup, leaving her eldest daughter Lucia to manage on her own. Mrs Gustavson was coming in to help, though, and, so far, the Loftfields' gifts of bread and broth were not being turned away, although no one seemed to have time to stand and chat anymore. Perhaps no one wanted to take the chance that Grace's madness was contagious, or perhaps it was just that the way Papa and Leo scowled at every man on the island was finally beginning to wear on their neighbors' patience.

Lucia Whitkoff, who had dark circles under her bright blue eyes, met Ingrid at the door with a broom in one hand and her infant brother balanced on her hip. Ingrid left one of the two jars on the kitchen table, and hurried away before Lucia had time to get really uncomfortable. She had no time to linger anyway. She had her own errand to complete, and she could not take long, or Mama would want to know where she'd been, and Ingrid was fast running out of lies.

The sun sparkled on the bay, turning the water silver and blue. Despite the warmth of the summer sun, Ingrid wrapped her shawl around her head, so that from the boats out on the lake, she'd be an anonymous woman with an anonymous bundle tucked under her arm. If Papa saw, if Leo saw . . . it didn't bear thinking about. But now was the time she had to come, because now was the time when the fishers' shacks were deserted, and there was no one to see her scurrying between them. No one but Avan.

We must bring the ghost's bones up from the lake. I am making a net for the purpose.

He'd delivered that message by Everett. Ingrid kept it tucked under her pillow as if it were a love letter. It was written on a scrap of brown paper with grease pencil in a bold, flowing hand, like none she had ever seen.

At the dark of the moon, we will go fishing. Come find me when you can.

But as she approached his rickety shack this morning, she did not see a plume of smoke rising from the tin chimney. Worry struck her. She rounded the hut to the door, and knocked for form's sake.

'Avan?' she whispered, and when there was no answer, pushed the door open.

Avan slumped in the hut's one chair, the great net he had been weaving spread out across his legs like a quilt. Ingrid gasped, almost losing her grip on the jar of soup she carried. Avan's hand twitched, scrabbling at a single knot, and even in the hut's gloom, she could see the blood staining his skin.

Quickly, Ingrid set the crock down by the door and ran forward. She pulled the net out from under Avan's hands, letting it fall in a heap onto the ground. As soon as the strings slipped from his fingers, his hands stilled, and fell limp at his sides. The weight of them threatened to drag him out of the chair, but Ingrid caught him under the armpits.

'Come, you must help me,' she grunted as she heaved him to his feet.

Avan didn't even groan, but he must have had a little strength in his legs, because he staggered beside Ingrid as she hefted him over to the rickety wooden cot that was his bed, and dropped him onto it. She snatched up his frying pan – there was nothing else – and ran out to the lake, scooping up some water to set on the stove. Upon opening the stove's door, she found three coals still glowing amid the ashes and was able to coax them to life with some of the tinder from the woodbox.

Avan groaned. Ingrid strode to the bedside, taking off her apron. She saw no cleaner cloth. His skin was fever hot against hers as she wiped away the blood from his tattered finger ends.

'What in God's name happened to you?' she murmured. He'd said the task would be hard. He'd stopped going out on the boats to save his strength. She'd become used to seeing Avan growing more pale, but this, this was gruesome.

Steam began to rise from the water on the stove. She washed his hands again in the hot water, cleaning away the scabs so they could bleed freely for awhile. She propped them up on her apron. She'd have to find something to use as bandaging. She surveyed the hut and saw rope, and sacking, and two chests, one bound in rope, the other bound in iron.

'Forgive the intrusion, if you will.' Ingrid opened the rope-bound chest and found a spare shirt and trousers, some linens and socks and four huge, worn but serviceable handkerchiefs.

'Thank goodness. I've enough explaining to do. If I came home without my apron or with my petticoats torn, I'd never be let out of the house again.'

She pulled the chair up beside the cot and wrapped one handkerchief over his fingers, making a crude mitten. As she did, she saw again how graceful his hands were, and she could not help but notice that his calluses were fresh, as on the hands of a boy who had just started out regularly in the boats, not like the ancient knobs that coated her father's and brother's hands. He had scars too, three long, white slashes on his palm, and a whole series of old nicks on his wrists.

What are you? she wondered, winding the second kerchief around the first and tying it tight to make a secure, if improvised, dressing. *What are you doing here at all?*

She picked up his left hand and felt the tips of her ears heating up. His hand was heavy and warm against hers, and from her secret self came the sudden wish to press the back of it against her cheek, to feel how that smooth skin would feel touching her face, how it would be to press her lips against it.

By the time she tied the second dressing off, she knew she was blushing furiously. She pressed her palms against her cheeks, willing herself to calm.

Then she saw Avan's eyes open and watching her, and all the blood in her heart rushed burning to her face.

'Keep still, Sir,' she said, rising swiftly to her feet and turning away. 'You need a cool cloth for that head . . .'

'No,' he croaked. 'Don't leave me.'

'I'll be back in a heartbeat.' She moved away, but hesitated.

'No,' he said again. 'Please. Stay here.'

Ingrid's heart thumped hard against her ribs. 'All right.' She pulled the chair back so she sat by his head. 'But you shouldn't talk . . .'

'Yes,' he said. 'I must. I must . . . come back. Too far gone,' he had to drag in several long breaths. 'Too long away. I must touch earth again.'

Ingrid frowned in incomprehension. 'What can I do?'

He rolled his eyes toward her and said quite seriously. 'Sing for me.'

Ingrid wanted to protest, but only for a moment. The time for questions would come later. She must have Avan strong and well to save Grace. So she licked her lips, and began.

'*Oh yes, my lads, we'll roll a-lee,*

'*Come down, you blood red roses, come down.*

'*We'll soon be far away from sea.*

'*Oh, you pinks and posies,*

'*Come down, you blood red roses, come down.*'

She did not look at him as the verses wound along, the slow, old song of a man coming home from the sea, sung to keep time while hauling on the ropes. She wanted to keep her mind on Grace's need, on how she might explain being away so long to Mama, and how she would get out of the house tonight, but her hands still tingled from touching Avan's hand, and she could not pull herself away from the sensation.

'*Come down, you blood red roses, come down . . .*'

'Thank you,' he said when her song was finished, and his voice sounded stronger. 'That cool cloth would be welcome now.'

Ingrid all but ran from the hut to fetch a fresh pan full of water.

Avan lay silent and patient as Ingrid sponged his face down with a rag she found by the stove. He had no cup so she held the hut's one tin bowl to his lips so that he could swallow some of the water down.

'Thank you,' he said again. 'Now, Ingrid, I must ask you to listen closely to me.'

Ingrid said nothing, she just leaned forward to better hear his rasping voice.

'The net is finished, but the working of it has shattered me. I thought myself strong enough, but I was not.' His voice was flat as he said it, but Ingrid had heard the disappointment, and the reproach for himself. 'If you want to save your sister, you must do as I tell you.'

'I will.'

'After dark you must take the net to the water's edge. You must have a fire going, a good one, with plenty of coals to make it hot. You must cast the net into the waters. The net will retrieve the dead man's bones onto the shore. You must cast them, net and all into the fire.'

Ingrid nodded.

'He will try to prevent you. You will have to be strong. He will work through your fear, and your cold.'

'I understand.' She spoke the words quickly, meaning only to use them to silence him. She was startled to realize that there was some truth behind them. This insanity had begun to make sense, the way a story of fairies or ghosts made its own sort of sense. As such stories had a deep familiarity to her, so all this had started to feel familiar. She felt at once reassured and disturbed by this realization.

Cloth brushed Ingrid's wrist as Avan reached for her. 'Your sister will be called tonight,' he said hoarsely. 'There is not enough iron in any world to keep her safe.'

'I understand,' she said again as she folded his arm fussily back across his chest. He did not need to be agitating himself right now. She was surely agitated enough for them both.

He did not protest, nor did he stir again. 'I will be there if I can.'

Ingrid just shook her head. 'You have done so much already. You have all my thanks.'

'I hope it is enough.' He turned his face away.

'Avan . . .' Ingrid rubbed her hands together. He turned toward her again. 'Avan, where are you from?'

Avan's mouth twitched as if he did not know whether to smile or frown. 'Isavalta,' he said.

'Isavalta,' Ingrid repeated the strange syllables. 'I've never heard of it. It must be far away.'

'It is.'

'What did you do there?' Ingrid was not sure why she had decided to quiz him, especially since a moment ago she had been convinced he should not agitate himself. Perhaps it was to convince herself of his reality. Perhaps part of her expected him to vanish away when all this was over, just another part of the ghost story in which she found herself. She already knew enough to know that if that happened she would be greatly saddened.

Whatever Avan might think of her questions, he answered mildly. 'I was hired by a great family to teach their eldest daughter.'

An image of Avan in a long-tailed black coat standing beside a little girl in ribbons and frills and a worktable piled with books flitted through Ingrid's mind. It felt unaccountably wrong, and yet she did not believe he lied. 'Why aren't you still there?'

The blanket rustled as Avan shrugged. 'The daughter got married, and I was no longer needed.'

'So you came here to work on the boats?'

'As you see.'

'It seems strange that you could not find another teaching position.'

'Yes, I imagine it must.' Ingrid knew he would answer any other question she asked, but she also knew that he hoped she would ask no more.

'I will find some place to stash the net.' Ingrid got to her feet. 'It would not be good if I were seen here after dark.'

Understanding and gratitude both glimmered in Avan's tired eyes. 'None of this has been good for you.'

'No. But I do not need to make it any worse.' She bent over the net where it lay and found one of its corners. She began to roll the great mass of knots up into the tidiest bundle she could manage. It was surprisingly heavy, despite the fact that the strings from which it had been made were far too delicate to contain any fish she knew of. The strings radiated out from their knots making patterns like sun-bursts, like snowflakes. She had never seen such a net. She felt somehow she could become lost in those patterns if she stared at them for too long.

'You must bear your sister great love.'

Ingrid bowed her head over the bundle in her arms. 'She is the one happy thing our family has ever made.' Then, heavily regretting those words, Ingrid strode toward the door. 'I shall do as you say tonight.'

She did not give him time to reply. She had stayed far too long already.

Ingrid stashed the net deep in a tangle of tall grass and fern. She marked the spot with three gray stones. She hurried over the bluff heading for home, snatching up branches of dry wood and pausing to pluck up wild thyme as she went so that her arms would not be empty, and her absence would appear less remarkable.

But she had barely reached sight of the family yard when Thad, her youngest brother, came running up the track.

'Papa's home.'

Ingrid's back stiffened and her step faltered, but she recovered. 'Well, it's early for him, isn't it?' she said as brightly as she could manage. 'Help me with this.' Thad held out his thin, nine-year-old arms dutifully and Ingrid loaded them with wood. He trotted around the house toward the back door. Relatively unencumbered, she opened the front door and strode into the house.

'So, is it you?' Papa's voice rumbled out of the back kitchen, and the man himself followed a bare instant later, with Mama and Leo in tow. 'And where have you been, Miss?'

'As I am sure Mama told you,' said Ingrid calmly. 'I have been taking soup down to Mrs Whitkoff.' She passed him as if nothing was wrong, laying the thyme down on the bare dining table.

'And is that all?' demanded Leo. 'Or do you have other goods to deliver?'

For a moment, Ingrid did nothing but breathe in the sharp clean scent of the wild herbs. Then, she stiffened her shoulders and turned to face her accuser. 'What wrong do you suspect me of?'

'Our sail tore out.' Papa started forward with his shoulders hunched up almost to his ears. 'We had to come in early. As we tacked around, we saw a woman going in and out of the fishers' huts. It was remarked by more than one how much she looked like you.'

Ingrid swallowed, her throat gone suddenly dry. *You knew this would come. You cannot pretend to be surprised.*

'The man Avan says he has a way to help Grace,' she said flatly. 'I sought only a remedy for my sister.' ,

'And what did he seek, eh?' sneered Leo.

Which was the final straw. 'Curb that evil tongue of yours, Leo, even if you cannot curb your thoughts.'

'Ingrid . . .' began Mama.

'No,' snapped Ingrid. 'I tried to tell you what was wrong with Grace, and you only worried about whether the neighbors would believe we had both kept our virginity safe.'

'Ingrid!' thundered Papa.

'Well, I will tell you what the neighbors think of that.' She barreled on, too hot and angry to stop. 'The neighbors don't care! Half of them are bastards of one stripe or the other! But for God knows what reason you have decided that Grace is wicked, and that I am implicated in her supposed wickedness because I care what becomes of her and you don't.'

'You will not speak so in this house!' Papa raised his heavy hand.

Ingrid did not even flinch. 'Go ahead,' she said. 'Strike me down, but I tell you this. That blow had better lay me in my grave next to Grace, because if it does not, I will leave this house and I will blacken our name from Sand Island to Bayfield and right down to Chicago.'

Mama had gone paper white. She moved forward, a slow, sleepwalker's motion that reminded Ingrid of watching Grace slip forward in the darkness.

'If I ever hear you speak so again in this house, mine will be the hands that throw you out into the dirt.'

'How can you?' Ingrid flung her hands open wide. 'She's your daughter.'

'Do you think for one instant I have forgotten?' spat Mama. 'I am responsible for her. I am responsible for whatever devilry has taken hold of her! God forgive me, this is my fault!' Mama buried her face in her hands. 'My fault!'

Ingrid wanted to feel sorry, she wanted to feel pity, but all she felt was tired. 'Listen to me. I am going out. I will return by morning. If all goes well, Grace's affliction will be lifted. After that you can do as you like with me. All I ask is that you consider that I might have been telling nothing but the truth.'

She meant to leave the house then, but even as she turned she realized she could not leave Grace here. Who knew what Papa and Leo would do when she was called out to the shore. So, instead, Ingrid stormed up the stairs to her bedroom.

Grace lay under the covers, as still as any corpse.

'Come, Little Sister,' said Ingrid gently. 'Let's get you dressed, shall we?'

Through the floorboards, Ingrid could hear the voices of her family raised in argument and blame. She tried in vain to shut them out as she moved about the room, gathering Grace's clean linen, her thickest skirt and layers of shawls. Grace's skin was horribly cold to the touch and Ingrid had to dress her as if she were a rag doll. Grace's eyelids did not even flutter under Ingrid's attentions, and nothing passed her lips but the sigh of her breath.

'Perhaps I should become a nurse,' muttered Ingrid as she sat Grace up. 'I seem to be making a profession of hauling the sick about with me.'

At the same time, she knew she would never be able to carry Grace all the way down to the beach. Biting her lip, Ingrid pulled the string holding the scrap of iron off from around Grace's neck and tossed it onto the bed.

As the iron thudded against the quilt, Grace's head jerked upright and her eyes flew open wide. Her gaze lighted for a moment on Ingrid, but then slipped past her to the door. Her hand tightened briefly on Ingrid's arm as she used Ingrid to pull herself to her feet. She took three faltering steps, and collapsed, measuring her own length on the floorboards.

Ingrid dropped at once to her knees beside Grace. Grace

lifted her bedraggled head and saw Ingrid, truly saw her for the first time in this whole hellish month.

'Help me, Ingrid,' rasped Grace. 'Help me go to him.'

'Yes,' said Ingrid, although the word choked her. 'We are going to him now.'

Ingrid raised Grace up, shocked at the strength of her sister's grip. One step at a time, they together made their way down the stairs to the front room. Their family stopped their arguing and stared in silent astonishment as Ingrid supported Grace to the door.

No one spoke. What was there left to say? No one would stop them. There would be time enough in the morning, if morning came, to worry about whether they would once again be admitted to their home.

The road to the lake's shore had never seemed so long. Grace stumbled over every rut. Children and old women came to their doorways to stare at their strange, limping progress. A child's voice laughed. Another's called a name. A clod of mud arced through the air and thudded softly at Ingrid's feet. It was of small consolation that this was followed quickly by the sound of a sharp rebuke and a ringing slap.

Ingrid did not allow her attention to waver. She kept her mind focused sharply on the road, and on Grace. Grace's eyes shone with an eager light. Her sunken mouth trembled. Ingrid knew that her lips would be shaping the name of her ghostly lover, if only she knew it.

What will I do if she decides to run into the lake? Ingrid wondered with sudden desperation. *How can I possibly stop her?*

But there was nothing for it but to continue on their way, one weary step at a time. Against her will, Ingrid found her thoughts trailing behind them, all the way back to their door. She could not have said which made her heart heavier; the fear that their family might follow, or the fear that they might not.

At long last, Ingrid and Grace stumbled onto the beach below the bluff. When they reached the sand, Ingrid let go of Grace, although her entire soul screamed at her not to do so. She had to see what Grace would do. Once free, Grace tottered forward a few steps and sank down to the sand, pulled up her knees against her chest and wrapped her arms around them.

'He will come for me,' she said. 'After dark. He says so. He sings so to me.'

'Well, we'll just have to wait,' said Ingrid with a brittle briskness. 'Will he object to a fire until then?'

If Grace heard, she had no answer. She just continued to stare hungrily out across the water, listening to a voice Ingrid could not hear.

At least she wasn't going anywhere, which would require that Ingrid sit with her. Activity allowed Ingrid to keep her mind occupied on things other than the coming night. She dug a pit in the sand with her hands and pieces of driftwood. She gathered driftwood and tinder, ranging as far afield as she dared to bring back fuel. She did not want to risk running out of wood. Her foraging also kept her from having to watch the sails from the returning boats, knowing that any one of them who looked toward the shore could see her and Grace, and would wonder about it. Oh, they were now surely the nine days' wonder of the island. Even if Mama and Papa took them back in when this was over, what then?

Ingrid Loftfield, I'm ashamed of you. How can you even be thinking of that now?

But she was. Evidently, something of her parents' teaching had sunk into her heart. She made herself sit back on her heels and look at Grace – bright, sunny, Grace – trapped by a dead man, lost in a ghost story. That was what mattered. That was all that mattered.

Ingrid squatted down beside the fire pit and lit her tinder.

Slowly, the sun lowered itself behind the island and the trees stretched their gray shadows across the beach. The sky and the water darkened to black and the stars, undimmed by any trace of moonlight, lit their own fires one by one. Ingrid's driftwood and pine burned down to white coals. She could feel the heat beating hard against her. At first, it was a comfort in the rapidly chilling air, but as she continued to lay fuel on the low, hot flames, the heat grew too much for her and she had to stand back several paces. *Surely, that is enough,* she thought, looking at the glowing nest of coals and feeling their heat against her face and the backs of her hands. *Surely that will burn whatever I may have to throw on it.*

'Ingrid.'

Ingrid whirled around to see Avan standing behind her. He leaned heavily on a pole of roughly trimmed hemlock, her makeshift bandages still swaddling his hands. Even in the dim light of the fire and the stars she could see he was far too pale.

'You are not well. You should not have come.'

'I fear I could not help myself,' he said ruefully. 'Bring the net. It is time.'

Ingrid retrieved the net from its hasty hiding place. As she brought the bundle to the edge of the water, she watched Avan walk widdershins around Grace. He seemed to be struggling under some great burden. She could hear his rasping breath even over the sound of the wind in the trees.

'Now, Ingrid. Now!'

With all her strength, Ingrid cast the net into the water. It spun into the air, fanning open to display its whirl of patterned snowflakes. It dropped onto the black water where it floated for a moment among the flecks of moonlight, and then sank from sight.

At that same moment, the ghost rose.

He shone like the stars and the white coals of Ingrid's fire. He should have been magnificent, but loneliness rolled from his presence in choking waves. He huddled frightened in the midst of his own light and it was all Ingrid could do to stand where she was and watch him, balanced on the lake's tiny, night-black waves. Abandoned, abandoned by God to the cold of the lake, and all he wanted was some small warmth. That was all. Surely, that was not too much.

Grace climbed to her feet. 'I am here. I am yours, as I promised.'

'No.' Avan spoke the word in a whisper, but nonetheless it carried across the water, and Ingrid knew the ghost heard it as clearly as she did. 'She is not yours.'

'You cannot keep her from me,' replied the ghost, lifting his dripping head. The holes where his eyes should have been were as black as the waves, and without any trace of moonlight in them.

'I have drawn my circle about Grace Hulda Loftfield,' said Avan heavily, and Ingrid had presence of mind enough left to think this a strange reply. 'I have walked five times around her and each circle is a wall of stone and locked with an iron key. The key is hidden in the egg of a duck, in the bottom of the spring, beneath the white stone, at the roots of the tree, on the Isle of Shukerepia, in the river of Zagovory, at the end of the world, on the shores of the Land of Death and Spirit.' Avan's voice faltered, but he straightened and began again. 'I have drawn my circle . . .'

'Grace!' cried the ghost. 'He cannot hold you. Come to me, my own! Come here now.'

Grace screamed as if she were being torn in two. Avan's voice droned on and on in his strange recitation. Ingrid felt as if all the air had become a riptide drawing her forward, and it was all she could do to stand against it. She didn't dare move to put her arms around Grace, because if she did, she might break the circle. But Grace screamed and screamed and would not stop, and the ghost called and Avan called and there was not enough air in the whole world to breathe because of the weight of their calling.

Then, the lake began to churn white with foam, and, impossibly, the net she had cast out rose again. Something bulky was tangled in its rope. Ingrid added her own cry to the cacophony and launched herself forward, grabbing the net and hauling it to shore. Bones, gray with rot, heavy with water and despair clacked dully against each other.

All the world fell suddenly silent, and it seemed that all light vanished. Ingrid gasped and clutched at the net. The bones clacked again, and she saw the flicker of her fire on the beach. How had it gotten so far away?

'Where do you go with my bones, woman?' asked a voice from the darkness.

'Away from here.' Ingrid grit her teeth and struggled toward the fire. The bones were so waterlogged she felt like she must be pulling half the lake behind her.

'You have no right.'

'I have every right. She's my sister.'

'Don't answer him,' said another voice, a tired voice, a weak voice, but compelling nonetheless. 'This way, keep walking. Don't let the bones touch you.'

'Give back my bones.'

'Don't answer. Walk toward me.'

'Give back my bones!'

'This way. You are almost here.'

The bones were so heavy, the drag so powerful. Ingrid was strong, but she was tired, and the burden hung awkwardly. Ingrid heaved the net up behind her. One wet, soft bone brushed Ingrid's skirt.

'*Give me my bones!*'

The cry reached through her like a hand and clenched itself around Ingrid's heart. Cold, instant and burning, tore through her flesh and veins and the pain seized her so hard she could not even scream.

'Mine!' shrieked the ghost. 'You steal all that is mine, mine, mine!'

'Ingrid! Ingrid Anna Loftfield! Come here!'

Name. Her name, it tugged, toward the voice, toward the fire. The fire she could see, the fire she had built. But she couldn't make it carrying the bones. They were too cold. She had to let them go. The cold squeezed her heart and the voice cried in her ears, 'Mine, mine, mine, mine!'

No, thought Ingrid desperately, as she took another step forward, and another. *Mine. My bones, my heart, my sister, my fire. Mine.*

'Thief!' cried the ghost.

'Thief!' croaked Ingrid in reply. Too cold. She shook. She couldn't hold the net any longer. It was heavy as the whole world and cold as death. She couldn't feel her fingers or her feet anymore. But was the fire closer? Was it close enough to warm her? If she could reach the fire, if only . . .

'Grace is here, Ingrid. She needs you.'

Yes. Grace. Grace needed her, needed the bones, needed the fire. The name sent a sliver of strength to Ingrid's collapsing heart. She could do this. She must. She dragged herself and her burden forward.

She couldn't breathe. Hands tightened around her throat, crushing her windpipe. Ingrid tried to scream and her hands dropped the net to rise to her neck and try to claw at her attacker, but she touched nothing but cold and air. She saw now, she saw the glowing, distorted face of the ghost, she saw the fire, just inches away, and she saw Grace straining against her prison, and she saw Avan drive his knife into the ghost's ribs.

The chokehold faltered, and Ingrid collapsed beside the net. The cold fell again, crushing, killing, and with the last of her strength, she shoved net and bones into the fire.

The flames exploded outward as if she had thrown a bomb. In that single instant, Avan raised his arms high in exultation, Grace threw herself backward from the water and the ghost dissolved in the circle of his own light. In the next heartbeat, the roar and the heat bowled Ingrid over until she lay flat on her back in the sand, blinking stupidly up at the stars.

Stars. She could see the stars. Hands, heart and throat tingled painfully with the memory of the clutching cold, but they were hers again. Ingrid got her hands under her and pushed herself upright.

'Ingrid! Oh my God, Ingrid!'

'Grace?'

It took her a moment to focus, and in that moment, Grace launched herself into Ingrid's arms, almost knocking her over again.

'Grace!' cried Ingrid. They clung to each other, laughing and hugging. Grace pulled back for a moment, and Ingrid saw her sister fully and completely in herself again. Her eyes shone with all the familiar spark. Ingrid hugged her close again, tears prickling her own eyes. 'My God, Grace, you're back. You're safe.'

'I knew you'd find me,' said Grace. 'Part of me was always trying to call to you, but I couldn't make any noise. His voice . . .' she shuddered. 'It was so loud.'

'Shhhh.' Ingrid stroked her fair hair. 'Over and done with now. Now there's only Papa to fear.'

'Tush,' said Grace lightly. 'I'll take care of that, don't you worry. We'll all be sitting around the table at breakfast, you'll see.'

'All . . .' Ingrid found her head had cleared enough to admit more than one thought at a time, and her eyes looked beyond Grace.

Avan stood at the very edge of the water. Ingrid could see nothing but his silhouette. She patted Grace's hands and got to her feet, pleased to find herself steady, if aching, and went to his side.

Another step and he'd have been in the water. Wavelets lapped around his boots. Both bandaged hands clenched the hemlock pole, and fresh blood stained the linen. In the faint glow from the remains of the fire she could see on his face the same straining look that had possessed Grace so recently.

'Avan?' she asked, although her throat had gone dry. 'Can you hear me?'

'Yes.' He shook himself and turned toward the shore, using the pole like a cane. 'Fear not for me. Your sister?'

'We both owe you . . . I could never begin to repay . . .'

Avan shook his head again, dismissing her words.

'Trust Ingrid to find me a genuine Finnish sorcerer.' Grace laughed again, but in the next breath she pressed her hand against her head, swaying dangerously. 'I don't think I'm well yet.'

'You've been in bed a month solid. It would be a wonder if you were not weak.' Ingrid took her arm, but she hesitated. Avan still hunched against his pole, staring across the water. She could not simply leave him. 'I must get my sister home. Can you walk?'

Avan straightened his back, and his grip on the pole loosened, answering her question better than words. 'I can,' he assured her. 'All is right.'

'I will come and look in on you in the morning.'

Avan opened his mouth, then closed it, seeming to think the better of his words, but then he did speak. 'I would be glad of that.'

With a shock, Ingrid realized she would too. 'Then I will,' was all she said before she turned and led Grace up the bluff.

Avanasy stood on the edge of the freshwater sea and stared out across the waves, doing nothing but lean on his makeshift staff and think over what had passed. He remembered the rush of freed power, the strangely savory struggle to raise magics buried deep, and the unrelenting determination of one woman.

'She's brave that one,' said a voice behind him.

'Yes.' Avanasy knew the voice. Once a soul had heard the voice of a spirit power, they did not forget it. If he turned around, there would be a large rabbit sitting on the sand, probably combing its ears, or otherwise looking harmless.

'Strong, too,' Nanabush went on. 'Tell you true, Magician, I did not think she'd manage.'

'I believe she could manage anything she set her mind to.'

'Pity about the family. They offer poor exchange to a giving heart.'

Avanasy turned from the water. The rabbit sat on the silver sands, its nose whiskers twitching to take in the scent and feel of the night wind. If anyone else had been close enough to see, they would have wondered indeed how a rabbit could cast a shadow in the shape of a fat man. 'She has a suitor,' Avanasy said, flatly. 'Why has she not accepted him?'

'The suitor isn't suited.' The rabbit shrugged. 'How much more reason can there be?' It cocked its head. 'Will you give her a better exchange?'

'I have nothing to give.'

'Nothing you can give or nothing you will give?' inquired Nanabush. 'What ghost calls you from the lake, Sorcerer?'

Medeoan. Medeoan moved somewhere beyond those waters, having banished him from her future. Out in the vastness of the universe, Isavalta, his home, turned on its own wheel, he having banished himself from its future. It turned and did not stop for his urging, or his leaving. It turned and did not look back. Which was the proper way. Which, indeed, was the only way.

'None.' Avanasy faced inland. His eyes easily found the track Ingrid had taken with her sister. Memory of her proud carriage, swift eyes and soft and gentle hands rose warmly and effortlessly in his mind. 'None at all.'

Chapter Four

The rains had come to Hastinapura. They poured down in steady sheets of water, turning all the world silver and slick. Every window and door of the Palace of the Pearl Throne had been thrown open to welcome the cool and damp. The myriad sounds of rain wormed through all the carved screens of black wood and lace-like ivory. The dancers in the temple changed their songs and sacred steps to honor Chirtrani who was the Mother of the Rains, and so the wheel turned within and without and the patterns were laid down afresh.

Chandra *tya* Achin Ireshpad knelt on a silken cushion in his private apartment. He stared out at the endless fall of the rain obscuring the usual view of the lush gardens and meditated on the nature of the palace and its patterns.

Patterns that served Hastinapura, keeping the land safe and in accord with the world shaped by the dances of the Seven Mothers. Patterns which served his brother Samudra even as Samudra served those patterns.

Patterns which should have served Chandra, had Samudra's greed not overwhelmed them both, had Samudra not distorted the flow of history.

Footsteps sounded lightly on the marble floor behind him. Chandra did not turn. He heard the rustle of cloth and a brief smacking sound as the floor was kissed.

'I am sent to say that the First of All Queens asks the Brother of her Heart to come sit beside her.'

Chandra stayed still and silent for a moment longer. The rain had its own patterns, woven by the falling drops. If one could understand all that complexity, the thousands of millions of droplets and their paths, one could surely understand the whole world. One could see how to return to an earlier point and rectify one's mistakes.

'I am sent to say . . .'

'Yes, yes, I hear,' Chandra sighed. 'You may tell the First of All Queens the Brother of her Heart follows.'

The slave kissed the floor again and scuttled away with a mouselike patter of sandals.

The First of All Queens. Chandra snorted as he rose smoothly, allowing his robe to fall neatly into place before he took his first step. Samudra kept only one true queen. Oh, there was a stable of concubines for appearances, girls and women taken on as part of treaties and to aid alliances with noble families. They lived well in the quarters, but it was known that Samudra visited them but rarely, choosing to prove his manhood in acts of destruction rather than generation.

By the time Chandra reached the hallway, the slave was long since vanished. The corridor's arches of black wood flew high overhead, contrasting with the walls of carved red stone and the white marble floors. It was said that when the palace had been built each vein of the marble had been scrutinized to make sure it would run in the correct direction to weave itself into the whole.

What few outsiders knew was that the palace itself formed a latticework of spells with the Pearl Throne at its heart. The order of the passages, the order of the day, the patrols of the soldiers, the dances of the worshippers, all combined to continuously renew the work of the thousand sorcerers who had built this edifice long centuries ago. Spells of protection, of wisdom, of peace, of prosperity, woven over and over again. His footsteps now, treading their way toward the throne room, worked their purpose to preserve the anointed Emperor, to bring him wisdom and to bring his realm stability. All that for Samudra.

The throne room itself was a lofty chamber. The ceiling was a series of high, narrow domes banded with gold, coral and crystal. Those domes were linked by ivory arches minutely carved with friezes and hymns of praise to the Mothers. The Pearl Throne waited empty atop its broad dais of ten steps of polished black marble veined with ghost white. Black pearls made up its base so it seemed to grow out of the shining stone, and black gave way to silver, to rose, to pink, to the purest shimmering white rising to frame the occupant of the golden cushions in a shining halo. Behind it, carved in the same red stone as the floor, the Seven Mothers, each one four times the size of a man, danced in bas-relief, their hands holding lotus, fruits, bowls and swords, the symbols of peace, progeny, plenty, and protection.

Chandra remembered the view from the throne. The vast chamber spread out at his feet, with all the ministers and their underlings kneeling patiently on the red stone. He remembered feeling the strength of the Mothers at his back and the strength of his dynasty rooted deep into the foundations of the palace. Nothing could touch him. Nothing could even reach him.

Until Samudra had completed his plan. Now Chandra stood level with the secretaries and ministers, even the soldiers guarding the entrances to the rooms and the gates to the women's quarters, and looked up, waiting for his turn to address the throne, to address his younger brother.

'The First of All Queens asks that you come sit near her now.'

Without the Emperor, the First of All Queens could not appear in public. So, a series of delicately carved sandalwood screens were erected next to the dais. A bench with red cushions had been placed beside the screens, along with a table arrayed with sherbet to drink and dainties to nibble.

As a member of the Imperial family, Chandra had only to bow from the waist to properly acknowledge the First of All Queens whom he had to designate as the Sister of his Heart. He saw nothing of her but shadows on the other side of the screen, and the occasional flash of gold and crimson.

'As I am commanded, so am I come, First of All Queens,' said Chandra smoothly.

'Such formality, Brother!' she exclaimed with mock surprise. 'Had you business to complete, you could have sent word.'

You know I have no business. Your husband, my brother, allows me none. 'What business could I have more important than waiting on the words of the First of All Queens?'

The Queen gave a sharp, impatient sigh, cut off short, and replaced by soothing words. 'I expect my Brother misses his son.'

'Prince Kacha does well in the far north,' he said. 'He sends his duties and his felicitations.'

'Which I am delighted to accept.' Cloth rustled, and the Queen's voice came closer. From the shadows, he thought she must have stepped nearer to the screen. 'But, is it not true that you are often dull, my brother? My husband is much away and has left little business for your attention.'

'I have all I need, First of All Queens.' *My brother generously permits my lungs to breathe and my heart to beat. He values my flesh enough to barter it away for his treaties with the northern barbarians. What more could I expect?*

'I do not believe that to be the truth.' The Queen's voice

was solemn, but without any note of accusation. Chandra felt curiosity rising in spite of himself. Could the woman be sincerely concerned about him? Was it possible Samudra had not completely drowned her sympathies? Perhaps there was room to work here.

'You have, I think, been too much alone since your wife died.'

Anger swiftly replaced curiosity. How dared this woman speak of Bandhura? His first wife, his true confidante, his help-mate? How dare she speak of any woman to him when she was the one who had deprived him of all his women? Bandhura had told him of the scene, of how this woman, who was just another woman then, had gone to the women's inner-most quarters, where the ones who waited on the Imperial pleasure were lodged, and announced that Samudra, and Samudra's line, would ascend to the Pearl Throne, and that all who so desired could take their places waiting on her, and on him now. And all of them had. All Chandra's wives proved themselves no better than the whores. All but Bandhura, who had stayed true and loyal, who had borne him his son to be vengeance for them both.

'There is a woman of my company, Abhilasha *ayka* Aditiela. Her dower is twelve towns in the south. She is young enough to bear many more children of your line. Further, she is fair and is skilled in all the sixty-four arts and sciences.'

Chandra couldn't believe what he was hearing. Marry? And marry one of the Queen's spies? She could not possibly believe . . .

'I have communicated my desire for the match at length to my husband, and he is agreeable. It shall be accomplished when the First Rain is over and the moon is again favorable. Our wedding gift to you shall be a new household complete in your capital town.'

Filled to brimming with your spies and lackeys so that I may not make any move without it being reported to you and my brother. You like not my presence in the shadow of the Pearl Throne to remind you of the wrong your husband did, so you must build me a coral prison with a wife for a jailer.

Chandra stood abruptly, unable to remain still any longer. 'Then I should compose a letter of greeting to my new bride.'

'Tell me this pleases you, Brother. I would not have it otherwise.'

Chandra forced a smile into his voice. 'It pleases me to do the will of the First of All Queens.'

'It is hard, Brother, to break a mourning that has been carried for so long, but let your heart be softened toward your new wife. Let her bring you peace.'

Chandra bowed. 'The First of All Queens is great in her wisdom. I will do my best.' *Probably you have found me some lowborn slut with the appetites of a cat in heat, thinking that, like my brother, I am counseled by the recipient of my cock and will soon be lulled into complaisancy.*

Again the Queen sighed. This time it was a reluctant, regretful sound. 'You may go now, Brother, if that is your wish. We will sit together again soon and speak more of these matters.'

'I await the Queen's word.' Officially excused, he straightened up and turned politely away so that he might not catch even a glimpse of the Queen's robe as she departed. He kept his pace even, his back straight, and his hands loose as he paced across the breadth of the throne room, following the ordained path to his apartment.

Inside, Yamuna waited for him. The brown skeleton of a man disdained the pillows and couches. Instead, he stood in front of the open window, his hands folded neatly in a position of patience and meditation. He could have stood so for hours, indeed for days, Chandra knew. He had more than once seen Yamuna do just that.

Chandra cursed futilely. He had hoped to have some time to himself, so that he might come to terms with what had just happened, and decide how to respond, and how to tell his *Agnidh*, his bound-sorcerer, what had occurred. But no, of course, Yamuna had heard of it the second it happened. It was part of his endless work.

'I dismissed the slaves,' said Yamuna, lowering his hands. He wore only a white cloth wrapped about his hips. His skin stuck tight to bone and muscle, giving the impression that all of the humors had long since been drained from him. One only had to look into his eyes, however, to see all the dreadful vitality that smoldered within his shrunken frame. Ascetic practice had burned away Yamuna's youth, but it had concentrated his soul. His right hand only was the hand of a young man. Chandra tried not to look at it. Chandra had not been present at the ceremony where Yamuna traded his hand for Kacha's hand, his eye for Kacha's eye, but the idea of it still could leave Chandra cold.

'I felt you would not want negligent ears to listen while we took counsel,' Yamuna was saying.

'Thank you.' Chandra sank onto his cushion. 'You are correct, as ever.'

'Do not speak to me as if I were your mindless brother or his strumpet wife,' snapped Yamuna. 'It is not seemly.'

I am to be wed to a spy of the Queen's, and now you are come to berate me. Chandra pressed his fingertips to his brow. *How did I fail to sever our bond when I had the Pearl Throne beneath me?*

'You did not think to argue with her, I suppose.' Yamuna did not sit, or bow, as he should have. He simply stood with the whole world at his back and looked down at his charge. 'Or suggest an alternate choice?'

'What choice is there? What woman could I name that she could not corrupt?'

'Then you should have told her you had decided to take an ascetic vow,' snapped Yamuna. 'In order to better purify your soul before the Mothers.'

'Then I will do so now.'

'Idiot!' The word slapped against Chandra. 'She will know you have spoken to me, and that this is not a true vocation. She will not accept it.'

'Then what does it profit to speak of what I could have done? The order has been given. I am to be married and sent away, and that is the end of it.' He shook his head. 'It changes nothing. The plan proceeds. Your link with Kacha is not severed.'

'So, you do remember that we are engaged in important work, and that the further you are sent from the throne, the fainter your power grows.' Yamuna snorted. 'Your son is in truth the best of you. I am glad I did not waste my right hand on such stuff as I see before me now.'

Which was finally too much to bear. Disregarding his robe and all his appearances, Chandra rose, meeting the sorcerer eye-to-eye. 'You forget yourself, Sorcerer, to chide me so.'

Yamuna did not flinch, did not even hesitate. 'All I forget is how you signed your throne over to your younger brother because you were afraid for your own skin,' said Yamuna, and his words were as cold and hard as the marble under their feet. 'Rather than face him in open battle, you sneak and skulk through the palace, looking for his bare buttock like a snake in the dark, and you force me to skulk beside you.'

'Stop!'

'And abandon my office, as you have abandoned yours?'

'I command you!'

'Then do so.' Yamuna dropped into a slave's obeisance in

front of him. 'I am, after all, yours to command. Tell me what
to do, Master. How shall we topple your brother? How shall
we rule the three empires when they tumble into our laps?'
Yamuna peered up at him from his mocking crouch,
prepared, to all appearances, to wait all year long for his
answer.

Chandra stared down at him. *I could strike your head off right
now, Old Man. No one would question me. Not even Samudra. You
are mine to do with as I will. I could rip your withered heart from your
chest and hurl it into the rain.*

And what would he do if that heart, once ripped free,
crawled obediently back to its master, as his hand had once
crawled away from him? What would Yamuna do to him then?

Inside himself, Chandra screamed at his impotence. How
much longer would he be ordered around by those who
should have obeyed his least word? He grit his teeth and stared
at the endlessly falling rain.

Not long, not long, he told himself, breathing the fresh, damp
air deeply. *Soon, the three empires will be yours. Yamuna will require
you to rule them. He thinks he sets a shadow on the Pearl Throne.
But he will learn differently.*

'If the Queen cannot be swayed, then this spy of hers must
be convinced to turn. Her death would be too conspicuous.'

'Very good, my Lord.' Yamuna rose from his mocking pose
and faced Chandra with the light of approval in his burning
eyes, one the eye of an ancient man, the other the eye of a hale
youth. 'You will permit yourself to be coaxed. The slaves and
the lackeys will hear you rage and soften by turns. And then
you will be turned by your bride, who shall be turned toward
you. I will provide the means.'

'And if they believe I am cowed, they will pay less attention
to my doings.'

'You show the beginnings of thought at last, Chandra.'

You, Old Man, will one day be stunned by the depths of my thought. I will enjoy seeing your face then.

Yamuna bowed humbly and departed, backing from the chamber, not turning his face from a member of the Imperial family, as if it was Prince Chandra who was finished with him, and not the other way around. When the slave closed the door between them, he straightened, turned silently on his heel and left, striding through the halls of ivory, coral and precious stone to his own chamber.

Chandra thought Yamuna did not see the hatred that blazed in his eyes, thought that Yamuna did not know the plans he harbored in his greedy and pathetic mind. Chandra thought he would one day humble Yamuna, in truth. Perhaps he even thought to kill his *Agnidh*. Well, let him think it. It kept that mind occupied and let him believe he was cunning. Chandra's vanity was as useful as his impotence.

Yamuna's private chamber waited at the summit of one of the palace's tall, narrow domes. A likeness of the summer sky curved overhead with the phases of the moon inlaid in mother of pearl. All the names of the Seven Mothers had been laid in ivory in the floor, so, it was said, that they might always pay attention to what happened within the chamber.

It was many years now since Yamuna had learned that was folly. The palace, so carefully designed and laid out to perpetuate its webwork of spells was nothing more than a cage of lies. The gods were wily beings, extorting their worship. They were expert and immortal bargainers, no better than the daemons who cowered under chains and treaties placed on them by the Ancients.

Well, soon the world would change. Soon, all the worlds would change.

For the moment, however, there were appearances to be maintained.

The smallest side chamber of Yamuna's apartment was lined with shelves, and the shelves were lined with jars of all shapes and sizes – tall, narrow jars of glass filled with smoky liquids; thick, squat alabaster jars that were impossibly cold to the touch; jars of red clay sealed with red wax; small obsidian jars the size of a child's hand that gleamed in the light; jars of cut crystal from the far north, jars of pure-white porcelain from Hung-Tse.

No slave tended these shelves. Yamuna had warned them all away years ago. No hand touched the jars save his own.

The vessel he reached for today was on the middle shelf; a graceful carafe carved of cinnabar, corked tightly and sealed with beeswax imprinted with three sigils known only to a handful of living men. Yamuna carried the jar to the center of the chamber and set it on the floor. Beside it he set a piece of blank parchment. Then, he cracked the beeswax seal, breaking the sigils, and pulled the stopper.

Yamuna stepped back. 'Your master calls you forth!'

There was no billow of smoke, nor any flash of light or peal of thunder. Such details were for children's tales. There was only silence, and cold, as the chill of death seeped from the jar where it had been confined. Slowly, it cocooned the room with cold. Only then did the dead man crawl forth.

Agnidh Harshul climbed painfully from his prison, cramped and crabbed, suffering from his cold confinement and having no choice but to suffer. In life, he had been a tall man, strong in his body and comfortable in his power. Pleased with his role as *Agnidh* to Prince Kacha, he had sought nothing beyond his service, a loyal son of the Mothers and a loyal scion of the Pearl Throne.

Kacha had killed him on the voyage to Isavalta, and Yamuna

had supplied both the poison and the locked box into which Kacha had placed his tongue, his seal, and one of his fingers to return to Yamuna so that Yamuna might conjure his soul into service, as he did now.

The dead man shivered before Yamuna, his raw hatred plain on his pained features. It meant nothing. He was bound and he must serve Yamuna's will. He had no choice.

'You will give me a letter,' said Yamuna to the dead man. 'A report of your activities in Isavalta. You will report on Kacha's satisfactory progress in his relations with the Imperial ministers. You will describe the coronation and how well he played his part in it.'

Death should have severed Harshul's bond with Kacha, but Yamuna's sorceries had re-established it. Even trapped as he was, Harshul touched Kacha, and he knew enough to compose what was needed, a false letter to lead the Emperor to believe that Harshul was alive and keeping his watchful eye on Kacha. Emperor Samudra must have no cause to question what was happening in Isavalta. He must be kept in ignorance as long as possible. When the war finally erupted, he would have to admit to one of two things: that he had lost control of a mere boy, or that he had been party to a coup.

Either admission would badly damage the Emperor's reputation, and make it that much harder for him to maintain his rule.

The dead man fought Yamuna's order, of course, but his struggle was as meaningless as his hatred. In the end, he knelt, as he must, and he shuddered with the effort of reaching across the veil that separated the solid and the ethereal. He breathed, if a dead man could be said to have breath, across the parchment, and the parchment filled with tight lines of words written in a precise hand the Emperor would recognize as Harshul's.

The ghost, trembling, straightened itself up. Yamuna retrieved the parchment, glancing it over to be sure it seemed complete enough.

'You may speak,' he told the ghost as he examined the missive. In life, Harshul had been gregarious. It pleased Yamuna to allow him speech now and again.

In death, Harshul's voice was as thick and cold as a mist over water. 'When you die, the Mothers will give you to me. I will be a daemon and I will feast on your soul for eternity.'

Yamuna folded the false missive with care and let himself smile at his slave. 'When I die you will be a shade, as impotent as you are now. You will never touch me. For I will never die.'

'You are mad, old man.' The bound spirit lacked the power to even speak Yamuna's name. 'All men return to the Mothers.'

'But I shall not remain a man.' Yamuna savored the words that he had so seldom spoken aloud. There was none to whom he could trust them. None but shades and slaves who could not utter a word unless it be by his own will. 'When Chandra is bound to the northern empire, so will I be bound, and its earth will know me, and the creatures of that earth will know me, and they will reveal to me the secrets of that land's wild heart, and how those barbarians can rise to divinity on their own wings when we must remain in the mud and dust, groveling at the feet of the sluts who call themselves the Seven Mothers.'

The shade said nothing, Yamuna did not wish it to. But even dead and bound as it was, it recoiled from him, and Yamuna took pleasure in the sight. It was a foolish pleasure, he knew, like a little boy tormenting insects, but it was there all the same. He would have to retreat for a series of days and perform penance to worm this petty pride from his heart. It was unworthy of one who would soon become a god, and as an impurity, it hampered his power and must be done away with.

But there were other matters to attend to first.

'Return to your prison, slave,' said Yamuna. 'I have no more need of you.'

The dead man would have screamed if he could, but Yamuna held him silent. So he turned, shaking violently, and crawled back into the jar. Yamuna replaced the stopper, applied fresh beeswax and remade the sigils before returning the jar to its place on the shelf in his workroom. There also, he closed up the missive with red wax and Harshul's own seal.

According to the most ancient sagas, the Seven Mothers bound together the souls of sorcerers so that they might preserve the life and order of the lands in their care. In exchange for power, place, and extended life, sorcerers were guardians, protectors and advisors to all who might have need of them. Their very footsteps would weave spells of protection across Hastinapura. Still, they must forever remember they were servants, not rulers. They might strive for any earthly power they could reach in service of their magic, but power beyond that was forbidden. Royalty was forbidden them. Immortality, divinity, these were never to be theirs.

Most sages said that such a transference was impossible. It was outside the order of nature.

But, reasoned Yamuna, if it was impossible, why was it forbidden? Why forbid a thing that could not be done?

Did not the Nine Elders of Hung-Tse work transformations of their own, turning their members into spirit powers? Did not the barbarians of the north have ones of divided souls who could turn themselves into gods through sacrifice?

No, it could not be impossible, only difficult. Perhaps it could not be done here in Hastinapura where all powers were catalogued and treated with and for. But in the wild north, where the powers did as they would, where disorder and chaos swirled together, what might he not harness? What might he not become? Worlds would come within his compass and not even the Mothers could forbid him anything his heart desired.

He smiled and tapped his fingers against his false letter. After dark, he would give the missive to one of his slaves, who would in turn go down to the city and find some Isavaltan captain or sailor who could be bribed to give the missive to one of the Pearl Throne's servants and say it had come from Vyshtavos for the Emperor. It would be delivered to the mountains where the Emperor Samudra waged his latest war, and Samudra would read the words and believe all was well in Isavalta.

Yamuna smiled out at the rain. In truth, all was well, but not in the manner which the Emperor believed.

'And where are the Mothers in all their power to tell you otherwise?' he asked the rain. When the rain had no answer, Yamuna laughed softly, and set about his other works.

'I am beginning to believe,' said Medeoan, rubbing her eyes, 'that either all my Lords Master are idiots, or they think I'm one.' She looked across the wide desk to Kacha who sat behind a pile of his own letters and papers. 'Listen to this.' She adjusted her voice to a fair imitation of an eastern accent. 'And I must further beg to inform Your Majesty Imperial that due to the unusual number of spring lambs born this year, additional pasturage has been allotted to nineteen shepherding families.' She lowered the paper and sighed in exasperation. 'Now why would I possibly need to know that?'

'Does Your Majesty Imperial wish to make any reply?' inquired Senoi, her fussy, officious, but very efficient first secretary. Even Kacha, who took such care in the appointment of her staff agreed he was the very man for the job.

Medeoan opened her mouth, but Kacha spoke first. 'Her

Majesty Imperial will answer that one in the morning,' he said, before he smiled across their desk at her. 'You're exhausted, Medeoan. Why do you not retire? I will finish what is needful here.'

She shouldn't, she knew. Attention to detail was important, and she could not pay attention to details if she did not know what they were. But even as she thought that, an enormous and undignified yawn forced its way out of her throat.

She stared at the mounds of paper still to be worked through. 'Perhaps I will retire,' she said sheepishly. 'But I'll expect you to review the remaining business with me thoroughly in the morning,' she added as she stood up.

'That I gladly will.' Kacha gave a half-bow.

Medeoan rounded the desk and bent to kiss her husband good night. 'And I expect you to attend me in my bed when you are finished,' she whispered into his ear.

'That I gladly will,' he replied just as softly and Medeoan smiled again at the mischievous light in his eyes.

With her ladies and the House Guard behind her, and pages scurrying before with lamps to light the way and herald her arrival, Medeoan traversed the corridors from her private study to her private apartments. She was tired, but she was cheerful. Another day successfully negotiated, thanks to Kacha's unflagging support and energy. As he had promised, together they were the autocrat of Isavalta.

She had been so frightened! Medeoan smiled now to think of her dread. Before her, the page girls opened her chamber doors and her ladies hurried in to light the lamps and coax the fire into more vigorous life. Had it not been for Kacha, she was certain she would not have even managed the coronation. Hours of ceremony, hours of standing and sitting and bowing and having the heavy golden regalia handed to her, taken away, blessed, anointed, kissed and handed back, and all the time she could think of nothing except her parents watching her from the Land of Death and Spirit and frowning at their reluctant, trembling child. But there was Kacha, beside her, more solid and more real than her fears. Kacha to attend to her with grave dignity, and to breathe such salacious comments in her ears about the ceremony's other participants that she could barely keep her countenance. That night, he had held her close and whispered reassurances to her, stroking her hair until her fears eased and she could sleep in peace.

In the weeks that had followed, all had continued as it had begun. Kacha remained always at her side, ever ready to help her plow through the endless petty work of empire. His counsel was always sober, and there was no point of her comfort, ease or service that he was not ready to oversee.

Medeoan sighed happily as she and her two head ladies moved behind the bed screens so that they could undress her for the night. She was happy. She had never imagined she would be happy as empress, but so it was, and it was because of Kacha.

Chekhania and Ragneda divested her of her outer coat and set to work on the laces of her dress and the catches of her jewels. They were competent, if inclined too much to giggle. She did miss Prathad and Vladka some days, but Prathad had been found in the hay barn with a sergeant of the House Guard and had to be dismissed in disgrace, and Vladka had been found taking bribes from one of the court lords to bear him tales of Medeoan's doings. How could she keep such a one with her, no matter how many years she had served? Vladka did not even have the strength of character to own her guilt in the end. She had just cried and begged and tried to say it was not so, even when she knew Kacha and Chekhania had brought Medeoan all the proof.

Medeoan raised her arms so Chekhania and Ragneda could

pull her nightdress over her head and lace it up. The covers on the bed were already turned down and the warming pans had been applied. Medeoan laid herself down and the ladies covered the braziers and drew the curtains, wishing her good night and departing to get themselves ready for bed.

Despite being tired, Medeoan found she was unable to compose herself to rest. She stared up at the shadowy canopy overhead, listening for Kacha's entrance into the chamber. But there were only the sounds of her ladies talking softly among themselves and making up their beds and changing into their own night clothes. A restlessness to have her husband beside her took hold of Medeoan. It was becoming a familiar sensation, and not a wholly unpleasant one. She imagined him walking down the corridors, wishing good night to those whose business kept them up late. He would return to his own chamber, where his waiting gentlemen would ready him for bed, and then he would come through the connecting door, and pull back her bed curtains, and then, and then . . .

A thought struck Medeoan, a happy bit of mischief. Always, Kacha came to her. What if, this time, she went to him? He would come behind his bed screens, thinking he would need to come find her, and there she would already be.

The idea pleased her, making her smile in the darkness. She decided at once to put thought into action and slipped out of her bed. The floor was chilly under her stockinged feet. She padded around the bed screens, and the ladies immediately sprang to their feet and ceased their activities; plaiting and brushing their hair, laying out their clothes, gossiping. Chekhania ran up to her at once, pale in her nightdress, but Medeoan waved her away.

'I shall be in the Emperor's chamber,' she announced.

Chekhania's hand flew to her mouth to smother the giggle that surely must be coming, and Medeoan saw the slightly scandalized delight in her eyes. Lifting her chin in a mockery of Imperial dignity, Medeoan turned and walked regally through the door and into Kacha's bedchamber.

The effect of her arrival there was as immediate as her unexpected appearance in her own room. The gentlemen were all still fully dressed, as their master had not yet retired for the night, but they too were engaged in their various activities; writing, reading, tending the fire, laying out wine and fruit, gossiping their own gossip. They stared for a moment at the sight of their Empress in her nightdress, but swiftly remembered to drop their eyes and make a reverence. Prithu, Kacha's head gentleman, a neat, dark-skinned man who had come with him from Hastinapura, approached Medeoan hesitantly, his eyes darting about the room, trying to look anywhere but at his partially dressed Empress, and reverenced nervously before her.

'Is there any way I can assist Your Majesty Imperial?'

'I have decided to await my husband here,' Medeoan said, amazed at how lofty her voice sounded. 'And you will not say anything about it, as I wish it to be a surprise. Do you understand?'

A look of extreme consternation crossed Prithu's face, but he reverenced again. 'I understand, Majesty Imperial.'

Medeoan felt she ought to pity the man. After all, where he came from, the women lived separately from their men, even their husbands. This must be extremely shocking for him. Somehow, that idea gave her little plan a whole new relish.

'If one word is spoken, I will be most displeased,' she announced, loud enough for the room in general to hear. Then, she gathered up her hems, retreated behind Kacha's bed screens, and slipped under the covers of his bed. Settling herself in, she had to cover her mouth, as Chekhania had, to smother her giggles.

Imagining Kacha's face, and his reaction to her mischief,

occupied Medeoan's mind pleasantly while she waited, listening to the muted, hesitant sounds of the gentlemen's voices and movements.

Then, at long last, she heard the outer door open, and the sounds of firm bootsteps, and the answering patter of quick steps from the gentlemen hurrying to meet their master.

'Mother's guts, Prithu, if I've had a more boring night, I don't know when it was,' said Kacha gruffly. There was a sound after that, probably him drinking a cup of sweet wine offered to him by Prithu. 'I've one matter to take care of first, then I must attend my lady wife.'

Medeoan clapped her hand over her mouth again, and forced down her own giggles.

'Majesty . . .' began Prithu, and Medeoan froze. Was he going to give her away?

'What?' answered Kacha impatiently.

'Majesty, perhaps you should attend the Empress directly. Perhaps your other business can wait . . .'

'Perhaps you should confine yourself to making sure my night clothes are brushed and ready. My wife likes to see me at my best.'

'But Majesty . . .'

If you do this, man, I will not be quick to forgive, thought Medeoan, quite miffed. He was going to spoil the whole joke.

The only answer was silence, and then Prithu saying, 'Yes, Majesty.' Medeoan found herself wondering what look or gesture Kacha had made to his servant.

She lay back then, secure in her nest and delighted in her mischief. Kacha would finish this last business, he would come around the screens and see her there, and then, and then . . .

Firelight flickered beyond the bed curtains. The noises of the servants settled to soft rustlings. Medeoan smiled in anticipation of the culmination of her jest. She smelled something sharp, not quite smoke, but not incense either.

Then, she felt it – the chilling of the air, the prickling in her skin that traveled deep into her bones. Magic. Nearby, someone was performing a working of will. She had given no orders, she knew of nothing needful . . .

Thoughts of danger shivered through Medeoan and she shot out of the bed.

'Kacha!' she cried as she dashed around the screens, and stopped in mid-stride.

She saw Kacha standing beside a brazier near his writing desk. He trembled hard, sweat pouring down his skin, his face in a wild grimace, torn between agony and ecstasy, and his hand, his withered right hand, thrust deep into the brazier's fire.

Shock froze Medeoan where she stood. As he gradually focused on Medeoan, a new emotion crept into his twisted visage – rage.

Medeoan couldn't think. Her vision blurred, refusing to see what was before her, she clutched at herself, seeking to still the sensation that told her against all reason that some strange magic was being worked here. Impossible, impossible. Kacha was no sorcerer. Kacha could not look at her with such hatred . . .

Medeoan fled. She turned and ran back to her room, slamming the door behind herself. Ignoring the startled flurry of questions from her ladies, she dashed toward the bed, like a child seeking safety from the night's terrors. She clambered through the curtains and huddled on the mattress, her hand pressed across her mouth, but now it was to suppress her screams.

It cannot have been . . . what did I see? Nothing, I cannot have . . . But it was a working, I felt it . . . I cannot . . . it was not . . . Fragments of thoughts, disjointed and purposeless, tumbled through her mind.

'Mistress . . .' came a tremulous voice beyond the curtain.

'Leave me be,' whispered Medeoan, wrapping her arms tightly around herself. 'Leave me be.'

'Yes, Mistress.'

She closed her eyes. Kacha's hand was in the fire. She had seen it. She had felt the magic coursing through the ether. These things were true, but could not be true.

What happened? What happened?

'Beloved?'

Kacha. His voice sounded so tender, so like himself. How could he have been that creature who looked at her with such rage?

'Beloved, let me look upon you.'

There was a rustle of cloth and the touch of flickering light upon her eyelids.

'Please, Medeoan. Look at me. Let me explain.'

Slowly, Medeoan opened her eyes, and there stood Kacha, framed by the heavy curtains, a lamp in his good hand. His face was as soft, as tender as it ever was when he gazed at her.

Medeoan licked her lips. 'What was that?' she whispered. 'What were you doing in there?'

Gingerly, as if unsure of his welcome, Kacha sat on the edge of the bed. He pushed the curtain back so that he could set the lamp down on the bedside table before he spoke.

'What you saw, Beloved, was what keeps my wounded hand,' he held up his scarred and withered limb, 'whole, if damaged, on my body.'

'There was magic there,' she said, her thoughts only reluctantly beginning to order themselves.

'The fire itself is magical. I must burn, each night, a series of sticks carved with runes, and give my hand over to the fire. This is the working of my father's sorcerer. If I did not do this, rot would have taken my hand long ago, and it would have been severed to save my life.' He looked shamefacedly down at his shriveled fingers. 'This is not a lovely thing, but it is better than no hand at all.'

'Why did you not tell me of this?' Medeoan's voice was harsh.

'Because this treatment is painful, and I . . . I do not always bear it as a man should. I did not want you to see me that way. I did not want you to worry,' his voice dropped to a whisper. 'I did not want you to pity me.'

She took his withered hand, and it was rough and crabbed as it always was. She had become well used to the touch of that hand. It wasn't even warm from the fire. The scars that ringed the wrist were as white and crooked against his dark skin as they had been before.

'This magic does not heal you,' she said.

He shook his head. 'It cannot. The damage was too severe by the time they were able to free me.'

She held his hand, willing herself to believe, willing herself to accept, but at the same time, her blood prickled with the sensation of shaping magic, of the working of will. It came from Kacha, and from Kacha's wounded hand, and she did not know why. If all was as he said, why would she feel this now that the spell was over and done? If he lied . . . but how could she even think that Kacha might lie to her?

'I'm sorry if I startled you, Beloved.' Kacha's good hand tucked under her chin and lifted her face until she must look into his deep eyes. 'I'm sorry I deceived you.'

She kissed him, hard and suddenly, surprising herself at the force of her gesture. Kacha stiffened, but only for a bare instant. Then, he wrapped his arms tightly around her, answering her urgency with his own. She needed the urgency, needed the rush of it, to wipe away her doubts, the lingering feeling of a spell where there should not have been any, to restore the unclouded peace in her heart that had always occupied the place where Kacha dwelled.

Morning came. Medeoan opened her eyes to see Kacha sleeping beside her. She liked to watch him as he dreamed. She liked the peace in his face and his tousled hair and the gentle sound of his breathing. Their mornings together were never long, so normally she would watch him and then she would press herself against him, and he would sigh in his sleep and roll over to embrace her, and she would revel in that as well.

This morning, she did not move toward him. Her eyes felt dry and too hot, as if she had just finished crying. She had slept only fitfully, for she could not stop the thoughts tumbling through her head.

Why would any sorcerer impose such a healing, not even a healing, such a spell, on a person? How could it be that this was the only way to keep Kacha's hand whole? She remembered too well the day Avanasy had called her from her studies and taken her out to the laundry sheds. Amidst the steam and the stench a woman lay on a pallet, screaming in her pain and writhing so her fellows were forced to hold her down. Her legs and both feet were a mass of burned and swollen flesh where a kettle had overturned and spilled a flood of boiling water over her. The stench from her roasted flesh sent Medeoan reeling.

Lord Sorcerer Iakush was already there. Avanasy ordered Medeoan to stand by the Mistress of the House, and the two men began to work. They had few tools at their disposal, and they had to work quickly, before the mere pain of her burns carried the woman away. Avanasy bound the woman's pain in a stone, the effort of it nearly making him swoon. Iakush plunged her legs into a basin of milk and herbs and then sprinkled more milk in a circle around her, weaving his spell as he made his circle. Perspiration sprang out on his forehead from the strength of his working and the heat of the room. Medeoan herself shivered from the waves of magic that rolled from the two men, cresting over the burned woman and crashing against Medeoan. No one else could feel anything. They could only stare and pray. Medeoan had been brought to watch and understand, and she tried to concentrate on the words Iakush spoke, on the touch of his working.

At last, at long last, a trembling Iakush knelt before the basin and drew out the woman's right leg. Even under the white film the milk left, Medeoan could see her flesh was whole and sound.

If an injury that should have killed a woman could be healed by two Isavaltan sorcerers, how could the sorcerers of the Hastinapuran court, who were rumored to be among the most powerful and extensively learned in the world, fail to make her husband's wounded hand whole? Medeoan had never asked herself the question before, and now she hated herself for the asking. She wanted to accept what she had been told with all her strength and soul, and yet she could not.

Was there some neglect? Some lie, some secret, some incompetence on the part of the sorcerer? Could that be true? Medeoan stared up at the canopy. There had been a sorcerer at her grandmother's court, a dark and charismatic man. He had been given the care and treatment of her ailing great-uncle, and had, it was later found, been deliberately keeping him ill to prolong his appointment. He'd been beheaded in the court-yard.

Could this Hastinapuran sorcerer be doing something similar to Kacha? Was that what was happening? Was Kacha being deliberately kept in pain by a worthless servant? The thought clenched Medeoan's jaw in anger.

'Beloved?' murmured Kacha sleepily.

Medeoan turned toward her husband, and felt her love for him, unquestioning and unquestionable, well up in her. He was being wronged, but, unschooled in magic as he was, how could he know?

The fingers of his good hand brushed her cheek. 'Your face was stern, Beloved. What were you thinking of?'

'Your hand, my husband.'

Kacha smoothed the coverlet over her stomach. 'I wish you would not. It is what it must remain. There is nothing to be done.'

Medeoan pushed herself up on her elbows. 'I'm not so certain, Kacha. I've seen miracles performed by Isavaltan sorcerers. It should not have been so impossible for a sorcerer to save your hand without this ... treatment you must undergo.'

Kacha shook his head ruefully. 'Everything that could be done, Yamuna did. He is my father's *Agnidh*, his bound-sorcerer. The life and protection of our family is his charge.'

Medeoan tried to choose her words with care. 'Kacha, is it possible that Yamuna ... did not do all that he might?'

'What do you mean, Medeoan?' Kacha frowned.

Carefully, Medeoan told him the story of her grand-mother's court sorcerer. Kacha listened, his face remaining grave.

'That might be a thing that could happen in Isavalta,' he said when she had finished. 'But it is not possible in the court of the Pearl Throne. Yamuna is bound to my family, by oaths and ceremonies. He cannot act against us. It is impossible. He would call down the wrath of the Seven Mothers if he did.' He tried to smile, and almost managed it. 'I must ask you to accept what I myself had to accept years ago, Beloved. My hand is ruined and its treatment is painful.' He kissed her gently on the forehead. 'Your concern speaks of love and I am glad of it, but try not to worry about it anymore.'

'I will do my best,' promised Medeoan.

Her best, however, did not take her very far. The question gnawed at her through the breakfast with Lord Master Kagnimir and his men. It occupied her through the Council meeting, and as she dictated her morning letters to her secretaries afterwards and tried to concentrate as they read back to her a report from the legal advisors her father had assembled in an attempt to begin to codify the laws of the empire.

It stayed with her even after Kacha rode out to welcome the new convoy of ships arriving from Hastinapura which were bearing the new ambassador from the Pearl Throne. Although Medeoan no longer had to watch him working with his weak and painful hand, the thought that he suffered repeatedly and needlessly would not leave her. But how could she make him believe that was so?

She would have to make sure he saw the proof with his own eyes. That would cause him pain, and she could not relish that thought, but the pain it would spare him would be much greater. After he saw how he had been wronged, he would allow her to bend her mind to the ways in which that wrong might be put right.

Medeoan left the papers and the laws and the blandly disapproving secretaries. Surrounded by her entourage, she returned to her private suite. Through a series of audience chambers, sitting rooms and private studies, she came to a small, unadorned inner door. There, she took a silver key from the bundle she carried at her waist and opened it smoothly. The ladies took up lit candles in tall holders, placed them on either side of the door and retreated immediately. Here was the one room in the palace where Medeoan alone was permitted to walk. This room held the Portrait of Worlds.

The Portrait of Worlds was no mere carving or daubing of paint on silk or canvas. It was a working clockwork model of all the worlds, mortal and immortal. Made of bronze, silver, copper and gems, it was a conglomeration of delicate spheres formed of wires and jewels, each turning on its silver spindle and each swinging in its separate stately orbit, all part of a great dance, its steps regulated by the fantastic clockwork that had taken a century to execute.

Unbidden, Medeoan's mind unleashed a flood of memories, all of them filled with Avanasy. Avanasy's loving voice as he described the Portrait, making her learn the names of its parts, their functions and the history of this immense and complex tool. Hours of study at Avanasy's side over the books written by the court sorcerers of the Portrait's various uses, and their discoveries concerning its nature and the further nature of the visions it might evoke and the barriers it might be used to bypass or uncover. Yet more hours of his patient, cautious tutelage so that she might work well and familiarly with the precious object her father had placed in her guardianship.

Now, as Medeoan stood before the Portrait, watching its intricate dance, she forced herself to consider, dispassionately, as Avanasy had always urged, the nature of her will, and how it might best be shaped. The sharpest knife was useless in a clumsy hand, he had always said.

Damn the man for all his words, for her being unable to set them aside no matter how hard she tried. Damn him for not staying beside her, especially now when she needed him.

Medeoan took a deep breath and pushed her anger aside. She must think now, and not waste her energies with useless curses or regret.

She would need something of Kacha's. That much was simple enough. She wore his ring on her hand. She would need a mirror in which to see the vision she hoped to call up.

She would need something to represent Hastinapura. Ideally, it should represent the Pearl Throne itself, as that palace was where the wrong had been inflicted. She would also need something to stand for the wound that was made and something to bind all these parts into a whole.

Tightening her jaw, Medeoan set to work.

In less than an hour, Medeoan stood again before the Portrait of Worlds. At its base she had laid out a scarf of precious scarlet cloth from Hastinapura, its weave so fine the scarf was translucent. On the cloth she had laid a silver mirror, and at the quarter points of the mirror she had placed a pearl from one of her pendants, a china hand broken from an ancient childhood toy, a brass dish of blood from the slaughtering shed, and, last of all, slipped from her middle finger, Kacha's ring. Beside the mirror waited a small bag she had filled with fine earth from the gardens.

The worlds of the Portrait swung over the mirror, the brass, copper and jewels reflected in its depths. Medeoan closed her eyes, making herself breathe deeply, and struggled to clear her mind. This was the true test of power, Avanasy had always said. It was one thing to perform a working that had been handed down the years, and carefully inscribed in books. It was quite another to meet the needs of the moment with only the materials to hand. There were those who never achieved the strength or the discipline.

As ready as she could be, Medeoan opened her eyes. She shook a small pile of the black, damp-scented earth into her palm and began sprinkling it in a circle around her mirror.

'I stand before all the worlds,' she said, drawing her magic from within and without. 'I am rooted in earth, in blood, in flesh and love. My eyes are open and my heart is open to the turning of the worlds. This is my word and my word is firm. The turning worlds will show me how Kacha *tya* Achin Ekulinjapad was wounded by Yamuna *dva* Ikshu Chitranipad. This is my word and my word is firm. The turning worlds will show me how Kacha *tya* Achin Ekulinjapad was wounded by Yamuna *dva* Ikshu Chitranipad.' She repeated the words again and again, pouring her circle of earth through her fingers and pouring her working through her spirit, weaving it into the required shape with earth and breath and the dance of all the worlds in front of her. She stared into the silver mirror, and watched the worlds swing and dip, turn and turn again, rest, and turn, anti-clockwise, forward, backward, up when they should have been down, turn and turn, and turn . . .

For a moment, shadows swirled in the silver mirror, then those shadows reached up to meet the turning worlds and draw them close. The vision swallowed all of Medeoan's senses, until the present world vanished and she was wholly and completely part of the past.

It was hot here, unbearably, oppressively hot. Medeoan struggled to breathe. It was as if she had suddenly been wrapped in a wet woolen blanket at the height of a summer's day. She stood with three men in a circular chamber, inlaid with ivory and decorated in the elaborate Hastinapuran fashion. Despite the heat, a fire burned brightly on a carved altar at the center of the chamber. The first man was wizened, skeletally thin and dressed only in a white robe. The second man was soft of face and body, but his dark eyes were harsh and hard. His hands shook slightly. *He's afraid,* Medeoan realized.

The third man was barely a man at all. It was Kacha, young and fierce and proud, just as he had been when he had first arrived in Isavalta.

No, not just. His face was unscarred, and his hands — Medeoan swallowed against some emotion she could not yet name – his hands were perfect; the strong, unmarked hands of a prince.

The heat had hidden it from her at first, but now that she became more accustomed to it, she could feel that the room throbbed with magic. This was no mere prickling of some random spell. It thrummed through Medeoan's blood making her stagger. She had never felt so much power. She would have thought a dozen sorcerers could not draw so much through themselves, and there was only one such here, and he held a black knife in his skinny hand.

'Are you ready, my Prince?' he asked. His voice was soft but strong, like the first wind that hints at a storm.

Kacha squared his shoulders. Medeoan's heart melted to see him so strong, so proud, but at the same time fear chilled her. What was happening here, in this room as filled with magic as it was filled with air?

Kacha lifted his right hand and laid it on the altar. The sorcerer, whom Medeoan was sure must be Yamuna, laid his own hand beside Kacha's.

'Hold your son, my Lord,' said Yamuna.

The second man, who must have been Chandra, Kacha's father, stepped hesitantly forward. He took his son's shoulders in his hands, but even Medeoan could see he gripped without strength. He had gone pale, and the perspiration that stood out on his forehead did not come entirely from the heat.

Yamuna raised the black knife, and he spoke again. This time the words were in some mellifluous tongue that Medeoan could not understand. She could, however, understand their effect full well. The magic that pressed so hard against her senses flared like the flames on the altar, brightening, intensifying, becoming so impossibly strong Medeoan felt certain the stone walls must burst because they could not contain it all.

The knife came down.

Yamuna did not scream. He did not even seem to flinch, not at the torrent of blood, not at the severed hand that had been his own lying curled and spasming like a dying insect on the altar.

Yamuna raised the knife again. Kacha lifted his chin.

Medeoan screamed, a high, hysterical, unbelieving scream, torn from her throat without thought of stopping. The shrill, wordless noise shattered her working, dropping the present and true world around her like a shroud.

'Mistress?' called a quavering voice. 'Mistress? Are you well?'

Medeoan's breath left her and she could scream no more. Her eyes opened of their own accord and she gasped for more air. She had fallen to her knees, she realized, and she now groveled at the base of the Portrait like some serf before an icon. The voice belonged to Chekhania, who could not enter this room without permission, and who must stand and fret outside.

'Mistress?'

Medeoan could not answer. She could not even pick herself up. She could only remain as she was, huddled on the floor, tears streaming down at the memory of what she had just seen.

But what *had* she seen? She didn't know. Not clearly. She had some vague intuitions, but she did not *know*. Could there be some benign explanation? Some reason, some oath extracted by his father that kept Kacha from telling her the truth of what had happened to his hand?

His father, Chandra, who had trembled during the working, as his son had not. Medeoan hid her face in her hands. Blood. Power and blood. The vision had been so filled with both. There had to be some explanation. There had to be some way this came out right.

'Mistress? Please . . .'

She had to get up. She had to pull herself together and to think, to think of the way that made what she had seen come out right. But she could not. Her strength was gone, drained by her working and by what she had seen.

'Help me,' she croaked. 'Chekhania. Help me.'

The waiting lady rushed into the Portrait room and lifted Medeoan to her feet. Medeoan had to put her hand on Chekhania's shoulder to steady herself. She had no strength in her legs at all.

'My bed,' she whispered. 'Get me to my bed.'

'Yes, Mistress.' The lady's voice was breathy with her concern. 'Shall I send for a surgeon, your sorcerer . . . ?'

Medeoan shook her head violently. 'Just get me to my bed.'

Chekhania supported her from the room to where Ragneda waited. Together, they laid Medeoan on her bed. They loosened her laces and brought a cloth for her head. Medeoan waved them away.

'Let me sleep,' she murmured. 'Just let me sleep.'

Unable to keep her eyes open a moment longer, Medeoan encased herself in a private darkness. She did not want to see her ladies, or her chamber, or anything but the answer she needed to understand what Kacha had done.

Help me, she prayed as her mind spiraled down into sleep. *Vyshemir, help me see what is true.*

But as she began to dream, it was not Vyshemir who came to her, it was her father. He appeared as she had known him in life: tall, distant, hawk-nosed and dark-bearded. His shroud draped around his shoulders like a cloak. He held out his hand to her and Medeoan took it without thought, in the manner of dreams, and without stopping to wonder how she had come again to be a little girl.

He held a finger to his lips, indicating a need for silence, and Medeoan nodded. Her father smiled approvingly and led her from her room, which had become her nursery, and down the corridors which became stairways leading down, which became the antechamber for the treasury rooms, which became the treasury warehouse itself, with its chests and its bags and its piles of wealth.

Father gestured for her to stand where she was. Medeoan stood quietly with her hands folded in front of her. Father reached down a small, flat chest, and Medeoan saw the mark graven on the lock. She knew this box, and she knew what it contained. It should have been locked up tight, for the thing inside was dangerous. But the box was not locked. Father opened it easily, and showed it to her, and it was empty.

In the moment she perceived this, she also saw Kacha with his mis-matched hands holding the silver girdle that had once been held within, and she knew that Yamuna saw what he did through Kacha's right eye, his eye that was from Yamuna as his hand was from Yamuna, and Yamuna's voice whispered approvingly in the back of his mind.

With this you will be able to control your wife.

'No,' whispered Medeoan. 'No!'

And the dream was gone, and Medeoan was awake in her bed, her heart pounding with fear.

Calm yourself, she ordered her heart, even as she clutched at the covers. *Be calm!*

A dream after a vision working was not unusual, even a clear and powerful one. It did not mean it was a true dream. It did not mean her father had been here. It did not, it did not, mean that Kacha had robbed the treasury of a powerful magical artifact.

He did not mean to use it against her. He did not. He could not. Medeoan squeezed her eyes shut again.

Come back. Come to me. Tell me my dream lied. Tell me!

But all such pleading without a working, was useless, and

she was too tired to even begin to attempt any such. Yet, she knew she would not be able to rest anymore without an answer. Although she felt like a guilty traitor to Kacha's love, she had to know. She had to prove to herself that it was all a lie.

Medeoan threw back her covers and climbed to her feet. The ladies came running in a bunch to reorder her clothes and flutter anxiously about her, asking what their Imperial mistress might require.

A surge of sudden anger washed through her. Anger at her father for not being here himself and leaving her only dreams. Anger, again, hot and fresh, at Avanasy for his betrayal and for leaving her alone. Anger at herself for not being able to trust Kacha absolutely and without question, which was what she desperately wanted.

Medeoan said not a word to her ladies. She just stood impatiently while they made her decent and then marched out of the apartment. She would do this quickly. She would find her answer and then she would be done. Then, she would find a way to apologize to Kacha for doubting him, and for not being able to rid her mind of a dream.

The ladies, guards and pages scrambled to keep pace with her. Fortunately, they had enough sense to keep silent. She led the entourage down the north staircase, with its pink marble and graceful pillars, down the secretary's stairs which were plain, gray stone worn smooth by generations of feet, down into the earth where the vaults waited.

'Mistress,' ventured Chekhania as the page girls hurried forward to announce her arrival to the soldiers guarding the treasure houses and the under-ministers of the treasury who kept count of it all. 'Mistress, if you could perhaps tell us what you wanted . . .'

Medeoan did not answer her. She just gripped her skirts

more tightly and kept her eyes straight ahead.

She strode up to the members of the House Guard who flanked the door of the main treasury. They needed no spoken command. They unbarred the door and stood back, giving her the soldier's reverence with their hands over their hearts.

The antechamber for the treasury was an undecorated stone room with two rows of copying desks, each manned by an under-minister with a huge ledger. As the door opened, all the servants of the storehouse leapt from their chairs and fell to their knees, properly respectful but obviously amazed at her presence.

'I require access to the treasury,' she barked out. 'Now.'

The First Under-Minister, who was a little gnome of a man weighed down by his gold chain of office, sprang to his feet, but did not seem to consider it polite to stand up straight in the Imperial presence. He fumbled with his ring that held a collection of keys that were almost as numerous as Medeoan's own, and unlocked the inner door. He reverenced as he stood aside, and Medeoan entered the dim storehouse.

Medeoan paused, trying to regain her composure, trying to calm her anger. She would do this swiftly. She would lay her doubts in their proper resting place. She would never again place more credence in dreams than she did in Kacha's word.

It was then she realized that her entire cluster of ladies had entered the storehouse behind her.

'Out of here,' Medeoan ordered. 'All of you. Out into the hallway.' They stared at her, as baffled as a flock of startled hens. 'Out!'

That got through to them. They grabbed up their skirts and scurried out the door, all their eyes wide in distress. Medeoan stared after them. How had she become surrounded by such a pack of fools?

You don't worry about Prathad? Beloved, you should, I've seen her with the guardsmen . . . Beloved, it grieves me to bring you this tale, but your lady, Vladka, has been carrying letters . . . Dismiss Chekhania? What for, Beloved? She looks so well beside you . . .

Medeoan shook her head violently to interrupt these unwanted memories.

It was cold in the treasury. Guards hurried in to light the waiting lamps and braziers, but their illumination was too feeble to warm the great stone chamber. Medeoan shivered and gazed around her. Some treasures waited out in the open. Sacks of silver coins gaped between the rows of chests that ran the length of the room. Ropes of pearls hung on hooks. Slabs of precious amber were stacked as high as Medeoan's waist in the far corners.

These were baubles, Medeoan knew. They were there to impress visitors whom the emperors needed to dazzle with the resources of Isavalta. Anything of true import waited safely locked in its chest and every chest was stacked in its appropriate place. Each chest was bound in metal, whether iron, copper, brass, or silver. Each had its separate lock, and each lock was graven with a symbol known only to the Lord Master Treasurer, or to members of the Imperial family.

'Close the door,' said Medeoan without looking behind her.

Someone obeyed. The clang reverberated against stone and metal, making the entire chamber ring. Medeoan hesitated where she was for a moment, her hand smoothing down the bundle of keys at her waist.

Come now, do what you must. You cannot stand here all day.

Down the years, her ancestors had collected, confiscated, commissioned, or been given many artifacts of powerful magic. These were locked in chests banded with silver and marked with Vyshemir's cup. Avanasy had spent many hours down here with her, teaching her the uses and histories of many of the objects. But there were some things that Avanasy was not allowed to know the use of. Some things about which even the Lord Sorcerer was kept in ignorance.

Medeoan paced up the left-hand aisle between the waiting boxes, each step carrying her further from the lights. Her mind could not help but imagine that her father walked beside her. She could almost hear the rustle of his kaftan, and the heavy wheeze of his breath.

'Reach me down that small one, Daughter,' he had said.

She had been twelve then, and had had to stand on tiptoe. Now, she had only to stretch out her arm to grasp the long, flat, box on top of the pile of teakwood chests. She set it down on top of a cedar casket that was bound in iron. The box she had retrieved was bound with silver and had a lock framed with a silver braid. She had a matching silver key on her ring. Her hand shook as she inserted the key into the lock.

'There are some things you must keep secret. You must whisper of them only in your own heart,' Father's voice told her solemnly from memory. 'This is one such. I pray you will never have to use it.'

He took out a girdle that seemed to be woven of pure silver. A hundred tassels shimmered in the lantern light. As Medeoan peered at it, she could see a series of runes had been woven into the band, silver on silver. The power of the thing was meant to be hidden. It was made to look harmless.

'This girdle was made with the empire,' her father said solemnly, laying the shimmering band back on its blue velvet lining. 'Its magic is strong. Anyone who wears it is placed in thrall to the one who ties it onto them. Their minds are clouded for as long as they wear the girdle and they can only do as they are told.' He closed the box. 'When you are Empress, should there ever be one you cannot act against openly, but whom you must silence, and you have no other means, this is yours to use.'

It will be there, insisted Medeoan to herself as she stared at the box and tried to still the trembling in her hands. *Of course it will be there.* The sorceress who had woven it was long dead. She had been old when she made it, and she had only told her mistress, Medeoan's grandmother, of its properties. How could Kacha, let alone Yamuna, even know of its existence? Her dream was false.

Medeoan inserted the key into the lock and turned it. The click of the lock seemed as loud as the clanging of the door that had shut her in here. She lifted the lid.

Medeoan stood amidst the wealth of her empire and stared at the one empty box with its blue velvet lining. Disbelief came first. It had to be the wrong chest. She had made a mistake. She had only seen it once, after all, and she had been little more than a child then.

But try as she might she could not make her heart believe that. Then came denial. Kacha was being deceived. There were traitors in the court, and at the foot of the Pearl Throne. They were using him for their own ends. She would root them out. They would be hanged in chains over a slow fire. They would be torn apart by horses. They would die, slowly and bloodily. All of them who dared to betray her. She would tell Kacha . . .

What could she possibly tell him? That she had used her magic to spy on him? That it had shown her . . . that it had shown her . . .

Grief then. Silent tears pouring down her cheeks, all unnoticed as her heart shattered. She could find no more reasons. She could form no more questions. She had been taught to trust her powers even more than she trusted her heart and her reason, and her powers had shown her too much.

Kacha was the traitor. He did serve his father, and his father's sorcerer, and their cause. He had lied to her, from the beginning, about everything. Avanasy had tried to warn her.

Avanasy. Medeoan's hand flew to her mouth to stifle a sob. Avanasy had tried to warn her and she had turned on him, and now only the gods knew where he was. She had severed herself from her only friend, and now what would she do? Now that Kacha, her lover, her husband, meant to make her his slave?

It was that thought that finally brought fear crashing down on Medeoan. She swayed, pressing her palm against her mouth. She could not cry out. She could not let anyone hear. Too many people already knew she had come here. If Kacha heard . . .

No. No. No. This was not happening. It could not be. She was wrong. She had made a mistake. Kacha loved her. She loved him. This was wrong.

Wrong, yes, but this time, she had not made a mistake. This knowledge was only the result of her mistakes.

Medeoan reached out and slammed the box lid shut. The sound echoed around the chamber for a long moment before it faded away. With trembling hands, she set the box back in its place, wood clattering against wood. In the silence that followed, she turned away from the box and walked out the door. She could not see. The whole world was a great blur of color. She moved like a puppet, with some exterior force directing her. She could not even order her own thoughts. A jumble of images filled her mind, memories of her father, her mother, of Kacha, and all his bright promises, his whispered words of love, his warm touch.

'Majesty Imperial, did you find all in order?'

Medeoan blinked. Slowly, she forced her eyes to focus in the direction from which the voice came. The First Under-Minister of the treasury had unusually small eyes, she noted, round and dark like a rat's. His shoulders hunched up around his ears, probably from leaning over his ledgers. How much had he been given to allow Kacha into the place where only she should have gone? What account did they keep together? Did it even matter now? All that mattered was that he was Kacha's creature, which now made him her enemy. Her enemy, and Isavalta's.

'Majesty Imperial?' The under-minister blinked rapidly several times.

'Yes,' said Medeoan. 'I found all that I needed.'

Chapter Five

Hours later, Medeoan slumped, exhausted into the one chair that waited in the room with the Portrait of Worlds.

She couldn't find the stolen girdle. She had taxed her skill and strength to its limits. She had tried every symbol, every word, every prayer she could think of and she still could not find it. Kacha or Yamuna had hidden it from her most searching eye, and she could not even see how that had been accomplished.

Yet she knew Kacha had it in his possession and at any unguarded moment he might slip it around her waist, tie it tight, and then her mind would no longer be her own. She would belong only to him, unable to think or to act but as he bid.

She bowed her head into her hands, pressing the heels of her palms against her eyes.

Help me, she prayed. *Vyshemir, help me. You also found your husband was your enemy, but I have no knife to use as you did. What do I do?*

'Beloved?'

Medeoan's head jerked up. Kacha's voice sounded from the other side of the door. Her heart hammered in her chest, and for a long moment, she didn't dare move. How could she face him? What could she say? She needed more time to think.

But she had no time. Kacha was outside, and she could not sit here with the locked door between them. If she did, he would know something was wrong.

Trembling, Medeoan got to her feet and opened the door.

Kacha stood there, the man she had loved so much for the past three years, and nothing about him had changed. He was still tall and strong, his face handsome and caring. He was so beautiful, despite his scars and his mismatched eyes. Even now, knowing all that she did, she yearned to throw herself into his arms and confess everything and ask what she should do. In that moment, she hated herself more than she could ever hate him. Despite all, Kacha was her friend as well as husband, her sole trusted advisor since Avanasy had left her.

Since I drove Avanasy away. Since I failed to believe in the one I should have trusted above all others.

'The ambassador from my uncle's court is safely here, Beloved,' he said, not moving from his place in the doorway. Even he would not come in here without an invitation. Not when he could be seen, anyway. 'I came to tell you so, and to see how your preparations were progressing for his reception, but your ladies tell me you have locked yourself in here all the day.'

She had to answer him. She could not simply stand here and stare. She must speak. One art had she learned in all its perfection from her parents. Medeoan could lie, effortlessly and without any change of demeanor. Now she found she could work that art against Kacha, to whom she had sworn she would never lie, and from whom she had believed she would never have to hide.

'I'm sorry, Kacha,' she said, taking both his hands, the one that belonged to him and the one that did not, lifting her face to kiss him softly, and dying inside to find that the touch of his kiss had not changed at all. 'I had a working which could not be attended to by the court sorcerers.' Which was true enough. 'I wanted to see to things myself.'

'And what working is this?' asked Kacha, his eyebrows rising.

She shook her head, smiling a little shyly. *Answer him, answer him,* she ordered herself desperately. Any doubt, any mystery and he would . . . he would . . .

She could not bring herself to think of the consequences directly, but the fear brought the lie she needed to her lips. 'I have been thinking about what you were saying to me the other day.' Medeoan smoothed her skirts down. 'That we must be sure of the loyalty of the Lords Master. I may have found a means to help us in those determinations.'

'Really?' Kacha sounded both impressed and wary. 'How would it work?'

Medeoan shrugged. 'I don't know that it can work yet, Kacha. I need some study in the library. Come to me tonight, and I will tell you all, I promise.'

His fingertips brushed her chin. 'I shall look forward to it.' He raised one finger in admonishment. 'But we must not neglect the ambassador. I will not have it reported back to my uncle that I have forgotten courtesy here in the north.'

Then, slowly, as she gazed at him, the realization came over her that she did have a knife to use against him. She was the Empress of Isavalta. She could have Kacha arrested and killed, or simply killed, and no one could question her. She could do it this instant, she could raise her voice to the men at arms who waited outside her door.

'What are you thinking, Beloved?' asked Kacha suddenly.

'I'm thinking of you,' said Medeoan honestly. 'And how you have surely forgotten nothing so vital as courtesy.'

His lips were warm, soft, and loving as he kissed her brow.

She felt the smile in that kiss and closed her eyes, hoping he would not see the pain that racked her.

And if she had him killed, what would Hastinapura do? What would his uncle who sat on the Pearl Throne do? Emperor Samudra would surely declare war. He would have to. Could Isavalta withstand such a war? She did not know. She had not spoken with the Master of War in . . . how long? She could not remember.

'Let me see to my study and to my wardrobe, Husband,' said Medeoan, keeping her smile about her mouth. 'We will speak again tonight.'

'That we surely will.' He reverenced to her with a wink and left then. Medeoan found she had to work hard for several moments just to continue breathing.

Fool, she cursed herself. *Fool! Now you have but a handful of hours, and what will you tell him at the end of them? What can you do?*

She looked around her chamber and the busy ladies, bent over their needlework or their books, pretending not to notice her until she gave an order. Any one of them might be a spy, or all of them. She did not truly know a single one. She was surrounded by strangers. She did not know her own Council anymore. She had allowed them all to be taken from her.

She had to get away from here, from this pit of spies, before Kacha could steal her mind. She had to find a way to hide herself, and in a place where he could not reach.

A plan came to her then, formed from old learning and the fog of desperation. A way to escape, a way to hide and a place to go.

But she could not do it alone. She would at the very least need one other ally. But who? Who was there?

For the hundredth time, her heart reached out to Avanasy, wishing desperately she had let her anger cool, that she had known he had remained in Isavalta, even to the end, even to the day of her wedding. If she had known, perhaps in her joy on the day she could have forgiven him, and he would be with her now . . .

Another memory came to her. A memory of the Commander of the House Guard standing before her, and telling her that Avanasy had not only defiantly stayed until the moment of her marriage, but that he had had help leaving the palace. A guard named Peshek. Did Her Majesty Imperial wish the man put to death?

No, no, she had replied, regally. *Let him not be punished. Today is a day of amnesty to all.*

Kacha had not been pleased when he heard, but he had let the matter lie.

So where was this Peshek, this man who had risked death to help Avanasy?

'I am repairing to the red library,' announced Medeoan to her ladies. 'Let the Commander of the House Guard attend me there.'

She whisked out of her apartments in their untrustworthy company, silently planning her escape.

The red library was housed in a much smaller chamber than the Imperial library that waited beside the god house. Its chamber was a blunt wedge lined with oaken shelves. Pillars of garnet-colored marble stood between them. Three arched windows overlooked the courtyard and let in the summer daylight. The ceiling had been painted with a replica of the astrologer's chart that was supposed to have predicted Medeoan's grandmother's rise to empress, and the floor was inlaid with stars in colored woods.

Like the room that held the Portrait, the red library was a

place she could enter alone without arousing suspicion. Here she could study in private among the grimoires, the books of shadows, the manuals of necromancy, and the ancient scrolls that the Isavaltan court sorcerers had collected or captured down the years.

Medeoan lifted a particular volume from the shelves. It was bound in white leather edged in blue ink. She laid it gently on one of the oaken tables. She had studied this book for months, with Avanasy at her shoulder. It was a book of spells that might be worked in cloth or thread. She began to turn the vellum pages, scanning the thick, black lettering and the precise drawings for the one she needed.

A knock sounded on the door.

'Come,' called Medeoan, hastily shutting the book.

A man in the blue coat and gilded armor of the House Guard marched into the room. One sweep of his eyes took in her solitary presence and at once he reverenced, not merely the soldier's bow from the waist, but the full reverence to the Imperial presence, down on both knees, his head bowed before her.

Medeoan rose. This was the man she had ordered the Commander to find. As he was, however, she could see nothing of him but a pair of broad shoulders under his uniform coat and his bowed back. 'Captain Peshek,' she said.

'Majesty Imperial,' he replied in acknowledgment, but without looking up, as was proper.

It was a propriety that did not help her at all now. She needed to see this man's eyes. She needed some hint as to how to judge him. 'Stand up, Captain. Look at me.'

Captain Peshek hesitated, but only for a heartbeat, and then did as he was bid. He had a good face under his helmet, Medeoan decided. It was lined by smiles as well as by wind and weather, and his eyes were open and cheerful. But handsome looks could blind the observer. She knew that too well now.

She did not have time to hedge or to engage in any sort of verbal dance. 'You are a friend of Lord Avanasy's, I believe.'

Would he admit it? His whole face went wary. 'Yes, Majesty Imperial.'

'Still? Despite his exile?'

He might well be answering for his position, if not his life, and the way he pulled himself to attention said he knew that. Would he deny the friendship in hopes of saving himself? Or would he acknowledge it and accept the consequences of his honesty?

'Yes, Majesty Imperial,' said Captain Peshek.

He said it without flinching or hesitation. Medeoan felt at least some of her knotted muscles loosen. 'I know he trusted you.'

Peshek said nothing. He just stood at rigid attention, his eyes straight ahead, waiting for orders, like the soldier he was.

'Because of that, I also will trust you.'

Peshek laid his hand over his heart. 'I live to serve, Majesty Imperial.'

Now she had to speak the words out loud, and once the words left her, it all became real and she could not explain away what had happened anymore. Medeoan clasped her hands in front of her to keep them from trembling.

'I am in danger, Captain Peshek.'

That startled him. He stared at her, confusion giving way rapidly to anger in his eyes. 'How, Majesty? From whom? I'll have . . .'

Medeoan shook her head. 'I can't tell you that. The less you know . . . it's my own fault . . . I . . .' she pulled herself together. 'Do you know where Lord Avanasy is?'

For the first time, Peshek hesitated. Why would he not? She had decided to trust him, but who was she? The one who had exiled Avanasy, who would have had him killed if she had caught him. Peshek had to decide how far he trusted her.

In the end, Peshek shook his head. 'No, Majesty Imperial. I don't know where he is. I'm sorry,' he said and Medeoan judged his regret to be sincere.

Medeoan bit her lip. 'He told you nothing of where he planned to go?'

'No, Majesty Imperial.'

'I see.' Medeoan circled the reading table. It had been a slim hope, but it had been all she had. The white grimoire lay on the table's polished surface, looking no more nor less dangerous than any other history or poem. Yet, in there lay her salvation, her promise of life. For that promise, however, she must ask for a sacrifice.

And you must do this now. You have only three days. In three days the household moved to the summer palace of Vaknevos. In three days she would be constantly in Kacha's company while they traveled, and her hopes for escape would come to nothing. That thought sent a chill through her bones.

Medeoan steeled herself. 'Captain,' she said as firmly as she could manage. 'I need you to bring me a girl, a drab, one newly brought into service if possible. This must be done quietly. The Mistress of the House must not know.' *No one must know. There must be no rumor, no gossip that can reach my husband's ears before I can have all my answers ready for him.*

Medeoan watched the question 'why?' form in Peshek's eyes, but he did not speak it. Instead, it seemed to Medeoan that he turned his mind to the logistics of his assignment. Peshek, she knew, had lived in Vyshtavos for almost as long as she had. He was familiar with its ways, in some areas more familiar with them than she, whose provinces were only great apartments and grand halls.

'The Mistress of the House spends the first part of every

day in her pantry reviewing the inventories,' said Captain Peshek, again laying his hand over his heart. 'If that meets with Her Majesty Imperial's approval, I shall bring the girl then.'

'In the morning, in two days' time,' said Medeoan. 'I will be walking by the canal. Bring her to me then. I remind you once more, this must be done quietly. No one must know.'

'Majesty Imperial.' Peshek pulled himself up to a posture of formal attention in acknowledgment of her orders.

Medeoan opened her mouth. She wanted to say something of her fear, of her fledgling plans. She wanted so much to have another heart beside her, as she had thought she had with Kacha, and as she had truly had with Avanasy. But Peshek, for all she must trust him, was not Avanasy, and would never be. So all she said was, 'Thank you, Captain Peshek. You may go.'

This time, he gave her the soldier's reverence, a deep bow with his hand over his heart. But he did not leave at once. 'Majesty Imperial?'

'Yes, Captain?' Medeoan rested her fingertips on the reading table, as if she might need to steady herself.

Peshek ventured a glance toward her face, but quickly recovered his discipline and dropped his gaze again. 'You may also trust Keeper Bakhar. He too is a friend of Lord Avanasy's.'

Bakhar. Thank goodness. I don't know if I could bear it if the attendant of the gods turned against me.

A thought struck her. Peshek would be a great help, but he could not provide all she needed. Nor could Keeper Bakhar. There would have to be a third. 'What of the Lord Sorcerer?'

Captain Peshek shifted his weight. 'Understand, Majesty, I am only a soldier, an unimportant member of the guard . . .'

'I understand, Captain.' Medeoan felt tired. She did not want to have to ask these questions.

'I do know Keeper Bakhar believes him to be loyal to you,' finished Peshek quickly.

'Thank you, Captain,' she said again, and again he reverenced. This time, however, he turned smartly on his heel and left, as protocol dictated.

Just this once, let me have judged a man rightly. Medeoan bowed her head. *I cannot do this alone.*

Two days. Only two days, and yet all of two days. It was just one more space of time to endure, she tried to tell herself. She had endured more, and for longer than this, playing her part as required. She could do anything for just two days.

Kacha held himself still while his waiting gentlemen stripped the heavy, Isavaltan finery from him, replacing it with a linen nightshirt and a plain, if voluminous, indigo velvet robe. The formal reception and subsequent feast for the new ambassador had lasted until well after dark, but he was not yet tired, which was just as well. There was more work to be done tonight.

On the whole, the reception had gone well. As Yamuna had predicted, Uncle Samudra had sent Girilal to act as the new ambassador. Girilal was a concession to old wounds at court, as he was known to have disapproved of the disruption of the succession Samudra had initiated. This disapproval could be worked on much more easily than Tanmay's loyalties. It had been a constant struggle to keep Tanmay from realizing that Harshul, Kacha's bound-sorcerer and Uncle Samudra's spy, had not reached Isavalta alive. That was not a report which could be permitted to reach the Pearl Throne.

Soon Kacha would find time to be alone with Girilal. He would make the new ambassador understand the situation here in Isavalta, and show him all the benefit his plans would bring to Hastinapura, including restoring the rightful line of succession. Ambassador Girilal would see the truth, and Kacha felt sure it would not take him long to do so.

Despite Kacha's confidence in his new ambassador, worry still gnawed at him. Medeoan had been too quiet, too withdrawn, this evening, as if she had something on her mind. But she had confided nothing to him. He must have this matter, whatever it might be, out of her soon. If she was ceasing to speak her whole mind to him, it might be the first sign she was slipping from his control, as Yamuna had said she might. If that were so, he would need to make use of the artifact Yamuna's magic and his bribery had ferreted out. The best time for that would be during the change of households, a time at which the Empress could become ill for so many different reasons, and during which the smallest number of people would have their eyes on her.

It must be done, Yamuna's voice had whispered to him. *It is better that it be done sooner. You have done well in cementing your alliances, my Prince. The lies are in place, and her power wanes. It is better it be done before she realizes what she has lost and struggles to regain it.*

Kacha waved his man away and tied the sash on his nightrobe himself. He did not wish to dispute Yamuna, who had been so right about so much, but Kacha wondered if Yamuna realized how frequently the rulers of Isavalta appeared in the public eye. Matters here were not as they were at home, where that which was most precious was most carefully concealed and protected. Here, the reasons for the Empress remaining confined were far fewer and would be examined much more closely. Here, many different sorcerers would be working to find the cure for any 'illness' which struck, as opposed to just one bound-sorcerer. Kacha was not certain Yamuna believed how close they had come to failure with the old Emperor and Empress. The court sorcerers and Medeoan had almost saved them, even at the bitter end. He had felt Yamuna's workings strain to hold against all the efforts of the Isavaltan magicians.

They would have to tread very carefully with Medeoan, and haste would only make the path more difficult to navigate.

Kacha turned to his man-servant. 'I've a mind to visit my lady wife. You may retire. I doubt your services will be required again tonight.'

The man was, of course, far too disciplined to so much as smile at that. He bowed low with his palms over his eyes, following the custom of Hastinapura. Kacha touched the man's head as he passed, giving his approval with that gesture for the man, and the other servants, to be about their business. He crossed the cold, stone apartment to the connecting door, knocked once and entered his wife's chamber.

The flock of ladies surrounding Medeoan were on their feet and performing deeply respectful reverences as soon as he appeared. Medeoan herself, sat by the fire, her head bent and her hand busy at some task he could not see. She did not look up as he entered.

'Beloved?' he inquired, as he moved softly forward. The worry that had touched him earlier drew closer.

Then, he felt the tingling in his right hand, and behind his right eye. Fear settled over him. Whatever Medeoan did, there was magic to it. She sat deep in concentration over some spell. As he approached, he could see she worked with a pair of weaving cards; thin, square pieces of wood with holes in their corners through which threads could be strung to make a small hand loom. The threads in question were very fine and glittered silver and gold in the firelight. As her hands manipulated the threads, her breath labored in her throat. This working was taking its toll on her strength.

What are you doing, Medeoan? thought Kacha as he sank into the chair beside her. The ladies, receiving no orders, rose from their reverences and set to the night's business of readying their mistress's bed. Kacha caught the lady Chekhania's eye, questioning. She replied with a small shake of her head. Whatever Medeoan did, his best spy among the ladies knew nothing of it.

Medeoan must have become aware of his presence because her breathing gradually eased, as did the uncomfortable tingling in Kacha's hand and eye. At last, her hands stilled their weaving and she lowered her work, looking up to smile at him.

'Forgive me, Beloved,' she said, dabbing at the sheen of perspiration that covered her brow. 'I am at a working here.'

'I guessed as much.' Kacha leaned close. His right hand twitched. She was weaving a golden band, about an inch across, shot through with silver. 'What is this you are making, Beloved?'

'Remember how I said I was thinking about how to be more certain of the loyalties of the Lords Master?' Medeoan fingered her work. She had not even completed four inches of whatever it was she labored over. 'When it is done, this will be a girdle which will help us in those determinations.'

'Really?' Kacha felt a stab of foreboding in the back of his right eye. 'How will it work?'

'At midsummer, when the new appointments are named, the loyalty oaths are renewed. We will declare that each Lord Master who takes the oath must wear the girdle as he does.' Medeoan touched the piece of weaving again, as if to check for flaws. 'If one is not sincere, the girdle will slip off his waist.' Her smile grew arch. 'Am I not clever? Is it not a good notion?'

Clever enough to be truly dangerous, if only you knew it. 'An excellent notion, Beloved,' he said, both surprised and pleased that she should have thought of such a thing. 'But will not such an open display of your power make your Lords Master nervous? You have said to me that they are not pleased at the thought they will be ruled over by a sorcerer.'

'They are not pleased that they will be ruled over by a man of Hastinapura either.' An unfamiliar note crept into Medeoan's voice. For a moment, she sounded fierce. 'But that is who has been set over them, and we must make sure that they know we are secure in our rule, and that there is no deceiving us.'

Kacha found himself answering her smile easily. Perhaps his earlier fears had been unfounded. That would be as well. Despite Yamuna's counsel of the need to hold her harmless, having Medeoan whole and articulate at his side would cause much less gossip and speculation than having her mute and bewildered. 'The midsummer appointments will thus allow us to take even better measure of our allies than I had thought.'

'Yes. No one will be able to hide from us,' she said firmly, laying her hand over his. 'You always know what to say. You will be able to find us some way to explain this so the Lords Master will not be too disturbed.'

'I will set my mind to it,' he assured her, stroking her arm lightly. 'But it is late. Shall we go to bed, you and I? We could discuss that, and many other things.'

Medeoan sighed and rubbed her eyes. 'You must forgive me, Beloved. This is a difficult sorcery. It will leave me profoundly weary. I wish to have it finished before we leave for Vaknevos, so that I am not overtaxed and a nuisance on the journey.' She shook her head ruefully. 'And if I am too often absent before the day itself, there will be talk we do not want.'

'All of this is well thought of. I will leave you to your work.' Kacha stood, and a new possibility occurred to him. 'Shall I make your excuses to the ambassador tomorrow?'

At that, Medeoan looked deeply relieved. 'Yes. Please. I am sure you can open whatever negotiations are required.'

Excellent, thought Kacha to himself. This would mean he could easily interview Girilal in private, and ascertain how best to approach him concerning the ultimate plans for Isavalta.

And perhaps now would be a good time to return to another matter.

'Beloved,' he said, letting his fingertips linger over hers. 'While you are of a mind to discuss the security of our rule, I would ask if you have reconsidered recalling Avanasy.'

Medeoan turned her face away, her cheeks turning red. 'Do you still believe . . .'

'I believe that while he is alive, he is a danger to you, my love. He knows your powers so well, he held your confidence for so long . . . who can say what he is doing with that knowledge? Beloved . . .' He touched her cheek, turning her back toward him. Her eyes were damp and her mouth was set in an unusually stern line. 'It is only when he is secured under the hand of those we know are loyal that you will be safe from him.'

And only when he is dead will we truly be sure of him, added Kacha to himself.

Medeoan took his hand, pressing it against her cheek. 'Very well, Husband,' she whispered.

Kacha smiled broadly and drew her to him, kissing her long and deeply. She clung to him with the desperate strength that possessed her when she gave in to him on some matter that pained her.

He disengaged her gently, keeping hold of both her hands. 'Shall I give the orders?' he asked gently.

She shook her head. 'I will see to it. This was my doing, let mine be the undoing.'

'I am as one of your guard.' Kacha rose and gave her a soldier's reverence. 'I live only to serve you.'

'I thought you lived to love me.' Medeoan pushed out her lower lip petulantly.

Knowing his part well, Kacha kissed that lip. 'That as well.

I shall seek my lonely bed this night, and let you get on with your good work.' He kissed her forehead for good measure, and left.

So, wife, you have bought yourself some time. Kacha paused by the door and looked back at Medeoan, who had already reclaimed her weaving. *And you have bought it for me as well. I thank you for both.*

But watch her, cautioned the voice that never seemed to leave the back of his mind. *Now more than ever, watch her closely. That girdle she weaves might be used as easily against you as against any.*

I've thought of that, answered Kacha silently. *It could also easily be taken from her to be my own tool when I bind her thoughts forever.*

In the morning, the household of Vyshtavos began in earnest to prepare itself for the annual move to the summer palace. Legions of scullions and house servants were loaded onto wagons under the watchful eye of the aides to the Mistress of the House. They were then sent to assist the workers already there in opening and preparing Vaknevos. Half of Medeoan's ladies and half of Kacha's gentlemen were sent ahead in barges to make sure the Imperial needs would be met without awkwardness or delay once the move was completed. Those who remained were doubly busy, not only in seeing to their masters, but in supervising the organizing and packing necessary for removing the Imperial couple to the summer palace, and for securing the belongings, furnishings and necessaries that must be left behind over the summer.

Dispatches had to be written, inventories had to be reviewed, orders and letters had to be conveyed to various parties. There was almost none among the Council and the high household who did not need to be spoken to.

A thing Medeoan was counting on. She was being watched, she was sure of it. Even when Kacha left her side to attend his own duties, she felt eyes staring at the back of her neck, reading over her shoulder, straining to catch every nuance of her work.

Could he tell what she truly did? Could Yamuna's hand and Yamuna's eye discern so much?

I am only tired, she tried to tell herself. *The working has been hard and slow, and that is what has me worried.*

The girdle was complete and lay in the basket with her sewing. Fatigue weighed Medeoan down. She had slept for only a handful of hours during the past two days, and it was only the thrumming of her nerves that kept her moving.

She had brought her entourage out onto the banks of the canal this morning by declaring that she and her ladies required some fresh air after all their time shut up indoors like bees trapped in their hive. Now, they sat in the willow grove, underneath the canopy that had been set up for them, their sewing on their laps and plates of white breads and fresh fruits before them. The birds sang and the wind blew fresh and strong across the grasses bringing them all the scents of early summer, and Medeoan could enjoy none of it.

Where is Peshek? she kept thinking as she stared at the linen in her lap. *Where is he?*

Unable to sit still any longer, Medeoan rose and began to stroll as calmly as she was able down the bank. The shadows of the willows played across her skin. Chekhania followed behind her in decorous silence. Beyond hearing the rustle of her skirts and her footsteps on the grass, Medeoan felt her there. She was watching Medeoan carefully, surely looking for something to report to Kacha.

Medeoan clenched her fists. She could not permit these fears to take over her mind. She had to be able to think clearly.

She needed all her wits about her for tomorrow.

'Mistress?' said Chekhania.

Medeoan turned, and as she did, she saw Captain Peshek walking across the lawn with a thin, gray girl beside him.

'Chekhania,' said Medeoan, despite her mouth becoming suddenly dry. 'Bring me my basket.'

'Mistress.' Chekhania reverenced and hurried to do as she was bid. Medeoan did not watch her. She kept her gaze on Peshek, and on the young woman whom he brought with him.

That she was not a true Isavaltan was the first thing that Medeoan saw. Her hair, where it showed under her headscarf, was coal black, as were her almond-shaped eyes. Her nose was long and straight and her skin had a dusky tone. Peshek had brought Medeoan a Tuukosov, a native of Tuukos, the dark island in the northern sea. That was well considered. The Tuukosov had few friends in Isavalta, so this girl would be missed less than even the lowest scullion of mainland birth.

'Drab' was a good term for the girl. She was bone thin and the sleeves of her gray shirt had been rolled up to expose knobbly wrists and elbows. Her headscarf had once been brightly and elaborately embroidered, but the colors had faded from many washings, and a number of threads had come loose, spoiling the symmetry of the design.

Peshek had a hand on the girl's shoulder for reassurance, but she trembled like a leaf in the wind. She stared mutely at Medeoan for a moment, and then recovered herself enough to drop to her knees.

'You may stand,' said Medeoan as gently as she could.

The girl, eyes wide with terror, looked at Peshek. In turn, Peshek took her hand, lifted the girl to her feet. He had left his helmet behind for this duty, and for the first time Medeoan got a look at his full face and was surprised at how handsome he truly was. Surely, he had charmed this girl into coming with him.

'What is your name?' Medeoan asked.

Again, the girl stared at Peshek, who nodded and gestured for her to speak.

'Eliisa Hahl,' the girl stammered. The name told Medeoan nothing. Had Eliisa been Isavaltan, her name would have said something of her heredity. But the Tuukosov took clan names instead of hereditary names and kept their family histories as if they were a dangerous secret. Still, Medeoan could tell this much, this was a poor girl, possibly an illegitimate girl, and certainly one who had never before been prized for what she knew.

Chekhania arrived with the sewing basket. Medeoan took it from her and motioned Chekhania away. The waiting lady stepped back a polite distance, but not so far, Medeoan noted, that she could not see all that occurred.

'Now, Eliisa, your Empress has a great favor to ask of you.' The words came awkwardly to Medeoan. This girl, this drab, was about her own age, and her eyes were filled with fear. The Empress gripped the rough handle of the basket. 'I am going to tie a girdle about your waist. It will do you no harm, but as I work, I must ask you to think of your life as it has been so far. Will you do that for me?'

Eliisa thudded back down on to her knees, her face hidden in her hands. Medeoan looked to Peshek, and Peshek took the girl's elbow, whispering gently in her ear. Probably, he was repeating Medeoan's promise that Eliisa would come to no harm. Of all the things she had said, Medeoan wished that one was not the lie.

Eliisa stood, visibly trembling. Medeoan set her basket down and drew out the shining girdle, taking a deep breath as she did. She ran the woven band through her fingers, breathing on its length, remembering the work of its making, and drawing up the magic in her soul. This was the completion of a spell that had been begun in those threads. She must concentrate. One silver girdle was to be her undoing. This one of gold would be her salvation.

Then she had it, the connection between the girdle of her working, and the workings of her inner self. She felt it. This was a part of her, it had been shaped and was being shaped by her will, her desire, her soul. Medeoan opened her eyes.

'I made this girdle of my hand, of silver and gold I made it,' she murmured as she walked around the girl, winding the waistband of the girdle twice around the drab's waist. The girl smelled of harsh soap, strong grease, sweat, and fear. The wool of her skirt and overshirt prickled Medeoan's delicate skin. Her body shook under the Empress's hands as Medeoan fastened the girdle about her. But the sorcery was stronger than Medeoan's senses and the current of it carried her past all other realizations. 'With my own hands I bind Eliisa Hahl to the girdle, and the girdle to the earth, and the mind and the soul and the heart of Eliisa shall be known to the work of my hands, to the hands that performed the work, to the soul that guided the hands.'

As Medeoan repeated the spell, Eliisa's trembling eased. She swayed from side to side with the rhythm of words she could only barely have heard. Finally, gently, as Medeoan's quick fingers tied the last knot in the girdle, Eliisa's knees crumbled and she slid gently to the ground. Medeoan dropped with her, cradling the girl's fall.

Slowly, the stupor of the sorceries fell away from Medeoan. She looked down and saw Eliisa's face. The girl's eyes were closed and she seemed to be in a deep and peaceful sleep.

Vyshko and Vyshemir grant you rest, Eliisa, thought Medeoan, smoothing the girl's headscarf. *And may they grant you swift return of what I have just stolen.*

Medeoan laid the girl on the cool grass as tenderly as she could manage. Swiftly, she undid the knot holding the girdle and drew it from Eliisa's waist. She dropped it into her sewing basket and closed the lid. It would not do for her to handle the girdle for too long, not yet anyway.

'Captain Peshek,' said Medeoan loud enough for Chekhania to clearly hear. 'You will see that this girl is dismissed and returned to her home.' Using her body as a shield, Medeoan slipped a small velvet bag from her sash and laid it on Eliisa's breast. Peshek knelt beside the prostrate girl and retrieved it. The gold inside clanked heavily as Peshek stowed the bag in his coat.

'Forgive me, Majesty Imperial, I . . .'

Medeoan did not let him finish his sentence. 'It is the shock of discovery, nothing more.' Another lie, but one Chekhania needed to hear.

Peshek reverenced as he was, on his knees, and this time asked no questions. Medeoan picked up her basket and turned her back on the girl and Peshek, using all her strength not to look back at them.

'Chekhania,' said Medeoan as the waiting lady fell into step behind her. 'I need you to take a message to the Emperor for me. You are to say to him, I have tested my working and it has performed perfectly. Do you understand?'

'Yes, Mistress Imperial. At once.' She reverenced quickly and hurried away over the lawn. Medeoan watched her leave, and from the corner of her eye, she saw Peshek cradling Eliisa in his arms and slowly bearing her away.

Medeoan set her jaw and turned away. She must not dawdle. She must return to her ladies so they could sit and sew together for a respectable length of time, a pretty picture of idleness and unconcern. Hopefully, sending Chekhania with a message to Kacha would reinforce her lies to him and continue the fiction of what the girdle was meant to be used for.

Now, though, there was one more thing to be done, one more wheel to be set in motion. After that, all she could do was wait for dark and what would come with it.

The morning passed slowly. Despite the myriad items demanding her attention once she and her ladies returned from their sojourn out of doors, Medeoan felt the time creep past her. But, at last, the midday meal was laid in the blue parlor so that she might dine in private, and so that, afterwards, she might have an audience with her Lord Sorcerer. Kacha was having his meal with Ambassador Girilal, and that gave her some freedom, although not much, for his eyes and ears were still with her.

Lord Iakush was prompt as ever, arriving just as the meal was being cleared away. The Lord Sorcerer was a precise, dark man, well but plainly dressed in a burgundy kaftan sashed and embroidered in black. He looked to be only a few years older than she herself, but Medeoan knew he was older than her father had been.

Lord Iakush knelt before her.

'Please rise,' she told him. 'Sit with me.' Iakush did as he was bid, and took the chair the footman positioned for him.

'Thank you, Majesty Imperial,' he said politely. Then, as was also polite, he waited for her to speak.

Medeoan glanced about. She was unaccustomed to taking note of her ladies, or the other servants. They were engaged with their own tasks, her ladies with their needlework, the footmen with clearing the meal and rearranging the room. There was no way to tell how well they were listening. Medeoan swallowed. She needed to speak. She needed to trust in her plan and her understanding. She could do nothing else.

She rubbed her hands together. 'I find myself in need of your counsel, Lord Sorcerer.'

Iakush spread his hands. 'I will be glad to offer what advice I can, Majesty Imperial.'

Medeoan leaned forward. She wanted to shout at the company to go away, to leave her in peace, to stop watching her. She controlled herself. 'I need to find Lord Avanasy, yet that seems to be beyond my power.'

'Need to find . . . ?' Lord Iakush, began, startled, but he recovered quickly. 'Her Majesty Imperial means to revoke the exile?'

Medeoan nodded and pressed her palms tightly together. 'That is what I want Lord Avanasy to believe, for it is the only way he will return here easily.'

Lord Iakush narrowed his eyes. 'I do not understand, Majesty Imperial.'

Why is this so hard? I lied to Kacha without effort. Why can I barely speak now?

Because I know who Kacha is now, and I do not know who this man is before me. In truth, she had avoided him as much as possible since her parents' funeral. She did not seem able to look at him without seeing him standing over their biers, saying the rites to keep their bodies safe in the earth.

Yet she did not replace him, even though Kacha had suggested it more than once. Remembering that, Medeoan gained courage.

'I have recently found evidence that Lord Avanasy was guilty of much more serious crimes than I had initially believed. I want him back here to answer for them directly, with his life.'

The Lord Sorcerer stiffened for a moment. She watched him attempting to relax himself, trying to think and assess what she might be leaving unsaid. 'If I may ask, Majesty Imperial . . .'

Medeoan stopped him with a gesture. 'No. You do not need to know what he has done, or has not done. You only need to tell me if you know where Lord Avanasy has taken himself?'

Iakush dropped his gaze, but Medeoan could see that it was not a mere show of humility. 'I only know rumors, Majesty Imperial.'

Medeoan nodded. Well enough. He did not flatter, or make claim to knowledge he did not have. Such signs were no guarantee of loyalty, but they would have to be enough. All her energies were diverted to keeping Kacha's suspicions quiet. She had not strength to search for Avanasy, even though it was Avanasy she most needed.

Medeoan reached down to the ring at her waist and unhooked the bronze key which wound the works of the Portrait of Worlds. 'Find him, Lord Sorcerer,' she said, holding out the key to him. 'Even if he has gone beyond the borders of the Land of Death and Spirit, find him. Tell him I have forgiven him. Tell him I am in need of him. Tell him I am in danger, for that was what he tried to make me believe before he was banished. Tell him what you must, but bring him back here. He must answer for what he has done.'

Medeoan watched Lord Iakush. His eyes were curious, he had questions he longed to ask, but he saw the key she held out to him. Handing such a key over was a sign of trust, and he was hungry for her trust. Her trust equaled power in the court and that key was a solid sign of that power. The position of a Lord Sorcerer under an empress who was herself touched by magic was a precarious one. However, he would do as she asked because he would believe that her request proved she needed him.

She would have to hope that later he would do it because

he understood what the truth of this meeting was.

'You will take him to Fortress Dalemar and await my representatives.'

Iakush received the key and reverenced, almost more to the object than to his Empress.

'I will do my best, Majesty Imperial,' he said, tucking the key into the safety of his broad, black sash.

'Find him, Lord Sorcerer,' she told him earnestly. 'I require his return.'

Iakush, recognizing the interview was at an end, knelt once more. She dismissed him and he left her there, alone with her servants and Kacha's spies.

One more day. Medeoan closed her eyes. *Only one more day. Then I will be free.*

Chapter Six

Summer deepened, and Sand Island grew warm and green. The mosquitoes rose in the marshes making morning and evening into special times of torture. There were a thousand hot, tedious tasks to be done, and the boats were always out, taking advantage of the long, calm days and the huge runs of fish. Grace was sunny, and as carelessly defiant as she had ever been. Her midnight wanderings were over, and no one in the house felt inclined to speak of them.

So far, it was a perfect match to all the other summers Ingrid had known. Nothing at all had changed.

And yet, everything had, because Avan had begun to call on her. The first time he came by at dusk, after the boats had come in and the evening meal had been cleared away. Ingrid had given him coffee in the back kitchen. There, they'd sat and talked about small things – Grace's health, how the fish were running, the nature and temperaments of the people on the island. The next time, he'd stopped by near dawn, just as the men were getting ready to go out. Papa and Leo had scowled when Ingrid invited him to sit down at the table and served out a portion of bread and porridge for his breakfast. But Avan had been unstintingly polite, asking their opinions on boats and nets, and the affairs of the town of Bayfield. Slowly, Avan found the thoughts Papa could not stand to keep to himself, and drew him out, word by word.

After that, his presence became part of the rhythm of her life. Mornings, he breakfasted with them. Evenings, when the work was done and the boats were back, he was there again, with her in the kitchen, talking in his low, strong voice of the events of the day, singing catches of songs with her, telling stories, laughing when she teased him for his ignorance of local custom and history. He spoke no more of ghosts or of magic, and Ingrid was content enough to let the subject lie.

Then, at night, when Grace snored softly beside her, Ingrid would lie awake and remember the touch of his hand against her skin. She wondered how it would be to have Avan beside her in the bed instead of her sister, and she both welcomed and feared the ache and the restless anticipation that rose in her.

August came. The blueberries and raspberries were quickly stripped from their branches by birds and by questing fingers. Now the blackberries were coming into season and the women and children of the island were out in force, baskets on hips, and wearing their thickest clothes despite the heat. The men forsook the water for the day to help cut and clear brush for the fuel it provided and to help keep the island safe from the wildfires that plagued the mainland.

Ingrid worked side-by-side with Grace, keeping one eye on the berry canes and one on the little ones, making sure they put almost as much into the baskets as they stuffed in their mouths. Mama was home by the stove, boiling the jams and syrups from the previous day's labors in field and garden.

She was not in the least surprised when a shadow fell across her and Avan's voice said, 'Good afternoon, Ingrid.'

She turned, smiling up at him. Summer had burned him brown as bark, making his dark-gold hair shine even more brightly than usual. He carried the long-handled scythe on his shoulder.

'Hello, Avan. How are you today?'

'Well, thank you.' He hesitated, looking hard at Grace and Ingrid's smallest siblings. 'I saw a good patch of berries as I came past. I . . . would be happy to show you the way.'

Which only caused Grace to giggle like a schoolgirl, without any attempt to hide it. Ingrid glowered at her.

'Oh, go on, Ingrid,' Grace waved her away. 'It's blackberries all the way through the marsh. If Papa asks, I'll swear on my life it is.'

Ingrid felt her cheeks burn, but nonetheless, she picked up the remaining empty basket. 'Thank you, Avan,' she said, giving Grace one last hard look. 'We can use all we can find.'

Avan tramped off through the thicket, and Ingrid followed on behind. Gradually, the noise of chattering women and children and the distant calls of men's voices fell away. The thicket turned to forest as the huge, ancient pines laid claim to the ground. The underbrush thinned, replaced by an unbroken carpet of brown needles. The calls of crows and humans all seemed equally far away. Ingrid and Avan were truly alone for the first time since Grace's haunting ended.

Ingrid felt her heart begin to pound. Her mind raced off in a hundred directions, trying to guess what would happen next, and how she should prepare for it. At last, Avan leaned his scythe against a tree trunk. He stared at it for a moment, and turned to face her.

'Ingrid . . .' he began. Ingrid felt her throat tighten, and tried to tell herself she was being foolish. There was nothing to fear. This was what she had hoped for. The fear, however, would not leave. 'I have some things I need to say to you,' he went on. 'I . . .' he stopped again, running a hand through his bright hair. 'I am blundering very badly. I must ask you to have patience.'

'Of course.' Ingrid hoped he did not hear how her own nervousness choked her.

'Thank you.' He looked around, saw nothing but tree roots and pine needles and shrugged irritably. 'Will you sit awhile with me?'

In answer, Ingrid sat in the cleft formed by the roots of one of the ancient pines, smoothing her skirt down across her knees, and silently cursing her berry-blackened fingers and disordered hair. She wanted to be beautiful. She wanted to be calm and poised. Instead she was sweaty, disheveled and frightened to her core that Avan was about to ask her to marry him, and equally frightened that he would not.

Avan sat in front of her, crossing his legs tailor fashion. 'Ingrid,' he said, as much to the ground as to her. 'Since we laid the ghost that troubled your sister, you have not asked me about my magics, or about how I came to possess them.'

Ingrid swallowed hard, willing her throat to open so she could speak normally. 'I thought you would tell me in your own good time.'

'And I thank you for trusting me so far.' The heel of his heavy boot scuffed the needles. 'Will you hear a story?'

'Yes.'

'Very well.' He looked up at her and took a deep breath, like someone about to speak a parlor piece they had memorized with great effort. 'Imagine if you will, that this whole world is like Sand Island, a single point of land in the midst of a vast sea. Imagine that it is not the only such island. There are others, an infinite number of others, each separate and complete in the sea, each alone without knowledge of its neighbors.

'Now imagine that one might sail that sea. If one had a

chart and the proper knowledge of boats, one might travel from island to island. It would not be an easy journey, for that sea is cold and treacherous, and the way is very long, but it could be done by one who was trained in its ways.'

Ingrid felt herself begin to stare. What was this? Was Avan mad after all? No, she could not believe it. This was a true thing he spoke of, like the ghost had been true, and the net he had made.

Ingrid cleared her throat. 'And on one of these islands there is a place called Isa . . . Isav . . .'

'Isavalta.' Avan's voice caressed the word, and Ingrid saw how loneliness dimmed his eye. 'Yes. It is a vast and northern land. Bigger even, I think, than your United States. Some call it grim and wild, but it has its beauties.' He bowed his head for a minute, remembering. It was that remembrance that wiped all thought of madness from Ingrid's mind. This was true. Every word of it.

'It is ruled by an emperor, and an empress. They had several children, but, as happens sometimes, two of them died, leaving only one, a girl, to inherit the throne.

'The girl, whose name was Medeoan, had been born a sorceress as well as a princess, and her parents wished her to be instructed in the ways of magic, and the powers of the spirits and the unseen folk. They summoned one of the masters of such knowledge to them, but he was an old man, even as sorcerers measured their years, and knew Grandfather Death waited nearby for him. So, he begged them to take his apprentice instead. It was thus the Emperor and Empress bound to their daughter a tutor who was a young man with more learning than wisdom. His name was Avanasy Finorasyn Goriainavin.'

Ingrid felt herself grow very still. Avan wasn't looking at her. He stared at the needle-covered ground.

'The young man was proud of his new post, and did his best, studying as well as teaching, advising and making friends in the court whenever he could. Soon, however, he found that his student was gravely troubled by her destiny. She did not want to rule. She feared the responsibilities of her birth. He tried to be a friend as well as a teacher to her, and so the years passed.' His voice dropped to a whisper. 'She was most fair as she grew, and powerful in her magics, and the tutor came to realize that in his secret heart, he was in love with her.'

Ingrid suddenly found it very hard to breathe.

'It was not a feeling which he could voice, nor even allow himself to think much about. So he buried it deeply, and things went on as they had always been.

'Then, the Emperor and Empress negotiated a marriage treaty around their daughter with the prince of a southern empire with which they sought alliance. Medeoan was distraught, but only because it was another thread binding her to the truth she disliked so. She had long known her marriage would be arranged to benefit Isavalta.

'The prince, Kacha, was brought to Isavalta so that he might learn its languages and customs before they married. He was handsome enough and he set himself to wooing his bride-to-be with great care and attention. They were both scions of powerful houses, both caught up in the political necessities of their realms. As such, they had much in common.

'At first, Avanasy was pleased to see friendship, and then love, growing between them. He was sad at the loss of his special relationship with Medeoan, but, he cheered himself with the thought that the one she must marry truly loved her.

'Then, he found, or thought he found, evidence that the prince was a spy, and a traitor. Kacha was being used by his father to conquer sovereign Isavalta, and possibly lead it into war. But when he tried to present his evidence to Medeoan, he found himself contradicted by the words and actions of the prince himself. Medeoan grew so angry with him for making accusations which in the end he could not prove, she ordered him banished from the boundaries of Isavalta.'

Avan grew quiet then, remembering. Ingrid didn't know what to say. She herself could scarcely remember how to breathe. She had thought the ghost the end of the strangeness in her life, now she found it was only the beginning.

'Was he, Prince Kacha, betraying the princess?'

Avan tilted his head back so he could stare at the branches and the sky overhead. 'I don't know.'

'And the sorcerer, this Avanasy, what did he do?'

'Cursed himself for a fool,' said Avan flatly. 'And realized that he was further gone with his impossible sentiment than he had realized. Had he been thinking clearly, he would have gone straight to the Emperor with what he knew, and the Emperor could have ordered the prince watched over by all the court sorcerers. But he did not do this.' A single muscle twitched in Avan's cheek. 'Instead he tried to prove himself the better man to the princess, and so brought about his own ruin.'

Ingrid opened her mouth, and closed it again. What on earth could she have possibly said?

'When Avanasy was certain he could not convince Medeoan to reverse the order of banishment, when he saw her finally married to Prince Kacha, he left,' Avan went on. 'Left Isavalta, and ultimately, left the world of his birth, because he could not stand to watch what he feared might be coming, and because he could not bear to face his foolishness and disgrace. He became a fisherman on an island in the middle of a lake, a world away from anything that he knew.' Avan lifted his gaze, and for the first time since he had begun his incredible story, he looked directly at Ingrid. 'He never thought to speak of any of these matters again to another living soul, but he fell in love, this time with a gracious woman whom he could court with honesty and a fully open heart, and he wished the lady to know the truth before he declared as much.'

Suddenly, Ingrid found she could not sit still. She rose to her feet and retreated a few steps. She might have run further if she had not felt a tree right at her back. It was too much for her to take in, and yet she did not know which overwhelmed her more, Avan's story, or his confession that he did love her.

Then she saw how he watched her, and how his face fell at her expression of bewilderment. Ingrid shook herself. She owed him better than this. She straightened her spine.

'Thank you for telling me,' she said. 'Thank you for trusting me.'

'You believe me, then?'

She nodded. 'Without the ghost and all that happened then, I might not. But having seen what I have, I cannot choose but to believe.'

'There are not many who would do so.' Avan stood. 'And the rest?'

And the rest? Ingrid looked at him. She remembered how she first saw him clearly in the firelight. She remembered how generously he had helped her and Grace. She remembered all the bright weeks of his patience, his humor, and his company. She felt again the ache and the anticipation that she knew lying alone in the darkness. And the rest?

'I think I loved you the moment I first saw you beside the fire. I was just not free to say so until now.'

Ingrid felt that with those words the whole world must change. Perhaps it did. Avan stood where he was, as if paralyzed by the sound of her voice. Then he took a step forward, two steps, three steps, until he stood right in front of her. He reached out one of his long, graceful hands and brushed it gently over her hair. Now it was Ingrid who found herself paralyzed. She felt as if she would never move again, unless he said that she should.

'I want to marry you, Ingrid,' he said, his voice hoarse with emotion. 'I want to build a house, a proper house, and bring you to it. I want to work with you and for you to build a good life. I want to sit beside the fire with you and sing and tell stories. I want to lie down beside you at night and wake up beside you in the morning. No,' he said as she opened her mouth and he held his fingertips just before her lips, not quite touching. 'There are two more things you need to know before you answer me.

'You know that I am a sorcerer. In the world into which I was born, magic is not merely a skill one can learn. It is tied to one's nature. There is a great deal of argument as to why that should be so, and what it means. What is known is that there are two consequences that come with the gift. The first is that the getting of children is very difficult for a sorcerer. The second is that we live very long lives, sometimes four or five times the length of other men. I do not know if these things remain true on this shore of the Land of Death and Spirit, but you deserve to know of them.' He stood back from her. 'If you need some time, or if you wish to turn away, I understand.'

Ingrid stayed where she was, trying to think. Life, life could end tomorrow or go on for a hundred years for either of them. There were a thousand accidents that could put an end to a person, and she had seen many of them at one time or another. Happiness was a matter of chance. The children . . . not to have children would be hard. Then again, that also was a matter of chance. There were women who brought four, five, six babies into the world and lost them all one by one. There were women who died trying to give birth to even one. It was all in God's hands, as was everything else. Had anything Avan told her really changed that?

But if Avan had told the truth, she should repay him in kind.

Ingrid drew in a breath heavy with the scent of pine resin and all the heat of summer. 'My father also came from a long ways off,' she said. 'From a place called Bavaria, as you may have heard. He traveled to Chicago and ended up working in the slaughterhouses. There, he met my mother, who was very beautiful, very young, and the daughter of a good family. They didn't approve of him. He was very poor, he was German, they were Irish.' She hung her head. 'That much I know for certain. The rest of this is only guesswork, letters, and gossip.

'My mother got in the family way without having married my father. Believing love would see them through, they ran away from their parents' anger and came up here to Bayfield, where no one knew them, and where no one was counting the days until she gave birth. I believe they worked hard at their lives, but something failed in the end. Maybe it happened when they began to have daughters, and they were afraid that those daughters might make the same mistakes that they had.' She shook her head. 'What I am trying to say is that I have no family who will speak to me, except for the ones you've met. I have no breeding or fortune, and I am in all likelihood a bastard.' She squared her shoulders and met his gaze. Let him see her, let him look long and hard at her – rumpled, berry-stained, her hands coarsened by hard work, her clothes much mended, and her skin brown from the sun. 'Can a man who has loved a princess settle for what he sees in front of him?'

But Avan only shook his head. 'If I were to marry you, I would not be settling,' he said, and his voice was as grave, as honest as it had been during the entire course of his narrative. 'I would be reaching so high that I might grasp the stars themselves. I have seen your bravery, your honesty, your love, your joy. It is nothing but the purest selfishness that makes me wish to bind all that you are to my side.'

Ingrid found she had no words. She could only cross the distance between them, stand on her toes and kiss him. He stiffened at her touch, startled, but in the next moment, wrapped his strong arms around her, answering her kiss, her love, with his own.

When at last they pulled away from each other, Avan looked her up and down as if he had never seen so wonderful and precious a thing before. 'I don't know what the customs are here,' he said shyly, softly touching her hair, her cheek, her shoulder. 'I don't know what is expected of me now. Should I make some gift . . . ?'

'You will have to speak to my father. He should give his consent.'

'And if he withholds it?'

Ingrid shrugged a little. 'I am of age, I'm free to marry whom I wish. But, it will be easier on us both if he consents.' She smiled. 'As for a gift, it is traditional that you give me a ring.'

He nodded with extreme seriousness. 'A ring. I will remember that.' He raised her right hand to his lips and kissed it gently. 'And I shall come to the house to speak with your father tonight. Now,' he added reluctantly straightening up, 'I think I had best return you to your sister.'

'Yes.' Then, she paused, an odd thought striking her. 'I don't . . . I . . . what should I call you?'

He appeared to consider her question gravely, but she saw the merry light in his blue eyes. 'In front of others, I think perhaps you should call me Avan, as that's how they know me. When we are alone, you may call me Avanasy, if you choose.'

'I'd like that. You'll have to teach me how to pronounce the rest later.'

'Willingly. Come now.' He shouldered his scythe easily. 'Your berries are spoiling in the sun, and your little sister is beginning to despair of your reputation.'

'Ha!' laughed Ingrid sharply. 'Despair is not what Grace is beginning to do, I'll wager you.'

But he was right otherwise, and Ingrid let him begin to walk her back. They made their way through the scrub and thickets silently, side-by-side, content for the moment just to be together. There would be time enough for everything else later.

When Grace saw them, she just grinned impishly and raised her brows. Ingrid made a show of cuffing her sister across the head, but Avan, Avanasy, did not even smile. He just gave them both a strange, formal bow, with one leg extended and both hands crossed over his breast. Then, he reclaimed his scythe and strolled easily away into the woods.

Ingrid stared after him, unable to take her eyes off the smooth motion of his body.

'Has something happened, Ingrid?' inquired Grace mildly.

'Not something,' answered Ingrid. 'Everything.'

'Ingrid!' Grace shrieked, and leapt forward, hugging Ingrid so hard, they both toppled over into the underbrush, barely missing the baskets of blackberries.

'Get off me, you idiot!' cried Ingrid, shoving her sister backward and making a great show of reordering her clothes and hair. 'A little dignity would only improve your character, Miss.'

Grace just laughed at her and plucked a leaf from her hair. 'I knew he would ask you. I knew it. When's it to be?'

'Would you keep your voice down!' snapped Ingrid, looking around. But little Thad and their sisters seemed to be out of earshot, and none of the neighbors had moved in. 'No one knows yet. He's got to talk to Papa. He'll come by tonight.'

'Perfect,' declared Grace. She began to pluck berries from the nearest bush, tossing them down into the basket without concern for whether they were crushed or not. 'You can be married in the fall, and then we can all move to Bayfield for the winter and . . .'

'"We?"' Now it was Ingrid's turn to arch her brows.

'Of course,' said Grace blithely, popping a couple of berries into her mouth. 'You can't set up housekeeping all on your own, you know. You're going to need my help.'

Ingrid turned her attention to the blackberry canes, carefully moving aside thorny green branches to hide her surprise, and her irritation. 'Mama is going to need help as well, you know.'

'And I know you won't leave me in that house,' said Grace with the blithe assurance that was so much a part of her. 'With Papa and Leo breathing down my neck all the time, and no Ingrid to stand up for me? It's unthinkable.'

Ingrid pulled a last few warm, sticky berries from the bush and dropped them into the basket. The warm delight that had come to her when she accepted Avan's proposal had fled, replaced by an unfamiliar frustration with her younger sister. Did Grace only see Ingrid's happiness in terms of how it would help her?

'We'll talk about this later,' said Ingrid, hefting her basket so she could move further into the thicket.

'Oh, Ingrid . . .' began Grace, but she did not finish her sentence, for at that moment, a man's horrible scream cut through the forest.

At once, Ingrid dropped her basket and hiked up her skirts to run for the trail and the direction from which the sound had come.

'Thad!' she shouted as she sprinted past her little brother. 'Get the girls home! Now!'

'Yes, Ingrid!' he called behind her, but she did not look to see that he obeyed. Ahead in the woods, the man cried out again and sobbed in his pain.

On the edge of the true woods, a cluster of people had gathered, their backs bent, their voices raised into an incomprehensible gabble. As Ingrid came crashing forward to join the crowd, crabbed Vale Anderson turned and saw her, and pulled his wife aside, opening a small lane for Ingrid. Others turned and saw her, and they also drew away.

Her heart in her mouth, and her blood suddenly singing in her ears, Ingrid moved forward through the crowd of faces that she had known since birth but suddenly could not see.

In front of her, Leo lay on the ground, his face ashen, knotted and straining in pain. Papa squatted by Leo's outstretched leg, his hands red with blood. A scythe lay on the ground nearby. More blood stained its blade.

Ingrid took in all this in a single heartbeat. In the next, she was on her knees by Leo, cradling his head in her apron and putting a stick between his teeth for him to bite down on. Papa had a knife out and was cutting through Leo's boot and trousers. Each movement brought a fresh cry of pain from her brother's throat.

'What on earth . . .' Grace's voice, then Grace herself pushed through the crowd. Ingrid looked up at her mutely, and then followed her gaze down to their brother's injured leg.

It was bad. The gash was just above his ankle, and went clear to the gray-white bone. Blood poured out like it could never be stopped.

'Mary Mother of God!' cried Grace, and she went whiter even than Leo. She stuffed her fist in her mouth to stifle what might have been a scream or a sob and, to Ingrid's shock, turned and fled.

Leo groaned again and his head pressed hard against her

apron. Ingrid grabbed his shoulders to hold him steady. Papa did not look up. He used the cloth cut from the trousers to tie off Leo's leg below the knee. The red flood slowed a little and Leo moaned against the biting stick.

Ingrid glanced around at her anxious neighbors, but the only face she could see clearly now was Avan's. She looked at him, a silent plea in her eyes. He understood at once, but only shook his head. There was nothing he could do.

No. There was something. 'Avan!' she cried. 'Get to Bayfield. Fetch the doctor!'

'At once,' said Avan, and he vanished from her sight.

Papa glanced at her sharply, but did not contradict her, or even glower. 'I need a hand here,' was all he said. 'We need to get him home.'

Four men surged forward to help lift her brother between them. One of them was Everett Lederle. Of course it was. In her shock and confusion, Ingrid found time to think, *Oh, Everett, I am sorry . . .*

The men tried to be gentle, but they had to hurry and they all knew it. The bleeding had slowed, but it had to be stopped, and soon. Each jolt of their footsteps ripped a fresh cry from Leo. Ingrid was selfishly glad to be able to run ahead fast enough that she outpaced the sound of her brother's screams, up the track to their house.

She half-expected Grace to have preceded her, but Mama was alone in the kitchen wielding a huge ladle and presiding over the steaming kettles on the stove when Ingrid burst in.

'Jesus and Mary, what's happened?' she cried as she saw Ingrid.

Ingrid, gasping for breath and pressing the heel of her hand against her side, told Mama. Mama shrieked and threw up her hands. The ladle fell to the floor with a clang and a clatter. Mama just ran from the room to throw open the front door.

'Ingrid! Get a basin of hot water, and we'll need all the clean sheets!'

'Yes, Mama!'

Ingrid moved as swiftly as she was able through the clouds of blackberry steam, but she suddenly felt unbelievably clumsy. Her hands shook as she poured boiling water from one of the iron kettles into an ancient and chipped shaving basin. Thad appeared in the kitchen, peering around the door.

'Take this up to Mama,' said Ingrid, shoving the basin into her little brother's hands. To her relief, she saw him carry it away with great care. *Where's Grace?* she wondered desperately at the same time. Her two littlest sisters peeked around the door. 'Girls, you stay in the yard, understand me?'

They vanished. Ingrid hurried into the front room and threw open the cedar chest, one of the family's few truly fine possessions. She scooped out an armful of fragrant, snow-white sheets, just as the men bearing Leo between them poured through the door.

'Upstairs,' directed Ingrid. And there was too much jostling and too many cries of, 'Careful, there!' before they were able to maneuver him up the narrow stairway. Leo himself made no sound. He must have fainted, for which Ingrid was grateful.

Mama waited beside the bed in the bare room Leo shared with Thad. Her face was white as the sheets Ingrid carried but she stayed steady as the men laid Leo on the bed. She shooed them all back and bent over her son, mopping away the blood and examining the gash. The men shuffled out of the room, murmuring their good wishes to Ingrid and Papa as they left. Everett brushed her arm in passing, and Ingrid, to her shame, found she could not look into his eyes.

'I need those sheets, Ingrid!' snapped Mama.

Then it was all blood and heat, and hot water and white sheets, and Mama stitching Leo's wound closed and Ingrid cradling his head, and hoping Thad would keep the little girls out of the way. They did not need to see this. Leo alternated between straining to hold still despite the pain and swooning from the same pain and loss of blood.

Then it was over and Leo was again in a faint and there was nothing to do but gather up the bloody sheets and the empty, rust-stained basin and lug the whole, stinking bundle down the stairs to the back kitchen.

The room was filled with the smell of burned blackberries. Ingrid nearly choked as she dumped the sheets into the washtub and hurried to throw open the stove and bank down the fire. Papa, seemingly oblivious to the stench, sat at the table, hunched over a cup that, from the smell, had probably held strong coffee not too long before.

'How's your brother?' he asked gruffly.

'I don't know,' admitted Ingrid, surveying the disaster on the stove. A kettle of syrup and another of preserves had boiled down into identical, thick, black, utterly inedible messes. A whole day's work gone. 'He's lost a lot of blood. The doctor will be able to say more.'

'You should not have involved that man Avan,' Papa grunted to his empty mug. 'It's none of his business.'

Ingrid strangled a sigh, telling herself that was a reflexive remark from Papa and meant nothing. It needed no reply. She took the still-hot coffee pot off the stove and poured what was left of its contents into Papa's mug.

'I'll get supper started,' she said, returning to the stove. She tried to give herself over to thoughts of the chore at hand. She'd set the kettles to soak and get at them with the wire brush after supper. There was still some stew from yesterday. A little water and it would stretch out just fine, with dumplings, and some of the fresh blackberries and what was left of the cream . . .

She wrapped a rag around the first kettle of burned black-berry essence and made ready to haul it out the back door.

'Your sister should have been here to tend to that,' announced Papa, gulping some coffee. 'Where is she?'

'I don't know.' Ingrid set the kettle outside the door. 'Thad!' she called to her younger brother. 'Get this filled with water, won't you? Be careful, it's still hot. I'll have another out shortly.'

She returned to the kitchen, only to find Papa glowering at her from under his heavy brows.

'Your sister's gone again and all you can say is you don't know where,' he snarled. 'Your brother can't keep his mind on his work and will probably have to have his foot off. By God, is there not one of my children who will do as they should?'

Ingrid set her jaw and concentrated on wrapping the dishrag tightly around the handle on the old Dutch oven.

'You'll pay attention when I speak to you, girl!' The exclamation was followed fast by the crash of Papa's hand coming down hard on the table-top.

Slowly, Ingrid turned. Her hands flexed, as if they wanted to curl into fists.

'You may be sure, Papa, I have heard every word you said.'

Papa rose slowly and fear stiffened Ingrid's spine. He stalked forward until he was a bare six inches from her and Ingrid knew he meant to hit her. His heavy hand itched to lash out at something, and she was nearest. At the same time, in his eyes, she saw fear and disappointment, fear for Leo, disappointment at his life and his lot, and his children. Oh, most especially his children, and all that had become of them lately.

'You'll mind your place, Ingrid Loftfield,' he said heavily. His breath was sour with coffee and worry. 'And you'll not speak to me again in that tone.'

Ingrid held her ground and her peace. There was nothing else she could do.

Papa's eyes searched hers for a long moment. What he found in her face, she could not tell. She could only see his anger growing cold and heavy, like a millstone around his neck. It seemed to be the only feeling he had left in him.

'Get about your work,' he grunted at last. 'It's time one of you did.'

With those words he pushed past her. She heard the front door open and close, and she let out the breath she didn't realize she had been holding.

Let it pass, she counseled herself. *Let it pass. It does no one any good, and it will soon be over. Soon.*

Soon she would be married to Avan, and in a house of her own. She lugged the Dutch oven out to set beside the back door. Soon, she would be well out of this, and Mama might cry and Papa might carp and Leo might glower, and it would be nothing at all to her, because she would have her own home, and she would love and be loved.

And how will Grace manage? Ingrid returned to the stove and squatted down in front of it. How will it be for her when there's no one to stand between her and Papa? She used the poker to uncover the embers and began laying tinder over them, watching the orange flames spring to life.

Grace will manage as she has managed everything else. Ingrid laid some larger sticks in the fire, and closed the stove door, letting them get on with the business of burning down to hot coals. *With a smile and wink. She'll be fine.* But even as she thought that, she glanced toward the back door. *But where is she?*

The sun slid slowly down behind the pines. Ingrid heated the stew and dropped in the fat, floury dumplings. She lit the lamp and took it upstairs to see if Mama needed anything. Leo still lay white and unconscious in his bed, the coverlets pulled up to his chin. Mama asked only for some fresh water to bathe his head, and Ingrid fetched it in a clean tin basin.

When she came back down to the kitchen, a shape stood in the shadows by the back door. Ingrid raised her lantern, and saw Grace standing there in the corner like a guilty child.

'Where have you *been*?' cried Ingrid. 'I've been out of my mind . . .'

'I'm sorry,' said Grace in a whisper. 'Is Leo . . . is he . . . ?'

'We don't know yet.' Ingrid set the lantern down on the table and turned back to the stove, picking up the worn wooden spoon. 'Avan's gone to fetch the doctor.' She peeked under the kettle lid to check the dumplings. 'And you didn't answer my question.'

'I'm sorry,' said Grace again. 'It was just . . . I was just upset, that's all.'

'We could have used your help.' Ingrid felt tired: tired, frightened and frustrated. 'Mama lost two kettles of jam and syrup because there was no one here to take care of them.'

'And don't you sound just like her,' answered Grace saucily. 'I've told you I'm sorry, and I am. I was just . . . sick.'

Ingrid set the spoon down carefully. Unfamiliar and unbidden, anger rose in her at her sister's careless tone. How could she stand there, having run out on her family when they needed her, when *Ingrid* needed her, and now come back, without a word as to what had happened to her, and with only a breezy little apology when . . .

Before Ingrid could even begin to find the words she wanted to speak to Grace, a light moved beyond the door, and a moment later it swung open, pushed by a drenched Avan, who held a mineral-oil lantern in his hand. Right behind him came Dr Nicholson clutching his black bag, his round figure swaddled in an oilskin that was still shedding rain water.

'Doctor,' Ingrid greeted him with a rush of gratitude for his presence, both because it meant help for Leo, and because it kept her from having to voice her feelings to Grace. 'I'm glad you've come. Has Avan . . .' she glanced at him.

'Aye, he's told me all,' said the doctor, brushing water from his sleeves. 'Where's the boy now?'

'I'll take you,' volunteered Grace, just as Ingrid opened her mouth. 'This way.'

Grace ushered the doctor up the stairs, leaving Ingrid standing alone with Avan.

'You look tired,' he said, setting his lantern down next to hers.

Ingrid wiped her hands on her apron, suddenly feeling awkward. 'It's been a hard day,' she answered. 'Thank you for bringing Dr Nicholson. Was it a hard sail?'

Avan shrugged. 'There'll be a blow tonight. We got in before the worst of it.'

Now that she listened, Ingrid could hear the wind rushing under the eaves. She'd been so wrapped up in her own gloom she hadn't even noticed before, hadn't even spared a thought for Avan except for how he would rescue her from her own troubles.

'What is it, Ingrid?' Avan asked quietly. He wanted to move toward her, she knew he did, but he did not dare here. Not when her father might come in any second. Nor could she move toward him, so there they stood, awkward as school-children on opposite sides of the kitchen table.

Ingrid shook her head, smoothing back her hair. It wasn't that she did not want to answer him, but she did not know how to begin. At the same time, she could not keep silent.

'Avan . . .' she began hesitantly. 'What we talked about before . . .'

'I had best wait until your brother has somewhat recovered,' he said for her. 'We met your father on the road. He wasn't pleased. I think he is not as used to me in his house as I would have hoped.'

Ingrid gave him a crooked smile. 'No. I'm afraid not.'

Avan reached out, and his fingertips brushed hers with fleeting warmth. 'Try not to worry, my love,' he whispered. 'All will yet be right.'

For the first time since he'd come in the door, Ingrid looked Avan fully in the eyes, and her heart melted once again with the love she saw there.

Grace chose just then to bustle back into the kitchen. 'Good news!' she cheered. 'The doctor says there's no reason for Leo to lose the leg. He says if we keep him warm and dry, and feed him on plenty of broth, he'll be sound again in no time.'

'That is good news,' said Avan, with a smile that was more for Ingrid than Grace.

'I knew it would all be well,' announced Grace with unexpected force. 'I *knew* it.'

Ingrid could think of nothing to say to that, considering Grace's behavior that afternoon, so instead she turned back to Avan. 'Will you stay for supper? We surely owe you that much.'

Avan just shook his head. 'Thank you, but I think not, considering all . . .'

'Oh, come now, Avan,' laughed Grace. 'Ingrid and I will manage Papa. You're welcome at the table.'

'I thank you, but I must take my leave.' He picked his lantern up. 'Good night, Miss Loftfield. Miss Grace.'

Ingrid followed him to the door. She could not have stopped herself. As she stood in the threshold, he turned, bent swiftly and kissed her, and then he turned and stumped down the path toward the gate, leaving Ingrid to stand there, her fingers touching her mouth and her heart brimming with warmth.

It would be all right. Leo would heal. Grace would come to see she must look after herself. Papa would relent, or he would not. It didn't matter. She was a grown woman. Avan loved her, truly loved her, and she loved him, and things would be all right. They would make them so, no matter what.

Chapter Seven

Kacha walked the moonlit gardens beside the Imperial canal. It had become his custom on the few nights he was not attending Medeoan to take the air in this fashion. His men followed at a discreet distance with such lanterns and other accouterments as might be required. Tonight, however, the moon was full, and he scarce needed any other light.

He liked these gardens underneath the moon. He liked the drooping willows shining with silver, and the soft grass and the scents of herbs and flowers. Here in the darkness, he could almost believe he was home again in Hastinapura, perhaps late in the wintertime when the air was dry and cool and the summer's blossoms had not yet woken. There was still the sound of water, and the trees made of silver and shadow. Here, he could almost feel content.

'Majesty?' Prithu, his head waiting gentleman, gave a small cough. Kacha turned. A cloaked figure glided across the lawn. From this distance, it was impossible to make out any detail regarding the approaching person, but Kacha smiled to himself. He had no doubt as to who this was.

The figure paused, as if uncertain what welcome he would offer. Kacha beckoned it forward and it knelt in reverence at his feet. Kacha reached out and pushed the fur and velvet hood back to reveal Chekhania, Medeoan's first waiting lady, and his finest ally in Vyshtavos.

'Good evening, Mistress,' he said, raising her to her feet.

'Good evening, Majesty Imperial.' She was a little breathless from hurrying, and even in the moonlight he could see that her cheeks were flushed.

'You have news for me?' he asked needlessly. Everything about her spoke of repressed excitement. Not only news, but important news, and Kacha had no doubt she was already anticipating how well she would be rewarded.

She did not answer, but glanced back at Kacha's men. They knew better than to come close during these meetings, but if Chekhania had a fault, it was that she enjoyed the drama of her position too much. Still, Kacha was inclined to humor her. He clasped her fingertips with his own, in the Isavaltan fashion, and walked her down the canal a little ways.

'Now, none can hear us,' he breathed, stepping close enough to feel the heat of her skin. 'Tell me what you've learned.'

'Majesty, I would have come to you sooner, but this is so grave, and so strange, I had to make certain it was the truth . . .'

'Tell me,' he said again. She smelled of musk and flowers, a scent, he was sure, she had chosen with care for this encounter, and he could not fault her choice.

She smiled, but still kept her eyes modestly turned down. 'The Empress plans to fly from Vyshtavos tomorrow.'

'What!' Kacha jerked backward. 'When did you learn this?'

'Yesterday,' she said, no longer so smiling. 'I heard it when I was with the Right Hand of the Keeper. He and I . . .' she delicately waved the end of the sentence away. 'Afterwards, when I was waiting for a good time to take my leave, I saw Captain Peshek come into the house and make confession to the gods, and as Your Majesty Imperial knows, he did meet with the Empress but lately.'

Kacha felt his demeanor grow cold as stone. 'Who else aids her in this plot?'

'I tremble to say that I don't know, yet.'

Kacha whirled away from Chekhania, his hands tightening into fists. So, for all Medeoan's protestations, she had given him nothing but pretty lies. Yamuna had been right. He had been more than right. Kacha should have watched her, should have insisted he stay by her, should not have given her a moment's peace . . .

I will hang Yamuna's spell about her neck for a noose, and pull her along behind me like a dog on a lead. I will teach her what it means to be a proper wife. I will . . .

Pain stabbed him from behind his right eye. Kacha grunted and slapped his hand over it. Slowly, with many deep breaths, he brought his anger under control. The pain eased, and he was able to lower his hand and think again.

This was not what he had expected. He had thought Medeoan might betray him, yes, but he had not even considered the idea that she might flee. He had expected her to try to win back her Council and her lords, and to cut him off from the instruments of power as he had cut her off. But simply to run away . . . he never would have considered that. Well, courage had never been Medeoan's strength. The question was, what to do about this. Should he use the girdle on her tonight? Or should he wait and catch her in the act? Or . . .

The fingers of his right hand grew warm. Yes. Yes. There was a way. He could see it clearly now. He could deal with Medeoan's actions and, thanks to Yamuna's foresight and excellent provision, he could deal with her Council. Yamuna and his own heart showed him how all might be done, and the picture pleased him well.

He faced Chekhania again, and found her a little pale, and a little anxious, properly afraid of her master's anger.

'You've done well, Chekhania,' he said, and to make sure she knew how well, he kissed her roughly. She melted at once into his arms, answering the kiss with a pleasing ardor. He pulled her down to the ground with him, his hands fumbling with her skirts, even as hers expertly sought the knot of his sash that she might open his coat.

Kacha laughed as he took her then, laughed for the passion and the future, and for how little Medeoan had sealed her own doom and with her own hands had given him all he desired.

The morning that the Imperial household was to move to its summer quarters dawned sweet and clear, full of the green scents of the season. Medeoan's waiting ladies pushed open what windows there were to let the warmth and sunshine wash through her stone room. A riot of noise rose from the courtyard as goods and people assembled to be borne down to the barges that Medeoan knew were waiting on the canal. Her dressing screens cut her off from the rest of the world, confining her in a tiny space with two of her ladies, with no room to move and nowhere to go. As her ladies dressed her in her best traveling clothes of light wool and linen, and girdled her around with the Imperial colors of blue and gold, she listened with a fluttering heart to the vibrant, busy sounds from outside.

Now was the time. All was in order. This morning she could make her escape, and, if she failed, then . . .

Then there was nothing to do but wait until Kacha decided to take away the last of her.

'Where is the Emperor, Chekhania?' asked Medeoan as the woman tied the final neat love knot.

'I believe he is supervising the assembly of your entourage, Majesty Imperial.' Chekhania stood back to inspect Medeoan and make sure that no piece of garment or ornamentation was missing. 'Shall I tell him that you request his presence?'

'No.' Medeoan's mouth had gone completely dry. Her words tasted thick with her own fear. 'Send a page to say I give him my best greetings on this fine morning, and that I shall meet him in the god house so that we may receive the blessing of Vyshko and Vyshemir for our journey.'

'Yes, Mistress Imperial.' Chekhania gave the abbreviated reverence her position allowed and hurried out the door to alert the page girl who waited there with the men at arms. Medeoan had hoped that the lady's brief departure would allow her to breathe easier, but instead her whole chest tightened.

'Master Senoi,' she called to her head secretary over the dressing screens. 'Go down to the pantries and make sure the Mistress of the House has prepared a complete inventory for His Majesty Imperial. He was remarking on the need for it the other day.'

'Mistress Imperial,' her man said to acknowledge the order. She heard the sound of his footsteps, and the door opened and closed again. A moment later, Chekhania returned.

'Your message is being delivered, Mistress Imperial.'

'Good.' Medeoan stepped out from behind the dressing screens, more so she would not have to look at Chekhania than anything else. 'Chekhania, you'll stay here with Ovsta and Dalidaand and see that the trunks are all packed and loaded properly. I do not trust some of these lackeys.' That made Chekhania smile, and Medeoan swore she was going to start preening any second now. Chekhania enjoyed her position, and any opportunity to lord it over her fellows.

How did I miss that vanity for so long? Medeoan's fingers

knotted themselves in her skirt. *Do not think of it now. You must think of what you will do next, and only that.*

'Ragneda, I want you to check the documents trunk off against the ledger. I do not wish any letters left behind. Report the results to His Majesty Imperial. Adeksii, come with me to the god house. We need to ask Vyshko and Vyshemir for a successful journey.'

With only a single lady behind her, Medeoan swept out into the corridor. Her men at arms formed up, two in front of her, two behind, but if they noticed her abbreviated entourage, they said nothing. But then again, what could they say? They were only soldiers, and she was the Empress. If she chose to wander the hallways stark naked, their duty would be to stay two in front and two behind and keep their eyes forward and their mouths silent.

All of Vyshtavos's grand corridors passed by her in a blur. The rhythmic tread of boots and the patter of shoes mixed together with the beating of her heart. Perhaps courtiers passed by and reverenced, perhaps a Lord Master moved forward to speak to her, she was not sure. Her sight strained past them, as if she were trying to see through the very walls of the palace to where Kacha was. She wanted to see if the loading of the barges kept him busy, or if he was even now on his way to the god house, and to her, to take her hand, and lead her down to the barge, to hold her prisoner with his constant gaze. He might already be there, waiting for her with his withered hand outstretched and his false smile. Medeoan swallowed as her stomach roiled. This was as cold as the hard frost of winter. She had never even considered that one day she might come to be afraid of Kacha, but so it was, for she now feared him more than she had ever feared a living thing.

At long last, the gilded doors of the god house loomed before her. The two men at arms who walked in the lead stepped forward to push the doors open and then stood back, saluting her with their hands over their hearts. Medeoan, her heart filling her throat, strode past them. For a moment, the dazzle of gold and candlelight kept her from looking around the room. First, she saw the gods on their pedestal, then she saw Keeper Bakhar ready and humble beside them. She bit down on her tongue to keep herself silent, and her gaze swept the painted and golden room. There was no one else there. She had been swift enough.

She approached the gods, her whole body trembling. With the deepest reverence, she kissed Vyshemir's hem.

'Help me,' she breathed soundlessly. 'Guide my steps and harden my heart. Lend me your courage, Vyshemir, for what I must now do.'

She stepped back and turned to her servitors. 'You may wait outside. I have matters to discuss with Keeper Bakhar.'

The lady and the soldiers reverenced, and backed out. The doors swung shut with a hollow thud, and Medeoan was alone with Bakhar. As simple as that.

'Quickly, Majesty,' whispered Keeper Bakhar, hurrying toward the vestment room. Medeoan gathered up her skirts and ran after him, her ears all the time straining to hear the doors open behind her, to hear Kacha's voice say, 'Beloved? What are you doing?'

'You must leave quickly once I am gone, Keeper,' said Medeoan, gripping his hand. 'Kacha will surely know you helped me.'

The Keeper's smile was grim and brief. 'He will not dare do anything to me at once, Majesty. If it becomes necessary, I will have time to make good my own escape.'

Keeper Bakhar threw open the vestment-room door and Medeoan darted through. The door shut at once, plunging her into darkness so quickly she pulled up short and blinked. Her eyes adjusted to show her the long wall hung with the formal garments of the Keeper and his underlings. Among the neat robes stood Captain Peshek.

'Majesty Imperial,' he whispered, reverencing quickly. 'We must get you changed.' He handed her a bundle of cloth.

'I can't alone,' she said helplessly. She hadn't even stopped to think of this before. It took two women the better part of an hour to get her into these clothes. It was physically impossible for her to remove them alone.

Captain Peshek bit his lip, his gaze darting between the room's four doors. 'I ask dispensation to commit a great liberty, Majesty.'

'You have it, Captain.'

'Then, Majesty, turn around.' Captain Peshek drew his knife.

Realizing what he meant to do, Medeoan put her back to him. She heard him suck in his breath, and a moment later, she was buffeted by a series of jerks and tugs. Laces snapped, cloth ripped, and her girdle snaked off from around her waist and slithered to the floor. If Kacha came in now, Peshek would be dead before she could order him spared.

'Try now, Mistress Imperial.'

Medeoan put her bundle on a nearby shelf and pushed the ruined finery from her shoulders. The cloth fell in a heap about her ankles, leaving her only her shift, stockings and shoes.

Trying not to think about the man in the room with her, Medeoan hopped over the crumpled cloth and undid the bundle she had been given. Inside was a rough woolen skirt, a gray blouse with sleeves that could be rolled up firmly past her elbows, a stained apron, and an embroidered headscarf that had seen many washings. With a start, she realized that the scarf was Eliisa's. She could not help but glance at

Captain Peshek, but he had turned away from her and all she saw was his rigid back. Well, she had stolen much more from the girl than this, why should she now balk at a piece of cloth?

Nonetheless, her scalp shivered as she tied the scarf in place.

A pair of black, scratchy stockings and scuffed, badly sewn shoes completed the disguise. Medeoan caught sight of her reflection in the polished brass mirror that served the keepers and had to stand and stare. Was that her? That thin, pale, wide-eyed drab? That was a powerful sorceress, and Empress of Eternal Isavalta?

'Mistress Imperial?' came Captain Peshek's urgent whisper.

Medeoan tore her eyes from her diminished reflection. 'You may turn around, Captain. I'm ready.'

Captain Peshek pivoted on his heel, saw her, and his eyes widened. In the next heartbeat, however, he recovered himself, and reverenced. 'This way, please, Mistress Imperial.'

He led her out the far door into an unadorned corridor where she, for all her life in the palace of Vyshtavos, had never walked. A skinny boy in rough, clean servant's clothes waited there, standing on one foot so that he could scratch his heel. When Peshek appeared, he lowered his foot hastily and reverenced.

'This is Sherosh,' said Peshek. 'He has no tongue, and cannot write, but he knows to show you out the servants' way. I will meet you beside the stables.'

Peshek did not reverence as he retreated, nor did Medeoan fail to notice that he had not used her title. The boy beside her probably did not even know who she was. He just faced her, as wide-eyed and curious as a puppy. Then he smiled, showing a row of ragged and dirty teeth, and took off running.

Suddenly a stranger in her home, Medeoan had no choice but to scurry after him. He led her down a bewildering array of windowless corridors that all seemed to be made of either aging plaster or dark wood. They passed other servants, some in livery, some in drab's clothes. No one stopped to notice her. Some cursed as she ran by, some bellowed, but no one stopped. No one knew her as their Empress.

Sherosh led her through the sculleries where the air was thick with the stench of slops and garbage and ringing with the clash of pots and kettles. A door, black with age, stood propped open to let in what relief the summer air could provide. Outside, it was only a little quieter, but it smelled even worse, if that were possible. This was the work yard with the sheds for the tanners, the dyers and the weavers, the smiths' great forges, the butchers' yard, and the brewers' hall. All conceivable smells of animals, living and dead, mixed with the smells of hot metal and hot mash.

The stables waited upwind of the work yard, so the horses would not be disturbed by the smells of work and slaughter. Reaching the relatively clean scent of well-kept horses was a relief.

A man waited in the shadow of the stable's western wall holding the reins of a scrawny yellow mule. His boots were worn, but his rough pantaloons and undyed kaftan were clean, and the brown sash around his waist was broad and neat. A moment later, Medeoan realized this man was Captain Peshek. She had never seen him out of uniform, and she found him as much altered as she herself was, from Imperial guardsman to peasant with a change of a costume.

'Good boy, Sherosh.' Peshek flipped a copper coin into the dust at the boy's feet. Sherosh dived for the coin and scooped it up without even breaking stride. He slapped his fist against his heart in a child's imitation of the soldier's reverence and took off for the scullery again.

'Now, Mistress,' said Peshek hastily. 'This mount is bad

tempered and inelegant, but it is inconspicuous. If you would
. . .' He cupped his hands for her foot.

Medeoan allowed herself to be helped onto the mule's
riding blanket. Peshek handed her the bundle she had
entrusted to him the previous evening. It contained some
money and the girdle she had woven of her magic and Eliisa's
memories. Even more importantly, it contained a plain
wooden box in which she had secreted her signet ring. With
that, she could still seal letters and decrees as the Empress of
Isavalta, no matter what clothes she wore.

The mule flapped its ears and snorted as Peshek grabbed
hold of its bridle and urged it forward. Medeoan clutched the
harness with one hand and her bundle with another. The
mule's backbone dug into her as the creature loped listlessly
across the hardpacked yard.

The shout will go up any moment. They've seen me. The
guardsmen have noticed. They'll have told Kacha. He's coming for me.

But no new voices shouted over the cacophony. The only
people who came and went were the artisans and the
bondsmen, and the apprentices with their baskets, bundles and
barrows.

Now Medeoan could see the unadorned iron of the rear
gates with their six men standing outside the guardhouse.

'Keep still and steady, Mistress,' murmured Peshek, halting
the mule. 'This will take but a moment.'

He walked forward, arms outstretched, hailing the other
men. They stiffened to attention, and then evidently recognized him, because they hailed him in return, slapping him on
the arm and clasping his wrists. With a wave of his hand, he
brought them close for some conference. Medeoan's ears rang.
How much did Kacha know? How far had his search gone?
What would he do when he found her? Whom could she trust
besides Peshek and Keeper Bakhar? Kacha would have them

killed immediately, and she was not sure she could stop it. How would she keep herself whole until Iakush found Avanasy and brought him back?

The soldier's conference continued, with several glances in her direction. Something, coins perhaps, passed between Peshek and the men on duty. Peshek then sauntered back to the mule. Behind him, the men swung the gates open.

'When you return, Mistress, you may want to consider having those men taken up,' he said quietly. 'They are too easily bribed.'

'What did you say to them?' she breathed as they passed between the gates and the soldiers. The men stared at her, measuring her with thin smiles on their faces.

'Nothing I would relish repeating to Your Reverence.' Peshek ducked his head.

And they were through. No voice cried out. Kacha's shout did not drift to her through the thick, warm summer air. No column of guards came at the double to seize Captain Peshek. There was only the wide, rutted road cutting through the park and leading to the outer walls, and beyond that, the city, and beyond that the whole wide world.

In that moment, Medeoan knew there would be no pursuit. Peshek's arrangements had worked, and they would walk out of the grounds and into the city. She should have felt relief, but she felt only strangling anger. Was she worth that little? Kacha did not even consider pursuing her? He thought he ruled so completely that he did not even have to consider her presence anymore.

You will learn differently, my false husband. And that presently.

Isavalta was hers, and if she had neglected it before, she would never do so again.

★   ★   ★

'Where is my Bride Imperial?'

Keeper Bakhar blinked down at him. The man who kept house for Isavalta's little gods was barrel-like in stature, obviously fond of the good life his office afforded.

'The Empress is not here, Majesty Imperial.'

'I see that,' said Kacha impatiently. The man was many things but not normally stupid. Suspicion formed in Kacha's mind. 'Where is she?'

The Keeper reverenced, giving at least the appearance of respect. 'I do not know, Majesty Imperial. She came here to await the blessing, but when you did not arrive, she left. I assumed it was to go in search of you.'

So, Kacha let out a sigh. *So. It has begun. The child has run away from home, thinking by her actions to leave me in disarray and confusion.*

Poor child.

'Very well,' said Kacha mildly. 'Should the Empress or any of her attendants come here, say that I will meet them in the courtyard.'

Again, the barrel-shaped keeper reverenced. 'As you command, Majesty Imperial.'

This time, Kacha caught the cold glitter in the man's eyes. He said nothing of it, however, and simply turned away, returning to the corridor where Medeoan's men at arms and sole waiting lady stood, having been given, he was sure, no orders to be elsewhere. They looked uncomfortable to say the least. Doubtlessly they were wondering what was taking their mistress so long. She was a pious lady, yes, but this was excessive.

Kacha turned to his nearest man and said in the court dialect of his home, 'Run to the Empress's chambers and have her lady Chekhania meet me in my own apartments.'

To Medeoan's servitors he said, 'You may wait for your

Mistress Imperial in the courtyard. We will be joining you there presently.'

Medeoan had all her personal attendants very well trained. They did not question him. They only reverenced, each according to their station, and left as ordered. Kacha found himself smiling at their retreating backs. In many ways, this was going to be simplicity itself.

'Come,' he said to Prithu and his men. 'We will return to the private apartments.'

The corridors of Vyshtavos were largely deserted now. Most of the servants and courtiers were already on their way to the summer palace. That household would be full and bustling, awaiting its Imperial masters.

Well, we shall not keep you waiting long, thought Kacha with satisfaction.

As he had instructed, Chekhania waited inside his apartments, beside the empty fire pit. She reverenced as he entered, and he came forward at once to take her hand and raise her up. He saw in her eyes the gesture had its intended effect and reminded her well of their previous night's sport.

'Now then, Chekhania,' he said gravely, still holding her hand. 'I must tell you, your Mistress Imperial has taken ill, but she must make the journey to Vaknevos, for there are none to care for her here. She must do so in complete quiet and seclusion. An enclosed litter, such that can be made a bower for her on the Imperial barge will be the answer, I believe. Can you arrange this?'

Chekhania did not quite lick her lips, but she wanted to, Kacha could see it in her eyes. She knew exactly what she was being asked to do, and how much it meant he trusted her. She reveled in that knowledge, and the sight of that pleased Kacha to his core. Such a one would do all he asked, and more, to keep her place of power. Oh, yes, he had chosen well in her.

'All will be as His Majesty Imperial commands,' said Chekhania solemnly.

'Excellent,' he said, giving her hand a secret squeeze. 'You may go.'

She reverenced again and left him to stand and smile at the empty air.

Run away, Medeoan, he thought. *Run far, run fast. When the time comes, Yamuna will find you, and I will bring you home in chains, and none will be the wiser.*

'We'll spend the night in the lockhouse. The keeper knows how to keep secrets as well as his lock. Many a man's put themselves up here.'

Medeoan nodded and clutched her bundle. Peshek led the skinny mule with great patience through Makashev's crowded streets. It was so strange, down here amid the jostling crowds. She had thought traveling anonymously through the traffic of foot and cart would be liberating, or at least familiar. She had, after all, lived all her life amidst a crowd of people. But the ones who had always surrounded her had been her people and there to serve her. Here, she was just another body, another obstruction. Carters hollered when Peshek could not hurry the stubborn mule along fast enough, and he shouted back. Gossiping women shouldered past her without a second glance. Herders screamed at them to make way for flocks of geese or drifts of sheep. Beggars spat and leered as she passed, holding up grubby palms. Several times, she barely escaped a deluge of filthy water dumped unceremoniously from an upper window.

So much noise and stench and mud. So many people, and not one of them knowing or caring who she was, and only Peshek to stand between her and the whole mass of them.

I can't do this, part of her shivered. *I don't know how.* She gripped the bundle tighter yet. *But I will.*

As bad as this was, the first part of their journey had been worse, for they had followed the Imperial canal, and Medeoan had had to bow her head and shut her eyes to keep from watching the barges, bright with pennants and heavy with the members and belongings of her household, row past. What if, despite all, someone recognized her? What if one of the guards Kacha had surely called out by now spied them on the bank? Fear had wrung tears from her eyes before Peshek turned them away from the canal, and Medeoan could breathe again, if only a little.

Now the sun was going down, and Medeoan was torn between exhaustion and a sort of wretched excitement.

'Here, Mistress,' Peshek said. 'Now we shall have some relief.'

He nodded indicating the way in front of them, and Medeoan looked up. At last, they had reached the city wall, and she could see the great gate standing open. A fresh breeze cut through the miasma of the city and Medeoan felt her heart lift a little.

It sank again instantly as she saw the ranks of the House Guard standing on either side of the gate. Of course, how foolish. The guards kept an eye on everyone leaving the city, as they did on all those entering. Surely they were looking out especially for her. Medeoan bowed her head and bit her lip.

The mule, however, never slowed. A shadow passed over her, and all the noise of their fellow travelers pulled together and concentrated for a moment. Then, the shadow passed, and all the sound spread out on the wind again. Medeoan raised her head.

They had passed through the gate. Ahead of them, the road spread out and branched. The carts and riders, the men and women under their yokes, the herders with their birds and beasts sprawled out, spilling like water from a stream into a pond.

'That simple,' murmured Medeoan. 'How can it be that simple?'

'It isn't, Mistress,' replied Peshek, thumping the mule's side to urge it onward at a better pace. 'The Emp . . . your husband can hardly sound a general alarm to say to all the world you are missing. Any search for you will be done quietly, and it will be under the auspices of the Commander of the House Guard, I promise you. We must take care to be in a safe house before dark.'

'As you say.' Medeoan shivered again. The sun was still high enough to give warmth, and indeed, the city streets had been stifling, but Medeoan remained cold. The countryside rolled gently away from the city walls, cut by the arrow-straight canals with their stone bridges. Suddenly profoundly tired, she longed for the comfort and ease of water travel, but she said nothing. Peshek had seen her safe so far. She must trust him just a little further.

Only a few buildings dotted the landscape immediately beyond the city walls, so the lock-keeper's house was easy to spot. It was a two-storied, clapboard structure with a steeply pitched roof waiting beside a broad stone arch of a bridge. As they approached, Medeoan could hear the rush of the water through the lock.

She must have passed the place a hundred times during her life, but she did not think she had ever truly seen it before. The house and the yard around it seemed neatly kept. The pens for the chickens and goats looked sturdy, as far as she could judge such things. The whitewash on the fence and house was fresh, and the door was gaily painted red with green knots and waves over all for protection and serenity.

As they approached the gate, a stout woman emerged, wiping her hands on her embroidered apron. Peshek halted the mule, and gestured for Medeoan to wait where she was. Accustomed now to doing as he said, Medeoan waited patiently while Peshek opened the gate and walked forward to greet the woman. They conversed for some minutes. Medeoan could hear none of it, but the woman's gaze kept darting from Peshek to Medeoan and back again.

At last, the stout lock-keeper's lady gave a harsh bark of laughter at something Peshek said and shouted inside the house. A little boy, as jug shaped as his mother, came running out. She pointed him at Medeoan, and he trotted up to take the mule's reins while Peshek followed close behind and took Medeoan's hand to help her down.

'It will have to be one room, Mistress,' said Peshek apologetically as he accompanied her up the dirt path to the house. 'They know me well here, so I cannot claim you as a sister.'

'Good greeting, Mistress,' boomed the woman as she looked Medeoan keenly up and down. 'You'll be tired after traveling all day with this ruffian, I'll be bound.' She cuffed Peshek affectionately. 'I've a room ready for you to take your ease, now. Come along with me.'

Without waiting for reply, she led them into the dim house. Medeoan had an impression of scrubbed wood, the smell of boiled vegetables and the rush of wind and water from outside. She climbed the narrow stairway that squeaked and creaked beneath her hostess. At the top, the woman stood aside and let Medeoan, followed by Peshek, enter the first room on the right.

There was not much to see. Medeoan turned around and took in the rough, whitewashed walls, the single bed with its lumpy pallet under the rough woolen blankets, the table and chair, the hearth and the stand for the chamber pot.

Peshek nodded to the hostess, who closed the door with a look that came very close to a leer.

'I'm sorry, Mistress,' said Peshek quickly. 'If there was anything better to be had . . .'

Medeoan waved her hand to cut him off. 'This will do very well, Captain,' she murmured. 'I owe you more than I can ever repay.'

Peshek bowed, his hand over his heart. 'I live to serve. We will wait here for a handful of days while I find us safe messengers to gather news and send out word to your loyal servitors.'

'Yes. Thank you.' Then, feeling utterly trivial and lost, she said, 'Is there any chance of supper?'

There was. Turnip stew, hard bread and dark beer, but Medeoan ate gratefully while their hostess laid a fresh fire in the hearth. When they were done and the crockery cleared outside the door, Peshek laid his knife, sword and knout within easy reach, took one of the blankets from the bed and rolled himself up in it so his body blocked the threshold and he faced the wall. It was as much privacy as he could afford her. Peshek would never leave her alone, even in a house he knew.

Medeoan unwrapped her headscarf, undid her apron and took off her clumsy shoes. Except for that, she laid herself under the covers, stockings and all. She stared into the darkness, willing herself to stay awake. Despite the long, terrifying day, staying awake proved to be quite easy. All the sounds were strange: the night birds, the call of the distant watch on the city walls, the lapping water. Peshek's heavy breathing was nothing like her ladies', and even less like Kacha's. The pallet's straw bit into her skin even through her clothes, and she had an ugly suspicion that that was not all that bit her. Without braziers to surround her bed, the room grew steadily colder, despite the fire, until Medeoan could see her own breath in the slices of moonlight the loose shutters allowed in.

The night deepened. Peshek's breathing grew slow and regular. The moonbeams lengthened on the floor. One by one, the birds outside grew silent, and Medeoan judged her time was right.

Slowly, so as to rustle the straw as little as possible, Medeoan reached for her bundle. Pulling it toward her, she spat on her two fingers and rubbed them against the knot tying the cloth. It fell open at once. The tiny pile of belongings inside seemed pathetic. How could she get by with so little?

Medeoan did not permit herself to dwell on it. Instead she drew out the god's eye amulet she had woven against this night. It really should be tied around Peshek's neck, but she did not trust herself to be able to slip it over his head without waking him. Nearby would have to do.

Medeoan wrapped the amulet's blue thong around the bedstead. Raising her magic, she breathed across the knot as she tied it.

'Night and Moon keep watch over Peshek Pachalkasyn Ursulvin and grant him sound sleep until you surrender the sky to Day and his sister Sun.'

The knot finished, she spat on it to seal it shut. She paused to listen. Peshek's breathing deepened and he began to snore.

Medeoan scrambled from her cold bed. Peshek did not stir. She took the sealed letter she had prepared for him and laid it on her pillow where he was sure to see it. Then, taking a deep breath, she lifted the gold and silver girdle out of the bundle.

Fixing her mind firmly on the need to reach the Heart of the World, Medeoan tied the girdle securely around her waist.

Eliisa Hahl cast a longing look around the room. It seemed a crime to abandon so stout a bed already paid for, and by a man who kept his hands to himself, of all the miracles! Still, there was no help for it. She reclaimed apron and scarf, and moved to tie up her bundle, and paused upon seeing her purse lying on the cloth. What fool had left so much money lying loose! As soon as she had time, she'd sew it into her waistband, but now there was nothing for it but to tie the purse up under her skirt and hope it would be safe enough.

The Captain lay across the threshold snoring in far too genteel a manner for a soldier. Well, he was an officer, after all. She leaned across him and pushed the door gently open. The Captain did not stir. Hiking her skirts high, Eliisa stepped over him. She closed the door, and nimbly hurried down the stairs, making no more noise than a cat.

So far and all's well, Eliisa thought as she emerged into the night. Her gaze skimmed the length of the canal and she briefly considered making off with one of the boats, but decided against it. There was no point in theft when there was money to pay the way. So, instead, she fastened her bundle to her girdle like a peddler woman and strode back toward the city.

Peshek woke, rubbing his hand hard across his eyes and face. The first thing he noticed was that it was full light, which was strange because he was long accustomed to waking before dawn. The second thing he noticed was that the Empress was not in her bed.

Peshek was beside the bed with his sword in his hand before he knew he had moved. His eye took in the tidy bed clothes, the flattened pillows, and the unlatched door, the knotted amulet on the bedpost, and the folded paper, and his heart froze.

'Oh, no, Majesty. Please, no.' Peshek had faced bandits, bears, and all manner of violent drunkards without fear, but now his hand shook as he picked up the folded paper and he found his mouth had gone completely dry.

Peshek broke the seal to open the letter. His breath catching in his throat, he read:

Loyal Captain Peshek,

Forgive the necessity of this ruse. It is the only way to hide my escape from my husband and the magics he has available to him. I may be found while I walk any of Isavalta's roads as myself, and I may also be found if I travel by sorcerous means through the Land of Death and Spirit.

You must go to Fortress Dalemar and await Avanasy. I have sent Lord Iakush to bring him home. Tell him what has happened. If all goes well I will send you word from the Heart of the World.

The letter was unsigned except for a crude sketch of a spread-winged eagle, the Imperial symbol.

Gods of my fathers, thought Peshek, clamping his fingers around the letter so it would not tumble to the floor. *What have I done?*

The autocrat, the embodiment of the Imperial, was the life and soul of Isavalta. When the keeper of the god house presented them to Vyshko and Vyshemir, they became Isavalta. Protecting their health and life was protecting the health and life of the land. Any order, all orders, no matter how incomprehensible, had to be followed, save one. Never was the autocrat to be left unguarded. Peshek had been taught this cardinal rule since he was ten years old and inducted into the House Guard by his father.

I should have stayed awake. I should never have closed my eyes.

But he had not. Which left only the question of what he should do next.

Carefully, Peshek refolded the missive. 'I should slit my own throat,' he muttered to the empty room.

Answering for what he had done before his gods and his ancestors certainly seemed a more attractive option right now than watching Isavalta fall to the hands of a foreign emperor.

But he had orders. The question was, which should he disregard — those orders he had just been given or the one order that stood above all others? Should he chase after the Empress, and be her guard, would she or no? Or should he obey her and go wait for Avanasy?

Now, my son, I will tell you a great truth about dealing with the nobles. His father's voice echoed back to him across the years. *You do what they tell you, but you never, ever get involved in their schemes. They know what they are doing, and you don't. You are shelter for them, like the walls of the palace. Do the palace walls mix themselves in the doings of their inhabitants? They do not. And you, my son, are surely as smart as a pile of stone.*

So, he had his orders. He would go wait for Avanasy. Avanasy could find the Empress in an instant if he needed to. Peshek had no magic in him, and knew no other sorcerer he trusted, and so had no choice.

Vyshko and Vyshemir watch out for her. Peshek buckled on his sword and knife, and tucked his knout into his belt. He wanted a shave, and food, but what he needed was a canal boat to Biradost, and a fast horse from there.

Be there, Avanasy. Don't fail us, or I'll have to spend eternity haunting you for it.

Chapter Eight

Iakush, the Lord Sorcerer of Isavalta, stood on the balcony of his private apartments in the summer palace of Vaknevos and gazed down the cliffs to the lake. The view was stunning. The lake lay like a great sapphire in the midst of a landscape of emerald velvet. Its breeze freshened the air, and as summer warmed it would prove to be lusciously cool in the torrid evenings. He always enjoyed the days here.

This day, however, he could not relax. Something was wrong, and he did not know what it was.

First, he had failed. Despite a full day closeted with the Portrait of Worlds, he had not been able to find Avanasy. Working with the Portrait was no easy matter, and required a deep familiarity with its ways, but still, he should have been able to find something. Even Avanasy, with all his cunning, could not have covered his tracks so completely. Now, the Portrait was miles away from him, and he would have to find some other way to carry out the Empress's orders.

Wrapping himself in his wounded pride, Iakush had meant to have a private word with Empress Medeoan as they journeyed, to assure her that he would find Avanasy and carry out her will. But he had not been able to see the Empress. Emperor Kacha would let none near her curtained litter where it had been placed on the raised deck of the barge, saying she needed complete quiet until the physicians met her at Vaknevos.

'Respectfully, Majesty,' Iakush had reverenced as best he could in the confined aisle of the rocking barge, 'I do have knowledge in the healing arts. I may be able to bring her ease from whatever troubles her.'

'I thank you for your concern,' the Emperor replied smoothly. 'But I believe rest is what will be most beneficial.'

'Majesty . . .' Iakush began again.

'I have said all I mean to, Lord Sorcerer.'

He had spoken the words mildly, but Iakush had heard them before, and knew better than to pursue the matter any further. So, he reverenced again, and made his way back down to the common benches that he shared with the other members of the Council of Lords. The Lords Master eyed him, but said nothing, and Iakush was content to have it so.

As he took his place on the padded bench and watched the banks of the canal pass, he noticed who did not travel on the barge. Not one of the Empress's waiting ladies was in evidence. Not even Chekhania, who traveled constantly at Empress Medeoan's side.

It was then that the first stirrings of disquiet settled into his blood. They stayed with him all the rest of the voyage, and even now, when his room was filled with the cheerful bustle of his servitors setting everything to rights and his eyes were filled with the beautiful and tranquil sight of the lake before him. Something was happening, something of which he was not being told, and it was happening too soon after the Empress had petitioned him to find Avanasy again to be mere chance.

'Lord Sorcerer?' called his man Cestimir. 'My Lord, you are summoned.'

Iakush turned. Beside Cestimir stood a boy in a kaftan of royal blue bound with a gold sash. The page boy reverenced and said, 'Lord Sorcerer, I am sent to say that the Council of Lords is summoned by His Majesty Imperial, and that your attendance is required.'

At those words, the disquiet that had filled Iakush turned still colder, and yet he could not have clearly said why. Perhaps it was because it was only the Emperor who convened the Council. That was a thing that had never happened before.

'Tell His Majesty Imperial I will not fail him.'

Again, the boy reverenced, and he hurried away. Iakush stared at the door as it closed behind the page. Then he turned his slow gaze to Cestimir, who stood ready for any order he might give.

But what order could he give? What provision could he make when he had no idea what was to come? He dismissed Cestimir with a wave to return to the business of unpacking.

What provision could he make? Against he knew not what or whom? A thought came to him, and he almost dismissed it, but the same cold disquiet made him reconsider.

There was a clothing press that Iakush had taken charge of himself during the journey and that had been set down beside his bed. Iakush unlocked it with a silver key and lifted the lid. Leaving his men to continue their chores, he removed his kaftan and his shirt. From the press, he lifted a shirt of blinding white linen. He had woven its cloth with his own hands, then cut and stitched that cloth. He slipped the shirt on over his head, fastening the buttons. Then, he put his kaftan back on, paying particular attention to how he tied his sash. Only then did he emerge from his chamber and stride down the corridor to the Council chamber in answer to the Emperor's summons.

The Council chamber of Vaknevos was a long, narrow room with a heavy table placed in its center and chairs on either side.

On the low dais at the far end waited two chairs of gilded wood for the Emperor and Empress. Iakush entered to find the Lords Master and the Emperor already assembled. His cautious gaze swept the room and found it as he remembered it, with one change only. A new carpet was spread across the floor. Iakush's eyes flickered to the other members of the Council. Probably none of them noticed. But then, none of them was a sorcerer. They knew about knots and weaving, and all their power, but they didn't comprehend it in their hands and their souls the way a sorcerer had to. They did not train themselves to notice every piece of cloth, of jewelry, or carving that came into their view. They did not automatically try to decipher the pattern they noted, to see if it was a danger, or a hindrance, or, perhaps, a help.

This carpet was blue and gold, so it looked very much in place in the Imperial Council room. Its pattern was nothing so blatant as interlocking circles or diamonds. The gold lines snaked through the bright-blue background like the outlines of a maze – seldom crossing, seldom touching, each line involved in its own swirls and waves, and yet all of them held together by the expanse of blue.

Iakush realized he had seen the carpet before. It had been one of the wedding gifts sent by Kacha's family before the ceremony. He had not paid it more than cursory attention then, but now he had to work to keep from staring at it. It could be magical. It could be complexly and powerfully magical. Iakush felt the soles of his feet begin to itch, and his knees protested the need to bend, to touch it even through the cloth of his pantaloons, as he made the Imperial reverence.

'Thank you, Lord Sorcerer Iakush,' said Emperor Kacha. 'Sit with us.'

'Thank you, Majesty Imperial.' Iakush stood and backed into the waiting chair, sitting beside weathered, broad Lord Master Seasta, Master of the Horse.

Emperor Kacha mounted the dais and took his own seat, facing them all, his hands, the strong hand and the weak hand, resting on the chair arms. Still, Iakush found his attention straying to the empty chair beside the Emperor.

'I have two pieces of news for you, my Lords Master, and I desire your counsel,' said Emperor Kacha in his clear, precise voice. 'The first is great good news for all of us, indeed for all of Eternal Isavalta. Her Majesty Imperial is with child.'

'But this is wonderful!' cried out Lord Master Tsepier. 'Vyshko and Vyshemir themselves must rejoice!'

The other Lords Master raised their voices in a clamor to sound their pious delight. Only Iakush sat still. His shirt cuffs had grown tight around his wrists, and the collar pressed close against his neck. Even his sash embraced him firmly.

Iakush struggled to keep his countenance. There was magic here. It was in place at this moment, seeping up from some prepared source to work its maker's will. That source most likely lay in the new carpet underfoot. Iakush could not help but feel a cold admiration for the sorcerer who sat before that carpet and tied knot after knot, securing his magic and his purpose in a thousand thousand strands of wool. Such power, such patience, even if worked by more than one hand. Perversely, Iakush found himself wishing to know how it had been done.

But who could be behind this magic? Avanasy? Was this the crime to which the Empress had alluded? No. Surely not. If she had known so much, the carpet would not be here . . .

Then who?

'Our Lord Sorcerer remains grave,' said the Emperor. 'He understands the deeper significance of this news.'

Iakush shook himself. Now was not the time for introspection. Now was the time to take careful stock of all the men around him, perhaps the Emperor most of all.

'Yes, Majesty Imperial,' Iakush said gravely. 'It is not easy for a sorcerer, male or female, to bring forth a child. No part of a sorcerer's soul touches the Land of Death and Spirit, which is the source of life's beginning, as well as its end. This severance gives us our magic and our long lives, but it also denies us the ability to pass life on to another. Frequently the females die in the attempt.' That silenced all the Lords, and settled them all back into their chairs.

Emperor Kacha nodded, his dark face a very mirror of sober thought. 'So Her Majesty Imperial has informed me, and that is the real reason I have called you here, instead of allowing the Keeper of the Emperor's God House to make the first announcement as is customary.' His withered hand waved toward the door. 'For the sake of her own health and that of her child, Her Majesty Imperial has chosen to go immediately into confinement. She will correspond closely with her court, of course, and read letters and petitions with great attention, as she has always done, but, she has asked me to say, there will be no more public appearances before she has been safely delivered of our child.'

The laces of Iakush's shirt drew themselves tight against his chest. He imagined the room thick with magic like some invisible perfume, with all the Lords Master breathing it in deeply. To what end?

'You will of course deliver our immediate congratulations,' announced fat Lord Master Goriain, Master of the Archives. 'Are we to assume His Majesty Imperial will be coordinating the receipt of the petitions?'

'I will, with your able assistance, of course, Lord Master Goriain. Your secretaries and scribes will be much required in the coming months.'

'I am here to serve.' His words were echoed by the other Lords Master, and Iakush knew what spell oozed from the carpet. Belief. Credulity. They would not question this sudden removal of the Empress from the public scene, and probably they would not remember that they had not questioned it. In their own memories, they would each have behaved ideally. They would have closely questioned the Emperor, satisfying themselves as to the truth and necessity of the situation. If the spell were thoroughly thought out, they might even remember having demanded to see her, and being escorted to her chamber. All that would build itself into their hearts and minds until no doubt remained.

Iakush felt his collar constrict until he had to suppress a cough. Oh, yes. The maker of this carpet was very good, very strong, and very careful. This spell would do at least that much to these men, and perhaps more.

And the purpose it served was Kacha's.

Iakush felt a burning rage rush through him. He wanted nothing more than to spring to his feet, his knife in his hand, to bring down this man who was doing this thing, who had done the gods only knew what to the anointed Empress.

But he could do nothing. He could only sit where he was and continue to listen to every poisonous word.

'Which brings me to the other piece of news,' said the Emperor. 'We have recently received word through the House Guard of a sorceress abroad in the land. She is mad, they think, or perhaps she is merely bold. She is claiming to be the Empress Medeoan, and making pronouncements in her name. Now, normally, such a thing would be ignored. She'd be picked up soon enough for vagrancy or some fraud, but I like not the timing of this appearance, nor does your Empress. She asks me to convey to you how urgently we wish this woman silenced. You will coordinate with the Lords Master of the oblasts, and she will be found and brought here before the Lord Sorcerer for judgment.' Emperor Kacha leveled his gaze fully on Iakush.

'And it will be a stern judgment, my Lord, will it not?'

Again Iakush shook himself. He felt as if his mind had been as tightly swaddled as his body. For all his protection, the spell leaked through, making concentration difficult. Of course what the Emperor said was true. Iakush had read the Empress's declaration. He knew her words and hand very well and . . .

No. That did not happen. That did not happen. We only sat and listened to the Emperor speak. That is all.

'It is unlawful for a sorcerer to impersonate any person of name,' Iakush said, choosing his words with care. He must not say too much, not now. His tongue might run away with him, clouding his mind yet further. He must speak only in absolutes. 'Should any who is not utterly mad have the temerity to say she is the Empress herself, it must surely be judged an act of treason.'

'Even if she be mad,' growled Lord Master Seasta, the muscles on his thick neck standing out from the force of his feeling. 'It were better she were killed on sight, than that she be allowed to spread lies and treason, especially at such a time.'

'There is much wisdom in those words, Lord Master Seasta,' mused the Emperor with a nod. 'What say you to that, Lord Sorcerer?'

Iakush could barely speak at all. His collar choked him, his own magic drawing close and trying to stave off the spell that permeated the air and wormed its way into his blood. 'With respect to His Majesty Imperial, I say that a thorough and openly witnessed examination will spark fewer rumors during this delicate time.' Delicate time, time of birthing, the Empress lying in surrounded by her doctors and ladies, as they had seen her, looking up at him, trusting him, finally, as she had once trusted Avanasy . . .

No. No. No. I never left this room. I never saw her. I see only Kacha, I know only that we are bespelled.

'That is also a worthy thought, Lord Sorcerer,' said the Emperor approvingly. 'I will relay this counsel to Her Majesty Imperial. In the meantime, my Lords Master, and my Lord Sorcerer, I ask you to spread word of these matters among your people, and take counsel with them. Tomorrow at this hour we will meet again. I will have Her Majesty Imperial's words, and we will together decide on the best plan of attack.'

Tell him I am in danger, Medeoan had ordered Iakush. Now he understood. She had couched that message as a lie to convince him to lure back Avanasy. Now, though, Iakush knew it to be no less than the truth. Avanasy's impending death sentence was the lie. She had done this thing not only so that he would obey her, but so that he could not betray her.

Iakush clenched his fist. She had not felt she could speak plainly to him, and whose fault was that? He had, after all, done nothing but stand by and watch as Avanasy was banished on a charge he had known could not be true. He'd been too bound up in his own search for power. Too much love of power was a danger for any sorcerer, and Iakush had fallen to it without even noticing.

That is what she tried to tell me. Tell him I need him.

He'd told himself then that it was Avanasy who had been greedy for power, that Medeoan would come to trust him, Iakush. She did trust him, she looked up to him, he'd seen her handwriting, heard her speak, weak but flushed with inner delight as women with child often became . . .

Iakush heaved himself awkwardly to his feet. Around him, the Lords Master made their reverences and departed in twos and threes, whispering urgently about what they had heard.

Vyshemir's knife, he told himself sternly, as he crossed his hands to reverence. *From here you will go retrieve Vyshemir's knife from Keeper Bakhar. Hold fast to that thought, Iakush, if no other.*

Vyshemir's knife was in the keeping of the Keeper of the

Emperor's God House, but in the hands of a sorcerer who knew the proper words to say, it could be used to cut away illusion and bring truth to light. It could save him now.

'Lord Sorcerer,' said the Emperor. 'Stay but a moment.'

Wants to keep me here. The Empress has some message . . . No. No. Vyshemir's knife. From here I must go get Vyshemir's knife.

'Majesty Imperial?' Iakush made himself turn, made himself stay on the carpet that reached out its magic to poison his thoughts. With an extreme effort of will, he made himself see Kacha. Kacha, not Medeoan. Kacha of Hastinapura. Kacha, son of Chandra. Kacha, who had been bargained away for peace, and was secretly harboring thoughts of conquest.

The Emperor had risen, and he walked casually down the dais to stand beside him. 'Her Majesty Imperial particularly asked that you look deeply into this matter.'

'I will do my best, Majesty Imperial.'

Emperor Kacha clapped Iakush on his shoulder, and steered him toward the door, forcing him to walk down the carpet. 'She knows well she is young in her power, and relies heavily on your judgment.'

Vyshemir's knife. Vyshemir's knife will cure me of this affliction, will open my eyes.

'She regrets that she has not said so before now, but her old teacher wounded her grievously, and she has not yet recovered from that.' Kacha paused in his stride and shook his head. 'She asks you to forgive her this failing, and says that when she is able, she wishes to continue her instructions under your guidance. She assures you that none other will be named Lord Sorcerer while you remain true.'

It would have been so easy to give in. With or without the enchantment, he could see that the Emperor was giving him a chance for the prestige and responsibility that he had longed for. He now spoke the words Iakush had ached with his whole being to hear since the death of the old Emperor and Empress.

It was in hope of those words that he had kept silent during the capricious exile of one who should have been as a brother.

And now she was saying them. Now, she finally saw his worth and his position was secure. Now, he would be able to . . . to . . .

No. Kacha speaks, not my Empress. The knife, the knife, the knife, I must go claim the knife.

'I am deeply honored, Majesty Imperial,' was all Iakush could make himself say.

Kacha faced him squarely, looking Iakush straight in his eyes, laying his hand again on Iakush's shoulder. 'I also am trusting you, Lord Sorcerer. Once my lineage is secure, there will be numerous preferments and titles to be awarded. The Empress needs no mere magical advisor. The duties, and the rewards of the office of Lord Sorcerer needs must become much greater during our reign.'

The pressure of the spell was almost unbearable. Iakush fought to keep himself from shuddering as his mind and soul were squeezed as if by an invisible hand. 'I live to serve.'

'To serve your master and mistress, the Emperor and Empress of Isavalta,' said Kacha. The Emperor did not blink as he watched Iakush.

Iakush forced his shoulders to straighten. 'I live, as we all do, to serve Eternal Isavalta.'

'As we all do, Lord Sorcerer,' said the Emperor. 'You may go now. I will expect you here tomorrow with your fellows.'

Iakush reverenced. Relief washed through him. He could get away from this. Vyshemir's knife would save him. It would cut away this enchantment and restore his right memories.

A cold pressure touched his side, and Iakush straightened, startled to see the Emperor right beside him.

'Did you think I would not know?' sneered Kacha. 'Did you think I would be sent here if I could not see?'

The Emperor stepped back, and Iakush felt something warm and wet against his shirt. His hand sought it automatically, and came away covered with something red. He stared at his stained hand mutely. What could this be? No wine had been served. He had spilled nothing. What could be so red?

The knot of his sash almost completely obscured the dagger's hilt.

'I should slit your throat,' said the Emperor casually. 'But you will be much easier to bury with a hidden wound. Far fewer people will have to be bemused. Now then, while you die, I will fetch you a physic. Perhaps you will live long enough to succumb to a fever.'

Blood. Still staring at his hand, Iakush dropped to his knees. But his knees would not hold him, and he sprawled against the carpet. Blood. His blood. Stabbed by the Emperor. Dying. He was dying in the thick puddle of his own blood.

Why? What had happened? He couldn't remember. He had been obeying the Empress. She had wanted him to go get Vyshemir's knife . . .

Vyshemir's knife. Proof against enchantment. The pain began now, lancing up his side, clenching jaw and throat, burning hotter than the blood that spilled. Enchantment. Emperor. Treason and greed, and blood, everywhere so much blood. He couldn't move, couldn't stop the pain or the blood. He was dying for his foolishness, dying for his Empress . . .

No, not for her. She was not here. She was elsewhere, and she had asked him to take word to Avanasy.

But he had no words, only blood.

With one trembling hand, Iakush reached out and drove his finger into the blood. Haltingly, he tried to spit, and managed to drool a little spittle into the redness. He stirred them together. He coughed for breath. Mortal blood, mortal breath. These were the sources of the greatest power a single sorcerer could give. It would be enough. It would have to be.

'Beyond life there is a forest,' he whispered, forcing his finger to move through the blood, drawing a wave that was the river, was a snake, was a ray of light, was all his hope borne on all his pain. 'Within the forest there is a river. At the end of the river is another shore. On the other shore, there walks Avanasy Finorasyn Goriainavin. Breath and blood, carry me to the river. Vyshko and Vyshemir carry me to the river's end. My heart's blood, my breath, my life, carry me to Avanasy.' He retched. Pain burned hotter than his blood, but he was so cold. His hand shook, and he could not feel it anymore, let alone make it move. The room was going gray.

'My heart's blood, my breath, my life, carry me to Avanasy Finorasyn Goriainavin. My heart's blood carry me . . .'

The room around him darkened, and vanished.

The Land of Death and Spirit is a land of eyes. This is the first thing taught to any sorcerer of Isavalta. It is not possible to pass through it unobserved. There is no true distance there, no true shadow and no true light. Anything may be shown to those who wish to see. The places that do not shift and change are few, and they offer nowhere to hide beyond the boundaries of the mortal world.

Inside a fence mended with bones, there stood a cottage on crooked, scaled, taloned legs. The cottage was called Ishbushka, and in it, an ancient witch with iron teeth sat at her loom of bones and spoke to her cat.

'What do you see?'

The cat sat on the windowsill, staring unblinking out the window. 'I see another sorcerer walking from Isavalta.' The cat twitched its tail. 'If this continues, soon Isavalta will have none of them left.'

The witch stilled her shuttle which was made of an ancient jaw bone. She perused the pattern of her weaving, reading what was written there in a language only she herself knew. 'What else do you see?'

'His blood flows red.' The cat turned and began to clean its shoulder nonchalantly. 'He has come early to the Land of Death, but the Grandfather waits for him. He will not reach the far shore.'

The witch grunted and laid her long, bony finger a moment on her weaving. She nodded, satisfied with what she saw. 'You will go to the Grandfather, Cat. You will send my greeting. You will ask him in my name to let the sorcerer pass.'

The cat used its paw to smooth down its ears. 'Grandfather Death will not be pleased to neglect one of his grandchildren so.'

'Say it is a delay only,' said the witch. 'This one has an important message that must be delivered. Say that in my name.'

The cat narrowed its emerald eyes as she gazed at her mistress. But the witch offered no explanation, and the cat asked no questions. She only leapt from the perch and silently padded out the cottage door.

The morning after Leo Loftfield was injured, Avanasy returned gladly to his work. It was something to occupy him until the sun set, for there was still plenty of brushwood to be cut and cleared. Even so, his mind was distracted enough that he abandoned the scythe as too dangerous and contented himself with bundling the cut brush and stacking wood. The news from Ingrid's home had been good. Leo would keep his leg, and was in fact awake, though he was still weak. Avanasy had stopped by the kitchen door this morning to speak a moment with Ingrid and say he would be back tonight. Perhaps it would be a good time to speak with her father, perhaps it would not, but he meant to sound the man out, so Ingrid's parents would know without a doubt that his intentions were honorable.

He would need to change his shirt before he went to visit the Loftfields, and wash, and shave. Should he bring the ring with him? Ingrid had not said. He would have it, in case. The ring waited at the bottom of his chest. His mother had given it to him when he had gone to be apprenticed. It was a golden band, set with coral and rubies. Perhaps it was too much for a fisherman's wife, but she would have it anyway. He would pass it off somehow, perhaps as an heirloom, or as paste, but he would tell Ingrid that it was real, and what its origins were. It would become one more tie between them. She'd smile when she saw it.

Or would she? It was beautiful, but in the Isavaltan fashion. Even riches were much plainer here. Perhaps she would only find it garish.

Avanasy had to laugh at himself. He was as nervous as a plowboy sending a bride-gift to a milkmaid's mother. It was ridiculous. Of course, Ingrid would smile, because it was a gift freely given, and that was her way.

'You're quiet,' said Everett Lederle, breaking in on his thoughts. Lederle worked beside him, gathering up newly trimmed branches and stacking them together to be bundled up and hauled away.

'Things on my mind,' answered Avanasy. He stepped on the pile of branches in front of him so he could more easily loop the twine around it and tie the bundle securely.

'Like Ingrid?'

Avanasy paid careful attention to the knot he was tying. 'And if it was?'

Everett said nothing to that. He just wrapped some twine around another bundle of brush and tied off his own knot. He pulled the clasp knife from his pocket and slit the twine. Then, he straightened to face Avanasy, the knife still held in his hand. 'She loves you,' he said flatly. 'Use her badly and I will hunt you down like a dog. Understand me?'

'Very well,' replied Avanasy, looking Everett in his face. The knife was nothing. Everett was not a man to use it without cause. Perhaps later, when some time had passed and wounds had healed, they could become friends. 'Maybe you should know I mean to go to her father tonight and ask for her hand.'

Everett drew in a long, low breath. He snapped the knife blade closed and returned it to his pocket. 'That's good then.'

Everett returned to his work without another word, and Avanasy bent to his own. The sun continued its long, slow trek across the sky, finally settling into Lake Superior and leaving no light left to work by. Avanasy shouldered his scythe once more and trooped back to the shore with the other itinerant fishers, his heart riding high with the memory of Ingrid's kiss. Part of him was greedy to know much more of her, but he was not that plowboy, and he could wait. Especially given what she had told him of her own birth, he could most definitely wait until they had been joined by the appropriate rites. There would be no shame for them. He would build her a proper house. They would wed and be feasted according to the expected custom. But then, ah, then, when once they were alone . . .

Savoring his imaginings, Avan pushed the door of his shack open. He smelled salt and copper, and for a moment did not realize how wrong that scent was. It smelled of the seashore. He froze. Lake Superior was freshwater, what was the scent of the sea doing here?

Something dark crouched in the center of his dirt floor.

Avan instantly took his scythe from his shoulder and hefted it.

'What are you?' he demanded.

'Avanasy,' grated a harsh voice. 'Please. Avanasy.'

The scythe thudded from Avanasy's suddenly numb hands. The voice spoke to him in the court language of Isavalta, and it belonged to Iakush, the Lord Sorcerer.

'My Lord Sorcerer.' Avanasy dropped to his knees. His eyes adjusted to the dimness and saw the dark stain spreading across Iakush's white shirt. Blood. It could not be anything else. Then he became aware of something else by the pricking of skin and soul. The Grandfather, Death, had walked into the room behind him, and he came for Iakush.

'Avanasy,' croaked Iakush again.

'What has happened?' Avanasy laid his hand against the wound, but pressure would do no good. Too much blood had already been lost. 'Tell me, Iakush.'

'Kacha. You were right from the first. Medeoan, Isavalta . . . all are in danger. Medeoan has fled, Kacha lies. He . . .' Iakush coughed. A stream of blood trickled from his slack mouth. 'He has magics at his command, Avanasy. I don't know how, but they are strong.' Death leaned closer. Avanasy felt the chill. 'Medeoan sent . . . Medeoan . . .' Another cough racked him. 'Ah, Grandfather, Grandfather, I hurt.'

'Medeoan sent you?' Avanasy grasped his shoulders. 'What of the Emperor? The Empress? Why have you left them?'

But Iakush just shuddered. Death was too close. Avanasy made a decision. He lifted his bloody hand to his mouth and breathed on it, then he pressed it against Iakush's lips.

'Blood to breath, Lord Iakush Vtoroisyn Gabravin,' he whispered, steeling himself. 'Yours to mine. My words, my breath, your blood, your words.'

Avanasy reached inside himself to find the magic he needed to shape the weaving of breath and blood, but it would not rise. He strained, reaching deep with all his strength, reaching out as far as he could for the last vestige of the magics that had brought Iakush this far. He shook to his core, but at last the magic rose, and the words wove it into shape.

Pain. Blinding, searing, strength-robbing pain. Avanasy doubled over above the Lord Sorcerer's body. The cold of loss and death shot through him, along with all the fear in Iakush's mind. But below that, he touched the Lord Sorcerer himself, and he felt recognition, and then relief.

The old Emperor and Empress are dead, Avanasy. I truly thought it was fever then, but now I think it was poison. Medeoan is Empress. She is fled. She sent me for you. She needs you, Avanasy. The rest of us have failed her. Kacha will kill her or worse, I fear. Then Hastinapura will rule us all. You must meet her at Fortress Dalemar.

They spasmed together, and Avanasy felt his heart squeezing itself to wring another drop of blood into his veins.

Let me go, Avanasy. I'm done and I cannot bear this anymore.

Avanasy lifted his hands away, and fell into darkness.

Eventually, Avanasy woke to night's cold and yet more darkness. A single shaft of silver moonlight squeezed through the plank boards of his walls and lit up his stack of kindling. Iakush lay beside him. The acrid stench of death filled the cabin until Avanasy could taste it. He struggled to his feet, weak as a kitten, and staggered out his doorway and down the shore.

'Hey, Avan! You all right?'

Avanasy only waved in response. Let whoever shouted think he was drunk. Let them think anything they wanted. He knelt, still shaking at the edge of the lake and vomited into the water until his stomach was shriveled and empty and his whole mouth bitter with gall. He pushed himself sideways to cleaner waters and drank, and washed his face.

Medeoan had fled. Medeoan was in danger, from Kacha.

He'd known it. He'd known it and he'd left her, abandoned his trust because he could not bear to face his own shame. Now, the Emperor and Empress were dead and Medeoan gone, and where was he? He stared out across the black lake. Playing fisherman in a village of drudges and rude mechanicals. Playing at a life to which he had no claim.

Oh, in Vyshko's name. Ingrid.

The moon was well up. It was late. He could not call on her tonight. She would think he had forgotten. She would think something had happened to him. That thought pulled him to his feet. She would think something had happened to him, and she would throw a shawl around her shoulders and she would . . .

Cursing his weakness, Avanasy stumbled back to his cabin. He threw open the door, nearly fell again but caught himself against the stove. Ingrid knelt beside Iakush's corpse. Even night's darkness could not disguise her from him. She lifted her head at his clumsy entrance and her face was as white as the moon.

'What happened?' she whispered fiercely. 'Who is this? I came . . . I thought . . . I thought crazy things when you didn't come. I thought maybe the ghost . . .'

Avanasy summoned all the strength that remained to him. He pushed himself upright and walked to the bed. He pulled off the single blanket and laid it across Iakush's body for a poor shroud. Ingrid rose slowly to her feet. Even in the faint moonlight he could see how her eyes glittered hard. He wanted to stand to face her, but his legs were already weakening. As slowly as he could manage, he sat in the rickety chair.

Ingrid said nothing. He ran both hands through his hair. She was waiting for him. She had waited for him all night to fulfill a promise he had no right to make.

'His name is Iakush,' said Avanasy. 'He was the Lord Sorcerer to the Imperial Court of Isavalta. He . . . Medeoan sent him to find me.'

'Why?'

'It seems I was right.'

She left the corpse and walked over to him, kneeling down so that they were eye-to-eye. 'Tell me.'

He did. He told her about coming back to find Iakush, and how he had delivered his message, and how Medeoan was gone, and his master and patron, the Emperor was dead. His strength failed him then, and to his shame, Avanasy found that all he could do was bow his head and begin to weep. He wept for his exile, and for his acceptance of it. He wept for his belief that he could begin a new life. He wept for the good man dead on the floor at his feet whom he lacked the strength to save. He pounded the chair with his fist and even the pain of it could not stop the tears.

Somewhere in the midst of this shameful weeping, Ingrid wrapped her arms around his shoulders and pulled him close, holding him while he poured out his grief.

'Jesus, Avan, what the hell's happened . . .' came a man's voice from the doorway.

'This is none of your business, Jan Iverksson,' snapped Ingrid. 'Go home.'

The sound of her harsh words reminded him where he truly was. Avanasy found his strength again and was able to force himself back into some semblance of composure.

'You should not be here.' He pushed himself back from her. 'Your family, they'll think . . .'

Ingrid sat on her heels and shrugged irritably. 'I'm here now, and there's nothing to be done about it. What are you going to do?'

Avanasy spread his hands hopelessly. 'I'm going back to Isavalta. I have to, Ingrid. My homeland is in danger.

Medeoan . . . she sent for me. She needs my help, and she is my Empress.'

'Of course,' said Ingrid, but he heard how hollow her voice was.

He slipped from the chair to kneel beside her and he took both her hands. They were so cold. He could not help but remember how warm they had been the previous afternoon, from the sun and from her delight at his proposal. 'I had no right to speak to you as I did,' he said. As he spoke, sudden, hard anger filled him. Why had this happened tonight? Why had Medeoan not sent for him yesterday? Or a month ago? Or a month before that? Why now?

'Did you mean it?' she asked steadily. 'That you wanted to marry me?'

'I did.'

'Do you mean it still?'

'With all my heart, Ingrid, I do.'

She was silent then for a long moment, and he saw her bite her lip. 'Then let me come with you.'

'Ingrid, no.'

'Yesterday, I agreed to become your wife, and when I said yes, I knew who you were and what your past was. I accepted it.'

'But not this, Ingrid.' He swept his hand out toward Iakush's corpse under its rough blanket. Iakush should have had a shroud of white linen and gold, and all he had was gray wool. 'You never accepted this.'

She stood, turning from him as she did, and walked away a few steps, her arms wrapped tightly around herself. Avanasy stood as well, but swayed on his feet. He realized that the fear that filled him was the fear that she would say he was right, that she would walk out of his house and leave him alone.

But she did not. She just turned around again to face him.

'Avan . . .' she began, but then she stopped, and started over. 'Avanasy, I never questioned how my life would be. I would help care for my family until one day I married someone from the island, or perhaps, if fate was especially bold, I would marry someone from Bayfield. Then, I would keep my own house and raise my own children.' Ingrid kicked at the dirt floor. 'And that would be that. It would be a good life, hard, but life always is.'

'You can do so still,' said Avanasy quietly. 'Nothing prevents you.'

Ingrid met his eyes. 'Do you honestly believe that?'

For a long moment, Avanasy did nothing but look into her moonlit gaze. He felt all the waves of his feeling swirl around them both – sorrow, regret, determination, fear, but all these pulled back and left only love.

'No,' he said at last. 'I do not believe that.'

'Well then?'

Avanasy folded his arms around her, pulling her into a hard embrace. He felt the thrill as Ingrid fell into it willingly, lifting her face to his kiss. She kissed back with a strength that left him dizzy with its heat. Avanasy kissed her cheek, her eyes, and buried his face against her shoulder, breathing her deeply. He held on, feeling the strength rushing between them – the strength of her body and the strength of his own heart which opened to her, and which, he knew, would never close to her again.

'I don't know what dangers there will be, Ingrid,' he said when he could speak again. 'I am exiled, and to return is to court death. If High Princess Medeoan . . . if the Empress has indeed fled her capital, very few will know that my exile is rescinded. I am long months away, and much has changed. I may no longer have friends where I go to look for them.'

'When must we go?' asked Ingrid, pulling back just far enough to see his face.

'I must go at first light, as soon as I can raise my sails.'

Her eyebrows lifted in astonishment. 'You have a boat of your own? Then why . . .'

'Do I work for others?' The corner of Avanasy's mouth twitched into a weak smile. 'It is not a boat for normal seas, at least, not entirely. I did not want to risk its sails being damaged in rough work while there was still a chance . . .' he paused, and then remembered himself and who he spoke to. 'While there was still a chance I might be summoned home again.'

Ingrid nodded and stepped back from him. 'But you're tired. You should get some rest.'

'I am, and it will get worse,' he admitted. 'This is no easy journey we undertake. But delay, even a few hours, may cost lives and loyalties.' He caught her gaze. 'Understand, Ingrid, this is not some squabble over fence lines that can be resolved in the court in Bayfield. This is the game of kings we are entering.'

Ingrid drew herself up. 'My father fought in a very bloody war, Sir. I know something of it. I have seen the dead myself, and fought for lives. You will not find me missish, or a fainting fool.'

Avanasy allowed himself a brief, real smile. 'That would be impossible.'

'I'll go back and get a few things together,' said Ingrid, picking up the shawl she had at some point discarded by the bed.

There was, Avanasy realized, one other thing that had to be said. 'Ingrid, your family, they'll believe you've run off with me.'

'They'll be right,' she said flatly. 'I am running off with you. We are just going a little farther than is customary.'

Knowing what this meant to her, and what it might cost, Avanasy held up his hand. 'Wait.'

He drew the iron key out from under his shirt and unlocked his chest. From the very bottom, he drew out a small linen bag.

'Everett would marry you in an instant, Ingrid,' he said as he straightened. 'There would be no need for you to be alone should you choose to stay.'

'Stop it, Avanasy.' She gripped his hand hard. 'You say that where we go life is difficult, and dangerous. What is life on this island?' She stabbed her finger toward the door. 'I could die tomorrow from a wave swamping a boat, from the cut of a knife, or from a fever, or when old Johnny Keeter gets drunk and takes it into his head to go on another of his tears. If I stay here without you, the only difference is the kind of danger I would be in, and that I would be alone for the rest of my life.' She released him. 'I am not romantic. Whatever this is we do together, it is not a fairy tale, but we will see it through.'

'Then, accept this my pledge.' He took the ring from the bag. Its gold and tiny rubies sparkled in the silver moonlight. 'I love you, Ingrid Loftfield. Let that be the one enduring truth between us, and let this be the sign of it.' He slipped the ring onto her third finger, as he had observed was the way such things were worn here.

She kissed him, the only pledge she had and far more dear to him than any scattering of rubies. Then, she threw her shawl over her head and hurried out the door to do what she must and swiftly return.

Avanasy ran his hand through his hair again, trying to bring order to his thoughts. He was beyond wondering what he was doing. All was set in motion, and now he must ride the tide of it.

Chapter Nine

So, the little Imperial cow has caught wind of her doom and strayed.
Yamuna stared down at the parchment before him, pulled
from the fire now and covered with Kacha's writing. He had
to admit, the boy had done well. His plan was sound, and the
beginning of it well-executed. The Council of Lords, for the
moment, believed what they had been told.

So, that much was done. Now, Medeoan must be found.
Her lords were not powerless yet, and she might still rally them
to her cause if she were not found and dealt with at once.

Yamuna's chamber possessed four balconies, one facing
each of the cardinal points of the compass. Yamuna stepped out
onto the one which faced north. The rain fell hard against his
leathery skin, but Yamuna ignored it. He pulled his knife from
his belt and stabbed the tip of it into the index finger of his
right hand. The pain was nothing, he had done himself much
greater injuries, and would again. The blood was needed, so he
released it, that was all. Then, he undid one of the hundred
spell braids that bound his long, white hair and from it pulled
out three white hairs. He twirled them in the fingers of his
right hand, spinning them into a single thread, bound tightly
with his blood, in the hand he had taken from Kacha.

'Kacha *tya* Achin Ekulinjapad, your blood calls, your flesh calls, my will calls, you will answer me,' said Yamuna clearly to the north. 'Kacha *tya* Achin Ekulinjapad, your blood calls, your flesh calls, my will calls. You will answer me.'

Yamuna closed his left eye, and through his right eye, which once had been Kacha's, he stared out past the rain, past the gray of the sky, past the veil of air and the curve of the earth, and he saw . . .

A silver wine cup, a rug, a stone floor, a pit with a fire burning brightly. He knew cold and night, and a young man's gnawing worry.

Where is she? The thought took up the whole of Kacha's mind. *What is she up to?* She had sworn him vows, and now she deserted him and her kingdom. A coward as well as a foolish child.

At least the carpet had worked. The palace was at the moment under his control, but that might not last. Kacha slammed down the wine cup. His servants jumped, but he waved them back as he rose to pace around the fire pit. His plan was good, it was sound, but she was out there, and who knew where. There was so much that might still go wrong . . .

All the secretaries were busy with announcements of the Empress's confinement, and missives about the false sorceress claiming her title. The Council Lords were preparing their own missives to the various magusates. There was nothing for him to do now but wait until Yamuna chose to, Yamuna chose to, Yamuna chose . . .

Come now, my Prince, the Sun's Own Son, walk with me. Say you go to see your wife.

The reflection of Kacha's face in a night-blackened window showed Yamuna the prince's sharp smile. The boy might be somewhat prone to his father's hysteria, but he knew the worth of his advisors, and he relished his role. He saw a single empire under the sway of the Pearl Throne stretching across the length of the continent, with himself as ruler as soon as his father might be gotten out of the way, and Yamuna was happy to give him that toy.

'I am going to consult with the Empress,' he announced. 'I need no company.'

Despite that, a ruler was seldom alone. The House Guard and footmen and waiting gentlemen all had to make sure doors were opened, lights lit or extinguished, movements announced, even if he did no more than walk through a door to the Empress's apartments, which adjoined his own.

Medeoan's outer apartment was an ideal of feminine tranquillity and gentle activity. The minor waiting ladies sat by the fire conscientiously bent over their needlework, if they were not engaged with books or letters. Every one of them duly laid aside their amusements and labors to kneel before their Emperor as he passed into the inner rooms. Some observed him slyly, covetously, or nervously, according to their own petty natures. Kacha made note of all such expressions against the time when they might prove useful.

The chief of Kacha's footmen knocked his staff against the carved door that led to the inner apartments which had been hastily converted from audience rooms to confinement rooms. After a moment, the door opened and Chekhania, whom he had caused to be raised to the position of head lady-in-waiting appeared. She reverenced politely to the footman.

'His Majesty Imperial requests an audience with the Empress Medeoan.'

'If His Majesty Imperial would deign to step within, I shall announce him at once to my Mistress Imperial.' Chekhania kept her gaze modestly on the floor as she spoke.

The males all stood aside then, allowing the Emperor to enter the inner chamber. Chekhania shut the door at once.

Such an excellent custom, confinement, Kacha thought,

knowing Yamuna would hear him. *So useful in so many ways.*

In Isavalta, once a woman entered confinement, no man could come into her presence, save her husband or her father. That meant none of the multitude of servants and gentlemen surrounding Kacha had to be bemused or bound, and only a few of the ladies around the Empress did, and then only those who, unlike Chekhania could not be bribed.

Here too there was gentle activity on every side, the endless round of reading, sewing and writing, tending to the chamber and to themselves, but if one looked into the ladies' faces, one could see a hollowness behind their eyes and a distance in their manner. These were divided souls in truth. Each had been severed from that half of their vitality that waited in the Land of Death and Spirit. Now, they could only wander lost in both worlds, ready to answer any order or command.

Which would all be given by Chekhania, and were limited indeed, as none of the ladies would be expected to appear in public until the Empress did.

So, Chekhania told them Medeoan lay in her bed, and they tended the empty bed as if she did. They brought it food, they changed its sheets, they brought braziers to warm it, read poetry to amuse it, and reverenced in its presence. All this they did gladly, for it gave them the purpose of living Yamuna's work had deprived them of.

'Does my Master Imperial wish to visit his wife or her works?' inquired Chekhania. She was a pale, plump woman, round of hip and bosom, and beautiful in the Isavaltan fashion. It was a fashion Kacha had grown to enjoy a great deal and his gaze lingered on her full breasts. He would enjoy the work of ensuring that she produced the infant that would be passed off as Medeoan's when the time came.

But now, you must see your wife's works, directed Yamuna, and Kacha told Chekhania so.

Chekhania reverenced again, and although there was no need, she led Kacha to the small door that waited past the inner apartments. The door should have been locked, but only Medeoan could touch the key, so of necessity it remained open. It did not matter. Chekhania was as good as any key in these guarded surroundings, now that the Lord Sorcerer had been disposed of.

To remind Chekhania of the various ways in which he appreciated her, Kacha paused before the inner door, wrapped his left hand around her neck, and kissed her hard. Yamuna permitted this for a long moment, for to keep Chekhania properly in her place she needed to believe the Emperor's lusts controlled him, and that by her treachery she was gaining real power.

Enough, said Yamuna at last, and Kacha released the woman and left her to mind the door.

Inside the chamber, Kacha had to light the braziers himself. No servant, even under normal circumstances, would be permitted in this room. As the firelight brightened, Yamuna, even from his great distance, found a moment to stop and admire the map table that dominated the chamber.

The Portrait of Worlds could not be duplicated, and it certainly could not be transported. So, a different tool had been created at the behest of the Isavaltan emperors. It was a table the length of the one that sat the Council of Lords which had been covered with a brass sheet. The brass was then etched with carefully drawn and divined lines and symbols that represented the worlds and their relationships, sketched out in the dance performed by the mechanisms of the Portrait. Because the brass did not move, this tool was not as delicate or precise as the Portrait, but it was here and it would serve.

It was said a sorcerer from the island of Tuukos had been smuggled in by Medeoan's grandmother to make this table. The

Tuukosov were known for drawing accurate and detailed astrological charts, and had, since their complete conquest by Isavalta, been forbidden to do so. Kacha, however, could well believe that such a canny woman would have had little trouble putting forbidden sorceries to work for the benefit of her new empire.

Seeing it through Kacha's eye, Yamuna had regretted the necessity of killing the Lord Sorcerer. He would have liked to have the man's secrets from him first, the secrets of this shining, engraved table, and most especially of the Portrait. Well, no matter. Avanasy would be found before all was done, that was not in doubt, and Avanasy could be made to tell the deeper spells concerning the detailed map and the exquisite mechanism. Until then, Yamuna's own skills could well answer.

Normally, some possession of Medeoan's would be required, but as Kacha was her husband, bound to her through the tightest of all bonds save that of birth, he himself could serve to weave the spell around.

Kacha was used to stilling himself so Yamuna could work. He did so now, positioning himself in front of the etched map of Isavalta at the center of the table. He relaxed himself, emptying his mind, making himself into the tool the sorcerer required.

Yamuna caused Kacha's right hand to take his left and place it palm down over the map of Isavalta. He reached inside himself, and pulled down his abundant magic, sending it outward across the bond of blood and flesh that tied him to Kacha. The power burned the young man, but he bore the pain proudly. Oh, it would be a pleasure to set him on the throne his father so coveted.

The spell itself had to be worked in the Isavaltan fashion to be most effective, but Yamuna had made a great study of their forms.

'This is my word.' Yamuna funneled the words to Kacha through the thoughts they shared, and Kacha, holding still under the burning that filled him inside, chanted them in time to his own heartbeat, weaving the words and the pain and the magic all into the pattern of the room. 'Upon the island of the sun there grows a tree, and upon that tree grows a branch, upon that branch sits a bird of gold and that bird has two eyes of silver. As those two eyes of silver see the whole of the world, so may I, Yamuna *dva* Ikshu Chitranipad who is Kacha *tya* Achin Ekulinjapad see Medeoan Edemskoidoch Nacheradavosh. May I see where she walks in all the worlds mortal and immortal, speaking and silent, waking and sleeping. This is my wish and this is my word, and my word is firm.'

Kacha burned, but he struggled against it, and he said the words again, and again. Yamuna stared, pushing the power through his resistant blood, willing their eye to see. For they must see. Alive or dead, the Map must show them. The spell commanded, there was no will here to resist. There must be a sign or signal, and it must come soon.

But Kacha cried out and his knees buckled, unable to stand against the pain, and Yamuna stilled the spell. Kacha dropped to the floor, panting, on hands and knees.

'How?' Kacha demanded through gritted teeth. 'She could not hide from you, you swore it. How then?'

Yamuna considered. The little cow obviously knew secrets he did not. She was powerful, and she was well taught.

Which gave him a new thought. It would take magic to vanish from the sight of the Map. Her teacher would surely know which spell she used, and where she might go.

Up. We must find Avanasy.

For a moment, Yamuna thought the prince was going to try to refuse. But Kacha gritted his teeth and heaved himself to his feet, held his palms outstretched over the Map, his whole body clenched to keep them there.

Yamuna would have preferred to have a possession of

Avanasy's for this. It would have made things easier on Kacha. He did not wish the boy damaged. But there was no time to go casting about the palace for something that might remain of Medeoan's former tutor.

This is my word. Upon the island of the sun there grows a tree, and upon that tree grows a branch, upon that branch sits a bird of gold . . .

Kacha screamed. Pain coursed through him, and more pain as the magic flowed through flesh that could not stand it and yet could not resist. Yamuna forced their right eye open and looked down upon the Map of Worlds, and he saw how the air shimmered and shone. Each beautifully rendered symbol that represented the myriad realms of the Silent Lands lit up in its turn – the Wheel, the Cup, the Wing, the Skull, the Fox – showing a passage through the Land of Death and Spirit. Here, the domain of the *lokai* had been passed by, here the fey, here the realm of Baba Yaga, and all had fetched up on a place marked with an etching of waves encased in two concentric circles. A nameless, mortal place, but now Yamuna knew its whereabouts, and Avanasy . . .

Hold just a little longer, my Prince, directed Yamuna as Kacha's scream forced itself out through clenched teeth. The fey lights hummed, a strange hinting resonance, and lit upon the map of Isavalta, and Yamuna's eye marked the spot, and in Hastinapura he threw back his head and laughed.

That laughter broke the spell, and Kacha reeled against the wall, barely missing a brazier, as he slumped there, sweating and shaking, but standing upright nonetheless.

'What did you see?' he gasped.

The teacher is planning to return, laughed Yamuna. *He has heard of his mistress's distress and means to come to her rescue. So, all we need do is be there to welcome him home and persuade him to tell us which way your wife has run.*

With that, Kacha saw the joke, and despite his pain, he too began to laugh.

It was full dark by the time Peshek reached his father's gates. He'd been half-afraid he would have to stop on the road somewhere, spending another night out in the open, but the moonlight had made it possible for him and his tired hired horse to pick out the way.

After a few minutes of shouting, the sleepy porter opened the window and squinted out at him without seeing him at all.

'Come, Labko, you know me,' he said impatiently. The hired horse danced uneasily under him. Peshek patted its neck. This was the most spirit the beast had shown since he'd mounted its sagging back.

Belated recognition widened the porter's eyes. 'Master Peshek.'

Labko's face vanished, and he shouted something indistinct. The shout was followed swiftly by a great creaking and grinding as the crank was turned and the great bolt was lifted so the gates could be cautiously pushed open. Peshek rode through as soon as there was room enough. A pair of boys wearing nothing but sandals and long-tailed shirts stared resentfully at him from under tousled hair. Peshek swung himself down onto the cobbles. He handed one of the boys his horse's reins and took the lantern the other held.

When his father had retired from service in the House Guard, he had been gifted with a thousand acres of land and twenty serfs by the Emperor. By that time, Peshek himself was already in the Guard, and, consequently, he had only visited the estate a handful of times; but he still knew his way across the yard and up the steps to the main door. Apparently his shouting had roused more than the porter, for the door opened as he approached and the rumpled servant looked at him like a startled rabbit before remembering to reverence.

'Is my father still awake?' Peshek asked.

'He is in his room, Sir,' the man stammered. It was more than suddenly being roused from sleep that unnerved him so, Peshek was sure, but he did not want to take the time to inquire. He needed to speak with his father at once.

He did take the time to stop at the gilded alcove that served as the god house and reverence to Ywane, who had gained his divinity when he hid the family from a warlord by burying them all and drawing them alive again from the earth. It would be wrong, now of all times, not to acknowledge his protection.

His father's house was a place of dark wood, well-fitted and beautifully carved, although he could only catch glimpses of the fine decorations as he marched through the narrow halls and up the zigzagging staircase with his flickering lantern. It was a new house, with fireplaces and chimneys rather than fire pits, and windows in every room. He could hear some vague noises of the servants stirring, but mostly the house was quiet and dark. He knew his father's door mainly because of the thin line of light that showed underneath it. Peshek knocked and did not wait for a reply before entering.

Pachalka Ursulsyn Rzhovin sat close to the low fire in a heavily carved chair. Peshek had a brief moment to regard his father and think that he had not changed much from when they had last met. His long face was a bit leaner under its gray beard and his hair was a bit whiter, but his body was still powerful as he pulled himself to his feet and crossed the room to the door in three strides.

And swung his fist against Peshek's jaw so hard that Peshek reeled backward and slammed hard against the wall.

'How dare you!' shouted Colonel Pachalka. 'How dare you come here after what you have done!'

'Father . . .' gasped Peshek when he could speak again. He tasted blood.

But Pachalka's fist came down again, and Peshek's head cracked back against the wooden panel.

'Traitor!' spat Pachalka. 'You betray your Empress, your family, your very gods! There are no words low enough for what you have become!'

'No, Father!' Peshek held up his hands. He could feel the warm thread of blood trickling down from his rapidly swelling lip. 'I swear . . .'

Pachalka lashed out again, but this time Peshek was ready for it and managed to block the blow with his forearm and shove his father backward, just far enough so he could dodge aside and put half the length of the room between himself and the old man.

Pachalka panted hard in his rage and Peshek seized the moment. 'Father, listen to me. I swear, all I have done, I have done in the Empress's name and at her command. I don't know who told you it was otherwise . . .'

'They came here looking for you not two days ago. Your own men. If I could have told them where you'd gone, I would have.' The words grated against Peshek's skin, all the more painful because his father spoke them. Pachalka's fists opened and closed at his sides, seizing on the empty air and strangling it, over and again.

'What did they tell you?' His lip was thickening and his words slurring, but at least his father was talking, not raining down more blows.

'That you left your post and your duty without leave.' Which was surely sin enough in the old soldier's eyes, and Pachalka all but spat as he said it. 'That you've been carrying messages for a band of traitors in their fine castles who would use the words of this madwoman roaming the countryside saying she's the true Empress to throw our rightful ruler down from her throne.' His breathing was harsh in the room and Peshek could see nothing of his face but shadows and the fire-light gleaming in his eyes, and for that moment he was glad. He did not want to see the fury twisting his father's visage as he looked at his son.

'Honored Father,' said Peshek, holding out his open hand. 'I swear on my mother's grave that it is not true. It is part of a web of lies being woven over Isavalta by Kacha and his allies here and in Hastinapura. I came here to tell you all. I beg you to hear me.'

Pachalka stood like a statue where he was, and for a long, agonizing series of heartbeats, Peshek thought his father would call down the servants to hold him fast. But then, Pachalka said softly and sternly, 'I am listening.'

Peshek could not hold back his sigh of relief. Ignoring the pain in his mouth and the iron taste of blood, Peshek told his father how the Empress had come to him in her need and what she had ordered him to do, and how he had done his best although he had agonized over it, but how he had seen where his duty lay, and how she had slipped from his charge, leaving him to spread word of her plight, and of Isavalta's, against her return.

Through it all, his father simply stood where he was. The shadows that veiled his face flickered as the fire danced in the hearth.

'Can you prove what you say?' he asked finally.

For an answer, Peshek untied his sash. With his knife, he slit the end of the cloth open and then he drew out the folded and wrinkled letter written in the Empress's hand, signed and sealed with the soaring eagle that was the Imperial crest. He watched as his father unfolded the letter and slowly, carefully, read its contents.

At last, Pachalka lifted his eyes from the paper, but did not look at Peshek. Instead, he stared for a long moment into emptiness. Then, with trembling hands, he handed it back to his son. Peshek found he could breathe again. If his father had not believed the letter to be genuine, he would have kept it to be used as evidence against Peshek at the martial tribunal.

His father's hands were still trembling, something, Peshek realized with a shock, he'd never seen before. Pachalka turned and retreated to the chair he'd occupied when Peshek first came in. A brass mug of something, probably beer, waited on a side table and Pachalka downed its contents in a single draft. When he set it down again, his hands no longer shook.

He turned to face Peshek again, hands and eyes steady and his shoulders straight and square.

'Forgive me, my son. I should have thought better of you.'

Peshek shook his head. 'There is nothing to forgive, Father. How could you doubt such honorable men? Especially when they told the truth. I did desert my post.'

'Will you sit, Peshek?' His father gestured to another chair.

'Gladly, Father.' Peshek dropped into the offered seat. In another moment he would have been the one trembling. He had not known he was so tired until this moment.

Pachalka returned to his chair. He was composed, but also more grave.

'I don't know how long I'll be able to shelter you, Peshek,' he said, his hand curling into a fist on the arm of his chair. 'It is known there is a reward for you, and one of the servants is sure to talk.'

'I thought as much,' Peshek sighed. 'In truth, it was one of the reasons I used the front door. I was hoping when I've said my piece, you might throw me out that same way.'

A knowing gleam lit his father's eye. 'And send Kabak to meet you and bring you back in secret.'

'As you say, Sir.'

'And what is this piece you wish to say to me?'

Peshek leaned forward, pitching his voice very low. 'The Empress will come back. The House Guard must be ready when she does.'

Pachalka did not flinch. 'But not before.'

'Unless other orders come, no.'

Silence settled over the room. The fire crackled and sparked in the hearth, but Peshek and his father remained silent, considering strategies, searching for possibilities, divining the difficulties, of which there were many.

'You had best go,' said Pachalka softly. 'It would not do for you to be here too long.' He stood. 'Ywane will guide you, my son, and after the moon has set, Kabak will meet you by the goose pond.'

And I will drag my father into a plot that could mean his death, thought Peshek as he embraced Pachalka, receiving the old man's kiss on his cheek. *And if I did any less, I truly would be guilty of betrayal.*

The house was dark when Ingrid stole back up the path to the front door. Fortunately, there was more than enough moonlight to see by, so she did not have to be bothered with a lantern. As softly as she could, she crept up the stairs to her bedroom, closing the door lightly behind herself.

'Ingrid, are you out of your mind?' came Grace's furious whisper. 'Where have you been?'

Ingrid nearly jumped out of her skin. She whirled around to see Grace sitting up in their bed, the covers drawn up around her chin against the chill. Even in the dim, silver light, Ingrid could see the anger on her face.

Ingrid put her hand over her heart, as if the pressure could slow its beating. 'Grace,' she began, hurrying to the bedside so she did not have to speak above a whisper. 'I've been to see Avana . . . Avan.'

Grace's eyes grew round. 'You are out of your mind,' she snapped. 'You almost have Papa won over. Are you going to throw it all away now?'

Ingrid lowered herself to sit on the edge of the bed. The springs creaked under her. 'Grace, listen to me. I'm going to ask you to believe something very difficult.'

'More difficult than a ghost?' asked Grace lightly.

'Yes.' She told her sister then, everything that Avanasy had told her. Grace sat as still as a statue, listening.

'You can't mean it,' whispered Grace when Ingrid had finally finished. 'You can't truly mean to go with him.'

Ingrid nodded. 'I do.' Those two words made it all real, and Ingrid felt an unexpected rush of freedom wash through her. This was her decision. For the first time in her whole life, she had made a choice for herself alone, and it felt fine. 'I've promised. I only came back to get some things, and to tell you. You will have to find something to tell Mama and Papa . . .'

'No, Ingrid.' Grace seized her hand. 'You can't leave me like this.'

Ingrid smiled sympathetically at her sister, patting her hand and setting it down on the quilts. 'If I married, I would leave you anyway,' she said reasonably.

'But not like this. You cannot leave me alone here. What am I going to do without you?'

'I know this is sudden, Grace, and I know it is strange, but I have given Avanasy my promise, and he has given me his,' She held out her hand so that Grace could see the ring.

Grace just struck her hand away. 'I'm supposed to be the flighty one. I'm the one who is supposed to get into trouble with men, not you, Ingrid. We need you. I need you.

Everything will fall apart if you're not here.' She wrapped her arms around her knees and looked away, her jaw working back and forth.

Ingrid could not believe what she was hearing. After all this time, after all they had been through together. They were sisters. They had always stood together, against Papa, against everything . . .

'Grace, I thought you would be happy for me.'

'How was I supposed to be happy with your running away in the middle of the night and leaving me here?'

'Grace . . .' Ingrid reached for her, but Grace jerked her whole body away.

'You don't even care what they're going to do to me when they wake up and find out you're gone,' she muttered.

Which was too much, even if she had upset Grace with the suddenness of her plans. That was just too much. 'How can you of all people, after everything that has happened, say I don't care?'

Grace wasn't looking at her. She just stared at the blank, dark wall and snapped, 'If you cared, you would persuade this Avan, or Avanasy, whatever he calls himself, to stay here.'

Bitter understanding crept into Ingrid's veins. She stood and turned away from her sister, rounding the foot of the bed to the linen press. 'I don't have time to sit here and argue with you, Grace.' She pulled out a fresh sheet and laid it on the bed. Her clean dress and petticoats came off their hooks, and fresh linens and the thickest wool stockings she owned came out of the dresser drawers.

'I can scream,' announced Grace. 'I can wake up everybody, and Papa will lock you in here.'

Ingrid couldn't bear to look at her sister. 'All my life,' she said, tying her bundle closed. 'All my life, I have looked after you. I have stood between Mama and Papa for you more times than I can count. I have asked for nothing from you until now. Why are you doing this?'

Grace crawled across the bed to Ingrid. She looked like a little child, kneeling there on the covers, wisps of hair coming loose from her fair braids. 'Because I can't lose you. Because I don't know how to live without you to lean on.'

'Then that is my fault,' breathed Ingrid, pressing both hands against her bundle. 'And I'm sorry. But I'm going. You're a good girl, Grace. You're smart. You'll manage.'

She lifted the bundle up and started for the door, biting her lip hard to keep back the tears. This was not the parting she had wanted from Grace. She had known it would be hard to say goodbye, but this reproach, this bitterness. It was too much, and she had to leave at once.

'Ingrid, I'm seeing things.'

Ingrid froze, her hand on the doorknob. 'What?'

'I'm seeing things. Since the night with the ghost. I've been seeing things, and I've been having dreams. Sometimes they come true.' She paused and her voice dropped even lower. 'I saw Leo's accident before it happened. I saw the scythe slip. That's why I was so upset when it happened. I think he . . . I think the ghost did something to me.'

Ingrid pivoted on her heel and stared at her sister who still crouched at the foot of their bed. 'Why didn't you tell me this before?'

Grace huddled in on herself again. 'I didn't want you to think I was going mad.'

'Grace, you should have told me.' Ingrid rushed to her and seized her shoulder. She could not help it. She had protected Grace for too many years to stay distant from her at this moment. 'We could have asked Avanasy. He would know.'

'We can go now. You can tell him . . .'

Ingrid saw the sudden light, the sudden hope that filled

Grace's face as she said that, and she realized what was truly happening here. Grace was trying to work on her. Anger sparked inside her. 'I don't believe this,' she said, pressing her hand against her forehead. 'I knew you were capable of saying anything to get your way with Papa and Mama, but I did not believe you would try this nonsense with me.'

'It's the truth. I swear.'

'Then it's too late,' Ingrid told her. 'I'm leaving. Now. This minute.' She turned away. She couldn't look at Grace anymore. Not like this. Not with all that was hanging in the air between them.

'They'll never let you in the house again,' said Grace desperately.

'Then you'll have to remember me in your prayers, as I'll remember you in mine.'

'You promised me, Ingrid.' Real anger touched Grace's voice, and it wrung Ingrid's heart. 'You promised you would always be here for me.'

Now. You must leave now, or you never will. Ingrid gripped her bundle more tightly. 'You promised me too,' she said without turning around. 'You promised me we would always be best friends. This is not the work of a friend.'

She left the house without pausing to close the door. Grace would see to it, or she would not. Ingrid ran down the track to the road, dashing the tears from her eyes.

She is only startled. When she has time to think it over, she will regret her words. She truly understands, she just does not want me to go. Later I will find some way to get word to her. Perhaps, when the troubles are over in this Isavalta it will be possible to send for her.

Clutching those thoughts like she clutched her bundle, Ingrid ran through the dying night to the docks.

The light of a single lantern guided her down the pier to Avanasy's boat. Avanasy himself was nothing but a silhouette in the false dawn, crouched on the deck coiling a rope. At the sound of her hurrying footsteps and her ragged breathing, he straightened up. Ingrid saw him fully in the lantern light and froze.

This was not Avan the fisherman who had sat so many evenings at her mother's kitchen table, drinking coffee and passing the time. This was a Cossack, this was a prince. He wore a wide-skirted coat of rich black. Two dozen silver buttons fastened the front of it. Elaborate silver embroidery adorned the high collar and wide cuffs. A cloth-of-silver sash circled his waist. There must have been a knife belt underneath that because she could see the sheath, with the dagger's handle protruding from the top of the sash. The coat's hem brushed the tops of polished leather boots, and worked leather gloves encased his hands. A peaked black cap with yet more silver embroidery covered his hair.

Ingrid stared, and for an awful moment felt every inch the poor, pale, country girl.

But the loving eyes were all Avanasy's, as was the welcoming hand that reached up to help her step into the boat.

'Is all well?' he asked.

'No,' she admitted. 'I had a scene with Grace. She is angry at me for leaving.'

Avanasy touched her shoulder. 'I'm sorry.'

'So am I.' *But I am glad you are not asking if I would rather stay.* Even as she thought that, she knew in her heart they were already well beyond such questions. 'Is there a hold? Let me stow my things.'

Avanasy nodded toward the hatch. 'Take the lamp. I must get us ready to cast off. The men will be coming soon, and we must be away before then.'

The men, and Papa with them, if Papa is not already on the way.
She climbed down the stout ladder. Ingrid had lived all her

life around boats, and she knew a well-made craft when she saw it. Avanasy's boat was clinker built, stout and strong. The cordage, casks and extra canvas were all neatly stowed. The chests from his cabin had been tied into place below one of the two bunks. Ingrid hung the lantern on a peg and stowed her own meager bundle in one of the cabinets built into the bow. This was a boat meant for fairly long journeys. Ingrid closed her mind against the idea of how long a journey she had just embarked upon. She reclaimed the lantern and returned to the deck.

Avanasy stood in the bow waiting for her. As she emerged he smiled, but still managed to look grave. 'Now there is one last thing I must require of you for this journey.'

'And that is?' Ingrid tried to keep her voice light, but was not sure how well she succeeded. This night had already asked a great deal from her, and she was beginning to feel weary with all her trying.

He paused for a moment, as if searching for the right words. 'The Land of Death and Spirit is a dangerous place, especially for those with divided souls, those with no magic in them. There are dangerous and jealous powers in that place, and there are some who are just mischievous. They will be attracted by the strength of your soul. They will try to lead you astray. You will see many things which are untrue.'

'Then I will have to keep my eyes closed,' said Ingrid simply.

Avanasy fumbled for a moment in the pocket of his beautiful black coat. 'That will not be enough. They will still find ways to reach you, and I will not be able to protect you, for I must concentrate on keeping us on course.' He brought out a small, stoppered vial. 'This will send you to sleep. That way, all you encounter will be as dreams, and will have no more power to hurt you than ordinary dreams do.'

Ingrid took the bottle from him, pulled out the stopper and

inhaled the scent. It was sharp, clean and medicinal, a strong smell of laudanum and alcohol, and things she could not name.

'If that's how it must be.' She tucked the vial into the pocket of her skirt. 'But let me stay awake as long as possible.'

'As long as possible,' agreed Avanasy. 'Now, we must away.'

Avanasy hopped down onto the pier and cast the ropes off. Ingrid coiled and stowed them as he did, and soon the boat was loose. Avanasy climbed back onto the deck, grasped the main line, and raised the canvas. The wind caught the dark sail a moment later, and they were off. Ingrid faced the shore as they pulled away. The docks remained empty and still. Papa had not come to fetch her back, neither had Grace.

Angry, although she could not have clearly said why, Ingrid stalked to the bow and faced the wind. It blew hard and cold in her face, setting her eyes stinging with tears. She welcomed it. This way she would not have to explain why she was crying. Behind her, she heard Avanasy working the ropes. A second sail rose over the first, and below her the deck creaked as they picked up speed.

She would not look back. Sand Island was not her home anymore. She stood steadily on the gently swaying deck and wrapped her arms around herself. She would not look back.

'Ingrid!' called Avanasy over the wind. 'I fear it is time.'

Ingrid took one last look at the gray waters of Lake Superior which had cradled her since her birth. Then, she turned on her heel and with the rocking gait of an experienced sailor, she strode to the stern. Avanasy stood at the tiller, one hand keeping it steady, the other feeling the tension in the main line. She took his face in both hands and kissed him, drinking in the promise as he returned her kiss and embraced her with one arm.

'When you wake, it will be to see the land of my birth,' he said.

'I look forward to the sight.' Ingrid smiled at him, and went below.

Neither of the bunks seemed to be claimed, so Ingrid sat herself down on the right-hand bed. She pulled the little bottle from her apron pocket, and stared at it for a moment, ashamed of the nervousness that fluttered in her breast.

Then, she pulled out the stopper and swallowed the thick liquid in one draft.

She had time enough to taste sweet honey and strong brandy before a wave of dizziness swept over her. She managed to lie back and swing her legs up, but a second wave overcame her and all the strength left her limbs. She was distantly aware of the clatter as the vial fell from her fingers to the deck, but she could do nothing about it. Sleep already wrapped her in an embrace as warm as any Avanasy could offer, and it pulled her close into its comforting darkness.

She lay oblivious for a time. Then it seemed to her that she sat up, wide awake, although she did not know why.

'Come out,' called a stranger's voice. 'Come out. You are summoned.'

The Land of Death and Spirit bloomed around Avanasy like a dream. Lake Superior and its wide gray waters were gone without a trace. Instead, he sailed up a broad brown river. The sails bellied full in a wind his skin did not feel. No sound came from his boat's timbers, nor did any come from the flowing waters, or the dark pines that towered on the mossy banks. These were the Silent Lands, the Shifting Lands, the homes of ghosts, the unborn, the never-born, and the eternal. No sorcerer crossed them in the flesh unless he was desperate. No sorcerer carried an unprotected, ordinary human through them unless he was insane.

Avanasy could not afford to think of that now. He had to keep all his mind fixed on his destination. In the mortal world, a sorcerer had to reach for his magic and use his will to shape it. Here, the magic reached for the sorcerer and tried to shape him. Here, the need was to hold one's soul steady, to be a rock in the stream of the Shifting Lands. A divided soul would feel the yearning, lonely tug of the half of itself that resided here and would travel far to ease that ache.

Small memories, his master had told him. *It is the tiniest, most intimate details of life that will make the links in the chain to pull you through the Silent Lands.*

So Avanasy remembered. He remembered the smell of the coal fire in his master Valerii's house late at night as Avanasy took down his instruction in the great vellum book. He remembered the taste of broth and dumplings in winter when he was a boy and had come back in from helping his father supervise the brewing sheds, and how the warmth of the good soup could be felt through and through. He remembered the day the *zhagravor*, the telling sorcerer, had wrapped the red sash around his waist and looked hard in his eyes and declared him sorcerer.

He remembered walking into the great hall at Vyshtavos, and how the Keeper of the Emperor's God House had barred his way, ceremonially challenging him, until Master Valerii gave his name and the keeper stood aside so that Avanasy might kneel before the Emperor and hear his charge.

'The High Princess, my beloved daughter Medeoan Edemskoidoch Nacheradavosh has been declared sorcerer. It is my express wish that she be trained in arts magical and the meaning of sorcery. Your master, Valerii Adrisyn Rhasovin, has said you are most suited to this charge. Will you accept the task?'

Protocol forbade him to look up at the monarch's face until

invited to stand and give counsel, so he gave his promise to the blue and gold carpeting and the tips of the Emperor's black velvet slippers. He remembered how his heart sang as he spoke of his loyalty and honor.

He remembered Medeoan as he first saw her. Twelve years old, pale-skinned and pale-haired, with too little flesh for her rapidly growing frame. 'Pinched' was the unflattering word that first came to his mind. She stood in the middle of the school room flanked by her graceful music tutor and fat mathematics tutor. He had time enough to see that much before he had to kneel and study the parquet floor. He remembered the patterns of pale stars laid out in the darker wood. He had a long time to become familiar with them before she bid him stand.

But then came the summer days in the gardens, and the winters by the fire, and discovering Medeoan's voracious mind and troubled heart. Hours in the red library poring over the volumes kept there, increasing his own knowledge and opening his own mind to the vastness of the world's possibilities that even his master could not teach him.

Memory on top of memory, long locked in the back of his own mind, all tumbling out in a flood, creating a current to draw them forward into Isavalta. He held his hand on the tiller to steady himself, but the tiller had no force in this river. There was only his heart and his concentration now, but after all those long months in a world where the magic was so stifled, even this amount of work felt like freedom.

Movement caught his eye, and despite Avanasy's deep concentration, his gaze flickered momentarily, and he saw Ingrid climb out of the hold.

'What!' he exclaimed, and his hold on the course and memory loosened dangerously.

Ingrid did not even pause at the sound of his voice. She

continued across the deck with a slow steady motion that was almost a glide.

'Ingrid!' Avanasy called desperately and he reached out as she passed him, unblinking. He saw his hand touch the cloth of her sleeve, but he felt nothing, nothing at all.

Illusion? Spirit? Avanasy's mind reeled, and he felt his hold on the course slip that much further.

Ingrid, or the seeming of Ingrid, did not pause when she reached the rail. She continued on, her stride unbroken, and then she was on the bank.

Avanasy could not believe what he was seeing. This must be a trick. Some fey spirit was trying to throw them off, trap them forever here in the Land of Death and Spirit. But as Ingrid vanished into the pine forest, his heart constricted, and he knew he could not hold his mind to the task without certainty.

He had to hurry, before his hold was gone, before he was awash in the unbroken and shifting sea that was the world around him.

Steeling himself, Avanasy lifted his hand from the tiller.

Remember Isavalta, he told himself as he crossed the deck. *Remember the hours at the loom weaving these sails. Remember how the threads cut even your toughened fingers. Remember the touch of the cotton dust in your throat. Remember.*

He started down the ladder. The boat rocked under him, gliding forward still on the current of his thoughts.

Remember the summer day you spent painting this boat. Remember how the sun beat down on your back and the strong smell of the paints in the heat. Remember how tired you were when you finished, but how proud. Your masterpiece. Remember how Master Valerii smiled and clapped you on the shoulder and you knew you'd done well.

It took a moment for his eyes to adjust to the gloom of the

hold, but when they did, he saw Ingrid lying still in her bunk and he wanted to shout with relief. He had almost been taken in by an illusion of the Silent Lands, but there she was, safe and whole.

Safe yes, but whole? nagged a little voice in the back of his head. *Are you certain?*

But how could she be otherwise? She had a divided soul. She was safely anchored, one foot in the mortal world and one in the Silent Lands. Asleep as she was, her spirit could not be moved. That was the law.

Despite this, Avanasy moved forward. He had to be sure. He could take no chances with Ingrid. In this place, she depended utterly on him.

Remember the first day in Master Valerii's house. Remember how you started at shadows, your boy's head filled with thoughts of ghosts and house-goblins. Remember how you were so afraid to open the big cupboard in the attic, and when you did you found it full of nothing more terrifying than the winter linens . . . .

Avanasy reached for Ingrid's hand, and found it cold. Fear rooted him to the deck. She breathed, he could see the rise and fall of her chest clearly, but she had gone cold as a corpse, and her sun-browned cheeks had lost all their color. Her white skin seemed to glow in the darkness.

She was not dead, but nor was she alive. Her vitality, her spirit, against all he knew to be possible, was gone, and he had seen it walk into the Land of Death and Spirit.

How? he wanted to howl. *How has this happened? Who has done this to you?*

No. No. He must stop. He must think, he must remember. He must hold their course, and he must let go. It was too much. Avanasy threw his head back, his jaw and fists clenched to hold in his screams, to try to keep his thoughts together.

He must find her. She would die left like this. He must

follow her spirit somehow. There must be a way.

Must be a way. Remember. Remember. Remember Isavalta. Ah, gods, gods, Ingrid, what have I brought you to? Stop. Remember. Remember your master's house. Remember his teaching, remember your study. It is all you both have now. Remember . . .

He had it. The ring. His promise given to her. He could follow that through the Shifting Lands. It would be a thin thread, but it would be enough. It would have to be.

His grip on his memories slid away just thinking about it. Too much to concentrate on. He could not guide the boat and walk the Silent Lands at the same time. He would have to let the boat slide into the mortal world, and it would have to take their bodies with it while their spirits both walked.

It was a grave risk. They could be so easily led astray. Ingrid might already be beyond him, in the grip of whatever great power could hail a divided soul from its body.

No. No, he could not believe that. There would still be something he could do. Some way to save her.

But even as he thought that, he felt his hold on the boat loosen yet further. The air around him seemed to thicken and grow warm, turning into a comfortable blanket into which it would be so easy to fall, fall and sleep, and let what would come bring itself and never worry about any of it . . .

Clamping down hard on his feelings, Avanasy pulled the ring from Ingrid's cold, unresisting hand. Then, as quickly as he could, he climbed the ladder and crossed the deck to the tiller.

Remember. Remember Medeoan's wedding, if you can remember nothing else. Remember the touch of the door under your hands. Remember the anger. Remember how you prayed.

Keeping tight rein on his thoughts, Avanasy sliced a length of rope off from one of the coils. He wound it around his left wrist, and bound his wrist to the tiller.

Remember how Medeoan's eyes blazed when she spoke the words of banishment. Remember how Kacha stood beside her, and how coldly he smiled. Remember the triumph you saw glittering in his unmatched eyes.

He pulled the knot closed as tightly as he could with his one free hand. Then, he laid his iron-bladed knife aside. He could not hold such a thing and do what he must. Instead, he clasped Ingrid's ring.

Avanasy closed his eyes and willed himself to relax. He let the warm vapors of the Shifting Lands enfold him. He abandoned will and memory, fear and anger. He must be a feather in the wind now. He must be light and air. No part of earth must he be. He must be free, a shadow, a thought, a dream, nothing at all.

Although he did not open his eyes, still Avanasy saw. He saw the wide, brown river. He saw the small, red boat with its white sails bellied in a wind he could not feel sailing with the current. He saw himself slumped over the tiller, but only for a moment. Boat and abandoned body vanished like mist at the touch of the sun. Back to Isavalta, if all was well, to drift upon the ocean, until he could make his way back.

Until we can make our way back, he told himself firmly.

He opened his shadow of a hand and in it found the memory of a ring. He let himself go further yet, unbound spirit, dream, vapor that he was, and he began to drift. Now it was the ring that provided the current. The ring would search out its mirror self in the Shifting Lands. The ring, his promise, would bring him to Ingrid.

All around Avanasy, the lands swayed and blurred. He had no true eyes to close in this form, but still, all turned to darkness, and he felt himself begin to fall.

* * *

Ingrid stepped onto the shore. All her clothing was perfectly dry. She did not remember having left the boat. She looked back, but all she saw behind her were the dark trunks of pine trees.

It's only a dream, she told herself. *There's nothing to fear.*

In the manner of dreams, Ingrid seemed to know exactly where she needed to go. She felt as if there were an invisible string tied to her waist and pulling her easily forward through the dark pine woods. Her feet made no sound as she walked over moss and fallen needles. She could see neither sun nor sky. She cast no shadow before or behind her. But none of that worried her. She knew which way she must go, and she was content to walk until she found her destination.

Ingrid did not know how long it was before the woods opened before her. She stepped easily from the thick forest into an open meadow lit by a pale, green light for which she could discern no source. The grass bent and waved in a wind she could not feel, but it made no noise at all as it moved. A round, green hill rose before her like a bubble from a pot of boiling water. On top of the hill stood a bright-red fox.

Ingrid hesitated. She had seen no other living creature since she had entered the wood. Her way, however, lay past the hill. She knew that, as she knew she must continue walking. She could not linger here. She turned from the hill and started toward the woods again.

But the fox was in front of her, and it was enormous.

Ingrid stopped short. Her heart thumped once. She distantly knew she was afraid, but she could do nothing. The fox stood before her, its head level with her own, its ears pricked up and alert, its whiskers twitching interestedly.

'Well now,' it said. 'What have we here?'

The sound of the fox's voice sent a cold thrill through her, as if it were a knife blade that touched her bare skin. She was still pulled forward, but at the same time she was rooted to the spot.

'I said,' the fox's tail swished back and forth, 'what have we here?'

'I . . . I don't know,' stammered Ingrid. 'I . . . I'm supposed to go that way.' She waved tremulously in the direction she was pulled. Without sun, without shadow, she had no way to give the direction a name. The pull, though, was becoming more insistent, almost a pain.

'Yes,' the Vixen narrowed her green eyes. 'Yes, you are. But perhaps I should not let you pass.' The Vixen whisked around Ingrid, more like a great cat than a fox. 'Perhaps I should keep you for myself.' She paused a moment, considering. 'But no. Then I would never know what she meant to do with you herself, you see. The Old Witch has hidden in her house for so long, none understand it. She has so many to serve her, what needs she with one more? What can you do that they cannot?' The Vixen lifted her muzzle, gazing closely at Ingrid's eyes, and Ingrid felt herself begin to tremble although she did not know why. 'Your eyes are sharp, but how sharp? Your sight may be your trouble, always showing you what you should not see.' She stepped away, contemplating Ingrid now with a sort of cool disinterest. 'Such eyes can plague a family down the generations. Such eyes can ruin kings and yet save kingdoms.' The Vixen sat back, her mouth hanging open so that she appeared to be laughing. 'But then, greed was ever a part of her nature. She may want you simply because she wants. Yes, I'm minded to let you go about her business for now, little woman. Perhaps she thinks you can bring back what she's lost.'

The Vixen was gone, as suddenly as she had appeared, and Ingrid was alone in the meadow under the pale-green light, utterly bewildered, except for the pulling that led her down a path she could not measure toward an end she could not guess.

It is a dream. I was promised. It is only a dream.

Because she could no longer bear to stand still, Ingrid continued forward into the dark trees again. The woods kept on without any end that she could see. Ingrid could not even feel the ground beneath her feet now. She might as well have been standing still while the woods flowed about her.

But slowly, gradually, the trees began to change. Maples and oaks intruded on the pines. A small creek ran silently between mossy banks. Ingrid stepped across it. On the other side, a birch tree pulled its branches back to let her pass. As it did, Ingrid saw a house swim into her vision as if from a fog.

It was a low, thatched building of gray stone. It looked as if it could be a cliff side, formed by wind and weather wearing away the soil, rather than an edifice built by human hands. A low stone fence surrounded it, and a winding stone path led to its door.

There was nothing in the least alarming about the place. It was an old homestead, well-tended and sturdy. Yet, Ingrid found herself hesitating beside the gate. The pull had released her. She was where she was supposed to be.

'Ingrid,' said a voice within the dark doorway. It was the same voice that had called her from the boat. 'Come in to me.'

Ingrid did not even think to disobey. She stepped across the threshold, and was suddenly dizzy, as if she had been swept up and carried some distance.

The inside of the cottage was as neat and as solid as the outside. The dim light that filtered through the doorway gave Ingrid the impression of heavy furniture carved of dark wood, a stone hearth without a fire, a broom, a dirt floor and in the far corner, an angular shadow that it took a moment for Ingrid to realize was a loom.

A shadow emerged from the darkness of the cottage and stepped into the square of pale, green light that fell through the cottage's single window. Dizziness took hold of Ingrid again, but it cleared swiftly and she saw the shadow had become a tall, slender woman. Years had etched themselves into her face, but each line held both beauty and strength. Her eyes were clear and filled with purpose. A waterfall of white hair, unbound like a girl's, hung down past her shoulders. She wore a simple black dress and held her capable hands folded neatly over a white apron.

Ingrid had never known either of her grandmothers, but what she felt now was a mix of longing and comfortable love that surely must be what she would have felt for them.

'You are a good child,' said the woman, nodding her approval. Her voice was melodious, nothing at all like the wild voice of the Vixen.

'Who are you?' asked Ingrid, her voice faltering. It seemed strange to speak after so much silence, and she sounded so clumsy to herself.

'I am grandmother and I am crone,' said the old woman. 'I am the one who sent for you and the one whom you heeded.'

'Yes,' said Ingrid, although she did not know why. Had she truly been expecting a name? That seemed presumptuous somehow.

'I called you here because I have a task that needs doing. I need you to hear me and to complete it.'

Ingrid hesitated. She yearned to do as she was told. She felt the gentle authority of this woman and, again like a child, she wished for her approval.

It's only a dream, she told herself. *What's wrong with giving a promise in a dream?*

'Ingrid.'

Ingrid turned to the window. Avanasy stood in the yard. The world seemed to ripple unpleasantly where he stood. The neat fence was at the same time pickets and bones. The gray stones were simultaneously skulls. The house rocked where it stood.

'Ingrid!' he called again. 'Come out to me!'

'Granddaughter, stay yet awhile,' said the woman behind her. 'Let the man cool his ardor for you while you attend your elders, as you should.'

'Yes, Grandmother.' But Ingrid's words had no force. Even as she spoke them, she felt herself drifting toward the door. The floor shifted and shuddered under her feet. Bones, she thought again. Why were there bones in the roofbeams and bones underfoot? She could not see them, but she knew they were there.

'Ingrid!' called Avanasy again.

'Bind you by the threshold, bind you by the word,' said the old woman behind her. 'Bind you by your promise to me.'

'But there was no promise,' said Ingrid vaguely, and the door fell open in front of her.

The house seemed to have grown stilts, for now she looked down a long stair at Avanasy.

He seemed insubstantial, somehow, as if he were nothing more than a shadow among shadows. Yet, she felt drawn to him, as she had been drawn to this house.

'Come away, Ingrid,' he held out his hand, beseeching. 'Come to me.'

'I will,' she assured him. 'But there is an old woman inside who needs my help.'

'No, Ingrid, she means to harm you.' Why could she not see clearly? This place had seemed so solid, such a part of the earth. Now it rocked under her like a restless boat, and all that was dark seemed to be bleached and white.

'How can she hurt me? This is only a dream. You told me so.'

Distress creased Avanasy's face. 'I was wrong.'

'Only a dream, Granddaughter,' said the old woman. 'Say you will help me and you will soon wake to your lover.'

'No!' cried Avanasy, starting forward. He stopped short, as if something blocked his way. 'Ingrid, promise her nothing until she tells you her name.'

'Name?' The world swam again. Avanasy drew further away, although he did not move. The doorway tipped and tilted, and Ingrid gripped the frame to steady herself, but the rocking would not cease.

'You go too far, Sorcerer,' said the old woman behind her, her voice suddenly stern and hard as stone, as bone. 'Leave her now and you will have her again when I am finished.'

'She has not told you her name, has she?' said Avanasy doggedly, oblivious to the distress he caused. 'Shall I tell you what it is?'

'Take care, Sorcerer,' the Grandmother's voice grew shrill and strange, and Ingrid shivered to hear it. 'Your flesh and your iron are far away. You may be compelled to stay here.'

'Then you will deal with me, Baba Yaga.'

At those words, the world split in two. The stone house and its gardens fell away on either side of Ingrid, leaving behind a room built of bones. Skulls and skeletons of a hundred different animals hung from rafter beams that curved like gigantic ribs. Human skulls framed the fireplace, gaping and grinning. Even the loom in the corner was built of the gruesome ivory. Where the Grandmother had stood so tall and strong now hunched a withered crone who was little more than a skeleton herself under her tattered black robe. Her lips drew back in a grimace of anger, exposing teeth of black iron, and she leaned on a stained and begrimed pestle.

Ingrid opened her mouth to scream but no sound came. Baba Yaga pointed one bony finger at her, and Ingrid felt the touch of it as if it pressed against her heart.

'Ingrid! Come to me!' cried Avanasy. 'Wish it so! Ingrid!'

Ingrid backed away even as Baba Yaga's hand curled shut. Ingrid knew the ancient witch meant to cradle her heart in that hand. As impossible as that was, it was also true, and fervently, desperately, she wished she was on Avanasy's boat, standing beside him, looking out across the banks.

And she knew the way. She felt it in her fingertips, a faint but certain tugging, and all she had to do was follow. Now she cried out as she turned and ran, and in a moment she was flying. All the world around her was a blur of blacks, browns and greens. She felt a pain in her side as if claws raked her, but it was brief, and she ran on, flying and running all at once.

And she saw herself, lying limp and corpse white in the little wooden bunk, and then there was darkness, and then she opened her eyes.

The boat rocked hard underneath her and for a dizzying moment, Ingrid thought she was still in the bone-framed house. But her hand gripped honest wood on the side of her bunk. Her stomach heaved hard with the motion of the vessel for the first time since she was a tiny child, and she had to swallow hard to keep it from spilling out.

What happened? Strange dreams. No, not dreams. Avanasy.

That thought rallied her sea legs and Ingrid threw back the blanket and ran to the ladder. Brisk wind smacked her face as soon as she emerged onto the deck. She had the vague impression of an iron-gray sea and a horizon that might have been the hazy coast or a bank of clouds.

Avanasy slouched beside the rudder, slack jawed and staring. Ingrid hurried to his side and saw the cord binding his hand to the tiller.

'Avanasy?' she called, but his eyes did not blink. She reached immediately for the cord, but hesitated. What if this was one of his spells? What would happen to him if she broke it? He had saved her from the Bony-Legged Witch, whether that had been a strange dream or a stranger reality, but what would she do if she now had to save him?

Ingrid sat back on her heels. Only the rise and fall of Avanasy's chest told her he still lived. She could not hear his breathing over the sound of the wind and water. She brushed back her hair where it whipped into her face. The wind was rising. The ropes creaked.

That she could do. She could trim the sails. She could keep the boat upright. She could pray.

The rigging was unfamiliar to her, but it was all neatly done, and it did not take her much looking to understand how the lines ran. She left the mainsail alone, but brought in the stemsail, lashing it tightly. The horizon had darkened. There was land out there, growing closer. That meant shoals, and coves and currents, none of which she knew. Ingrid bit her lip.

Here I am in this new world, and I am useless. Tears stung her eyes. *What do I do, Avanasy?*

She yearned hard for her answer, and in response came an unaccountable sensation of floating, of drifting far too free, like a boat without mooring. There was danger in this, she knew that too, but still she reached. There was so much out there . . . the answers . . . Avanasy.

No, Ingrid.

Ingrid's eyes snapped open. She had not even realized she had closed them. She had leaned out over the gunwale, and she did not remember that either.

Had that been Avanasy? Or the wind? What was happening?

She wanted to reach out again, but realized that in another moment she would have fallen right over the side.

She remembered the last time she had seen Avanasy so incapacitated. He'd asked her to sit by him, to sing, to bring him back into the world.

Ingrid pushed aside all thought of feeling foolish and steeled herself. She put her arms around him, laying her hands over his.

'Here I sit on Buttermilk hill
'Who could blame me cry my fill?
'Every tear would turn a mill,
'Johnny's gone for a soldier . . .'

She sang of loss, and of sorrow, of a woman who had given everything and was left alone, and she felt whole, rooted impossibly through the deck to the surging ocean, and she felt Avanasy stir.

'Oh my baby, oh my love,
'Gone the rainbow, gone the dove,
'Your father was my only love . . .'

'Ah!' Avanasy cried out. His head snapped up and for a terrible instant his whole body went rigid with pain. His spasm swung the tiller wildly and Ingrid tightened her hands over his automatically to bring it around again.

Avanasy cried out again, but Ingrid could make nothing of his words. She could only hold him close. In a moment, he subsided, and blinked slowly.

'Ingrid?'

She opened her mouth to answer him, but before she could speak, he seized her face with his free hand, bringing her forward to kiss her hard and desperately on the mouth.

'I'm sorry,' he whispered as he released her. 'I'm so sorry, Ingrid. I didn't know.'

'Know what, Avanasy? What happened?'

'I can't tell you. Not yet. We need earth and stone under us for those words, not shifting water.'

'What . . .'

'Trust me in this, Ingrid. Please.'

Ingrid closed her mouth, her spine stiffening. Avanasy did

not look at her. He instead lifted his knife from where it lay and cut himself free. In another moment, he was busy with line, canvas and tiller. Ingrid sat on the stern bench, scant inches from him, but she felt as if she were suddenly miles away.

The wind blew through her shawl and dress, and she shivered from the cold. She did not clearly know what had happened, but this much she did know. In the space of this moment, all had somehow changed.

The house of bones that bore the name Ishbushka turned on its great, scarred legs. Its windows opened like blank and bleary eyes on the shifting world around it. Beyond the ragged fence of bones that marked its territory, the Vixen sat on her haunches and watched.

'So, you will send another to do your work for you?' The Vixen's tail swished back and forth. She spoke softly, but she knew Ishbushka's mistress heard every word. 'She is an unnatural thing, to be sure, but did you really think you could hide her from me?'

The house stopped its restless motion and bent its monstrous legs to kneel on the ground. The rotted door fell open toward the Vixen, who did not even blink. In the doorway stood Baba Yaga, leaning on her pestle, her tattered black robes clinging to her bony frame.

'You have stolen what is mine,' rasped the Old Witch. 'I will have it back.'

The Vixen yawned. 'Prove that I have stolen it then. Call me out according to the law.' She let her mouth hang open in a wide grin. 'But then, you would have to leave your house, wouldn't you?'

Baba Yaga bared her iron teeth. 'You think you've won this

game. You do not even see the next move, let alone the end of it. You have no idea how far my power reaches.'

'At the moment, I'd say it reaches to the edge of your charming yard.' The Vixen flicked her tail again. 'As I'm sitting here quite undisturbed.'

'Think that, then,' sneered Baba Yaga. 'You've thought many a more foolish thing.'

Ishbushka's door shut and the house heaved itself back to its taloned feet to resume its alert and watchful turning. The Vixen gazed at it awhile longer, her own lips drawn back to show just a gleam of her sharp, yellow teeth.

You think I do not see the end of this? she thought. *Are you certain you know which game I am playing?*

And she was gone.

Chapter Ten

Avanasy would not look at her.

For her own part, Ingrid found herself remaining determinedly silent. She wrapped her arms around herself and concentrated on the approaching shoreline. It was a rocky coast, as gray as the ocean and about as inviting. A thin border of stunted and twisted trees surmounted the cliffs. As they sailed closer, Ingrid could see the shore was ragged with countless tiny coves and points. An excellent place for catching shellfish, or for smuggling, but an awful place for boats.

Still, Avanasy seemed to know the shore well. He adjusted the sails with precision for the erratic wind and was an expert hand with the tiller. No wonder Papa had found him such a good sailor, if these were the waters he learned in.

But he still would not look at her.

The land curved around to the port side. Gradually, Ingrid saw that one of the broader cliffs was topped with a mass of stone that had a more regular shape than the tumbled boulders they had been seeing. It was a fortress, squat and massive, with fat turrets obviously meant for keeping watch over the ocean.

'That is Fortress Dalemar,' said Avanasy, shouting to be heard over the wind and the water. 'When we have landed, I hope to gain us news from there.'

Ingrid did not answer him, and she found herself wondering what reason there could be for her own black mood. A whole new world spread out before her. Avanasy sat beside her and she wore his ring on her finger. Whatever had happened during their strange crossing, it was over. They were safe on a sea that was obviously familiar to Avanasy, who was an excellent sailor. He had promised her an explanation soon enough. Where was her patience? What was the matter with her?

The truth was, she felt torn. Not between excitement and fear, or any other two emotions she could name. Rather, she felt as if some physical force were literally tugging at her insides, separating out some vitality from the core of her, and it was wrong, this feeling. She knew it. Yet, who was she to say that it was not just the sensation of being taken to a new world? There was no way to tell, until she could ask Avanasy, and Avanasy would not answer until they reached land, and he showed no signs of steering them to harbor just yet.

They sailed around another sharp point, close enough for Ingrid to see the breakers rolling against the rocky beach. In the tiny cove, sheltered by the point, a cluster of people were at work. Some sorted through heaps of seaweed, some cast nets into pools, confirming her thoughts about shellfish. The workers all straightened up as the boat came into view, raising their hands.

'Do they know you?' asked Ingrid.

'I hope not,' answered Avanasy. 'It is custom, and good luck, to bless any sail that is sighted.'

'Ah.'

They lapsed into silence again.

At last, Avanasy sailed them through a channel between the rocky shore and, judging from the way the waves broke against them, what must have been some ragged shallows. This cove was wider than the first, and some sand actually showed between the stones, but the cliffs behind it were high and unbroken, and the way in was narrow. The piles of seaweed on the beach told Ingrid that this was low tide, yet this inviting cove was deserted, probably because of the risky entry.

Avanasy sailed them up close to the shore, and finally tossed out the anchor. Without being asked, Ingrid took in the mainsail and lashed it down. Avanasy climbed out into the shallows and gave her his hand. Ingrid pulled off her boots, knotted the laces so they could be slung about her neck, stuffed her stockings into the boots, hiked her skirts up around her knees and took his hand. Together they waded to shore.

'I am sorry this is all the welcome I can give you to my home,' said Avanasy.

Ingrid looked about her. Sheltered now at least somewhat from the driving wind, Ingrid felt the sun warm her face and shoulders. Seabirds wheeled overhead, giving calls to each other that were as familiar to her as the feel of the sand under her feet and the bright summer blue of the sky overhead. Unaccountably, the feeling of being pulled apart vanished, and Ingrid found herself able to smile.

'I like the view,' she said. 'But I believe you must speak to your carpenter about that draft.'

Solemnly, Avanasy bowed to her, stretching out one leg and folding his hands over his breast. 'As my lady wishes.'

They laughed together then, and that laugh was as welcome as the warmth of the sun on her shoulders.

'Can you tell me what happened now?' she asked.

Avanasy sighed and rested his foot against a stone. 'Yes, and no.'

Ingrid swallowed another burst of impatience. 'How is that?'

He stared over the gray waters for a moment, ordering his

thoughts. 'One of the dangers of the passage through the Land of Death and Spirit is that the powers that live there may take . . . notice. They may have use for mortal life, or they may simply desire trouble or blessing. I had thought, asleep as you were, you were safe from interference. A sleeping mind moves more swiftly and more lightly than a waking one, and is far less likely to be noticed, or to be of interest if it is noticed.' He ran one hand through his dark-gold hair. 'But perhaps you did not sleep deeply enough, or, perhaps the Old Witch was looking for someone . . .' He shook his head, anger creasing his brow. 'I cannot say more clearly, and I wish I could. Whatever the case, she was able to lure you from the safety of the boat.' His frown grew sharper. 'What I do not understand is how she was able to make you walk as spirit. She should not have been able to separate soul from flesh.'

'I should hope not,' said Ingrid, growing chill despite the warm sun.

'There exists natural law, even in the Silent Lands. There are things which cannot be done.'

'And you know all those laws?'

'No, Ingrid. I don't.'

'Ah.'

He knelt in front of her, taking her left hand in his. 'Should I have turned you away, Ingrid? Left you on the shores of your own world?'

She touched his lovely cheek. 'No. I would not have let you in any case.' She squared her shoulders. 'Assuming there is no more immediate danger from that witch, what do we do now?'

'We secure the boat more firmly and walk to the nearest village. There I should be able to barter for news from the fortress. I may even still have friends there.'

'A sensible plan,' said Ingrid, getting to her feet. 'Shall we begin?'

'You are not tired? Or hungry?'

'No. I feel remarkably well.'

Again, Avanasy frowned.

'I should not feel so well, should I?'

'In truth, Ingrid, I do not know.'

His words sent a thrill of fear through Ingrid, but she pushed it aside. What would come would come. She was past caution now. Her decision had been made back on Sand Island, a whole world away.

So, Ingrid knotted her skirts into her waistband and together they returned to the boat, unshipped the mast, gathered their belongings, such as they were, into bundles that could be slung over their shoulders. Finally, they drew a canvas over the hatch. As he tightened the lashings, Avanasy breathed out some words Ingrid could not understand and spat on the last knot. For a moment, he closed his eyes, and Ingrid saw a look of peace steal over him. When he opened his eyes and saw her staring, he actually blushed.

'It has been a long time since magic came easily to me,' he said by way of explanation. 'There is . . . joy in it.'

'You did . . . you made a spell, just then?'

He nodded. 'A small protection on the boat. Nothing complex or truly secure. We do not have the time. But if the boat is meddled with in any way, I will know.'

Remember the ghost, said Ingrid to herself, as she felt her face wrinkle. *Remember all you have seen.*

'You want to know if there is truth in what I say. Despite all, you cannot quite believe that it is magic which you have seen.'

'I'm sorry, Avanasy.'

'There is no need. For all you know this is dream and superstition, and the habits of a lifetime are hard to loosen. But I may give you proof yet, as soon as we are back on shore.'

Once more they clambered over the side and splashed through the chilly ocean waters to the shore. Ingrid put down her things so she could wring out her skirts. She glanced up and saw the sun was high in the sky. She hoped it would give enough warmth to dry out her clothes, or she would be far too cold, far too quickly.

While Ingrid drew her stockings and boots back on, Avanasy set his pack on a stone and from it brought out a strip of brightly braided cloth.

'I made this when I reached Sand Island, and kept it afterwards, because the making was so hard.' He ran the braid through his fingers. 'With it, I can grant you an understanding of the language of Isavalta.'

'What will you need to do?'

'Give me your hand, and I will show you.'

So Ingrid held out her hand, and Avanasy began to speak. His words were rhythmic and rich, all clipped, hard consonants and round vowels. The sound of the chant made Ingrid feel absolutely still inside. Still chanting, Avanasy wrapped the end of the braid around her right wrist, once, twice, three times. Then, he wrapped the other around his own wrist. His voice reached in her, and through her, it pulled her close, even as his hand pulled her close, and yet at the same time left her feeling incredibly distant.

Then, he kissed her full and openly on the mouth. For a startling moment, she felt his warm breath filling her lungs. In the next moment, he released her and stepped back. Ingrid pressed her hand hard against her chest.

'How does my lady?'

'Well, I thank you.' Her hand flew to her mouth. Those syllables that had tumbled out of her bore no relation to English. They were all hard consonants and round vowels.

She stared at him, both amazed and a little frightened.

'Can I still speak . . .'

'As surely as I can speak both languages,' he said, this time in English.

'That's a mercy,' she said, and then hastened to reassure him. 'Not that I thought you had taken anything from me . . .' she hesitated. 'I am simply not used . . .'

But Avanasy only smiled and shook his head. 'Give yourself time, Ingrid. I must ask for time as well. I have worked very hard to put my old life behind me.' He looked ruefully down at the embroidered cuff of his black coat. 'I will need time to find my way again.'

Ingrid took his arm. 'Then we will find it together.'

He smiled the bright smile that she had come to love, and arm-in-arm they began to pick their way up the rocky beach. Their wet boots skidded and tripped over the round stones, but they only laughed and clung more tightly to each other for balance. Ingrid felt an unfamiliar warmth creep over her. She had not realized it could be enough simply to *be* with Avanasy. That love could, for a time, be satisfied just by being in the presence of the one who was beloved. Every lover, she supposed, found out this truth, and every lover, she supposed, found it a great surprise.

Eventually, the cliffs broke, and Ingrid could see that someone had wedged stones and branches in the break to make a kind of rough trail leading upward. Despite this, it was still a scramble to reach the top. When they emerged again onto level ground, Ingrid was breathless, soaked with perspiration and salt spray, and her back had begun to ache.

Without the cliffs, the world opened around her, an undulating plain under the misty bowl of the sky. A single crabbed and crooked tree stood sentry on the cliff's edge. The land around them was covered with thin grasses and dotted here and there with bright, red flowers. At their feet, a faint track wound through the grass toward a series of shadowed mounds that Ingrid took to be some sort of village. To the right, she saw a dark rise that looked like a distant forest. To the left, she thought she could just barely make out the outlines of the fortress they had seen from the sea.

Avanasy inhaled the salt-scented air deeply. Then, he bent and plucked up one of the blossoms and presented it to Ingrid with a courtly bow.

'It is called heartsfoil,' he said as she took it. 'It is said to awaken passion.' Now his smile reminded her of all that they had not yet done, and she felt a different warmth grow inside her.

Without a word, Ingrid tucked the blossom behind her ear and took his arm again. Together, they started down the track, their gaits easy and long, despite their recent climb. It felt good to be in the open air and on level ground again.

Might as well be on our way back from a picnic, thought Ingrid absurdly.

But the thought gave her a moment's pause. 'Isn't it a risk to travel this openly? You said you were an exile.'

Avanasy scanned the land around them as well, picking out landmarks he recognized, Ingrid supposed, and regaining a feel for the place. The ceaseless breeze blew his hair back from his brow. 'It is, but it is less of a risk than acting furtively, and I have the best disguise I might at this time.'

'What is that?'

'You, Ingrid.' He rubbed her hand where it lay in the crook of his arm. 'If any are watching for my return, they will be watching for a single traveler.'

'Ah, so that's why you brought me.' Ingrid pushed her lip out into a pout. 'And here I am thinking you've fallen for my feminine wiles.'

'My grasp of your language is not complete,' Avanasy said

with an air of complete sobriety. 'I believe you will have to explain that phrase to me.'

Ingrid tossed her hair back. 'Ha! You wish that I would.'

'I do.'

They laughed again. Ingrid felt light, and free, traveling a strange track in a strange country with a man she knew so little of, and yet it was a marvel, all of it. For the first time in her life, she was not watched. Neither Mama nor Papa could catch word of what she did. There would be no shouts, no tears, no dreaded guilt and threats of blows. There was only the wind and the cries of seabirds in the distance. Her family was, quite literally, a world away, and she was free to do exactly as she would. She did not even have to think of looking after Grace, although thoughts of Grace stirred some of the old guilt that lay slumbering in the back of her mind.

Still, something pricked at her.

'Avanasy? This village, will there . . . will there be someone, a minister, or a magistrate, or some such . . .'

'To marry us?' he finished for her.

Ingrid nodded, blushing furiously. 'It's a foolish thing to bring up now, I know, but . . . I . . . you promised, and I trust you, of course, but I . . .'

He squeezed her arm gently. 'The village will have a god house, and the house will have a keeper. The keeper will be able to see us married.'

'I know it must seem ludicrous to you, Avanasy. I've come this far, but . . .'

'It is my wish to take you to wife, Ingrid, before man and the gods, and the law as well. I wish there to be no bar between us. Not ever.'

'I don't think there ever could be.'

Silence seemed enough after that.

The village that was their destination approached only

slowly. By the time they reached it, Ingrid's skirt had dried itself completely and fresh perspiration trickled down her back. She began to hope sincerely that a long, cool drink of fresh water would be available when they found human company again.

The settlement screened itself from the ceaseless winds that scoured the grasslands with a wall of stone. No guard kept the gate, however, and they were able to pass through without impediment. Ingrid felt suddenly nervous, and she had to stop herself from pulling closer to Avanasy. This would, after all, be her first meeting with other people in this strange land, and she had no idea what would be considered polite here. The fear of making herself or Avanasy ridiculous loomed very large indeed.

Still, not everything was strange. The round, stone houses with their grass roofs were silent and empty. This was, after all, a fishing village and it was a fine day. Everyone who could walk would be at work in some fashion.

The smell of smoke drifted on the wind. In silent accord they disengaged their arms and followed the scent to the rear of the village. There, old women tended huge iron kettles full of something steaming that smelled of the sea. Brown-skinned, fair-haired children ran between the kettles. They were of various ages, although none older than eight at the most, Ingrid guessed. Some played, some attempted to sort heaps of drying seaweed into piles under the eyes of the stooped old grandmothers.

The first grandmother to see them hissed a warning to the others and all chatter, all motion, stopped. Avanasy and Ingrid approached under the silent stare of a dozen strangers, and inside Ingrid felt her stomach tighten. The steam from the kettles seemed to flicker and shimmer in air gone suddenly still.

Avanasy gave them all his courtly bow. 'A good greeting to you all on this good day,' he said.

One of the women put down the huge wooden paddle she had been using to stir the kettle. She had a face like a dried apple, but blue eyes that were bright and sharp. A worn scarf covered in faded embroidery hid her hair.

'A good greeting and a good welcome to you, Stranger,' she replied, wiping her hand on an apron that had long ago been embroidered to match her scarf. 'And to your lady.'

'Thank you,' said Ingrid, bobbing a curtsy. She hoped it would be appropriate. The steam flickered strangely before her eyes again. She blinked.

'We were hoping we might find a roof to shelter us for the night,' Avanasy went on. 'We've come a long way, and have a long way to go yet.'

The wrinkled woman wiped her hands again. Her face had gone sour, but she glanced at her fellows, looking for what? Approval? Or the opposite? It was hard to tell with all the steam . . .

Something's wrong. Ingrid wiped her eyes. *Why can't I see?*

'We are a poor village,' the woman was saying. 'We have little comfort to offer such folk as yourself.'

'We do not have any wish to impose,' Avanasy replied as Ingrid lifted her gaze again. 'And will gladly lend our hands to what we can while we are here. I have some skills . . .'

Ingrid did not hear the end of Avanasy's polite speech. A man had appeared behind the children who had all clustered together to stare at the strangers. His tunic and pantaloons hung loosely on his bony frame, and he reached out to gently stroke the hair of the tallest of the boys.

He had no eyes. Like the ghost that had tried to drown Grace, his eyes were only empty sockets staring down at the young boy.

Ingrid's hand went to her throat which had suddenly closed itself up tight.

'Ingrid?'

'Is something wrong, Mistress?' inquired the leader of the women, in an icily polite voice.

The ghost laid its hand on the boy's shoulder. The child, who looked all of seven years old, didn't seem to notice anything as he drew closer to the others, staring uneasily at Ingrid.

What do I do? What do I say? It's a ghost. Oh, God, what does it want?

'Ingrid, tell me what is happening,' said Avanasy. In English. Oh, of course, of course. This way they could speak in private even in front of this whole assemblage.

'There's a ghost,' she said quickly. 'With the tall boy.'

'A ghost?' Avanasy repeated, stunned. 'You see a ghost? You're sure?'

'It's got no eyes. It's like the one who tried to take Grace.' She knuckled her eyes, uncertain whether she wished she could see the thing more clearly, or whether she could make it vanish. 'It's standing right behind him. It's got both hands on his shoulders.'

'I think we've nothing for you here,' said the headwoman edgily. 'You two had best be going.'

Avanasy swung around to face her. 'Forgive me, Mother,' he said. 'Has there been fever in your village? Any mortal illness?'

The headwoman frowned. 'And what business is that of yours?'

'Because it has not left you yet.' Avanasy strode into the crowd of children, who scattered like a flock of sparrows. He dropped to one knee in front of the tall boy. One of the grandmothers came instantly to stand behind the boy, laying both hands on his shoulders, just as the ghost had. Ingrid could still see the ghost, its features superimposed over those of the ancient living woman, turning her eyes hollow and her skin deathly gray. Ingrid shuddered.

'There's nothing to fear, lad,' Avanasy tried to reassure the boy, who just shrank backward against the grandmother's apron. 'I just wish to . . .'

'Leave him,' snapped the headwoman. She hefted the great wooden paddle in her hand, and Ingrid saw what an excellent club it would make. 'You've no business . . .'

But Avanasy cocked his head up toward her. 'His father died of fever recently, didn't he?'

The headwoman opened her mouth and closed it again. 'How did you know that?'

'His ghost is here,' said Avanasy simply, flatly. 'It may mean the boy is to be dealt the same fate.'

The grandmother gave out a shriek and hugged the boy tightly to her. The ghost had moved to her right, and was now staring at Ingrid with its black and empty eyes. Pleading? Warning? Ingrid couldn't tell.

The headwoman did not put her paddle down. 'If you're some mountebank . . .'

'I promise you, Mother, I am not. I am a sorcerer, and I can furnish proof of that, if you require. I also promise that if this boy is ill, I can help him.'

The headwoman set her jaw, and laid aside the paddle, balancing it on the kettle's rim. She marched forward and grabbed the boy by the shoulder. Startled, the boy squeaked but the grandmother – his grandmother? – let him go. The headwoman turned the boy roughly to face her while she crouched down in front of him. She seized his pointed chin and turned his face sharply this way and that. She reached up under his hair and felt the back of his neck, and then she thrust her wrinkled, callused hand down his shirt and felt about under his arms, ignoring the way he squirmed. Whatever she felt made her blanch, and she shoved the boy's tunic up to expose his bony ribs and sunken stomach; even at a distance, Ingrid could see splotches of red making a rough circle on his summer brown skin.

'Dimska's tears, no!' cried the grandmother. One of the little girls shrieked, and darted away behind the kettles, soon all the children were screaming and running away, leaving the little boy dazed in his grandmother's embrace and the old women shouting for the children to stop that nonsense!

'Take him home, Edka,' said the headwoman to the grandmother. 'We'll send for his mother.'

'But I'm not sick!' protested the boy. 'I promise I'm not. I feel fine!'

'Of course you do,' murmured his grandmother. 'This is nothing. It will pass.' But she was looking up at the headwoman as she spoke and her eyes were bright with tears. 'Come, help me home, Tiri,' she said to the boy. 'I need my tea.'

Dutifully, but with a rebellious, frightened frown, the boy took his grandmother's arm and let her lean on him as she shuffled toward the cluster of huts. The ghost, its head and shoulders drooped in what Ingrid could only believe was an attitude of misery, moved to follow them.

The women had drawn the children back, clustering around them like so many birds around their chicks, as if their bodies alone could ward off what they had just seen. The headwoman, however, rounded on Avanasy.

'What are you? What do you know of this?'

'I told you, Mother,' said Avanasy without even blinking. 'I am a sorcerer. I can help you, I promise it. It is possible that the boy need not die, nor anyone else.'

Two bright pink spots appeared on the woman's wrinkled cheeks. 'Last winter, we had a man come here. He said he was a sorcerer too. Had plenty of fine tricks to prove what he said. Said he could dose all the goats against the winter dropsy, and he did too, and took plenty of pennies for his trouble, and this spring, what do we have? Not a kid born alive, and no milk fit to drink.'

Avanasy's face hardened. It looked to Ingrid as if he wanted to curse, but he controlled himself. 'I ask no fee for my work,' he said doggedly. 'I ask only that you let me do what I can for the boy, and for your people.'

The woman's face darkened with her internal struggle. The other women huddled together, whispering and darting glances at Ingrid and Avanasy. She scanned them and their children, seeking for other traces of ghost or smoke, and saw none, much to her relief.

'And her?' said the headwoman suddenly, pointing at Ingrid. 'What will she take?'

Pride drew Ingrid's shoulders back. 'Nothing I am not freely given, I assure you, Mother,' she said.

That silenced the headwoman, but did not lighten her expression at all. 'Well, I don't know,' she said flatly. 'It'll have to be talked over. You can stay till it's decided.'

'Thank you, Mother,' said Avanasy gravely.

'Ara!' snapped the headwoman to another of the grand-mothers. 'Stop fussing, old woman, and take these two to the god house.'

A particularly ancient woman, bent almost double under her dowager's hump, broke away from the others and hobbled past them without a word. Avanasy bowed once more to the headwoman. Taking this as her cue, Ingrid curtsied again. Together they followed the ancient dame toward the center of the village.

Ingrid found she could not tell one of the round, stone huts from another, until Ara led them around to a threshold that had been painted red. Ara stood aside, gazing at them sourly as Avanasy thanked her. She did not wait about as he and Ingrid entered the gloomy hut.

When Ingrid's eyes adjusted to the dim interior, she saw a single round room with an altar in its center. The altar was a simple affair; carefully piled stones surmounted by a polished wooden plinth holding a plaque that looked to be worked brass or bronze, on which the figure of a weeping woman had been painted. She stood ankle deep in the foaming tide and a pair of gray seals raised their heads to her.

There was little else to see; some bales, baskets and folded blankets, a table and two chairs, a hearth built against one wall with a stack of firewood beside it.

'This, I imagine, is Dimska of the tears,' said Avanasy. He bent and kissed the icon. 'We should leave some gift as well.' He drew his pouch from his sash and brought out a pair of copper coins which he laid at the icon's base.

Ingrid realized she was staring. She blinked and looked away, but not soon enough. Avanasy smiled at her.

'This is very strange for you, isn't it?'

Ingrid nodded. 'Although I'm not certain what my trouble is. My family was never one for church, not really. Mother had us all baptized, and she read the Bible at Easter and Christmas, but that was the end of it.'

'To honor the divine in one form, Ingrid, is to honor all its forms. Here, the divine is Dimska,' he gestured toward the icon, 'who performed some great miracle that helped her people.'

Ingrid nodded. 'It's just one more thing to get used to, I suppose.' She shook herself. 'Avanasy, what happened out there? What did I really see? What's happening to me?' She shivered again. She couldn't help it. It was wrong, what she had seen, where she was, everything that was happening. It was all wrong, although she could not have said why.

Avanasy was beside her at once, wrapping his arms around her and pulling her close. 'Ingrid, I'm sorry. I did not foresee anything of this kind, and I should have.' He held her for a moment, and Ingrid let herself be held, letting his warmth enfold her and ease the shivering that crawled up and down her skin.

'Magic in your world is buried deeply. For it to make an appearance at all, it must be strong, but I had, I have, no good measure for how strong. What plagued your sister on your shores was in your world nothing more than a restless spirit. On this shore, it would have been a monster, a lord of the storms and hurricane. There, it touched you and left no effect. Here . . .'

'Here I'm beginning to see things.' She pulled away from him and stared out the door, looking at the tiny slice of the village it showed her; gray walls, pale roofs, gray sky, gray and stony ground. 'Oh God, and Grace tried to warn me.'

'What?'

'Before I left . . . as I was leaving actually. I thought . . . I did not take her seriously. Not really. I thought she was trying to trick me into staying, which she was . . .' Ingrid shook her head. 'Grace told me she was beginning to see things, that she'd had a premonition of Leo's accident.' She drew in a long, shaky breath. 'She thought the ghost might have done something to her.'

In the distance, she could hear the faint sound of women's voices calling and children answering. Other than that, the world was hushed.

'Probably it was not done deliberately,' said Avanasy. 'The touch of the immortal can affect the mortal being. It can bring . . . changes.'

'Changes like the second sight?' Ingrid clutched the doorframe more tightly. She could not bring herself to turn around, but she could not say why.

'Yes.'

'Is that all that's happened to me?'

'I don't know,' said Avanasy softly. 'I don't even know that I have correctly interpreted what has happened. I am far from my books and my tools.'

Ingrid nodded and bit her lip. She felt him move close behind her, but she still did not turn to look at him. She continued to stare out at the tiny piece of gray world. By straining her ears, she could just hear the sea, an eternal rushing sound that would never grow silent. She could smell its salt on the wind.

Something was happening inside her. She could feel it stirring in her blood and her bones. She had no name for it and no way to perceive what she might be at its finish. Fear gripped her, and anger at her willingness to come so far in such ignorance, for all she knew her love for Avanasy was real and that to let him leave alone would have broken her heart. And yet, and yet . . .

'You can't see ghosts?'

'Not without a great deal of preparation, no.'

'But you can help that boy?'

'Yes, if they let me.' Avanasy was very close behind her. She could feel him, close enough to touch, but not willing to do so. He would not want to feel her pull away from him. She knew that.

'And if I hadn't seen what I saw?'

'We might have been gone before he was ill enough for them to ask for help from a stranger, especially since they've been so robbed before.'

Ingrid let out a long, slow sigh. 'Well, that's something then.'

'Is it enough?'

Ingrid turned to face the man whose ring she wore. Even

in the dim light she could see the worry and hope warring with each other in his face. 'For now,' she said honestly. 'You will have to give me time, Avanasy. This is . . . unexpected is far too faint a word.'

He took her hand then and kissed it softly. 'Just remember, my heart, that you are not alone. Tell me always how it is with you, and we will come to understand this new thing together.'

'I promise,' she assured him.

He leaned forward to kiss her and she tilted her mouth up to meet his, but all at once, the world seemed filled with the sound of tramping boots and the shouting of coarse voices.

'I believe our hosts are coming home.'

As Ingrid watched the fishers flowing into their village, she was struck by the familiarity of the scene. Oh, the clothes and the faces were strange, but the attitudes – the combination of dour weariness and neighborly joviality was a thing she had witnessed all her life. Men and women called out to each other, split up to enter their homes, joked with their fellows, greeted or scolded their children, or simply stretched their backs and shoulders before stooping to enter their own doorways.

Eventually, an older man, with a gray beard that now had only a few threads of what must have been its original golden color, made his way to the god house. He glanced at Ingrid and Avanasy with one appraising blue eye.

'So. I was told you'd be here.'

Avanasy made his bow and Ingrid curtsied, but the man ignored both gestures, instead moving straight to the altar and the icon. He bowed first, laying down a small cache of shells and what Ingrid was sure were pearls. Then he kissed the icon, his eyes reverently closed. Only then did he turn to face the strangers.

'I fear you've had a thin welcome,' he said, cocking his head toward Avanasy.

'I have heard of your troubles, Keeper . . .'

'Hajek Ragdoksyn Kraichinivin,' he said, tucking his thumbs into his sash. 'And who are you, Sorcerer?'

Avanasy hesitated for a moment, and then evidently decided that the risk of the truth was less than the risk of a lie. 'I am Avanasy Finorasyn Goriainavin, and with me is Ingrid Loftfield.' Ingrid nodded to the keeper, who looked her up and down with a face gone suddenly hostile.

'A Tuukosov?' he demanded.

Avanasy touched Ingrid's arm to reassure her and shook his head. 'No, Good Keeper. She is from an island much further away than that.'

The keeper's expression relaxed at once. 'Malan'ia's calling for a parley about the two of you. I think she's hoping you'll be run out for a pair of frauds.' He pursed his lips. 'She's even muttering you brought the fever on young Iakhnor.'

'Then he has got the first flush of it?' asked Avanasy quietly.

Hajek nodded. 'So she says. I must go there now and offer Dimska's words of blessing.' He plucked one of the pearls from the altar and tucked it into his sash.

As the man turned, Avanasy said, 'And what do you think of us, Keeper?'

'Ah.' Hajek held up one thick finger. 'I think you have to be who you say, or you're a great fool to be giving out that name.' His grin showed a scattering of crooked teeth clinging to his pink gums. 'Yes, I know it well, and you thought I might. But we're loyal to the true Empress here.' His voice went suddenly grim. 'We are her people, and none other's, especially not that Hastinapuran bull who calls himself Emperor.' For a moment, Ingrid thought Hajek might spit, but he refrained, probably because of the house he was in. Instead, he just shook his head, his bearded face gone sour. 'If it's the fire and snow with Iakhnor, I'll have you sent for, and then we'll see.'

He left them there, striding out into the fading daylight, calling to people they could not see and receiving their hails in return.

'What has happened?' murmured Avanasy to his retreating back. 'What have they said? What are they doing?' His fist clenched.

'Can't you find out?' ventured Ingrid. 'Some spell . . .' it felt odd to say the word in perfect seriousness.

Avanasy shook his head, pacing to the far side of the hut. 'Scrying without the proper tools is an uncertain business. You might see the past, or the future, or, more likely, nothing at all.' He tapped the wall with his fist. 'And the proper tools can take months to create. The best take years. There was so much I could not bring with me, and so little I believed I'd need,' he added absently and Ingrid knew he was talking because he could not bear the thoughts silence would bring. 'At least part of me believed she would call me back within a few weeks, when her anger had passed. When that call did not come . . .' he shrugged. 'I did not believe I would have any need for such divinations again.'

They were silent for a moment, then Ingrid rubbed her arms. The evening was turning chill, as was only to be expected with the constant ocean wind. 'Why did the keeper say the boy had fire and snow?' she asked, changing the subject and feeling something of a coward for doing so. She knew who Avanasy was, and what had brought him to her. She could surely stand to hear him speak about it when he needed to. Surely.

'It's the local name for the fever,' he answered, circling the hut to the hearth. 'The victim turns red and white from the fever, spots and swelling.' He crouched down next to the woodpile. 'I think Dimska will not begrudge us some warmth in her house.' He reached for some kindling, but before he could lay it in the hearth, Hajek's voice sounded from outside the house.

'Sorcerer!' he called. 'Sorcerer, come quick!'

Avanasy was on his feet and out the door in the next heart-beat and Ingrid hiked up her skirts to follow fast behind him. Keeper Hajek swung around as soon as he saw them, stomping off between the scattering of round huts to one bright with flickering light and full of murmuring voices.

Hajek, Avanasy, and Ingrid had to push their way through the mass of people to get inside. It seemed as if the entire village had crammed itself into the hut to stare. The boy, Iakhnor, lay on a pallet in front of the hearth where the fire had been built up so high Ingrid feared the chimney might catch fire.

It could not have been more than two hours since they had seen the boy as wide-eyed and spry as the other young children. The change was terrifying. He lay wrapped in a blanket in front of the fire, his skin as white as paper except for fist-sized blotches of red on his cheeks and neck. Sweat poured in rivers from his face and yet he shivered constantly as if from some awful ague. A stout woman, her hair covered by an embroidered cloth, knelt beside him and buried her face in her hands, rocking back and forth while all her neighbors stood about solemn-faced and watched the boy perspiring his life away.

The ghost was there too. He stood beside the woman, but all his attention was on the boy, waiting for that last moment when the child would depart with him, Ingrid was sure of it.

'Ingrid,' murmured Avanasy, and Ingrid knelt beside the woman, wrapping her arms around her.

'Shhh,' she said, stroking the woman's head. 'Shhh, it will be all right. It will be all right.' Useless words. This woman's child was dying and it would not be all right, but the woman buried her face in Ingrid's shoulder, and sobbed and Ingrid held her, and that was all that could be done. Avanasy laid his hand on Iakhnor's head, and then his heart. He looked at the red weals, the blazing fire, and the whole village crowded in to see the contagion.

'I will need a birch pole with the bark still on it,' he said to Hajek. 'And a strip of red cloth, and salt. As much as you can bring me.'

'For what?' snapped the old woman to whom they had spoken when they first arrived. Malan'ia, Keeper Hajek had said her name was. She pushed her way to the front of the crowd. 'What will that do, Sorcerer?'

'Of itself, nothing, Mistress,' said Avanasy, working to keep his voice even. His hand still lay on Iakhnor's chest, and even over his mother's cries, Ingrid could hear the boy's breath becoming ragged. Jesus and Mary, it was taking his tiny body so fast. And they were all in here, breathing the bad air. Oh, God this was going to be a disaster.

'If I can begin before sundown,' said Avanasy firmly, 'it can allow me to drive this illness from the whole village.'

'Lies,' Malan'ia snorted. 'The boy wants sweating and beating with birch branches to stir the fever from his blood. That's all.'

Avanasy rose. Ingrid saw how hard and still he held his face as he towered over the shrunken woman. 'Mistress Malan'ia,' he said softly, but his words stilled all other voices in the hut – even the woman Ingrid cradled fell silent. 'I grieve for your losses and if I could find the one who lied so to you and yours, believe me, I would make him regret his works more than you ever could. But if I do not work quickly, by morning the boy will be dead and half your people will be ill. If I fail, you may deliver my bones to Dimska for judgment if you choose, but if I am to have any chance at success, I must begin now.'

'Burnah, you've some untrimmed birch waiting in your shed, haven't you?' asked Keeper Hajek mildly. 'And Daliunda, didn't your good man bring you home a red petticoat from the market at Musetsk?'

'He did,' said a woman's voice from the back of the crowd.

'Good,' said Hajek firmly. 'The rest of you, you will bring all the salt in your homes to the god house, and if any grain is left behind, Dimska will know it.' With that, he marched from the house.

His words might have been a spell in and of themselves, for all at once, the crowd poured out the door, each person rushing to their own home to search out what was needed. Only one wizened woman stayed behind to kneel carefully next to Ingrid and Iakhnor's mother.

'I'll take her now,' she said, kindly. 'I'm old, and if I'm to be cursed, I can be spared.'

It was doubtful the mother even knew she was being passed from one set of arms to the other. She simply sagged against the old woman, insensible in her grief.

Avanasy bowed over the boy for one more moment, his lips moving in prayer, or perhaps in promise, before he rose. 'Ingrid, I'll need your help.'

'What did she mean?' asked Ingrid as she followed him out into the sharpening night wind. 'If she's to be cursed?'

'It is believed that the mother of a dying child can pass the curse on,' he said, weaving a path back toward the god house. 'That was why no one would stand by her, lest in her frenzy, she say their name and strike them down with the illness.'

Ingrid wanted to proclaim that for superstitious nonsense, but here, who was she to say?

'Ingrid, I have a delicate question to ask you.' Avanasy halted and turned toward her.

'What is it?'

He dropped his voice to the lightest whisper. 'Are you a virgin?'

Ingrid felt all her blood rush to her face. 'Avanasy!'

'Forgive me, but it is important. As part of the spell, a ring of salt must be sowed around the village, and the salt must be dropped from the hands of a virgin woman.'

Ingrid tried to swallow her discomfort, but it was difficult. 'Yes,' she said finally. 'I could do it.'

'Thank you.'

The god house now had a steady stream of people trickling in and out through its low doorway. Each person carried a covered dish or a little cloth bundle. These they laid on the altar before kissing the icon and receiving a nod of approval from the keeper. As they departed, the villagers still glanced sideways at Avanasy and Ingrid and the suspicion Ingrid saw there tightened her throat. Avanasy did not seem to notice. He frowned up at the sky which was fading from pale gray to the color of slate with the coming night.

'Time enough but barely,' he muttered. 'Ingrid, see if the keeper has a container that can hold all the salt, and fill it. No one must touch it but you from now on.'

'I understand,' she said, although in truth she did not. She was operating on trust. This was Avanasy's world, and his work, and that would have to be enough for right now.

Once inside the god house, they found a birch branch leaning beside the hearth with the red petticoat laid beside it. Avanasy claimed them at once, drawing his knife to trim the branch into a pole and to slice the petticoat to ribbons. At Ingrid's query, Keeper Hajek produced an earthen soup pot and Ingrid began pouring the coarse and lumpy salt into it as fast as she could open bundles and dishes. The light was fading rapidly, and she could feel the tension thickening in the air.

She caught glimpses of Avanasy as she worked. He sat

cross-legged, his eyes distant, his hands busy wrapping strips of red cloth around the birch pole so that they crossed each other, and crossed again, making a complex pattern, bright red against the white bark. But she could have sworn he did not see what he did. His lips moved the entire time, working on some pattern of their own with breath and word that she could not hear.

At last, Avanasy stood. 'Come,' he said to her, and his voice was hollow. He was not there, not truly. His magic, his working, had laid hold of him and he was in a place beyond. Perhaps he was in the Land of Death and Spirit. Ingrid had no way to know.

She rested the pot of salt against her hip and followed him.

The entire village lined the rough path toward the cliff, but Ingrid was ready for their stares, and simply lifted her chin. Avanasy took no notice of them at all. His eyes were locked rigidly ahead of him, and his hand clutched the birch pole.

When they passed through the gate and stood just outside the rough wall, Avanasy rested the birch pole on the ground. He had sharpened one end, Ingrid now saw, so that it dug into the dirt.

'Sow the salt into the line I draw,' he said in his pale, hollow voice. 'We must go twelve times around the village. We must not stop or falter, no matter what you see or hear, or the working will not hold.'

'Yes,' said Ingrid. It was all she could say. This was so strange, so incomprehensible, all she could do was agree, and keep following.

Slowly, Avanasy began to drag the sharpened birch pole through the dirt. 'I call out Triaseia, who is the maiden with the unbound hair, who is the daughter of the red *rusalki*, who is the one who has taken hold in Dimska's place. I call out Triaseia who makes Iakhnor shake, by my heart and by my breath, by Dimska, Vyshko and Vyshemir. I call her out and I forbid her entry, by the transparent line I draw, by white birch and red cloth and salt sown by maiden's hands.'

Avanasy's words were hollow no more. They were heavy with purpose and fell like stones through the air that had gone suddenly and inexplicably still. Ingrid forced herself to concentrate on her strange task and scooped up a fistful of salt, allowing the grains to trickle in a tiny snowfall into the furrow Avanasy's staff plowed. They settled into the dark earth, becoming all but invisible. She could not look up to see how far she and Avanasy had traveled in their circuit, or what would be coming next. She had to keep her eyes on the furrow stretching out before her and let her salt fall carefully down. In all the world there existed only the salt, Avanasy's heavy, droning words, and the furrow, fading from her sight in the gathering dark.

But then she heard a rushing wail, as if all the sounds of sea and wind had suddenly returned, and her eyes lifted them-selves to see a woman, like a ghost but more solid, and pale as death. The ends of her hair swept the ground unhindered by any ribbon and her dress fluttered without any sash to bind it in a wind Ingrid could not feel. Her fingers raked the air, reaching for Avanasy, reaching for Ingrid herself, and Ingrid's chest tightened.

Then the woman vanished, and Ingrid saw they were again at the gates of the town.

'I call out Ogneia,' said Avanasy, without pause, without any change to his tone or the weight of his words. 'Who is the maiden with the unbound hair, who is the daughter of the red *rusalki*, who is the one who has taken hold in Dimska's place. I call out Ogneia who makes Iakhnor burn, by my heart and by my breath, by Dimska, Vyshko and Vyshemir. I call her out and I forbid her entry, by the transparent line I draw, by white birch and red cloth and salt sown by maiden's hands.'

Time vanished, sense of place and self vanished. The moon must have risen, because she could see the furrow stand out as a black line against the silver ground. The salt glowed white as it showered down from her fist. She should have been cold. She should have been tired, but she was aware of these things only dimly. The words carried her forward, the words and her task. Salt was lifted from bowl to hand to be poured into the dark line of the soil. The salt rubbed her hand until it was so tender she imagined she could feel every grain that spilled through her fingers. The pale maidens – Ledia, Gneteia, Grynusha, Glukheia, and all their sisters – with their ghost-locks and their wails that sounded like the sea, appeared one by one, hooking their clawed fingers into the wind itself in their fury, only to vanish, dragged into the earth by the weight of Avanasy's working.

Then, after a time that might have been a few hours or a few hundred years for all Ingrid could tell, they came again to the gates, again a pale maiden rose and choked on the air and drowned in earth, and Avanasy did not move on. He stood, leaning on the birch staff, and Ingrid blinked stupidly up at him, dazed by her efforts, by all she had seen and by the magic.

Together their knees buckled and, slowly, almost carefully, they fell to the ground, slumping forward to lean against each other. As the darkness took hold of her, Ingrid was aware of Avanasy's breathing and of three words. 'It is done.'

After that, for a time, there was nothing else. Then, it seemed to Ingrid she must be dreaming, for she stood at the edge of the village, just beyond the salted furrow, and she watched while the fishers flowed out of their huts. Under the direction of Keeper Hajek, they lifted herself and Avanasy up and carefully bore them away, leaving her alone there in the night.

Then, she heard a noise, and she turned and saw a man on horseback. He wore chainmail and a thick coat and carried a pennant in his right hand, and all about him was as red as blood or sunset. He looked down on her for a long moment, but she could not distinctly see his face. She opened her mouth to speak, but she could form no words.

The man wheeled his horse around and urged it into a trot until they were both lost in the darkness. Curiosity washed through Ingrid to know where he had gone, and she moved to follow, but then, just as strong, she felt a tugging in her heart, calling her back to the village, back across the salt furrow, back to sleep and herself, and the world swam and was dark again.

Baba Yaga stood at the door of her house, Ishbushka. Two huge, black dogs flanked her. Ishbushka's taloned legs were for the moment still as its mistress watched the lands out beyond her mended fence of bone.

Eventually, the thin and dying birch tree that stood beyond her gate drew back its branches. From behind it rode a blood-red horse guided by a rider who himself was dressed in the same red and who carried a plain red pennant in his gloved fist.

The gate in the bone fence swung open to admit him. The rider walked his horse up to Ishbushka's ragged and splintered steps. He stood in his stirrups and bowed low to the witch. In turn, she bared her iron teeth to him.

'What did you see?' she asked.

'The woman's spirit is housed securely enough by her flesh when the sun is in the sky,' he replied. 'But at night, its will is to fly free.'

'Good,' said the witch, laying one crabbed hand on her dog's head. 'Very good.'

Chapter Eleven

'You are certain, Old Woman?'

Garrison Commander Mareshka was in a black mood. The dispatches coming out of Vaknevos spelled nothing good. The Empress in confinement. The border patrols being stepped up. The garrison forts all being ordered to inspect and repair their walls, and to prepare to receive new levies of men. Something was in the wind, and it did not bode well for what had, so far, been his quiet command.

Pirates and smugglers did not as a rule favor these waters. There were too few people to help shelter them, or to buy what they brought. Those that came were ready to pay for safe passage. His men were in general surly, but he'd never met a crew of bored soldiers that weren't. He kept them as busy as he could with regular patrols and drills, and made sure the rotations for supply duty out to Manesk, the nearest town big enough to have both liquor and women freely available, were regular.

He was not in the least pleased to have been roused from his bed by his over-lieutenant saying there was a fisherwoman in the keep swearing up and down that the traitor Avanasy was asleep in her village.

'He gave his name to the keeper of our god house,' she said.

She, withered old creature that she was, did not seem in the least tired. She held her chin high and her back straight with the force of her righteousness. 'He has given a display of his power. It is the sorcerer. I will swear to it.'

'No need,' Mareshka waved his hand, ending the gesture by clapping it over his mouth to stifle a yawn. 'Who did you tell before coming here?'

The woman's wrinkled chin rose a little bit higher. 'No one. I am here alone.'

'Then if we bring him in, and it is him, yours alone is the reward.' Mareshka tried to brush a few of the wrinkles out of his uniform coat.

'Keep it,' spat the old woman, and the force of her tone made Mareshka look up in surprise. 'Just get him away from us.'

Curiosity narrowed Mareshka's eyes. 'What's he done to you, old woman?'

'He is a sorcerer.' Anger burned in her words. 'That is enough.'

As you please. Mareshka shrugged and turned in his chair toward his over-lieutenant, who had stood at ease beside the door during the entire conversation. 'Over-Lieutenant Dajik, you will pick four men. Make sure they carry cold iron. Mistress Malan'ia will guide you to her village . . .'

'Not I.' The old woman stepped away. 'I must get back before light. There are fools who will turn on me if they know what I have done here.'

Mareshka shrugged again. 'You will take her directions to her village,' he amended. 'You will arrest Lord Avanasy, and you will bring him back here.'

'He has a woman with him,' Malan'ia warned. 'She's as clever and glib as he is.'

'And you will bring any companions he has as well,'

Mareshka said smoothly to his over-lieutenant. 'Is there anything else I should know, Mother?' He let his voice take on an edge, hoping the vindictive creature would realize this was her one chance to give him complete information, or things might not be so pleasant for her.

In response, the woman folded her arms across her breast and bent her knees in a peasant's reverence. 'That's all, Master,' she said.

It had better be. 'Very well. Over-Lieutenant, you have your orders, and you will see that Mother Malan'ia is escorted to the gate.'

'Sir.' Dajik put his hand over his heart and bowed. Then he stepped smartly back, pushing open the door to allow Malan'ia to stride through with remarkable speed for one so old.

When they were gone, Mareshka yawned hugely and knuckled his eyes. Out past the door, he heard the rumble of Dajik's voice, probably giving orders to his under-lieutenant to get Malan'ia out of the fort. So, he waited.

As he suspected, a moment later, Dajik knocked and walked back into the office.

'Yes, Over-Lieutenant?' inquired Mareshka, folding his hands across his stomach.

'Sir.' Dajik reverenced again. 'Sir, I just wanted ...' Mareshka raised his eyebrows and waited. 'Do you honestly believe we will catch Avanasy napping in some fishing village?'

Mareshka lifted one corner of his mouth in a slight smile. 'I believe if we do, you and I will find ourselves with commendations and bonuses for our trouble. If not, it will let us see how some of your men do going into a village to drag out someone who may be more popular there than they are.'

'Do you think he's being willingly harbored, Sir?' Dajik's brow wrinkled.

'I think our fishwife did not want her neighbors to know

what she was doing for a reason,' Mareshka replied. 'You have your orders, Over-Lieutenant.'

'Sir.'

Dajik left, and this time Mareshka heard his boots marching down the hallway. Mareshka sighed and rubbed his eyes again. With all that was ringing around his head, it probably wasn't worth returning to bed to toss and turn for the few hours of darkness that were left. Instead, he took himself out into the stone hallway, up a narrow, curving stairway and out onto the battlements. The salt wind from the ocean hit him on the back of his neck, making him shiver, and at the same time bringing him instantly awake. The night's patrol saluted him smartly with their pikes as they marched by, and Mareshka answered the gesture with his hand over his heart.

Mareshka turned inland. The stars still shone brightly overhead, but the moon had long since set. Dawn was a thin, white line on the horizon. Mareshka leaned his hands on the parapet and gazed across the dark carpet of the land, trying to guess what was happening. It smelled strongly like war. But war against whom? And what was it that brought Avanasy back into Isavalta just when the Empress had retired from public view? Mareshka shivered again, but more from his thoughts than from the wind this time. It smelled strongly like war, and that war smelled bad.

In a little while, he heard the rumble and creak of the gates cranking open. A cluster of men on horseback, four of them bearing lanterns, rode out, heading due east along the rutted road. As their hoofbeats faded, the gates cranked shut, and quiet fell again.

Mareshka stared out into the coming dawn for awhile longer, turning his uncomfortable thoughts over in his head. Then, because there was nothing else to do, he turned and went back down the stairs.

As a result, he did not see the single rider emerge from the rubble by the cliff's edge and follow slowly and carefully after his men.

Ingrid woke alone to a dim room, a raging thirst and utter confusion. For a long, tense moment she recognized nothing around her. The shadows were all the wrong shape and why was she wrapped in blankets on the floor instead of in bed with Grace?

Fragments of memory surfaced gradually. The voyage and its dreams, which were not dreams, the village, Avanasy and the magic.

Where is Avanasy?

Ingrid disentangled herself from the rough blankets and got to her feet, appalled to find her knees weak enough to tremble underneath her.

'Good morning, Mistress.' Keeper Hajek ducked through the doorway, toting a bucket in his gnarled hands. 'I have brought us water.'

Ingrid thought she might fall to her knees in gratitude as Hajek handed her a clay dipper. She drank ladle after ladle from the bucket before she felt her thirst begin to ebb.

'Thank you, Keeper Hajek,' she was finally able to say. 'Do you know where Avanasy is?'

'He is with Iakhnor.' Hajek took a deep draft from the dipper.

'How is the boy this morning?'

Hajek lowered the dipper to reveal a large grin. 'The boy is complaining because his mother is keeping him in bed another day. The fever's tokens have vanished.'

Relief and unexpected pride washed through Ingrid. 'That's wonderful.'

'You and Lord Avanasy have surely saved us all, Mistress,' he told her, setting the bucket aside and wiping the water from his beard. 'It was Dimska herself who sent you to us.'

Lord Avanasy? thought Ingrid absurdly. *There is something he neglected to tell me.*

Even as that thought spread another smile on her face, Avanasy entered the god house. The dim light did not hide his own pleased grin.

'Lord Avanasy?' she inquired, in English.

'It is only an honorary title,' he replied with a dismissiveness Ingrid found a bit too lofty to be entirely trusted.

Before Ingrid could make any further remark on the subject, Hajek said, 'Will you break bread with me before Dimska today, Lord Avanasy? The village will wish to thank you publicly tonight, I am certain.'

Avanasy looked to Ingrid, but Ingrid just raised her eyebrows to indicate this was his decision. 'I do thank you, Keeper,' he said, 'but I fear we must be gone before the evening falls.'

'I am sorry for it,' said the keeper. 'But not surprised to hear it. Still, let me help you break your fast.'

Breakfast turned out to be thick black bread toasted on the hearth together with a potted paste made of dried and salted fish. All this was washed down with drafts of cool water. The meal tasted strange to Ingrid, but she was now as hungry as she had been thirsty before, and was not in the mood to decline any food, even if she could have done so without giving offense.

After they had eaten for a time in polite silence, Avanasy turned to Hajek. 'Good Keeper, you recognized my name when I gave it . . .'

'The garrison sends men down here every so often.' Hajek jerked his chin in the general direction of the coast and the fortress. 'They buy our catch and salt. Sometimes they drop a bit of news. More often they grumble in our hearing and we take our news that way.'

'Have you had any news from Vyshtavos?' He was doing his best to keep the strain of worry out of his voice, and not entirely succeeding.

Keeper Hajek made a face around his current mouthful as if he was keeping down a laugh. But then he swallowed and regained his countenance. 'Precious little of that sort reaches this far, Lord. We were, of course, commanded to pray for the Empress and the new heir . . .'

'What!' cried Avanasy.

Hajek blinked. 'The Empress is with child. She has gone into her confinement.'

Avanasy's whole face tightened, and Ingrid knew he did not believe what he had just been told. She remembered what he said about the difficulty for sorcerers to get children.

'Is there any other news?' Avanasy went on, his voice hard.

'There's been some . . .'

Before Hajek could finish what he meant to say, a boy rushed through the door. He bowed hastily to the icon and ran up to the keeper.

'What is it?' asked Hajek.

'Soldiers,' panted the boy. 'Riding fast.'

Hajek wiped the crumbs from his beard. 'I doubt they're in that much of a hurry for fresh fish . . .' He stood. 'Perhaps, Master, Mistress, you should stay here. We will meet them at the wall.'

Hajek put a hand on the boy's shoulder and steered him out the door.

Ingrid rose together with Avanasy and they followed the keeper as far as the door.

'You believe this will be for us then?' she asked him softly in English as they waited in the shadows.

Avanasy nodded. 'But what that means depends on who it is.'

Which was no sort of reassurance, but Ingrid was certain Avanasy knew that.

Outside the low arch of the doorway, the morning was bright and cloudless. It might even have been hot, if it were not for the constant ocean wind. Only a few voices drifted through the village. Ingrid realized she must have been very soundly asleep, for she had not heard what had surely been the considerable noise of the village rising early to go work their nets.

In the far distance, she could just make out the rhythmic thudding of hoofbeats on turf. If they had been riding fast, as the child reported, they did not do so now. There was more than one horse, but they moved at a steady walk.

Perspiration prickled the back of Ingrid's neck.

Keeper Hajek's voice raised itself on the wind, possibly in greeting. Ingrid could not make out the words. Another man's voice answered. Avanasy pressed his hands against the wall as if that could help him hear better.

'Three of them, at least,' he murmured. 'I cannot hear the names.'

Ingrid strained her own ears. The men's voices lifted and lowered, as if in easy conversation.

'They don't sound as if they're making demands,' she ventured.

'Yet.' Avanasy's jaw worked back and forth. 'If only there was some way . . .'

But he was not allowed to finish his wish.

'Will you come out then, my Lord?' inquired a man's polite voice. 'And whoever's in there with you. I charge you in the Empress's name.'

Ingrid's heart leapt into her throat, choking her. It was so neat, she could see at once what had happened. While some of the soldiers had kept Hajek busy talking at the gate, others had circled around the back of the village, crept between the houses, and found the place where the strangers were most likely to be sheltered. Overhearing their whispered conversation, the soldiers ordered the strangers out.

For all the anger and self-reproach in Avanasy's eyes, there was nothing to be done. The god house had only one door and no windows at all.

Shoulder-to-shoulder, they walked out into the sunlight.

Three soldiers met them with swords drawn. They had taken care to stand so their shadows would not cross into the line of sight of the threshold and give away their presence. They were all brown from sun and wind. Two had golden hair showing underneath their helmets and heavy beards concealing their faces. The third was younger and slighter. His beard was neatly trimmed along the line of his pointed chin and his eyes glittered as he looked Avanasy and Ingrid over.

Uniform seemed to be woolen coats with chainmail over all and breastplates over that. The rows of braid and brass buttons on cuffs and collars were probably indications of rank. Leather gloves covered their hands, and worn leather boots their legs, just below the round steel caps that protected their knees. Their swords were clean and straight, and glinted in the sun and Ingrid suddenly felt very keenly that her neck was quite bare.

'Thank you, my Lord,' said the one with the trimmed beard. 'It is best to do these things quietly, don't you agree?'

In reply, Avanasy drew himself up to his full height. 'Over-Lieutenant, I have been summoned back to Isavalta by Imperial order. The errand is urgent, and must not be hindered.'

'And my commander will be happy to examine any documents you carry to prove your assertions,' said the over-lieutenant, sounding like the soul of reason. 'In the meantime, my orders are to return you and any companions you may have,' his eyes raked Ingrid over, 'to our fortress. So, if you will be so good as to walk with us, and to remain quiet.' He gestured with his free hand, indicating that they should start toward the rear of the village.

Avanasy's fists opened and closed, but they were unarmed, and the soldiers surrounded them. He brushed his fingertips against the back of Ingrid's hand, as if to reassure himself that she remained solid, and they turned and walked as they were ordered. One soldier took up position on either side of them, and the over-lieutenant brought up the rear.

Avanasy held his head and shoulders proudly as they were marched through the village, but his eyes were never still. They darted this way and that, looking for a way out of this, Ingrid was certain. She tried to do the same, but all she seemed able to see were the glinting swords in the hands of the armored men that flanked them. Her mouth had gone as dry as dust and her brains seemed to have fled.

But if they were unarmed, they were not unnoticed. Their escort led them around another hut, and straight into the grandmothers. Two of them carried the big wooden bats used for stirring the kettles. Another pair carried a kettle between them full of steaming green water that smelled of seaweed. The others, maybe half a dozen old women, just stood like stones, blocking the way and making no noise at all.

Which left Ingrid wondering where the children were.

'Good morning, Honored Grandmother,' said the over-lieutenant. 'How do I find you on this fine morning?'

'You've two guests of ours there,' said one of the old women, a squat creature, wrinkled and brown as the stump of a tree. It was then Ingrid noticed that Malan'ia was also nowhere to be seen. 'We're here to say you'd best leave them be.'

'Grandmother, I honor your respect for the laws of hospitality,' the over-lieutenant replied seriously. Beside Ingrid, the bearded soldier shifted uneasily. His eyes seemed to be counting the old women, and taking in the long wooden bats, and the steaming iron kettle. 'But these two are wanted for questioning. If they've done nothing, they'll be back with you soon, you may be sure of it.'

'You'd best leave them be,' repeated the old woman. 'There's no trouble wanted here.'

'You old fools!' cried a different voice.

Ingrid began to realize what a warren this village really was. A place of dark doorways and careful ears, where anyone might appear from anywhere. Apparently the soldiers did too, because the new voice made them all jump.

Malan'ia stormed out from one of the doorways. 'What are you doing?' she shrilled. 'Do you want to see the entire village burned to the ground?' She planted herself squarely between the villagers and the soldiers. 'Burned for a sorcerer?' she sneered. 'Have your brains all turned to sea foam? Do we need that much more trouble? Let them pass!'

The squat woman narrowed her eyes. 'Malan'ia, it may be you'd better stand back too.'

'Stand back and what?' demanded Malan'ia, hands planted on hips. 'Let you kill us all? Let you wipe our home away into memory? Get along with you, all you old fools! This has nothing to do with us!'

'Be advised by your good friend here, Grandmother. We're taking our leave, and our prisoners now.'

The over-lieutenant tried to start forward. The squat woman stepped into his path. The flanking soldiers drew in closer to Avanasy and Ingrid. Ingrid heard the blood singing in her ears. Malan'ia, with a snort of derision, raised the back of her hand to the squat woman and slapped her full across the face.

At the same time, Avanasy grabbed the soldier beside him, and using his sword arm as a lever, swung the man around and sent him careening into the over-lieutenant.

'Run!' he shouted to Ingrid.

But Ingrid had no intention of doing such a thing. Her flanking soldier lunged for her, and she dove forward, measuring her length on the ground and rolling sideways. As she did, the two old women with the kettle hefted it in one motion and flung its contents straight in the soldier's face. He reeled back screaming as the boiling water drenched him and the weed wrapped his hands and face. He fell, clawing at the green mass that clung to his face, searing his skin and blinding him.

Ingrid scrambled to her feet. For an instant, she saw Avanasy facing the over-lieutenant with one of the paddles in his hands. In the next heartbeat, Malan'ia was on her, pushing and pinching, with sharp elbows and sharp fingers. Ingrid staggered backwards, and tried to shove the old woman aside, but she was tougher and more wiry than Ingrid had given her credit for, and she just pushed back, sending Ingrid stumbling toward the remaining soldier, before the other woman reached her, and pulled her, cursing, back.

'Let them go, damn you! You'll have us all put to the sword for a *sorcerer*!'

The second soldier wrapped one brawny arm around Ingrid from behind. She kicked back, but her shoes found nothing but armor and leather.

Avanasy parried the over-lieutenant's blows with the stout paddle, but splinters flew with each cut. Only the length of the thing kept the over-lieutenant back, and it would not hold much longer.

'Sorcerer!' the soldier bellowed. 'I've got your woman!'

Avanasy swung around, and the over-lieutenant pulled his

sword back to aim a fresh blow. Ingrid cried out in warning, but at the same moment, she heard the sound of galloping hooves.

The soldier wrenched Ingrid around toward the sound. The over-lieutenant hesitated just long enough and Avanasy dodged the blow. The old women screamed, scattering like leaves, and another soldier on horseback plunged between the huts.

He held no sword, but a pike, and he bore down on Avanasy. Ingrid screamed. She could not help it. But the blow did not catch Avanasy. Instead, it sent the over-lieutenant spinning and crying out, dropping into the dust, his sword falling from his hand.

The rider wheeled his roan horse around in a tight and expert circle. The soldier behind Ingrid tightened his grip until she could barely breathe, dragging her back from the rider. The edge of his sword pressed against her belly.

'Let her go,' said Avanasy, his voice low and dangerous as he picked up the sword dropped by the fallen over-lieutenant. His gaze never left the soldier.

The rider closed in beside Avanasy, his pike lowered and ready. Ingrid could make out nothing of his face in the shadow of his helmet, but his coat was bright blue and its trimmings were gold.

The wind carried yet another new roar, over the perpetual sound of the ocean. The sound of men's angry voices, a lot of them, and Ingrid suddenly knew where the children had gone. Their grandmothers had sent them scampering down the cliffs to call back the fishermen, the young men with strong backs and arms, carrying nets and hooks and perhaps even spears for their work. Horses neighed and voices cursed, and yet more voices roared, and the soldier holding Ingrid swung her around yet again, and she felt his grip slacken.

Ingrid threw herself sideways, lunging with all her weight, and trusting desperately to her woolen petticoats to keep the edge of the sword from her flesh. She fell again into the dust, skinning her palms and banging her chin so hard it rattled her teeth. Hooves started behind her and she rolled again in time to see the soldier trying to flee from the horseman, and taking the blow from the pike straight in his back so he too went sprawling in the dust. This time the old women got him, falling on him, rolling him over, kicking and beating wherever there was enough bare flesh to make a target. The over-lieutenant staggered to his feet, but the horseman wheeled around again and charged back. This time the over-lieutenant took the blow on his helmet, fell backwards, and stayed down.

Evidently satisfied with his work, the rider stilled his horse, and patted its neck as he dismounted. His free hand worked the straps on his helmet and he pulled it off.

As soon as the sunlight touched his face, Avanasy gave a delighted shout.

'Peshek!' Avanasy ran forward and clasped the man's shoulder.

'Avanasy!' The rider grinned in return. 'Still don't know when to run, do you?'

'It would seem not.' Avanasy laughed with him, sounding happier than he had since they arrived in the village.

'And who is this good lady?' The man, Peshek, turned toward her.

Ingrid had never seen a man as straightforwardly handsome as Peshek. His hair was a rich chestnut, his eyes were summer blue. His face was strong and open and his shoulders broad. All about him hung an air of easy confidence. Despite herself, Ingrid felt her cheeks begin to redden as he regarded her.

'She is Ingrid Loftfield of Sand Island in the United States of America, and she is to be my wife, Peshek. So, you may keep those rogue's eyes to yourself,' he added with a mock growl.

'Wife!' Peshek exclaimed, genuinely startled. 'What . . .' he stopped himself. 'Well,' he amended. 'I knew there was no woman of Isavalta good enough for Avanasy. My greetings and my duty, Mistress.' Peshek bowed to her with his hand over his heart.

'Thank you, Sir,' said Ingrid, curtsying. 'Your timing is excellent.'

'And you are not the first woman to tell him so.' Avanasy laughed again. 'Quick, Peshek, come stand here by me. I think a second rescue is coming.'

Sure enough, the tide of village men boiled around the houses, coming from all directions to cut off any retreat, and what they found was Ingrid, Avanasy, Peshek, the horse, which danced back nervously, the old women, and the fallen soldiers. Peshek grabbed his horse's reins and patted the animal's nose to soothe it.

Two of the fishers with wicked-looking iron hooks in their hands started forward from the crowd.

'I beg you, put up your arms,' said Avanasy, stepping into their path. 'This man is a friend and helped us in our need.' Grumbling, the fishers fell back, but their suspicious eyes did not leave Peshek.

All of which was too much for Malan'ia.

'You've slain us all!' she cried, shedding tears even as she glared around at her neighbors. 'Just see if you haven't! How long do you think it will be before the garrison sends out a search for this lot!' She swept out her hands to indicate the fallen soldiers. The over-lieutenant lay still as death. The unin-jured man gazed around with wide and nervous eyes, but did not seem to think it wise to move.

Malan'ia spat on the ground and stumped back into her house.

'I think you will not need to look far to see how the garrison knew you were here,' murmured Peshek very softly, stroking his horse's nose again. Then, he raised his voice. 'I fear she is right. I saw their horses making straight back to the fort. If they are found without their riders, a search party will go out immediately.'

Keeper Hajek made his way to the head of the crowd of fishers, saying, 'If we send some men out now, we might still be able to catch them.'

'That will help for awhile,' agreed Peshek. 'But not for long. The best course for the three of us is to be gone from here.'

Hajek nodded. He pointed to one cluster of fishermen who all carried stout ropes over their shoulders. 'Get you out and find those horses if you can.' To another group he said, 'Take these three out of sight, and then you'd better see to the others by the gate.' The men growled their affirmation, and with three of them to a soldier, they hauled them out of sight. The rest of the village parted to let the men through, and muttered uneasily among themselves. Ingrid caught Malan'ia's name spoken several times, and the tone used was not friendly.

Apparently, Hajek heard it too. 'Friends, friends,' he called. 'There's work to be done, and if we're missed from the cliffs, suspicions will rise fast and high.'

Hajek stepped smartly up to Avanasy and Ingrid and bowed in front of them, adding a nod for Peshek, who returned it gravely. The rest of the village followed suit, all of them bowing with great solemnity, leaving Ingrid feeling like the guest of honor at a huge country wedding. As Hajek led his people away, their voices lifted high in song.

'Let the waves roll, let the wind roar,
'You've brought me home, from many's the shore.
'Your eyes light the moon, your tears fill the sea,
'Your hands hold my heart, your voice calls to me.'

A question filled Ingrid as the villagers departed to their tasks. She was sure she did not want to know the answer, but she could not stop herself from asking, 'What will they do with the soldiers?'

'They will make sure the men do not follow us,' said Avanasy flatly, and his cold voice told Ingrid all she needed to know. 'Come, Ingrid. Let us get our things. We'll take shelter beneath the cliffs. There'll be a moon tonight and we can sail out after dark.'

Ingrid tried to catch Avanasy's eye, to get some reassurance from his voice or his manner, but there was none. He was distant from her, although they walked side-by-side with Peshek leading his horse behind them. His mind was on his Empress and thoughts of the danger to the empire, and she would have to try to wait him out with as much patience as she could muster. But she did not feel content to wait. Something pulled at her, some restlessness like the sensation left over from a bad dream made her uneasy inside, and she could not give it a name.

Avanasy watched Ingrid sink into her own silence, and he regretted it. He wanted to speak comfort to her, but he had not words. A day and a night in Isavalta, and he had already condemned five men to death for carrying out their lawful orders. The first casualties of the war to come.

No, Iakush came before them, and I'll lay all I own down that even he was not the first.

Peshek waited outside the god house with his horse while Avanasy and Ingrid went inside to pick up their bundles and sling them over their shoulders again. Avanasy took this heart-beat of privacy to touch Ingrid's arm and look into her eyes. She returned a small smile that held no more than a spark of warmth, but there was no time now to inquire as to just what troubled her. He would have to trust to her patience a little longer.

There was no question of Peshek's horse being able to negotiate the path that had brought Avanasy and Ingrid up to the village, so they were forced to head eastward along the coastline, until the cliffs gentled into hills, and then trek back over sand and stone, following the waterline as the waves ebbed and surged at their right hand.

At last, with much coaxing for the skittish, tired horse, they made their way around the rocky point to the cove that sheltered Avanasy's boat. Salt stung his lips and sand grated against his skin. Ingrid looked wan, and even Peshek's banter had ceased to make her smile.

Peshek seemed to have already forgotten the men left behind, but that was ever his way. He lived for now and for what was to come. The past was over and done with as soon as it happened. He did as he must, loved as he would, and never labored under any shadow. Avanasy sometimes envied him, and sometimes grew exasperated for his carelessness. Added to all that, he suspected that the nagging that teased at his insides as he watched Peshek coax Ingrid with his light words – telling her of the pleasant sights that Isavalta held – was the first mild stirring of jealousy.

Which was so ridiculous, he had to laugh, grimly and silently, at himself.

'Well,' announced Peshek, gazing at the narrow cove about him. 'Not so fine as your other country home, Avanasy, but I'm sure all the fresh air is most healthful.'

'It wants a woman's touch,' replied Ingrid. 'And a fire. I'll see if there's driftwood to be found. I'm sure you two need to talk.' Before Avanasy could offer advice or caution, she plonked her bundle onto a boulder and started down the shoreline again, pausing here and there to pick up what drift-wood she found.

While Ingrid wandered farther afield, Peshek busied himself with his horse, uncinching the animal's tack and laying it aside. Relieved of its bridle, the horse began to nose among the rocks, in case there was some shred of edible greenery to be found.

'She's a fair one, Avanasy,' he said cheerfully, as he bent down to take up the horse's near hoof and check for stones. 'But I'd stay on the right side of her tongue if I were in your shoes.'

'If you were in my shoes, you'd have wedded her and bedded her months since, rascal that you are,' joked Avanasy in answer, but his humor did not last long. 'Peshek, what has happened? Is the Empress truly with child? The Lord Sorcerer said nothing of it.'

Peshek shook his head, and straightened up. 'Nothing so simple. Where is Lord Iakush? I cannot believe he stayed away when all is falling apart.'

'He's dead, Peshek. Kacha killed him.'

Peshek's face turned thunderous, and he spat. 'Not the first and not the last by a long chalk,' he muttered with grim prophecy. 'The Empress is not with child. She is fled her palace, and all that comes out of there are Kacha's lies.'

Avanasy's cheeks paled as Peshek told him how he had taken the disguised Empress from Vaknevos, and how he had been charmed to sleep and she had escaped his custody.

'She bids you meet her at the Heart of the World. I know no more than that.' Peshek turned away again, laying both hands on his horse's mane. The creature snorted and stamped one hoof. Despite his attempt to hide it, Avanasy clearly saw the shame that filled Peshek. 'I am glad you are back with us, Avanasy,' he said.

Avanasy thumped his thigh with his fist. 'How is he able to do this! Kacha is no sorcerer, yet magic comes under his hands. Only through magic could he deceive the entire Council and put Medeoan to flight.'

'And it is not possible all the Council Lords are traitors,' added Peshek. 'Fools, perhaps, scheming, perhaps, but most of them believe in the empire.'

'Which is why they are Council Lords.' Avanasy stared past his friend toward the rushing gray ocean. The foam-crested waves spoke in their wordless, unceasing voices and gave him no answers at all. 'This is a deep plot, Peshek, and it was set in motion well before Kacha was sent to wed Medeoan. Why did I let her send me away?'

'Because you are of more use to her alive than dead, wherever you might be, and you knew that.' He shook his head. 'Still, the news is not all bad.' Peshek went on to tell Avanasy of his meeting with his father, and how word was spreading to find the truly loyal.

Avanasy blew out a sigh to the dimming air. 'I should have known you would not be idle. This will be good news to give to the Empress when I reach her.'

'So I hoped.' Peshek pulled on the fingers of his gloves for a moment. Then, he said in a low voice, 'A wife, Avanasy? In truth?'

'We have not been prayed over yet, but, yes, I have given her my pledge.'

'Was that wise? The Empress . . . now that Kacha has betrayed her, she's going to turn back to you, and . . .'

Avanasy held up his hand. 'No more, Peshek.'

'Avanasy, you are not a fool.'

'No. But there are things that may not be spoken of. Not even here in the middle of nowhere. I fell in love. I made a promise. I did not believe I would ever be welcomed back, and when I was sent for, I could not abandon her.' His eyes instantly searched the mouth of the cove for Ingrid, but did not see her. It was just as well. This was not a conversation he wanted her to hear.

'And what will you do when you face our Mistress Imperial again?' inquired Peshek mildly.

'What I must. But I will not desert Ingrid, Peshek. She holds my heart.'

Peshek simply shrugged at this, and changed the subject. 'Can you get us to the Heart of the World?'

Avanasy nodded once. 'I can, but I won't be taking you, Friend Peshek.'

'And why not?' Peshek's voice filled with mock indignation.

'Because we need to know the true state of things among the Lords Master and at the court, and there must be someone utterly trustworthy who can carry that news between those who join with your father. I cannot find out so much and still reach the Empress, but you can.'

For the first time, hesitation crept into Peshek's manner. 'You cannot believe they do not know what I have done.'

'I'm counting on it,' Avanasy told him, making sure Peshek could see his whole face, so that the soldier would know Avanasy was not asking this of him lightly. 'It is how you will know friend from foe.'

'So, I am to walk into the wasps' nest and count their numbers for you?'

'Yes.'

Peshek sighed. 'Are there any other miracles you wish me to perform?'

'No, that should be sufficient, and I thank you.'

Neither man laughed, but neither did they look away from each other.

'For what it is worth, and in spite of what you've just asked of me,' Peshek smiled wryly, 'I am glad you have come back.'

'It is worth more than you know.' Avanasy leaned one foot against a stone. 'I had scarce hoped to find so good a friend so soon upon my return.'

They clasped hands then, but only for a moment before Peshek turned his eyes to the sky. 'There's little enough daylight left. I'd best be getting on.'

Without another word, Peshek picked up his saddle and settled it back onto his horse. The beast snorted and danced in annoyance at being encumbered again so soon, but Peshek went about the business of cinching girth and harness with a practiced hand.

'How shall I get word to you, all the way out there in the Heart of the World?' he asked.

'I'll send a bird to you. Speak your message to it, and that message will be borne to me.'

Peshek turned, one foot in the stirrup and both hands on the saddle, ready to hoist himself onto the horse's back. 'You are in earnest, aren't you?'

Avanasy nodded, and Peshek just whistled as he mounted and gathered up his reins. 'What a marvelous thing to be a sorcerer. Good luck to you, Avanasy. Send your bird soon.'

With the slightest touch of the reins and a soft click of Peshek's tongue, the horse started forward, careful of the loose stones. Avanasy watched horse and rider pick their cautious way along the waterline, leaving footprints on the darkened sand, and his heart lifted a little, despite all. If there was anyone he could have hoped to find upon his return, other than Medeoan herself, Peshek was that one.

Be strong, Medeoan, Avanasy thought, gazing out across the ocean, which had dimmed to charcoal gray in the shadows of the cliffs. *Wherever you are, I will be with you soon, and together we will restore you to your place.*

He felt the boat through his spell of protection rather than saw it clearly anymore. They should get aboard. Once the moon rose, they could be on their way.

And Ingrid should have been back with whatever firewood she'd found ages ago. With that thought, Avanasy realized how cold the wind off the water had become. His cheeks and hands tingled, and, for a moment, his breath drew sharply.

He clambered over boulders and stones that were little more than lumps of shadow in the deepening night, following the direction Ingrid had taken and cursing himself for forgetting her, even for an instant. He pulled himself over the outcropping that protruded from the cliff, and stood for a moment, taking the measure of the rocky land and dark water all under the sky that had dimmed to indigo.

In the distance he saw a figure, and realized that not even in the darkness could he mistake Ingrid's silhouette. She stood with her arms folded and her head tilted upward to gaze at the cloudless heavens.

Relief as much as exertion warmed Avanasy, as he picked his way to her side.

'And how fares my lady?'

'I shall have to learn a whole new sky full of stars,' she answered him without looking down. 'Otherwise how will I know which way I'm going?'

Worry stirred inside Avanasy. 'Do you feel lost already?'

'I feel useless,' she rubbed her arms. 'You were there talking strategy and politics and . . .' She broke her words off. 'I am wondering if after all I should have imitated a fisherman's wife and simply waited for you to come home from the sea.'

Avanasy stroked her arms, seeking to bring her both warmth and reassurance as he pulled her close to his chest. 'Does it mean anything to you if I say that I'm glad you did not wait?'

'It does,' she said, but her shoulders did not relax. 'Something is wrong, Avanasy.'

'Many things are wrong, Ingrid,' he said, brushing his fingertips across her hair. 'Which thing do you mean in particular?'

'Something is wrong with me.'

'How do you mean?' He turned her around to face him so that he might look in her eyes. The falling night had become cold again. 'Are you ill?'

'I wish I knew.' She pressed her fist against her stomach. 'Something is gnawing at me, Avanasy. It is not worry, it is not regret, it is not loneliness. It is something physical. I first felt it out on the water. Now it has come back, and I cannot make it go away.'

Avanasy laid his hand on her forehead. 'No fever. I feel no magic at work here, and yet, there is something, you're right.' He frowned. 'Ingrid, think. When you were with the Bony-Legged Witch, did you take anything from her, or did you give her anything? It does not matter how ineffable it was. Did you exchange anything other than words?'

Ingrid shook her head, but even as she did, she winced. 'I thought it might be my time of the month, but . . .' she winced again and grasped his hand. 'Avanasy, what is happening?'

Ingrid's knees collapsed. Avanasy caught her as she fell, suddenly unconscious as a stone. He had to bite back his cry. Swiftly, he scooped her up in his arms and carried her back away from the waterline. As he did, he saw Ingrid's silhouette, quite separate from her body, standing out against the darkness. In the next moment, it dissolved into nothingness.

'No. This is not possible.' He laid Ingrid tenderly on a bare patch of sand, felt for pulse, felt for breath, but he could find neither. The blush remained on her cheeks, and her eyes moved underneath her lids, but she did not breathe and she was now cold from much more than the wild ocean wind.

Somehow, something had pulled her soul from her body.

This was not possible. Ingrid was a divided soul. Her flesh could be led astray, but her spirit was rooted firmly in both worlds and could not be moved. In the Land of Death and Spirit it was just barely conceivable for her to be so separated, especially by as strong a power as Baba Yaga, but in the world of flesh? Avanasy had never even heard any legend of such a thing. It was the mortal's body that was vulnerable, and the sorcerer's soul. That was the way of it.

'No time, no time,' rasped Avanasy to himself. However it had been done, it had been done, and he had to call her back. But he had so little to work with. A promise might be enough to bind them in the Silent Lands, but not here.

Avanasy drew his knife. Blood was the first and last resource of any sorcerer, his master had told him. His blood, and hers, his breath, and his magic, those would reach her however far away she had been taken.

He rested the blade against his arm, and in front of him the darkness shifted. It rippled, bowed, distorted and reformed. Avanasy rose slowly so that he stood over Ingrid's still form, shifting his grip on the knife, ready to strike out instead of down.

A horse and rider stood in front of him now. Both were as black as the darkness from which they had been shaped. Avanasy could see no face under the rider's obsidian helmet. He rested a black javelin against his black stirrup, and from it a black pennant flapped in the salt wind.

'Sorcerer,' said the rider. 'I bring you a message from my mistress.'

Avanasy felt his heart constrict as he realized who faced him. Baba Yaga, the Witch with the Iron Teeth, commanded the service of three knights. She called them her Black Night, her Red Sun, and her Bright Day. They were her spies, and her messengers.

'What does your mistress want with this woman?' There could be no other reason for this creature to be here. Baba Yaga had taken her away. Again.

Ingrid, Ingrid, I was too slow and too stupid. What have I done?

The faceless knight spoke. 'She bids me say that as long as you do not interfere, and as long as the woman does her bidding, neither of you will be harmed, and she will be returned to you.'

'Your mistress has no right to interfere with the soul of this woman.'

'She does not interfere. The woman was broken in twain before she ever came here. My mistress merely waited for her spirit to work itself free.' The horse stood unnaturally still under its rider, more akin to a carved statue than a living beast. 'You should be grateful to my mistress, Sorcerer,' said the rider in a tone that was both arrogant and casual. 'Without her, the woman's spirit would have simply drifted away.'

But what could have done this? Avanasy clenched his teeth to keep the question from bursting forth. *It is against all the laws of flesh or spirit.*

Except that Ingrid came from a world that followed different laws. Heedless in his own need for her, desperate too in his need to return to Medeoan, he had not even considered that some hurt from her encounter with the drowned man would be harmless in her world and yet would show as a gaping wound in Isavalta.

Fool, fool, fool! Avanasy's teeth ground together. With a force of will he managed to set all that aside. At his feet, Ingrid's skin glowed white in the darkness. He could not let anger at himself cloud his mind.

'It is a grand statement,' he told the knight. 'By what does your mistress swear?'

The knight's helmet tipped back, just a little, as if he lifted his head to look down his nose at Avanasy's presumption. 'She swears by nothing. Who are you to require an oath from the Old Witch?'

'No one,' he admitted. 'But if she does not swear, how may I trust her?'

The pennant snapped once, sharply in the wind. It was a sound like a branch breaking. 'She has sent her messenger, Man. Let that be enough for you.'

'Then,' said Avanasy, feeling the weight of his iron knife in his hand, 'let her messenger stay until my wife is returned to me.'

'This woman is not your wife.'

Avanasy should have been afraid, and he knew it. This was the servant of a true power. This was no bogle or spirit of the roof tree to be bribed with a bowl of milk and pretty compliments. This one could kill him if it would. Its mistress could haunt his dreams and send him mad in the darkness.

But Ingrid lay still as death at his feet, and no other fear could touch him. 'I say that she is my wife, and I say that you will stay until she is returned to me.'

'You are arrogant, Sorcerer. You forget yourself.'

'Forgive me,' he inclined his head without taking his eyes off the shadowy presence. 'Perhaps it is only that I have been too long from Isavalta. Nonetheless, you will stay. If your mistress will not swear, you will stay.'

'I have no more words for you.' The rider wheeled his horse around.

Avanasy charged. Knife first, he leapt for the horse's reins. The animal reared and a heavy hoof struck Avanasy's shoulder, felling him to the ground, but his grip held and he swung down his blade. The iron cut through the fabulous cloth the rider wore and stuck fast. The horse reared again, but the rider could not be ripped free from the iron blade and he fell, heavy and silent, to the ground beside Avanasy.

Avanasy, pain burning through his shoulder, ground the knife in deeper until the rider hissed like a snake. He struck out, but his blows had no force. The cold iron that impaled him drained him of strength. The horse, acting for all the world like a mortal beast, bolted into the darkness and was lost to his sight. Perhaps it had gone home to its mistress. Good. Then he would not have to waste effort crafting a message for her.

'Now,' he said to his prisoner. 'We will wait together, you and I, and when your mistress returns what is mine, I will return what is hers.'

'You are a fool, Man.' The rider's voice was thick with unaccustomed pain. 'You will pay for this, and pay again.'

'I know it well,' answered Avanasy. 'In the meantime, we will wait.'

Overhead, the night turned and Avanasy held his grip on the iron knife. Beside him, Ingrid lay cold and motionless, and all of Avanasy's soul cried out to her.

Come home, my love. Come back to me.

Ingrid watched herself fall unconscious into Avanasy's arms. She watched his eyes widen with alarm as he caught her.

Avanasy! cried Ingrid. *Avanasy!*

But she could make no sound, and, all unbidden, she felt herself drift away like smoke.

No! No! She tried to scream, tried to dig her heels in, but she had no sense of place. No touch of the world seemed to reach her. She was air and vapor, and the wind blew her away into the night, out over the seas, faster than thought, until she could not see land, until she could not see stars.

Avanasy!

But for all the force of will in it, her cry was soundless. Darkness of earth and darkness of sky merged, and Ingrid was nowhere. From blackness thick as sleep, dreams emerged, strange flashes of images. She saw a young man and woman wearing clothes stained and wrinkled from long travel. They shouted at each other with heartbreaking fury. She saw herself as a child, holding onto the waistband of Grace's skirt so Grace could lean out over the edge of a bluff and spread her arms onto the wind coming off the lake pretending she could fly. She saw herself as she was, standing on the deck of an unfamiliar ship, leaning too far over the gunwale and reaching down for Avanasy who stood on the shore.

And she saw a stranger, a young woman with auburn hair and strong features that reminded her sharply of Avanasy. The woman stood beside a trio of gravestones and struggled not to weep. Ingrid's heart went out instantly to the stranger, but she could not tell why.

The images all faded, and instead a formless light shone from the darkness. Ingrid started and tried with all her strength to reach it. She found she could move, but it was like wading through syrup. The light was bright as the sun and slowly it took shape. Now it was a horse and rider, both shining so brightly Ingrid felt she should not have been able to look at them. They trotted away from her. Unable to bear the idea of being left alone in the darkness any longer, Ingrid strained forward, reaching with all the force she possessed, and the light grew brighter, and brighter yet, until the darkness retreated, and Ingrid could see.

She stood under an ancient birch tree, its branches tossing this way and that, although Ingrid could feel no breeze. A brook ran fresh and free at her feet, but it made no sound. On the other side stood a woman in working clothes and thick boots. Ingrid looked into her brown eyes and saw . . . herself.

The woman on the other side of the brook was Ingrid's double. Hair for hair, thread for thread. Ingrid realized she should have been afraid, but she could not be. All she felt was anger radiating at her from her twin, or, was this more than a twin? Avanasy had spoken of Ingrid as a divided soul, with a portion of herself in the Land of Death and Spirit. Was this that place again? Was this her other self?

If it was, then this other Ingrid was steeped in fury, but not at Ingrid – at the force that brought her here. It was a violation, it was wrong. Her other self lifted her hand, in greeting, in warning or in blessing, Ingrid could not tell. The other did not speak, and Ingrid could find no voice in her throat.

'You'd better go in,' said someone behind her.

Ingrid jerked her head around. Behind her, a cat sat on a fence of ancient pickets much mended with human bones. The cat washed its paw and smoothed down its ears, and looked up at Ingrid with an expression of impossible intelligence.

Behind the cat waited another impossibility. A house, a thatched cottage, ancient and covered with the stains of years, but it turned on a pair of taloned and scaled legs, each as thick around as Ingrid's own waist. It was a thing out of nightmare, and Ingrid shrank away from it. At the same time, she recognized it. This was what Avanasy had shown her when she thought she stood in a pleasant stone cottage with an old woman who might have been her grandmother.

This was Baba Yaga's house.

Ingrid felt her other self at her back, straining to reach her, but the brook ran between them, and she could not cross. She pressed her fist against her forehead. She wanted no more of this – this unaccountable knowledge drifting into her head from outside. She wanted her voice, she wanted to understand in the normal way. She wanted herself, alone and solid. She wanted to weep, but she could not cry any more than she could speak.

'You'd better go inside,' said the cat, tucking its legs underneath itself as it settled down on the gate post. 'You would not like what she sends out to fetch you.'

Ingrid's own anger pushed out all other feeling. What was happening? How dare she . . . interfere like this?

But I will not find out here.

Knife-edged warning reached Ingrid from her other self. If she went inside she would be trapped. This was different from last time. The other's knowledge filled her. Avanasy's ring would not pull her out again.

Ingrid tightened her will and strode up to the gate of bones. With painful slowness, as if its hinges were rusted past redemption, it opened for her. The cat watched her with disinterested eyes as she moved as close as she dared to the house, turning on its monstrous, crooked legs, its talons gouging the ground.

She stood there, watching it turn slowly and silently, impossible, ridiculous and terrifying all at once.

You know I'm here, she thought toward its owner. *I will not come into your parlor, Spider. If you want me, you must come out.*

A wave of contempt as palpable as a raw wind engulfed Ingrid, and she withered under the force of it, but not completely, for her other self made a wall for her back. She was supported and sheltered by that other. Not much, but enough, just enough so that she could stay where she was and resist.

After a long moment, the house ceased its restless turning. Carefully, the scarred and scaled legs bent until its steps touched the ground, and the door fell open toward Ingrid. She felt as if she were looking into some terrible open maw.

Baba Yaga squatted in the threshold, as gaunt and tattered as the spirit of famine. She leaned on her filthy pestle that was as thick around as both of Ingrid's arms. Two huge black mastiffs waited at her side. Both bared their yellow fangs, and Ingrid could feel their growls, low and sullen, vibrating through the air.

'I have need of you, Woman,' she said, and Ingrid could see the black iron of her teeth as she spoke.

Ingrid stiffened. This place was all bone and blood, and she was in danger. She knew that. But she also knew boundaries had been crossed here, and wrong had been done. It made a difference.

'So I gathered,' she said simply, and tried to hold back her relief at being able to speak. The witch's regard seemed to have made her more solid, more real in this place of horrors and fancies, and that idea sent a tremor of fear through Ingrid.

'I will not be brooked.' The witch thumped her pestle on the floor, and the whole house shuddered. 'Aid me and you will have aid in return. Cross me and you will be held until you yield. There is nothing else.'

'What could you possibly need me for?' Ingrid spread her hands.

'You will find me the Vixen and bring back what she has stolen from me. When that is done, you may depart.'

'I don't even know what you're talking about.'

'Nonetheless. You will do this thing I ask.'

The words fell against Ingrid like a weight, pressing her down until it was a struggle to think of anything else. Images of foxes and meadows, and a round green hill flashed unbidden through her mind, and she remembered with crystal clarity the creature who had spoken to her when she was here before, who had sent her off to the Old Witch, just to see what would happen. She knew all at once that her other half could lead her to the Vixen again, and she would do this thing because the Old Witch bid her, and because she could do nothing else.

But there was the crossing of boundaries, that bit of wrong, that bit of freedom.

'No,' said Ingrid.

Baba Yaga pointed one long, crooked finger at Ingrid. On either side of her, the mastiffs raised their hackles. 'I give you this last warning, Woman. I know your name, I know your future and your past. I see the warp and woof of your tapestry life. Without me, your death is sure. Think carefully before you wake my anger.'

It couldn't be true, what she said. It couldn't be and yet it might be. Her other self feared that the witch spoke too much truth, and the wall that sheltered Ingrid faltered.

It was too much, it was too strange and the fear of it too great. Despite that, she would not place herself in the power of this creature, this hag. She could not. But she could not move.

Then the witch's head went up as if she had caught some strange scent. She bared her iron teeth in a death's head grin.

'So, your man thinks to take a hostage. Thinks to have and keep what is mine in exchange for you.'

Avanasy? Some caution outside herself kept Ingrid from saying his name out loud.

Baba Yaga snapped her teeth and they came together with a hollow clang.

'You try my patience, you two. This is the second time you have refused me and he has tried to pull you from me. Very well.' She turned her black, black gaze on Ingrid, and for a moment Ingrid felt she would burn to a cinder from the heat of it. 'There will be a third time, and you will beg to do my bidding, for only I know how to cage the Firebird. Go freely. I am done with you. Now, you may see if you can find your own way home.'

At those words, Ingrid found she could not stay still. The dogs advanced, snarling. The house lifted itself up onto its legs, and without feeling her own movement, she was outside the gate, which swung shut with the slow straining of dry and rusted hinges.

And they all faded away, leaving her alone beside a brook in a piney wood staring at her own double.

Avanasy? she choked. Her voice was gone again. What substance she had possessed had dissolved, leaving behind only vapor and desperate sensibility.

What am I to do? she thought toward her double, and knew that other self was consumed with anxiety. *Why can't you speak to me?*

For a moment, she thought to cross the brook that separated them, but as soon as it entered her mind, the thought filled her with loathing. To go closer to her reflection was even more wrong than being here in the first place. She did not know why this was so, only that it was.

Ingrid wished she could cry. She wished she could scream, but all releases seemed denied her. Already, she was drifting, pulled by some current she could not feel. It was as if the bank flowed and the brook stayed still.

No! she steeled herself again. *No!*

That denial seemed to root her in place, at least for a moment. It occurred to Ingrid that if she failed to will herself some destination, her destination might be chosen for her, and who knew what else was out here. There might be things even worse than Baba Yaga.

Ingrid lifted her eyes to her other self, and gathered her determination. She willed that she should turn, that she should follow the current of the brook at her feet. Her other self turned with her, and together, side-by-side in the silence that this spirit land enforced, they began to travel downstream.

★   ★   ★

Avanasy ached. His hand ached from holding his knife. His shoulder burned from the blow it had taken. His soul ached from seeing Ingrid still and lifeless on the sands.

His prisoner did not struggle, but he pulled. His body pulled against the iron knife that held him pinned, and his encased spirit pulled against Avanasy's command enforced by that iron. He pulled toward his mistress, and his mistress would know it soon, if she did not already. Grimly, Avanasy held on, because to let go would be to leave Ingrid alone. Overhead, the stars wheeled toward morning, and his pain settled into his bones, and he still held on.

Then, the rider lifted his head as if he heard a distant sound.

'Your woman is free,' he said. 'You may not hold me any longer.'

'But she has not returned,' croaked Avanasy. His hand had begun to go numb with cold and effort. All he could feel now was the pain that throbbed in time to his heartbeat.

'My mistress did not take her,' sneered the knight. 'And now my mistress does not hold her. You have no more right to me, and even your iron cannot claim me.'

The pull which Avanasy had fought all night turned into a sudden wrench, and Avanasy cried out, but he could not hold on and the rider tore himself free. Before Avanasy could stumble to his feet to try to strike out again, the knight snatched his black javelin up from the ground where it had fallen, and was gone.

For a moment, Avanasy only stared at the suddenly empty night. Then, he roared out in wordless frustration and stabbed his knife deep into the ground. But it changed nothing. Ingrid's body still lay abandoned.

He crawled to her side and cradled her head against his chest. He had to think. He must think clearly. Where could she be now? What path could she have taken? The rider said Baba

Yaga had not pulled her forth. This must be true or by the laws that governed bargains between the mortal world and the Land of Death and Spirit he would not have been able to break the hold Avanasy had placed on him. All the magics Avanasy knew were for binding that which was already together. He knew no spell to call a spirit back into its body. Not a divided spirit. Even if he could go in search of her, could he find her in the vastness of the Silent Lands? Did he have the strength to walk that road now?

'Oh, Ingrid,' he breathed as he held her yet more tightly. 'I will try. I must. But, love, help me to find you.'

Ingrid felt the current again, a gentle undertow to her awareness. At first, she tried to clench herself against it, but then she realized this current had a familiar touch. She looked across at her other self and that other self nodded once.

Avanasy.

Ingrid pushed forward. The world around her had grown thick and sluggish again. She was no longer the vapor she had been, but neither was she yet solid. Movement was difficult, even with the current. She had weight now, but not flesh. Will, but not strength, and she was growing tired.

Help me. Love, reach for me. Please, I'm here.

Soft, so soft Avanasy almost did not feel it, Ingrid's breath blew across his hand. He froze, his heart pounding, but no other breath came. He chafed her wrist gently. 'Here, love, here, please, I am here.'

He pressed two fingers against her wrist, and felt the tiniest trace of living warmth. Beyond that, there was the flutter of a heartbeat, and another. But that was all.

'Yes. Here.' He drew her even closer. 'Here.'

Her breath touched his cheek again, and her chest rose and fell, once, and again.

'Yes.' He kissed her mouth, breathing into her with his breath, and willing her with all his strength to find her way home.

Weight and form, distant but real. Ingrid felt her sluggish blood in the netting of her veins, the frame of her bones and the binding of her sinews. But it was all too far away, and she was so tired. What had she done to become so tired? She could not reach out, but she knew where her hands were. She could not cry out, even though now she knew where her voice lay. She was weighted down with weariness and fear, struggling through a world that grew thicker with each passing instant.

Then, then, she felt Avanasy's kiss, and she felt her being, flesh and spirit, yearn to respond, though she did not know how.

But the weight was hers, and the will was hers, and she could feel her hand. She would raise her hand, she would touch him. She would hold him. She would.

Avanasy, almost not believing what he saw, watched, filled with hope and fear, as Ingrid's hand struggled to lift itself.

'Yes,' he kissed her again. 'Yes, love. Come back to me.'

Ingrid felt herself sinking into the ground, into the weight of her flesh, into the sluggish flow of her own blood, and into Avanasy's embrace. She was still so cold, so far away, and yet she felt the warmth of her bones gathering around her. She could raise her hand now, she could touch his cheek, and feel its warmth and roughness underneath her palm as her hand traced its way down his back to his shoulder to his arm to his hand where he held her. She kissed him, she held him close, for if he let her go now she would fly away again.

'Hold me, hold me,' she said, and she knew she spoke with her true voice. Avanasy gathered her close in his arms, kissing her endlessly, taking her breath, breathing again into her. She felt him weary, and in pain, yet she also knew his desire quickened his blood, as her desire quickened hers, growing insistent, pulling her home, and she embraced herself and him, wrapping his hands around her so he might caress her, the warmth and strength of his touch bringing her closer to him still.

She had no other thought – no care for propriety, or fear of abandonment. She wished him close, wished no barrier between them, and he knew her need and he laid her down and covered her and she was able to wrap herself around him so that they could lie close, and closer yet, and she knew nothing but joy, and she opened her eyes and she saw Avanasy and she was whole and alive and for that one moment they were together in life and love, and the morning star shone down from a brightening sky, and Ingrid knew this was all the blessing that they would ever need.

For awhile after that she slept. She woke at last to the dawn, and the feel of Avanasy stroking her hair. She turned to look up at him, and found him gazing down at her, and his cheeks were wet with tears.

'You found me,' she rasped, her voice dry in her throat.

Avanasy shook his head. 'No, you found your own way. I think it must be ever so with you.'

She took his hand to still it and also to pull herself up. She was covered in sand, and hungry as a bear, but she didn't care. 'Do you know what happened?'

'I think I do. I think the touch of the ghost that troubled your sister loosened your soul from your body.'

Not even reflex made her say that was impossible. She was far beyond doubting any word he spoke of sorceries and spirit. 'But . . . why now? It's been months.'

'Until now you have not been in a place where magic and spirit dwelled openly, and I brought you here without thought.'

'Can you . . . undo this?'

'No,' he said simply and bitterly. 'Not yet. I do not understand it. It should not be possible. I would have to consult with . . . others. A way may be found. Until then, though, I think I can bind you together so that the danger is at least lessened.'

'Then we had better do that. I do not want to see that . . . old witch again anytime soon, thank you very much.' She wondered if she should tell him what Baba Yaga had said, about seeing her future and her past, but she looked into his eyes and saw how much he already blamed himself for what was happening, and how real his pain, physical and spiritual, was. She decided to wait.

There would be, after all, time enough for that worry when these present troubles were over.

Chapter Twelve

The House Guard captain gave his horse its head, guiding the animal only with his knees while he raised his javelin. As the horse raced by the posts that had been set up on Vaknevos's great, green lawn, the captain neatly spitted the small brass rings hanging from their threads – one, two, three, four. He missed the fifth, but wheeled the horse tightly around and sent it galloping back to capture it. Holding his javelin high for the roar of approval from the assembled nobles and courtiers, he walked his sweating horse up to the dais with the Imperial canopy, reverenced from the saddle, and dropped the rings into a heap of similar trinkets at the Emperor's feet.

Kacha acknowledged the gesture with a bow of his head. At his back, the Lords Master laughed over their various wagers. Ambassador Girilal, for whose benefit this display had ostensibly been arranged, applauded politely before reaching again for the tiny cup of clear, peppery liquor set out on the refreshment tray for him. Girilal was developing quite a taste for the stuff, Kacha noted. It was a taste that should perhaps be nurtured.

Out on the lawn, the servants had hung fresh rings from the waiting posts. The invited guests who did not merit a spot on the dais milled about behind the temporary fences of blue and gold ribbons while other servitors dispensed drinks and dainties among them. When all was ready, Nausha, the Commander of the Imperial House Guard, raised his hand sending the next officer charging out.

'These seem a well-trained and disciplined group,' remarked Girilal. 'I confess, I am quite impressed.'

'I was myself when I first saw them,' Kacha acknowledged. The officer on the field had tossed aside his pike with its catch of rings and drawn his sword. Riding back down the lawn at full tilt, he clove a spitted apple neatly in twain as he thundered past.

Kacha lifted his cup to the officer as he wheeled the horse again to take aim at another set of apples already stuck into place. 'We have taken great care to keep them actively employed so that they will be ready for whatever may come.'

'A wise policy,' said Girilal blandly. 'Especially in a land known for its fractious provinces.'

Kacha pursed his lips. On the field, the officer slashed left and right, never once missing his mark. The cheers rose up to shake the day. 'Not so fractious as you might believe. This empire offers great advantages in peace and security for those who accept their part in her.'

'And, of course, they nurture great love for their Empress.' Girilal nodded toward the empty chair that stood at Kacha's left side. 'And her soon-to-be heir.'

'Of course,' acknowledged Kacha, and his right hand twitched. Girilal was probing, but for what?

The officer on the field finished his run and rode his sweating horse sedately past the Imperial dais to make his reverence and receive the nod of approval in return. Behind them, there was more laughter, and more wagers proposed and accepted. They were content, his Council Lords. Regular meetings in the room fitted out with Yamuna's carpet kept their minds calm. The ranks of the House Guard swelled, and the newer officers could be safely charged with keeping order among the oblasts and the cities. Eventually, they could be trusted with more extensive duties, should such be necessary. There were whispers, here and there, of potential difficulties that would have to be dealt with, if what was to come could not sufficiently distract the troublemakers.

On the lawn, the set-up for the next run was complete. The Council Lords finished their current round of betting to watch the next officer. Girilal reached again for his liquor cup.

In that moment of relative stillness, a very different cry rang out across the lawn. This was no soldier's bellow as he charged, no shout of triumph from a betting noble. This was a harsh, rattling cry torn from a worn throat desperate to be heard.

'News! News!'

Hoofbeats thudded across the lawn. Exclamations rose from the assembled crowd. Commander Nausha barked two orders and a rank of mounted officers assembled themselves in front of the dais while the armed guard that flanked the Emperor and the Council came at once to attention, their hands slapping onto the pommels of their swords.

A single rider careened across the lawn. Foam flew from the horse's mouth, and the rider slumped low across its neck as if he lacked the ability to hold himself upright. Yet, he mustered the strength to cry again.

'News! Majesty Imperial! News!'

Commander Nausha rapped out another order and the front rank of horsemen moved forward to intercept the rider, but Kacha got to his feet.

'Hold!' he called. 'Let him approach!'

Another order rang out. Smartly, the mounted ranks parted to let the stranger enter the Imperial presence, but none of the soldiers on the dais removed their hands from their swords, nor did Commander Nausha relax at all.

As the rider drew nearer, it could be seen that he wore the black coat and green trim of the Sol'uyche oblast, one of the most southern provinces. His boots were caked with mud, and more mud spattered his coat and helmet. He had lost one glove and that hand where it clenched the reins had been slashed and battered and fresh blood oozed out between the scabs.

The crowd on the lawn were completely still. Only the horses stamped and shifted restlessly, jingling their harnesses and snorting out their disapproval.

The rider halted his trembling, sweating horse and lifted a paper-white face to Kacha and the assemblage on the dais. He tried to lift his naked hand to make the reverence, but Kacha waved the gesture away.

'Majesty Imperial,' the man gasped. 'I am come from the border. From Miateshcha. My commander sent me across into Hung-Tse to see . . .' he tried to draw a deep breath and it ended in a rattling cough. 'Hung-Tse is sending its troops to the border. I overheard a band of raiders. They said . . .' again, his words were lost in a racking cough. 'They said there would soon be no work for them to do, because the soldiers of the Heart of the World would level all before them.' He managed to take one shaky breath. 'I have ridden many days to bring you word, Majesty Imperial . . .'

The man's strength gave out at last, and he slumped forward over his horse's neck. Commander Nausha glanced at Kacha for permission, which Kacha gave with a sharp nod. Nausha ordered forward a clutch of soldiers who gently slipped the rider off his horse and bore him away. Another took charge of the trembling beast and led it after its master. Its head hung so low that its mane all but brushed the ground.

But Kacha had no time to think more on the fallen rider. Behind him, the voices of the Council were lifting from murmurs to demands for explanation. The crowd on the field sounded like the surging of the ocean.

He lifted his voice to carry across the field. 'This is grave news indeed. The Empress must be alerted at once. But be sure,' he raised his hands. 'No threat to Isavalta will go un-answered!'

'Strike them down!' shouted someone from the crowd.

Kacha suppressed a smile. 'All enemies to Isavalta will be struck down and they will never rise!'

A cheer started, softly at first, but it rose and gathered strength and broke upon the summer air. 'Strike!' cried a voice. 'Strike them down!' shouted another.

'Let them die!'

'Kill them all!'

The cheer turned into an ugly thunder of voices and Kacha made no move to be heard over it. Instead he spoke to Commander Nausha. 'Disperse the crowd gently, and call your men back to the barracks. You will be summoned to the Council room shortly. My Lords Master,' he turned to the men behind him. 'Meet us in the Council room within the hour. I must go to the Empress.' He looked to Girilal. 'Be so good as to walk with me, Ambassador. There are things we must speak of at once.'

He took the ambassador's elbow. The Council Lords, their faces ranging from worried to furious, stood back and rever-enced while Kacha led Girilal down the dais's steps.

Once they were away from the Council and striding across the grass toward Vaknevos with the honor guards a prudent distance away, Girilal drew close to Kacha and whispered low in Kacha's ear.

'I will ask you plainly, Son of the Throne. What are you doing?' Girilal used the court language of Hastinapura, and the first title Kacha had been given at his birth.

'With all reverence, Learned Sir,' replied Kacha, just as softly and in the same tongue, 'your meaning is not plain to me.'

'That man came at a time too convenient for it to be a coincidence,' replied Girilal in the same, even whisper. He might have been speaking of some rare and beautiful bird he did not wish to frighten away. 'And at a time when you were displaying the military prowess of your new realm. I ask you again, Son of the Throne, by all the names of the Seven Mothers, what are you doing?'

'Ridding Isavalta and Hastinapura of a common enemy.' Kacha had to work to keep his smile from his face. He had not meant to tell Girilal of this so soon, but the man had forced the issue. It was best he hear the bones of it, and then Kacha could see how he would respond, now, before a communiqué indicating unease could be written to the Pearl Throne.

'Think on it,' he went on, folding his hands behind his back. His right hand twitched again. The part of him that was Yamuna did not like this course, but neither did it actively interfere. 'If Isavalta goes to war, the resources of Hung-Tse will be sorely taxed. They will no longer be able to support the invaders my uncle battles against. He will then be able to harry their southern borders as we take the north. The central lands will be ours to divide, and there will be no bar to the peace and prosperity between us.'

Girilal narrowed his eyes, as if seeking to see beneath Kacha's skin to find what truth lay there. 'And has your uncle approved of this plan?'

Here came the risk. 'Not my uncle, no.'

Despite his wish to appear casual, Kacha found himself watching the ambassador intently. Girilal did not know it, but what he said next might determine the length of his life. Sweat prickled Kacha's scalp. The ambassador would make an excellent and useful ally, but if he could not see . . . well, one additional death would not be that much more difficult to hide, especially as a war was about to begin.

'No, it is not something of which your uncle would approve.' Girilal fastened his gaze on the approaching walls of Vaknevos. 'There are many important things to which he has given no credence.'

Kacha felt himself relax. 'Fortunately, we are discussing the affairs of Isavalta, and not of Hastinapura. It is not the Pearl Throne which decides actions here.'

'So, the Empress agrees with your plan?'

'The Empress has left all in my hands.' Which was very much the truth.

Girilal walked beside him in silence for a time, digesting his thoughts with care. Kacha tried not to watch him too closely, to give him some room in which to think. To frighten him now would be to lose all. If Girilal decided his duty was to the one on the throne, then their alliance was over before it had begun, and he would have to ask Yamuna how best to deal with a man who had seemed to hold so much promise. But, if his alliance was to the throne itself, and the proper order . . .

'Then, I suppose,' said Girilal at last, 'it remains for me to ask the Son of the Throne how my office may assist in this hopeful plan.'

Now Kacha could smile with ease, as he felt the future Yamuna had taught him to dream of come that much closer.

Yamuna arrived in Devang on foot, the only proper way to approach such a place. Although he had been there a hundred times or more, he leaned upon his staff and took a moment to simply stare.

Once, Devang had been the greatest of all temples. Every bit of it had been carved from the cliffs that towered high on all sides – the obelisks, the reliefs, the altars under their stone canopies, and the niches where the acolytes had trained and worshipped. All were of a single piece growing out of the smooth, red stone floor. It had been seven generations in the making, and now none even came here. It was a place of ghosts and daemons, a place of old gods and goddesses conquered and cast down by the Seven Mothers before Ajitabh bowed down before them and rose up again in their names to lead the founding of the Pearl Throne.

Now the conquered received their sacrifice only when the Mothers were done, and no one came to this temple but the tribes of monkeys to house themselves in the niches. And Yamuna.

The red stone reflected all the heat of the sun, turning the ancient temple into an oven. Yamuna walked unhesitatingly into the blazing heat. All around him, the squawks and calls of the monkey tribes filled the air. One of the creatures sat on the central obelisk, gazing down at him. A family groomed each other on the eastern altar. Another pair squabbled by the lone fountain that still bubbled from the earth to spill across the barren stone. The place smelled strongly of heat and animals.

But for all that, the place had been made for power. Great things could still be accomplished here by one who knew the proper rites.

Monkeys screamed at each other in alarm as Yamuna strode into their midst. They scattered like leaves in the wind to the mouths of their niches where they might squeal their insults at him in safety. For a moment, they reminded him very much of Chandra.

'I will not permit this!' Chandra had shouted at him, red-faced and shaking in his anger. 'Your place is with me!'

'It is your wedding night,' replied Yamuna coolly. 'I cannot see how you would need my help for what must be done.'

'You would send me alone to my exile in a house of spies,' he sulked.

'You have your work to do there.' Yamuna produced an amber bracelet carved with serpents, symbols of wisdom and fidelity twined around each other. 'When you arrive, you will give your bride this for her wrist, and you will put this,' he held up a small clay vial stoppered tightly with wax, 'in her tea as soon as you are able. Take care that you do not yourself inhale any steam from that tea. When all is done, she will not be able to keep any secret from us.' *From me.* Chandra had grasped the trinkets as greedily as the monkeys around Yamuna now grasped their fruit rinds. 'The preparations I go to make now will help ensure that while Samudra and his queen may believe they spy on us, their eyes will be clouded while ours see clearly.'

All of which had been more than enough to satisfy Chandra. Escaping Samudra's subtle traps was not so easy.

He had been summoned to the Emperor's balcony the morning after the wedding rites. A dainty breakfast had been spread on low tables beside the bathing pool. The Emperor, the Father of the Throne, Samudra the Usurper, sat on cushions of rose and gold silk, indecently close to his queen who had been draped in silks and linens all the colors of flame. Servants clad in white paced silently back and forth, filling goblets and removing plates. All the while Samudra's bound-sorcerer, the woman Hamsa, stood as still as the pillar that shaded her, one hand resting lightly on her staff. The Queen's bound-sorcerer was nowhere to be seen, a fact Samudra noted with disquiet as he knelt and bowed his head to the tiled floor.

'*Agnidh* Yamuna,' said the Emperor in a perfectly friendly fashion. 'Rise. Sit with us. There are matters we would discuss with you.'

Hoping his silence would be taken for respectful humility, Yamuna lifted himself from the obeisance and knelt on the sky-blue cushion the servant set down for him. A few slices of bread, thick with candied fruit, and a goblet of tangerine juice were placed in front of him, for it was known that as part of his asceticism, Yamuna ate only the simplest and plainest of foods. He was not one like *Agnidh* Hamsa to gorge himself whenever the opportunity arose.

'We wanted to take this opportunity before you leave with Chandra to thank you, Yamuna, for your loyal service to our family,' Samudra went on.

Yamuna bowed his head. What was running through the usurper's mind? What did he want?

'I did not succeed the throne under favorable circumstances,' Samudra went on. 'I do not deny it. I have since tried my best to make peace within the palace as well as without.'

Samudra was a soldier. His mind worked at all problems as if they were campaigns. Yet, he had convinced more than one enemy to surrender without bloodshed using the promise of a liberal treaty in place of a long siege. He knew well how to flatter, and when to use a soft word while laying his naked sword across his lap for the enemy to see. It was Samudra who left his brother, and Yamuna, alive, when all around him, including the Queen, urged that they be killed.

'The wisdom of the Father of the Throne is well known,' murmured Yamuna piously.

The Queen's eyes flashed, seeing the platitude plainly for what it was. Yamuna did not care. Whatever plan they had concocted between them, Samudra would not permit her to disrupt it through something so trifling as anger.

'Yamuna, I have known you as long as I have known any. You have been with my brother his whole life, as Hamsa has been with me. I know your service does not come easily to you, and it comes less so now that *Agnidh* Hamsa has taken your place beside the throne to do the rites of empire and sacrifice in your place.'

Yamuna glanced sharply at Hamsa who did not even raise an eyebrow to indicate that she saw him. Not that Hamsa had ever deigned to take much note of him since her part in Samudra's . . . ascension.

'I accept my place.' Yamuna told the lie smoothly and without inflection. He had, after all, said it often enough. 'I do the office the Mothers have given me.'

'I can break your bond with Chandra.'

Yamuna's head jerked up. Samudra's face was perfectly open, and perfectly frank. The Queen raised a gilded goblet in a slight toast to Yamuna, before she drank, watching him carefully over the bejeweled rim.

'I am bound to the life of Chandra *tya* Achin Ireshpad,' said Yamuna firmly. 'It is a thing fixed and cannot be broken.'

'Yes, it can.'

Samudra was too much of a soldier to recline on his pillows, but he did lean back a little, letting Yamuna get a good look at the full length of him. He sat, straight, cross-legged and calm, with an Imperial bearing Chandra could never have managed. His hands rested on his knees. It did not take much work for Yamuna to imagine the sword lying under them.

'*Agnidh* Hamsa has found the way. There are bonds that my word as Emperor, Father of the Throne, the one who is joined to the land, may break. This is one of them.'

To his shame, Yamuna felt his mouth go dry as he realized what Samudra was truly offering him. Freedom. Were his bond broken, he could walk away from Chandra, from the Pearl Throne, and from all the petty cares that clustered in its shadows. He could step into the sunlight and go where he would. He could even walk into the northern lands on his own, and seek out his destiny there without having to coax and crawl before Chandra and his son.

Freedom.

Yamuna had to swallow before he could make himself speak clearly. 'But such a thing could not come without a price.'

'There will be no further price.' Samudra shook his head. 'You are dissatisfied with your service. You do not like your place in the shadow of the throne, and you will like the south-lands even less. That is enough. You have proven true when your master most needed you, and I am willing to reward that fidelity by releasing you now.'

Yamuna's heart beat hard within his chest. Samudra was not lying. Not he. Oh, he was not above a ruse and deep deception when it suited him, but not like this. Not a bald lie to an enemy's face.

What do you want? Yamuna thought, working to keep his expression bland. He added another thought. *What do you know?*

Then, he saw it. *You know your brother to be harmless and inef-fectual. That is why you let him live when you could have killed him. For all you would do, you would not shed family blood without true need. You will get him out of the court, you will give him women to keep him watched and sated, and you will send me away. You know he has ideas of regaining the throne.* Despite all, Yamuna felt his eyes narrow. *And you know where they come from.*

If my bond is broken, if I leave him, the last true danger to your rule is gone for good.

But what did Yamuna care for any of that? The politics of empire meant nothing to him. They were but the means to an end, and Samudra had just offered to remove all need for them.

Freedom.

Yamuna laid his staff down at the fountain's edge. The

monkeys there proved reluctant to desert their territory and splashed and scrambled to the far side, shrieking insults at him as he stripped off his loin cloth and sandals. The water ran clean and pure into the red stone basin, warmed by sun above and stone below. Yamuna scooped the clear water into his hands and used it to wash the dust from his body. He poured more water over his head and combed his fingers through his hair and beard to clean them as well. He rinsed his mouth and spat, startling the monkeys again and making them leap and scream in frustration, waving their arms at him, plainly saying, 'go away, go away!' The male leaned across the edge of the fountain, baring his teeth and growling low in his throat, but he made no move to attack.

Very like Chandra. Yamuna rewrapped his cloth and picked his staff back up. *His fall was not undeserved.*

Well, Yamuna, what will you do?

Those were the words the Queen had spoken to him on the sun-drenched balcony. The break in the rains was quite welcome, and all were enjoying it. To all appearances, she was a leisurely lady, stretched across her embroidered pillows, picking at the dainties before her with her right hand and listening without too much attention to the business of her husband.

It was a ruse, and those who believed her wits were not as sharp as her husband's swords often learned of their mistake far too late.

'Father of the Throne,' said Yamuna, stalling for time. 'You ask me to break the oath of a lifetime with the words of a moment.'

'It is not breaking an oath to be lawfully released from it.' Samudra nodded toward Hamsa. 'Tell him what you have found, *Agnidh.*'

Hamsa turned her head toward Yamuna, as if she were just

becoming aware that any conversation was taking place before her.

'When the Mothers came to bless the Pearl Throne built by Ajitabh, first of the Emperors, they brought with them the laws that the Emperor must obey, and the laws in which the Emperor must be obeyed.'

I know this as well as you, Woman. But Yamuna sat silently.

'Among these laws is the prescription that, as the Emperor is father over all born in the shadow of the Pearl Throne, his alone are the hands that finally hold all oaths and contracts made to the throne and the Imperial family.' Her eyes glittered amber in the sunlight. 'All oaths.'

Was it true then? Was there no bar to his leaving Chandra to fend for himself, to walking away, to devoting himself to study and asceticism until his ends were reached, until he could stand in the northlands and call down the Mothers, god to god?

'I beg you, Father.' Yamuna bowed down and covered his face with his hands. 'Give me time to think, and leave to seek solitude to take my heart's counsel.'

'Of course,' said Samudra amiably. 'You may give us your answer tomorrow.'

So, Yamuna had come here, to this place of old power and chittering monkeys, to seek his answers and understand what he must do. If he needed the bond that Chandra and Kacha's formal conquest would bring in order to find his divinity, then he could not free himself. But if he did not . . .

Past the fountain, Devang became a plaza with curving walls that were the towering red cliffs, carved with reliefs of the gods; playing games, calling down storms, healing the sick, sitting in judgment over the daemons. The only other decoration had been carved into the smooth floor.

It was a sun wheel, a pattern of concentric circles and radiating arms. Each circle was filled with meticulously carved planets and stars along with their ruling gods and elements. It was so large it was difficult to take in all at once down here in the plaza. One had to scale the cliffs and look down on it to see its true sweep.

This was what Yamuna had come here to find. Years of study and searching through the oldest texts and tablets had led him to believe that this was part of a weaving, one that could allow the skilled to see into the future, one of the most difficult of the sorcerous arts. He had traced a trail of hints and possibilities, from ancient acolytes, to worn carvings on pillars that marked ancient cities and shrines, to one great, black pillar of iron that was supposed to mark the spot where the gods stood to create Hastinapura from the surrounding ocean.

From his small travel bag, Yamuna pulled a tiny vial made of obsidian. In it was a liquid it had taken him a lifetime's work to distill. Patient skill and patient magic had been woven into this liquor to bring it properly into being, and now he would use what was left to make this last, most important decision.

The sun wheel spread out before him, its carvings as elaborate as the pattern woven into the finest carpet. Yamuna cracked the seal on the vial and pulled out the stopper.

Gently, reverently, he stepped onto the first circle of the wheel. He held the vial before him, and tipped one drop of the golden distillation onto the burning red stone. Its rich, heady scent rose up at once.

'I give you to drink of the fruits of the trees,' he said, walking forward so that the soles of his feet pressed the liquor into the stone. It was slick and hot underfoot and its perfume wafted about him. Another careful drop, another careful step. 'I give you to drink of the flowers of the field and the blood of life.' Yamuna kept his words steady, matching them in time to his steps, and his offering of the sacred liquor. It was not easy. The scent soaked into his mind as the strong liquor soaked into his skin, turning him dizzy and making him feel far too light. The heat began to burn his much-toughened soles, but he held himself firmly. This was a weaving of the most delicate kind. Although it was built on a foundation of stone, all was done in air, the least solid of all the elements. He must not miss a single step or syllable.

'I give you to drink of fire and water, of earth and air. I give you to drink of the world, of all that is present and past. I give you to drink of myself. I walk the paths of stone and I pour out all I have that you might drink. Only show me, show me what is yet to come. Show me, show me if I may accept what is offered and gain what it is I seek.'

Heat beat down. The air felt strangely dry for this season of rains. It seemed to grate against every pore. The scent of the liquor was too thick to be mere vapor. It was a tactile curtain, thick and binding, pressing against him, smothering his breath and making his footsteps unsteady. But he did not feel afraid. He felt buoyant, as if any step might lift him off the ground and allow him to fly freely away. The sensation made it difficult to see. His own hands and voice felt far away. The scented curtain surrounded him and supported him. It was a rich veil between him and the world, removing all care, all responsibility, lifting him into the air, dissolving him from flesh and the cares of the flesh, the world of the flesh, winding and binding him into a new world, where he himself was nothing but a vapor.

In this new world, the wheels that had been beneath his feet turned freely in the golden light of the sun. All the eternal forces which drove mortal destinies were visible. Each of the figures danced within its own sphere, the gods at their wars and their justice, the symbols turning like the wheels themselves, pausing to point this way, then that, to bestow fortune or tragedy in the dramas unfolding around them.

As a vapor, Yamuna wafted calmly over the turning wheels, until one of the symbols stilled before him. It was an empty throne. It pulled at him, airy being that he was, and he saw himself sitting on it. The gods crowded around his feet, ready to greet him as great among them. His left hand held a lotus, his right held a sword, and he knew himself to be powerful, even as the immortal reckon power. He tossed up the lotus and as it fell, he sliced it neatly in two with his sword and the petals rained down upon the old gods who lifted their hands to catch them, accepting his bounty, and he knew that beyond the range of his golden vision the Seven Mothers saw all this and grew unquiet.

Yamuna drifted closer to this vision, this turn of the wheel that promised him all he sought, and he saw that around his neck was a golden collar, and from the collar dangled the severed end of a golden chain. His broken oath, his freedom from Chandra, brought him to this throne. Yamuna saw all this and rejoiced.

But the wheels kept turning. The throne turned under Yamuna, the sword turned, the severed lotus turned, and all the dancers moved, but Yamuna did not move, and their turning toppled him from his seat, and lotus and sword fell, and pierced his side. Yamuna saw himself sprawled at the feet of the gods, impaled upon his own sword, covered in the petals of the lotus, his hand stretching out toward the other end of his chain as if seeking to join the two together again.

The wheels turned and the world turned, and their current caught up the vapor that was Yamuna and spun it wildly around until all became a blur of red and gold, heat and heady perfume, senseless, swirling, spinning ever faster until the force of its fury cast Yamuna out, back into his flesh, falling hard against the unmoving sun wheel where he had begun.

Yamuna tasted blood where he had bitten his tongue. More

blood trickled down his split chin onto the carved wheels where he sprawled, darkening and hardening quickly in the baking sun. He felt as parched as a stone himself, but he could not move. All force of will and strength of body had been wrung from him, and he had no choice but to lie unsheltered in the sun until they returned.

But he had seen what he needed to see. If he severed his chain, if he allowed his vow to be annulled, he would bring his destruction.

So, my little Prince Chandra, it would appear I need you yet awhile longer.

At last, burning from the heat of the sun above and the heat of the stone below, Yamuna made himself move. He crawled one painful inch at a time back toward the fountain. The sound of the cool, trickling water sent tremors through his frame. The monkeys, chased away by his magics, had returned now, and they hooted and screamed at him. Aware that he was much weakened, perhaps even dying, they grew bold and scampered close to shriek at him before running back to the safety of their niches. He crawled forward, concentrating only on moving his arms and legs. At last, he fell into the fountain's shallow trough. Water cascaded over him like the blessings of paradise. He lay in the fresh water, drinking with his mouth and with his pores, until the burning lessened and he was able to stand without shaking, and reclaim his meager clothing, which he had laid beside his pouch and staff.

Dressed again, but feeling only a little stronger, Yamuna knelt in the shadow cast by the temple. He opened his pouch and took a little bread to eat with fresh drafts from the fountain. Then, he brought out another bottle. This one was a squat, ungainly jar of red clay, the exact color of the stone around him. Yamuna had made the vessel using clay from a spring close to Devang and he had carved the weaving patterns that covered its sides with his own hands. More red clay, carved with a representation of the sun wheel at his feet, sealed the jar tightly.

Yamuna took a deep breath. This would not take much strength, which was fortunate, as he did not have much to give, but it would require a show of strength. He crossed his legs, stiffened his spine so that he sat up straight, and fixed his face in a stern attitude.

Then, he swiftly cracked the seal and cast the jar away.

The air above the jar blurred and warped. Opaque figures formed slowly, as if they pulled their constituent elements from the surrounding ether. They grew red and gold, like the surrounding sun-baked stone. They lengthened and separated into a crowd of four, all standing on sinewy legs, on taloned feet. Torsos, armored and chained, thickened and sprouted terrible arms that ended in clawed hands clutching spears and curved swords. Fangs as curved as those blades protruded from gaping lips. Sail-shaped ears hung with gold turned in Yamuna's direction, as did the terribly alert, round, yellow eyes. Wings, heavy with feathers the color of old blood, spread from their shoulders.

The first among them, the tallest, with the most terrible eyes, roared out a wordless challenge and rushed toward Yamuna, shaking his weapons and raising his wings to blot out the sun so that all Yamuna could see was a shadow in the shape of a nightmare. He did not permit himself to flinch, even as the daemon stabbed its spear down at his heart and his eyes, at his hands and his private parts. The daemon could not harm him. The invisible bonds that restrained it were too well forged.

At last, the daemon seemed to have vented its immediate rage and it retired, snarling to its fellows.

'Why have you called us?' demanded the daemon, its voice heavy with its hatred.

'Because I have need of your eyes and your wings,' Yamuna replied calmly. 'I need you to see Avanasy Finorasyn Goriainavin.'

'What if we do see?' growled the first of the daemons.

'Then you will tell me what you see.'

'And if we do not see?'

Yamuna narrowed his eyes just a little. 'You will see.' *You will see because I can't find the little straying cow. But she will have recalled her teacher, and where he is, she will be.*

The first of the daemons snarled. He turned west, away from Yamuna and his fellows. His wide, yellow eyes stared steadily out through Devang's gate, searching, Yamuna knew, the whole world beyond.

'The man Avanasy Finorasyn Goriainavin sails south down the coast of Isavalta,' said the daemon slowly. 'He stands on the deck of a small boat. There is a woman at the tiller.'

'Who is the woman?' snapped Yamuna.

The daemon squinted. 'She has no name in this world. I know her not.'

'What else?'

'He is waiting for something. He speaks to the woman of it.' The daemon's sail-shaped ear twitched. 'He waits for a crow. The bird is a messenger between him and his man in Isavalta. He hopes it will find them before they reach the Heart of the World.' The daemon's wings shook themselves restlessly. 'That is what I see.'

The Heart of the World! The little cow had taken shelter with the Nine Elders? Yamuna considered. It was not so foolish a move as it might first appear. The Heart of the World was well protected against both force and magic. She could not be readily reached there, and she could warn the Nine Elders and their Emperor somewhat at least of what came toward them, removing the advantage of surprise. It might, in fact, be a swifter way to gain aid for her cause than sending her messengers hither and thither about her provinces trying to determine who was still loyal to her, especially if she had trusted spies still in Isavalta who could do that for her.

Well, well, there is a brain in that head after all. Yamuna permitted a small nod in deference to the child's scramblings. She would fail in the end, but at least she would put up a fight.

'You will allow that crow to meet with this man in Isavalta, and then you will bring it to me along with whatever message it carries,' said Yamuna to the daemons. 'You will also find the sorcerer Avanasy, and kill him and all who are with him.' There would be little Medeoan could do if she were cut off from her aides and information, and now that they knew where she was, they could watch movements down the coast all the more carefully. As soon as his strength was restored, he must send a message to Kacha.

The daemons growled, a long, low noise that he felt trembling through his torso.

'You ask too much of us, Man,' said the first of them. 'Take what we have seen and be content.'

Worry rippled through Yamuna's blood. If the daemons challenged him now, it was possible they might break free from his grip. The spell was strong, but he was weak, and he did not know how much of the working he could call on. He could not let it come to that.

'I still hold your chains,' he said coldly. 'I could at this moment bury you deep in the earth and you would not be able to move until I so ordered. But I am not such a master. You will do as I say because if you do not, you will suffer, and you know this.' His mouth twitched, as though he were about to smile. 'You remember other times you have suffered.'

The first of the daemons shrank back. Yamuna held himself very still. Like most of their kind, these four were inherently cowards. Terrible and powerful, but cowards all the same. When

Yamuna had first bound them to him, he had not done so out of immediate need, but because need might arise. He had driven them deep into the earth first, and left them there, snarling and howling. When he had finally pulled them forth, they were firmly his, cowed by fear of imprisonment in an element that was no part of their being, and so gave them no succor, only pain.

They remembered that imprisonment now. He saw it in their eyes, and in the way they pulled their heavy wings close about themselves.

'We will do as you say,' the first daemon told him.

'Good.' Yamuna nodded. 'Then go.'

The four daemons raised their arms, and lifted from the ground in a rattling flurry of wings and hot wind. In a heart-beat, they were gone and Yamuna was left alone with his exhaustion and a stark sense of relief.

It had almost been too much. He had almost failed.

It does not matter, he told himself, taking a long breath to purge the tremors beginning again in his limbs. *I did not fail, and now I know not only that I must stay bound to Chandra for this little while longer, I know where the Isavaltan Empress has hidden herself, and I can turn her shelter into her prison.*

Yamuna moved his gaze to the sun wheel again. *What does it matter that I am bound for awhile longer? Only the gods are truly free, and once I have that freedom for myself, nothing else will matter. Nothing at all.*

Eliisa paid off the canal boat's pilot with the three copper coins she had carefully counted out from her stash the night before. Thankfully, he took them without comment, slipping them into his sash, and nodding her farewell. The night before he'd suggested a way she might save the fee, and she'd been afraid she'd have to fight him off before the trip was over. But it had not come to that, and now she was safe in Camaracost.

If 'safe' was the word for it. Even thinking the name brought a sour taste to her mouth. Camaracost was a market town, a port town. Anything could be bought here, be it a passage to Hung-Tse, or a girl for the kitchens of a fine house.

She wondered for a moment if Mother still lived inside the city walls. She dismissed the idea. She could not idle here. If she was lucky, it was a market day, and she could see who was about doing the buying and the selling.

The streets by the canals were warrens of warehouses and storage barns. The best could be told by the hired guards standing alert at the doors in their clean kaftans and broad sashes. The worst slouched in the shadows near the open drains, either unattended, or watched over by greasy men with greasy eyes that glided over her as she strode past.

Noise and distant memory guided Eliisa's feet. Soon, she found herself in better, if more crowded, streets. Wooden houses, some two and three stories high, with brightly painted doors and roofs, crowded up to the cobbles. They left barely enough room for three grown men to walk abreast, let alone for the carts and mule trains that tried to squeeze through the streets.

Finally, the narrow thoroughfares opened onto the public square. The city's gilded god house shone in its center, and around it flocked all the crowds, noise, and smell of a bustling market. Stalls and tents filled the square the way the merchants' voices filled the air. Eliisa plunged into the crowd without hesitation. Housewives and husbandmen jostled shoulders with servants and agents for the noble houses. Men in the bright silks of Hastinapura haggled over baskets of nuts and bags of spices. Money-changers weighed and counted. Scribes recorded bargains and set the Lord Master's seal upon bills of goods and sales to show that the taxes had been duly paid. There were even men of Hung-Tse here, in long coats of plain, undyed cotton with jet buttons, pacing quietly through the throng, their sharp eyes darting this way and that.

They might be just who she wanted. If they were not, perhaps they could lead her to the ones she did.

As in all other transactions, however, appearing eager was a sure way to get cheated. Eliisa wished she had a basket so that she would look more like she was on an errand for some mistress. But, as it was, she kept most of her attention on the stalls she passed, fingering grains and dried beans. Sniffing suspiciously at the summer's first fruits, she was able to see the two men of Hung-Tse arguing with a seller from Hastinapura over sacks of cinnamon and peppercorns, judging by the smell the wind brought her. Eliisa bought herself a portion of black bread and liver sausage from a sharp-eyed biddy and squeezed into a corner between a stall and a house to eat it. The foreigners argued, haggled and dickered in a mix of languages, with much waving of hands and beating of breasts. At last, though, they bowed to each other, each in the fashion of his own country, and the shorter of the two men from Hung-Tse left his partner to write up the contract of sale and see to the proper seals while he stepped back into the stream of the crowd.

Eliisa smiled. Now it only remained to see which ship was his. The captain, whoever he might be, would surely not be averse to a little extra money, and another pair of hands in the galley.

Munching the last of her meal, Eliisa followed the foreigner through the crowds. He knew the ways of the market well, and crossed the center of the square nearest the god house where the crowds were thinner. On market days, beggars were permitted to cluster around the sides of the god house with their bowls to see what charity was to be had. They smelled even more strongly than the stalls of the spice merchants in the heat. As she passed, Eliisa caught the eye of one of the god house keeper's assistants who frowned at her. Ducking her head, Eliisa fished one of her remaining pennies out of her girdle and tossed it into one of the brass bowls that waited at the foot of the stairs. Supposedly, it garnered the good will of the gods as a charitable act. Eliisa was not so sure of herself that she was ready to turn down a little extra luck.

Eliisa followed her guide to the edge of town where the canals emptied into the bay. The world took on the smell of fish. Because it was summer, the docks were a forest of masts and sails. Tiny fishing boats bobbed between huge, sharp-keeled, oceangoing vessels. It was to one of these that her guide went. Eliisa marked the ship. It had a scratched, black hull, but the knotwork paint was bright and the wind nets hanging from its sides were whole and stout, and might even have been woven by an actual sorcerer. It was a prosperous ship, and Eliisa smiled. The voyage aboard that craft might even be fun, or at least comfortable.

'Now, then, my girl,' said a voice behind her. 'You're going to come along and explain yourself. I've many a question to put to you.'

Eliisa's throat closed and she turned. Behind her stood a soldier. He did not wear the gray and red livery of Camaracost's Lord Master. He wore the bright blue and gold of the Imperial House Guard.

'I don't have to go anywhere with you,' she snapped, trying to keep the tremor from her voice. 'I have my papers. I am free.'

'You're not, and you do,' replied the soldier, darting his eyes sideways so that Eliisa could not help but turn her head to see the two other guards waiting at the end of the dock. 'Come, my girl. You're wanted.'

'But why? They let me go!'

'That's not for me to say or you to ask.' His hand closed lightly around her elbow, with the clear implication that he could hold her much harder should she decide to struggle.

Eliisa's mouth hardened, and she knew there was something she could do about this, but she did not move. Instead, she remained quiet while the soldier, an over-sergeant, by the braid on his cuffs and the brass buttons on his kaftan, walked her back to the pair of under-sergeants that waited for them.

'Next time, my girl, if you want to stay hidden, do not pay off the local gods in Imperial coin.'

Eliisa's mouth went dry. 'What do they want me for?' she asked again. The over-sergeant had not released her and she had to step smartly to keep up as the under-sergeants marched them over the bridge and between the long tables where the fishermen unloaded and scaled their catch. The cobbles were slick with blood and the smell made Eliisa's head spin even worse than her sudden capture did. Despite that, she could not help but note the dark hair and features of the fishers, which told her they were probably all from the Island of Tuukos, as her mother had been.

A bent man struggling under a yoke of buckets filled with fish heads and guts staggered into the road. One of the under-sergeants reached out to cuff the old man and the blow knocked him off balance. The man sprawled onto the street, pouring guts and scales all across the soldiers' boots. He mumbled his apologies, and tried to scramble out of the way, but slipped in his own mess so that one of the under-sergeants tripped over the yoke and hit the ground beside him, cursing.

'Under-Sergeant!' shouted the soldier beside her, and his grip on Eliisa loosened, just a little.

Eliisa twisted hard and threw herself sideways. The sudden motion startled the soldier and Eliisa yanked herself free and ran, skidding on the slick cobbles but keeping her feet. She had more experience on wet slates than the House Guard. They must not catch her. They must not. She only barely knew why, but they must not.

Eliisa dodged between the tables, tossing one over as she passed, earning shouts and curses from the fishers working there as she splashed their wares all across the muddy street.

Then, a fresh set of hands grabbed her. Before she could think to struggle, they shoved her into a pile of empty pickling barrels. A fish-smelling tarp dropped over Eliisa and the barrels, cutting off all light. But by then she was recovered enough to understand she must hold quite still. Outside, something was piled on top of her shelter, pressing the canvas down until it rested against her skull.

Boots ran by. Voices shouted and argued. Someone brushed her canvas and Eliisa bit down hard on her lip. She tried to breathe quietly in the choking, fish-scented darkness. The sounds outside faded away, but she still did not move. The heat sent rivulets of sweat trickling down her cheeks and neck, but she didn't dare shift herself to wipe them away. Her right foot went to sleep.

Just as she thought she would surely faint from the heat and lack of air, a corner of the canvas peeled back to let in painfully bright light and the silhouette of a human head.

'Come out, Daughter,' said a man's voice, and Eliisa started. He was speaking in the language of Tuukos. No one had spoken that to her since she was five or six. Since her mother had signed her into service. It was like hearing a voice from a dream.

Stiff, and blinking hard, Eliisa crawled out of her stinking shelter. As she straightened up, she saw how badly she had lost track of time. The sun had already sunk behind the tallest houses, and the shadows lengthened across the water turning the bright-green bay to somber gray. Eliisa's hand flew to her mouth as her eyes sought out the water level as measured against the dock pilings. The tide had turned. Her ship might have already sailed.

'Calm yourself, Daughter,' said a lithe little man at her side. It was only by the bright-red cuffs on his rough, woolen smock that she recognized him as the man with the yoke who had tripped up the soldiers. She had thought him old, but now that he stood upright she saw he had not yet even reached his middle years. He added something more which she could not understand.

'I'm sorry, Father.' She tried to answer him in Tuukosov, but her tongue fumbled the words badly. 'I don't understand anymore.'

A woman nearby with a face like an old apricot spat and muttered something angrily. The only word Eliisa caught was 'Isavaltans.'

'Never mind, Daughter.' The man spoke slowly, as to a child, and patted her arm with his thick, callused hand. 'What did your parents name you?'

'Eliisa.'

'Well, Eliisa, it's no good you standing here in the street. You had best come along with us.'

'Thank you, Father, but I must . . .'

'That ship you were so intent on is still there,' he said kindly, but firmly. 'You'd best come with us.'

Eliisa swallowed her next words. The stubby woman frowned hard at her, and she remembered she should not be questioning her elders. So, she just nodded. She was too tired to do otherwise. Besides, she had to get somewhere she could be alone, and take her girdle off. It was important, but she couldn't remember why. Thinking in Tuukosov seemed to push the Isavaltan words out of her head.

'Good,' said the little man. 'I am Finon. The woman there is Ilta. We'll see you safe stowed among your own for the night.'

'Then, my girl,' said Ilta, taking her arm even more firmly than the over-sergeant had and steering her toward the docks, 'you can tell us what the House Guard wanted with you.'

'I don't know,' answered Eliisa stubbornly. 'I was let go. I've got the paper. It's sealed. I can go anywhere in the oblast.'

'And where in the oblast would you be going on that tall ship?' mused Finon.

'That's my business,' snapped Eliisa in Isavaltan. Ilta pinched her elbow hard. 'Hey!'

'Mind your manners, Girl. You've Isavaltan blood in you by the look of you. If it shows stronger than your clean blood, we may just hand you back to them.'

Eliisa swallowed. Here it came. Half-blood. Mother wouldn't have given her over else.

'Now, then, Ilta,' said Finon, his dark eyes glittering. 'She's still wearing the patterns, isn't she? Still knows her name, doesn't she? Give her time to remember herself. How long have you been with them, Daughter?'

Them. The Isavaltans, with their bright hair and pale eyes. Daemons who came out to the Holy Island and slaughtered the people and tried to drive out the True Ways by killing every sorcerer of the pure blood they could find. She'd heard all the stories when she was a child, and had held them close, even after Mother had signed her away. 'I was six when I was sold.'

'Huh. Your blood father should have starved himself first,' said Ilta.

'He was a soldier, Mother said,' muttered Eliisa to the cobbles. 'Isavaltan.'

She didn't have to say any more. They understood how she had come into the world, and Ilta spat again.

The warm summer darkness swiftly enclosed the bay. Ilta and Finon walked her past the tall ships and the tugs and the Isavaltan fishing vessels, to a cluster of boats the like of which she hadn't seen in years. They had square sterns and dark, square sails. Each was painted red, black and green with lettering stretched out and run together until it looked like knotwork, but each pattern was really a spell written out for the individual craft, taken from its name and blessed, if not painted, by a sorcerer.

Guttering lanterns hung from spars. The boats had been tied together in a cluster, and Eliisa knew there would be planks stretched between them to make walking from one to the other easier. The tiny fleet was, for the time being, a tiny village, huddled in the shadows and hoping the Isavaltans would not take notice of it tonight.

Finon led them to one of the boats. By the lantern light, Eliisa could see that it was painted bright green all over. That meant this was the headman's boat. Eliisa swallowed and hoped she could remember her manners. It would not do to anger these people. They knew knives and darkness. She could vanish so easily down here. Why had she agreed to come?

Because you had no choice, she reminded herself sharply as she tried to reassemble her courage.

Eliisa had lost the trick of the boats along with most of her blood's tongue, so she was forced to scramble clumsily over the side, even though Finon extended his hands to help her. The boat's deck was wide and its gear tidily stowed. Voices drifted down from the bow. Up by the galley, a pair of lanterns showed a gathering of solemn men and women, their heads together as they conferred. Finon removed his round cap and stepped forward, not seeming to notice the rocking motion of the deck. The gathering parted to reveal a young man sitting on a carved bench. Eliisa sucked in a breath. There was only one reason so young a man would be sitting when so many elders were standing. He was not a headman. He was a sorcerer.

Her heart sank within her and Eliisa tried to hang back, but it was far too late. Ilta was already pulling her forward, and Finon had raised his hand in salute to the sorcerer.

'We've rescued this daughter of the Holy Island from the guard,' he said, speaking slowly for Eliisa's benefit. 'With your blessing, I'll take her to my boat for sanctuary.'

Ilta pushed Eliisa forward. The sorcerer looked young, but he could have been any age. Sorcerers lived two and three times as long as normal men. His thick, black hair swept back from his high forehead, and his black eyes glittered in the lamplight. Here was one who knew his own power. As his gaze raked her from head to foot, Eliisa also knew that his power, at least here among these people, was considerable.

'Who taught you to tie your girdle in such a fashion, Little Sister?' the sorcerer asked. He had a smooth voice. It was easier to understand him than either Finon or Ilta.

Eliisa started to shrug, but caught herself. 'My mother, I suppose, Honored Brother,' she said, remembering to speak softly and keep her eyes cast down. Looking too long upon a sorcerer was bad luck, they said. They could draw your soul out through your eyes.

'Did your mother have power then?'

'No, Honored Brother.'

'Strange she should know that knot to teach you. It is a spell knot. Much in favor among the Isavaltans.'

Reflexively, Eliisa covered the knot with her hand, shrinking back as she did. 'I did not know, Honored Brother. Perhaps I learned it in the scullery. I was there a long time.'

'That could very well be,' said the sorcerer. 'There's many a scrap of knowledge in such a place.' He put his hand under her chin and tilted it up so she could see he smiled at her, and Eliisa felt herself relax a little.

A moment later, she heard fabric tearing, and her girdle thudded to the deck. Pain stabbed her heart and the whole world swam in front of her eyes as the spell snapped in two, and Eliisa vanished.

Medeoan stared at the knife in the sorcerer's hand. All around her, the Tuukosov had gone completely silent. The sorcerer stepped back, but made no move to sheathe the knife.

'Or perhaps, that knowledge has been too well remembered.'

There were no shouts, only mutters in the language she could not understand now that Eliisa had left her. Ilta, the woman who had been just barely willing to give one of her own the benefit of the doubt, raised her hand and would have brought it down against Medeoan's face, but the sorcerer stopped her with a sharp gesture.

'Who are you?' he asked in Isavaltan.

Medeoan lifted her chin. 'I thank you for saving me from the guard. I wish no quarrel, or trouble. I want only to be on my way.'

'That was not the question I asked,' said the sorcerer. He still had the knife out, and yet he also held back his countrymen with his word. 'Answer me truthfully, for you know that I can have the truth at any time.'

'I am taking myself away from my husband's home,' said Medeoan. 'He wants me back. Surely, you do not need to know any more than that. You do not want to be able to give answers to the guard.'

The sorcerer nodded thoughtfully. 'That is a reasonable thought, especially for an Isavaltan woman. It is still, however, not what I asked.'

Then Finon, who had been standing very still, moved over to the sorcerer. He murmured something, and the sorcerer's eyes widened. He touched Finon's hand and whispered back in his own language. Medeoan felt her throat tighten. An attempt to run would be useless, she would just have to bargain for time, until she was left alone and could contrive some weaving to help her escape. They were on the water, that would help with any magic of motion and uncertainty.

'Ilta,' the sorcerer said. Then he added something in his own language. Ilta's face went grim, and she grabbed Medeoan's elbow, with no pretense at gentleness this time.

'Come,' she barked and dragged Medeoan toward the boat's hatch. Medeoan saw the sorcerer watching her carefully while Finon murmured in his ear.

She had no opportunity to see anything else, for Ilta was stuffing her down into the boat's dark, fish-scented hold. At least there was somewhat more air to breathe here than there had been under the canvas. She heard Ilta moving about and then saw the spark and soft glow as a tin lantern was lit.

'Sit,' growled Ilta, stationing herself at the ladder leading to the deck. 'Make any other move and I will give you reason to regret it.'

Medeoan could not make out any benches or bunks in the shadows, so she picked a small cask and sat, folding her hands on her knees. Overhead she heard the sounds of many voices, rising and falling. They were all of them stern, and angry. That much she needed no language to understand. One glance at Ilta showed that she had no intention of leaving Medeoan alone. Probably that was on the orders of the sorcerer. Medeoan bridled at her confinement. There were so many things in this hold she could use to free herself, if she had the chance. There were ropes, and cloths, there was fire and there was water. Nothing would be easy, but so much could be done.

Once again, she found herself missing Avanasy. Not that she believed he would have automatically known what to do in this bizarre situation, but because she did not wish to be alone here. It was Avanasy she had always turned to when she did not want to be alone. Until Kacha had come, of course. Until Kacha had filled her heart with his lies and driven her to this. She could die here tonight, her throat slit by a crowd of peasants and dark sorcerers, and no one would ever know. Kacha would rule Isavalta, and she would have failed her parents and her land.

Anger shifted her weight and stiffened her spine. Ilta straightened up instantly in warning. Medeoan forced herself to stay calm. Her fingers idly smoothed down her apron. Her apron, her headscarf. Medeoan swallowed. Her headscarf with its bands of embroidery. Ilta stood in the lantern light, and Medeoan was surely lost in shadow. The embroidered threads she wore were faded and worn, and surely some of them were loosened. Anything she could make from such threads would only be a small weaving, but if she could make herself concentrate, it might be enough.

Sighing heavily, Medeoan pulled off her scarf and ran her hand through her hair.

Ilta made no move. Above her the voices continued on, now louder, now softer, debating her fate.

'I truly do not mean you any harm,' said Medeoan, drawing the scarf through her fingers. 'I just want to be on my way.'

Ilta only glared at her. Under her searching thumb, Medeoan found the crinkled end of a knot that had come loose. Overhead, someone pounded the deck to emphasize their point.

'I have no family who would pay for my return.' Medeoan plucked at the thread. It came blessedly loose from the fabric. She plucked at it again, and a little more unraveled from the patterns woven to keep Eliisa safe.

'You think we are bandits then?' sneered Ilta. 'You think we have no pride? That shame is for your people, not mine.'

'Then what do you want from me?' A bit more thread unraveled under her restless fingers. 'I'm worth nothing, I know nothing.'

'To begin with,' said the sorcerer's voice, 'we want to know what happened to the girl whose life you used.'

The sorcerer climbed down the ladder. He was tall, and for a Tuukosov he was slender, but that was all Medeoan could see. She crumpled her scarf in both hands.

'Ilta,' he said, and added a string of words. The woman ducked her head in acquiescence, and made her way up the ladder, while the sorcerer strode forward.

'Now, then,' he said, taking a seat on another cask. 'Let us not mince words, you and I. You are a sorceress. No other hand wove that girdle or bound it to you.'

Medeoan said nothing. The sorcerer reached out and took the scarf from her hands. It did not take him long to find the loosened thread and hold it up for inspection.

'Finon tells me the Isavaltan soldiers are all running about like rats looking for an insane sorceress who is claiming to be the Empress Medeoan, and that she is to be brought in for high treason and sowing dissent.'

He looked down his long nose at Medeoan, who felt herself go still as stone. Was that their plan? They had her own people, her own soldiers, sworn to her until death, planning to drag her in as a madwoman to be put to the question? How *dare* they!

Medeoan wanted to hang her head and cry, but she did not move. How dare they do anything else? But what had they done to hide her absence? What lie had Kacha dreamed up for this one?

'You do not act like one who has lost their wits to the moon,' said the sorcerer, toying with the loosened thread. 'But, so Finon tells me, you do look like the Empress Medeoan. Who is, as chance would have it, also a sorceress, and a powerful one at that.'

Medeoan turned her face to the darkness. She was out of lies. Her disguise was broken and her own people were in search of her. How could she convince soldiers, common soldiers who had never been to court, who she was? Could she take shelter with the Lord Master? Where did his loyalties lie? All this assumed she could even find a way to leave this tiny boat.

'But how could the Empress Medeoan be here?' went on the sorcerer, winding the loose thread around his finger. 'When all know she is in her confinement waiting to give birth to an heir for the glory of Eternal Isavalta.'

Medeoan's head snapped up. Confinement! That was their lie! Who assisted them? That treacherous crowd of hens Kacha had surrounded her with? Oh, she was a fool, a *fool* and she almost deserved to die for what she had allowed to happen.

'So.' The thread snapped abruptly in the sorcerer's hand. 'So,' he said again, and the soft whisper was like a laugh. 'They say the world moves in patterns woven on fate's own loom, but I had not truly believed that before this moment.' He stood up, and reverenced to her. 'Majesty, you must forgive me if I take some time to decide what should be done now. There are many among my people who would like to see you dead, and would be only too glad to do the deed.' He looked down at the scarf he held. 'No more of spells, Majesty, please. I will not be far away, and I will feel any such workings. I have no wish to bind your hands.'

He left her then, and she heard the hatch close. She stood at once, and in the dim lantern light, began to search the hold. It was packed with casks and crates, cages and nets, but there were no portals, and no other hatch. Medeoan looked around at all the lengths of cord, and thought that the boots she heard pacing the deck must belong to the sorcerer. He had not even told her his name, damn the arrogance of him. The Tuukosov were ever arrogant. It was their nature, Father said, and why they had to be watched so closely. Yet, when Kacha's murderous plans had come to fruition, Father had been at work negotiating with the Tuukosov nobility, such as they were, with an eye to increasing the freedom of the island. Perhaps that had been a mistake. Medeoan sat back down and rested her head in her hand. Or perhaps not. That mercy might be what now kept her alive.

A swift spell could be finished before the sorcerer came down the hatch, which was surely battened down. But a swift spell would carry little power. A powerful spell would take time. There had to be a way. Whole nets were made of strings of single knots. There had to be a way, a way to build on small bindings, windings and entanglements. There had to be a way . . .

In the darkness of the hold, alone and exhausted, Medeoan fell asleep.

'Empress.' A hand shook her roughly. Medeoan started awake, instantly ashamed and afraid. The face of the man Finon looked down at her.

'Come on. Hush.' He beckoned to her and began climbing the ladder.

Medeoan gathered up her skirts to follow. 'What are you . . .'

'Getting you out of here, Empress.' He lifted the hatch and peered into the darkness. 'Come, quietly.'

Medeoan closed her mouth and followed him up the ladder, setting her boots lightly on the rungs. Out in the moonlight and the fresh wind, she could see the deck cluttered with sleeping bodies. Finon stepped nimbly between them, moving toward the bow. Medeoan followed as best she could. Fortunately, the sleepers seemed used to people walking among them, and none woke.

Finon slipped over the rail down into a dinghy with its broad oars neatly shipped. He reached up for Medeoan and she allowed him to help her down onto the bench beside him. She knew enough to scramble out of Finon's way so that he could grasp the oars and push off from the sorcerer's boat, dipping one oar and then the other silently into the gentle waves, steering them deftly through the larger craft.

'I've seen the master of the *Gull's Wing*,' Finon whispered as they pulled away from the docks. 'He's willing to take you aboard, and quietly, provided you've money to pay. Have you money, Empress?'

Medeoan nodded.

'Good.'

Finon said nothing else. The oars clacked and splashed as he worked them, and their boat pulled past the end of the dock. Finon turned them parallel to the shore and pulled harder, heading for the berth of the *Gull's Wing*.

'Why . . .' she began.

'Do not ask that question, Empress,' said Finon through his teeth. 'You might not want the answer.'

Medeoan held her peace. She did not wish this man to change his mind. After another moment's silence, however, Finon said, 'I have seen my cousins, my blood kin, beaten in the streets for failing to bow to the Imperial flag. I have seen friends burned out of their houses under suspicion of harboring rebels.' He did not look at her, he kept his gaze on the water past her shoulder. 'What will be done to us if it is found we murdered the Empress of Isavalta?' He sucked on his teeth for a moment as he worked the oars in steady strokes. 'Though there are those who say it would be justice.'

'Such as your sorcerer?'

Finon chuckled. 'Do you really believe I could have taken you out of there with such ease without Valin Kalami's permission?' He shook his head. 'Kalami knows the reality of our place in the world. He knows that we must bow before we break.'

Medeoan was silent for a moment. Who was the Lord Master of Tuukosov? Direshk, wasn't it? When had she last seen a letter from him? Had she ever? She had never asked the secretaries for any such thing, she was sure of that. How well did he carry out her father's new policies?

Medeoan suppressed a laugh. Here she was, a peasant in a peasant's boat, wondering about matters of high policy. She didn't even know if she'd live to reach the next shore, let alone to take her place under the Imperial canopy again.

Nonetheless, she said, 'I will not forget this.'

'See that you don't, Empress.'

There was nothing she could say to that. Finon steered the boat to the end of a dock and shipped the oars again. 'This is as far as I go. The *Gull's Wing* has the third berth. The night watch knows to listen for your hail. They know you by the name Eliisa.'

Medeoan hesitated for a moment and then reached into her waistband, bringing out a silver coin. 'Take this coin to the fortress of Dalemar,' she said. 'Ask for Captain Peshek. Tell him what has passed. He will see you safe in some new position. Tell him it is my order.'

But Finon just waved the coin away. 'Save your favors, Empress. But do not forget them.'

'But those others . . .'

'Are my people. I'll deal with them. I just ask that you remember what happened here today.' He sucked on his teeth again. 'It may be one day I turn up at your high palace, and it may be I have someone with me who needs a place as badly as you needed shelter. Then I'll take my Empress's boon, and be glad of it.'

Medeoan nodded. 'Tell me your full name then, so I can remember.'

'Finon Pasi,' he replied, staring intently at her with his dark eyes. 'I will hold your promise, Empress.'

Of all the things that had happened in the long, hard day, that one stung her pride. 'You will not have to,' she said, drawing herself up. 'For I hold it myself and Vyshko and Vyshemir have heard me speak.'

Finon made no answer, he only bowed where he sat. Medeoan accepted the gesture with a nod. Then, she turned and clambered up the ladder to the dock, hurrying toward the ship that would take her to Hung-Tse and the Heart of the World.

I must succeed now, she told herself. *I have made promises in the name of the rule Imperial. I cannot fail now. Vyshko and Vyshemir have heard me speak in their stead.*

There, alone in the darkness, surrounded by tall ships and fleeing from her own soldiers, Medeoan at last felt them, the bonds of empire of which her father had spoken. Shackle and support, he'd called them, and he'd been right.

Medeoan felt her shoulders square themselves as she hurried forward into the night.

Chapter Thirteen

T'ien, the great city that held the Heart of the World, was a city of walls. Walls sheltered it from the outside world. Walls separated its quarters from each other. Walls lined its streets and hid its gardens. Walls held its garrisons and their broad tops provided pathways for its soldiers. Walls cradled its markets and squares.

Medeoan sat hunched in the shadow of one of the beige, stone walls, nursing her sore feet and trying to feel fortunate. Her ship had arrived without incident. No one on board had questioned or molested her. She had been able to perform the tasks assigned, not as well as Eliisa could have, but she got by, and she was safe and sound in the city that held the Heart of the World.

All that was left was the question of how she was to approach the Heart's gate. She could not simply walk up, tattered and unattended, and announce she was the Empress of Isavalta. She did not have enough money left in her waistband to buy even a decent wardrobe, let alone the regal one she should have worn. She could not hire a single bodyguard.

But neither could she appear weak before the Nine Elders. She could not be seen to beg.

'I am so tired,' she whispered. 'Vyshemir, help me, I am so tired.'

Tired of moving, tired of wondering what was being

whispered behind her, tired of being so constantly afraid. Even if she could have acquired the proper materials to weave herself another disguise, Medeoan did not believe she could have concentrated long enough to complete the spell.

Medeoan lowered her head into her hands and scrubbed her scalp to try to wake herself up. This was useless. She had to try. She had to find some way. She could not simply sit here and wait for some spy of Kacha's to find her. If he could even be bothered. She leaned her head against the wall. The Empress of Isavalta, lost in a foreign land in a servant's clothes. Why go looking for her? She had put herself out of the way most efficiently. Kacha could consolidate his power over her empire and birthright without hindrance.

That thought rekindled Medeoan's anger. If for no other reason, if not for duty of birth or the gods or her parents' deaths, she would see Kacha crawl to prove she was not to be taken lightly, to prove she was no longer lulled by his warm words or warmer touch, that she would not forgive him, even if he begged. She would only spit on him and order him put to death . . .

So why can I not stop missing him?

She did miss him. She missed his touch, his scent, looking into his eyes and seeing the light within them. Part of her knew that she would miss those things until the day she died, and that part wept.

'Now then, here's a pretty lady all alone.'

Medeoan jerked her chin down. A man stood in front of her. His robe was plain, black cotton with wide cuffs of deep blue that no one but the Imperial family would be allowed to wear in Isavalta. His burlap pack made a hump for his left shoulder. He wore his hair in a long pony-tail, as was the fashion for the men of Hung-Tse, and his eyes twinkled as he smiled at her.

Medeoan mustered what she hoped was a haughty stare. Evidently it was close enough, for the man shrank backward in a pose of mock cowardice.

'Such ice! Such power! I shall surely be struck to pieces with another such glance!' He peered at her from behind his hands. 'Perhaps the pretty lady will accept a gift? To show that we are indeed friends?' When Medeoan did not move or answer, he lowered his hand. 'A poor sorcerer am I,' he said, waving his left hand about in the air. 'A poor sorcerer of limited gifts who must carry his own pack along the roads and under the shadows of walls, but even such a poor sorcerer as I may give a gift to a pretty lady.' He opened his hand to show a fold of silk. Deftly, he knotted the silk, and pulled the knot close, and through, and opened the silk again, and inside lay a delicate summer flower with petals the color of ripe peaches.

With a flourish, the man made the silk vanish, and handed Medeoan the flower. To her surprise, she felt herself smile.

'Thank you,' she said, inhaling the sweet scent. 'But I have nothing to give you.'

'Ah, but perhaps you do,' he smiled. 'Perhaps the pretty lady will allow me to ply my arts on her behalf. A horoscope? To tally the lovers that will surely be lining up before her door? An amulet of good luck? My powers are humble, to be sure, but they will serve, they will serve.'

'They will serve to make a pretty trick for a sad day,' Medeoan answered. 'But no further.'

'The pretty lady assumes because my workings are humble, they are not sound,' said the man, his voice for the first time growing peevish.

'There was no true working made here,' Medeoan said sternly. During the moment of creation, a sorcerer could feel a spell being created, especially if it was being completed nearby. 'You know that, as do I. Thank you for the flower, Man. I have no coin to spare.'

'Then may someone teach you what it is to give your best for nothing,' he spat and stalked away, hitching his lumpy pack up higher on his shoulder.

'It's already happened,' she whispered to his back and his flower.

Still, it was a pleasant trick. Even as she thought that, a fresh idea tickled at the back of her mind. A trick. Could such a trick get her into the palace? She was already in disguise. Eliisa was gone from her, but she still retained some knowledge that the girl's presence had left in her mind. If she could just get inside the walls, then she would be able to find her way. She knew the customs of palaces, and of servants, as well as of nobles. All she had to do was get herself inside.

Medeoan, hope and energy restored, climbed to her feet and strode briskly down the street, following the path the trickster had taken.

The walls guarding the five palaces that formed the Heart of the World were, at first glance, painted a bright, solid yellow. Only after staring at them for a long time could Medeoan discern the patterns made with delicate brushstrokes and enormous skill. Dragons, whiskered unicorns, phoenixes, tortoises, horses, oxen, and cranes all had been woven together, layer upon layer, picture upon picture, to create a net of protective spells that stretched out on all sides, sealing the Emperor away from any dangers.

But such walls must have gates, for the servants as well as for the nobles, and although she knew the Heart of the World held orchards, gardens and fish ponds as well as palaces, its extensive grounds were not enough to feed all its occupants. Food, at the very least, had to be brought in.

Medeoan bought herself a scrub brush and a bucket, and now she knelt outside the tall, yellow walls, slowly scrubbing at the bricks in the street, keeping one eye on the western gate, the servants' small gate. It had a complement of six guards, which was changed regularly, for no one charged with the Emperor's safety was foolish enough to believe that a servant could not bring harm to their master. But still, she could see that in the steady stream of traffic flowing in and out some carts and some pack animals were searched more thoroughly than others. Could she follow such a servant, and be smuggled inside in a bag or a basket? She shook her head. She was beginning to think like a tale in an opera, but still, it might work, and it might be less risky than an attempt at bribery. Medeoan dunked her brush in her bucket and turned her attention briefly to her bricks, so as not to be caught staring too long at the Imperial gate.

A mule tender, an empty hay cart and a detachment of soldiers all paraded out from the gate. Medeoan squinted up at the driver. He was a pudgy man in a good green coat, and a broad-brimmed straw hat to protect himself from the sun.

Follow him, she told herself. *See where he goes, how he is regarded. See where your chance is.*

She dropped her brush into the bucket with a splash and a thunk and staggered to her feet. Her right leg had gone numb from spending the entire morning kneeling on bricks. She would have thought her shipboard labors would have hardened her to such tasks, but not yet, evidently.

She shook her leg, and tried to rub some feeling back into it, when a shadow fell across her.

'Well, here's a pretty lady all alone.'

Medeoan could not stop herself from looking up. In front of her stood the mountebank, the false sorcerer. He still wore his black coat with its blue cuffs, but his pack was gone and he carried himself straight and proud, all trace of mischievous twinkle gone from his black eyes. Around him stood six soldiers, the saffron sashes around their waists and gold trim around their helmets marking them as members of the Heart's guard.

'Take her,' ordered the false sorcerer.

One of the soldiers reached for her. Medeoan swung her bucket, a pathetic weapon at best, and doused him over with muddy water, but the bucket itself only clanked against his armored coat, and he swatted it angrily away. Before she could run, another of them caught her from behind, seizing both her wrists. She twisted, trying to kick out, but he held her fast. Another of them moved forward, and Medeoan screamed as she saw the iron shackles ready to close about her wrists.

'No!'

But her cries did no more good than her struggles, and the soldier snapped the shackles shut, twisting the iron key in the lock that sealed them, and then turning with a bow to present the key to the false sorcerer.

'Who are you?' demanded Medeoan. 'How dare you!'

'I am the one who has found a foreign sorceress,' he replied mildly. 'And I dare for I serve the Nine Elders and through them the Emperor Himself. If she speaks again, you may strike her,' he said to the soldier to Medeoan's left.

'Sir,' he bowed.

'Bring her.'

The soldier pushed Medeoan, who stumbled forward, too startled to protest. The shackles weighted her hands down in front of her. The short chain that held them together rattled. The false sorcerer, the Imperial official, walked ahead of her without a backward glance.

The yellow walls with their iron-studded gates passed by,

and Medeoan had her wish. She almost laughed. She was inside the Heart of the World.

All she saw before her was another yellow wall, as cunningly and delicately painted as the first. It was thicker, though, and she guessed by the narrow slits of windows in its sides and the sentries on its top that it held its own garrison. The two walls made a narrow lane that her nightmarish escort now marched her along. Her hair had come loose and wisps fluttered into her face, but she didn't dare raise her hands to brush them aside.

After what seemed an age, they came to a portcullis in the inner wall. The six guards there raised their spears and swords in salute to her party. Medeoan had to stop herself from giving a reflexive and regal nod in return. Again she almost laughed. This was indeed becoming a bad dream.

Medeoan only caught a glimpse of the great tiled courtyard that lay beyond the inner wall. The Imperial official unlocked a door on the right-hand side of the passage and the soldiers marched Medeoan into the wall.

The world at once became cool and dim. Single beams of light filtered through the slit windows, and a pair of lanterns hung on either side of an iron-banded door that the official unlocked with a key he drew out of his robe. Medeoan blinked hard, trying to will her eyes to adjust, and she succeeded well enough to see the beginnings of a stairway leading down into the earth and darkness.

'No,' she said, hanging back. 'You don't . . .'

A heavy hand came down, and pain exploded in Medeoan's head, making her see stars. Reeling, she barely felt herself shoved forward. She stumbled and would have fallen, had someone not caught her up under her arm and, pinching her painfully, hauled her forward.

Slowly, the dizzying pain receded and Medeoan realized she

was once again on level ground. Her vision stilled and cleared enough for her to see she was being led down a stone corridor lit at intervals by copper lanterns hung from the ceiling. Ahead, the corridor opened into a square room dominated by a table of chipped black wood behind which waited a crooked stick of an old man who wore a black coat that matched that of the Imperial official who led Medeoan's escort. The two men bowed to one another and spoke together, too fast and too soft for Medeoan to follow. The stick-figure official sniffed and wrote something down on the paper scroll that was spread out before him. Another soldier came forward and grabbed Medeoan's chain, jerking her forward. She opened her mouth, to try to protest or explain, but the memory of the last blow was too fresh, and she shut it again.

The new soldier dragged her into another square corridor, lit by more lamps, but this one was lined with iron doors. An eerie silence filled Medeoan's ears. The guard's square-toed shoes did not even make any noise against the dusty stone floor. One door in the left-hand wall stood open. The soldier tweaked Medeoan's chain, and she stumbled inside. The door swung shut without even a whisper from the hinges, cutting off all light. As if from a great distance, Medeoan heard a lock click.

Then there was only silence, and the sound of her own shallow breathing in the absolute darkness.

A tear trickled from her eye, tickling her cheek with its slow descent. It was followed by another, and another, until a stream of them ran down her face. But she could not raise her hands. The chains were too heavy. All she could do was stand and weep until her strength failed her and she fell to her knees, weeping still, until at last the darkness wrapped itself tight around her mind and she knew no more.

* * *

The god house of Vaceta was seldom empty during the summer. Much of the prosperity of the town came from the fact that the court was in residence, and its merchants as well as those who tended its fields trooped in and out to ask the god that their sons, their daughters or they themselves might be noticed by some member of the household staff and signed to indenture for the summer, earning a year's wages in a few months, and a reputation for having served the Imperial household, which would last for a good deal longer than a year. Courtiers not housed in Vaknevos itself also had need of their houses, their staffs, their artisans and servants. While not as good as an Imperial appointment, they were still more secure than the hit-and-miss life of one bound to no house, and therefore much sought after. It seemed that the entire town was more engaged in offering prayers or giving thanks than it was in the business of the day.

Peshek found it easy to settle in under the shadow of one of the carved pillars and wait without being noticed or remarked upon.

Vaceta did not have anything like the Imperial budget for gilding their god house, but they had made up for it by employing the best of their woodworkers to carve the interior into a haven of bounty. The supporting pillars were trees laden with apples and pears. The arched roof held friezes of all manner of artisans at their trades. The walls showed reliefs of farmers reaping and gathering in plentiful fields accompanied by fat-cheeked children lifting sheaves of grain or baskets of vegetables to the sky.

Cezta, the god of the city, stood on his pillar, a fresh, green branch in one hand and the other raised in blessing. Supposedly, he had gained his divinity during a famine by going out into a field and feeding his own blood to the soil. The next day, the grain waved fresh and green in the summer sun, and Cezta was gone.

But it was not Cezta Peshek had come to beg the aid of. Once every ten days or so while the court was in its summer home, the Keeper of the Emperor's God House would come to Cezta's god house, to call on the keeper and extend the courtesies and the blessings of Vyshko and Vyshemir. Peshek had been hanging about the doorways and market places for days waiting to overhear when the visit might be expected. Now that the day had finally arrived, all that was left was to wait and see if Keeper Bakhar had managed to survive at his post.

Peshek forced himself to exercise again the patience he had spent the recent days practicing. Since leaving his father's house, he had traveled on foot, mostly at night, pausing here and there to work a day in a field or barn for a meal or a night's lodging, so that he might be taken for nothing but an unattached laborer, no one to rouse suspicion, or even comment, except from maids, and not infrequently, matrons with good eyes and lively minds.

He had tried to plan for what to do if Bakhar were no longer the keeper, but his mind could not seem to address the problem. He could only wonder what could have been done to the keeper, and what the keeper would have said before it was completed.

The doors to the god house opened again. Peshek let his eyes flicker up from their reverent attitude, and his heart leapt. Bakhar strode into the dim house, accompanied by the men who bore the titles of Right Hand and Left Hand. All three were dressed in the simple, belted blue robes Bakhar favored for non-ceremonial occasions. Bakhar's only adornments were the small gold symbols on his belt's end; a cup, a knife and a pike.

Peshek pushed past a knot of worshippers, hurrying toward the central aisle. Bakhar walked forward toward Cezta to pay his respects. The local keeper came out of the back, and opened his arms wide in a gesture of welcome. Bakhar lifted his hand in return. Peshek hurried forward, and collided straight into the Left Hand, who in turn collided with Bakhar.

'Clumsy . . . !' began the Left Hand, but a glance from the keeper checked his exclamation.

'I'm so sorry!' gasped Peshek, stepping back just a little and folding his hands to reverence to the keeper. 'Forgive me, Sir, please . . .'

'That's perfectly all right . . .' began Bakhar. Peshek lifted his head and met the keeper's eyes. Recognition and surprise flickered swiftly across the other man's visage. '. . . My son,' Bakhar went on smoothing down his robe. 'No harm.'

Reverencing humbly, and keeping his head ducked lest the Left Hand and Right Hand should chance to recognize him, Peshek retreated down the aisle and out the doors. The summer sun was painfully bright after spending the better part of a day inside the dim god house, but the fresh breeze was more than welcome.

Fortunately, there were not many loiterers around the god-house steps to notice him cross the street and settle himself into the shadowy niche between two houses across the way. This time, though, he found it hard to make himself wait. The man he needed was but two dozen feet away, separated from him by a few wooden walls. The keeper had seen him. If he couldn't get back in there quietly, his best chance at good information would shortly be beyond his reach, again, and there would be nothing for it but more delay and yet more waiting in shadows. Peshek's palms began to itch with impatience.

At last, a small troop of men with muddy boots and undyed kaftans strode up the street and turned toward the god house. Peshek ducked out of his hiding place and joined their number, affording himself an anonymous entry back into the holy place after his rather public exit.

Peshek queued up with the farmers to kiss the hem of the god's robe, as was proper. As he put his lips to the bright, green fabric, he glanced toward the back of the house. There stood Bakhar in quiet conference with the local keeper, a far slighter man with a mournful face and stubby hands.

But did Bakhar see him? Peshek bit his lip and stepped sideways to make way for the other worshippers. After a bad moment wondering what to do, he dropped to one knee facing Cezta's image and bowed his head, making himself the picture of a poor man with many cares, praying for succor from this most prosperous god, and, at the same time, putting himself directly in Keeper Bakhar's line of sight.

The move had its intended effect. After only a few heart-beats, a hand touched his shoulder, and Peshek looked up to see Bakhar standing over him.

'I see your heart is heavy, my son,' Bakhar said. 'Would you care to come and talk a little? Perhaps together we can under-stand how Cezta, under the hands of Vyshko and Vyshemir, touches your life.'

'Thank you, Good Keeper,' said Peshek, keeping his voice low and his face solemn.

'Come with me.'

Peshek rose and followed Bakhar into the niche that each god house in Isavalta kept for Vyshko and Vyshemir. Their representations were carved into an alcove above a curving shelf meant for offerings. Two low stools had been placed there to accommodate any who needed to stay and meditate for a long period.

Bakhar kissed his fingers, and laid them on the carved folds of the gods' robes and then reverenced. Peshek did the same. As he did, he stole a glance at the keeper. The man had aged since Peshek had last seen him. Tired lines ran down his cheeks and his normally serene eyes had grown uneasy.

'You take a chance being here,' whispered Bakhar as Peshek straightened up. 'But I am glad beyond words to see you. Tell me quickly, how fares the Empress?'

'I wish I could tell you,' muttered Peshek, his gaze darting around the niche and the greater house, just to make sure no one had strayed too near. 'She has fled to the Heart of the World, and, as much as it pains me, I have orders other than to accompany her. I can tell you she has help on the way. Avanasy has returned.'

Bakhar closed his eyes and let out a long sigh. 'I had not dared to hope, but I could not believe he would stay away at such a time.'

'Avanasy says that Lord Iakush gave his life to warn him as to what was happening.' Peshek rubbed his hands together.

This time, Bakhar's sigh was heavy. 'I wondered. It's been given out the Lord Sorcerer died of a hemorrhage in his spleen. No one will speculate though, on what might have caused that hemorrhage, and his body was not allowed to lie in state before burial.' Bakhar's hand strayed to the golden icons on his belt. 'You've heard what happened at the games for the Hastinapuran ambassador?'

Peshek sat himself on one of the padded stools, rubbing his scalp and face. 'I've heard something dramatic happened, but the rumors in the streets have doubtlessly improved greatly on reality.'

Peshek listened grimly while Bakhar told him of the arrival of the lone, tattered soldier right in the middle of the martial display, and his declaration of Hung-Tse's treachery.

'Is what this man said true?' he asked when the keeper's soft voice fell silent.

Bakhar shook his head. 'I have not been able to learn for

certain, but I doubt it.' His whole face hardened. 'Kacha has already orchestrated far more difficult displays.'

'And where stand the Council? Do they all accept Kacha's story of early confinement and an impending heir?'

'To a man. Kacha has done something to them. I smell magics here, but I cannot find the source. Kacha is no sorcerer himself, nor did he bring one from Hastinapura. He barely holds any conference with the sorcerers who remain at court, so who is aiding him and how?' Bakhar's gaze rested on the images of Vyshko and Vyshemir for a long moment. 'Avanasy might be able to tell us, but Avanasy is needed elsewhere.'

'Except that Avanasy was asking the same questions.' Peshek's fist tightened. 'So, the Empress has no friend left at court?'

'None I am certain could be trusted with the truth.'

For the first time, Peshek heard the strain in the keeper's voice, and he realized suddenly that since the Empress's flight, Bakhar had been even more alone than he himself had. He reached out and touched the other man's arm.

'How is it you remain above suspicion?'

Bakhar's mouth twisted into a humorless smile. 'By pretending to be a foolish old man concerned with nothing outside my god house. Kacha is juggling so many intrigues right now, I believe he is content to let that facade stand.' Again, he looked to the gods, reaching out from their alcove, their weapons held high. 'But what luck have you had?'

'My father is sounding out the lords he believes will hear the truth and keep it close to themselves. I am to meet his messenger shortly. If all goes well, we will soon have arms to back our answer to Kacha's declarations.'

'You have brought me the first good news I've had in many days.' Bakhar smoothed his beard down. He looked as tired as Peshek felt. *We are not either of us meant for intrigue,* thought

Peshek. *Not truly.* 'I will begin to move beyond the house as much as I am able. Perhaps I can find the source of what has blinded so many shrewd men.'

'Do your best, Good Keeper,' said Peshek getting to his feet. 'Send what word you can to my father. If any know where to find me, he will.' Remembering his role, Peshek reverenced in the peasant fashion. 'I will send your news to Avanasy. Perhaps he can puzzle this out from a distance, or at least tell us where to begin looking.'

Bakhar touched Peshek's brow in blessing. 'Vyshko walks strong beside you, my son.'

There was nothing more to be said. Head ducked, shoulders rounded, Peshek left the house for the broad, cobbled street and the summer sun. As soon as his eyes had adjusted again to the brightness, he set off down the street, heading for the city's wooden walls and the south gates. He wound his way quickly and confidently through the crowded streets, the carts and mules, the goose-herders and the men toiling under heavy sacks.

Then, faintly, he heard a rhythmic sound that made him pause, causing a woman struggling along with a huge basket to curse and shoulder her way past him. Peshek listened. Under all the thousand sounds of the busy city, he heard it again. A steady, rhythmic tramping that could have but one source; the boots of many soldiers.

No sooner had Peshek identified the sound, than a faint but imperious voice from a man as yet unseen called out, 'Clear the way! Clear the way for the House Guard Imperial!'

Groans and cursing broke out from the crowds. Carters whipped their animals, trying to get them off to one side. All around, beasts and people jostled one another, noisy with their complaints, seeking some side-street or alley that would get them away from the crush. But Peshek heard another noise as he strove to keep the pressure of the crowd from pushing him down the alley at his back. Along the street, cheers swelled growing louder with each heartbeat, as did the sound of marching feet.

Up ahead, the street bent in a broad curve. Peshek craned his neck along with the rest to try to see who was coming. At last, a broad shadow filled the bend, and then the ranks of the House Guard marched into view.

They were decked out as brightly as for any Imperial review. Gilded armor shone in the sun, as did the tips of the pikes. Blue coats were flawless. They marched in stride, rank on rank, their armor and arms jingling in metallic counterpoint.

Officers on horseback flanked the foot soldiers, and Peshek stared in dismay at faces he knew. Habat, whose nose was as crooked as an old man's back from the number of times it had been broken. Maccek, with whom he'd fought over one of the weaver girls in the sheds and gotten far too drunk with an hour afterwards when they both found out she preferred Over-Lieutenant Oal. Rzhova, who still owed him two days' pay from their last game of dice.

Stop! he wanted to shout at him. *Stop! You don't know what you're doing! Come with me! I'll show you the enemy!*

But he was alone in the cheering crowd. They'd heard the stories come down from Vaknevos, and they believed. Why shouldn't they?

'Cut the heart right out of them!' shouted a man to Peshek's right.

'Captain! Captain!' cried another man with a sack of charcoal on his back. 'Give 'em two for me!'

Rzhova turned his head and began to reverence genially to the crowd, and then he froze, and Peshek had a single heartbeat to realize he'd been a fool.

Here he stood, at least half a head taller than those around him, close enough to the grand parade to recognize the faces of old comrades.

Close enough to be recognized by them.

He had only enough time to turn to run before Rzhova shouted, 'Peshek, you traitor!'

The press of bodies before him suddenly became a solid wall. Peshek swore and tore at shoulders and coats, shoving people sideways as far as he could. He could feel the crowd stirring behind him to try to let Rzhova ride through. He was sure he heard the rasp of a sword being drawn. Peshek slammed his shoulder against a portly man who tried to grab his arms. That broke the wall of bodies just far enough and Peshek fled down the stinking alley. In the space of another breath, hoofbeats clattered after him.

Peshek didn't dare look back. He pelted ahead as fast as he could, but his boots skittered on the garbage that littered the cobbles. Twice he stumbled, and almost fell. He slammed his shoulder against a door, seeking to find a way into one of the houses, only to find it solidly barred.

'Coward!' shouted Rzhova. 'Make your stand!'

Clutching his shoulder, Peshek turned. Rzhova, tall and terrible on horseback bore down on him, standing in the stirrups, sword held high. Peshek bit back a cry of terror and got ready to duck if he could.

All at once, another harsh scream cut the air. Peshek jerked around, thinking it was another soldier. Instead, a black bird dove down, making him duck his head. Rzhova hollered and flung up his arm to protect his eyes as the bird went straight for him, cawing fiercely.

Peshek did not wait to see what would happen next. He took off running down the alley again, praying that Vyshko really did walk strong beside him, and that He had made it hard enough for the other officers to get their horses through the crowds that there would be no one waiting for Peshek at the end of the alley. Behind him, the crow squawked angrily and Rzhova cursed, and the horse's hooves clopped as the animal danced, but none of those sounds grew closer.

Several sacks of chaff and straw waited by the alley's mouth. Peshek snatched a pair up as he ran past, hoisting one onto each shoulder and plunging straight for the middle of the crowd. The continuous roll of voices, the brays and snorts of animals, and the creaking of overburdened carts filled up the world and Peshek could make out no other noise. Flanked by his sacks, he could only see a narrow slice of what was ahead of him. The sacks itched his cheeks, and their must and dust tickled his nose. But he heard no shouts for him to halt, and the only clopping of hoofs came from reluctant mules and flocks of sheep.

At last, Peshek spied another alley. He slowly worked his way to the edge of the crowd, tossed down his sacks and slumped momentarily against the corner of the house. From the cool and dirty smell coming up from the narrow way, this one led to the canals. Good. From there he could get his bearings again and maybe find a boatman for hire. It would be the quickest way out of the city.

While all this flashed through his mind, two sharp caws sounded overhead. A glossy black crow perched on the eaves of the house Peshek leaned against. With a clatter of wings, the bird dropped onto the sack that Peshek had just discarded.

There was absolutely no doubt in Peshek's mind that this bold creature was the same one that had saved him from Rzhova. Pushing aside all feelings of foolishness, Peshek crouched down until his head was level with the crow's. It regarded him first with one round eye, then the other, then it cawed again.

'I owe you my thanks, Master Crow,' murmured Peshek,

reaching out with one finger to stroke the shining feathers. The bird cawed again, outraged at the familiarity and hopped backwards.

'Your pardon, your pardon,' Peshek murmured, drawing his hand back at once. 'And may I assume you are the messenger my friend Avanasy promised to send?'

The bird cawed once more and puffed its feathers out proudly.

'Your timing, Sir, is impeccable.' Peshek rested his forearms on his knees. 'You may tell our friend . . .'

It was only then that the enormity of what he had seen and heard engulfed him. Until this instant, he'd had no time to consider what it meant. But now he grew cold as his thoughts ordered themselves. Isavalta was going to war against Hung-Tse, and the Empress was traveling toward the Heart of the World. If she reached Hung-Tse's Emperor, she would be taken hostage at once and held for ransom. Kacha would never pay such a ransom, because that would mean he would have to admit that she was not in confinement in Vaknevos after all. If she could not be ransomed . . . Peshek closed his eyes. Hung-Tse would not waste their time on her.

'Tell him urgently that the Empress must not go to the Heart of the World. Kacha has mobilized for war against Hung-Tse, and she is sure to be taken hostage by the Nine Elders.'

The crow bobbed its head several times, as if to reassure Peshek that it understood. Then, it shook itself once and leapt into the sky, spreading its wings and flying off over the rooftops. Peshek watched, wishing for a long, vain moment that he could do the same.

'And if I've been here talking to someone's tame crow, what a complete ass I'll have made of myself,' he muttered as he straightened up. He pushed the thought aside at once. That was

Avanasy's messenger. He would reach the Empress in time. Peshek had done his part there. He would have to trust to Avanasy's skill to manage affairs in the Heart of the World. His whole purpose must be to raise what troops he could to stop the unlawful war that Kacha sought to start.

Resuming his soldier's bearing for the first time in days, Peshek marched down the alleyway.

Cai-Yun leapt from the sedan that had carried her to her uncle's house with no thought for decorum. She left it to her bodyguard to pay the bearers who had brought her and instead hurried through the gate and up the garden path to the verandah. There, her two old servants bowed to her, but this once she passed them by without a word. She had news that could not wait.

Fortunately, Uncle was in his study, sitting calmly at the low table that served as his desk, working on a letter. Her abrupt and undignified entrance made him pause, the ink brush poised in mid-stroke, and look up at her with raised eyebrows.

'I have come from meeting Zhang Sung, Uncle,' said Cai-Yun breathlessly, kneeling down in front of him. 'You were right. He was worth every coin, and all my flirtations. He . . .'

Uncle raised his free hand and set down his ink brush before it could drip on his carefully written letter. 'Pause for breath, Beloved Niece. You will be fainting on the mat before you finish this tale.'

Cai-Yun did pause, and struggled to slow her breathing and regain her calm. When she was no longer panting like a horse, she bowed to Uncle, who bowed in return. Thus composed, she said, more slowly and more properly, 'He tells me there is an Isavaltan prisoner in the cells below the Heart of the World.'

'An Isavaltan?' Uncle savored the word, as Cai-Yun knew he would. 'This is indeed interesting. Does Zhang Sung know who this Isavaltan is?'

Cai-Yun limited her triumph to a flash of her eyes. 'A woman. A sorceress.'

Uncle's eyebrows lifted again. 'Well, well, a sorceress. And at a time when we have word that the Isavaltans are chasing a mad sorceress about the countryside for impersonating their Empress. This is indeed interesting news.'

Cai-Yun searched her uncle's face, even though by now she knew well he would show her nothing he did not wish her to see. Still, the lilt in his words made her believe that this news was more than interesting. It was welcome.

Uncle moved the brush to the shallow dish of water beside the stone and grinder so that the ink would not harden and ruin the bristles. 'Niece, I have a task for you.'

She was not surprised. 'How can I assist my uncle?'

'I believe someone will soon be coming to retrieve this Isavaltan sorceress. I would speak with them when they do.' Uncle stood and lifted a casket down from the shelf behind him. It opened easily under his hands, although Cai-Yun knew from the painful experience of childhood that if she had tried to lift that same lid, her fingers would smart for a week.

From the casket, Uncle drew a silken bag, and from the bag he took an amulet of jade carved in the shape of a dragon with a fox's head and cunning eyes.

'I suggest you go to the river docks. This amulet will help bring you and such as seek the sorceress together.' Uncle handed the precious object to Cai-Yun who took it with a bow and concealed it in her sleeve.

'I will do my best.'

'I know you will,' Uncle replied, a hint of pride in his placid voice. His eyes shone and Cai-Yun felt an answering warmth run through her. 'Understand, this may be the beginning of something much greater. If we act swiftly and with good information, you and I, Niece, will strike such a blow against the Nine Elders that they will never recover.'

Chapter Fourteen

A sharp, swift pain in her stomach woke Medeoan. She cried out and rolled over, clutching her side. Light flared in the darkness and she shrank from it. Gradually, she could see the soldiers had carried in a table and chair, and the little stick of a man who had ordered her put in this cell sat before her, a fresh scroll laid out before him. Two guards flanked him. A third stood beside Medeoan, and she realized his square-toed shoe must be the source of the pain in her side. Her anger flared, but she kept her mouth shut.

'Can you understand me?' asked the stick-figure official.

'Very well, thank you,' croaked Medeoan. Her throat burned, her head spun. Despite the pain from the kick, her stomach cramped up with hunger. How long had she been left here in this hole?

The official noted something down. 'Stand.'

Medeoan gritted her teeth and made herself get to her feet. Her knees shook, but she remained upright. They would not see her grovel. They had already seen too much of her weakness.

'Who are you?' the official asked, without even looking up at her. His pen was busy on the scroll, but from this distance Medeoan could not make out what he wrote.

Medeoan drew herself up as straight as she could. This brief moment, at least, she was going to enjoy.

'I am the Empress of Isavalta.'

She expected a blow, and steeled herself for it, but none came. The skinny official just tightened his mouth into a smirk.

'It is at least a creative lie,' he said. 'Who are you?'

Let him see it. Medeoan let her anger blaze in her eyes. She remembered standing before the throne, she remembered the coronation and the oaths of loyalty. She remembered looking out the window of Vyshtavos and seeing her lands spread out before her. 'I am Medeoan Edemskoidoch Nacheradavosh, the Empress of Eternal Isavalta, the Heir of Vyshemir, the Prince of the Northern Marches, and the Autocrat of Tuukos,' she said in her own tongue. 'And you will address me properly, or the Heart of Heaven and Earth will know why.'

The skinny official blinked slowly. How much did he understand? Was she just speaking gibberish to him? Did they now believe her to be a madwoman?

Slowly, the skinny official set down his pen. He stood, and then he bowed, not deeply, but he did bow. Medeoan inclined her head in response.

'I must look into this matter,' he said, gathering up his scroll. 'Stay with Her Majesty.'

He left then, and two of the guards went with him. They closed the door behind themselves, leaving Medeoan in the cell with the third guard, who positioned himself by the door, and assumed an attitude of attention.

Medeoan did not bother to try to speak to him. She claimed the official's chair. Her guard made no remark. He did not even look at her. So, she got ready to wait.

Hunger thinned Medeoan's blood. She tried to be grateful for the light and the chair, but that did not last long. What was the skinny man doing? How could he look into this matter? She had arrived in secret, at least she hoped she had. He either believed her or he did not. If he did not, her trouble deepened. If he did, he should have her taken out of here. Immediately. She should at least be provided with food and clean clothes. Whatever else she was, she had declared herself to be an empress, and there were rules of treatment.

After an unendurably long time, the cell door swung open again. Medeoan started at the sudden, silent movement, but forced herself to remain seated, and simply look up.

As expected, the skinny official stepped back into the cell. This time, in addition to the soldiers, he was accompanied by a second, taller man in a long scarlet coat. His black hair was rolled into a bun rather than hanging down as a braid. A serpentine green dragon had been tattooed onto his right cheek. The loops and twists of its body probably wove some permanent protection or silence into his being.

A sorcerer then, probably of the outer court, or he would also have been wearing a cap to match his coat, and would have had more than one visible tattoo.

'You are the one who claims to be the Empress of Isavalta?' he said in the language of Medeoan's home.

'I claim nothing,' replied Medeoan. 'I speak the truth.'

He blinked. 'You will, however, agree it is a truth that must be verified.'

'That depends entirely on the means of verification.'

The sorcerer stepped forward, and held out his hand. His palm had also been tattooed, this time with a brown snake twisting itself into a pattern that, Medeoan was sure, matched that of the dragon on his face.

'You will take my hand.'

Medeoan hesitated. Avanasy had required her to become familiar with the common symbols and patterns of magic in

Hung-Tse and Hastinapura. The snake was wisdom, but it was also cleverness, and truthfulness. She had no protection about her. What could he compel her to say?

Still, she had little choice. Medeoan lifted her chained wrists. She grasped the sorcerer's hand, and found it cold and callused from his workings. With his free hand, the sorcerer raised her chin so that he could look into her eyes. Medeoan bit back the rebuke that rose at this familiarity.

The sorcerer began to chant. It was a high, tonal language, like the tongue she knew, but not the same. Whether this was some ancient dialect or some sorcerer's secret, she could not tell. All she knew was she felt the cold prickling of a spell being worked. It traveled down her skin from her scalp and reached inside her, through flesh to her veins and her blood, and crawled along her bones. She felt the sorcerer draw toward her, although her outward senses told her neither he nor she had moved.

Who are you? he asked, although she heard no words. *Who are you?*

Unbidden, a hundred images rose in Medeoan's mind. Her mother holding her hand and telling her a great prince never cries, looking up and up the high dais to where her father sat, a god enthroned in gold, her parents dead under their shrouds, looking into Kacha's eyes on her wedding day, looking into Avanasy's eyes as she banished him from her land. Too many, too fast, the images tumbled over each other; Kacha in her arms, her coronation, her parents in their grave, Kacha in her bed, Avanasy staring at her, his whole face full of betrayal . . .

'Enough!' shouted Medeoan. With all the strength she had left, she tore free of the sorcerer's grip. The prickling faded instantly, but Medeoan was seized with an icy trembling that she could not control.

The sorcerer too was shaking, and Medeoan was secretly

glad she had been able to cause him some discomfort as repayment for what he had just done to her. It was a long moment before he was able to harden his face and regain control. None of the other men said a word. Medeoan could not even hear them breathe.

'Yes,' said the sorcerer at last. 'It is enough.' He turned to the skinny official. 'Release Her Majesty Imperial.'

The skinny official bowed immediately and deeply. He pulled out his ring of keys and unlocked Medeoan's shackles. She stood, letting the chains fall rattling to the floor without looking at them. They were beneath her notice, as was the raw chafing on her wrists.

'If Her Majesty Imperial will follow me,' the sorcerer bowed, although not as deeply as the skinny official had.

Medeoan nodded. She hoped her face was strong, for she did not trust her voice. Her body felt weak, weak from hunger and thirst, from fear and relief, and from the working that had passed through her.

The sorcerer straightened up and paced through the door. Medeoan followed, and the soldiers formed up at her back.

Medeoan knew from childhood lessons that the Heart of the World was laid out in a pattern of nine squares containing five palaces. Each of the four outer palaces was surrounded by four walls, and had two adjoining gardens. One palace was for the Imperial women, one was for the high level administrators and bureaucrats. Another was for foreign ambassadors and hostage guests. The fourth was for the Dowager Empress and her family.

The fifth palace waited at the center of the great complex. This was the true Heart, the home of the Emperor, who was 'the Heart of Heaven and Earth,' and the Imperial protectors, the Nine Elders. It was to this palace that the sorcerer led her. The final yellow gate opened for them and they stepped out into a courtyard so huge that Medeoan was willing to swear it could have held all of Vyshtavos and still had room left over. Across the expanse of pale sandstone, Medeoan saw the scarlet and emerald wings of the Heart spreading out so far she could not take them in with a single glance. In the center rose a great, gilded tower with more windows than she could easily count looking out across the land of Hung-Tse.

Medeoan tried to keep her composure. She worked hard not to gape at the pillars of carnelian and jade that flanked the palace's entranceway. More pillars, these scarlet, with gilded tops and bases, held up the soaring golden roof. Instead of tapestries, the broad hall was hung with silken banners. Some had been painted with images of the four protectors; the dragon, the phoenix, the unicorn and the tortoise. Others carried pictograms woven together so fancifully they could not be anything but spells. More silk covered the polished floor they walked. Beneath the silk, the wood was so dark, it could not have been anything but lacquered mahogany.

They did not stop at any of the doors they passed. None of the guards in their shimmering black armor made any move as they passed.

The hall ended at a gate of carved wood that had been polished until it shone like silk. Medeoan's eyes automatically traced the carving. She found the spells woven into the carving and knew that despite its delicate appearance, this gate was stronger than any she had yet passed through.

Before the gate stood a single figure. Medeoan thought it was a man, but it was difficult to tell. The figure wore a long, enveloping robe of deep blue embroidered all over with sinuous dragons of so many colors that they dazzled Medeoan's eyes. More dragons covered his folded hands. Curving lines and graceful clouds had been tattooed all across his face, turning his skin into a living mask. It was by these signs that Medeoan knew she stood before the Minister of Air.

Her escort knelt, pressing their hands and their foreheads against the floor. Medeoan remained standing. Properly, the Minister should have knelt to her. The fact he remained standing sent a shiver of warning through her. All was not going smoothly yet.

'If Her Majesty Imperial will consent to come with me,' said the Minister in perfect High Isavaltan. He had a rich, mellifluous voice that nonetheless set Medeoan's skin to pricking. Even in his words there was an undercurrent of power, and he was but one of nine.

'Lead on,' said Medeoan stiffly. Hunger and uncertainty both gnawed at her. What manner of reception would she have beyond this deceptive gate? How would she be able to stand up to it?

The Minister of Air turned and bowed to the gate, holding his hands out so his left hand covered his right fist. At this gesture, the gate pulled open of its own accord. The Minister stepped through, without looking back to see if Medeoan followed. Medeoan straightened her shoulders and walked past her still-kneeling escort into the audience chamber.

Like everything else about the Heart of the World, the audience chamber had been built on a grand scale. Life-sized statues of the gods and the powers with their swords and spears raised, or their arms lifted to bar the entrance of any unwelcome thing, stood guard between elaborately carved pillars of cinnabar. At the center of the chamber rose a dais with ten stone steps. The Emperor himself sat on a simple platform of lacquered wood. His robe was unadorned saffron and his hair was rolled high on his head and lacquered until it shone like the platform on which he sat. His skin was clear brown and his eyes black, and he was younger than Medeoan thought he would be, almost as young as she. Beside him stood a man in white with his hands neatly folded. This was the Imperial Voice, Medeoan knew. The Emperor could never be heard to speak by any other, lest his words be captured and used to weave a spell against him.

Five steps below the Emperor stood the remaining eight of the Nine Elders.

Medeoan swallowed the temptation to giggle nervously. At least they took her seriously. Avanasy had told her that the way one measured how Hung-Tse regarded a threat was to see how many of the Nine Elders stood between the Emperor and any ambassador or messenger. All Nine were seldom present at once.

One minister for each of the five elements, Medeoan remembered; earth, air, fire, water and metal. One for each of the directions; north, south, east and west. The Emperor himself was the fifth direction; center.

So, as the Minister of Air mounted the dais to stand with his colleagues and turn toward her, the whole world faced Medeoan.

Mindful of her position as an unwelcome guest, Medeoan folded her hands over her breast and reverenced deeply to the assemblage in front of her.

'I am most grateful to my Brother Emperor for receiving me into his Heart,' she said in her best court manner. Her words echoed briefly around the still chamber, and were quickly swallowed by the vast space.

The Emperor nodded and gestured to his Voice.

'I greet my Sister Empress, and I ask her to accept my sorrow and deep respect for her departed parents.'

Medeoan reverenced again. 'My thanks to my Brother Emperor.'

'Your refreshment has been arranged for. Please, take your ease and eat and drink.'

At those words, Medeoan almost collapsed with relief. But,

she forced herself to remain standing while silent servitors in black robes with white hems and cuffs swept forward, bringing with them a chair and table of carved wood. Still others laid out a tray covered with small bowls of cold dainties, a ceramic beaker of clear wine and another of water, and a pair of small cups to accompany the drinks. A maid bowed before Medeoan offering a bowl of steaming water and a clean towel.

All done under the eyes of the Emperor and the Nine Elders. Medeoan's eyes narrowed. This had the feel of a subtle insult somehow, but she could not unearth its meaning. So, she rinsed her hands and dabbed them dry. She sat in the presented chair, and ate from each of the bowls. It was all she could do not to fall upon the food like a dog, but a lifetime of training helped her keep her dignity.

'Again, I thank my Brother Emperor,' she said when she could make herself stop eating. 'The courtesies of the Heart of the World are as legendary as its wealth. Now I see those legends spoke nothing but the purest truth.'

The Emperor nodded briefly and turned to his Voice again. Medeoan saw his hand move swiftly, making some sign or signal for the Voice to interpret.

'I wonder what grave circumstances have occurred that cause one of my Sister Empress's station to be wandering alone and in common garb in the open streets of the city.'

Here it was. Here was where she had to pull her mind together. She'd had plenty of time on the voyage and wandering the streets to think of what to say, and now was her time to speak.

Medeoan rose to her feet. The eyes of all Nine of the Elders tracked her as she did.

'It has been said, and wisely, that the enemy of my enemy is my friend,' said Medeoan, pitching her voice to carry. The room would hear her, the Emperor would hear her. She would make them listen. 'I do not pretend that there has not long been great trouble between Isavalta and Hung-Tse. My Brother feels we have wronged him, and we feel that my Brother has wronged us. This is ever the way of empire.' Father had spoken those words, but he had said them to the ambassador from Hastinapura. Medeoan had sat at his side that day, still and quiet, and wishing she was somewhere else. 'But when a common threat arises, it is also the way of the wise in the empire to set aside reckoning for those wrongs and attend to the business of survival.'

The Emperor's eyes narrowed, and he gestured to his Voice. 'Do you say there is a threat to Hung-Tse?'

'I do.'

'And the name of this threat?'

'Hastinapura.'

Much to Medeoan's consternation, the Nine Elders all laughed. Even the Emperor smiled.

'That there is danger to the south of our borders is not news,' said the Voice. 'Perhaps it is because our Sister Empress is so young she finds it noteworthy.'

Medeoan forced herself to wait until the last of the laughter had died away. 'The danger of a bear sleeping in its den is far different from the danger of a bear hunting and hungry.'

'You say that Hastinapura plans to attack us?'

'They seek to use treachery to overthrow Isavalta, with whom they have a treaty. If this is accomplished, will they leave at peace Hung-Tse with whom they have an active quarrel? Kacha . . .' she stumbled over the name, 'has broken the treaty my father entered into with the bonds of our marriage. He is supported by powerful magics and more powerful lies. Because of them, my own lords may not be trusted. But,' she raised her finger, 'long is the memory of Hung-Tse, and subtle are the ways of my Brother Emperor and his protectors. If we together end this ignoble and unclean overthrow of the right order, the benefits to both our lands will be manifold.'

The Emperor and the Nine Elders were silent for a long time. Medeoan's heart beat hard in her chest, driven by uncertainty. Did they believe? Did they hear the promise in that last statement?

At last, the Emperor waved his hand to his Voice.

'But none of this explains why my Sister Empress has come here alone and in such disguise.'

For which there was no choice but to lie. She could not have them know that Isavalta had already fallen. 'There are some matters that may be spoken of only between princes. What messenger could I trust with such a letter? Whose magics could I safely employ? The efficiency and perception of the Heart of the World are known to all. I knew I would be brought before my Brother Emperor before it was too late.'

Silence again, and she and the Emperor looking across a gulf into each other's eyes. She felt a sudden stab of envy for her 'brother,' comfortable on his dais surrounded by advisors he could trust. *One day,* she tried to tell herself. *One day, it shall be so with me.*

Then, the Emperor turned away, making his signs to his Voice. Medeoan wished fervently her tutors had thought to teach her this language of the Emperor's hand, so that she might know for certain what was being said.

The Voice spoke. 'I hear the words of my Sister Empress of Isavalta and they are grave and worthy of much thought. I ask that she accept the hospitality of the Heart of the World while I take counsel with the Nine Elders so that I may give to her a worthy answer.'

Hospitality. A bed, a bath, a true meal. Medeoan kept her face still and solemn. 'I accept willingly. I only ask that my Brother Emperor understand that this matter is most urgent, and delay for leisurely debate only allows the treacherous to further their plans.'

'I assure my Sister Empress that I am quite aware of the urgency of her words, and she will not have to wait long for my answer.'

Medeoan reverenced, and the Emperor bowed in acknowledgment. The Minister of Air left his fellows and walked her back to the inner gate. All the time, she felt the eyes of the others on her, and she could almost hear the air whispering around her. What were they thinking? What were they planning? Medeoan's jaw tightened. She needed to find out.

Medeoan expected to be conducted to the foreigner's palace, but instead, she was taken to the Palace of the Autumn, and there was greeted by the Dowager Empress, Dieu Han, as soon as she stepped through the gilded doors.

'Ah! My Daughter, how pale you look! It is a shame upon my son and my house that he kept you talking so long!' She wagged her head to express the strength of her emotion. 'Come, come, let me show you your rooms. Let me summon your attendants. You must be faint from all your trials!'

Or, at least, that was what Medeoan could make out from her speech. The woman talked fast and moved constantly, and if she was old enough to have mothered the Emperor, she did not look it. Her face appeared only gently lined and her hair was as black as his. She looked more like his sister than his mother, and Medeoan found herself wondering if the woman was a sorceress. She did not know. She could not remember her father, or anyone else, talking about the Dowager.

Dieu Han took Medeoan's arm with comfortable familiarity and steered her through the scarlet and sienna corridors, sending servants scurrying in every direction with rapid-fire orders, so that by the time they reached the 'poor, very poor', as she called it, chamber set aside for Medeoan, the room was open to the warm sun and fresh air of the early afternoon. Fresh flowers bloomed in the basins, a cold meal of roasted meats and chilled rice was waiting along with tea and wine, and even a small pot of coffee. 'It is much favored in your country, is it not?' asked the Dowager anxiously. 'There is so little comfort here to offer such a visitor.'

In truth, her activity and her orders left Medeoan a little dizzy. But at last she was satisfied that Medeoan had all the food she could possibly desire beside her, and that the water for washing was just the right temperature, and the robes laid out were of sufficiently good quality. Medeoan was used to being waited on, but not like this. Her hair and body were washed for her. She was swiftly dressed in rich silken robes. Her plates were prepared and brought to her by servants who knelt with each offering. Even her cups were held for her so that she could sip from them.

The Dowager sat beside her, supervising the service, and making small talk about the weather, the history of the palace and the silliness of waiting ladies, but Medeoan soon found herself less and less able to answer without suppressing progressively energetic yawns.

'But there, you are tired,' said Dieu Han at last. 'I am as guilty as the Emperor of keeping you talking.' And she sent the women running to ready the teakwood bed with its smooth sheets and coverlets, and herself escorted Medeoan to its side. Medeoan laid down, and her eyes closed at once. She was asleep so fast, she did not even hear Dieu Han order the ladies out, nor did she see the woman searching her clothing before it was handed over to the serving women to be stored away.

★　　★　　★

Medeoan woke to an oddly familiar scene. Around her hung the curtains of a great, carved bed. Beyond them she could see a peaceful and well-organized apartment with the waiting ladies bowed over their sewing and their letters. So much the same, and yet so utterly different. Medeoan had grown up with stone and darkness. This place, palace though it was, was so airy and filled with light she wondered briefly how it did not fly away when the winds were strong. The light had reddened to evening, and Medeoan realized she had been asleep for hours.

'Ah, good, you are awake.' Medeoan sat up as Dieu Han rose from her place by a low, rosewood table and bustled to the bedside. 'First, you must eat, then we must talk.'

Medeoan's stomach grumbled, despite also tightening at the tone the Dowager gave her final words, but she only nodded her agreement.

More tea and wine, and another light meal of rice, cured fish and fruit was laid out by the silent, efficient ladies, with many orders from the Dowager. Medeoan ate and drank hungrily, learning quickly that she was not to reach for the dishes or the cups, but indicate with a flick of her finger what she wanted. It seemed to her excessive, but she was not going to show herself to be any less sophisticated than this silk-clad and lacquered woman in front of her.

'Now then, my dear child,' said the Dowager. 'I must tell you, the Emperor has taken me much into his confidence on matters concerning you, quizzing me most closely on your behavior and demeanor.'

Medeoan felt the muscles in the back of her neck begin to knot up. 'As is to be expected. I would surely do the same if my guards brought my Brother Emperor into my great hall, alone and dressed in a peasant's clothes.'

'To be sure, to be sure.' The Dowager patted her hand. 'But there is more to it than that. He does not like Isavaltans, and never has, and looks on you with suspicion, be your face and heart ever so open.'

Now Medeoan's eyes narrowed. 'And what would he say to you if he knew you were telling me these things?'

The Dowager waved Medeoan's words away. 'What could he say? He has given me charge of you, to house as I see fit. I may hold such conversation with you as I choose, and I choose to advise you that undue discretion may jeopardize all you would accomplish here. You must be open, and confident. The Emperor will in no way support a usurper unseating his Sister Empress, but he must be convinced yet that that is what has happened here.'

'I assure you, Mother, I mean to be nothing but honest with my Brother Emperor.'

'Good,' she pronounced the word with firm satisfaction. 'I told him it would be so.'

Medeoan looked down at her porcelain wine cup, and studied the letters written in red and gold on its side. They had been cleverly drawn to resemble a field of waving grasses. Since she could not pick the cup up, she couldn't examine them closely. She only saw the occasional character that made sense, such as 'truth,' or 'peace,' or 'heart.'

'Forgive me for asking such a question, Mother,' she said. 'But if the Emperor has these reservations, why do you not share them?'

The Dowager sighed. 'Perhaps I should. Perhaps I would be wiser if I did, but I will tell you, in the last year, my daughter, Mei Lin, was given in marriage to a king in the southern states. It was a good match for Hung-Tse, but less so I fear for my daughter. I can do very little to help her, but in her place, my mother's heart urges me to help you.'

The older woman spoke with such feeling, Medeoan's tired heart longed to reach out to her, but she held it in check. She had no proof, no reason to believe anything Dieu Han said, and she had lived too long among sycophants to immediately accept protestations of sympathy. Most of the time.

A plan formed in Medeoan's mind.

'Mother,' she said, setting her cup down. 'It grieves me to hear of your daughter parted from you. You have been very good to me, and perhaps I can now return your courtesy.'

Was that wariness that flashed past the Dowager's dark eyes? 'In what way, Daughter?'

Medeoan chose her words with care. 'I am sure you know that I have some humble gifts of spirit,' Medeoan used Hung-Tse's phrase for sorcery. 'If you can give me something of your daughter's, and a mirror, I can show you how she does at this moment. It may ease your worries for her.'

The Dowager hesitated. 'Thank you, Daughter. Your offer is gracious. But you may put yourself in danger with the Nine Elders, who will surely be aware of any such casting within the Heart of the World . . .'

Now it was Medeoan's turn to wave words away. 'Should they inquire, you will be able to reassure them. Indeed, they will be able to make their own examination of all I do. It is not a complex working, nor, in truth, a very subtle one.'

Yes, she looked wary. She was not entirely the worried mother then. How far would she persist in that game?

The Dowager reached her decision. 'I will return in a few moments.' She rose, and swept from the room, surrounded by her gaggle of ladies.

That surprised Medeoan – she had expected some of the ladies to be sent running. Did the Dowager need to alert the Elders as to what was about to happen? Send a message to the Emperor? Either of those things were possible. It was also possible there was some casket or drawer that needed to be unlocked by the Dowager's own hand. Such things were not common in Vyshtavos, but they were not unknown either.

Medeoan forced herself to be patient. If she could just wait a little while longer, she would have her means for gaining real information that she could indeed trust. She wandered about the apartment, examining the blooming flowers in their bowls of water, the finely executed landscapes with their attendant poems painted on lengths of translucent paper. She exclaimed with approval over the work of the waiting ladies, who responded by clapping their hands over their faces in a way that made her think of Kacha, and caused her to turn away.

At last, the Dowager returned. With a furtive expression, she handed over to Medeoan a circular mirror of polished silver and a hair comb that had been beautifully etched with a chain of blossoms.

'Thank you, Mother,' said Medeoan as she accepted them. 'These will do admirably.' Especially since the comb still had one long, black hair entwined in its teeth. 'I will need to borrow some of your ladies' sewing thread as well, and then we may begin.'

The ladies worked exclusively with silk, which was perhaps too fine a thread for this spell, but it would certainly serve. Medeoan arrayed the cut threads in the lap of her robe and began to weave them into a net, with the red threads knotted together to make the left half and the blue to make the right. All the while she breathed deeply, drawing the magic out and calling it in.

'I stand on the isle of the world, and the sun shines down upon me. The sun sees all that is, all that has been and all that will be. Mei Lin stands on the isle of the world, and the sun shines down upon Mei Lin. The sun sees all that is, all that has been and all that will be.' The spell flowed strongly from her, and the weaving caught the words and the magic and gave them the needed shape. It felt surprisingly good. In this, at least, she was sure of what she did. 'I will see Mei Lin as the sun sees Mei Lin. I will see all that is, and all that is true for Mei Lin. This is my wish and this is my word, and my word is firm.'

With the final word, she wove the net through the teeth of the comb, and laid the mirror down in the net's center. She breathed across the smooth silver, all her work done for now. Now, she had only to wait and watch, along with the Dowager.

At first, the mirror reflected her face, and the Dowager's where she leaned over to see. After a few, brief heartbeats, the shining surface of the mirror clouded over, as if obscured by fog. Then, the fog cleared, and Medeoan no longer saw her own face. Instead, she saw a garden of willow trees with a carefully constructed stream trickling over rounded stones and golden roots. A young woman, Mei Lin, who appeared to be perhaps a year or two older than Medeoan, sat on a curved bench on the bank. A cluster of waiting ladies laid out a picnic in a silken pavilion nearby. It was a peaceful, busy scene, but, for some reason, it made the Dowager frown.

Then, Mei Lin turned her head, probably at the sound of someone's approach. Her face lit up, and she rose gracefully to her feet. A man stepped into the mirror's view. He also was young, and, Medeoan supposed, handsome after the fashion of Hung-Tse. His robe was of good green and white cloth and he smiled to see Mei Lin. Instead of bowing he folded his arms around her so they might embrace and kiss.

Oddly embarrassed, Medeoan turned her face away.

'The fool!' spat the Dowager. 'Oh, the little fool!'

Before Medeoan could move, the Dowager snatched up the mirror. She drew her hand back as if she meant to hurl it across the room, but at the last moment, she recovered her composure and set it down. Medeoan did not miss the way her hand shook performing that simple act.

'I'm sorry, Mother,' said Medeoan softly. 'I did not know . . .'

But I do now. Your daughter has a lover, and this jeopardizes her position, and possibly yours.

'No, you could not.' The Dowager bit off the words, plainly struggling to regain control of herself. 'You will excuse me. There is something I must do.'

The Dowager and her ladies swept from the room, leaving Medeoan alone with her servants. Only when the door closed did Medeoan allow the smile she had been holding in to show itself. Vyshemir bless Mei Lin in her inconstancy, she thought. The shock delivered to Dieu Han had meant the woman left comb, stray hair, mirror and completed net with Medeoan. She had been wondering how she might keep hold of them without arousing attention.

Now, Dowager, we shall see in what regard you are held by your son, and in what regard he holds me.

What she was about to do was dangerous, but she could not leave herself without information. The lies that might cover it were many, but might not be easily believed. Still, she must take the risk.

Around her, the ladies sewed or read passively. One rose to tend the small stove where the water heated for tea. By all appearances they were ignoring her, but Medeoan knew this could not be so. Like her ladies back home, they had to be ready for any soft summons. But unlike her ladies back home, Medeoan knew no way to get rid of them.

So, to screen herself as best she could, Medeoan got up and folded the items she had been left with into her robe's voluminous sleeves. Casually, as if she only meant to stretch her legs, she wandered out onto the apartment's sun porch. One of the ladies immediately responded by fetching a pillow for the low wooden bench. Another placed a steaming cup of tea within easy reach. Both then retired at once to the company of their fellows.

Medeoan sat in the place that had been prepared and sipped

the tea. The sun was pleasantly warm against her skin, and she would have loved to spend the evening just dozing in this spot bathed in the rich perfumes that wafted to her from the gardens beyond.

Instead, she spilled her booty into her lap. She picked up the comb and gently disentangled the single hair from its teeth. Then, gingerly, she began to twine it into the center of her net, calling up her magic as softly as she could.

'As daughter is bound to mother, so is my sight bound to Dieu Han,' she whispered, winding the hair around the silken strands. 'As daughter's heart is hidden from mother, so is my sight hidden from those in the Heart of the World.' She spoke the spell again, and again, as she delicately knotted the hair to bind it firmly into her net.

Then, as she had before, she laid the silver mirror across the net in her lap and breathed across its smooth surface.

This time when the mirror cleared, Medeoan saw the throne room. The Emperor sat on his dais as before, with the Nine Elders ranged before him. But this time, the Elders faced inward, and from Medeoan's view, it seemed she sat at their center in a chair made of some dark wood with elegantly carved arms, for she now saw through the eyes of the Dowager Empress Dieu Han.

The Emperor signed to his Voice. It seemed that he could not speak aloud even to his mother. Medeoan leaned close to her mirror. Very faintly, she heard the words, 'What have you to tell us, Mother?'

Dieu Han dropped her eyes briefly. 'Little, my son. I found no charms about her person, nor any one thing I could easily say was enchanted. There was no possession she seemed to cling to. I found only a few coins, and no jewels at all.'

Medeoan repressed a spasm of anger. She had in truth expected to be searched.

The Emperor nodded and his Voice said, 'This is also the word of the jailer who held her.' The Voice paused thoughtfully as the Emperor did the same. 'Did she speak at all of her hopes or fears?'

'Not yet, but I believe she may, if I am given time.'

So, you are my hostess and my spy. Well, I cannot truly be surprised at that either. Medeoan bit her lip and bent closer.

Now one of the Elders spoke. This one wore robes that gleamed with threads of copper, silver and gold, and was tattooed with squares and angles overlaid with serpents coiled together. This was the Minister of Metal. 'Time is not something we have, if what she says is true,' said the Minister. From the depth of the voice, Medeoan decided this minister was male.

'It does not matter what truth she speaks,' Dieu Han said with a dismissive wave. 'What we know is that Isavalta is grown unstable and this must threaten us to the north.'

'Must it?' inquired the Minister of Air, who had greeted Medeoan so politely when she arrived. 'If Isavalta falls again into a pack of squabbling kingdoms, we may safely regard them with indifference.'

The Emperor tapped his fingers on his knee, the first stray movement Medeoan had seen him make. It was a long moment before he signed again. 'Unless she speaks the truth and Hastinapura seeks to seize them all,' said the Voice.

Another Elder spoke. This one was all in blue, like the Minister of Air, and sparkling fishes chased the dragons on both robe and skin – the Minister of Water.

'Let Hastinapura try. We are still surrounded by enemies. What matter if there are one or two? While Hastinapura strengthens itself in Isavalta, we will be able to gather our own strength to meet whatever challenge may come.'

'But how far along is this plan?' asked the Minister of Air.

'It is possible that the Isavaltan Empress did not leave as voluntarily as she claims. If they have already driven out their own Empress . . .'

'That is a key point.' Dieu Han raised her finger. 'It may be Isavalta is already conquered. It may be Isavalta is but a prelude for greater conquests.'

All looked toward the Emperor who signed to his Voice with energy. 'I am finding it difficult to believe so much of our Brother Emperor Samudra. All his letters have been crisp and direct, saying he wishes no quarrel, that he has quarrels enough of his own to contend with.'

'There are more powers in Hastinapura than Emperor Samudra,' Dieu Han reminded him.

'You do not believe Chandra may have a hand in this?'

Oh believe that much, thought Medeoan as her grip tightened on the mirror. The scents of summer and the touch of the fresh wind seemed incongruous. She was in a closed chamber, surrounded by pillars of cinnabar and statues of gods.

Dieu Han turned her head a little so she could regard the Emperor owlishly from one eye. 'It is Chandra whose son was sent to bed the Isavaltan Empress.'

'You think he seeks to invade his own land from the north?'

'He spoke with great feeling of a single empire when he was a young prince,' said the Minister of the North whose robes were white as snow and embroidered over with broad winged geese and beautifully stylized gulls. 'Our reports on this matter are most reliable.'

The Emperor considered this for a moment. 'But he does not hold the Pearl Throne.'

'That may make him safer for this work,' said the Minister of Metal slowly, as if testing a fresh idea. 'All the blame must go to his brother Samudra who does sit on the throne.'

All in the chamber fell silent for a long moment. Medeoan

felt sweat prickling the back of her neck, even though it was not that warm. Tension tightened her throat and snatched at her breath.

'There is another possibility,' said Dieu Han finally.

The Emperor cocked his head. 'What is that?'

'It is all a trap.'

No. Medeoan felt herself go cold. *No. That's not what is happening. You cannot believe that.*

The Elders did not stir. If she had spoken so in Council in Isavalta, every Lord Master would have been shouting at once. As it was, the Emperor just regarded her coolly and signed to his Voice. 'How so, Mother?'

Dieu Han rubbed the chair arm with her palm as she put her thoughts in order. 'This little girl, this sorceress, with her tale of woe and wrong. What if she seeks to trick us into committing our armies and our protection, and we lead them into the waiting arms of her forces? We are weak. We cannot here, in this room, pretend that we are not. What if the Isavaltans have discovered that weakness and seek to maneuver us into a war we cannot win?'

Vyshemir protect me, Medeoan licked her lips. *I spoke only the truth. You cannot believe I did any less.*

'It is an elaborate ruse, if ruse it is,' said the Minister of Air.

'Of course it is.' Dieu Han spread her hands. 'Would a simple plan suffice?'

'Her father spoke of exchanging emissaries, and quelled the pirates in Hastinapura's waters,' the Minister of the North reminded them.

'Her father is dead, and she may now be ruled by her husband. We also have reliable reports from Vyshtavos, about how she seldom conducts any business, how all her thoughts are given to her own pleasures and none to her rule. The Emperor is Chandra's son. It may be he has persuaded his bride to yield her unwanted power to him.'

No, no, no, Medeoan wanted to shout out her frustration. *I told you the truth!*

'But why come alone?' asked the Minister of Metal. 'Why in this state?'

'Because there is a limit to what one may safely carry through the Land of Death and Spirit,' replied the Minister of Fire whose scarlet robes and tattooed skin were covered with representations of the phoenix. 'To arrive swiftly and secretly, she must have used the routes through the Silent Lands, otherwise our spies surely would have had word of her departure. Could she sail through the Land of Death and Spirit with an escort of mortal soldiers? It would be dangerous. Could she take her court sorcerers into her confidence? It is not likely. We would know if her escort consisted only of magicians, and be alerted.'

Again the Emperor tapped his knee. 'These thoughts are unwelcome, but they are worthy. They must be given careful consideration.'

'Thoughts will only scatter us like leaves in autumn,' said Dieu Han firmly. 'We must have facts.'

The Minister of the North bowed her head. 'Vyshtavos is well protected. Even we may not see within its walls.'

'There are other places, and other eyes than our own, that may be trusted,' said the Minister of Metal. His heavy robes glinted in the light, rivaling the draperies of the gods around them. 'We must know how the ships and soldiers move in Isavalta. If there is to be danger in this year, they cannot now be idle, for their summer is short and their winter is long, and they must strike quickly before the ice comes so that they may have secure garrisons for the winter. Whether or not Medeoan is involved in the plan, if they mean to attack, they will now be on the move.'

At these words, the Emperor frowned. 'Minister of Earth, if the Isavaltans do mean to attack, how well may we withstand them?'

The Minister of Earth was robed in green. Tortoises adorned his robes and skin, picked out in sienna and sparkling gold. 'Not well, Your Majesty. Our dealings with Hastinapura and the pirate fleets have left us drained, as the Isavaltans surely knew. If we now must face war from the north . . .' he shook his head.

As the Isavaltans surely knew? Tears pricked the corners of Medeoan's eyes. *As Kacha surely knew. Oh, Vyshko. Vyshemir. What if this is true? What if this is his plan?*

The Emperor nodded. 'Very well. If it cannot be open conflict, what means can we employ?'

There was silence for a long moment before the Minister of the North said, 'We must invoke one of the great protectors.'

'Not yet,' said the Minister of the South. Her robes were scarlet like those of the Minister of Fire, and her phoenixes pursued white cranes across the cloth and her skin. 'We must try to treat first with our enemies in Hastinapura. Then we must consider that the pirates may be turned to war on Isavalta.'

'For what payment?' countered the Minister of Air. 'Will you return the islands of K'ien and Shai to Hastinapura's mercy, which is their capital demand? Will you hand them those bases and fortifications, those walls over which they may look with greed at the Heart of the World?'

Again the Elders fell into their profound silence. Medeoan found herself wishing they would shout, would argue, would *do* something, not just stand there like ciphers believing she came as the pawn of their enemy.

Oh, but you do come as that pawn, whispered a treacherous

little voice in the back of her head. *If Kacha's moving troops to the southern border, what else could you be doing here?*

Furrows creased the Emperor's brow. At length, a tiny smile appeared on his face. 'Perhaps you should have chosen another for the throne, Mother. Look where I have led the Heart of the World.'

'I do not regret my choice, my son.' Dieu Han drew herself up straight. 'If danger threatens from many directions, then it must be met at each turning. If there is conflict at the foot of the Pearl Throne, expose it. If Isavalta threatens the north, break it. If the child Medeoan is a treasure, keep her.'

'There is wisdom in what you say, Mother. Very well.' The Voice hardened, growing even more imperious. 'Let our eyes be turned toward Isavalta to see what there is to be seen. As we strive for that understanding, let a letter be drafted to the Emperor of Hastinapura protesting this attack by his representative in Isavalta. If we cannot muster mortal protection, we will summon the immortal.'

'And Medeoan?' inquired Dieu Han.

'Will be moved into the Heart where she may be kept more closely.'

Medeoan could not stand to listen anymore. She tossed the mirror and her spell-net aside, burying her face in her hands for a moment before she remembered the watchful, silent ladies behind her. She straightened up at once, but did not turn to look into her chamber. Medeoan did not want them to see her face, for she could feel that her chin trembled as badly as her hands as the full weight of her folly tumbled down on her head.

Since her second brother had died of his fever, Medeoan had wanted to run away from her destiny. She had imagined a free life, one where she lived away from politics, able to enjoy her days and her companions without worrying whether it was her rank that made them stay beside her. Her parents had worked hard to train her for her appointed role, and she had responded by isolating herself from all those around her. All except Avanasy, and then Kacha.

So, what did I do when danger truly threatened? Medeoan ground her teeth together until the pain ran through her jaw. *I thought of nothing but to run away. I did not think to find a counter to the spell Kacha would place on me. I did not think to gather my own loyal followers, no. I ran, and now I will be put under lock and key as strong as any Kacha could have devised for me, and I have left Isavalta without friend or protector under the hand of a bloody usurper!*

She knotted all the muscles in her neck to keep her head from falling forward as the tears began to trickle down her cheeks. *What have I done? Oh, Vyshemir, what have I done?*

But there was no time for despair. She wiped her eyes quickly. She was about to be placed under arrest. They would be on their way shortly. They would take from her every means she had to work her will. Without sorcery, she would never be let out until Kacha paid a ransom for her, or until whatever conflict that might come between Isavalta and Hung-Tse had reached a resolution, and that might take years. She could not leave Isavalta alone under a false power. She could never leave Isavalta alone again.

Medeoan quickly snatched up the spell-net from where it lay beside the cup of tea, the mirror, and the comb. The spell woven into it would not be of much use should she need to escape, but the silken threads could be reknotted to provide the base for some more elaborate working. She wadded the net up into a fine ball, and then tucked it as deeply under the elaborate braid that held her hair in place as she could. A quick glance in the mirror showed her no trace of colored silk showing under her golden hair.

A breeze at her back and the rustle of cloth told her the chamber door had opened. Medeoan rose and turned, as calmly and smoothly as she could manage.

Dieu Han entered the room, with the Minister of Air standing impassively beside her. With them came six guards with their long-handled axes and their black, lacquered armor trimmed in Imperial saffron.

'What is this?' demanded Medeoan. 'What has happened?'

'Oh, Daughter,' sighed Dieu Han, shaking her head. 'I told you to be open with my son.'

The Minister of Air gestured once, and the soldiers moved forward to surround Medeoan.

She feared they might return her to the cells she had been held in before, but instead, they took her into the very center of the Heart, placing her in a small chamber in the gilded tower. The room was bare stone with only a leather mattress resting on the floor. There was a window, low enough for her to look out of, so she could see the expanse of stone walls that surrounded her and the constant patrols of guards that traversed their battlements.

They took her clothes away and left her a shift of leather. They cut her hair. Medeoan almost cried out as they did. But they seized her braid and sheared it off right at the base of her skull. Her heart rose to her throat, but the maids had done their work too well; the braiding closest to her scalp held tight and the hidden netting did not fall.

Then they left her, taking her shorn braid with them.

Alone, Medeoan's first thought was to undo her few remaining pins and pull her netting free. She clutched it in her hands. As little as it was, it was her only weapon, her only chance. They had left her nothing else but her ragged hair and the blood in her veins.

The leather shift chafed her skin as she moved to the

window. She looked out on the neat walls and their guards moving as precisely as if they were driven by clockwork. She saw the splendid gardens and the majestic gates and beyond them the teeming city dissected by its own walls.

Loneliness settled like a stone into her heart. All she had in the world to aid her was a tangle of silken threads. And Avanasy. If Avanasy were here. If Iakush had found him. If, if, if . . .

Medeoan bowed her head. She would not weep. Even in such circumstances, she was a great prince, and she would not weep anymore.

Avanasy, you will find me. You have never let me down. You will find me and we will be free, and together we will return to free Isavalta. My land. I have been shown the error of my ways, and I will never flee from my land again.

Chapter Fifteen

The time on the water acquired its own rhythm, and Ingrid found herself coming to relish it. She and Avanasy shared the work of canvas and tiller, fishing with drag lines for whatever the ocean felt like offering. She liked his boat and soon learned its strange rigging and its easy ways. In the evening, they would anchor off the coast. While they remained in Isavalta, if one of his maps showed there to be a village nearby, one or the other of them would hike inland to hear the news and barter for bread and other provisions. Although Ingrid found herself missing any number of things – sugar, coffee, white flour, more than one change of linen – the days still felt sweet.

Nights were spent cradled in each other's arms and that was the sweetest of all.

Only two things kept the time from being perfect. The first was Avanasy's growing anxiety to reach their destination. Every day he would scan the skies, looking for the messenger from Peshek. Every day his face would grow just a little more grave as the messenger failed to appear.

The second flaw was Ingrid's dreams.

As soon as they had left the cove below Hajek's village and reached the open water, Avanasy had given her the tiller and sail and gone below. Ingrid sailed them across calm seas in a steady wind, and wished that there was a little more for her to do so she would not have to wonder so much about what had happened to her, what would happen next, and how Avanasy was going to do what he needed to if he was going to have to keep worrying about her.

An hour or so later, Avanasy returned to the deck, looking tired but satisfied. In his hand he held a delicate, complex braid made of colored cloth, canvas threads and several strands of his hair, and hers. He tied his creation securely around her right wrist, and kissed the knot when he was finished.

'It should be a girdle, or a sash, but I have no time to weave you such before dark.' He met her eyes anxiously. 'How do you feel?'

Ingrid considered, searching inside herself for an honest answer. 'As if something has eased,' she said. 'At least for now.'

'Good.' Avanasy kissed her. 'Good.'

She knew he did not sleep that night for watching over her, and, in truth, she was hard pressed to give herself over to oblivion, but at last fatigue won out. She slept, and she stayed within herself, though she was seized with a straining and stretching, as if she were struggling against the bond that held body and soul together. It was the same every night after that. She would see things, fleeting as shadows in the darkness, and would feel them pausing to stare at her; a knight all dressed in red; the Vixen, who was the size of a cart horse; a snake, a tortoise, a huge chestnut horse, a dragon, a beautiful bird with trailing wings.

She would tell Avanasy of her dreams, and he would frown and reconsecrate her wristlet.

'They are spirit powers,' he told her. 'You are seeing into the Land of Death and Spirit, and it is looking back at you. I don't like it.'

Neither did Ingrid, in truth, but there was nothing to be

done. Avanasy said there would be help in Hung-Tse, perhaps even from the Nine Elders, depending on what Medeoan had been able to accomplish. Ingrid would be whole again, he swore, and with that, she worked hard to let herself be content.

It was their tenth day on the water. Ingrid was taking her turn at the tiller. It was a good day with a clear sky and only a few hazy clouds. The sea was blue, the swells were high but regular and the wind stiff and steady and smelling only of warm salt. The seabirds sported lazily over the low green coast.

Avanasy stood by the mast, one hand shading his eyes as he stared toward land. Then, he pointed toward an oddly cleft rise, where it looked like a single hill had been split open with a giant axe.

'Ngar-Chen,' he said. 'That puts us about a day out from the mouth of the Sze-Leng river. From there we will be able to find our way to the Heart of the World. There may even be a river boat, if we are lucky.' He came to stand beside her, one hand wrapping itself around the gunwale, the other touching the line, as if testing its tension. 'Grant that we have not been too long.'

'Whatever we find, we'll deal with it then,' said Ingrid. 'Your Empress arrived safely, you know that much.'

Avanasy nodded absently. He had tried several times over the past days to work a spell which would allow him to see Empress Medeoan, and possibly to pass a message to her, but there had been little success, even though his efforts would leave him drained and shaking. He had nothing of hers to create a bond between them, he told Ingrid when he had recovered from his first attempt, and working with the unshaped elements was chancy at best. He had been able to find traces that led him to believe she had reached the Heart of the World in safety, but beyond that he could see nothing.

'The Nine Elders will not permit prying eyes near their Emperor,' he had said ruefully.

The wind shifted, tugging at line and canvas. Ingrid, in response, shifted her grip on the tiller and checked the ropes. All seemed well to her, but Avanasy had straightened up, and turned his gaze from the shore to the open sea.

'What is it?' she asked.

'I don't know. Something . . .' he lifted his head, as if he had caught a sudden sound, or scent. 'Something new . . .'

Ingrid stared in the same direction, but saw nothing. All the sounds of sea and wind seemed the same.

'Ingrid, take us into shore,' said Avanasy. 'I do not like this.'

Ingrid did not question or protest. She trimmed the sail and swung the tiller around, steering them toward the green land. She badly wanted to see what Avanasy was staring at as he watched the open water past her shoulder, but her business was the boat, and she needed to keep a sharp eye out for breakers that would mark any shoals or other shallows.

Then it seemed to Ingrid that the day grew dimmer, and something was lost. In another minute she knew what it was. The seabirds had fallen silent.

'Vyshemir defend!' Avanasy leapt over benches and gear, to reach the port rail.

Ingrid risked a look back, and her grip slipped from the tiller.

They flew behind the boat, faster than the wind, for they were gaining. They were huge and ungainly, shaped more like apes than men. Their wings blocked out the sun, and they were armed. What light there was outlined spears and swords in their huge fists.

'God in Heaven,' was all she could breathe.

'Get us in, Ingrid,' cried Avanasy, drawing his knife. 'I'll hold them off, but we must get to land!'

Ingrid forced her eyes back down. *Work the ropes, raise the sail, steer the tiller, watch the shore, watch for breakers. Don't look back, don't look back.* She forced these words through her, although her mind was awash with panic. What were those things? What did they want? Oh, God, how could Avanasy face them all down with just a knife?

Shadows swooped over the boat, and despite all her resolve, Ingrid had to look.

Avanasy did not hold his knife now. Both his palms were cut and the blood ran red down his hands as he lifted them to the wind. He cried aloud, harsh words Ingrid could not understand and the daemon — what else could it be? — responded with a laugh like the low roll of thunder and swooped closer. Light glinted on red skin and black armor and cruel yellow fangs. Fear left Ingrid dizzy, but Avanasy didn't move.

All at once, the wind blew hard, making the boat buck against the waves. It scattered the daemons. The nearest shouted in his frustration and dove down on them again, and again the wind blew him back. But it also strained the canvas and made the ropes creak dangerously. A wave rolled over the rail, and Ingrid leaned all her weight against the tiller. The boat fought her, torn between Avanasy's wind and the natural actions of the waves.

Avanasy, pale as death in the bright sun, snatched up a length of rope in his bloody hands. Shouting again, he tied a knot in its length. One of the daemons arched its back, screeching in what Ingrid could only believe was pain. It plummeted into the sea, tossing up a fountain of brine. For a moment, the wind stilled, and Ingrid was able to haul hard on the tiller and swing the boat about, aiming the prow for a cleft in the shore that she prayed would make a harbor.

Avanasy staggered, the motion of the boat sending him

reeling against the rail. The chief of the daemons laughed again and whirled his sword over his head, bringing it flashing down as if he meant to cleave rope and sail. Ingrid hauled hard on the line and the boat heeled over, its rail skimming the water, and the sword missed by a bare inch. Avanasy slid to the deck, but braced himself against the bench.

'This is my wish,' Ingrid heard him grate, his hand curling around one of the belaying pins. 'This is my word, and my word is firm, my word is firm, my word is firm!'

He lifted the pin high, raising himself to his feet, and in his hand it was a pin no more. It was an axe on a long pole, and as the daemon swooped close again he swung it out and their weapons rang together with a mighty clash. The daemon shrieked and fell back, beating the air with its wings. It dove again, and again Avanasy parried, and it was all Ingrid could do to keep her seat and make herself watch the water, but when her eyes dropped again, she saw what she feared more than any impossible monster.

Breakers.

Rocks, shallows, shoals, it didn't matter, the safe cove she had steered them toward had no safe entrance. Immediately, Ingrid leaned forward to bring in the canvas, to swing the boom and bring them about, but the daemons had seen, and they dropped low behind the boat, their great wings fanning the wind and driving the little boat forward, toward the breakers.

'Avanasy!'

Avanasy saw, and swung his axe through the air, cutting at wind and wings. The daemons shrieked and fell back, giving Ingrid a moment's respite to haul the sail down, but the boat still surged forward, and the breakers were far too close. She searched the pattern of them desperately, watching for a clear space, or at least a strong wave to carry them over whatever lay beneath.

She spied their chance, or what she hoped was their

chance, a place in the swell where the waves seemed to surge through rather than smash against the shallows. She leaned hard on the tiller, aiming the boat and praying hard to whatever gods watched over sailors here.

One of the daemons dropped in front of the boat. Ingrid did not let herself flinch. The way was too narrow, she had to hold steady. Avanasy gripped the rail with one hand and raised his axe, shouting to the sky. The daemon shook as if buffeted by heavy blows, and it fell back.

At that moment the boat shuddered, and the tiller ripped itself momentarily from Ingrid's hands, but it was enough to lose her mark. The other two daemons rose grinning from the side, and she had just time enough to realize they had battered themselves against the boat before the surge drove them onto the rocks.

The world filled with a hideous splintering, crashing and roaring. Thrown backwards, Ingrid tumbled into the surf, dragged down instantly into the swell by her heavy skirts. Her hands clamped around the stern rail, barely able to hang on. A daemon dove grinning toward her. She screamed and dropped down into the water, and the world was suddenly blue-gray and silent; her lungs strained and saltwater stung her eyes. Waves shoved her hard forward and she struggled to swim, expecting any second to be snatched into the air. But no grip seized her, other than the water, relentlessly surging, weighting her too heavily down. She thought of Grace and for a moment despaired.

But her foot found the ragged bottom and she kicked upward at the same time as a wave tumbled her forward, dashing her against a shelf of rock and knocking all the air from her lungs just as her head broke the surface, allowing her to scream her pain and fear.

The waves rolled her over again, driving her onto the

pebbly shoal and then dragging her back out again. Scrabbling with hands and knees, Ingrid managed to gain a little purchase and forced her head and shoulders above water. Saltwater burned in her eyes as she struggled upright so she could see.

And she saw Avanasy. He stood up to his waist in the surging water, his axe over his head. The daemons wheeled above him, but they did not come close. Avanasy slashed the air with his axe, again, and again. With each slash, the daemons pulled closer together, as if bound by invisible ropes. Avanasy cried once more, and the daemons fell. Not in a straight line, not into the sea, but in an impossible arc, to vanish into the forest that covered the coast.

At that same moment, Avanasy's arms dropped, and he fell forward into the surf. With a cry of her own, Ingrid launched herself to his side to try to catch him, but her own strength was failing her, and she could only prop him up against her shoulder. But his eyes were open, and he was breathing, and it was enough.

'Come, come,' she croaked, her throat harsh with salt and sand. 'We must get to shore.'

Avanasy mustered a nod and together, leaning on each other, they labored to the shore, half swimming at times, sometimes with Ingrid dragging Avanasy, sometimes with Avanasy dragging her. At last, the waves pushed them forward and left them stranded on the stony beach, collapsed and panting, bleeding and bruised, two lost creatures of the sea left upon land to die.

The sun was hot and the water they had escaped from was harsh. Eventually, thirst became a stronger force than exhaustion, and Ingrid was able to push herself upright. Avanasy already sat up, hunched over his own knees, facing inland. He had been white before. He was gray now, and his breath was a sickening rattle.

'We need to find water,' rasped Ingrid.

Avanasy just shook his head. 'We need to find the daemons.'

'Why?' was all the answer Ingrid could make.

'I've bound them. They pull at me. If I don't transfer the bond . . . If I don't make some bargain, or bind them to some element, they'll break free, and they'll set on us again. I've not much strength left, and they'll know it.'

The thought of facing those monsters again made Ingrid shudder, but she would not leave Avanasy alone, not while he was shivering despite the bright sun.

She made herself swallow and say, 'Do you know where they are?'

'All too well.' He tightened his sinews and stood, and Ingrid stood with him.

This coast was as different from the place they had first come ashore in Isavalta as it was possible to be. That place had been all gray stones and gray cliffs. Here, there rose a thick forest beyond the beach. Salt wind twisted the trees, leaving them stooped and kinked like arthritic old men. From inside, she could hear the daemons, their thrashing and their shrieking like the sound of tortured metal. Beads of sweat stood out on Avanasy's forehead as they entered the wood, but he walked with determination.

The further they ventured from the sea, the straighter the trees became, and the pebble-strewn shore gave way to loam, dead leaves, ferns and rich moss. The noise did not pause or abate. If anything it grew more riotous. Avanasy staggered, and Ingrid caught him by the arm, lending what little strength she had to his support. He squeezed her hand, and they went on through the green dimness toward the unearthly clamor.

'You will be bound,' said Avanasy through his clenched teeth. 'I will it so, you will be bound.'

At last, the trees pulled away from a stony clearing. The daemons waited there, shaking their weapons and straining their wings at the sky. Their leader, or so Ingrid thought of him, due to the rings of gold in his ears, beat the ground with his spear as if he could force it to let them go.

'Be still!' ordered Avanasy.

And they were still, but even so, Ingrid could see them quivering as they strained against the order. Even restrained as they were, they were terrifying. Fangs curled from their mouths and talons from their hands and feet. The constant wind rattled the scales of their armor like the leaves of the trees. Their yellow eyes were the size of saucers, and a rotten, burning smell clung to them that went straight to the back of Ingrid's throat, choking off her breath.

The chief of the four monsters snarled at Avanasy. 'You transgress, Man. We may not be twice bound.'

'You may be bound until the end of time if I so declare it,' answered Avanasy. 'The roots in the earth beneath us can be called on to bind you tightly. The air can weave a net to hold you close.'

'Such boasts, such brags. You have not the strength.'

'You are bound to me with blood shed between us. If I transfer that bond, what can you do?' Avanasy's voice turned dangerous. 'You are creatures of fire, air and metal. I will bind you here with earth and water, by earth and water, under earth and water, between earth and water, I will bind, and my binding will be as firm as my word, as strong as my blood . . .'

Beneath the daemons, the earth began to move. Runnels of dirt ran up their legs like reaching fingers, swaddling their skin and exposing the bare tree roots. The roots themselves writhed and parted, revealing dark holes beneath the trees. Ingrid smelled a sudden gust of sea wind from the opened hole. Avanasy had gone freshly white with effort, but his voice did not falter. The daemons screamed, their cries of pain shuddering the wood and filling the air with heat and the scent of burning. It did them no good, and terror joined pain in their screams. Avanasy put out one hand to steady himself against a tree, but he worked grimly on, his spell never faltering, although his voice began to soften. The daemons looked like living statues of sand now, and the weight of the earth heaping itself over them began to bear them down, into the opening caves and the scent of the sea.

'No!' cried one of the daemons. 'Please, Master, no!'

'Mercy!' cried another, and its cry now was as heartbreaking as it had been horrible before.

Only then did Avanasy cease his slow chant, and for a moment, all the world held still.

'Mercy?' said Avanasy, softly, dangerously. 'Why should I show mercy to the ones who sought my blood and the blood of my wife?'

'We were ordered, Master,' wailed the leader of them all. 'We bear you no ill. Set us free, bind us no more, and we will leave you and yours in peace.'

'Ordered by whom?'

'We know no name.'

'Do not lie to me. What is his name?'

'Yamuna, Yamuna, Master, now let us go! Let us leave each other in peace!'

Slowly, Avanasy shook his head. 'It is not enough. Not for the hurt you would have dealt us.' And he began his chant again, and relentlessly the weight of the earth pressed the daemons to the ground.

'Please!' gasped the leader, forced to his knees. 'Master, please. What is your price?'

Again, Avanasy halted the spell, and the whole world was still for a moment. 'You will never again plague any under my protection, and you will carry us safely to the Heart of the World.'

'We cannot, we cannot.'

'Then be you buried,' said Avanasy implacably. 'For I cannot leave you free.'

The one of them nearest the pit began to howl, struggling against the earth that bound him like a shroud, to no avail. The hole simply widened, yawning like a mouth about to receive a morsel.

'Mercy, mercy!' cried the daemon chief. 'It shall be as you say!'

'Swear it,' said Avanasy.

'I swear, I swear!' gibbered the daemon. 'Spare us the earth!'

'By what do you swear?'

'By my own eyes, by the fire that birthed me!' screamed the daemon.

At that, Avanasy nodded. 'It is enough.' He knelt, laying his bloodstained hands flat upon the ground. He murmured something Ingrid could not hear, and all at once, the earthen shrouds fell from the daemons, the grains scattering like the dust they were. The ground heaved once more, and the tree roots closed over the pit again, lacing themselves into a tight, natural net.

Avanasy did not get to his feet. Rather than have to look at the creatures that faced her with their fangs and their wild yellow eyes, Ingrid crouched beside him. 'Are you all right?'

'No,' he answered flatly. 'But it does not matter. Help me up.'

Ingrid tightened her jaw around all of her questions and helped Avanasy to stand. The chief of the daemons did not seem able to look him in the eyes. It bowed its head and its great wings slumped until they dragged the ground.

'You have doomed us, Man,' he growled. 'When would you have us fulfill our bond?'

'Now,' said Avanasy. He looked toward Ingrid, and Ingrid could not keep her trepidation from her eyes.

'How can we do this? How can we trust them?'

'They are bound to me now. They cannot harm or disobey,' Avanasy said with utter conviction. He moved close to her and gripped Ingrid's forearms. 'Hold tight to me, Ingrid, and do not be afraid.'

'Come now, Master,' growled their chief.

Freed from Avanasy's spell, the daemons showed no further sign of weakness. In a single moment, they surrounded Ingrid and Avanasy, and their wings rose up until the sun was blocked by the blood-red feathers. Ingrid bit her tongue to keep silent. Then there came a great rush of air, and the ground fell away from underneath her feet.

Ingrid had little time to imagine what such a flight would be like, but if she had had a thousand years, she never would have anticipated the reality of it. She could not see anything. The world was the rushing of wind, red, gold and black shadows, the stench of burning and Avanasy's hands gripping her arms. The heat was stifling. Her feet dangled loosely, and she had to fight to keep from kicking out in a vain attempt to find some footing.

Then, it was over, and it was only she and Avanasy, their backs against a sandstone wall, and the docks of a busy river spreading out before them. Ingrid realized she was soaked with sweat and stench and her hands had gone completely numb. Avanasy looked like death itself, but at the same time, his limbs seemed steady while Ingrid's felt weak as water.

'Come,' his voice rasped in his throat. 'Let us sit for a moment here.'

Still holding tightly to each other, they settled themselves stiffly at the base of the wall. Avanasy gently extricated himself from Ingrid's grip and laid her hands in her own lap. For awhile she was content just to sit and feel the warmth that was no more than sunlight touch her skin, and draw some sensibility back into her hands, even if it was only pins and needles. Indeed, it seemed as if she might never will herself to movement again. But, gradually, as the world stayed steady and the familiar sensation of wind in her hair and on her face proved it would not change suddenly into the breath of a daemon in black and gold armor, Ingrid found thoughts once again beginning to coalesce inside her battered mind.

'Where are the . . . daemons?' she asked.

Avanasy let his head fall back to rest against the wall so that he stared up at the summer-blue sky with its drifting clouds.

'Perhaps gone back to their home in the Silent Lands. But more likely, they have fled to try to avoid the summons from their other master, which will surely come.' He watched the clouds slowly shifting their shapes overhead. 'I cannot imagine Yamuna will be pleased.'

'Who is Yamuna?'

'Each member of the royal family in Hastinapura is assigned a sorcerer as a protector and advisor. Yamuna serves Chandra, who is father to Kacha, the one who was married to the Empress of Isavalta.'

'They know you have returned then.'

Avanasy bowed his head and ran his hand through his hair. 'So it would seem. I have not been as subtle as I thought.'

'But these will not come again.'

'Not these. They are bound by their oaths to me now.'

'Can't they break those oaths?'

Avanasy shook his head. 'They cannot. It would put them in my power again.'

'How so?'

Avanasy's smile was thin. 'It is one of the mysteries between this world and the Land of Death and Spirit. An oath between a mortal and a spirit or a power is not as an oath between mortal and mortal. Words between us have powers of their own. They can wound, they can tie, they can break. The arguments about why this is so are extensive, they fill books and scrolls of great antiquity. The only point which cannot be argued is that this is the truth.'

Ingrid stared out across the docks. She had not imagined a river could be so broad. Even the Mississippi could not match this watercourse for girth. The ships waiting at the piers came in all sizes. There were huge galleons with four masts and three tiers of portholes. There were lean three-masted cutters with knife-sharp prows for cutting through the waves with all speed. Sloops and smacks and dories of all descriptions crowded in the shadows of the larger vessels. Bare-chested men in broad, peaked hats worked in and around their vessels, singing, swearing and shouting by turns. These were surely the common sailors, decided Ingrid. They carried huge bundles on their backs, or tightly packed baskets on shoulder-yokes. The air was full of the smell of tar, sweat and spices. Despite the strangeness of dress and the sight of so many sails, the place felt strangely familiar to Ingrid. It reminded her sharply of the port at Bayfield.

Between the shirtless men worked men in short coats and wide trousers, mostly of white or unbleached cloth with colored bands around the cuffs and hems for trimming, but here and there was one dressed in solid black or bright green or sapphire blue. These men stood in groups, talking, or supervised the unloading of ships and the loading of carts, or sat at trestle tables beside ships' gangways weighing samples of goods or reviewing what Ingrid supposed were bills of goods.

But all these sights and sounds were not enough to drive the question that had formed inside her out of her mind. 'So, if I had promised that . . . Baba Yaga that I would carry out the task she gave me . . .'

'You would have been bound to her by that promise until the task had been completed, yes. If you had tried to break that promise, your life itself could have been forfeit to her.'

'Oh.'

Ingrid was silent for a time, breathing in air that smelled of spices, fish and garbage. Then, another thought occurred to her. 'But surely those daemons were sent to murder us.'

'They were.'

'Did they not break a promise then by failing to do so?'

'They did. Which is why they have fled. At the time, they feared me more than they feared Yamuna.' He rubbed his forehead. 'I was gambling, I confess, that they were among those breeds not noted for their courage, and that they might indeed have been coerced.' He lifted his eyes again. 'If they had given their oaths freely, nothing short of their annihilation would have saved us.'

To that, Ingrid made no reply. At her silence, Avanasy's face fell. 'It is a dangerous place I have brought you to, Ingrid. But these are dangers beyond what I anticipated. I am sorry.'

She shook her head. 'It was my decision.' She tried to smooth down her filthy dress. 'Now, where are we and how are we to make ourselves decent enough to be seen here?'

He smiled at her sudden practicality. The expression brought a more healthy color to his cheeks, which her heart lifted to see.

'I have some gold,' he said. 'Not much, but some. We can change it for local coin easily enough, which in turn will buy us a bath and whatever else is needful. As for where we are . . .' with a grunt, Avanasy got himself to his feet, and extended his hand to Ingrid to help her do the same. 'We are in T'ien, the city that holds the Heart of the World.'

Together they waded into the busy crowd surrounding the river docks. The warm, damp air was made heavier by the presence of so many bodies surrounding them. Although Avanasy said he had only been to Hung-Tse three times in his life on errands for the Emperor of Isavalta, he spoke the language well. So too, apparently, did Ingrid, for he had imparted that understanding to her through his enchantment. She could understand the language of the sailors and the wharfmen in all its rough color as they worked their way down past the piers and the warehouses.

Finally, Avanasy found what he was looking for. He touched Ingrid's forearm and gestured for her to wait by the seawall. She nodded and backed away while he strolled onto the docks toward a man in a white coat with narrow green lapels and deep cuffs who sat behind a table weighing out what looked from Ingrid's vantage point like thimbles of tarnished silver. He looked up at the sound of Avanasy's voice, and from the men's expressions, Ingrid felt confident that a period of pleasantries and bargaining was about to begin.

She let her attention wander to the business of the port. A rhythmic song rang out as sailors hoisted heavy loads aboard one of the galleons. A cart loaded with live chickens in their coops turned a corner in a flurry of feathers and frantic clucking. A drunken man wove his way unsteadily through the throng clutching a wineskin to his bosom. Ingrid rolled her eyes. That was a recipe for disaster in this crowd.

Disaster was not long in coming. The drunk, rather than choosing the path of least resistance, seemed determined to force his way through the thickest part of the traffic. He was shouldered off to one side, and then the other, but before he had gone many yards he collided straight into one of the few women who walked near the docks, sending up a spurt of clear liquor between them, which drew a laugh from the passers-by. The woman drew back in an obvious attempt to regain both distance and dignity. The drunkard himself batted at the woman's robe, in either an assault, or an attempt to wipe away the dampness. Angrily, the woman pushed him away, shouting something that was lost in the general laughter and noise of the crowd. But, even as she did, traffic began to flow around her again. One man brushed against her, and Ingrid saw his hand reach quickly into her sash, and secrete something in his own sleeve.

'Thief!' shouted Ingrid, before she even had time to think. She jerked herself upright and leveled an accusing finger at the man. 'Thief!'

A general shout rose from the crowd. Some drew back and others surged forward, and the thief himself tried to dart into the crowd. Ingrid leapt forward, putting herself squarely in his path, and grabbing his sleeve as he tried to push past her.

'Let me go!' he shouted. 'Are you mad? Let go!'

But the assaulted woman reached into her sash, and found her property missing.

'Thief!' she echoed Ingrid's cry. 'Thief! That man has my purse!'

Then it was not just Ingrid who held him. Two of the passing sailors seized the thief roughly by the shoulders, pulling him from Ingrid's grip. Avanasy was suddenly beside her, urging her back. A third sailor with a moth tattooed in blue on his shoulder searched the thief roughly, coming up with a bag of scarlet leather.

'My purse!' cried the woman, running forward to snatch it from the sailor's hand.

The crowd did not take this declaration well, and the shouts turned ugly. The thief was shoved from hand to hand and his pleas were lost under the general roar. But someone's grip must have slipped, because the thief darted through a cluster of sailors, and pelted up the alleyway between two warehouses, the mob in hot pursuit behind him.

'Are you all right?' Avanasy asked Ingrid.

Before she could answer, the assaulted woman stepped up to them and bowed deeply, holding both hands before her, palms pressed together as if for prayer.

'May your sharp eyes be blessed,' she said breathlessly. 'I and my family are in your debt.'

Ingrid glanced sideways at Avanasy, her eyebrows raised, but she quickly recovered herself and curtsied to the woman. 'You're welcome. Anyone would have done the same.'

'But anyone did not,' replied the woman, straightening up. She was a slender woman, a few inches shorter than Ingrid. Her eyes were almond shaped, and of a rich almond-brown hue in her round face. Her black hair had been piled high on her head and bound with peach-colored ribbon that exactly matched the skirts and cuffs of her robe. 'I am Cai-Yun Shen. May I have the honor of knowing to whom I owe the return of my property?'

Caution nibbled at the edge of Ingrid's mind. 'I am Ingrid,' she said. 'And this is my husband Avan.'

Cai-Yun looked from one of them to the other, but did not ask about their abbreviated names. 'And you are strangers to this province?'

'Travelers only,' said Avanasy.

'Then please allow me to extend to you the hospitality of my family's house. My uncle will be pleased to personally thank you both.'

Ingrid felt her face begin to warm, and opened her mouth to protest she had not done so much, but felt Avanasy's gently warning touch on her shoulder.

'The honor would be ours,' he said to Cai-Yun. Then, to Ingrid, in English he added, 'Hospitality is not something we can lightly refuse here. It would be a grave insult.'

Ingrid nodded her understanding. At that same moment, she thought she saw Cai-Yun's eyes narrow ever so slightly. What disconcerted her? Was it the language? Why would that be?

But all Cai-Yun said was, 'Then if you will please follow me.'

'Gladly,' said Ingrid, despite her troubled propriety. They were still filthy, covered with the residue of their travels. The idea of entering a decent home in this condition did not leave her at ease.

But Cai-Yun did not seem to notice, and Avanasy walked with his head up, apparently unconcerned. Ingrid tried to put it out of her own mind and pay attention to the sights passing by them. She soon came to realize she was in a city far larger than any she had ever been in. For all she knew, the place might be as big as Chicago. The narrow streets were filled with people and lined with houses of stone and wood with tiled roofs, some as many as three stories high. The tallest and the richest rose behind walls of carved and painted stone, and Ingrid saw the tops of rich, green trees, leading her to believe the walls enclosed gardens as well as homes.

They had not been walking many minutes before Cai-Yun stopped before one of these private walls. The opening in it was a narrow, dark, wooden door carved all over with patterns that might have been swirls of wind, or might have been winding ribbons. She would not have given them a second thought, except she heard Avanasy's sharp intake of breath at the sight of them.

Inside the gate, as Ingrid had thought, there was a garden. It was a lush, green lawn overshadowed by drooping trees with leaves of all shades of green and red. Rich ferns and reeds clustered about still, brown ponds blooming with lilies and purple flags.

Beyond the garden waited a house Ingrid could only describe as grand, which made her shabbiness feel even more apparent. Two stories tall and far broader than it was high, it was a beautiful building of painted wood with wide, red lacquered eaves, covered with flowing decorations of green and gold. Rather than windows, it seemed that whole panels of the walls folded back like screens to open the rooms to the sea breezes that drifted over the walls.

Avanasy's eyes looked about ready to fall from his head, he was staring so hard as they walked up the flagstone path. 'If these sigils are real, this place is protected by more magics than the Imperial winter home in Isavalta,' he murmured.

Ingrid wanted to ask him why anyone would guard their home so heavily, but Cai-Yun was watching them again with her narrowed eyes, so Ingrid responded with a smile.

'What beautiful gardens you have,' she said. 'My husband was just remarking on them.'

Cai-Yun smiled, apparently satisfied. 'They are indeed lovely. I have spent many peaceful hours here, and am always glad to return when I have been away.'

'You travel a great deal then, Lady?' inquired Avanasy.

'My family makes its living by ships,' answered Cai-Yun, a trifle coolly, Ingrid thought. 'I have sailed some distance with them.'

They had reached the verandah now. Two servants, a man and a woman in identical coats and trousers of unbleached cotton with black cuffs, opened the doors and bowed deeply.

'Welcome, Mistress,' said the woman to Cai-Yun. 'Your uncle has been awaiting your return and asks that you join him in his library at once.'

'Gladly, Shien. Now, these two travelers are my honored guests. You and Du will show them to a good apartment and see that they are brought clean clothes and all that they will need to refresh themselves.' She spoke with the casual ease of one used to command. 'As they are northerners, you will see them housed together.' She blinked up at Avanasy. 'That is customary for a husband and wife in your land, is it not?'

Avanasy did not frown, not quite, but a flicker of suspicion crossed his face. 'It is,' he acknowledged, and Ingrid wondered what he was thinking.

'Welcome to this house, Master, Mistress,' said Du. 'If you will come with us please.'

'I will relate the full story to my uncle,' said Cai-Yun. 'He will be anxious to meet you and thank you for your vigilance.'

'I'm just glad I could help,' murmured Ingrid, and she was glad to be able to turn quickly away to follow the old servants.

The inside of the house, at least on the first floor, seemed composed of only a few separate rooms. The rest of the space seemed to be broken by gleaming wooden pillars and screens of carved wood or painted silk. Ingrid felt as if she was in some grand pavilion rather than a true house.

Up the broad, shallow stairs the rooms were smaller, with solid walls and doors. Du and Shien led them down a corridor to the far corner of the house, opening a pair of doors to reveal a room of rose-colored wood and water-blue silk. The two servants bustled about, opening the broad windows and sheltering them with intricately carved screens. Du hurried to fetch water while Shien opened a rosewood press and laid out two sets of robes, one white and green, one white and blue. Black sashes accompanied each robe. As Du returned with water for the porcelain ewers, Shien also laid out towels, soaps, combs and brushes in such profusion that Ingrid was not sure she could decipher uses for them all.

It took some doing to convince the pair that she really wanted them to wait outside during their ablutions, but Ingrid was firm. She apologized repeatedly for her coarse and foreign ways, but she shooed them out just the same. She wanted a moment to think, and to catch her breath with Avanasy. She did not want to be fussed over by a stranger.

At last, however, Shien closed the door behind herself murmuring that she would see to their meal, and bowing to Ingrid's thanks. The door shut, Ingrid let out a sigh of relief and set about stripping her filthy dress off down to her petticoats. She had peeled off her outer layer and tossed it aside, only to look up and see Avanasy smiling at her.

'What is that for?' she inquired with mock stiffness.

'You. A world away from your home, and you are stopping thieves, graciously smoothing our entrance into the homes of the wealthy, and ordering servants about, and yet I believe you think nothing of it.'

Ingrid shrugged, pouring water from a ewer into a basin. The faint scent of jasmine rose from the cascade. 'Compared to what I have seen you do today, it's a small thing.'

'No,' he came to stand next to her, his hands resting on her shoulders. 'It is a great thing indeed.' As if to prove what he said, he kissed her lingeringly, a gesture Ingrid willingly accepted.

'Do you have any idea where we might be?' she asked when they parted. With towel and soap, she set about scrubbing her face, neck and arms. The water turned from clear to gray with distressing speed.

'If I am not mistaken,' said Avanasy, filling his own basin, 'this house belongs to a pirate.'

'A pirate?' repeated Ingrid, lifting her dripping face in surprise.

Avanasy nodded, stripping off his shirt and laying it aside with Ingrid's dress. 'They are a plague on Hung-Tse, and most embarrassingly on T'ien and the Heart of the World, but they flourish, well-paid and well-protected.'

'You don't sound as if you believe we are in much danger.'

'I don't. They have their own honor in many ways, and judging from our Lady Cai-Yun's reaction, whatever was in that purse was valuable to the master of this house. I think we will be safer here than we could have been in hired rooms and public baths, and much less observed.'

'It is no worse than daemons, I suppose,' admitted Ingrid, bending once again to her wash.

But she heard no indication that Avanasy was doing the same. 'Ingrid, what is wrong?' he asked softly.

For a time, Ingrid did not answer. She washed her neck and arms, wrung out the towel, folded it onto the side of the basin, picked up a fresh towel and began to dry herself.

'I don't know,' she admitted. 'I . . . It's all so strange. As soon as I think I know what to expect, everything seems to change, and I know nothing. I even find . . . I wonder . . .' she bit her lip. She had not meant to say so much.

'What?' asked Avanasy, drawing close. 'Wondering perhaps how much you know of your husband?'

She could not look at him. 'I don't want to feel this way, I swear to you, Avanasy . . .'

He just shook his head to silence her. 'It would be strange indeed if you did not. You have seen me threaten torture and murder against my enemies. You have been swept from one land to another with barely a word, and you have been torn in two since you came here.' He ran his fingers lightly over the braided wristlet. 'What sane woman would not have doubts about what she had done?'

'And what do we do about it, then?'

'We trust,' said Avanasy. 'We hold close. We keep to the hope that this chaos must end and the world will be righted again.'

Ingrid knew her smile was wan. 'I will do my best.'

'As will I.' Avanasy picked up his own towel. 'And we will

speak more tonight, but I think now we must finish our washing. I fear poor Shien and Du will be fretting outside the door for not being allowed to do their jobs.'

Ingrid set her hair in order and Avanasy finished his wash. Then they attempted to help each other on with the robes, which looked so tidy when Shien laid them out, but proved to consist of acres of cloth that had to be carefully folded, wrapped and tied. After several laughing attempts to get them on, they retired to opposite sides of the room behind separate screens and called for the servants. As Avanasy suspected, they were just outside the door. Shien bustled in behind Ingrid's changing area and in moments had her wrapped and tied neatly in the thick, clean, cloth so that the robe fell in graceful folds from her shoulders and her waist.

Now that her charge was dressed to her satisfaction, Shien busied herself with setting out the numerous diminutive bowls and cups that were evidently required for their meal. Each dish held just a taste of some delicacy: a few pieces of fresh melon, a piquant vegetable pickle, cold rice flavored with jasmine, some shelled nuts, a few small steamed rolls. The cups held various teas and liquors. It all seemed incredibly exotic to Ingrid, as she sat at the low table and allowed Shien to help her to various samplings while Du helped Avanasy, and yet at the same time it was an undeniably refreshing way to eat on an afternoon that was becoming increasingly sweltering.

When the last dish was emptied and cleared away, and Ingrid had sipped the last of the orange-blossom water, Shien bowed low again, and said she had been instructed to take them down to the study to meet their host.

The food and wine had mellowed Ingrid, but not enough to erase her apprehension. What sort of hospitality had they accepted? Avanasy's reassurances notwithstanding, she knew something of banditry and even piracy; while such men might have honor, it was of a notably expedient sort.

The study was in a well-shaded corner of the house on the lower floor. Cai-Yun stood outside its screened entrance and dismissed Shien with brief thanks and a wave as they arrived to stand in front of her. Cai-Yun led them around the screen into a spacious and beautiful room. Its many low tables were spread with maps or piled with scrolls or folios of thin paper. In the midst of these tools of scholarship sat a man whom Ingrid assumed must be the master of the house. He appeared to be a man just entering middle age with sharp cheek bones and keen eyes. His black hair had been bound into a neat braid at the back of his head, and unlike most of the other men of this country he wore a thin beard that outlined his jaw. His robe was almost a reverse of the one Avanasy wore, solid blue with white cuffs and sash.

Cai-Yun bowed to the seated scholar. 'Uncle, may I introduce to you Ingrid and her husband Avan. It was Ingrid who saved our family property and my honor this morning. Mistress Ingrid, Master Avan, may I introduce my Uncle Lien Jinn.'

Lien Jinn bowed without rising. 'Please accept my thanks. My niece was on an errand for me to meet a ship of mine that had come in. What you saved was much more than a maiden's pocket money.' He gestured toward two chairs that looked to Ingrid to be little more than low platforms with thin pillows on them. 'Will you sit with me?'

'Gladly, Sir,' answered Avanasy. He was holding his face oddly, as if trying to keep some unwanted expression at bay. He and Ingrid settled themselves cross-legged on the seats while Cai-Yun stationed herself at her uncle's right hand. 'I have only rarely had occasion to enjoy the fabled hospitality of T'ien, and my wife not at all. I am humbled by its extent.'

'Your words warm my poor heart,' answered Lien solemnly.

'I was most struck by the beauty·of your home,' Avanasy went on. 'Great care has been taken in its construction, and its protection.'

'What peace can there be if a man's family is not safe?' Now it was Lien who narrowed his eyes, and it was easy to see the family resemblance between him and Cai-Yun.

'This is wisdom.' Avanasy nodded. 'Your own children are grown then?'

'My ancestors deemed my role should be to look after the health and well-being of my brothers' families.'

'Having seen how you provide for strangers, I have no doubt your family is in excellent hands,' said Ingrid, beginning to get a feel for the rhythm of this conversation.

'It is a blessing to be able to help those who are far from their homes.' Lien's face grew shrewd. 'And I cannot help but believe you are both very far from your home.'

'Not so far as I have been,' answered Avanasy. 'But not so near as I would be.'

'You did not wish to travel then?' Lien inquired mildly. Ingrid noted that although she sat silently, Cai-Yun was watching both her and Avanasy, like a cat might watch a mousehole, not blinking, missing nothing. Looking for lies under the pleasantries, Ingrid was sure of it. Looking for what might be hidden by words.

Avanasy sighed. 'In truth, no. We find we have become seekers, my wife and I.'

'And what is it you seek?'

'Something valuable, which was removed from its rightful place.'

'Ah.' Lien nodded sagely, as if Avanasy had spoken with perfect clarity. 'This is a common problem. It must be very valuable for you to have traveled so far.'

'It is unique.'

'I thought it must be. It may be I am in a position to help you.'

'Indeed?' Avanasy's eyebrows shot up in mock surprise. 'We would be most grateful for any help that could be offered.'

'It happens in the course of trade that I occasionally hear of valued movables, and may be able to bend my humble skills toward negotiating its retrieval.'

'I fear it is not only retrieval which we must concern ourselves with, but return. While I hope those who have it will return it willingly once certain conditions can be met, I fear they may not, in which case, they may pursue it.'

Cai-Yun frowned openly at this, but the light of curiosity sparked in her uncle's eyes. 'This enterprise could lead you to some expense, I think, my friend, as well as trouble.'

Avanasy bowed his head. 'It can, and it has, but I am under obligation.'

'Ah, yes. I thought as much. Isavalta is noted for its dedication to duty.'

'And you, Mistress, what are your people noted for?' asked Cai-Yun lightly.

'Stubbornness, Mistress,' answered Ingrid, which earned her a laugh. 'And an inability to keep our opinions to ourselves.'

'Have you an opinion on this matter then, Mistress?'

Ingrid decided to risk it. 'It is my opinion that the master of the house already knows who we are, and has some idea of what it is we seek. I believe he is taking our measure, for which I cannot fault him, but I think it would be beneath all our dignities to begin bargaining over the fate of nations like a fishwife over fish.'

Lien laughed out loud. 'Well spoken, Mistress. Well spoken. What do you say, Avan? Do we bargain thus? Or do we open our books each to the other and show what we know?'

'I would not presume to tell the master what to do in his

own home. But I do find myself reminded of a legend they tell in my homeland.'

Lien's eyes glittered. 'I would be most interested to hear it.'

'I was trained by the sorcerer Valerii. When it came time for me to leave my master, he gave me many gifts. The most precious of these was the secret of making sail-cloth that could catch the wind that blows between the worlds and enable a boat to sail between mortal shores and the Land of Death and Spirit. He told me the secret of its making had been won by a sorcerer from south of our home. This sorcerer, it seems, loved a young woman who was chosen to enter the Heart of the World as a concubine. But she continued to write to him, so the story goes, and he to her, swearing he would find a way to spirit them both away without even the Nine Elders being able to follow.

'My master went on to say that this sorcerer walked across the Land of Death and Spirit and, through immense patience and cleverness, won the secret of making the sail-cloth from the Old Witch herself. But when he returned to his home, it was only to find that his love had been discovered and made to drink poison for her transgressions. The sorcerer vowed vengeance upon the Emperor and all his heirs, and he has been taking that vengeance ever since, as slowly and as patiently as he took the secret he needed from the Old Witch.'

Lien's eyes glittered. 'So. You know rather more than I would have told you left to my own devices, Master Avan.'

'Avanasy,' Avanasy corrected him, and there was no look of surprise on Lien's face. 'I believe Mistress Ingrid is correct. The time has come for us to call things by their proper names.'

'And while we are so doing, what would you have of me?'

'Beyond a night's shelter, nothing, if all is well.'

'And if it is not?'

'Safe transport for myself, my wife and one other to a

destination of our choosing, safe transport that the Nine Elders cannot follow.'

'This item you seek, it is valuable to the Nine Elders.'

Avanasy nodded. 'If they are so inclined, they will find it a treasure great enough to buy the peace of an empire.'

The smile on Lien's face then was thin, and filled with greed, but his words were cautious. 'I shall consider your words carefully. We will speak again at the evening meal. In the meantime, I invite you to treat my house as if it were your own. Niece, show them the gardens.'

'Gladly, Uncle.' She bowed to him even as she rose.

'The peace of an empire?' inquired Lien as they turned to go.

'Perhaps,' said Avanasy. 'If they have chosen safety over honor.'

At those words, Lien's face turned utterly bitter. 'That has ever been their choice in the past. I think we may easily rely on them to do so again.'

Chapter Sixteen

The temple city of Durah was normally a place of solemn monks, prayer fires and the smells and smokes of sacrifice. Pilgrims filed up the narrow way to pay what coins they had to the priests and pray at the feet of the Mothers for guidance or deliverance. Today, however, the way was blocked by vigilant soldiers and those pilgrims who did not wish to return home waited in a makeshift camp at the bottom of the cliff. More soldiers crowded the alleys and twisted walkways between the temples and dormitories, pitching their own tents and adding the smoke of their cooking fires to the sacred smoke rising in tribute to the gods and the Mothers.

Emperor Samudra *tya* Achin Ireshpad, Holder of the Pearl Throne, Beloved of the Seven Mothers, Warrior of the Gods, the Uniter and the Deliverer, having prostrated himself for a suitable time in the highest temple and having in addition paid for a seven-fold sacrifice and added a gift for the high priest, was given a priest's house to use as his headquarters, and not too grudgingly either.

The house's great room had been cleared of most of its furniture and appointments. In their place, great maps had been unrolled and laid on the floor, decked out with copper markers indicating where the enemy troops were last known to be stationed. The latest news from the scouts was not good. The invaders from the north, the Huni, had dug themselves into the mountain fastnesses, and showed no sign of being willing to come out for a fight. Indeed, why should they? All they needed to do was wait for winter to descend upon the mountains and fill the passes with snow and ice. It was still early enough in the year to start a siege, but a siege would have costs, and not all of them would be paid on the battlefield.

The true problem lay in not having an accurate count of the enemy, nor a good idea of the state of their supplies. His generals were questioning some of the local villagers even now in other, quieter rooms, but so far they were not getting good answers. Shepherds could count rams and ewes accurately, but to them five soldiers were the same as five thousand; too many for safety.

'We could parley, Majesty,' suggested General Makul, seeing Samudra frowning at the delicately drawn maps and the copper coins. 'Draw them out and take their measure across the negotiating table.'

'And have them think we are weak,' growled Samudra.

'The better to know how weak they are,' replied Makul calmly. He knew the growl to be purely reflexive, a mark of Samudra's disappointment more than anything else. This had been meant to be a brief campaign. The march from the Pearl Throne had been accomplished quickly. He had believed that the rout of the Huni here might be the same. The Huni in these mountains were known to be fat and careless, convinced Samudra's attentions lay elsewhere. It should have been a quick fight, with Samudra and his men home in time to supervise the tallies from the harvests and deal with Chandra, Yamuna and their antics, all the time having let Hung-Tse know that their days of holding the land that belonged to the Seven Mothers were almost done.

But the Huni had been warned, and when Samudra arrived, they were long gone.

'Would they parley, do you think?' he mused, rubbing his chin.

'I think they would sneer. I think they would bluster,' Makul replied. 'And I think they would be glad of a chance to do so to Your Majesty's face.'

'I think that some of our scouts led by a well-paid shepherd might keep watch at such a time in a hidden place, to observe their comings and goings so we might better know how they can be winkled out of their shells.'

'Your Majesty thinks wisely and well,' replied the general gravely.

Samudra let the flattery pass with a smile. 'What do you think, Hamsa?' He lifted his head to his sorceress.

Hamsa stood in the corner of the room in front of a fire of smoldering sandalwood and incense. She balanced herself neatly on one foot, with one hand raised above her head, her fingers cupped in the sign of supplication to Jalaja, first of the Seven Mothers. She had been standing so for three days and three nights using prayer, smoke, strength and sacrifice to bind her magic into shape. She sought to see into the warp and weft of time, to see what was possible and what was not, at least as far – as she would have been the first to remind him – as the Mothers would permit. Despite her fierce concentration on matters beyond the flesh, he knew she heard him, for it was the consequences of what was said in this room that she was meant to see.

'I think . . .' she murmured, her voice slurred with trance and fatigue. 'I think I see a ravine in the foothills where a tributary to the river Harsha cuts sharp through the rocks.' She swayed just a little on her one leg. 'I think I see a man's broken body at the bottom. His horse lies beside him for the ravens and the wolves. He came fast and far, that man, and he had a message.'

'What message?' demanded Samudra. Inside he cursed. What this ill-starred expedition did not need was more complexity.

'Gone,' said Hamsa thickly. She did not look at him, but stared straight ahead, seeing further than any untouched human might. 'Consigned to the fire, blocked, blotted, ashes . . .' She swayed again, like a young willow in the wind, bending so that Samudra sucked in his breath, but still she remained upright. 'For that message could not reach the Emperor, or all would be lost, lost . . .'

'Do you see the message, *Agnidh* Hamsa?' asked Samudra quietly, uncertain whether she would even hear him where she had gone.

'In the fire,' she whispered, her words swaying in rhythm with her body. 'In the fire, first and last, beginning and ending. It was in the fire, it is in the fire, it will be in the fire, ever in the fire . . .' She shuddered violently, and Makul started forward, but Samudra stopped him with a touch on the arm. Samudra disliked magic. He shied away from it when possible. But he knew enough to know Hamsa had gone from a trance to an active working, and to interrupt could be perilous, to both the sorcerer and the mortal attempting the intervention.

'In the fire,' Hamsa said again, bending forward from her waist, still balanced on only one leg, breathing the scented smoke deeply, weaving her spell of breath, smoke, sacrifice and words. 'Fire, flame, ash, smoke, message to the mighty, message in the fire, in the flame, in the ash, in the smoke, in the fire, in the fire, in the fire . . .'

Hamsa lowered the hand she had held cupped over her head for three days and reached it unhesitating into the bright flames. When she drew it out again, she held a piece of sealed paper in her fingers.

'There,' she whispered, and let it fall to the floor. Immediately, she herself sank down to sit on the flagstones, arms and legs folded, eyes closed, and lungs laboring to keep breathing. This too was the way of things. Samudra motioned to the waiting servants. They knew what to do. Water, bread and fruit would be placed beside her so that she could regain her strength as soon as she was ready to rejoin the human world; but first, there was the message, which Makul had already retrieved from the floor.

What he had taken for paper was in fact white silk, tied with a saffron ribbon and sealed with saffron wax, the sort that was only used by one person; the Emperor of Hung-Tse.

Samudra slit the ribbon with his knife and unrolled the silk. The characters had been painted in red and black ink with a minute brush, and the whole of it was finished with the yellow dragon seal of the Heart of Heaven and Earth. Samudra allowed himself to sit and spread the letter out before him. He could read the language of Hung-Tse, but not as quickly as he would have liked. For such a letter, no translator could properly be called, not yet. However it came to him, this message was from ruler to ruler and must be treated with respect.

So, slowly, he read:

To the Emperor Samudra tya *Achin Ireshpad, Revered and Respected, Father of the Pearl Throne and Son of the Seven Mothers, we send greeting.*

It is not our wish to speak to you with anger, but for the care in which we hold our sacred lands, our borders allotted to us by the will of Heaven and of men, we must protest the injustices that have their origin in the blood of the Pearl Throne.

The northern border of Hung-Tse is assaulted, the leader of the assault is the nephew of the Pearl Throne, Kacha tya *Achin*

Ekulinjapad. He moves to attack without provocation, without warning and without lawful reason. We would appeal to the lawful Empress of Isavalta and bring forth our suit to her, but it has come to our ears that she has been driven forth from her own court.

We ask you to appeal to the filial responsibility of your nephew to stop this unwarranted and unjust attack on our lands and peoples. Whatever are the lawful quarrels of our empires one to one, to break and reform the power of the north must lead to a war so complete that powers will fall and be broken under its wheel. As a man of prudence and martial wisdom, you surely see this and will not desire such an outcome.

Samudra felt the blood draining drop by drop from his cheeks.

'What is this?' he whispered. 'What is this!' he shouted, staring at the letter as if it had burst back into flames. 'War, war with Hung-Tse and Isavalta and Kacha at its head! What *is* this!'

'The truth,' said Hamsa before Makul could even open his mouth. The sorceress lifted her head. Even across the room, Samudra could hear her breath wheezing in her lungs. 'The Mothers forefend, Majesty, but it is the truth.'

'How did we not know? Why did Kacha's bound-sorcerer not write to me or to the Queen?'

Hamsa had to take several rattling breaths before she was able to answer. 'I don't know. The *Agnidh* Harshul may have been corrupted.'

'Or he may have been killed,' said Makul grimly.

'And the letters forged?' demanded Samudra. 'How? By whom? I know Harshul, and Kacha does not have the mind for this, let alone the skill.' *At least I believed he did not, I believed he was safe to send as pledge and prize. Oh, Mothers, what have I done?*

'Those are questions that should be put to the Prince

Chandra,' said Makul. 'I cannot believe that the son acts without his father's blessing.'

'Yamuna,' breathed Hamsa. She coughed, and reached a trembling hand toward the water bowl that had been placed out for her. She dipped her fingertips in the water and sucked them dry. 'I saw . . . as I saw the history of the missive, I saw . . . Ah, forgive me, Majesty.' Coughs racked her, shuddering her bony frame. A servant knelt beside her, lifting the bowl to her lips that she might drink. Samudra waited. He had seldom seen Hamsa so drained. The effort it was costing her to speak was as great as if she had been wounded to the heart in battle. As much as his blood wanted immediate answers, he held himself in check.

'The missive came from the Heart of the World to the Pearl Throne,' rasped Hamsa. Her head drooped. The wheezing in her chest did not lessen. 'The First of All Queens saw the seal and sent it on, unopened, with a courier. But Yamuna's spies . . . Yamuna saw . . .' she shuddered again, and again the servant held up the bowl, and Hamsa drank deeply. 'Yamuna laid a curse on the pass and his servants hurried to the spot to find the courier dead and they burned the missive. They should not have,' she smiled weakly. 'They should have left it whole. If it had remained separate from the element of fire, I would not have been able to call it forth.'

Yamuna's spies? Yamuna saw? Samudra stared at the sorceress. Not Chandra? Yamuna was but a servant in this matter, and a foolishly loyal one at that. He detested his service, and yet would not take freedom when it was offered in a sanctioned bargain. Samudra had to admit himself completely unable to understand why the sorcerer's answer had been no.

Yamuna's spies. Yamuna saw.

An almost unthinkable, and certainly unwelcome, idea stole

slowly into Samudra's mind. Could it be that Yamuna already had such freedom as he desired?

Could it be that Chandra had come to allow himself to be ruled by the one who was bound to serve him? Could this plot be Yamuna's rather than Chandra's?

It went wholly against the order of the world. It was worse than treason, it was sacrilege, a defiance of the patterns laid down by the Seven Mothers. Jalaja herself declared it was only by observance of the sacred dance of life that Hastinapura would remain safe. Such reversal, such removal . . .

And yet there were those who said that Samudra himself had done exactly the same thing. He was the younger brother. It was not his place to rule, not while Chandra lived. Had he not removed himself from his proper place in the dance in search of a higher position?

No. Hastinapura would have been nibbled away by the Huni under Chandra. The Mothers meant this for me. All the signs portended . . .

This was Samudra's private agony. He feared that in badgering Chandra into relinquishing the Pearl Throne he had truly saved Hastinapura for the Mothers, but that he himself had truly violated the order of the world. What could this be but another consequence of his transgression?

'Rest now, *Agnidh* Hamsa. Surely you have earned it,' said Samudra aloud.

'Thank you, Majesty.' Hamsa's head sank onto her breast as she fell into her meditations again, or perhaps it was only that she fell into simple exhaustion.

'Make up a pallet for the *Agnidh* so that she does not have to be moved,' Samudra ordered the servants. 'And stay by her in case she wakes and has need.' Beside him, Makul opened his mouth. Samudra held up his hand to keep the general silent. 'Have your scribe craft a message to the Huni asking for a parley. Choose us a reliable courier, a reliable scout and the most reliable shepherd you can buy. If you have need of me, I will be out walking in the night for awhile.'

'Majesty,' Makul bowed with his palms pressed over his eyes, and then hurried away to carry out his orders, shouting for his scribe Ikshu as he went.

Samudra did not stay long after Makul had gone. He left the servants scuttling to take care of Hamsa, left the soldiers standing at attention waiting for any orders he or Makul might give, left the maps and the copper counters, and emerged into the dry, chilly air of the mountain evening. The sky blazed orange and copper, and the land falling away from the cliff where the Temple City perched was nothing but a carpet of shadows.

It was one of the luxuries when he was campaigning that there were times he could be alone, as he never could when he was only the Emperor. Samudra stood for a moment on the steps of his borrowed house and breathed in the thin mountain air and the smoke from both profane and holy fires. He listened to the shouts and clatter that were as much a part of a soldier's camp as the patrols and the tents. Then he strode up the narrow way to the Temple of the Seven Mothers.

The temple stood at the highest point of the city. Seven narrow, tiered domes surmounted the building, stretching like searching fingers toward Heaven. Seven broad, shallow steps led up to arched doors carved all over with scenes from the great epics, scenes of gods and heroes and the Mothers' intervention in their deeds. As this was not the hour for any rite or observance, the doors were closed. Samudra pushed them open and entered the temple.

The way to the sanctuary was not straight. The progressively larger chambers and the narrow corridors that connected them were precisely measured and laid out according to the ancient formulas. As the paths in the Palace of the Pearl Throne caused all to constantly reweave the patterns of protection and prosperity, here the pilgrims and the priests alike walked the patterns of generation that were the mortal representation of the Mothers' eternal dance.

The sanctuary opened before him. Its chamber stood under the largest dome, which created a ceiling that rose tier upon tier over the circular chamber. Dominating all the carvings and all the altars to lesser gods and their many aspects, were the statues of the Seven. Carved four times a man's size, they danced eternally around the central fire that smelled of the heady herbs that might set a man to dreaming if he stayed too long in his meditations. Summer blossoms in many colors draped and crowned the Mothers and petals lay scattered around their feet.

Samudra dropped to his knees, prostrating himself before the images.

I am sorry. I am sorry. I truly believed I was only doing what you desired.

Chandra had played at ruling as if it were a garden sport. He had ordered lavish palaces built. He had filled the women's quarters with skilled and exotic beauties and offered them freely to his favorites. He had feasted himself and those women and favorites liberally, and had ordered the ministers and administrators about like a petulant child giving orders to slaves. Through it all, Samudra had stood by and watched. It was not his place, he told those who came to him, to speak of taking the throne. His place was to be a soldier, to defend Hastinapura. That was his role.

He had held to that, until the day the Huni moved. They marched unimpeded down from their holds in the northern mountains, occupying first a few valleys, then a few cities, then three whole provinces, and Chandra refused to let Samudra take his armies north to meet them. They would not be able to hold such vast tracts, Chandra said with a wave of his scented hand. They would soon withdraw.

But they did not, and at last, Chandra was forced to act. But he still did not send Samudra who had trained all his life for this fight, and who was adept in the arts of war. No, he himself would be carried to the fight, an umbrella over his head and a naked sword at his side.

He was captured three days after the ridiculous, limping battle was joined, and immediately sent word back to the Pearl Throne that he should be ransomed, whatever the cost.

Samudra could not stand it anymore. He consulted the best astrologers, he spent long hours with Hamsa, making her draw him out fortune after fortune. All said the same thing; if Chandra were allowed to rule, Hastinapura would collapse. The thought of the Pearl Throne falling to ruin inflamed him. It could not be permitted.

Samudra traveled in secret to Chandra's camp. He dressed himself in women's clothes and went to the Huni commander, begging to be allowed to see Chandra, his 'dear husband.' His plea was granted, and Samudra killed the Huni commander with a hidden dagger and escaped, slinging Chandra over his saddle bow when Chandra would not move quickly enough.

When he had Chandra safely back in the camp, and had made sure the story of the rescue was spreading fast, he presented Chandra with his demands: Chandra would leave the camp, Samudra would pursue the war; when Samudra returned to the Pearl Throne, Chandra would turn over the rule to Samudra. In return, Samudra would not rise up against him, and he would grant Chandra his life.

Chandra snarled, Chandra barked, Chandra threatened. Samudra stood silently before him while the shouts of praise bearing his name, not Chandra's, rang through the camp, more than loud enough to be heard in the Imperial pavilion. In the end, Chandra tried to bribe, and then he begged, and Yamuna stood to one side in the pavilion and watched it all. Chandra finally agreed and Samudra marched away to his own quarters. Hamsa did not sleep that night, nor for many nights afterward, waiting, wary, for whatever attack Chandra might order Yamuna to launch.

But from that quarter, no attack came.

Or so he had thought then.

After a time, Samudra sat back on his heels, gazing up at the Mothers whose images had been before him all his life. Jalaja, Queen of Heaven; Daya, Queen of Earth; Ela, Queen of Mercy; Harsha, Fertility; Indu, War; Chitrani, the Rains and Waters; Vimala, Destruction.

'Yamuna,' he whispered to them. 'I did not look for him. I looked long and hard at my brother, but Yamuna is a servant. He vowed to serve you, and us. How could I believe he had come to rule? Even Chandra could not permit himself to be so ruled. It never even crossed my mind.' He bowed his head. 'And I believed myself to be such a fine soldier, a great planner, and I failed to take the true measure of the traitor in my own house, and now his son has begun a war I do not know if I can stop.' He lifted his eyes. 'We cannot have chaos in the north. We cannot have Hung-Tse uncontained. I am committed here, my brother is days away with his master, and his son is out of reach in the north. So many pieces so far away. Mothers, how do I guide the patterns on this board where all the players are out of my reach?'

Samudra sat in the silence of the temple, alone with the Mothers and the heat and scent of the sacred fire. If the priests came and went, he did not hear them, sunken as he was in his own thoughts. At last, slowly, the layers of anger, worry and reproach peeled themselves away, and he saw into his own memories, and found the answer waiting there.

Samudra prostrated himself once more to the Mothers, and got stiffly to his feet. He had no idea how long he had sat in his meditations. But it was cold now, and when he stepped outside, the moon was well up. He breathed in the air made chill by the deepening night and returned to his borrowed residence.

Hamsa had been carried to a side chamber and laid on a pallet of blankets. A fire smoldered in the hearth, and her body servant slept beside her. Samudra looked down on his sorceress and noted how drawn her face was from the day's exertions. Still, he was not surprised when her eyes fluttered slowly open. She had ever known when he needed her.

'Majesty,' she croaked, and reached for her staff to help her stand.

Both Hamsa and the servant, who was also now wide awake, struggled to rise. He waved his hand to keep them both down on their beds. Hamsa obeyed, lying back on her pillows, but her servant scuttled backward, moving herself off to a polite distance so her presence might not intrude on their conference.

'Hamsa.' Samudra settled down cross-legged next to her. 'You have done me good service today.'

She bowed her head humbly, but he saw the deprecating twinkle in her tired eyes.

'I am afraid I will have to ask yet more of you.'

'I stand, or lie,' she gestured toward her pallet ruefully. 'Ready to serve however I can.'

'I was taking counsel with the Mothers,' he said, rubbing his hands slowly together. 'And they reminded me of my coronation, when you told me certain things. You told me that you could curse an enemy of Hastinapura, no matter how great the distance.'

Hamsa shook her head. 'I cannot,' she said. 'But you can, Majesty.'

'I am no sorcerer.'

'No, but you are lord, bound to the land and the heavens through your anointing and your sacrifices. I can make a working that will give your will force and weight in the ethereal realms, but it must be your will, and your words must form part of that working.'

Sámudra considered this in silence for a long moment. 'It is a difficult undertaking then?'

Hamsa nodded.

'Will there be a price?'

Again, the sorceress nodded. 'Normally, it would be mine, but, in this case, my price will only be partial payment.' She met his eyes, her face set and serious, an expression he knew well from his childhood, when she was trying to drum in some particularly difficult lesson. 'Because it is your will that sets this thing in motion, you too must pay. Some day, in the future, you may lose what you hold dear because of what this curse sets in motion.'

Again, Samudra turned over her words silently. 'Will it be Hastinapura I lose?'

'I cannot say, Majesty. I think not. But it could be a child, or your queen, or your life. It will be a high price, that much I can be certain of.'

Samudra continued to rub his palms slowly together, as if he could feel the shape of the truth between them. 'I do not like magic,' he said at last.

Hamsa smiled. 'I know.'

'It is imprecise, and it has too many hidden costs. The powers play their own games in the Silent Lands, and no man may know how their dice are cast.'

'These are true things, Majesty,' Hamsa agreed soberly, but

he could still see the ghost of a smile on her face. These were matters they had spoken of often before.

'But even if I sent a missive to the Queen this instant and bid her act against Yamuna, even if I sent to Kacha in the north and bid him stop this nonsense, it would be tens of days before any action could be taken.'

'Even with my help, yes, Majesty.'

He was talking himself into an unpleasant task, and he knew it. Hamsa knew it as well, and she, as usual, simply let him do it.

'Hastinapura itself is at stake,' he said. 'If Isavalta is fractured, the Huni and Hung-Tse will begin seizing territory in the north. With new men and new resources, the Huni will be bolstered and we will never root them out, and they will expand again, like the poisonous weeds they are.' He growled the last words, letting anger shore up his resolve. 'I do not have time to deal with Chandra myself, yet he must be dealt with, and now, and your magics are all I have to cross such distances in such times.'

'I can have all ready in two days, Majesty,' was all Hamsa said. Her voice held no tremor or hesitation, but all Samudra had to do was look at her to see how close to utter exhaustion she was. Neither of them spoke of that. Neither of them ever would.

'Thank you, Hamsa.' Samudra stood and bowed to her, giving her the salute of trust, with his palms over his eyes. She returned the gesture, and he left her to go seek his own bed, although it was a long time before he found sleep there.

Two days later, Samudra had received a message from the Huni saying they would deign to meet him, and an additional message from Makul's chosen spy saying there was a break in the mountain pass that might be exploited by a small force of men as part of a larger attack. Both missives were highly welcome and allowed Samudra to spend time with his maps and his generals, deep in thoughts and plans that he understood well. This, in turn, kept his thoughts diverted from the Temple of the Mothers. Hamsa had disappeared in there the morning after he had laid out her task, and he had not seen her since.

Hamsa had been a part of his life since he was an infant. She had been chosen by the most learned sorcerers and astrologers his father's court held as the one who would best be able to serve and support him in his life as High Prince, as it was thought. She had cared for him alongside his nurses. She had taught him alongside his other tutors. She had saved his life more than once with her art when he was a young and reckless warrior, chafing at watching Chandra, spoilt, spineless and careless on his father's throne. She, even more than the priests, had presided over the horse sacrifice that had bound him to throne and land, and set the seal on his rightful claim to the throne.

He had set old and dear friends to tasks that might take their lives before, but not like this. Never like this.

It was evening again, with the dim, orange sun just balanced on the rim of the world, when Hamsa's woman servant knelt in the map room and said, 'It is time, Majesty.'

Without a word, Samudra rose from his place at the table and left the house while his generals and servants bowed around him. He followed Hamsa's servant up to the Temple of the Mothers and through the winding corridors to the sanctuary.

Inside, heat struck Samudra even before the light did. All seven of the dedicated fires leapt up waist-high from the fire pits. The central fire burned just as fiercely. Even over the incense and sandalwood, he could smell the sweat of the priests, two for each Mother. A hump-shouldered bullock stood beside the central fire, its tether held by three acolytes in pure white tunics. In the center of it all, her skin glistening in the light and heat of the sacred fires, stood Hamsa. One hand clutched her staff. The other clutched a curved, bronze knife.

Samudra knelt, prostrating himself to both the Mothers and Hamsa. When he rose again, Hamsa nodded once and drew back her shoulders. Samudra recognized the gesture. Hamsa was calling on her magic.

Hamsa lifted her staff from the ground. An acolyte ran forward to take it from her. Unsupported, on legs as thin as twigs, she walked to the bullock, which bellowed nervously. Samudra saw how glassy the sorceress's eyes were. Wherever her mind was, it was a great distance away.

Hamsa laid her free hand on the bullock's shoulder. With one swift, clean gesture, she slashed the knife against its neck. Blood, dark and fresh from the vein, poured freely into the great stone bowl that waited for it. The bullock bellowed and the acolytes tightened their hold, patting its neck and murmuring to it soothingly as it fell to its knees, breathing in the steam from its own swiftly draining blood.

Hamsa gave her knife to an acolyte, and held her cupped hands under the flowing blood. She anointed herself: head, hands, and the soles of her feet. When she arose again, her face was terrible and her eyes as bright and hard as diamonds, and Samudra knew that by her working Hamsa had become an aspect of Vimala, the Mother of Destruction.

Hamsa began to dance. Slowly, she circled the central fire, leaving bloody footprints behind her. Her arms waved high over her head, weaving new patterns in the air as if she were painting the stars with her stained hands. Gradually, her steps grew quicker, wilder. She touched each Mother, each priest, bringing them all, heartbeats, breath, pulse of life, into her dance. She laid both hands on the bullock, gathering up even its death into her working. All was done in silence, with no sound but the slap of her feet against the stones, the ragged breathing of the witnesses, the dying of the bull, the crackle of the fires, and yet, as Samudra's ears strained against the near silence, he seemed to hear a deeper music – a rushing that was neither the wind outside, nor the blood in his veins, although he heard both. This was a deeper pulse, a rhythm more strange and more compelling, and yet more terrifying. It was too great, too strong, too wild, like Hamsa's blood-stained dance in front of his eyes. It called to the depths of his heart, and his heart knew it would swallow him whole.

But all at once, Hamsa stopped stock-still before him. She lifted his hands, pressing them between hers, and her eyes were wild with that rhythm they both felt to their cores.

'Speak, Lord of Men,' she cried. 'Speak Son of the Land. I will hear your words.'

But the voice was not Hamsa's. Samudra knew this and dropped to his knees before the goddess. 'Curse him, Mother,' he whispered. His breath did not wish to leave his body, lest it be pulled free and drowned by the rhythm pulsing through him. 'Let the works of Yamuna *dva* Ikshu Chitranipad turn in his hand and cut him to the heart. Make his greatest weakness his only support. Blind him with his own sight, drive him out with his own folly.'

'It is heard, and all is accepted,' said the voice that spoke through Hamsa. She let go of his hands and rose to her feet, her arms stretched over her head. 'It is spoken and may not now be undone.'

Again, the dance took her, tracing its bloody trail on the stones, around the fires, around the priests and their acolytes, and the Mothers in their watchfulness, around the dying bullock and its spilled blood. Over and over the pattern repeated, filling Samudra with its wild rhythm until he felt he must burst. It was too strange, too strong. It surrounded him, bound him, called him through the stones of the temple and the stones of the cliff beneath them. He could not move, could not think, could not breathe, there was only the rhythm and the dance and it was inside him and outside him, it was everything and all, and he was everything and all.

Without a sound, Hamsa stepped into the central fire, her arms raised, her face ecstatic, and the flames enfolded her in a lover's embrace, and she was gone.

The spell broke like a string snapping. Samudra shuddered, his strength failing, and pitched over onto his face. Gasping from pain and shock, he pushed himself upright. He saw the room, the blazing fires, the bemused priests, the dead bull, and Hamsa's staff in the hands of a dazed acolyte.

She was gone. Samudra passed a shaking hand in front of his eyes. Of course. He should have seen this was how it must end. How could she remain part of the mortal world once she had danced with the Mothers? She had surely known this, even though she had not told him.

And I did not ask. Samudra pushed himself, shaking, to his feet. Every person in the sanctuary stared at him, none of them fully themselves yet.

'Let the funerary rites be prepared for *Agnidh* Hamsa,' Samudra said to the priests, a little amazed that his voice had returned to him. 'Call me when all is in readiness.'

'Majesty.' All bowed, but Samudra did not stay to acknowledge their obeisance. He teetered around and staggered for the door.

Out on the broad steps, he breathed deeply of the night air, his fists clenching and unclenching, trying to find something to grasp for support. But there was nothing. His support had gone, burned alive in the Mother's fire. Gone because his need had used her up.

'Brother,' he whispered to the night. 'Chandra, I would have let you live. I gave your son position and power. I gave you land and freedom when my advisors said I should have you trampled to death. But the Mothers say we must bear our brother's burdens, and I tried, Brother, I tried.' He swallowed. The servants would remember their duty and be behind him in another moment. 'But you would break apart the realm like a child's toy, and for that you will pay. For that, and for Hamsa, you will pay.'

There, in the darkness, where none could see, the Emperor of Hastinapura wept for his loss.

The Vixen sat on a wooden throne, on the crest of her green hill, underneath the spreading thorn tree. She was not currently a fox, but a woman of sleek and strong build, red-haired and green-eyed, wearing a garment of gray fur belted with black. A cluster of foxes, red, white and gray, lay at her feet. Thus, she prepared to greet her visitor.

The second woman came on foot. Brown-skinned, black-eyed, she wore little besides the ropes of pearls around her neck and the sword belt at her waist. More pearls bound her black hair high on her head. Her footsteps left behind bloody prints on the grass.

The Vixen made no move to hinder the woman as she climbed the green hill and came to stand in the shadow of the thorn tree. They looked into each other's eyes for a moment, before the woman bowed courteously, and the Vixen nodded to receive the gesture.

'Welcome, Mother,' said the Vixen mildly. 'How is it I have come to merit a visit from so illustrious a personage?'

'I am come with a message from my sisters.' The Vixen's voice held the wild tones of the green wood. This woman spoke coldly, like the winds of autumn.

'I am most interested to hear it.' The Vixen gestured with one hand, indicating the woman might sit if she felt so inclined.

The woman sat cross-legged upon the ground, drawing her sword from her belt and laying it across her knees. The blade was black and had an edge so keen, even the Vixen's eyes could scarcely see it. One of the red foxes at her feet pricked up its ears and lifted its head, alert to the warning of that drawn blade.

'It has been seen that soon the Old Witch will send an ambassador to you to reclaim that which you stole.'

The corner of the Vixen's mouth quirked up in a crooked smile. 'Yet I insist I stole nothing. The Old Witch wounds me to the heart.' She laid her long white hand on her bosom. 'To think that she believes I would wrong her in that fashion.'

The woman did not blink at these words. 'My sisters and I say that we would be grateful if the ambassador were able to find what she will seek.'

'Would you?' The Vixen raised her eyebrows. 'And how would this gratitude be expressed?'

'Your help would be remembered,' said the woman, her words as solid as stones. 'We would swear it so.'

'Hmmmm . . .' the Vixen leaned her chin in her hand. 'Gratitude from you seven. You who seek to bring permanent order to your lands, grateful to me. Tempting,' she admitted. Then she straightened and shook her head. 'No. It is too much. I cannot give what I do not have.'

The woman's dark eyes glowed. 'What then, pray, can you give?'

The Vixen considered. Her gaze lingered for a moment on

the naked sword with its keen edge. A gray fox lifted its head and curled its lip back, showing a gleam of fang. She reached down idly and scratched its ears, calming it so that it once again curled up.

'Why would you wish to do a favor for the Old Witch?' she asked. 'She has no claim on you, or your sisters.'

'Our lands are troubled by a little man who walks too tall.' The woman gripped the hilt of her sword. A dangerous light sparked in the Vixen's green gaze, but the woman moved no further. 'He has begun a chain of dangers that will crash down over that which is ours. If the ambassador returns the Old Witch what has been lost, the little man will fall.'

'May fall,' the Vixen corrected her. 'Nothing is set. Not where I can see. Your little man is most resourceful.'

The woman bridled at those words, but did not move to contradict them. 'Will you do this thing we ask?'

'No,' said the Vixen. The woman lifted the sword a fraction of an inch from her lap. One white fox rose to its feet, its tail bristling.

The Vixen just smiled. 'But I will give this ambassador a chance. One chance, for a price. If she succeeds, she may have what she wants. If she fails . . .' the Vixen shrugged. 'Then you too will have to be resourceful.'

The woman laid her sword back down. As she did, the white fox lowered its hackles, but did not sit.

'What price?' asked the woman.

'A favor, from your oldest sister. A favor of my choosing, to be granted without questions or restrictions.'

'You ask a great thing.' The woman's voice rasped in the still air.

'As do you,' replied the Vixen calmly. 'Especially for one who has come to my place of power to call me a thief.'

The Vixen watched the woman bridle at this, and smiled as

she struggled to hold back her rage. But need and, more likely, the warnings of her sisters, kept her hand from her sword.

'Very well. A favor, without questions or restrictions. It shall be so.'

'Then this ambassador from the Old Witch will have her one chance,' replied the Vixen. Her smile spread so that all her shining teeth showed. 'Then we will see what may happen, Mother Vimala. Then we will most certainly see.'

'Well?' said Chandra, looking up from the pile of pillows where he lounged on the balcony. 'What news have you?'

The rains poured down in solid sheets outside, obscuring the gardens with a curtain of silver and filling the world with the scent of fresh water. This was the beginning of the Second Rains. Samudra had timed Chandra's wedding, and the beginning of his campaign, nicely. The brief respite that separated the First Rains from the Second had given the Emperor enough time to march his army inland, beyond the floods. It had also given him enough time to see his elder brother sent to the far south with his new bride and his household of spies.

Chandra had never been able to wait well. Every day he summoned Yamuna to him and demanded to know how things proceeded in the north. Not even a full month had passed, and already his exile seemed to chafe at him beyond endurance.

Yamuna looked down his nose at his master, and considered lying. No, he decided. It would be more humiliating should he have to retract his words later.

'The quest did not succeed,' he said blandly.

Chandra stared at him, as if he could not believe what he heard. For a time, the drumming of the rain on the balcony's arched roof sounded very loud.

'My servants who failed me have been punished,' said Yamuna, his memory filling with the sound of the daemons' screams as the earth pulled them down. 'They will have no further opportunity to make such mistakes.'

'In the meantime, Avanasy is still alive, and the Empress is still out of our control, and has her best advisor hurrying toward her,' sneered Chandra. 'Excellently managed, *Agnidh* Yamuna. For all your machinations, you have accomplished exactly nothing.' Disgusted, he turned back toward the rain.

Yamuna held himself very still. They were not truly alone. Slaves still moved about the interior apartment. If any of those were ears for Samudra, they had already heard too much. It was very like Chandra to have forgotten such a salient fact at this moment.

'Son of the Throne,' said Yamuna, slowly and deliberately, so that Chandra turned one eye to look at him. 'I must beg your leave to undertake a quest of my own.' *I must, for I must remain bound to you, whether I wish it or no. The gods have declared that your success is the determinant for my own.*

Chandra narrowed his eyes at Yamuna. His gaze flickered left, looking through the archways to the apartments beyond, this time noting the slaves who were there, and actually remembering which master they might truly serve. As he did, an unexpected smile flickered across his face, before his bland mask of disinterest and disdain settled back in place.

'Yes,' he said. 'Undertake your quest. You have good leave.'

He settled himself back down to watch the steady fall of rain, and did not even look as Yamuna knelt to him and rose again to take his leave.

That flicker of a smile haunted Yamuna's thoughts as he returned to his own apartments. It was a strange expression, sly and unfamiliar, and indicative of hidden thoughts.

Was it possible Chandra would attempt to plot his own

coup while Yamuna was gone? It would be a disaster. It would ruin all. Chandra had no mind for subtlety. He was merely a petulant child who wanted his brother's pretty toy. When the plot was discovered, which it would surely be, Samudra would have no choice but to execute his brother, and without Chandra, weak support that he was, Yamuna's own plans would crumble.

But Avanasy must be stopped. The little Empress could not be allowed to regain power in Isavalta. Alone, she was helpless, she had proven that often enough. But with a powerful and subtle sorcerer to aid her . . . Yamuna knew full well how that could make the weakest of men an enemy to be feared.

No. Without a servant he could trust, he himself must take care of Avanasy. There was no choice. He must go swiftly and swiftly return.

Yamuna proceeded through his outer apartments, paying no heed to the servants there, still putting the place in order for their master. The innermost door he unlocked with a key and a word. He closed the door carefully behind himself.

This chamber was much less fine than the one where he had worked in the Palace of the Pearl Throne. Arches and domes with their inlays of coral and ivory were here replaced by simple carvings of gray and red stone surmounted by a wooden dome with seven tiers, each tier, of course, dedicated to one of the Mothers. Yamuna did not spare them a thought.

The only furnishings in the chamber thus far were four chests which Yamuna had carried there himself. No other hand would touch them, as no other foot would tread in this place that was his alone. For the bare moment he stopped to think on it, he did not believe those who served him were sorry to obey this order.

Yamuna's touch and five more words opened the first chest.

There, packed in straw, were one quarter of his precious vials and bottles. Some glinted dully in the watery daylight. The most delicate, however, had been wrapped first in white linen.

Yamuna lifted one of the linen bundles out, brushing a few wisps of straw from the cloth. Inside lay a small, faceted bottle, the color of garnet. If he peered closely through the translucent crystal, he could see the contents swirling and blurring like contained smoke.

Despite its wrapping and despite the warmth of the day, the sides of the bottle were cold to the touch.

A curse waited inside that bottle, a curse made into a solid thing so that it did not have to be woven again, no more blood had to be shed, no detection had to be risked. The bottle simply had to be opened with the name of the one for whom the curse was intended. The closer one came, the more quickly this solid, pulsating thing would envelop them and suck away their fortunes, their good destiny, their love and, at last, their life. Applied to Avanasy, it would not kill at once. It would allow him to live, hobbled and increasingly impaired. His advice would sour, as would his commitments. If he reached Medeoan, he would do her more harm than good.

Yamuna laid the bottle carefully inside a pouch of soft deerskin leather that he tied firmly about his neck. The pouch hung against the hollow of his throat. Already, he could feel its intense chill seeping through the leather wrapping. It was not a thing that was healthy to hold for long, but he must endure it for the present.

He lifted out another jar. This one was alabaster, opaque and milk white. The stone was smooth to his eye, but strangely rough under his hands. It seemed almost wasteful to reach into his hoard twice like this, but this was the time against which he had laid by this stock of workings. He would spend it all in pursuit of his destiny. After that, it would no longer matter. He would, when his godhood was achieved, see what an infinitesimally small effort it had been.

Unlike the vial at his throat, the jar of alabaster was warm. He had bargained heavily for this jar when he was still a young man, giving away a small fortune and a large secret to possess it. The seal was of white clay engraved with symbols even Yamuna could not read. Once it was opened, he would not be able to close it again, or duplicate what lay within. This jar was made by priests in the furthest of the southern islands who worshipped gods they would not name. Not even Yamuna could squeeze their secrets from them.

Setting the jar on the floor, Yamuna drew his knife and cracked the seal. He lifted the heavy lid. An odor of iron and old copper wafted up. He laid the lid aside. The jar brimmed with deep, red blood, still fresh and liquid, even though the jar had been sealed over two hundred years before.

Yamuna reached into the warm blood, and after a moment, his fingers found the soft treasure it concealed and nourished. He drew out a small bird, just barely fledged. It struggled hard against the clutch of his fingers to stretch its wings and gain its freedom.

It smelled of flesh, of blood and of heat. Its heart beat frantically against his hand.

Yamuna took the frightened nestling into his mouth and swallowed it whole.

A shock of pain ran through him so strong that he saw darkness and stars. Even Yamuna could not stand against the fire and doubled over, clutching his stomach. His bones snapped within him, the jagged ends rearranging. Yamuna clamped his jaw down to keep from crying out, and felt his teeth shatter and sink into his gums as his jaw lengthened and the flesh around it peeled away. His joints popped as they dislocated and reformed. Too many changes, too much pain.

Yamuna roared in agony, even as he felt the first of the feathers pushing through his skin.

After that, he lost track of all but pain.

When the pain ended, Yamuna was gone. There was only a white crane huddled on the polished floor beside an alabaster jar, empty except for a thin coating of red-brown dust on its inner surface. The crane blinked and flopped its wings clumsily so it could stand on its slender legs. Strutting delicately, as was the nature of its kind, it stepped out onto the broad balcony. Heedless of the rain, the crane launched itself into the air. Wheeling on the wind, it flapped its great wings and turned toward the north.

Kacha reviewed the lists showing the levies of men with growing satisfaction. Barbarians these northerners might be, but that turned out to have its advantages. They were ever ready when it came to a fight. As they marched south, the army grew stronger. More lords arrived at the heads of columns of men, many of them trained, with letters and lists from their Lords Master, pledging their allegiance to the Empress in this 'great and long-overdue action.' All were placed under the command of officers of the House Guard, and the ranks swelled.

He had thought long and hard before deciding to lead the campaign himself. So much required careful control at the summer palace. But, he reasoned, if he hoped to continue to rule in his own name, he must prove his manhood. He could not be seen to be sitting idle while Isavaltan men went out to fight. So, he had crafted his permission from the Empress to go and lead the troops, and had ridden out at their head.

Now, he sat in a stone room in one of Isavalta's many coast-line fortresses. On the fields outside had sprung acres of tents like summer wheat. When he went out into the fresh air, the world was filled with shouts, the ring of the armorer's hammer, the sounds of horses and the tramp of boots. He imagined the noise reaching down the peninsula and across the sea to Hung-Tse, making their own border guards quake. Kacha smiled at the image.

This had proved to be the right decision. He was able here to gain the trust of the truly powerful men of the empire, and the news from Vaknevos was all good. Chekhania reported that the status of the 'Empress' continued healthful, and that her belly swelled daily and she glowed with impending mother-hood, meaning their child was alive and lively in her womb, readying himself to be born and take his place in the world. Ambassador Girilal held a number of conferences with the Council Lords who were jointly acting in regency until the Empress would finish her confinement. The bemusements held. Yamuna's magics and Chekhania's cooperation allowed him still to see into the palace. She had developed a real talent for imitating Medeoan's style in her messages to the Council.

A dull ache began behind Kacha's right eye, a reminder that despite all, Yamuna was not easy. Yamuna believed that Medeoan had taken refuge in the Heart of the World, but no word of confirmation had been received, nor had definite news that her ally Avanasy had died. Several popular and prominent landlords had not sent their levies yet, and their reasons why were slow in coming and vague when they arrived. Most notable among these was Pachalka Ursulsyn Rzhovin, father of the House Guard captain Peshek who had disappeared with Medeoan. Peshek had also not been found.

These were little things against the might of the army in the camp surrounding him, but little things might be enough to change the course of empires. Kacha had studied enough history to know that much.

The head secretary coughed politely. 'Majesty Imperial? Did you wish to continue?'

Kacha rubbed his eye, but it did nothing to lessen the ache. No voice whispered to him from the back of his mind, no compulsion radiated to him from his withered right hand. He felt alone for the first time in years, and the sensation frightened him.

'No,' he said abruptly to the secretaries. 'I do not wish to continue. Take what you have and get the documents fair copied as soon as possible. Send someone to find General Alike.'

'Majesty Imperial.' The four secretaries reverenced and gathered up their sheaves of paper, scuttling out the door like the flock of old women that they were. The ache behind his eye deepened, but it remained only an ache.

If you want something, Yamuna, you are going to have to give me a better sign than this. Kacha lifted his silver tankard and found it empty, likewise the pitcher beside it. Only the smell of beer remained.

'Boy!' he shouted and the waiting page ran in. Kacha stuffed the pitcher into the boy's hands. No other instruction was needed. The child reverenced and ran out again, nearly colliding with General Alike as the man reached the door.

Alike sidestepped the page and let the door close behind him. He gave the soldier's reverence. 'You sent for me, Majesty Imperial?'

'I am concerned about the levies, General,' said Kacha, as he beckoned Alike to take a chair. 'Specifically, I am concerned about who has not delivered them yet.'

'We do have men enough for the actions we have planned before winter.' Alike sat stiffly, unwilling to relax his formal posture even for a moment. Alike was a square man, not overly tall, but broad and solid with thick hands, hardened from their life's work. His kaftan of Imperial blue strained at the seams, giving Kacha the impression that the man had not worn it much before being called up on these actions. He preferred, doubtlessly, some less cumbersome, more well-worn coat when not in the presence of his autocrat. He also firmly believed that Hung-Tse was a constant danger to Eternal Isavalta, and so had been more than ready to answer when Kacha called.

'That is not the point, General,' said Kacha, pushing himself fully upright in his chair. The ache continued, becoming a low throb in his bones. 'I am concerned that a traitor's father has not yielded up his men, as is his duty.'

'Lord Pachalka was a member of the House Guard. He knows his duty.' Alike spoke the words as if he were saying Pachalka knew the sun would rise tomorrow. Duty was an unalterable fact with him.

'Captain Peshek was also a member of the guard,' answered Kacha evenly. 'Despite that, he ran off with some scullery maid in complete breach of that same duty.' That reminder made the stalwart man drop his gaze.

The page boy chose that moment to return with the pitcher of beer. With a child's extra care, he filled Kacha's tankard. Kacha gave him a nod, and he filled another for the general. Alike accepted the beer, but did not drink. Kacha took several swallows of the black brew, only to find it did nothing for his ache.

'Now.' Kacha leaned forward. The movement sharpened the pain in his eye. 'I do not wish to trouble Her Majesty Imperial with this. You will select a detail of men, and I will grant them police powers. They will go investigate the reasons for Pachalka's lateness. If necessary, they will make an example of him and his, and they will collect the levies after that. Is this clear?'

Alike set down his untouched tankard and laid his thick hand over his heart. 'Yes, Majesty Imperial.'

Kacha nodded. 'You may go.'

The general rose and reverenced one more time. When he left, Kacha found himself briefly, and unusually, alone in a room, and uncertain of what to do next. The promise of direct action against Pachalka had no more eased the pain in his eye than the beer had.

What is it you want, Yamuna? Why do you not take my hand? What is wrong? Kacha rubbed his eye again. Well, tonight he would light a fire and he would communicate with Yamuna directly. He would surely find then that Avanasy was dead and all was well.

In the meantime, he would make sure the search for Peshek was stepped up, along with the inquiries from the spies in Hung-Tse as to who had seen a foreign sorceress, or sorcerer, just in case.

Kacha frowned and took another long pull at the beer. All was in hand, and it would remain so. He would make certain of that.

Chapter Seventeen

Medeoan had lost track of the days. She only knew there had been too many of them. The leather shift which was her only clothing had chafed welts under her arms. Some of them were beginning to bleed. The silent women who were sent in to search her every day saw the weals, and did nothing. Not even ointment was permitted her. She was brought regular meals of fairly good food: fresh meats, pastries, rices and vegetables, well, if plainly prepared, but she ate under their watchful gaze, and all that was brought in was removed again as soon as she was finished. A chamber pot was provided at these times so she could do what was needful, but not even that was left to her when she was alone.

With the first meal each morning came the search. Her shift was removed and inspected. The leather mattress was turned over and examined closely for any irregularity in the stitching, in case she had managed to use her fingers to loosen the gut and get at the ticking or conceal something inside. The bare room was inspected. Medeoan's cropped hair was rifled. Only when all was found to be in order did they permit Medeoan to sit and break her fast.

After her guards departed, it had become Medeoan's custom to sit in the window for a time, looking down at the gardens and across the walls to the city. She watched the green sea of trees waving below her and the flights of distant birds. After the first few days, she realized that it was becoming increasingly unlikely that she would be released alive. True, she was not being treated quite as a common prisoner. She was not in chains, but would the Nine Elders really want their honor impinged by stories of how they treated the lawful empress of another realm? No. They meant to make her a prisoner for life, and they were the ones who would determine how long her life would be.

When she was sure her guards were going to stay outside, when she heard no footsteps coming or going in the narrow hallway just beyond her door, she would leave her window and push her mattress away from its corner.

To her eye, it was easy to see the circle of braided silk plastered to the floor with a mixture of blood and less pleasant things. Inside the circle lay a delicately formed weaving of blonde hairs. It looked like a short chain of flowers, their stems wound and knotted together to hold them in place.

Sitting cross-legged on the floor, Medeoan pulled three more hairs from her head. She had ceased to wince at this small pain. She wet them with her spittle and twirled them together to make a slender thread. Then, she took a deep breath and carefully, tentatively, she drew up her magic. She did not seek to release a river, which she normally would, especially for so complex a spell as she created now, but only a soft trickle. If her power rose too strongly, the Nine Elders would feel it. They would come and search her chamber with magic and find this working, her one chance at escape.

Concentrating, and attempting to relax at the same time, she spun the single new thread into the weaving, and that was all. To do more than that at one sitting was to invite detection. She laid her working back in its circle of protection, repeating the spell that caused it to be so overlooked.

'I Medeoan, servant of Vyshko and Vyshemir, place my working with a stone barrier about it, closed with a stone door, locked with three times nine locks and three times nine keys, with one key and one lock let no one cross this barrier, no bird fly over it, no eye light on it.'

She replaced the mattress. Then, there was nothing to do but return to her window to wait and watch until the next meal. She had so often wished to be left alone, not to be princess or empress. Now, she had that wish, and she was locked up in a single room without any sort of help. Her captors attempted to make her nothing and nobody. But even they had not succeeded. She was still the Empress of Isavalta. She was still Medeoan the sorceress, and she would make them remember that before the end.

And Avanasy will come for me.

She held fast to that hope most of all. As the sun crept across the sky, her only measure of the hours, she would picture him coming to the Heart of the World, and to her. Sometimes, in her dreams, he arrived at night, alone and stealthy, and they eluded the guards and their magics flew them over the walls. Sometimes he arrived with Peshek and a legion of loyal soldiers, leading a proud horse, and she would mount it in broad daylight and ride in triumph back to Isavalta, where Kacha would kneel at her feet and beg for mercy. He would find none. She might, she thought sometimes, choose to keep him in the dungeons long enough for a public trial, but then he would die. She would have him beheaded in the courtyard as befitted his rank and crimes.

Each day, she found it a little easier to think of Kacha without longing, and with a clearer view as to who he was and what he had truly done to her. It was his fault she was prisoner here, locked away and struggling for her freedom. She would see this added to the list of his crimes that would be read out at his trial. If she chose to give him a trial. If she did not simply choose to have Peshek, or some other loyal guard, run him through the moment she saw him again. That would prevent him from using his honeyed words to try to soften her heart toward him, not that it would work, but she was not certain she wished to hear him try.

Then there would only be her and Avanasy. She would make him Lord Sorcerer for his loyal service to her. She would have it published and proclaimed that it was only Kacha's treachery that had caused him to be banished. She would rule Isavalta wisely and well, just as her father had wished, and Avanasy would be chief among her advisors, and she would never turn him away again.

And perhaps, in time, he would become more than advisor, more than teacher and friend.

This dream she permitted herself to dwell on only occasionally, even though she found it warmed her in a way no other plan could. She had to remind herself that she did not know what state Avanasy would be in when he returned. He might be angry with her for a time for not valuing his loyalty more highly, for throwing him aside for a traitor. It might take time for him to forgive her, but they would have that time. There would be so much to do. Starting with renewing the loyalty oaths of all the Lords Master. Then it would probably be necessary to appoint a new Council, as Kacha could not be acting alone at this point. The traitors would have to be tried and sentenced before any other work could be done. Then . . . then . . . then . . .

Dreaming her unfamiliar dreams of empire, Medeoan smiled out across the walls of the Heart of the World, worked her magics and learned to bide her time.

★   ★   ★

In the end, Ingrid and Avanasy traveled to the Heart of the World in fine style. Lien hired them a troop of guards, and saw that both Ingrid and Avanasy were properly outfitted with silk robes and riding in a sedan chair carried by six bearers. Avanasy had thought they should ride horseback to the gates in Isavaltan fashion, but Ingrid had had to admit she had never been on a horse in her life, so it was the sedan.

They did not go unannounced. Three days before, a hired messenger had accompanied the hired guards into the Heart of the World bearing a courteous message written on translucent rice paper naming Avanasy and Ingrid as messengers from the Empress of Isavalta who begged an audience with the Emperor of Hung-Tse so that they might deliver the Empress's 'sagacious and urgent words.' Two days ago, a message sealed in saffron ribbons had been returned, fixing the time for their arrival.

Avanasy was barely able to sleep the night before. Ingrid, awake with her own worries, had seen him pacing the gardens and gone down to join him. They said nothing to each other, only walked side-by-side across the lawns silvered by moonlight. They had not been able to discover any news of Medeoan. Lien had consulted his numerous sources carefully. Cai-Yun had taken Ingrid with her visiting the ladies of several rich and possibly noble families, all of whom had relatives serving or living in the palaces of the Heart, but her discreet questions of these ladies yielded nothing.

Was Medeoan here, incognito? It was possible, but there should be servants' gossip if that was true. Had she yet to arrive? What could have held her up? Her route should have been more direct than theirs, even with their magical aid.

Had she died? Had she been captured? Was Isavalta now truly in the hands of the usurper? Ingrid knew the thoughts rang around Avanasy's head, and she had no answers for him.

But first and foremost among them was, is my charge, my student, safe?

To make matters even worse, there was still no word from Peshek.

So they walked, and they held hands, and they looked at the moon reflected in the still garden pools. They held each other close as the night wore away, parting at dawn with a soft kiss to prepare for the day ahead.

Now, the eastern gates of the Heart of the World stood open before them. Soldiers in black lacquered armor with saffron sashes stood rank on rank, some holding colorful pennants, some holding poles tipped by wicked-looking hooked blades or spears. In the center of the martial display stood two . . . people. Ingrid could not readily identify whether they were male or female, their features were so obscured by a myriad of garish tattoos. The person on the right seemed to be marked mostly in veins of green and brown. The person on the left had been decorated in sharply angled stripes of copper, silver and gold. They both wore heavy robes of an identical cut and style of wrapping, save that the right-hand person wore a rich emerald covered all over with embroidered tortoises, and the left was in what appeared to be cloth of silver with copper trimming.

'The Minister of Earth and the Minister of Metal,' murmured Avanasy to Ingrid. 'Two of the Nine Elders. We are indeed honored, and the Heart is indeed suspicious of us.'

The sedan's bearers halted inside the gate, set their conveyance upon the ground and bowed to the ministers who stood solemnly before them. The ministers did not even nod to acknowledge this gesture, but kept their gazes fixed steadily on Avanasy as he helped Ingrid out of the chair so that they in their turn could stand before these representatives of the Emperor and bow. Ingrid held her hands before her as Avanasy had instructed, and bowed no lower than he did, such gestures being serious matters of etiquette here. The ministers bowed in return in perfect unison with the soldiers who stood guard behind them.

'We have been instructed by the most elevated, the Heart of Heaven and Earth, to say that you are welcome to the Heart of the World on behalf of your mistress and his Sister Empress, Medeoan Edemskoidoch Nacheradavosh,' said the Minister of Metal.

'Please return our thanks to His Reverend Majesty,' replied Avanasy. They had not yet straightened up and Ingrid was beginning to feel the strain in her back. 'For the grace of this welcome and his willingness to receive these humble messengers.'

The pleasantries having been delivered, it was all right to stand straight again. The two ministers turned gracefully and the guards parted for them. In perfect step, they walked through the great gates. Ingrid glanced at Avanasy with raised brows. He just gestured for her to walk beside him and together they entered the Heart of the World.

Until that moment, Ingrid had been feeling fairly comfortable with what was happening to her. Now, with the great palace spread before her and the impassive soldiers in their black and saffron armor escorting them up the expanse of stone, she felt a sudden fraud; a rough, country girl done up in borrowed silks like a caricature in a bad pantomime. Her mouth had gone dry and she had the unaccountable desire to hike up her skirts and run. It occurred to her that this was exactly the effect this splendid vista was supposed to inspire. The thought did nothing to put the strength back in her spine.

After what seemed an age of walking and watching the spreading scarlet and emerald palace with its great golden tower approach, they reached the beautifully lacquered doors.

Yet more soldiers bowed before the two ministers who led them, and then drew the doors open to allow them admittance to a great, pillared hallway hung with elegant paintings executed on pale paper.

Ingrid worked hard to keep her mouth closed before the splendor that opened before her as she stepped across the threshold. As soon as her thin-soled shoes touched the polished floor, however, the air swam in front of Ingrid's eyes, and the whole world changed.

The palace was full of ghosts.

Gaunt and gray, they lined the corridor, watching all the passers-by with their blank eyes. Some were bloody, some held their mouths slack, some bore burns or brands on their shadowy flesh. Some were blank-eyed maidens who wept bloody tears and wiped them away with their long, black hair. If she could have heard their wailing, Ingrid was certain she would have been deaf in an instant.

Ingrid felt she could not breathe for the press of them. If the ministers could see them, they gave no sign as they continued serenely down the wide hall. The ghosts reached out to them as they passed, some beseeching, some cursing and crying, others kneeling in respect or desperate humility, Ingrid could not tell.

Avanasy's hand brushed hers, and Ingrid jerked her gaze sideways to look at him. His face was fixed straight ahead, but his eyes flickered.

What is it? he was asking. She must have hesitated without being aware of it, or her distress must show in her features.

'Ghosts,' she breathed the word in English, hoping no one heard her speak.

Avanasy sucked in a breath, but did not look at her. They could not afford any conversation right now, especially not any that could be perceived as secret. Ingrid struggled to school her features into a calm blank, but she could not tell if she succeeded at all.

In truth, she could barely see her way because her gaze kept getting caught by the lonely, empty eyes of the dead. They seemed barely aware of her, and relief at this realization almost buckled her knees. All their attention was on the ministers. Watching them in their shuddering, pitiful crying, mouthing their pain in an attempt to shout it, Ingrid suddenly understood what had moved Grace to make her promises to the drowned sailor lost in the grip of Lake Superior, and this was worse, hundreds of times worse, because there were so many more dead.

All Ingrid's attention being taken up by the crowds of dead, she barely noticed that they had reached the end of the corridor, or that the interior gates had opened onto a grand room that was even more opulent than the corridor they had just passed down, with pillars of semi-precious stone and elaborately enameled statues of stern and beautiful beings she could not take for anything but gods standing guard with their weapons raised. But again, these were all things she barely noticed, for the dead were here too. Some of these were soldiers standing around the base of the dais, rank on rank of ghostly troops ready, it seemed, to defend the young man in the saffron robe who sat at the top of the curving steps next to an older man robed completely in white. Others of the dead were old men, young men and boys, some as young as three or four, all of whom wore a robe identical to the young man sitting on the dais. In attendance with them were dozens of women, their robes and elaborately styled hair heavy with ornamentation. None of these cried as did the ghosts in the corridor. These whispered among themselves, pointing to the ministers, and to Avanasy, and to Ingrid. Some looked concerned. Some merely shook their heads.

The two ministers mounted the steps halfway up the dais and turned to face Ingrid and Avanasy. It was only then that she saw there was another minister already there. This one was robed and marked in white with gulls and snow geese the prominent motif for the decoration. This, Ingrid assumed, must be the Minister of the North.

She only had a bare moment to note all this before she remembered what she was supposed to be doing at this time. Both she and Avanasy knelt and pressed their hands and foreheads against the cool, silky-smooth floor. Under her breath, Ingrid counted to thirty. Part of her was sorry the time was so short. Huddled face down like this, she could not see a single one of the pale, attentive dead.

But beside her she heard the rustle of silk as Avanasy stood, and so she had to stand herself. The ghosts around them all looked stern or disdainful, and Ingrid felt herself withering under their blank-eyed attention.

As she had been told would happen, the Emperor made a series of elaborate signs to the old man in white who was the Imperial Voice. As he did, all the ghosts filling the great chamber stilled themselves and seemed to strain to listen.

'We extend our welcome and hospitality to the messengers who have come at the word of my Sister Empress, Medeoan Edemskoidoch Nacheradavosh of Eternal Isavalta, and I am now well disposed to hear the missive they carry.'

Avanasy had considered long and hard what he would need to say at this moment. Even so, Ingrid saw the flicker of uncertainty in his eyes. Fear took her, because the ghosts saw it too, and they whispered to each other, pointing and smiling cruelly behind their hands.

Despite that flicker, and despite what Ingrid knew he would have to say next, Avanasy's voice rang out clear and steady.

'Esteemed and Reverend Majesty, I must speak to you with slow and reluctant words. I must speak of treachery and the usurpation of rightful power. I must also speak of a danger to both the Heart of the World and Eternal Isavalta.'

None of the audience, living or dead, moved for a moment. Then the Emperor made his signs to the Voice.

'This prologue is indeed grave. Let us hear your words.'

So, Avanasy told them. He told them what he knew about Kacha's treachery and his plans for war. He told them rather more than he knew about the rallying of the loyal Lords Master raising their own armies to fight the usurper. With an utterly straight face, he told them about the Empress being escorted across the borders by her loyal followers to take counsel with her Brother Emperor and how she desired to speak with him about how their powers could be combined for the protection and prosperity of not only their realms, but of the right order of the world.

All this time, Ingrid watched the ghosts. They stood still as Avanasy spoke of Kacha. At first, Ingrid thought they were listening attentively, but then, she saw how their pale faces were set. Bored. The dead heard Avanasy's dire warnings, and they were bored. When he spoke of the loyal nobles of Isavalta rallying to the cause of their mistress, the dead smirked and whispered back and forth to each other. Ingrid imagined she heard the rustle of ethereal voices. When Avanasy spoke of the Empress being escorted by her followers, the ghosts began to laugh. They were not merry laughs, for their faces were hard and cruel. Their hollow eyes squinted, and would have rolled, she was sure, if they had orbs still in their sockets. They pointed at Avanasy, and they mouthed silent jeers. It was all Ingrid could do to stand rigid among the crowd of taunting dead, their hands waving in gestures of mockery, the jibes she could not hear passing back and forth between them. Her ears burned with anger, shame, and the reflexive effort of straining to hear what could never become audible to her.

Her fists and jaw clenched, she could not help it. She forced her eyes to look ahead of her, to focus on the living who stood on the dais, the one place in the great room that was free of the jeering ghosts. It was only then she noticed that the Minister of Earth was staring straight at her.

Ingrid, unable to endure another searching presence, dropped her own gaze to the floor, studying the polished boards at her feet. But she knew they were there, the ghosts, the ministers, the Emperor, the Voice. They knew something was wrong, with her, and by extension with Avanasy. She could not stand steady in the face of the dead's mockery and the living's inquiry, and her failure was ruining all of Avanasy's careful planning.

Ingrid forced her head up in time to see that the ghosts had sobered, and were again straining toward their Emperor, who was, in turn, signaling his Voice as to what was to be said next. The Minister of Earth, however, still had his (her?) gaze pinned to Ingrid. She made herself watch the Emperor and his Voice.

'We are most concerned by what you have told us. You may be assured that we will be at once deploying members of our personal guard to watch the roads down the peninsula so that the Empress may be properly greeted and escorted when she arrives in Hung-Tse. In the meantime, you will be given quarters where you may rest and take refreshment while we consider what else may be done regarding these most serious tidings.'

Avanasy bowed and, barely in time, Ingrid remembered to do the same. Four servants, who had gone unnoticed by Ingrid, the living lost among the dead, stepped sedately forward and bowed to them. Avanasy nodded in acknowledgment, and they followed the quartet out of the throne room.

All the way, Ingrid could feel the eyes of the living and the dead staring at her back.

Returning to the hallways was agony. At least the haunts in the throne room had seemed composed, as if they accepted their fate. The dead who lingered in the corridors were in torment. Tears and blood both streaked their faces and hands. They wailed to heavens that seemed to have long ago ceased to hear them, and reached out to the living who never could. Some, to Ingrid's horror, seemed to realize she could see them, and they fell on their knees, reaching up to her, mouthing their pleas. She wanted so much to shrink against Avanasy, to have him shield her from the desperate, tortured spirits, but she could not. There were living beings in the corridor – men, mostly, in fine robes, or soldiers in armor, going to and fro about their own business, but most definitely taking note of the two foreigners and their escort. She could not show such overt weakness yet, but neither could she repress the tremors seizing hold of her.

The corridors seemed endless, an interminable stretch of painted pillars, gilding and works of art Ingrid could barely discern for the press of the dead. Her resolve ebbed with every step. She wanted to throw herself on the floor with her eyes shut and her hands pressed over her ears. She wanted to scream and scream until someone made these hideous visions vanish.

Then at last, at *last*, the servants stopped in front of a green door painted over with gilded sigils.

'Honored Sir, Honored Lady, in deference to the customs of your nation . . .' there seemed to be a small deprecative sneer in the voice, but Ingrid could not be sure, her head was reeling so badly. Next to the servant, the ghost of a crone reached out her crabbed hand, trying to pluck at his sleeve, her mouth shaping one word over and over. 'We have been instructed to see you housed together,' he was saying. Bowing low, he pushed the door open.

The first thing Ingrid saw about the room was that no ghosts stood within. She practically ran across the threshold before she remembered she was still watched and recovered herself enough to stand up straight and look about with something like detachment.

Thankfully, this chamber seemed to be designed with comfort more than grandeur in mind. The low, carved benches were laden with pillows. The hangings on the walls were pleasant landscapes of lakes and mountains. Feather mattresses had been piled high on the beautiful bedframe, and curtains of sapphire silk hung from the canopy. A fresh breeze and the scents of flowers and ripening-fruit told her that the lace-like wooden screens against the far wall concealed open windows, or possibly doors to a verandah. Ingrid's chest loosened and she found she could breathe normally again.

Avanasy stepped up beside her, his own gaze sweeping the room, and nodding with approval at what he saw, particularly the plates of dainties laid out on one of the tables.

'This will be quite satisfactory,' he said in the same utterly confident tone he had used before the Emperor. 'We will send for you if we have need.'

The chief among the servants blinked in surprise. Ingrid knew enough now to understand how strange the dismissal would sound to him. Nonetheless, he and his fellows simply bowed without other comment and slipped out the door.

No sooner did the door close behind them than Ingrid collapsed onto the nearest bench, pressing her palms against her eyes.

'Vyshemir's knife!' exclaimed Avanasy, coming at once to sit beside her. 'What is it, Ingrid?'

'Ghosts,' she said. She couldn't look up, not even at him. She had seen too much and needed to be in darkness for awhile. 'This place is full of them. Hundreds of them. They're

. . . they're in pain, Avanasy. They're crying, and they're begging and I can't hear them. I can't ask them what they want.'

Avanasy's arms wrapped tightly around her and drew her close to his chest, holding her safe from all that she had seen. She relaxed into his embrace. She had thought she might cry when this moment came, but she did not. Fear and pity had drained her dry for the moment, and she needed no more than Avanasy's warmth to sustain her.

When at last she was able to push herself away and look Avanasy in the face, she said, 'I wanted to tell you, there were ghosts in the throne room. I think some of them were old emperors, and there were soldiers, and some women. I don't know who they were, but when you started talking about Medeoan being escorted here, they all started laughing. Not kindly either.' She shuddered remembering their mocking gestures and pointing fingers. 'It was as if they were making fun of us.'

Avanasy let out a long, slow breath. He pushed his hair back from his forehead. 'So, I did feel it. Medeoan is already here.'

Ingrid felt her brow furrow with perplexity. 'Surely not. They would have told us.'

'Not if they are keeping her prisoner.' Avanasy rose swiftly and crossed the room. He folded back one of the elaborately carved screens and revealed a stretch of lawn trimmed with drooping trees and brightly colored blossoms. It ended in a high wall painted with saffron and bordered in black. Several wooden gates had been set into the stone, all of them solidly closed. Avanasy's shoulders slumped and then stiffened as he gazed at that well-built wall. 'When a spell is being worked, a sorcerer nearby can feel the making of it. I know the touch of Medeoan's working quite well.' Ingrid could hear the soft smile in his voice, but it faded quickly. 'While we stood before the Emperor, I thought, for just the briefest instant, I felt that touch. This place is such a warren of spells and workings being constantly employed to protect the people within ... I thought I must have imagined it among all the other currents, but no, I did not.' He turned and his face was grim. 'The Empress came here before us, and the Emperor and the Nine Elders are holding her captive until they can decide what to do with her.'

'What should we do?' asked Ingrid softly.

Avanasy looked over his shoulder at the high wall and the closed gates. 'I don't know,' he murmured. 'Yet.'

Pa K'un, the Heart of Heaven and Earth, sat in the summer garden, to all appearances contemplating the small waterfall where it ran over the perfectly rounded gray stones. The sound of it was pleasant, especially when mixed with the rustle of the leaves around him and the warmth of the summer sun on his skin. The servants, secretaries, soldiers and Elders had retired to various discreet distances, which gave him rare and welcome room to think for himself.

His thoughts, however, were far more troubled than the chattering water in front of him. Counts of troops, of supplies, of moneys, of stores whirled through his head, and they were far from enough to repel a determined invasion. He held what would be a valuable hostage under normal circumstances, but if the goal of the enemy's game was conquest, even the anointed Empress would not be hostage enough.

Now there came these two 'messengers,' also with tales of usurpation. They came in the name of the Empress of Isavalta, but obviously had no idea where she was. The first of them, Lord Avanasy, was a known name, and was a close advisor and tutor to the Empress before her marriage, but then was sent into exile. Which led to the question, did he truly come in the

Empress's name, or did he secretly serve the usurper?

The silent woman who accompanied him in the station of his wife was a complete unknown, but the Elders felt an oddness about her, as of someone who might not be a power, but who had most certainly been touched by power.

There had been no answer yet from his missive to Hastinapura, and Pa K'un found himself beginning to fear what that answer might hold. For the first time in several years, he felt himself too young for his sacred office.

Movement off to the right caught his eye. He turned, and saw Dieu Han, the Dowager Empress, kneel on the grass before him. She performed the obeisance carefully, conscious of the fall of her silken sleeves and of the gold and jade ornaments adorning her lacquered hair.

'Please rise, Honored Mother,' said Pa K'un, torn between relief, as she was the one person to whom he could speak of these matters freely, and annoyance, as he wanted to think more, and knew she would have her own firm opinions on what should be done next. 'Sit with me.' Here in the garden, he could speak without the Voice. This earth was sacred and plowed deep with spells of peace and protection long before the first stone of the Heart of the World was laid. Even the Minister of Air acknowledged that no malevolent magic could be brought to bear here.

Dieu Han rose as gracefully as she had knelt, giving her robes time to settle back into their proper lines. A pair of servants instantly slipped forward with a low chair for her and placed it behind her where she might sit without having to rudely glance away from the Emperor.

Pa K'un contemplated the Dowager. She was not his blood mother. She had not been the mother of the two emperors before him, both of whom had died when they were still boys. Her blood son had been Jian Ayd Cao whom she bore to

Emperor Seong Kyung Cao when she still bore the more humble title of Beloved Companion, and was only the first among the concubines in the women's palace. Emperor Seong had at once raised her to be Empress, and she bore the change, they said, with all appropriate dignity. But Emperor Seong had died in battle against feuding overlords, and Emperor Jian had died of a fall in the arms of a careless nurse when he was only three. That left Dieu Han as Dowager, with the responsibility to choose the next Emperor, with the guidance of the gods and the Nine Elders, of course. Should such advice lead her to one who was under the age of manhood, then she also had the ruling of Hung-Tse as regent until the Imperial boy could rule in his own name.

Pa K'un was not so foolish as to believe it was mere coincidence or divine will that had led Dieu Han to choose three young boys in a row. Nor was it accidental that he was the first to have survived past sixteen. He had ever been diligent about making sure his 'mother's' wishes were attended to, and that her voice was always heard in Council. Never forgetting other facts, Dieu Han could be an excellent advisor on certain matters. This might well be one of them.

'So, Honored Mother,' said Pa K'un, 'how do you think we should dispose of these northern visitors?'

The set of Dieu Han's jaw and the glint in her dark eyes told Pa K'un that she was not in the mood to waste words on ceremony. 'My son, you must let them escape.'

Pa K'un blinked. He had been expecting an audacious answer, but nothing like this. 'And why should I do this thing, Honored Mother?'

'Because,' replied Dieu Han in a voice that was little more than a whisper, 'when the Empress of Isavalta is gone, it will force the Nine Elders to do what they will not do otherwise – summon one of the four guardians to protect us all.'

Pa K'un took a moment to let the implications of that suggestion settle in. The possibility had been raised before, when last he had spoken with Dieu Han in the throne room, as a matter of fact. He had given it lip service then, but now he forced himself to consider it seriously.

None of the immortal guardians had been summoned in three hundred years. To do so was to demand the sacrifice of one of the Nine Elders. If that was not reason enough to give one pause, there was also the well-documented fact that such a summoning could be a two-edged sword. The four guardians would indeed protect Hung-Tse from her enemies, but once summoned, they had been known to decide that one of those enemies was a rash and careless emperor.

A fact which Dieu Han was as aware of as he.

'I may not order such a thing,' he said, reminding the Dowager of another fact which she also knew perfectly well. 'The Nine Elders are preeminent in the magical defense of Hung-Tse. In this area, even I may not interfere.'

'Which is why the northerners must escape,' murmured Dieu Han without even the show of demure deference to her Emperor. 'We may be honest here, you and I, my son. Hung-Tse is weak. We know this. Hastinapura, the pirates, the rebels in the east and our own lords all assail our defenses. There has been too much strife for too long and we are a hollow land. We cannot wait for our enemies to make this discovery.'

'You are very sure of this, Honored Mother.'

'I have outlived three emperors to choose you for the throne, my son. I may outlive you. We cannot know what the future holds, but I am growing old, and I have seen the way of things for a long time.'

The Emperor regarded her steadily, understanding full well what she had said, and what she had not said. Around them, the wind blew in the leaves, the waterfall chattered, and the warmth and scents of summer wafted on the breeze, yet it seemed to Pa K'un he sat in the middle of a profound stillness.

'It would be a thing which must be most carefully accomplished,' he said slowly.

'As you say, my son.' Dieu Han finally let some deference creep into her tone, if only because she knew she must not push him too boldly now that he appeared to be leaning toward agreement. 'The orders must be given only to those whose loyalty is beyond question.'

'Do you know of any such?'

'I do.' The confidence in her voice was absolute.

She played a dangerous game. There were so many possibilities, and once the guardian was summoned, it would be in no one's control, not even the gods'. The guardian would surely defeat the invaders on the northern border, but what else would it do? It might decide Pa K'un was weak and unfit, and devour him, leaving Dieu Han to choose yet another emperor and regain the rule of Hung-Tse.

But it might also decide that Dieu Han had played one too many games with the sacred rule, and there would be no more Dowager in Hung-Tse.

If this was a gamble, it was one of legendary proportions. Pa K'un carefully considered the state of readiness his generals had outlined to him again, and again, he saw how badly short it fell. He had inherited a much-weakened empire, and he could not be the only one to see that much of that weakness was attributable to the woman who sat across from him and all her cleverness. How long had she planned this? Why should she desire it? Or was it that she finally realized that she had brought Hung-Tse to the brink by all her years of surreptitious rule?

Pa K'un gazed at the woman who had adopted him as her son. It was not possible that her face paint had been poorly applied, so the shadows under her eyes must be real. Perhaps she was afraid. They were weak. He knew that, and she might know it better than he.

He would have to accept her wager, and pray hard to be granted a pure heart as he did.

'Then, Honored Mother,' he said, forcing his voice to stay steady as he did. 'I will trust you to see this thing properly done.'

The Dowager Empress slipped from her chair to her knees, making the departing obeisance. Her gold, jade and silk sparkled in the clear light. Holding herself still as she did, she might have been some beautifully carved statue. 'You honor me, my son.'

'But Mother,' he went on. 'Have a care when you contemplate which of us will live the longest. My gratitude at you placing me upon the throne is great, but I am no longer a boy. I have held the seat for some years now, and there is every sign I may hold it for many years yet.'

'That is my only wish for you, my son,' she murmured piously.

'I thank you, Honored Mother,' he replied. 'You may now go. I wish to be alone awhile yet.'

She rose and left him. Pa K'un watched her gliding away among the carefully tended willows and drooping lilies.

And thus the thing is set in motion, he thought, and permitted himself to shiver despite the warmth of the day. *We play with the dice of lives and empires, Honored Mother, and we know not what is truly stirring in the hearts of the Isavaltans or their kings. Oh gods, oh spirit of my father, let my throw be true.*

There is no such thing as a warm night on guard.

Ferin Zarnotasyn Ferinivin, over-lieutenant of the Imperial

House Guard tucked his poleax under his arm and clapped his hands together, trying to get some blood circulating through his fingers. His leather gloves seemed to be holding the cold in more than they were keeping it out. In the darkness, he could hear his fellow guards giving each other the watch word as they patrolled the edges of the encampment in the light of the campfires and the slender moon. Most of them worked in twos and threes. Ferin had the dubious distinction of a lonely outrider's post, gleefully assigned to him by his bull's ass of a captain who liked the southern Emperor's ideas of camp discipline. What was a dice game to anyone? A man had to do *something* with his time. There was only so much sitting around a man could bear.

Make sure to tell Rasina he was lucky they didn't catch him with that woman. Probably have had the balls off him for that. Ferin stripped off his right glove and blew on his fingers.

Damn, we're too far south for it to be this cold.

To his left, the woods rustled. Ferin broke off his train of thought, and lowered his poleax to a ready position. No need to get upset if it was just a fox, but no excuse not to be ready in case it wasn't.

The rustling continued. Whatever was out there, it was far too big for a fox, and too bold for a deer.

'Come out and be recognized,' Ferin called into the darkness, straining his eyes to see further, but there was nothing but shadows.

After another moment's rustling, an indistinct figure emerged from the underbrush. It took Ferin a minute to realize what he was seeing was a thick kaftan with a hood pulled down low to disguise the face underneath it.

What Ferin did not see was any weapon. That, however, did not ease his mind at all.

'Friend or foe?' he demanded. *And you'd better speak your*

*Isavaltan pure, friend. Any Hung accents and I'm having your head
off here.*

'Friend,' came back a man's voice, muffled badly by the
deep hood.

'What's the word?'

The stranger hesitated and Ferin tightened his grip on his
axe.

'The word is that the night you made Over-Sergeant, Ferin
Zarnotasyn Ferinivin, you decided you were going to celebrate in Voislava's house, no matter what anyone tried to tell
you about that particular whore's den being a thieves' den as
well. You got so drunk, you passed out and woke up to find
out the women had stolen your purse, all your gear, stripped
you naked and left you out in the street for the dawn patrol to
find, and if you hadn't had good friends in the foot guard at
the time, you would have lost your new rank as well.'

Ferin choked. There were two men who knew that story.
One of them was still guarding Vaknevos. The other . . .

'Peshek?' whispered Ferin despite the disbelief that filled him.

The hooded figure nodded.

'Vyshko's pike!' Ferin reached out to clasp his friend's hand,
but stopped in the midst of the gesture. 'What are you doing
here?' he demanded in a harsh whisper. 'Are you out of your
mind? They'll kill you if they catch you!'

'You should kill me here and now, Ferin,' replied Peshek
steadily. He moved sideways just a little to let the moonlight
filter under his hood. It was Peshek all right. There was no
mistaking that face, or those blue eyes that held their spark of
mischief even at such a time as this. 'I'm a traitor after all.'

Ferin spat. 'Pah. Not a man believes that.'

The corner of Peshek's mouth twisted into a smile. 'Tell
that to the ones that have been chasing me halfway across
Isavalta.'

'Not a man who knows you then.' Ferin looked sharply left and right to make sure no one was approaching. 'But what in the name of Vyshko's bones *are* you doing here?'

'Recruiting.' Peshek's smile faded and his partly lit face became a mask of perfect seriousness. 'Starting with you, I hope.'

'Recruiting?' Ferin gaped at him. 'Who? For what?'

'For the Empress's army.'

Ferin pulled back. He could see enough of Peshek's face to see the man was perfectly sober, and that he meant what he said. Could it be true after all? Could Peshek, Peshek, of all men, son of one of the best commanders there ever was, truly have turned traitor?

'The Empress's army is here.' Ferin planted the butt of his poleax on the ground for emphasis.

'No,' replied Peshek, gravely. 'This is Kacha's army. The Empress's army is with me, and my father.'

Again, Ferin's gaze shifted left, then right. The other patrols sounded reassuringly far away. If he were caught at this moment, what he'd be staring at would be a lot worse than a cold patrol. 'Peshek, I think maybe you should get out of here, now.'

Peshek didn't move. 'Do you think I'd be here if I couldn't prove what I say?' he asked with his familiar, light confidence. 'Will you hear me, Ferin?'

Vyshko's bones. I should be calling for the men. I should give you a count of three to get your fool self out of here. I should.

But he did not. 'I'll hear you, but only if you talk fast.'

'I'll do my best.' Peshek reached into his sash, and despite all he knew of the man, Ferin automatically stiffened, ready to dodge sideways should metal flash in the moonlight. If Peshek noticed, he said nothing, he just pulled out a folded piece of paper and held it out for Ferin.

Ferin took the paper, squinting closely at it to decipher the broken seal. At last, he made out the spread wings of the Imperial eagle.

'Where did you get this?'

'From the Empress.'

Ferin opened the letter and read the brief words it contained. As he did, Peshek began to speak in a steady whisper, telling him of being summoned to the red library, of the Empress's fear for her life, of how he and the Keeper of the Emperor's God House had helped Her Majesty Imperial flee toward the Heart of the World, of how he had carried out his orders by meeting Lord Avanasy, whose treason was also a ruse, and sending him on after the Empress. How he continued to serve by raising an army to stop the one now led by Emperor Kacha.

'He's nothing but a southern usurper,' muttered Peshek. 'I know not what he's done to the Council of Lords, but he has strong magics supporting him. This whole business of the confinement is a lie to explain why the Empress does not appear in public anymore. I'll bet my head that they'll say she died suddenly in childbed, probably with the heir, when her time comes.'

Ferin looked down at the letter again. The paper crackled between his fingers. 'And that is why we could not find this madwoman sorceress, although we scoured the country for her.'

Peshek nodded. 'This war is not the Empress's. This war is the southerner's.'

Ferin looked away from Peshek toward the camp. The fires flickered between the trees. The noise of voices had abated as those not on watch took to their tents, if they were lucky enough to have such, or rolled themselves in blankets to get what sleep they could on the unforgiving ground.

'What's the mood of the camp?' asked Peshek.

Ferin shrugged. 'Good enough. No one likes the southern Emperor, that's certain, but they do like the idea of taking a bite out of the Hung.'

Peshek fell silent. Ferin kept looking toward the fires. He did not want to think about this. This was not the sort of choice he should have to make. He knew where his orders came from and where his loyalties lay. Before Peshek had come with this . . . story of his, Ferin would not have questioned any of that, any more than he would have questioned his need to breathe. But if what Peshek said was true, then it was Ferin himself who was the traitor right now, not Peshek. But if he was being led astray . . .

'Do you believe what I'm telling you, Ferin?' asked Peshek finally.

The night wind blew cold against his cheeks, and Ferin inhaled the scents of wood smoke and pine resin. 'I don't know.' It was the only answer he could give.

'I think you do.' Ferin did not turn to look at him. He did not want to see Peshek's face right now. He did not want to hear these words anymore. But Peshek continued. 'And I'm going to prove it to you. At the Padinogen passage, my men and I are going to attack the baggage trains. If you don't believe me, warn your commanders. Send out search parties. If you do believe . . . come away with us, and let it be known why you're going.'

'Start a camp rumor for you,' he snorted. 'And then desert.'

'Yes. Because it won't be desertion. It will be returning to the proper service of the Empress.'

Ferin said nothing. He did not know what reply to make. His head swam with the implications of what he had heard, and of the fact that he had been willing to stand here and listen.

'I'll take my letter back now.'

Ferin turned, startled. He had forgotten he still held the thing. He stared at the pale paper. He could no longer make out the words. He should keep it. Show it to his commanders. It was a forgery. It must be. What Peshek told him was ridiculous. It would mean Isavalta had been conquered by Hastinapura, without anybody knowing the thing had happened.

Ferin folded the paper and handed it back to Peshek, who took it without a word and stowed it in his sash. The two men looked into each other's eyes for a long moment. Ferin knew Peshek saw all the disquiet inside him. Peshek, on the other hand, looked back at him with nothing but calm certainty.

The sound of tramping boots and crackling scrub broke the moment. Peshek drew his hood down and plunged back into the woods.

'Vyshko's balls,' growled a familiar voice. S't'pan. His relief was here. The big man loomed in the darkness. 'What was all that racket?'

Ferin blinked and straightened up. Peshek was already well out of sight. 'A fox,' he said. 'Nothing more.'

Chapter Eighteen

'The Reverend Person of the Dowager Empress, Dieu Han, requests the company of the Lady Ingrid in the Autumn Garden.'

Ingrid shook herself to avoid staring. She had not realized until she heard the voice that the person clad in black armor and sashed in saffron bowing deeply before her was a woman.

She glanced back at Avanasy who sat at one of the room's low tables where he was, to all appearances, puzzling over a silken scroll recounting Hung-Tse's recent history. Avanasy raised his brows, somewhat in surprise, and nodded, which was the gesture she expected.

'Of course I will come,' Ingrid told the woman soldier. 'When should I be ready?'

'Her Reverend Personage requests that you accompany me as soon as is convenient.'

Which, of course, could not mean anything but now. 'Certainly,' said Ingrid, self-consciously smoothing down the jade and black robe she wore. 'I am ready.'

Ingrid exchanged a parting glance with Avanasy. They had not spoken much during the past day. Avanasy had been absorbed in delicate magics, trying to find some way to reach out past the room they were in without alerting the Nine Elders. Ingrid, in an attempt to give him the freedom he needed to concentrate, had roamed the little space of garden outside their rooms, and watched the guards walk by on the walls, and tried hard not to feel trapped.

They had heard nothing from the Emperor, or the Nine Elders.

Now, the woman soldier led Ingrid across the garden to one of the wall's arched doorways. She produced an iron key and unlocked the portal. The wall, it seemed, was actually a pair of walls that made a cool, dim tunnel. She could hear the footsteps of the patrols overhead. The soldier stood back as Ingrid entered, locking the door behind them. Ingrid felt her heart speed up, and hoped her sudden attack of nerves did not show in her face.

'This way, Honored Lady.'

The soldier led her off to the right, so they were following the sound of marching. Ingrid could see nothing except her escort's yellow sash. Even as her eyes adjusted, there was little to make out but beige stone and a dusty floor. The dust tickled her nose and she suppressed a sneeze. It seemed a strange way to take an honored guest, and Ingrid's unease grew stronger.

Nothing was made better by the occasional ghost standing beside this or that door. They drew to attention as her escort passed them, and saluted her with pale hands. Ingrid tried to keep her eyes on the living woman's heels.

At last, she stopped them in front of one of the doors in the left-hand wall. Two ghosts stood on guard here, big and grim, pale and hollow-eyed, surrounded by the smell of old dust. Ingrid could discern nothing from them. Was this a trap? What truly lay beyond that door?

Her escort produced a second key, this one smaller and more highly polished than the first. She unlocked the new door smoothly, and a shaft of sunlight shot through. She stepped back and bowed again, and Ingrid, blinking, walked out into the welcome daylight.

When she could see clearly again, she knew why this place was called the Autumn Garden. The carefully trimmed trees had leaves the color of burgundy and rich brandy. Gold, orange and claret chrysanthemums bloomed in profusion. Tiny yellow flowers, of a sort similar to those her mother called 'eggs and butter', bloomed in the grass. White lace blooms and tall stalks tufted with purple swayed above beds of low, red-leafed plants around the garden pools where herons and storks stood tall and graceful in the brown water. One blue heron looked at Ingrid and stretched its great wings, flapping them in the gentle breeze, but it did not fly, and Ingrid realized those wings must have been clipped.

There was no question as to where she was supposed to go. Toward the center of the garden, a great pavilion had been erected. In keeping with its surroundings, it was made of burnt orange cloth that Ingrid supposed was silk.

The woman soldier accompanied her across the neat lawn to the pavilion. In its shade a sienna cloth had been spread, and some of the low, dark furniture that the people of Hung-Tse seemed to delight in had been set up. Serving women moved to and fro, laying out dishes, taking up cloths, brushing away the occasional leaf or insect that had strayed into the tent.

In the tallest carved chair sat the woman who must be the Reverend Person of the Dowager Empress Dieu Han. She was thin and straight, like a willow wand, and something in her dark eyes told Ingrid she was just as tough. Saffron embroidery ornamented her white and sapphire robe. Combs of jade and gold decorated her lustrous black hair. Her face had been made up white and red, but Ingrid could see the faint wrinkles around her mouth and on her brow that no cosmetic could hide. The woman was not nearly so young as she was being made to appear.

As soon as she entered the pavilion's shadow, Ingrid began the deep bow with her hands held before her that she hoped was a polite and appropriate greeting, but she was not permitted to finish it. The Dowager rose swiftly and grasped both Ingrid's hands, a familiar gesture that seemed so out of place among these formal people that Ingrid started.

'Honored Lady Ingrid, I am so glad you have come.' The Dowager drew Ingrid back with her and set her into a low, curving seat next to her own chair. 'I apologize for the dirty route you had to take to come here, but I needed to speak to you at once, and I wanted as few eyes as possible to see you arrive.'

Ingrid's gaze flickered to the serving women. The Dowager did not miss the gesture.

'All my ladies are bound to silence by more than oaths,' she said gravely. 'They can say nothing without leave.'

In many ways this was not a terribly reassuring statement, but Ingrid said nothing of it. 'What is so urgent . . .' she groped for an appropriate title, 'Majesty?'

The Dowager had obviously heard the hesitation, but she nodded in what Ingrid hoped was approval of her choice of words. 'I am afraid, Lady Ingrid.'

'Afraid?' was all Ingrid could think to say. Here? In this walled place surrounded by soldiers?

'The Emperor, my son, is speeding the doom of Hung-Tse.'

Is he? Ingrid knew her shock showed plainly on her face. 'I don't understand, Majesty.'

'He holds the Empress of Isavalta in humiliating captivity,' the Dowager breathed the words as if afraid after all they might be overheard. 'He will not give her up. He violates the order of nature and the laws of man by so treating a fellow monarch.

No good can come of this.' She trembled, just a little. 'No good at all.'

Ingrid licked her lips, trying to compose herself. She badly wished Avanasy were here instead. This was not the sort of conversation she was adept at.

'But, Majesty, why is he doing this?' she asked. 'Surely the Empress Medeoan told him what was happening in Isavalta.'

The Dowager ducked her head. 'He is doing it because he can. It pleases him to be able to hold so powerful a person to his pleasure.' She glanced up, shamefaced. 'My son is new to the throne, and he is in love with his own power. I did not guide him well enough when he was young. I . . .' She glanced away, but not before Ingrid saw the tremor around her mouth. When she collected herself, she went on. 'I want only what is right for Hung-Tse. I fear that if Empress Medeoan is not released soon, she will have her own reasons for continuing the war against us when she regains the throne. Indeed, she has ample cause now.' The Dowager swallowed. 'But if you and your lord tell her it was only the whim of a young man, that Hung-Tse itself is not her enemy, then perhaps you may cool her blood and avert what can only bring disaster to both our countries.'

Ingrid sat silently for a moment, trying to absorb all that had just been said. The scents of the Autumn Garden wafted around her. The gowns of the serving women rustled like the leaves of the trees as they moved about their tasks.

'But how can we tell her anything?' she asked at last. 'We cannot even reach her.'

The Dowager leaned forward, clasping Ingrid's hand again. 'Peik Shing who brought you here is one of my personal guard. She has found out where your Empress is secreted. She can take you there. It will have to be done swiftly, tonight if possible. Rumors fly faster than wrens in the Heart. I have taken all the precautions I can, but they will not be enough. The whispers will begin soon, and then the guard will be changed, or the Empress will be moved.'

And if we're caught? Ingrid did not ask that question. She said. 'Very well. I must speak to . . . Lord Avanasy.' It was the first time she had used the title in something other than jest, and the words sounded strange to her ears. 'How may we get a message to you?'

'You cannot,' said the Dowager flatly. 'Peik Shing will come to your windows at midnight. If you are not ready then, this will not happen. There will be no second chance.'

Ingrid nodded, and despite the heat of the day, goose pimples pricked her arms. 'Thank you for this, Majesty.'

Again, Dieu Han dipped her gaze. 'I want only what is best for my land,' she murmured to her hands where they lay in her lap. 'And for my son.' She looked up and around, but not at Ingrid. 'Peik Shing will take you back now.' The Dowager gestured over Ingrid's head.

Peik Shing marched up smartly and bowed to her mistress. Ingrid got to her feet, and she also bowed, both grateful for what the Dowager had told her and frightened for what was to come. But there was truly no choice. Unless Avanasy had formed some other plan, this was their chance.

Ingrid found herself so thoroughly distracted as Peik Shing led her back through the walls, she barely noticed the soldiers' ghosts as she passed. Her mind was too busy turning over the conversation she had just had, turning it over and over, trying to find what might lie hidden beneath it.

She had made no progress on this task by the time Peik Shing opened the door that led to the bit of garden attached to the rooms she and Avanasy had been housed in. The woman bowed and shut the door before Ingrid could stammer her thanks. She heard the iron key turn in its lock, securing the door to what Ingrid could only think of now as their cage.

'What happened?' asked Avanasy behind her.

Ingrid whirled around to face him, opened her mouth, and closed it again. 'I don't know.'

'Tell me.'

Ingrid did. They sat on one of the stone benches that had been set beneath the willows and she described her encounter with the Empress, repeating the dialog as accurately as she could. When she was finished, Avanasy's face remained quietly grave, but Ingrid could feel the tension humming through him.

'Could it be as she says?' Ingrid asked.

'It could be,' Avanasy acknowledged. 'But it could also be a trap of some kind. For whom, and for what purpose I cannot begin to guess.'

She watched the way his fingers slowly curled into fists, quite sure he was not even conscious of the gesture. 'But we have no choice, do we?' she said, knowing the words were true as she spoke them. 'This is our single chance to find her, trap or no.'

Avanasy turned his face away. 'I should have left you with Lien.'

'I would not have stayed,' she answered him simply. 'We are well past that sort of wishing, Avanasy.'

That brought a smile to him. 'I think I was past it when I first met you, despite all I knew.'

'So then.' Ingrid took his hand and smoothed his fingers out until they lay gently in hers. 'We wait.'

Time did not pass easily. Avanasy went back to his scrolls, and Ingrid joined him, listening to him read, and taking in some elementary lessons in deciphering the language. Despite this, it seemed an eternity until the servants carried in the evening meal. Still no message came from the Emperor or his ministers. The Dowager sent no fresh word, which Ingrid took to be a sign that their plan remained unchanged and, hopefully, undiscovered.

Gradually, the evening deepened and the servants returned to light the lamps, screen off the windows and ready them for bed. As a fortunate consequence of Ingrid and Avanasy being lodged together, the servants, men for Avanasy and women for Ingrid, chose to retire modestly to the outer rooms where they would not have to observe a custom they found uncomfortable.

Night deepened. The moon rose over the walls, highlighting the patrols that continued across their tops without stopping for so small a thing as darkness. Avanasy extinguished the lamps, and they lay in the bed, side-by-side, with no chance of sleep coming to either of them.

Then, as Ingrid was watching the moonbeams creep across the floor and wondering how much longer midnight could be in coming, something scratched softly at one of the wooden window screens. Avanasy was on his feet in an instant. He carefully folded back the screen and Peik Shing entered the room, little more than a shadow in her black armor.

She carried a bulky package in her arms. 'You must put these on, Lord, Lady, and quickly.'

Avanasy slit open the knot that tied the package and its cloth fell open to reveal two identical coats of plain black cloth, with black sashes and round black caps. Ingrid wanted to ask questions, but Peik Shing was already glancing about anxiously, first at the door leading to the outer room where the servants slept, with one ear alert for any call from within, and then at the darkened wall where another patrol would soon be passing by. Seeing this, Ingrid held her tongue and managed to struggle into her coat. Avanasy tied off her sash and she performed the same service for him. Fortunately, the pillbox cap was large enough for Ingrid to bundle her hair underneath it, allowing her to pass for a young man at a casual glance, in bad light.

Peik Shing beckoned them silently to follow her. One by one they slipped out into the garden. Avanasy took a minute to fold the screen back into place behind them. Then, casually, they strolled across the lawn. Ingrid felt precious time crawling like ants across her skin, but she knew that should there be eyes watching now, hurrying figures were more likely to raise suspicions than those that might simply be out for a stroll due to sleeplessness.

Once again, Peik Shing opened the door in the wall. It would have been pitch black inside, but small lanterns had been hung every few yards, giving a dim light. This time, she turned to the left, and in another few feet, turned again, leading them down an earthen staircase into a completely different set of corridors. The air around them grew damp and there was no smell but that of old earth. Peik Shing walked rapidly, navigating the twists and turns of the place without hesitation.

The place is a rabbit warren, Ingrid realized, as she hurried behind Avanasy. *If she means to lose us down here, she'll have an easy job of it.*

Soon, however, they came to another, longer staircase, of the same beige stone as the walls. They climbed its length to reach yet another door. This one Peik Shing did not unlock. Instead, she gave the same soft, scratching knock as she had outside the window. Only silence followed and Ingrid's heart hammered hard. Then came a muffled reply that Ingrid could not make out.

'Friend,' rasped Peik Shing. 'Open up, Ayd.'

There followed the sound of sliding bolts and heavy hinges. The door swung open, and another soldier, this one a man, squinted at Peik Shing.

'What are you doing?' he demanded in a hoarse whisper. 'Who are these?'

'Heart's business, I promise you, Ayd.' Peik Shing held up her right hand to swear. 'Let me through?'

Ayd looked at Ingrid and Avanasy, and then back at Peik Shing. 'All right, as it's you,' he growled. 'But if aught of this comes back, I'm not giving up my place to save you, understand?'

'Perfectly. Come, friends.' Peik Shing slid past the other soldier, and Ingrid and Avanasy followed suit.

Open air touched them. They had come out on top of one of the walls. Ingrid could see the wonderful outlines of the Heart of the World clearly in the moonlight. Peik Shing did not give them time to stand and admire the view, however. She hustled them down an outer stair into the great stone courtyard.

As soon as her shoes touched the paving stones, Peik Shing's entire manner changed. She assumed a martial stance with her back and shoulders ramrod straight. She did not walk swiftly before them now, she marched at a steady pace. Walking so openly sent fear to choke off Ingrid's breath. There was no place to hide here, no way to run should they be spotted, no one to turn to except Peik Shing, who might be on a mission of her own.

The guards at the main doors closed ranks as they approached. Ingrid was sure they were caught. But Peik Shing flashed them some sigil – Ingrid saw a graven gold disk in her palm – and the other guards drew back.

Inside, the ghosts watched them even more closely than the guards had. Hollow eyes weeping blood followed them, hands clawed for them, in beseeching and in warning, thought Ingrid, although that could have been her imagination. She made herself watch Peik Shing's back, but the movements of the dead kept catching at the corners of her eyes, and tears began to form from the effort of trying not to see.

The end of the corridor opened into a broad rotunda. A black spiral stair rose from the wooden floor, winding up around gilded walls hung with silk. Not one ghost stood upon those stairs.

'Cold iron,' murmured Avanasy in wonder. 'I've never seen so much in one place.'

Peik Shing marched them up the steps. Their soft-soled shoes made each stair ring like faint and distant bells. Below them, the dead reached up their hands and mouthed incomprehensible words.

Ingrid counted four stories passing by them as their path spiraled higher and higher. She breathed more easily here, despite the dizzying height. It was easy not to look down, not to see the ghosts below.

On the fifth story, Peik Shing led them onto the surrounding balcony with its fantastically carved rail. Ingrid thought she recognized a few of the signs Avanasy had showed her worked into their design. Corridors opened at the points of the compass. Still, there were no ghosts. But Ingrid found no comfort in the cold and empty place. Peik Shing picked one corridor and led them down its dim length. The open window at the end let in some of the moonlight, but there was no other illumination. Ingrid saw exactly where they were going. Doors opened on the left and the right at regular intervals, but only the left-hand door at the end was decorated by a pair of guards.

Peik Shing stopped in front of the guards who might have been her sisters in their black armor and yellow sashes. She flashed the golden sigil she carried again.

'The Dowager has sent these two doctors to inspect the prisoner,' she declared.

The right-hand soldier frowned and squinted at Ingrid and Avanasy. 'At this time of night?'

'She is concerned. There have been signs that the prisoner does not thrive. These honored physicians have traveled far and are concerned enough by the reports they have heard that they ask to see her at once.'

The left-hand soldier glanced at her partner. 'I've seen no such signs.'

'You're not a doctor trained in northern medicine,' snapped back Peik Shing. 'Perhaps you'd care to go wake the Reverend Person of the Dowager and tell her that in your opinion the prisoner is fine and her orders may be disregarded.'

Right Hand looked at Left Hand for a long moment. Ingrid's heart rose to fill the base of her throat. Left Hand watched Peik Shing for some wavering in her expression. None came. Reluctantly, Left Hand turned and lifted first one, then the other, heavy bar that blocked the door. She next unlocked it with a key taken from under her breastplate, pulling the door open and standing aside. Peik Shing also stood aside, and Ingrid and Avanasy walked alone into the bare room.

The door slammed shut behind them.

A single figure shot up from the mattress that lay in the corner. Avanasy stood where he was, amazed or bewildered. Then, he reached up one hand, pulled off his cap and walked into the patch of moonlight the room's open window allowed in.

'Avanasy?' the young woman breathed. She took a step forward, then another, trembling and staring as if she could not believe what she saw. Then, all at once, she ran forward and threw her arms around his neck, burying her face against his shoulder. 'I knew you would find me!' Ingrid barely heard the muffled exclamation. 'I knew it.'

Gently, Avanasy extricated himself, stepping back, just a little so the young woman had to stand on her own, but he did not let go of her hands. Then, slowly, and with dignity, he knelt before her.

She was slight, this young Empress. Her fair hair had been cropped off and now stuck out wild and ragged in all directions. Dark circles ringed her blue eyes. Despite all, Ingrid could see the bloom of her beauty, and understood easily how a man who spent much time in her confidence could come to be distracted as Avanasy had confessed to being. Nothing she could name as jealousy stirred in her though as she watched the man she called her husband kneel, only an odd, straining sadness.

Remembering how custom here called for so many salutes and bows, Ingrid also knelt.

The Empress Medeoan did not even seem to see her.

'You heard then?' she said to Avanasy, looking down at both their hands. 'Iakush found you?'

'Yes, Majesty Imperial,' Avanasy replied. 'But he gave his life to do so.'

Ingrid saw no flicker of emotion pass across the Empress's face as she heard this. 'Stand,' she told Avanasy. 'There is no time for ceremony here.'

'No, Majesty.' Avanasy rose quickly, and Ingrid stood with him. It was only then that the Empress truly noticed her. Medeoan's expression was nonplused. Ingrid might have been a goat or a ghost, for all the sense the Empress seemed able to make of her presence.

Avanasy licked his lips. 'This is Ingrid Loftfield, Majesty. She returned with me from the far shore of the Silent Lands. She has been of great help to me in my quest to find you again.'

He did not say 'she is my wife,' and Ingrid's sadness deepened, but she just bobbed a curtsy for the Empress.

Medeoan's gaze raked her over, evidently still uncertain as to what this stranger was doing here.

'You are most welcome,' she said quickly, and Ingrid tried to tell herself the lack of warmth was due to circumstances, which would be natural enough.

'Avanasy, have you a way out?' asked the Empress.

'A guard outside says she'll guide us.'

'I have a better way.' The Empress's blue eyes gleamed, and all at once she looked very young. She ran to the leather mattress that was the room's only furnishing and flipped it aside. Ingrid retreated to the door, listening. She heard no running feet, no cries or even conversation. Surely that must mean they were still undiscovered.

She glanced back. The Empress held up something for Avanasy's inspection. At first, it seemed to be nothing more than a flat mat of hair, but, as she stared, she saw it was a wreath of flowers, woven, obviously, from Medeoan's own shorn locks. Avanasy as he gazed at it seemed nothing short of stunned.

He took the thing from the Empress's fingers and laid it flat on his palm. 'Is it complete?' he asked in an awed whisper.

'No,' the Empress answered. 'But it should serve, and it means we will not have to trust one of theirs.'

As she spoke, a single knock sounded against the door, followed fast by the faint sound of boots against a wooden floor.

'Whatever it is,' breathed Ingrid, 'you'd best do it quickly. Our time is up.'

'Let them see the mettle of the Empress of Isavalta,' said Avanasy. 'Call for the place of Lien to receive us.'

The young woman's shoulders straightened. She turned to the window. Ingrid caught just a glimpse of her expression, at once proud, mischievous and vengeful.

'The sky is held in place by twelve apple trees,' she intoned.

'The trees are held up by three pillars. Beneath each pillar is a green snake. The first is named Shkurapeia. The second is named Poliukha. The third is Liukha. I beg you, Liukha, Poliukha, Shkurapeia, loan me the strength of your pillars to hold up the moonlight under my feet. I beg you, Liukha, Poliukha, Shkurapeia, let me and mine walk safely to the place of Lien under your ever-watchful gaze. I beg you in the name of divine Vyshemir, vengeful Vyshko and in the name of their daughter Medeoan Edemskoidoch Nacheradavosh!'

Medeoan tossed the woven wreath of hair out into the darkness. For a moment, Ingrid saw it, dark against the waning moonlight. Then, impossibly, the wreath began to unravel. The golden strands glowed, catching up the silver light in themselves, stretching out as if spun by fantastic spiders into arching, shining webwork that spanned from the windowsill to the dark distance.

Gasps of wonder from below. More shouts. Hammering at the door. All urged Ingrid to motion, but all she could do was stand and stare. With all she had seen so far, nothing equaled this bright miracle.

'Hurry, Majesty,' said Avanasy. 'Ingrid, come quickly.'

There was no way she could brace the door against the hammering, so Ingrid ran to Avanasy's side. He cupped his hands and held them to help boost the Empress onto the windowsill. The young woman bit her lip and murmured something, perhaps a prayer, perhaps another spell. She stepped onto the bridge of gossamer and moonlight. For a moment, Ingrid's lungs refused to draw air.

But it held. The shining span of fairy tales and impossibilities held as strong as mortared brick under the Empress's bare feet. Eyes ahead, and lips still moving, Medeoan strode up the gentle arch, her shadow standing out stark and black on its glowing surface.

'Ingrid.'

Behind her, the door splintered. She jumped hard at the sudden shock of noise, and scrambled up onto the sill. She could see the ground plainly through the thin veil of maiden's hair and moonlight, dozens of yards below. The door crashed open, wood cracking and iron bands slamming against stone.

Jesus, Mary and Joseph. Ingrid hiked up her skirts, fixed her gaze on the Empress's back, and ran.

The moonlight bridge did not yield the least bit under her hurrying feet, but nor did it make any sound. She ran in eerie silence, hearing only her own breathing and the diminishing shouts of the soldiers who had broken into the cell. The motion of her black shadow caught her eye, but she forced herself not to look. If she looked down now, she would be lost, and she knew it.

Something whistled past her ear. Ingrid screamed and involuntarily jerked sideways. A familiar, welcome hand clapped onto her shoulder, righting her balance, and she saw the arrow arch past, falling to earth on the right of the glowing span.

Avanasy looked down at her, and his face was hard with strain. She said nothing, but took his hand, and together they ran. In a few strides they reached the Empress, Avanasy catching her with his other hand. Another arrow whistled through the night. Ingrid ducked, but Avanasy didn't even flinch. He just strode on, holding them solidly anchored on either side of him.

Then she heard another voice call out. This was no soldier shouting orders or profanities. This was a voice like thunder, like storm wind. She could make out nothing of what it said, but around her the air shivered with sympathetic vibration.

The night exploded into a cloud of shrieks and battering, clawing things. Ingrid threw up her hands, to beat the hundreds of tiny shadows off, to keep them from her eyes. They screamed back at her in a million tiny voices. Birds, she realized, as her hands flailed out. Birds, with beaks pecking and claws catching her flesh, scrapes and pinpoints of pain setting her blood flowing. Wings and feet snarled themselves in her hair, pulling on it from the roots. They battered at her clothing, tugging at it as if they sought to tear it from her body. She couldn't see, and she couldn't move for fear of putting a foot wrong and plunging to the ground. She crouched down, beating out feebly, only to have her fingers bitten over and again.

'Disperse!' roared Avanasy over the din and pain. 'By blood and moon's fire, I order you be gone!'

The birds screamed again in one last wrenching chorus. Something wet touched Ingrid's cheek, but the birds were gone. She risked a look up. Avanasy stood tall in the moonlit darkness. Dark blood ran down his hand, and his chest heaved from trying to draw enough air. Ingrid realized it was a spatter of blood that had touched her. She pulled herself to her feet. She wanted to get away from here, she wanted to be on the ground again. She had had enough of miracles, and she wanted this over. For that there was only one course. She caught Avanasy's sleeve again, and they ran once more, all three of them, across the gossamer road into darkness.

But the world below was not done with them yet. Another arrow, this one shining like the bridge beneath their feet, shot straight up, several yards ahead of them, arching high over their heads. At first, Ingrid thought it trailed a rope that would ensnare them, but then she saw how the 'rope' shimmered and gleamed. Then, she felt the heat of it.

Fire. A bow of fire arched across the moonlight bridge. A few seconds later, another arrow shot up, this one through the weaving of the bridge itself, and then down again. Medeoan balked, and Avanasy drew back, and a second bow of fire joined the first at a ninety-degree angle.

'What are they doing?' demanded Medeoan. 'I can feel heat . . .'

'Breaking the bridge?' Avanasy knuckled his eyes. 'There's something but I cannot tell what.'

'You can't see it?' cried Ingrid. Two more arrows whistled through the night, one more from below, trailing another rope of fire to arch across the bridge, the other from straight behind, making Medeoan leap sideways, coming down perilously close to the edge of the bridge.

'What is it, Ingrid?'

Before she could answer, something tugged at her skirt. Looking down automatically, Ingrid saw an arrow sticking out from her billowing coat, and even as Avanasy yanked it free, another shining arrow shot up, adding another strand to the net of fire in front of them.

And she saw what they were doing. The arrows from behind and the net before. If they stayed where they were, they'd be picked off like birds on a branch. If they ran forward blindly, they'd be burned to death. If they jumped . . . they would be shattered on the ground.

'It's a net,' said Ingrid, her words choking her. 'Mary Mother of God, it's fire.'

'I can't see it!' shouted Medeoan. Frustration and fear tore at her words.

'Nor can I,' replied Avanasy calmly, and Ingrid could feel how much that calm was costing him. Another arrow whistled overhead, but barely. 'But I feel the heat. Ingrid, you'll have to lead us.'

Ingrid bit the inside of her cheek and tasted blood. She snatched up her hems in one hand and Avanasy's hand in the other. Another arrow arched overhead, trailing its rope of fire behind it, adding another strand to the web. Moonlight and firelight blended starkly together, dazzling her eyes and making her skin shine red and white.

'Step exactly as I do.'

Swallowing so much fear she felt heart and belly would split open from the pressure, Ingrid strode forward. Another arrow, another strand of fire shot up straight in front of her, and she had to jump back. She could hear the sizzle of the magical flames now, and their heat licked at her skin, breaking a sweat out on her brow. She dodged the fiery strand, and the next, and the next. Cloth ripped near her, and she knew another arrow had come too close. Behind her, Avanasy cursed, and Medeoan cursed. Ingrid did not look back. She dodged under the last arch and looked out and saw nothing but the unbroken bridge ahead. The impossible span of moonlight suddenly seemed the safest thing she had ever known and she ran, forgetting Avanasy's hand, forgetting the young woman they had come so far to save, forgetting everything but the need to get away from the arrows and the fire, she bolted into the darkness, her only guide the shining road at her feet.

Slowly, slowly, she realized the moonlight arch had begun to slope down. Her bedazzled eyes could make out some landmarks ahead of her; trees lifting from the darkness, and another light. A lantern held high by a man waiting at the foot of their bridge.

Lien. The man was Lien and the trees were in Lien's garden. They had made it.

The glow of moonlight gave way to the springy darkness of grass. Gasping with relief, Ingrid missed her step and tumbled to the ground. The cool dampness of night's dew bathed the hundred small wounds she had taken. She lay there panting for just a moment, not caring for the dampness soaking rapidly through her fine silken clothing, before

Avanasy's arms scooped her up and pulled her close, pressing his body tightly against hers for a long moment.

Eventually, Ingrid and Avanasy were able to loosen their hold on each other, and turn toward the others. The first thing Ingrid saw was the utter shock on Medeoan's face. Suddenly ashamed, she took another step back. She could not read the look on Avanasy's face, and did not at this time care to try. Instead, she looked up in the direction from which they had come.

The bridge of moonlight was already gone. No trace of it lingered to shine against the night sky.

'Was it a dream?'

Avanasy shook his head. 'No dream, but a working of great skill.' Pride filled his voice. 'Majesty Imperial, may I make known to you our host, Lien Jinn, and his niece Cai-Yun Shen.'

Lien and Cai-Yun bowed deeply. The Empress blinked dazedly in the lantern light. She seemed reluctant to take her gaze from Avanasy's face. Her bewilderment tightened Ingrid's throat. But at last, she gestured to Lien and Cai-Yun to stand.

Something was wrong with Lien, but it took Ingrid a moment to realize what it was. Instead of his silken robe, the old sorcerer wore only a short coat of unbleached cotton with dark cuffs and short trousers to match. A dark cap covered his hair and he wore sandals on his feet instead of his soft shoes.

'I thank you for your hospitality to my advisor . . . advisors,' the Empress was saying. 'And now to myself. I am in your debt.'

'Your Majesty Imperial honors my home with your presence,' Lien bowed. 'But I fear we may not stay. The Nine Elders have many ways to track such sorceries, and may already be on their way here. We must be gone as soon as possible.'

Ingrid swayed on her feet. As bad as she felt, Medeoan

looked close to collapse. Avanasy hurried to the Empress's side and held out his arm so she could steady herself against him.

'Of course,' said Medeoan. 'Is conveyance ready?'

'This way, please.'

He set off into the depths of the garden at a pace Ingrid felt she could not possibly match. She was damp, cold and filthy, she had been dragged through dark tunnels by soldiers, shot at by sorcerers, and now her husband was back together with the woman he . . . she could barely bring herself to think of it at this moment. She wanted to stamp her foot, to screech her disapproval, to refuse to move until she could get some sleep in a bed. Any bed.

She did none of these things. She gathered up the hems of her ridiculous silken robe and set off after Lien as best she could. Avanasy shot her a worried glance, but did not reach for her. Both his hands were occupied in supporting the fainting Empress and keeping her moving forward.

The garden passed them in a blur of shadows with flashes of lantern light on pale leaves and silver pools. They reached the back wall, and Lien paused at the arched gate. He laid his hand on the latch and spoke three words Ingrid could not understand. The latch snicked open, and Lien led them out into a tiny back lane. Moonlight and lantern light showed Ingrid a black canal and a sharp-prowed boat moored to an iron post.

Lien blew out the lantern, leaving them only moonlight to see by. It took Ingrid a moment to realize the old man standing at the long steering oar was Du, and Shien was hunched by the high gunwale.

'Go below, please. Shien will show you where.'

As Avanasy and Shien helped the unsteady Empress aboard, Lien turned to Cai-Yun and grasped both her hands, saying something soft and urgent that Ingrid could not make out. She had just time enough to see the young woman nod before Avanasy motioned to her, and she had to clamber over the rail and onto the deck. There was no time to survey the little craft. Shien was already leading them to the stern ladder and down below decks.

Only one covered lantern lit the hold. Ingrid could make out nothing but bundles and stacks of shadow. Shien stepped nimbly between them and beckoned that they should follow.

They obeyed, with considerably less grace. Ingrid barked her shins several times against unidentifiable objects, bit her tongue to keep from exclaiming, and wished for her usual thick skirts and petticoats.

'In here, please, Master, Mistresses,' whispered Shien.

She gestured down. It took Ingrid a moment, but she realized the old woman was gesturing toward a hole in the lower deck. It was a smuggler's hold.

Ingrid saw at once what she was to do, and she balked. They had done enough, and all her nerve had left her. She felt hollow and her limbs began to shake. The idea of being shut up in the tiny, black hold, even with Avanasy's presence for support and comfort, filled her with revulsion.

But there was Avanasy, helping Shien to lower the Empress, whose skin glowed white as a ghost's in the faint light. Ingrid heard her bumping and shuffling below. Avanasy stretched his hand out to Ingrid.

What was there to do? She took his hand, and felt how warm it was, even though her own was so cold, and let herself be lowered into the smuggler's hold.

It was pitch black inside. She put up her hand and found the upper deck barely three feet above the lower. She had to lie flat on her back in the straw that had been strewn on the hull boards in order to fit. She heard the Empress's echoing breath off to the right, so she shifted herself to the left to make

room for Avanasy to climb down and stretch himself out.
Shien laid the planking back into place. Ingrid had just time
enough to see the planks had padded backs, both to muffle any
sound from below and so they would not sound unusually
hollow if thumped, before Shien settled them down, cutting
off all light.

Ingrid lay where she was. Overhead, she heard Shien's soft
footsteps and the sound of something heavy being dragged
and thumped into place. They were sealed in now. She swallowed against the panic that tried to rise in her throat. More
soft footsteps crossed the upper deck. Then that sound was
gone. The straw was rough against her back, and the cold and
damp began to sink in, raising goose bumps across every inch
of her. The hold smelled of old seawater and mildew. The
breathing of all three of them sounded far too loud in the
confined space.

'Well.' Ingrid drew a deep but shaky breath to prove to
herself that there was plenty of air, and to help pull her tattered
nerves back together. 'They do say there's nothing like traveling first class.'

'I must ask you later what you mean by that,' answered
Avanasy gravely. 'Majesty? Are you well?'

'As well as I can be,' the Empress whispered in reply.
'Although I am beginning to have second thoughts about
Hung-Tse's reputation for hospitality.' The lightness of her tone
quickly faded. 'Avanasy, do you know where they will take us?'

As if her words were a signal, the boat rocked sharply under
them, and began to slide through the water, in the direction
which Ingrid's feet pointed. She tried to remember which way
that was, and failed. Little waves slapped the hull underneath
them. The cold seemed to deepen, but perhaps that was only
her imagination.

'We'll go down to the river docks, I think,' murmured

Avanasy. Their confinement seemed to forbid speaking in normal tones. 'Lien has access to . . . grander ships there. It is my hope he will be able to sail us directly back to Isavalta.'

'Vyshemir grant your hope is correct.'

There was no more to be said. They lay still in the darkness, packed like sardines in a strange, cold tin. The boat rocked steadily, the waves and the slow creaking of the boards making a gentle counterpoint to the steady splash of the steering oar. Were it not for the fact that she was now soaked to the skin from bilge water, Ingrid believed she might have fallen asleep. As it was, she just fell into a kind of waking doze, her mind trying to sense something of the boat's speed, and trying in vain to measure time to guess how far they had come, and how far they might have to go.

Avanasy's hand brushed hers, ice cold now, but Ingrid grasped it gratefully anyway. A small traitorous part of herself wondered if he held onto the Empress with his other hand, and then she wondered why it should matter, which brought back the strange sadness she had felt in the tower room.

Time must have passed, but how much of it she could not tell. Her skin went numb. She could barely feel Avanasy's hand now. She tried to wriggle her toes to get some blood flowing, but it was no good.

Then came the sounds of footsteps, and Ingrid almost cried out in relief, but fast on the heels of the footsteps came the tramp of boots. Ingrid choked herself off. She had enough sensation left to her to feel Avanasy tense beside her. Her bloodless fingers gripped his hand.

Scraps of sound filtered through the padded boards. A woman's voice, high and querulous. That must have been Shien. A man's baritone that might have been Lien, or Du, or a stranger, answered. The boots clumped up and down the decks, shoving heavy burdens this way and that. Something that might have been a spear butt thumped against the deck above Ingrid's right shoulder.

They were going to hear her heartbeat. They were going to hear her breathing. She tried to hold her breath, tried to quiet her heart, to be wood and stone here in the cold.

Something heavy was shoved aside directly overhead. Ingrid bit down on her lip until she tasted blood. The boots clomped, the spear butt thumped. Shien spoke again, and a stranger's bass rumble answered. The baritone that might have been Lien or Du spoke, and the bass barked out a sharp reply, and the spear butt came down right over Ingrid's face, making her whole body jolt. She squeezed her eyes shut like a child desperate not to be seen.

The baritone said something else, and the words were followed by a faint, new noise. After a moment, Ingrid recognized it – the chink of metal, possibly of coins. Was Lien paying a tax, or perhaps a bribe? Would it work? Her throat closed. All was silent for a moment. Then, the baritone rapped out some order, and more burdens were dragged across the deck. Tears leaked out of Ingrid's eyes and she began to shake again.

But then, miraculously, the boots all trooped away toward her head, where the stern ladder was. Footsteps padded after them, and blessed, blessed silence fell around them again.

Tears of gratitude ran down Ingrid's cheeks to mix with the bilge water, and she did not care. She wept in silence as the boat started to move again, and the steering oar splashed once more down into the water.

It was too much. The sudden release from terror robbed Ingrid of consciousness. Whether she fainted or simply fell at last into sleep, she could not have said. For a time, however, the world went away.

★   ★   ★

Light struck Ingrid's eyes. She would have cringed but she could not move. Shadows moved overhead. They reached down long arms, grabbed Avanasy and hoisted him out of the smuggler's hold.

'Careful, you wastrels!' shrilled Shien's voice.

Then the arms reached out for Ingrid. Powerless to resist, or even to question, Ingrid was lifted like a sack of grain and set upright on the deck. She could not even feel her knees, let alone stiffen them to stand, but fortunately, Shien seemed to guess her condition and the old woman was there beside her, wrapping an arm around Ingrid's shoulder to support her weight as she slumped down.

'Carefully!' Shien barked again.

Ingrid could see at least a little now. Two men in loose shirts and short trousers bent down and raised the Empress up from the hold. Avanasy sat on a bench nearby. As she was lifted, he struggled to rise, and failed.

'Bring them with me,' snapped Shien. 'And *gently*, you louts, that lady is of quality.'

One of the two men began to snigger, but his companion stopped him with a glower. Shien moved toward the ladder, and Ingrid had no choice but to stumble along with her.

Climbing onto the upper deck was a nightmare. Sensation came back to Ingrid as pins and needles stabbing her skin from the inside. Shien, stronger than she looked, hauled Ingrid bodily up the ladder to stand blinking stupidly in the first gray light of dawn.

They were back at the docks. There was no mistaking the noise or the smell of the place. Shadowy sailing ships rose up on either side of the small boat. Shien steered Ingrid toward the starboard rail, where Du was helping Avanasy to a rope ladder lowered from the side of one of the larger vessels. His hands shook badly, but he managed to hang on while sailors at the top hauled the ropes up, pulling Avanasy with them.

To her shame, Ingrid whispered, 'I don't think I can.'

'You will,' said Shien with gentle practicality. 'Because you must.'

The sailors let the ladder slither back down over the side. Shien guided Ingrid up to it and folded her hands around the rungs. Ingrid made her left foot step up and rest on the rope, then her right. She dangled there for a moment, and her hands clamped down reflexively. The sailors began to pull, and she gasped, but did not scream.

In less time than she would have thought, she was on the deck of the ship, being helped over the rail and standing next to Avanasy so the ladder could be let down once more for the Empress.

Somewhat more composed, and at least able to stand on her own, although the pins and needles still plagued her, and the ruined, sodden silk clung to her back like a wet rag, Ingrid was able to look about her. The ship was a big one for its kind; a four master, and elaborately rigged. The quarter deck rose up proudly from the stern, and even in the dim light she could see the long arm of the tiller. Shouted orders filled the air. Men and boys swarmed up the rigging, loosening furled canvas, which came down like a snowfall. Others lashed it into place on the yard arms, plainly getting ready to sail as soon as the captain gave the order.

The sailors lifted the Empress over the side, and set her swaying on the deck. Avanasy moved toward her, but Shien came over the rail under her own steam a moment later and caught the young woman before she could fall. She looked dazed. However bad the recent trip had been for Ingrid, for the Empress it had obviously been worse, and Ingrid felt a stab of pity for her.

A man ran down from the quarter deck, and as he

approached, Ingrid recognized him as Lien, still in his short coat and sandals. The sorcerer bowed hastily.

'I apologize for the mode of bringing you here, but it was necessary. Let my men conduct you below. We will be underway in moments.'

He signaled for a sailor, an officer in all probability. The man was slender and taller than most Ingrid had seen in Hung-Tse. His coat was short and practical in cut, but brilliant green in color and its buttons sparkled silver. He bowed and led them all, with Shien supporting the Empress, to a ladder beneath the quarter deck, and down past the second deck to the third. By Ingrid's mental measure, they were only just down to the waterline, and she saw the ladder went further down yet, so there must be at least one more deck beneath them, possibly two.

They went no lower, however. The officer conducted them toward the bow. They passed doors on both port and starboard. The officer opened one of the starboard doors, bowing to the Empress. Shien led her through, and closed them in. Then, the officer opened a port door. Avanasy bowed his own thanks, and he and Ingrid filed into the cabin.

It was small, which Ingrid had expected, but it was also snug and dry. Two cozy bunks had been built into the wall. A gracefully carved table and high-backed bench stood under an unlit tin lantern. What illumination there was came from two portholes with glass so thick they turned the light watery.

Ingrid managed to take two steps toward the bench before the strength that had supported her this far failed and she collapsed. Avanasy caught her and they sank to the deck together. They knelt there for a time, doing nothing but holding onto each other, reminding themselves that the other was solid and real.

Eventually, by silent, mutual consent, they pulled themselves to their feet again. A carved chest had been lashed into one corner. Avanasy investigated the contents and pulled out Ingrid's ordinary clothes, the thick skirt, apron, petticoats and stockings she had missed so recently. Avanasy's black coat, trousers and boots were also inside.

Groaning with relief, Ingrid shucked her ruined silk and dressed in her clean, familiar clothing. Avanasy also reclaimed his traveling clothes, and when he turned to face her, he looked more comfortable than she had seen him in days. But at the same time, his face was troubled.

'Ingrid,' he took her hand and sat them both down on the carved bench. 'Lien will be sailing us through the Land of Death and Spirit to return us to Isavalta as swiftly as possible. This . . .' he touched the spell braid on her wrist, 'will only provide you with some protection. You must not be asleep when we cross the veil.'

She nodded. 'You'll warn me when that's to happen?'

'I will, but I must leave you for a time. I . . .'

He stood there for a moment, his hand against the smooth wood, as if looking for words in the pattern of the grain.

When he did not find them, Ingrid said, 'If you want to go see the Empress, you should.'

That turned him around. 'Ingrid . . .' He stopped and started again. 'I don't wish you to have cause to doubt my love for you.'

'I don't,' she said, and she meant it, but she did not speak further. She did not say how she still felt the sadness she had known the moment she first saw Avanasy and his young Empress together. For in that moment she had seen not how much Avanasy loved Empress Medeoan, but how much love shone from the young woman for him.

Did Avanasy still love Medeoan as other than pupil and monarch? Looking at him now, she saw that he did, but she could not bring herself to fear that love. She was too numb to do anything but accept that it was so. Later, she knew, she would have to weep, or rage, or do some other thing that she might regret in time, but now, she could do nothing but look at the man who was her husband and see the truth.

'Go,' she told him. 'Say what you must.'

Avanasy crossed the distance between them in three swift strides. He kissed her long and lingeringly on the mouth, and left her there. That kiss, that love, was as true as the other, and she knew that as well, but that knowledge did nothing to stir the numbness that had settled over her heart.

Sad, tired and still bewildered by all that had happened, Ingrid found she had no trouble at all creeping beneath the covers on the lower bunk and falling gratefully into oblivion.

Avanasy stood outside the door that led to Medeoan's cabin, trying to calm himself. He could scarcely number the emotions swirling through him. He felt like a nervous schoolboy. He felt like a courtier who knows they are out of favor. He felt like a parent who wanted desperately to comfort their child, but knew they had no comfort to offer. He told himself he was too tired for this, and surely Medeoan was as well. He wanted to run and take shelter in Ingrid's arms until they reached the shores of Isavalta. He wanted to know that Medeoan had already gone to sleep so that he would not have to do this thing.

He raised his hand and softly knocked.

Shien opened the door a moment later. Behind her he saw the soft glow of morning through thick glass.

'Has Her Majesty Imperial retired?' he asked.

'Not yet,' replied Shien. 'I will see if she will grant you admittance.'

She closed the door, leaving Avanasy alone with his inner

turmoil for a seemingly endless moment. Above, the capstan ground as it turned to the rhythm of stamping feet. The ship around him strained as shouts rose from a variety of throats.

Shien returned to the doorway and beckoned him inside.

Medeoan sat on the lower of two bunks, wrapped in a woolen blanket. Underneath, he glimpsed a robe of bright blue cotton, of a shade very close to the Imperial blue she should have been wearing. Avanasy had no doubt Lien had specifically arranged for that. Her bright, cropped hair had been loosened and brushed. She looked far too thin, and too pale.

Shien ducked out the door and closed it again behind her. Medeoan did not look up at her departure. She just stared at the deck and rubbed her thin, wounded hands together.

What have you been through, Medeoan? Avanasy wanted to blurt out. He did not. He simply knelt, as was proper before his Empress. The deck rocked under him and Avanasy swayed gracelessly as the ship slowly slipped forward.

The motion lifted Medeoan's head. She glanced toward the ceiling and the sounds of men's orders and creaking ropes. Then, she finally seemed to see him there, kneeling in reverence before her.

'There is no need for such between us, Avanasy,' she said, running a hand through her badly shorn locks. 'I would have thought that much you would remember.'

'I've forgotten nothing,' he said, getting to his feet again. 'Including the fact that you are now Empress of Eternal Isavalta.'

'Such an empress as the world has never seen,' she snorted. 'Crop-headed, imprisoned, alone . . .'

'Never alone,' he said, moving to her side.

'Oh, but I was.' She gazed up at him, and he saw the dark circles under her eyes. 'You will never know . . . I'm sorry,

Avanasy. I should have known you would not betray me. This is my fault.'

Hearing the dejection in her words, Avanasy knelt again, but this time it was so he could look directly into Medeoan's eyes. They were underway. The ship rocked with its own easy motion as they moved out into the bay. They were making good their escape. His heart should have been lifting, but guilt grown old weighed it down.

'No. The fault is mine. I should have gone to your father with what I suspected. I should have . . .'

She smiled and straightened up a little, shaking her head to stop his words. 'There are so many things we both should have done.' She ran both hands through her shorn hair again. 'I should have found a lady in the Heart of the World who knows how to cut hair!'

They laughed a little at that, but too soon Medeoan grew serious again. 'He did not take the crown,' she said, staring out of the tiny porthole. 'I gave it to him.'

'No, Medeoan.'

'Yes, Avanasy.' Her face hardened. 'All I could think to do was run, and I did. I left Isavalta in his hands. I *gave* it to him.' She spat the words. 'Because I was such a child, I couldn't understand, I couldn't accept who I truly was. I stood at the foot of my father's throne and I swore to Vyshemir and Vyshko I would protect Isavalta, that I would be a true daughter, and at the first opportunity, I abandoned them.'

'The gods forgive, Medeoan,' he said, laying a hand on the edge of her bunk, as close as he dared come to touching her. 'They know it was not them you ran from. They will welcome your return.'

'Yes.' She was not looking at him. She looked out the portal at the green-brown river and the brightening sky. Avanasy was not sure what she saw there, but it turned her expression to stone. 'We will return together, and together we will make Kacha rue what he has done to Isavalta, and to me.'

It was then Avanasy saw the depths of the bitterness that had taken hold in Medeoan. Imprisonment had only fostered it. It had begun with Kacha, whom she had truly loved, and who had committed betrayal on top of betrayal. She had a right to her anger, he could not say otherwise, but it chilled him to the heart to see the hard light it sparked in her eyes.

'Medeoan, thinking too much on blame will not help you do what must be done,' he ventured.

She smiled mirthlessly. 'I am sure you are right. But it is past time I opened my eyes . . .' she shook herself, and did not finish the phrase. 'So, tell me, Avanasy, where have you been, and who is this woman you are traveling with?'

All that Avanasy had thought of saying crowded into his mind at that moment – the evasions, the careful words, the partial and easier truths – but he pushed the babble of it aside. Instead, he settled into the cabin's one chair and told her, fully and deliberately, of his time on Sand Island, of his life as a fisher, which at least made her smile, of the ghost and of Ingrid and her sister. He told her how Iakush, dying, found him there, and how he determined at once to return, but could not leave Ingrid behind.

'She is worthy of you then, Avanasy?' asked Medeoan softly.

'More than I am of her, I sometimes think.' He could not help but smile as he thought of her warmth and courage again.

Medeoan touched his hand. 'What else?'

Relieved that the moment he had dreaded had passed so easily, Avanasy spun the tale to the end, bringing her news of Peshek's continued bravery and his quest to raise a loyal army in Isavalta, of the certainty that Kacha meant to war with Hung-Tse, and how that war had probably already begun.

Medeoan's jaw worked itself back and forth. 'He plays this game with my land?' she rasped. 'With my people now? In my name?' She spat the final word. 'And then, after all, he would blame me for his wars! I won't leave enough of him left for his mother to mourn!'

The force of her words rocked Avanasy back.

'We need to be home,' she announced. 'We need to find Peshek, and then Kacha.'

'Lien speeds us on our way. There is no one better able to sail through the Land of Death and Spirit.'

An unfamiliar, calculating expression crossed her face. 'Avanasy, could he raise more than one crew of men?'

'I believe he can.'

'Good. We will speak to him as soon as we are safe in Isavalta. His men could come in useful to whatever force Peshek has managed to raise.' She stood, and as the morning's watery light flickered across her, Avanasy saw how very much she looked like her father. 'You will stand beside me then.'

'As ever, Majesty Imperial,' he bowed his head, and this time she did not reject the gesture.

'Thank you.' Even those words sounded stern. 'There is nothing to be done at this moment. You should try to sleep. I'll need you awake when we arrive.'

Avanasy rose and gave a formal reverence. 'You should also sleep.'

'I'll try, I promise,' she said, sounding a little more like the child he remembered. Avanasy let himself be content with that and showed himself out the door.

In the passage, he lifted his eyes to the gods. *Vyshko, Vyshemir, protect your daughter. She is ready to become what she must be, but I beg you, do not let her forget what she should be.*

★　★　★

'They are gone. We have failed.' Anh Thao, the Minister of the North, spoke the words. She, with the other Nine Elders, knelt on the dais, a gesture of apology and an admission of guilt all at once.

'We have searched the house of the pirate Lien, but they have already been taken away,' added Shaiming, the Minister of Metal. 'Nothing has been learned from questioning his niece.'

Pa K'un held himself still and silent, letting the Nine Elders bask for a moment in his disapproval. Then, when he judged that moment had lasted long enough, he signed swiftly to his Voice. Seeing him ready to speak, the Nine Elders stood.

'We must turn our minds to what may be done about this invasion,' the Voice intoned solemnly. 'And we must do so now. We have intelligence that tells us the Isavaltans hasten toward Erh Huan. They mean to attack there, and if they do not have plans to attack soon by sea, they are fools.'

'If the story the three from Isavalta told is true . . .' began the Minister of the North, but Pa K'un cut her off with a gesture.

'If it is true, then the security of Hung-Tse will be the Isavaltans' last consideration. The Empress will return with her advisors to try to take her own land back. It may be she will be able to do so swiftly, but can we rely on that? Their winter comes early and hard. If she must stage a pitched campaign, she will not be able to do so until the spring thaw. That will give the usurper time to dig in on our borders, and prepare at home for her assault, if he has not already begun to do so.' The Voice spoke sternly, in good reflection of the Emperor's mood. 'And if she has lied to us, and works with her Hastinapuran husband rather than against him, she has escaped with whatever information or advantage her magics were able to procure. No, Ministers, we have no choice. We must act swiftly.'

He did not say it. He was not permitted to say it. But as he gazed at the nine solemn faces before him, he knew they saw the direction in which his words led.

Xuan, the Minister of Fire, walked up a single step of the dais, and knelt.

'I am ready,' he said.

The other eight said nothing at first. Xuan remained where he was, bent in obeisance and offering, ready to sacrifice all to make good his failure and to protect the Heart of the World.

'Let it be done,' whispered Chi Tahn, the Minister of Water.

'Let it be done,' whispered En Lai, the Minister of Earth.

'Let it be done,' whispered Shaiming, the Minister of Metal.

Eight times the words echoed around the throne room. As the ministers spoke, the air seemed to thicken with the force of their resolve, until the hairs on the back of Pa K'un's head stood up, and it seemed that the very images of the gods must shiver from the strength of it.

Pa K'un signed to his Voice. 'Can it be done now?'

'It can,' answered the Minister of Air. 'It has been prepared for these many years.'

The Voice looked to the Emperor, and Pa K'un nodded.

'Then I also say, let it be done.'

The eight of the Elders who still stood all bowed in unison. 'Will Your Majesty deign to come with us?'

Again, Pa K'un inclined his head. With this as the signal, the Voice beckoned to the bearers with their black coats and saffron caps. They mounted the dais from the rear, carrying their poles which were their badge of office. The poles were fitted into slots on the side of his throne and the Emperor was lifted onto the shoulders of his servants. Already, the soldiers were assembled at the foot of the dais that he might have a proper escort.

The Nine Elders stood aside so that Pa K'un preceded them down the dais steps. As a result, the Emperor had no opportunity to see how bravely the Minister of the Fire walked toward his destiny.

There was only one place for such magic as this. The ministers and the Imperial escort proceeded up the winding stairs of the Heart's central tower, the Heart's Spear. Only those who had the privilege of mounting the final stair could tell that the last chamber was opened to the moon and stars. The silver light flooded down and filled the circular room with its polished floor inlaid in gold and ivory with maps of the heavens and ringed round with signs of protection for Hung-Tse.

In the center of the chamber waited a stone altar the size and shape of a millstone, its top blackened by years of fires and its sides carved with prayers to the gods and the Imperial ancestors. As his bearers lowered him, Pa K'un read those prayers, and wondered if any of the boys who had sat here before him would hear if he spoke those prayers aloud. He wondered if they would bless or curse him if they could.

The Minister of Fire stepped forward and knelt before the altar. He bowed and kissed the ground before it, remaining in the position of obeisance to pray. Then, at last, he stood straight, and stepped into the center of the altar. He stood there, still and seemingly unafraid, but Pa K'un could not believe that was so. He remembered his investiture as Emperor. He had schooled himself to sit perfectly still through the hours of chants and formal declarations. He had appeared calm and strong, or so he had been told, but inside he had felt weak, despite knowing it was a glorious thing that happened to him.

Even in the moonlight, Xuan's tattoos shimmered brightly as if he were living flame himself rather than just flesh and blood.

The Minister of Earth and the Minister of the South joined

their fellows in the circle. Each carried a shining bundle reverently in their arms. Xuan lifted his chin just a little higher. Then, he inclined his head once.

The rest of the Nine Elders bowed in return. Then, they all lifted their voices, and together, they began to sing.

Pa K'un had studied many languages, but the spell tongue of the Nine Elders was known to them alone. It was never written down, and was only passed on when a new Elder was chosen and invested with the robes, markings and name of the previous sorcerer who had held the office, and then it was passed on by magic. That particular ceremony had not been required, the Emperor knew, for three hundred years. But then, neither had this one.

The nine voices rose higher, became more commanding. Even Pa K'un could feel the air shiver as the song wove the Elders' will into corporeal form. It grew bitterly cold for a moment, then, slowly, the temperature began to rise, as if the song reached up to the stars themselves and pulled down their fire.

En Lai, the Minister of Earth, broke the circle, still singing, high, ringing harmonies that soared above the other tones. He stepped onto the altar. The Minister of Fire did not move, did not look at him. En Lai lifted the burden he carried and draped it around Xuan's shoulders.

It was a robe, stiff with golden embroidery. Phoenixes soared across scarlet cloth. They raised their trailing wings in triumph. They stretched their necks out in song. They spread their long tails out to wrap around Xuan's body so that they encompassed him completely.

En Lai bowed again, and slowly, Pa K'un thought lovingly, tied the golden sash and returned to the circle.

The song deepened, strengthened, drawing its power from the stones beneath as well as the stars above. The night grew warmer still. Pa K'un felt sweat begin to prickle his scalp and the back of his neck.

On the altar, Xuan sagged under the weight of the song of power and the robe that bound him. The song did not cease, but grew louder and stronger yet. Pa K'un, for all his years of training, could barely hold himself still. He had ordered this thing, but now he wanted to flee it. This was wrong. This tore at the fabric of what was and what must be. This power was too great, this song too loud. The gods heard this sound, and they answered, and their answers were not kind.

The Minister of the South stepped onto the altar with her burden. Xuan, no longer able to stand on his own, sagged against her. She bore his weight sturdily, singing her thread of this terrible, powerful web, and laid her burden across Xuan's face. It was a mask, made of gold and etched with delicate feathers. It was a bird's face she bound with scarlet ribbons over Xuan's own. He arched his back from the weight and the pain and the burden of the song that pressed against him, but he made no sound. The Minister of the South returned to the circle, and Xuan collapsed in a heap of gold and beauty onto the stone.

The Elders' song grew louder yet. Pa K'un felt he could not stand it a moment longer. He must clap his hands over his ears, he must scream, he must leap up and break the circle. He must stop this. It was wrong, wrong. The song would tear the world open. It would shatter night and day around them. It was too huge, too loud, too terrible to be contained.

The Emperor shot to his feet, and at that exact moment, the Phoenix rose from the altar.

It was dazzling. It shone like the sun as it lifted its wings, each feather a tongue of flame. The blue of the heart of the flame burned in its eyes. Pa K'un felt he must be blinded if he looked too long, but he could not turn his face away from the power and the unearthly beauty of this creature that rose, graceful as smoke, into the night sky, dimming the stars themselves with its blaze. It uttered one cry that pierced Pa K'un's ears through to his heart, and it flew, a star of impossible proportions rising from the earth instead of falling from the heavens, toward the north.

Only when its blaze had faded could Pa K'un breathe again. He fell back on his chair, his strength gone. The after-images of the Phoenix flickered brightly across his vision. At some point, he could not have said when, the Elders had ceased to sing. They clasped hands now, bowing toward the empty altar. There were only eight of them in that circle. Xuan, the Minister of Fire, was gone.

Pa K'un gathered himself back into the approved position of calm reflection, then, he too bowed toward the empty altar.

Thank you, Xuan, for your sacrifice. Thank you, immortal one, for answering our call. If there is a price, I will pay, but I beg you, burn these invaders from our door.

As his prayer winged skyward, a fierce cry echoed in the distance. Pa K'un knew then he had been heard, and he could not help but tremble.

unable to maintain a winter siege, would get what they could through the pirate harassment and attack the Isavaltan coast. Having thus tied up and weakened Hung-Tse's navy, which was their true strength, Kacha would, come spring, start the real press, on land, down the Miateshcha peninsula, and up from the south. Because, by next year, his father in Hastinapura would be brought into the battle, and Hung-Tse would be facing its worst nightmare. They would be besieged from north and south, and for all the size of their lands, they would not be able to survive that for long.

The only question truly was, did the Heart of the World realize yet what was happening to them? And if they did, what would they do? The armies of Hung-Tse, Peshek did not fear overmuch. He was a soldier, and he had faced them. Isavalta could match them, not easily, perhaps, but it could be done. But the Nine Elders would not be idle, and their powers . . . Isavalta had nothing to match that, and how then would those men down there suffer? The Nine Elders were said to be able to call down armies of daemons from the clear blue sky, or to be able to open the earth at your feet and swallow you whole.

It was this thought that steeled Peshek toward what must be done. This would work only once, and they must do it now. On the other side of the pass waited Raichik's plains, and there they would have to move to much more dangerous night raids, swift hit-and-run efforts. Even though Lord D'rno was promising them help in the form of two score of his famous horses and was also swearing to help get news of Kacha's treachery spread among his men who had already been levied, if they were going to do serious damage, here and now was when it must happen. After this, Kacha would post better guard, but as it was, why should he order any but the most perfunctory of watches? They were, after all, still safely in the borders of Isavalta, in the oblast of a Lord Master who had demonstrated his unquestioning loyalty to the Imperial throne.

Peshek squinted toward the east. The masses of men were thinning, giving way to the slower and more cumbersome supply and baggage carts.

This was wrong. These were Isavaltans. These were members of the House Guard, whose only crime was obeying the orders that had come down from the Imperial hand.

Peshek crawled backward from his perch to where Ferin waited for him. Ferin's raised eyebrows asked the only question there could be, and Peshek's nod gave the only answer needed.

They had chosen this overlook because it was heavily forested. It gave them cover for when Kacha's advance scouts rode through, and it gave them the raw materials for their work. Ferin raised his hand in signal to the nearest crew of men, and that signal traveled all down the ridge line. The men crouched behind the great piles of pitch and resin-soaked brush that they had spent the past few days gathering. Each team set to work with their flint and steel, starting up a tiny fire, little more than a spark on the end of a taper.

Peshek raised his hand. Farin raised his. Peshek flattened himself down, and scanned the pass. The first of the baggage carts passed under the first of the waiting brush piles. He could hear the faint echo of the driver cursing the mules as they struggled with the stony ground. At last, the beasts pulled him clear of the obstacles. A knot of boys ran up and began clearing the stones away for the next cart. Peshek swallowed. He had forgotten the boys. How could he have done so? The second cart entered the pass, and the third, and the fourth.

Now. It had to happen now. Peshek closed his eyes, and swung his arm down.

He smelled the smoke instantly as the nurtured sparks were

applied to the brush, with the pitch-soaked logs underneath. The crewmen scrambled back quickly and took up the long-handled pushes they had fashioned. The dry brush caught clean and fast, the flames rising up and the heat reaching down.

The smell of it was strong, and reached the bottom of the pass quickly. Heads lifted, and spied the fire, and voices shouted out, but the carts could not be quickly turned, and no archers were in position. Peshek gave the signal to Ferin, and Ferin gave it to the men.

They pushed the piles of tarred and burning brush down onto Kacha's baggage train. The burning bundles fell like stars, trails of sparks shining in their wakes. For a moment, it was beautiful.

Then they landed, at the feet of the mules, who reared and stamped, struggling at their traces and screaming in their mindless, animal voices; at the feet of the horses, who bucked and ran, beyond the control of any rider; onto the carts, that erupted with fresh flame at once; on the heads and backs of the men, who screamed even louder than the animals and threw themselves to the ground trying to smother the flames; onto the boys, who, lacking any experience or discipline, simply ran, and took the fire with them down the train. The stench soon grew worse than the screams.

But there was no time to wait. Already the fire crews had retired, making their retreat to the rendez-vous. A man had Peshek's horse, and he mounted swiftly, charging down the ridge line to join the other raiders cascading down the shallower pass toward the far end of the train. Someone among Kacha's men had organized a response, and arrows flew up toward the raiders, and were met with an answering volley from Peshek's own men. Lit torches flared in their hands, and pikes and swords were held at the ready.

He noted that absently, as the majority of his concentration was occupied trying to keep his horse and himself upright as they charged down a slope that was still steeper than he would have liked to see. The arrows whistled overhead, and the shouts of the hale and ready mixed with the screams of the burning.

'Medeoan!' shouted Peshek, and his men, as agreed, took up the cry. 'Medeoan! Empress Medeoan!'

They poured down the slope into the baggage train. The flames roared high in the narrow pass, cutting the baggage train off from the majority of the army. Peshek rode hard down the line, swinging his sword at those who challenged him, knocking them off balance or out of the way, long enough for the men behind him to thrust their torches into the baggage carts and spread the fire further yet.

'Medeoan! Empress Medeoan!'

Shouts, flames, screams of horse and man, all blurred into one incomprehensible roar. The burning of tar, wood and flesh assailed his nostrils and the smoke stung his eyes and wrung tears out to trail along his face. Heat pounded at his back and right side. The guards in the train managed to assemble themselves for their own charge. Screaming their own battle cries, they rode head-on into Peshek's company.

Peshek could spare no thought for what was happening behind him. Men reared up before him, swords or pikes jabbing and slashing, and it was heat and noise, and only instinct and reflex to keep him alive.

Fight through, fight through, fight through. The words sang in his mind as he slashed at the men he should have been fighting beside. He pushed his horse forward, wading through the fray. *Fight through!* That was the order, that was the plan. Fight through and get out the other side, and run for it. Ignore the screams, ignore the way your arm is beginning to ache, don't see the faces, see the weapons, knock them aside, thrust, parry, hit hard, take down the horse and the man goes with it, ignore the arrows, ignore the flames, ignore the screams . . .

All at once the way in front of him opened to the sloping and stony apron that was the mouth of the pass, and Peshek drove his knees into his horse's side. The animal launched itself forward, streaking free down the remaining slope, galloping hard to leave the smells of smoke and battle far behind.

Peshek found himself grinning. He sheathed his sword and gripped the reins with both hands, hearing the other hoofbeats behind him.

They'd done it, they'd done it. They'd done serious damage to the baggage train, they'd slowed the march while the fire was dealt with and the damage assessed. They had maybe weakened Kacha's force, not just by the dead and wounded they'd left behind, but by the men who might be sent out to find them.

If they were pursued, let it be so. They could deal with any such, especially if they were given a moment to talk, to show their proofs and make their pursuers believe. Then they would be that much stronger, and Kacha that much weaker.

'Vyshko's name! What is it?'

A heartbeat after he heard that shout, the whole world changed. The light turned orange. A rush like the roar of the sea filled the sky accompanied by a scream that grated Peshek's bones and left him deaf. Then all was heat and a light of blood and brass overhead. Peshek tried to rein in his horse, but the animal bucked and fought, and it was all Peshek could do to keep his seat. He looked up, and the heat beating down from the sky felt as if it would singe his face.

And he saw the Firebird swoop down low over the pass. His jaw hung loose and his hands went slack around the reins. His horse lost no time. It charged, and Peshek was on his back on the ground before he knew what had happened. He pushed himself upright, and not even the pain of his fall could make him look away. The whole of his mind was filled with the sight of the creature of living flame. Even as it flew away, he could feel its heat against his skin. Fear and wonder left him paralyzed. It was coming for him now. He was vaguely aware he ought to run, ought to warn, but he could do nothing but stare at the wonder and deadly beauty that filled the sky.

Then, he heard the screams of Kacha's army begin.

Peshek didn't think. He scrambled to his feet and stumbled into a run. The world around him shivered with heat, and his lungs protested the need to breathe the burning air. The last of his men galloped past, in the other direction. A few saw him, and shouted. A few more turned around, and he heard the hoofbeats as they raced on with him, until he topped the stony rise.

The heat sent him reeling backward, both hands held up in a futile attempt to ward it off. The whole world was on fire, a blazing, roaring, curtain of red, gold, and white. It boiled up the mountainsides, not even the stone could stop it. Men and animals screamed and were silenced. Smoke black as tar poured into the sky, and the Firebird, magnificent and terrible, rode it high, shrieking in its triumph. Peshek could see nothing but its fire, feel nothing but its heat. Pain seeped into his skin, his throat, his eyes. He turned and he ran.

He had no conscious thought, he could not even pray, he could only run, away from the fire, away from its cause. A hot wind blew over him, and Peshek's gaze lifted without his willing it to. The Firebird streaked above him, and dove again.

'No!' screamed Peshek. 'No!'

But more men began to scream, and more smoke rose ahead of him, and more heat and more deadly red light leapt into being.

Fire raging ahead and fire raging behind, Peshek threw

himself at the hillside, scrambling for purchase on the stones that were already growing hot from the Firebird's blaze. He had to get above the fire. That was his only hope. Had to get above, had to get away, had to find a way to help his men, his men who were screaming and dying, whose deaths he could smell and taste as burning flesh in his mouth.

No, no, no, Vyshko, Vyshemir, no!

He couldn't see. He couldn't hear. Heat burned his hands, but fear was stronger than pain, and he lunged forward again and again, a wild animal acting only on the desperation of instinct.

Impossibly, the ground under him grew level. Peshek drew another lungful of burning air, and turned to run again, but a thin bush in front of him burst into fresh flame. Shock took his balance and he fell, and he saw yet more fire on his coat. Peshek screamed and rolled, beating at the flames, the smoke and the stench of his own burning filling his lungs now. He burned inside, he burned outside. Pain engulfed him utterly, and all the world went black.

Eventually, Peshek heard a voice.

'So, the Nine Elders have played their highest card,' said the voice. 'We must have scared them badly.'

Pain. There was nothing in the whole world but pain, and this strange voice. Like a child that will reach out to whatever help may be at hand, Peshek lifted his head and tried to open his eyes. He could, but only barely, and the attempt was agony.

For a second, he saw a thin, brown man. He seemed to have a blaze of red at his throat. Then he had to drop his head again, and there was only darkness and pain.

'Yet, he will still come back to you. You reek of him, Man,' said the voice. 'And where he is, she will be, and once this fire is burned out, we cannot have them trying to make whole what has been broken, can we?' There was a smile in the voice,

Peshek realized. He wanted to move, to beg for water, or for a knife, if that was the only way to end his pain.

'So, we will wait.'

'Ingrid.'

The gentle voice dragged Ingrid reluctantly back from the deep place she had gone. She peeled open her eyes. Avanasy sat on the edge of her bunk, his hand warm against her arm. She had not thought it possible to see him looking any more tired than he had when he had left her to go speak with the Empress, but he did now. The dark circles under his eyes made his face look hollow.

Ingrid pushed herself up onto her elbows and brushed her tousled hair back. She had gone to sleep without braiding it, she noted ruefully, and would be brushing the tangles out for days.

Odd how it's the little things that bother one at such a time . . .

'How is the Empress?' she asked.

Avanasy shook his head, and his face grew just a little more pinched. 'She is . . . much changed. Kacha has wounded her deeply, and I think her confinement has not been good for her.' His eyes grew distant for a moment, but then he shook himself. 'But, it is time for you to be awake. Lien readies us for the crossing.'

'I'd like to see it.' Ingrid pushed back the covers.

'Very well.' Avanasy gave her his hand and helped her out of the bunk. She brushed down her skirts and apron and together they climbed to the upper deck.

Up top, the wind was stiff and sharp, and whipped her hair into her eyes. Ingrid pushed it back and followed Avanasy's gaze with her own up to the quarter deck. Lien stood tall and alone, staring out ahead into the misty morning. The ship sailed easily with the current, the rush of water blending with the rush of the wind. The banks with their burdens of buildings and walls slipped past on either side. She could see a few other vessels in the distance, both before and behind, their sails blending with the morning mists. Overhead, the taut canvas of their own sails bellied in the wind, giving the ship wings.

Now Ingrid saw that those sails were more than the plain white canvas she was used to. Each had been painted with complex red sigils, woven together into rings and knots. She could make nothing of them other than that they seemed well done, but the expression on Avanasy's face as he took them in was something close to awe.

'He's going to take them in awake,' he murmured. 'This ship must have a crew of a hundred men, and he's going to take them all through the Land of Death and Spirit wide awake. I would have said it was impossible, but this . . .' he gestured toward the sigils. 'No wonder he has been able to defy the Nine Elders for so long.'

On the quarter deck, Lien raised his hand. He might have shouted something, Ingrid thought she heard his voice, but the wind snatched his words away. Ahead of them, the green river and the bright sky seemed dimmed and she wondered if they were sailing into a genuine fog. The edges of the world blurred and whitened. The wind dropped, but the sails stayed impossibly full.

The whiteness brightened and at the same time, all sound dimmed. The pitch and roll of the ship eased, changing into an even glide, as if they sailed across a garden pond, and all the river turned to flat, white mist. There was no more wind.

Ingrid sucked in a breath of air suddenly grown chill and thin. The silence pressed against her ears, making them ring as she strained to hear some sound beyond the beating of her heart. The men in the rigging and on the deck did not seem to have noticed a thing. They went obliviously about their business, but as one shirtless sailor passed Ingrid she saw his eyes as fixed as glass. Whatever Lien did, it blinded them. They could see nothing of the strangeness beyond the ship, and so, in these Silent Lands, could not be seduced or frightened by any of it.

Avanasy fingered the braid Ingrid wore on her wrist, as if to reassure himself that it was still sound.

This time Ingrid felt no tugging, no strange separation of self. She felt whole and solid, almost as if she were stone in this world of mist. Was this how Avanasy felt? Was this what it was to be a sorcerer here? Or was this something else? A spell-wrought rooting that kept her severed soul tied to the deck, like a water cask or a bundle of cotton.

That thought chafed at her, although she could not have said why. She did not want to leave, to roam in the white mists that swirled before and behind, where she would surely lose herself and all that she was. She could not possibly want that. She wanted to stay beside Avanasy, to see this business she had helped start through to the end, and then . . . and then . . .

She wanted to see whatever came next, of course. She did not want to vanish into the mists. Whatever it was. Avanasy loved her. Truly. The Empress was an old love from other days. She was his wife.

Her fist closed around her ring.

Around them, the mists parted enough for her to make out patches of green beyond the whiteness. Round, green islands rose from the shifting snow-white fog. Each had a single tree growing from it, and each seemed to Ingrid more beautiful than any garden she had ever seen. She meant to take a step toward the rail, but Avanasy gripped her arm and shook his head, and she stayed where she was, her fingers still wrapped hard around her ring.

From the quarter deck Lien waved to them, gesturing for

them to come join him. Avanasy moved aside so that Medeoan, and then Ingrid, could precede him up the ladder to stand with Lien on a far-too-steady deck.

'Who is it you seek to meet?' asked the sorcerer captain. 'Is there a name?'

Medeoan looked to Avanasy. 'Peshek Pachalkasyn Ursulvin,' he answered. 'And Vyshko grant that he has lived long enough,' Ingrid heard him add under his breath.

Still with one hand on the rail, Lien stared out past the prow of the great ship. The mists and the green hills moved around them. Here and there, a dark tree floated in the whiteness. Ingrid forced herself not to look. She did not wish to see what birds nested in such trees.

'I sense him,' said Lien softly, his gaze distant and clouded. 'Yes, I sense him. But we may not sail where he is.'

'You promised . . .' began Medeoan.

With painful slowness, Lien turned to focus on her. 'We must walk,' he said reasonably.

'But your ship . . .' began Avanasy. The sailors went placidly about their duties, unseeing, uncaring. Even Ingrid understood his concern. How long would that last without their master's will to follow?

'Will act as if becalmed until I call them forth again,' replied Lien serenely.

Avanasy had to struggle to keep his jaw from falling open. 'You can do such a thing?'

Lien smiled faintly. 'How is it you think I've eluded the Emperor's navy and the Nine Elders all these years? This has been all my study, the full focus of my art.' His eyes were calm as he spoke, but his voice was grim. 'I pay, and I pay heavily, but I have what I want.'

'Master Lien,' said Avanasy, and Ingrid heard the awe in his voice, 'you should be one of the Nine Elders.'

'You would not wish such a fate on me if you knew of what you spoke.' He wearily waved Avanasy's words away.

A tremor of uncertainty ran through Ingrid. Whatever it was he did, it clearly cost him some effort. How much more did Lien have to give? Would they be able to make it out of these twisting mists?

But if Lien felt any such doubts, he did not show them. He only faced forward, and began to chant. His voice was high and thin, oddly loud in the silent world that surrounded them. It chilled Ingrid, and filled her with disquiet, although she could not have said why.

Then, faintly, blessedly, a sound touched her ear. A distant rushing, like the sea, or a crowd of voices heard from a long way off.

The sound of the living world. It could not be anything else.

Slowly, the mist darkened. The rushing noise separated. Ingrid could make out the sound of wind in the trees, a crackle, like dust falling, and the sharp sound of fires burning.

Lien held out his hand to Medeoan. She took it, and held out hers to Avanasy. Avanasy caught up Ingrid's hand in his firm, familiar grip, and took the Empress's hand.

Lien walked forward. Disdainful of the wooden sides of the ship, he strode straight ahead. Ingrid closed her eyes and let herself be pulled along, following the tug of Avanasy's hand.

Ingrid's shoes touched solid ground, and the cool air around her turned warm. She breathed out a sigh of relief, and opened her eyes.

And she looked out to see the charred remains of a scraggly forest and a rocky hillside that looked down onto a ravine filled with blackened stone and plumes of gray smoke. The myriad, terrible scents of burning assailed her nose. She clapped her hand against her mouth and stumbled backward, and fell.

A man groaned, and Ingrid suppressed a scream. A mound

of ash moved, and was not ash, but a man, a man burned black and red who looked up at her with startling blue eyes.

'Vyshemir's knife! Peshek!' cried Avanasy, falling to his knees and raising a cloud of ash.

Peshek? Ingrid's mind refused to encompass it for a moment. This ruined man was Peshek.

The ruined man reached out to Avanasy, his ravaged throat struggling to croak out a few sounds.

'No, Peshek, no.' Avanasy's own voice cracked. 'Lie still, lie still. I'll help you, but you must . . .'

'There you are,' said a new voice. 'I've been waiting.'

Ingrid scrambled to her feet. Avanasy rose more slowly, as a man's form emerged from the shadows.

He was lean and brown. Ashes turned his bare feet gray, and more ash settled in his braided hair.

Avanasy moved at once to stand in front of Medeoan and Ingrid.

'Who are you?' he demanded.

Medeoan stepped around him, her eyes wide. 'Yamuna.'

The lean man bowed, palms over his eyes, and an air of complete mockery made more terrible by the destruction around them, and by Peshek still as death at their feet. Ingrid saw that his hands were mismatched. One of them was smooth and strong, the hand of a much younger man.

'I am flattered so illustrious a one would recognize so humble a servant as myself.' Yamuna straightened up. 'Your husband has sought long and hard for you, Majesty, but I fear you are a little late in returning.' He smiled toward the cloud of smoke that hung in the distance. Ingrid could smell nothing but burning, and her throat itched from the smoke and ash they had to breathe even here.

Medeoan went white. She swayed for a bare instant, and murmured a single word. 'Kacha.'

Yamuna smiled. 'Yes, poor, young Kacha. The Nine Elders were more frightened by his maneuvers than he realized, and played their highest card against him.'

'Highest . . .'

'No,' croaked Lien. 'No.'

'Yes, old man,' said Yamuna with mock solemnity. 'They chose to summon one of the four immortal guardians, and the one they selected was the Phoenix.'

'The Phoenix?' stammered Medeoan. 'They brought the Firebird into the world?'

'And it is not pleased with your realm.' Yamuna pursed his lips and shook his head at the smoke, even as his dark eyes gleamed.

'You did this.' Medeoan clenched her fists. 'Your magic allowed all this!'

'So it did,' agreed Yamuna. 'And now, my magic will allow me to make an end of you, as well as your man here.' He held up a bottle of scarlet glass, and a chill swept across Medeoan's skin. She glanced at Avanasy's face, and saw how he groped for a spell, for a defense against whatever magic was to come. Yamuna raised his arm. Medeoan lifted her hands, as did Lien.

Ingrid leapt. She tackled Yamuna with all her weight and they fell together. She rolled over, coming up on top of the skinny old man, clutching the wrist of his impossibly young hand in both of hers. He snarled and struggled, but she hung grimly on. His fingers loosened from around the bottle, and it fell.

It dropped into Avanasy's outstretched hand. Avanasy stumbled forward, handing it to Lien, who received it quickly. Yamuna screamed and Ingrid screamed, but she had been distracted and he threw her off, causing her to hit the ground hard, and take in a lungful of ash. Choking and sputtering, she forced herself to her feet. Yamuna was already standing.

Avanasy snatched up a pike that lay beside a dead man. Ingrid heard the hiss as the hot metal touched his flesh, and now he too screamed, but he wheeled around. Avanasy charged forward, and the pike spitted flesh and bone and heart.

Yamuna fell without a sound.

Avanasy dropped the pike and stood over the body, panting for a long moment. Ingrid moved to his side, as did Medeoan, but he did not seem aware of them. Ingrid's lungs and eyes burned, and she knew he felt the same, but she also knew that his heat did not only come from outside. It came from the rage that would not be quieted by the death of this enemy. This man's whole world should burn for what he had done, what he was doing to Peshek, and Medeoan, and himself, and Isavalta, and to her, to Ingrid.

'There is no time for this, Master Avanasy,' said Lien's voice, sounding far sharper than Ingrid had yet heard it.

They all turned, and Ingrid saw thunder and fear in Lien's face.

'The Phoenix has been unleashed. We must get away from here at once.'

'No!' cried Medeoan before Avanasy could speak a word. 'Master Lien, if this is the Firebird, it flies in Isavalta. I cannot leave my people . . .'

'There is nothing you can do!' Lien shouted in reply. 'It is one of the four immortal guardians. It will fly until it has destroyed Hung-Tse's enemies.' He swallowed hard. His face had gone deathly pale. 'I must return home. I must warn Cai-Yun . . .'

'Master.' Avanasy's wounded hand curled up. 'Do not lose your way.'

'You don't understand.' Lien pulled himself roughly from Avanasy's grasp. 'The Phoenix will seek out Hung-Tse's enemies. After Isavalta, who is a greater enemy than myself?

Than my niece who aids my vengeance out of loyalty? I must get her to safety . . .' What little color she had faded from the Empress's cheeks. 'No,' whispered Medeoan. She knotted her fists and grit her teeth hard.

Avanasy turned to say something to the Empress, but Ingrid did not hear it. Her ears were ringing and her eyes were filled up with memory – the house of bones on its taloned legs, the famine-thin hag with her black iron teeth, the growling dogs, the watching cat. Ingrid's hand flew to her mouth. She began to tremble. Despite the golden heat radiating from overhead, the world about her had gone suddenly cold, and she could do nothing but shiver.

'Ingrid, what is it?' Avanasy stretched his hand out toward her.

'The . . . Old Witch,' gasped Ingrid from between her fingers. 'Oh, God, Oh, Mary, she told me. She told me she knew how to cage the Firebird.'

Avanasy gaped. 'She said this?'

Ingrid nodded, pressing her hand against her mouth as if she were about to be sick. Gently, Avanasy urged her to sit. She thumped clumsily onto the ground, raising up a cloud of soot, unable to look anywhere but straight ahead, unable to see anything but Baba Yaga.

'You have spoken with the Bony-Legged Witch?' said Medeoan, sounding half angry, half disbelieving.

Again, Ingrid nodded. 'She . . . called me to her. She has something she wants me to do. She said . . . she said that I would come to her a third time, that I would beg to be allowed to do this thing, because only she knew how to cage the Firebird.'

'Is this true?' the Empress demanded of Avanasy.

'Yes.' Avanasy dropped to one knee at Ingrid's side. 'Oh, Ingrid, why did you not tell me?'

Ingrid let her hand fall into her lap. 'I meant to. At first, I didn't want to add to your worries. Then, so much was happening . . .' she gestured vaguely at Lien and the Empress. 'As foolish as it sounds, I forgot.'

'No. It is not foolish. It is easy to forget what happens in the Land of Death and Spirit. It is as when we walk in dreams.' He took her hand. 'Do not reproach yourself.'

'What did the Old Witch want of you?' asked Medeoan flatly.

Ingrid shook her head. 'I'm not sure. I can't remember clearly. Something that had been stolen from her . . .' She tried to concentrate, but the memories slipped through her mind's fingers like water. 'I don't know anymore. I'm sorry.'

'It doesn't matter,' said Avanasy. 'We know the knowledge exists. We will seek it out.'

'None of this matters,' said Lien, his cold voice cutting across whatever else might be said. 'It is too late. The Phoenix has flown ahead of us. It has already burned the army of Isavâlta.'

Ingrid thought Medeoan was going to faint. The Empress swayed on her feet, as white as the mists surrounding them.

Avanasy gripped the Empress's hand. 'We can still save Isavalta. We will . . .'

'You will stay to die!' shouted Lien. 'Do you not hear me! The Phoenix will not permit your empire to survive. Your capital may already be on fire, you can't know. We cannot wait here for you to come to your senses. I will not leave my child . . . my niece to its judgment.'

'How do I find the Old Witch?' Ingrid asked, putting out one hand to push herself to her feet.

Avanasy covered her hand with his free one. 'Ingrid, no. I can't let you do this. I don't know what going alone into the Silent Lands will do to you. I have not had time to understand

the whole of your ... divided state. If you attempt this,'
Avanasy's voice dropped to an urgent whisper, 'you may not be
able to return to the mortal world. I will go and bargain with
the Old Witch.'

'With what?' said Ingrid. 'I'm the one she wants. What else
do you have to give her?'

She knew nothing of Isavalta, except for some coastline and
one fishing village. She had no obligations there, no family,
except Avanasy, and Avanasy said she did not need to do this
thing, that another way could be found. She could let that
happen. She did not need to go back to that place, to face that
... hag again. She did not need to acknowledge the split in
herself before Avanasy could heal her. It did not have to
happen.

Yet, even as she told herself that as firmly as she could, she
knew she lied. She knew what wild fires were. She had seen
them on the mainland, the after-effects of the loggers' efforts.
She had seen smoke blackening the sky and smelled the
choking stench. She had heard the screams.

No, she knew nothing of Isavalta, but she knew very well
what had been visited upon the Isavaltans.

'There is no other way, Avanasy,' said the Empress.

Avanasy's face creased, at first Ingrid thought from anger,
but then she knew it was from the effort to hold that anger
back. 'You would order this from one who is not even subject
to you?'

The Empress did not flinch at this question. 'I am not
ordering her, she is freely offering.'

'Do I have to take this off?' Ingrid asked, touching the
braid on her wrist. 'Or can I just ... go as I am?'

Avanasy wanted to protest. He wanted to rage, Ingrid was
sure of it, but she also saw how terribly he knew that there was
no other choice. Whatever must be done to cage the Firebird,

it would surely involve magic, and strong magic at that. Even she could see that much. If he drained himself white to gain the secret of this working, the Empress would be left alone to do what must be done afterwards, and that could not be allowed either.

'No,' he said sorrowfully. 'If the Old Witch wants you, she will take you. All you need to do is speak her name. Do not remove the braid. It will, I think, lessen the disorientation and difficulty you will have as you move through the Silent Lands.' His fingers trailed gently around her wrist. 'And as with the ring, the binding of the spell will help bring you back to me.'

'I will set vigil for you myself,' announced Lien. 'If you can do this thing, you will be saving my family's lives.'

'Well, then.' Ingrid faced Avanasy, and smoothed down her apron. 'I'd best get on with it.'

But Avanasy's eyes glistened brightly. He grasped both of Ingrid's hands and drew them up close to his chest. She could feel his heart beating hard and frightened, even underneath his woolen coat. 'Listen to me, Ingrid. Courtesy is all where you are going. Do not fail to be polite, to anyone or anything. Accept nothing until you know the conditions under which it is given. Refuse nothing that is freely given, and trust your heart over your eyes.'

'I'll remember,' she told him gravely.

'I love you.'

'I'll remember that as well.' She kissed him softly, feeling afresh how the warmth of his mouth was like no other heat there could be. Not even the fire still smoldering around her could burn her so deeply.

Then, she let go of his hands and walked away from him. She faced the blackened forest. The sooty wind teased at her disheveled hair.

'Baba Yaga!' she cried out, as if she stood at the back door of her father's house calling one of her little siblings in for supper. 'I know you're out there! I'll do what you want if you'll tell me how to cage the Firebird. Do you hear me, Baba Yaga?'

There was no transition. Ingrid was simply elsewhere and she did not understand how it could be so. Bewildered she stared about her, and her confusion only deepened.

This was not the Land of Death and Spirit as she had seen it before. These were not the dense pine forests lit by the directionless glow. These were ordinary pine trees, hedged by fern and bramble. Birds called to one another overhead and mosquitoes whined uncomfortably near. High summer had passed, and the green leaves of the underbrush paled toward autumn's yellow. The wind smelled of pine resin and fresh water, and she knew where she was.

She was home. This was Sand Island. She was sure of it. If she headed south, she would come to her family's house. How had she come to be home so suddenly? What had gone wrong?

Ingrid didn't know what to do. She had expected the fairyland, and the insistent tugging telling her where to go. Not to be home, not to be alone.

Because no other idea came to her, she hiked up her skirts and trudged southward. She moved only because she could not stand still in the middle of the woods. Her mind was so awhirl with astonishment, she had no clear idea whether she thought movement itself could bring her answers, or whether it was merely an instinctual reaction to get clear of the mosquitoes the frost had not yet come to kill.

In the distance, she heard someone humming a familiar tune. Ingrid broke into a run, shoving aside the brush and brambles with her elbows. There, in a small clearing, stood

Grace, smiling her sunny smile and breaking dead branches into kindling.

'Grace!' cried Ingrid, running up to her sister's side.

Grace turned and looked at her mildly, with no surprise or ruffling of her expression at all. 'Hello, Ingrid. What are you doing here?'

'Grace, I'm home,' Ingrid panted. 'I'm back.'

'Why?'

'Wh . . . why?' Ingrid could only stammer in surprise.

'Yes, why?'

Ingrid stared at her sister. Grace just smiled, the sunny, careless smile that Ingrid knew so well.

Why am I here? Ingrid rubbed her forehead. The sun warmed her shoulders. The scents and sights she had known all her life surrounded her. She had been away, she knew that, and there had been good reason, but now . . . now . . .

'I came home,' she said uncertainly.

'Well good,' said Grace. 'You can help me carry this.' She handed Ingrid a bundle of kindling wood.

'Yes, all right.' Ingrid's hands closed around the deadwood. It smelled of earth and bark and pricked her hands. She tucked the bundle under one arm. Grace hoisted her own bundle onto her shoulder and took Ingrid's hand. Ingrid had forgotten what her sister's touch felt like, that warm, light palm. Grace was a grown woman, but walking with her still felt like walking with a child, cheerful, careless, enjoying the moment.

Grace swung their arms, and began to sing. '*An old man come courtin' me, fa-la-la-loodle!*

'*An old man come courtin' me, hi-derry-down!*'

Ingrid grinned. They had sung this one together so often, she joined in instantly.

'*An old man come a-courtin' me, all for to marry me,*

'*Maids when you're young, never wed an old man!*'

Grace began to giggle, and Ingrid could not help herself. She began to laugh as well. It was so good here, so simple, walking with her sister, all forgiven, heading for home and hearth with nothing more complicated than a bundle of firewood to carry.

'*It's when that we went to church, fa-la-la-loodle . . .*'

Ingrid faltered for a moment. What had needed to be forgiven? What had she done?

'Look,' Grace broke off the song. 'There's Leo.'

Leo stood beneath a birch tree, his scythe raised. Fresh cut brush lay in heaps at his feet.

'Be careful!' Ingrid cried at once, although she didn't know why.

Leo swung the scythe down; it tore through the tangle of brush and saplings, laying them flat on the ground.

'So, you've turned up at last, have you?' he said, bringing the scythe around again. 'I don't suppose you remembered to think of your family while you were gone?'

No, she hadn't. She had been too busy, with . . . all that needed doing. She had been . . . on the mainland? In Bayfield? Further? Had she gone to Chicago? Ingrid shook her head. It was wrong to return without a gift, that much was clear. But what did she have? She had left so much behind already.

She groped in her apron pocket, and brought out a spear tip. She did not remember placing it there, but it didn't matter. Leo would like this.

'Here, Leo,' she said, extending it. 'This is for you.'

He shouldered the scythe and took the spear tip. He held it up to the light as if it were a coin of dubious quality.

'Well, all right then,' he said, pocketing the shining piece of metal. 'Better get on, the both of you. Mama's waiting.' He jerked his thumb over his shoulder in the direction of home.

Grace took Ingrid's hand again. 'That was a good gift, sister.'

'Yes.' Ingrid fell into step beside her. She felt lighter and emptier at the same time. But she was happy. She was walking and singing with her sister. She was going home.

'It's when we were walkin' home, fa-la-la-loodle!
'It's when we were walkin' home, hi-derry-down!
'It's when we were walkin' home, he let me walk alone.
'Maids when you're young, never wed an old man!'

'Look,' said Grace suddenly. 'There's Papa.'

Ingrid looked, and there was Papa standing in the clearing with his gun. A rustling filled the long, blanched grasses and Papa aimed and shot, the gun sounding horribly loud in the still afternoon.

What a strange time to be hunting rabbits, thought Ingrid, perplexed. *Rabbits are all underground in the middle of the day.*

'What are you hunting, Papa?' she asked.

Papa cracked open his shot gun and reloaded the breech. 'What's been lost,' he said tersely. 'What are you hunting, young woman?'

'What's been stolen,' answered Ingrid promptly. *But why? What does that mean?*

Papa just grunted and sighted along the barrel of his shot gun again. 'And what have you brought home for your father?'

Ingrid dug in her other apron pocket. This time, she brought out a tiny golden statue of a long-tailed bird in flight.

'Here, Papa.' She handed it to him carefully, suddenly afraid she might drop the precious thing. She could not lose this. It was precious, but she didn't know why, or where it had come from, or how it had come to be part of her.

Part of me? This is part of me?

Papa snatched the golden icon off her palm and turned it over, examining its workmanship before he tucked it into his shirt pocket. 'I suppose that'll do,' he grunted, not looking at them, but staring off across the clearing. 'Get along, both of you. Mama's waiting.'

Grace took her hand and led her away, even as the grasses began to rustle again, and another shot exploded through the warm air.

'Grace,' said Ingrid as her sister took her hand again. 'What's happening?'

'We're going to see Mama,' said Grace with a grin. This time, her teeth, bared as she smiled, seemed unaccountably sharp.

'It's when that we went to bed, fa-la-la-loodle!
'It's when that we went to bed, hi-derry-down!
'It's when that we went to bed, he lay as if he were dead.
'Maids when you're young, never wed an old man!'

But this time Ingrid did not join in. She felt too hollow for singing. Where was she? She was with Leo, and with Papa, and with Grace, but what was with herself? She hunted what had been stolen, but she was led away to Mama. How was she to look for it if she was being led to Mama?

'Look,' said Grace. 'There's Mama.'

Ingrid looked. She saw the back of their house, with the outbuildings and the chicken coop. Mama stood beside the big, iron laundry kettle, stirring it with the long, well-worn paddle. But no steam rose from the kettle. In the next moment, Ingrid saw why. No fire burned underneath the pot.

'Well, you're here at last,' said Mama grimly. 'Lay the fire, you two.'

Ingrid knelt beside the kettle and laid down her bundle of wood. 'Mama, why are you stirring before the fire's lit?'

'I'm keeping fresh a past that's gone missing,' she answered. 'Why are you wandering loose in the woods?'

'I'm looking for a heart that's been stolen,' said Ingrid, laying out the wood to be ready for the fire. *Why? Why? I don't understand. Why am I saying these things? Why am I here?*

She stared at the pile of sticks. *What is happening?*

'Light the fire, Ingrid,' said Grace, sitting back on her haunches and grinning at Ingrid with her oddly pointed teeth.

Ingrid automatically reached in her pocket for matches, but her pocket was empty. 'I can't,' she said muzzily. 'I must have given it away.'

Grace shook her head and clucked her tongue. Above them, Mama stirred the kettle relentlessly. The liquid inside sloshed, making the sides of the great kettle ring.

'You should not have given so much,' Mama grumbled. 'I dare say you didn't even bring anything for your poor mother.'

Ingrid searched her pockets, unaccountably frightened, but there was nothing to be found.

'I'm sorry,' she stammered. 'Really. I didn't mean . . .'

'Oh, Ingrid,' sighed Grace. 'Whatever are we going to do with you? You have so much, and know so little of anything you carry. You'll waste it all on trivialities, and never know what you could have been.'

'Nothing else for it, then,' muttered Mama.

'No, I'm afraid not.' Grace's eyes glinted. She snapped her fingers, and a fire sprang to life underneath the kettle. But the fire wasn't . . . right. It should have burned red and gold. Ingrid was sure of it. Grace's fire burned bright green. She had seen such light elsewhere. Where? It was important. Where had she seen that light?

'In you get,' said Grace cheerfully.

'What?' Ingrid scrambled to her feet, her heart pounding hard.

'If you've nothing else to give, you must give yourself.' Mama's paddle stirred the thick, black liquid in steady, even strokes. It had already begun to steam. 'In you get.' She nodded toward the kettle.

'No! Mama, Grace, no!' Ingrid backed away. She'd die in

that darkness, she'd drown. She'd lose what little of herself she had left, the tiny spark inside her would be snuffed out. She knew it, and she didn't know what else to do.

'Nothing else for it,' rumbled Papa's voice behind her. Ingrid swung around. Papa emerged from the woods, his gun tucked casually under his arm, and a brace of birds slung over his shoulder. Leo walked beside him, his scythe held in both hands ready to swing up. 'You didn't bring enough.'

'You never did,' said Mama to the black liquid. 'Tries, and tries, and it's never enough for her, is it? Would have been enough for anyone else, but not for her, oh no. Can't let go, can't let it be enough, ever. Well, now you're called on to give the last, my girl.'

'You've always offered that much, but no one's ever taken you up on it, have they?' Grace's eyes were very green, and slanted in her face.

Not right. Too much wrong here. She stared around at Mama, at Papa, at Leo. Then she saw the blade of Leo's scythe wasn't steel. It was stone, stained dark with something that was not tree resin.

'Why are you doing this?' she cried. '*Why?*'

'Because you won't stop,' said Leo, stepping closer.

'Because you can't be stopped.' Papa stepped away from Leo, blocking Ingrid's path.

'Because there are limits to any power,' said Mama without breaking the pace of her endless stirring.

'Because you've been divided and remade into something new,' said Grace pleasantly. 'Unnatural thing that you are, you cannot be held back in any of the usual ways, as you fall under none of the usual provinces. She knew that. Now.' Grace's eyes shone green with the same light that came from the strange fire under Mama's kettle. 'In you get.'

She? She? Ingrid backed away, but there was nowhere to

go. Grace, strangely altered as she was, stood behind her. The rest of her family surrounded her, pressed against her, herding her toward the great, dark steaming kettle.

'Still afraid.'

'In the end always afraid. So ready to give, until the end, then there is only fear.'

'No!' shouted a new voice. Ingrid jerked her head around.

Everett Lederle, his blue Union army cap askew on his head and his clasp knife open in his hand. 'Ingrid, here! Run!'

'Everett!' Ingrid cried, and leapt toward him, pushing past her family in one burst of speed until she was beside him, her arms thrown around his neck in gratitude. 'Mary Mother of God, Everett. How did you know?'

'Don't worry about it.' Everett wrapped one arm around her waist. He brandished his knife at her family who stood clustered around Mama's kettle. The green light gleamed in their eyes and caught the smooth stone of Leo's scythe blade. 'I've got you safe now. None of them will touch you while you're with me.'

But why should they stay back? Ingrid swallowed and pulled away just a little. Leo had his scythe, and Papa had a gun. All Everett had was his tiny knife. *Why stay away?*

'Everett, what's happening?'

'I don't know. We just need to get out of here. We'll figure it out later.' He grasped her hand and tugged her toward the house. 'Come on.'

But Ingrid held her ground. 'Everett, I have to find . . . There's something stolen and I have to find it.'

'I know, I know.' He patted her hand. 'But not here, Ingrid. You're not safe. We have to get away.'

Grace's eyes glowed and she stepped forward. 'Yes, run away, Ingrid. Do.' Her teeth, yellow now, and shining like her eyes, snapped.

'Take her away from here, ungrateful girl,' muttered Mama, stirring, constantly stirring. 'Get her out of my sight.'

'Yes. Do.' Now Leo took a step forward, hefting his strange, stained, stone scythe.

'Ingrid, please,' said Everett, retreating before Leo's fierce grin, pulling her back toward the safety of the house. 'Let's go!'

Papa lifted his gun.

She should run, she knew it. The ones who faced her were dangerous. She knew that with all her heart. Everett was safe. He would protect her and keep her close, as he had always sought to do. Why didn't she run? What held her here?

Trust your heart over your eyes, said a voice in her memory. Whose voice? What memory? She didn't know. Her head swam. Papa put his gun to his shoulder. Everett yanked on her hand, almost pulling her off her feet. He wanted to save her, to keep her close, to keep her from drowning in Mama's kettle, that was somehow the source of all this danger. She had been led here, and now she was being torn away from here by these people who were not quite her family. But Everett was Everett still. Wasn't he?

Ingrid looked up into Everett's eyes. They were blue as she remembered. His grip was as strong as she had always known it would be.

The knife he carried had a blade of stone like Leo's scythe.

'Please, Ingrid,' he said desperately. 'There's no more time! Let me get you out of here!'

'No more time,' repeated Ingrid.

And she ran.

She tore herself from Everett's grip and she charged toward her family. She knocked Papa's gun away. Leo's scythe swished past her. Grace stretched out clawed hands, and Mama lifted her paddle, but Ingrid did not break her stride. She dove forward, flinging herself headlong into the steaming kettle.

Ingrid fell into darkness. Nothing touched her, no heat, no

cold, no air, no light. She fell, flailing her limbs, and there was no light above or below, only emptiness and falling as in a nightmare, but she did not wake. She screamed, but the sound went nowhere, and still she fell.

Just as she thought for sure she must faint, the fall was over. There was no sensation of landing, just of ceasing to fall. She stood, she thought. There seemed to be some uneven surface underfoot, and she seemed to be whole and unhurt, but she could see nothing. Blackness as thick as blindness surrounded her.

'So,' said a voice Ingrid was sure she should have known. 'Not afraid enough.'

Two eyes opened in the darkness. They were huge and green and slanted. Animal's eyes, feral and cunning. Grace's eyes as Ingrid had last seen them in the face of the apparition who had been Grace and yet could not have been.

Her throat closed, and Ingrid swallowed hard.

'You cannot see, Little Woman?' inquired the voice. 'How very rude of me.'

There was a soft pop, as if someone had snapped their fingers. Green fire sprang up before Ingrid. She blinked hard and stumbled backward.

When she could look again, she saw a gigantic fox lounging on the other side of the fire. The light in her eyes was the same light that filled the green flames that burned without fuel between them. All of Ingrid's memories came back in a single wave, of where she had seen this green light before, of who she was and why she had come to this strange place, and how this must be the Silent Lands, and who waited on the other shore for her.

'I beg your pardon.' Ingrid's voice shook. The Vixen's mouth fell open, laughing. Her rank scent filled the place where Ingrid stood. The green fire illuminated only a small space around them. She thought this might be a cave, but she could not be sure. 'I did not mean to intrude, I only . . .'

'I know what you want, Little Woman.' The Vixen nodded her head toward Ingrid's feet. 'And you have won it. I give it to you freely.'

Ingrid looked down. At her feet, in a small hollow of rough stone, gleamed a golden ball about the size of Ingrid's fist. She picked it up, marveling at its great weight and cool smooth skin as it lay in her hand.

She was looking for what had been stolen. She was looking for a heart that had been taken. She knew that, although she did not fully understand how. In that same way of understanding, she knew this golden ball held what she needed.

'Why . . .' she began, and then she stopped. Questions might be dangerous here. They might be considered rude. The answers might have conditions she could not meet.

'Why did I take it?' The Vixen cocked her head. 'Why do I give it back now?' She lifted one great paw and scratched her chin thoughtfully. 'Perhaps one day when the Old Witch had gone about some errand, she left her heart behind, as she is wont to do from time to time. Perhaps someone crept into her window and stole it then. Perhaps they meant it as a joke, or perhaps they meant it in earnest, for without her heart, without knowing who held it or what they might do with it, how could the Old Witch go about her business? How could she even dare to leave the safety of her house?' The Vixen's eyes gleamed dangerously. 'For she has much power and many enemies, the Old Witch does.'

Ingrid swallowed again, and clutched the golden ball close to her chest.

'But perhaps there was a little man who aspired to divinity and I was asked by one whom I'm glad to have owe me a favor to stop his plans.' The Vixen grinned. 'Perhaps I saw the future and it amused me to help it come about. Perhaps I just saw an opportunity to anger the Old Witch. It could be all these things, or none of them.' Her teeth were white, and very sharp. 'What would you give to know the answer to that riddle, Little Woman?'

Courtesy is all where you are going. Avanasy had said that to her. How could she have forgotten, even for an instant. Ingrid pushed the guilt away. This was not the time.

'Thank you for your hospitality,' she said, dropping a curtsy to the Vixen. 'I am very much afraid that it is time for me to go.'

'Perhaps,' laughed the Vixen, swishing her tail back and forth. 'Take care of what you've been given, Little Woman, and take care of your daughter while you can.'

'I . . .' began Ingrid. But she stopped. She had meant to say, 'I have no daughter,' but standing knee deep in memories freshly brought back to her, she realized she could not remember when her time had last come. So much had been happening, she had completely lost track of her days.

Was she carrying Avanasy's child? She could well be. One hand went automatically to her belly.

The Vixen threw back her head and let out a snarling, growling laugh that went straight through to Ingrid's bones. 'Go, Little Woman, get away with you, before I decide perhaps I'd like to keep you here.' Eyes and teeth flashed in the light of the green flames. 'Or your daughter.'

Grabbing up her hems, Ingrid turned and ran. The Vixen's growling laugh followed fast behind her, and she had no thought but to get away from it. She stumbled through the darkness, the golden ball held tight to her bosom. Gradually, she saw light up ahead. It was strange and diffuse, and certainly not daylight, but she followed it anyway, because she had no other guide.

At last, Ingrid stumbled out into the odd, pale light of the Land of Death and Spirit. Ahead of her lay a green meadow surrounded by the dark piney woods she remembered. Behind her rose a smooth, green hill like a bubble from a pot of water. A single thorn tree grew from its crown, spreading its branches up to the sunless sky. She knew this place. She had been here before.

Ingrid saw no movement from the dark cave mouth from which she had emerged, but she hurried on toward the piney woods anyway.

The only question being, which way do I go? She looked around for the river, for her other self, and saw only the dark tree trunks in every direction.

Something pushed at her palm. Ingrid stared at her hand where it held the golden ball. The ball stirred against her and pushed outward, as if seeking release.

Slowly, uncertainly, Ingrid set the ball onto the grass. It glinted for a moment in the pale, greenish light, and then it began to roll toward the woods. With nothing else to do, Ingrid followed.

She followed the ball into the darkness that gathered under the pine trees. The thick carpet of needles should have crunched underfoot, but it did not. She followed the ball across the narrow brook that ran silently over the rounded stones that lined its bed. The water did not wet her shoes or the trailing hem of her skirt.

She followed it until the trees changed from pine to oaks and maples, and she saw the lone, crooked birch tree that spread its branches as if to bar her way. The golden ball rolled unhesitatingly beneath it, and the branches sagged, defeated, to let Ingrid past.

Ahead stood the fence mended with bones. The cat perched on top of it, ears alert. The bone gate swung open for the golden ball, and Ingrid followed. She was owed for this and that knowledge removed her fear as she stood in the torn and savaged yard before the house on its scarred and taloned legs, turning and with each step gouging up great chunks of mud.

The golden ball stopped and Ingrid waited, her hands folded neatly over her apron. Slowly, the house stopped turning and knelt so that its splintered steps touched the ground and its door could fall open.

Baba Yaga stood in the doorway, leaning on her stained pestle. Eagerly, the golden ball skipped up the steps and hopped into her hand. Baba Yaga caught it firmly in one skinny claw. With the other, she rapped on it with her knuckles. The gold cracked open and fell away. Inside lay an egg, smooth and white and gleaming. Baba Yaga cracked that too. The white spilled away leaving something red and blue and pulsing in her crabbed hand. Baba Yaga looked at the thing hungrily for a moment, then tucked it inside her tattered black robe, as if she were tucking away a full purse or a precious locket.

When she drew out her hand again, Baba Yaga smiled, a rictus grin that exposed all her black, iron teeth. Ingrid shuddered but held her ground. The Old Witch set aside her pestle, and did a thing Ingrid had never seen her do before. She walked down the steps of her house.

As she came nearer, bone thin and bent, her eyes nearly as hollow as a ghost's, Ingrid felt her nerve fail her. Her knees began to shake and she wanted more than anything to run away, but she could not. Baba Yaga held her pinned with her dark gaze.

The Old Witch stood before her now. Ingrid should have been able to feel her breath, but could not. She smelled a dry, musty scent, like old dust, like bones.

In a single, swift motion, Baba Yaga kissed Ingrid on the

mouth. Ingrid staggered back, only just keeping her balance. Her mouth filled with the tang of cold iron.

And she knew how to cage the Firebird. She knew it like she knew her own name. She could forget everything else, and she would remember this, she was sure of it.

Ingrid thought to stammer out her thanks, but one glance from Baba Yaga silenced her utterly.

'You have been paid your price, now go. I have business to which I must attend.' There was a quality in those words that made Ingrid shiver. She was about to speak up to say she did not know which way to go, but the world around her was already fading. She did not feel herself being dragged, so much as all that was around her seemed to be rushing away, wrinkling, like a cloth pulled from a table. She screamed, because she feared another long fall into darkness.

Ingrid woke.

Chapter Twenty

She might not have moved at all. She was in the burned forest on the hillside. Lien knelt beside Peshek's racked body, but . . . Ingrid blinked and looked again. Peshek was ruined no more. His skin was red and blistered, but no longer blackened. His breath did not rattle in his chest as he lay on the scant bed of coats that had been spread for him. He would live. She could tell that in an instant. 'Magic.'

'And neatly done,' replied Lien. Ingrid jumped. She had not realized she had spoken aloud. 'She is powerful, your Empress.'

Ingrid's first instinct was to say, 'She's not mine,' but she stopped those words. 'Where are they?'

'I sent them down,' he nodded toward the pass where the smoke still hung heavy in the air. 'To see if any lived yet there.'

Ingrid swallowed hard. 'I must find them.' Her blood rushed in her veins, and she knew the sensation to be from the knowledge the Old Witch had given her. She must pass it on and quickly. This was not a secret she was meant to hold.

'Then we will go.' Lien stood. 'You have your answers?'

'I do.' Despite the need for movement that sang inside her, she glanced down at Peshek where he lay, dead to the world. 'Shouldn't you stay . . .'

'All that can be done for him has been done. We will

return.' His voice was stone. He was making his choice. He could not worry about Peshek, because his niece was in a danger he knew better than any of them. Ingrid wanted to berate him, but could not. She just tucked up her hems in her waistband and started down the hillside toward the center of the devastation.

It was a long walk. The wind blew hot and heavy with ash. It was difficult to breathe without coughing. The stones were black with soot. Ingrid's eyes and lungs burned, but she kept slogging forward, the strength of the secret she carried urging her onward. Lien paced quietly beside her, and she was very glad for the presence of another being.

Then, at last, they crested the rise, and looked down on the real horror.

The army had been caught in the blaze with nowhere to flee. Men and beasts had died where they stood, and now were nothing but charred black sticks that once were bones. The stench was unspeakable. Ingrid's hand went immediately to her face, and she had to choke down her bile.

'Come, Mistress,' said Lien, but even his voice shook. 'Come. We must keep going.'

And they did. They waded through the ash and ruin. Ingrid blocked her mouth and nose with her apron held crumpled in both hands. It brought only a small measure of relief. Heat nibbled at her skin and horror nibbled at her mind.

Avanasy and the Empress were easy to find as the only bits of color in a world turned black and gray with death. They stood near the far edge of the worst of the destruction. This must have been the head of the procession. Medeoan looked down at something. It was a hand, an arm, sticking grotesquely out of the soot that had once been a man. It was as burned and as black as all the rest of the dead Ingrid had tried not to see, but Medeoan seemed to see something different about it. She lifted her robe of blackened silk and aimed a swift and vicious kick at the pathetic remains, shattering it into flakes of ash. Then she turned away, and Avanasy put his hand on her shoulder.

'I believe,' murmured Lien. 'The Empress has found her husband.'

Ingrid found a small piece of herself that had not been numbed by her smoldering surroundings and felt pity for the young woman. To be so betrayed . . . could even what she saw now be worse than that?

At last, the sound of their approach reached Avanasy. He looked around quickly, and when he saw Ingrid, his face lit up with a joy incongruous to see in the midst of this burned world, but even so, her heart answered with an equal joy.

'I knew you would find your way!' he cried as he wrapped his arms around her, covering her soot-smudged face with his kisses. 'I knew, I always knew. Oh, Ingrid . . .' They kissed, long and deep then, and when he pulled away, Avanasy looked startled.

'Did the Old Witch give you what we need?'

Medeoan had come up behind Avanasy, her face cold as stone. Whether it was from the devastation of her people, or from what she had just seen between Ingrid and Avanasy, Ingrid could not tell.

'Yes,' Avanasy answered for her, his voice thick with wonder. 'Yes, she did, and Ingrid has given it to me.'

'I would have warned you, if you had given me a moment,' she said, an odd gaiety taking hold in her now that her burden was lifted and Avanasy was before her, whole and sound.

'What must we do?' demanded the Empress. 'How do we begin?'

Avanasy's eyes flicked back and forth, as if he were drawing out some deep memory. 'We need a forge, or a crucible. We need gold and blood to shape the cage, and . . .' he froze, and under his coating of grime, he paled. 'Mortal breath.'

Medeoan bowed her head. 'Of course,' she sighed. 'It would be so, for such a thing, it would be so.'

Despite the heat, Ingrid shivered. 'I don't understand.' She had carried the knowledge inside her, yes, but she had been a vessel only. It was Avanasy who knew what these things brought from the Silent Lands meant.

'Mortal breath.' Avanasy was not looking at her. He was looking at Medeoan where she stood, turned away, her arms wrapped around herself. 'Is the last breath. The dying breath.'

Whatever Ingrid had thought to say died in her throat. Avanasy turned back toward her, his eyes soft.

'Oh, no, Avanasy. You won't . . . you wouldn't . . .'

He took both her hands. 'Ingrid, I'm going to ask you to leave.'

'No.' She gripped him, hard. 'No. Avanasy, listen to me. I'm with child. We're going to have a baby.'

Avanasy's face went completely blank for a moment, as if he could not understand a word that she said. Then, he swept her into his arms and held her so closely she could scarcely breathe.

'Oh, Ingrid,' he breathed against her shoulder. 'Oh, my heart.'

'You can't send me away now. You can't die.' Because he would do it. She had no doubts. He would not let the Empress be the one to sacrifice herself. He would never do such a thing.

'I will only do what I must, Ingrid,' he said, but the soft words had all the force of an oath. Then he drew away, and looked her steadily in the eyes. 'But you must be safe. That is what will sustain me. If I can think on you and our child without fear, I will live. But I cannot do that while this battle may touch you. I beg you, go home. Let Master Lien return you to Sand Island. Wait for me there. I will come for you as soon as I can.'

'But the Firebird may be finished,' she said, grasping at straws. 'Perhaps this is all it was sent to do . . .'

'No, Mistress,' said Lien. Ingrid started. She had forgotten how close he stood. 'The Phoenix will not stop at so little when the whole of an empire has been arrayed against Hung-Tse.'

So little? Ingrid wanted to cry and sweep her hands out to encompass the devastation, but she could only stand and tremble for a moment while the implications of Lien's words sank into her.

'Think of our child, Ingrid,' whispered Avanasy. 'Take our child to safety.'

Ingrid kissed Avanasy then, all other doubts, all other fears drowned in the terrible knowledge that she might never see him again.

When she drew back, he wrapped his arms still more tightly around her and pulled her against him again. 'I will come back to you,' he said, and she felt his breath warm against her cheek as he spoke. 'I swear it, by all that is in me, I swear it.'

She nodded. She did not trust her voice. Avanasy released her and turned to Lien.

'Lien, will you return her to her home? You can then go back to Hung-Tse and take your niece to safety, in case we fail.'

'If you fail, there will in truth be no safety for us,' replied Lien, looking stooped and aged with his new head of white hair. 'But for what she has tried, I will carry Mistress Ingrid to her home.'

'Can we go now?' asked Ingrid, her voice breaking, as she had known it would. 'I can't . . . I don't want . . .'

'Go, Ingrid,' said Avanasy. 'Go and let me know that you are safe.'

She did not say goodbye. She did not look back. She turned on her heel and marched away through the ruin of what had been an army. Lien was beside her, and he took her hand. She did not resist him. He began to chant, to draw on his power, but all she could feel was the touch of Avanasy's lips against hers. All she could think of was the sound of his voice.

She barely noticed when the world faded away from around her.

Medeoan stood at Avanasy's side and tried not to be impatient. One moment, Ingrid and Lien walked through the ruins. The next moment, they were gone. It was not until the wind blew again and raised a whorl of hot ash where they had stood that Avanasy was able to turn away.

She saw the pain in his eyes, and had to resist the urge to shout at him. *What of Isavalta?* she wanted to cry. *What of me?*

But she saw the ravage his emotions had wrought on his face and held her tongue.

'Come, Majesty,' said Avanasy roughly. 'We must see what we can salvage.'

The work was as grim, as hard and as filthy as she imagined it would be. The ash was greasy with grisly fat making what debris there was slick. The stench filled her to the brim. She wrapped her sleeves around her hands to try to stave off the smoldering heat, but it did not work well. She would have blisters soon.

But she went on. All the ruination around her reminded her of Lien's words. This could be Vyshtavos. It could be Camaracost, or Biradost. It could be the whole of Isavalta from Tuukos to Miateshcha, wherever the Firebird decided to fly.

She glanced at the horizon, again and again, terrified at the thought that she would see fresh plumes of smoke.

At last, she and Avanasy, filthy, wheezing and burning with heat and with thirst, assembled what they had been able to find. Avanasy had ranged back along where they thought the baggage train had been and found the smith's cart with its small forge and anvil. They righted it as best they could, but could not move it, so they would perform their working beside it. Medeoan had guessed that Kacha would not be far from the war chest his army carried, and she was right. Some of the gold was only partially melted, and she was able to retrieve the misshapen bits of still-hot metal in the skirts of her robe.

They would need blood as well, but there was no shortage of ways to let that flow.

Behind them, the last rays of the sun shone over the hills. Medeoan imagined she could hear the distant rush of wings that was the Firebird.

Stop! she wanted to cry out. *If you want to fight Isavalta, you will come to me!*

She wiped her brow and tried to calm such thoughts. They would call the Firebird to them soon enough. Avanasy, his voice rough with thirst and ash, had told her what they must do. Pain made his face haggard, but he still held himself still and strong.

He had split open a blackened cart rail and found its center still burned red. Carefully, he took that spark of fire and applied it to the heap of charcoal underneath the iron brazier that was what was left of the portable forge. Medeoan held her breath, and concentrated, and pushed the ruined world, the world where the Firebird roamed at will, away. In this world, her world, there was only Avanasy and the spreading flames, lapping at the half-burned splinters they used for kindling, and the charcoaled wood they had laid on top. In this world there was only the fire and Avanasy's injured hands.

Avanasy's hands that had held Ingrid's face so gently before he kissed her farewell.

Stop that. There is no place for that here. You are not a child. You are Empress, and he serves you. That is all you require.

'Now, Medeoan.'

Relief washed over her at those words. As Avanasy stood and stepped back, Medeoan knelt in front of the fire. Individual flames danced in front of her eyes, in all their shades of gold. Each one could be a feather in the Firebird's plumage, or each one a bar in its cage. It was up to her. This, at last, was one thing she could do for her people, her empire, and for herself.

Medeoan steeled herself. She reached out until the heat of the flames became too much for her already seared and tender skin. With a supreme effort she shut out the sensations of the world one by one – the hot wind, the scents of smoke and burning, the crackle as yet another bone or bracing broke and fell – until all that remained was the pounding of her own heart. She reached down deep, past that familiar rhythm, past the surge of her breath, past the current of her blood and into her spirit. There she drew up the magic cradled there until it flowed freely down her fingertips and into the fire. The barrier of their heat dissolved, and she pushed past it as easily as if it had been cool well-water, until she cupped the flames in her hands.

They were soft to hold, and smooth and delicate as the petals of the rarest flower. Her fingers stroked them lovingly and her magic willed them to grow, to spread, to become white with heat and life. The flames responded to her urgings, turning from individual petals into silken sheets of pure white light. She was aware of the heat in some distant part of her mind but it was of no significance. This fire was hers and could do her no harm. It could only serve. Not even the Phoenix could wrest this fire from her.

She felt the touch of Avanasy's magic even before she glimpsed him kneeling beside her. He was cool and strong, as he ever had been, earth and metal to her fire and air. She welcomed the touch of him, the solid, familiar and loved, yes, loved, presence beside her. The manifestation of her spirit that was her magic opened and made room for his, the pair of them twining together even as he lifted the charred board where they had laid the lumps of gold and emptied them into her fire.

Magic, fire and hands caught the gold. Guided by her will and her work, the flames encircled the gold, claiming its shape, softening it to the texture of molten glass. Avanasy drizzled their pitiful store of water, claimed from a stream nearby, into the crucible, sending up great clouds of steam, and only increasing the greed of Medeoan's fire, and then he bent close, so close his mouth almost touched her fingers, and he breathed out, long and cool across the molten gold.

Medeoan caught the gold and their magic up and her fingers began to spin it into threads, long, hair-fine and pure, as strong as steel and as pliable as flax. In her mind, she fixed the image of the cage, a filigree thing of shining gold, made of all these threads, woven together by sorcery, skill and need. It would be made of all the elements of the world summoned together, and the work of her hands. Her fingers moved, and her mind moved and the gold took shape.

All at once, she saw the Firebird. Burning bright and deadly, she saw it streaking across the pale-blue sky on its own mission. She gasped and her fingers snapped the thread they held in two. The heat bit hard into her skin and her magic faltered.

But there was Avanasy, to catch the broken thread and cup her hands again. He breathed across her fingertips and the heat receded. His power swirled around her, supporting her like bones, like the bars of a golden cage, their cage, the Firebird's cage.

Together, they spun the molten gold. Together they wove the bars of her fire and Avanasy's breath and their mingled blood and in the midst of raging war and the flood of magics, Medeoan felt she at last knew the meaning of her own love.

The mind of the Phoenix burned bright with thoughts of vengeance. The invaders dared to wake its anger, dared to approach the threshold of its home and flail at its people. They would know the fire and they would know a generation of fear. The Phoenix opened its mouth and cried aloud to let its people know they were not abandoned.

Fire gripped Avanasy. Its spirit dragged his down into the flames, spinning it with the gold flames, weaving it into bars. He was the cage, was the fire, was the spell, reaching up and out to find the Firebird. It burned bright. He hungered after it, longed to hold it close. It was his purpose, his need for being. He would give his all to encompass that wildness.

Ingrid. Think also of Ingrid and your child. She waits for you, and you must hold on.

But, oh, how the bird soared free in its beauty, and how brightly it burned, how the gold shimmered with its own fire, and it pulled him, pulled breath from his body, pulled will from his soul.

And Medeoan needed him, and Isavalta needed him.

The cage rose before him, impossibly balanced on the crucible, open like a filigree flower, reaching, waiting.

'Now,' whispered Medeoan. 'Now.'

She plunged her hands and her magic deep into the fire.

Vyshemir, I never knew her true strength. She caught him up as easily as a handful of chaff and flung him into the air. He soared free on the gout of flame, his own power the connection between flame and cage, and the flame sought its living avatar, and flashed toward the Phoenix, and touched the bird, and merged as it must, for that was the nature of the world.

And Avanasy, suspended between earth and sky began to pull.

I can't breathe. I can't breathe. I am stretched too far. There is too much heat. I can't breathe.

I must breathe. I must live.

Ingrid waited for him. He had to live to cross to her, to carry her home. She carried their child.

Avanasy breathed, and, with all the strength of purely human need, pulled.

The Firebird was impossibly huge. The sun never burned so brightly, nor in so many colors of flame. Its cry was sharper than the screams of the dying, more thunderous than the wood that exploded at the merest brush of its wings. It was vengeance, it was protection. It was fire in all its forms set loose. It cast no shadow, for it was nothing but light.

It surely must consume the world.

But then, the Firebird paused in its flight, hovering over the darkening plains. Then it spread its wings and loosed a strange, new cry. Fire leapt up from the ranges it had left, fresh fire, strange fire. The new flame stretched out and it and the bird's fiery plumage melted into one.

Then the Firebird began to sink.

★　★　★

No! screamed the Firebird.

Medeoan started, and almost dropped the weaving again. She had not expected the creature to have a voice.

The heat of it was volcanic. It seared the skin on her face and scalp. Medeoan felt she must burst into flame at any second. Her fire seemed such a slender thread by comparison, but it held, and it dragged the great Phoenix down to her cage.

Their cage. Avanasy clung tightly to the delicate bars, holding the weaving together with magic and will as the bird fell closer, pulled by her fire.

Stop! You have no right to interfere! screamed the bird inside her mind.

'I am the Empress of Isavalta!' cried out Medeoan. 'I will protect my own!'

The Firebird shrank and shriveled, its fire fading as her flame bound it ever more tightly. Now it was the size of a swan, then a crane, a heron, a great golden eagle. Now, it was the size of a hawk, and Medeoan's flame pulled it down into the waiting cage that balanced atop the crucible.

It was then Medeoan felt it. The real burning. Not the physical fire that blistered her skin and singed her hair. She felt the burning inside, the fire that stretched from the center of the earth to the stars and the sun, the single flame at the heart of all fire. It lanced through her like pain and elation, and she knew all at once what she was trying to bind.

She caught sight of Avanasy beside her, gripping the cage. His skin cracked with heat and his face was blistered. His brows were a single smear of ash, and pain turned him gray, but he held. His knees buckled under him, but still he held, and still he breathed out, a single long exhalation into the smoke and steam of her fire, swirling around the immortal bird, penetrating it, and binding it fast.

The Firebird was only the size of a raven now, and

Medeoan grasped the woven gold and bent the bars over its head. It flailed, striking out with wings and beak, and her hands burned where it touched and she screamed with the pain, but Avanasy cooled her flesh with his breath and she held her flames in control, and the cage began to weave itself closed under her fingers.

You will pay for this, screamed the Firebird. *Life and blood and realm I will have from you. You will pay with your whole life for this act!*

Medeoan shaped the gold and fire together, weaving them into a ring to hold the bars, to suspend the cage. But in the flicker of the flame she thought she saw images. She saw a young man, and she saw herself, impossibly aged, holding the tasseled girdle up before him. She saw Ingrid, no, not Ingrid, the girl had Avanasy's face, standing before her, her expression full of bitter gall. She saw herself dying on a couch, alone, in the cold, and the Firebird soaring free over a stone tower.

It doesn't matter. Nothing matters but what I do now. Medeoan drew on the last of her strength. Pain and blood and breath and magic, she drew out all she had, and sealed the ring, and the cage closed and the fire winked out.

For one heartbeat, triumph raged through Medeoan's blood. Then, Avanasy, still bound to her by all the strength of their working, crumpled to the ground.

'Avanasy!' shrieked Medeoan, falling to her knees on the scorched earth beside him. Avanasy lay in the midst of the destruction, his skin white against the black ash, his golden hair filthy. He couldn't seem to breathe. He could only choke and gasp.

She had known from the beginning this act would take a life to complete, but now that the moment came, she could not let him go.

'No,' she seized his hand. 'No, you cannot leave me. Not now.'

But she was so tired. Weariness dragged at every muscle. Her throat cried out with a thirst that could never be slaked, and behind her, the bird and its miraculous cage burned so brightly, she could feel it pulsing in her blood, sapping what little strength remained to her.

But Avanasy could not die. Not now. Now that she knew where her heart lay, now that he had saved her and all of Isavalta.

Slowly, Avanasy reached out with his free hand. 'Please,' he whispered. 'Medeoan, help me.'

Medeoan leaned across him. She looked in his eyes and she saw the love that was there even as their light died. She kissed him, open mouthed, breathing her life, her magic into him. Bound as they were, this they could share. Source to source, spirit to spirit, she could give this to him, and she would, for their work, their need, their love. She pushed her magic hard into his heart, willing it strength to beat.

And she found Ingrid there. Not herself, the stranger.

Shock and rage threw Medeoan backwards, all but severing the connection between them. Avanasy's whole frame convulsed, and his throat gasped hard for air. His whole back arched as he struggled to breathe. She stared at him, heart beating hard, skin burning from what waited behind her, unable to believe that now, when they had been heart to heart, now when she had been willing to share with him her mortal breath, he still loved a stranger, a peasant, a nothing.

Avanasy collapsed, the struggle finally becoming too much. Only his hand clenched itself. He was dying. She felt him ebbing, his spirit pulled away from his body by Grandfather Death, even as their cage had pulled the Firebird down.

She saw then, in one blinding instant, how she could make all right. If Avanasy lived, if she gave her future to him, the

Firebird's hideous prophecy could not come true. Isavalta could stand free and strong. She could do as Vyshemir herself did and give her life for her realm and go to the Land of Death and Spirit in Avanasy's place.

She could give him back to his lover.

The thought made her hesitate, and she watched Avanasy's hand curl tight once more, and then the fingers loosened, and his head rolled sideways. Medeoan cried out and threw herself forward, but she was too weak. His strength had been sustaining her, and she could only fall beside him. She pushed herself up, and tried to reach him, to kiss him, to breathe into him, to say she was sorry, that he must forgive her, that she was not thinking of herself, not really, that she loved him, that she needed him beside her.

'Don't go,' she breathed the words into his mouth, reaching inside herself for the last of her strength, searching her sorcery for the barest thread of their connection. 'Don't leave me.' She pressed her mouth against his, and breathed out the last of herself.

Blackness swirled around her then, and Medeoan slipped forward to meet it.

Ingrid dozed on the deck of Lien's ship surrounded by the white mists of the Land of Death and Spirit. Mindful of the warnings and dangers, she had tried hard to stay awake, but the day and the parting had been too much, and her mind and soul sought a relief that she had no strength left to deny.

'Ingrid.'

Ingrid was dreaming. She knew it. The cabin deck was warm with sunlight and she could see waves sparkling over the side, but there was no sun here. She sailed no real ocean. She dreamed and she should wake herself.

But it was a wonderful dream, for Avanasy knelt beside her, gazing at her with eyes full of love.

She reached out to take his hand, but although he was there and she could see him, she could not touch him.

'Come closer,' she said, in the manner of dreams.

'I'm here beside you,' he told her. 'Where I'll be forever.'

'But I can't touch you.'

'No. Not yet.'

'Soon.'

'Not for years to come, Ingrid. For you must live now.'

Cold dread seized her, and she tried to tell herself this was only a dream. Nothing more, but part of her knew that was a lie.

'No, Avanasy. Be here. You can't . . . you can't . . .'

Avanasy was silent. He reached out to stroke her hair, but she felt nothing at all.

'You promised.'

'It was not for lack of love, Ingrid, I swear.'

'No,' she said, with a rock-hard certainty. 'Not alone. Not without you.' Her fingers found the wristlet he had made for her, and began tearing at the knot.

'Stop, Ingrid. Don't do this.'

'I am not going to live without you,' she said doggedly. 'You're all I have.'

'And you are all our babe has now.'

Ingrid stilled her hand.

'You must live for her, and for yourself, Ingrid. You must see her living into the world, for all our sakes.'

'Say you'll be beside me. Say you will be there with us.'

'As close as I can be, Ingrid. As close as I am allowed.'

'Don't leave me,' she whispered, reaching again, and failing to touch him, yet again.

'I love you, Ingrid. Carry that with you always. Tell our daughter that.'

He was fading like a ghost, like a dream, he was pulling away from her.

'No! Avanasy! No!'

And she was awake and on her feet, staring out at the swirling mists and green islands, and strange dark trees, and the whole empty world between worlds.

Ingrid bowed her head and began to weep. Her tears fell into the mist, and were gone.

Epilogue

Lien's men rowed her ashore in the early morning, and left her on the sand of Eastbay. As soon as their boat returned to the ship, the ship raised sail, and vanished from her sight.

It was cold, and the trees were bare. November already maybe. Maybe only October. It didn't matter. It was cold and the wind bit hard at her bones.

Ingrid entered Avanasy's shack and sat in his chair. She could not think. She was numb. All she could do was sit and stare at the empty stove, and remember how he had lain in the now-empty bed and let her sing him back to the world.

Eventually, cold overcame even numbness, and Ingrid found matches in a tin can, and some tinder, and some kindling, and with only a little trouble, managed to light the stove. On a shelf, there was coffee, and tins of beans, and some others of beef. She ate some of the beans, and returned to Avanasy's chair, and curled up in it, watching the fire through the grate in the old stove.

She lived for two or three days that way, doing no more than absolutely necessary to keep body and soul together. She did not weep. She could not seem to remember how.

Then, one morning – she had lost count of the mornings – as she knelt to light the stove, she heard a footstep outside, and the door swung open.

'Ingrid?'

Still on her knees, Ingrid turned, and saw Everett standing in the doorway.

She rose, but could find nothing to say.

Everett pulled off his cap and stepped inside. 'I heard you'd been seen.'

'Did you?' Ingrid smoothed down her worn and filthy dress.

Everett took another tentative step toward her. 'Your family is saying they won't have you back.'

'I'm not surprised.' It was hard, but she made herself think of her family, of how she had come to be in this place. 'Did you speak with Grace?'

Everett shook his head. 'She's gone to Bayfield.'

Ingrid laid her hand on the edge of the warming stove. 'She's better off there.'

Silence hung between them while Ingrid stared past Everett to the doorway, wondering if her paralysis was because she wanted Everett to go, or she wanted Avanasy to come for her.

'Ingrid, you can't stay here.'

Ingrid shrugged. 'It's only for a few days,' she lied, 'until I can convince the tug to take me across to Bayfield. I'll find work.'

'Where?' asked Everett. 'It's all over how you ran off.'

'If no one will have me in Bayfield, then I'll just have to go further.' She couldn't meet his eyes. She did not want to see how earnestly he looked at her. She did not want to see love on another man's face.

'You could come with me,' he said.

Now it was Ingrid's turn to shake her head. 'You don't want me, Everett.'

'I've never wanted anyone else.' He did not move closer to her. He relied on his words to reach her. He had no idea how far they had to travel.

Better to end this now. Ingrid laid her hand against her belly. 'I'm pregnant, Everett.'

'I don't care.'

Those soft words caused Ingrid to finally raise her eyes and look directly at him. A good man. He had always been such a good man. Even now, as he stood ready to forgive her so much, she could feel only regret, only grief, and love for another.

'Come with me,' urged Everett. 'If not for your own sake, then for the baby's.'

The baby. Yes, she had to think of the baby, her baby, Avanasy's baby. What would life be like for it born a bastard, even more of an outcast than it needed to be?

Everett held out his hand.

'I don't know if I will ever love you, Everett.'

'But you don't know that you won't,' Everett answered.

His faith was warming, like a fire at her back. He believed. He believed if he loved her enough that the dry tinder of her heart would catch fire. Maybe he was right. They could hope. Even now, they could still hope. If there was hope, then what she did was not a lie. Her child would be born healthy and alive to a loving mother and father, and then one day, one day she would find a way to return to Isavalta, just for a little while, just so the child would know that part of its heritage, would know at least the land of its father. Then, she would return to Everett whom she would have learned to love. If she could hold tight to that hope, then this was not a lie. If she could hold tight to that hope she could find some corner of her heart that could hold love for Everett as well as for Avanasy.

Ingrid gave Everett her hand, answering his soft smile with her own as he took her arm and led her to his home.

★   ★   ★

Medeoan entered the long pavilion with her entourage behind her. A gleaming trestle table had been placed in the center. At either side sat the representatives of Hung-Tse — generals in lacquered armor, scholars in modest black and white coats, and, at the far end, two of the Nine Elders: the Minister of Earth and the Minister of the North.

They had left the carved chair at the foot of the table for her. Prathad pulled it out for her and Medeoan sat, letting her ladies adjust her trains and sleeves, while the Council Lords and secretaries arrayed themselves behind her with their caskets and scrolls and other small burdens.

Captain Peshek, in his crisp coat and gleaming breastplate, stood at Medeoan's right hand.

Peasants had found them both. Peshek had been carried from the ruin. Medeoan, they had not dared touch because of the Firebird caged beside her. When she had woken, with the ones who had found her and the keeper of their village god house as a ragged escort, she had carried cage and captive to their Lord's estate. He had not doubted who she was, and, no matter whom he had followed before, he knelt to her and her cage now and sent instant word to the Lord Master, who knelt himself, and proclaimed his fealty.

Later, she would sort out who had remained true, who had been bemused by Kacha and Yamuna, and who had truly betrayed. For now, it was enough that they obeyed and gave her what men were left to march in procession to the next fortress, the next manor, the next Lord and Lord Master. Word flew ahead of her, the tale of betrayal and duplicity, and the countryside turned out to cheer her return at the head of her growing guard.

She kept the cage covered.

When they finally reached Vaknevos, the whole of the palace turned out to greet her. With Yamuna's death, the spells he had laid with Kacha's help had broken and the newly freed seized the traitors, or the supposed traitors, and offered them up to her in exchange for forgiveness. They waited in the cells for her judgment, all except one.

The woman Chekhania sailed in chains to Hastinapura, her belly big with Kacha's bastard. The Hastinapuran ambassador's head in a jar of honey was her accompaniment.

That left the Hung-Tse army, massing at Miateshcha, and their navy gathering its strength in the southern sea. So, she had made her arrangements, and had ridden here to meet with the representatives of Hung-Tse. She'd had to come herself; until she'd had time to investigate what had happened in her absence, there was no way to know who she could really trust.

The Minister of the North bowed her head in acknowledgment of Medeoan's arrival. 'We thank Your Majesty Imperial for appearing before us. We are certain that this recent misunderstanding between yourself and the Heart of Heaven and Earth can be quickly resolved and appropriate reparation made.'

She looked from one minister to the other. Their faces behind their tattoos were bland, but their eyes were not easy. They were wondering, she knew, why she lived. She should have been dead. She should have been ash and char.

'Ministers of the Heart of the World,' she replied evenly. 'I am not here to speak of reparations. I am here to confirm that Isavalta has no lawful quarrel with Hung-Tse. Our armies have been removed and disbanded and we hope soon to exchange ambassadors with the Heart of the World. We expect that our Brother Emperor will give similar orders as soon as you carry my word back to him.' She gestured to her chief secretary who walked to the ministers and handed over a scroll bound with sapphire ribbons and sealed with red wax.

The Minister of the North received the missive in silence.

'We are of course delighted to hear that Your Majesty Imperial has understood that this quarrel previously standing between our empires has no basis in the laws of earth or heaven,' said the Minister of Earth. 'But, it is Hung–Tse that was attacked and . . .'

Medeoan did not let him finish. 'We will not speak of attacks, Minister. We will not speak of damages or reparations. We have withdrawn. You will withdraw. That is all.'

'It is Hung–Tse that was attacked,' the Minister of Earth repeated. 'You have acknowledged that this attack was unlawful. That entitles Hung–Tse to reparations from Isavalta.'

Medeoan looked to Peshek. Peshek turned to the Commander of the House Guard who handed him the object covered with black cloth that he carried. Peshek set the object in front of Medeoan.

All the representatives of Hung–Tse shifted uneasily at their end of the table.

Medeoan pulled away the black cloth, revealing a curved jar of purest crystal. Inside lay a single feather that at first glance appeared to be perfectly formed of shining gold, but if one looked longer and more closely, one saw how lights of orange, red and white played along its length.

She lifted the curved jar from its base. The air touched the feather, and it burst at once into a single gout of flame that burned for an instant, and was gone.

The two sorcerers of Hung–Tse let their gaze linger on the now empty jar, and then slowly lifted their gaze to meet Medeoan's.

Medeoan replaced the crystal jar on its base, and Peshek lifted it away.

'We will not speak of attacks,' she said. 'We will not speak of reparations. We have withdrawn our forces. Hung–Tse will also withdraw. That is all.'

Medeoan left the pavilion. Her grooms had her horse waiting for her, and she mounted. Without looking behind even to see if her escort followed, she rode back across the plain to the encampment that had been made around her banner with the golden Imperial eagle on its bright blue field.

At one time, she might have found her tent cramped and uncomfortable, for all its carpets and finely made furniture. No longer. She had known far rougher accommodation. Prathad hurried about, directing the other ladies, all new, and all chosen by her, to take her outer coat, to fetch small beer and refreshment and to do all else that was needful for the maintenance of their empress.

A shadow crossed the entrance of the tent. Medeoan glanced back and saw Captain Peshek waiting to be acknowledged.

'Come in, Peshek.'

Peshek entered and knelt. She nodded and waved him to a chair, which he did not accept as she still stood.

'Majesty, I do not mean to question your judgment, but was that . . .'

'Wise?' she finished for him. 'Perhaps not, but it will do. They will spend this night trying to understand what has happened to the Firebird and how we came to possess any fragment of it. When they understand that their guardian is no longer free to protect their borders, they will withdraw, and we will have peace.' She sat, slumping as far into her chair as her layers of clothing permitted. She closed her eyes briefly. 'That is enough.'

'Yes, Majesty.'

She heard movement and looked to see Prathad setting the tray with wine and dainties beside her. The lady poured two goblets full, handing one to Medeoan and one to Peshek.

Medeoan did not drink. She just looked at the dark depths of the wine. 'Lien said Ingrid arrived safely home.'

'Yes, Majesty,' replied Peshek.

'She is carrying Avanasy's child, Peshek.'

'Yes, Majesty.'

She swirled her cup gently. 'I want to send for her, when we know we have found all the real traitors and that our borders are safe. Avanasy's child should be raised in Isavalta. He should be given the honors due to him as the Avanasin.'

Peshek was silent for a moment. Then, he said, 'I miss him too, Majesty.'

She looked up at him then, and saw how bright his blue eyes were. Lien's healing had worked well, and his scars were almost completely gone. He was again the handsome, loyal soldier who had taken her to safety when she was so beset.

'His life is part of Isavalta now,' she said. 'It is because of him that we have a chance to be safe in our borders. Our task is to see that what he has begun is completed.'

Peshek laid his hand over his heart, his blue eyes sparkling. 'I live to serve, Majesty.'

She lifted the wine cup to him and smiled, feeling a thread of warmth working its way through the chill of her soul. 'As do we all, Peshek. Isavalta will in truth be the Eternal.'

But even as she spoke those words, Medeoan knew that the Firebird, away in its cage, locked in the cells of Vaknevos, heard, and cried out its defiance.

The Empress of Isavalta shivered and turned her face away.